ROBERT LUDLUM
The Bourne Trilogy

Also by Robert Ludlum

The Janson Directive
The Sigma Protocol
The Prometheus Deception
The Matarese Countdown
The Cry of the Halidon
The Apocalypse Watch
The Scorpio Illusion
The Road to Omaha
Trevayne
The Icarus Agenda
The Aquitaine Progression
The Parsifal Mosaic
The Road to Gandolfo
The Matarese Circle
The Holcroft Covenant
The Chancellor Manuscript
The Gemini Contenders
The Rhinemann Exchange
The Matlock Paper
The Osterman Weekend
The Scarlatti Inheritance

The Covert-One Novels

The Cassandra Compact (with Philip Shelby)
The Hades Factor (with Gayle Lynds)

Robert Ludlum

The Bourne Trilogy

The Bourne Identity
The Bourne Supremacy
The Bourne Ultimatum

First published in Great Britain in 2003 by
Orion
An imprint of Orion Books Ltd
Orion House, 5 Upper St Martin's Lane, London WC2H 9EA

An Hachette Livre UK Company

9 10

ISBN 978-0-7528-6039-8 (hardback)

A CIP catalogue record for this book is available from the British Library

Typeset at The Spartan Press Ltd,
Lymington, Hants

Printed and bound in Great Britain by
Clays Ltd, St Ives plc

www.orionbooks.co.uk

Contents

The Bourne Identity

For Glynis
A very special light we all adore.
With love and deep respect.

THE NEW YORK TIMES
FRIDAY, 11 JULY 1975
FRONT PAGE

DIPLOMATS SAID TO BE LINKED
WITH FUGITIVE TERRORIST
KNOWN AS CARLOS

Paris, 10 July – France expelled three high-ranking Cuban diplomats today in connection with the world-wide search for a man called Carlos, who is believed to be an important link in an international terrorist network.

The suspect, whose real name is thought to be Ilich Ramirez Sanchez, is being sought in the killing of two French counter-intelligence agents and a Lebanese informer at a Latin Quarter apartment on 27 June.

The three killings have led the police here and in Britain to what they feel is the trail of a major network of international terrorist agents. In the search for Carlos after the killings, French and British policemen discovered large arms caches that linked Carlos to major terrorism in West Germany and led them to suspect a connection between many terrorist acts throughout Europe.

REPORTED SEEN IN LONDON

Since then Carlos has been reported seen in London and in Beirut, Lebanon.

ASSOCIATED PRESS
MONDAY, 7 JULY 1975
SYNDICATED DISPATCH

A DRAGNET FOR ASSASSIN

London (AP) – Guns and girls, grenades and good suits, a well-stuffed wallet, airline tickets to romantic places and nice apartments in half a dozen world capitals. This is the portrait emerging of a jet-age assassin being sought in an international manhunt.

The hunt began when the man answered his doorbell in Paris and shot dead two French intelligence agents and a Lebanese informer. It has put four women into custody in two capitals, accused of offences in his wake. The assassin himself has vanished – perhaps in Lebanon, the French police believe.

In the past few days in London, those acquainted with him have described him to reporters as good looking, courteous, well educated, wealthy and fashionably dressed.

But his associates are men and women who have been called the most dangerous in the world. He is said to be linked with the Japanese Red Army, the Organization for the Armed Arab Struggle, the West German Baader-

Meinhof gang, the Quebec Liberation Front, the Turkish Popular Liberation Front, separatists in France and Spain and the Provisional wing of the Irish Republican Army.

When the assassin travelled – to Paris, to the Hague, to West Berlin – bombs went off, guns cracked and there were kidnappings.

A breakthrough occurred in Paris when a Lebanese terrorist broke under questioning and led two intelligence men to the assassin's door on 27 June. He shot all three to death and escaped. Police found his guns and notebooks containing 'death lists' of prominent people.

Yesterday the London *Observer* said police were hunting for the son of a Venezuelan Communist lawyer for questioning in the triple slaying. Scotland Yard said, 'We are not denying the report', but added there was no charge against him and he was wanted only for questioning.

The *Observer* identified the hunted man as Ilich Ramirez Sanchez, of Caracas. It said his name was on one of the four passports found by French police when they raided the Paris flat where the slayings took place.

The newspaper said Ilich was named after Vladimir Ilyich Lenin, founder of the Soviet state, and was educated in Moscow and speaks fluent Russian.

In Caracas, a spokesman for the Venezuelan Communist Party said Ilich is the son of a seventy-year-old Marxist lawyer living 450 miles west of Caracas, but 'neither father nor son belong to our party'.

He told reporters he did not know where Ilich was now.

Book 1

1

The trawler plunged into the angry swells of the dark, furious sea like an awkward animal trying desperately to break out of an impenetrable swamp. The waves rose to Goliathan heights, crashing into the hull with the power of raw tonnage; the white spray caught in the night sky cascaded down over the deck under the force of the night wind. Everywhere there were the sounds of inanimate pain, wood straining against wood, ropes twisting, stretched to the breaking point. The animal was dying.

Two abrupt explosions pierced the sounds of the sea and the wind and the vessel's pain. They came from the dimly lit cabin that rose and fell with its host body. A man lunged out of the door grasping the railing with one hand, holding his stomach with the other.

A second man followed, the pursuit cautious, his intent violent. He stood bracing himself in the cabin door; he raised a gun and fired again. And again.

The man at the railing whipped both his hands up to his head, arching backwards under the impact of the fourth bullet. The trawler's bow dipped suddenly into the valley of two giant waves lifting the wounded man off his feet; he twisted to his left unable to take his hands away from his head. The boat surged upwards, bow and midships more out of the water than in it, sweeping the figure in the doorway back into the cabin, a fifth gunshot fired wildly. The wounded man screamed, his hands now lashing out at anything he could grasp, his eyes blinded by blood and the unceasing spray of the sea. There was nothing he could grab, so he grabbed at nothing; his legs buckled as his body lurched forward. The boat rolled violently leeward and the man whose skull was ripped open plunged over the side into the madness of the darkness below.

He felt rushing cold water envelop him, swallowing him, sucking him under, and twisting him in circles, then propelling him up to the surface – only to gasp a single breath of air. A gasp and he was under again.

And there was heat, a strange moist heat at his temple that seared through the freezing water that kept swallowing him, a fire where no fire should burn. There was ice, too; an icelike throbbing in his stomach and his legs and his chest, oddly warmed by the cold sea around him. He felt these things, acknowledging his own panic as he felt them. He could see his own body turning and twisting, arms and feet working frantically against the pressures of the whirlpool. He could feel, think, see, perceive panic and struggle – yet strangely there was peace. It was the calm of the observer, the uninvolved observer, separated from the events, knowing of them but not essentially involved.

Then another form of panic spread through him, surging through the heat and the ice and the uninvolved recognition. He could not submit to peace! Not yet! It would happen any second now; he was not sure what it was, but it *would happen.* He had to *be* there!

He kicked furiously, clawing at the heavy walls of water above, his chest bursting. He broke surface, thrashing to stay on top of the black swells. Climb up! *Climb up!*

A monstrous rolling wave accommodated; he was on the crest, surrounded by pockets of foam and darkness. *Nothing.* Turn! *Turn!*

It happened. The explosion was massive; he could hear it through the clashing waters and the wind, the sight and the sound somehow his doorway to peace. The sky lit up like a fiery diadem and within that crown of fire, objects of all shapes and sizes were blown through the light into the outer shadows.

He had won. Whatever it was, he had won.

Suddenly, he was plummeting downwards again, into an abyss again. He could feel the rushing waters crash over his shoulders, cooling the white hot heat at his temple, warming the ice cold incisions in his stomach and his legs and . . .

His *chest.* His chest was in agony! He had been struck – the blow crushing, the impact sudden and intolerable. It happened again! *Let me alone. Give me peace.*

And again!

And he clawed again, and kicked again . . . until he felt it. A thick, oily object that moved only with the movements of the sea. He could not tell what it was, but it was there and he could feel it, hold it.

Hold it! It will ride you to peace. To the silence of darkness . . . and peace.

The rays of the early sun broke through the mists of the eastern sky, lending glitter to the calm waters of the Mediterranean. The skipper of the small fishing boat, his eyes bloodshot, his hands marked with rope burns, sat on the stern gunwale smoking a Gauloise, grateful for the sight of the smooth sea. He glanced over at the open wheelhouse; his younger brother was easing the throttle forward to make better time, the single other crewman checking a net several feet away. They were laughing at something and that was good; there had been nothing to laugh about last night. Where had the storm come from? The weather reports from Marseilles had indicated nothing; if they had he would have stayed in the shelter of the coastline. He wanted to reach the fishing grounds eighty kilometres south of La Seyne-sur-mer by daybreak, but not at the expense of costly repairs, and what repairs were not costly these days?

Or at the expense of his life, and there were moments last night when that was a distinct consideration.

'*Tu es fatigué, mon frère!*' his brother shouted, grinning at him. '*Vas te coucher! Je suis très capable!*'

'Yes, you are,' he answered, throwing his cigarette over the side and sliding down to the deck on top of a net. 'A little sleep won't hurt.'

It was good to have a brother at the wheel. A member of the family should always be the pilot on the family boat; the eyes were sharper. Even a brother who spoke with the smooth tongue of a literate man as opposed to his own coarse words. Crazy! One year at the university and his brother wished to start a *compagnie.* With a single boat that had seen better days many years ago. Crazy. What good did his books do last night? When his *compagnie* was about to capsize.

He closed his eyes, letting his hands soak in the rolling water on the deck. The salt of the sea would be good for the rope burns. Burns received while lashing equipment that did not care to stay put in the storm.

'*Look!* Over there!'

It was his brother; apparently sleep was to be denied by sharp family eyes.

'What is it?' he yelled.

'Port bow! There's a man in the water! He's holding on to something! A piece of debris, a plank of some sort.'

The skipper took the wheel, angling the boat to the right of the figure in the water, cutting the engines to reduce the wake. The man looked as though the slightest motion would send him sliding off the fragment of wood he clung to, his hands were white, gripped around the edge like claws, but the rest of his body was limp – as limp as a man fully drowned, passed from this world.

'Loop the ropes!' yelled the skipper to his brother and the crewman. 'Submerge them around his legs. *Easy* now! Move them up to his waist. Pull gently.'

'His hands won't let go of the plank!'

'Reach down! Pry them up! It may be the death lock.'

'No. He's alive . . . but barely, I think. His lips move, but there's no sound. His eyes also, though I doubt he sees us.'

'The hands are free!'

'Lift him up. Grab his shoulders and pull him over. *Easy,* now!'

'Mother of God, look at his head!' yelled the crewman. 'It's split open.'

'He must have crashed it against the plank in the storm,' said the brother.

'No,' disagreed the skipper, staring at the wound. 'It's a clean slice, razorlike. Caused by a bullet; he was shot.'

'You can't be sure of that.'

'In more than one place,' added the skipper, his eyes roving over the body. 'We'll head for Île de Port Noir; it's the nearest island. There's a doctor on the waterfront.'

'The Englishman?'

'He practises.'

'When he can,' said the skipper's brother. 'When the wine lets him. He has more success with his patients' animals than with his patients.'

'It won't matter. This will be a corpse by the time we get there. If by chance he lives, I'll charge him for the extra petrol and whatever catch we miss. Get the kit; we'll bind his head for all the good it will do.'

'Look!' cried the crewman. 'Look at his eyes.'

'What about them?' asked the brother.

'A moment ago they were grey – as grey as steel cables. Now they're blue!'

'The sun's brighter,' said the skipper, shrugging. 'Or, it's playing tricks with your own eyes. No matter, there's no colour in the grave.'

Intermittent whistles of fishing boats clashed with the incessant screeching of the gulls; together they formed the universal sounds of the waterfront. It was late afternoon, the sun a fireball in the west, the air still and too damp, too hot. Above the piers and facing the harbour was a cobblestone street and several blemished white houses, separated by overgrown grass shooting up from dried earth and sand. What remained of the verandas were patched lattice-work and crumbling stucco supported by hastily implanted piles. The residences had seen better days a number of decades ago when the residents mistakenly believed Île de Port Noir might become another Mediterranean playground. It never did.

All the houses had paths to the street, but the last house in the row had a path obviously more trampled than the others. It belonged to an Englishman who had come to Port Noir eight years before under circumstances no one understood or cared to; he was a doctor and the waterfront had need of a doctor. Hooks, needles, and knives were at once means of livelihood and instruments of incapacitation. If one saw *le médecin* on a good day, the sutures were not too bad. On the other hand, if the stench of wine or whisky was too pronounced, one took one's chances.

Ainsi soit-il. He was better than no one.

But not today; no one used the path today. It was Sunday and it was common knowledge that on any Saturday night the doctor was roaring drunk in the village, ending the evening with whatever whore was available. Of course, it was also granted that during the past few Saturdays the doctor's routine had altered; he had not been seen in the village. But nothing ever changed that much; bottles of Scotch whisky were sent to the doctor on a regular basis. He was simply staying in his house; he had been doing so since the fishing boat from La Ciotat had brought in the unknown man who was more corpse than man.

Dr Geoffrey Washburn awoke with a start, his chin, settled into his collar bone, causing the odour of his mouth to invade his nostrils; it was not pleasant. He blinked, orienting himself, and glanced at the open bedroom door. Had his nap been interrupted by another incoherent monologue from his patient? No; there was no sound. Even the gulls outside were mercifully quiet; it was Île de Port Noir's holy day, no boats coming in to taunt the birds with their catches.

Washburn looked at the empty glass and the half-empty bottle of whisky on the table beside his chair. It was an improvement. On a normal Sunday both would be empty by now, the pain of the previous night having been spiralled out by the Scotch. He smiled to himself, once again blessing an older sister in Coventry who made the Scotch possible with her monthly stipend. She was a good girl, Bess was, and God knew she could afford a hell of a lot more than she sent him, but he was grateful she did what she did. And one day she would stop, the money would stop, and then the oblivions would be achieved with the cheapest wine until there was no pain at all. Ever.

He had come to accept that eventuality . . . until three weeks and five days ago when the half-dead stranger had been dragged from the sea and brought to his door by fishermen who did not care to identify themselves. Their errand was one of mercy, not involvement. God would understand, the man had been shot.

What the fishermen had not known was that far more than bullets had invaded the man's body. And mind.

The doctor pushed his gaunt frame out of the chair and walked unsteadily to the window overlooking the harbour. He lowered the blind, closing his eyes to block out the sun, then squinted between the slats to observe the activity in the street below, specifically the reason for the clatter. It was a horse-drawn cart, a fisherman's family out for a Sunday drive. Where the hell else could one see such a sight? And then he remembered the carriages and the finely groomed geldings that carried tourists through London's Regent's Park during the summer months; he laughed out loud at the comparison. But his laughter was short-lived, replaced by something unthinkable three weeks ago. He had given up all hope of seeing England again. It was possible that might be changed now. The stranger could change it.

Unless his prognosis was wrong, it would happen any day, any hour or minute. The wounds to the legs, stomach and chest were deep and severe, quite possibly fatal were it not for the fact the bullets had remained where they had lodged, self-cauterized and continuously cleansed by the sea. Extracting them was nowhere near as dangerous as it might have been, the tissue primed, softened, sterilized, ready for an immediate knife. The cranial wound was the real problem, the penetration was subcutaneous, but it appeared to have bruised the thalamus and hippocampus fibrous regions. Had the bullet entered millimetres on either side the vital functions would have ceased; they had not been impeded, and Washburn had made a decision. He went dry for thirty-six hours, eating as much starch and drinking as much water as was humanly possible. Then he performed the most delicate piece of work he had attempted since his dismissal from Macleans Hospital in London. Millimetre by agonizing millimetre he had brush-washed the fibrous areas, then stretched and sutured the skin over the cranial wound, knowing that the slightest error with brush, needle or clamp would cause the patient's death.

He had not wanted this unknown patient to die for any number of reasons. But especially one.

When it was over and the vital signs remained constant, Dr Geoffrey Washburn went back to his chemical and physiological appendage. His bottle. He had got drunk and he had remained drunk, but he had not gone over the edge. He knew exactly where he was and what he was doing at all times. Definitely an improvement.

Any day now, any hour perhaps. The stranger would focus his eyes and intelligible words would emerge from his lips.

Even any moment.

*

The words came first. They floated in the air as the early morning breeze off the sea cooled the room.

'Who's there? Who's in this room?'

Washburn sat up in the cot, moved his legs quietly over the side, and rose slowly to his feet. It was important to make no jarring note, no sudden noise or physical movement that might frighten the patient into a psychological regression. The next few minutes would be as delicate as the surgical procedures he had performed; the doctor in him was prepared for the moment.

'A friend,' he said softly.

'Friend?'

'You speak English. I thought you would. American or Canadian is what I suspected. Your dental work didn't come from the UK or Paris. How do you feel?'

'I'm not sure.'

'It will take a while. Do you need to relieve your bowels?'

'What?'

'Take a crapper, old man. That's what the pan's for beside you. The white one on your left. When we make it in time, of course.'

'I'm sorry.'

'Don't be. Perfectly normal function. I'm a doctor, *your* doctor. My name is Geoffrey Washburn. What's yours?'

'What?'

'I asked you what your name was.'

The stranger moved his head and stared at the white wall streaked with shafts of morning light. Then he turned back, his blue eyes levelled at the doctor. 'I don't know.'

'Oh, my *God*.'

'I've told you over and *over* again. It will take *time*. The more you fight it, the more you crucify yourself, the worse it will be.'

'You're drunk.'

'Generally. It's not pertinent. But I can give you clues, if you'll *listen*.'

'I've listened.'

'No you *don't*; you turn away. You lie in your cocoon and pull the cover over your mind. Hear me again.'

'I'm listening.'

'In your coma – your *prolonged* coma – you spoke in three different languages. English, French and some goddamned twangy thing I presume is Oriental. That means you're multi-lingual; you're at home in various parts of the world. Think *geographically*. What's most comfortable for you?'

'Obviously English.'

'We've agreed to that. So what's most *un*comfortable?'

'I don't know.'

'Your eyes are round, not sloped. I'd say obviously not Oriental.'

'Obviously.'

'Then why do you *speak* it? Now, think in terms of *association*. I've written down words; listen to them. I'll say them phonetically. *Ma – kwa. Tam – Kwan. Kee – sah.* Say the first thing that comes to mind.'

'Nothing.'

'Good show.'

'What the hell do you want?'

'Something. *Anything.*'

'You're drunk.'

'We've agreed to that. Consistently. I also saved your bloody life. Drunk or not, I *am* a doctor. I was once a very good one.'

'What happened?'

'The patient questions the doctor?'

'Why not?'

Washburn paused, looking out of the window at the waterfront. 'I was drunk,' he said. 'They said I killed two patients on the operating table because I was drunk. I could have got away with one. Not two. They see a pattern very quickly, God bless them. Don't ever give a man like me a knife and cloak it in respectability.'

'Was it necessary?'

'Was what necessary?'

'The bottle.'

'Yes, damn you,' said Washburn softly, turning from the window. 'It was and it is. And the patient is not permitted to make judgments where the physician is concerned.'

'Sorry.'

'You also have an annoying habit of apologizing. It's an overworked protestation and not at all natural. I don't for a minute believe you're an apologetic person.'

'Then you know something I don't know.'

'About you, yes. A great deal. And very little of it makes sense.'

The man sat forward in the chair. His open shirt fell away from his taut frame, exposing the bandages on his chest and stomach. He folded his hands in front of him, the veins in his slender, muscular arms pronounced. 'Other than the things we've talked about?'

'Yes.'

'Things I said while in coma?'

'No, not really. We've discussed most of that gibberish. The languages, your knowledge of geography – cities I've never or barely heard of – your obsession for avoiding the use of names, names you want to say but won't; your propensity for confrontation – attack, recoil, hide, run – all rather violent, I might add. I frequently strapped your arms down, to protect the wounds. But we've covered all that. There are other things.'

'What do you mean? What are they? Why haven't you told me?'

'Because they're physical. The outer shell, as it were. I wasn't sure you were ready to hear. I'm not sure now.'

The man leaned back in the chair, dark eyebrows below the dark brown hair joined in irritation. 'Now it's the physician's judgment that isn't called for. I'm ready. What are you talking about?'

'Shall we begin with that rather acceptable looking head of yours? The face, in particular.'

'What about it?'

'It's not the one you were born with.'

'What do you mean?'

'Under a thick glass, surgery always leaves its mark. You've been altered, old man.'

'Altered?'

'You have a pronounced chin; I daresay there was a cleft in it. It's been removed. Your upper left cheekbone – your cheekbones are also pronounced, conceivably Slavic generations ago – has minute traces of a surgical scar. I would venture to say a mole was eliminated. Your nose is an English nose, at one time slightly more prominent than it is now. It was thinned ever so subtly. Your very sharp features have been softened, the character submerged. Do you understand what I'm saying?'

'No.'

'You're a reasonably attractive man but your face is more distinguished by the category it falls into than by the face itself.'

'Category?'

'Yes. You are the prototype of the white Anglo-Saxon people see every day on the better cricket fields, or the tennis court. Or the bar at Mirabel's. Those faces become almost indistinguishable from one another, don't they? The features properly in place, the teeth straight, the ears flat against the head – nothing out of balance, everything in position and just a little bit soft.'

'Soft?'

'Well, "spoiled" is perhaps a better word. Definitely self-assured, even arrogant, used to having your own way.'

'I'm still not sure what you're trying to say.'

'Try this then. Change the colour of your hair, you change the face. Yes, there are traces of discoloration, brittleness, dye. Wear glasses and a moustache, you're a different man. I'd guess you were in your middle to late thirties, but you could be ten years older, or five younger.' Washburn paused, watching the man's reactions as if wondering whether or not to proceed. 'And speaking of glasses, do you remember those exercises, the tests we did a week ago?'

'Of course.'

'Your eyesight's perfectly normal; you have no need of glasses.'

'I didn't think I did.'

'Then why is there evidence of prolonged use of contact lenses about your retinas and lids?'

'I don't know. It doesn't make sense.'

'May I suggest a possible explanation?'

'I'd like to hear it.'

'You may not.' The doctor returned to the window and peered absently outside. 'Certain types of contact lenses are designed to change the colour of the eyes. And certain types of eyes lend themselves more readily than others to the device. Usually those that have a grey or bluish hue; yours are a cross.

Hazel-grey in one light, blue in another. Nature favoured you in this; often no alteration was required.'

'Required for what?'

'For changing your appearance. Very professionally, I'd say. Visas, passports, driver's licences – switched at will. Hair: brown, blond, auburn. Eyes – can't tamper with the eyes – green, grey, blue? The possibilities are far-ranging, wouldn't you say? All within that recognizable category in which the faces are blurred by repetition.'

The man got out of the chair with difficulty, pushing himself up with his arms, holding his breath as he rose. 'It's also possible that you're reaching. You could be way out of line.'

'The traces are there, the markings. That's evidence.'

'Interpreted by you, with a heavy dose of cynicism thrown in. Suppose I had an accident and was patched up? That would explain the surgery.'

'Not the kind you had. Dyed hair and the removal of clefts and moles aren't part of a restoration process.'

'You don't *know* that!' said the unknown man angrily. 'There are different kinds of accidents, different procedures. You weren't there; you can't be certain.'

'Good! Get furious with me. You don't do it half often enough. And while you're mad, *think*. What were you? What *are* you?'

'A salesman . . . an executive with an international company, specializing in the Far East. That could be it. Or a teacher . . . of languages. In a university somewhere. That's possible, too.'

'Fine. Choose one. Now!'

'I . . . I *can't*.' The man's eyes were on the edge of helplessness.

'Because you don't believe either one.'

The man shook his head. 'No. Do you?'

'No,' said Washburn. 'For a specific reason. Those occupations are relatively sedentary and you have the body of a man who's been subjected to physical stress. Oh, I don't mean a trained athlete or anything like that; you're no jock, as they say. But your muscle tone's firm, your arms and hands used to strain and quite strong. Under other circumstances, I might judge you to be a labourer, accustomed to carrying heavy objects, or a fisherman, conditioned by hauling in nets all day long. But your range of knowledge, I daresay your intellect, rules out such things.'

'Why do I get the idea that you're leading up to something? Something else.'

'Because we've worked together, closely and under pressure, for several weeks now. You spot a pattern.'

'I'm right then?'

'Yes. I had to see how you'd accept what I've just told you. The previous surgery, the hair, the contact lenses.'

'Did I pass?'

'With infuriating equilibrium. It's time now; there's no point in putting it off any longer. Frankly, I haven't the patience. Come with me.' Washburn preceded the man through the living-room to the door in the rear wall that led to the dispensary. Inside, he went to the corner and picked up an antiquated projector, the shell of its thick round lens rusted and cracked. 'I had this brought in with the supplies from Marseilles,' he said, placing it on the small desk and inserting the plug into the wall socket. 'It's hardly the best equipment, but it serves the purpose. Pull the blinds, will you?'

The man with no name or memory went to the window and lowered the blind; the room was dark. Washburn snapped on the projector's light; a bright square appeared on the white wall. He then inserted a small piece of celluloid behind the lens.

The square was abruptly filled with magnified letters.

Die Bank Gemeinschaft
11 Bahnhofstrasse. Zürich.
Zero–seven—seventeen–twelve—zero–
fourteen—twenty-six–zero.

'What is it?' asked the nameless man.

'Look at it. Study it. *Think.*'

'It's a bank account of some kind.'

'Exactly. The printed letterhead and address is the bank; the handwritten numbers take the place of a name, but insofar as they *are* written out, they constitute the signature of the account holder. Standard procedure.'

'Where did you get it?'

'From you. This is a very small negative, my guess would be half the size of a thirty-five millimetre film. It was implanted – surgically implanted – beneath the skin above your right hip. The numbers are in your handwriting; it's your signature. With it you can open a vault in Zürich.'

2

They chose the name Jean-Pierre. It neither startled nor offended anyone, a name as common to Port Noir as any other.

And books came from Marseilles, six of them in varying sizes and thicknesses, four in English, two in French. They were medical texts, volumes that dealt with the injuries to the head and mind. There were cross-sections of the brain, hundreds of unfamiliar words to absorb and try to understand. *Lobes occipital* and *temporal*, the *cortex* and the connecting fibres of the *corpus callosum*; the *limbic system* – specifically the *hippocampus* and *mamillary bodies* that together with the *fornix* were indispensable to memory and recall. Damaged, there was amnesia.

There were psychological studies of emotional stress that produced *stagnate hysteria* and *mental aphasia*, conditions which also resulted in partial or total loss of memory. Amnesia.

Amnesia.

'There are no rules,' said the dark-haired man, rubbing his eyes in the inadequate light of the table lamp. 'It's a geometric puzzle; it can happen in any combination of ways. Physically or psychologically – or a little of both. It can be permanent or temporary, all or part. No *rules*!'

'Agreed,' said Washburn, sipping his whisky in a chair across the room. 'But I think we're getting closer to what happened. What I *think* happened.'

'Which was?' asked the man apprehensively.

'You just said it: "a little of both". Although the word "little" should be changed to "massive". Massive shocks.'

'Massive shocks to what?'

'The physical *and* the psychological. They were related, interwoven – two strands of experience, or stimuli, that became knotted.'

'How much sauce have you had?'

'Less than you think; it's irrelevant.' The doctor picked up a clipboard filled with pages. 'This is your history – your new history – begun the day you were brought here. Let me summarize. The physical wounds tell us that the situation in which you found yourself was packed with psychological stress, the subsequent hysteria brought on by at least nine hours in the water, which served to solidify the psychological damage. The darkness, the violent movement, the lungs barely getting air; these were the instruments of hysteria. Everything that preceded it – the hysteria – had to be erased so you could cope, survive. Are you with me?'

'I think so. The head was protecting itself.'

'Not the head, the mind. Make the distinction; it's important. We'll get back to the head, but we'll give it a label. The brain.'

'All right, Mind, not head . . . which is really the brain.'

'Good.' Washburn flipped his thumb through the pages on the clipboard. 'These are filled with several hundred observations. There are the normal medical notes – dosage, time, reaction, that sort of thing – but in the main they deal with *you*, the man himself. The words you use, the words you react to; the phrases you employ – when I can write them down – both rationally and when you talk in your sleep and when you were in coma. Even the way you walk, the way you talk or tense your body when startled or seeing something that interests you. You appear to be a mass of contradictions; there's a subsurface violence almost always under control, but very much alive. There's also a pensiveness that seems painful for you, yet you rarely give vent to the anger that pain must provoke.'

'You're provoking it now,' interrupted the man. 'We've gone over the words and the phrases time and time again . . .'

'And we'll continue to do so,' broke in Washburn, 'as long as there's progress.'

'I wasn't aware any progress had been made.'

'Not in terms of an identity or an occupation. But we *are* finding out what's most comfortable for you, what you deal with best. It's a little frightening.'

'In what way?'

'Let me give you an example.' The doctor put the clipboard down and got out of the chair. He walked to a primitive cupboard against the wall, opened a drawer and took out a large automatic hand gun. The man with no memory tensed in his chair; Washburn was aware of the reaction. 'I've never used this, not sure I'd know how to, but I do live on the waterfront.' He smiled, then suddenly, without warning, threw it to the man. The weapon was caught in midair, the catch clean, swift, and confident. 'Break it down; I believe that's the phrase.'

'What?'

'Break it down. *Now.*'

The man looked at the gun, and then, in silence, his hands and fingers moved expertly over the weapon. In less than thirty seconds it was completely dismantled. He looked up at the doctor.

'See what I mean?' said Washburn. 'Among your skills is an extraordinary knowledge of firearms.'

'*ArmyFührer . . .' asked the man, his voice intense, once more apprehensive.*

'Extremely unlikely,' replied the doctor. 'When you first came out of coma, I mentioned your dental work. I assure you it's not military. And, of course, the surgery, I'd say, would totally rule out any military association.'

'Then *what*?'

'Let's not dwell on it now; let's go back to what happened. We were dealing with the mind, remember? The psychological stress, the hysteria. Not the physical brain but the mental pressures. Am I being clear?'

'Go on.'

'As the shock recedes, so do the pressures, until there's no fundamental need to protect the psyche. As this process takes place your skills and talents will come back to you. You'll remember certain behaviour patterns; you may live them out quite naturally, your surface reactions instinctive. But there's a gap and everything in those pages tell me that it's irreversible.' Washburn stopped and went back to his chair and his glass. He sat down and drank, closing his eyes in weariness.

'Go *on*,' whispered the man.

The doctor opened his eyes, levelling them at his patient. 'We return to the head, which we've labelled the brain. The *physical* brain with its millions upon millions of cells and interacting components. You've read the books; the fornix and the limbic system, the hippocampus fibres and the thalamus; the callosum and especially the lobotomic surgical techniques. The slightest alteration can cause dramatic changes. That's what happened to you. The damage was *physical*. It's as though blocks were rearranged, the *physical* structure no longer what it was.' Again Washburn stopped.

'*And*,' pressed the man.

'The recessed psychological pressures will allow – *are* allowing – your skills and talents to come back to you. But I don't think you'll ever be able to relate them to anything in your past.'

'*Why*? Why not?'

'Because the physical conduits that permit and transmit those memories have been altered. Physically rearranged to the point where they no longer function as they once did. For all intents and purposes, they've been destroyed.'

The man sat motionless. 'The answer's in Zürich,' he said.

'Not yet. You're not ready; you're not strong enough.'

'I will be.'

'Yes, you will.'

The weeks passed; the verbal exercises continued as the pages grew and the man's strength returned. It was mid-morning of the nineteenth week, the day bright, the Mediterranean calm and glistening. As was the man's habit he had run for the past hour along the waterfront and up into the hills; he had stretched the distance to something over twelve miles daily, the pace increasing daily, the rests less frequent. He sat in the chair by the bedroom window, breathing heavily, sweat drenching his undershirt. He had come in through the back door, entering the bedroom from the dark hallway that passed the living-room. It was simply easier; the living-room served as Washburn's waiting area and there were still a few patients with cuts and gashes to be repaired. They were sitting in chairs looking frightened, wondering what *le médecin*'s condition would be that morning. Actually, it wasn't bad. Geoffrey Washburn still drank like a mad Cossack, but these days he stayed on his horse. It was as if a reserve of hope had been found in the recesses of his own destructive fatalism. And the man with no memory understood; that hope was tied to a bank in Zürich's Bahnhofstrasse. Why did the street come so easily to mind?

The bedroom door opened and the doctor burst in, grinning, his white coat stained with his patient's blood.

'I did it!' he said, more triumph in his words than clarification. 'I should open my own hiring hall and live on commissions. It'd be steadier.'

'What are you talking about?'

'As we agreed, it's what you need. You've *got* to function on the outside, and as of two minutes ago Monsieur Jean-Pierre No-Name is gainfully employed! At least for a week.'

'How did you do that? I thought there weren't any openings.'

'What was about to be opened was Claude Lamouche's infected leg. I explained that my supply of local anaesthetic was very, *very* limited. We negotiated; you were the bartered coin.'

'A week?'

'If you're any good, he may keep you on.' Washburn paused. 'Although that's not terribly important, is it?'

'I'm not sure any of this is. A month ago, maybe, but not now. I told you, I'm ready to leave. I'd think you'd want me to. I have an appointment in Zürich.'

'And I'd prefer you function the very best you can at that appointment. My interests are extremely selfish, no remissions permitted.'

'I'm ready.'

'On the surface, yes. But take my word for it, it's vital that you spend prolonged periods of time on the water, some of it at night. Not under controlled conditions, not as a passenger, but subjected to reasonably harsh conditions – the harsher the better, in fact.'

'Another test?'

'Every single one I can devise in this primitive hole of Port Noir. If I could conjure up a storm and a minor shipwreck for you, I would. On the other hand, Lamouche is something of a storm himself; he's a difficult man. The swelling in his leg will go down and he'll resent you. So will others; you'll have to replace someone.'

'Thanks a lot.'

'Don't mention it. We're combining two stresses. At least one or two nights on the water, if Lamouche keeps to schedule – that's the hostile environment which contributed to your hysteria – and exposure to resentment and suspicion from men around you – symbolic of the initial stress situation.'

'Thanks again. Suppose they decide to throw me overboard? That'd be your ultimate test, I suppose, but I don't know how much good it would do if I drowned.'

'Oh, there'll be nothing like that,' said Washburn, scoffing.

'I'm glad you're so confident. I wish I were.'

'You can be. You have the protection of my absence. I may not be Barnard or DeBakey, but I'm all these people have. They need me; they won't risk losing me.'

'But you want to leave. I'm your passport out.'

'In ways unfathomable, my dear patient. Come on, now. Lamouche wants you down at the dock so you can familiarize yourself with his equipment.

You'll be setting out at four o'clock tomorrow morning. Consider how beneficial a week at sea will be. Think of it as a cruise.'

There had never been a cruise like it. The skipper of the filthy, oil-soaked fishing boat was a foul-mouthed rendering of an insignificant Captain Bligh, the crew a quartet of misfits who were undoubtedly the only men on Port Noir willing to put up with Claude Lamouche. The regular fifth member was a brother of the chief netman, a fact impressed on the man called Jean-Pierre within minutes after leaving the harbour at four o'clock in the morning.

'You take food from my brother's table!' whispered the netman angrily between rapid puffs on an immobile cigarette. 'From the stomachs of his children!'

'It's only for a week,' protested Jean-Pierre. It would have been easier – far easier – to offer to reimburse the unemployed brother from Washburn's monthly stipend but the doctor and his patient had agreed to refrain from such compromises.

'I hope you're good with the nets!'

He was not.

There were moments during the next seventy-two hours when the man called Jean-Pierre thought the alternative of financial appeasement was warranted. The harassment never stopped, even at night – especially at night. It was as though eyes were trained on him as he lay on the infested deck mattress, waiting for him to reach the brinks of sleep.

'You! Take the watch! The mate is sick. You fill in.'

'Get up! Philippe is writing his memoirs! He can't be disturbed.'

'On your feet! You tore a net this afternoon. We won't pay for your stupidity. We've all agreed. Mend it now!'

The nets.

If two men were required for one flank, his two arms took the place of four. If he worked beside one man, there were abrupt hauls and releases that left him with the full weight, a sudden blow from an adjacent shoulder sending him crashing into the gunwale and nearly over the side.

And Lamouche. A limping maniac who measured each kilometre of water by the fish he had lost. His voice was a grating, static-prone bullhorn. He addressed no one without an obscenity preceding his name, a habit the patient found increasingly maddening. But Lamouche did not touch Washburn's patient; he was merely sending the doctor a message: *Don't ever do this to me again. Not where my boat and my fish are concerned.*

Lamouche's schedule called for a return to Port Noir at sundown on the third day, the fish to be unloaded, the crew given until four the next morning to sleep, fornicate, get drunk, or, with luck, all three. As they came within sight of land, it happened.

The nets were being doused and folded at midships by the netman and his first assistant. The unwelcome crewman they cursed as *Jean-Pierre Sangsue* scrubbed down the deck with a long-handled brush. The two remaining crew heaved buckets of sea water in front of the brush, more often than not drenching *the leech* with truer aim than the deck.

A bucketful was thrown too high, momentarily blinding Washburn's patient, causing him to lose his balance. The heavy brush with its metal-like bristles flew out of his hands, its head up-ended, the sharp bristles making contact with the kneeling netman's thigh.

'*Sacre diable!*'

'*Je regrette,*' said the offender casually, shaking the water from his eyes.

'The hell you are!'

'I said I was sorry,' replied the man called Jean-Pierre. 'Tell your friends to wet the deck, not me.'

'My friends don't make me the object of their stupidity!'

'They were the cause of mine just now.'

The netman grabbed the handle of the brush, got to his feet, and held it out like a bayonet. 'You want to play, leech?'

'Come on, give it to me.'

'With pleasure, leech. Here!' The netman shoved the brush forward, downward, the bristles scraping the patient's chest and stomach, penetrating the cloth of his shirt.

Whether it was the contact with the scars that covered his previous wounds, or the frustration and anger resulting from three days of harassment, the man would never know. He only knew he had to respond. And his response was as alarming to him as anything he could imagine.

He gripped the handle with his right hand, jamming it back into the netman's stomach, pulling it forward at the instant of impact; simultaneously, he shot his left foot high off the deck, ramming it into the netman's throat.

'*Tao!*' The guttural whisper came from his lips involuntarily; he did not know what it meant.

Before he could understand, he had pivoted, his right foot now surging forward like a battering ram, crashing into the netman's left kidney.

'*Che-sah!*' he whispered.

The netman recoiled, then lunged towards him in pain and fury, his hands outstretched like claws. 'Pig!'

The patient crouched, shooting his right hand up to grip the netman's left forearm, yanking it downwards, then rising, pushing his victim's arm up, twisting it at its highest arc clockwise, yanking again, finally releasing it while jamming his heel into the small of the netman's back. The Frenchman sprawled forward over the nets, his head smashing into the wall of the gunwale.

'*Mee-sah!*' Again he did not know the meaning of his silent cry.

A crewman grabbed his neck from the rear. The patient crashed his left fist into the pelvic area behind him, then bent forward, gripping the elbow to the right of his throat. He lurched to his left; his assailant was lifted off the ground, his legs spiralling in the air as he was thrown across the deck, his face impaled between the wheels of a winch.

The two remaining men were on him, fists and knees pummelling him, as the captain of the fishing boat repeatedly screamed his warnings.

'*Le médecin! Rappelons le médecin! Doucement!*' The doctor! Remember the doctor! Easy!

The words were as misplaced as the captain's appraisal of what he saw. The patient gripped the wrist of one man, bending it down, twisting it counter-clockwise in one violent movement; the man roared in agony. The wrist was broken.

Washburn's patient viced the fingers of his hands together, swinging his arms up like a sledgehammer, catching the crewman with the broken wrist at the midpoint of his throat. The man somersaulted off his feet and collapsed on the deck.

'*Kwa-sah!*' The whisper echoed in the patient's ears.

The fourth man backed away, staring at the maniac who simply looked at him.

It was over. Three of Lamouche's crew were unconscious, severely punished for what they had done. It was doubtful that any would be capable of coming down to the docks at four o'clock in the morning.

Lamouche's words were uttered in equal parts, astonishment and contempt. 'Where you come from I don't know, but you will get off this boat.'

The man with no memory understood the unintentional irony of the captain's words. *I don't know where I came from, either.*

'You can't stay here now,' said Geoffrey Washburn, coming into the darkened bedroom. 'I honestly believed I could prevent any serious assault on you. But I can't protect you when you've done the damage.'

'It was provoked.'

'To the extent it was inflicted? A broken wrist and lacerations requiring sutures on one man's throat and face and another's skull. A severe concussion, and an undetermined injury to a kidney? To say nothing of a blow to the groin that's caused a swelling of the testicles? I believe the word is overkill.'

'It would have been just plain "kill" and I would have been the dead man, if it'd happened any other way.' The patient paused, but spoke again before the doctor could interrupt. 'I think we should talk. Several things happened; other words came to me. We should talk.'

'We should, but we can't. There isn't time. You've got to leave now. I've made arrangements.'

'Now?'

'Yes. I told them you went into the village, probably to get drunk. The families will go looking for you. Every able-bodied brother, cousin and in-law. They'll have knives, hooks, perhaps a gun or two. When they can't find you, they'll come back here. They won't stop until they *do* find you.'

'Because of a fight I didn't *start*?'

'Because you've injured three men who will lose at least a month's wages between them. And something else that's infinitely more important.'

'What's that?'

'The insult. An off-islander proved himself more than a match for not one, but three respected fishermen of Port Noir.'

'*Respected?*'

'In the physical sense. Lamouche's crew is considered the roughest on the waterfront.'

'That's ridiculous.'

'Not to them. It's their honour . . . Now, hurry, get your things together. There's a boat in from Marseilles; the captain's agreed to stow you, and drop you a half-mile offshore north of La Ciotat.'

The man with no memory held his breath. 'Then it's time,' he said quietly.

'It's time,' replied Washburn. 'I think I know what's going through your mind. A sense of helplessness, of drifting without a rudder to put you on a course. I've been your rudder, and I won't be with you; there's nothing I can do about that. But believe me when I tell you, you are *not* helpless. You *will* find your way.'

'To Zürich,' added the patient.

'To Zürich,' agreed the doctor. 'Here. I've wrapped some things together for you in this oilcloth. Strap it around your waist.'

'What is it?'

'All the money I have, some two thousand francs. It's not much, but it will help you get started. And my passport for whatever good it will do. We're about the same age and it's eight years old; people change. Don't let anyone study it. It's merely an official paper.'

'What will you do?'

'I won't ever need it if I don't hear from you.'

'You're a decent man.'

'I think you are, too . . . As I've known you. But then I didn't know you before. So I can't vouch for that man. I wish I could, but there's no way I can.'

The man leaned against the railing, watching the lights of Île de Port Noir recede in the distance. The fishing boat was heading into darkness, as he had plunged into darkness nearly five months ago.

As he was plunging into another darkness now.

3

There were no lights on the coast of France, only the wash of the dying moon outlined the rocky shore. They were two hundred yards from land, the fishing boat bobbing gently in the cross-currents of the inlet. The captain pointed over the side.

'There's a small stretch of beach between those two clusters of rock. It's not much, but you'll reach it if you swim to the right. We can drift in another thirty, forty feet, no more than that. Only a minute or two.'

'You're doing more than I expected. I thank you for that.'

'No need to. I pay my debts.'

'And I'm one?'

'Very much so. The doctor in Port Noir sewed up three of my crew after that madness five months ago. You weren't the only one brought in, you know.'

'The storm? You know me?'

'You were chalk white on the table, but I don't know you and I don't want to know you. I had no money then, no catch; the doctor said I could pay when my circumstances were better. You're my payment.'

'I need papers,' said the man, sensing a source of help. 'I need a passport altered.'

'Why speak to me?' asked the captain. 'I said I would put a package over the side north of La Ciotat. That's all I said.'

'You wouldn't have said that if you weren't capable of other things.'

'I will *not* take you into Marseilles. I will *not* risk the patrol boats. The Sûreté has squadrons all over the harbour, the narcotics teams are maniacs. You pay *them* or you pay twenty years in a cell!'

'Which means I can get papers in Marseilles. And you can help me.'

'I did not say that.'

'Yes, you did. I need a service and that service can be found in a place where you won't take me – still the service is there. You said it.'

'Said what?'

'That you'll talk to me in Marseilles – if I can get there without you. Just tell me where.'

The skipper of the fishing boat studied the patient's face, the decision was not made lightly, but it was made. 'There's a café on rue Sarasin, south of Old Harbour. *Le Bouc de Mer*. I'll be there tonight between nine and eleven. You'll need money, some of it in advance.'

'How much?'

'That's between you and the man you speak with.'

'I've got to have an idea.'

'It's cheaper if you have a document to work with; otherwise one has to be stolen.'

'I told you. I've got one.'

The captain shrugged. 'Fifteen hundred, two thousand francs. Are we wasting time?'

The patient thought of the oil-cloth packet strapped to his waist. Bankruptcy lay in Marseilles, but so did an altered passport, a passport to Zürich. 'I'll handle it,' he said, not knowing why he sounded so confident. 'Tonight, then.'

The captain peered at the dimly lit shoreline. 'This is as far as we can drift. You're on your own now. Remember, if we don't meet in Marseilles, you've never seen me and I've never seen you. None of my crew has seen you, either.'

'I'll be there. *Le Bouc de Mer*, rue Sarasin, south of Old Harbour.'

'In God's hands,' said the skipper, signalling a crewman at the wheel; the engines rumbled beneath the boat. 'By the way, the clientele at *Le Bouc* are not used to the Parisian dialect. I'd rough it up if I were you.'

'Thanks for the advice,' said the patient as he swung his legs over the gunwale and lowered himself into the water. He held his knapsack above the surface, legs scissoring to stay afloat. 'See you tonight,' he added in a louder voice, looking up at the black hull of the fishing boat.

There was no one there; the captain had left the railing. The only sounds were the slapping of the waves against the wood and the muffled acceleration of the engines.

You're on your own now.

He shivered and spun in the cold water, angling his body towards the shore, remembering to sidestroke to his right, to head for a cluster of rocks on the right. If the captain knew what he was talking about, the current would take him into the unseen beach.

It did; he could feel the undertow pulling his bare feet into the sand, making the last thirty yards the most difficult to cross. But the canvas knapsack was relatively dry, still held above the breaking waves.

Minutes later he was sitting on a dune of wild grass, the tall reeds bending with the offshore breezes, the first rays of morning intruding on the night sky. The sun would be up in an hour; he would have to move with it.

He opened the knapsack and took out a pair of boots and heavy socks along with rolled-up trousers and a coarse denim shirt. Somewhere in his past he had learned to pack with an economy of space; the knapsack contained far more than an observer might think. Where had he learned that? Why? The questions never stopped.

He got up and took off the British walking shorts he had accepted from Washburn. He stretched them across the reeds of grass to dry; he could discard nothing. He removed his undershirt and did the same.

Standing there naked on the dune he felt an odd sense of exhilaration mingled with a hollow pain in the middle of his stomach. The pain was fear, he knew that. He understood the exhilaration, too.

He had passed his first test. He had trusted an instinct – perhaps a compulsion – and had known what to say and how to respond. An hour ago he was without an immediate destination, knowing only that Zürich was his objective, but knowing, too, that there were borders to cross, official eyes to satisfy. The eight-year-old passport was so obviously not his own that even the dullest immigration clerk would spot the fact. And even if he managed to cross into Switzerland with it, he had to get out; with each move the odds of his being detained were multiplied. He could not permit that. Not now; not until he knew more. The answers were in Zürich, he had to travel freely, and he had homed in on a captain of a fishing boat to make that possible.

You are not *helpless. You* will *find your way.*

Before the day was over he would make a connection to have Washburn's passport altered by a professional, transformed into a licence to travel. It was the first concrete step, but before it was taken there was the consideration of money. The two thousand francs the doctor had given him were inadequate, they might not even be enough for the passport itself. What good was a licence to travel without the means to do so? Money. He had to get money. He had to think about that.

He shook out the clothes he had taken from the knapsack, put them on, and shoved his feet into the boots. Then he lay down on the sand, staring at the sky, which progressively grew brighter. The day was being born and so was he.

He walked the narrow stone streets of La Ciotat, going into the shops as much to converse with the clerks as anything else. It was an odd sensation to be part of the human traffic, not an unknown derelict dragged from the sea. He remembered the captain's advice and gutturalized his French, allowing him to be accepted as an unremarkable stranger passing through town.

Money.

There was a section of La Ciotat that apparently catered to a wealthy clientele. The shops were cleaner and the merchandise more expensive, the fish fresher and the meat several cuts above that in the main shopping area. Even the vegetables glistened; many exotic, imported from Northern Africa and the Middle East. The area held a touch of Paris or Nice set down on the fringes of a routinely middle-class coastal community. A small café, its entrance at the end of a flagstone path, stood separated from the shops on either side by a manicured lawn.

Money.

He walked into a butcher's shop, aware that the owner's appraisal of him was not positive, nor the glance friendly. The man was waiting on a middle-aged couple, who from their speech and manner were domestic servants at an outlying estate. They were precise, curt and demanding.

'The veal last week was barely passable,' said the woman. 'Do better this time, or I'll be forced to order from Marseilles.'

'And the other evening,' added the man, 'the Marquis mentioned to me that the lamb chops were much too thin. I repeat, a full three centimetres.'

The owner sighed and shrugged, uttering obsequious phrases of apology and assurance. The woman turned to her escort, her voice no less commanding than it was to the butcher.

'Wait for the packages and put them in the car. I'll be at the grocer's; meet me there.'

'Of course, my dear.'

The woman left, a pigeon in search of further seeds of conflict. The moment she was out the door her husband turned to the shopowner, his demeanour entirely different. Gone was the arrogance; a grin appeared.

'Just your average day, eh, Marcel?' he said, taking a packet of cigarettes from his pocket.

'Seen better, seen worse. Were the chops really too thin?'

'My God, no. When was *he* last able to tell? But she feels better if I complain, you know that.'

'Where is the Marquis of the Dungheap now?'

'Drunk next door, waiting for the whore from Toulon. I'll come down later this afternoon, pick him up and sneak him past the Marquise into the stables. He won't be able to drive his car by then. He uses Jean-Pierre's room above the kitchen, you know.'

'I've heard.'

At the mention of the name Jean-Pierre, Washburn's patient turned from the display case of poultry. It was an automatic reflex, but the movement only served to remind the butcher of his presence.

'What is it? What do you want?'

It was time to degutturalize his French. 'You were recommended by friends in Nice,' said the patient, his accent more befitting the *Quai d'Orsay* than *Le Bouc de Mer*.

'Oh?' The shopowner made an immediate reappraisal. Among his clientele, especially the younger ones, there were those who preferred to dress in opposition to their status. The common Basque shirt was even fashionable these days. 'You're new here, sir?'

'My boat's in for repairs; we won't be able to reach Marseilles this afternoon.'

'May I be of service?'

The patient laughed. 'You may be to the chef; I wouldn't dare presume. He'll be around later and I do have some influence.'

The butcher and his friend laughed. 'I would think so, sir,' said the shopowner.

'I'll need a dozen ducklings and, say, eighteen chateaubriands.'

'Of course.'

'Good. I'll send our master of the galley directly to you.' The patient turned to the middle-aged man. 'By the way, I couldn't help overhearing . . . no, please don't be concerned. The Marquis wouldn't be that jackass d'Ambois, would he? I think someone told me he lived around here.'

'Oh no, sir,' replied the servant. 'I don't know the Marquis d'Ambois. I was referring to the Marquis de Chambord. A fine gentleman, sir, but he has problems. A difficult marriage, sir. Very difficult, it's no secret.'

'Chambord? Yes, I think we've met. Rather short fellow, isn't he?'

'No, sir. Quite tall, actually. About your size, I'd say.'

'Really?'

The patient learned the various entrances and inside staircases of the two-storey café quickly – a produce delivery man from Roquevaire unsure of his new route. There were two sets of steps that led to the first floor, one from the kitchen, the other just beyond the front entrance in the small foyer; this was the staircase used by patrons going to the upstairs washrooms. There was also a window through which an interested party outside could see anyone who used this particular staircase, and the patient was sure that if he waited long enough he would see two people doing so. They would undoubtedly go up separately, neither heading for a washroom but, instead, to a bedroom above the kitchen. The patient wondered which of the expensive cars parked on the quiet streets belonged to the Marquis de Chambord. Whichever, the middle-aged manservant in the butcher's shop need not be concerned; his employer would not be driving it.

Money.

The woman arrived shortly before one o'clock. She was a windswept blonde, her large breasts stretching the blue silk of her blouse, her long legs tanned, striding gracefully above spiked heels, thighs and fluid hips outlined beneath the tight-fitting white skirt. Chambord might have problems but he also had taste.

Twenty minutes later he could see the white skirt through the window; the girl was heading upstairs. Less than sixty seconds later another figure filled the window frame; dark trousers and a blazer beneath a white face cautiously lurched up the staircase. The patient counted off the minutes; he hoped the Marquis de Chambord owned a watch.

Carrying his canvas knapsack as unobtrusively as possible by the straps, the patient walked down the flagstone path to the entrance of the restaurant. Inside, he turned left in the foyer, excusing himself past an elderly man trudging up the staircase, reached the first floor and turned left again down a long corridor that led towards the rear of the building, above the kitchen. He passed the washrooms and came to a closed door at the end of the narrow hallway where he stood motionless, his back pressed into the wall. He turned his head and waited for the elderly man to reach the washroom door and push it open while unzipping his trousers.

The patient – instinctively, without thinking, really – raised the soft knapsack and placed it against the centre of the door panel. He held it securely in place with his outstretched arms, stepped back and, in one swift movement, crashed his left shoulder into the canvas, dropping his right hand as the door sprang open, gripping the edge before the door could smash into a wall. No one below in the restaurant could have heard the muted forced entry.

'*Nom de Dieu!*'

'*Mère de Christ!*'

'*Qui est là? . . .*'

'*Silence!*'

The Marquis de Chambord spun off the naked body of the blonde woman, sprawling over the edge of the bed onto the floor. He was a sight from a comic opera, still wearing his starched shirt, the tie knotted in place, and on his feet black silk, knee-length socks; but that was all he wore. The woman grabbed the covers, doing her best to lessen the indelicacy of the moment.

The patient issued his commands swiftly. 'Don't raise your voices. No one will be hurt if you do exactly as I say.'

'My wife hired you!' cried Chambord, his words slurred, his eyes barely in focus. 'I'll pay you more!'

'That's a beginning,' answered Dr Washburn's patient. 'Take off your shirt and tie. Also the socks.' He saw the glistening gold band around the Marquis's wrist. 'And the watch.'

Several minutes later the transformation was complete. The Marquis's clothes were not a perfect fit, but no one could deny the quality of the cloth or the original tailoring. Also, the watch was a Gérard-Perrégaux, and Chambord's wallet contained over thirteen thousand francs. The car keys were also impressive; they were set in monogrammed heads of sterling silver with the familiar big cat device.

'For the love of God, give me your clothes!' said the Marquis, the implausibility of his predicament penetrating the haze of alcohol.

'I'm sorry, but I can't do that,' replied the intruder, gathering up both his own clothes and those of the blonde woman.

'You can't take *mine*!' she yelled.

'I told you to keep your voices down.'

'All right, all *right*,' she continued, 'but you *can't* . . .'

'Yes, I can.' The patient looked around the room; there was a telephone on a desk by a window. He crossed to it and yanked the cord out of the socket. 'Now no one will disturb you,' he added, picking up the knapsack.

'You won't go free, you know!' snapped Chambord. 'You won't get away with this! The police will find you!'

'The police?' asked the intruder. 'Do you really think you should call the police? A formal report will have to be made, the circumstances described. I'm not so sure that's such a good idea. I think you'd be better off waiting for that fellow to pick you up later this afternoon. I heard him say he was going to get you past the Marquise into the stables. All things considered, I honestly believe that's what you should do. I'm sure you can come up with a better story than what really happened here. I won't contradict you.'

The unknown thief left the room, closing the damaged door behind him.

You are not *helpless. You will* find your way.

So far he had and it was a little frightening. What had Washburn said? That his skills and talents would come back . . . *but I don't think you'll ever be able to relate them to anything in your past.* The past. What kind of past was it that produced the skills he had displayed during the past twenty-four hours? Where had he learned to maim and cripple with lunging feet, and fingers entwined into hammers? How did he know precisely where to deliver the blows? Who had taught him to play upon the criminal mind, provoking and evoking a reluctant commitment? How did he zero in so quickly on mere implications, convinced beyond doubt that his instincts were right? Where had he learned to discern instant extortion in a casual conversation overheard in a butcher's shop? More to the point, perhaps, was the simple decision to carry out the crime. My God, how *could* he?

The more you fight it, the more you crucify yourself, the worse it will be.

He concentrated on the road and on the mahogany dashboard of the Marquis de Chambord's Jaguar. The array of instruments were not familiar; his past did not include extensive experience with such cars. He supposed that told him something.

In less than an hour he crossed a bridge over a wide canal and knew he had reached Marseilles. Small square houses of stone, angling like blocks up from the water; narrow streets and walls everywhere – the outskirts of the old harbour. He knew it all, and yet he did not know it. High in the distance, silhouetted on one of the surrounding hills, were the outlines of a huge cathedral, a statue of the Virgin seen clearly atop its steeple. *Notre-Dame de la Garde.* The name came to him; he had seen it before – and yet he had not seen it.

Oh, Christ! *Stop it!*

Within minutes he was in the pulsing centre of the city, driving along the crowded rue Cannebière, with its proliferation of expensive shops, the rays of the afternoon sun bouncing off expanses of tinted glass on either side, and on either side enormous pavement cafés. He turned left, towards the harbour, passing warehouses and small factories and fenced-off areas that contained cars prepared for transport north to the showrooms of Saint-Étienne, Lyons and Paris. And to points south across the Mediterranean.

Instinct. Follow instinct. For nothing could be disregarded. Every resource had an immediate use; there was value in a rock if it could be thrown, or a vehicle if someone wanted it. He chose a lot where the cars were both new and used, but all expensive; he parked at the kerb and got out. Beyond the fence was a small cavern of a garage, mechanics in overalls laconically wandering about carrying tools. He walked casually around inside until he spotted a man in a thin pin-striped suit whom instinct told him to approach.

It took less than ten minutes, explanations kept to a minimum, a Jaguar's disappearance to North Africa guaranteed, with the filing of engine numbers.

The silver monogrammed keys were exchanged for six thousand francs, roughly one-fifth the value of Chambord's car. Then Dr Washburn's patient found a taxi and asked to be taken to a pawnbroker – but not an establishment that asked too many questions. The message was clear; this was Marseilles. And half an hour later the gold Gérard-Perrégaux was no longer on his wrist, having been replaced by a Seiko chronograph and eight hundred francs. Everything had a value in relationship to its practicality; the chronograph was shockproof.

The next stop was a medium-sized department store in the south-east section of rue Cannebière. Clothes were chosen off the racks and shelves, paid for and worn out of the fitting rooms, an ill-fitting dark blazer and trousers left behind.

From a display on the floor, he selected a soft leather suitcase; additional garments were placed inside with the knapsack. The patient glanced at his new watch; it was nearly five o'clock, time to find a comfortable hotel. He had not really slept for several days; he needed to rest before his appointment in the rue Sarasin, at a café called *Le Bouc de Mer*, where arrangements could be made for a more important appointment in Zürich.

He lay back on the bed and stared at the ceiling, the wash of the streetlamps below causing irregular patterns of light to dance across the smooth white surface. Night had come rapidly to Marseilles, and with its arrival a certain sense of freedom came to the patient. It was as if the darkness were a gigantic blanket, blocking out the harsh glare of daylight that revealed too much too quickly. He was learning something else about himself: he was more comfortable in the night. Like a half-starved cat he would forage better in the darkness. Yet there was a contradiction, and he recognized that, too. During the months in Île de Port Noir, he had craved the sunlight, hungered for it, waited for it each dawn, wishing only for the darkness to go away.

Things were happening to him; he was changing.

Things *had* happened. Events that gave a certain lie to the concept of foraging more successfully at night. Twelve hours ago he was on a fishing boat in the Mediterranean, an objective in mind and two thousand francs strapped to his waist. Two thousand francs, something less than five hundred American dollars according to the daily rate of exchange posted in the hotel lobby. Now he was outfitted with several sets of acceptable clothing and lying on a bed in a reasonably expensive hotel with something over twenty-three thousand francs in a Louis Vuitton wallet belonging to the Marquis de Chambord. Twenty-three thousand francs . . . nearly six thousand American dollars.

Where had he come from that he was able to do the things he did?

Stop it!

The rue Sarasin was so ancient that in another city it might have been considered a landmark, a wide brick alley connecting streets built centuries later. But this was Marseilles; ancient co-existed with old, both uncomfortable with the new. The rue Sarasin was no more than two hundred yards long, frozen in time between the stone walls of waterfront buildings, devoid of streetlights, trapping the mists that rolled off the harbour. It was a back street conducive to brief meetings between men who did not care for their conferences to be observed.

The only light and sound came from *Le Bouc de Mer*. The café was situated roughly in the centre of the alley, its premises once a nineteenth-century office building. A number of cubicles had been taken down to allow for a large bar-room and tables; an equal number were left standing for less public appointments. These were the waterfront's answer to those private rooms found at restaurants along La Cannebière, and, as befitting their status, there were curtains, but no doors.

The patient made his way between the crowded tables, cutting his way through the layers of smoke, excusing himself past lurching fishermen and drunken soldiers and red-faced whores looking for beds to rest in as well as a few francs. He peered into a succession of cubicles, a crewman looking for his companions – until he found the captain of the fishing boat. There was another man at the table. Thin, pale-faced, narrow eyes peering up like a curious ferret's.

'Sit down,' said the dour skipper. 'I thought you'd be here before this.'

'You said between nine and eleven. It's quarter to eleven.'

'You stretch the time, you can pay for the whisky.'

'Be glad to. Order something decent, if they've got it.'

The thin, pale-faced man smiled. Things were going to be all right.

They were. The passport in question was, naturally, one of the most difficult in the world to tamper with, but with great care, equipment and artistry, it could be done.

'How much?'

'These skills – and equipment – do not come cheap. Twenty-five hundred francs.'

'When can I have it?'

'The care, the artistry, they take time. Three or four days. And that's putting the artist under great pressure; he'll scream at me.'

'There's an additional one thousand francs if I can have it tomorrow.'

'By ten in the morning,' said the pale-faced man quickly. 'I'll take the abuse.'

'And the thousand,' interrupted the scowling captain. 'What did you bring out of Port Noir? Diamonds?'

'Talent,' answered the patient, meaning it but not understanding it.

'I'll need a photograph,' said the connection.

'I stopped at an arcade and had this made,' replied the patient, taking a small square photograph out of his shirt pocket. 'With all that expensive equipment I'm sure you can sharpen it up.'

'Nice clothes,' said the captain, passing the print to the pale-faced man.

'Well tailored,' agreed the patient.

The location of the morning rendezvous was agreed upon, the drinks paid for, and the captain slipped five hundred francs under the table. The conference was over; the buyer left the cubicle and started across the crowded, raucous, smoke-layered bar-room towards the door.

It happened so rapidly, so suddenly, so completely unexpectedly, there was no time to think. Only *react.*

The collision was abrupt, casual, but the eyes that stared at him were not casual; they seemed to burst out of their sockets, widening in disbelief, on the edge of hysteria.

'No! Oh my God, *no*! It *cannot* . . .' The man spun in the crowd; the patient lurched forward, clamping his hand down on the man's shoulder.

'Wait a minute!'

The man spun again, thrusting the V of his outstretched thumb and fingers up onto the patient's wrist, forcing the hand away. '*You*! You're *dead*! You could not have *lived*!'

'I lived. What do you *know*?'

The face was now contorted, a mass of twisted fury, the eyes squinting, the mouth open, sucking air, baring yellow teeth that took on the appearance of an animal's teeth. Suddenly, the man pulled out a knife, the snap of its recessed blade heard through the surrounding din. The arm shot forward, the blade an extension of the hand that gripped it, both surging in towards the patient's stomach. 'I know I'll finish it!' whispered the man.

The patient swung his right forearm down, a pendulum sweeping aside all objects in front of it. He pivoted, lashing his left foot up, his heel plunging into his attacker's pelvic bone.

'*Che-sah.*' The echo in his ears was deafening.

The man lurched backwards into a trio of drinkers as the knife fell to the floor. The weapon was seen; shouts followed, men converged, fists and hands separating the combatants.

'Get out of here!'

'Take your argument somewhere else!'

'We don't want the police in here, you drunken bastards!'

The angry coarse dialects of Marseilles rose over the cacophonic sounds of *Le Bouc de Mer*. The patient was hemmed in; he watched as his would-be killer threaded his way through the crowd, holding his groin, forcing a path to the entrance. The heavy door swung open, the man raced into the darkness of rue Sarasin.

Someone who thought he was dead – wanted him dead – knew he was alive.

4

The economy class section of Air France's Caravelle to Zürich was filled to capacity, the narrow seats made more uncomfortable by the turbulence that buffeted the plane. A baby was screaming in its mother's arms; other children whimpered, swallowing cries of fear as parents smiled with tentative reassurances they did not feel. Most of the remaining passengers were silent, a few drinking their whisky more rapidly than obviously was normal. Fewer still were forcing laughter from tight throats, false bravado that emphasized their insecurity rather than disguising it. A terrible flight was many things to many people, but none escaped the essential thoughts of terror: encased in a metal tube thirty thousand feet above the ground, he was vulnerable. With one elongated, screaming dive he could be plummeting downwards into the earth. And there were fundamental questions that accompanied the essential terror. What thoughts would go through one's mind at such a time? How would one react?

The patient tried to find out; it was important to him. He sat next to the window, his eyes on the aircraft's wing, watching the broad expanse of metal bend and vibrate under the brutalizing impact of the winds. The currents were clashing against one another, pounding the man-made tube into a kind of submission, warning the microscopic pretenders that they were no match for the vast infirmities of nature. One ounce of pressure beyond the flex-tolerance and the wing would crack, the lift-sustaining limb torn from its tubular body, shredded into the winds; one burst of rivets and there would be an explosion, the screaming plunge to follow.

What would he do? What would he think? Other than the uncontrollable fear of dying and oblivion, would there be anything else? That's what he had to concentrate on; that was the *projection* Washburn kept emphasizing in Port Noir. The doctor's words came back to him.

Whenever you observe a stress situation – and you have the time – do your damnedest to project yourself into it. Associate as freely as you can, let words and images fill your mind. In them you may find clues.

The patient continued to stare out of the window, consciously trying to raise his unconscious, fixing his eyes on the natural violence beyond the glass, distilling the movement, silently doing his 'damnedest' to let his reactions give rise to words and images.

They came – slowly. There was the darkness again, and the sound of rushing wind, ear-shattering, continuous, growing in volume until he thought his head would burst. His head . . . The winds were lashing the left side of his head and face, burning his skin, forcing him to raise his left shoulder for protection . . . Left shoulder. Left *arm.* His arm was raised, the gloved fingers of his left hand gripping a straight edge of metal, his right holding a . . . a strap; he was holding onto a strap, waiting for something. A signal . . . a flashing light or a tap on the shoulder, or both. A signal. It *came.* He plunged. Into the darkness, into the void, his body tumbling, twisting, swept away into the night sky. He had . . . parachuted!

'*Êtes-vous malade?*'

His insane reverie was broken; the nervous passenger next to him had touched his left arm – which was raised, the fingers of his hand spread, as if resisting, rigid in their locked position. Across his chest his right forearm was pressed into the cloth of his jacket, his right hand gripping the lapel, bunching the fabric. And on his forehead were rivulets of sweat; it had happened. The something-else had come briefly – insanely – into focus.

'*Pardon,*' he said, lowering his arms. '*Un réve,*' he added meaninglessly.

There was a break in the weather, the Caravelle stabilized. The smiles on the harried stewardesses' faces became genuine again; full service was resumed as embarrassed passengers glanced at one another.

The patient observed his surroundings but reached no conclusions. He was consumed by the images and the sounds that had been so clearly defined in his mind's eye and ear. He had hurled himself from a plane . . . at night . . . signals and metal and straps intrinsic to his leap. He *had* parachuted. *Where? Why?*

Stop crucifying yourself!

If for no other reason than to take his thoughts away from the madness, he reached into his breast pocket, pulled out the altered passport and opened it. As might be expected the name *Washburn* had been retained; it was common enough and its owner had explained that there were no flags out for it. The *Geoffrey R.*, however, had been changed to *George P.*, the eliminations and space-line blockage expertly accomplished. The photographic insertion was expert, too; it no longer resembled a cheap print from a machine in an amusement arcade.

The identification numbers, of course, were entirely different, guaranteed not to cause an alarm in an immigration computer. At least, up until the moment the bearer submitted the passport for its first inspection; from that time on it was the buyer's responsibility. One paid as much for this guarantee as for the artistry and the equipment, for it required connections within Interpol and the immigration clearing houses. Customs officials, computer specialists and clerks throughout the European border networks were paid on a regular basis for this vital information, they rarely made mistakes. If and when they did, the loss of an eye or an arm was not out of the question, such were the brokers of false papers.

George P. Washburn. He was not comfortable with the name; the owner of the unaltered original had instructed him too well in the basics of projection and association. *George P.* was a side-step from *Geoffrey R.*, a man who had been eaten away by a compulsion that had its roots in escape – escape from identity. That was the last thing the patient wanted; he wanted more than his *life* to know who he was.

Or did he?

No matter. The answer was in Zürich. In Zürich there was . . .

'*Mesdames et messieurs. Nous commençons notre descente vers l'aéroport de Zürich.*'

He knew the name of the hotel. *Carillon du Lac.* He had given it to the taxi driver without thinking. Had he read it somewhere? Had the name been one of those listed in the Welcome-to-Zürich folders placed in the elasticized pockets in front of his seat in the plane?

No. He knew the lobby; the heavy, dark, polished wood was familiar . . . somehow. And the huge plate-glass windows that looked out over Lake Zürich. He had been here *before*; he had stood where he was standing now – in front of the marble-topped counter – a long time ago.

It was all confirmed by the words spoken by the clerk behind the desk. They had the impact of an explosion.

'It's good to see you again, sir. It's been quite a while since your last visit.'

Has it? How long? Why don't you call me by my name? For God's sake. I don't know you! I don't know me! Help me! Please, help me!

'I guess it has,' he said. 'Do me a favour, will you? I sprained my hand; it's difficult to write. Could you fill in the registration and I'll do my damnedest to sign it?' The patient held his breath. Suppose the polite man behind the counter asked him to repeat his name, or the spelling of his name?

'Of course.' The clerk turned the card around and wrote. 'Would you care to see the hotel doctor?'

'Later, perhaps. Not now.' The clerk continued writing, then lifted up the card, reversing it for the guest's signature.

Mr J. Bourne. New York, NY, USA.

He stared at it, transfixed, mesmerized by the letters. He had a name – part of a name. And a country as well as a city of residence.

J. Bourne. *John? James? Joseph?* What did the *J* stand for?

'Is something wrong, Herr Bourne?' asked the clerk.

'Wrong? No, not at all.' He picked up the pen, remembering to feign discomfort. Would he be expected to write out a first name? No; he would sign exactly as the clerk had printed.

J. Bourne.

He wrote the name as naturally as he could, letting his mind fall free, allowing whatever thoughts or images that might be triggered come through. None did; he was merely signing an unfamiliar name. He felt nothing.

'You had me worried, mein Herr,' said the clerk. 'I thought perhaps I'd made a mistake. It's been a busy week, a busier day. But then, I was quite certain.'

And if he had? Made a mistake? Mr J. Bourne of New York City, USA did not care to think about the possibility. 'It never occurred to me to question your memory . . . Herr Strossel,' replied the patient, glancing up at the

On-Duty sign on the left wall of the counter; the man behind the desk was the Carillon du Lac's assistant *Leiter.*

'You're most kind.' The assistant manager leaned forward. 'I assume you'll require the usual conditions of your stay with us?'

'Some may have changed,' said J. Bourne. 'How did you understand them before?'

'Whoever telephones or inquires at the desk is to be told you're out of the hotel, whereupon you're to be informed immediately. The only exception is your firm in New York. The Treadstone Seventy-one Corporation, if I remember correctly.'

Another name! One he could trace with an overseas call. Fragmentary shapes were falling into place. The exhilaration began to return.

'That'll do. I won't forget your efficiency.'

'This is Zürich,' replied the polite man, shrugging. 'You've always been exceedingly generous, Herr Bourne. *Vorwärts! Schnell!*'

As the patient followed the bell boy into the elevator, several things were clearer. He had a name and he understood why that name came so quickly to the Carillon du Lac's assistant manager. He had a country and a city and a firm that employed him – *had* employed him, at any rate. And whenever he came to Zürich certain precautions were implemented to protect him from unexpected, or unwanted visitors. That was what he could not understand. One either protected oneself thoroughly or one did not bother to protect oneself at all. Where was any real advantage in a screening process that was so loose, so vulnerable to penetration? It struck him as second-rate, without value, as if a small child were playing hide-and-seek. *Where am I? Try and find me. I'll say something out loud and give you a hint.*

It was not professional, and if he had learned anything about himself during the past forty-eight hours it was that he *was* a professional. Of what he had no idea, but the status was not debatable.

The voice of the New York operator faded sporadically over the line. Her conclusion, however, was irritatingly clear. And final.

'There's no listing for any such company, sir. I've checked the latest directories as well as the private telephones and there's no Treadstone Corporation – and nothing even resembling Treadstone with numbers following the name.'

'Perhaps they were dropped to shorten . . .'

'There's *no* firm or company with that name, sir. I repeat, if you have a first or second name, or the type of business the firm's engaged in, I might be of further help.'

'I don't. Only the name, Treadstone Seventy-one, New York City.'

'It's an odd name, sir. I'm sure if there were a listing it would be a simple matter to find it. I'm sorry.'

'Thanks very much for your trouble,' said J. Bourne, replacing the phone. It was pointless to go on; the name was a code of some sort, words relayed by a caller that gained him immediate access to a hotel guest not so readily accessible. And the words could be used by anyone regardless of where he had placed the call; therefore the location of New York might well be meaningless. According to an operator five thousand miles away it was.

The patient walked to the bureau where he had placed the Louis Vuitton wallet and the Seiko chronograph. He put the wallet in his pocket and the watch on his wrist; he looked in the mirror and spoke quietly.

'You are J. Bourne, citizen of the United States, resident of New York City, and it's entirely possible that the numbers "zero–seven—seventeen–twelve—zero–fourteen—twenty-six–zero" are the most important things in your life.'

The sun was bright, filtering through the trees along the elegant Bahnhofstrasse, bouncing off the windows of the shops and creating blocks of shadows where the great banks intruded on its rays. It was a street where solidity and money, security and arrogance, determination and a touch of frivolity all coexisted; and Dr Washburn's patient had walked along its pavements before.

He strolled into the Bürkliplatz, the square that overlooked the Zürichsee, with its numerous quays along the waterfront bordered by gardens that in the heat of summer became circles of bursting flowers. He could picture them in his mind's eye; images were coming to him. But no thoughts, no memories.

He doubled back into the Bahnhofstrasse, instinctively knowing that the Gemeinschaft Bank was a nearby building of off-white stone; it had been on the opposite side of the street on which he had just walked; he had passed it deliberately. He approached the heavy glass doors and pushed the centre plate forward. The right-hand door swung open easily and he was standing on a floor of brown marble; he had stood on it before, but the image was not as strong as others. He had the uncomfortable feeling that the Gemeinschaft was to be avoided.

It was not to be avoided now.

'*Puis-je vous aider, monsieur?*' The man asking the question was dressed in a cutaway, the red *boutonnière* his symbol of authority. The use of French was explained by the client's clothes; even the subordinate gnomes of Zürich were observant.

'I have personal and confidential business to discuss,' replied J. Bourne in English, once again mildly startled by the words he spoke so naturally. The reason for the English was twofold: he wanted to watch the gnome's expression at his error, and he wanted no possible misinterpretation of anything said during the next hour.

'Pardon, sir,' said the man, his eyebrows arched slightly, studying the client's topcoat. 'The lift to your left, first floor. The receptionist will assist you.'

The receptionist referred to was a middle-aged man with close-cropped hair and tortoiseshell glasses; his expression was set, his eyes rigidly curious. 'Do you currently have personal and confidential business with us, sir?' he asked, repeating the new arrival's words.

'I do.'

'Your signature, please,' said the official, holding out a sheet of Gemeinschaft stationery with two blank lines centred in the middle of the page.

The client understood; no name was required. *The hand-written numbers take the place of a name . . . they constitute the signature of the account holder. Standard procedure.* Washburn.

The patient wrote out the numbers, relaxing his hand so the writing would be free. He handed the stationery back to the receptionist, who studied it, rose from the chair and gestured to a row of narrow doors with frosted glass panels. 'If you'll wait in the fourth room, sir, someone will be with you shortly.'

'The fourth room?'

'The fourth door from the left. It will lock automatically.'

'Is that necessary?'

The receptionist glanced at him, startled. 'It is in line with your own request, sir,' he said politely, an undertone of surprise beneath his courtesy. 'This is a three-zero account. It's customary at the Gemeinschaft for holders of such accounts to telephone in advance so that a private entrance can be made available.'

'I know that,' lied Washburn's patient with a casualness he did not feel. 'It's just that I'm in a hurry.'

'I'll convey that to Verifications, sir.'

'Verifications?' Mr J. Bourne of New York City, USA, could not help himself; the word had the sound of an alarm.

'Signature Verifications, sir.' The man adjusted his glasses; the movement covered his taking a step nearer his desk, his lower hand inches from a console. 'I suggest you wait in Room Four, sir.' The suggestion was not a request; it was an order, the command in the praetorian's eyes.

'Why not? Just tell them to hurry, will you?' The patient crossed to the fourth door, opened it and walked inside. The door closed automatically; he could hear the click of the lock. J. Bourne looked at the frosted panel; it was no simple pane of glass, for there was a network of thin wires webbed beneath the surface. Undoubtedly if cracked, an alarm would be triggered; he was in a cell, waiting to be summoned.

The rest of the small room was panelled and furnished tastefully, two leather armchairs next to each other opposite a miniature couch flanked by antique tables. At the far end was a second door, startling in its contrast; it was made of grey steel. Up-to-date magazines and newspapers in three languages were on the tables. The patient sat down and picked up the Paris edition of the *Herald-Tribune.* He read the printed words but absorbed nothing. The summons would come any moment now; his mind was consumed by thoughts of manoeuvre. Manoeuvre without memory, only by instinct.

Finally, the steel door opened, revealing a tall slender man with aquiline features and meticulously groomed grey hair. His face was patrician, eager to serve an equal who needed his expertise. He extended his hand, his English refined, mellifluous under his Swiss intonation.

'So very pleased to meet you. Forgive the delay; it was rather humorous, in fact.'

'In what way?'

'I'm afraid you rather startled Herr Koenig. It's not often a three-zero account arrives without prior notice. He's quite set in his ways, you know; the unusual ruins his day. On the other hand, it generally makes mine more pleasant. I'm Walther Apfel. Please, come in.'

The bank officer released the patient's hand and gestured towards the steel door. The room beyond was a V-shaped extension of the cell. Dark panelling, heavy comfortable furniture and a wide desk, that stood in front of a wider window overlooking the Bahnhofstrasse.

'I'm sorry I upset him,' said J. Bourne. 'It's just that I have very little time.'

'Yes, he relayed that.' Apfel walked around the desk, nodding at the leather armchair in front. 'Do sit down. One or two formalities and we can discuss the business at hand.' Both men sat; the instant they did so the bank officer picked up a white clipboard and leaned across his desk, handing it to the Gemeinschaft client. Secured in place was another sheet of stationery, but instead of two blank lines there were ten, starting below the letterhead and extending to within an inch of the bottom border. 'Your signature, please. A minimum of five will be sufficient.'

'I don't understand. I just did this.'

'And very successfully. Verification confirmed it.'

'Then why again?'

'A signature can be practised to the point where a single rendition is acceptable. However, successive repetitions will result in flaws if it's not authentic. A graphological scanner will pick them up instantly; but then I'm sure that's no concern of yours.' Apfel smiled as he placed a pen at the edge of the desk. 'Nor of mine, frankly, but Koenig insists.'

'He's a cautious man,' said the patient, taking the pen and starting to write. He had begun the fourth set when the banker stopped him.

'That will do; the rest really is a waste of time.' Apfel held out his hand for the clipboard. 'Verifications said you weren't even a borderline case. Upon receipt of this, the account will be delivered.' He inserted the sheet of paper into the slot of a metal case on the right side of his desk and pressed a button; a shaft of bright light flared and then went out. 'This transmits the signatures directly to the scanner,' continued the banker. 'Which, of course, is programmed. Again, frankly, it's all a bit foolish. No one forewarned of our precautions would consent to the additional signatures if he were an impostor.'

'Why not? As long as he'd gone this far, why not chance it?'

'There is only one entrance to this office, conversely one exit. I'm sure you heard the lock snap shut in the waiting room.'

'And saw the wire mesh in the glass,' added the patient.

'Then you understand. A certified impostor would be trapped.'

'Suppose he had a gun?'

'You don't.'

'No one searched me.'

'The lift did. From four different angles. If you had been armed, the machinery would have stopped between the first and second floors.'

'You're all cautious.'

'We try to be of service.' The telephone rang. Apfel answered. 'Yes? . . . Come in.' The banker glanced at his client. 'Your account file's here.'

'That was quick.'

'Herr Koenig signed for it several minutes ago; he was merely waiting for the scanner release.' Apfel opened a drawer and took out a ring of keys. 'I'm sure he's disappointed. He was quite certain something was amiss.'

The steel door opened and the receptionist entered carrying a black metal container, which he placed on the desk next to a tray that held a bottle of Perrier and two glasses.

'Are you enjoying your stay in Zürich?' asked the banker, obviously to fill in the silence.

'Very much so. My room overlooks the lake. It's a nice view, very peaceful, quiet.'

'Splendid,' said Apfel, pouring a glass of Perrier for his client. Herr Koenig left; the door was closed and the banker returned to business.

'Your account, sir,' he said, selecting a key from the ring. 'May I unlock the case, or would you prefer to do so yourself?'

'Go ahead. Open it.'

The banker looked up. 'I said unlock, not open. That's not my privilege, nor would I care for the responsibility.'

'Why not?'

'In the event your identity is listed, it's not my position to be aware of it.'

'Suppose I wanted business transacted? Money transferred, sent to someone else?'

'It could be accomplished with your numerical signature on a withdrawal-form.'

'Or sent to another bank – outside Switzerland? For me.'

'Then a name would be required. Under those circumstances an identity would be both my responsibility and my privilege.'

'Open it.'

The officer did so. Dr Washburn's patient held his breath, a sharp pain forming in the pit of his stomach. Apfel took out a sheaf of statements held together by an outsized paper clip. His banker's eyes strayed to the right-hand column of the top pages, his banker's expression unchanged, but not totally. His lower lip stretched ever so slightly, creasing the corner of his mouth; he leaned forward and handed the pages to their owner.

Beneath the Gemeinschaft letterhead the typewritten words were in English, the obvious language of the client:

> Account: Zero-Seven—Seventeen-Twelve—Zero-Fourteen—Twenty-six-Zero
> Name: Restricted to Legal Instructions and Owner
> Access: Sealed Under Separate Cover.
> Current Funds on Deposit . . . 11,850,000 Francs

The patient exhaled slowly, staring at the figure. Whatever he *thought* he was prepared for, nothing prepared him for this. It was as frightening as anything he had experienced during the past five months. Roughly calculated the amount was over four million American dollars.

$4,000,000.00!

How? Why?

Controlling the start of a tremble in his hand, he leafed through the statements of entry. They were numerous, the sums extraordinary, none less than 300,000 francs, the deposits spaced every five to eight weeks apart, going back twenty-three months. He reached the bottom statement, the first. It was a transfer from a bank in Singapore and the largest single entry. Two million, seven hundred thousand Malaysian dollars converted into 5,175,000 Swiss francs.

Beneath the statement he could feel the outline of a separate envelope, far shorter than the page itself. He lifted up the paper; the envelope was rimmed with a black border, typewritten words on the front:

Identity:	Owner Access
Legal Restrictions:	Access – Registered Officer, Treadstone Seventy-one Corporation, Bearer Will Produce Written Instructions From Owner. Subject To Vertifications.

'I'd like to check this,' said the client.

'It's your property,' replied Apfel. 'I can assure you it has remained intact.'

The patient removed the envelope and turned it over. A Gemeinschaft seal was pressed over the borders of the flap; none of the raised letters had been disturbed. He tore the flap open, took out the card, and read:

Owner:	Jason Charles Bourne
Address:	Unlisted
Citizenship:	USA.

Jason Charles Bourne.

Jason.

The J was for Jason! His name was *Jason Bourne.* The *Bourne* had meant nothing, the *J.* Bourne still meaningless, but in the combination Jason *and* Bourne, obscure tumblers locked into place. He could accept it; he *did* accept it. He was Jason Charles Bourne, American. Yet he could feel his chest pounding; the vibration in his ears was deafening, the pain in his stomach more acute. *What was it? Why did he have the feeling that he was plunging into the darkness again, into the black waters again?*

'Is something wrong?' asked Walther Apfel.

Is something wrong, Herr Bourne?

'No. Everything's fine. My name's Bourne. Jason Bourne.'

Was he shouting? Whispering? He could not tell.

'My privilege to know you, Mr Bourne. Your identity will remain confidential. You have the word of an officer of the Bank Gemeinschaft.'

'Thank you. Now, I'm afraid I've got to transfer a great deal of this money, and I'll need your help.'

'Again, my privilege. Whatever assistance or advice I can render, I shall be happy to do so.'

Bourne reached for the glass of Perrier.

The steel door of Apfel's office closed behind him; within seconds he would walk out of the tasteful ante-room cell, into the reception room and over to the lifts. Within minutes he would be on the Bahnhofstrasse with a name, a great deal of money and little else but fear and confusion.

He had done it. Dr Geoffrey Washburn had been paid far in excess of the value of the life he had saved. A teletype transfer in the amount of 3,000,000 Swiss francs had been sent to a bank in Marseilles, deposited to a coded account that would find its way to Île de Port Noir's only doctor, without Washburn's name ever being used or revealed. All Washburn had to do was to get to Marseilles, recite the codes, and the money was his. Bourne smiled to himself, picturing the expression on Washburn's face when the account was turned over to him. The eccentric, alcoholic doctor would have been overjoyed with ten or fifteen thousand pounds; he had more than a million dollars. It would either ensure his recovery or his destruction; that was his choice, his problem.

A second transfer of 4,000,000 francs was sent to a bank in Paris on the rue Madeleine, deposited in the name of Jason C. Bourne. The transfer was expedited by the Gemeinschaft's twice-weekly pouch to Paris, signature cards in triplicate sent with the documents. Herr Koenig had assured both his superior and the client that the paper would reach Paris in three days.

The final transaction was minor by comparison. One hundred thousand francs in large bills were brought to Apfel's office, the withdrawal slip signed in the account holder's numerical signature.

Remaining on deposit in the Gemeinschaft Bank were 3,215 Swiss francs, a not inconsequential sum by any standard.

How? Why? From where?

The entire business had taken an hour and twenty minutes, only one discordant note intruding on the smooth proceedings. In character, it had been delivered by Koenig, his expression a mixture of solemnity and minor triumph. He had rung Apfel, was admitted, and had brought a small, black-bordered envelope to his superior.

'*Une fiche*,' he had said in French.

The banker had opened the envelope, removed a card, studied the contents, and had returned both to Koenig. 'Procedures will be followed,' he had said.

Koenig had left.

'Did that concern me?' Bourne had asked.

'Only in terms of releasing such large amounts. Merely house policy.' The banker had smiled reassuringly.

The lock clicked. Bourne opened the frosted glass door and walked out into Herr Koenig's personal fiefdom. Two other men had arrived, seated at opposite ends of the reception room. Since they were not in separate cells behind opaque glass windows, Bourne presumed that neither had a three-zero account. He wondered if they had signed names or written out a series of numbers, but he stopped wondering the instant he reached the lift and pressed the button.

Out of the corner of his eye he perceived movement. Koenig had shifted his head, nodding at both men. They rose as a lift door opened. Bourne turned; the man on the right had taken a small radio out of his overcoat pocket; he spoke into it – briefly, quickly.

The man on the left had his right hand concealed beneath the cloth of his raincoat. When he pulled it out he was holding a gun, a black .38 calibre automatic pistol with a perforated cylinder attached to the barrel. A silencer.

Both men converged on Bourne as he backed into the deserted lift.

The madness began.

5

The lift doors started to close; the man with the hand-held radio was already inside, the shoulders of his armed companion angling between the moving panels, the weapon aimed at Bourne's head.

Jason leaned to his right – a sudden gesture of fear – then abruptly, without warning, swept his left foot off the floor, pivoting, his heel plunging into the armed man's hand, sending the gun upwards, reeling the man backwards out of the enclosure. Two muted gunshots preceded the closing of the doors, the bullets embedding themselves in the thick wood of the ceiling. Bourne completed his pivot, his shoulder crashing into the second man's stomach, his right hand surging into the chest, his left pinning the hand with the radio. He hurled the man into the wall. The radio flew across the lift; as it fell words came out of its speaker.

'*Henri! Ça va? Maintenant, l'ascenseur?*'

The image of another Frenchman came to Jason's mind. A man on the edge of hysteria, disbelief in his eyes; a would-be killer who had raced out of *Le Bouc de Mer* into the shadows of the rue Sarasin less than twenty-four hours ago. *That* man had wasted no time sending his message to Zürich: the one they thought was dead was alive. Very much alive. *Kill him!*

Bourne grabbed the Frenchman in front of him now, his left arm around the man's throat, his right hand tearing at the man's left ear. 'How *many*?' he asked in French. 'How many are there down there? Where *are* they?'

'Find out, *pig*!'

The lift was halfway to the ground-floor lobby.

Jason angled the man's face down, ripping the ear half out of its roots, smashing the man's head into the wall. The Frenchman screamed, sinking to the floor. Bourne rammed his knee into the man's chest; he could feel the holster. He yanked the overcoat open, reached in, and pulled out a short-barrelled revolver. For an instant, it occurred to him that someone had deactivated the scanning machinery in the lift. *Koenig.* He would remember; there'd be no amnesia where Herr Koenig was concerned. He jammed the gun into the Frenchman's open mouth.

'Tell me or I'll blow the back of your skull off!' The man expunged a cry; the weapon was withdrawn, the barrel now pressed into his cheek.

'Two. One by the lifts, one outside on the pavement, by the car.'

'What *kind* of car?'

'Peugeot.'

'*Colour?*' The lift was slowing down, coming to a stop.

'Brown.'

'The man in the lobby. What's he *wearing*?'

'I don't know . . .'

Jason cracked the gun across the man's temple. 'You'd better remember!'

'A black coat!'

The lift stopped; Bourne pulled the Frenchman to his feet; the doors opened. To the left, a man in a dark raincoat and wearing an odd-looking pair of gold-rimmed spectacles, stepped forward. The eyes beyond the lenses recognized the circumstances; blood was trickling down across the Frenchman's cheek. He raised his unseen hand, concealed by the wide pocket of his raincoat, another silenced automatic levelled at the target from Marseilles.

Jason propelled the Frenchman in front of him through the doors. Three rapid spits were heard; the Frenchman shouted, his arms raised in a final, guttural protest. He arched his back and fell to the marble floor. A woman to the right of the man with the gold-rimmed spectacles screamed, joined by several men who called to no one and everyone for *help*, for the *police*.

Bourne knew he could not use the revolver he had taken from the Frenchman. It had no silencer; the sound of a gunshot would mark him. He shoved it into his topcoat pocket, side-stepped the screaming woman and grabbed the uniformed shoulders of the lift attendant, whipping the bewildered man around, throwing him into the figure of the killer in the dark raincoat.

The panic in the lobby mounted as Jason ran towards the glass doors of the entrance. The *boutonnière*-ed greeter who had mistaken his language an hour and a half ago was shouting into a wall telephone, a uniformed guard at his side, weapon drawn, barricading the exit, eyes riveted on the chaos, riveted suddenly on *him*. Getting out was instantly a problem. Bourne avoided the guard's eyes, directing his words to the guard's associate on the telephone.

'The man wearing gold-rimmed glasses!' he shouted. 'He's the one! I saw him!'

'*What?* Who are you?'

'I'm a friend of Walther Apfel! *Listen* to me! The man wearing gold-rimmed glasses, in a black raincoat. Over there!'

Bureaucratic mentality had not changed in several millennia. At the mention of a superior officer's name, one followed orders.

'Herr Apfel!' The Gemeinschaft receptionist turned to the guard. 'You heard him! The man wearing glasses. Gold-rimmed glasses!'

'Yes, sir!' The guard raced forward.

Jason edged past the receptionist to the glass doors. He shoved the door on the right open, glancing behind him, knowing he had to run again, but not knowing if a man outside on the pavement, waiting by a brown Peugeot, would recognize him and fire a bullet into his head.

The guard had run past a man in a black raincoat, a man walking more slowly than the panicked figures around him, a man wearing no glasses at all. He accelerated his pace towards the entrance, towards Bourne.

Out on the pavement, the growing chaos was Jason's protection. Word had gone out of the bank; wailing sirens grew louder as police cars raced up the

Bahnhofstrasse. He walked several yards to the right, flanked by pedestrians, then suddenly ran, wedging his way into a curious crowd taking refuge in a shopfront, his attention on the cars at the kerb. He saw the Peugeot, saw the man standing beside it, his hand ominously in his overcoat pocket. In less than fifteen seconds, the driver of the Peugeot was joined by the man in the black raincoat, now replacing his gold-rimmed glasses, adjusting his eyes to his restored vision. The two men conferred rapidly, their eyes scanning the Bahnhofstrasse.

Bourne understood their confusion. He had walked with an absence of panic out through the Gemeinschaft's glass doors into the crowd. He had been prepared to run, but he had *not* run, for fear of being stopped until he was reasonably clear of the entrance. No one else had been permitted to do so – and the driver of the Peugeot had not made the connection. He had *not* recognized the target identified and marked for execution in Marseilles.

The first police car reached the scene as the man in the gold-rimmed spectacles removed his raincoat, shoving it through the open window of the Peugeot. He nodded to the driver, who climbed in behind the wheel and started the engine. The killer took off his delicate glasses and did the most unexpected thing Jason could imagine. He walked rapidly back towards the glass doors of the Bank, joining the police who were racing inside.

Bourne watched as the Peugeot swung away from the kerb and sped off down the Bahnhofstrasse. The crowd in the shopfront began to disperse, many edging their way towards the glass doors, craning their necks around one another, rising on the balls of their feet, peering inside. A police officer came out, waving the curious back, demanding that a path be cleared to the kerb. As he shouted, an ambulance careened around the north-west corner, its horn joining the sharp, piercing notes from its roof, warning all to get out of its way; the driver nosed his outsized vehicle to a stop in the space created by the departed Peugeot. Jason could watch no longer. He had to get to the Carillon du Lac, gather his things and get out of Zürich, out of Switzerland. To Paris.

Why Paris? Why had he insisted that the funds be transferred to *Paris*? It had not occurred to him before he sat in Walther Apfel's office, stunned by the extraordinary figures presented him. They had been beyond anything in his imagination – so much so that he could only react numbly, instinctively. And instinct had evoked the city of Paris. As though it were somehow vital. *Why?*

Again, no time . . . He saw the ambulance crew carry a stretcher through the doors of the bank. On it was a body, the head covered, signifying death. The significance was not lost on Bourne; save for skills he could not relate to anything he understood, he was the dead man on that stretcher.

He saw an empty taxi at the corner and ran towards it. He had to get out of Zürich; a message had been sent from Marseilles, yet the dead man was alive. Jason Bourne was alive. Kill him. Kill Jason Bourne!

God in heaven, *why*?

He was hoping to see the Carillon du Lac's assistant manager behind the front desk, but he was not there. Then he realized that a short note to the man – what was his name? Stossel? Yes, Stossel – would be sufficient. An explanation for his sudden departure was not required and five hundred francs would easily take care of the few hours he had accepted from the Carillon du Lac – and the favour he would ask of Herr Stossel.

In his room he threw his shaving equipment into his suitcase, checked the pistol he had taken from the Frenchman, leaving it in his overcoat pocket, and sat down at the desk; he wrote out the note for *Herr Stossel, Ass't Mgr.* In it he included a sentence that came easily – almost too easily.

. . . *I may be in contact with you shortly relative to messages I expect will have been sent to me. I trust it will be convenient for you to keep an eye out for them, and accept them on my behalf.*

If any communication came from the elusive Treadstone Seventy-one, he wanted to know about it. This was Zürich; he would.

He put a five-hundred-franc note between the folded stationery and sealed the envelope. Then he picked up his suitcase, walked out of the room, and went down the hall to the bank of lifts. There were four; he touched a button and looked behind him, remembering the Gemeinschaft. There was no one there; a bell pinged and the red light above the third lift flashed on. He had caught a descending machine. Fine. He had to get to the airport just as fast as he could; he had to get out of Zürich, out of Switzerland. A message had been delivered.

The lift doors opened. Two men stood on either side of an auburn-haired woman; they interrupted their conversation, nodded at the newcomer – noting the suitcase and moving to the side – then resumed talking as the doors closed. They were in their mid-thirties and spoke French softly, rapidly, the woman glancing alternately at both men, alternately smiling and looking pensive. Decisions of no great import were being made. Laughter intermingled with semi-serious interrogation.

'You'll be going home then after the summations tomorrow?' asked the man on the left.

'I'm not sure. I'm waiting for word from Ottawa,' the woman replied. 'I have relations in Lyons; it would be good to see them.'

'It's impossible,' said the man on the right, 'for the steering committee to find ten people willing to summarize this God-forsaken conference in a single day. We'll all be here another week.'

'Brussels will not approve,' said the first man grinning. 'The hotel's too expensive.'

'Then by all means move to another,' said the second with a leer at the woman. 'We've been waiting for you to do just that, haven't we?'

'You're a lunatic,' said the woman. 'You're both lunatics, and that's *my* summation.'

'You're not, Marie,' interjected the first. 'A lunatic, I mean. Your presentation yesterday was brilliant.'

'It was nothing of the sort,' she said. 'It was routine and quite dull.'

'No, no!' disagreed the second. 'It was superb; it had to be. I didn't understand a word. But then I have other talents.'

'Lunatic . . .'

The lift was braking; the first man spoke again. 'Let's sit in the back row of the hall. We're late anyway and Bertinelli is speaking – to little effect, I suggest. His theories of enforced cyclical fluctuations went out with the finances of the Borgias.'

'Before then,' said the auburn-haired woman, laughing. 'Caesar's taxes.' She paused, then added, 'If not the Punic Wars.'

'The back row then,' said the second man, offering his arm to the woman. 'We can sleep. He uses a slide projector; it'll be dark.'

'No, you two go ahead, I'll join you in a few minutes. I really must send off some cables and I don't trust the telephone operators to get them right.'

The doors opened and the threesome walked out of the lift. The two men started diagonally across the lobby together, the woman towards the front desk. Bourne fell in step behind her, absently reading a sign on a triangular stand several feet away.

Welcome To:
Members of The Sixth World Economic Conference

Today's Schedule:
1:00 p.m.: The Hon. James Frazier, MP United Kingdom. ***Suite 12***
6:00 p.m.: Dr Eugenio Bertinelli, Univ. of Milan, Italy. ***Suite 7.***
9:00 p.m.: Chairman's Farewell Dinner. ***Hospitality Suite.***

'Room Five-zero-seven. The operator said there was a cablegram for me.'

English. The auburn-haired woman now beside him at the counter spoke English. But then she had said she was 'waiting for word from Ottawa'. A Canadian.

The desk clerk checked the slots and returned with the cable. 'Doctor St Jacques?' he asked, holding out the envelope.

'Yes. Thanks very much.'

The woman turned away, opening the cable, as the clerk moved in front of Bourne. 'Yes, sir?'

'I'd like to leave this note for Herr Stossel.' He placed the Carillon du Lac envelope on the counter.

'Herr Stossel will not return until six o'clock in the morning, sir. In the afternoons, he leaves at four. Might I be of service?'

'No, thanks. Just make sure he gets it, please.' Then Jason remembered: this was Zürich. 'It's nothing urgent,' he added, 'but I need an answer. I'll check with him in the morning.'

'Of course, sir.'

Bourne picked up his suitcase and started across the lobby towards the hotel's entrance, a row of wide glass doors that led to a circular drive fronting the lake. He could see several taxis waiting under the floodlights of the canopy; the sun had gone down; it was night in Zürich. Still, there were flights to all points of Europe until well past midnight . . .

He stopped walking, his breath suspended, a form of paralysis sweeping over him. His eyes did not believe what else he saw beyond the glass doors. A brown Peugeot pulled up in the circular drive in front of the first taxi. Its door opened and a man stepped out – a killer in a black raincoat, wearing thin, gold-rimmed spectacles. Then from the other door another figure emerged, but it was not the driver who had been at the kerb on the Bahnhofstrasse, waiting for a target he did not recognize. Instead, it was another killer, in another raincoat, its wide pockets recesses for powerful weapons. It was the man who had sat in the reception room on the first floor of the Gemeinschaft Bank, the same man who had pulled a .38 calibre pistol from a holster beneath his coat. A pistol with a perforated cylinder on its barrel that silenced two bullets meant for the skull of the quarry he had followed into an elevator.

How? How could they have found him? . . . Then he remembered and felt sick. It had been so innocuous, so casual!

Are you enjoying your stay in Zürich? Walther Apfel had asked while they were waiting for a minion to leave and be alone again.

Very much so. My room overlooks the lake. It's a nice view, very peaceful, quiet.

Koenig! Koenig had heard him say his room looked over the lake. How many hotels had rooms overlooking the lake? Especially hotels a man with a three-zero account might frequent. Two? Three? . . . From unremembered memory names came to him: *Carillon du Lac, Baur au Lac, Eden au Lac.* Were there others? No further names came. How easy it must have been to narrow them down! How easy it had been for him to say the words. How stupid!

No time. Too *late.* He could see through the row of glass doors; so, too, could the killers. The second man had spotted him. Words were exchanged over the hood of the Peugeot, gold-rimmed spectacles adjusted, hands placed in outsized pockets, unseen weapons gripped. The two men converged on the entrance, separating at the last moment, one on either end of the row of clear glass panels. The flanks were covered, the trap set; he could not race outside.

Did they think they could walk into a crowded hotel lobby and simply *kill* a man?

Of course they could! The crowds and the noise were their cover. Two, three, *four* muted gunshots fired at close range would be as effective as an ambush in a crowded square in daylight, escape easily found in the resulting chaos.

He could not let them get near him! He backed away, thoughts racing through his mind, outrage paramount. How *dared* they? What made them think he would not run for protection, scream for the *police*? And then the answer was clear, as numbing as the question itself. The killers knew with certainty that which he could only surmise. He could not seek that kind of protection – he could not seek the police. For Jason Bourne, all the authorities had to be avoided . . . Why? Were they seeking *him*?

Jesus Christ, why?

The two opposing doors were opened by outstretched hands, other hands hidden, around steel. Bourne turned; there were lifts, doorways, corridors – a roof and cellars; there had to be a dozen ways out of the hotel.

Or were there? Did the killers now threading their way through the crowds know something else he could only surmise? Did the Carillon du Lac have only two or three exits? Easily covered by men outside, easily used as traps themselves to cut down the lone figure of a running man.

A lone man; a lone man was an obvious target. But suppose he was *not* alone? Suppose someone was with him? Two people were not one, but for one alone an extra person was camouflage – especially in crowds, especially at night, and it *was* night. Determined killers avoided taking the wrong life, not from compassion but for practicality; in any ensuing panic the real target might escape.

He felt the weight of the gun in his pocket but there was not much comfort in knowing it was there. As at the bank, to use it – to even display it – was to mark him. Still, it was there. He started back towards the centre of the lobby, then turned to his right where there was a greater concentration of people. It was the pre-evening hour during an international conference, a thousand tentative plans being made, rank and courtesan separated by glances of approval and rebuke, odd groupings everywhere.

There was a marble counter against the wall, a clerk behind it checking pages of yellow paper with a pencil held like a paintbrush. *Cablegrams.* In front of the counter were two people, an obese elderly man and a woman in a dark red dress, the rich colour of the silk complementing her long titian hair . . . Auburn hair. It was the woman in the lift who had joked about *Caesar's taxes* and the *Punic Wars,* the doctor who had stood beside him at the hotel desk, asking for the cable she knew was there.

Bourne looked behind him. The killers were using the crowds well, excusing themselves politely but firmly through, one on the right, one on the left, closing in like two prongs of a pincer attack. As long as they kept him in sight, they could force him to keep running blindly, without direction, not knowing which path might lead to a dead end where he could run no longer. And then the muted spits would come, pockets blackened by powder burns . . .

Kept him in sight?

The back row then . . . We can sleep. He uses a slide projector; it'll be dark.

Jason turned again and looked at the auburn-haired woman. She had completed her cable and was thanking the clerk, removing a pair of tinted, horn-rimmed glasses from her face, placing them in her purse. She was no more than eight feet away.

Bertinelli is speaking, to little effect I suggest.

There was no time for anything but instinctive decisions. Bourne shifted his suitcase to his left hand, walked rapidly over to the woman at the marble counter, and touched her elbow, gently, with as little alarm as possible.

'Doctor? . . .'

'I beg your pardon?'

'You *are* Doctor? . . .' He released her, a bewildered man.

'St Jacques,' she completed, using the French *Senh* for Saint. 'You're the one in the lift.'

'I didn't realize it was you,' he said. 'I was told you'd know where this Bertinelli is speaking.'

'It's right on the board. Suite Seven.'

'I'm afraid I don't know where it is. Would you mind showing me? I'm late and I've got to take notes on his talk.'

'On Bertinelli? Why? Are you with a Marxist newspaper?'

'A neutral pool,' said Jason, wondering where the phrases came from. 'I'm covering for a number of people. They don't think he's worth it.'

'Perhaps not, but he should be heard. There are a few brutal truths in what he says.'

'I lost so I've got to find them. Maybe you can point them out.'

'I'm afraid not. I'll show you the room, but I've a phone call to make.' She snapped her purse shut.

'Please. *Hurry!*'

'What?' She looked at him, not kindly.

'Sorry, but I *am* in a hurry.' He glanced to his right; the two men were no more than twenty feet away.

'You're also rude,' said the St Jacques woman coldly.

'*Please.*' He restrained his desire to propel her forward, away from the moving trap that was closing in.

'It's this way.' She started across the floor towards a wide corridor carved out of the left rear wall. The crowds were thinner, prominence less apparent in the back regions of the lobby. They reached what looked like a velvet-covered tunnel of deep red, doors on opposite sides, lighted signs above them identifying *Conference Room One, Conference Room Two.* At the end of the hallway were double doors, the gold letters to the right proclaiming them to be the entrance to *Suite Seven.*

'There you are,' said Marie St Jacques. 'Be careful when you go in; it's probably dark. Bertinelli lectures with slides.'

'Like a movie,' commented Bourne, looking behind him at the crowds at the far end of the corridor. He was *there*; the man with gold-rimmed spectacles was excusing himself past an animated trio in the lobby. He was *walking into the hallway*, his companion right behind him.

'. . . a considerable difference. He sits below the stage and pontificates.' The St Jacques woman had said something and was now leaving him.

'What did you say? A stage?'

'Well, a raised platform. For exhibits usually.'

'They have to be brought in,' he said.

'What does?'

'Exhibits. Is there an exit in there? Another door?'

'I have no idea, and I really must make my call. Enjoy the *professore.*' She turned away.

He dropped the suitcase and took her arm. At the touch, she glared at him. 'Take your hand off me, please.'

'I don't want to frighten you, but I have no choice.' He spoke quietly, his eyes over her shoulder; the killers had slowed their pace, the trap sure, about to close. 'You have to come with me.'

'Don't be ridiculous!'

He viced the grip around her arm, moving her in front of him. Then he pulled the gun out of his pocket, making sure her body concealed it from the men thirty feet away.

'I don't want to use this. I don't want to hurt you, but I'll do both if I have to.'

'My *God* . . .'

'Be *quiet.* Just do as I say and you'll be fine. I have to get out of this hotel and you're going to help me. Once I'm out, I'll let you go. But not until then. Come on. We're going in there.'

'You *can't* . . .'

'Yes, I can.' He pushed the barrel of the gun into her stomach, into the dark silk that creased under the force of his thrust. She was terrified into silence, into submission. 'Let's go.'

He stepped to her left, his hand still gripping her arm, the pistol held across his chest inches from her own. Her eyes were riveted on it, her lips parted, her breath erratic. Bourne opened the door, propelling her through it in front of him. He could hear a single word shouted from the corridor.

'*Schnell!*'

They were in darkness, but it was brief; a shaft of white light shot across the room, over the rows of chairs, illuminating the heads of the audience. The projection on the faraway screen on the stage was that of a graph, the grids marked numerically, a heavy black line starting at the left, extending in a jagged pattern through the lines to the right. A heavily accented voice was speaking, amplified by a loudspeaker.

'You will note that during the years of 'seventy and 'seventy-one, when specific restraints in production were self-imposed – I repeat, *self*-imposed – by these leaders of industry, the resulting economic recession was far less severe than in – Slide Twelve, please – the so-called paternalistic regulation of the marketplace by government interventionists. The next slide, please.'

The room went dark again. There was a problem with the projector; no second shaft of light replaced the first.

'Slide Twelve, please!'

Jason pushed the woman forward, in front of the figures standing by the back wall, behind the last row of chairs. He tried to judge the size of the lecture hall, looking for a red light that could mean escape. He saw it! A faint reddish glow in the distance. *On* the stage, *behind* the screen. There were no other exits, no other doors but the entrance to Suite Seven. He had to reach it; he had to get them to that exit. On that stage.

'*Marie! Ici!*' The whisper came from their left, from a seat in the back row.

'*Non, ma chérie! Je suis tout près.*' The second whisper was delivered by the shadowed figure of a man standing directly in front of Marie St Jacques. He had stepped away from the wall, intercepting her.

Bourne pressed the gun firmly into the woman's rib cage, its message unmistakable. She whispered without breathing, Jason grateful that her face could not be seen clearly. 'Please, let us by,' she said in French. '*Please.*'

'What's this? Is he your cablegram, my dear?'

'An old friend,' whispered Bourne.

A shout rose over the increasingly louder hum from the audience. 'May I please have *Slide Twelve! Per cortesia!*'

'We have to see someone at the end of the row,' continued Jason, looking behind him. The right-hand door of the entrance opened; in the middle of a shadowed face, a pair of gold-rimmed glasses reflected the dim light of the corridor. Bourne edged the girl past her bewildered friend, forcing him back into the wall, whispering an apology.

'Sorry, but we're in a hurry!'

'You're damned rude, too!'

'Yes, I know.'

'Slide *Twelve! Che cosa! Impossibile!*'

The beam of light shot out from the projector; it vibrated under the nervous hand of the operator. Another graph appeared on the screen as Jason and the woman reached the far wall, the start of the narrow aisle that led down the length of the hall to the stage. He pushed her into the corner, pressing his body against hers, his face against her face.

'I'll *scream*,' she whispered.

'I'll shoot,' he said. He peered around the figures leaning against the wall; the killers were both inside, both squinting, shifting their heads like alarmed rodents, trying to spot their target among the rows of faces.

The voice of the lecturer rose like the ringing of a cracked bell, his diatribe brief but strident. '*Ecco!* For the sceptics I address here this evening – and that is most of you – here is statistical proof! Identical in substance to a hundred other analyses I have prepared. Leave the marketplace to those who live there. Minor excesses can always be found. They are a small price to pay for the general good.'

There was a scattering of applause, the approval of a definite minority. Bertinelli resumed a normal tone and droned on, his long pointer stabbing at the screen emphasizing the obvious – his obvious. Jason leaned back again; the gold spectacles glistened in the harsh glare of the projector's side light, the killer who wore them touching his companion's arm, nodding to his left, ordering his subordinate to continue the search on the left side of the room; he would take the right. He began, the gold rims growing brighter as he side-stepped his way in front of those standing, studying each face. He would reach the corner, reach *them*, in a matter of seconds. Stopping the killer with a gunshot was all that was left; and if someone along the row of those standing moved, or if the woman he had pressed against the wall went into panic and shoved him . . . or if he missed the killer for any number of reasons, he was trapped. And even if he hit the man, there was another killer across the room, certainly a marksman.

'Slide *Thirteen*, if you please.'

That was it. *Now!*

The shaft of light went out. In the blackout, Bourne pulled the woman from the wall, spun her in her place, his face against hers. 'If you make a sound, I'll kill you!'

'I believe you,' she whispered, terrified. 'You're a maniac.'

'Let's go!' He pushed her down the narrow aisle that led to the stage fifty feet away. The projector's light went on again; he grabbed the girl's neck, forcing her down into a kneeling position as he, too, knelt down behind her. They were concealed from the killers by the rows of bodies sitting in the chairs. He pressed her flesh with his fingers; it was his signal to keep moving, crawling . . . slowly, keeping down, but *moving.* She understood; she started forward on her knees, trembling.

'The conclusions of this phase are irrefutable,' cried the lecturer. 'The profit motive is inseparable from productivity incentive, but the adversary roles can never be equal. As Socrates understood, the inequality of values is constant. Gold simply is not brass or iron; who among you can deny it? Slide Fourteen, if you please!'

The darkness again. *Now.*

He yanked the woman up, pushing her forward, towards the stage. They were within three feet of the edge.

'*Che cosa?* What is the matter, please? Slide *Fourteen*!'

It had happened! The projector was jammed again; the darkness was extended again. And there on the stage in front of them, above them, was the red glow of the exit sign. Jason gripped the girl's arm viciously. 'Get up on that stage and run to the exit! I'm right behind you; you stop or cry out, I'll shoot.'

'For God's sake, let me go!'

'Not yet.' He meant it; there was another exit somewhere, men waiting outside for the target from Marseilles. 'Go on! *Now.*'

The St Jacques woman got to her feet and ran to the stage. Bourne lifted her off the floor, over the edge, leaping up as he did so, pulling her to her feet again.

The blinding light of the projector shot out, flooding the screen, washing the stage. Cries of surprise and derision came from the audience at the sight of the two figures, the shouts of the indignant Bertinelli heard over the din.

'*Affronto! Insultante! Ecco, Comunisti!*'

And there were other sounds – three – lethal, sharp, sudden. Cracks of a muted weapon – weapons; wood splintered on the moulding of the proscenium arch. Jason hammered the girl down and lunged towards the shadows of the narrow wing space, pulling her behind him.

'*Da ist er!*'

'*Der Projektionsapparat!*'

A scream came from the centre aisle of the hall as the light of the projector swung to the right, spilling into the wings – but not completely. Its beam was intercepted by receding upright flats that masked the offstage area; *light, shadow, light, shadow.* And at the end of the flats, at the rear of the stage, was the exit. A high, wide metal door with a crush bar against it.

Glass shattered; the red light exploded, a marksman's bullet blew out the sign above the door. It did not matter, he could see the gleaming brass of the crush bar clearly.

The lecture hall had broken out in pandemonium. Bourne grabbed the woman by the cloth of her blouse, yanking her beyond the flats towards the door. For an instant, she resisted; he slapped her across the face and dragged her beside him until the crush bar was above their heads.

Bullets spat into the wall to their right; the killers were racing down the aisles for accurate sightlines. They would reach them in seconds, and in seconds other bullets, or a single bullet, would find its mark. There were enough shells left, he knew that. He had no idea how or why he knew, but he *knew*. By sound he could visualize the weapons, extract the clips, count the shells.

He smashed his forearm into the crush bar of the exit door. It flew open and he lunged through the opening, dragging the kicking St Jacques woman with him.

'*Stop it*!' she screamed. 'I won't go any farther! You're *insane*! Those were gunshots!'

Jason slammed the large metal door shut with his foot. 'Get up!'

'*No!*'

He lashed the back of his hand across her face. 'Sorry, but you're coming with me. Get *up*! Once we're outside, you have my word. I'll let you go.' But where was he going now? They were in another tunnel, but there was no carpet, no polished doors with lighted signs above them. They were . . . in some kind of deserted loading area, the floor was concrete; and there were two, pipe-framed freight dollies next to him against the wall. He had been right: exhibits used on the stage of Suite Seven had to be brought in by lorry, the exit door high enough and wide enough to accommodate large displays.

The *door*! He had to block the door! Marie St Jacques was on her feet; he held her as he grabbed the first dolly, pulling it by its frame in front of the exit door, slamming it with his shoulder and knee until it was lodged against the metal. He looked down; beneath the thick wooden base were footlocks on the wheels. He jammed his heel down on the front lever lock, and then the back one.

The girl spun, trying to break his grip as he stretched his leg to the end of the dolly; he slid his hand down her arms, gripped her wrist, and twisted it inward. She screamed, tears in her eyes, her lips trembling. He pulled her alongside him, forcing her to the left, breaking into a run, assuming the direction was towards the rear of the Carillon du Lac, hoping he'd find the exit. For there and only there he might need the woman; a brief few seconds when a couple emerged, not a lone man running.

There was a series of loud crashes, the killers were trying to force the stage door open but the locked freight dolly was too heavy a barrier.

He yanked the girl along the cement floor; she tried to pull away, kicking again, twisting her body again from one side to the other; she was over the edge of hysteria. He had no choice; he gripped her elbow, his thumb on the inner flesh, and pressed as hard as he could. She gasped, the pain sudden and excruciating; she sobbed, expelling breath, allowing him to propel her forward.

They reached a cement staircase, the four steps edged in steel, leading to a pair of metal doors below. It was the loading dock; beyond the doors was the Carillon du Lac's rear parking area. He was almost there. It was only a question of appearances now.

'Listen to me,' he said to the rigid, frightened woman. 'Do you want me to let you go?'

'Oh God, yes! *Please!*'

'Then do exactly as I say. We're going to walk down these steps and out of that door like two perfectly normal people at the end of a normal day's work. You're going to link your arm in mine and we're going to walk slowly, talking quietly, to the cars at the far end of the parking area. And we're both going to laugh – not loudly, just casually – as if we were remembering funny things that happened during the day. Have you got that?'

'Nothing funny at all has happened to me during the past fifteen minutes,' she answered in barely audible monotone.

'Pretend that it has. I may be trapped; if I am I don't care. Do you understand?'

'I think my wrist is broken.'

'It's not.'

'My left arm, my shoulder. I can't move them; they're throbbing.'

'A nerve ending was depressed, it'll pass in a matter of minutes. You'll be fine.'

'You're an animal.'

'I want to live,' he said. 'Come on. Remember, when I open the door, look at me and smile, tilt your head back, laugh a little.'

'It will be the most difficult thing I've ever done.'

'It's easier than dying.'

She put her injured hand under his arm and they walked down the short flight of steps to the platform door. He opened it and they went outside, his hand in his topcoat pocket gripping the Frenchman's pistol, his eyes scanning the loading dock. There was a single bulb encased in wire mesh above the door, its spill defining the concrete steps to the left that led to the pavement below; he led his hostage towards them.

She performed as he had ordered, the effect macabre. As they walked down the steps, her face was turned to his, her terrified features caught in the light. Her generous lips were parted, stretched over her white teeth in a false, tense smile; her wide eyes were two dark orbs, reflecting primordial fear, her tear-stained skin taut and pale, marred by the reddish splotches where he had hit her. He was looking at a face of chiselled stone, a mask framed by dark red hair that cascaded over her shoulders, swept back by the night breezes – moving, the only living thing about the mask.

Choked laughter came from her throat, the veins in her long neck pronounced. She was not far from collapsing, but he could not think about that. He had to concentrate on the space around them, on whatever movement – however slight – he might discern in the shadows of the large parking area. It was obvious that these back, unlit regions were used by the Carillon du Lac's employees; it was nearly 6:30, the night shift well immersed in its duties. Everything was still, a smooth black field broken up by rows of silent vehicles, ranks of huge insects, the dull glass of the headlamps a hundred eyes staring at nothing.

A scratch. Metal had scraped against metal. It came from the right, from one of the cars in a nearby row. Which *row*? Which *car*? He tilted his head back as if responding to a joke made by his companion, letting his eyes roam across the windows of the cars nearest to them. Nothing . . .

Something? It was there but it was so small, barely seen . . . so bewildering.

A tiny circle of green, an infinitesimal glow of green light. It moved . . . as they moved.

Green. Small . . . *light*? Suddenly, from somewhere in a forgotten past the image of crosshairs burst across his eyes. His *eyes* were looking at two thin intersecting lines! *Crosshairs!* A scope . . . the *infra-red scope of a rifle.*

How did the killers know? Any number of answers. A handheld radio had been used at the Gemeinschaft; one could be in use now. He wore an overcoat; his hostage wore a thin silk dress and the night was cool. No woman would go out like that.

He swung to his left, crouching, lunging into Marie St Jacques, his shoulder crashing into her stomach, sending her reeling back towards the steps. The muffled cracks came in staccato repetition; stone and asphalt exploded all around them. He dived to his right, rolling over and over again the instant he made contact with the pavement, yanking the pistol from his overcoat pocket. Then he sprang again, now straight forward, his left hand steadying his right wrist, the gun centred, aimed at the window with the rifle. He fired three shots.

A scream came from the dark open space of the stationary car; it was drawn out into a cry, then a gasp, and then nothing. Bourne lay motionless, waiting, listening, watching, prepared to fire again. Silence. He started to get up . . . but he could not. Something had *happened.* He could barely *move.* Then the pain spread through his chest, the pounding so violent he bent over, supporting himself with both hands, shaking his head, trying to focus his eyes, trying to reject the agony. His left shoulder, his lower *chest* – below the ribs . . . his left *thigh* – above the knee, below the hip, the locations of his previous wounds, where dozens of stitches had been removed over a month ago. He had damaged the weakened areas, stretching tendons and muscles not yet fully restored. Oh, *Christ*! He had to get up; he had to reach the would-be killer's car, pull the killer from it, and get *away.*

He whipped his head up, grimacing with the pain, and looked over at Marie St Jacques. She was getting slowly to her feet, first on one knee, then on one foot, supporting herself on the outside wall of the hotel. In a moment she would be standing, then running. Away.

He could not let her go! She would race screaming into the Carillon du Lac; men would come, some to take him . . . some to kill him. He had to stop her!

He let his body fall forward and started rolling to his left, spinning like a wildly out-of-control manikin, until he was within four feet of the wall, four feet from her. He raised his gun, aiming at her head.

'Help me up,' he said, hearing the strain in his voice.

'What?'

'You heard me! Help me *up.*'

'You said I could go! You gave me your word!'

'I have to take it back . . .'

'No, *please.*'

'This gun is aimed directly at your face, Doctor. You come here and help me get up or I'll blow it off.'

*

He pulled the dead man from the car and ordered her to get behind the wheel. Then he opened the rear door and crawled into the back seat out of sight.

'Drive,' he said. 'Drive where I tell you.'

6

Whenever you're in a stress situation yourself – and there's time, of course – do exactly as you would do when you project yourself into one you're observing. Let your mind fall free, let whatever thoughts and images that surface come cleanly. Try not to exercise any mental discipline. Be a sponge; concentrate on everything and nothing. Specifics may come to you, certain repressed conduits electrically prodded into functioning.

Bourne thought of Washburn's words as he adjusted his body into the corner of the seat, trying to restore some control. He massaged his chest, gently rubbing the bruised muscles around his previous wound; the pain was still there, but not as acute as it had been minutes ago.

'You can't just tell me to drive!' cried the St Jacques woman. 'I don't know where I'm going!'

'Neither do I,' said Jason. He had told her to stay on the lakeshore drive; it was dark and he had to have time to think. If only to be a sponge.

'People will be *looking* for me,' she exclaimed.

'They're looking for me, too.'

'You've taken me against my will. You struck me. Repeatedly.' She spoke more softly now, imposing a control on herself. 'That's kidnapping, assault . . . those are serious crimes. You're out of the hotel, that's what you said you wanted. Let me go and I won't say anything. I promise you!'

'You mean you'll give me your word?'

'*Yes!*'

'I gave you mine and took it back. So could you.'

'You're different. I *won't*. No one's trying to kill me! Oh *God*! *Please!*'

'Keep driving.'

One thing was clear to him. The killers had seen him drop his suitcase and leave it behind in his race for escape. That suitcase told them the obvious: he was getting out of Zürich, undoubtedly out of Switzerland. The airport and the station would be watched. And the car he had taken from the man he had killed – who had tried to kill him – would be the object of a search.

He could not go to the airport or to the station; he had to get rid of the car and find another. Yet he was not without resources. He was carrying 100,000 Swiss francs, and more than 16,000 French francs, the Swiss currency in his passport case, the French in the wallet he had stolen from the Marquis de Chambord. It was more than enough to buy him secretly to Paris.

Why Paris? It was as though the city were a magnet, pulling him to her without explanation.

You are not helpless. You will find your way . . . Follow your instincts, reasonably, of course.

To Paris.

'Have you been to Zürich before?' he asked his hostage.

'Never.'

'You wouldn't lie to me, would you?'

'I've no *reason* to! *Please.* Let me stop. Let me *go*!'

'How long have you been here?'

'A week. The conference was for a week.'

'Then you've had time to get around, do some sightseeing.'

'I barely left the hotel. There *wasn't* time.'

'The schedule I saw on the board didn't seem very crowded. Only two lectures for the entire day.'

'They were guest speakers; there were never more than two a day. The majority of our work was done in conference . . . small conferences. Ten to fifteen people from different countries, different interests.'

'You're from Canada?'

'I work for the Canadian government . . .'

'The "doctor" is not medical then.'

'Economics. McGill University. Pembroke College, Oxford.'

'I'm impressed.'

Suddenly, with controlled stridency, she added, 'My superiors expect me to be in contact with them. *Tonight.* If they don't hear from me, they'll be alarmed. They'll make inquiries; they'll call the Zürich police.'

'I see,' he said. 'That's something to think about, isn't it?' It occurred to Bourne that throughout the shock and the violence of the last half hour, the St Jacques woman had not let her handbag out of her hand. He leaned forward, wincing as he did so, the pain in his chest suddenly acute again. 'Give me your bag.'

'What?' She moved her hand quickly from the wheel, grabbing the bag in a futile attempt to keep it from him.

He thrust his right hand over the seat, his fingers grasping the leather. 'Just drive, Doctor,' he said as he lifted the purse off the seat and leaned back again.

'You have no *right* . . .' She stopped, the foolishness of her remark apparent.

'I know that,' he replied, opening the handbag, turning on the reading lamp, moving the bag into its spill. As befitted the owner, it was well organized. Passport, wallet, a purse, keys and assorted notes and messages in the rear pockets. He looked for a specific message; it was in a yellow envelope given to her by the clerk at the Carillon du Lac's front desk. He found it, lifted the flap, and took out the folded paper. It was a cablegram from Ottawa.

> *Daily reports first rate. Leave granted. Will meet you at airport Wednesday 26th. Call or cable flight. In Lyons, do not miss Beau Meunière. Cuisine superb.*
>
> *Love, Peter*

Jason put the cable back. He saw a small book of matches, the cover a glossy white, scroll writing on the front. He picked it out and read the name. *Kronehalle.* A restaurant . . . A restaurant. Something bothered him; he did not know what it was but it was there. Something about a *restaurant.* He kept the matches, closed the bag and leaned forward, dropping it on the front seat. 'That's all I wanted to see,' he said, settling back into the corner, staring at the matches. 'I seem to remember your saying something about "word from Ottawa". You got it; the twenty-sixth is over a week away.'

'Please . . .'

The supplication was a cry for help; he heard it for what it was but could not respond. For the next hour or so he needed this woman, needed her as a lame man needed a crutch or, more aptly, as one who could not function behind a wheel needed a driver. But not in this car.

'Turn around,' he ordered. 'Head back to the Carillon.'

'To the . . . hotel?'

'Yes,' he said, his eyes on the matches, turning them over and over in his hand under the light of the reading lamp. 'We need another car.'

'*We?* No, you *can't*! I won't go any . . .' Again she stopped before the statement was made, before the thought was completed. Another thought had obviously struck her; she was abruptly silent as she swung the wheel until the car was facing the opposite direction on the dark lakeshore road. She pressed the accelerator down with such force that the car bolted; the tyres span under the sudden burst of speed. She depressed the pedal instantly, gripping the wheel, trying to control herself.

Bourne looked up from the matches at the back of her head, at the long dark red hair that shone in the light. He took the gun from his pocket and once more leaned forward directly behind her. He raised the weapon, moving his hand over her shoulder, turning the barrel and pressed it against her cheek.

'Understand me clearly. You're going to do exactly as I tell you. You're going to be right at my side and this gun will be in my pocket. It will be aimed at your stomach, just as it's aimed at your head right now. As you've seen, I'm running for my life, and I won't hesitate to pull the trigger. I want you to understand.'

'I understand.' Her reply was a whisper. She breathed through her parted lips, her terror complete. Jason removed the barrel of the gun from her cheek; he was satisfied.

Satisfied and revolted.

Let your mind fall free . . . The matches. What was it about the matches? But it was not the matches, it was the restaurant – not the *Kronehalle,* but a *restaurant.* Heavy beams, candlelight, black . . . triangles on the outside. White stone and black triangles. Three? . . . *Three black triangles.*

Someone was there . . . at the restaurant with three triangles in front. The image was so clear, so vivid . . . so disturbing. What *was* it? Did such a place even exist?

Specifics may come to you . . . certain repressed conduits . . . prodded into functioning.

Was it happening now? *Oh, Christ, I can't stand it!*

He could see the lights of the Carillon du Lac several hundred yards down the road. He had not fully thought out his moves, but was operating on two assumptions. The first was that the killers had not remained on the premises. On the other hand, Bourne was not about to walk into a trap of his own making. He knew two of the killers; he would not recognize others if they had been left behind.

The main parking area was beyond the circular drive, on the left side of the hotel. 'Slow down,' Jason ordered. 'Turn into the first drive on the left.'

'It's an exit,' protested the woman, her voice strained. 'We're going the wrong way.'

'No one's coming out. Go on! Drive into the parking area, past the lights.'

The scene at the hotel's canopied entrance explained why no one paid attention to them. There were four police cars lined up in the circular drive, their roof lights revolving, conveying the aura of *emergency.* He could see uniformed police among the crowds of excited hotel guests; they were asking questions as well as answering them, checking off names of those leaving in cars, dark-suited hotel clerks at their sides.

Marie St Jacques drove across the parking area beyond the floodlights and into an open space on the right. She turned off the engine and sat motionless, staring straight ahead.

'Be very careful,' said Bourne, rolling down his window. 'And move slowly. Open your door and get out, then stand by mine and help me. Remember, the window's open and the gun's in my hand. You're only two or three feet in front of me; there's no way I could miss if I fired.'

She did as she was told, a terrified automaton. Jason supported himself on the frame of the window and pulled himself to the pavement. He shifted his weight from one foot to another, mobility was returning. He could *walk.* Not well, and with a limp, but he *could walk.*

'What are you going to do?' asked the St Jacques woman, as if she were afraid to hear his answer.

'Wait. Sooner or later someone will drive a car back here and park it. No matter what happened in there, it's still dinner time. Reservations were made, parties arranged, a lot of it business; those people won't change their plans.'

'And when a car does come, how will you take it?' She paused, then answered her own questions. 'Oh, my God, you're going to kill whoever's driving it.'

He gripped her arm, her frightened, chalk-white face inches away. He had to control her by fear, but not to the point where she might slip into hysterics. 'If I have to I will, but I don't think it'll be necessary. Parking attendants bring the cars back here. Keys are usually left on the visors or under the seats. It's just easier.'

Headlight beams shot out from the dark in the circular drive; a small coupé entered the area, accelerating once into it, the mark of an attendant driver. The car came directly towards them, alarming Bourne until he saw the empty space nearby. But they were in the path of the headlights; they had been seen.

Reservations for the dining room . . . A restaurant. Jason made his decision; he would use the moment.

The attendant got out of the coupé, and placed the keys under the seat. As he walked to the rear of the car, he nodded at them, not without curiosity. Bourne spoke in French.

'Hey, young fellow! Maybe you can help us.'

'Sir?' The attendant approached them haltingly, cautiously, the events in the hotel obviously on his mind.

'I'm not feeling so well, too much of your excellent Swiss wine.'

'It will happen, sir.' The young man smiled, relieved.

'My wife thought it would be a good idea to get some air before we left for town.'

'A good idea, sir.'

'Is everything still crazy inside? I didn't think the police officer would let us out until he saw that I might be sick all over his uniform.'

'Crazy, sir. They're everywhere . . . We've been told not to discuss it.'

'Of course. But we've got a problem. An associate flew in this afternoon and we agreed to meet at a restaurant, only I've forgotten the name. I've been there but I just can't remember where it is or what it's called. I do remember that on the front there were three odd shapes . . . a design of some sort, I think. Triangles, I believe.'

'That's the *Drei Alpenhäuser*, sir. The . . . *Three Chalets*. It's in a sidestreet off the Falkenstrasse.'

'Yes, of course, that's it! And to get there from here we . . .' Bourne trailed off the words, a man with too much wine trying to concentrate.

'Just turn left out of the exit, sir. Stay on the Uto Quai for about six kilometres, until you reach a large pier, then turn right. It will take you into the Falkenstrasse. Once you pass Seefeld, you can't miss the street or the restaurant. There's a sign on the corner.'

'Thank you. Will you be here a few hours from now, when we return?'

'I'm on duty until two this morning, sir.'

'Good. I'll look for you and express my gratitude more concretely.'

'Thank you, sir. May I get your car for you?'

'You've done enough, thanks. A little more walking is required.' The attendant saluted, and started for the front of the hotel. Jason led Marie St Jacques towards the coupé, limping beside her. 'Hurry up. The keys are under the seat.'

'If they stop us, what will you do? That attendant will see the car go out; he'll know you've stolen it!'

'I doubt it. Not if we leave right away, the minute he's back in that crowd.'

'Suppose he *does*?'

'Then I hope you're a fast driver,' said Bourne, pushing her towards the door. 'Get in.' The attendant had turned the corner; he suddenly hurried his pace! Jason took out the gun, and limped rapidly around the bonnet of the coupé, supporting himself on it while pointing the pistol at the windscreen. He opened the passenger door and climbed in beside her. 'Goddamn it, I said get the keys!'

'All *right* . . . I can't *think*.'

'Try harder!'

'Oh, *God* . . .' She reached below the seat, stabbing her hand around the carpet until she found the small leather case.

'Start the engine, but wait until I tell you to back out.' He watched for headlight beams to shine into the area from the circular drive; it would be a reason for the attendant to have suddenly broken into a near run; a car to be parked. They did not come; the reason could be something else. Two unknown people in the parking area. 'Go ahead. Quickly. I want to get out of here.' She threw the gear into reverse; seconds later they approached the exit into the lakeshore drive. 'Slow down,' he commanded. A taxi was swinging into the curve in front of them.

Bourne held his breath and looked through the opposite window at the Carillon du Lac's entrance; the scene under the canopy explained the attendant's sudden decision to hurry. An argument had broken out between the police and a group of hotel guests. A queue had formed for names to be checked before leaving the hotel, the resulting delays angered the innocent.

'Let's go,' said Jason, wincing again, the pain shooting through his chest. 'We're clear.'

It was a numbing sensation, eerie and uncanny. The three triangles were as he had pictured them: thick dark wood raised in bas-relief on white stone. Three equal triangles, abstract renditions of chalet roofs in a valley of snow so deep the lower storeys were obscured. Above the three points was the restaurant's name in Germanic letters. Drei Alpenhäuser. Below the base line of the centre triangle was the entrance, double doors that together formed a cathedral arch, the hardware massive rings of iron common to Alpine châteaux.

The surrounding buildings on both sides of the narrow brick street were restored structures of a Zürich and a Europe long past. It was not a street for cars; instead one pictured elaborate coaches drawn by horses, drivers sitting high in mufflers and top hats, and gas lamps everywhere. It was a street filled with the sights and sounds of forgotten memories, thought the man who had no memory to forget.

Yet he *had* had one, vivid and disturbing. Three dark triangles, heavy beams and candlelight. He had been right; it was a memory of Zürich. But in another life.

'We're here,' said the woman.

'I know.'

'Tell me what to *do*,' she cried. 'We're going past it.'

'Go to the next corner and turn left. Go round the block, then drive back through here.'

'Why?'

'I wish I knew.'

'What?'

'Because I said so.' *Someone was there . . . at that restaurant. Why didn't other images come? Another image. A face.*

They drove down the street past the restaurant twice more. Two separate couples and a foursome went inside; a single man came out, heading for the Falkenstrasse. To judge from the cars parked on the kerb, there was a medium-sized crowd at the Drei Alpenhäuser. It would grow in number as the next two hours passed, most of Zürich preferring its evening meal nearer ten-thirty than eight. There was no point in delaying any longer; nothing further came to Bourne. He could only sit and watch and hope something *would* come. *Something.* For something had; a book of matches had evoked an image of reality. Within that reality there was a truth he had to discover.

'Pull over to your right, in front of the last car. We'll walk back.'

Silently, without comment or protest, the St Jacques woman did as she was told. Jason looked at her; her reaction was too docile, inconsistent with her previous behaviour. He understood. A lesson had to be taught. Regardless of what might happen inside the Drei Alpenhäuser, he needed her for a final contribution. She had to drive him out of Zürich.

The car came to a stop, tyres scraping the kerb. She turned off the engine and began to remove the keys, her movement slow, too slow. He reached over and held her wrist; she stared at him in the shadows without breathing. He slid his fingers over her hand until he felt the key case.

'I'll take those,' he said.

'Naturally,' she replied, her left hand unnaturally at her side, poised by the panel of the door.

'Now get out and stand by the bonnet,' he continued. 'Don't do anything foolish.'

'Why should I? You'd kill me.'

'Good.' He reached for the handle of the door exaggerating the difficulty. The back of his head was to her; he snapped the handle down.

The rustle of fabric was sudden, the rush of air more sudden still; her door crashed open, the woman half out into the street. But Bourne was ready; a lesson had to be taught. He spun around, his left arm an uncoiling spring, his hand a claw, gripping the silk of her dress between her shoulder blades. He pulled her back into the seat and, grabbing her by the hair, yanked her head towards him until her neck was stretched, her face against his.

'I won't do it again!' she cried, tears welling at her eyes. 'I *swear* to you I won't!'

He reached across and pulled the door shut, then looked at her closely, trying to understand something in himself. Thirty minutes ago in another car he had experienced a degree of nausea when he had pressed the barrel of the gun into her cheek, threatening to take her life if she disobeyed him. There was no such revulsion now; with one overt action she had crossed over into another territory. She had become an enemy, a threat; he could kill her if he had to, kill her without emotion because it was the practical thing to do.

'*Say* something!' she whispered. Her body went into a brief spasm, her breasts pressing against the dark silk of her dress, rising and falling with the agitated movement. She gripped her own wrist in an attempt to control herself; she partially succeeded. She spoke again, the whisper replaced by a monotone. 'I said I wouldn't do it again and I won't.'

'You'll try,' he replied quietly. 'There'll come a moment when you think you can make it, and you'll try. Believe me when I tell you you can't, but if you try again I will have to kill you. I don't want to do that, there's no reason for it, no reason at all. Unless you become a threat to me, and in running away before I let you go you do just that. I can't allow it.'

He had spoken the truth as he understood the truth. The simplicity of the decision was as astonishing to him as the decision itself. Killing was a practical matter, nothing else.

'You say you'll let me go,' she said. 'When?'

'When I'm safe,' he answered. 'When it doesn't make any difference what you say or do.'

'When will that be?'

'An hour or so from now. When we're out of Zürich and I'm on my way to somewhere else. You won't know where or how.'

'Why should I believe you?'

'I don't care whether you do or not.' He released her. 'Pull yourself together. Dry your eyes and comb your hair. We're going inside.'

'What's in there?'

'I wish I knew,' he said, glancing through the rear window at the door of the Drei Alpenhäuser.

'You said that before.'

He looked at her, at the wide brown eyes that were searching his. Searching in fear, in bewilderment. 'I know. Hurry up.'

There were thick beams running across the high Alpine ceiling, tables and chairs of heavy wood, deep booths and candlelight everywhere. An accordion player moved through the crowd, muted strains of Bavarian *Musik* coming from his instrument.

He had seen the large room before, the beams and the candlelight printed somewhere in his mind, the sounds recorded also. He had come here in another life. They stood in the shallow foyer in front of the *maître d'hôtel*'s station; he greeted them.

'*Haben Sie einen Platz reserviert, mein Herr?*'

'If you mean have I a reservation, I'm afraid not. But you were highly recommended. I hope you can fit us in. A booth, if possible.'

'Certainly, sir. It's the early sitting; we're not yet crowded. This way, please.'

They were taken to a booth in the nearest corner, a flickering candle in the centre of the table. Bourne's limp and the fact that he held on to the woman, dictated the closest available location. Jason nodded to Marie St Jacques; she sat down, and he slid into the booth opposite her.

'Move against the wall,' he said, after the *maître* had left. 'Remember, the gun's in my pocket and all I have to do is raise my foot and you're trapped.'

'I said I wouldn't try.'

'I hope you don't. Order a drink; there's no time to eat.'

'I couldn't eat.' She gripped her wrist again, her hands visibly trembling. 'Why isn't there time? What are you waiting for?'

'I don't know.'

'Why do you keep *saying* that? "I don't know." "I wish I knew." Why did you come here?'

'Because I've been here before.'

'That's no answer!'

'There's no reason for me to give you one.'

A waiter approached. The St Jacques woman asked for wine; Bourne ordered Scotch, needing the stronger drink. He looked round the restaurant, trying to concentrate 'on everything and nothing'. A sponge. But there was only nothing. No images filled his mind; no thoughts intruded on his absence of thought. *Nothing.*

And then he saw the face across the room. It was a large face set in a large head, above an obese body pressed against the wall of an end booth, next to a closed door. The fat man stayed in the shadows of his observation point as if they were his protection, the unlit section of the floor his sanctuary. His eyes were riveted on Jason, equal parts fear and disbelief in his stare. Bourne did not know the face, but the face knew him. The man brought his fingers to his lips and wiped the corners of his mouth, then shifted his eyes, taking in each diner at every table. Only then did he begin what was obviously a painful journey around the room towards their booth.

'A man's coming over here,' he said over the flame of the candle. 'A fat man, and he's afraid. Don't say anything. No matter what he says, keep your mouth shut. And don't look at him; raise your hand, rest your head on your elbow casually. Look at the wall, not him.'

The woman frowned, bringing her right hand to her face; her fingers trembled. Her lips formed a question, but no words came. Jason answered the unspoken.

'For your own good,' he said. 'There's no point in his being able to identify you.'

The fat man edged round the corner of the booth. Bourne blew out the candle, throwing the table into relative darkness. The man stared him down and spoke in a low, strained voice.

'*Leiber Gott!* Why did you *come* here? What have I done that you should do this to me?'

'I enjoy the food, you know that.'

'Have you no *feelings*? I have a family, a wife and children. I did only as I was told. I gave you the envelope; I did not look inside, I know nothing!'

'But you were paid, weren't you?' asked Jason instinctively.

'Yes, but I said *nothing*. We never met, I never described you. I spoke to no one!'

'Then why are you afraid? I'm just an ordinary patron about to order dinner.'

'I beg you. *Leave.*'

'Now I'm angry. You'd better tell me why.'

The fat man brought his hand to his face, his fingers again wiping the moisture that had formed around his mouth. He angled his head, glancing at the door, then turned back to Bourne. 'Others may have spoken, others may know who you are. I've had my share of trouble with the police, they would come directly to me.'

The St Jacques woman lost control; she looked at Jason, the words escaping. 'The police . . . They were the *police*.'

Bourne glared at her, then turned back to the nervous fat man. 'Are you saying the police would harm your wife and children?'

'Not in themselves – as you well know. But their interest would lead others to me. To my family. How many are there that look for you, mein Herr? And what *are* they that do? You need no answer from me; they stop at nothing – the death of a wife or a child is nothing. *Please.* On my life, I've said nothing. *Leave.*'

'You're exaggerating.' Jason raised his drink to his lips, a prelude to dismissal.

'In the name of Christ, don't *do* this!' The man leaned over, gripping the edge of the table. 'You wish proof of my silence, I give it to you. Word was spread throughout the *Verbrecherwelt.* Anyone with any information whatsoever should call a number set up by the Zürich police. Everything would be kept in the strictest confidence; they would not lie in the *Verbrecherwelt* about that. Rewards were ample, the police in several countries sending funds through Interpol. Past misunderstandings might be seen in new judicial lights.' The conspirator stood up, wiping his mouth again, his large bulk hovering above the wood. 'A man like myself could profit from a kinder relationship with the police. Yet I did nothing. In spite of the guarantee of confidentiality, I did nothing at all!'

'Did anyone else? Tell me the truth; I'll know if you're lying.'

'I know only Chernak. He's the only one I've ever spoken to who admits having even seen you. But you know that; the envelope was passed through him to me. He'd never say anything.'

'Where's Chernak now?'

'Where he always is. In his flat on the Löwenstrasse.'

'I've never been there. What's the number?'

'You've never been? . . .' The fat man paused, his lips pressed together, alarm in his eyes. 'Are you testing me?'

'Answer the question.'

'Number 37. You know it as well as I do.'

'Then I'm testing you. Who gave the envelope to Chernak?'

The man stood motionless, his dubious integrity challenged. 'I have no way of knowing. Nor would I ever inquire.'

'You weren't even curious?'

'Of course not. A goat does not willingly enter the wolf's cave.'

'Goats are sure-footed; they've got an accurate sense of smell.'

'And they are cautious, mein Herr. Because the wolf is faster, infinitely more aggressive. There would be only one chase. The goat's last.'

'What was in the envelope?'

'I told you, I did not open it.'

'But you know what was in it.'

'Money, I presume.'

'You *presume*?'

'Very well. Money. A great deal of money. If there was any discrepancy, it had nothing to do with me. Now *please*, I *beg* you. Get *out* of here!'

'One last question.'

'*Anything*. Just leave!'

'What was the money for?'

The obese man stared down at Bourne, his breathing audible, sweat glistening on his chin. 'You put me on the rack, mein Herr, but I will not turn away from you. Call it the courage of an insignificant goat who has survived. Every day I read the newspapers. In three languages. Six months ago a man was killed. His death was reported on the front page of each of those papers.'

7

They circled the block, emerging on the Falkenstrasse, then turned right towards the Limmat Quai and the Grossmünster. The Löwenstrasse was across the river, on the west side of the city. The quickest way to reach it was to take the Münster Bridge to the Nuschelerstrasse; the avenues intersected, according to a couple who had been about to enter the Drei Alpenhäuser.

Marie St Jacques was silent, holding onto the wheel as she had gripped the straps of her handbag during the madness at the Carillon, somehow her connection with sanity. Bourne glanced at her and understood.

. . . a man was killed, his death reported on the front pages of each of those papers.

Jason Bourne had been paid to kill, and the police in several countries had sent funds through Interpol to convert reluctant informers, to broaden the base of his capture. Which meant that other men had been killed . . .

How many are there that look for you, mein Herr? And what are they that do? . . . They stop at nothing – the death of a wife or a child is nothing!

Not the police. Others.

The twin bell towers of the Grossmünster rose in the night sky, floodlights creating eerie shadows. Jason stared at the ancient structure; as so much else he knew it but did not know it. He had seen it before, yet he was seeing it now for the first time.

I know only Chernak . . . The envelope was passed through him to me . . . Löwenstrasse. Number 37. You know it as well as I do.

Did he? Would he?

They drove over the bridge into the traffic of the newer city. The streets were crowded, cars and pedestrians vying for supremacy at every intersection, the red and green signals erratic and interminable. Bourne tried to concentrate on nothing . . . and everything. The outlines of the truth were being presented to him, shape by enigmatic shape, each more startling than the last. He was not at all sure he was capable – *mentally* capable – of absorbing a great deal more.

'*Sie! Fräulein. Ihre Scheinwerfer! Und Sie signalisieren. Unrechter Weg!*'

Jason looked up, a hollow pain knotting his stomach. A patrol car was beside them, a policeman shouting through his open window. Everything was suddenly clear . . . clear and infuriating. The St Jacques woman had seen the police car in the side view mirror; she had extinguished the headlights and slipped her hand down to the indicator, flipping it for a left turn. A *left* turn into a one-way street whose arrows at the intersection clearly defined the traffic heading *right*! And turning left by bolting in front of the police car would result in several violations: the absence of headlights, perhaps even a premeditated collision; they would be stopped, the woman free to scream.

Bourne snapped the headlights on, then leaned across the girl, one hand disengaging the directional signal, the other gripping her arm where he had gripped it before.

'I'll kill you, Doctor,' he said quietly, then shouted though the window at the police officer. 'Sorry! We're a little confused! Tourists! We want the next block!'

The policeman was barely two feet away from Marie St Jacques, his eyes on her face, evidently puzzled by her lack of reaction.

The light changed. 'Ease forward. Don't do anything stupid,' said Jason. He waved at the police officer through the glass. 'Sorry again!' he yelled. The policeman shrugged, turning to his partner to resume a previous conversation.

'I *was* confused,' said the girl, her soft voice trembling. 'There's so much traffic . . . Oh, *God*, you've broken my arm! . . . You *bastard*.'

Bourne released her, disturbed by her anger; he preferred fear. 'You don't expect me to believe you, do you?'

'My arm?'

'Your confusion.'

'You said we were going to turn left soon; that's all I was thinking about.'

'Next time look at the traffic.' He moved away from her but did not take his eyes off her face.

'You *are* an animal,' she whispered, briefly closing her eyes, opening them in fear, it had come back.

They reached the Löwenstrasse, a wide avenue where low buildings of brick and heavy wood stood sandwiched between modern examples of smooth concrete and glass. The character of nineteenth-century flats competed against the utilitarianism of contemporary neuterness, they did not lose. Jason watched the numbers, they were descending from the middle eighties, with each block the old houses more in evidence than the highrise apartments, until the street had returned in time to that other era. There was a row of neat three-storey flats, roofs and windows framed in wood, stone steps and railings leading up to recessed doorways washed in the light of carriage lamps. Bourne recognized the unremembered; the fact that he did so was not startling, but something else was. The row of houses evoked another image, a very strong image of another row of flats, similar in outline but oddly different. Weathered, older, nowhere near as neat or scrubbed . . . cracked windows, broken steps, incomplete railings – jagged ends of rusted iron. Farther away, in another part of . . . Zürich, yes they *were* in Zürich. In a small district rarely if ever visited by those who did not live there, a part of the city that was left behind, but not gracefully.

'*Steppdeckstrasse*,' he said to himself, concentrating on the image in his mind. He could see a doorway, the paint a faded red, as dark as the red silk dress worn by the woman beside him. 'A boarding house . . . in the Steppdeckstrasse.'

'*What?*' Marie St Jacques was startled. The words he uttered alarmed her; she had obviously related them to herself and was terrified.

'Nothing.' He took his eyes off the dress and looked out of the window. 'There's Number 37,' he said, pointing to the fifth house in the row. 'Stop the car.'

He got out first, ordering her to slide across the seat and follow. He tested his legs and took the keys from her.

'You can walk,' she said. 'If you can walk, you can *drive*.'

'I probably can.'

'Then let me go! I've done everything you've wanted.'

'And then some,' he added.

'I won't say anything, can't you *understand* that? You're the last person on earth I ever want to see again . . . or have anything to *do* with. I don't want to be a witness, or get involved with the police, or make statements, or *anything*! I don't want to be a part of what you're a part of! I'm frightened to death . . . that's your protection, don't you *see*? Let me go, *please*.'

'I can't.'

'You don't believe me.'

'That's not relevant. I need you.'

'For *what*?'

'For something very stupid. I don't have a driver's licence. You can't hire a car without a driver's licence and I've got to hire a car.'

'You've got *this* car.'

'It's good for maybe another hour. Someone's going to walk out of the Carillon du Lac and want it. The description will be radioed to every police car in Zürich.'

She looked at him, dead fear in the glass of her eyes. 'I don't want to go up there with you. I heard what that man said in the restaurant. If I hear any more you'll kill me.'

'What you heard makes no more sense to me than it does to you. Perhaps less. Come on.' He took her by the arm, and put his free hand on the railing so he could climb the steps with a minimum of pain.

She stared at him, bewilderment and fear converged in her look.

The name *M. Chernak* was under the second letter box, with a bell beneath. He did not ring it, but pressed the adjacent four buttons. Within seconds a cacophony of voices sprang out of the small, dotted speakers asking in Schweitzerdeutsch who was there. But someone did not answer, he merely pressed a buzzer which released the lock. Jason opened the door, pushing Marie St Jacques in front of him.

He moved her against the wall and waited. From above came the sounds of doors opening, footsteps walking towards the staircase.

'*Wer ist da?*'

'*Johann?*'

'*Wie bitte?*'

Silence. Followed by words of irritation. Footsteps were heard again; doors closed.

M. Chernak was on the second floor, *Flat 2C*. Bourne took the girl's arm, limped with her to the staircase and started the climb. She was right, of course. It would be far better if he were alone, but there was nothing he could do about that; he did need her.

He had studied road maps during the weeks in Port Noir: Lucerne was no more than an hour away, Bern two and a half or three. He could head for either one, dropping her off in some deserted spot along the way, and then disappear. It was simply a matter of timing; he had the resources to buy a hundred connections. He needed only a conduit out of Zürich and she was it.

But before he left Zürich he had to know; he had to talk to a man named . . .

M. Chernak. The name was to the right of the doorbell. He sidestepped away from the door, pulling the woman with him.

'Do you speak German?' Jason asked.

'No.'

'Don't lie.'

'I'm not.'

Bourne thought, glancing up and down the short hallway, 'Ring the bell. If the door opens just stand there. If someone answers from inside, say you have a message – an urgent message – from a friend at the Drei Alpenhäuser.'

'Suppose he – or she – says to slide it under the door?'

Jason looked at her. 'Very good.'

'I just don't want any more violence. I don't want to *know* anything or *see* anything. I just want to . . .'

'I know,' he interrupted. 'Go back to Caesar's taxes and the Punic Wars . . . If he – or she – says something like that, explain in a couple of words that the message is verbal and can only be delivered to the man who was described to you.'

'If he asks for that description?' said Marie St Jacques icily, analysis momentarily pre-empting fear.

'You've got a good mind, Doctor,' he said.

'I'm precise. I'm frightened; I told you that. What do I do?'

'Say to hell with them, someone else can deliver it. Then start to walk away.'

She moved to the door and rang the bell. There was an odd sound from within. A scratching, growing louder, constant. Then it stopped and a deep voice was heard through the wood.

'*Was ist los?*'

'I'm afraid I don't speak German,' said the St Jacques woman

'*Englisch.* What is it? Who are you?'

'I have an urgent message from a friend at the Drei Alpenhäuser.'

'Shove it under the door.'

'I can't do that. It isn't written down. I have to deliver it personally to the man who was described to me.'

'Well, that shouldn't be difficult,' said the voice. The lock clicked and the door opened.

Bourne stepped away from the wall, into the doorframe.

'You're *insane*!' cried a man with two stumps for legs, propped up in a wheelchair. 'Get *out*! Get away from here!'

'I'm tired of hearing that,' said Jason, pulling the girl inside and closing the door.

It took no pressure to persuade Marie St Jacques to remain in a small windowless bedroom while they talked; she did so willingly. The legless Chernak was close to panic, his ravaged face chalk white, his unkempt grey hair matted about his neck and forehead.

'What do you *want* from me?' he asked. 'You swore the last transaction was our final one! I can do no more, I cannot take the risk. Messengers have *been* here. No matter how cautious, how many times removed from your sources, they have *been here*! If one leaves an address in the wrong surroundings, I'm a dead man!'

'You've done pretty well for the risks you've taken,' said Bourne, standing in front of the wheelchair, his mind racing, wondering if there was a word or a phrase that could trigger a flow of information. Then he remembered the envelope. *If there was any discrepancy, it had nothing to do with me.* A fat man at the Drei Alpenhäuser.

'Minor compared to the magnitude of those risks.' Chernak shook his head; his upper chest heaved; the stumps that fell over the chair moved obscenely back and forth. 'I was content before you came into my life, mein Herr, for I *was* minor. An old soldier who made his way to Zürich – blown up, a cripple, worthless except for certain facts stored away that former comrades paid meagrely to keep suppressed. It was a decent life, not much, but enough. Then *you* found me . . .'

'I'm touched,' broke in Jason. 'Let's talk about the envelope – the envelope you passed to our mutual friend at Drei Alpenhäuser. Who gave it to you?'

'A messenger. Who else?'

'Where did it come from?'

'How would *I* know? It arrived in a box, just like the others. I unpacked it and sent it on. It was *you* who wished it so. You said you could not come here any longer.'

'But you opened it.' A statement.

'Never!'

'Suppose I told you, there was money missing.'

'Then it was not paid; it was not in the envelope!' The legless man's voice rose. 'However, I don't believe you. If that were so, you would not have accepted the assignment. But you did accept that assignment. So why are you here now?'

Because I have to know. Because I'm going out of my mind. I see things and I hear things I do not understand. I'm a skilled, resourceful . . . vegetable! Help me!

Bourne moved away from the chair; he walked aimlessly towards a bookcase where there were several upright photographs recessed against the wall. They explained the man behind him. Groups of German soldiers, some with alsatians, posing outside barracks and by fences . . . and in front of a high-wire gate with part of a name showing. *DACH* . . .

Dachau.

The man behind him. He was moving! Jason turned; the legless Chernak had his hand in the canvas bag strapped to his chair; his eyes were on fire, his ravaged face contorted. The hand came out swiftly, in it a short-barrelled revolver, and before Bourne could reach his own, Chernak fired. The shots came rapidly, the icelike pain filling his left shoulder, then head – oh *God*! He dived to his right, spinning on the rug, shoving a heavy floor lamp towards the cripple, spinning again until he was at the far side of the wheelchair. He crouched and lunged, crashing his right shoulder into Chernak's back, sending the legless man out of the chair as he reached into his pocket for the gun.

'They'll pay for your corpse!' screamed the deformed man, writhing on the floor, trying to steady his slumped body long enough to level his weapon. 'You won't put me in a coffin! I'll see you there! Carlos will pay! By Christ, he'll pay!'

Jason sprang to the left and fired. Chernak's head snapped back, his throat erupting in blood. He was dead.

A cry came from the door of the bedroom. It grew in depth, low and hollow, an elongated wail, fear and revulsion weaved into the chord. A woman's cry . . . of course, it was a woman! His hostage, his conduit out of Zürich! Oh, *Jesus*, he could not focus his eyes! His temple was in agony!

He found his vision, refusing to acknowledge the pain. He saw a bathroom, the door open, towels and a basin and a . . . mirrored cabinet. He ran in, pulled the mirror back with such force that it jumped its hinges, crashing to the floor, shattered. *Shelves.* Rolls of gauze and plaster and . . . they were all he could grab. He had to get out . . . *gunshots*; gunshots were alarms. He had to get out, take his hostage, and get away! The bedroom, the *bedroom.* Where was it?

The cry, the wail . . . follow the cry! He reached the door and kicked it open. The woman . . . his hostage – what the hell was her *name*? – was pressed against the wall, tears streaming down her face, her lips parted. He rushed in and grabbed her by the wrist, dragging her out.

'My *God*, you killed him!' she cried. 'An old man with no . . .'

'Shut *up*!' He pushed her towards the door, opened it and shoved her into the hallway. He could see blurred figures in open spaces, by railings, inside rooms. They began running, disappearing; he heard doors slam, people shout. He took the woman's arm with his left hand; the grip caused shooting pains in his shoulder. He propelled her to the staircase and forced her to descend with him, using her for support, his right hand holding the gun.

They reached the lobby and the heavy door. 'Open it!' he ordered, she did. They passed the row of letterboxes to the outside entrance. He released her briefly, opening the door himself, peering out into the street, listening for sirens. There were none. 'Come *on*!' he said, pulling her out to the stone steps and down to the pavement. He reached into his pocket, wincing, taking out the car keys. 'Get in!'

Inside the car he unravelled the gauze, bunching it against the side of his head, blotting the trickle of blood. From deep inside his conscious, there was a strange feeling of relief. The wound was a graze; the fact that it had been his head had sent him into panic, but the bullet had not entered his skull. It had *not* entered; there would be no return to the agonies of Port Noir.

'Goddamn it, start the car! Get *out* of here!'

'Where? You didn't say where.' The woman was not screaming; instead she was calm. Unreasonably calm. Looking at him . . . was she looking at him?

He was feeling dizzy again, losing focus again. 'Steppdeckstrasse . . .' He heard the word as he spoke it, not sure the voice was his. But he could picture the doorway. Faded dark-red paint, cracked glass . . . rusted iron. 'Steppdeckstrasse,' he repeated.

What was wrong? Why wasn't the engine running? Why didn't the car move forward. Didn't she *hear* him?

His eyes were closed; he opened them. The *gun*! It was on his lap; he had set it down to press the bandage . . . she was hitting it, *hitting* it! The weapon crashed to the floor, he reached down and she pushed him, sending his head into the window. Her door opened and she leaped out into the street and began running. She was running away! His hostage, his conduit was racing up the Löwenstrasse!

He could not stay in the car; he dared not try to drive it. It was a steel trap, marking him. He put the gun in his pocket with the roll of plaster, and grabbed the gauze, clutching it in his left hand, ready to press it against his temple at the first recurrence of blood. He got out and limped as fast as he could down the pavement.

Somewhere there was a corner, somewhere a taxi. *Steppdeckstrasse.*

Marie St Jacques kept running in the middle of the wide, deserted avenue, in and out of the spills of the street lamps, waving her arms at the cars in the Löwenstrasse. They sped by her. She turned in the wash of headlights behind her, holding up her hands, pleading for attention; the cars accelerated and passed her by. This was Zürich, and the Löwenstrasse at night was too wide, too dark, too near the deserted park and the river Sihl.

The men in one car, however, were aware of her. Its headlights were off, the driver inside having seen the woman in the distance. He spoke to his companion in Schweitzerdeutsch.

'It could be her. This Chernak lives only a block or so down the street.'

'Stop and let her come closer. She's supposed to be wearing a silk . . . it's her.'

'Let's make certain before we radio the others.'

Both men got out of the car, the passenger moving discreetly around the boot to join the driver. They wore conservative business suits, their faces pleasant, but serious, businesslike. The panicked woman approached; they walked rapidly into the middle of the street. The driver called out.

'*Fräulein! Was ist los?*'

'Help me!' she screamed. 'I . . . I don't speak German. *Nicht sprechen.* Call the police! The . . . *Polizei*!'

The driver's companion spoke with authority, calming her with his voice.

'We are with the police,' he said in English. '*Züriche Sicherheit.* We weren't sure, Miss. You *are* the woman from the Carillon du Lac?'

'*Yes!*' she cried. 'He wouldn't let me go! He kept hitting me, threatening me with his gun! It was horrible!'

'Where is he now?'

'He's hurt. He was shot. I ran from the car . . . he was in the car when I ran!' She pointed down the Löwenstrasse. 'Over there. Two blocks, I think – in the middle of the block. A coupé, a grey coupé! He has a gun.'

'So do we, Miss,' said the driver. 'Come along, get in the back of the car. You'll be perfectly safe; we'll be very careful. Quickly, now.'

They approached the grey coupé, coasting, headlights extinguished. There was no one inside. There were, however, people talking excitedly on the pavement and up the stone steps of Number 37. The driver's associate turned and spoke to the frightened woman pressed into the corner of the rear seat.

'This is the residence of a man named Chernak. Did he mention him? Did he say anything about going in to see him?'

'He *did* go; he made me come with him! He *killed* him! He killed that crippled old man!'

'*Radioapparat! Schnell*,' said the associate to the driver, as he grabbed a microphone from the dashboard. The car bolted forward; the woman gripped the front seat.

'What are you *doing*? A man was killed back there!'

'And we must find the killer,' said the driver. 'As you say, he was wounded; he may still be in the area. This is an unmarked vehicle and we could spot him. We'll wait, of course, to make sure the inspection team arrives, but our duties are quite separate.' The car slowed down, sliding into the kerb several hundred yards from Number 37 Löwenstrasse.

The associate had spoken into the microphone while the driver had explained their official position. There was static from the dashboard speaker, then the words, '*Aufenthalt. Zwanzig Minuten.*'

'Our superior will be here shortly,' the associate said. 'We're to wait for him. He wishes to speak with you.'

Marie St Jacques leaned back in the seat, closing her eyes, expelling her breath. 'Oh, *God*, I wish I had a drink!'

The driver laughed, nodded to his companion. The associate took out a pint bottle from the glove compartment and held it up, smiling at the woman. 'We're not very chic, Miss. We have no glasses or cups but we do have brandy. For medical emergencies, of course. I think this is one now. Please, our compliments.'

The St Jacques woman smiled back and accepted the bottle. 'You're two very nice people, and you'll never know how grateful I am. If you ever come to Canada, I'll cook you the best French meal in the province of Ontario.'

'Thank you, Miss,' said the driver.

Bourne studied the bandage on his shoulder, squinting at the dull reflection in the dirty, streaked mirror, adjusting his eyes to the dim light of the filthy room. He had been right about the Steppdeckstrasse, the image of the faded red doorway accurate, down to the cracked window panes and rusted iron railings. No questions had been asked when he rented the room in spite of the fact that he was obviously hurt. However, a statement had been made by the *Vermieter* when Bourne paid him.

'For something more substantial a doctor can be found who keeps his mouth shut.'

'I'll let you know.'

The wound was not that severe; the plaster would hold it until he found a doctor somewhat more reliable than one who practised surreptitiously in the Steppdeckstrasse.

If a stress situation results in injury, be aware of the fact that the damage may be as much psychological as physical. You may have a very real revulsion to pain and bodily harm. Don't take risks, but if there's time, give yourself a chance to adjust. Don't panic . . .

He had panicked; areas of his body had frozen. Although the penetration in his shoulder and the graze at his temple were real and painful, neither was serious enough to immobilize him. He could not move as fast as he might wish or with the strength he knew he had, but he could move deliberately. Messages were sent and received, brain to muscle and limb, he could function.

He would function better after a rest. He had no conduit now; he had to be up long before daybreak and find another way out of Zürich. The Steppdeckstrasse *Vermieter* on the first floor liked money; he would wake up the slovenly landlord in an hour or so.

He lowered himself on the sagging bed and lay back on the pillow, staring at the naked lightbulb in the ceiling, trying not to hear the words so he could rest. They came anyway, filling his ears like the pounding of kettledrums.

A man was killed . . .

But you did accept that assignment . . .

He turned to the wall, shutting his eyes, blocking out the words. Then other words came and he sat up, sweat breaking out on his forehead.

They'll pay for your corpse! . . . Carlos will pay! By Christ, he'll pay!

Carlos.

A large limousine pulled up in front of the coupé and parked at the kerb. Behind them, at 37 Löwenstrasse, the patrol cars had arrived fifteen minutes ago, the ambulance less than five. Crowds from surrounding flats lined the pavement near the staircase, but the excitement was muted now. A death had occurred, a man killed at night in this quiet section of the Löwenstrasse. Anxiety was uppermost; what had happened at Number 37 could happen at 32 or 40 or 53. The world was going mad, and Zürich was going with it.

'Our superior has arrived, Miss. May we take you to him, please?' The associate got out of the car and opened the door for Marie St Jacques.

'Certainly.' She stepped out onto the pavement and felt the man's hand on her arm; it was so much gentler than the hard grip of the animal who had held the barrel of a gun to her cheek. She shuddered at the memory. They approached the rear of the limousine; and she climbed inside. She sat back in the seat and looked at the man beside her. She gasped, suddenly paralysed, unable to breathe, the man beside her evoking a memory of terror.

The light from the street lamps was reflected off the thin gold rims of his spectacles.

'*You!* . . . You were at the hotel! You were one of them!'

The man nodded wearily; his fatigue apparent. 'That's right. We're a special branch of the Zürich police. And before we speak further, I must make it clear to you that at no time during the events of the Carillon du Lac were you in any danger of being harmed by us. We're trained marksmen; no shots were fired that could have struck you, a number withheld because you were too close to the man in our sights.'

Her shock eased, the man's quiet authority reassuring. 'Thank you for that.'

'It's a minor talent,' said the official. 'Now, as I understand, you last saw him in the front seat of the car back there.'

'Yes. He was wounded.'

'How seriously?'

'Enough to be incoherent. He held some kind of bandage to his head, and there was blood on his shoulder – on the cloth of his coat, I mean. Who is he?'

'Names are meaningless; he goes by many. But as you've seen, he's a killer. A brutal killer, and he must be found before he kills again. We've been hunting him for several years. Many police from many countries. We have an opportunity now none of them has had. We know he's in Zürich, and he's wounded. He would not stay in this area, but how far can he go? Did he mention how he expected to get out of the city?'

'He was going to rent a car. In my name, I gather. He doesn't have a driver's licence.'

'He was lying. He travels with all manner of false papers. You were an expendable hostage. Now, from the beginning, tell me everything he said to you. Where you went, whom he met, whatever comes to mind.'

'There's a restaurant, the Drei Alpenhäuser, and a large fat man who was frightened to death . . .' Marie St Jacques recounted everything she could remember. From time to time the police official interrupted, questioning her about a phrase or reaction, or a sudden decision on the part of the killer. Intermittently he removed his gold spectacles, wiping them absently, gripping the frames as if the pressure controlled his irritation. The interrogation lasted nearly twenty-five minutes; then the official made his decision. He spoke to his driver.

'*Drei Alpenhäuser. Schnell!*' He turned to Marie St Jacques. 'We'll confront that man with his own words. *His* incoherence was quite intentional. He knows far more than he said at the table.'

'Incoherence . . .' She said the word softly, remembering her own use of it. 'Steppdeck . . . Steppdeck*strasse.* Cracked windows, rooms.'

'What?'

' "A boarding house in the Steppdeckstrasse." That's what he said. Everything was happening so fast but he *said* it. And just before I jumped out of the car, he said it again. *Steppdeckstrasse.*'

The driver spoke. '*Der Alte ist verrückt.* Steppdeckstrasse *gibt es!*'

'I don't understand,' said Marie St Jacques.

'It's a rundown section that has not kept up with the times,' replied the official. 'The old fabric mills used to be there. A haven for the less fortunate . . . and others. *Los!*' he ordered.

They drove off.

8

A crack. Outside the room. Snaplike, echoing off into a sharp coda, the sound penetrating, diminishing in the distance. Bourne opened his eyes.

The staircase. The staircase in the filthy hall outside his room. Someone had been walking up the steps and had stopped, aware of the noise his weight had caused on the warped, cracked wood. A normal boarder at the Steppdeckstrasse rooming house would have no such concern.

Silence.

Crack. Now closer. A risk was taken, timing paramount, speed the cover. Jason spun off the bed, grabbing the gun that was by his head, and lunged to the wall by the door. He crouched, hearing the footsteps – one man – the runner, no longer concerned with sound, only with reaching his destination. Bourne had no doubt what it was; he was right.

The door crashed open; he smashed it back, then threw his full weight into the wood, pinning the intruder against the doorframe, pummelling the man's stomach, chest and arm into the recessed edge of the wall. He pulled the door back and lashed the toe of his right foot into the throat below him, reaching down with his left hand, grabbing blond hair and yanking the figure inside. The man's hand went limp; the gun in it fell to the floor, a long-barrelled revolver with a silencer attached.

Jason closed the door and listened for sounds on the staircase. There were none. He looked down at the unconscious man. Thief? Killer? What was he? *Police?* Had the *Vermieter* of the boarding house decided to overlook the code of the Steppdeckstrasse in search of a reward? Bourne rolled the intruder over and took out a wallet. Second nature made him remove the money, knowing it was ludicrous to do so; he had a small fortune on him. He looked at the various credit cards and driver's licence; he smiled, but then his smile disappeared. There was nothing funny, the names on the cards were different names, the name on the licence matching none. The unconscious man was no police officer.

He was a professional, come to kill a wounded man in the Steppdeckstrasse. Someone had hired him. *Who?* Who could possibly know he was *there*?

The woman? Had he mentioned the Steppdeckstrasse when he had seen the row of neat houses, looking for Number 37? . . . No, it was not she; he may have said something, but she would not have understood. And if she had, there'd be no professional killer in his room; instead, the rundown boarding house would be surrounded by police.

The image of a large fat man perspiring above a table came to Bourne. That same man had wiped the sweat from his protruding lips and had spoken of the *courage of an insignificant goat – who had survived.* Was this an example of his survival technique? Had he known about the Steppdeckstrasse? Was he aware of the habits of the patron whose sight terrified him? Had he *been* to the filthy rooming house? Delivered an envelope there?

Jason pressed his hand to his forehead and shut his eyes. *Why can't I remember? When will the mists clear? Will they ever clear?*

Don't crucify yourself . . .

Bourne opened his eyes, fixing them on the blond man. For the briefest of moments he nearly burst out laughing; he had been presented with his exit visa from Zürich, and instead of recognizing it, he was wasting time tormenting himself. He put the wallet in his pocket, wedging it behind the Marquis de Chambord's, picked up the gun and shoved it into his belt, then dragged the unconscious figure over to the bed.

A minute later the man was strapped to the sagging mattress, gagged by a torn sheet wrapped around his face. He would remain where he was for hours, and in hours Jason would be out of Zürich, compliments of a perspiring fat man.

He had slept in his clothes. There was nothing to gather up or carry, except his overcoat. He put it on, and tested his leg, somewhat after the fact, he reflected. In the heat of the past few minutes he had been unaware of the pain; it was there, as the limp was there, but neither immobilized him. The shoulder was not in as good shape. A slow paralysis was spreading; he had to get to a doctor. His head . . . he did not want to think about his head.

He walked out into the dimly lit hallway, pulled the door closed and stood motionless, listening. There was a burst of laughter from above; he pressed his back against the wall, gun poised. The laughter trailed off; it was a drunk's laughter – incoherent, pointless.

He limped to the staircase, held onto the railing, and started down. He was on the top floor of the four-storey building, having insisted on the highest room when the phrase *high ground* had come to him instinctively. *Why had it come to him? What did it mean in terms of renting a filthy room for a single night? Sanctuary?*

Stop it!

He reached the first-floor landing, creaks in the wooden staircase accompanying each step. If the *Vermieter* came out of his flat below to satisfy his curiosity, it would be the last thing he satisfied for several hours.

A noise. A scratch. Soft fabric moving briefly across an abrasive surface. Cloth against wood. Someone was concealed in the short stretch of hallway between the end of one staircase and the beginning of another. Without breaking the rhythm of his walk, he peered into the shadows; there were three recessed doorways in the right wall, identical to the floor above. In one of them. . .

He took a step closer. Not the first; it was empty. And it would not be the last, the bordering wall forming a *cul de sac*, no room to move. It had to be the second, *yes*, the second doorway. From it a man could rush forward, to his left or right, or throwing a shoulder into an unsuspecting victim, sending his target over the railing, plunging down the staircase.

Bourne angled to his right, shifting the gun to his left hand and reaching into his belt for the weapon with a silencer. Two feet from the recessed door, he heaved the automatic in his left hand in the shadows as he pivoted against the wall.

'*Was?* . . .' An arm appeared; Jason fired once, blowing the hand apart. "*Ahh!*' The figure lurched out in shock, incapable of aiming his weapon. Bourne fired again, hitting the man in the thigh; he collapsed on the floor, writhing, cringing. Jason took a step forward and knelt, his knee pressing into the man's chest, his gun at the man's head. He spoke in a whisper.

'Is there anyone else down there?'

'*Nein!*' said the man wincing in pain. '*Zwei* . . . two of us only. We were paid.'

'By whom?'

'You know.'

'A man named Carlos?'

'I will not answer that. Kill me first.'

'How did you know I was here?'

'Chernak.'

'He's dead.'

'Now. Not yesterday. Word reached Zürich: you were alive. We checked everyone . . . everywhere. Chernak knew.'

Bourne gambled. 'You're lying!' He pushed the gun into the man's throat. 'I never told Chernak about the Steppdeckstrasse.'

The man winced again, his neck arched. 'Perhaps you did not have to. The Nazi pig had informers everywhere. Why should the Steppdeckstrasse be any different? He could describe you. Who else could?'

'A man at the Drei Alpenhaüser.'

'We never heard of any such man.'

'Who's "we"?'

The man swallowed, his lips stretched in pain. 'Businessmen . . . only businessmen.'

'And your service is killing.'

'You're a strange one to talk. But, *nein.* You were to be taken, not killed.'

'Where?'

'We would be told by radio. Car frequency.'

'Terrific,' said Jason flatly. 'You're not only second-rate, you're accommodating. Where's your car?'

'Outside.'

'Give me the keys.' The radio would identify it.

The man tried to resist; he pushed Bourne's knee away and started to roll into the wall. '*Nein!*'

'You haven't got a choice.' Jason brought the handle of the pistol down on the man's skull. The Swiss collapsed.

Bourne found the keys – there were three in a leather case – took the man's gun, and put it into his pocket. It was a smaller weapon than the one he held in his hand and had no silencer, lending a degree of credence to the claim that he was to be taken, not killed. The blond man upstairs had been acting as the point, and therefore needed the protection of a silenced gunshot should wounding be required. But an unmuffled report could lead to complications; the Swiss on the first floor was a back-up, his weapon to be used as a visible threat.

Then why was he *on* the first floor? Why hadn't he followed his colleague? On the staircase? Something was odd, but there was no accounting for tactics, nor the time to consider them. There was a car outside on the street and he had the keys for it.

Nothing could be disregarded. The third gun.

He got up painfully, and found the automatic he had taken from the Frenchman in the lift at the Gemeinschaft Bank. He pulled up his left trouser leg and inserted the gun under the elasticized fabric of his sock. It was secure.

He paused to get his breath and his balance, then crossed to the staircase, aware that the pain in his left shoulder was suddenly more acute, the paralysis spreading more rapidly. Messages from brain to limb were less clear. He hoped to God he could drive.

He reached the fifth step and abruptly stopped, listening as he had listened barely a minute ago for sounds of concealment. For a scratch of cloth or a quiet intake of breath. There was nothing, the wounded man may have been tactically deficient, but he had told the truth. Jason hurried down the staircase. He would drive out of Zürich – somehow – and find a doctor – somewhere.

He spotted the car easily. It was different from the other shabby automobiles on the street. Outsized, well-kept, and he could see the bulge of an antenna base riveted into the boot. He walked to the driver's side and ran his hand around the panel and left front mudguard; there was no alarm device.

He unlocked the door, then opened it, holding his breath in case he was wrong about the alarm; he was not. He climbed in behind the wheel, adjusting his position until he was as comfortable as he could be, grateful that the car had automatic gears. The large weapon in his belt inhibited him. He placed it on the seat beside him, then reached for the ignition, assuming the key that had unlocked the door was the proper one.

It was not. He tried the one next to it, but it, too, would not fit. For the boot, he assumed. It was the third key.

Or was it? He kept stabbing at the opening. The key would not enter; he tried the second again; it was blocked. Then the first. None of the keys would fit into the ignition! Or were the messages from brain to limb to fingers too garbled, his co-ordination too inadequate? Goddamn it! Try *again*!

A powerful light came from his left, burning his eyes, blinding him. He grabbed for the gun, but a second beam shot out from the right; the door was yanked open and a heavy torch crashed down on his hand, another hand taking the weapon from the seat.

'Get *out*!' The order came from his left, the barrel of a gun pressed into his neck.

He climbed out, a thousand coruscating circles of white in his eyes. As vision slowly came back to him, the first thing he saw was the outline of two circles. Gold circles, the spectacles of the killer who had hunted him throughout the night. The man spoke.

'They say in the laws of physics that every action has an equal and opposite reaction. The behaviour of certain men under certain conditions is similarly predictable. For a man like you one sets up a gauntlet, each combatant told what to say if he falls. If he does not fall, you are taken. If he does, you are misled, lulled into a false sense of progress.'

'It's a high degree of risk,' said Jason. 'For those in the gauntlet.'

'They're paid well. And there's something else – no guarantee, of course, but it's there. The enigmatic Bourne does not kill indiscriminately. Not out of compassion, naturally, but for a far more practical reason. Men remember when they've been spared; he infiltrates the armies of others. Refined guerrilla tactics applied to a sophisticated battleground. I commend you.'

'You're a horse's ass.' It was all Jason could think to say. 'But both your men are alive, if that's what you want to know.'

Another figure came into view, led from the shadows of the building by a short, stocky man. It was the woman; it was Marie St Jacques.

'That's him,' she said softly, her look unwavering.

'Oh, my God . . .' Bourne shook his head in disbelief. 'How was it done, Doctor?' he asked her, raising his voice. 'Was someone watching my room at the Carillon? Was the lift timed, the others shut down? You're very convincing. And I thought you were going to crash into a police car.'

'As it turned out,' she replied, 'it wasn't necessary. These are the police.'

Jason looked at the killer in front of him; the man was adjusting his gold spectacles. 'I commend you,' he said.

'A minor talent,' answered the killer. 'The conditions were right. You provided them.'

'What happens now? The man inside said I was to be taken, not killed.'

'You forget. He was told what to say.' The Swiss paused. 'So this is what you look like. Many of us have wondered during the past two or three years. How much speculation there's been! How many contradictions . . . He's tall, you know; no, he's of medium height. He's blond; no, he has dark black hair. Very light blue eyes, of course; no, quite clearly, they are brown. His features are sharp; no, they're really quite ordinary, can't pick him out in a crowd. But nothing was ordinary. It was all *extra*ordinary.'

Your features have been softened, the character submerged. Change your hair, you change your face . . . Certain types of contact lenses are designed to alter the colour of the eyes . . . Wear glasses, you're a different man. Visas, passports . . . switched at will.

The design was there. Everything fitted. Not all the answers, but more of the truth than he wanted to hear.

'I'd like to get this over with,' said Marie St Jacques stepping forward. 'I'll sign whatever I have to sign – at your office, I imagine. But then I really must get back to the hotel. I don't have to tell you what I've been through tonight.'

The Swiss glanced at her through his gold-rimmed glasses. The stocky man who had led her out of the shadows took her arm. She stared at both men, then down at the hand that held her.

Then at Bourne. Her breathing stopped, a terrible realization becoming clear. Her eyes grew wide.

'Let her go,' said Jason. 'She's on her way back to Canada. You'll never see her again.'

'Be practical, Bourne. She's seen *us.* We two are professionals; there are rules.' The man flicked his gun up under Jason's chin, the barrel pressed once more into Bourne's throat. He ran his left hand about his victim's clothes, felt the weapon in Jason's pocket and took it out. 'I thought as much,' he said, and turned to the stocky man. 'Take her in the other car. The Limmat.'

Bourne froze. Marie St Jacques was to be killed, her body thrown into the Limmat River.

'Wait a minute!' Jason stepped forward; the gun was jammed into his neck, forcing him back into the bonnet of the car. 'You're being stupid! She works for the Canadian government. They'll be all over Zürich.'

'Why should that concern you? You won't be here.'

'Because it's a waste!' cried Jason. 'We're professionals, remember?'

'You bore me.' The killer turned to the stocky man. '*Machen Sie mal los! Der Guisan Quai.*'

'Scream your goddamn head off!' shouted Jason. 'Start yelling! Don't stop!'

She tried, the scream cut short by a paralysing blow to her throat. She fell to the pavement as her would-be executioner dragged her towards a small nondescript black car.

'*That* was stupid,' said the killer, peering through his gold-rimmed spectacles into Bourne's face. 'You only hasten the inevitable. On the other hand, it will be simpler now. I can free a man to tend to our wounded. Everything's so military, isn't it? It really is a battlefield.' He turned to the man with the flashlight. 'Signal Johann to go inside. We'll come back for them.'

The torch was switched on and off twice. A fourth man, who had opened the door of the small car for the condemned woman, nodded. Marie St Jacques was thrown into the rear seat, the door slammed shut. The man named Johann started for the concrete steps, nodding now at the executioner.

Jason felt sick as the engine of the small car was gunned and it bolted away from the kerb into the Steppdeckstrasse, the twisted chrome bumper disappearing into the shadows of the street. Inside that car was a woman he had never seen in his life . . . before three hours ago. And he had killed her. 'You don't lack for soldiers,' he said.

'If there were a hundred men I could trust, I'd pay them willingly. As they say, your reputation precedes you.'

'Suppose *I* paid you. You were at the bank; you know I've got funds.'

'Probably millions, but I wouldn't touch a franc note.'

'Why? Are you afraid?'

'Most assuredly. Wealth is relative to the amount of time one has to enjoy it. I wouldn't have five minutes.' The killer turned to his subordinate. 'Put him inside. Strip him. I want photographs taken of him naked – before and after he leaves us. You'll find a great deal of money on him; I want him holding it. I'll drive.' He looked again at Bourne. 'Carlos will get the first print. And I have no doubt that I'll be able to sell the others quite profitably on the open market. Magazines pay outrageous prices.'

'Why should "Carlos" believe you? Why should *anyone* believe you? You said it: no one knows what I look like.'

'I'll be covered,' said the Swiss. 'Sufficient unto the day. Two Zürich bankers will step forward identifying you as one Jason Bourne. The same Jason Bourne who met the excessively rigid standards set by Swiss law for the release of a numbered account. It will be enough.' He spoke to the gunman. '*Hurry!* I have cables to send. Debts to collect.'

A powerful arm shot over Bourne's shoulder, vicing his throat in a hammerlock. The barrel of a gun was jolted into his spine, pain spreading throughout his chest as he was dragged inside the car. The man holding him was a professional; even without his wounds it would have been impossible to break the grip. The gunman's expertise, however, did not satisfy the bespectacled leader of the hunt. He climbed behind the wheel and issued another command.

'Break his fingers,' he said.

The arm lock briefly choked off Jason's air as the barrel of the gun crashed down repeatedly on his hand – *hands.* Instinctively, Bourne had swung his left hand over his right, protecting it. As the blood burst from the back of his left, he twisted his fingers, letting it flow between them until both hands were covered. He choked his screams; the grip lessened; he shouted.

'My hands! They're broken!'

'*Gut.*'

But they were not broken, the left was damaged to the point where it was useless; not the right. He moved his fingers in the shadows; his hand was intact.

The car sped down the Steppdeckstrasse and swung into a side street, heading south. Jason collapsed back in the seat, gasping. The gunman tore at his clothes, ripping his shirt, yanking at his belt. In seconds his upper body would be naked; passport, papers, cards, money no longer his, all the items intrinsic to his escape from Zürich taken from him. It was now or it was not to be. He screamed.

'My *leg*! My goddamned leg!' He lurched forward, his right hand working furiously in the dark, fumbling under the cloth of his trouser leg. He felt it. The handle of the automatic.

'*Nein!*' roared the professional in the front. '*Watch* him!' He knew; it was instinctive knowledge.

It was also too late. Bourne held the gun in the darkness of the floor, the powerful soldier pushed him back. He fell with the blow, the automatic now at his waist, pointed directly at his attacker's chest.

He fired twice; the man arched backwards. Jason fired again, his aim sure, the heart punctured, the man fell over into the recessed jump seat.

'Put it *down*!' yelled Bourne, swinging the automatic over the rounded edge of the front seat, pressing the barrel into the base of the driver's skull. '*Drop* it!'

His breathing erratic, the killer let the gun fall. 'We will talk,' he said, gripping the wheel. 'We are professionals. We will talk.' The large automobile lurched forward, gathering speed, the driver increasing pressure on the accelerator.

'Slow down!'

'What is your answer?' The car went faster. Ahead were the headlights of traffic; they were leaving the Steppdeckstrasse district, entering the busier city streets. 'You want to get out of Zürich. I can get you out. Without me, you can't. All I have to do is spin the wheel, crash into the pavement. I have nothing whatsoever to lose, Herr Bourne. There are police everywhere up ahead. I don't think you want the police.'

'We'll talk,' lied Jason. Everything was timing, split-second timing. There were now two killers in a speeding enclosure that was in itself a trap. Neither killer was to be trusted, both knew it. One had to make use of that extra half-second the other would not take. Professionals. 'Put on the brakes,' said Bourne.

'Drop your gun on the seat next to mine.'

Jason released the weapon. It fell on top of the killer's, the ring of heavy metal proof of contact. 'Done.'

The killer took his foot off the accelerator, transferring it to the brake. He applied the pressure slowly, then in short stabs so that the large automobile pitched back and forth. The jabs on the pedal would become more pronounced, Bourne understood this. It was part of the driver's strategy, balance a factor of life and death.

The arrow on the speedometer swung left: *30 kilometres, 18 kilometres, 9 kilometres.* They had nearly stopped, it was the moment for the extra half-second of effort – balance a factor, life in balance.

Jason grabbed the man by the neck, clawing at his throat, yanking him up off the seat. Then he raised his bloody left hand and thrust it forward, smearing the area of the killer's eyes. He released the throat, surging his right hand down towards the guns on the seat. Bourne gripped a handle, shoving the killer's hand away; the man screamed, his vision blurred, the gun out of reach. Jason lunged across the man's chest, pushing him down against the door, elbowing the killer's throat with his left arm, grabbing the wheel with his bloody palm. He looked up through the windscreen and turned the wheel to the right, heading the car towards a pyramid of rubbish on the pavement.

The car ploughed into the mound of debris – a huge, somnambulant insect crawling into garbage, its appearance belying the violence taking place inside its shell.

The man beneath him lunged up, rolling on the seat. Bourne held the automatic in his hand, his fingers jabbing for the open space of the trigger; he found it. He bent his wrist and fired.

His would-be executioner went limp, a dark red hole in his forehead.

In the street, men came running towards what must have looked like a dangerously careless accident. Jason shoved the dead body across the seat, and climbed over behind the wheel. He pushed the gearshift into reverse; backed awkwardly out of the debris, over the kerb and into the street. He rolled down his window, calling out to the would-be rescuers as they approached.

'Sorry! Everything's fine! Just a little too much to drink!'

The small band of concerned citizens broke up quickly, a few making gestures of admonition, others running back to their escorts and companions. Bourne breathed deeply, trying to control the involuntary trembling that seized his entire body. He pulled the gear into drive; the car started forward. He tried to picture the streets of Zürich from a memory that would not serve him.

He knew vaguely where he was – where he had been – and more important, he knew more clearly where the Guisan Quai was in relationship to the Limmat.

Machen Sie mal los! Der Guisan Quai!

Marie St Jacques was to be killed on the Guisan Quai, her body thrown into the river. There was only one stretch where the Guisan and the Limmat met; it was at the mouth of Lake Zürich, at the base of the western shore. Somewhere in an empty car park or a deserted garden overlooking the water, a short, stocky man was about to carry out an execution ordered by a dead man. Perhaps by now the gun had been fired, or a knife plunged into its mark; there was no way to know, but Jason knew he had to find out. Whoever and whatever he was, he could not walk away blindly.

The professional in him, however, demanded that he swerve into the dark wide alley ahead. There were two dead men in the car; they were a risk and a burden he could not tolerate. The precious seconds it would take to remove them could avoid the danger of a traffic policeman looking through the windows and seeing death.

Thirty-two seconds was his guess; it had taken less than a minute to pull his would-be executioners from the car. He looked at them as he limped around the bonnet to the door. They were curled up obscenely next to each other against a filthy brick wall. In darkness.

He climbed behind the wheel and backed out of the alley.

Der Guisan Quai!

9

He reached an intersection, the traffic light red. *Lights.* On the left, several blocks east, he could see lights arching gently into the night sky. A bridge! The Limmat! The signal turned green; he swung the car to the left.

He was back on the Bahnhofstrasse; the start of the General-Guisan Quai was only minutes away. The wide avenue curved around the water's edge, river-bank and lakefront merging. Moments later, on his left was the silhouetted outline of a park, in summer a stroller's haven, now dark, devoid of tourists and citizens. He passed an entrance for vehicles; there was a heavy chain across the white pavement, suspended between two stone posts. He came to a second, another chain prohibiting access. But it was not the same; something was different, something odd. He stopped the car and looked closer, reaching across the seat for the torch he had taken from his would-be executioner. He snapped it on, and shot the beam over the heavy chain. What was it? What was different?

It was not the chain. It was *beneath* the chain. On the white pavement kept spotless by maintenance crews. There were tyre marks, at odds with the surrounding cleanliness. They would not be noticed during the summer months; they were now. It was as if the filth of the Steppdeckstrasse had travelled too well.

Bourne switched off the torch and dropped it on the seat. The pain in his battered left hand suddenly fused with the agony in his shoulder and his arm; he had to push all pain out of his mind, he had to curtail the bleeding as best he could. His shirt had been ripped; he reached inside and ripped it further, pulling out a strip of cloth which he proceeded to wrap around his left hand, knotting it with teeth and fingers. He was as ready as he would ever be.

He picked up the gun – his would-be executioner's gun – and checked the clip: full. He waited until two cars had passed him, he extinguished the headlights and made a U-turn, parking next to the chain. He got out, instinctively testing his leg on the pavement, then favouring it as he limped to the nearest post and lifted the hook off the iron circle protruding from the stone. He lowered the chain, making as little noise as possible, and returned to the car.

He pulled at the gearshift, gently pressed the accelerator, then released it. He was now coasting into the wide expanse of an unlit parking area, made darker by the abrupt end of the white entrance road and the start of a field of black asphalt. Beyond, two hundred-odd yards in the distance, was the straight dark line of the sea wall, a wall that contained no sea but, instead, the currents of the Limmat as they poured into the waters of Lake Zürich. Farther away were the lights of the boats, bobbing in stately splendour. Beyond these were the stationary lights of the Old City, the blurred floodlights of darkened piers. Jason's eyes took everything in, for the distance was his backdrop; he was looking for shapes in front of it.

To the right. The *right.* A dark outline darker than the wall, an intrusion of black on lesser black – obscure, faint, barely discernible, but there. A hundred yards away . . . now ninety, eighty-five, he cut the engine and brought the car to a stop. He sat motionless by the open window, staring into the darkness, trying to see more clearly. He heard the wind coming off the water; it covered any sound the car had made.

Sound. A *cry.* Low, throated . . . delivered in fear. A harsh slap followed, then another, and another. A scream was formed, then swallowed, broken echoing off into silence.

Bourne got out of the car silently, the gun in his right hand, the torch awkward in the bloody fingers of his left. He walked towards the obscure black shape, each step, each limp a study in silence.

What he saw first was what he had seen last when the small black car had disappeared in the shadows of the Steppdeckstrasse; the shining metal of the twisted chrome bumper; it glistened now in the night light.

Four slaps in rapid succession, flesh against flesh, blows maniacally administered, received with muted screams of terror. Cries terminated, gasps permitted, thrashing movement part of it all. Inside the car!

Jason crouched as best he could, side-stepping round the boot towards the right rear window. He rose slowly then, suddenly, using sound as a weapon of shock, shouted as he switched on the powerful torch.

'*You move, you're dead!*'

What he saw inside filled him with revulsion and fury. Marie St Jacques' clothes were torn away, shredded into strips. Hands were poised like claws on her half-naked body, kneading her breasts, separating her legs. The executioner's organ protruded from the cloth of his trousers; he was inflicting the final indignity before he carried out the sentence of death.

'Get *out*, you *son of a bitch*!'

There was a massive shattering of glass; the man raping Marie St Jacques saw the obvious. Bourne could not fire the gun for fear of killing the girl; he had spun off the woman, crashing the heel of his shoe into the window of the small car. Glass flew out, sharp fragments blanketing Jason's face. He closed his eyes, limping backwards to avoid the spray.

The door swung open; a blinding spit of light accompanied the explosion. Hot, searing pain spread through Bourne's right side. The fabric of his coat was blown away, blood matting what remained of his shirt. He squeezed the trigger, only vaguely able to see the figure rolling on the ground; he fired again, the bullet detonating the surface of the asphalt. The executioner had rolled and lurched out of sight . . . into the darker blackness, unseen.

Jason knew he could not stay where he was; to do so was his own execution. He raced, dragging his leg, to the cover of the open door.

'Stay *inside*!' he yelled to Marie St Jacques; the woman had started to move in panic. 'Goddamn it! Stay in there!'

A gunshot; the bullet embedded in the metal of the door. A running figure was silhouetted above the wall. Bourne fired twice, grateful for an expulsion of breath in the distance. He had wounded the man; he had not killed him. But the executioner would function less well than he had sixty seconds ago.

Lights. Dim lights . . . squared, frames! What was it? What *were* they? He looked to the left and saw what he could not possibly have seen before. A small brick structure, some kind of dwelling by the sea wall. Light had been turned on inside. A watchman's station; someone inside had heard the gunshots.

'*Was ist? Ist da jemand?*' The shouts came from the figure of a man – a bent-over old man – standing in a lighted doorway. Then the beam of a torch pierced the blacker darkness. Bourne followed it with his eyes, hoping it would shine on the executioner.

It did. He was crouched by the wall. Jason stood up and fired; at the sound of his gun, the beam swung over to him. *He* was the target; two shots came from the darkness, a bullet ricocheting off a metal strip in the window. Steel punctured his neck; blood erupted.

Racing footsteps. The executioner was running towards the source of the light.

'*Nein!*'

He had reached it; the figure in the doorway was lashed by an arm that was both his leash and his cage. The beam went out; in the light of the windows Jason could see the killer pulling the watchman away, using the old man as a shield, dragging him back into darkness.

Bourne watched until he could see no more, his gun raised helplessly over the bonnet. He was helpless, his body draining.

There was a final shot, followed by a guttural cry and, once again, racing footsteps. The executioner had carried out a sentence of death, not on the condemned woman, but on an old man. He was running; he had made his escape.

Bourne could run no longer; the pain had finally immobilized him, his vision too blurred, his sense of survival exhausted. He lowered himself to the pavement. There was nothing; he simply did not care.

Whatever he was, let it be. Let it be.

The St Jacques woman crawled out of the car, holding her clothes, every move made in shock. She stared at Jason, disbelief, horror and confusion coming together in her eyes.

'Go on,' he whispered, hoping she could hear him. 'There's a car back there, the keys are in it. Get out of here. He may bring others, I don't know.'

'You came for me,' she said, her voice echoing through a tunnel of bewilderment.

'Get *out*! Get in that car and go like hell, Doctor. If anyone tries to stop you, run him down. Reach the police . . . Real ones, with uniforms, you damn fool.' His throat was so hot, his stomach so cold. Fire and ice; he'd felt them before. Together. Where was it?

'You saved my life . . .' She continued in that hollow tone, the words floating in the air. 'You came for me. You came *back* for me, and saved . . . my . . . life.'

'Don't make it what it wasn't.' *You are incidental, Doctor. You are a reflex, an instinct born of forgotten memories, conduits electrically produced by stress. You see, I know the words . . . I don't care any more. I hurt – oh my God, I hurt.*

'You were free. You could have kept going, but you didn't. You came back for me.'

He heard her through mists of pain. He saw her, and what he saw was unreasonable – as unreasonable as the pain. She was kneeling beside him, touching his face, touching his head. *Stop it! Do not touch my head! Leave me.*

'Why did you do that?' It was her voice, not his.

She was asking him a question. Didn't she understand? He could not answer her.

What was she doing? She had torn a piece of cloth and was wrapping it around his neck . . . and now another, this larger, part of her dress. She had loosened his belt and was pushing the soft smooth cloth down into the boiling hot skin on his right hip.

'It wasn't *you*.' He found words and used them quickly. He wanted the peace of darkness – as he had wanted it before but could not remember when. He could find it if she left him. 'That man . . . he'd seen me. He could identify me. It was him. I wanted *him*. Now *get out*!'

'So could half a dozen others,' she replied, another note in her voice, 'I don't believe you.'

'Believe me!'

She was standing above him now. Then she was not there. She was gone! She had left him! The peace would come quickly now, he would be swallowed up in the dark crashing waters and the pain would be washed away. He leaned back against the car and let himself drift with the currents of his mind.

A noise intruded. A motor, rolling and disruptive. He did not care for it; it interfered with the freedom of his own particular sea. Then a hand was on his arm. Then another, gently pulling him up.

'Come on,' said the voice. 'Help me.'

'Let go of me!' The command was shouted; he had shouted it. But the command was not obeyed. He was appalled; commands should be obeyed! Yet not always; something told him that. The wind was there again, but not a wind in Zürich. In some other place, high in the night sky. And a signal came, a light flashed on, and he leaped up whipped by furious new currents.

'All right. You're all right,' said the maddening voice that would not pay attention to his commands. 'Lift your foot up. *Lift* it! . . . That's right. You did it. Now, inside the car. Ease yourself back . . . slowly. That's right.'

He was falling . . . *falling* in the pitch black sky. And then the falling stopped, everything stopped, and there was stillness; he could hear his own breathing. And footsteps, he could hear footsteps . . . and the sound of a door closing, followed by the rolling, disruptive noise beneath him, in front of him . . . somewhere.

Motion, swaying in circles. Balance was gone and he was falling again, only to be stopped again, another body against his body, a hand holding him, lowering him. His face felt cool; and then he felt nothing. He was drifting again, currents gentler now, darkness complete.

There were voices above him, in the distance, but not so far away. Shapes came slowly into focus, lit by the spill of table lamps. He was in a fairly large room, and on a bed, a narrow bed, blankets covering him. Across the room were two people, a man in an overcoat and a woman . . . dressed in a dark red skirt beneath a white blouse. Dark red, as the hair was . . .

The St Jacques woman? It *was* she, standing by a door talking to a man holding a leather bag in his left hand. They were speaking French.

'Rest, mainly,' the man was saying. 'If you're not accessible to me, anyone can remove the sutures. They can be taken out in a week, I'd say.'

'Thank you, Doctor.'

'Thank *you*. You've been most generous. I'll go now. Perhaps I'll hear from you, perhaps not.'

The doctor opened the door and let himself out. When he was gone the woman reached down and slid the bolt in place. She turned and saw Bourne looking at her. She walked slowly, cautiously, towards the bed.

'Can you hear me?' she asked.

He nodded.

'You're hurt,' she said, 'quite badly; but if you stay quiet, it won't be necessary for you to get to a hospital. That was a doctor . . . obviously. I paid him out of the money I found on you; quite a bit more than might seem usual, but I was told he could be trusted. It was your idea, incidentally. While we were driving, you kept saying you had to find a doctor, one you could pay to keep quiet. You were right. It wasn't difficult.'

'Where are we?' He could hear his voice; it was weak, but he could hear it.

'A village called Lenzburg, about twenty miles outside Zürich. The doctor's from Wohlen; it's a nearby town. He'll see you in a week, if you're here.'

'How? . . .' He tried to raise himself, but the strength wasn't there. She touched his shoulder; it was an order to lie back down.

'I'll tell you what happened, and perhaps that will answer your questions. At least I hope so, because if it doesn't, I'm not sure I can.' She stood motionless, looking down at him, her tone controlled. 'An animal was raping me – after which he had orders to kill me. There was no way I was going to live. In the Steppdeckstrasse, you tried to stop them, and when you couldn't, you told me to scream, to keep screaming. It was all you could do, and by shouting to me, you risked being killed at that moment yourself. Later, you somehow got free – I don't know how, but I know you were hurt very badly doing so – and you came back to find me.'

'Him,' interrupted Jason. 'I wanted *him*.'

'You told me that, and I'll say what I said before. I don't believe you. Not because you're a poor liar, but because it doesn't conform with the facts. I work with statistics, Mr Washburn, or Mr Bourne, or whatever your name is. I respect observable data and I can spot inaccuracies; I'm trained to do that. Two men went in that building to find you, and I heard you say they were both alive. They could identify you. And there's the owner of the Drei Alphenhäuser; he could too. Those are the facts, and you know them as well as I do . . . No, you came back to find me. You came back and saved my life.'

'Go on,' he said, his voice gaining strength. 'What happened?'

'I made a decision. It was the most difficult decision I've ever made in my life. I think a person can only make a decision like that if he's nearly *lost* his life by an act of violence, his life saved by someone else. I decided to help you. Only for a while – for just a few hours, perhaps – but I would help you get away.'

'Why didn't you go to the police?'

'I almost did, and I'm not sure I can tell you why I didn't. Maybe it was the rape, I don't know. I'm being honest with you. I've always been told it's the most horrible experience a woman can go through. I believe it now . . . And I heard the anger – the disgust – in your own voice when you shouted at him. I'll never forget that moment as long as I live, as much as I may want to.'

'The police?' he repeated.

'That man at the Drei Alpenhäuser said the police were looking for you. That a telephone number had been set up in Zürich.' She paused. 'I couldn't give you to the police. Not then. Not after what you did.'

'Knowing what I am?' he asked.

'I know only what I've heard, and what I've heard doesn't correspond with the injured man who came back for me and offered his life for mine.'

'That's not very bright.'

'That's the one thing I am, Mr Bourne – I assume it's Bourne; it's what he called you. *Very* bright.'

'I hit you. I threatened to kill you.'

'If I'd been you, and men were trying to kill *me*, I probably would have done the same – if I were capable.'

'So you drove out of Zürich?'

'Not at first, not for a half hour or so. I had to calm down, reach my decision. I'm methodical.'

'I'm beginning to see that.'

'I was a wreck, a mess; I needed clothes, hairbrush, make-up. I couldn't walk anywhere. I found a telephone booth down by the river, and there was no one around, so I got out of the car and called a colleague at the hotel . . .'

'The Frenchman? The Belgian?' interrupted Jason.

'No. They'd been at the Bertinelli lecture, and if they had recognized me up on the stage with you, I assumed they'd given my name to the police. Instead, I called a woman who's a member of our delegation; she loathes Bertinelli and was in her room. We've worked together for several years and we're friends. I told her that if she heard anything about me to disregard it, I was perfectly all right. As a matter of fact, if anyone asked about me, she was to say I was with a friend for the evening – for the night, if pressed. That I'd left the Bertinelli lecture early.'

'Methodical,' said Bourne.

'Yes.' Marie allowed herself a tentative smile. 'I asked her to go to my room – we're only two doors away from each other and the night maid knows we're friends. If no one was there she was to put some clothes and make-up in my suitcase and come back to her room. I'd call her in five minutes.'

'She just accepted what you said?'

'I told you, we're friends. She knew I was all right, excited perhaps, but all right. And that I wanted her to do as I asked.' Marie paused again. 'She probably thought I was telling her the truth.'

'Go ahead.'

'I called her back and she had my things.'

'Which means the two other delegates didn't give your name to the police. Your room would have been watched, sealed off.'

'I don't know whether they did or not. But if they did, my friend was probably questioned quite a while ago. She'd simply say what I told her to say.'

'She was at the Carillon, you were down at the river. How did you get your things?'

'It was quite simple. A little tacky, but simple. She spoke to the night maid, telling her I was avoiding one man at the hotel, seeing another outside. I needed my overnight case and could she suggest a way to get it to me. To a car . . . down at the river. An off-duty waiter brought it to me.'

'Wasn't he surprised at the way you looked?'

'He didn't have much of a chance to see anything. I opened the boot, stayed in the car, and told him to put it in the back. I left a ten-franc note on the spare tyre.'

'You're not methodical, you're remarkable.'

'Methodical will do.'

'How did you find the doctor?'

'Right here. The *concierge*, or whatever he's called in Switzerland. Remember, I'd wrapped you up as best I could, reduced the bleeding as much as possible. Like most people, I have a working knowledge of first aid; that meant I had to remove some of your clothing. I found the money and then I understood what you meant by finding a doctor you could pay. You have thousands and thousands of dollars on you. I know the rates of exchange.'

'That's only the beginning.'

'What?'

'Never mind.' He tried to rise again; it was too difficult. 'Aren't you afraid of me? Afraid of what you've done?'

'Of course I am. But I know what you did for me.'

'You're more trusting than I'd be under the circumstances.'

'Then perhaps you're not that aware of the circumstances. You're still very weak and I have the gun. Besides, you don't have any clothes.'

'None?'

'Not even a pair of shorts. I've thrown everything away. You'd look a little foolish running down the street in a plastic money belt.'

Bourne laughed through his pain, remembering La Ciotat and the Marquis de Chambord. 'Methodical,' he said.

'Very.'

'What happens now?'

'I've written out the name of the doctor and paid a week's rent for the room.

The *concierge* will bring you meals starting at noon today. I'll stay here until mid-morning. It's nearly six o'clock; it should be light soon. Then I'll return to the hotel for the rest of my things and my airline tickets, and do my best to avoid any mention of you.'

'Suppose you can't? Suppose you were identified?'

'I'll deny it. It was dark. The whole place was in panic.'

'Now you're *not* being methodical. At least, not as methodical as the Zürich police would be. I've got a better way. Call your friend and tell her to pack the rest of your clothes and settle your bill. Take as much money as you want from me and grab the first plane to Canada. It's easier to deny long-distance.'

She looked at him in silence, then nodded. 'That's very tempting.'

'It's very logical.'

She continued to stare at him a moment longer, the tension inside her building, conveyed by her eyes. She turned away and walked to the window, looking out at the earliest rays of the morning sun. He watched her, feeling the intensity, knowing its roots, seeing her face in the pale orange glow of dawn. There was nothing he could do; she had done what she felt she had to do because she had been released from terror. From a kind of terrible degradation no man could really understand. From death. And in doing what she did, she had broken all the rules. She whipped her head towards him, her eyes glaring.

'Who *are* you?'

'You heard what they said.'

'I know what I saw! What I *feel*!'

'Don't try to justify what you did. You simply did it, that's all. Let it be.'

Let it be. Oh, God, you could have let me be. And there would have been peace. But now you have given part of my life back to me, and I've got to struggle again, face it again.

Suddenly, she was standing at the foot of the bed, the gun in her hand. She pointed it at him and her voice trembled. 'Should I undo it then? Should I call the police and tell them to come and take you?'

'A few hours ago I would have said go ahead. I can't bring myself to say it now.'

'Then who are you?'

'They say my name is Bourne. Jason Charles Bourne.'

'What does that mean? "They say"?'

He stared at the gun, at the dark circle of its barrel. There was nothing left but the truth – as he knew the truth.

'What does it mean?' he repeated. 'You know almost as much as I do, Doctor.'

'What?'

'You might as well hear it. Maybe it'll make you feel better. Or worse, I don't know. But you may as well, because I don't know what else to tell you.'

She lowered her gun. 'Tell me what?'

'My life began five months ago on a small island in the Mediterranean called Île de Port Noir . . .'

The sun had risen to the midpoint of the surrounding trees, its ray filtered by windblown branches, streaming through the windows and mottling the walls with irregular shapes of light. Bourne lay back on the pillow, exhausted. He had finished; there was nothing more to say.

Marie sat across the room in a leather armchair, her legs curled up under her, cigarettes and the gun on a table to her left. She had barely moved, her gaze fixed on his face; even when she smoked, her eyes never wavered, never left his. She was a technical analyst, evaluating data, filtering facts as the trees filtered the sunlight.

'You kept saying it,' she said softly, spacing out her next words. '"I don't know." . . . "I wish I knew." You'd stare at something, and I was frightened. I'd ask you, what was it? What were you going to do? And you'd say it again, "I wish I knew." My God, what you've been through . . . What you're *going* through.'

'After what I've done to you, you can even think about what's happened to me?'

'They're two separate lines of occurrence,' she said absently, frowning in thought.

'Separate? . . .'

'Related in origin, developed independently; that's economics nonsense . . . And then on the Löwenstrasse, just before we went up to Chernak's flat, I begged you not to make me go with you. I was convinced that if I heard any more you'd kill me. That's when you said the strangest thing of all. You said . . . "What you heard makes no more sense to me than it does you. Perhaps less . . ." I thought you were insane.'

'What I've got is a form of insanity. A sane person remembers. I don't.'

'Why didn't you tell me Chernak tried to kill you?'

'There wasn't time and I didn't think it mattered.'

'It didn't at that moment – to you. It did to me.'

'Why?'

'Because I was holding onto an outside hope that you wouldn't fire your gun at someone who hadn't tried to kill you first.'

'But he did. I was wounded.'

'I didn't know the sequence; you didn't tell me.'

'I don't understand.'

Marie lit a cigarette. 'It's hard to explain, but during all the time you kept me hostage, even when you hit me, and dragged me and pressed the gun into my stomach and held it against my head – God knows, I was terrified – but I thought I saw something in your eyes . . . Call it reluctance. It's the best I can come up with.'

'It'll do. What's your point?'

'I'm not sure. Perhaps it goes back to something else you said in the booth at the Drei Alpenhäuser. That fat man was coming over and you told me to stay against the wall, cover my face with my hand. "For your own good," you said. "There's no point in his being able to identify you." '

'There wasn't.'

'For your own good. That's not the reasoning of a pathological killer. I think I held onto that – for my own sanity, maybe – that and the look in your eyes.'

'I still don't get the point.'

'The man with the gold-rimmed glasses who convinced me he was the police, said you were a brutal killer who had to be stopped before he killed again. Had it not been for Chernak I wouldn't have believed him. On either point. The police don't behave like that; they don't use guns in dark, crowded places. And you were a man running for your life – *are* running for your life – but you're not a killer.'

Bourne held up his hand. 'Forgive me, but that strikes me as a judgment based on false gratitude. You say you have a respect for facts – then look at them. I repeat: you heard what they said – regardless of what you think you saw and feel – you heard the words. Boiled down, envelopes were filled with money and delivered to me to fulfil certain obligations. I'd say those obligations were pretty clear, and I accepted them. I had a numbered account at the Gemeinschaft Bank containing over four million dollars. Where did I get it? Where does a man like me – with the obvious skills I have – get that kind of money?' Jason stared at the ceiling. The pain was returning, the sense of futility also. 'Those are the facts, Dr St Jacques. It's time you left.'

Marie rose from the chair and crushed out her cigarette. Then she picked up the gun and walked towards the bed. 'You're very anxious to condemn yourself, aren't you?'

'I respect facts.'

'Then if what you say is true, *I* have an obligation, too, don't I? As a law-abiding member of the social order I must call the Zürich police and tell them where you are.' She raised the gun.

Bourne looked at her. 'I thought . . .'

'Why not?' she broke in. 'You're a condemned man who wants to get it over with, aren't you? You lie there talking with such finality, with, if you'll forgive me, not a little self-pity, expecting to appeal to my . . . what was it? False gratitude? Well, I think you'd better understand something. I'm not a fool; if I thought for a minute you're what they say you are, I wouldn't be here and neither would you. Facts that cannot be documented aren't facts at all. You don't have facts, you have conclusions, your own conclusions based on statements made by men you know are garbage.'

'And an unexplained bank account with over four million dollars in it. Don't forget that.'

'How could I? I'm supposed to be a financial whiz. That account may not be explained in ways that you'd like, but there's a proviso attached that lends a considerable degree of legitimacy to it. It can be inspected – probably invaded – by any certified director of a corporation called something-or-other. Seventy-one. That's hardly an affiliation for a hired killer.'

'The corporation may be named, it isn't listed.'

'In a telephone book? You *are* naïve . . . But let's get back to you. Right now. Shall I really call the police?'

'You know my answer. I can't stop you, but I don't want you to.'

Marie lowered the gun. 'And I won't. For the same reason you don't want me to. I don't believe what they say you are any more than you do.'

'Then what do you believe?'

'I told you, I'm not sure. All I really know is that seven hours ago I was underneath an animal, his mouth all over me, his hands clawing me . . . and I knew I was going to die. And then a man came back for me – a man who could have kept running – but who came back for me and offered to die in my place. I guess I believe in him.'

'Suppose you're wrong?'

'Then I'll have made a terrible mistake.'

'Thank you. Where's the money?'

'On the bureau. In your passport case and wallet. Also the name of the doctor and the receipt for the room.'

'May I have the passport, please? That's the Swiss currency.'

'I know.' Marie brought them to him. 'I gave the *concierge* three hundred francs for the room and two hundred for the name of the doctor. The doctor's services came to four hundred and fifty, to which I added another hundred and fifty for his co-operation. Altogether I paid out eleven hundred francs.'

'You don't have to give me an account,' he said.

'You should know. What are you going to do?'

'Give you money so you can get back to Canada.'

'I mean afterwards.'

'See how I feel later on. Probably pay the *concierge* to buy me some clothes. Ask him a few questions. I'll be all right.' He took out a number of large bills and held them out for her.

'That's over fifty thousand francs.'

'I've put you through a great deal.'

Marie St Jacques looked at the money, then down at the gun in her left hand. 'I don't want your money,' she said, placing the weapon on the bedside table.

'What do you mean?'

She turned and walked back to the armchair, turning again to look at him as she sat down. 'I think I want to help you.'

'Now wait a minute . . .'

'Please,' she interrupted. 'Please don't ask me any questions. Don't say anything for a while.'

Book 2

10

Neither of them knew when it happened, or, in truth, whether it had happened. Or, if it had, to what lengths either would go to preserve it, or deepen it. There was no essential drama, no conflicts to overcome or barriers to surmount. All that was required was communication, by words and looks, and, perhaps as vital as either of these, the frequent accompaniment of quiet laughter.

Their living arrangements in the room at the village inn were as clinical as they might have been in the hospital ward it replaced. During the daylight hours Marie took care of various practical matters such as clothes, meals, maps and newspapers. On her own she had driven the stolen car ten miles south to the town of Reinach where she had abandoned it, taking a taxi back to Lenzburg. When she was out Bourne concentrated on rest and mobility. From somewhere in his forgotten past he understood that recovery depended upon both and he applied rigid discipline to both; he had been there before . . . before Port Noir.

When they were together they talked, at first awkwardly, the thrusts and parries of strangers thrown together and surviving the shock waves of cataclysm. They tried to insert normality where none could exist, but it was easier when they both accepted the essential abnormality: there was nothing to say not related to what had happened. And if there was, it would begin to appear only during those moments when the probing of what-had-happened was temporarily exhausted, the silences springboards to relief, to other words and thoughts.

It was during such moments that Jason learned the salient facts about the woman who had saved his life. He protested that she knew as much about him as he did, but he knew nothing about her. Where had *she* sprung from? Why was an attractive woman with dark red hair and skin obviously nurtured on a farm somewhere pretending to be a Doctor of Economics.

'Because she was sick of the farm,' Marie replied.

'No kidding? A farm, really?'

'Well, a small ranch would be more like it. Small in comparison to the king-sized ones in Alberta. In my father's time, when a Canute went west to buy land, there were unwritten restrictions. Don't compete in size with your betters. He often said that if he'd used the name St James rather than St Jacques, he'd be a far wealthier man today.'

'He was a rancher?'

Marie had laughed. 'No, he was an accountant who *became* a rancher by way of a Vickers bomber in the war. He was a pilot in the Royal Canadian Air Force. I guess once he saw all that sky, an accounting office seemed a little dull.'

'That takes a lot of nerve.'

'More than you know. He sold cattle he didn't own on land he didn't have before he bought the ranch. French-to-the-core, people said.'

'I think I'd like him.'

'You would.'

She had lived in Calgary with her parents and two brothers until she was eighteen, when she went to McGill University in Montreal and the beginnings of a life she had never contemplated. An indifferent student who preferred racing over the fields on the back of a horse to the structured boredom of a convent school in Alberta, discovered the excitement of using her mind.

'It was really as simple as that,' she told him. 'I'd looked at books as natural enemies, and suddenly here I was in a place surrounded by people who were caught up in them, having a marvellous time. Everything was talk. Talk all day, talk all night – in classrooms and seminars, in crowded booths over pitchers of beer. I think it was the talk that turned me on. Does that make sense to you?'

'I can't remember, but I can understand,' Bourne said. 'I have no memories of college or friends like that, but I'm pretty sure I was there.' He smiled. 'Talking over pitchers of beer is a pretty strong impression.'

She smiled back. 'And I was pretty impressive in that department. A strapping girl from Calgary with two older brothers to compete with, could drink more beer than half the university boys in Montreal.'

'You must have been resented.'

'No, just envied.'

A new world had been presented to Marie St Jacques, she never returned to her old one. Except for prescribed mid-term holidays, prolonged trips to Calgary grew less and less frequent. Her circles in Montreal expanded, the summers taken up with jobs in and outside the university. She gravitated first to history, then reasoned that most of history was shaped by economic forces – power and significance had to be paid for – and so she tested the theories of economics. And was consumed.

She remained at McGill for five years, receiving her master's degree and a Canadian Government Fellowship to Oxford.

'That was a day, I can tell you. I thought my father would have an apoplectic fit. He left his precious cattle to my brothers long enough to fly east to talk me out of it.'

'Talk you out of it? Why? He was an accountant; you were going after a doctorate in economics.'

'Don't make *that* mistake,' Marie exclaimed. 'Accountants and economists are natural enemies. One views trees, the other forests, and the visions are usually at odds, as they should be. Besides, my father's not simply Canadian, he's French-Canadian. I think he saw me as a traitor to Versailles. But he was mollified when I told him that a condition of the fellowship was a commitment to work for the government for a minimum of three years. He said I could "serve the cause better from within". Vive Québec, vive la France!'

They both laughed.

The three-year commitment to Ottawa was extended for all the logical reasons: whenever she thought of leaving, she was promoted, given a larger office and an expanded staff.

'Power corrupts, of course,' she smiled, 'and no one knows it better than a ranking bureaucrat whom banks and corporations pursue for a recommendation. But I think Napoleon said it better. "Give me enough medals and I'll win you any war." So I stayed. I enjoy my work immensely. But then it's work I'm good at and that helps.'

Jason watched her as she talked. Beneath the controlled exterior there was an exuberant, childlike quality about her. She was an enthusiast, reining in her enthusiasm whenever she felt it becoming too pronounced. Of course she was good at what she did; he suspected she never did anything with less than her fullest application. 'I'm sure you are – good, I mean – but it doesn't leave much time for other things, does it?'

'What other things?'

'Oh, the usual. Husband, family, house with a white picket fence.'

'They may come one day, I don't rule them out.'

'But they haven't.'

'No. There were a couple of close calls, but no brass ring. Or diamond, either.'

'Who's Peter?'

The smile faded. 'I'd forgotten. You read the cable.'

'I'm sorry.'

'Don't be. We've covered that . . . Peter? I adore Peter. We lived together for nearly two years, but it didn't work out.'

'Apparently he doesn't hold any grudges.'

'He'd better not!' She laughed again. 'He's director of the section, hopes for a cabinet appointment soon. If he doesn't behave himself, I'll tell the Department of Treasury what he doesn't know and he'll be back as an SX-Two.'

'He said he was going to pick you up at the airport on the twenty-sixth. You'd better cable him.'

'Yes, I know.'

Her leaving was what they had not talked about, they had avoided the subject as though it were a distant eventuality. It was not related to what-had-happened, it was something that was going to be. Marie had said she wanted to help him, he had accepted, assuming she was driven by false gratitude into staying with him for a day or so – and he was grateful for that. But anything else was unthinkable.

Which was why they did not talk about it. Words and looks had passed between them, quiet laughter evoked, comfort established. At odd moments there were tentative rushes of warmth and they both understood and backed away. Anything else *was* unthinkable.

So they kept returning to the abnormality, to what-had-happened. To him more than to them, for he was the irrational reason for their being together . . . together in a room at a small village inn in Switzerland. Abnormality. It was not part of the reasonable, ordered world of Marie St Jacques, and because it was not, her orderly, analytical mind was provoked. Unreasonable things were to be examined, unravelled, explained. She became relentless in her probing, as insistent as Geoffrey Washburn had been on the Île de Port Noir, but without the doctor's patience. For she did not have the time; she knew it and it drove her to the edges of stridency.

'When you read the newspapers, what strikes you?'

'The mess. Seems it's universal.'

'Be serious. What's familiar to you?'

'Almost everything, but I can't tell you why.'

'Give me an example.'

'This morning. There was a story about an American arms shipment to Greece and the subsequent debate in the United Nations; the Russians protested. I understand the significance, the Mediterranean power struggle, the Middle East spillover.'

'Give me another.'

'There was an article about East German interference with the Bonn government's liaison office in Warsaw. Eastern bloc, western bloc; again I understood.'

'You see the relationship, don't you? You're politically – *geo*politically – receptive.'

'Or I have a perfectly normal working knowledge of current events. I don't think I was ever a diplomat. The money at the Gemeinschaft would rule out any kind of government employment.'

'I agree, still you're politically aware. What about maps? You asked me to buy you maps. What comes to mind when you look at them?'

'In some cases names trigger images, just as they did in Zürich. Buildings, hotels, streets . . . sometimes faces. But never names. The faces don't have any.'

'Still you've travelled a great deal.'

'I believe I have.'

'You *know* you have.'

'All right, I've travelled.'

'How did you travel?'

'What do you mean, how?'

'Was it usually by plane, or by car – not taxis but driving yourself?'

'Both, I think. Why?'

'Planes would mean greater distances more frequently. Did people meet you? Are there faces at airports, hotels?'

'Streets,' he replied involuntarily.

'Streets? Why streets?'

'I don't know. Faces met me in the streets . . . and in quiet places. Dark places.'

'Restaurants? Cafés?'

'Yes. And rooms.'

'Hotel rooms?'

'Yes.'

'Not offices? Business offices?'

'Sometimes. Not usually.'

'All right. People met you. Faces. Men? Women? Both?'

'Men mostly. Some women, but mostly men.'

'What did they talk about?'

'I don't know.'

'Try to remember.'

'I can't. There aren't any voices; there aren't any words.'

'Were there schedules? You met people, that means you had appointments. They expected to meet you and you expected to meet them. Who scheduled those appointments? Someone had to.'

'Cables. Telephone calls.'

'From whom? From where?'

'I don't know. They would reach me.'

'At hotels?'

'Mostly, I imagine.'

'You told me the assistant manager at the Carillon said you *did* receive messages.'

'Then they came to hotels.'

'Something-or-other Seventy-one?'

'Treadstone.'

'*Treadstone.* That's your company, isn't it?'

'It doesn't mean anything. I couldn't find it.'

'Concentrate!'

'I *am.* It wasn't listed. I called New York.'

'You seem to think that's so unusual. It's not.'

'Why *not*?'

'It could be a separate in-house division, or a blind subsidiary – a corporation set up to make purchases for a parent company whose name would push up a negotiating price. It's done every day.'

'Who are you trying to convince?'

'*You.* It's entirely possible that you're a roving negotiator for American financial interests. Everything points to it: funds set up for immediate capital, confidentiality open for corporate approval, which was never exercised. These facts, plus your own antenna for political shifts, point to a trusted purchasing agent, and quite probably a large shareholder or part owner of the parent company.'

'You talk awfully fast.'

'I've said nothing that isn't logical.'

'There's a hole or two.'

'Where?'

'That account didn't show any withdrawals. Only deposits. I wasn't buying, I was selling.'

'You don't know that; you can't remember. Payments can be made with shortfall deposits.'

'I don't even know what that means.'

'A treasurer aware of certain tax strategies would. What's the other hole?'

'Men don't try to kill someone for buying something at a lower price. They may expose him; they don't kill him.'

'They do if a gargantuan error has been made. Or if that person has been mistaken for someone else. What I'm trying to tell you is that you can't be what you're not! No matter what anyone says.'

'You're that convinced.'

'I'm that convinced. I've spent three days with you. We've talked, I've listened. A terrible error *has* been made . . . Or it's some kind of conspiracy.'

'Involving what? *Against* what?'

'That's what you have to find out.'

'Thanks.'

'Tell me something. What comes to mind when you think of money?'

Stop it! Don't do this! Can't you understand? You're wrong. When I think of money I think of killing.

'I don't know,' he said. 'I'm tired. I want to sleep. Send your cable in the morning.'

It was well past midnight, the beginning of the fourth day, and still sleep would not come. Bourne stared at the ceiling, at the dark wood that reflected the light of the table lamp across the room. The light remained on during the nights; Marie simply left it on, no explanation sought, none offered.

In the morning she would be gone and his own plans had to crystallize. He would stay at the inn for a few more days, call the doctor in Wohlen and arrange to have the stitches removed. After that, Paris. The money was in Paris, and so was something else; he knew it, he felt it. A final answer; it was in Paris.

You are not helpless. You will find your way.

What would he find? A man named Carlos? Who was Carlos and what was he to Jason Bourne?

He heard the rustle of cloth from the couch against the wall. He glanced over, startled to see that Marie was not asleep. Instead, she was looking at him, staring at him really.

'You're wrong, you know,' she said.

'About what?'

'What you're thinking.'

'You don't know what I'm thinking.'

'Yes, I do. I've seen that look in your eyes, seeing things you're not sure are there, afraid that they may be.'

'They have been,' he replied. 'Explain the Steppdeckstrasse. Explain a fat man at the Drei Alpenhäuser.'

'I can't, but neither can you.'

'They were there. I saw them and they were there.'

'Find out why. You can't be what you're not, Jason. Find out.'

'Paris,' he said.

'Yes, Paris.' Marie got up from the couch. She was in a soft yellow nightgown, nearly white, pearl buttons at the neck; it flowed as she walked towards the bed in her bare feet. She stood beside him, looking down, then raised both her hands and began unbuttoning the top of the gown. She let it fall away as she sat on the bed, her breasts above him. She leaned towards him, reaching for his face, cupping it, holding him gently, her eyes as so often during the past few days unwavering, fixed on his. 'Thank you for my life,' she whispered.

'Thank you for mine,' he answered feeling the longing he knew she felt, wondering if an ache accompanied hers, as it did his. He had no memory of a woman and, perhaps because he had none she was everything he could imagine, everything and much . . . much more. She repelled the darkness for him. She stopped the pain.

He had been afraid to tell her. And she was telling him now it was all right, if only for a while for an hour or so. For the remainder of that night, she was giving him a memory because she too longed for release from the coiled springs of violence. Tension was suspended, comfort theirs for an hour or so. It was all he asked for, but God in heaven, how he *needed* her.

He reached for her breast and pulled her lips to his lips, her moisture arousing him, sweeping away the doubts.

She lifted the covers and came to him.

She lay in his arms, her head on his chest, careful to avoid the wound in his shoulder. She slid back gently, raising herself on her elbows. He looked at her; their eyes locked, and both smiled. She lifted her hand, pressing her index finger over his lips, and spoke softly.

'I have something to say and I don't want you to interrupt. I'm not sending the cable to Peter. Not yet.'

'Now, just a *minute.*' He took her hand from his face.

'Please, don't interrupt me. I said "not yet". That doesn't mean I won't send it, but not for a while. I'm staying with you. I'm going to Paris with you.'

He forced the words. 'Suppose I don't want you to.'

She leaned forward brushing her lips against his cheek. 'That won't wash. The computer just rejected it.'

'I wouldn't be so certain, if I were you.'

'But you're not me, and I know the way you held me, and tried to say so many things you couldn't say. Things I think we both wanted to say to each other for the past several days. I can't explain what's happened. Oh, I suppose it's there in some obscure psychological theory somewhere, two reasonably intelligent people thrown into hell together and crawling out . . . together. And maybe that's all it is. But it's there just now and I can't run away from it. I can't run away from you. Because you need me, and you gave me my life.'

'What makes you think I need you?'

'I can do things for you that you can't do for yourself. It's all I've thought about for the past two hours.' She raised herself further, naked beside him. 'You're somehow involved with a great deal of money, but I don't think you know a debit from an asset. You may have before, but you don't now. I do. And there's something else. I have a ranking position with the Canadian government. I have clearance and access to all manner of inquiries. And protection. International finance is rotten and Canada has been raped. We've mounted our own protection and I'm part of it. It's why I was in Zürich. To observe and report alliances, not to discuss abstract theories.'

'And the fact that you have this clearance, this access, can help me?'

'I think it can. And embassy protection, that may be the most important. But I give you my word that at the first sign of violence, I'll send the cable and get out. My own fears aside, I won't be a burden to you under those conditions.'

'At the first sign,' repeated Bourne, studying her. 'And I determine when and where that is?'

'If you like. My experience is limited. I won't argue.'

He continued to hold her eyes, the moment long, magnified by silence. Finally, he asked, 'Why are you doing this? You just said it. We're two reasonably intelligent people who crawled out of some kind of hell. That may be all we are. Is it worth it?'

She sat motionless. 'I also said something else; maybe you've forgotten. Four nights ago a man who could have kept running came back for me and offered to die in my place. I believe in that man. I think more than he does. That's really what I have to offer.'

'I accept,' he said, reaching for her. 'I shouldn't, but I do. I need that belief very badly.'

'You may interrupt now,' she whispered, lowering the sheet, her body coming to his. 'Make love to me, I have needs too.'

Three more days and nights went by, filled by the warmth of their comfort, the excitement of discovery. They lived with the intensity of two people aware that change would come. And when it came, it would come quickly; so there were things to talk about which could not be avoided any longer.

Cigarette smoke spiralled above the table, joining the steam from the hot, bitter coffee. The *concierge*, an ebullient Swiss whose eyes took in more than his lips would reveal, had left several minutes before, having delivered the *petit déjeuner* and the Zürich newspapers. Jason and Marie sat opposite each other; both had scanned the news.

'Anything in yours?' asked Bourne.

'That old man, the watchman at the Guisan Quai, was buried the day before yesterday. The police still have nothing concrete. "Investigation in progress," it says.'

'It's a little more extensive here,' said Jason, shifting his paper awkwardly in his bandaged left hand.

'How is it?' asked Marie, looking at the hand.

'Better. I've got more play in the fingers now.'

'I know.'

'You've got a dirty mind.' He folded the paper. 'Here it is. They repeat the things they said the other day. The shells and blood scrapings are being analysed.' Bourne looked up. 'But they've added something. Remnants of clothing; it wasn't mentioned before.'

'Is that a problem?'

'Not for me. My clothes were bought off a rack in Marseilles. What about your dress? Was it a special design or fabric?'

'You embarrass me; it wasn't. All my clothes are made by a woman in Ottawa.'

'It couldn't be traced then?'

'I don't see how. The silk came from a bolt a C-Six in our section brought back from Hong Kong.'

'Did you buy anything at the shops in the hotel? Something you might have had on you. A kerchief, a pin, anything like that?'

'No. I'm not much of a shopper that way.'

'Good. And your friend wasn't asked any questions when she checked out?'

'Not by the desk, I told you that. Only by the two men you saw me with in the elevator.'

'From the French and Belgian delegations.'

'Yes. Everything was fine.'

'Let's go over it again.'

'There's nothing to go over. Paul – the one from Brussels – didn't see anything. He was knocked off his chair to the floor and stayed there. Claude – he tried to stop us, remember? – at first thought it was me on the stage, in the light, but before he could get to the police he was hurt in the crowd and taken to the infirmary.'

'And by the time he might have said something,' interrupted Jason, recalling her words, 'he wasn't sure.'

'Yes. But I have an idea he knew my main purpose for being at the conference; my presentation didn't fool him. If he did, it would reinforce his decision to stay out of it.'

Bourne picked up his coffee. 'Let me have *that* again,' he said. 'You were looking for . . . alliances?'

'Well, hints of them, really. No one's going to come out and say there are financial interests in his country working with interests in that country so they can buy their way into Canadian raw materials or any other market. But you see who meets for drinks, who has dinner together. Or sometimes it's as dumb as a delegate from, say, Rome – whom you know is being paid by Agnelli – coming up and asking you how serious Ottawa is about the declaration laws.'

'I'm still not sure I understand.'

'You should. Your own country's very touchy about the subject. Who owns what? How many American banks are controlled by OPEC money? How much industry is owned by European and Japanese consortiums? How many hundreds of thousands of acres have been acquired by capital that's fled England and Italy and France? We all worry.'

'We do?'

Marie laughed. 'Of course. Nothing makes a man more nationalistic than to think his country's owned by foreigners. He can adjust in time to losing a war – that only means the enemy was stronger – but to lose his economy means the enemy was smarter. The period of occupation lasts longer, and so do the scars.'

'You've given these things a lot of thought, haven't you?'

For a brief moment, the look in Marie's eyes lost its edge of humour; she answered him seriously. 'Yes, I have. I think they're important.'

'Did you learn anything in Zürich?'

'Nothing startling,' she said. 'Money's flying all over the place; syndicates are trying to find internal investments where bureaucratic machineries look the other way.'

'That cablegram from Peter said your daily reports were first rate. What did he mean?'

'I found a number of odd economic bedfellows who I think may be using Canadian figureheads to buy up Canadian properties. I'm not being elusive, it's just that they wouldn't mean anything to you.'

'I'm not trying to pry,' countered Jason, 'but I think you put *me* in one of those beds. Not with respect to Canada, but in general.'

'I don't rule you out; the structure's there. You could be part of a financial combine that's looking for all manner of illegal purchases. It's one thing I can put a quiet trace on, but I want to do it over a telephone. Not words written out in a cable.'

'Now I'm prying. What do you mean and how?'

'If there's a Treadstone Seventy-one behind a multinational corporate door somewhere, there are ways to find which company, which door. I want to call Peter from one of those public telephone stations in Paris. I'll tell him that I ran across the name Treadstone Seventy-one in Zürich and it's been bothering me. I'll ask him to make a CS – a covert search – and say that I'll call him back.'

'And if he finds it . . . ?'

'If it's there, he'll find it.'

'Then I get in touch with whoever's listed as the "certified directors" and surface.'

'Very cautiously,' added Marie. 'Through intermediaries. Myself, if you like.'

'Why?'

'Because of what they've done. Or *not* done, really.'

'Which is?'

'They haven't tried to reach you in nearly six months.'

'You don't know that – *I* don't know that.'

'The bank knows it. Millions of dollars left untouched, unaccounted for, and no one has bothered to find out why. That's what I can't understand. It's as though you were being abandoned. It's where the mistake could have been made.'

Bourne leaned back in the chair, looking at his bandaged left hand, remembering the sight of the weapon smashing repeatedly downward in the shadows of a racing car in the Steppdeckstrasse. He raised his eyes and looked at Marie. 'What you're saying is that if I was abandoned, it's because that mistake is thought to be the truth by the directors at Treadstone.'

'Possibly. They might think you've involved them in illegal transactions – with criminal elements – that could cost them millions more. Conceivably risking expropriation of entire companies by angry governments. Or that you joined forces with an international crime syndicate, probably not knowing it. Anything. It would account for their not going near the bank. They'd want no guilt by association.'

'So, in a sense, no matter what your friend Peter learns, I'm still back at square one.'

'*We're* back, but it's not square one, more like four-and-a-half to five on a scale of ten.'

'Even if it were nine, nothing's really changed. Men want to kill me and I don't know why. Others could stop them but they won't. That man at the Drei Alpenhäuser said Interpol has its nets out for me, and if I walk into one I don't have any answers. I'm guilty as charged because I don't know what I'm guilty of. Having no memory isn't much of a defence, and it's possible that I have no defence, period.'

'I refuse to believe that, and so must you.'

'Thanks . . .'

'I *mean* it, Jason. Stop it.'

Stop it. How many times do I say that to myself? You are my love, the only woman I have ever known, and you believe in me. Why can't I believe in myself?

Bourne got up, as always testing his legs. Mobility was coming back to him, the wounds less severe than his imagination had permitted him to believe. He had made an appointment that night with the doctor in Wohlen to remove the stitches. Tomorrow change would come.

'Paris,' said Jason. 'The answer's in Paris. I know it surely as I saw the outline of those triangles in Zürich. I just don't know where to begin. It's crazy. I'm a man waiting for an image, for a word or a phrase – or a book of matches – to tell me something. To send me somewhere else.'

'Why not wait until I hear from Peter? I can call him tomorrow; we can be in Paris tomorrow.'

'Because it wouldn't make any difference, don't you see? No matter what he came up with, the one thing I need to know wouldn't be there. For the same reason Treadstone hasn't gone near the bank. *Me.* I have to know why men want to kill me, why someone named Carlos will pay . . . what was it . . . a fortune for my corpse.'

It was as far as he got, interrupted by the crash at the table. Marie had dropped her cup and was staring at him, her face white, as if the blood had drained from her head. 'What did you just say?' she asked.

'What? I said I have to know . . .'

'The *name.* You just said the name *Carlos.*'

'That's right.'

'In all the hours we've talked, the days we've been together, you never *mentioned* him.'

Bourne looked at her, trying to remember. It was true; he had told her everything that had come to him, yet somehow he had omitted Carlos . . . almost purposely, as if blocking it out.

'I believe I didn't,' he said. 'You seem to know. Who's Carlos?'

'Are you trying to be funny? If you are, the joke's not very good.'

'I'm not trying to be funny. I don't think there's anything to be funny about. Who's Carlos?'

'My God, you don't know,' she said, studying his eyes. 'It's part of what was taken from you.'

'Who is *Carlos*?'

'An assassin. He's called the assassin of Europe. A man hunted for twenty years, believed to have killed between fifty and sixty political and military figures. No one knows what he looks like . . . but it's said he operates out of Paris.'

Bourne felt a wave of cold going through him.

The taxi to Wohlen was an English Ford belonging to the *concierge*'s son-in-law. Jason and Marie sat in the back seat, the dark countryside passing swiftly outside the windows. The stitches had been removed, replaced by soft bandages held by wide strips of plaster.

'Get back to Canada,' said Jason softly, breaking the silence between them.

'I will, I told you that. I've a few more days left. I want to see Paris.'

'I don't want you in Paris. I'll call you in Ottawa. You can make the Treadstone search yourself and give me the information over the phone.'

'I thought you said it wouldn't make any difference. You had to know the *why*; the *who* was meaningless until you understood.'

'I'll find a way. I just need one man; I'll find him.'

'But you don't know where to begin. You're a man waiting for an image, for a phrase, or a book of matches. They may not be there.'

'Something will be there.'

'Something *is*, but you don't see it. I *do*. It's why you need me. I know the words, the methods. You don't.'

Bourne looked at her in the rushing shadows. 'I think you'd better be clearer.'

'The banks, Jason. Treadstone's connections are in the banks. But not in the way that you might think.'

The stooped old man in the threadbare overcoat, black beret in hand, walked down the far left aisle of the country church in the village of Apajon, ten miles south of Paris. The bells of the evening Angelus echoed throughout the upper regions of stone and wood; the man held his place at the fifth row and waited for the ringing to stop. It was his signal; he accepted it, knowing that during the pealing of the bells another, younger man – as ruthless as any man alive – had circled the small church and studied everyone inside and outside. Had that man seen anything he did not expect to see, anyone he considered a threat to his person, there would be no questions asked, simply an execution. That was the way of Carlos and only those who understood that their lives could be snuffed out because they themselves had been followed accepted money to act as the assassin's messenger. They were all like himself, old men from the old days, whose lives were running out, months remaining limited by age, or disease, or both.

Carlos permitted no risks whatsoever, the single consolation being that if one died in his service – or by his hand – money would find its way to old women, or the children of old women, or their children. It had to be said: there was a certain dignity to be found in working for Carlos. And there was no lack of generosity. This was what his small army of infirm old men understood; he gave a purpose to the ends of their lives.

The messenger clutched his beret and continued down the aisle to the row of confessional booths against the left wall. He walked to the fifth booth, parted the curtain and stepped inside, adjusting his eyes to the light of a single candle that glowed from the other side of the translucent drape separating priest from sinner. He sat down on the small wooden bench and looked at the silhouette in the holy enclosure. It was as it always was, the hooded figure of a man in a monk's habit. The messenger tried not to imagine what that man looked like; it was not his place to speculate on such things.

'Angelus Domini,' he said.

'Angelus Domini, child of God,' whispered the hooded silhouette. 'Are your days comfortable?'

'They draw to an end,' replied the old man, making the proper response, 'but they are made comfortable.'

'Good. It's important to have a sense of security at your age,' said Carlos. 'But to business. Did you get the particulars from Zürich?'

'The owl is dead; so are two others, possibly a third. Another's hand was severely wounded; he cannot work. Cain disappeared. They think the woman is with him.'

'An odd turn of events,' said Carlos.

'There's more. The one ordered to kill her has not been heard from. He was to take her to the Guisan Quai; no one knows what happened.'

'Except that a watchman was killed in her place. It's possible she was never a hostage at all, but instead, bait for a trap. A trap that snapped back on Cain. I want to think about that . . . In the meantime, here are my instructions. Are you ready?'

The old man reached into his pocket and took out the stub of a pencil and a scrap of paper. 'Very well.'

'Telephone Zürich. I want a man in Paris by tomorrow who has seen Cain, who can recognize him. Also, Zürich is to reach Koenig at the Gemeinschaft, and tell him to send his tape to New York. He's to use the post office box in Village Station.'

'Please,' interrupted the aged messenger. 'These old hands do not write as they once did.'

'Forgive me,' whispered Carlos. 'I'm preoccupied and inconsiderate. I'm sorry.'

'Not at all, not at all. Go ahead.'

'Finally, I want our team to take rooms within a block of the bank on the rue Madeleine. This time the bank will be Cain's undoing. The pretender will be taken at the source of his misplaced pride. A bargain price, as despicable as he is . . . Unless he's something else.'

11

Bourne watched from a distance as Marie passed through customs and immigration in Bern's airport, looking for signs of interest or recognition from anyone in the crowd that stood around Air France's departure area. It was four o'clock in the afternoon, the busiest hour for flights to Paris, a time when privileged businessmen hurried back to the City of Light after dull company chores at the banks of Bern. Marie glanced over her shoulder as she walked through the gate; he nodded, waited until she had disappeared, then turned and started for the Swiss Air Lounge. *George P. Washburn* had a reservation on the 4.30 plane to Orly.

They would meet later at a café Marie remembered from visits during her Oxford days. It was called Au Coin de Cluny on the boulevard Saint-Michel, several blocks from the Sorbonne. If by any chance it was no longer there, Jason would find her around nine o'clock on the steps of the Cluny Museum.

Jason would be late, nearby but late. The Sorbonne had one of the most extensive libraries in all Europe and somewhere in that library were back issues of newspapers. University libraries were not subject to the working hours of government employees; students used them during the evenings. So would he as soon as he reached Paris. There was something he had to learn.

Every day I read the newspapers. In three languages. Six months ago a man was killed, his death reported on the front page of each of those newspapers. So said a fat man in Zürich.

He left his suitcase at the library cloakroom and walked to the first floor, turning left towards the arch that led to the huge reading room. The *Chambre des Journals* was in this annexe, the newspapers on spindles placed in racks, the issues going back precisely one year from the day's date.

He walked along the racks, counting back six months, lifting off the first ten weeks' worth of papers beyond that date a half a year ago. He carried them to the nearest vacant table and without sitting down flipped through from front page to front page, issue to issue.

Great men had died in their beds, while others had made pronouncements; the dollar had fallen, gold risen; strikes had crippled, and governments had vacillated between action and paralysis. But no name had been killed who warranted headlines; there was no such incident – no such assassination.

Jason returned to the racks and went back further. Two weeks, twelve weeks, twenty weeks. Nearly eight months. Nothing.

Then it struck him; he had gone *back* in time, not forward from that date six months ago. An error could be made in *either* direction; a few days or a week, even two. He returned the spindles to the racks, and pulled out the papers from four and five months ago.

Aeroplanes had crashed and revolutions had erupted bloodily; holy men had spoken only to be rebuked by other holy men; poverty and disease had been found where everyone knew they could be found, but no man of consequence had been killed.

He started on the last spindle, the mists of doubt and guilt clearing with each turn of a page. Had a sweating fat man in Zürich lied? Was it all a lie? *All* lies? Was he somehow living a nightmare that could vanish with . . .

AMBASSADEUR LELAND EST MORT A MARSEILLES!

The thick block letters of the headline exploded off the page hurting his eyes. It was not imagined pain, not invented pain, but a sharp ache that penetrated his sockets and seared through his head. His breathing stopped, his eyes rigid on the name, LELAND. He knew it; he could picture the face, actually *picture* it. Thick brows beneath a wide forehead, a blunt nose centred between high cheekbones and above curiously thin lips topped by a perfectly groomed grey moustache. He knew the face, he knew the man. And the man had been killed by a single shot from a high-powered rifle fired from a waterfront window. Ambassador Howard Leland had walked down a Marseilles pier at five o'clock in the afternoon. His head had been blown off.

Bourne did not have to read the second paragraph to know that Howard Leland had been Admiral H. R. Leland, United States Navy, until an interim appointment as Director of Naval Intelligence preceded his ambassadorship to the Quai d'Orsay in Paris. Nor did he have to reach the body of the article where motives for the assassination were speculated upon to know them; he knew them. Leland's primary function in Paris was to dissuade the French government from authorizing massive arms sales – in particular fleets of Mirage jets – to Africa and the Middle East. To an astonishing degree he had succeeded, angering interested parties at all points in the Mediterranean. It was presumed that he had been killed for his interference; a punishment which served as a warning to others. Buyers and sellers of death were not to be hindered.

And the seller of death who had killed him would have been paid a great deal of money, far from the scene, all traces buried.

Zürich. A messenger to a legless man; another to a fat man in a crowded restaurant off the Falkenstrasse.

Zürich.

Marseilles.

Jason closed his eyes, the pain now intolerable. He had been picked up at sea five months ago, his port-of-origin assumed to have been Marseilles. And if Marseilles, the waterfront had been his escape route, a boat hired to take him into the vast expanse of the Mediterranean. Everything fitted too well, each piece of the puzzle sculpted into the next. How could he know the things he knew if he were not that seller of death from a window on the Marseilles waterfront?

He opened his eyes, pain inhibiting thought, but not all thought, one decision as clear as anything in his limited memory. There would be no rendezvous in Paris with Marie St Jacques.

Perhaps one day he would write her a letter, saying the things he could not say now. If he was alive and could write a letter; he could not write one now. There could be no written words of thanks or love, no explanations at all; she would wait for him and he would not come to her. He had to put distance between them; she could not be involved with a seller of death. She had been wrong, his worst fears accurate.

Oh, *God.* He could picture Howard Leland's face, and there was no photograph on the page in front of him! The front page with the terrible headline that triggered so much, confirmed so many things. The date. *Thursday, 26 August. Marseilles.* It was a day he would remember as long as he could remember for the rest of his convoluted life.

Thursday, 26 August . . .

Something was wrong. What was it? What *was* it? Thursday? . . . Thursday meant nothing to him. The twenty-sixth of August? . . . The twenty-*sixth*? It could *not be* the twenty-*sixth*! The twenty-sixth was wrong! He had heard it over and over again. Washburn's diary – his patient's *journal.* How often had Washburn gone back over every fact, every phrase, every day and point of progress? Too many times to count. Too many times not to remember!

You were brought to my door on the morning of Tuesday, August twenty-fourth, at precisely eight-twenty o'clock. Your condition was . . .

Tuesday, 24 August.

August 24.

He was not in Marseilles on the twenty-sixth! He could not have fired a rifle from a window on the waterfront. He was not the seller of death in Marseilles; he had not killed Howard Leland!

Six months ago a man was killed . . . But it was not six months; it was close to six months but *not* six months. And he had not killed that man; he was half dead in an alcoholic's house on Île de Port Noir.

The mists were clearing, the pain receding. A sense of elation filled him; he had found one concrete lie! If there was one there could be others!

Bourne looked at his watch; it was quarter past nine. Marie had left the café; she was waiting for him on the steps of the Cluny Museum. He replaced the spindles in their racks, then started towards the large cathedral door of the reading room, a man in a hurry.

He walked up the boulevard Saint-Michel, his pace accelerating with each stride. He had the distinct feeling that he knew what it was to have been given a reprieve from hanging and he wanted to share that rare experience. For a time he was out of the violent darkness, beyond the crashing waters, he had found a moment of sunlight – like the moments and the sunlight that had filled a room in a village inn – and he had to reach the one who had given them to him. Reach her and hold her and tell her there was hope.

He saw her on the steps, her arms folded against the March wind that swept off the boulevard. At first, she did not see him, her eyes searching the tree-lined street. She was restless, anxious, an impatient woman afraid she would not see what she wanted to see, frightened that it would not be there.

Ten minutes ago he would not have been.

She saw him. Her face became radiant, the smile emerged and it was filled with life. She rushed to him as he raced up the steps towards her. They came together and for a moment neither said anything, warm and alone on the Saint-Michel.

'I waited and *waited*,' she breathed finally. 'I was so afraid, so worried. Did anything happen? Are you all right?'

'I'm fine. Better than I've been in a long time.'

'What?'

He held her by the shoulders. '"Six months ago a man was killed . . ." Remember?'

The joy left her eyes. 'Yes, I remember.'

'I didn't kill him,' said Bourne. 'I couldn't have.'

They found a small hotel in the crowded centre of Montparnasse. The lobby and the rooms were threadbare, but there was a pretence to forgotten elegance that gave it an air of timelessness. It was a quiet resting place set down in the middle of a carnival, hanging onto its identity by accepting the times without joining them.

Jason closed the door, nodding to the white-haired bell boy whose indifference had turned to indulgence upon the receipt of a twenty-franc note.

'He thinks you're a provincial deacon flushed with a night's anticipation,' said Marie. 'I hope you noticed I went right to the bed.'

'His name is Hervé, and he'll be very solicitous of our needs. He has no intention of sharing the wealth.' He crossed to her and took her in his arms. 'Thanks for my life,' he said.

'Any time, my friend.' She reached up and held his face in her hands. 'But don't keep me waiting like that again. I nearly went crazy; all I could think of was that someone had recognized you . . . that something terrible had happened.'

'You forget, no one knows what I look like.'

'Don't count on that; it's not true. There were four men in the Steppdeckstrasse, including that bastard on the Guisan Quai. They're alive, Jason. They saw you.'

'Not really. They saw a dark-haired man with bandages on his neck and head, who walked with a limp. Only two were near me; the man on the first floor and that pig on the Guisan. The first won't be leaving Zürich for a while; he can't walk, and he hasn't much of a hand left. The second had the beam of the torch in his eyes; it wasn't in mine.'

She released him, frowning, her alert mind questioning. 'You can't be sure. They were there, they did see you.'

Change your hair . . . you change your face. Geoffrey Washburn, Île de Port Noir.

'I repeat, they saw a dark-haired man in shadows. How good are you with a weak solution of peroxide?'

'I've never used it.'

'Then I'll find a shop in the morning. The Montparnasse is the place for it. Blonds have more fun, isn't that what they say?'

She studied his face. 'I'm trying to imagine what you'll look like.'

'Different. Not much, but enough.'

'You may be right. I hope to God you are.' She kissed his cheek, her prelude to discussion. 'Now, tell me what happened. Where did you go? What did you learn about that . . . incident six months ago?'

'It wasn't six months ago, and because it wasn't I couldn't have killed him.' He told her everything, save for the few brief moments when he thought he would never see her again. He did not have to; she said it for him.

'If that date hadn't been so clear in your mind, you wouldn't have come to me, would you?'

He shook his head. 'Probably not.'

'I knew it. I felt it. For a minute, while I was walking from the café to the museum steps, I could hardly breathe. It was as though I were suffocating. Can you believe that?'

'I don't want to.'

'Neither do I, but it happened.'

They were sitting, she on the bed he in the single armchair close by. He reached for her hand. 'I'm still not sure I should be here . . . I *knew* that man, I *saw* his face, I was *in* Marseilles forty-eight hours before he was killed!'

'But you didn't kill him.'

'Then why was I there? Why do people think I *did*? Christ, it's *insane*!' He sprang up from the chair, pain back in his eyes. 'But then I forgot. I'm not sane, am I? Because I've forgotten . . . Years, a lifetime.'

Marie spoke matter-of-factly, no compassion in her voice. 'The answers will come to you. From one source or another, finally from yourself.'

'That may not be possible. Washburn said it was like blocks rearranged, different tunnels . . . different windows?' Jason walked to the window, bracing himself on the sill, looking down on the lights of Montparnasse. 'The views aren't the same; they never will be. Somewhere out there are people I know, who know me. A couple of thousand miles away are other people I care about and don't care about . . . Or, oh *God*, maybe a wife and children, I don't know. I keep spinning around in the wind, turning over and over and I can't get down to the ground. Every time I try I'm thrown back up again.'

'Into the sky?' asked Marie.

'Yes.'

'You've jumped from a plane,' she said, making a statement.

Bourne turned. 'I never told you that.'

'You talked about it in your sleep the other night. You were sweating; your face was flushed and hot and I had to wipe it with a towel.'

'Why didn't you say anything?'

'I did, in a way. I asked you if you were a pilot, or if flying bothered you. Especially at night.'

'I didn't know what you were talking about. Why didn't you press me?'

'I was afraid to. You were very close to hysterics, and I'm not trained in things like that. I can help you try to remember, but I can't deal with your unconscious. I don't think anyone should but a doctor.'

'A doctor? I was with a doctor for damn near six months.'

'From what you've said about him, I think another opinion is called for.'

'I don't!' he replied, confused by his own anger.

'Why not?' Marie got up from the bed. 'You need help, my darling. A psychiatrist might . . .'

'*No!*' He shouted in spite of himself, furious with himself. 'I won't do that. I *can't*.'

'Please, tell me why?' she asked calmly, standing in front of him.

'I . . . I . . . can't do it.'

'Just tell me why, that's all.'

Bourne stared at her, then turned and looked out of the window again, his hands on the sill again. 'Because *I'm* afraid. Someone lied, and I was grateful for that more than I can tell you. But suppose there aren't any more lies, suppose the rest is true. What do I do then?'

'Are you saying you don't want to find out?'

'Not that way.' He stood up and leaned against the window frame, his eyes still on the lights below. 'Try to understand me,' he said. 'I have to know certain things . . . enough to make a decision . . . but maybe not everything. A part of me has to be able to walk away, disappear. I have to be able to say to myself, what was isn't any longer, and there's a possibility that it *never* was because I have no memory of it. What a person can't remember didn't exist . . . for him.' He turned back to her. 'Why I'm trying to tell you is that maybe it's better this way.'

'You want evidence, but not proof, is that what you're saying?'

'I want arrows pointing in one direction or the other, telling me whether to run or not to run.'

'Telling *you*. What about *us*?'

'That'll come with the arrows, won't it? You know that.'

'Then let's find them,' she replied.

'Be careful. You may not be able to live with what's out there. I mean that.'

'I can live with you. And I mean that.' She reached up and touched his face. 'Come on. It's barely five o'clock in Ontario, and I can still reach Peter at the office. He can start the Treadstone search . . . and give us the name of someone here at the embassy who can help us if we need him.'

'You're going to tell Peter you're in Paris?'

'He'll know it anyway from the operator, but the call won't be traceable to this hotel. And don't worry, I'll keep everything "in-house", even casual. I came to Paris for a few days because my relatives in Lyons were simply too dull. He'll accept that.'

'Would he know someone at the embassy here?'

'Peter makes it a point to know someone everywhere. It's one of his more useful but less attractive traits.'

'Sounds like he will.' Bourne got their coats. 'After your call we'll have dinner. I think we could both use a drink.'

'Let's go past the bank on rue Madeleine. I want to see something.'

'What can you see at night?'

'A telephone box. I hope there's one nearby.'

There was. Diagonally across the street from the entrance.

The tall blond man wearing tortoise-shell glasses checked his watch under the afternoon sun on the rue Madeleine. The pavements were crowded, the traffic in the street unreasonable, as most traffic was in Paris. He entered the telephone box and untangled the telephone which had been hanging free of its cradle, the line knotted. It was a courteous sign to the next would-be user that the phone was out of commission; it reduced the chance that the box would be occupied. It had worked.

He glanced at his watch again; the time span had begun. Marie inside the bank. She would call within the next few minutes. He took several coins from his pocket, put them on the ledge, and leaned against the glass panel, his eyes on the bank across the street. A cloud diminished the sunlight and he could see his reflection in the glass. He approved of what he saw, recalling the startled reaction of a hairdresser in Montparnasse who had sequestered him in a curtained booth while performing the blond transformation. The cloud passed, the sunlight returned, and the telephone rang.

'It's you?' asked Marie St Jacques.

'It's me,' said Bourne.

'Make sure you get the name and the location of the office. And rough up your French. Mispronounce a few words so he knows you're American. Tell him you're not used to the telephones in Paris. Then do everything in sequence. I'll call you back in exactly five minutes.'

'Clock's on.'

'What?'

'Nothing. I mean, let's go.'

'All right . . . The clock is on. Good luck.'

'Thanks.' Jason depressed the lever, released it, and dialled the number he had memorized.

'La Banque de Valois. *Bonjour.*'

'I need assistance,' said Bourne, continuing with the approximate words Marie had told him to use. 'I recently transferred sizeable funds from Switzerland on a pouch-courier basis. I'd like to know if they've cleared.'

'That would be our Foreign Services Department, sir. I'll connect you.'

A click, then another female voice. 'Foreign Services.'

Jason repeated his request.

'May I have your name, please?'

'I'd prefer speaking with an officer of the bank before giving it.'

There was a pause on the line. 'Very well, sir. I'll switch you to the office of Vice-President d'Amacourt.'

Monsieur d'Amacourt's secretary was less accommodating, the bank officer's screening process activated, as Marie had predicted. So Bourne once more used Marie's words. 'I'm referring to a transfer from Zürich, from the Gemeinschaft Bank on the Bahnhofstrasse, and I'm talking in the area of several figures. Monsieur d'Amacourt, if you please. I have very little time.'

It was not a secretary's place to be the cause of further delay. A perplexed first vice-president got on the line.

'May I help you?'

'Are you d'Amacourt?' asked Jason.

'I am Antoine d'Amacourt, yes. And who, may I ask, is calling?'

'Good! I should have been given your name in Zürich. I'll make certain next time certainly,' said Bourne, the redundancy intended, his accent American.

'I beg your pardon? Would you be more comfortable speaking English, monsieur?'

'Yes,' replied Jason, doing so. 'I'm having enough trouble with this damn phone.' He looked at his watch; he had less than two minutes. 'My name's Bourne, Jason Bourne, and eight days ago I transferred four million francs from the Gemeinschaft Bank in Zürich. They assured me the transaction would be confidential . . .'

'All transactions are confidential, sir.'

'Fine. Good. What I want to know is, has everything cleared?'

'I should explain,' continued the bank officer, 'that confidentiality excludes blanket confirmations of such transactions to unknown parties over the telephone.'

Marie had been right, the logic of her trap became clearer to Jason.

'I would hope so, but as I told your secretary I'm in a hurry. I'm leaving Paris in a couple of hours and I have to put everything in order.'

'Then I suggest you come to the bank.'

'I know *that*,' said Bourne, satisfied that the conversation was going precisely the way Marie had foreseen. 'I just wanted everything ready when I got there. Where's your office?'

'On the main floor, Monsieur. At the rear, beyond the gate, centre door. A receptionist is there.'

'And I'll be dealing only with you, right?'

'If you wish, although any officer . . .'

'Look, mister,' exclaimed the ugly American, 'we're talking about millions of francs!'

'Only with me, Monsieur Bourne.'

'Fine. Good.' Jason put his fingers on the cradle bar. He had fifteen seconds to go. 'Look, it's two-thirty-five now . . .' He pressed down twice on the lever, breaking the line, but not disconnecting it. 'Hello? Hello?'

'I am here, Monsieur.'

'Damn phones! Listen, I'll . . .' He pressed down again, now three times in rapid succession. '*Hello? Hello?*'

'Monsieur, please, if you'll give me your telephone number.'

'Operator? Operator!?'

'Monsieur Bourne, please . . .'

'I can't hear you!' *Four seconds, three seconds, two seconds.* 'Wait a minute. I'll call you back.' He held the lever down, breaking the connection. Three more seconds elapsed and the phone rang; he picked it up. 'His name's d'Amacourt, office on the main floor, rear, centre door.'

'I've got it,' said Marie, hanging up.

Bourne dialled the bank again, inserted coins again. '*Je parlais avec Monsieur d'Amacourt quand le téléphone coupe . . .*'

'*Je regrette, monsieur.*'

'Monsieur Bourne?'

'D'Amacourt?'

'Yes, I'm so terribly sorry you've having such trouble. You were saying? About the time?'

'Oh, yeah. It's a little after two-thirty. I'll get there by three o'clock.'

'I look forward to meeting you, Monsieur.'

Jason reknotted the phone, letting it hang free, then left the box and walked quickly through crowds to the shade of a shopfront canopy. He turned and waited, his eyes on the bank across the way, remembering another bank in Zürich and the sound of sirens on the Bahnhofstrasse. The next twenty minutes would tell whether Marie was right or not. If she was, there would be no sirens on the rue Madeleine.

The slender woman in the wide-brimmed hat that partially covered the side of her face hung up the public phone on the wall to the right of the bank's entrance. She opened her bag, removed a compact and ostensibly checked her make-up, angling the small mirror first to the left, then to the right. Satisfied, she replaced the compact, closed her bag, and walked past the tellers' cages towards the rear of the main floor. She stopped at a counter in the centre, picked up a chained ballpoint pen, and began writing aimless numbers on a form that had been left on the marble surface. Less than ten feet away was a small, brass-framed gate, flanked by a low wooden railing that extended the width of the lobby. Beyond the gate and the railing were the desks of the lesser executives and behind them the desks of the major secretaries – five in all – in front of five doors in the rear wall. Marie read the name painted in gold script on the centre door.

M. A. R. d'Amacourt. Affaires Étrangères
Premier Vice-Président

It would happen any moment now – if it was going to happen, if she was right. And if she was, she had to know what M. A. R. d'Amacourt looked like; he would be the man Jason would reach. Reach him and talk to him, but not in the bank.

It happened. There was a flurry of controlled activity. The secretary at the desk in front of d'Amacourt's office rushed inside with her note pad, emerged thirty seconds later, and picked up the phone. She dialled three digits – an inside call – and spoke, reading from her pad.

Two minutes passed; the door of d'Amacourt's office opened and the vice-president stood in the frame, an anxious executive concerned over an unwarranted delay. He was a middle-aged man with a face older than his age, but striving to look younger. His thinning dark hair was singed and brushed to obscure the bald spots; his eyes were encased in small rolls of flesh, attesting to long hours with good wine. Those same eyes were cold, darting eyes, evidence of a demanding man wary of his surroundings. He barked a question to his secretary; she twisted in her chair, doing her best to maintain her composure.

D'Amacourt went back inside his office without closing the door, the cage of an angry cat left open. Another minute passed; the secretary kept glancing to her right, looking at something – *for* something. When she saw it, she exhaled, closing her eyes briefly in relief.

From the far left wall, a green light suddenly appeared above two panels of dark wood; a lift was in use. Seconds later the door opened and an elderly elegant man walked out carrying a small black case not much larger than his hand. Marie stared at it, experiencing both satisfaction and fear; she had guessed right. The black case had been removed from a confidential file inside a guarded room, and signed out by a man beyond reproach or temptation – the elderly figure making his way past the ranks of desks towards d'Amacourt's office.

The secretary rose from her chair, greeted the senior executive, and escorted him into d'Amacourt's office. She came out immediately, closing the door behind her.

Marie looked at her watch, her eyes on the sweep-second hand. She wanted one more fragment of evidence, and it would be hers shortly if she could get beyond the gate, with a clear view of the secretary's desk. If it was going to happen, it would happen in moments, the duration brief.

She walked to the gate, opening her bag, and smiling vacuously at the receptionist who was speaking into her phone. She mouthed the name d'Amacourt with her lips to the bewildered receptionist, reached down and opened the gate. She moved quickly inside, a determined if not very bright client of the Valois Bank.

'*Pardon, madame.*' The receptionist held her hand over the telephone, rushing her words in French, 'Can I help you?'

Again Marie pronounced the name with her lips – now a courteous client late for an appointment and not wishing to be a further burden to a busy employee. 'Monsieur d'Amacourt. I'm afraid I'm late. I'll just go and see his secretary.' She continued up the aisle toward the secretary's desk.

'*Please*, Madame' called out the receptionist. 'I must announce . . .'

The hum of electric typewriters and subdued conversations drowned her words. Marie approached the stern-faced secretary, who looked up, as bewildered as the receptionist.

'Yes? May I help you?'

'Monsieur d'Amacourt, please.'

'I'm afraid he's in conference, Madame. Do you have an appointment?'

'Oh, yes, of course,' said Marie, opening her bag again.

The secretary looked at the typed schedule on her desk. 'I'm afraid I don't have anyone listed for this time.'

'Oh, my word!' exclaimed the confused client of the Valois Bank. 'I just noticed. It's for tomorrow, not today! I'm *so* sorry.'

She turned and walked rapidly back to the gate. She had seen what she wanted to see, the last fragment of evidence. A single button was lighted on d'Amacourt's telephone; he had bypassed his secretary and was making an outside call. The account belonging to Jason Bourne had specific, confidential instructions attached to it which were not to be revealed to the account holder.

Bourne looked at his watch in the shade of the canopy; it was eleven minutes to three. Marie would be back by the telephone at the front of the bank, a pair of eyes inside. The next few minutes would give them the answer; perhaps she already knew it.

He edged his way to the left side of the shop window, keeping the bank's entrance in view. A clerk inside smiled at him, reminding him that all attention should be avoided. He pulled out a packet of cigarettes, lit one and looked at his watch again. Eight minutes to three.

And then he saw them. *Him.* Three well-dressed men walking rapidly up rue Madeleine, talking to one another, their eyes, however, directed straight ahead. They passed the slower pedestrians in front of them, excusing themselves with a courtesy that was not entirely Parisian. Jason concentrated on the man in the middle. It was *him.* A man named Johann!

Signal Johann to go inside. We'll come back for them. A tall gaunt man wearing gold-rimmed spectacles had said the words in the Steppdeckstrasse. *Johann.* They had sent him here from Zürich; he had seen Jason Bourne. And that told him something: There *were* no photographs.

The three men reached the entrance. Johann and the man on his right went inside; the third man stayed by the door. Bourne started back to the telephone box; he would wait four minutes and place his last call to Antoine d'Amacourt.

He dropped his cigarette outside the box, crushed it under his foot, and opened the door.

'*Regardez!*' A voice came from behind.

Jason spun around, holding his breath. A nondescript man with a stubble of a beard pointed at the box. '*Pardon?*'

'*Le téléphone. Il n'opère pas. La corde est en noeud.*'

'*Oh? Merci. Maintenant, j'essayerais. Merci bien.*'

The man shrugged and left. Bourne stepped inside; the four minutes were up. He took the coins from his pocket – enough for two calls – and dialled the first.

'*La Banque de Valois. Bonjour.*'

Ten seconds later d'Amacourt was on the phone, his voice strained. 'It is you, Monsieur Bourne? I thought you to say you were on your way to my office?'

'A change of plans, I'm afraid. I'll have to call you tomorrow.' Suddenly, through the glass panel of the booth, Jason saw a car swing into a space across the street in front of the bank. The third man who was standing by the entrance nodded to the driver.

'. . . I can do?' d'Amacourt had asked a question.

'I beg your pardon?'

'I asked if there was anything I can do. I have your account; everything is in readiness for you here.'

I'm sure it is, Bourne thought; the ploy was worth a try. 'Look, I have to get over to London this afternoon. I'm taking one of the shuttle flights, but I'll be back tomorrow. Keep everything with you, all right?'

'To London, Monsieur?'

'I'll call you tomorrow. I have to find a cab to Orly.' He hung up and watched the entrance of the bank. In less than half a minute, Johann and his companion came running out; they spoke to the third man, then all three climbed into the waiting car.

The killers' escape car was still in the hunt, on its way now to Orly Airport. Jason memorized the number on the licence plate, then dialled his second call. If the pay phone in the bank was not in use, Marie would pick it up before the ring had barely started. She did.

'Yes?'

'See anything?'

'A great deal. d'Amacourt's your man.'

12

They moved about the shop, going from counter to counter. Marie, however, remained near the wide front window keeping a perpetual eye on the entrance of the bank across rue Madeleine.

'I picked out two scarves for you,' said Bourne.

'You shouldn't have,' answered Marie. 'The prices are far too high.'

'It's almost four o'clock. If he hasn't come out by now, he won't until the end of office hours.'

'Probably not. If he were going to meet someone, he would have done so by now. But we had to know.'

'Take my word for it, his friends are at Orly, running from shuttle to shuttle. There's no way they can tell whether I'm on one or not, because they don't know what name I'm using.'

'They'll depend on the man from Zürich to recognize you.'

'He's looking for a dark-haired man with a limp, not me. Come on, let's go into the bank. You can point out d'Amacourt.'

'We can't do that,' said Marie, shaking her head. 'The cameras on the ceilings have wide-angle lenses. If they ran the tapes they could spot you.'

'A blond-haired man with glasses?'

'Or me. I was there; the receptionist or his secretary could identify me.'

'You're saying it's a regular cabal in there. I doubt it.'

'They could think up any number of reasons to run the tapes.' Marie stopped; she clutched Jason's arm, her eyes on the bank beyond the window. 'There he is! The one in the overcoat with the black velvet collar, d'Amacourt.'

'Pulling at his sleeves?'

'Yes.'

'I've got him. I'll see you back at the hotel.'

'Be careful. Be *very* careful.'

'Pay for the scarves; they're at the counter at the back.'

Jason left the store, wincing in the sunlight beyond the canopy, looking for a break in the traffic so he could cross the street; there was none. D'Amacourt had turned right and was strolling casually; he was not a man in a rush to meet anyone. Instead, there was the air of a slightly squashed peacock about him.

Bourne reached the corner and crossed with the light, falling behind the banker. D'Amacourt stopped at a news-stand to buy an evening paper. Jason held his place in front of a sporting goods shop, then followed as the banker continued down the block.

Ahead was a café, windows dark, entrance heavy wood, thick hardware on the door. It took no imagination to picture the inside; it was a drinking place for men, and for women brought with men other men would not discuss. It was as good a spot as any for a quiet discussion with Antoine d'Amacourt. Jason walked faster, falling in stride beside the banker. He spoke in the awkward, anglicized French he had used on the phone.

'*Bonjour, monsieur. Je . . . pense que vous . . . êtes Monsieur d'Amacourt.* I'd say I was right, wouldn't you?'

The banker stopped. His cold eyes were frightened, remembering. The peacock shrivelled further into his tailored overcoat. '*Bourne?*' he whispered.

'Your friends must be very confused by now. I expect they're racing all over Orly Airport, wondering, perhaps, if you gave them the wrong information. Perhaps on purpose.'

'*What?*' The frightened eyes bulged.

'Let's go inside here,' said Jason, taking d'Amacourt's arm, his grip firm. 'I think we should have a talk.'

'I know absolutely nothing! I merely followed the demands of the account. I am not *involved*!'

'Sorry. When I first talked to you, you said you wouldn't confirm the sort of bank account I was talking about on the phone; you wouldn't discuss business with someone you didn't know. But twenty minutes later you said you had everything ready for me. That's confirmation, isn't it? Let's go inside.'

The café was in some ways a miniature version of Zürich's Drei Alpenhäuser. The booths were deep, the partitions between them high and the light dim. From there, however, the appearances veered; the café on rue Madeleine was totally French, carafes of wine replacing steins of beer. Bourne asked for a booth in the corner; the waiter accommodated.

'Have a drink,' said Jason. 'You're going to need it.'

'You presume,' replied the banker coldly. 'I'll have a whisky.'

The drinks came quickly, the brief interim taken up with d'Amacourt nervously extracting a packet of cigarettes from under his form-fitting overcoat. Bourne struck a match, holding it close to the banker's face. Very close.

'*Merci.*' D'Amacourt inhaled, removed his cigarette, and swallowed half the small glass of whisky. 'I'm not the man you should talk with,' he said.

'Who is?'

'An owner of the bank, perhaps. I don't know, but certainly not me.'

'Explain that.'

'Arrangements were made. A privately held bank has more flexibility than a publicly owned institution with stockholders.'

'How?'

'There's greater latitude, shall we say, with regard to the demands of certain clients and sister banks. Less scrutiny than might be applied to a company listed on the Bourse. The Gemeinschaft in Zürich is also a private institution.'

'The demands were made by the Gemeinschaft?'

'Requests . . . demands . . . yes.'

'Who owns the Valois?'

'Who? Many, a consortium. Ten or twelve men and their families.'

'Then I have to talk to you, don't I? I mean it'd be a little foolish my running all over Paris tracking them down.'

'I'm only an executive. An employee.' D'Amacourt swallowed the rest of his drink, crushed out his cigarette and reached for another. And the matches.

'What are the arrangements?'

'I could lose my position, Monsieur!'

'You could lose your life,' said Jason, disturbed that the words came so easily to him.

'I'm not as privileged as you *think*.'

'Nor as ignorant as you'd like me to believe,' said Bourne, his eyes wandering over the banker across the table. 'Your type is everywhere, d'Amacourt. It's in your clothes, the way you wear your hair, even your walk; you strut too much. A man like you doesn't get to be the *vice-président* of the Valois bank without asking questions; you cover yourself. You don't make a smelly move unless you can save your own ass. Now, tell me what those arrangements were. You're not important to me, am I being clear?'

D'Amacourt struck a match and held it beneath his cigarette while staring at Jason. 'You don't have to threaten me, Monsieur. You're a very rich man. Why not pay me?' The banker smiled nervously. 'You're quite right, incidentally. I did ask a question or two. Paris is not Zürich. A man of my station must have words if not answers.'

Bourne leaned back, revolving his glass, the clicking of the ice cubes obviously annoying to d'Amacourt. 'Name a reasonable price,' he said finally, 'and we'll discuss it.'

'I'm a reasonable man. Let the decision be based on value, and let it be yours. Bankers the world over are compensated by grateful clients they have advised. I would like to think of you as a client.'

'I'm sure you would.' Bourne smiled, shaking his head at the man's sheer nerve. 'So we slide from bribe to gratuity. Compensation for personal advice and service.'

D'Amacourt shrugged. 'I accept the definition and, if ever asked, would repeat your words.'

'The arrangements?'

'Accompanying the transfer of our funds from Zürich was *une fiche plus confidentielle*.'

'*Une fiche?*' broke in Jason, recalling the moment in Apfel's office at the Gemeinschaft when Koenig came in saying the words. 'I heard it once before. What is it?'

'A dated term, actually. It comes from the middle nineteenth century when it was a common practice for the great banking houses – primarily the Rothschilds – to keep track of the international flow of money.'

'Thank you. Now what is it specifically?'

'Separate sealed instructions to be opened and followed when the account in question is called up.'

'"Called up"?'

'Funds removed or deposited.'

'Suppose I'd just gone to a teller, presented a bank book, and asked for money?'

'A double asterisk would have appeared on the transaction computer. You would have been sent to me.'

'I was sent to you anyway. The operator gave me your office.'

'Irrelevant chance. There are two other officers in the Foreign Services Department. Had you been connected to either one, the *fiche* would have dictated that you still be sent to me. I am the senior executive.'

'I see.' But Bourne was not sure that he did see. There was a gap in the sequence; a space needed filling. 'Wait a minute. You didn't know anything about a *fiche* when you had the account brought to your office.'

'Why did I ask for it?' interrupted d'Amacourt, anticipating the question. 'Be reasonable, monsieur. Put yourself in my place. A man calls and identifies himself, then says he is "talking about millions of francs". *Millions.* Would you not be anxious to be of service? Bend a rule here and there?'

Looking at the seedily elegant banker, Jason realized it was the most unstartling thing he had said. 'The instructions. What were they?'

'To begin with a telephone number, unlisted, of course. It was to be called, all information relayed.'

'Do you remember the number?'

'I make it a point to commit such things to memory.'

'I'll bet you do. What is it?'

'I must protect myself, Monsieur. How else could you have got it? I pose the question . . . how do you say it? . . . rhetorically.'

'Which means you have the answer. How *did* I get it? If it ever comes up.'

'In Zürich. You paid a very high price for someone to break not only the strictest regulation on the Bahnhofstrasse, but also the laws of Switzerland.'

'I've got just the man,' said Bourne, the face of Koenig coming into focus. 'He's already committed the crime.'

'At the Gemeinschaft? Are you *joking*?'

'Not one bit. His name is Koenig; his desk is on the first floor.'

'I'll remember that.'

'I'm sure you will. The number?' D'Amacourt gave it to him. Jason wrote it on a paper napkin. 'How do I know this is accurate?'

'You have a reasonable guarantee. I have not been paid.'

'Good enough.'

'And as long as value is intrinsic to our discussion, I should tell you that it is the second telephone number, the first was cancelled.'

'Explain that.'

D'Amacourt leaned forward. 'A photostat of the original *fiche* arrived with the accounts-courier. It was sealed in a black case, accepted and signed for by the senior keeper-of-records. The card inside was validated by a partner of the Gemeinschaft, countersigned by the usual Swiss notary; the instructions were simple, quite clear. In all matters pertaining to the account of Jason C. Bourne, a transatlantic call to the United States was to be placed immediately, the details relayed . . . Here the card was altered, the number in New York deleted, one in Paris inserted and initialled.'

'New York?' interrupted Bourne. 'How do you know it was New York?'

'The telephone area code was parenthetically included, spaced in front of the number itself; it remained intact. It was two-one-two. As first vice-president, Foreign Services, I place such calls daily.'

'The alteration was pretty sloppy.'

'Possibly. It could have been made in haste, or not thoroughly understood. On the other hand, there was no way to delete the body of the instructions without renotarization. A minor risk considering the number of telephones in New York. At any rate, the substitution gave me the latitude to ask a question or two. Change is a banker's anathema.' D'Amacourt fingered his glass.

'Care for another?' asked Jason.

'No, thank you. It would prolong our discussion.'

'You're the one who stopped.'

'I'm thinking, Monsieur. Perhaps you should have in mind a vague figure before I proceed.'

Bourne studied the man. 'It could be five,' he said.

'Five what?'

'Five figures.'

'I shall proceed. I spoke to a woman . . .'

'A woman? How did you begin?'

'Truthfully. I was the vice-president of the Valois, and was following instructions from the Gemeinschaft in Zürich. What else was there to say?'

'Go on.'

'I said I had been in communication with a man claiming to be Jason Bourne. She asked me how recently, to which I replied a few minutes. She was then most anxious to know the substance of our conversation. It was at this point that I voiced my own concerns. The *fiche* specifically stated that a call should be made to New York, not Paris. Naturally, she said it was *not* my concern, and that the change was authorized by signature, and did I care for Zürich to be informed that an officer of the Valois refused to follow the Gemeinschaft instructions?'

'Hold it,' interrupted Jason. 'Who was she?'

'I have no idea.'

'You mean you were talking all this time and she didn't tell you? You didn't ask?'

'That is the nature of the *fiche*. If a name is proffered, well and good. If it is not, one does not inquire.'

'You didn't hesitate to ask about the telephone number.'

'Merely a device; I wanted information. You transferred four million francs, a sizeable amount, and were, therefore, a powerful client with, perhaps, *more* powerful strings attached to him . . . One balks, then agrees, then balks again only to agree again; that is the way one learns things. Especially if the party one is talking to displays anxiety. I can assure you, she did.'

'What did you learn?'

'That you should be considered a dangerous man.'

'In what way?'

'The definition was left open. But the fact that the term was used was enough for me to ask why the Sûreté was not involved. Her reply was extremely interesting. "He is beyond the Sûreté, beyond Interpol," she said.'

'What did that tell you?'

'That it was a highly complicated matter with any number of possibilities, all best left private. Since our talk began, however, it now tells me something else.'

'What's that?'

'That you really should pay me well for I must be extremely cautious. Those who look for you are also, perhaps, beyond the Sûreté, beyond Interpol.'

'We'll get to that. You told this woman I was on my way to your office?'

'Within the quarter-hour. She asked me to remain on the telephone for a few moments, that she would be right back. Obviously she made another call. She returned with her final instructions. You were to be detained in my office until a man came to my secretary inquiring about a matter from Zürich. And when you left you were to be identified by a nod or a gesture; there could be no error. The man came, of course, and, of course, you never arrived, so he waited by the tellers' cages with an associate. When you phoned and said you were on your way to London, I left my office to find the man. My secretary pointed him out and I told him. The rest you know.'

'Didn't it strike you as odd that I had to be identified?'

'Not so odd as intemperate. A *fiche* is one thing – telephone calls, faceless communications – but to be involved directly, in the open, as it were, is something else again. I said as much to the woman.'

'What did she say to you?'

D'Amacourt cleared his throat. 'She made it clear that the party she represented – whose stature was, indeed, confirmed by the *fiche* itself – would remember my co-operation. You see, I withhold nothing . . . Apparently they don't know what you look like.'

'A man was at the bank who saw me in Zürich.'

'Then his associates do not trust his eyesight. Or, perhaps, what he thinks he saw.'

'Why do you say that?'

'Merely an observation, Monsieur; the woman was insistent. You must understand, I strenuously objected to any overt participation; that is *not* the nature of the *fiche*. She said there was no photograph of you. An obvious lie, of course.'

'Is it?'

'Naturally. All passports have photographs. Where is the immigration officer who cannot be bought, or duped. Ten seconds in a control room, a photograph of a photograph; arrangements can be made. No, they committed a serious oversight.'

'I see they did.'

'And you,' continued d'Amacourt, 'just told me something else. Yes, you really must pay me very well.'

'What did I just tell you?'

'That your passport does not identify you as Jason Bourne. Who are you, Monsieur?'

Jason did not at first answer; he revolved his glass again. 'Someone who may pay you a lot of money,' he said.

'Entirely sufficient. You are simply a client named Bourne. And I must be cautious.'

'I want that telephone number in New York. Can you get it for me? There'd be a sizeable bonus.'

'I wish I could. I see no way.'

'It might be raised from the *fiche* card. Under a low-power scope.'

'When I said it was deleted, Monsieur, I did not mean it was crossed out. It was *deleted*, it was *cut* out.'

'Then someone has it in Zürich.'

'Or it has been destroyed.'

'Last question,' said Jason, anxious now to leave. 'It concerns you, incidentally. It's the only way you'll get paid.'

'The question will be tolerated, of course. What is it?'

'If I showed up at the Valois without calling you, without telling you I was coming, would you be expected to make another telephone call?'

'Yes. One does not disregard the *fiche*; it emanates from powerful board rooms. Dismissal would follow.'

'Then how do *we* get *our* money?'

D'Amacourt pursed his lips. 'There is a way. Withdrawal *in absentia*. Forms filled out, instructions by letter, identification confirmed and authenticated by an established firm of attorneys. I would be powerless to interfere.'

'You'd still be expected to make the call, though.'

'It's a matter of timing. Should a lawyer with whom the Valois has had numerous dealings call me requesting that I prepare, say, a number of cashier's cheques drawn upon a foreign transfer he has ascertained to have been cleared, I would do so. He would state that he was sending over the completed forms, the cheques, of course, made out to "Bearer", not an uncommon practice in these days of excessive taxes. A messenger would arrive with the letter during the most hectic hours of activity, and my secretary – an esteemed, trusted employee of many years – would simply bring in the forms for my counter-signature and the letter for my initialling.'

'No doubt,' interrupted Bourne, 'along with a number of other papers you were to sign.'

'Exactly. I would *then* place my call, probably watching the messenger leave with his briefcase as I did so.'

'You wouldn't, by any remote chance, have in mind the name of a law firm in Paris, would you? Or a specific attorney?'

'As a matter of fact, one just occurred to me.'

'How much will he cost?'

'Ten thousand francs.'

'That's expensive.'

'Not at all. He was a judge on the bench, an honoured man.'

'What about you? Let's refine it.'

'As I said, I'm reasonable, and the decision should be yours. Since you mentioned five figures, let us be consistent with your words. Five figures, commencing with five. Fifty thousand francs.'

'That's outrageous!'

'So is whatever you've done, Monsieur Bourne.'

'*Une fiche plus confidentielle*,' said Marie, sitting in the chair by the window, the late afternoon sun bouncing off the ornate buildings of Montparnasse outside. 'So that's the device they've used.'

'I can impress you, I know where it comes from.' Jason poured a drink from the bottle on the bureau and carried it to the bed; he sat down, facing her. 'Do you want to hear?'

'I don't have to,' she answered, gazing out of the window, preoccupied. 'I know exactly where it comes from and what it means. It's a shock, that's all.'

'Why? I thought you expected something like this.'

'The results, yes, not the machinery. A *fiche* is an archaic stab at legitimacy, almost totally restricted to private banks on the Continent. American, Canadian and UK laws forbid its use.'

Bourne recalled d'Amacourt's words; he repeated them. '"It emanates from powerful board rooms," that's what he said.'

'He was right.' Marie looked over at him. 'Don't you see? I knew that a flag was attached to your account. I assumed that someone had been bribed to forward information. That's not unusual; bankers aren't in the front ranks for canonization. But this is different. That account in Zürich was established – at the very beginning – with the *fiche* as part of its activity. Conceivably with your own knowledge.'

'Treadstone Seventy-one,' said Jason.

'Yes. The owners of the bank had to work in concert with Treadstone. And considering the latitude of your access, it's possible you were aware that they did.'

'But someone *was* bribed. Koenig. He substituted one telephone number for another.'

'He was well paid, I can assure you. He could face ten years in a Swiss prison.'

'Ten? That's pretty stiff.'

'So are the Swiss laws. He had to be paid a small fortune.'

'Carlos,' said Bourne. '*Carlos . . . Why?* What am I to *him*? I keep asking myself. I say the name over and over and over again! I don't *get* anything, nothing at all. Just a . . . a . . . I don't know. *Nothing*.'

'But there's something, isn't there?' Marie sat forward. 'What is it, Jason? What are you thinking of?'

'I'm not thinking . . . I don't know.'

'Then you're *feeling*. *Something*. What is it?'

'I don't know. Fear, maybe . . . Anger, nerves. I don't *know*.'

'*Concentrate!*'

'Goddamn it, do you think I'm *not*? Do you think I *haven't*? Have you any idea what it's *like*?' Bourne stiffened, annoyed at his own outburst. 'Sorry.'

'Don't be. Ever. These are the hints, the clues you have to look for – *we* have to look for. Your doctor friend in Port Noir was right; things come to you, provoked by other things. As you yourself said, a book of matches, a face, or the front of a restaurant. We've seen it happen . . . Now, it's a name, a name you avoided for nearly a week while you told me everything that had happened to you during the past five months down to the smallest detail. Yet you never mentioned Carlos. You should have, but you didn't. It *does* mean something to you, can't you see that? It's stirring things inside you; they want to come out.'

'I know.' Jason drank.

'Darling, there's a famous bookshop on the boulevard Saint-Germain that's run by a magazine freak. A whole floor is crammed with back issues of old magazines, thousands of them. He even catalogues subjects, indexes them like a librarian. I'd like to find out if Carlos is in that index. Will you do it?'

Bourne was aware of the sharp pain in his chest. It had nothing to do with his wounds; it was fear. She saw it and somehow understood; he felt it and could not understand. 'There are back issues of newspapers at the Sorbonne,' he said, glancing up at her. 'One of them put me on cloud nine for a while. Until I thought about it.'

'A lie was exposed. That was the important thing.'

'But we're not looking for a lie now, are we?'

'No, we're looking for the truth. Don't be afraid of it, darling. I'm not.'

Jason got up. 'Okay. Saint-Germain's on the schedule. In the meantime, call that fellow at the embassy.' Bourne reached into his pocket and took out the paper napkin with the telephone number on it; he had added the numbers of the licence plate on the car that had raced away from the bank on rue Madeleine. 'Here's the number d'Amacourt gave me, also the licence of that car. See what he can do.'

'All right.' Marie took the napkin and went to the telephone. A small, spiral-hinged notebook was beside it; she flipped through the pages. 'Here it is. His name is Dennis Corbelier. Peter said he'd call him by noon today, Paris time. And I could rely on him; he was as knowledgeable as any attaché in the embassy.'

'Peter knows him, doesn't he? He's not just a name from a list.'

'They were classmates at the University of Toronto. I can call him from here, can't I?'

'Sure. But don't say where you are.'

'I'll tell him the same thing I told Peter,' Marie picked up the phone. 'That I'm moving from one hotel to another but don't know which yet.' She got an outside line, then dialled the number of the Canadian Embassy on the avenue Montaigne. Fifteen seconds later she was talking with Dennis Corbelier, attaché.

Marie got to the point of her call almost immediately. 'I assume Peter told you I might need some help.'

'More than that,' replied Corbelier, 'he explained that you were in Zürich. Can't say I understood everything he said, but I got the general idea. Seems there's a lot of manoeuvring in the world of high finance these days.'

'More than usual. The trouble is no one wants to say who's manoeuvring whom. That's my problem.'

'How can I help?'

'I have a licence plate and a telephone number, both here in Paris. The telephone's unlisted; it could be awkward if I called.'

'Give them to me.' She did. '*A mari usque ad mare*,' Corbelier said, reciting the national motto of their country. 'We have several friends in splendid places. We trade favours frequently, usually in the narcotics area, but we're all flexible. Why not have lunch with me tomorrow? I'll bring what I can.'

'I'd like that, but tomorrow's no good. I'm spending the day with an old friend. Perhaps another time.'

'Peter said I'd be an idiot not to insist. He says you're a terrific lady.'

'He's a dear, and so are you. I'll call you tomorrow afternoon.'

'Fine. I'll go to work on these.'

'Talk to you tomorrow, and thanks again.' Marie hung up and looked at her watch. 'I'm to call Peter in three hours. Don't let me forget.'

'You really think he'll have something so soon?'

'He *does!* He started last night by calling Washington. It's what Corbelier just said; we all trade off. This piece of information here for that one there, a name from our side for one of yours.'

'Sounds vaguely like betrayal.'

'The opposite. We're dealing in money, not missiles. Money that is illegally moving around, outflanking laws that are good for all our interests. Unless you want the sheikhs of Arabi owning Grumman Aircraft. *Then* we're talking about missiles . . . after they've left the launching pads.'

'Strike my objection.'

'We've got to see d'Amacourt's man first thing in the morning. Figure out what you want to withdraw.'

'All of it.'

'*All?*'

'That's right. If you were the directors of Treadstone, what would you do if you learned that four million Swiss francs were missing from a corporate account?'

'I see!'

'D'Amacourt suggested a series of cashier's cheques made out to the bearer.'

'He said that? Cheques?'

'Yes. Something wrong?'

'There certainly is. The numbers of those cheques could be punched on a fraud tape and sent to banks everywhere. You have to *go* to a bank to redeem them, payments would be stopped.'

'He's a winner, isn't he? He collects from both sides. What do we do?'

'Accept half of what he told you, the bearer part. But not cheques. Bonds. Bearer bonds of various denominations. They're far more easily brokered.'

'You've just earned dinner,' said Jason, reaching down and touching her face.

'I tries to earn my keep, sir,' she replied, holding his hand against her cheek. 'First dinner, then Peter . . . and then a bookshop in Saint-Germain.'

'A bookshop in Saint-Germain,' repeated Bourne, the pain coming to his chest again. *What was it? Why was he so afraid?*

They left the restaurant on the boulevard Raspail and walked to the telephone complex on rue de Vaugirard. There were glass booths against the walls and a huge circular counter in the centre of the floor where clerks filled out slips, assigning booths to those placing calls.

'The traffic is very light, Madame,' said the clerk to Marie. 'Your call should go through in a matter of minutes. Number twelve, please.'

'Thank you. Booth twelve?'

'Yes, Madame. Directly over there.'

As they walked across the crowded floor to the booth, Jason held her arm. 'I know why people use these places,' he said. 'They're a hundred and ten times quicker than a hotel phone.'

'That's only one of the reasons.'

They had barely reached the booth and lighted cigarettes when they heard the two short bursts of the bell inside. Marie opened the door and went in, her spiral-hinged notebook and a pencil in her hand. She picked up the receiver.

Sixty seconds later Bourne watched in astonishment as she stared at the wall, the blood draining from her face, her skin chalk white. She began shouting, and dropped her bag, the contents scattering over the floor of the small booth; the notebook was caught on the ledge, the pencil broken in the grip of her hand. He rushed inside, she was close to collapse.

'This is Marie St Jacques in Paris, Lisa. Peter's expecting my call.'

'*Marie?* Oh, my God . . .' The secretary's voice trailed off, replaced by other voices in the background. Excited voices, muted by a cupped hand over the phone. Then there was a rustle of movement, the phone being given to or taken by another.

'Marie, this is Alan,' said the first assistant director of the section. 'We're all in Peter's office.'

'What's the matter, Alan? I don't have much time; may I speak to him, please?'

There was a moment of silence. 'I wish I could make this easier for you, but I don't know how. Peter's dead, Marie.'

'He's . . . *what*?'

'The police called a few minutes ago; they're on their way over.'

'The *police*? What happened? Oh God, he's *dead*? What *happened*?'

'We're trying to piece it together. We're studying his phone log, but we're not supposed to touch anything on his desk.'

'His desk . . . ?'

'Notes or memos, or anything like that.'

'Alan! Tell me what *happened*!'

'That's just it, we don't know. He didn't tell any of us what he was doing. All we know is that he got two phone calls this morning from the States, one from Washington, the other from New York. Around noon he told Lisa he was going to the airport to meet someone flying up. He didn't say who . . . The police found him an hour ago in one of those tunnels used for freight. It was terrible; he was shot. In the throat . . . Marie? *Marie*?'

The old man with the hollow eyes and the stubble of a white beard, limped into the dark confessional booth, blinking his eyes repeatedly, trying to focus on the hooded figure beyond the opaque curtain. Sight was not easy for this eighty-year-old messenger. But his mind was clear; that was all that mattered.

'Angelus Domini,' he said.

'Angelus Domini, child of God,' whispered the hooded silhouette. 'Are your days comfortable?'

'They draw to an end but they are made comfortable.'

'Good . . . Zürich?'

'They found the man from the Guisan Quai. He was wounded, they traced him through a doctor known to the *Verbrecherwelt.* Under severe interrogation he admitted assaulting the woman. Cain came back for her; it was Cain who shot him.'

'So it was an arrangement, the woman and Cain.'

'The man from the Guisan Quai does not think so. He was one of the two who picked her up on the Löwenstrasse.'

'He's also a fool. He killed the watchman?'

'He admits it and defends it. He had no choice in making his escape.'

'He may not have to defend it; it could be the most intelligent thing he did. Does he have his gun?'

'Your people have it.'

'Good. There is a prefect in the Zürich police. That gun must be given to him. Cain is elusive, the woman far less so. She has associates in Ottawa; they'll stay in touch. We trap her, we trace him. Is your pencil ready?'

'Yes, Carlos.'

13

Bourne held her in the close confines of the glass booth, gently lowering her to the seat that protruded from the narrow wall. She was shaking, breathing in swallows and gasps, her eyes glazed, coming into focus as she looked at him.

'They killed him. They *killed* him! My God, what did I *do*? *Peter*.'

'You didn't *do* it! If anyone did it, *I* did. Not you. Get that through your head.'

'Jason, I'm *frightened*. He was half a world away . . . and they *killed* him!'

'Treadstone?'

'Who else? There were two phone calls, Washington . . . New York. He went to the airport to meet someone and he was *killed*.'

'How?'

'Oh, Jesus Christ . . .' Tears came to Marie's eyes. 'He was shot. In the throat,' she whispered.

Bourne suddenly felt a dull ache, he could not localize it, but it was there, cutting off air. 'Carlos,' he said, not knowing why he said it.

'What?' Marie stared up at him. 'What did you say?'

'Carlos,' he repeated softly. ' A bullet in the throat. Carlos.'

'What are you trying to say?'

'I don't know.' He took her arm. 'Let's get out of here. Are you all right? Can you walk?'

She nodded, closing her eyes briefly, breathing deeply. 'Yes.'

'We'll stop for a drink, we both need it. Then we'll find it.'

'Find what?'

'A bookshop on Saint-Germain.'

There were three back issues of magazines under the *Carlos* index. A four-year-old edition of the international *Time*, and two Paris issues of *Le Globe*. They did not read the articles inside the shop; instead they bought all three and took a taxi back to the hotel in Montparnasse. There they began reading. Marie on the bed, Jason in the chair by the window. Several minutes passed, and Marie bolted up.

'It's here,' she said, fear in both her face and voice.

'Read it.'

' "A particularly brutal form of punishment is said to be inflicted by Carlos and/or his small band of soldiers. It is death by a gunshot in the throat, often leaving the victim to die in excruciating pain. It is reserved for those who break the code of silence or loyalty demanded by the assassin, or others who have refused to divulge information" . . .' Marie stopped, incapable of reading further. She lay back and closed her eyes. 'He wouldn't tell them and he was killed for it. Oh, my *God* . . .'

'He couldn't tell them what he didn't *know*,' said Bourne.

'But *you* knew!' Marie sat up again, her eyes open. 'You knew about the gunshot in the throat! You *said* it!'

'I said it. I knew it. That's all I can tell you.'

'*How?*'

'I wish I could answer that. I can't.'

'May I have a drink?'

'Certainly.' Jason got up and went to the bureau. He poured two small glasses of whisky and looked over at her. 'Do you want me to call for some ice? Hervé's on; it'll be quick.'

'No. It won't be quick enough.' She slammed the magazine down on the bed and turned to him. On him, perhaps. 'I'm going *crazy*!'

'Join the party of two.'

'I want to believe you, I *do* believe you. But I . . . I . . .'

'You can't be sure,' completed Bourne. 'Any more than I can.' He brought her the glass. 'What do you want me to say? What can I say? Am I one of Carlos's soldiers? Did I break the code of silence or loyalty? Is that why I knew the method of execution?'

'*Stop* it!'

'I say that a lot to myself. "Stop it." Don't think; try to remember but somewhere along the line put the brakes on. Don't go too far, too deep. One lie can be exposed only to raise ten other questions intrinsic to that lie. Maybe it's like waking up after a long drunk, not sure whom you fought with or slept with, or . . . Goddamn it . . . killed.'

'No! . . .' Marie drew out the word. 'You are *you.* Don't take that away from me.'

'I don't want to. I don't want to take it away from myself.' Jason went back to the chair and sat down, his face turned to the window. 'You found . . . a method of execution. I found something else. I knew it, just as I knew about Howard Leland. I didn't even have to read it.'

'Read what?'

Bourne reached down and picked up the four-year-old issue of *Time.* The magazine was folded open to a page on which there was a sketch of a bearded man, the lines rough, inconclusive, as if drawn from an obscure description. He held it out for her.

'Read it,' he said. 'It starts on the left, under the heading, "*Myth or Monster*". Then I want to play a game.'

'A game?'

'Yes. I've read only the first two paragraphs; you'll have to take my word for that.'

'All right.' Marie watched him, bewildered. She lowered the magazine into the light and read.

MYTH OR MONSTER

For over a decade, the name 'Carlos' has been whispered in the back streets of such diverse cities as Paris, Tehran, Beirut, London, Cairo and Amsterdam. He is said to be the supreme terrorist in the sense that his commitment is to murder and assassination in themselves, with no apparent political ideology. Yet there is concrete evidence that he has undertaken profitable executions for such extremist radical groups as the PLO and Baader-Meinhof, both as teacher and profiteer. Indeed, it is through his infrequent gravitation to, and the internal conflicts within, such terrorist organizations that a clearer picture of 'Carlos'' is beginning to emerge. Informers are coming out of the bloodied spleens and they talk.

Whereas tales of his exploits give rise to images of a world filled with violence and conspiracy, high-explosives and higher intrigues, fast cars and faster women, the facts would seem to indicate at least as much Adam Smith as Ian Fleming. 'Carlos' is reduced to human proportions and in the compression a truly frightening man comes into focus. The sado-romantic myth turns into a brilliant, blood-soaked monster who brokers assassination with the expertise of a market analyst, fully aware of wages, costs, distribution and the divisions of underworld labor. It is a complicated business and 'Carlos' is the master of its dollar value.

The portrait starts with a reputed name, as odd in its way as the owner's profession. Ilich Ramirez Sanchez. He is said to be a Venezuelan, the son of a fanatically devoted but not very prominent Marxist attorney (the Ilich is the father's salute to Vladimir Ilyich Lenin and partially explains 'Carlos'' forays into extremist terrorism) who sent the young boy to Russia for the major part of his education, which included espionage training at the Soviet compound in Novgorod. It is here that the portrait fades briefly, rumor and speculation now the artists. According to these, one or another committee in the Kremlin that regularly monitors foreign students for future infiltration purposes saw what they had in Ilich Sanchez and wanted no part of him. He was a paranoid who saw all solutions in terms of a well-placed bullet or bomb; the recommendation was to send the youth back to Caracas and disassociate any and all Soviet ties with the family. Thus rejected by Moscow, and deeply antithetical to western society, Sanchez went about building his own world, one in which he was the supreme leader. What better way than to become the apolitical assassin whose services could be contracted for by the widest range of political and philosophical clients?

The portrait becomes clearer again. Fluent in numerous languages including his native Spanish as well as Russian, French and English, Sanchez used his Soviet training as a springboard for refining his techniques. Months of concentrated study followed his expulsion from Moscow, some say under the tutelage of the Cubans, Che Guevara in particular. He mastered the science and handling of all manner of weaponry and explosives; there was no gun he could not break down and reassemble blindfolded, no explosive he could not analyse by smell and touch and know how to detonate in a dozen different ways. He was ready; he chose Paris as his base of operations and the word went out. A man was for hire who would kill where others dared not.

Once again the portrait dims as much for lack of birth records as anything else. Just how old is 'Carlos'? How many targets can be attributed to him and how many are myth – self-proclaimed or otherwise? Correspondents based in Caracas have been unable to unearth any birth certificates anywhere in the country for an Ilich Ramirez Sanchez. On the other hand, there are thousands upon thousands of Sanchezes in Venezuela, hundreds with Ramirez attached; but none with an Ilich in front. Was it added later, or is the omission simply further proof of 'Carlos' ' thoroughness? The consensus is that the assassin is between thirty-five and forty years of age. No one really knows.

A GRASSY KNOLL IN DALLAS?

But one fact not disputed is that the profits from his first several kills enabled the assassin to set up an organization that might be envied by an operations analyst of General Motors. It is capitalism at its most efficient, loyalty and service extracted by equal parts fear and reward. The consequences of disloyalty are swift in coming – death – but so, too, are the benefits of service – generous bonuses and huge expense allowances. The organization seems to have hand-picked executives everywhere; and this well-founded rumor leads to the obvious question. Where did the profits initially come from? Who were the original kills?

The one most often speculated upon took place thirteen years ago in Dallas. No matter how many times the murder of John F. Kennedy is debated, no one has ever satisfactorily explained a burst of smoke from a grassy knoll three hundred yards away from the motorcade. The smoke was caught on camera; two open police radios on motorcycles recorded noise(s). Yet neither shell casings nor footprints were found. In fact, the only information about the so-called grassy knoll at that moment was considered so irrelevant that it was buried in the FBI-Dallas investigation and never included in the Warren Commission Report. It was provided by a bystander, K. M. Wright of North Dallas, who when questioned made the following statement:

'Hell, the only son of a bitch near there was old Burlap Billy, and he was a couple of hundred yards away.'

The 'Billy' referred to was an aged Dallas tramp seen frequently panhandling in the tourist areas; the 'Burlap' defined his penchant for wrapping his shoes in coarse cloth to play upon the sympathies of his marks. According to our correspondents, Wright's statement was never made public.

Yet six weeks ago a captured Lebanese terrorist broke under questioning in Tel Aviv. Pleading to be spared execution, he claimed to possess extraordinary information about the assassin 'Carlos'. Israeli intelligence forwarded the report to Washington; our Capitol correspondents obtained excerpts.

Statement: 'Carlos was in Dallas in November 1963. He pretended to be

Cuban and programmed Oswald. He was the back-up. It was his operation.'

Question: 'What proof do you have?'

Statement: 'I heard him say it. He was on a small embankment of grass beyond a ledge. His rifle had a wire shell-trap attached.'

Question: 'It was never reported; why wasn't he seen?'

Statement: 'He may have been, but no one would have known it. He was dressed as an old man, with a shabby overcoat, and his shoes were wrapped in canvas to avoid footprints.'

A terrorist's information is clearly not proof, but neither should it always be disregarded. Especially when it concerns a master assassin, known to be a scholar of deception, who had made an admission that so astonishingly corroborates an unknown unpublished statement about a moment of national crisis never investigated. That, indeed, must be taken seriously. As so many others associated – even remotely – with the tragic events in Dallas, 'Burlap Billy' was found dead several days later from an overdose of drugs. He was known to be an old man drunk consistently on cheap wine; he was never known to use narcotics. He could not afford them.

Was 'Carlos' the man on the grassy knoll? What an extraordinary beginning for an extraordinary career! If Dallas really was his 'operation' how many millions of dollars must have been funnelled to him? Certainly more than enough to establish a network of informers and soldiers that is a corporate world unto itself.

The myth has too much substance; Carlos may well be a monster of flesh and too much blood.

Marie put down the magazine. 'What's the game?'

'Are you finished?' Jason turned from the window.

'Yes.'

'I gather a lot of statements were made. Theory, suppositions, equations.'

'Equations?'

'If something happened here and there was an effect over there, a relationship existed.'

'You mean connections,' said Marie.

'All right, connections. It's all there, isn't it?'

'To a degree, you could say that. It's hardly a legal brief; there's a lot of speculation, rumour, and second-hand information.'

'There *are* facts, however.'

'Data.'

'Good. Data. That's fine.'

'What's the game?' Marie repeated.

'It's got a simple title. It's called "Trap".'

'Trap who?'

'Me.' Bourne sat forward. 'I want you to ask me questions. Anything that's in there. A phrase, the name of a city, a rumour, a fragment of . . . data. *Anything*. Let's hear what my responses are. My *blind* responses.'

'Darling, that's no proof of . . .'

'*Do* it!' ordered Jason.

'All right.' Marie raised the issue of *Time*. 'Beirut,' she said.

'Embassy,' he answered. 'CIA station head posing as an attaché. Gunned down in the street. Three hundred thousand dollars.'

Marie looked at him. 'I remember,' she began.

'I *don't*!' interrupted Jason. 'Go on.'

She returned his gaze, then went back to the magazine. 'Baader-Meinhof.'

'Stuttgart. Regensburg. Munich. Two kills and a kidnapping, Baader accreditation. Fees from . . .' Bourne stopped, then whispered in astonishment, 'US sources. Detroit . . . Wilmington, Delaware.'

'Jason, what are . . . ?'

'Go *on. Please.*'

'The name, Sanchez.'

'The *name* is Ilich Ramirez Sanchez,' he replied. 'He is . . . Carlos.'

'Why the Ilich?'

Bourne paused, his eyes wandering. 'I don't know.'

'It's Russian, not Spanish. Was his mother Russian?'

'No . . . *yes.* His mother. It had to be his mother . . . I think. I'm not sure.'

'Novgorod.'

'Espionage compound. Communications, cyphers, frequency traffic. Sanchez is a graduate.'

'Jason, you read that here!'

'*I did not* read it! *Please.* Keep going!'

Marie's eyes swept back to the top of the article. 'Tehran.'

'Eight kills. Divided accreditation – Khomeini and PLO. Fee, two million. Source: South-west Soviet sector.'

'Paris,' said Marie quickly.

'All contracts will be processed through Paris.'

'What contracts?'

'*The* contracts . . . Kills.'

'Whose kills? Whose contracts?'

'Sanchez's . . . Carlos's.'

'Carlos? Then they're Carlos's contracts, *his* kills. They have nothing to do with you.'

'Carlos's contracts,' said Bourne, as if in a daze. 'Nothing to do with . . . me,' he repeated, barely above a whisper.

'You just said it, Jason. None of this has anything to do with you!'

'*No!* That's not *true*!' Bourne shouted, lunging up from the chair, holding his place, staring down at her. '*Our* contracts,' he added quietly.

'You don't know what you're saying!'

'I'm responding! Blindly! It's why I had to come to Paris!' He spun round and walked to the window, gripping the frame. 'That's what the game is all about,' he continued. 'We're not looking for a lie, we're looking for the truth, remember? Maybe we've found it, maybe the game revealed it.'

'This is no valid test! It's a painful exercise in incidental recollection. If a magazine like *Time* printed this, it would have been picked up by half the newspapers in the world. You could have read it anywhere.'

'The fact is I retained it.'

'Not entirely. You didn't know where Ilich came from, that Carlos's father was a Communist attorney in Venezuela. They're salient points, I'd think. You didn't mention a *thing* about the Cubans. If you had, it would have led to the most shocking speculation written here. You didn't say a *word* about it!'

'What are you talking about?'

'Dallas,' she said. 'November, 1963.'

'Kennedy,' replied Bourne.

'That's it? Kennedy?'

'It happened then.' Jason stood motionless.

'It did, but that's not what I'm looking for.'

'I know,' said Bourne, his voice once again flat, as if speaking in a vacuum. 'A grassy knoll . . . Burlap Billy.'

'You *read this*!'

'No.'

'Then you heard it before, read it before!'

'That's possible, but it's not relevant, is it?'

'*Stop it*, Jason!'

'Those words again. I wish I could.'

'What are you trying to *tell* me? You're *Carlos*?'

'God, no. Carlos wants to kill me, and I don't speak Russian, I know that.'

'Then *what*?'

'What I said at the beginning. The game. The game is called "trap-the-soldier".'

'A soldier?'

'Yes. One who defected from Carlos. It's the only explanation, the only reason I know what I know. In all things.'

'Why do you say defect?'

'Because he *does* want to kill me. He has to; he thinks I know as much about him as anyone alive.'

Marie had been crouching on the bed; she swung her legs over the side, her hands at her sides. 'That's a *result* of defecting. What about the *cause*? If it's true, then you did it, became . . . became . . .' She stopped.

'All things considered, it's a little late to look for a moral position,' said Bourne, seeing the pain of acknowledgement on the face of the woman he loved. 'I could think of several reasons, clichés. How about a falling out among thieves . . . killers.'

'Meaningless!' cried Marie. 'There's not a shred of evidence!'

'There's buckets of it and you know it. I could have sold out to a higher bidder, or stolen huge sums of money from the fees. Either would explain the account in Zürich.' He stopped briefly, looking at the wall above the bed, feeling, not seeing. 'Either would explain Howard Leland, Marseilles, Beirut, Stuttgart . . . Munich. Everything. All the unremembered facts that want to come out. And one especially. Why I avoided his name, why I never mentioned him. I'm frightened. I'm afraid of him.'

The moment passed in silence; more was spoken of than fear. Marie nodded. 'I'm sure you believe that,' she said, 'and in a way I wish it were true. But I don't think it is. You want to believe it because it supports what you just said. It gives you an answer . . . an identity. It may not be the identity you want, but God knows it's better than wandering blindly through that awful labyrinth you face every day. Anything would be, I guess.' She paused. 'And *I* wish it were true because then we wouldn't be here.'

'What?'

'*That*'s the inconsistency, darling. The number or symbol that doesn't fit in your equation. If you *were* what you say you were, and afraid of Carlos – and heaven knows you should be – Paris would be the last place on earth you'd feel compelled to go to. We'd be somewhere else; you said it yourself. You'd run away; you'd take the money from Zürich and disappear. But you're not doing that; instead, you're walking right back into Carlos's den. That's not a man who's either afraid *or* guilty.'

'There isn't anything else. I came to Paris to find out; it's as simple as that.'

'Then run away. We'll have the money in the morning; there's nothing stopping you – us. That's simple, too.' Marie watched him closely.

Jason looked at her, then turned away. He walked to the bureau and poured himself a drink. 'There's still Treadstone to consider,' he said defensively.

'Why any more than Carlos? There's your real equation. Carlos and Treadstone. A man I once loved very much was killed by Treadstone. All the more reason for us to run, to survive.'

'I'd think you'd want the people who killed him exposed,' said Bourne. 'Make them pay for it.'

'I do. Very much. But others can find them. I have priorities and revenge isn't at the top of the list. *We* are. You and I. Or is that only my judgment? My feelings.'

'You know better than that.' He held the glass tighter in his hand and looked over at her. 'I love you,' he whispered.

'Then let's *run*!' she said, raising her voice almost mechanically, taking a step towards him. 'Let's forget it all, *really* forget, and run as fast as we can, as far *away* as we can! Let's *do* it!'

'I . . . I,' Jason stammered, the mists interfering, infuriating him. 'There are . . . *things*.'

'What things? We love each other, we've found each *other*! We can go anywhere, be *anyone*! There's nothing to stop us, is there?'

Bourne could feel sweat breaking out on his forehead, and there was a hollowness in his throat. 'Nothing to stop us.' He could hardly hear his own voice. 'I have to think.

'What's there to think about?' pressed Marie, taking another step, forcing him to look at her. 'There's only *you* and *me*, isn't there?'

'Only you and me,' he repeated softly, the mists now closing in, suffocating him. 'I know. I know. But I've got to think. There's so much to learn, so much that has to come out.'

'Why is it so important?'

'It . . . just is.'

'Don't you *know*?'

'Yes . . . No, I'm not sure. Don't ask me now.'

'If not now, *when*? When *can* I ask you? When will it pass? Or will it ever?!'

'*Stop* it!' he suddenly roared, slamming the glass down on the wooden tray. 'I can't run! I won't! I've got to stay here! I've got to *know*!'

Marie rushed to him, putting her hands first on his shoulders, then on his face, wiping away the perspiration. 'Now you've said it. Can you hear yourself, darling? You can't run because the closer you get, the more maddening it is for you. And if you did run, it would only get worse. You wouldn't have a life, you'd live a nightmare. I know that.'

He reached for her face, touching it, looking at her. 'Do you?'

'Of course. But you had to say it, not me.' She held him, her head against his chest. 'I had to force you to . . . The funny thing is that I *could* run. I could get on a plane with you tonight and go wherever you wanted, disappear and not look back, happier than I've ever been in my life. But you couldn't do that. What is – or isn't – here in Paris would eat away at you until you couldn't stand it any more. That's the crazy irony, my darling. I could live with it, but you couldn't.'

'You'd just disappear?' asked Jason. 'What about your family, your job, all the people you know?'

'I'm neither a child nor a fool,' she answered quickly. 'I'd cover myself somehow, but I don't think I'd take it very seriously. I'd request an extended leave for medical and personal reasons. Emotional stress, a breakdown; I could always go back, the department would understand.'

'Peter?'

'Yes.' She was silent for a moment. 'We went from one relationship to another, the second more important to both of us, I think. He was like an imperfect brother you want to succeed in spite of the flaws, because underneath there was such decency.'

'I'm sorry. I'm truly sorry.'

She looked up at him. 'You have the same decency. When you do the kind of work I do decency becomes very important. It's not the meek who are inheriting the earth, Jason, it's the corruptors. And I have an idea that the distance between corruption and killing is a very short step.'

'Treadstone Seventy-one?'

'Yes. We were both right. I do want them exposed, I want them to pay for what they've done . . . And you can't run away.'

He brushed his lips against her cheek and then her hair and held her. 'I should throw you out,' he said. 'I should tell you to get out of my life. I can't do it, but I know damned well I should.'

'It wouldn't make any difference if you did. I wouldn't go, my love.'

The lawyer's suite of offices was on the boulevard de la Chapelle, the book-lined conference room more a stage setting than an office; everything was a prop, and in its place. Deals were made in that room, not contracts. As for the lawyer himself, a dignified white goatee and silver pince-nez above an aquiline nose could not conceal the essential graft in the man. He even insisted on conversing in poor English, for which, at a later date, he could claim to have been misunderstood.

Marie did most of the talking, Bourne deferring, client to advisor. She made her points succinctly, altering the cashier's cheques to bearer bonds, payable in dollars, in denominations ranging from a maximum of twenty thousand to a minimum of five. She instructed the lawyer to tell the bank that all series were to be broken up numerically in threes, international guarantees with every fifth lot of certificates. Her objective was not lost on the attorney; she so complicated the issuing of the bonds that tracing them would be beyond the facilities of most banks or brokers. Nor would such banks or brokers take on the added trouble or expense; payments were guaranteed.

When the irritated, goateed lawyer had nearly concluded his telephone conversation with an equally disturbed Antoine d'Amacourt, Marie held up her hand.

'Pardon me, but Monsieur Bourne insists that Monsieur d'Amacourt also include two hundred thousand francs in cash, one hundred thousand to be included with the bonds and one hundred to be held by Monsieur d'Amacourt. He suggests that the second hundred thousand be divided as follows. Seventy-five thousand for Monsieur d'Amacourt and twenty-five thousand for yourself. He realizes that he is greatly in debt to both of you for your advice, and the additional trouble he has caused you. Needless to say, no specific record of breakdown is required.'

Irritation and disturbance vanished with her words, replaced by an obsequiousness not seen since the court of Versailles. The arrangements were made in accordance with the unusual – but completely understandable – demands of Monsieur Bourne and his esteemed advisor.

A leather attaché case was provided by Monsieur Bourne for the bonds and the money; it would be carried by an armed courier who would leave the bank at 2:30 in the afternoon and meet Monsieur Bourne at 3:00 on the Pont Neuf. The distinguished client would identify himself with a small piece of leather cut from the shell of the case which, when fitted in place, would prove to be the missing fragment. Added to this would be the words: 'Herr Koenig sends greetings from Zürich.'

So much for the details. Except for one, which was made clear by Monsieur Bourne's advisor.

'We recognize that the demands of the *fiche* must be carried out to the letter, and fully expect Monsieur d'Amacourt to do so,' said Marie St Jacques. 'However, we also recognize that the timing can be advantageous to Monsieur Bourne, and would expect no less than that advantage. Were he not to have it, I'm afraid that I, as a certified – if for the present, anonymous – member of the International Banking Commission, would feel compelled to report certain aberrations of banking and legal procedures as I have witnessed them. I'm sure that won't be necessary; we're all very well paid, *n'est-ce pas, monsieur?*'

'*C'est vrai, madame!* In banking and law . . . indeed, as in life itself . . . timing is everything. You have nothing to fear.'

'I know,' said Marie.

Bourne examined the grooves of the silencer, satisfied that he had removed the particles of dust and fluff that had gathered with non-use. He gave it a final, wrenching turn, depressed the magazine release and checked the clip. Six shells remained; he was ready. He shoved the weapon into his belt and buttoned his jacket.

Marie had not seen him with the gun. She was sitting on the bed, her back to him, talking on the telephone to the Canadian Embassy attaché, Dennis Corbelier. Cigarette smoke curled up from an ashtray next to her notebook; she was writing down Corbelier's information. When he had finished, she thanked him and hung up the phone. She remained motionless for two or three seconds, the pencil still in her hand.

'He doesn't know about Peter,' she said, turning to Jason. 'That's odd.'

'Very,' agreed Bourne. 'I thought he'd be one of the first to know. You said they looked over Peter's telephone logs; he'd placed a call to Paris, to Corbelier. You'd think someone would have followed up on it.'

'I hadn't even considered that. I was thinking about the newspapers, the wire services. Peter was . . . was found eighteen hours ago, and regardless of how casual I may have sounded, he was an important man in the Canadian government. His death would be news in itself, his murder infinitely more so . . . It wasn't reported.'

'Call Ottawa tonight. Find out why.'

'I will.'

'What did Corbelier tell you?'

'Oh, yes.' Marie shifted her eyes to the notebook. 'The licence plate in rue Madeleine was meaningless, a car rented at De Gaulle airport to a Jean-Pierre Larousse . . .'

'John Smith,' interrupted Jason.

'Exactly. He had better luck with the telephone number d'Amacourt gave you but he can't see what it could possibly have to do with anything. Neither can I, as a matter of fact.'

'It's that strange?'

'I think so. It's a private line belonging to a fashion house on Saint-Honoré. *Les Classiques.*'

'A fashion house? You mean a studio?'

'I'm sure it's got one, but it's essentially an elegant dress shop. Like the House of Dior, or Givenchy. *Haute couture.* In the trade, Corbelier said, it's known as the "House of René". That's Bergeron.'

'Who?'

'René Bergeron, a designer. He's been around for years, always on the fringes of a major success. I know about him because my little lady back home copies his designs.'

'Did you get the address?'

Marie nodded. 'Why didn't Corbelier know about Peter? Why doesn't everybody?'

'Maybe you'll learn when you call. It's probably as simple as time zones, too late for the morning editions here in Paris. I'll pick up an afternoon paper.' Bourne went to the wardrobe for his overcoat, conscious of the hidden weight in his belt. 'I'm going back to the bank. I'll follow the courier to the Pont

Neuf.' He put on the coat, aware that Marie was not listening. 'I meant to ask you, do these fellows wear uniforms?'

'Who?'

'Bank couriers.'

'That would account for the newspapers, not the wire services.'

'I beg your pardon?'

'The difference in time. The papers might not have picked it up, but the wire services would have. And embassies have teletypes; they would have known about it. It *wasn't* reported, Jason.'

'You'll call tonight,' he said. 'I'm going.'

'You asked about the couriers. Do they wear uniforms?'

'I was curious.'

'Most of the time, yes. They also drive armoured vans, but I was specific about that. If a van was used it was to be parked a block from the bridge, the courier to proceed on foot.'

'I heard you, but I wasn't sure what you meant. Why?'

'A bonded courier's bad enough, but he's necessary; bank insurance requires him. A van is simply too obvious; it could be followed too easily. You won't change your mind and let me go with you?'

'No.'

'Believe me, nothing will go wrong; those two thieves wouldn't permit it.'

'Then there's no reason for you to be there.'

'You're maddening.'

'I'm in a hurry.'

'I know. And you move faster without me.' Marie got up and came to him. 'I do understand.' She leaned into him, kissing him on the lips, suddenly aware of the weapon in his belt. She looked into his eyes. 'You are worried, aren't you?'

'Just cautious.' He smiled, touching her chin. 'It's an awful lot of money. It may have to keep us for a long time.'

'I like the sound of that.'

'The money?'

'No. Us.' Marie frowned. 'A safety deposit box.'

'You keep talking in *non-sequiturs.*'

'You can't leave negotiable certificates worth over a million dollars in a Paris hotel room. You've got to get a deposit box.'

'We can do it tomorrow.' He released her, turning for the door. 'While I'm out, look up Les Classiques in the phone book and call the regular number. Find out how late it's open.' He left quickly.

Bourne sat in the back seat of a stationary taxi, watching the front of the bank through the windscreen. The driver was humming an unrecognizable tune, reading a newspaper, content with the fifty-franc note he had received in advance. The cab's motor, however, was running; the passenger had insisted upon that.

The armoured van loomed in the right rear window, its radio antenna shooting up from the centre of the roof like a tapered bowsprit. It parked in a space reserved for authorized vehicles directly in front of Jason's taxi. Two small red lights appeared above the circle of bullet-proof glass in the rear door. The alarm system had been activated.

Bourne leaned forward, his eyes on the uniformed man who climbed out of the side door and threaded his way through the crowds on the pavement towards the entrance of the bank. He felt a sense of relief; the man was not one of the three well-dressed men who had come to the Valois yesterday.

Fifteen minutes later the courier emerged from the bank, the leather attaché case in his left hand, his right covering an unlatched holster. The jagged rip on the side of the case could be seen clearly. Jason felt the fragment of leather in his shirt pocket; if nothing else it was the primitive combination that made a life beyond Paris, beyond Carlos, possible. If there was such a life and he could accept it without the terrible labyrinth from which he could find no escape.

But it was more than that. In a man-made labyrinth one kept moving, running, careening off walls, the contact itself a form of progress, if only blind. His personal labyrinth had no walls, no defined corridors through which to race. Only space, and swirling mists in the darkness that he saw so clearly when he opened his eyes at night and felt the sweat pouring down his face. Why was it always space and darkness and high winds? Why was he always plummeting through the air at night? A parachute. Why? Then other words came to him; he had no idea where they were from, but they were there and he heard them.

What's left when your memory's gone? And your identity, Mr Smith?

Stop it!

The armoured van swung into the traffic on rue Madeleine. Bourne tapped the driver on the shoulder. 'Follow that truck, but keep at least two cars between us,' he said in French.

The driver turned, alarmed. 'I think you have the wrong taxi, monsieur. Take back your money.'

'I'm with the company, you damn fool. It's a special assignment.'

'Regrets, Monsieur. We will not lose it.' The driver plunged diagonally forward into the combat of traffic.

The van took the quickest route to the Seine, going down side streets, turning left on the Quai de la Rapée towards the Pont Neuf. Then within what Jason judged to be three or four blocks of the bridge, it slowed down, hugging the kerb as if the courier had decided he was too early for his appointment. But, if anything, Bourne thought, he was running late. It was six minutes to three, barely enough time for the man to park and walk the one prescribed block to the bridge. Then why had the van slowed down? Slowed down? No, it had stopped, it wasn't moving! *Why?*

The traffic? . . . Good God, *of course*, the traffic!

'Stop here,' said Bourne to the driver. 'Pull over to the kerb. Quickly!'

'What is it, Monsieur?'

'You're a very fortunate man,' said Jason. 'My company is willing to pay you an additional one hundred francs if you simply go to the front window of that van and say a few words to the driver. Do you want the hundred?'

'*What*, Monsieur?'

'Frankly, we're testing him. He's new. Do you want the hundred?'

'I just go to the window and say a few words?'

'That's all. Five seconds at the most, then you can go back to your taxi and drive off.'

'There's no trouble? I don't want trouble.'

'My firm's among the most respectable in France. You've seen our trucks everywhere.'

'I don't know . . .'

'Forget it!' Bourne reached for the handle of the door.

'What are the words?'

Jason held out the hundred francs. 'Just these: "Herr Koenig. Greetings from Zürich." Can you remember those?'

' "Koenig. Greetings from Zürich." What's so difficult?'

'Good. Let's go. I'll be right behind you.'

'You? Behind me?'

'That's right.' They walked rapidly towards the van, hugging the right side of their small alley in the traffic as cars and trucks passed them in starts and stops on their left. The van was Carlos's trap, thought Jason. The assassin had bought his way into the ranks of the armed couriers. A single name and a rendezvous revealed over a monitored radio frequency could bring an under-paid messenger a great deal of money. *Bourne. Pont Neuf.* So simple. This particular courier was less concerned with being prompt than in making sure the soldiers of Carlos reached the Pont Neuf in time. Paris traffic was notorious; anyone could be late. Jason stopped the taxi driver, holding in his hand two additional two-hundred franc notes; the man's eyes were riveted on them.

'*Monsieur?*'

'My company's going to be very generous. This man must be disciplined for gross infractions. After you say, "Herr Koenig. Greetings from Zürich," simply add, "The schedule's changed. There's a fare in my taxi who must see you." Have you got that?'

The driver's eyes returned to the franc notes. 'What's difficult?' He took the money.

They edged their way along the side of the van, Jason's back pressed against the wall of steel, his right hand concealed beneath his overcoat, gripping the gun in his belt. The driver approached the window and reached up, tapping the glass.

'You inside! Herr Koenig! Greetings from Zürich!' he yelled.

The window was rolled down, no more than an inch or two. 'What *is* this?' a voice yelled back. 'You're supposed to be at the Pont Neuf, Monsieur!'

The driver was no idiot; he was also anxious to leave as rapidly as possible. 'Not me, you jackass!' he shouted through the din of the surrounding, perilously close traffic. 'I'm telling you what I was told to say! The schedule's been changed. There's a man back there who says he has to see you!'

'Tell him to hurry,' said Jason, holding a final fifty-franc note in his hand, beyond sight of the window.

The driver glanced at the money, then back up at the courier. 'Be quick about it! If you don't see him right away you'll lose your job!'

'Now, get out of here!' said Bourne. The driver turned and ran past Jason, grabbing the franc note as he raced back to his taxi.

Bourne held his place, suddenly alarmed by what he heard through the cacophony of pounding horns and gunning engines in the crowded street. There were voices from inside the van, not one man shouting into a radio, but two shouting at each other. The courier was not alone; there was another man with him.

'Those were the words! You heard them!'

'He was to come *up* to you. He was to show himself.'

'Which he will *do*. And present the piece of leather which must fit exactly! Do you expect him to do that in the middle of the street filled with traffic?'

'I don't like it!'

'You paid me to help you and your people find someone. Not to lose my job! I'm going!'

'It *must* be the Pont Neuf!'

'Kiss my ass!'

There was the sound of heavy footsteps on the metal floorboards. 'I'm coming with you!'

The panel door opened; Jason spun behind it, his hand still under his coat. Below him a child's face was pressed against the glass of a car window, the eyes squinting, the young features contorted into an ugly mask, fright and insult the childish intent. The swelling sound of angry horns, blaring in counterpoint, filled the street; the traffic had come to a standstill.

The courier stepped off the metal ledge, the attaché case in his left hand. Bourne was ready; the instant the courier was on the street, he slammed the panel back into the body of the second man, crashing the heavy steel into a descending kneecap and an outstretched hand. The man screamed, reeling backwards inside the van. Jason shouted at the courier, the jagged scrap of leather in his free hand.

'I'm Bourne! Here's the fragment! And you keep that gun in its holster or you won't just lose your job, you'll lose your life, you son of a bitch!'

'I meant no harm, Monsieur! They wanted to find you! They have no interest in your delivery, you have my *word* on it!'

The door crashed open; Jason slammed it again with his shoulder, then pulled it back to see the face of Carlos's soldier, his hand on the weapon in his belt.

What he saw was the barrel of a gun, the black orifice of its opening staring him in the eyes. He spun back, aware that the split-second delay in the gunshot that followed was caused by a burst of shrill ringing that exploded out of the armoured van. The alarm had been tripped, the sound deafening, riding over the dissonance in the street; the gunshot seemed muted by comparison, the eruption of asphalt below not heard.

Once more Jason hammered the panel. He heard the impact of metal against metal; he had made contact with the gun of Carlos's soldier. He pulled his own from his belt, dropped to his knees in the street, and pulled the door open.

He saw the face from Zürich, the killer they had called Johann, the man they had brought to Paris to recognize him. Bourne fired twice; the man arched backwards, blood spreading across his forehead.

The courier! The attaché case!

Jason saw the man; he had ducked below the tailgate for protection, his weapon in his hand, screaming for help. Bourne leaped to his feet and lunged for the extended gun, gripping the barrel, twisting it out of the courier's hand. He grabbed the attaché case and shouted.

'No harm, *right*? Give me that, you bastard!' He threw the man's gun under the van, got up, and plunged into the hysterical crowds on the pavement.

He ran wildly, blindly, the bodies in front of him the movable walls of his labyrinth. But there was an essential difference between this gauntlet and one he lived in every day. There was no darkness; the afternoon sun was bright, as blinding as his race through the labyrinth.

14

'Everything's here,' said Marie. She had collated the certificates by denominations, the stacks and the franc notes on the desk. 'I told you it would be.'

'It almost wasn't.'

'What?'

'The man they called Johann, the one from Zürich. He's dead. I killed him.'

'Jason, what *happened*?'

He told her. 'They counted on the Pont Neuf,' he said. 'My guess is that the back-up car got caught in traffic, broke into the courier's radio frequency, and told them to delay. I'm sure of it.'

'Oh God, they're everywhere.'

'But they don't know where *I* am,' said Bourne, looking into the mirror above the bureau, studying his blond hair while putting on the tortoiseshell glasses. 'And the last place they'd expect to find me at this moment – if they conceivably thought I knew about it – would be a fashion house on Saint-Honoré.'

'Les Classiques?' asked Marie, astonished.

'That's right. Did you call it?'

'Yes, but that's insane!'

'Why?' Jason turned from the mirror. 'Think about it. Twenty minutes ago their trap fell apart; there's got to be confusion, recriminations, accusations of incompetency, or worse. Right now, at *this moment*, they're more concerned with each other than with me; nobody wants a bullet in his throat. It won't last long; they'll regroup quickly, Carlos will make sure of that. But during the next hour or so while they're trying to piece together what happened, the one place they won't look for me is a relay-drop they haven't the vaguest idea I'm aware of.'

'Someone will recognize you!'

'Who? They brought in a man from Zürich to do that and he's dead. They're not sure what I look like.'

'The courier. They'll take him; he saw you.'

'For the next few hours he'll be busy with the police.'

'D'Amacourt. The lawyer!'

'I suspect they're halfway to Normandy or Marseilles or, if they're lucky, out of the country.'

'Suppose they're stopped, caught?'

'Suppose they are? Do you think Carlos would expose a drop where he gets messages? Not on your life. Or his.'

'Jason, I'm frightened.'

'So am I. But not of being recognized.' Bourne returned to the mirror. 'I could give a long dissertation about facial classifications and softened features, but I won't.'

'You're talking about the evidences of surgery. Port Noir. You told me.'

'Not all of it.' Bourne leaned against the bureau, staring at his face. 'What colour are my eyes?'

'*What?*'

'No, don't look at me. Now, tell me, what colour are my eyes? Yours are brown with speckles of green; what about mine?'

'Blue . . . bluish. Or a kind of grey, really . . .' Marie stopped. 'I'm not really sure. I suppose that's dreadful of me.'

'It's perfectly natural. Basically they're hazel, but not all the time. Even I've noticed it. When I wear a blue shirt or tie, they become bluer; a brown coat or jacket, they're grey. When I'm naked, they're strangely nondescript.'

'That's not so strange. I'm sure millions of people are the same.'

'I'm sure they are. But how many of them wear contact lenses when their eyesight is normal?'

'Contact . . . ?'

'That's what I said,' interrupted Jason. 'Certain types of contact lenses are worn to change the colour of the eyes. They're most effective when the eyes are hazel . . . When Washburn first examined me there was evidence of prolonged usage. It's one of the clues, isn't it?'

'It's whatever you want to make of it,' said Marie. 'If it's true.'

'Why wouldn't it be?'

'Because the doctor was more often drunk than sober. You've told me that. He piled conjecture on top of conjecture, heaven knows how often warped by alcohol. He was never specific. He *couldn't* be.'

'He was about one thing. I'm a chameleon, designed to fit a flexible mould. I want to find out whose; maybe I can now. Thanks to you I've got an address. Someone there may know the truth. Just *one man*, that's all I need. One person I can confront, break if I have to . . .'

'I can't stop you, but for God's sake be careful. If they do recognize you, they'll kill you.'

'Not there they won't; it'd be rotten for business. This is Paris.'

'I don't think that's funny, Jason.'

'Neither do I. I'm counting on it very seriously.'

'What are you going to do? I mean, how?'

'I'll know better when I get there. See if anyone's running around looking nervous or anxious or waiting for a phone call as if his life depended on it.'

'Then what?'

'I'll do the same as I did with d'Amacourt. Wait outside and follow whoever it is. I'm this close, I won't miss. And I'll be careful.'

'Will you call me?'

'I'll try.'

'I may go crazy waiting. Not knowing.'

'Don't wait. Can you deposit the bonds somewhere?'

'The banks are closed.'

'Use a large hotel; hotels have vaults.'

'You have to have a room.'

'Take one. At the Meurice, or the Georges Cinq. Leave the case at the desk, but come back here.'

Marie nodded. 'It would give me something to do.'

'Then call Ottawa. Find out what happened.'

'I will.'

Bourne crossed to the bedside table and picked up a number of five-thousand franc notes. 'A bribe would be easier,' he said. 'I don't think it'll happen, but it could.'

'It could,' agreed Marie, and then in the same breath continued, 'Did you hear yourself? You just rattled off the names of two hotels.'

'I heard.' He turned and faced her. 'I've been here before. Many times. I lived here, but not in those hotels. In out-of-the-way streets, I think. Not very easily found.'

The moment passed in silence, the fear electric.

'I love you, Jason.'

'I love you, too,' said Bourne.

'Come back to me. No matter what happens, come back to me.'

The lighting was soft and dramatic, pinpoint spotlights shining down from the dark brown ceiling, bathing mannequins expensively dressed in pools of flattering yellows. The jewellery and accessories counters were lined with black velvet, silks of bright red and green tastefully flowing above the midnight sheen, glistening eruptions of gold and silver caught in the recessed frame lights. The aisles curved graciously in semi-circles, giving an illusion of space that was not there, for Les Classiques, though hardly small, was not a large emporium. It was, however, a beautifully appointed shop on one of the most costly strips of real estate in Paris. Fitting rooms with doors of tinted glass were at the rear, beneath a balcony where the offices of management were located. A carpeted staircase rose on the right beside an elevated switchboard in front of which sat an oddly out-of-place middle-aged man dressed in a conservative business suit, operating the console, speaking into a mouthpiece that was an extension of his single earphone.

The staff were mostly women, tall, slender, gaunt of face and body, living postmortems of former fashion models whose tastes and intelligence carried them beyond their sisters in the trade, other practices no longer feasible. The few men in evidence were also slender; reedlike figures emphasized by form-fitting clothes, gestures rapid, stances balletically defiant.

Light romantic music floated out of the dark ceiling, quiet crescendos abstractly punctuated by the beams of the miniature spotlights. Jason wandered through the aisles, studying mannequins, touching the fabric, making his own appraisals. They covered his essential bewilderment. Where was the confusion, the anxiety he expected to find at the core of Carlos's message centre? He glanced up at the open office doors and the single corridor that bisected the small complex. Men and women walked casually about as they did on the main floor, every now and then stopping one another, exchanging pleasantries or scraps of relevantly irrelevant information. Gossip. Nowhere was there the slightest sense of urgency; no sign at all that a vital trap had exploded in their faces, an imported killer – the only man in Paris who worked for Carlos and could identify the target – shot in the head, dead in the back of an armoured van on the Quai de la Râpée.

It was incredible, if only because the whole atmosphere was the opposite of what he had anticipated. Not that he expected to find chaos, far from it; the soldiers of Carlos were too controlled for that. Still, he had expected *something.* And here there were no strained faces, or darting eyes, no abrupt movements that signified alarm. Nothing whatsoever was unusual; the elegant world of *haute couture* continued to spin in its elegant orbit, unmindful of events that should have thrown its axis off balance.

Still, there was a private telephone somewhere and someone who not only spoke for Carlos but was also empowered to set in motion three killers on the hunt. A woman . . .

He saw her; it had to be her. Halfway down the carpeted staircase, a tall imperious woman with a face that age and cosmetics had rendered into a cold mask of itself. She was stopped by a reedlike male clerk who held out a salesbook for the woman's approval; she looked at it, then glanced down at the floor, at a nervous, middle-aged man by a nearby jewellery counter. The glance was brief, but pointed, the message clear. *All right,* mon ami, *pick up your bauble but pay your bill soon. Otherwise you could be embarrassed next time. Or worse. I might call your wife.* In milliseconds, the rebuke was over; a smile as false as it was broad cracked the mask, and with a nod and a flourish the woman took a pencil from the clerk and initialled the sales slip. She continued down the staircase, the clerk following, leaning forward in further conversation. It was obvious he was flattering her; she turned on the bottom step, touching her crown of streaked dark hair and tapped his wrist in a gesture of thanks.

There was little placidity in the woman's eyes. They were as aware as any pair of eyes Bourne had ever seen, except perhaps behind gold-rimmed glasses in Zürich.

Instinct. She was his objective; it remained how to reach her. The first moves of the pavane had to be subtle, neither too much nor too little but warranting attention. She had to come to him.

The next few minutes astonished Jason, which was to say he astonished himself. The term was 'role-playing', he understood that, but what shocked him was the ease with which he slid into a character far from himself – as he knew himself. Where minutes before he had made appraisals, he now made inspections, pulling garments from their individual racks, holding the fabrics up to the light. He peered closely at stitchings, examined buttons and button holes, brushed his fingers across collars, fluffing them up, then letting them fall. He was a judge of fine clothes, a schooled buyer who knew what he wanted and rapidly disregarded that which did not suit his tastes. The only items he did not examine were the price tags; obviously they held no interest for him.

The fact that they did not prodded the interest of the imperious woman who kept glancing over in his direction. A sales clerk, her concave body floating upright on the carpet, approached him; he smiled courteously, but said he preferred to browse by himself. Less than thirty seconds later he was behind three mannequins, each dressed in the most expensive designs to be found in Les Classiques. He raised his eyebrows, his mouth set in silent approval as he squinted between the plastic figures at the woman beyond at the counter. She whispered to the clerk who had spoken to him; the former model shook her head, shrugging.

Bourne stood arms akimbo, billowing his cheeks, his breath escaping slowly as his eyes shifted from one mannequin to another; he was an uncertain man about to make up his mind. And a potential client in that situation, especially one who did not look at prices, needed assistance from the most knowledgeable person in the vicinity; he was irresistible. The regal woman touched her hair, and gracefully negotiated the aisles towards him. The pavane had come to its first conclusion; the dancers bowed, preparing for the gavotte.

'I see you've gravitated to our better items, Monsieur,' said the woman in English, a presumption obviously based on the judgment of a practised eye.

'I trust I have,' replied Jason. 'You have an interesting collection here, but one does have to ferret, doesn't one?'

'The ever-present and inevitable scale of values, Monsieur. However, all our designs are exclusive.'

'*D'accord, madame.*'

'*Ah, vous parlez français?*'

'*Un peu.* Passably.'

'You are American?'

'I'm rarely there,' said Bourne. 'You say these are made for you alone?'

'Oh, yes. Our designer is under exclusive contract; I'm sure you've heard of him. René Bergeron.'

Jason frowned. 'Yes, I have. Very respected, but he's never made a breakthrough, has he?'

'He will, Monsieur. It's inevitable; his reputation grows each season. A number of years ago he worked for St Laurent, then Givenchy. Some say he did far more than *cut* the patterns if you know what I mean.'

'It's not hard to follow.'

'And how those cats try to push him in the background! It's disgraceful! Because he adores women; he flatters them and does not make them into little boys, *vous comprenez*?'

'*Facilement.*'

'He'll emerge worldwide one day soon and they'll not be able to touch the hems of his creations. Think of these as the works of an emerging master, Monsieur.'

'You're very convincing. I'll take these three. I assume they're in the size twelve range.'

'Indeed, Monsieur, but they will be fitted, of course.'

'I'm afraid not, but I'm sure there are decent dressmakers in Cap Ferrat.'

'*Naturellement*,' conceded the woman quickly.

'Also . . .' Bourne hesitated, frowning again. 'While I'm here, and to save time, select a few others for me along these lines. Different prints, different cuts, but related, if that makes sense.'

'Very *good* sense, Monsieur.'

'Thanks, I appreciate it. I've had a long flight from the Bahamas and I'm exhausted.'

'Would Monsieur care to sit down then?'

'Frankly Monsieur would care for a drink.'

'It can be arranged, of course . . . As to the method of payment, Monsieur . . .?'

'*Encaisse*, I think,' said Jason, aware that the exchange of merchandise for hard currency would appeal to the overseer of Les Classiques. 'Cheques and accounts are like spoors in the forest, aren't they?'

'You are as wise as you are discriminating.' The rigid smile cracked the mask again, the eyes in no way related. 'About that drink, why not my office? It's quite private; you can relax and I shall bring you selections for your approval.'

'Splendid.'

'As to the price range, Monsieur?'

'*Les meilleurs, madame.*'

'*Naturellement.*' A thin white hand was expended. 'I am Jacqueline Lavier, managing partner of Les Classiques.'

'Thank you.' Bourne took the hand without offering a name. One might follow in less public surroundings, his expression said, but not at the moment. For the moment, money was his introduction. 'Your office? Mine's several thousand miles from here.'

'This way, Monsieur.' The rigid smile appeared once more, breaking the facial mask like a sheet of progressively cracked ice. Madame Lavier gestured towards the staircase. The world of *haute couture* continued, its orbit uninterrupted by failure and death on the Quai de la Râpée.

That lack of interruption was as disturbing to Jason as it was bewildering. He was convinced the woman walking beside him was the carrier of lethal commands that had been aborted by gunfire an hour ago, the orders having been issued by a faceless man who demanded obedience or death. But there was not the slightest indication that a strand of her perfectly groomed hair had been disturbed by nervous fingers, no pallor on the chiselled mask that might be taken for fear. Yet there was no one higher at Les Classiques, no one else who would have a private number in a very private office. Part of an equation was missing . . . but another had been disturbingly confirmed.

Himself. The chameleon. The charade had worked; he was in the enemy's camp convinced beyond doubt that he had not been recognized. The whole episode had a *déjà vu* quality about it. He had done such things before, experienced the feelings of similar accomplishment before. He was a man running through an unfamiliar jungle, yet somehow *instinctively* knowing his way, sure of where the traps were and how to avoid them. The chameleon was an expert.

They reached the staircase and started up the steps. Below, on the right, the conservatively dressed, middle-aged operator was speaking quietly into the extended mouthpiece, nodding his grey-haired head almost wearily, as if assuring the party on the line that *their* world was as serene as it should be.

Bourne stopped on the seventh step, the pause involuntary. The back of the man's head, the outline of the cheekbone, the sight of the thinning grey hair – the way it fell slightly over the ear; he had seen that man before! Somewhere. In the past, in the *unremembered* past, but remembered now in darkness . . . and with flashes of light. Explosions, mists; buffeting winds followed by silences filled with tension. What was it? *Where* was it? Why did the pain come to his eyes again? The grey-haired man began to turn in his swivel chair; Jason looked away before they made contact.

'I see Monsieur is taken by our rather unique switchboard,' said Madame Lavier. 'It's a distinction we feel sets Les Classiques apart from the other shops on Saint-Honoré.'

'How so?' asked Bourne, as they proceeded up the steps, the pain in his eyes causing him to blink.

'When a client calls Les Classiques, the telephone is not answered by a vacuous female, but instead by a cultured gentleman who has all our information at his fingertips.'

'A nice touch.'

'Other gentlemen think so,' she added. 'Especially when making telephone purchases they would prefer to keep confidential. There are no spoors in our forest, Monsieur.'

They reached Jacqueline Lavier's spacious office. It was the lair of an efficient executive, scores of papers in separate piles on the desk, an easel against the wall holding water-colour sketches, some boldly initialled, others left untouched, obviously unacceptable. The walls were filled with framed photographs of the Beautiful People, their beauty too often marred by gaping mouths and smiles as false as the one on the mask of the inhabitant of the office. There was a bitch quality in the perfumed air; these were the quarters of an ageing, pacing tigress, swift to attack any who threatened her possessions or the sating of her appetites. Yet she was disciplined; all things considered, an estimable liaison to Carlos.

Who was that man on the switchboard? Where had he seen him?

He was offered a drink from a selection of bottles; he chose brandy.

'Do sit down, Monsieur. I shall enlist the help of René himself, if I can find him.'

'That's very kind, but I'm sure whatever you choose will be satisfactory. I have an instinct about taste, yours is all through this office. I'm comfortable with it.'

'You're too generous.'

'Only when it's warranted,' said Jason, still standing. 'Actually, I'd like to look at the photographs. I see a number of acquaintances, if not friends. A lot of these faces pass through the Bahamian banks with considerable frequency.'

'I'm sure they do,' agreed Lavier, in a tone that bespoke regard for such avenues of finance. 'I shan't be long, Monsieur.'

Nor would she, thought Bourne, as Les Classiques' partner swept out of the office. Mme Lavier was not about to allow a tired, wealthy man too much time to think. She would return with the most expensive designs she could gather up as rapidly as possible. Therefore, if there was anything in the room that could shed light of Carlos's intermediary – or on the assassin's operation – it had to be found quickly. And, if it was there it would be on or around the desk.

Jason circled behind the imperial chair in front of the wall, feigning amused interest in the photographs, but concentrating on the desk. There were invoices, receipts and overdue bills, along with dunning letters of reprimand awaiting Lavier's signature. An address book lay open, four names on the page; he moved closer to see more clearly. Each was the name of a company, the individual contacts bracketed, his or her positions underlined. He wondered if he should memorize each company, each contact. He was about to do so when his eyes fell on the edge of an index card. It was only the edge; the rest was concealed under the telephone itself. And there was something else – dull, barely discernible. A strip of transparent tape, running along the edge of the card, holding it in place. The tape itself was relatively new, recently stuck over the heavy paper and the gleaming wood; it was clean, no smudges or coiled borders or signs of having been there very long.

Instinct.

Bourne picked up the telephone to move it aside. It rang, the bell vibrating through his hand, the shrill sound unnerving. He replaced it on the desk and stepped away as a man in shirtsleeves rushed through the open door from the corridor. He stopped, staring at Bourne, his eyes alarmed but noncommittal. The telephone rang a second time; the man walked rapidly to the desk and picked up the receiver.

'*Allo?*' There was silence as the intruder listened, head down, concentration on the caller. He was a tanned, muscular man of indeterminate age, the sun-drenched skin disguising the years. His face was taut, his lips thin, his close-cropped hair thick, dark brown and disciplined. The sinews of his bare arms moved under the flesh as he transferred the phone from one hand to the other, speaking harshly. '*Pas ici maintenant. Je ne sais pas la réponse. Appelez encore.*' He hung up and looked at Jason. '*Où et Jacqueline?*'

'A little slower, please,' said Bourne, lying in English. 'My French is limited.'

'Sorry,' replied the bronzed man. 'I was looking for Madame Lavier.'

'The owner?'

'The title will suffice. Where is she?'

'Depleting my funds.' Jason smiled, raising his glass to his lips.

'Oh? And who are you, Monsieur?'

'Who are *you*?'

The man studied Bourne. 'René Bergeron.'

'Oh, Lord!' exclaimed Jason. 'She's looking for *you*. You're very *good*, Mr Bergeron. She said I was to look upon your designs as the work of an emerging master.' Bourne smiled again. 'You're the reason I may have to wire the Bahamas for a great deal of money.'

'You're most kind, Monsieur. And I apologize for barging in.'

'Better that you answered that phone than me. Berlitz considers me a failure.'

'Buyers, suppliers, all screaming idiots. To whom, Monsieur, do I have the honour of speaking?'

'Briggs,' said Jason, having no idea where the name came from, astonished that it came so quickly, so naturally. 'Charles Briggs.'

'A pleasure to know you.' Bergeron extended his hand; the grip was firm. 'You say Jacqueline was looking for me?'

'On my behalf, I'm afraid.'

'I shall find her.' The designer left quickly.

Bourne moved quickly to the desk, his eyes on the door, his hand on the telephone. He moved it to the side, exposing the index card. There were two telephone numbers, the first recognizable as a Zürich exchange, the second obviously Paris.

Instinct. He had been right, a strip of transparent tape the only sign he had needed. He stared at the numbers, memorizing them, then moved the telephone back into place, and stepped away.

He had barely managed to clear the desk when Madame Lavier swept back into the room, a half dozen dresses over her arm. 'I met René on the steps. He approves of my selections most enthusiastically. He also tells me your name is Briggs, Monsieur.'

'I would have told you myself,' said Bourne, smiling back, countering the pout in Lavier's voice. 'But I don't think you asked.'

' "Spoors in the forest", Monsieur. Here, I bring you a feast!' She separated the dresses, placing them carefully over several chairs. 'I truly believe these are among the finest creations René has brought us.'

'Brought you?' replied Jason. 'He doesn't work here then?'

'A figure of speech; his studio's at the end of the corridor, but it is a holy sacristy. Even I tremble when I enter.'

'They're magnificent,' continued Bourne, going from one to another. 'But I don't want to overwhelm her, just pacify her,' he added, pointing out three garments. 'I'll take these.'

'A fine selection, Monsieur Briggs!'

'Box them with the others, if you will.'

'Of course. She is, indeed, a fortunate lady.'

'A good companion, but a child. A spoiled child, I'm afraid. However, I've been away a lot and haven't paid much attention to her, so I feel I should make peace. It's one reason I sent her to Cap Ferrat.' He smiled, taking out his Louis Vuitton wallet. '*La facture, s'il vous plait?*'

'I'll have one of the girls expedite everything.' Mme Lavier pressed a button on the intercom next to the telephone. Jason watched closely, prepared to comment on the call Bergeron had answered in the event the woman's eyes settled on a slightly out-of-place phone. '*Envoyez Janine ici avec les vêtements sur comptoir cinq. Aussi la facture.*' She stood up. 'Another brandy, Monsieur Briggs?'

'*Merci bien.*' Bourne extended his glass; she took it and walked to the bar. Jason knew the time had not yet arrived for what he had in mind; it would come soon – as soon as he parted with money – but not now. He could, however, continue building a foundation with the managing partner of Les

Classiques. 'That fellow, Bergeron,' he said, 'you say he's under exclusive contract to you?'

Madame Lavier turned, the glass in her hand. 'Oh, yes. We are a closely knit family here.'

Bourne accepted the brandy, nodded his thanks, and sat down in an armchair in front of the desk. 'That's a constructive arrangement,' he said pointlessly.

The tall, gaunt clerk he had first spoken to came into the office, a salesbook in her hand. Instructions were given rapidly, figures entered, the garments gathered and separated as the salesbook exchanged hands. Lavier held it out for Jason's perusal. '*La facture*,' she said.

Bourne shook his head, dismissing inspection. '*Combien?*' he asked.

'*Vingt mille soixante francs, monsieur*,' answered the Les Classiques partner, watching his reaction with the expression of a large, wary bird.

There was none. Jason merely removed six five-thousand franc notes and handed them to her. She nodded and gave them in turn to the slender salesgirl, who walked cadaverously out of the office with the dresses.

'Everything will be packaged and brought up here with your change.' Lavier went to her desk and sat down. 'You're on your way to Ferrat, then. It should be lovely.'

He had paid; the time had come. 'A last night in Paris before I go back to kindergarten,' said Jason, raising his glass in a toast of self-mockery.

'Yes, you mentioned that your friend is quite young.'

'A child is what I said, and that's what she is. She's a good companion, but I think I prefer the company of more mature women.'

'You must be very fond of her,' contested Lavier, touching her perfectly coiffed hair, the flattery accepted. 'You buy her such lovely – and, frankly – expensive things.'

'A minor price considering what she might try to opt for.'

'Really.'

'She's my wife, my third to be exact, and there are appearances to be kept in the Bahamas. But all that's neither here nor there; my life's quite in order.'

'I'm sure it is, Monsieur.'

'Speaking of the Bahamas, a thought occurred to me a few minutes ago. It's why I asked you about Bergeron.'

'What is that?'

'You may think I'm impetuous; I assure you I'm not. But when something strikes me, I like to explore it . . . Since Bergeron's yours exclusively, have you ever given any thought to opening a branch in the islands?'

'The Bahamas?'

'And points south. Into the Caribbean, perhaps.'

'Monsieur, Saint-Honoré by itself is often more than we can handle! Untended farmland generally goes fallow, as they say.'

'It wouldn't have to be tended; not in the way that you think. A concession here, one there, the designs exclusive, local ownership on a percentage-franchise basis. Just a boutique or two, spreading, of course, cautiously.'

'That takes considerable capital, Monsieur Briggs.'

'Key prices, initially. What you might call entrance fees. They're high, but not prohibitive. In the finer hotels and clubs it usually depends on how well you know the managements.'

'And you know them?'

'Extremely well. As I say, I'm just exploring, but I think the idea has merit. Your labels would have a certain distinction. Les Classiques, Paris, Grand Bahama . . . Caneel Bay, perhaps.' Bourne swallowed the rest of his brandy. 'But you probably think I'm crazy. Consider it just talk . . . Although I've made a dollar or two on risks that simply struck me on the spur of the moment.'

'Risks?' Jacqueline Lavier touched her hair again.

'I don't give ideas away, Madame, I generally back them.'

'Yes, I understand. As you say, the idea does have merit.'

'I think so. Of course, I'd like to see what kind of agreement you have with Bergeron.'

'It could be produced, Monsieur.'

'Tell you what,' said Jason. 'If you're free, let's talk about it over drinks and dinner. It's my only night in Paris.'

'And you prefer the company of more mature women,' concluded Jacqueline Lavier, the mask cracked into a smile again, the white ice breaking beneath eyes now more in concert.

'*D'accord, madame.*'

'It can be arranged,' she said, reaching for the phone.

The phone. Carlos.

He would break her, thought Bourne. *Kill her if he had to. He would learn the truth.*

Marie walked through the crowd towards the box in the telephone complex on rue Vaugirard. She had taken a room at the Meurice, left the attaché case at the front desk and sat alone in the room for exactly twenty-two minutes. Until she could not stand it any longer. She had sat in a chair facing a blank wall thinking about Jason, about the madness of the last eight days that had propelled her into an insanity beyond her understanding. Jason. Considerate, frightening, bewildered Jason Bourne. A man with so much violence in him, and yet, oddly, so much compassion. And too terribly capable in dealing with a world ordinary men knew nothing about. Where *had* he sprung from, this love of hers? Who had taught him to find his way through the dark back streets of Paris, Marseilles and Zürich . . . as far away as the Orient, perhaps? What was the Far East to him? How did he know the languages? What *were* the languages? Or language?

Tao.

Che-sah.

Tam Quan.

Another world, and she knew nothing of it. But she knew Jason Bourne, or the man called Jason Bourne, and she held on to the decency she knew was there. Oh, *God*, how she loved him so!

Ilich Ramirez Sanchez. *Carlos.* What *was* he to Jason Bourne?

Stop it, she had screamed at herself while in that room alone. And then she had done what she had seen Jason do so many times: she had lunged up from the chair, as if the physical movement would clear the mists away – or allow her to break through them.

Canada. She had to reach Ottawa and find out why Peter's death – his *murder* – was being handled so secretly, so *obscenely*! It did not make sense; she objected with all her heart. For Peter, too, was a decent man, and he had been killed by indecent men. She would be told why or she would expose that death – that murder – herself. She would scream out loud to the world she *knew* and say *Do Something!*

And so she had left the Meurice, taken a cab to the rue de Vaugirard, and placed the call to Ottawa. She waited now outside the booth, her anger mounting, an unlit cigarette creased between her fingers. When the bell rang, she could not take the time to crush it out.

It rang. She opened the glass door and went inside.

'Is this you, Alan?'

'Yes,' was the curt reply.

'Alan, what the *hell* is going on? Peter was *murdered*, and there hasn't been a single word in any newspaper, or on any broadcast! I don't think the embassy even knows! It's as though no one cared! What are you people *doing*?'

'What we're told to do. And so will you.'

'*What?* That was *Peter*! He was *your* friend! Listen to me, Alan . . .'

'*No!*' The interruption was harsh. '*You* listen. Get out of Paris. *Now!* Take the next direct flight back here. If you have any problems the embassy will clear them, but you're to talk *only* to the ambassador, is that understood?'

'No!' screamed Marie St Jacques. 'I don't understand! Peter was killed and nobody cares! All you're saying is bureaucratic bullshit! Don't get involved; for *God's sake*, don't *ever* get involved!'

'Stay out of it, Marie!'

'Stay out of *what*? That's what you're not telling me, isn't it? Well, you'd *better* . . .'

'I can't!' Alan lowered his voice. 'I don't know. I'm only telling you what I was told to tell you.'

'By whom?'

'You can't ask me that.'

'I *am* asking!'

'Listen to me, Marie. I haven't been home for the past twenty-four hours. I've been waiting here for the last twelve for you to call. Try to understand me, I'm not *suggesting* you come back. Those are orders from your government.'

'*Orders?* Without explanations?'

'That's the way it is . . . I'll say this much. They want you out of there; they want him isolated . . . That's the way it is.'

'Sorry, Alan! That's *not* the way it is! Good-bye!' She slammed the receiver down, then instantly gripping her hands to stop the trembling. *Oh, my God, she loved him so . . . and they were trying to kill him. Jason, my Jason, they all want you killed. Why?*

*

The conservatively-dressed man at the switchboard snapped the red toggle that blocked the lines, reducing all incoming calls to a busy signal. He did so once or twice an hour, if only to clear his mind and expunge the empty inanities he had been required to mouth during the past minutes. The necessity to cut off all conversation usually occurred to him after a particularly tedious one; he had just had it. The wife of a Deputy trying to conceal the outrageous price of a single purchase from her husband by breaking it up into several. *Enough!* He needed a few minutes to *breathe.*

The irony struck him. It was not that many years ago when others sat in front of the switchboards for *him.* At his companies in Saigon and in the communications room of his vast plantation in the Mekong Delta. And here he was now in front of someone else's switchboard in the perfumed surroundings of Saint-Honoré. The English poet said it best: there were more preposterous vicissitudes in life than a single philosophy could conjure.

He heard laughter on the staircase and looked up. Jacqueline was leaving early, no doubt with one of her celebrated and fully bank-rolled acquaintances. There was no question about it, Jacqueline had a talent for removing gold from a well-guarded mine, even diamonds from De Beers. He could not see the man with her; he was on the other side of Jacqueline, his head oddly turned away.

Then for an instant he did see him; their eyes made contact; it was brief and explosive. The grey-haired switchboard operator suddenly could not breathe; he was suspended in a moment of disbelief, staring at a face, a head, he had not seen in years! And then almost always in darkness, for they had worked at night . . . died at night.

Oh, my *God*, it was *him*! From the living – dying – nightmares thousands of miles away. It *was* him!

The grey-haired man rose from the switchboard as if in a trance. He pulled the mouthpiece-earphone off and let it drop to the floor. It clattered as the board lit up with incoming calls that made no connections, answered only by discordant hums. The middle-aged man stepped off the platform, and side-stepped his way quickly towards the aisle to get a better look at Jacqueline Lavier and the ghost that was her escort. The ghost who was a killer – above all men he had ever known, a *killer*. They said it might happen, but he had never believed them; he believed them now! It *was* the *man.*

He saw them both clearly. Saw *him.* They were walking down the centre aisle towards the entrance. He had to stop them. Stop *her*! But to rush out and yell would mean death. A bullet in the head, instantaneous.

They reached the doors; *he* pulled them open, ushering her out to the pavement. The grey-haired man raced out from his hiding place, across the intersecting aisle and down the front window. Out in the street *he* had flagged a taxi. He was opening the door, motioning Jacqueline to get inside. Oh, *God*! She was going!

The middle-aged man turned and ran as fast as he could towards the staircase. He collided with two startled customers and a salesgirl, pushing all three violently out of his way. He raced up the steps, across the balcony and down the corridor, to the open studio door.

'René! René!' he shouted, bursting inside.

Bergeron looked up from his sketchboard, astonished. 'What is it?'

'That man with Jacqueline! Who is he? How long has he been here?'

'Oh? Probably the American,' said the designer. 'His name's Briggs. A fatted calf; he's done very well by our grosses today.'

'Where did they go?'

'I didn't know they went anywhere.'

'She left with him!'

'Our Jacqueline retains her touch, no? And her good sense.'

'Find them! Get her!'

'Why?'

'He *knows*! He'll kill her!'

'What?'

'It's him! I'd swear to it! That man is Cain!'

15

'The man is Cain,' said Colonel Jack Manning bluntly, as if he expected to be contradicted by at least three of the four civilians at the Pentagon conference table. Each was older than he, and each considered himself more experienced. None was prepared to acknowledge that the army had obtained information where his own organization had failed. There was a fourth civilian but his opinion did not count. He was a member of the Congressional Oversight Committee, and as such to be treated with deference, but not seriously. 'If we don't move *now*,' continued Manning, 'even at the risk of exposing everything we've learned, he could slip through the nets again. As of eleven days ago, he was in Zürich. We're convinced he's still there. And, gentlemen, it *is* Cain.'

'That's quite a statement,' said the balding, bird-like academic from the National Security Council as he read the summary page concerning Zürich given to each delegate at the table. His name was Alfred Gillette, an expert in Personnel Screening and Evaluation, and he was considered by the Pentagon to be bright, vindictive, and with friends in high places.

'I find it extraordinary,' added Peter Knowlton, an associate director of the Central Intelligence Agency, a man in his middle fifties who perpetuated the dress, the appearance, and the attitude of an Ivy League of thirty years ago. 'Our sources have Cain in Brussels, *not* Zürich, at the same time – eleven days ago. Our sources are rarely in error.'

'*That's* quite a statement,' said the third civilian, the only one at that table Manning really respected. He was the oldest there, a man named David Abbott, a former Olympic swimmer whose intellect had matched his physical prowess. He was in his late sixties now, but his bearing was still erect, his mind as sharp as it had ever been, his age, however, betrayed by a face lined from the tensions of a lifetime he would never reveal. He knew what he was talking about, thought the colonel. Although he was currently a member of the omnipotent Forty Committee, he had been with the CIA since its origin in the OSS. The Silent Monk of Covert Operations had been the sobriquet given him by his colleagues in the intelligence community. 'In my days at the agency,' continued Abbott, chuckling, 'the sources were as often in conflict as in agreement.'

'We have different methods of verification,' pressed the associate director. 'No disrespect, Mr Abbott, but our transmissions equipment is literally instantaneous.'

'That's equipment, not verification. But I won't argue; it seems we have a disagreement. Brussels or Zürich.'

'The case for Brussels is airtight,' insisted Knowlton firmly.

'Let's hear it,' said the balding Gillette, adjusting his glasses. 'We can return to the Zürich summary, it's right in front of us. Also, *our* sources have some input to offer, although it's not in conflict with Brussels or Zürich. It happened over six months ago.'

The silver-haired Abbott glanced over at Gillette. 'Six months ago? I don't recall NSC having delivered anything about Cain six months ago.'

'It wasn't totally confirmed,' replied Gillette. 'We try not to burden the Committee with unsubstantiated data.'

'That's also quite a statement,' said Abbott, not needing to clarify.

'Congressman Walters,' interrupted the colonel, looking at the man from Oversight, 'do you have any questions before we go on?'

'Hell, yes,' drawled the congressional watchdog from the state of Tennessee, his intelligent eyes roaming the faces, 'but since I'm new at this, you go ahead so I'll know where to begin.'

'Very well, sir,' said Manning, nodding at the CIA's Knowlton. 'What's this about Brussels eleven days ago?'

'A man was killed in the Place Fontainas, a covert dealer in diamonds between Moscow and the West. He operated through a branch of Russolmaz, the Soviet firm in Geneva that brokers all such purchases. We know it's one way Cain converts his funds.'

'What ties the killing to Cain?' asked the dubious Gillette.

'Method, first. The weapon was a long needle, implanted in a crowded square at noontime with surgical precision. Cain's used it before.'

'That's quite true,' agreed Abbott. 'There was a Rumanian in London somewhat over a year ago; another only weeks before him. Both were narrowed to Cain.'

'Narrowed but not confirmed,' objected Colonel Manning. 'They were high-level political defectors; they could have been taken by the KGB'

'Or by Cain with far less risk to the Soviets,' argued the CIA man.

'*Or* by Carlos,' added Gillette, his voice rising. 'Neither Carlos nor Cain is concerned about ideology; they're both for hire. Why is it every time there's a killing of consequence, we ascribe it to Cain?'

'Whenever we do,' replied Knowlton, his condescension obvious, 'it's because informed sources unknown to each other have reported the same information. Since the informants have no knowledge of each other there could hardly be collusion.'

'It's all too pat,' said Gillette disagreeably.

'Back to Brussels,' interrupted the colonel. 'If it was Cain, why would he kill a broker from Russolmaz? He used him.'

'A covert broker,' corrected the CIA director. 'And for any number of reasons according to our informants. The man was a thief, and why not? Most of his clients were too; they couldn't very well file charges. He might have cheated Cain, and if he did, it'd be his last transaction. Or he could have been foolish enough to speculate on Cain's identity; even a hint of what would call for the needle. Or perhaps Cain simply wanted to bury his current traces. Regardless, the circumstances plus the sources leave little doubt that it was Cain.'

'There'll be a lot more when I clarify Zürich,' said Manning. 'May we proceed to the summary?'

'A moment, please.' David Abbott spoke casually while lighting his pipe. 'I believe our colleague from the Security Council mentioned the occurrence related to Cain that took place six months ago. Perhaps we should hear about it.'

'Why?' asked Gillette, his eyes owl-like beyond the lenses of his rimless glasses. 'The time factor removes it from having any bearing on Brussels *or* Zürich. I mentioned that, too.'

'Yes, you did,' agreed the once-formidable Monk of Covert Services. 'I thought, however, any background might be helpful. As you also said, we can return to the summary; it's right in front of us. But if it's not relevant, let's get on with Zürich.'

'Thank you, Mr Abbott,' said the colonel. 'You'll note that eleven days ago, on the night of February twenty-seventh, four men were killed in Zürich. One of them was a watchman in a parking area by the Limmat River, it can be presumed that he was not involved in Cain's activities, but caught in them. Two others were found in an alley on the west bank of the city, on the surface unrelated murders, except for the fourth victim. He's tied in with the dead men in the alley – all three part of the Zürich–Munich underworld – and is, without question, connected to Cain.'

'That's this Chernak,' said Gillette, reading the summary. 'At least, I assume it's Chernak. I recognize the name, and associate it with the Cain file somewhere.'

'You should,' replied Manning. 'It first appeared in a G-Two report eighteen months ago, and cropped up again a year later.'

'Which would make it six months ago,' interjected Abbott, softly, looking at Gillette.

'Yes, sir,' continued the colonel. 'If there was ever an example of what's called the scum-of-the-earth, it was Chernak. During the war he was a Czechoslovakian recruit at Dachau, a tri-lingual interrogator as brutal as any guard in the camp. He sent Poles, Slovaks and Jews to the showers after torture sessions in which he extracted – and manufactured – "incriminating" information Dachau's commandants wanted to hear. He went to any length to curry favour with his superiors and the most sadistic cliques were hard pressed to match his exploits. What they didn't realize was that *he* was cataloguing *theirs.* After the war he escaped, got his legs blown off by an undetected land mine, and still managed to survive very nicely on his Dachau extortions. Cain found him and used him as a go-between for payments on his kills.'

'Now just want a minute!' objected Knowlton strenuously. 'We've been over this Chernak business before. If you recall, it was the agency that first uncovered him; we would have exposed him long ago if State hadn't interceded on behalf of several powerful, anti-Soviet officials in the Bonn government. You *assume* Cain's used Chernak; you don't know it for certain any more than *we* do.'

'We do now,' said Manning. 'Seven and a half months ago, we received a tip about a man who ran a restaurant called the Drei Alpenhäuser; it was reported that he was an intermediary between Cain and Chernak. We kept him under surveillance for weeks, but nothing came of it; he was a minor figure in the Zürich underworld, that was all . . . We didn't stay with him long enough.' The colonel paused, satisfied that all eyes were on him. 'When we heard about Chernak's murder, we gambled. Five nights ago two of our men hid in the Drei Alpenhäuser after the restaurant closed. They cornered the owner and accused him of dealing with Chernak, working for Cain; they put on a hell of a show. You can imagine their shock when the man broke, literally fell to his knees begging to be protected. He admitted that Cain was in Zürich the night Chernak was killed; that, in fact, he had seen Cain that night and Chernak had come up in the conversation. Very negatively.'

The military man paused again, the silence filled by a slow soft whistle from David Abbott, his pipe held in front of his crag-lined face. 'Now, that *is* a statement,' said the Monk quietly.

'Why wasn't the Agency informed of this tip you received seven months ago?' asked the CIA's Knowlton abrasively.

'It didn't prove out.'

'In your hands; it might have been different in ours.'

'That's possible. I admitted we didn't stay with him long enough. Manpower's limited; which of us can keep up a non-productive surveillance indefinitely?'

'We might have shared it, if we'd known.'

'And we could have saved you the time it took to build the Brussels file, if we'd been told about that.'

'Where did the tip come from?' asked Gillette, interrupting impatiently, his eyes on Manning.

'It was anonymous.'

'You *settled* for that?' The bird-like expression on Gillette's face conveyed his astonishment.

'It's one reason the initial surveillance was limited.'

'Yes, of course, but you mean you never dug for it?'

'Naturally, we did,' replied the colonel testily.

'Apparently without much enthusiasm,' continued Gillette angrily. 'Didn't it occur to you that someone over at Langley, or on the Council, might have helped, might have filled in a gap? I agree with Peter. We should have been informed.'

'There's a reason why you weren't.' Manning breathed deeply; in less military surroundings it might have been construed as a sigh. 'The informant made it clear that if we brought in any other branch, he wouldn't make contact again. We felt we had to abide by that; we've done it before.'

'What did you say?' Knowlton put down the summary page and stared at the Pentagon officer.

'It's nothing new, Peter. Each of us sets up his own sources, protects them.'

'I'm aware of that. It's why you weren't told about Brussels. Both drones said to keep the army out.'

Silence. Broken by the abrasive voice of the Security Council's Alfred Gillette. 'How often is "we've done it before", Colonel?'

'What?' Manning looked at Gillette, but was aware that David Abbot was watching both of them closely.

'I'd like to know how many times you've been told to keep your sources to yourself. I refer to Cain, of course.'

'Quite a few, I guess.'

'You guess?'

'Most of the time.'

'And you, Peter? What about the Agency?'

'We've been severely limited in terms of in-depth dissemination.'

'For *God's* sake, what's *that* mean?' The interruption came from the least expected member of the conference; the congressman from Oversight. 'Don't misunderstand me, I haven't begun yet. I just want to follow the language.' He turned to the CIA man. 'What the hell did you just say? "In-depth *what*?" '

'Dissemination, Congressman Walters; it's throughout Cain's file. We risked losing informants if we brought them to the attention of other intelligence units. I assure you, it's standard.'

'It sounds like you were test-tubing a heifer.'

'With about the same results,' added Gillette. 'No cross-pollenization to corrupt the strain. And, conversely, no cross-checking to look for patterns of inaccuracy.'

'Some nice turns of phrase,' said Abbott, his craggy face wrinkled in appreciation, 'but I'm not sure I understand you.'

'I'd say it's pretty damned clear,' replied the man from National Security, looking at Colonel Manning and Peter Knowlton. 'The country's two most active intelligence branches have been fed information about Cain – for the past *three years* – and there's been no pooling for origins of fraud. We've simply received all information as *bona fide* data, stored and accepted as valid.'

'Well, I've been around a long time – perhaps too long, I concede but there's nothing here I haven't heard before,' said the Monk. 'Sources are shrewd and defensive people, they guard their contacts jealously. None are in the business of charity, only for profit and survival.'

'I'm afraid you're overlooking my point.' Gillette removed his glasses. 'I said before that I was alarmed that so many recent assassinations have been attributed to Cain – attributed *here* to Cain – when it seems to me that the most accomplished assassin of our time – perhaps in history – has been relegated to a comparatively minor role. I think that's *wrong*. I think Carlos is the man we should be concentrating on. What happened to *Carlos*?'

'I question your judgment, Alfred,' said the Monk. 'Carlos's time has passed, Cain's moved in. The old order changes; there's a new and, I suspect, far more deadly shark in the waters.'

'I can't agree with that,' said the man from National Security, his owl-eyes boring into the elder statesman of the intelligence community. 'Forgive me,

David, but it strikes me as if Carlos himself was manipulating this committee. To take the attention away from himself, making us concentrate on a subject of much less importance. We're spending all our energies going after a toothless sand shark while the hammerhead roams free.'

'No one's forgetting Carlos,' objected Manning. 'He's simply not as active as Cain's been.'

'Perhaps,' said Gillette icily, 'that's exactly what Carlos wants us to believe. And, by God, we believe it!'

'Can you doubt it?' asked Abbott. 'The record of Cain's accomplishments is staggering.'

'Can I doubt it?' repeated Gillette. 'That's the question, isn't it? But can any of us be sure? That's also a valid question. We now find that both the Pentagon and the Central Intelligence Agency have been literally operating independently of each other, without even conferring as to the accuracy of their sources.'

'A custom rarely breached in this town,' said Abbott, amused.

Again the congressman from Oversight interrupted. 'What are you trying to say, Mr Gillette?'

'I'd like more information about the activities of one Ilich Ramirez Sanchez. That's . . .'

'Carlos,' said the congressman. 'I remember my reading. I see. Thank you. Go on, gentlemen.'

Manning spoke quickly. 'May we get back to Zürich, please. Our recommendation is to go after Cain now. We can spread the word in the *Verbrecherwelt*, pull in every informer we have, request the co-operation of the Zürich police. We can't afford to lose another day. The man in Zürich *is* Cain!'

'Then what was Brussels?' The CIA's Knowlton asked the question as much of himself as anyone at the table. 'The method was Cain's, the informants unequivocal. What was the purpose?'

'To feed you false information *obviously*,' said Gillette. 'And before we make any dramatic moves in Zürich, I suggest that *each* of you comb the Cain files and recheck every source given you. Have your European stations pull in every informant who so miraculously appeared to offer information. I have an idea you might find something you didn't expect; the fine Latin hand of Ramirez Sanchez.'

'Since you're so insistent on clarification, Alfred,' interrupted Abbott, 'why not tell us about the unconfirmed occurrence that took place six months ago. We seem to be in a quagmire here; it might be helpful.'

For the first time during the conference, the abrasive delegate from the National Security Council seemed to hesitate. 'We received word around the middle of August from a reliable source in Aix-en-Provence that Cain was on his way to Marseilles.'

'*August*?' exclaimed the colonel. 'Marseilles? That was Leland! Ambassador Leland was shot in Marseilles. In August!'

'But Cain didn't fire that rifle. It was a Carlos kill; that *was* confirmed. Bore markings matched with previous assassinations, three descriptions of an unknown dark-haired man on the third and fourth floors of the waterfront warehouse carrying a satchel. There was never any doubt that Leland was murdered by Carlos.'

'For Christ's sake,' roared the officer. 'That's after the fact, *after* the kill! No matter whose, there was a contract out on Leland, hadn't that occurred to you? If we'd known about Cain, we might have been able to cover Leland. He was military property! Goddamn it, he might be alive today!'

'Unlikely,' replied Gillette calmly. 'Leland wasn't the sort of man to live in a bunker. And given his life style, a vague warning would have served no purpose. Besides, had our strategy held together, warning Leland would have been counter-productive.'

'In what way?' asked the Monk harshly.

'It's your fuller explanation. Our source was to make contact with Cain during the hours of midnight and three in the morning in the rue Sarasin on August twenty-third. Leland wasn't due until the twenty-fifth. As I say, had it held together we would have taken Cain. It didn't; Cain never showed up.'

'And your *source* insisted on co-operating solely with *you*,' said Abbott. 'To the exclusion of all others.'

'Yes,' nodded Gillette, trying but unable to conceal his embarrassment. 'In our judgment, the risk to Leland had been eliminated – which in terms of Cain turned out to be the truth – and the odds for capture greater than they'd ever been. We'd finally found someone willing to come out and identify Cain. Would any of you have handled it any other way?'

Silence. This time broken by the drawl of the astute congressman from Tennessee.

'Jesus Christ Almighty . . . what a bunch of bullshitters!'

Silence terminated by the thoughtful voice of David Abbott.

'May I commend you, sir, on being the first honest man sent over from the Hill. The fact that you are not overwhelmed by the rarefied atmosphere of these highly classified surroundings is not lost on any of us. It's refreshing.'

'I don't think the congressman fully grasps the sensitivity of . . .'

'Oh, shut up, Peter,' said the Monk. 'I think the congressman wants to say something.'

'Just for a bit,' said Walters, 'I thought you were all over twenty-one; I mean, you *look* over twenty-one, and by then you're supposed to know better. You're supposed to be able to hold intelligent conversations, exchange information while respecting confidentiality, and look for common solutions. Instead, you sound like a bunch of kids jumping on a goddamn carousel, squabbling over who's going to get the cheap brass ring. It's a hell of a way to spend taxpayers' money.'

'You're oversimplifying, Congressman,' broke in Gillette. 'You're talking about a utopian fact-finding apparatus. There's no such thing.'

'I'm talking about reasonable men, sir. I'm a lawyer and before I came up to this godforsaken circus I dealt with ascending levels of confidentiality every day of my life. What's so damn new about them?'

'And what's your point?' asked the Monk.

'I want an explanation. For over eighteen months I've sat on the House Assassination Subcommittee. I've ploughed through thousands of pages, filled with hundreds of names and twice as many theories. I don't think there's a suggested conspiracy or a suspected assassin I'm not aware of. I've lived with those names and those theories for damn near two years, until I didn't think there was anything left to learn.'

'I'd say your credentials were very impressive,' interrupted Abbott.

'I thought they might be; it's why I accepted the Oversight chair. I thought I could make a realistic contribution, but now I'm not so sure. I'm suddenly beginning to wonder what I *do* now.'

'Why?' asked Manning apprehensively.

'Because I've been sitting here listening to the four of you describe an operation that's been going on for three years, involving networks of personnel and informants and major intelligence posts throughout Europe – all centred on an assassin whose "list of accomplishments" is staggering. Am I substantively correct?'

'Go on,' replied Abbott quietly, holding his pipe, his expression rapt. 'What's your question?'

'Who is he? Who the hell is this Cain?'

16

The silence lasted precisely five seconds, during which time eyes roamed other eyes, several throats were cleared and no one moved in his chair. It was as if a decision was being reached without discussion; evasion was to be avoided. Congressman Efrem Walters, out of the hills of Tennessee by way of the Yale *Law Review*, was not to be dismissed with facile circumlocution that dealt with the esoterica of clandestine manipulations. Bullshit was out.

David Abbott put his pipe down on the table, the quiet clatter his overture. 'The less public exposure a man like Cain receives the better it is for everyone.'

'That's no answer,' said Walters. 'But I assume it's the beginning of one.'

'It is. He's a professional assassin – that is, a trained expert in wide-ranging methods of taking life. That expertise is for sale, neither politics nor personal motivation any concern to him whatsoever. He's in business solely to make a profit and his profits escalate – in direct ratio to his reputation.'

The congressman nodded. 'So by keeping as tight a lid as you can on that reputation you're holding back free advertising.'

'Exactly. There are a lot of maniacs in this world with too many real or imagined enemies who might easily gravitate to Cain if they knew of him. Unfortunately, more than we care to think about already have; to date thirty-eight killings can be directly attributed to Cain, and some twelve to fifteen are probabilities.'

'That's his list of "accomplishments"?'

'Yes. And we're losing the battle. With each new killing his reputation spreads.'

'He was dormant for a while,' said Knowlton of the CIA. 'For a number of months recently we thought he might have been taken himself. There were several probables in which the killers themselves were eliminated; we thought he might have been one of them.'

'Such as?' asked Walters.

'A banker in Madrid who funnelled bribes for the Europolitan Corporation for government purchases in Africa. He was shot from a speeding car on the Paseo de la Castellana. A chauffeur-bodyguard gunned down both driver and killer; for a time we believed the killer was Cain.'

'I remember the incident. Who might have paid for it?'

'Any number of companies,' answered Gillette, 'who wanted to sell gold-plated cars and indoor plumbing to instant dictators.'

'What else? Who else?'

'Sheikh Mustafa Kalig in Oman,' said Colonel Manning.

'He was reported killed in an abortive coup.'

'Not so,' continued the officer. 'There was no attempted coup; G-Two informants confirmed that Kalig was unpopular, but the other sheikhs aren't fools. The coup story was a cover for an assassination that could tempt other professional killers. Three troublesome nonentities from the Officer Corps were executed to lend credence to the lie. For a while, we thought one of them was Cain; the timing corresponds to Cain's dormancy.'

'Who would pay Cain for assassinating Kalig?'

'We asked ourselves that over and over again,' said Manning. 'The only possible answer came from a source who claimed to know, but there was no way to verify it. He said Cain did it to prove it could be done. By him. Oil sheikhs travel with the tightest security in the world.'

'There are several dozen other incidents,' added Knowlton. 'Probables that fall into the same pattern where highly protected figures were killed and sources came forward to implicate Cain.'

'I see.' The congressman picked up the summary page for Zürich. 'But from what I gather you don't know who he is.'

'No two descriptions have been alike,' interjected Abbott. 'Cain's apparently a virtuoso at disguise.'

'Yet people have seen him, talked to him. Your sources, the informants, this man in Zürich; none of them may come out in the open to testify, but surely you've interrogated them. You've got to have come up with a composite, with *something*.'

'We've come up with a great deal,' replied Abbott, 'but a consistent description isn't part of it. For openers, Cain never lets himself be seen in daylight. He holds meetings at night, in dark rooms or alleyways. If he's ever met more than one person at a time – as Cain – we don't know about it. We've been told he never stands, he's always seated – in a dimly lit restaurant, or a corner chair, or parked car. Sometimes he wears heavy glasses, sometimes none at all; at one rendezvous he may have dark hair, at another white or red or covered by a hat.'

'Language?'

'We're closer here,' said the CIA director, anxious to put the Company's research on the table. 'Fluent English and French, and several Oriental dialects.'

'Dialects? What Dialects? Doesn't a language come first?'

'Of course. It's root-Vietnamese.'

'*Viet?* . . .' Walters leaned forward. 'Why do I get the idea that I'm coming to something you'd rather not tell me?'

'Because you're probably quite astute at cross-examination, sir.' Abbott struck a match and lit his pipe.

'Passably alert,' agreed the congressman. 'Now, what is it?'

'Cain,' said Gillette, his eyes briefly, oddly, on David Abbott. 'We know where he came from.'

'Where?'

'Out of South-east Asia,' answered Manning, as if sustaining the pain of a knife wound. 'As far as we can gather, he mastered the fringe dialects so as to be understood in the hill country along the Cambodian and Laos border routes, as well as in rural North Vietnam. We accept the data; it fits.'

'With what?'

'Operation Medusa.' The colonel reached for a large, thick manilla envelope on his left. He opened it and removed a single folder from among several inside; he placed it in front of him. 'That's the Cain file,' he said, nodding at the open envelope. 'This is the Medusa material, the aspects of it that might in any way be relevant to Cain.'

The Tennessean leaned back in his chair, the trace of a sardonic smile creasing his lips. 'You know, gentlemen, you slay me with your pithy titles. Incidentally, that's a beaut; it's very sinister, very ominous. I think you fellows take a course in this kind of thing. Go on, Colonel. What's this Medusa?'

Manning glanced briefly at David Abbott, then spoke. 'It was a clandestine outgrowth of the search-and-destroy concept, designed to function behind enemy lines during the Vietnam war. In the late 'sixties and early 'seventies, units of American, French, British, Australian and native volunteers were formed into teams to operate in territories occupied by the North Vietnamese. Their priorities were the disruption of enemy communications and supply lines, the pinpointing of prison camps and, not the least, the assassination of village leaders known to be co-operating with the Communists, as well as the enemy commanders whenever possible.'

'It was a war-within-a-war,' broke in Knowlton. 'Unfortunately, racial appearances and languages made participation infinitely more dangerous than, say, the German and Dutch undergrounds, or the French Resistance in World War Two. Therefore, occidental recruitment was not always as selective as it might have been.'

'There were dozens of these teams,' continued the colonel, 'the personnel ranging from old line Navy chiefs who knew the coastlines to French plantation owners whose only hope for reparations lay in an American victory. There were British and Australian drifters who'd lived in Indochina for years, as well as highly motivated American army and civilian intelligence career officers. Also, inevitably, there was a sizeable faction of hard-core criminals. In the main, smugglers – men who dealt in running guns, narcotics, gold and diamonds throughout the entire South China Sea area. They were walking encyclopaedias when it came to night landings and jungle routes. Many we employed were runaways or fugitives from the States, a number well-educated, all resourceful. We needed their expertise.'

'That's quite a cross-section of volunteers,' interrupted the congressman. 'Old line Navy and Army; British and Australian drifters, French colonials, and platoons of thieves. How the hell did you get them to work together?'

'To each according to his greeds,' said Gillette.

'Promises,' amplified the colonel. 'Guarantees of rank, promotions, pardons, outright bonuses of cash, and in a number of cases opportunities to steal funds . . . from the operation itself. You see, they all had to be a little crazy; we understood that. We trained them secretly, using codes, methods of transport, entrapment and killing – even weapons Command Saigon knew nothing about. As Peter mentioned, the risks were incredible, capture resulting in torture and execution; the price was high and they paid it. Most people would have called them a collection of paranoics, but they were geniuses where disruption and assassination were concerned. Especially assassination.'

'What was the price?'

'Operation Medusa sustained over ninety per cent casualties. But there's a catch – among those who didn't come back were a number who never meant to.'

'From that faction of thieves and fugitives?'

'Yes. Some stole considerable amounts of money from Medusa. We think Cain is one of those men.'

'Why?'

'His *modus operandi.* He's used codes, traps, methods of killing and transport that were developed and specialized in the Medusa training.'

'Then for Christ's sake,' broke in Walters, 'you've got a direct line to his identity. I don't care where they're buried – and I'm damn sure you don't want them made public – but I assume records were kept.'

'They were, and we've extracted them all from the clandestine archives, inclusive of this material here.' The officer tapped the file in front of him. 'We've studied everything, put rosters under microscopes, fed facts into computers – everything we could think of. We're no further along than when we began.'

'That's incredible,' said the congressman. 'Or incredibly incompetent.'

'Not really,' protested Manning. 'Look at the man; look at what we've had to work with. After the war, Cain made his reputation throughout most of East Asia, from as far north as Tokyo down through the Philippines, Malaysia and Singapore, with side trips to Hong Kong, Cambodia, Laos and Calcutta. About two and a half years ago reports began filtering in to our Asian stations and embassies. There was an assassin for hire; his name was Cain. Highly professional, ruthless. These reports started growing with alarming frequency. It seemed that with every killing of note, Cain was involved. Sources would phone embassies in the middle of the night, or stop attachés in the streets, always with the same information. It was Cain, Cain was the one. A murder in Tokyo; a car blown up in Hong Kong; a narcotics caravan ambushed in the Triangle; a banker shot in Calcutta; an ambassador assassinated in Moulmein, a Russian technician or an American businessman killed in the streets of Shanghai itself. Cain was everywhere, his name whispered by dozens of trusted informants in every vital intelligence sector. Yet no one – not one single person in the entire east Pacific area – would come forward to give us an identification. Where were we to begin?'

'But by this time, hadn't you established the fact that he'd been with Medusa?' asked the Tennessean.

'Yes. Firmly.'

'Then with the individual Medusa dossiers, damn it!'

The colonel opened the folder he had removed from the Cain file. 'These are the casualty lists. Among the white occidentals who disappeared from Operation Medusa – and when I say disappeared, I mean vanished without a trace –

are the following. Seventy-three Americans, forty-six French, thirty-nine and twenty-four Australians and British respectively, and an estimated fifty white male contacts recruited from neutrals in Hanoi and trained in the field – most of *them* we never knew. Over two hundred and thirty possibilities; how many are blind alleys? Who's alive? Who's dead? Even if we learned the name of every man who actually survived, who is he now? What is he? We're not even sure of Cain's nationality. We think he's American, but there's no proof.'

'Cain's one of the side issues contained in our constant pressure on Hanoi to trace MIAs,' explained Knowlton. 'We keep recycling these names with the division lists.'

'And there's a catch with that, too,' added the army officer. 'Hanoi's counter-intelligence forces broke and executed scores of Medusa personnel. They were aware of the operation, and we never ruled out the possibility of infiltration. Hanoi knew the Medusans weren't combat troops; they wore no uniforms. Accountability was never required.'

Walters held out his hand. 'May I?' he said, nodding at the stapled pages.

'Certainly.' The officer gave them to the congressman. 'You understand, of course, that those names still remain classified, as does the Medusa Operation itself.'

'Who made that decision?'

'It's an unbroken executive order from successive presidents based on the recommendation of the Joint Chiefs of Staff. It was supported by the Senate Armed Services Committee.'

'That's considerable fire-power, isn't it?'

'It was felt to be in the national interest,' said the CIA man.

'In this case, I won't argue,' agreed Walters. 'The spectre of such an operation wouldn't do much for the glory of Old Glory. We don't train assassins, much less field them.' He flipped through the pages. 'And somewhere here just happens to be an assassin we trained and fielded and now can't find.'

'We believe that, yes,' said the colonel.

'You say he made his reputation in Asia but moved to Europe. When?'

'About a year ago.'

'Why? Any ideas?'

'The obvious, I'd suggest,' said Peter Knowlton. 'He over-extended himself. Something went wrong and he felt threatened. He was a white killer among Orientals, at best a dangerous concept; it was time for him to move on. God knows his reputation *was* made; there'd be no lack of employment in Europe.'

David Abbott cleared his throat. 'I'd like to offer another possibility based on something Alfred said a few minutes ago.' The Monk paused and nodded deferentially at Gillette. 'He said that we had been forced to concentrate on a "toothless sand shark while the hammerhead roamed free". I believe that was the phrase, although my sequence may be wrong.'

'Yes,' said the man from National Security. 'I was referring to Carlos, of course. It's not Cain we should be after. It's Carlos.'

'Of course, Carlos. The most elusive killer in modern history, a man many of us truly believe has been responsible – in one way or another – for the most tragic assassinations of our time. You were quite right, Alfred, and, in a way, I was wrong. We cannot afford to forget Carlos.'

'Thank you,' said Gillette. 'I'm glad I made my point.'

'You did. With me, at any rate. But you also made me think. Can you imagine the temptation for a man like Cain, operating in the steamy confines of an area rife with drifters and fugitives and regimes up to their necks in corruption? But he must have envied Carlos; how he must have been jealous of the faster, brighter, more luxurious world of Europe. How often did he say to himself, "I'm better than Carlos". No matter how cold these fellows are, their egos are immense. I suggest he went to Europe to find that better world . . . and to dethrone Carlos. The pretender, sir, wants to take the title. He wants to be champion.'

Gillette stared at the Monk. 'It's an interesting theory.'

'And if I follow you,' interjected the congressman from Oversight, 'by tracking Cain we may come up with Carlos.'

'Exactly.'

'I'm not sure *I* follow,' said the CIA director, annoyed. 'Why?'

'Two stallions in a paddock,' answered Walters. 'They tangle.'

'A champion does not give up the title willingly,' Abbott reached for his pipe. 'He fights viciously to retain it. As the congressman says, we continue to track Cain, but we must also watch for other spoors in the forest. And when and if we find Cain, perhaps we should hold back. Wait for Carlos to come after him.'

'Then take both,' added the military officer.

'Very enlightening,' said Gillette.

The meeting was over, the members in various stages of leaving. David Abbott stood with the Pentagon colonel who was gathering together the pages of the Medusa folder; he had picked up the casualty sheets, prepared to insert them.

'May I take a look?' asked Abbott. 'We don't have a copy over at Forty.'

'Those were our instructions,' replied the officer, handing the stapled pages to the older man. 'I thought they came from you. Only three copies. Here, at the Agency, and over at the Council.'

'They did come from me.' The silent Monk smiled benignly. 'Too damn many civilians in my part of town.'

The colonel turned away to answer a question posed by the congressman from Tennessee. David Abbott did not listen; instead his eyes sped rapidly down the columns of names; he was alarmed. A number had been crossed out, accounted for. Accountability was the one thing they should not allow! Ever! Where *was* it? He was the only man in that room who knew the name, and he could feel the pounding in his chest as he reached the last page. The name was there!

Bourne, Jason C. – Last known station: Tam Quan.

What in God's name *had happened?*

René Bergeron slammed down the telephone on his desk; his voice only slightly more controlled than his gesture. 'We've tried every café, every restaurant and bistro she's ever frequented!'

'There's not a hotel in Paris that has him registered,' said the grey-haired switchboard operator, seated at a second telephone by a drawing board. 'It's been more than two hours now; she could be dead. If she's not, she might well wish she were.'

'She can only tell him so much,' mused Bergeron. 'Less than we could; she knows nothing of the old men.'

'She knows enough; she's called Parc Monceau.'

'She's relayed messages; she's not certain to whom.'

'She knows why.'

'So does Cain, I can assure you. And he would make a grotesque error with Parc Monceau.' The designer leaned forward, his powerful forearms tensing as he locked his hands together, his eyes on the grey-haired man. 'Tell me, again, everything you remember. Why are you so sure he's Bourne?'

'I don't know that. I said he was Cain. If you've described his methods accurately, he's the man.'

'Bourne *is* Cain. We found him through the Medusa records. It's why you were hired.'

'Then he's Bourne, but it's not the name he used. Of course, there were a number of men in Medusa who would not permit their real names to be used. For them, false identities were guaranteed; they had criminal records. He would be one of those men.'

'Why him? Others disappeared. You disappeared.'

'I could say because he was here in Saint-Honoré and that should be enough. But there's more, much more. I watched him function. I was assigned to a mission he commanded; it was not an experience to be forgotten, nor was he. That man could be – *would* be – your Cain.'

'Tell me.'

'We parachuted at night into a sector called Tam Quan, our objective to bring out an American named Webb who was being held by the Viet Cong. We didn't know it, but the odds against survival were monumental. Even the flight from Saigon was horrendous; gale-force winds at a thousand feet, the aircraft vibrating as if it would fall apart. Still, he ordered us to jump.'

'And you did?'

'His gun was pointed at our heads. At each of us as we approached the hatchway. We might survive the elements, not a bullet in our skulls.'

'How many were there of you?'

'Eight.'

'You could have taken him.'

'You didn't know him.'

'Go on,' said Bergeron, concentrating; immobile at the desk.

'Seven of us regrouped on the ground; two, we assumed, had not survived the jump. It was amazing that I did. I was the oldest and hardly a bull, but I knew the area; it was why I was sent.' The grey-haired man paused, shaking his head at the memory. 'Less than an hour later we realized it was a trap. We were pinned down by enemy gunfire for two nights and a day, running like lizards through the jungle . . . And during the nights, he went out alone through the mortar explosions and the grenades. To kill. Always coming back before dawn to force us closer and closer to the base camp. I thought at the time, sheer *suicide*.'

'Why did you do it? He had to give you a reason; you were Medusans, not soldiers.'

'He said it was the only way to get out alive and there was logic to that. We were far behind the lines; we needed the supplies we could find at the base camp – if we could take it. He said we had to take it, we had no choice. If any argued, he'd put a bullet in his head, we knew it . . . On the third night we took the camp and found the man named Webb more dead than alive, but breathing. We also found the two missing members of our team, very much alive and stunned at what had happened. A white man and a Vietnamese; they'd been paid by the Cong to trap us – trap him, I suspect.'

'Cain?'

'Yes. The Vietnamese saw us first and escaped. Cain shot the white man in the head. He just walked up to him and blew his head off.'

'He got you back? Through the lines?'

'Four of us, yes, and the man named Webb. Five men were killed. It was during that terrible journey back that I thought I understood why the rumours might be true – that he was the highest paid recruit in Medusa.'

'In what sense?'

'He was the coldest man I ever saw, the most dangerous, and utterly predictable. I thought at the time it was a strange war for him; he was a Savonarola, but without religious principle, only his own odd morality which was centred on himself. All men were his enemies – the leaders in particular – and he cared not one whit for either side.' The middle-aged man paused again, his eyes on the drawing board, his mind obviously thousands of miles away and back in time. 'Remember, Medusa was filled with diverse and desperate men. Many were paranoid in their hatred of Communists – kill a Communist and Christ smiled, odd examples of Christian teaching. Others – such as myself – had fortunes stolen from us by the Viet Minh; the only path to restitution was if the Americans won the war. France had abandoned us at Dien Bien Phu. But there were dozens who saw that fortunes could be made from Medusa. Pouches often contained fifty to seventy-five thousand American dollars. A courier siphoning off half during ten, fifteen runs could retire in Singapore or Kuala Lumpur, or set up his own narcotics network in the Triangle. Apart from the exorbitant pay – and frequently the pardoning of past crimes – the opportunities were unlimited. It was in this group that I placed that very strange man. He was a modern-day pirate in the purest sense.'

Bergeron unlocked his hands. 'Wait a minute. You used the phrase, "a mission he commanded". There were military men in Medusa; are you sure he wasn't an American officer?'

'American, to be sure, but certainly not an army man.'

'Why?'

'He hated everything military. His scorn for Command Saigon was in every decision he made; he considered the army fools and incompetents. At one point orders were radioed to us in Tam Quan. He broke off the transmission and told a regimental general to have sex with himself – he would not obey. An army officer would hardly do that.'

'Unless he was about to abandon his profession,' said the designer. 'As Paris abandoned you and you did the best you could, stealing from Medusa, setting up your own hardly patriotic activities – wherever you could.'

'My country betrayed me before I betrayed her, René.'

'Back to Cain. You say Bourne was not the name he used. What was it?'

'I don't recall. As I said, for many, surnames were not relevant. He was simply "Delta" to me.'

'Mekong?'

'No, the alphabet, I think.'

'"*Alpha, Bravo, Charlie . . . Delta*",' said Bergeron pensively in English. 'But in many operations the code word "Charlie" was replaced by . . . "Cain", because "Charlie" had become synonymous with the Cong. "Charlie" became "Cain"!'

'Quite true. So Bourne dropped back a letter and assumed Cain. He could have chosen "Echo" or "Foxtrot" or "Zulu". Twenty-odd others. What's the difference? What's your point?'

'He chose Cain deliberately! It was symbolic! He wanted it clear from the beginning.'

'Wanted what clear?'

'That Cain would replace Carlos. *Think*. "Carlos" is Spanish for Charles – *Charlie.* The code word "Cain" was substituted for "Charlie" – *Carlos.* It was his intention from the start. Cain would replace Carlos. And he wanted Carlos to know it.'

'*Does* Carlos?'

'Of course! Word goes out in Amsterdam and Berlin, Geneva and Lisbon, London and right here in Paris. Cain is available; contracts can be made, his price lower than Carlos's fee. He erodes! He constantly erodes Carlos's stature.'

'Two matadors in the same ring. There can only be one.'

'It will be Carlos. We've trapped the puffed-up sparrow. He's somewhere within two hours of Saint-Honoré.'

'But *where*?'

'No matter. We'll find him. After all, he found us. He'll come back; his ego will demand it. And then the eagle will sweep down and catch the sparrow. Carlos will kill him.'

The old man adjusted his single crutch under his left arm, parted the black curtain, and stepped into the confessional. He was not well; the pallor of death was on his face, and he was glad the figure in the priest's habit beyond the transparent curtain could not see him clearly. The assassin might not give him further work if he looked too worn to carry it out; he needed work now. There were only weeks remaining and he had responsibilities. He spoke.

'Angelus Domini.'

'Angelus Domini, child of God,' came the whisper. 'Are your days comfortable?'

'They draw to an end, but they are made comfortable.'

'Yes . . . I think this will be your last job for me. It is of such importance, however, that your fee will be five times the usual. I hope it will be of help to you.'

'Thank you, Carlos. You know, then.'

'I know. This is what you must do for it, and the information must leave this world with you. There can be no room for error.'

'I have always been accurate. I will go to my death being accurate now.'

'Die in peace, old friend. It's easier . . . You will go to the Vietnamese Embassy and ask for an attaché named Phan Loc. When you are alone, say the following words to him: "Late March, 1968 Medusa, the Tam Quan sector. Cain was there. Another also." Have you got that?'

' "Late March, 1968 Medusa, the Tam Quan sector. Cain was there. Another also." '

'He'll tell you when to return. It will be in a matter of hours.'

17

'I think it's time we talked about *une fiche plus confidentielle* out of Zürich.'

'My God . . . !'

'I'm not the man you're looking for.'

Bourne gripped the woman's hand, holding her in place, preventing her from running into the aisles of the crowded, elegant restaurant in Argenteuil, twenty miles outside Paris. The pavane was over, the gavotte finished. They were alone; the velvet booth a cage.

'Who *are* you?' The Lavier woman grimaced, trying to pull her hand away, the veins in the cosmeticized neck pronounced.

'A rich American who lives in the Bahamas. Don't you believe that?'

'I should have known,' she said, 'no charges, no cheque . . . only cash. You didn't even look at the bill.'

'Or the prices before that. It's what brought you over to me.'

'I was a fool. The rich always look at prices, if only for the pleasure of dismissing them.' Lavier spoke while glancing round, looking for a space in the aisles, a waiter she might summon. Escape.

'Don't,' said Jason, watching her eyes. 'It'd be foolish. We'd both be better off if we talked.'

The woman stared at him, the bridge of hostile silence accentuated by the hum of the large, dimly-lit, candelabra'd room and the intermittent eruptions of quiet laughter from the nearby tables. 'I ask you again,' she said. 'Who are you?'

'My name isn't important. Settle for the one I gave you.'

'Briggs? It's false.'

'So's Larousse and that's on the lease of a hired car that picked up three killers at the Valois bank. They missed there. They also missed this afternoon at the Pont Neuf. He got away.'

'Oh, *God*!' she cried, trying to break away.

'I said *don't*!' Bourne held her firmly, pulling her back.

'If I scream, Monsieur?' The powdered mask was cracked with lines of venom now, the bright red lipstick defining the snarl of an ageing, cornered rodent.

'I'll scream louder,' replied Jason. 'We'd both be thrown out, and once outside I don't think you'll be unmanageable. Why not talk? We might learn something from each other. After all, we're employees, not employers.'

'I have nothing to say to you.'

'Then I'll start. Maybe you'll change your mind.' He lessened his grip cautiously. The tension remained on her white, powdered face, but it, too, was lessened as the pressure of his fingers was reduced. She was ready to listen. 'You paid a price in Zürich. We paid, too. Obviously more than you did. We're after the same man; we know why *we* want him.' He released her. 'Why do you?'

She did not speak for nearly half a minute, instead, studying him in silence, her eyes angry yet frightened. Bourne knew he had phrased the question accurately; for Jacqueline Lavier not to talk to him would be a dangerous mistake. It could cost her her life if subsequent questions were raised.

'Who is "we"?' She asked.

'A company that wants its money. A great deal of money. He has it.'

'He did not earn it, then?'

Jason knew he had to be careful, he was expected to know far more than he did. 'Let's say there's a dispute.'

'How could there be? Either he did or he did not, there's hardly a middle ground.'

'It's my turn,' said Bourne. 'You answered a question with a question and I didn't avoid you. Now, let's go back. Why do you want him? Why is the private telephone of one of the better shops in Saint-Honoré put on a *fiche* in Zürich?'

'It was an accommodation, Monsieur.'

'For whom?'

'Are you mad?'

'All right, I'll pass on that for now. We think we know anyway.'

'Impossible!'

'Maybe, maybe not. So it was an accommodation . . . To kill a man?'

'I have nothing to say.'

'Yet a minute ago when I mentioned the car, you tried to run. That's saying something.'

'A perfectly natural reaction.' Jacqueline Lavier touched the stem of her wine glass. 'I arranged for the rental. I don't mind telling you that because there's no evidence that I did so. Beyond that I know nothing of what happened.' Suddenly she gripped the glass, her mask of a face a mixture of controlled fury and fear. 'Who *are* you people?'

'I told you. A company that wants its money back.'

'You're interfering! Get out of Paris! Leave this alone!'

'Why should we? We're the injured party; we want the balance sheet corrected. We're entitled to that.'

'You're entitled to nothing!' spat Mme Lavier. 'The error was yours and you'll pay for it!'

'Error?' He had to be *very* careful. It was here – right below the hard surface – the eyes of the truth could be seen beneath the ice. 'Come off it. Theft isn't an error committed by the victim.'

'The error was in your *choice*, Monsieur. You chose the wrong man.'

'He stole millions from Zürich,' said Jason. 'But you know that. He took millions, and if you think you're going to take them from him – which is the same as taking them from us – you're very much mistaken.'

'We want no money!'

'I'm glad to know it. Who's "we"?'

'I thought you said you knew.'

'I said we had an idea. Enough to expose a man named Koenig in Zürich, d'Amacourt here in Paris. If we decide to do that, it could prove to be a major embarrassment, couldn't it?'

'Money? *Embarrassment?* These are *not issues.* You are consumed with stupidity, all of you! I'll say it again. Get out of Paris. Leave this alone! It is not your concern any longer.'

'We don't think it's yours. Frankly, we don't think you're competent.'

'*Competent?*' repeated Lavier, as if she did not believe what she had heard.

'That's right.'

'Have you any idea what you're *saying*? Whom you're *talking* about?'

'It doesn't matter. Unless you back off, my recommendation is that we come out loud and clear. Mock up charges – not traceable to us, of course. Expose Zürich, the Valois. Call in the Sûreté, Interpol . . . anyone and anything to create a manhunt – a massive manhunt.'

'You *are* mad. And a fool!'

'Not at all. We have friends in very important positions; we'll get the information first. We'll be waiting at the right place at the right time. We'll take him.'

'You *won't* take him. He'll disappear again! Can't you *see* that? He's in Paris and a network of people he cannot know are looking for him. He may have escaped once, twice; but not a third time! He's trapped now. We've trapped him!'

'We don't want you to trap him. That's not in our interests.' It was almost the moment, thought Bourne. Almost, but not quite, her fear had to match her anger. She had to be detonated into revealing the truth. 'Here's our ultimatum, and we're holding you responsible for conveying it – otherwise you'll join Koenig and d'Amacourt. Call off your hunt tonight. If you don't we'll move first thing in the morning; we'll start shouting. Les Classiques'll be the most popular store in Saint-Honoré, but I don't think it'll be the right people.'

The powdered face cracked. 'You wouldn't *dare*! How *dare* you? Who are you to say this?!'

He paused, then struck. 'A group of people who don't care much for your Carlos.'

The Lavier woman froze, her eyes wide, stretching the taut skin into scar tissue. 'You *do* know,' she whispered. 'And you think you can oppose him? You think you're a match for Carlos?'

'In a word, yes.'

'You're *insane*! You don't give ultimatums to Carlos!'

'I just did.'

'Then you're dead. You raise your voice to *anyone* and you won't last the day. He has men everywhere; they'll cut you down in the street.'

'They might if they knew who to cut down,' said Jason. 'You forget. No one does. But they know who you are. And Koenig, and d'Amacourt. The minute we expose you you'd be eliminated. Carlos couldn't afford you any longer. But no one knows me.'

'*You* forget, Monsieur. I *do*.'

'The least of my worries. Find me . . . after the damage is done and before the decision is made regarding your own future. It won't be long.'

'This is *madness*. You come out of nowhere and talk like a madman! You *cannot* do this!'

'Are you suggesting a compromise?'

'It's conceivable,' said Jacqueline Lavier. 'Anything is possible.'

'Are you in a position to negotiate it?'

'I'm in a position to convey it . . . far better than I can an ultimatum. Others will relay it to the one who decides.'

'What you're saying is what I said a few minutes ago; we can talk.'

'We can talk, Monsieur,' agreed Mme Lavier, her eyes fighting for her life.

'Then let's start with the obvious.'

'Which is?'

Now. The truth.

'What's Bourne to Carlos? Why does he want him?'

'What's *Bourne?* . . .' The woman stopped, venom and fear replaced by an expression of absolute shock. '*You* can ask *that*?'

'I'll ask it again,' said Jason, hearing the pounding echoes in his chest. 'What's Bourne to Carlos?'

'He's Cain! You know it as well as we do. He was your error, your choice! You chose the wrong man!'

Cain. He heard the name and the echoes erupted into cracks of deafening thunder. And with each crack, pain jolted him, bolts searing one after another through his head, his mind and body recoiling under the onslaught of the name. Cain. *Cain!* The mists were there again. The darkness, the wind, the explosions.

Alpha, Bravo, Cain, Delta, Echo, Foxtrot . . . Cain, Delta. Delta, Cain. Delta . . . Cain.

Cain is for *Charlie.*

Delta is for *Cain!*

'What is it? What's wrong with you?'

'Nothing.' Bourne had slipped his right hand over his left wrist, gripping it, his fingers pressed into his flesh with such pressure he thought his skin might break. He had to do *something*; he had to stop the trembling, lessen the noise, repulse the pain. He had to *clear his mind*. The eyes of the truth were staring at him; he could not look away. He was there, he was home, and the cold made him shiver. 'Go on,' he said, imposing a control on his voice that resulted in a whisper; he could not help himself.

'Are you ill? You're very pale and you're . . .'

'I'm fine,' he interrupted curtly. 'I said, go *on*.'

'What's there to tell you?'

'Say it all. I want to hear it from you.'

'Why? There's nothing you don't know. You chose Cain. You dismissed

Carlos; you think you can dismiss him now. You were wrong then and you are wrong now.'

I will kill you. I will grab your throat and choke the breath out of you. Tell me! For Christ's sake, tell me! At the end, there is only my beginning! I must know it.

'That doesn't matter,' he said. 'If you're looking for a compromise – if only to save your life – tell me why we should listen. Why is Carlos so adamant . . . so paranoid . . . about Bourne? Explain it to me as if I hadn't heard it before. If you don't, those names that shouldn't be mentioned will be spread all over Paris, and you'll be dead by the afternoon.'

Lavier was rigid, her alabaster mask set. 'Carlos will follow Cain to the ends of the earth and kill him.'

'We know that. We want to know why?'

'He has to. Look to yourself. To people like you.'

'That's meaningless. You don't know who we are.'

'I don't have to. I know what you've done.'

'Spell it out!'

'I did. You picked Cain over Carlos, that was your error. You chose the wrong man. You paid the wrong assassin.'

'The wrong . . . assassin.'

'You were not the first, but you will be the last. The arrogant pretender will be killed here in Paris, whether there is a compromise or not.'

'We picked the wrong assassin . . .' The words floated in the elegant, perfumed air of the restaurant. The deafening thunder receded, angry still but far away in the storm clouds; the mists were clearing, circles of vapour swirling around him. He began to see, and what he saw were the outlines of a monster. Not a myth, but a monster. Another monster. There were two.

'Can you *doubt* it?' asked the woman. 'Don't interfere with Carlos. Let him take Cain; let him have his revenge.' She paused, both hands slightly off the table; Mother Rat. 'I promise nothing, but I *will* speak for you, for the loss your people have sustained. It's possible . . . only possible, you understand . . . that your contract might be honoured by the one you should have chosen in the first place.'

'The one we should have chosen . . . Because we chose the wrong one.'

'You see that, do you not, Monsieur? Carlos should be *told* that you see it. Perhaps . . . only perhaps . . . he might have sympathy for your losses if he were convinced you saw your error.'

'That's your compromise?' said Bourne flatly, struggling to find a line of thought.

'Anything is possible. No good can come from your threats, I can tell you that. For any of us, and I'm frank enough to include myself. There would be only pointless killing; and Cain would stand back laughing. You would lose not once, but twice.'

'If that's true . . .' Jason swallowed, nearly choking as dry air filled the vacuum in his dry throat, 'then I'll have to explain to my people why we . . . chose . . . the . . . wrong man.' *Stop it! Finish the statement. Control yourself.* 'Tell me everything you know about Cain.'

'To what purpose?' Lavier put her fingers on the table, her bright red nail polish ten points of a weapon.

'If you chose the wrong man, then we had the wrong information.'

'You heard he was the equal of Carlos, no? That his fees were more reasonable, his apparatus more contained, and because fewer intermediaries were involved there was no possibility of a contract being traced. Is this not so?'

'Maybe.'

'Of course it's so. It's what everyone's been told and it's all a lie. Carlos's strength is in his far-reaching sources of information, *infallible* information. In his elaborate system of reaching the right person at precisely the right moment prior to a kill.'

'Sounds like too many people. There were too many people in Zürich, too many here in Paris.'

'All blind, Monsieur. Every one.'

'Blind?'

'To put it plainly. I've been part of the operation for a number of years, meeting in one way or another dozens who have played their minor roles – none is major. I have yet to meet a single person who has even spoken to Carlos, much less has any idea who he is.'

'That's Carlos. I want to know about Cain. What *you* know about Cain.' *Stay controlled. You cannot turn away. Look at her. Look at her!*

'Where shall I begin?'

'With whatever comes to mind first. Where did he come from?' *Do not look away!*

'South-east Asia, of course.'

'Of course . . .' *Oh, God.*

'From the American Medusa, we know that . . .'

Medusa! The winds, the darkness, the flashes of light, the pain . . . The pain ripped through his skull now; he was not where he was, but where he had been. A world away in distance and time. The pain. Oh, Jesus! The pain . . .

Tao!

Che-sah!

Tam-Quan!

Alpha, Bravo, Cain . . . Delta.

Delta . . . Cain!

Cain is for Charlie.

Delta is for Cain!

'What is it?' The woman looked frightened; she was studying his face, her eyes roving, boring into his. 'You're perspiring. Your hands are shaking. Are you having an attack?'

'It passes quickly.' Jason pried his hand away from his wrist and reached for a napkin to wipe his forehead.

'It comes with the pressures, no?'

'With the pressures, yes . . . Go on. There isn't much time; people have to be reached, decisions made. Your life is probably one of them. Back to Cain. You say he came from the American . . . Medusa.'

'*Les mécaniciens du Diable*,' said Lavier. 'It was the nickname given Medusa by the Indo-China colonials – what was left of them. Quite appropriate, don't you think?'

'It doesn't make any *difference* what I think. Or what I know. I want to hear what *you* think, what *you* know about *Cain*.'

'Your attack makes you rude.'

'My impatience makes me impatient! You say we chose the wrong man; if we did we had the wrong information. *Les mécaniciens du Diable*. Are you implying that Cain is French?'

'Not at all, you test me poorly. I mentioned that only to indicate how deeply we penetrated Medusa.'

' "We" being the people who work for Carlos.'

'You could say that.'

'I will say that. If Cain's not French, what is he?'

'Undoubtedly American . . .'

Oh, God!

'Why?'

'Everything he does has the ring of American audacity. He pushes and shoves with little or no finesse, taking credit where none is his, claiming kills when he had nothing to do with them. He has studied Carlos's methods and connections like no other man alive. We're told he recites them with total recall to potential clients, more often than not putting himself in Carlos's place, convincing fools that it was *he*, not Carlos, who accepted and fulfilled the contracts.' Lavier paused. 'I've struck a chord, no? He did the same with you – your people – yes?'

'Perhaps . . .' Jason reached for his own wrist again, as the statements came back to him. Statements made in response to clues in a dreadful game.

Stuttgart. Regensburg, Munich. Two kills and a kidnapping, Baader accreditation. Fees from US sources.

Tehran? Eight kills. Divided accreditation – Khomeini and PLO. Fee, two million. South-west Soviet sector.

Paris? . . . All contracts will be processed through Paris.

Whose contracts?

Sanchez . . . Carlos.

'. . . always such a transparent device.'

The Lavier woman had spoken; he had not heard it. 'What did you say?'

'You were remembering, yes? He used the same device with you – your people. It's how he gets his assignments.'

'Assignments?' Bourne tensed the muscles in his stomach until the pain brought him back to the table in the dining room in Argenteuil. 'He gets assignments, then,' he said pointlessly.

'And carries them out with considerable expertise; no one denies him that. His record of kills is impressive. In many ways, he is second to Carlos – not his equal, but far above the ranks of *les guérilleros*. He's a man of immense skill, extremely inventive, a trained lethal weapon out of Medusa. But it is his arrogance, his lies at the expense of Carlos that will bring him down.'

'And that makes him American? Or is it your bias? I have an idea you like

American money, but that's about all they export that do you do like.' *Immense skill; extremely inventive; a trained lethal weapon . . . Port Noir, La Ciotat, Marseilles, Zürich, Paris. Oh, Jesus!*

'It is beyond prejudice, Monsieur. The identification is positive.'

'How did you get it?'

Lavier touched the stem of her wine glass, her red-tipped index finger curling around it. 'A discontented man was bought in Washington.'

'Washington?'

'The Americans also look for Cain – with an intensity approaching Carlos's, I suspect. Medusa has never been made public and Cain might prove to be an extraordinary embarrassment. This discontented man was in a position to give us a great deal of information, including the Medusa records. It was a simple matter to match the names with those in Zürich. Simple for Carlos, not for anyone else.'

Too simple, thought Jason, not knowing why the thought struck him. 'I see,' he said.

'And you? How did you find him? Not Cain, of course, but Bourne.'

Through the mists of anxiety, Jason recalled another statement. Not his, but one spoken by Marie. 'Far simpler,' he said. 'We paid the money to him by means of a shortfall deposit into one account, the surplus diverted blindly into another. The numbers could be traced; it's a tax device.'

'Cain permitted it?'

'He didn't know it. The numbers were paid for . . . as you paid for different numbers – telephone numbers – on a *fiche*.'

'I commend you.'

'It's not required, but everything you know about Cain is. All you've done so far is explain an identification. Now, go on. Everything you know about this man Bourne, everything you've been told.' *Be careful. Take the tension from your voice. You are merely . . . evaluating data. Marie, you said that. Dear, dear Marie. Thank God you're not here.*

'What we know about him is incomplete. He's managed to remove most of the vital records, a lesson he undoubtedly learned from Carlos. But not all; we've pieced together a sketch. Before he was recruited into Medusa, he was apparently a French-speaking businessman living in Singapore, representing a collective of American importers from New York to California. The truth is he had been dismissed by the collective, which then tried to have him extradited back to the States for prosecution; he had stolen hundreds of thousands from it. He was known in Singapore as a recluse, very powerful in contraband operations and extraordinarily ruthless.'

'Before that,' interrupted Jason, feeling again the perspiration breaking out on his hairline. 'Before Singapore. Where did he *come* from?' *Be careful! The images! Oh, Christ, he could see the streets of Singapore, Prince Edward Road, Kim Chuan, Boon Tat Street, Maxwell, Cuscaden. Oh, God!*

'Those are the records no one can find. There are only rumours, and they are meaningless. For example, it was said that he was a defrocked Jesuit, gone mad; another speculation was that he had been a young, aggressive investment banker caught embezzling funds in concert with several Singapore banks.

There's nothing concrete, nothing that can be traced. Before Singapore, nothing.'

You're wrong, there was a great deal. But none of that is part of it . . . There is a void, and it must be filled, and you can't help me. Perhaps no one can; perhaps no one should.

'So far, you haven't told me anything startling,' said Bourne, 'nothing relative to the information I'm interested in.'

'Then I don't know what you want! You ask me questions, press for details, and when I offer you answers you reject them as immaterial. What *do* you want?'

'What do you know about Cain's . . . work? Since you're looking for a compromise, give me a reason for it. If our information differs, it would be over what he's done, wouldn't it? When did he first come to your attention? Carlos's attention? *Quickly!*'

'Two years ago,' said Mme Lavier, disconcerted by Jason's impatience, annoyed, frightened. 'Word came out of Asia of a white man offering a service astonishingly similar to the one provided by Carlos. He was swiftly becoming an industry. An ambassador was assassinated in Moulmein; two days later a highly regarded Japanese politician was killed in Tokyo prior to a debate in the Diet. A week after that a newspaper editor was blown out of his car in Hong Kong, and in less than forty-eight hours a banker was shot on a street in Calcutta. Behind each one, Cain. Always Cain.' The woman stopped, appraising Bourne's reaction. He gave none. 'Don't you see? He was *everywhere.* He raced from one kill to another, accepting contracts with such rapidity that he had to be indiscriminate. He was a man in an enormous hurry, building his reputation so quickly that he shocked even the most jaded professionals. And no one doubted that *he* was a professional, least of all Carlos. Instructions were sent: find out about this man, learn all you can. You see, Carlos understood what none of us did, and in less than twelve months he was proved correct. Reports came from informers in Manila, Osaka, Hong Kong and Tokyo. Cain was moving to Europe, they said; he would make Paris itself his base of operations. The challenge was clear, the gauntlet thrown. Cain was out to destroy Carlos. He would become the *new* Carlos, his services *the* services required by those who sought them. As *you* sought them, Monsieur.'

'Moulmein, Tokyo, Calcutta . . .' Jason heard the names coming from his lips, whispered from his throat. Again they were floating, suspended in the perfumed air, shadows of a past forgotten. 'Manila, Hong Kong . . .' He stopped, trying to clear the mists, peering at the outlines of strange shapes that kept racing across his mind's eye.

'These places and many others,' continued Lavier. 'That was Cain's error, his error still. Carlos may be many things to many people, but among those who have benefited from his trust and generosity, there is loyalty. His informers and hirelings are not so readily for sale, although Cain has tried time and again. It is said that Carlos is swift to make harsh judgments, but, as they also say, better a Satan one knows, than a successor one doesn't . . . What Cain did not realize – does not realize now – is that Carlos's network is a vast one. When Cain moved to Europe, he did not know that his activities were uncovered in Berlin, Lisbon, Amsterdam . . . as far away as Oman.'

'Oman,' said Bourne involuntarily. 'Sheikh Mustafa Kalig,' he whispered, as if to himself.

'Never proved,' interjected the Lavier woman defiantly. 'A deliberate smokescreen of confusion, the contract itself a fiction. He took credit for an internal murder; no one could penetrate that security. A lie!'

'A lie,' repeated Jason.

'So many lies,' added Mme Lavier contemptuously. 'He's no fool, however; he lies quietly, dropping a hint here and there, knowing that they will be exaggerated into substance in the telling. He provokes Carlos at every turn, promoting himself at the expense of the man he would replace. But he's no match for Carlos; he takes contracts he cannot fulfil. You are only one example, we hear there have been several others. It's said that's why he stayed away for months, avoiding people like yourselves.'

'Avoiding people . . .' Jason reached for his wrist; the trembling had begun again, the sound of distant thunder vibrating in far regions of his skull. 'You're . . . sure of that?'

'Very much so. He wasn't dead, he was in hiding. Cain botched more than one assignment; it was inevitable. He accepted too many in too short a time. Yet whenever he did, he followed an abortive kill with a spectacular, unsolicited one, to uphold his stature. He would select a prominent figure and blow him away, the assassination a shock to everyone, and unmistakably Cain's. The ambassador travelling in Moulmein was an example; no one had called for his death. There were two others that we know of – a Russian commissar in Shanghai and more recently a banker in Madrid . . .'

The words came from the bright red lips working feverishly in the lower part of the powdered mask beside him. He heard them; he had heard them before. He had *lived* them before. They were no longer shadows, but remembrances of that forgotten past. Images and reality were fused. She began no sentence he could not finish, nor could she mention a name or a city or an incident with which he was not instinctively familiar.

She was talking about . . . him.

Alpha, Bravo, Cain, Delta . . .

Cain is for Charlie, and Delta is for Cain.

Jason Bourne was the assassin called Cain.

There was a final question, his brief reprieve from darkness two nights ago at the Sorbonne. Marseilles. 23 August.

'What happened in Marseilles?' he asked.

'*Marseilles?*' The Lavier woman recoiled. 'How *could* you? What lies were you told? What *other* lies?'

'Just tell me what happened.'

'You refer to Leland, of course. The ubiquitous ambassador whose death *was* called for – paid for, the contract accepted by Carlos.'

'What if I told you that there are those who think Cain was responsible?'

'It's what he wanted *everyone* to think! It was the ultimate insult to Carlos – to steal the kill from him. Payment was irrelevant to Cain; he only wanted to show the world – our world – that he could get there first and do the job for which Carlos had been paid . . . But he didn't, you know. He had nothing to do with the Leland kill.'

'He was there.'

'He was trapped. At least, he never showed up. Some said he'd been killed, but since there was no corpse, Carlos didn't believe it.'

'How was Cain supposedly killed?'

Mme Lavier retreated, shaking her head in short, rapid movements. 'Two men on the waterfront tried to take the credit, tried to get paid for it. One was never seen again; it can be presumed Cain killed him, if it *was* Cain. They were dock garbage.'

'What was the trap?'

'The *alleged* trap, Monsieur. They claimed to have got word that Cain was to meet someone in the rue Sarasin a night or so before the assassination. They say they left appropriately obscure messages in the street and lured a man they were convinced was Cain down to the piers, to a fishing boat. Neither trawler nor skipper were seen again, so they may have been right, but as I say, there was no proof. Not even an adequate description of Cain to match against the man led away from the Sarasin. At any rate, that's where it ends.'

You're wrong. That's where it began. For me.

'I see,' said Bourne, trying again to infuse naturalness into his voice. 'Our information's different naturally. We made a choice on what we thought we knew.'

'The *wrong* choice, Monsieur. What I've told you is the truth.'

'Yes, I know.'

'Do we have our compromise, then?'

'Why not?'

'*Bien.*' Relieved, the woman lifted the wine glass to her lips. 'You'll see, it will be better for everyone.'

'It . . . doesn't really matter now.' He could barely be heard, and he knew it. What did he say? What had he just *said*? Why did he *say* it? . . . The mists were closing in again, the thunder getting louder; the pain had returned to his temples. 'I mean . . . I mean, as you say, it's better for everyone.' He could feel – *see* – the Lavier's woman's eyes on him, studying him. 'It's a reasonable solution.'

'Of course it is . . . You are not feeling well?'

'I said it was nothing; it'll pass.'

'I'm relieved. Now, would you excuse me for a moment?'

'No!' Jason grabbed her arm.

'*S'il vous plaît, monsieur.* The powder room, that is all. If you care to, stand outside the door.'

'We'll leave. You can stop on the way.' Bourne signalled the waiter for the bill.

'As you wish,' she said, watching him.

He stood in the darkened corridor between the spills of light that came from recessed lamps in the ceiling. Across the way was the ladies' room, denoted by small, uncapitalized letters of gold that read *les femmes.* Beautiful people – stunning women, handsome men – kept passing by; the orbit was similar to that of Les Classiques. Jacqueline Lavier was at home.

She had also been in the ladies' room for nearly ten minutes, a fact that would have disturbed Jason had he been able to concentrate on the time. He could not; he was on fire. Noise and pain consumed him, every nerve ending raw, exposed, the fibres swelling, terrified of puncture. He stared straight ahead, a history of dead men behind him. The past was in the eyes of the truth; they had sought him out and he had seen them. Cain . . . *Cain* . . . *Cain!*

He shook his head and looked up at the black ceiling. He had to function; he could not allow himself to keep falling, plunging into the abyss filled with darkness and high wind. There were decisions to make . . . No, they were made; it was a question now of implementing them.

Marie. Marie? Oh, God, my love, we've been so wrong!

He breathed deeply and glanced at his watch – the chronometer he had traded for a thin gold piece of jewellery belonging to a marquis in the south of France. *He is a man of immense skill, extremely inventive* . . . There was no joy in that appraisal. He looked across at the ladies' room.

Where was Jacqueline Lavier? Why didn't she come out? What could she hope to accomplish by remaining inside? He had had the presence of mind to ask the *maître* if there was a telephone in the ladies' room; the man had replied negatively, pointing to a box by the entrance. The Lavier woman had been at his side; she heard the answer, understanding the inquiry.

There was a blinding flash of light. He lurched backwards recoiling into the wall, his hands in front of his eyes. The pain! Oh, *Christ!* His eyes were on *fire*!

And then he heard the words, spoken through the polite laughter of well-dressed men and women walking casually about the corridor.

'In memory of your dinner at Roget's, Monsieur,' said an animated hostess, holding a press camera by its vertical flashbar. 'The photograph will be ready in a few minutes. Compliments of Roget.'

Bourne remained rigid, knowing that he could not smash the camera, the fear of another realization sweeping over him. 'Why me?' he asked.

'Your fiancée requested it, Monsieur,' replied the girl, nodding her head towards the ladies' room. 'We talked inside. You are most fortunate, she is a lovely lady. She asked me to give you this.' The hostess held out a folded note; Jason took it as she pranced away towards the restaurant entrance.

Your illness disturbs me, as I'm sure it does you, my new friend. You may be what you say you are, and then again you may not. I shall have the answer in a half hour or so. A telephone call was made by a sympathetic diner, and that photograph is on its way to Paris. You cannot stop it any more than you can stop those driving now to Argenteuil. If we, indeed, have our compromise, neither will disturb you – as your illness disturbs me – and we shall talk again when my associates arrive.

It is said that Cain is a chameleon, appearing in various guises, and most convincing. It is also said that he is prone to violence and to fits of temper. These are an illness, no?

He ran down the dark street in Argenteuil after the receding roof light of the taxi; it turned the corner and disappeared. He stopped, breathing heavily, looking in all directions for another; there was none. The doorman at Roget's had told him a cab would take ten to fifteen minutes to arrive; why had not Monsieur requested one earlier? The trap was set and he had walked into it.

Up ahead! A light, another taxi! He broke into a run. He had to stop it; he had to get back to Paris. To Marie.

He was back in a labyrinth, racing blindly, knowing, finally, there was no escape. But the race would be made alone; that decision was irrevocable. There would be no discussion, no debate, no screaming back and forth – arguments based on love and uncertainty. For the certainty had been made clear. He knew who he was . . . what he had been; he was guilty as charged – as suspected.

An hour or two saying nothing. Just watching, talking quietly about anything but the truth. Loving. And then he would leave; she would never know when and he could never tell her why. He owed her that; it would hurt deeply for a while, but the ultimate pain would be far less than that caused by the stigma of Cain.

Cain!

Marie. Marie! What have I done?

'Taxi! Taxi!'

18

Get out of Paris! Now! Whatever you're doing, stop it and get out! . . . Those are orders from your government . . . They want you out of there. They want him isolated.

Marie crushed out her cigarette in the ashtray on the bedside table, her eyes falling on the four-year-old issue of *Time*, her thoughts briefly on the terrible game Jason had forced her to play.

'I won't listen!' she said to herself out loud, startled at the sound of her own voice in the empty room. She walked to the window, the same window he had faced, looking out, frightened, trying to make her understand.

I have to know certain things . . . enough to make a decision but maybe not everything. A part of me has to be able . . . to run, disappear. I have to be able to say to myself, what was isn't any longer, and there's a possibility that it never was because I have no memory of it. What a person can't remember didn't exist . . . for him.

'My darling, my darling. Don't let them *do* this to you!' Her spoken words did not startle now, for it was as though he were there in the room, listening, heeding his *own* words, willing to run, disappear . . . with her. But at the core of her understanding, she knew he could not do that; he could not settle for a half-truth, or three-quarters of a lie.

They want him isolated.

Who were *they*? The answer was in Canada and Canada was cut off, another trap.

Jason was right about Paris; she felt it, too. Whatever it was was here. If they could find *one person* to lift the shroud and let him see for himself he was being manipulated, then other questions might be manageable, the answers no longer pushing him towards self-destruction. If he could be convinced that whatever unremembered crimes he had committed, he was a pawn for a much greater single crime, he might be able to walk away, disappear with her. Everything *was* relative. What the man she loved had to be able to say to himself was not that the past no longer existed, but that it had, and he could live with it, and put it to rest. That was the rationalization he needed, the conviction that whatever he had been was far less than his enemies wanted the world to believe, for they would not use him otherwise. He was the Judas goat, his death to take the place of another's. If he could only *see* that; if she could only convince him. And if she did not, she would lose him. They would take him; they would kill him.

They.

'Who *are* you?' she screamed at the window, at the lights of Paris outside. '*Where* are you?'

She could feel a cold wind against her face as surely as if the panes of glass had melted, the night air rushing inside. It was followed by a tightening in her throat, and for a moment she could not swallow . . . could not breathe. The moment passed and she breathed again. She was afraid; it had happened to her before, on their first night in Paris, when she had left the café to find him on the steps of the Cluny. She had been walking rapidly down Saint-Michel when it happened, the cold wind, the swelling of the throat . . . at that moment she had not been able to breathe. Later she thought she knew why; at that moment also, several blocks away inside the Sorbonne, Jason had raced to a judgment that in minutes he would reverse – but he had reached it then. He had made up his mind he would not come to her.

'Stop it!' she cried. 'It's crazy,' she added, shaking her head, looking at her watch. He had been gone over five hours; where was he? *Where was he?*

Bourne got out of the taxi in front of the seedily-elegant hotel in Montparnasse. The next hour would be the most difficult of his briefly remembered life – a life that was a void before Port Noir, a nightmare since. The nightmare would continue, but he would live it alone; he loved her too much to ask her to live it with him. He would find a way to disappear, taking with him the evidence that tied her to Cain. It was as simple as that; he would leave for a non-existent rendezvous, and not return. And some time during the next hour he would write her a note.

> *It's over. I've found my arrows. Go back to Canada and say nothing for both our sakes. I know where to reach you.*

The last was unfair – he would never reach her – but the small feathered hope had to be there, if only to get her on a plane to Ottawa. In time – with time – their weeks together would fade into a darkly kept secret, a cache of brief riches to be uncovered and touched at odd quiet moments. And then no more, for life was lived for active memories; the dormant ones lost meaning. No one knew that better than he did.

He passed through the lobby, nodding at the *concierge* who sat on his stool behind the marble counter, reading a newspaper. The man barely looked up, noting only that the intruder belonged.

The lift rumbled and groaned its way up to the fourth floor. Jason breathed deeply and reached for the gate; above all he would avoid dramatics, no alarms raised by words or by looks. The chameleon had to merge with his quiet part of the forest, one in which no spoors could be found. He knew what to say; he had thought about it carefully, as he had the note he would write.

'Most of the night walking around,' he said, holding her, stroking her dark red hair, cradling her head against his shoulder . . . and aching, 'chasing cadaverous salesgirls, listening to animated nonsense and drinking coffee disguised as sour mud. Les Classiques was a waste of time; it's a zoo. The monkeys and the peacocks put on a hell of a show, but I don't think anyone really knows anything. There's one outside possibility, but he could simply be a sharp Frenchman in search of an American mark.'

'He?' asked Marie, her trembling diminished.

'A man who operated the switchboard,' said Bourne, repelling images of blinding explosions and darkness and high winds as he pictured the face he did not know but he knew so well. That man now was only a device; he pushed the images away. 'I agreed to meet him around midnight at the *bastringue* on rue de Hautefeuille.'

'What did he say?'

'Very little, but enough to interest me. I saw him watching me while I was asking questions. The place was fairly crowded so I could move around pretty freely, talk to the employees.'

'Questions? What questions did you ask?'

'Anything I could think of. Mainly about the manager, or whatever she's called. Considering what happened this afternoon, if she were a direct relay to Carlos she should have been close to hysterics. I saw her. She wasn't; she behaved as if nothing had happened except a good day in the shop.'

'But she *was* a relay, as you call it. D'Amacourt explained that. The *fiche*.'

'Indirect. She gets a phone call and is told what to say before making another call herself.' Actually, Jason thought, the invented assessment was based on reality. Jacqueline Lavier was, indeed, an indirect relay.

'You couldn't just walk around asking questions without seeming suspicious,' protested Marie.

'You can,' answered Bourne, 'if you're an American writer doing an article on the boutiques in Saint-Honoré for a national magazine.'

'That's very good, Jason.'

'It worked. No one wants to be left out.'

'What did you learn?'

'Like most of those kinds of places, Les Classiques has its own clientele, all wealthy, most known to each other and with the usual marital intrigues and adulteries that go with the scene. Carlos knew what he was doing; it's a regular answering service over there, but not the kind listed in a phone book.'

'People told you that?' asked Marie, holding his arms, watching his eyes.

'Not in so many words,' he said, aware of the shadows of her disbelief. 'The accent was always on this Bergeron's talent, but one thing leads to another. You can get the picture. Everyone seems to gravitate to that manager. From what I've gathered, she's a font of social information, although she probably couldn't tell me anything except that she did someone a favour – an accommodation – and that someone will turn out to be someone else who did another favour for another someone. The source could be untraceable, but it's all I've got.'

'Why the meeting tonight at the *bastringue*?'

'He came over to me when I was leaving and said a very strange thing.' Jason did not have to invent this part of the lie. He had read the words on a note in an elegant restaurant in Argenteuil less than an hour ago. 'He said, "You may be who you say you are, and then again, you may not." That's when he suggested a drink later on, away from Saint-Honoré.' Bourne saw her doubts receding. He had done it; she accepted the tapestry of lies. And why not? He was *a man of immense skill and extremely inventive.* The appraisal was not loathsome to him; he *was* Cain.

'He may be the one, Jason. You said you only needed one; he could be it!'

'We'll see.' Bourne looked at his watch. The countdown to his departure had begun; he could not look back. 'We've got almost two hours. Where did you leave the attaché case?'

'At the Meurice, I'm registered there.'

'Let's pick it up and get some dinner. You haven't eaten, have you?'

'No . . .' Marie's expression was quizzical. 'Why not leave the case where it is? It's perfectly safe, we wouldn't have to worry about it.'

'We would if we had to get out of here in a hurry,' he said almost brusquely, going to the bureau. *Everything was a question of degree now, traces of friction gradually slipping into speech, into looks, into touch. Nothing alarming, nothing based in false heroics; she would see through such tactics. Only enough so that later she would understand the truth when she read his words. 'It's over. I've found my arrows . . .'*

'What's the matter, darling?'

'Nothing.' The chameleon smiled. 'I'm just tired and probably a little discouraged.'

'Good heavens, why? A man wants to meet you confidentially late at night, a man who operates a switchboard. He could lead you somewhere! And you're convinced you've narrowed Carlos's contact down to this woman; she's bound to be able to tell you *something* – whether she wants to or not. In a macabre way, I'd think you'd be elated.'

'I'm not sure I can explain it,' said Jason, now looking at her reflection in the mirror. 'You'd have to understand what I found there.'

'What you found?' A question.

'What I found.' A statement. 'It's a different world,' continued Bourne, reaching for the bottle of Scotch and a glass, 'different people. It's soft and beautiful and frivolous, with lots of tiny spotlights and dark velvet. Nothing's taken seriously except gossip and indulgence. Any one of those giddy people – including that woman – could be a relay for Carlos and never know it, never even suspect it. A man like Carlos would use such people; anyone like him would, including *me* . . . That's what I found. It's discouraging.'

'And unreasonable. Whatever you believe, those people make very conscious decisions. That indulgence you talk of demands it; they think. And you know what *I* think? I think you *are* tired, and hungry, and need a drink or two. I wish you could put off tonight; you've been through enough for one day.'

'I can't do that,' he said sharply.

'All right, you can't,' she answered defensively.

'Sorry, I'm edgy.'

'Yes. I know.' She started for the bathroom. 'I'll freshen up and we can go . . . Pour yourself a stiff one, darling. Your teeth are showing.'

'Marie?'

'Yes?'

'Try to understand. What I found there upset me. I thought it would be different. Easier.'

'While you were looking, I was waiting, Jason. Not knowing. That wasn't easy either.'

'I thought you were going to call Canada. Didn't you?'

She held her place for a moment. 'No,' she said. 'It was too late.'

The bathroom door closed; Bourne walked to the desk across the room. He opened the drawer, took out stationery, picked up the ballpoint pen, and wrote the words.

It's over. I've found my arrows. Go back to Canada and say nothing for both our sakes. I know where to reach you.

He folded the stationery, inserted it into an envelope, holding the flap open as he reached for his wallet. He took out both the French and the Swiss notes, slipping them behind the folded paper, and sealed the envelope. He wrote on the front:

Marie.

He wanted so desperately to add:

My love, my dearest love.

He did not. He could not.

The bathroom door opened. He put the envelope in his jacket pocket. 'That was quick,' he said.

'Was it? I didn't think so. What are you doing?'

'I wanted a pen,' he answered, picking up the ballpoint. 'If that fellow has anything to tell me I want to be able to write it down.'

Marie was by the bureau; she glanced at the dry, empty glass. 'You didn't have your drink.'

'I didn't use the glass.'

'I see. Shall we go?'

They waited in the corridor for the rumbling lift, the silence between them awkward, in a real sense unbearable. He reached for her hand. At the touch she gripped his, staring at him, her eyes telling him that her control was being tested and she did not know why. Quiet signals had been sent and received, not loud enough or abrasive enough to be alarms, but they were there and she heard them. It was part of the countdown, rigid, irreversible, prelude to his departure.

Oh, God, I love you so. You are next to me and we are touching and I am dying. But you cannot die with me. You must not. I am Cain.

'We'll be fine,' he said.

The metal cage vibrated noisily into its recessed perch. Jason pulled the brass grille open, then suddenly swore under his breath.

'Oh, Christ, I forgot!'

'What?'

'My wallet. I left it in the bureau drawer this afternoon in case there was any trouble in Saint-Honoré. Wait for me in the lobby.' He gently swung her through the gate, pressing the button with his free hand. 'I'll be right down.' He closed the grille; the brass latticework cutting off the sight of her startled eyes. He turned away and walked rapidly back towards the room.

Inside, he took the envelope out of his pocket and placed it against the base of the lamp on the bedside table. He stared down at it, the ache unendurable.

'Good-bye, my love,' he whispered.

Bourne waited in the drizzle outside the Hotel Meurice on the rue de Rivoli, watching Marie through the glass doors of the entrance. She was at the front desk, having signed for the attaché case which had been handed to her over the counter. She was now obviously asking a mildly astonished clerk for her bill, about to pay for a room that had been occupied less than six hours. Two minutes passed before the bill was presented. Reluctantly; it was no way for a guest at the Meurice to behave. Indeed, all Paris shunned such inhibited visitors.

Marie walked out onto the pavement, joining him in the shadows and the mist-like drizzle to the left of the canopy. She gave him the attaché case, a forced smile on her lips, a slight breathless quality in her voice.

'That man didn't approve of me. I'm sure he's convinced I used the room for a series of quick tricks.'

'What did you tell him?' asked Bourne.

'That my plans had changed, that's all.'

'Good, the less said the better. Your name's on the registration card. Think up a reason why you were there.'

'Think up? . . . *I* should think up a reason?' She studied his eyes, the smile gone.

'I mean we'll think up a reason. Naturally.'

'Naturally.'

'Let's go.' They started walking towards the corner, the traffic noisy in the street, the drizzle in the air fuller, the mist denser, the promise of heavy rain imminent. He took her arm – not to guide her, not even out of courtesy – only to touch her, to hold a part of her. There was so little time.

I am Cain. I am death.

'Can we slow down?' asked Marie sharply.

'What?' Jason realized he had been practically running; for a few seconds he had been in the labyrinth, racing through it, careening, feeling, and not feeling. He looked up ahead and found an answer. At the corner an empty cab had stopped by a garish news-stand, the driver shouting through an open window to the dealer. 'I want to catch that taxi,' said Bourne, without breaking stride. 'It's going to rain like hell.'

They reached the corner, both breathless as the empty cab pulled away, swinging left into rue de Rivoli. Jason looked up into the night sky, feeling the wet pounding on his face, unnerved. The rain had arrived. He looked at Marie in the gaudy lights of the news-stand; she was wincing in the sudden down-pour. No. She was not wincing; she was staring at something . . . staring in disbelief, in shock. In *horror*. Without warning, she screamed, her face contorted, the fingers of her right hand pressed against her mouth. Bourne grabbed her, pulling her head into the damp cloth of his overcoat; she would not stop screaming.

He turned, trying to find the cause of her hysterics. Then he saw it, and in that unbelievable split half-second he knew the countdown was aborted. He had committed the final crime; he could not leave her. Not now, not yet.

On the first ledge of the news-stand was an early morning tabloid, black headlines electrifying under the circles of light:

Slayer in Paris
Woman Sought in Zürich Killings
Suspect in Rumoured Theft of Millions

Under the screaming words was a photograph of Marie St Jacques.

'Stop it!' whispered Jason, using his body to cover her face from the curious newsdealer, reaching into his pocket for coins. He threw the money on the counter, grabbed two papers, and propelled her down the dark, rain-soaked street.

They were both in the labyrinth now.

Bourne opened the door, and led Marie inside. She stood motionless, looking at him, her face pale and frightened, her breathing erratic, an audible mixture of fear and anger.

'I'll get you a drink,' said Jason, going to the bureau. As he poured, his eyes strayed to the mirror and he had an overpowering urge to smash the glass, so despicable was his own image to him. What the hell had he *done*? Oh God!

I am Cain. I am death.

He heard her gasp and span around, too late to stop her, too far away to lunge and tear the awful thing from her hand. Oh, *Christ*, he had forgotten! She had found the envelope on the bedside table, and was reading his note. Her single scream was a searing, terrible cry of pain.

'*Jasonnnn!* . . .'

'Please! No!' He raced from the bureau and grabbed her. 'It doesn't matter! It doesn't count any more!' He shouted helplessly, seeing the tears welling in her eyes, streaking down her face. '*Listen* to me! That was before, not *now*.'

'You were leaving! My God, you were *leaving* me!' Her eyes went blank, two blind circles of panic. 'I knew it! I *felt* it!'

'I *made* you feel it!' he said, forcing her to look at him. 'But it's over now. I won't leave you. *Listen* to me. I *won't leave* you!'

She screamed again. 'I couldn't *breathe*! . . . It was so cold!'

He pulled her to him, enveloping her. 'We have to begin again. Try to understand. It's different now – and I can't change what was – but I won't leave you. Not like this.'

She pushed her hands against his chest, her tear-stained face angled back, begging, 'Why, Jason? *Why*?'

'Later. Not now. Don't say anything for a while. Just hold me; let me hold you.'

*

The minutes passed, hysteria ran its course and the outlines of reality came back into focus. Bourne led her to the chair; she caught the sleeve of her dress on the frayed lace. They both smiled as he knelt beside her, holding her hand in silence.

'How about that drink?' he said finally.

'I think so,' she replied, briefly tightening her grip on his hand as he got up from the floor. 'You poured it quite a while ago.'

'It won't go flat.' He went to the bureau and returned with two glasses half filled with whisky. She took hers. 'Feeling better?' he asked.

'Calmer. Still confused . . . frightened, of course. Maybe angry, too, I'm not sure. I'm too afraid to think about that.' She drank, closing her eyes, her head pressed back against the chair. 'Why did you do it, Jason?'

'Because I thought I had to. That's the simple answer.'

'And no answer at all. I deserve more than that.'

'Yes, you do, and I'll give it to you. I have to now because you have to hear it; you have to understand. You have to protect yourself.'

'Protect . . . ?'

He held up his hand, interrupting her. 'It'll come later. All of it, if you like. But the first thing we have to do is know what happened – not to *me*, but to *you*. That's where we have to begin. Can you do it?'

'The newspaper?'

'Yes.'

'God knows, I'm interested,' she said, smiling weakly.

'Here.' Jason went to the bed where he had dropped the two papers. 'We'll both read it.'

'No games?'

'No games.'

They read the long article in silence, an article that told of death and intrigue in Zürich. Every now and then Marie gasped, shocked at what she was reading; at other times she shook her head in disbelief. Bourne said nothing. He saw the hand of Ilich Ramirez Sanchez. *Carlos will follow Cain to the ends of the earth. Carlos will kill him.* Marie St Jacques was expendable, a baited decoy that would die in the trap that caught Cain.

I am Cain. I am death.

The article was, in fact, two articles – an odd mixture of fact and conjecture, speculations taking over where evidence came to an end. The first part indicted a Canadian government employee, a female economist, Marie St Jacques. She was placed at the scene of three murders, her fingerprints confirmed by the Canadian government. In addition, police found a hotel key from the Carillon du Lac, apparently lost during the violence on the Guisan Quai. It was the key to Marie St Jacques' room, given to her by the hotel clerk who remembered her well – remembered what appeared to him to be a guest in a highly disturbed state of anxiety. The final piece of evidence was a handgun discovered not far from the Steppdeckstrasse, in an alley close by the scene of two other killings. Ballistics held it to be the murder weapon, and again there were fingerprints, again confirmed by the Canadian government. They belonged to the woman, Marie St Jacques.

It was at this point that the article veered from fact. It spoke of rumours along the Bahnhofstrasse that a multi-million-dollar theft had taken place by means of a computer manipulation dealing with a numbered, confidential account belonging to an American corporation called Treadstone Seventy-one. The bank was also named; it was of course the Gemeinschaft. But everything else was clouded, obscure, more speculation than fact.

According to 'unnamed sources', an American male holding the proper codes transferred millions to a bank in Paris, assigning the new account to specific individuals who were to assume rights of possession. The assignees were waiting in Paris and, upon clearance, withdrew the millions and disappeared. The success of the operation was traced to the American's obtaining the accurate codes to the Gemeinschaft account, a feat made possible by penetrating the bank's numerical sequence related to year, month and day of entry, standard procedure for confidential holdings. Such an analysis could only be made through the use of sophisticated computer techniques and a thorough knowledge of Swiss banking practices. When questioned, an officer of the bank, Herr Walther Apfel, acknowledged that there was an on-going investigation into matters pertaining to the American company, but pursuant to Swiss law, 'the bank would make no further comment. To anyone.'

Here the connection with Marie St Jacques was clarified. She was described as a government economist extensively schooled in international banking procedures, as well as a skilled computer programmer. She was suspected of being an accomplice, her expertise necessary to the massive theft. And there *was* a male suspect; she was reported to have been seen in his company at the Carillon du Lac.

Marie finished the article first and let the paper drop to the floor. At the sound, Bourne looked over from the edge of the bed. She was staring at the wall, a strange pensive serenity having come over her. It was the last reaction he expected. He finished reading quickly, feeling depressed and hopeless – for a moment, speechless. Then he found his voice and spoke.

'Lies,' he said, 'and they were made because of me, because of who and what I am. Smoke you out, they find me. I'm sorry, sorrier than I can ever tell you.'

Marie shifted her eyes from the wall and looked at him. 'It goes much deeper than lies, Jason,' she said. 'There's too much truth for lies alone.'

'*Truth?* The only truth is that you were in Zürich! You never touched a gun, you were never in an alley near the Steppdeckstrasse, you didn't lose a hotel key, and you never went near the Gemeinschaft.'

'Agreed, but that's not the truth I'm talking about.'

'Then what is?'

'The Gemeinschaft, Treadstone Seventy-one, Apfel. Those are true and the fact that any of them were mentioned – especially Apfel's acknowledgment – is incredible. Swiss bankers are cautious men. They don't defy the law, not this way; the sentences are too severe. The statutes pertaining to banking confidentiality are among the most sacrosanct in Switzerland. Apfel could go to prison for years for saying what he did, for even alluding to such an account, much less confirming it by name. Unless he was ordered to say what he did by an authority powerful enough to contravene the laws.' She stopped, her eyes straying to the wall again. 'Why? Why was the Gemeinschaft or Treadstone or Apfel ever made part of the story?'

'I told you. They want me and they know we're together. Carlos knows we're together. Find you, he finds me.'

'No, Jason, it goes beyond Carlos. You really *don't* understand the laws in Switzerland. Not even a Carlos could cause them to be flouted this way.' She looked at him, but her eyes did not see him; she was peering through her own mists. 'This *isn't* one story, it's *two.* Both are constructed out of lies, the first connected to the second by tenuous speculation – *public* speculation – on a banking crisis that would *never* be made public, unless and until a thorough and *private* investigation proved the facts. And that second story – the patently false statement that millions were stolen from the Gemeinschaft – was *tacked* on to the equally false story that I'm wanted for killing three men in Zürich. It was *added.* Deliberately.'

'Explain that, please.'

'It's there, Jason. Believe me when I tell you that; it's right in front of us.'

'What is?'

'Someone's trying to send us a message.'

19

The heavy army car sped south on Manhattan's East River Drive, headlights illuminating the swirling remnants of a March snowfall. The major in the back seat dozed, his long body angled into the corner, his legs stretched out diagonally across the floor. In his lap was a briefcase, a thin nylon cord attached to the handle by a metal clamp, the cord itself strung through his right sleeve and down his inner tunic to his belt. The security device had been removed only twice in the past nine hours. Once during the major's departure from Zürich, and again with his arrival at Kennedy Airport. In both places, however, US government personnel had been watching the customs clerks – more precisely, watching the briefcase. They were not told why; they were simply ordered to observe the inspections, and at the slightest deviation from normal procedures – which meant any undue interest in the briefcase – they were to intervene. With weapons, if necessary.

There was a sudden, quiet ringing; the major snapped his eyes open and brought his left hand up in front of his face. The sound was a wrist alarm; he pressed the button on his watch and squinted at the second radium dial of his two-zoned instrument. The first was on Zürich time; the second, New York; the alarm had been set twenty-four hours ago, when the officer had received his cabled orders. The transmission would come within the next three minutes. That is, thought the major, it would come if Iron Ass was as precise as he expected his subordinates to be. The officer stretched, awkwardly balancing the briefcase, and leaned forward, speaking to the driver.

'Sergeant, turn on your scrambler to fourteen-thirty megahertz, will you please?'

'Yes, sir.' The sergeant flipped two switches on the radio panel beneath the dashboard, then twisted the dial to the 1430 frequency. 'There it is, Major.'

'Thanks. Will the microphone reach back here?'

'I don't know. Never tried it, sir.' The driver pulled the small plastic microphone from its cradle and stretched the spiral cord over the seat. 'Guess it does,' he concluded.

Static erupted from the speaker, the scrambling transmitter electronically scanning and jamming the frequency. The message would follow in seconds. It did.

'Treadstone? Treadstone, confirm, please.'

'Treadstone receiving,' said Major Gordon Webb. 'You're clear. Go ahead.'

'What's your position?'

'About a mile south of the Triboro, East River Drive,' said the major.

'Your timing is acceptable,' came the voice from the speaker.

'Glad to hear it. It makes my day . . . sir.'

There was a brief pause, the major's comment not appreciated. 'Proceed to one-four-zero, Seven-one East. Confirm by repeat.'

'One-four-zero, East Seventy-first.'

'Keep your vehicle out of the area. Approach on foot.'

'Understood.'

'Out.'

'Out.' Webb snapped the transmission button in place and handed the microphone back to the driver. 'Forget that address, Sergeant. Your name's on a very short file now.'

'Gotcha, Major. Nothing but static on that thing anyway. But since I don't know where it is and these wheels aren't supposed to go there, where do you want to be dropped off?'

Webb smiled. 'No more than two blocks away. I'd go to sleep in the gutter if I had to walk any further than that.'

'How about Lex and Seventy-second?'

'Is that two blocks?'

'No more than three.'

'If it's three you're a private.'

'Then I couldn't pick you up later, Major. Privates aren't cleared for this duty.'

'Whatever you say, Captain.' Webb closed his eyes. After two years, he was about to see Treadstone Seventy-one for himself. He knew he should feel a sense of anticipation; he did not. He felt only a sense of weariness, of futility. *What had happened?*

The incessant hum of the tyres on the tarmac below was hypnotic, but the rhythm was broken by sharp intrusions where concrete and wheels were not compatible. The sounds evoked memories of long ago, of screeching jungle noises woven into a single tone. And then the night – that night – when blinding lights and staccato explosions were all around him, telling him he was about to die. But he did not die; a miracle wrought by a man had given his life back to him . . . and the years went on, that night, those days never to be forgotten. *What the hell had happened?*

'Here we are, Major.'

Webb opened his eyes, his hand wiping the sweat that had formed on his forehead. He looked at his watch, gripped his briefcase and reached for the handle of the door.

'I'll be here between twenty-three-hundred and twenty-three-thirty hours, Sergeant. If you can't park, just cruise around and I'll find you.'

'Yes, sir.' The driver turned in his seat. 'Could the major tell me if we're going to be driving any distance later?'

'Why? Have you got another fare?'

'Come on, sir. I'm assigned to you until you say otherwise, you know that. But these heavy-plated trucks use gas like the old-time Shermans. If we're going far I'd better fill it.'

'Sorry.' The major paused. 'Okay. You'll have to find out where it is, anyway, because I don't know. We're going to a private airfield in Madison, New Jersey. I have to be there no later than O-one-hundred hours.'

'I've got a vague idea,' said the driver. 'At twenty-three-thirty, you're cutting it pretty close, sir.'

'Twenty-three-hundred, then. And thanks.' Webb got out of the car, closed the door, and waited until the brown vehicle entered the flow of traffic on Seventy-second Street. He stepped off the kerb and headed south to Seventy-first.

Four minutes later he stood in front of a well-kept brownstone house, its muted, rich design in concert with those around it in the tree-lined street. It was a quiet street, a monied street – *old* money. It was the last place in Manhattan a person would suspect of housing one of the most sensitive intelligence operations in the country. And as of twenty minutes ago, Major Gordon Webb was one of only eight or ten people in the country who knew of its existence.

Treadstone Seventy-one.

He climbed the steps, aware that the pressure of his weight on the iron grids embedded in the stone beneath him triggered electronic devices that in turn activated cameras, producing his image on screens inside. Beyond this, he knew little, except that Treadstone Seventy-one never closed; it was operated and monitored twenty-four hours a day by a select few, identities unknown.

He reached the top step and rang the bell, an ordinary bell, but not for an ordinary door, the major could see that. The heavy wood was riveted to a steel plate behind it, the decorative iron designs in actuality the rivets, the large brass knob disguising a hot-plate that caused a series of steel bolts to shoot across into steel receptacles at the touch of a human hand when the alarms were on. Webb glanced up at the windows. Each pane of glass, he knew, was an inch thick, capable of withstanding the impact of .30 calibre shells. Treadstone Seventy-one was a fortress.

The door opened and the major involuntarily smiled at the figure standing there, so totally out of place did she seem. She was a petite, elegant-looking, grey-haired woman with soft aristocratic features and a bearing that bespoke monied gentility. Her voice confirmed the appraisal; it was mid-Atlantic, refined in the better finishing schools and at innumerable polo matches.

'How good of you to drop by, Major. Jeremy wrote us that you might. Do come in. It's such a pleasure to see you again.'

'It's good to see you again, too,' replied Webb, stepping into the tasteful foyer, finishing his statement when the door was closed, 'but I'm not sure where it was we met before.'

The woman laughed. 'Oh, we've had dinner ever so many times.'

'With Jeremy?'

'Of course.'

'Who's Jeremy?'

'A devoted nephew who's also your devoted friend. Such a nice young man; it's a pity he doesn't exist.' She took his elbow as they walked down a long hallway. 'It's all for the benefit of neighbours who might be strolling by . . . Come along now, they're waiting.'

They passed an archway that led to a large living-room; the major looked inside. There was a grand piano by the front windows, harp beside it; and everywhere – on the piano and on polished tables glistening under the spill of subdued lamps – were silver-framed photographs, mementos of a past filled with wealth and grace. Sailing boats, men and women on the decks of ocean liners, several military portraits . . . and yes, two candid shots of someone mounted for a polo match. It was a room that belonged in a brownstone on this street.

They reached the end of the hallway; there was a large mahogany door, bas-relief and iron ornamentation part of its design, part of its security. If there was an infra-red camera, Webb could not detect the whereabouts of the lens. The grey-haired woman pressed an unseen bell; the major could hear a slight hum.

'Your friend is here, gentlemen. Stop playing poker and go to work. Snap to, Jesuit.'

'Jesuit?' asked Webb, bewildered.

'An old joke,' replied the woman. 'It goes back to when you were probably playing marbles and snarling at little girls.'

The door opened and the aged but still erect figure of David Abbott was revealed. 'Glad to see you, Major,' said the one-time Silent Monk of Clandestine Services, extending his hand.

'Good to be here, sir.' Webb shook hands. Another elderly, imposing-looking man came up beside Abbott.

'A friend of Jeremy's, no doubt,' said the man, his deep voice edged with humour. 'Dreadfully sorry time precludes proper introductions, young fellow. Come along, Margaret. There's a lovely fire upstairs.' He turned to Abbott. 'You'll let me know when you're leaving, David?'

'Usual time for me, I expect,' replied the Monk. 'I'll show these two how to ring you.'

It was then that Webb realized there was a third man in the room; he was standing in the shadows at the far end, and the major recognized him instantly. He was Elliot Stevens, senior aide to the President of the United States – some said his *alter ego.* He was in his early forties, slender, wore glasses and had the bearing of unpretentious authority about him.

'. . . it'll be fine.' The imposing older man who had not found time to introduce himself had been speaking; Webb had not heard him, his attention on the White House aide. 'I'll be waiting.'

'Till next time,' continued Abbott, shifting his eyes kindly to the grey-haired woman. 'Thanks, Sister Meg. Keep your habit pressed down.'

'You're still wicked, Jesuit.'

The couple left, closing the door behind them. Webb stood for a moment, shaking his head and smiling. The man and woman of One-four-zero, Seven-one East belonged to the room down the hall just as that room belonged in the brownstone, all a part of the quiet, monied, tree-lined street. 'You've known them a long time, haven't you?'

'A lifetime, you might say,' replied Abbott. 'He was a yachtsman we put to good use in the Adriatic runs for Donovan's operations in Yugoslavia.

Mikhailovich once said he sailed on sheer nerve, bending the worst weather to his will . . . and don't let Sister Meg's graciousness fool you. She was one of Intrepid's girls, a piranha with very sharp teeth.'

'They're quite a story.'

'It'll never be told,' said Abbott, closing the subject. 'I want you to meet Elliot Stevens. I don't think I have to tell you who he is. Webb, Stevens. Stevens, Webb.'

'That sounds like a law firm,' said Stevens amiably walking across the room, hand extended. 'Nice to know you, Webb. Have a good trip?'

'I would have preferred military transport. I hate those damned commercial airlines. I thought a customs agent at Kennedy was going to slice the lining of my suitcase.'

'You look too respectable in that uniform,' laughed the Monk. 'You're obviously a smuggler.'

'I'm still not sure I understand the uniform,' said the major, carrying his briefcase to a long hatch table against the wall and unclipping the nylon cord from his belt.

'I shouldn't have to tell you,' answered Abbott, 'that the tightest security is often found in being quite obvious on the surface. An army intelligence officer, prowling around undercover in Zürich at this particular time could raise alarms.'

'Then I don't understand, either,' said the White House aide, coming up beside Webb at the table, watching the major's manipulations with the nylon cord and the lock. 'Wouldn't an obvious presence raise even more shrill alarms? I thought the assumption of undercover was that discovery was less probable.'

'Webb's trip to Zürich was a routine consulate check, pre-dated on the G-Two schedules. No one fools anybody about those trips; they're what they are and nothing else. Ascertaining new sources, paying off informants. The Soviets do it all the time; they don't even bother to hide it. Neither do we. frankly.'

'But that *wasn't* the purpose of his trip,' said Stevens, beginning to understand. 'So the obvious conceals the unobvious.'

'That's it.'

'Can I help?' The presidential aide seemed fascinated by the briefcase.

'Thanks,' said Webb. 'Just pull the cord through.'

Stevens did so. 'I always thought it was chains around the wrist,' he said.

'Too many hands cut off,' explained the major, smiling at the White House man's reaction. 'There's a steel wire running through the nylon.' He freed the briefcase and opened it on the table, looking around at the elegance of the furnished library-den. At the rear of the room was a pair of French windows that apparently led to an outside garden, the outline of a high stone wall seen dimly through the panes of thick glass. 'So this is Treadstone Seventy-one. It isn't the way I pictured it.'

'Pull the curtains again, will you please, Elliot?' Abbott said. The presidential aide walked to the French windows and did so. Abbott crossed to a bookcase, opened the cabinet beneath it, and reached inside. There was a quiet whirr; the entire bookcase came out of the wall and slowly revolved to the left. On the other side was an electronic radio console, one of the most sophisticated Gordon Webb had seen. 'Is this more what you had in mind?' asked the Monk.

'Jesus . . .' The major whistled as he studied the dials, calibrations, cable patches and scanning devices built into the panel. The Pentagon war rooms had far more elaborate equipment, but this was the miniaturized equal of most well-structured intelligence stations.

'I'd whistle, too,' said Stevens, standing in front of the dense curtain. 'But Mr Abbott already gave me my personal sideshow. That's only the beginning. Five more buttons and this place looks like a Strategic Air Command base in Omaha.'

'Those same buttons also transform this room back into a graceful East Side library.' The old man reached inside the cabinet; in seconds the enormous console was replaced by bookshelves. He then walked to the adjacent bookcase, opened the cabinet beneath and once again put his hand inside. The whirring began; the book case slid out, and shortly in its place were three tall filing cabinets. The Monk took out a key and pulled out a file drawer. 'I'm not showing off, Gordon. When we're finished, I want you to look through these. I'll show you the switch that'll send them back. If you have any problems, our host will take care of everything.'

'What am I to look for?'

'We'll get to it; right now I want to hear about Zürich. What have you learned?'

'Excuse me, Mr Abbott,' interrupted Stevens. 'If I'm slow, it's because all this is new to me. But I was thinking about something you said a minute ago about Major Webb's trip.'

'What is it?'

'You said the trip was predated on the G-Two schedules.'

'That's right.'

'Why? The major's obvious presence was to confuse Zürich, not Washington. Or was it?'

The Monk smiled. 'I can see why the President keeps you around. We've never doubted that Carlos has bought his way into a circle or two – or ten – in Washington. He finds the discontented men and offers them what they do not have. A Carlos could not exist without such people. You must remember, he doesn't merely sell death, he sells a nation's secrets. All too frequently to the Soviets, if only to prove to them how rash they were to expel him.'

'The President would want to know that,' said the aide. 'It would explain several things.'

'It's why you're here, isn't it?' said Abbott.

'I guess it is.'

'And it's a good place to begin for Zürich,' said Webb, taking his briefcase to an armchair in front of the filing cabinets. He sat down, spreading the folders inside the case at his feet, and took out several sheets of paper. 'You may not doubt Carlos is in Washington, but I can confirm it.'

'Where? *Treadstone?*'

'There's no clear proof of that, but it can't be ruled out. He found the *fiche.* He altered it.'

'Good God, how?'

'The how I can only guess; the who I know.'

'Who?'

'A man named Koenig. Until three days ago he was in charge of primary verifications at the Gemeinschaft Bank.'

'Three days ago? Where is he now?'

'Dead. A freak accident on a road he travelled every day of his life. Here's the police report; I had it translated.' Abbott took the papers, and sat down in a nearby chair. Elliot Stevens remained standing; Webb continued. 'There's something very interesting there. It doesn't tell us anything we don't know, but there's a lead I'd like to follow up.'

'What is it?' asked the Monk, reading. 'This describes the accident. The curve, speed of vehicle, apparent swerving to avoid a collision.'

'It's at the end. It mentions the killing at the Gemeinschaft, the bolt that got us off our asses two weeks ago.'

'It does?' Abbott turned the page.

'Look at it. Last couple of sentences. See what I mean?'

'Not exactly,' replied Abbott, frowning. 'This merely states that Koenig was employed by the Gemeinschaft where a recent homicide took place . . . and he had been a witness to the initial gunfire. That's all.'

'I don't think it is "all",' said Webb. 'I think there was more. Someone started to raise a question, but it was left hanging. I'd like to find out who has his red pencil on the Zürich police reports. He could be Carlos's man; we know he's got one there.'

The Monk leaned back in the chair, his frown unrelieved. 'Assuming you're right, why wasn't the entire reference deleted?'

'Too obvious. The killing *did* take place, Koenig *was* a witness; the investigating officer who wrote up the report might legitimately ask why.'

'But if he had speculated on a connection wouldn't he be just as disturbed that the speculation was deleted?'

'Not necessarily. We're talking about a bank in Switzerland. Certain areas are officially inviolable, unless there's proof.'

'Not always. I understand you were very successful with the newspapers.'

'*Un*officially. I appealed to prurient journalistic sensationalism, and – although it damn near killed him – got Walther Apfel to corroborate halfway.'

'Interruption,' said Elliot Stevens. 'I think this is where the Oval office has to come in. I assume by the newspapers you're referring to the Canadian woman.'

'Not really. That story was already out; we couldn't stop it. Carlos is wired into the Zürich police; they issued that report. We simply enlarged on it and tied her to an equally false story about millions having been stolen from the Gemeinschaft.' Webb paused and looked at Abbott. 'That's something we have to talk about; it may not be false after all.'

'I can't believe that,' said the Monk.

'I don't *want* to believe it,' replied the major. 'Ever.'

'Would you mind backing up?' asked the White House aide, sitting down opposite the army officer. 'I have to get this very clear.'

'Let me explain,' broke in Abbott, seeing the bewilderment on Webb's face. 'Elliot's here on orders from the President. It's the killing at the Ottawa airport.'

'It's an unholy mess,' said Stevens bluntly. 'The Prime Minister damn near told the President to take our stations out of Nova Scotia. He's one angry Canadian.'

'How did it come down?' asked Webb.

'Very badly. All they know is that a ranking economist at the Department of Finance made discreet inquiries about an unlisted American corporation and got himself killed for it. To make matters worse, Canadian Intelligence was told to stay out of it; it was a highly sensitive US operation.'

'Who the hell did *that*?'

'I believe I've heard the name Iron Ass bandied about here and there,' said Monk.

'General Crawford? Stupid son of a bitch . . . Stupid ironassed son of a bitch!'

'Can you imagine?' interjected Stevens. '*Their* man gets killed and *we* have the gall to tell them to stay out.'

'He was right, of course,' corrected Abbott. 'It had to be done swiftly, no room for misunderstanding. A clamp had to be put on instantly, the shock sufficiently outrageous to stop everything. It gave me time to reach MacKenzie Hawkins – Mac and I worked together in Burma; he's retired, but they listen to him. They're co-operating now and that's the important thing, isn't it?'

'There are other considerations, Mr Abbott,' protested Stevens.

'They're on different levels, Elliot. We working stiffs aren't on them; we don't have to spend time over diplomatic posturing. I'll grant you those postures are necessary, but they don't concern us.'

'They do concern the President, sir. They're part of his every working-stiff day. And that's why I have to go back with a very clear picture.' Stevens paused, turning to Webb. 'Now, please, let me have it again. Exactly what did you do and why? What part did we play regarding this Canadian woman?'

'Initially not a goddamn thing; that was Carlos's move. Someone very high up in the Zürich police is on Carlos's payroll. It was the Zürich *police* who mocked up the so-called evidence linking her to the three killings. And it's ludicrous; she's no killer.'

'All right, all right,' said the aide. 'That was Carlos. Why did he do it?'

'To flush out Bourne. The St Jacques woman and Bourne are together.'

'Bourne being this assassin who calls himself Cain, correct?'

'Yes,' said Webb. 'Carlos has sworn to kill him. Cain's moved in on Carlos all over Europe and the Middle East, but there's no photograph of Cain, no one really knows what he looks like. So by circulating a picture of the woman – and let me tell you, it's in every damn newspaper over there – someone may spot her. If she's found, the chances are that Cain – Bourne – will be found too. Carlos will kill them both.'

'All right. Again, that's Carlos. Now what did *you* do?'

'Just what I said. Reached the Gemeinschaft and persuaded the bank into confirming the fact that the woman might – just *might* – be tied with a massive theft. It wasn't easy, but it was their man Koenig who'd been bribed, not one of our people. That's an internal matter; they wanted a lid on it. Then I called the papers and referred them to Walther Apfel. Mysterious woman, murder, millions stolen; the editors leaped at it.'

'For Christ's sake, *why*?' shouted Stevens. 'You used a citizen of another country for a US intelligence strategy! A service staff employee of a closely allied government. Are you out of your minds? You only exacerbated the situation. You sacrificed her!'

'You're wrong,' said Webb. 'We're trying to save her life. We've turned Carlos's weapon against him.'

'How?'

The Monk raised his hand. 'Before we answer we have to go back to another question,' he said. 'Because the answer to *that* may give you an indication of how restricted the information must remain. A moment ago I asked the major how Carlos's man could have found Bourne – found the *fiche* that identified Bourne as Cain. I think I know, but I want him to tell you.'

Webb leaned forward. 'The Medusa records,' he said quietly, reluctantly.

'Medusa . . . ?' Stevens's expression conveyed the fact that Medusa had been the subject of early White House confidential briefings. 'They're buried,' he said.

'Correction,' intruded Abbott. 'There's an original and two copies and they're in vaults at the Pentagon, the CIA and the National Security Council. Access to them is limited to a select group, each one among the highest ranking members of his unit. Bourne came out of Medusa; a cross-checking of those names with the bank records would produce his name. Someone gave them to Carlos.'

Stevens stared at the Monk. 'Are you saying that Carlos is . . . wired into . . . men like that? It's an extraordinary charge.'

'It's the only explanation,' said Webb.

'But why would Bourne ever use his own name?'

'It was necessary,' replied Abbott. 'It was a vital part of the portrait. It had to be authentic; everything had to be authentic. Everything.'

'Authentic?'

'Maybe you'll understand now,' continued the major. 'By tying the St Jacques woman into millions supposedly stolen from the Gemeinschaft Bank, we're telling Bourne to surface. He knows it's false.'

'Bourne to *surface*?'

'The man called Jason Bourne,' said Abbott, getting to his feet and walking slowly towards the drawn curtains, 'is an American intelligence officer. There is no Cain, not the one Carlos believes. He's a lure, a trap for Carlos: that's who he is. Or was.'

The silence was brief, broken by the White House man. 'I think you'd better explain. The President has to know.'

'I suppose so,' mused Abbott, parting the curtains, looking absently outside. 'It's an insoluble dilemma, really. Presidents change, different men with different temperaments and appetites sit in the Oval office. However, a long-range intelligence strategy doesn't change, not one like this. Yet an offhand remark over a glass of whisky in a post-presidential conversation, or an egotistical phrase in a memoir, can blow that same strategy right to hell. There isn't a day that we don't worry about those men who have survived the White House.'

'*Please*,' interrupted Stevens. 'I ask you to remember that I'm here on the orders of *this* President. Whether you approve or disapprove doesn't matter. He has the right by law to know, and in his name I insist on that right.'

'Very well,' said Abbott still looking outside. 'Three years ago we borrowed a page from the British. We created a man who never was. If you recall, prior to the Normandy invasion British Intelligence floated a corpse into the coast of Portugal, knowing that whatever documents were concealed on it would find their way to the German Embassy in Lisbon. A life was created for that dead body; a name, a naval officer's rank; schools, training, travel orders, driver's licence, membership cards of exclusive London clubs, and half a dozen personal letters. Scattered throughout were hints, vaguely worded allusions and a few very direct chronological and geographical references. They all pointed to the invasion taking place a hundred miles away from the beaches at Normandy and six weeks off the target date in June. After panicked checks were made by German agents all over England controlled, incidentally and monitored by MI5 – the High command in Berlin bought the story and shifted a large part of their defences. As many were lost, thousands upon thousands of lives were saved by that man who never was.' Abbott let the curtain fall into place and walked wearily back to his chair.

'I heard the story,' said the White House aide. 'And?'

'Ours was a variation,' said the Monk, sitting down wearily. 'Create a living man, a quickly established legend, seemingly everywhere at once, racing all over South-east Asia, outdoing Carlos at every turn, especially in the area of sheer numbers. Whenever there was a killing, or an unexplained death, or a prominent figure involved in a fatal accident, there was Cain. Wherever there was violence and homicide, we tied in Cain. Reliable sources – paid informants known for accuracy – were fed his name: embassies, listening posts, entire intelligence networks were repeatedly funnelled reports that concentrated on Cain's rapidly expanding activities. His "kills" were mounting every month, sometimes it seemed weekly. He was everywhere . . . and he *was*. In all ways.'

'You mean this Bourne was?'

'Yes. He spent months learning everything there was to learn about Carlos, studying every file we had, every known and suspected assassination with which Carlos was involved. He pored over Carlos's tactics, his methods of operation, everything. Much of *that* material has never seen the light of day and probably never will. It's explosive – governments and international combines would be at one another's throats. There was literally nothing Bourne did not know – that could be *known* – about Carlos. And then he'd show himself, always with a different appearance, speaking any of several languages, talking about things to selected circles of hardened criminals that only a professional killer would talk about. Then he'd be gone, leaving behind bewildered and often frightened men and women. They had seen Cain; he existed, and he was ruthless. That was the image Bourne conveyed.'

'He's been underground like this for *three years*?' asked Stevens.

'Yes. He moved to Europe, the most accomplished white assassin in Asia, graduate of the infamous Medusa, challenging Carlos in his own backyard. And in the process he saved four men marked by Carlos, took credit for others Carlos had killed, mocked him at every opportunity . . . always trying to force him out in the open. He's spent nearly three years living the most dangerous sort of life a man can live, the kind of existence few men ever know. Most would have broken under it; and that possibly can never be ruled out.'

'What kind of man is he?'

'A professional,' answered Gordon Webb. 'Someone who had the training and the capability, who understood that Carlos had to be found, stopped.'

'But three *years* . . . ?'

'If that seems incredible,' said Abbott, 'you should know that he submitted to surgery. It was like a final break with the past, with the man he was in order to become a man he wasn't. I don't think there's any way a nation can repay a man like Bourne for what he's done. Perhaps the only way is to give him the chance to succeed, and, by God, I intend to do that.' The Monk stopped for precisely two seconds, then added, 'If it *is* Bourne.'

It was as if Elliot Stevens had been struck by an unseen hammer. 'What did you say?' he asked.

'I'm afraid I've held this to the end. I wanted you to understand the whole picture, before I described the gap. It may *not* be a gap, we just don't know. Too many things have happened that make no sense to us, but we don't *know*. It's the reason why there can be absolutely no interference from other levels, no diplomatic sugar pills that might expose the strategy. We could condemn a man to death, a man who's given more than any of us. If he succeeds, he can go back to his own life, but only anonymously, *only* without his identity ever being revealed.'

'I'm afraid you'll have to explain that,' said the astonished presidential aide.

'Loyalty, Elliot. It's not restricted to what's commonly referred to as the "good guys". Carlos has built up an army of men and women who are devoted to him. They may not know him but they revere him. If Bourne is exposed, that army will spread out and kill him. However, if he can take Carlos – or trap Carlos so we can take him – then vanish, he's home free.'

'But you say he may *not* be Bourne!'

'I said we don't know. It *was* Bourne at the bank, the signatures were authentic. But is it Bourne now? The next few days will tell us.'

'If he surfaces,' added Webb.

'It's delicate,' continued the old man. 'There are so many variables. If it isn't Bourne – or if he's turned – it could explain the call to Ottawa, the killing at the airport. From what we can gather, the woman's expertise *was* used to withdraw the money in Paris. All Carlos had to do was make a few inquiries at the Canadian Department of Finance. The rest would be child's play for him. Kill her contact, panic her, cut her off and use her to contain Bourne.'

'Were you able to get word to her?' asked the major.

'I tried and failed. I had Mac Hawkins call a man who also worked closely with the St Jacques woman, a man named Alan somebody-or-other. He instructed her to return to Canada immediately. She hung up on him.'

'God*damn* it!' exploded Webb.

'Precisely. If we could have got her back, we might have learned so much. She's the key. Why is she with him? Why he with her? Nothing makes sense.'

'Less so to me!' said Stevens, his bewilderment turning into anger. 'If you want the President's co-operation – and I promise nothing – you'd better be clearer.'

Abbott turned to him. 'Six months ago Bourne disappeared,' he said. 'Something happened: we're not sure what, but we can piece together a probability. He got word into Zürich that he was on his way to Marseilles, Later – too late – we understood. He'd learned that Carlos had accepted a contract on Howard Leland, and Bourne tried to stop it . . . Then nothing: he vanished. Had he been killed? Had he broken under the strain? Had he . . . given up?'

'I can't accept that,' interrupted Webb. 'I won't accept it.'

'I know you won't,' said the Monk. 'It's why I want you to go through that file. You know his codes; they're all in there. See if you can spot any deviations in Zürich.'

'*Please!*' broke in Stevens. 'What do you *think*? You must have found something concrete, something on which to base a judgment! I need that, Mr Abbott. The President needs it.'

'I wish to heaven I had,' replied the Monk. 'What have we found? Everything and nothing . . . Two years and ten months of the most carefully constructed deception in our records. Every false act documented, every move defined and justified: each man and woman informants, contacts, sources – given faces, voices, stories to tell. And every month, every week just a little bit closer to Carlos . . . Then nothing. Silence. Six months' vacuum.'

'Not *now*,' countered the President's aide. 'That silence was broken. By whom?'

'That's the basic question, isn't it?' said the old man, his voice tired. 'Months of silence, then suddenly an explosion of unauthorized, incomprehensible activity. The account penetrated, the *fiche* altered, millions transferred – by all appearances, stolen. Above all, men killed and traps set for other men. But for whom, *by* whom?' The Monk shook his head wearily. 'Who *is* the man out there?'

20

The limousine was parked between two street lamps, diagonally across from the heavy ornamental doors of the brownstone house. In the front seat sat a uniformed chauffeur; such a driver at the wheel of such a vehicle was not an uncommon sight on the tree-lined street. What was unusual, however, was the fact that two other men remained in the shadows of the deep back seat, neither making any move to get out. Instead, they watched the entrance of the brownstone, confident that they could not be picked up by the infra-red beam of a scanning camera.

One man adjusted his glasses, the eyes beyond his thick lenses owl-like, flatly suspicious of most of what they surveyed. Alfred Gillette, Director of Personnel Screening and Evaluation for the National Security Council, spoke. 'How gratifying to be there when arrogance collapses. How much more so to be the instrument.'

'You really dislike him, don't you?' said Gillette's companion, a heavy-shouldered man in a black raincoat whose accent derived from a Slavic language somewhere in Europe.

'I loathe him. He stands for everything I hate in Washington. The right schools, houses in Georgetown, farm in Virginia, quiet meetings at their *clubs.* They've got their tight little world and you don't break in – they run it all. The *bastards.* The superior, self-inflated *gentry* of Washington. They use other men's intellects, other men's work, wrapping it all into decisions bearing their imprimatures. And if you're on the outside, you become part of that amorphous entity, a "damn fine staff".'

'You exaggerate,' said the European, his eyes on the brownstone. 'You haven't done badly there. We never would have contacted you otherwise.'

Gillette scowled. 'If I haven't done badly, it's because I've become indispensable to too many like David Abbott. I have in my head a thousand facts they couldn't possibly recall. It's simply easier for them to place me where the questions are, where problems need solutions. *Director* of Personnel Screening and Development! They created that title, that post, for me. Do you know why?'

'No, Alfred,' replied the European, looking at his watch, 'I don't know why.'

'Because they don't have the patience to spend hours poring over thousands of résumés and dossiers. They'd rather be dining at Sans Souci, or preening in front of Senate committees, reading from pages prepared by others – by those unseen, unnamed "damn fine staffs".'

'You're a bitter man,' said the European.

'More than you'll know. A lifetime doing the work those bastards should have done for themselves. And for what? A title and an occasional lunch where my brains are picked between the shrimps and the entrée. By men like the supremely arrogant David Abbott; they're nothing without people like me.'

'Don't underestimate the Monk. Carlos doesn't.'

'How could he? He doesn't know what to evaluate. Everything Abbott does is shrouded in secrecy; no one knows how many mistakes he's made. And if any come to light, men like me are blamed for them.'

The European shifted his gaze from the window to Gillette. 'You're very emotional, Alfred,' he said coldly. 'You must be careful about that.'

The bureaucrat smiled. 'It never gets in the way, I believe my contributions to Carlos bear that out. Let's say I'm preparing myself for a confrontation I wouldn't avoid for anything in the world.'

'An honest statement,' said the heavy-shouldered man.

'What about you? You found me.'

'I knew what to look for.' The European returned to the window.

'I mean *you.* The work you do. For Carlos.'

'I have no such complicated reasoning. I come out of a country where educated men are promoted at the whim of morons who recite Marxist litany by rote. Carlos, too, knew what to look for.'

Gillette laughed, his flat eyes close to shining. 'We're not so different after all. Change the bloodlines of our eastern establishment for Marx and there's a distinct parallel.'

'Perhaps,' agreed the European, looking again at his watch. 'It shouldn't be long now. Abbott always catches the midnight shuttle, his every hour accounted for in Washington.'

'You're sure he'll come out alone?'

'He always does, and he certainly wouldn't be seen with Elliot Stevens. Webb and Stevens will also leave separately; twenty-minute intervals is standard for those called in.'

'How did you find Treadstone?'

'It wasn't so difficult. You contributed, Alfred; you were part of a damn fine staff.' The man laughed, his eyes on the brownstone. 'Cain was out of Medusa, you told us that, and if Carlos's suspicions are accurate, that meant the Monk, *we* knew *that*; it tied him to Bourne. Carlos instructed us to keep Abbott under twenty-four-hour surveillance; something had gone wrong. When the gunshots in Zürich were heard in Washington, Abbott got careless. We followed him here. It was merely a question of persistence.'

'That led you to Canada? To the man in Ottawa?'

'The man in Ottawa revealed himself by looking for Treadstone. When we learned who the girl was we had the Department of Finance watched, her section watched. A call came from Paris; it was she, telling him to start a search. We don't know why, but we suspect Bourne may be trying to blow Treadstone apart. If he's turned, it's one way to get out and keep the money. It doesn't matter. Suddenly, this section head no one outside the Canadian government had ever heard of was transformed into a problem of the highest priority. Intelligence communiqués were burning the wires. It meant Carlos was right; *you* were right, Alfred. There is no Cain. He's an invention, a trap.'

'From the beginning,' insisted Gillette. 'I told you that. Three years of false reports, sources unverified. It was all there!'

'From the beginning,' mused the European. 'Undoubtedly the Monk's finest creation . . . until something happened and the creation turned. Everything's turning; it's all coming apart at the seams.'

'Stevens's being here confirms that. The President insists on knowing.'

'He has to. There's a nagging suspicion in Ottawa that a section head at the Department of Finance was killed by American Intelligence.' The European turned from the window and looked at the bureaucrat. 'Remember, Alfred, we simply want to know what happened. I've given you the facts as we've learned them; they're irrefutable and Abbott cannot deny them. But they must be presented as having been obtained independently by your own sources. You're appalled. You demand an accounting; the entire intelligence community has been duped.'

'It *has*,' exclaimed Gillette. 'Duped and *used*. No one in Washington knows about Bourne, about Treadstone. They've excluded everyone; it *is* appalling. I don't have to pretend. Arrogant *bastards*!'

'Alfred,' cautioned the European, holding up his hand in the shadows, 'do remember whom you're working for. The threat cannot be based on emotion, but on cold professional outrage. He'll suspect you instantly; you must dispel those suspicions just as swiftly. *You* are the accuser, not him.'

'I'll remember.'

'Good.' Headlight beams bounced through the glass. 'Abbott's taxi is here. I'll take care of the driver.' The European reached to his right and flipped a switch beneath the armrest. 'I'll be in my car across the street, listening.' He spoke to the chauffeur. 'Abbott will be coming out any moment now. You know what to do.'

The chauffeur nodded. Both men got out of the limousine simultaneously. The driver walked around the bonnet as if to escort a wealthy employer to the south side of the street. Gillette watched through the rear window, the two men stayed together for several seconds, then separated, the European heading for the approaching cab, his hand held up, a note between his fingers. The taxi would be sent away; the caller's plans had changed. The chauffeur had raced to the north side of the street and was now concealed in the shadows of a staircase two doors away from Treadstone Seventy-one.

Thirty seconds later Gillette's eyes were drawn to the door of the brownstone. Light spilled through as an impatient David Abbott came outside, looking up and down the street, glancing at his watch, obviously annoyed. The taxi was late and he had a plane to catch; precise schedules had to be followed. Abbott walked down the steps, turning left on the pavement, looking for the cab, expecting it. In seconds he would pass the chauffeur. He did, both men well out of camera range.

The interception was quick, the discussion rapid. In moments, a bewildered David Abbott climbed inside the limousine, and the chauffeur walked away into the shadows.

'You!' said the Monk, anger and disgust in his voice. 'Of all people, *you*.'

'I don't think you're in any position to be disdainful . . . much less arrogant.'

'What you've *done*! How *dare* you? Zürich. The Medusa records. It was you!'

'The Medusa records, yes. Zürich, yes. But it's not a question of what *I've* done; it's what you've done. We sent our own men to Zürich, telling them what to look for. We found it. His name is Bourne, isn't it? He's the man you call Cain. The man you invented!'

Abbott kept himself in check. 'How did you find this house?'

'Persistence. I had you followed.'

'You had *me* followed? What the hell did you think you were *doing*?'

'Trying to set a record straight. A record you've warped and lied about, keeping the truth from the rest of us. What did you think *you* were doing?'

'Oh, my God, you damn fool!' Abbott inhaled deeply. 'Why did you do it? Why didn't you come to me yourself?'

'Because you'd have done nothing. You've manipulated the entire intelligence community. Millions of dollars, untold thousands of man hours, embassies and stations fed lies and distortions about a killer that never existed. Oh, I recall your words; what a challenge to Carlos. What an irresistible *trap* it was! Only we were your pawns too, and as a responsible member of the Security Council I resent it deeply! You're all alike. Who elected you God so you could break the rules – no, not just the rules, the *laws* – and make us look like fools?'

'There was no other way,' said the old man wearily, his face a drawn mass of crevices in the dim light. 'How many know? Tell me the truth.'

'I've contained it. I gave you that.'

'It may not be enough. Oh, *Christ*!'

'It may not last, *period*,' said the bureaucrat emphatically. 'I want to know what happened.'

'What happened?'

'To this grand strategy of yours. It seems to be . . . falling apart at the seams.'

'Why do you say that?'

'It's perfectly obvious. You've lost Bourne, you can't find him. Your Cain has disappeared with a fortune banked for him in Zürich.'

Abbott was silent for a moment. 'Wait a minute. What put you onto it?'

'You,' said Gillette quickly, the prudent man rising to the baited question. 'I must say I admired your control when that ass from the Pentagon spoke so knowingly of Operation Medusa . . . sitting directly across from the man who created it.'

'History.' The old man's voice was strong now. 'That wouldn't have told you anything.'

'Let's say it was rather unusual for you not to *say* anything. I mean, who at that table knew more about Medusa than you? But you didn't say a word and that started me thinking. So I objected strenuously to the attention being paid to this assassin, Cain. You couldn't resist, David. You had to offer a very plausible reason to continue the search for Cain. You threw Carlos into the hunt.'

'It was the truth,' interrupted Abbott.

'Certainly it was; you knew when to use it, and I knew when to spot it. Ingenious. A snake pulled out of Medusa's head, groomed for a mythical title. The contender jumps into the champion's ring to draw the champion out of his corner.'

'It was sound, sound from the beginning.'

'Why not? As I say, it was ingenious, even down to every move made by his own people against Cain. Who better to relay those moves to Cain than the one man on the Forty Committee who is given reports on every covert operations conference. You used us *all*!'

The Monk nodded. 'Very well. To a point you're right, there've been degrees of abuse – in my opinion, totally justified – but it's not what you think. There are checks and balances; there always are, I wouldn't have it any other way. Treadstone is comprised of a small group of men among the most trustworthy in the government. They range from Army G-Two to the Senate, from the CIA to Naval Intelligence, and now, frankly, the White House. Should there be any true abuse, there's not one of them that would hesitate to put a stop to the operation. None has ever seen fit to do so, and I beg you not to do so, either.'

'Would I be made part of Treadstone?'

'You *are* part of it now.'

'I see. What happened? Where is Bourne?'

'I wish to God we knew. We're not even sure it *is* Bourne.'

'You're not even sure of *what*?'

'I see. What happened? Where is Bourne?'

'I wish to God we knew. We're not even sure it is Bourne.'

'You're not even sure of what?'

The European reached for the switch on the dashboard and snapped it off. 'That's it,' he said. 'That's what we had to know.' He turned to the chauffeur beside him. 'Quickly, now. Get back behind the staircase. Remember, if one of them comes out, you have precisely three seconds before the door is closed. Work fast.'

The uniformed man got out first; he walked up the pavement towards Treadstone Seventy-one. From one of the adjacent brownstones, a middle-aged couple were saying loud good-byes to their hosts, the chauffeur slowed down, reached into his pocket for a cigarette and stopped to light it. He was now a bored driver, whiling away the hours of a tedious vigil. The European watched, then unbuttoned his raincoat and withdrew a long, thin revolver, its barrel enlarged by a silencer. He released the safety catch, shoved the weapon back into his holster, got out of the car and walked across the street towards the limousine. The mirrors had been angled so that, by staying in the blind spot, there was no way either man inside could see him approach. The European paused briefly beside the boot, then swiftly, hand extended, lunged for the right front door, opened it and spun inside, levelling his weapon over the seat.

Alfred Gillette gasped, his left hand surging for the door handle; the European snapped the four-way lock. David Abbott remained immobile, staring at the invader.

'Good evening, Monk,' said the European. 'Another, whom I'm told often assumes a religious habit, sends you his congratulations. Not only for Cain, but for your household personnel at Treadstone. The Yachtsman, for instance. Once a superior agent.'

Gillette found his voice; it was a mixture of a scream and a whisper. 'What *is* this? Who *are* you?' he cried, feigning ignorance.

'Oh come now, old friend. That's not necessary,' said the man with the gun. 'I can see by the expression on Mr Abbott's face that he realizes his initial doubts about you were accurate. One should always trust one's first instincts, shouldn't one, Monk . . . ? You were right, of course. We found another discontented man; your system reproduces them with alarming rapidity. He, indeed, gave us the Medusa files, and they did, indeed, lead us to Bourne.'

'What are you doing?!' screamed Gillette. 'What are you *saying*?'

'You're a bore, Alfred. But you were always part of a damn fine staff. It's too bad you didn't know which staff to stay with; your kind never do.'

'*You!* . . .' Gillette rose bodily off the seat, his face contorted.

The European fired his weapon, the spit echoing briefly in the soft interior of the limousine. The bureaucrat slumped over, his body crumbling to the floor against the door, owl-eyes wide in death.

'I don't think you mourn him,' said the European.

'I don't,' said the Monk.

'It *is* Bourne out there, you know. Cain turned; he broke. The long period of silence is over. The snake from Medusa's head decided to strike out on his own. Or perhaps he was bought. That's possible too, isn't it? Carlos buys many men, the one at your feet now, for example.'

'You'll learn nothing from me. Don't try.'

'There's nothing to learn. We know it all. Delta, Carlos . . . Cain. But the names aren't important any longer; they never were, really. All that remains is the final isolation – removing the man-monk who makes the decisions. You, Bourne is trapped. He's finished.'

'There are others who make decisions. He'll reach them.'

'If he does, they'll kill him on sight. There's nothing more despicable than a man who's turned, but in order for a man to turn there has to be irrefutable proof that he was yours to begin with. Carlos has the proof; he *was* yours, his origins as sensitive as anything in the Medusa files.'

The old man frowned; he was frightened, not for his life, but for something infinitely more indispensable. 'You're out of your mind,' he said. 'There is no proof.'

'That was the flaw, *your* flaw. Carlos is thorough; his tentacles reach into all manner of hidden recesses. You needed a man from Medusa, someone who had lived and disappeared. You chose a man named Bourne because the circumstances of his disappearance had been obliterated, eliminated from every existing record – or so you believed. But you didn't consider Hanoi's own field personnel who had infiltrated Medusa; those records exist. On 25

March 1968, Jason Bourne was executed by an American Intelligence officer in the jungles of Tam Quan.'

The Monk lunged forward; there was nothing left but a final gesture, a final defiance. The European fired.

The door of the brownstone opened. From the shadows beneath the staircase, the chauffeur smiled. The White House aide was being escorted out by the Yachtsman, and the killer knew that meant the primary alarms were off. The three-second span was eliminated.

'So good of you to drop by,' said the Yachtsman shaking hands.

'Thank you very much, sir.'

These were the last words either man spoke. The chauffeur aimed above the brick-walled railing, pulling the trigger twice, the muffled reports indistinguishable from the myriad if distant sounds of the city. The Yachtsman fell back inside; the White House aide clutched his upper chest, reeling into the door frame. The chauffeur spun around the wall and raced up the steps, catching Stevens's body as it plummeted down. With bullet-like strength, the killer lifted the White House man off his feet, hurling him back through the door into the foyer beyond the Yachtsman. Then he turned to the interior border of the heavy, steel-plated door. He knew what to look for; he found it. Along the upper moulding, disappearing into the wall, was a thick cable, stained the colour of the doorframe. He closed the door part way, raised his gun and fired into the cable. The spit was followed by an eruption of static and sparks; the security cameras were blown out, screens everywhere now dark.

He opened the door to signal; it was not necessary. The European was walking rapidly across the quiet street. Within seconds he had climbed the steps and was inside, glancing around the foyer and the hallway – and at the door at the end of the hall. Together both men lifted a rug from the foyer floor, the European closing the door on its edge, welding cloth and steel together so that a two-inch space remained, the security bolts still in place. No back-up alarms could be raised.

They stood erect in silence; both knew that if the discovery was going to be made, it would be made quickly. It came with the sound of an upstairs door opening, followed by footsteps and words that floated down the staircase in a cultured female voice.

'Darling! I just noticed, the damn camera's on the fritz. Would you check it, please?' There was a pause; then the woman spoke again. 'On second thought why not tell the Jesuit?' Again the pause, again with precise timing. 'Don't bother then, darling. I'll tell David!'

Two footsteps. Silence. A rustle of cloth. The European studied the stairwell. A light went out. David Jesuit . . . Monk!

'*Get her!*' he roared at the chauffeur, spinning around, his weapon levelled at the door at the end of the hallway.

The uniformed man raced up the staircase; there was a gunshot; it came from a powerful weapon – unmuffled, unsilenced. The European looked up; the chauffeur was holding his shoulder, his coat drenched with blood, his pistol held out, spitting repeatedly up the well of the stairs.

The door at the end of the hallway was yanked open, the major standing there in shock, a file folder in his hand. The European fired twice; Gordon Webb arched backwards, his throat torn open, the papers in the folder flying out behind him. The man in the raincoat raced up the steps to the chauffeur; above, over the railing, was the grey-haired woman, dead, blood spilling out of her head and neck. 'Are you all right? Can you move?' asked the European.

The chauffeur nodded. 'The bitch blew half my shoulder off, but I can manage.'

'You *have* to!' commanded his superior, ripping off his raincoat. 'Put on my coat. I want the Monk in here! Quickly!'

'Jesus! . . .'

'*Carlos* wants the Monk in here!'

Awkwardly the wounded man put on the black raincoat and made his way down the staircase around the bodies of the Yachtsman and the White House aide. Carefully, in pain, he let himself out of the door and down the front steps.

The European watched him, holding the door, making sure the man was sufficiently mobile for the task. He was; he was a bull whose every appetite was satisfied by Carlos. The chauffeur would carry David Abbott's corpse back into the brownstone, no doubt supporting it as though helping an ageing drunk for the benefit of anyone in the street; and then he would somehow contain his bleeding long enough to drive Alfred Gillette's body across the river, burying him in a swamp. Carlos's men were capable of such things; they were all bulls. Discontented bulls who had found their own causes in a single man.

The European turned and started down the hall; there was work to do. The final isolation of the man called Jason Bourne.

It was more than could be hoped for, the exposed files a gift beyond belief. Included were folders containing every code and method of communication ever used by the mythical Cain. Now not so mythical, thought the European, as he gathered the papers together. The scene was set, the four corpses in position in the peaceful, elegant library, David Abbott was arched in a chair, his dead eyes in shock, Elliot Stevens at his feet; the Yachtsman was slumped over the hatch table, an overturned bottle of whisky in his hand, while Gordon Webb sprawled on the floor, clutching his briefcase. Whatever violence had taken place, the setting indicated that it had been unexpected; conversations interrupted by abrupt gunfire.

The European walked around in suede gloves, appraising his artistry, and it *was* artistry. He had dismissed the chauffeur, wiped every door handle, every knob, every gleaming surface of wood. It was time for the final touch. He walked to a table where there were brandy glasses on a silver tray, picked one up and held it to the light; as he expected; it was spotless. He put it down, and took out a small, flat, plastic case from his pocket. He opened it and removed a strip of transparent tape, holding it, too, up to the light. There they were, as clear as portraits – for they were portraits, as undeniable as any photograph.

They had been taken off a glass of Perrier, removed from an office at the Gemeinschaft Bank in Zürich. They were the fingerprints of Jason Bourne's right hand.

The European picked up the brandy glass and, with the patience of the artist he was, pressed the tape around the lower surface, then gently peeled it off. Again he held the glass up; the prints were seen in dull perfection against the light of the table lamp.

The European carried the glass over to a corner of the parquet floor and dropped it. He knelt down, studied the fragments, removed several, and brushed the rest under the curtain.

They were enough.

21

'Later,' said Bourne, throwing their suitcases on the bed. 'We've got to get out of here.'

Marie sat in the armchair. She had read the newspaper article again, selecting phrases, repeating them. Her concentration was absolute; she was consumed, more and more confident of her analysis.

'I'm right, Jason. Someone *is* sending us a message!'

'We'll talk about it later; we've stayed here too long as it is. That newspaper'll be all over this hotel in an hour and the morning papers may be worse. It's no time for modesty; you stand out in a hotel lobby, and you've been seen in this one by too many people. Get your things.'

Marie stood up, but made no other move. Instead, she held her place and forced him to look at her. 'We'll talk about several things later,' she said firmly. 'You were leaving me, Jason, and I want to know why.'

'I told you I'd tell you,' he answered, without evasion, 'because you have to know and I mean that. But right now I want to get out of here. Get your things, goddamn it!'

She blinked, his sudden anger having its effect. 'Yes, of course,' she whispered.

They took the lift down to the lobby. As the worn marble floor came into view, Bourne had the feeling they were in a cage, exposed and vulnerable; if the machine stopped, they would be taken. Then he understood why the feeling was so strong. Below on the left was the front desk, the *concierge* sitting behind it, a pile of newspapers on the counter to his right. They were copies of the same tabloid Jason had put in the attaché case Marie was now carrying. The *concierge* had taken one; he was reading it avidly; poking a toothpick between his teeth, oblivious to everything but the *nouvelles scandaleuses.*

'Walk straight through,' said Jason. 'Don't stop, just go right to the door. I'll meet you outside.'

'Oh, my God! . . .' she whispered, seeing the *concierge.*

'I'll pay him as quickly as I can.'

The sound of Marie's heels on the marble floor was a distraction Bourne did not want. The *concierge* looked up as Jason moved in front of him, blocking his view.

'It's been very pleasant,' he said in French, 'but I'm in a great hurry. I have to drive to Lyons tonight. Just round out the figure to the nearest five hundred francs. I haven't had time to leave gratuities.'

The financial distraction accomplished its purpose. The *concierge* reached his totals quickly; he presented the bill. Jason paid it and bent down for the suitcases, glancing up at the sound of surprise that exploded from the *concierge's* gaping mouth. The man was staring at the pile of newspapers on his right, his eyes on the photograph of Marie St Jacques. He looked over at the glass doors of the entrance; Marie stood on the pavement. The *concierge* shifted his astonished gaze to Bourne; the connection was made, the man inhibited by sudden fear.

Jason walked rapidly towards the glass doors, angling his shoulder to push them open, glancing back at the front desk. The *concierge* was reaching for a telephone.

'Let's go!' he cried to Marie. 'Look for a cab!'

They found one on rue Lecourbe, five blocks from the hotel. Bourne feigned the role of an inexperienced American tourist, employing the inadequate French that had served him so well at the Valois Bank. He explained to the driver that he and his *belle amie* wanted to get out of central Paris for a day or so, somewhere they could be alone. Perhaps the driver could suggest several places and they would choose one.

The driver could and did. 'There's a small inn outside Les Moulineux Billancourt, called Maison Quadrillage,' he said. 'Another in Ivry-sur-Seine, you might like. It's very private, Monsieur. Or perhaps the Auberge du Coin in Montrouge; it's between the two and very discreet.'

'Let's take the first,' said Jason. 'It's the first that came to your mind. How long will it take?'

'No more than fifteen, twenty minutes, Monsieur.'

'Good.' Bourne turned to Marie and spoke softly. 'Change your hair.'

'What?'

'Change your hair, Pull it up or push it back, I don't care, but change it. Move out of sight of his mirror. Hurry up!'

Several moments later Marie's long auburn hair was pulled severely back, away from her face and neck, fastened with the aid of a mirror and hairpins into a tight chignon. Jason looked at her in the dim light.

'Wipe off your lipstick. All of it.'

She took out a tissue and did so. 'All right?'

'Yes. Have you got an eyebrow pencil?'

'Of course.'

'Thicken your eyebrows; just a little bit. Extend them about a quarter of an inch; curve the ends down just a touch.'

Again she followed his instructions. 'Now?' she asked.

'That's better,' he replied, studying her. The changes were minor but the effect major. She had been subtly transformed from a softly elegant, striking woman into a harsher image. At the least, she was not on first sight the woman in the newspaper photograph and that was all that mattered.

'When we reach Billancourt,' he whispered, 'get out quickly, and turn your back. Don't let the driver see you.'

'It's a little late for that, isn't it?'

'Just do as I say.'

Listen to me. I am a chameleon called Cain and I can teach you many things I do not care to teach you, but at the moment I must. I can change my colour to accommodate any backdrop in the forest, I can shift with the wind by smelling it. I can find my way through the natural and man-made jungles. Alpha, Bravo, Charlie, Delta . . . Delta is for Charlie and Charlie is for Cain. I am Cain. I am death. And I must tell you who I am and lose you.

'My darling, what is it?'

'What?'

'You're looking at me; you're not breathing. Are you all right?'

'Sorry,' he said, glancing away, breathing again. 'I'm working out our moves. I'll know better what to do when we get there.'

They arrived at the inn. There was a parking area bordered by a post-and-rail fence on the right; several late diners came out of the lattice-framed entrance in front. Bourne leaned forward in the seat.

'Let us off inside the parking area, if you don't mind,' he ordered, offering no explanation for the odd request.

'Certainly, Monsieur,' said the driver, nodding his head, then shrugging, his movements conveying the fact that his passengers were, indeed, a cautious couple.

The rain had subsided, returning to a mistlike drizzle. The taxi drove off. Bourne and Marie remained in the shadows of the foliage at the side of the Inn until it disappeared. Jason put the suitcases down on the wet ground. 'Wait here,' he said.

'Where are you going?'

'To phone for a taxi.'

The second taxi took them west into the Montrouge district. This driver was singularly unimpressed by the stern-faced couple who were obviously from the provinces, and probably seeking cheaper lodgings. When and if he picked up a newspaper and saw a photograph of a French-Canadienne involved with murder and theft in Zürich, the woman in his back seat now would not come to mind.

The Auberge du Coin did not live up to its name. It was not a quaint village inn situated in a secluded nook of the countryside. Instead, it was a large, flat, two-storey structure a quarter of a mile off the main road. If anything, it was reminiscent of motels that blight the outskirts of cities the world over; commercially guaranteeing the anonymity of their guests. It was not hard to imagine weekly appointments by the score that were best attributed to erroneous registrations.

So they registered erroneously and were given a plastic room where every accessory worth over twenty francs was bolted into the floor or attached with headless screws to lacquered Formica laminate. There was, however, one positive feature to the place; an ice machine down the hall. They knew it worked because they could hear it. With the door closed.

'All right, now. Who would be sending us a message?' asked Bourne, standing, revolving the glass of whisky in his hand.

'If I knew, I'd get in touch with them,' she said, sitting at the small desk, chair turned, legs crossed, watching him closely. 'It could be connected with why you were running away.'

'If it was, it was a trap.'

'It was no trap. A man like Walther Apfel didn't do what he did to accommodate a trap.'

'I wouldn't be so sure of that.' Bourne walked to the single plastic armchair and sat down. 'Koenig did; he marked me right there in the waiting room.'

'He was a bribed foot-soldier, not an officer of the bank. He acted alone. Apfel couldn't.'

Jason looked up. 'What do you mean?'

'Apfel's statement had to be cleared by his superiors. It was made in the name of the bank.'

'If you're so sure, let's call Zürich.'

'They don't want that. Either they haven't the answer, or they can't give it. Apfel's last words were that they "would have no further comment. To anyone." That too, was part of the message. We're to contact someone else.'

Bourne drank; he needed the alcohol for the moment was coming when he would begin the story of a killer named Cain. 'Then we're back to whom?' he said. 'Back to the trap.'

'You think you know who it is, don't you?' Marie reached for her cigarettes on the desk. 'It's why you were running, isn't it?'

'The answer to both questions is yes.' *The moment had come. The message was sent by Carlos! I am Cain and you must leave me! I must lose you. But first there is Zürich and you have to understand.* 'That article was planted to find me.'

'I won't argue with that,' she broke in, surprizing him with the interruption. 'I've had time to think; they know the evidence is false – so patently false it's ridiculous. The Zürich police fully expect me to get in touch with the Canadian Embassy now . . .' Marie stopped, the unlit cigarette in her hand. 'My God, Jason, that's what they want us to do!'

'Who wants us to do?'

'Whoever's sending us the message. They know I have no choice but to call the embassy, get the protection of the Canadian government. I didn't think of it because I've already *spoken* to the embassy, to what's his name – Dennis Corbelier, and he had absolutely nothing to tell me. He only did what I asked him to do; there was nothing else. But that was *yesterday* . . . Not *today*, not *tonight*.' Marie started for the telephone on the bedside table.

Bourne rose quickly from the chair and intercepted her, holding her arm. 'Don't,' he said firmly.

'Why not?'

'Because you're wrong.'

'I'm *right*, Jason! Let me prove it to you.'

Bourne moved in front of her. 'I think you'd better listen to what I have to say.'

'No!' she cried, startling him. 'I don't want to hear it. Not now!'

'An hour ago in Paris it was the only thing you wanted to hear. *Hear* it!'

'*No!* An hour ago I was dying! You'd made up your mind to run. *Without* me. And I know now it will happen over and *over* again until it stops for you. You hear words, you see images, and fragments of things come back to you that you can't understand, but because they're there you condemn yourself! You always *will* condemn yourself until someone proves to you that whatever you were . . . there are others *using* you, who will *sacrifice* you! But there's also someone else out there who wants to help you, help us! That's the message! I know I'm right. I want to prove it to you. *Let* me!'

Bourne held her arms in silence, looking at her, her lovely face filled with pain and useless hope, her eyes pleading. The terrible ache was everywhere within him. Perhaps it was better this way; she would see for herself and her fear would make her listen, make her understand. There was nothing for them any longer. *I am Cain* . . . 'All right, you can make the call, but it's got to be done my way.' He released her and went to the telephone; he dialled the Auberge du Coin's front desk. 'This is room three-four-one. I've just heard from friends in Paris; they're coming out to join us in a while. Do you have a room down the hall for them . . . ? Fine. Their name is Briggs, an American couple. I'll come down and pay in advance and you can let me have the key . . . Splendid. Thank you.'

'What are you *doing*?'

'Proving something to you,' he said. 'Get me a dress,' he continued. 'The longest one you've got.'

'What?'

'If you want to make your call, you'll do as I tell you.'

'You're crazy.'

'I've admitted that,' he said, taking trousers and a shirt from his suitcase. 'The dress, please.'

Fifteen minutes later, Mr and Mrs Briggs' room, six doors away and across the hall from three-four-one, was in readiness. The clothes had been properly placed, selected lights left on, others not functioning because the bulbs had been removed.

Jason returned to their room; Marie was standing by the telephone. 'We're set.'

'What have you done?'

'What I wanted to do; what I had to do. You can make the call now.'

'It's very late. Suppose he isn't there?'

'I think he will be. If not, they'll give you his home phone. His name was on the telephone logs in Ottawa; it had to be.'

'I suppose it was.'

'Then he will have been reached. Have you gone over what I told you to say?'

'Yes, but it doesn't matter; it's not relevant. I know I'm not wrong.'

'We'll see. Just say the words I told you. I'll be right beside you listening. Go ahead.'

She picked up the phone and dialled. Seven seconds after she reached the embassy switchboard, Dennis Corbelier was on the line. It was quarter past one in the morning.

'Christ almighty, where *are* you?'

'You were expecting me to call then?'

'I was hoping to hell you would! This place is in an uproar. I've been waiting here since five o'clock this afternoon.'

'So was Alan. In Ottawa.'

'Alan who? What are you talking about? Where the hell *are* you?'

'First, I want to know what you have to tell me.'

'*Tell* you?'

'You have a message for me, Dennis. What is *it*?'

'What is *what*? What message?'

Marie's face went pale. 'I didn't kill anyone in Zürich. I wouldn't . . .'

'Then for God's sake,' interrupted the attaché, 'get *in* here! We'll give you all the protection we can. No one can *touch* you here!'

'Dennis, *listen* to me! You've been waiting there for my call, haven't you?'

'Yes, of course.'

'Someone *told* you to wait, isn't that true?'

A pause. When Corbelier spoke, his voice was subdued. 'Yes, he did. They did.'

'What did they tell you?'

'That you need our help. Very badly.'

Marie resumed breathing. 'And they want to help us?'

'By us,' replied Corbelier, 'you're saying he's with you, then?'

Bourne's face was next to hers, his head angled to hear Corbelier's words. He nodded.

'Yes,' she answered. 'We're together, but he's out for a few minutes. It's all lies; they told you that, didn't they?'

'All they said was that you had to be found, protected. They *do* want to help you; they want to send a car for you. One of ours. Diplomatic.'

'Who are they?'

'I don't know them by name: I don't have to. I know their rank.'

'Rank?'

'Specialists, FS-Five. You don't get much higher than that.'

'You trust them?'

'My God, yes! They reached me through Ottawa. Their orders came from Ottawa!'

'They're at the embassy now?'

'No, they're out-posted.' Corbelier paused, obviously exasperated. 'Jesus *Christ*, Marie, where *are* you?'

Bourne nodded again, she spoke.

'We're at the Auberge du Coin in Montrouge. Under the name of Briggs.'

'I'll get that car to you right away.'

'No, Dennis!' protested Marie, watching Jason, his eyes telling her to follow his instructions. 'Send one in the morning. First thing in the morning – four hours from now, if you like.'

'I can't *do* that! For your own sake.'

'You have to; you don't understand. He was trapped into doing something and he's frightened he wants to run. If he knew I called you, he'd be running now. Give me time. I can persuade him to turn himself in. Just a few more hours. He's confused, but underneath he knows I'm right.' Marie said the words looking at Bourne.

'What kind of a son of a bitch is he?'

'A terrified one,' she answered. 'One who's being manipulated. I need the time. Give it to me.'

'*Marie* . . . ?' Corbelier stopped. 'All right, first thing in the morning. Say . . . six o'clock. And, Marie, they want to help you. They can help you.'

'I know. Good night.'

'Good night.'

Marie hung up. 'Now, we'll wait,' Bourne said.

'I don't know what you're proving. Of course he'll call the FS-Fives, and of course they'll show up here. What do you expect? He as much as admitted what he was going to do, what he thinks he has to do.'

'And these diplomatic FS-Fives are the ones sending us the message?'

'My guess is they'll take us to whoever is. Or if those sending it are too far away, they'll put us in touch with them. I've never been surer of anything in my professional life.'

Bourne looked at her. 'I hope you're right, because it's your whole life that concerns me. If the evidence against you in Zürich isn't part of any message, if it was put there by experts to find me – if the Zürich police *believe* it – then I'm that terrified man you spoke about to Corbelier. No one wants you to be right more than I do. But I don't think you are.'

At three minutes past two, the lights in the motel corridor flickered and went out, leaving the long hallway in relative darkness, the spill from the stairwell the only source of illumination. Bourne stood by the door of their room, pistol in hand, the lights turned off, watching the corridor through a crack between the door's edge and the frame. Marie was behind him, peering over his shoulder, neither spoke.

The footsteps were muffled, but there. Distinct, deliberate, two sets of shoes cautiously climbing the staircase. In seconds, the figures of two men could be seen emerging out of the dim light. Marie gasped involuntarily; Jason reached over his shoulder, his hand gripping her mouth harshly. He understood; she had recognized one of the two men, a man she had seen only once before. In Zürich's Steppdeckstrasse, minutes before another had ordered her execution. It was the blond man they had sent up to Bourne's room, the expendable scout brought now to Paris to spot the target he had missed. In his left hand was a small pencil light, in his right a long-barrelled gun, swollen by a silencer.

His companion was shorter, more compact, his walk not unlike an animal's tread, shoulders and waist moving fluidly with his legs. The lapels of his overcoat were pulled up, his head covered by a narrow-brimmed hat, shading his unseen face. Bourne stared at this man; there was something familiar about him, about the figure, the walk, the way he carried his head. What was it? What *was* it? He *knew* him.

But there was not time to think about it; the two men were approaching the door of the room reserved in the name of Mr and Mrs Briggs. The blond man held his pencil light on the numbers, then swept the beam down towards the knob and the lock.

What followed was mesmerizing in its efficiency. The stocky man held a ring of keys in his right hand, placing it under the beam of light, his fingers selecting a specific key. In his left hand he gripped a weapon, its shape in the spill revealing an out-sized silencer for a heavy-calibred automatic, not unlike the powerful German Sternlicht Luger favoured by the Gestapo in World War Two. It could cut through webbed steel and concrete, its sound no more than a romantic cough, ideal for taking enemies of the state at night in quiet neighbourhoods, nearby residents unaware of any disturbances, only of disappearance in the morning.

The shorter man inserted the key, turned it silently, then lowered the barrel of the gun to the lock. Three rapid coughs accompanied three flashes of light; the wood surrounding any bolts shattered. The door fell free; the two killers rushed inside.

There were two beats of silence, then an eruption of muffled gunfire, spits and white flashes from the darkness. The door was slammed shut; it would not stay closed, falling back as louder sounds of thrashing and collision came from within the room. Finally, a light was found; it was snapped on briefly, then shot out in fury, a lamp sent crashing to the floor, glass shattering. A cry of frenzy exploded from the throat of an infuriated man.

The two killers rushed out, weapons levelled, prepared for a trap, bewildered that there was none. They reached the staircase and raced down as a door to the right of the invaded room opened. A blinking guest peered out, then shrugged and went back inside. Silence returned to the darkened hallway.

Bourne held his place, his arm around Marie St Jacques. She was trembling, her head pressed into his chest, sobbing quietly, hysterically in disbelief. He let the minutes pass, until the trembling subsided and deep breaths replaced the sobs. He could not wait any longer; she had to see for herself. See completely, the impression indelible; she had to finally understand, *I am Cain. I am death.*

'Come on,' he whispered.

He led her out into the hall, guiding her firmly towards the room that was now his ultimate proof. He pushed the broken door open and they walked inside.

She stood motionless, both repelled and hypnotized by the sight. In an open doorway on the right was the dim silhouette of a figure, the light behind it so muted only the outline could be seen, and only when the eyes adjusted to the strange admixture of darkness and glow. It was the figure of a woman in a long gown, the fabric moving gently in the breeze of an open window.

Window. Straight ahead was a second figure, barely visible but there, its shape an obscure blot indistinctly outlined by the wash of light from the distant highway. Again, it seemed to move, brief, spastic flutterings of cloth – of arms.

'Oh, God,' said Marie, frozen. 'Turn on the lights, Jason.'

'None of them work,' he replied. Only two table lamps; they found one. He walked across the room cautiously and reached the lamp he was looking for, it was on the floor against the wall. He knelt down and turned it on; Marie shuddered.

Strung across the bathroom door, held in place by threads torn from a curtain, was her long dress, rippling from an unseen source of wind. It was riddled with bullet holes.

Against the far window, Bourne's shirt and trousers had been tacked to the frame, the panes by both sleeves smashed, the breeze rushing in, causing the fabric to move up and down. The white cloth of the shirt was punctured in a half-dozen places, a diagonal line of bullets across the chest.

'There's your message,' said Jason. 'Now you know what it is. And now I think you'd better listen to what I have to say.'

Marie did not answer him. Instead, she walked slowly to the dress, studying it as if not believing what she saw. Without warning, she suddenly spun around, her eyes glittering, the tears arrested. 'No! It's wrong! Something's terribly *wrong*! Call the embassy.'

'What?'

'Do as I say. *Now!*'

'Stop it, Marie. You've got to understand.'

'No, goddamn you! *You've* got to understand! It wouldn't happen this way. It *couldn't.*'

'It did.'

'Call the embassy! Use that phone over there and call it now! Ask for Corbelier. *Quickly*, for God's sake! If I mean anything to you, do as I ask!'

Bourne could not deny her. Her intensity killing both herself and him. 'What do I tell him?' he asked, going to the telephone.

'Get him first! *That's* what I'm afraid of . . . oh, *God*, I'm frightened!'

'What's the number?'

She gave it to him; he dialled, holding on interminably for the switchboard to answer. When it finally did, the operator was in panic, her words rising and falling, at moments incomprehensible. In the background, he could hear shouts, sharp commands voiced rapidly in English and in French. Within seconds he learned why.

Dennis Corbelier, Canadian attaché, had walked down the steps of the embassy on the avenue Montaigne at 1.40 in the morning and had been shot in the throat. He was dead.

'There's the other part of the message, Jason,' whispered Marie, drained, staring at him. 'And now I'll listen to anything you have to say. Because there *is* someone out there trying to reach you, trying to help you. A message *was* sent, but not to us, not to me. Only to you, and only you were to understand it.'

22

One by one the four men arrived at the crowded Hilton Hotel on Sixteenth Street in Washington, DC. Each went to a separate lift, taking it two or three floors above or below his destination, walking the remaining flights to the correct level. There was no time to meet outside the limits of the District of Columbia; the crisis was unparalleled. These were men of Treadstone Seventy-one – those that remained alive. The rest were dead, slaughtered in a massacre on a quiet, tree-lined street in New York.

Two of the faces were familiar to the public, one more than the other. The first belonged to the ageing senator from Colorado, the second was Brigadier-General I. A. Crawford – Irwin Arthur, freely translated as Iron Ass – acknowledged spokesman for Army Intelligence and defender of the G-Two data banks. The other two men were virtually unknown, except within the corridors of their own operations. One was a middle-aged naval officer, attached to Information Control, 5th Naval District. The fourth and last man was a forty-six-year-old veteran of the Central Intelligence Agency, a slender, coiled spring of anger who walked with a cane. His foot had been blown off by a grenade in South-east Asia; he had been a deep cover agent with the Medusa operation at the time. His name was Alexander Conklin.

There was no conference table in the room; it was an ordinary double bedroom with the standard twin beds, a couch, two armchairs and a coffee table. It was an unlikely spot to hold a meeting of such consequence, there were no spinning computers to light up dark screens with green letters, no electronic communications equipment that would reach consoles in London or Paris or Istanbul. It was a plain hotel room, devoid of everything but four minds that held the secrets of Treadstone Seventy-one.

The senator sat at one end of the couch, the naval officer at the other. Conklin lowered himself into an armchair, stretching his immobile limb out in front of him, the cane between his legs, while Brigadier-General Crawford remained standing, his face flushed, the muscles of his jaw pulsing in anger.

'I've reached the President,' said the senator, rubbing his forehead, the lack of sleep apparent in his bearing. 'I had to; we're meeting tonight. Tell me everything you can, each of you. You begin, General. What in the name of God happened?'

'Major Webb was to meet his car at twenty-three-hundred hours on the corner of Lexington and Seventy-second Street. The time was firm, but he didn't show up. By twenty-three-thirty the driver became alarmed because of the distance to the airfield in New Jersey. The sergeant remembered the address – mainly because he'd been told to forget it – drove round and went to the door. The security bolts had been jammed, and the door just swung open; all the alarms had been shorted out. There was blood on the foyer floor, the dead woman on the staircase. He walked down the hall into the operations room and found the bodies.'

'That man deserves a very quiet promotion,' said the naval officer.

'Why do you say that?' asked the senator.

Crawford replied. 'He had the presence of mind to call the Pentagon and insist on speaking with covert transmissions, domestic. He specified the scrambler frequency, the time and the place of reception, and said he had to speak with the sender. He didn't say a word to anyone until he got me on the phone.'

'Put him in the War College, Irwin,' said Conklin grimly, holding his cane. 'He's brighter than most of the clowns you've got over there.'

'That's not only unnecessary, Conklin,' admonished the senator, 'but patently offensive. Go on, please, General.'

Crawford exchanged looks with the CIA man. 'I reached Colonel Paul McClaren in New York, ordered him over there, and told him to do absolutely nothing until I arrived. I then phoned Conklin and George here, and we flew up together.'

'I called a Bureau print team in Manhattan,' added Conklin. 'One we've used before, and can trust. I didn't tell them what we were looking for, but I told them to sweep the place and give what they found only to me.' The CIA man stopped, lifting his cane in the direction of the naval officer. 'Then George fed them thirty-seven names, all men whose prints we knew were in the FBI files. They came up with the one set we didn't expect, didn't want . . . didn't believe.'

'Delta's,' said the senator.

'Yes,' concurred the naval officer. 'The names I submitted were those of anyone – no matter how remote – who might have learned the address of Treadstone, including, incidentally, all of us. The room had been wiped clean; every surface; every knob, every glass – except one. It was a broken brandy glass, only a few fragments in the corner under a curtain, but it was enough. The prints were there: third and index fingers, right hand.'

'You're absolutely positive?' asked the senator slowly.

'The prints can't lie, sir,' said the officer. 'They were there, moist brandy still on the fragments. Outside this room, Delta's the only one who knows about Seventy-first Street.'

'Can we be sure of that? The others may have said something.'

'No possibility,' interrupted the brigadier-general. 'Abbott would never have revealed it and Elliot Stevens wasn't given the address until fifteen minutes before he got there, when he called from a phone booth. Beyond that, assuming the worst, he would hardly ask for his own execution.'

'What about Major Webb?' pressed the senator.

'The major,' replied Crawford, 'was radioed the address by me after he landed at Kennedy Airport. As you know, it was a G-Two frequency and scrambled. I remind you, he also lost his life.'

'Yes, of course.' The ageing senator shook his head. 'It's unbelievable. *Why?*'

'I should like to bring up a painful subject,' said Brigadier-General Crawford. 'At the outset, I was not enthusiastic about the candidate. I understood David's reasoning and agreed he was qualified, but if you recall, he wasn't my choice.'

'I wasn't aware we had that many choices,' said the senator. 'We had a man – a qualified man, as you agreed – who was willing to go in deep cover for an indeterminate length of time, risking his life every day, severing all ties with his past. How many such men exist?'

'We might have found a more balanced one,' countered the brigadier. 'I pointed that out at the time.'

'You pointed out,' corrected Conklin, 'your own definition of a balanced man, which *I*, at the time, pointed out was a crock.'

'We were *both* in Medusa, Conklin,' said Crawford, angrily yet reasonably. 'You don't have exclusive insight. Delta's conduct in the field was continuously and overtly hostile to command. I was in a position to observe that pattern somewhat more clearly than you.'

'Most of the time he had every right to be. If you'd spent more time in the field and less in Saigon you would have understood that. *I* understood it.'

'It may surprise you,' said the brigadier, holding his hand up in a gesture of truce, 'but I'm not defending the gross stupidities often rampant in Saigon, no one could. I'm trying to describe a pattern of behaviour that could lead to the night before last on Seventy-first Street.'

The CIA man's eyes remained on Crawford; his hostility vanished as he nodded his head. 'I know you are. Sorry. That's the crux of it, isn't it? It's not easy for me; I worked with Delta in half a dozen sectors, was stationed with him in Phnom-Penh before Medusa was even a gleam in the Monk's eye. He was never the same after Phnom-Penh; it's why he went into Medusa, why he was willing to become Cain.'

The senator leaned forward on the couch. 'I've heard it, but tell me again. The President has to know everything.'

'His wife and two children were killed on a pier in the Mekong River, bombed and strafed by a stray aircraft – nobody knew which side's – the identity never uncovered. He hated that war, hated everybody in it. He snapped.' Conklin paused, looking up at the brigadier. 'And I think you're right, General. He snapped again. It was in him.'

'What was?' asked the senator sharply.

'The explosion, I guess,' said Conklin. 'The dam burst. He'd gone beyond his limits and the hate took over. It's not hard, you have to be very careful. He killed those men, that woman, like a madman on a deliberate rampage. None of them expected it, except perhaps the woman who was upstairs and probably heard the shouts . . . He's not Delta any more. We created a myth called Cain, only it's not a myth any longer. It's really him.'

'After so many months . . .' The senator leaned back, his voice trailing off. 'Why did he come back? From where?'

'From Zürich,' answered Crawford. 'Webb was in Zürich and I think he's the only one who could have brought him back. The "why" we may never know unless he expected to catch all of us there.'

'He doesn't know who we are,' protested the senator. 'His only contacts were the Yachtsman, his wife and David Abbott.'

'And Webb, of course,' added the general.

'Of course,' agreed the senator. 'But not at Treadstone, not even him.'

'It wouldn't matter,' said Conklin, tapping the rug once with his cane. 'He knows there's a board; Webb might have told him we'd all be there, reasonably expecting that we would. We've got a lot of questions – six months' worth, and now several million dollars. Delta would consider it the perfect solution. He could take us and disappear. No traces.'

'Why are you so certain?'

'Because, one, he was *there*,' replied the intelligence man, raising his voice. 'We have his prints on a glass of brandy that wasn't even finished. And, two, it's a classic trap with a couple of hundred variations.'

'Would you explain that?'

'You remain silent,' broke in the general, watching Conklin, 'until your enemy can't stand it any longer and exposes himself.'

'And we've become the enemy? *His* enemy?'

'There's no question about it now,' said the naval officer. 'For whatever reasons, Delta's turned. It's happened before – thank heaven, not very often. We know what to do.'

The senator once more leaned forward on the couch. 'What *will* you do?'

'His photograph has never been circulated,' explained Crawford. 'We'll circulate it now. To every station and listening post, every source and informant we have. He has to go somewhere, and he'll start with a place he knows, if only to buy another identity. He'll spend money; he'll be found. When he is, the orders will be clear.'

'You'll bring him in at once?'

'We'll kill him,' said Conklin simply. 'You don't bring in a man like Delta, and you don't take the risk that another government will. Not with what he knows.'

'I can't tell the President that! There are laws.'

'Not for Delta,' said the agent. 'He's beyond the law. He's beyond salvage.'

'Beyond . . .'

'That's right, Senator,' interrupted the general. 'Beyond salvage. I think you know the meaning of the phrase. You'll have to make the decision whether or not to define it for the President. It might be better to . . .'

'You've got to explore *everything*,' said the senator, cutting off the officer. 'I spoke to Abbott last week. He told me a strategy was in progress to reach Delta. Zürich, the bank, the naming of Treadstone; it's all part of it, isn't it?'

'It is, and it's over,' said Crawford. 'If the evidence on Seventy-first Street isn't enough for you, that should be. Delta was given a clear signal to come in. He didn't. What more do you want?'

'I want to be absolutely certain!'

'I want him dead.' Conklin's words, though spoken softly, had the effect of a sudden, cold wind. 'He not only broke all the rules we each set down for ourselves – no matter what – but he sunk into the pits. He reeks; he *is* Cain. We've used the name Delta so much – not even Bourne, but Delta – that I think we've forgotten. Gordon Webb was his brother. Find him. Kill him.'

Book 3

23

It was ten minutes to three in the morning when Bourne approached the Auberge du Coin's front desk, Marie continuing directly to the entrance. To Jason's relief, there were no newspapers on the counter, but the night clerk behind it was from the same mould as his predecessor in the centre of Paris. He was a balding, heavy-set man with half-closed eyes, leaning back in a chair, his arms folded in front of him, the weary depression of his interminable night hanging over him. But this night, thought Bourne, would be one he'd remember for a long time to come – quite apart from the damage to an upstairs room which would not be discovered until morning. A night clerk in Montrouge must have his own transportation.

'I've just called Rouen,' said Jason, his hands on the counter, an angry man, furious with uncontrollable events in his personal world. 'I have to leave at once and need to rent a car.'

'Why not?' snorted the man, getting out of the chair. 'What would you prefer, Monsieur? A golden chariot or a magic carpet?'

'I beg your pardon?'

'We rent rooms, not cars.'

'I *must* be in Rouen before morning.'

'Impossible. Unless you find a taxi crazy enough to take you at this hour.'

'I don't think you understand. I could sustain considerable losses and embarrassment if I'm not at my office by eight o'clock. I'm willing to pay generously . . .'

'You have a problem, Monsieur.'

'Surely there's someone here who would be willing to lend me his car for, say . . . a thousand, fifteen hundred francs.'

'A thousand . . . *fifteen hundred*, Monsieur?' The clerk's half-closed eyes widened until his skin was taut. 'In cash, Monsieur?'

'Naturally. My companion would return it tomorrow evening . . .'

'There's no rush, Monsieur.'

'I beg your pardon? Of course, there's really no reason why I couldn't hire a taxi. Confidentiality can be paid for.'

'I wouldn't know where to *reach* one,' interrupted the clerk in persuasive frenzy. 'On the other hand, my Renault is not so new, perhaps, and perhaps, not the fastest machine on the road, but it is a serviceable car, even a worthy car . . .'

The chameleon had changed his colours again, had been accepted again for someone he was not. But he knew now who he was and he understood.

Daybreak. But there was no warm room at a village inn, no wallpaper mottled by the early light streaking through a windown, filtered by the weaving leaves outside. Rather, the first rays of the sun spread up from the east, crowning the French countryside, defining the fields and hills of St Germain-en-Laye. They sat in the small car parked off the shoulder of a deserted back road, cigarette smoke curling out through the partially open windows.

He had begun that first narrative three weeks before in Switzerland with the words: *My life began six months ago on a small island in the Mediterranean called Île de Port Noir.*

He had begun this with a quiet declaration: *I'm known as Cain.*

He had told it all, leaving out nothing he could remember, including the terrible images that had exploded in his mind when he had heard the words spoken by Jacqueline Lavier in the candelabra'd restaurant in Argenteuil. Names, incidents, cities . . . assassinations.

Medusa.

'Everything fitted. There wasn't anything I didn't know, nothing that wasn't somewhere in the back of my head, trying to get out. It was the truth.'

'It *was* the truth,' repeated Marie.

He looked closely at her. 'We were wrong, don't you see?'

'Perhaps. But also right. You were right, and I was right.'

'About what?'

'You. I have to say it again, calmly and logically. You offered your life for mine before you knew me; that's not the decision of the man you've described. If that man existed, he doesn't any longer.' Marie's eyes pleaded, while her voice remained controlled. 'You said it, Jason. "What a man can't remember doesn't exist. For him." Maybe that's what you're faced with. Can you walk away from it?'

Bourne nodded; the dreadful moment had come. 'Yes,' he said. 'But alone. Not with you.'

Marie inhaled on her cigarette, watching him, her hand trembling. 'I see. That's your decision, then?'

'It has to be.'

'You will heroically disappear so I won't be tainted.'

'I have to.'

'Thank you very much, and who the hell do you think you are?'

'What?'

'Who the *hell* do you think you *are*?'

'I'm a man they call Cain. I'm wanted by governments – by the police – from Asia to Europe. Men in Washington want to kill me because of what they think I know; an assassin named Carlos wants me shot in the throat because of what I've done to him. Think about it for a moment. How long do you think I can keep running before someone in one of those armies out there finds me, traps me, *kills* me? Is that the way you want your life to end?'

'Good God, no!' shouted Marie, something obviously very much on her analytical mind. 'I intend to rot in a Swiss prison for fifty years, or be hanged for things I never did in Zürich!'

'There's a way to take care of Zürich. I've thought about it, I can do it.'

'How?' She stabbed out her cigarette in the ashtray.

'For God's sake, what *difference* does it make? A confession. Turning myself in, I don't know yet, but I can *do* it! I can put your life back together. I *have* to put it back!'

'Not *that* way.'

'Why not?'

Marie reached for his face, her voice now soft once more, the sudden stridency gone. 'Because I've just proved my point again. Even the condemned man – so sure of his own guilt – should see it. The man called Cain would never do what you just offered to do. For anyone.'

'I *am* Cain!'

'Even if I were forced to agree that you were, you're not now.'

'The ultimate rehabilitation? A self-induced lobotomy? Total loss of recall? That happens to be the truth, but it won't stop anyone who's looking for me. It won't stop him – them – from pulling a trigger.'

'That happens to be the worst, and I'm not ready to concede it.'

'Then you're not looking at the facts.'

'I'm looking at two facts you seem to have disregarded. I can't. I'll live with them for the rest of my life because I'm responsible. Two men were killed in the same brutal way because they stood between you and a message someone was trying to send you. Through me.'

'You saw Corbelier's message. How many bullet holes were there? Ten, fifteen?'

'Then he was used! You heard him on the phone and so did I. He wasn't lying; he was trying to help us. If not you, certainly me.'

'It's . . . possible.'

'*Anything*'s possible! I have no answers, Jason, only discrepancies, things that can't be explained – that *should* be explained. You haven't once, *ever*, explained or displayed a *need* or a *drive* for what you say you might have been! And without those things a man like that couldn't be. Or you couldn't be *him*.'

'I'm him.'

'Listen to me. You're very dear to me, my darling, and that could blind me, I know it. But I also know something about myself. I'm no wide-eyed flower child; I've seen a share of this world, and I look very hard and very closely at those who attract me. Perhaps to confirm what I like to think are my values – and they *are* values. Mine, nobody else's.' She stopped for a moment and moved away from him. 'I've watched a man being tortured – by himself and by others – and he won't cry out. You may have silent screams, but you won't let them be anyone else's burden but your own. Instead, you probe and dig and try to understand. And that, my friend, is not the mind of a cold-blooded killer, any more than what you've done and want to do for me. I don't know what you were before, or what crimes you're guilty of, but they're not what you believe – what others want you to believe. Which brings me back to those values I spoke of. I know myself. I couldn't love the man you say you are.

I love the man I know you are. You just confirmed it again. No killer would make the offer you just made. And that offer, sir, is respectfully rejected.'

'You're a goddamn fool!' exploded Jason. 'I can help you; you can't help me! Leave me *something* for Christ's sake!'

'I won't! Not that way! . . .' Suddenly Marie broke off. Her lips parted. 'I think I just did,' she said, whispering.

'Did what?' asked Bourne angrily.

'Gave us both something.' She turned back to him. 'I just said it; it's been there a long time. "What others want you to believe . . .".'

'What the hell are you talking about?'

'Your crimes . . . what others want you to believe are your crimes.'

'They're there. They're mine.'

'Wait a minute. Suppose they were there but they *weren't* yours? Suppose the evidence was planted – as expertly as it was planted against me in Zürich – but it belongs to someone else. Jason, you don't *know* when you lost your memory.'

'Port Noir.'

'That's when you began to build one, not when you lost it. *Before* Port Noir; it could explain so much. It could explain *you*, the contradiction between you and the man people think you are.'

'You're wrong. Nothing could explain the memories – the images – that come back to me.'

'Maybe you just remember what you've been told,' said Marie. 'Over and over and over again. Until there was nothing else. Photographs, recordings, visual and aural stimulae.'

'You're describing a walking, functioning vegetable who's been brainwashed. That's not me.'

She looked at him, speaking gently. 'I'm describing an intelligent, very ill man whose background conformed with what other men were looking for. Do you know how easily such a man might be found? They're in hospitals everywhere, in private sanatoriums, in military wards.' She paused, then continued quickly. 'That newspaper article told another truth. I'm reasonably proficient with computers; anyone doing what I do would be. If I were looking for a curve-example that incorporated isolated factors, I'd know how to do it. Conversely, if someone was looking for a man suffering from amnesia, whose background incorporated specific skills, languages, racial characteristics, the medical data banks could provide candidates. God knows, not many in your case; perhaps only a few, perhaps only one. But one man was all they were *looking* for, all they *needed*.'

Bourne glanced at the countryside, trying to pry open the steel doors of his mind, trying to find a semblance of the hope she felt. 'What you're saying is that I'm a reproduced illusion,' he said, making the statement flatly.

'That's the end effect, but it's not what I'm saying. I'm saying it's possible you've been manipulated. Used. It would explain so much.' She touched his hand. 'You tell me there are times when things want to burst out of you – blow your head apart.'

'Words – places, names – they trigger things.'

'Jason, isn't it possible they trigger the false things? The things you've been told over and over again, but you can't relive. You can't see them clearly, because they're *not* you.'

'I doubt it. I've seen what I can do. I've done them before.'

'You could have done them for other reasons! . . . *Goddamn you*, I'm fighting for my life! For *both* our lives! . . . All right! You can think and feel. Think *now, feel* now! Look at me and tell me you've looked inside yourself, inside your thoughts and feelings, and you know without a doubt you're an assassin called Cain! If you can do that – *really* do that – then bring me to Zürich, take the blame for everything, and get out of my *life*! But if you can't, stay with me and let me help you. And love me, for God's sake. *Love* me, Jason.'

Bourne took her hand, holding it firmly, as one might an angry, trembling child. 'It's not a question of feeling or thinking. I saw the account at the Gemeinschaft; the entries go back a long time. They correspond with all the things I've learned.'

'But that account, those entries, could have been created yesterday, or last week, or six months ago! Everything you've heard and read about yourself could be part of a pattern designed by those who want you to take Cain's place! You're *not* Cain, but they want you to think you are, want others to think you are! But there's someone out there who knows you're not Cain and he's trying to tell you . . . I have my proof, too. My lover's alive, but two friends are dead because they got between you and the one who's sending you the message, who's trying to save your life. They were killed by the same people who want to sacrifice you to Carlos in place of Cain . . . You said before that everything fitted. It didn't, Jason, but *this* does! It explains *you.*'

'A hollow shell who doesn't even own the memories he thinks he has? With demons running around inside kicking hell out of the walls? It's not a pleasant prospect.'

'Those aren't demons, my darling. They're parts of you – angry, furious, screaming to get out because they don't belong in the shell you've given them.'

'And if I blow that shell apart, what'll I find?'

'Many things. Some good, some bad, a great deal that's been hurt. But Cain won't be there, I promise you that. I believe in you, my darling. Please don't give up.'

He kept his distance, a glass wall between them. 'And if we're wrong? Finally wrong? What then?'

'Leave me quickly. Or kill me. I don't care.'

'I love you.'

'I know. That's why I'm not afraid.'

'I found two telephone numbers in Lavier's office. The first was for Zürich, the other here in Paris. With any luck, they can lead me to the one number I need.'

'New York? Treadstone?'

'Yes. The answer's there. If I'm not Cain, someone at that number knows who I am.'

*

They drove back to Paris on the assumption that they would be far less obvious among the crowds of the city than in an isolated country inn. A blond-haired man wearing tortoise-shell glasses and a striking but stern-faced woman, devoid of make-up and with her hair pulled back like an intense graduate student at the Sorbonne, were not out of place in Montmartre. They took a room at the Terrasse on the rue de Maistre, registering as a married couple from Brussels.

In the room, they stood for a moment, no words necessary for what each was seeing and feeling. They came together, touching, holding, closing out the abusive world that refused them peace, that kept them balancing on taut wires next to each other, high above a dark abyss; if either fell, it was the end for both.

Bourne could not change his colour for the immediate moment. It would be false, and there was no room for artifice. 'We need some rest,' he said. 'We've got to get some sleep. It's going to be a long day.'

They made love. Gently, completely, each with the other in the warm, rhythmic comfort of the bed. And there was a moment, a foolish moment, when adjustment of an angle was breathlessly necessary and they laughed. It was a quiet laugh, at first even an embarrassed laugh, but the observation was there, the appraisal of foolishness intrinsic to something very deep between them. They held each other more fiercely when the moment passed, more and more intent on sweeping away the awful sounds and the terrible sights of a dark world that kept them spinning in its winds. They were suddenly breaking out of that world, plunging into a much better one where sunlight and blue water replaced the darkness. They raced towards it feverishly, furiously, and then they burst through and found it.

Spent, they fell asleep, their fingers entwined.

Bourne woke first, aware of the horns and the engines in the Paris traffic below in the streets. He looked at his watch; it was ten past one in the afternoon. They had slept nearly five hours, probably less than they needed, but it was enough. It *was* going to be a long day. Doing what, he was not sure; he only knew that there were two telephone numbers that had to lead him to a third. In New York.

He turned to Marie, breathing deeply beside him, her face – her striking, lovely face – angled down on the edge of the pillow, her lips parted, inches from his lips. He kissed her and she reached for him, her eyes still closed.

'You're a frog and I'll make you a prince,' she said in a sleep-filled voice. 'Or is it the other way around?'

'As expanding as it may be, that's not in my present frame of reference.'

'Then you'll have to stay a frog. Hop around, little frog. Show off for me.'

'No temptations. I only hop when I'm fed flies.'

'Frogs eat flies? I guess they do. Shudder; that's awful.'

'Come on, open your eyes. We've both got to start hopping. We've got to start hunting.'

She blinked and looked at him. 'Hunting for what?'

'For me,' he said.

From a telephone booth on the rue Lafayette, a reverse charge call was placed to a number in Zürich by a Mr Briggs. Bourne reasoned that Jacqueline Lavier would have wasted no time sending out her alarms; one must have been flashed to Zürich.

When he heard the ring in Switzerland, Jason stepped back and handed the phone to Marie. She knew what to say.

She had no chance to say it. The international operator in Zürich came on the line.

'We regret that the number you have called is no longer in service.'

'It was the other day,' broke in Marie. 'This is an emergency, operator. Do you have another number?'

'The telephone is no longer in service, Madame. There is no alternative number.'

'I may have been given the wrong one. It's most urgent. Could you give me the name of the party who had this number?'

'I'm afraid that's not possible.'

'I told you; it's an emergency! May I speak with your superior, please?'

'He would not be able to help you. This number is an unpublished listing. Good afternoon, Madame.'

The connection was broken. 'It's been disconnected,' she said.

'It took too goddamn long to find that out,' replied Bourne, looking up and down the street. 'Let's get out of here.'

'You think they could have traced it *here*? In Paris? To a public phone?'

'Within three minutes an exchange can be determined, a district pinpointed. In four, they can narrow the blocks down to half a dozen.'

'How do you *know* that?'

'I wish I could tell you. Let's go.'

'*Jason.* Why not wait out of sight? And watch?'

'Because I don't know what to watch for and they do. They've got a photograph to go by; they could station men all over the area.'

'I don't look anything like the picture in the papers.'

'Not you. Me. Let's go!'

They walked rapidly within the erratic ebb and flow of the crowds until they reached the boulevard Malesherbes ten blocks away, and another telephone box, this with a different exchange from the first. This time there were no operators to go through; this was Paris. Marie stepped inside, coins in her hand and dialled; she was prepared.

But the words that came over the line so astonished her:

'*La résidence du General Villiers. Bonjour? . . . Allo? Allo?*'

For a moment Marie was unable to speak. She simply stared at the telephone. '*Je regrette,*' she whispered, '*un faux numéro.*' She hung up.

'What's the matter?' asked Bourne, opening the glass door. 'What happened? Who was it?'

'It doesn't make sense,' she said. 'I just reached the house of one of the most respected and powerful men in France.'

24

'André François Villiers,' repeated Marie, lighting a cigarette. They had returned to their room at the Terrasse to sort things out, to absorb the astonishing information. 'Graduate of St Cyr, hero of the Second World War, a legend in the Resistance, and, until his break over Algeria, de Gaulle's heir-apparent. Jason, to connect such a man with Carlos is simply unbelievable.'

'The connection's there. Believe it.'

'It's almost too difficult. Villiers is old-line honour-of-France, a family traced back to the seventeenth century. Today he's one of the senior deputies in the National Assembly – politically to the right of Charlemagne, to be sure – but very much a law-and-order army man. It's like linking Douglas MacArthur to a Mafia hit man. It *doesn't* make sense.'

'Then let's look for some. What was the break with de Gaulle?'

'Algeria. In the early 'sixties, Villiers was part of the OAS – one of the Algerian colonels under Salan. They opposed the Evian agreements that gave independence to Algeria, believing it rightfully belonged to France.'

' "The mad colonels of Algiers," ' said Bourne, as with so many words and phrases, not knowing where they came from, or why he said them.

'That means something to you?'

'It must, but I don't know what it is.'

'*Think,*' said Marie. 'Why should the "mad colonels" strike a chord with you? What's the first thing that comes to your mind? Quickly!'

Jason looked at her helplessly, then the words came. 'Bombings . . . infiltrations. *Provocateurs.* You study them; you study the mechanisms.'

'*Why?*'

'I don't know.'

'Are decisions based on what you learn?'

'I guess so.'

'What kind of decisions? You decide *what*?'

'Disruptions.'

'What does that mean to you? Disruptions.'

'I don't know! I can't think!'

'All right . . . all right. We'll go back to it some other time.'

'There isn't time. Let's get back to Villiers. After Algeria, what?'

'There was a reconciliation of sorts with de Gaulle; Villiers was never directly implicated in the terrorism, and his military record demanded it. He returned to France – was welcomed, really – a fighter for a lost but respected cause. He resumed his command, rising to the rank of general before going into politics.'

'He's a working politician, then?'

'More a spokesman. An elder statesman. He's still an entrenched militarist, still fumes over France's reduced military stature.'

'Howard Leland,' said Jason. 'There's your connection to Carlos.'

'How? Why?'

'Leland was assassinated because he interfered with the Quai D'Orsay's arms build-ups and exports. We don't need anything more.'

'It seems incredible, a man like that . . .' Marie's voice trailed off; she was struck by recollection. 'His son was murdered. It was a political thing, about five or six years ago.'

'Tell me.'

'His car was blown up on the rue du Bac. It was in all the papers everywhere. *He* was the working politician, like his father a conservative, opposing the socialists and Communists at every turn. He was a young member of parliament, an obstructionist where government expenditure was concerned, but actually quite popular. He was a charming aristocrat.'

'Who killed him?'

'The speculation was Communist fanatics; he'd managed to block some legislation or other that favoured the extreme left wing. After he was murdered, the ranks fell apart and the legislation was passed. Many think that's why Villiers left the army and stood for the National Assembly . . . That's what's so improbable, so contradictory. After all, his son *was* assassinated; you'd think the last person on earth he'd want to have anything to do with would be a professional assassin.'

'There's also something else. You said he was welcomed back to Paris because he was never *directly* implicated in the terrorism . . .'

'If he was,' interrupted Marie, 'It was buried. They're more tolerant of passionate causes over here where patriotism and the bed are concerned. And he was a legitimate hero, don't forget that.'

'But once a terrorist, always a terrorist, don't you forget that.'

'I can't agree. People change.'

'Not about some things. No terrorist ever forgets how effective he's been; he lives on it.'

'How would you know that?'

'I'm not sure I want to ask myself right now.'

'Then don't.'

'But I am sure about Villiers. I'm going to reach him.' Bourne crossed to the bedside table and picked up the telephone book. 'Let's see if he's listed or if that number's private. I'll need his address.'

'You won't get near him. If he's Carlos's connection, he'll be guarded. They'll kill you on sight; they have your photograph remember?'

'It won't help them. I won't be what they're looking for . . . Here it is. Villiers, AF. Parc Monceau.'

'I still can't believe it. Just knowing whom she was calling must have put the Lavier woman in shock.'

'Or frightened her to the point where she'd do anything.'

'Doesn't it strike you as odd that she'd be given that number?'

'Not under the circumstances. Carlos wants his drones to know he isn't kidding. He wants Cain.'

Marie stood up. 'Jason? What's a "drone"?'

Bourne looked up at her. 'I don't know . . . Someone who works blind for somebody else.'

'Blind? Not seeing?'

'Not knowing. Thinking he's doing one thing when he's really doing something else.'

'I don't understand.'

'Let's say I tell you to watch for a car at a certain street corner. The car never shows up, but the fact that you're there tells someone else who's watching for you that something else has happened.'

'Arithmetically, an untraceable message.'

'Yes, I guess so.'

'That's what happened in Zürich. Walther Apfel was a drone. He released that story about the theft not knowing what he was really saying.'

'Which was?'

'It's a good guess that you were being told to reach someone.'

'Treadstone Seventy-one,' said Jason. 'We're back to Villiers. Carlos found me in Zürich through the Gemeinschaft. That means he had to know about Treadstone; it's a good chance that Villiers does too. If he doesn't, there may be a way of getting him to find out for us.'

'How?'

'His name. If he's everything you say he is, he thinks pretty highly of it. The honour-of-France coupled with a pig like Carlos might have an effect. I'll threaten to go to the police, to the papers.'

'He'd simply deny it. He'd say it's outrageous.'

'Let him. It isn't. That was his number in Lavier's office. Besides, any retraction will be on the same page as his obituary.'

'You still have to get to him.'

'I will. I'm part chameleon, remember?'

The tree-lined street in Parc Monceau seemed familiar somehow, but not in the sense that he had walked it before. Instead, it was the atmosphere. Two rows of well-kept stone houses, doors and windows glistening, metalwork shining, steps washed clean, the lighted rooms beyond filled with hanging plants. It was a monied street in a wealthy section of the city, and he knew he had been exposed to one like it before, and that exposure *had* meant something.

It was 7:35 in the evening, the March night cold, the sky clear and the chameleon dressed for the occasion. Bourne's blond hair was covered by a cap, his neck concealed beneath the collar of a jacket that spelled out the name of a messenger service across the back. Slung over his shoulder was a canvas strap attached to a nearly empty satchel; it was the end of this particular messenger's run. He had two or three stops to make, perhaps four or five if he thought they were necessary; he would know in a moment. The envelopes were not really envelopes at all, but brochures advertising the pleasures of the Bâteau Mouche, picked up from a hotel lobby. He would select at random several houses near General Villiers's residence and deposit the brochures in letter boxes. His eyes would record everything they saw, one thing sought above everything else. What kind of security arrangements did Villiers have? Who guarded the general and how many were there?

And because he had been convinced he would find either men in cars or other men walking their posts, he was startled to realize there was no one. André François Villiers, militarist, spokesman for his cause, and the prime connection to Carlos, had no external security arrangements whatsoever. If he was protected, that protection was solely within the house. Considering the enormity of his crime, Villiers was either arrogant to the point of carelessness or a damn fool.

Jason climbed the steps of an adjacent residence, Villiers's door no more than twenty feet away. He deposited the brochure in the slot, glancing up at the windows of Villiers's house, looking for a face, a figure. There was no one.

The door twenty feet away suddenly opened. Bourne crouched, thrusting his hand beneath his jacket for his gun, thinking *he* was a damn fool; someone more observant than he had spotted him. But the words he heard told him it wasn't so. A middle-aged couple – a uniformed maid and a dark-jacketed man – were talking in the doorway.

'Make sure the ashtrays are clean,' said the woman. 'You know how he dislikes ashtrays that are stuffed full.'

'He drove this afternoon,' answered the man. 'That means they're full now.'

'Clean them in the garage; you've got time. He won't be down for another ten minutes. He doesn't have to be in Nanterre until eight-thirty.'

The man nodded, pulling up the lapels of his jacket as he started down the steps. 'Ten minutes,' he said aimlessly.

The door closed and silence returned to the quiet street. Jason stood up, his hand on the railing, watching the man hurry down the pavement. He was not sure where Nanterre was, only that it was a suburb of Paris. And if Villiers was driving there himself, and if he was alone, there was no point in postponing confrontation.

Bourne shifted the strap on his shoulder and walked rapidly down the steps, turning left on the pavement. Ten minutes.

Jason watched through the windscreen as the door opened and General André François Villiers came into view. He was a medium-sized, barrel-chested man in his late sixties, perhaps early seventies. He was hatless, with close-cropped grey hair and a meticulously-groomed white chin beard. His bearing was unmistakably military, imposing his body on the surrounding space, entering it by breaking it, invisible walls collapsing as he moved.

Bourne stared at him, fascinated, wondering what insanities could have driven such a man into the obscene world of Carlos. Whatever the reasons, they had to be powerful, for *he* was powerful. And that made him dangerous – for he was respected and had the ears of his government.

Villiers turned, speaking to the maid and glancing at his wristwatch. The woman nodded, closing the door, as the general walked briskly down the steps and around the bonnet of a large saloon to the driver's side. He opened the door and climbed in, then started the engine and rolled slowly out into the middle of the street. Jason waited until the saloon reached the corner and turned right; he eased the Renault away from the kerb and accelerated, reaching the intersection in time to see Villiers turn right again a block east.

There was a certain irony in the coincidence, an omen if one could believe in such things. The route General Villiers chose to the outlying suburb of Nanterre included a stretch of back road in the countryside nearly identical to the one in St Germain-en-Laye where twelve hours ago Marie had pleaded with Jason not to give up – his life or hers. There were stretches of pasture land, fields that fused into the gently rising hills; but instead of being crowned by early light, these were washed in the cold, white rays of the moon. It occurred to Bourne that this stretch of isolated road would be as good a spot as any on which to intercept the returning general.

It was not difficult for Jason to follow at distances up to a quarter of a mile, which was why he was surprised to realize he had practically caught up with the old soldier. Villiers had suddenly slowed down and was turning into a gravelled drive cut out of the woods, the parking area beyond illuminated by floodlights. A sign, hanging from two chains on a high-angle post, was caught in the spill.

L'Arbalète. The general was meeting someone for dinner at an out-of-the-way restaurant, not *in* the suburb of Nanterre but close by. In the country.

Bourne drove past the entrance and pulled off the shoulder of the road, the right side of the car covered by foliage; he had to think things out . . . he had to control himself. There was a fire in his mind; it was growing, spreading. He was suddenly consumed by an extraordinary possibility.

Considering the shattering events – the enormity of the embarrassment experienced by Carlos last night at the motel in Montrouge, it was more than likely that André Villiers had been summoned to an out-of-the-way restaurant for an emergency meeting. Perhaps even with Carlos *himself.* If that was the case, the premises would be guarded, and a man whose photograph had been distributed to those guards would be shot the instant he was recognized. On the other hand, the chance to observe a nucleus belonging to Carlos – or Carlos himself – was an opportunity that might never come again. He had to get inside L'Arbalète. There was a compulsion within him to take the risk. *Any* risk! It was crazy! But then he was not sane. Sane as a man with a memory was sane. *Carlos. Find Carlos! God in heaven, why?*

He felt the gun in his belt; it was secure. He got out and put on his overcoat, covering the jacket with the lettering across the back. He picked up a narrow-brimmed hat from the seat, the cloth soft, angled down on all sides; it would cover his hair. Then he tried to remember if he had been wearing the tortoise-shell glasses when the photograph was taken in Argenteuil. He had not; he had removed them at the table when successive bolts of pain had seared through his head, brought on by words that told him of a past too familiar, too frightening to face. He felt his shirt pocket; the glasses were there if he needed them. He pressed the door closed and started for the woods.

The glare of the restaurant floodlights filtered through the trees, growing brighter with each several yards, less foliage to block the light. Bourne reached the edge of the short patch of forest, the gravelled parking area in front of him. He was at the side of the rustic restaurant, a row of small windows running the length of the building, flickering candles beyond the glass illuminating the figures of the diners. Then his eyes were drawn to the first floor – although it did not extend the length of the building but only halfway, the rear section an open terrace. The enclosed part, however, was similar to the ground floor. A line of windows, a bit larger, perhaps, but still in a row, and again glowing with candles. Figures were milling about, but they were different from the diners below.

They were all men. Standing, not sitting; moving casually, glasses in hands, cigarette smoke spiralling over their heads. It was impossible to tell how many – more than ten, less than twenty, perhaps.

There *he* was, crossing from one group to another, the white beard a beacon, switching on and off as it was intermittently blocked by figures nearer the windows. General Villiers had, indeed, driven out to Nanterre for a meeting, and the odds favoured a conference that dealt with the failures of the past forty-eight hours, failures that permitted a man named Cain to remain alive.

The odds. What were the odds? Where were the guards? How many, and where were their stations? Keeping behind the edge of the woods, Bourne side-stepped his way towards the front of the restaurant, bending branches silently, his feet over the underbrush. He stood motionless, watching for men concealed in the foliage or in the shadows of the building. He saw none, and retraced his path, breaking new ground until he reached the rear of the restaurant.

A door opened, the spill of light harsh, and a man in a white jacket emerged. He stood for a moment, cupping his hands, lighting a cigarette. Bourne looked to the left, to the right, above to the terrace; no one appeared. A guard stationed in the area would have been alarmed by the sudden light ten feet below the conference. There were no guards outside. Protection found – as it had to be at Villiers's house in Parc Monceau – within the building itself.

Another man appeared in the doorway, also wearing a white jacket, but with the addition of a chef's hat. His voice was angry, his French laced with the guttural dialect of Gascony. 'While you piss off, we sweat! The pastry cart is half empty. Fill it. *Now*, you bastard!'

The pastry man turned and shrugged; he crushed out his cigarette and went back inside, closing the door behind him. The light vanished, only the wash of the moon remained, but it was enough to illuminate the terrace. There was no one there, no guard patrolling the wide double doors that led to the inside room.

Carlos. Find Carlos. Trap Carlos. Cain is for Charlie, and Delta is for Cain.

Bourne judged the distance and the obstacles. He was no more than forty feet from the rear of the building, ten or twelve below the railing that bordered the terrace. There were two vents in the exterior wall, vapour escaping from both and next to them a drainpipe that was within reach of the railing. If he could scale the pipe and manage to get a toehold in the lower vent, he would be able to grab a rung of the railing and pull himself up to the terrace. But he could do none of this wearing the overcoat; he took it off, placing it at his feet, the soft-brimmed hat on top and covered both with undergrowth. Then he stepped to the edge of the woods and raced as quietly as possible across the gravel to the drainpipe.

In the shadows he tugged at the fluted metal: it was strongly in place. He reached as high as he could, then sprang up, gripping the pipe, his feet pressed into the wall, pedalling one on top of the other until his left foot was parallel to the first vent. Holding on, he slipped his foot into the recess, and propelled himself further up the drain. He was within eighteen inches of the railing; one surge launched from the vent and he could reach the bottom rung.

The door crashed open beneath him, white light shooting across the gravel into the woods. A figure plummeted out, weaving to maintain its balance, followed by the white-hatted chef who was screaming.

'You piss-ant! You're drunk, that's what you are! You've been drunk the whole shit-filled night! Pastries all over the dining-room floor . . . everything a mess. Get out, you'll not get a *sou*!'

The door was pulled shut, the sound of a bolt unmistakably final. Jason held onto the pipe, arms and ankles aching, rivulets of sweat breaking out on his forehead. The man below staggered backwards, making obscene gestures repeatedly with his right hand for the benefit of the chef who was no longer there. His glazed eyes wandered up the wall, settling on Bourne's face. Jason held his breath as their eyes met; the man stared, then blinked, and stared again. He shook his head, closing his lids, then opened them wide, taking in the sight he was not entirely sure was there. He backed away, lurching into a sideslip and a forward walk, obviously deciding that the apparition halfway up the wall was the result of his pressured labours. He weaved around the corner of the building, a man more at peace with himself for having rejected the foolishness that had assaulted his eyes.

Bourne breathed again, letting his body slump against the wall in relief. But it was only for a moment; the ache in his ankle had descended to his foot, a cramp forming. He lunged, grabbing the iron bar that was the base of the railing with his right hand, whipping his left up from the drainpipe, joining it. He pressed his knees into the tiles and pulled himself slowly up the wall until his head was over the edge of the terrace. It was deserted. He kicked his right leg up to the ledge, his right hand reaching for the wrought-iron top; balanced, he swung over the railing.

He was on a terrace used for dining in the spring and summer months, a tiled floor that could accommodate ten to fifteen tables. In the centre of the wall separating the enclosed section from the terrace were the wide double doors he had seen from the woods. The figures inside were now motionless, standing still, and for an instant Jason wondered whether an alarm had been set off – whether they were waiting for him. He stood immobile, his hand on his gun; nothing happened. He approached the wall, staying in the shadows.

Once there, he pressed his back against the wood and edged his way towards the first door until his fingers touched the frame. Slowly, he inched his head up to the pane of glass level with his eyes and looked inside.

What he saw was both mesmerizing and not a little frightening. The men were in lines – three separate lines, four men to a line – facing André Villiers, who was addressing them. Thirteen men in all, twelve of them not merely standing, but standing at attention. They were old men, but not merely old men; they were old soldiers. None wore uniforms; instead in each lapel they wore ribbons, regimental colours above decorations for valour and rank. And if there was one all-pervasive note about the scene, it, too, was unmistakable. These were men used to command – used to power. It was in their faces, their eyes, in the way they listened – respect rendered but not blindly, judgment ever present. Their bodies were old, but there was strength in that room. Immense strength. That was the frightening aspect. If these men belonged to Carlos, the assassin's resources were not only far-reaching, they were extraordinarily dangerous. For these were not ordinary men; they were seasoned professional soldiers. Unless he was grossly mistaken, thought Bourne, the depth of experience and range of influence in that room was staggering.

The mad colonels of Algiers, what was left of them? Men driven by memories of a France that no longer existed, a world that was no more, replaced by one they found weak and ineffectual. Such men could make a pact with Carlos, if only for the covert power it gave them. Strike. Attack. Dispatch. Decisions of life and death that were once a part of their fabric brought back by a force that could serve causes they refused to admit were no longer viable. Once a terrorist, always a terrorist, and assassination was the raw core of terror.

The general was raising his voice; Jason tried to hear the words through the glass. They became clearer.

'. . . our presence will be felt, our purpose understood. We are together in our stand, and that stand is immovable; we *shall* be heard! In memory of all those who have fallen – our brothers of the tunic and the cannon – who laid down their lives for the glory of France. We shall force our beloved country to remember, and in their names to remain strong, *lackey to no one*! Those who oppose us will know our anger. In this, too, we are united. We pray to Almighty God that those who have gone before us have found peace, for we are still in conflict . . . Gentlemen. I give you our Lady. Our France.'

There was a murmur of muttered approvals, the old soldiers remaining rigidly at attention. And then another voice was raised, the first five words sung singly, joined at the sixth by the rest of the group.

Allons, enfants de la patrie,
Le jour de gloire est arrivé . . .

Bourne turned away, sickened by the sight and the sounds inside that room. Lay waste in the name of glory; the death of fallen comrades perforce demands further death. It is required; and if it means a pact with Carlos, so be it.

What disturbed him so? Why was he suddenly swept by feelings of anger and futility? What triggered the revulsion he felt so strongly? And then he knew. He hated a man like André Villiers, despised the men in that room. They were all old men who made war, stealing life from the young . . . and the very young.

Why were the mists closing in again? Why was the pain so acute? There was no time for questions, no strength to tolerate them. He had to push them out of his mind, and concentrate on André François Villiers, warrior and warlord, whose causes belonged to yesterday but whose pact with an assassin called for death today.

He would trap the general. Break him. Learn everything he knew and probably kill him. Men like Villiers robbed life from the young and the very young. They did not deserve to live. *I am in my labyrinth again, and the walls are embedded with spikes. Oh, God, they hurt.*

Jason climbed over the railing in the darkness and lowered himself to the drainpipe, each muscle aching. Pain, too, had to be erased. He had to reach a deserted stretch of road in the moonlight and trap a broker of death.

25

Bourne waited in the Renault two hundred yards east of the restaurant entrance, the motor running, prepared to race ahead the instant he saw Villiers drive out. Several others had already left, all in separate cars. Conspirators did not advertise their association, and these old men were conspirators in the truest sense. They had traded whatever honours they had earned for the lethal convenience of an assassin's gun and an assassin's organization. Age and bias had robbed them of reason, as they had spent their lives robbing life . . . from the young and the very young.

What was it? Why won't it leave me? Some terrible thing is deep inside me, trying to break out, trying I think to kill me. The fear and the guilt sweep through me . . . but of what and for what I do not know. Why should these withered old men provoke such feelings of fear and guilt . . . and loathing?

They were war. They were death. On the ground and from the skies. From the skies . . . from the skies. Help me, Marie. For God's sake, help me!

There it was. The headlights swung out of the drive, the long black chassis reflecting the wash of the floodlights. Jason kept his own lights off as he pulled out of the shadows. He accelerated down the road until he reached the first curve, where he switched on the headlights and pressed the pedal to the floor. The isolated stretch of countryside was roughly two miles away; he had to get there quickly.

It was ten past eleven and, as three hours before, the fields swept into the hills, both bathed in the light of the March moon, now in the centre of the sky. He reached the area; it *was* feasible. The shoulder was wide, bordering a pasture, which meant that both cars could be pulled off the road. The immediate objective, however, was to get Villiers to stop. The general was old but not feeble; if the tactic were suspect, he would break over the grass and race away. Everything was timing, and a totally convincing moment of the unexpected.

Bourne swung the Renault around in a U-turn, waited until he saw the headlights in the distance, then suddenly accelerated, swinging the wheel violently back and forth. The car careened over the road – an out-of-control driver, incapable of finding a straight line, but nevertheless speeding.

Villiers had no choice; he slowed down, as Jason came racing insanely towards him. Then abruptly, when the two cars were no more than twenty feet from colliding, Bourne spun the wheel to the left, braking as he did so, sliding into skid, tyres screecbing. He came to a stop, the window open, and raised his voice in an undefined cry. Half shout, half scream; it could have been the vocal explosion of an ill man or a drunk man, but the one thing it was not was threatening. He slapped his hand on the frame of the window and was silent, crouching in the seat, his gun on his lap.

He heard the door of Villiers's saloon open and peered through the steering wheel. The old man was not visibly armed; he seemed to suspect nothing, relieved only that a collision had been avoided. The general walked through the beams of the headlights to the Renault's left window, his shouts anxious, his French the interrogating commands of Saint Cyr.

'What's the meaning of this? What do you think you're *doing*? Are you all right?' His hands gripped the base of the window.

'Yes, but you're not,' replied Bourne in English, raising the gun.

'*What?* . . .' The old man gasped, standing erect. 'Who are you and what is this?'

Jason got out of the Renault, his left hand extended above the barrel of the weapon. 'I'm glad your English is fluent. Walk back to your car. Drive it off the road.'

'And if I refuse?'

'I'll kill you right now. It wouldn't take much to provoke me.'

'Do these words come from the Red Brigades? Or the Paris branch of the Baader-Meinhof?'

'Why? Could you countermand them if they did?'

'I spit at them! And you!'

'No one's ever doubted your courage, General. Walk to your car.'

'It's not a matter of courage!' said Villiers, without moving. 'It's a question of logic. You'll accomplish *nothing* by killing me, less by kidnapping me. My orders are firm, fully understood by my staff and my family. The Israelis are absolutely right! There can be no negotiations with terrorists. Use your gun, *garbage*! Or get *out* of here!'

Jason studied the old soldier, suddenly profoundly uncertain, but not about to be fooled. It would be in the furious eyes that stared at him. One name soaked in filth coupled with another name heaped with the honours of his nation would cause another kind of explosion; it would be in the eyes.

'Back at that restaurant, you said France shouldn't be a lackey to anyone. But a general of France became someone's lackey. General André Villiers, messenger for Carlos . . . Carlos's contact, Carlos's soldier, Carlos's lackey.'

The furious eyes did grow wide, but not in any way Jason expected. Fury was suddenly joined by hatred, not shock, not hysteria, but deep, uncompromising abhorrence. The back of Villiers's hand shot up, arching from his waist, the crack against Bourne's face sharp, accurate, painful. It was followed by a forward slap, brutal, insulting, the force of the blow reeling Jason back on his feet. The old man moved in, blocked by the barrel of the gun but unafraid, undeterred by its presence, intent only on inflicting punishment. The blows came one after another, delivered by a man possessed.

'*Pig!*' screamed Villiers. 'Filthy, *detestable pig! Garbage!*'

'I'll shoot! I'll *kill* you! Stop it!' But Bourne could not pull the trigger. He was backed into the small car, his shoulders pressed against the roof. Still the old man attacked, his hands flying out, swinging up, crashing down.

'Kill me if you *can*, if you dare! Dirt! *Filth!*'

Jason threw the gun to the ground, raising his arms to fend off Villiers's assault. He lashed his left hand out, grabbing the old man's right wrist, then his left, gripping the left forearm that was slashing down like a broadsword. He twisted both violently, bending Villiers into him, forcing the old soldier to stand motionless, their faces inches from each other, the old man's chest heaving.

'Are you telling me you're *not* Carlos's man? Are you denying it?'

Villiers lunged forward, trying to break Bourne's grip, his barrel-like chest smashing into Jason. 'I *revile* you! *Animal!*'

'*Goddamn* you, yes or no!'

The old man spat in Bourne's face, the fire in his eyes now clouded, tears welling. 'Carlos killed my son,' he said in a whisper. 'He killed my only son on the rue du Bac. My son's life was blown up with five sticks of dynamite on the *rue du Bac!*'

Jason slowly reduced the pressure of his fingers. Breathing heavily, he spoke as calmly as he could.

'Drive your car into the field and stay there. We have to talk, General. Something's happened you don't know about, and we'd both better learn what it is.'

'*Never!* Impossible! It could not happen!'

'It happened,' said Bourne, sitting with Villiers in the front seat of his car.

'An incredible mistake has been made! You don't know what you're saying!'

'No mistake, and I do know what I'm saying because I found the number myself. It's not only the right number, it's a magnificent cover. Nobody in his right mind would connect you with Carlos, especially in light of your son's death. Is it common knowledge he was Carlos's kill?'

'I would prefer different language, Monsieur.'

'Sorry. I mean that.'

'Common knowledge? Among the Sûreté, a qualified yes. Within military intelligence and Interpol, most certainly. I read the reports.'

'What did they say?'

'It was presumed that Carlos did a favour for his friends from his radical days. Even to the point of allowing them to appear silently responsible for the act. It was politically motivated, you know. My son was a sacrifice, an example to others who opposed the fanatics.'

'Fanatics?'

'The extremists were forming a false coalition with the socialists, making promises they had no intention of keeping. My son understood this, exposed it and initiated legislation to block the alignment. He was killed for it.'

'Is that why you retired from the army and stood for election?'

'With all my heart. It is customary for the son to carry on for the father . . .' The old man paused, the moonlight illuminating his haggard face. 'In this matter, it was the father's legacy to carry on for the son. He was no soldier, nor I a politician, but I am no stranger to weapons and explosives. His causes were moulded by me, his philosophy reflected my own, and he was killed for these things. My decision was clear to me. I would carry our beliefs into the political arena and let his enemies contend with me. The soldier was prepared for them.'

'More than one soldier, I gather.'

'What do you mean?'

'Those men back there at the restaurant. They looked as if they ran half the armies in France.'

'They did, Monsieur. They were once known as the angry young commanders of Saint Cyr. The Republic was corrupt, the army incompetent, the Maginot a joke. Had they been heeded in their time, France would not have fallen. They became the leaders of the Resistance; they fought the Boche and Vichy all through Europe and Africa.'

'What do they do now?'

'Most live on pensions, many obsessed with the past. They pray to the Virgin that it will never be repeated. In too many areas, however, they see it happening. The army is reduced to a sideshow. Communists and socialists in the Assembly are for ever eroding the strength of the services. The Moscow apparatus runs true to form: it does not change with the decades. A tree society is ripe for infiltration and, once infiltrated, the changes do not stop until that society is remade in another image. Conspiracy is everywhere; it cannot go unchallenged.'

'Some might say that sounds pretty extreme itself.'

'For what? Survival? Strength? Honour? Are these terms too anachronistic for you?'

'I don't think so. But I can imagine a lot of damage being done in their names.'

'Our philosophies differ and I don't care to debate them. You asked me about my associates and I answered you. Now, please, this incredible misinformation of yours. It's appalling. You don't know what it's like to lose a son, to have a child killed.'

The pain comes back to me and I don't know why. Pain and emptiness, a vacuum in the sky . . . from the sky. Death in and from the skies. Jesus, it hurts. It. What is it?

'I can sympathize,' said Jason, his hands gripped to stop the sudden trembling. 'But it fits.'

'Not for an instant! As you said, no one in his right mind would connect me to Carlos, least of all the killer pig himself. It's a risk he would not take. It's unthinkable.'

'Exactly. Which is why you're being used; it is unthinkable. You're the perfect relay for final instructions.'

'Impossible! How?'

'Someone at your number is in direct contact with Carlos. Codes are used, certain words spoken, to get that person on the line. Probably when you're not there, possibly when you are. Do you answer the telephone yourself?'

Villiers frowned. 'Actually, I don't. Not that number. There are too many people to be avoided and I have a private line.'

'Who does answer it?'

'Generally the housekeeper, or her husband who serves as part butler, part chauffeur. He was my driver during my fast years in the army. If not either of them, my wife, of course. Or my aide, who often works at my office at the house; he was *my* adjutant for twenty years.'

'Who else?'

'There is no one else.'

'Maids?'

'None permanent; if they're needed, they're hired for an occasion. There's more wealth in the Villiers name than in the banks.'

'Cleaning woman?'

'Two. They come twice a week and not always the same two.'

'You'd better take a closer look at your chauffeur and the adjutant.'

'Preposterous! Their loyalty is beyond question.'

'So was Brutus's, and Caesar outranked him.'

'You can't be serious . . .'

'I'm goddamned serious! And you'd better believe it. Everything I've told you is the truth.'

'But then you haven't really told me very much, have you? Your name, for instance.'

'It's not necessary. Knowing it could only hurt you.'

'In what way?'

'In the very remote chance that I'm wrong about the relay – and that possibility barely exists.'

The old man nodded the way old men do when repeating words that have stunned them to the point of disbelief. His lined face moved up and down in the moonlight. 'An unnamed man traps me on a road at night, holds me under a gun and makes an obscene accusation – a charge so filthy I wish to kill him – and he expects me to accept his word. The word of a man without a name, with no face I recognize, and no credentials offered other than the statement that Carlos is hunting him. Tell me why should I believe this man?'

'Because,' answered Bourne. 'He'd have no reason to come to you if *he* didn't believe it was the truth.'

Villiers stared at Jason. 'No, there's a better reason. A while ago you gave me my life. You threw down your gun, you did not fire it. You could have. Easily. You chose, instead, to plead with me to talk.'

'I don't think I pleaded.'

'It was in your eyes, young man. It's always in the eyes. And often in the voice, but one must listen carefully. Supplication can be feigned, not anger. It is either real or it's a posture. Your anger was real . . . as was mine.' The old man gestured towards the small Renault ten yards away in the field. 'Follow me back to Parc Monceau. We'll talk further in my office. I'd swear on my life that you're wrong about both men, but then as you pointed out, Caesar was blinded by false devotion. And indeed he did outrank me.'

'If I walk into that house and someone recognizes me, I'm dead. So are you.'

'My aide left shortly past five o'clock this afternoon, and the chauffeur, as you call him, retires no later than ten to watch his interminable television. You'll wait outside while I go in and check. If things are normal, I'll summon you; if they're not, I'll come back out and drive away. Follow me again. I'll stop somewhere and we'll continue.'

Jason watched closely as Villiers spoke. 'Why do you want me to go back to Parc Monceau?'

'Where else? I believe in the shock of unexpected confrontation. One of those men is lying in bed watching television in a room on the second floor. And there's another reason. I want my wife to hear what you have to say. She's an old soldier's woman and she has antennae for things that often escape the officer in the field. I've come to rely on her perceptions, she may recognize a pattern of behaviour once she hears you.'

Bourne had to say the words. 'I trapped you by pretending one thing, you can trap me by pretending another. How do I know Pare Monceau isn't a trap?'

The old man did not waver. 'You have the word of a general of France, and that's all you have. If it's not good enough for you, take your weapon and get out.'

'It's good enough,' said Bourne. 'Not because it's a general's word, but because it's the word of a man whose son was killed on the rue du Bac.'

The drive back into Paris seemed far longer to Jason than the journey out. He was fighting images again, images that caused him to break out into sweat. And pain, starting at his temples, sweeping down through his chest, forming a knot in his stomach – sharp bolts pounding until he wanted to scream.

Death in the skies . . . from the skies. Not darkness, but blinding sunlight. No winds that batter my body into further darkness, but instead silence and the stench of jungle and . . . river banks. Stillness followed by the screeching of birds and the screaming pitch of machines. Birds . . . machines . . . racing downwards out of the sky in blinding sunlight. Explosions. Death. Of the young and the very young.

Stop it! Hold the wheel! Concentrate on the road but do not think! Thought is too painful and you don't know why.

They entered the tree-lined street in Parc Monceau. Villiers was a hundred feet ahead, facing a problem that had not existed several hours ago. There were many more cars in the street now, parking at a premium.

There was, however, one sizeable space on the left, opposite the general's house, it could accommodate both their cars. Villiers thrust his hand out of the window, gesturing for Jason to pull in behind him.

And then it happened. His eyes were drawn by a light in a doorway, his focus suddenly rigid on the figures in the spill; the recognition of one so startling and so out of place he found himself reaching for the gun in his belt.

Had he been led into a trap after all? Had the word of an officer of France been *worthless*?

Villiers was manoeuvring his car into place. Bourne spun round in the seat, looking in all directions; there was no one coming towards him, no one closing in. It was *not* a trap. It was something else, part of what was happening about which the old soldier knew nothing.

For across the street at the top of the steps of Villiers's house stood a youngish woman – a striking woman – in the doorway. She was talking rapidly, with small anxious gestures, to a man standing on the top step, who kept nodding as if accepting instructions. That man was the grey-haired, distinguished-looking switchboard operator from Les Classiques. The man whose face Jason knew so well, yet did not know. The face that had triggered other images . . . images as violent and as painful as those which had ripped him apart during the past half hour in the Renault.

But there was a difference. This face brought back the darkness and torrential winds in the night sky, explosions coming one after another, sounds of a staccato gunfire echoing through the myriad tunnels of a jungle.

Bourne pulled his eyes away from the door and looked at Villiers through the windscreen. The general had switched off his headlights and was about to get out of the car. Jason released the clutch and rolled forward until he made contact with the saloon's bumper. Villiers whipped around in his seat.

Bourne extinguished his own headlights and turned on the small inside roof light. He raised his hand – palm downward – then raised it twice again, telling the old soldier to stay where he was. Villiers nodded, and Jason switched off the light.

He looked back at the doorway. The man had taken a step down, stopped by a last command from the woman; Bourne could see her clearly now. She was in her middle to late thirties, with short dark hair, stylishly cut, framing a face that was bronzed by the sun. She was a tall woman, statuesque, actually, her figure tapered, the swell of her breasts accentuated by the sheer, close-fitting fabric of a long white dress that heightened the tan of her skin. Villiers had not mentioned her, which meant she was not part of the household. She was a visitor who knew when to come to the old man's home, it would fit the strategy of relay-removed-from-relay. And that meant she had a contact in Villiers's house. The old man had to know her, but how well? The answer obviously was not well enough.

The grey-haired switchboard operator gave a final nod, descended the steps and walked rapidly down the street. The door closed, the light of the carriage lamps shining on the deserted staircase and the glistening black door with its brass metalwork.

Why did those steps and that door mean something to him? Images. Reality that was not real.

Bourne got out of the Renault, watching the windows, looking for the movement of a curtain; there was nothing. He walked quickly to Villiers's car; the front window was rolled down, the general's face turned up, his thick eyebrows arched in curiosity.

'What in heaven's name are you doing?' he asked.

'Over there, at your house,' said Jason, crouching on the pavement. 'You saw what I just saw.'

'I believe so. And?'

'Who was the woman? Do you know her?'

'I would hope to God I did. She's my wife.'

'Your *wife*?' Bourne's shock was on his face. 'I thought you said . . . I thought you said she was an *old* woman. That you wanted her to listen to me because over the years you'd learned to respect her judgement. In the field, you said. That's what you *said*.'

'Not exactly. I said she was an *old soldier's* woman. And I do, indeed, respect her judgment. But she's my second wife – my very much younger second wife – but every bit as devoted as my first, who died eight years ago.'

'Oh, my God . . .'

'Don't let the disparity of our ages concern you. She is proud and happy to be the second Madame Villiers. She's been a great help to me in the Assembly.'

'I'm sorry,' whispered Bourne. 'Christ, I'm sorry.'

'What about? You mistook her for someone else? People frequently do: she's a stunning girl. I'm quite proud of her.' Villiers opened the door as Jason stood up on the pavement. 'You wait here,' said the general, 'I'll go inside and check; if everything's normal, I'll open the door and signal you. If it isn't, I'll come back to the car and we'll drive away.'

Bourne remained motionless in front of Villiers, preventing the old man from stepping forward. 'General, I've got to ask you something. I'm not sure how, but I have to. I told you I found your number at a relay drop used by Carlos. I didn't tell you where, only that it was confirmed by someone who admitted passing messages to and from contacts of Carlos.' Bourne took a breath, his eyes briefly on the door across the street, 'Now I've got to ask you a question, and please think carefully before you answer. Does your wife buy clothes at a shop called Les Classiques?'

'In Saint-Honoré?'

'Yes.'

'I happen to know she does not.'

'Are you sure?'

'Very much so. Not only have I never seen a bill from there, but she's told me how much she dislikes its designs. My wife is very knowledgeable in matters of fashion.'

'Oh, Jesus.'

'What?'

'General, I can't go inside that house. No matter what you find, I can't go in there.'

'Why not? What are you saying?'

'The man on the steps who was talking to your wife. He's from the drop; it's Les Classiques. He's a contact to Carlos.'

The blood drained from André Villiers's face. He turned and stared across the tree-lined street at his house, at the glistening black door and the brass fittings that reflected the light of the carriage lamps.

The pockmarked beggar scratched the stubble of his beard, took off his threadbare beret and trudged through the bronze doors of the small church in Neuilly-sur-Seine.

He walked down the far right aisle under the disapproving glances of two priests. Both clerics were upset; this was a wealthy parish and, biblical compassion notwithstanding, wealth did have its privileges. One of them was to maintain a certain status of worshipper – for the benefit of other worshippers – and this elderly, dishevelled derelict hardly fitted the mould.

The beggar made a feeble attempt to genuflect, sat down in a pew in the second row, crossed himself and knelt forward, his head in prayer, his right hand pushing back the left sleeve of his overcoat. On his wrist was a watch somewhat in contradistinction to the rest of his apparel. It was an expensive digital, the numbers large and the readout bright. It was a possession he would never be foolish enough to part with, for it was a gift from Carlos. He had once been twenty-five minutes late for confession, upsetting his benefactor, and had no other excuse but the lack of an accurate timepiece. During their next appointment, Carlos had pushed it beneath the translucent scrim separating sinner from holy man.

It was the hour and the minute. The beggar rose and walked towards the second booth on the right. He parted the curtain and went inside.

'Angelus Domini.'

'Angelus Domini, child of God.' The whisper from behind the black cloth was harsh. 'Are your days comfortable?'

'They are made comfortable . . .'

'Very well,' interrupted the silhouette. 'What did you bring me? My patience draws to an end. I pay thousands – *hundreds* of thousands – for incompetence and failure. What happened in Montrouge? Who was responsible for the lies that came from the embassy in the Montaigne? Who *accepted* them?'

'The Auberge du Coin was a trap, yet not one for killing. It is difficult to know exactly what it was. If the attaché named Corbelier repeated lies, our people are convinced he was not aware of it. He was duped by the woman.'

'He was duped by Cain! Bourne traces each source, feeding each one false information, thus exposing each and confirming the exposure. But why? To whom? We know what and who he is now, but he relays nothing to Washington. He refuses to surface.'

'To suggest an answer,' said the beggar, 'I would have to go back many years, but it's possible he wants no interference from his superiors. American intelligence has its share of vacillating autocrats, rarely communicating fully with one another. In the days of the cold war, money was made selling information three and four times over to the same stations. Perhaps Cain waits until he thinks there is only one course of action to be taken, no different strategies to be argued by those above.'

'Age hasn't dulled your sense of manoeuvre, old friend. It's why I called upon you.'

'Or perhaps,' continued the beggar, 'he really has turned. It's happened.'

'I don't think so, but it doesn't matter. Washington thinks he has. The Monk is dead, they're all dead at Treadstone. Cain is established as the killer.'

'The Monk?' said the beggar. 'A name from the past; he was active in Berlin, in Vienna. We knew him well, from a distance and healthier for it. There's your answer, Carlos. It was always the Monk's style to reduce the numbers to as few as possible. He operated on the theory that his circles were infiltrated, compromised. He must have ordered Cain to report only to him. It would explain Washington's confusion, the six months of silence.'

'Would it explain ours? For six months there was no word, no activity.'

'A score of possibilities. Illness, exhaustion, brought back for new training. Even to spread confusion to the enemy. The Monk had a cathedral full of tricks.'

'Yet before he died he said to an associate that he did *not* know what had happened. That he wasn't even certain the man *was* Cain.'

'Who was the associate?'

'A man named Gillette. He was our man, but Abbott couldn't have known it.'

'Another possible explanation. The Monk had an instinct about such men. It was said in Vienna that David Abbott would distrust Christ on the mountain and look for a bakery.'

'It's possible. Your words are comforting; you look for things others do not look for.'

'I've had far more experience; I was once a man of stature. Unfortunately I pissed away the money.'

'You still do.'

'A profligate, what can I tell you?'

'Obviously something else.'

'You're perceptive, Carlos. We should have known each other in the old days.'

'Now you're presumptuous.'

'Always. You know that I know you can swat my life away at any moment you choose, so I must be of value. And not merely with words that come from experience.'

'What have you to tell me?'

'This may not be of great value, but it is something. I put on respectable clothes and spent the day at the Auberge du Coin. There was a man, an obese man – questioned and dismissed by the Süreté – whose eyes were too unsteady; and he perspired too much. I had a chat with him, showing him an official NATO identification I had made in the early 'fifties. It seems he negotiated the rental of his car at three o'clock yesterday morning. To a blond man in the company of a woman. The description fits the photograph from Argenteuil.'

'A rental?'

'Supposedly. The car was to be returned within a day or so by the woman.'

'It will never happen.'

'Of course not, but it raises a question, doesn't it? Why would Cain go to the trouble of obtaining a car in such a fashion?'

'To get as far away as possible as rapidly as possible.'

'In which case the information *has* no value,' said the beggar. 'But then there are so many ways to travel faster less conspicuously. And Bourne could hardly trust an avaricious night clerk; he might easily look for a reward from the Süreté. Or anyone else.'

'What's your point?'

'I suggest that Bourne could have obtained that car for the sole purpose of following someone here in Paris. No loitering in public where he might be spotted, no rented cars that could be traced, no frantic searches for elusive taxis. Instead, a simple exchange of licence plates and a nondescript black Renault in the crowded streets. Where would one begin to look?'

The silhouette turned. 'The Lavier woman,' said the assassin softly. 'And everyone else he suspects at Les Classiques. It's the only place he has to start. They'll be watched, and within days – hours perhaps – a nondescript black Renault will be seen and he'll be found. Do you have a full description of the car?'

'Down to three dents in the left rear bumper.'

'Good. Spread the word to the old men. Comb the streets, the garages, the parking areas. The one who finds it will never have to look for work again.'

'Speaking of such matters . . .'

An envelope was slipped between the taut edge of the curtain and the blue felt of the frame. 'If your theory proves right, consider this a token.'

'I am right, Carlos.'

'Why are you so convinced?'

'Because Cain does what you would do, what I would have done – in the old days. He must be respected.'

'He must be killed,' said the assassin. 'There's symmetry in the timing. In a few days it will be the twenty-fifth of March. On 25 March 1968, Jason Bourne was executed in the jungles of Tam Quan. Now, years later – nearly to the day – another Jason Bourne is hunted, the Americans as anxious as we are to see him killed. I wonder which of us will pull the trigger this time.'

'Does it matter?'

'I want him,' whispered the silhouette. 'He was never real and that's his crime against me. Tell the old men that, if any find him, to get word to Parc Monceau but do nothing. Keep him in sight, but do *nothing*! I want him alive on the twenty-fifth of March. On 25 March I'll execute him myself, and deliver his body to the Americans.'

'The word will go out immediately.'

'Angelus Domini, child of God.'

'Angelus Domini,' said the beggar.

26

The old soldier walked in silence beside the younger man down the moonlit path in the Bois de Boulogne. Neither spoke for too much had already been said – admitted, challenged, denied and reaffirmed. Villiers had to reflect and analyse, to accept or violently reject what he had heard. His life would be far more bearable if he could strike back in anger, attack the lie and find his sanity again. But he could not do that with impunity; he was a soldier and to turn away was not in him.

There was too much truth in the younger man. It was in his eyes, in his voice, in his every gesture that asked for understanding. The man without a name was not lying. The ultimate treason was in Villiers's house. It explained so many things he had not dared to question before. An old man wanted to weep.

For the man without a memory there was little to change or invent; the chameleon was not called upon. His story was convincing because the most vital part was based in the truth. He had to find Carlos, learn what the assassin knew, there would be no life for him if he failed. Beyond this he would say nothing. There was no mention of Marie St Jacques, or the Île de Port Noir, or a message being sent by person or persons unknown, or a walking hollow shell that might or might not be someone he was or was not – who could not even be sure that the fragments of memories he possessed were really his own. None of this was spoken of.

Instead, he recounted everything he knew about the assassin called Carlos. That knowledge was so vast that during the telling Villiers stared at him in astonishment, recognizing information he knew to be highly classified, shocked at new and startling data that was in concert with a dozen existing theories, but to his ears never before put forth with such clarity. Because of his son, the general had been given access to his country's most secret files on Carlos and nothing in those records matched the younger man's array of facts.

'This woman you spoke with in Argenteuil, the one who telephones my house, who admitted being a courier to you . . .'

'Her name is Lavier,' Bourne interrupted.

The general paused. 'Thank you . . . She saw through you, she had your photograph taken.'

'Yes.'

'They had no photograph before?'

'No.'

'So as you hunt Carlos, he in turn hunts you. But you have no photograph; you only know two couriers, one of which was at my house.'

'Yes.'

'Speaking with my wife.'

'Yes.'

The old man turned away, the period of silence had begun.

They came to the end of the path where there was a miniature lake. It was bordered with white gravel, benches spaced every ten to fifteen feet, circling the water like a guard of honour surrounding a grave of black marble. They walked to the second bench. Villiers broke his silence.

'I should like to sit down,' he said. 'With age there comes a paucity of stamina. It often embarrasses me.'

'It shouldn't,' said Bourne, sitting down beside him.

'It shouldn't,' agreed the general, 'but it does.' He paused for a moment, adding quietly, 'Frequently in the company of my wife.'

'That's not necessary,' said Jason.

'You mistake me.' The old man turned to the younger. 'I'm not referring to the bed. There are simply times when I find it necessary to curtail activities – leave a dinner party early, absent myself on weekends to the Mediterranean, or decline a few days on the slopes in Gstaad.'

'I'm not sure I understand.'

'My wife and I are often apart. In many ways we live quite separate lives, taking pleasure, of course, in each other's pursuits.'

'I still don't understand.'

'Must I embarrass myself further?' said Villiers. 'When an old man finds a stunning young woman anxious to share his life, certain things are understood, others not so readily. There is, of course, financial security and in my case a degree of public exposure. Creature comforts, entry into the great houses, easy friendship with the celebrated, it's all very understandable. In exchange for these things, one brings a beautiful companion into his home, shows her off among his peers – a form of continuing virility, as it were. But there are always doubts.' The old soldier stopped for several moments, what he had to say was not easy for him. 'Will she take a lover?' he continued softly. 'Does she long for a younger, firmer body, one more in tune with her own? If she does, one can accept it – even be relieved, I imagine – hoping to God she has the sense to be discreet. A cuckolded statesman loses his constituency faster than a sporadic drunk, it means he's fully lost his grip . . . There are other worries. Will she abuse his name? Publicly condemn an adversary whom one is trying to win over? These are the inclinations of the young, they are manageable, part of the risks in the exchange . . . But there is one underlying doubt that if proved justified cannot be tolerated. And that is if she is part of a design. From the beginning.'

'You've felt it then?' asked Jason quietly.

'Feelings are not reality!' shot back the old soldier vehemently. 'They have no place in observing the field.'

'Then why are you telling me this?'

Villiers's head arched back, then fell forward, his eyes on the water. 'There could be a simple explanation for what we both saw tonight. I pray there is, and I shall give her every opportunity to provide it.' The old man paused again. 'But in my heart I know there isn't. I knew it the moment you told me about Les Classiques. I looked across the street at the door of my house, and suddenly a number of things fell painfully into place. For the past two hours I have played the devil's advocate, there is no point in continuing. There was my son before there was this woman.'

'But you said you trusted her judgment. That she was a great help to you.'

'True. You see, I wanted to trust her, desperately wanted to trust her. The easiest thing in the world is to convince yourself that you're right. As one grows old it is easier still.'

'What fell into place for you?'

'The very help she gave me, the very trust I placed in her.' Villiers turned and looked at Jason. 'You have extraordinary knowledge about Carlos. I've studied those files as closely as any man alive, for I would give more than any man alive to see him caught and executed, I alone the firing squad. And swollen as they are, those files do not approach what you know. Yet your concentration is solely on his kills, his methods of assassination. You've overlooked the other side of Carlos. He not only sells his gun, he sells a country's secrets.'

'I know that,' Bourne said. 'It's not the side . . .'

'For example,' continued the general, as if he had not heard Jason. 'I have access to classified documents dealing with France's military and nuclear security. Perhaps five other men – all above suspicion – share that access. Yet with damning regularity we find that Moscow has learned this, Washington that, Peking something else.'

'You discussed those things with your wife?' asked Bourne, surprised.

'Of course not. Whenever I bring such papers home, they are placed in a vault in my office. No one may enter that room except in my presence. There is only one other person who has a key, one other person who knows the whereabouts of the alarm switch. My wife.'

'I'd think that would be as dangerous as discussing the material. Both could be forced from her.'

'There was a reason. I'm at the age when the unexpected is a daily occurrence; I commend you to the obituary pages. If anything happened to me she is instructed to telephone the Brevet Militaire, go down to my office and stay by that vault until the security personnel arrive.'

'Couldn't she simply stay by the door?'

'Men of my years have been known to pass away at their desks.' Villiers closed his eyes. 'All along it was she. The one house, the one place no one believed possible.'

'Are you sure?'

'More than I dare admit to myself. She was the one who insisted on the marriage. I repeatedly brought up the disparity of our ages but she would have none of it. It was the years together, she claimed, not those that separated our birth dates. She offered to sign an agreement renouncing any claim to the Villiers estate and, of course, I would have none of that, for it was proof of her commitment to me. The adage is quite right; the old fool is the complete fool. . . . Yet there were always the doubts; they came with the trips, with the unexpected separations.'

'Unexpected?'

'She has many interests, for ever demanding her attention. A Franco-Swiss museum in Grenoble, a fine arts gallery in Amsterdam, a monument to the Resistance in Boulogne-sur-Mer, an idiotic oceanography conference in Marseilles. We had a heated argument over that one. I needed her in Paris; there were diplomatic functions. I had to attend and I wanted her with me. She would not stay. It was as though she were being ordered to be here and there and somewhere else at a given moment.'

Grenoble – near the Swiss border, an hour from Zürich. Amsterdam. Boulogne-sur-Mer – on the Channel, an hour from London. Marseilles . . . Carlos.

'When was the conference in Marseilles?' asked Jason.

'Last August, I believe. Towards the latter part of the month.'

'On 24 August at five o'clock in the afternoon, Ambassador Howard Leland was assassinated on the Marseilles waterfront.'

'Yes, I know,' said Villiers. 'You spoke of it before. I mourn the passing of the man, not his judgments.' The old soldier stopped; he looked at Bourne. 'My *God*,' he whispered. 'She had to be with him. Carlos summoned her and she came to him. She *obeyed*.'

'I never went this far,' said Jason. 'I swear to you I thought of her as a relay – a blind relay. I never went this far.'

Suddenly, from the old man's throat came a scream – deep and filled with agony and hatred. He brought his hands to his face, his head arched back once again in the moonlight; and he wept.

Bourne did not move; there was nothing he could do. 'I'm sorry,' he said.

The general regained control. 'And so am I,' he replied finally. 'I apologize.'

'No need to.'

'I think there is. We will discuss it no further. I shall do what has to be done.'

'Which is?'

The soldier sat erect on the bench, his jaw firm. 'You can ask that?'

'I have to ask it.'

'Having done what she's done is no different from having killed the child of mine she did not bear. She pretended to hold his memory dear. Yet she was and is an accomplice to his murder. And all the while she committed a second treason against the nation I have served throughout my life.'

'You're going to kill her?'

'I'm going to kill her. She will tell me the truth and she will die.'

'She'll deny everything you say.'

'I doubt it.'

'That's crazy!'

'Young man, I've spent over half a century trapping and fighting the enemies of France, even when they were Frenchmen. The truth will be heard.'

'What do you think she's going to do? Sit there and listen to you and calmly agree that she's guilty?'

'She'll do nothing calmly. But she'll agree; she'll proclaim it.'

'Why *would* she?'

'Because when I accuse her she'll have the opportunity to kill me. When she makes the attempt, I will have my explanation, won't I?'

'You'd take that risk?'

'I must take it.'

'Suppose she doesn't make the attempt, doesn't try to kill you?'

'That would be another explanation,' Villiers said. 'In that unlikely event, I should look to my flanks if I were you, Monsieur.' He shook his head. 'It will not happen. We both know it, I far more clearly than you.'

'Listen to me,' insisted Jason. 'You say there was your son first. *Think* of *him*! Go after the killer, not the accomplice. She's an enormous wound for you, but he's a greater wound. Get the man who killed your son! In the end, you'll get both. Don't confront her; not yet! Use what you *know* against Carlos. Hunt him with me. No one's ever been this close.'

'You ask more than I can give,' said the old man.

'Not if you think about your *son*. If you think of *yourself*, it is! But not if you think of the rue du Bac!'

'You are excessively cruel, Monsieur.'

'I'm right and you know it.'

A high cloud floated by in the night sky, briefly blocking the light of the moon. Darkness was complete; Jason shivered. The old soldier spoke, resignation in his voice.

'Yes, you are right,' he said. 'Excessively cruel and excessively right. It's the killer, not the whore, who must be stopped. How do we work together? Hunt together?'

Bourne closed his eyes briefly in relief. 'Don't do anything. Carlos must be looking for me all over Paris. I've killed his men, uncovered a drop, found a contact. I'm too close to him. Unless we're both mistaken your telephone will become busier and busier. I'll make sure of it.'

'How?'

'I'll intercept a half a dozen employees of Les Classiques. Several clerks, the Lavier woman, Bergeron maybe, and certainly the man at the switchboard. They'll talk. And so will I. That phone of yours will be busy as hell.'

'But what of me? What do I do?'

'Stay at home. Say you're not feeling well. And whenever that phone rings, stay near whoever else answers. Listen to the conversation, try to pick up codes, question the servants as to what was said to them. You could even listen in. If you hear something, fine, but you probably won't. Whoever's on the line will know you're there. Still, you'll frustrate the relay. And depending upon where your wife is . . .'

'The whore is,' broke in the old soldier.

'. . . in Carlos's hierarchy, we might even force him to come out.'

'Again, how?'

'His lines of communication will be disrupted. The secure, unthinkable relay will be interfered with. He'll demand a meeting with your wife.'

'He would hardly announce the whereabouts.'

'He has to tell *her*!' Bourne paused, another thought coming into focus. 'If the disruption is severe enough, there'll be that one phone call, or that one person you don't know coming to the house, and shortly after, your wife will tell you she has to go somewhere. When it happens insist she leave a number where she can be reached. Be firm about it; you're not trying to stop her from going, but you *must* be able to reach her. Tell her anything – use the relationship *she* developed. Say it's a highly sensitive military matter you can't talk about until you get a clearance. Then you want to discuss it with her before you render a judgment. She might jump at it.'

'What will it serve?'

'She'll be telling you where she is. Maybe where Carlos is. If not Carlos, certainly others closer to him . . . Then reach me. I'll give you a hotel and a room number. The name on the register is meaningless, don't bother about it.'

'Why don't you give me your real name?'

'Because if you ever mentioned it – consciously or unconsciously – you'd be dead.'

'I'm not senile.'

'No, you're not. But you're a man who's been hurt very badly. As badly as a person can be hurt, I think. *You* may risk your life; I won't.'

'You're a strange man, Monsieur.'

'Yes . . . If I'm not there when you call, a woman will answer. She'll know where I am. We'll set up timing for messages.'

'A woman?' The general drew back. 'You've said nothing about a woman, or anyone else.'

'There is no one else. Without her I wouldn't be alive. Carlos is hunting both of us; he's tried to kill both of us.'

'Does she know about me?'

'Yes. She's the one who said it couldn't be true. That you couldn't be allied with Carlos. I thought you were.'

'Perhaps I'll meet her.'

'Not likely. Until Carlos is taken – if he *can* be taken – we can't be seen with you. Of all people, not you. Afterwards – if there is an afterwards – you may not want to be seen with us. With me. I'm being honest with you.'

'I understand that and I respect it. In any event, thank this woman for me. Thank her for thinking I could be no part of Carlos.'

Bourne nodded. 'Can you be sure your private line isn't tapped?'

'Absolutely. It is swept on a regular basis, all the telephones restricted by the Brevet are.'

'Whenever you expect a call from me, answer the phone and clear your throat twice. I'll know it's you. If for any reason you can't talk, tell me to call your secretary in the morning. I'll call back in ten minutes. What's the number?'

Villiers gave it to him. 'Your hotel?' asked the general.

'The Terrasse. Rue de Maistre, Montmartre. Room Four-twenty.'

'When will you begin?'

'As soon as possible. Noon today.'

'Be like a wolf pack,' said the old soldier, leaning forward, a commander instructing his officer corps. 'Strike swiftly.'

27

'She was *so* charming, I simply *must* do something for her,' cried Marie in ebullient French into the telephone. 'Also for the sweet young man; he was of such help. I tell you, the dress was a *succès fou*! I'm *so* grateful.'

'From your descriptions, Madame,' replied the cultured male voice on the switchboard at Les Classiques, 'I'm sure you mean Janine and Claude.'

'Yes, of course. Janine and Claude, I remember now. I'll drop each a note with a token of my thanks. Would you by any chance know their last names? I mean, it seems so crass to address envelopes simply to "Janine" and "Claude". Rather like sending missives to servants, don't you think? Could you ask Jacqueline?'

'It's not necessary, Madame. I know them. And may I say that Madame is as sensitive as she is generous. Janine Dolbert and Claude Oréale.'

'Janine Dolbert and Claude Oréale,' repeated Marie, looking at Jason. 'Janine is married to that cute pianist, isn't she?'

'I don't believe Mademoiselle Dolbert is married to anyone.'

'Of course. I'm thinking of someone else.'

'If I may, Madame, I didn't catch *your* name.'

'How silly of me!' Marie thrust the phone away and raised her voice. 'Darling, you're back, and so soon! That's marvellous. I'm talking to those lovely people at Les Classiques . . . Yes, right away, my dear.' She pulled the phone to her lips. 'Thank you *so* much. You've been *very* kind.' She hung up.

'If you ever decide to get out of economics,' said Jason, poring through the Paris telephone book, 'go into sales. I bought every word you said.'

'Were the descriptions accurate?'

'To a cadaver and a very limp wrist. Nice touch, the pianist.'

'It struck me that if she were married, the phone would be in her husband's name . . .'

'It isn't,' interrupted Bourne. 'Here it is. Dolbert, Janine, rue Losserand.' Jason wrote down the address.

'Oréale, that's with an *O*, isn't it? Not *Au*.'

'I think so.' Marie lit a cigarette. 'You're really going to go to their homes?'

Bourne nodded. 'If I picked them up in Saint-Honoré, Carlos will have it watched.'

'What about the others? Lavier, Bergeron, whoever-he-is on the switch-board.'

'Tomorrow. Today's for the groundswell.'

'The what?'

'Get them all talking. Running around saying things that shouldn't be said. By closing time, word will be spread through the store by Dolbert and Oréale. I'll reach the two others tonight, they'll call Lavier and the man at the switchboard. We'll have the first shock wave and then the second. The general's phone will start ringing this afternoon. By morning the panic should be complete.'

'Two questions,' said Marie, getting up from the edge of the bed and coming towards him. 'How are you going to get two employees away from Les Classiques during working hours? And what people will you get tonight?'

'Nobody lives in a deep freeze,' replied Bourne, looking at his watch. 'Especially in *haute couture*. It's eleven-fifteen now; I'll reach Dolbert's apartment by noon and get the *concierge* to call her at work. He'll tell her to come home right away. There's an urgent, very personal problem she'd better deal with.'

'What problem?'

'I don't know, but who hasn't got one?'

'You'll do the same with Oréale?'

'Probably even more effective.'

'You're outrageous, Jason.'

'I'm deadly serious,' said Bourne, his finger once again sliding down a column of names. 'Here he is. Oréale, Claude Giselle. No comment. Rue Racine. I'll reach him by three: when I'm finished he'll head right back to Saint-Honoré and start screaming.'

'What about the other two? Who are they?'

'I'll get names from either Oréale or Dolbert, or both. They won't know it, but they'll be giving me the second shock wave.'

Jason stood in the shadows of the recessed doorway in rue Losserand. He was fifteen feet from the entrance to Janine Dolbert's small apartment house where moments before a bewildered and richer *concierge* had obliged a well-spoken stranger by calling Mademoiselle Dolbert at work and telling her that a gentleman in a chauffeured limousine had been around twice asking for her. He was back again; what should the *concierge* do?

A small black taxi pulled up to the kerb and an agitated, cadaverous Janine Dolbert literally jumped out. Jason rushed from the doorway, intercepting her on the pavement, only teet from the entrance.

'That was quick,' he said, touching her elbow. 'So nice to see you again. You were very helpful the other day.'

Janine Dolbert stared at him, her lips parted in recollection, then astonishment. '*You.* The American,' she said in English. 'Monsieur Briggs, isn't it? Are you the one who . . . ?'

'I told my chauffeur to take an hour off. I wanted to see you privately.'

'Me? What could you possibly wish to see me about?'

'Don't you know? Then why did you race back here?'

The wide eyes beneath the short bobbed hair were fixed on his, her pale face paler in the sunlight. 'You're from the House of Azur, then?' she asked tentatively.

'I could be.' Bourne applied a bit more pressure to her elbow. 'And?'

'I've delivered what I promised. There will be nothing more, we agreed to that.'

'Are you sure?'

'Don't be an idiot! You don't know Paris *couture*. Someone will get furious with someone else and make bitchy comments in your own studio. What strange deviations! And when the autumn line comes out, with you parading half of Bergeron's designs before *he* does, how long do you think I can stay at Les Classiques? I'm Lavier's number two girl, one of the few who has access to her office. You'd better take care of me as you promised. In one of your Los Angeles shops.'

'Let's take a walk,' said Jason, gently propelling her. 'You've got the wrong man, Janine. I've never heard of the House of Azur and haven't the slightest interest in stolen designs – except where the knowledge can be useful.'

'Oh, my God! . . .'

'Keep walking.' Bourne gripped her arm. 'I said I wanted to talk to you.'

'About what? What do you want from me? How did you get my name?' The words came rapidly now, the phrases overlapping. 'I took an early lunch hour and must return at once; we're very busy today. *Please*, you're hurting my arm.'

'Sorry.'

'What I said; it was foolishness. A lie. On the floor, we've heard rumours; I was testing you. *That's* what I was doing, I was testing you!'

'You're very convincing. I'll accept that.'

'I'm *loyal* to Les Classiques. I've always been loyal.'

'It's a fine quality, Janine. I admire loyalty. I was saying that the other day to . . . what's his name? . . . that nice fellow on the switchboard. What *is* his name? I forget.'

'Philippe,' said the salesgirl, frightened, obsequious. 'Philippe d'Anjou.'

'That's it. Thank you.' They reached a narrow, cobblestone alleyway between two buildings. Jason guided her into it. 'Let's step in here for a moment, just so we're off the street. Don't worry, you won't be late. I'll only take a few minutes of your time.' They walked ten paces into the narrow enclosure. Bourne stopped; Janine Dolbert pressed her back against the brick wall. 'Cigarette?' he asked, taking a packet from his pocket.

'Thank you, yes.'

He lighted it for her, noting that her hand trembled. 'Relaxed now?'

'Yes . . . No, not really. What do you want, Monsieur Briggs?'

'To begin with, the name's not Briggs, but I think you know that.'

'I don't. Why should I?'

'I was sure Lavier's number one girl would have told you.'

'Monique?'

'Use last names, please. Accuracy's important.'

'Brielle, then,' said Janine frowning curiously. 'Does she know you?'

'Why not ask her?'

'As you wish. What *is* it, Monsieur?'

Jason shook his head. 'You really *don't* know, do you? Three-quarters of the employees at Les Classiques are working with us and one of the brightest wasn't even contacted. Of course it's possible someone thought you were a risk; it happens.'

'*What* happens? What risk? Who *are* you?'

'There isn't time now. The others can fill you in. I'm here because we've never received a report from you, and yet you speak to prime customers all day long.'

'You *must* be clearer, Monsieur.'

'Let's say I'm the spokesman for a group of people – American, French, English, Dutch – closing in on a killer who's murdered political and military leaders in each of our countries.'

'*Murdered?* Military, political . . .' Janine's mouth gaped, the ash of her cigarette breaking off, spilling over her rigid hand. 'What *is* this? What are you *talking* about? I've heard none of this!'

'I can only apologize,' said Bourne softly, sincerely. 'You should have been contacted several weeks ago. It was an error on the part of the man before me. I'm sorry, it must be a shock to you.'

'It is a shock, Monsieur,' whispered the salesgirl, her concave body tensed, a bent, lacquered reed against the brick. 'You speak of things beyond my understanding.'

'But now *I* understand,' interrupted Jason. 'Not a word from you about anyone. Now it's clear.'

'It's not to me.'

'We're closing in on Carlos. The assassin known as Carlos.'

'*Carlos?*' The cigarette fell from Dolbert's hand, the shock complete.

'He's one of your most frequent customers, all the evidence points to it. We've narrowed the probabilities down to eight men. The trap is set for some time in the next several days, and we're taking every precaution.'

'Precaution . . . ?'

'There's always the danger of hostages, we all know that. We anticipate gunfire, but it will be kept to a minimum. The basic problem will be Carlos himself. He's sworn never to be taken alive; he walks the streets wired up to explosives calculated to be in excess of a thousand-pound bomb. But we can handle that. Our marksmen will be on the scene; one clean shot to the head and it'll be all over.'

'*Un coup de feu . . .*'

Suddenly Bourne looked at his watch. 'I've taken up enough of your time. You've got to get back to the shop and I have to get back to my post. Remember, if you see me outside, you don't know me. If I come into Les Classiques, treat me as you would any rich client. *Except* if you've spotted a customer you think may be our man; then don't waste time telling me . . . Again, I'm sorry about all this. It was a breakdown in communications, that's all. It happens.'

'*Une rupture . . .*?'

Jason nodded, turned in place, and began walking rapidly out of the alleyway towards the street. He stopped and glanced back at Janine Dolbert.

She was comatose against the wall; for her the elegant world of *haute couture* was spinning wildly out of orbit.

Philippe d' Anjou. The name meant nothing to him, but Bourne could not help himself. He kept repeating it silently, trying to raise an image . . . as the face of the grey-haired switchboard operator gave rise to such violent images of darkness and flashes of light. *Philippe d' Anjou.* Nothing, Nothing at all. Yet there had been something, something that caused Jason's stomach to knot, the muscles taut and inflexible, a flat panel of hard flesh constricted . . . by the darkness.

He sat by the front window and the door of a coffee shop on the rue Racine, prepared to get up and leave the moment he saw the figure of Claude Oréale arrive at the doorway of the ancient building across the street. His room was on the fourth floor, in a flat he shared with two other young men, reached only by climbing a worn, angular staircase. When he did arrive, Bourne was sure he would not be walking.

For Claude Oréale, who had been so effusive with Jacqueline Lavier on another staircase in Saint-Honoré, had been told by a toothless landlady over the phone to get his worthless self quickly back to rue Racine and put a stop to the screaming and smashing of furniture that was taking place in his flat. Either he would stop it, or the gendarmes would be called; he had ten minutes to show up.

He did so in eight. His slight frame, encased in a Pierre Cardin suit – rear flap fluttering in the head wind – could be seen racing up the pavement from the Métro exit two blocks south. He avoided collisions with the agility of an out-of-shape broken field runner trained by the Ballet Russe. His thin neck was thrust forward several inches in front of his waistcoated chest, his long dark hair a flowing mane parallel to the pavement. He reached the entrance and gripped the railing, leaping up the steps and plunging into the shadows of the foyer.

Jason walked rapidly out of the coffee shop and raced across the street. Inside, he ran to the ancient staircase then started up the cracked steps. From the third-floor landing, he could hear the pounding on the door above.

'*Ouvrez. Ouvrez! Vite, nom de Dieu! . . .*'

Oréale stopped, the silence within perhaps more frightening than anything else.

Bourne climbed the remaining steps until he could see Oréale between the bars of the railing and the floor. The clerk's frail body was pressed into the door, his hands on either side, fingers spread, his ear against the wood, his face flushed. Jason shouted in guttural, bureaucratic French as he rushed up into view.

'Sûreté! Stay exactly where you are, young man. Let's not have any unpleasantness. We've been watching you and your friends. We know about the darkroom.'

'No!' screamed Oréale. 'It has nothing to do with me, I swear it! . . . *Darkroom?*'

Bourne raised his hand. 'Be quiet. Don't shout so!' He immediately followed his commands by leaning over the railing and looking below.

'You can't involve *me*!' continued the clerk 'I'm not involved! I've told them over and over again to get rid of it all! One day they'll kill themselves. Drugs are for idiots! . . . My God, it's quiet. I think they're dead!'

Jason stood up from the railing and approached Oréale, his palms raised. 'I told you to shut up,' he whispered harshly. 'Get inside there and be quiet! This was all for the benefit of that old bitch downstairs.'

The clerk was transfixed, his panic suspended in silent bysteria. '*What?*'

'You've got the key,' said Bourne. 'Open up and get inside.'

'It's bolted,' replied Oréale. 'It's always bolted at these times.'

'You damn *fool*, we had to *reach* you! We had to get you here without anyone knowing why. Open that door. *Quickly!*'

Like the terrified rabbit he was, Claude Oréale fumbled in his pocket and found the key. He unlocked the door and pushed it open as a man might enter a storage vault filled with mutilated corpses. Bourne propelled him through the doorframe, stepped inside and closed the door.

What could be seen of the flat belied the rest of the building. The fair-sized living room was filled with sleek, expensive furniture, dozens of red and yellow velvet pillows scattered about on couches, chairs and the floor. It was almost an erotic room, a luxurious sanctuary in the midst of debris.

'I've only got a few minutes,' said Jason. 'No time for anything but business.'

'Business?' asked Oréale, his expression paralysed. 'This . . . this darkroom? *What* darkroom?'

'Forget it. You had something better going.'

'What *business*?'

'We received word from Zürich, and we want you to get it to your friend Lavier.'

'Madame Jacqueline? My *friend*?'

'We can't trust the phones.'

'What phones? The word? *What* word?'

'Carlos is right.'

'Carlos? Carlos who?'

'The assassin.'

Claude Oréale screamed. He brought his hand up to his mouth, bit the knuckle of his index finger, and screamed. 'What are you *saying?*'

'Be *quiet*!'

'Why are you saying it to *me*!'

'You're number five. We're counting on you.'

'Five *what*? *For* what?'

'To help Carlos escape the net. They're closing in. Tomorrow, the next day, perhaps the day after that. He's to stay away; he's *got* to stay away. They'll surround the shop, marksmen every ten feet. The crossfire will be murderous; if he's in there, it could be a massacre. Every one of you. Dead.'

Oréale screamed again, his knuckle red. 'Will you *stop* this! I don't know what you're talking about! You're a maniac and I won't hear another word – I haven't heard *anything*. Carlos, crossfire . . . massacres! God, I'm suffocating . . . I need air!'

'You'll get money. A lot of it, I imagine. Lavier will thank you. Also d'Anjou.'

'*D'Anjou.* He loathes me! He calls me a peacock, insults me every chance he gets.'

'It's his cover, of course. Actually, he's very fond of you – perhaps more than you know. He's number six.'

'What are these *numbers*? Stop talking numbers!'

'How else can we distinguish between you, allocate assignments? We can't use names.'

'*Who* can't?'

'All of us who work for Carlos.'

The scream was ear-shattering as the blood trickled from Oréale's finger. 'I won't *listen*! I'm a couturier, an *artist*!'

'You're number five. You'll do exactly as we say or you'll never see this passion pit of yours again.'

'*Aunghunn!*'

'Stop screaming! We appreciate you; we know you're all under a strain. Incidentally, we don't trust the bookkeeper.'

'Trignon?'

'First names only. Obscurity's important.'

'Pierre, then. He's hateful. He deducts for telephone calls.'

'We think he's working for Interpol.'

'*Interpol?*'

'If he is, you could all spend ten years in prison. *You'd* be eaten alive, Claude.'

'*Aunghunn!*'

'Shut up! Just let Bergeron know what we think. Keep your eyes on Trignon, especially during the next two days. If he leaves the store for any reason watch out. It could mean the trap's closing.' Bourne walked to the door, his hand in his pocket. 'I've got to get back, and so do you. Tell numbers one to six everything I told you. It's vital the word is spread.'

Oréale screamed again, hysterically again. 'Numbers! Always *numbers*! What *number*? I'm an artist, not a number!'

'You won't have a face unless you get back there as fast as you got here. Reach Lavier, d'Anjou, Bergeron. As quickly as you can. Then the others.'

'*What* others?'

'Ask number two.'

'Two?'

'Dolbert. Janine Dolbert.'

'*Janine.* Her too?'

'That's right. She's two.'

The salesman flung his arms wildly above him in helpless protest. 'This is *madness*! Nothing makes sense!'

'Your life does, Claude,' said Jason simply. 'Value it . . . I'll be waiting across the street. Leave here in exactly three minutes. And don't use the phone; just leave and get back to Les Classiques. If you're not out of here in three minutes I'll have to return.' He took his hand out of his pocket. In it was his gun.

Oréale expunged a lungful of air, his face ashen as he stared at the weapon.

Bourne let himself out and closed the door.

The telephone rang on the bedside table. Marie looked at her watch; it was 8:15 and for a moment she felt a sharp jolt of fear. Jason had said he would call at 9:00. He had left La Terrasse after dark, around 7:00, to intercept a salesgirl named Monique Brielle. The schedule was precise, to be interrupted only in emergency. Had something happened?

'Is this room Four-twenty?' asked the deep male voice on the line.

Relief swept over Marie; the man was André Villiers. The general had called late in the afternoon to tell Jason that panic had spread throughout Les Classiques; his wife had been summoned to the phone no less than six times over the span of an hour and a half. Not once, however, had he been able to listen to anything of substance: whenever he had picked up the phone, serious conversation had been replaced by innocuous banter.

'Yes.' said Marie. 'This is Four-twenty.'

'Forgive me, we did not speak before.'

'I know who you are.'

'I'm also aware of you. May I take the liberty of saying thank you.'

'I understand. You're welcome.'

'To substance. I'm telephoning from my office, and, of course, there's no extension for this line. Tell our mutual friend that the crisis has accelerated. My wife has taken to her room, claiming nausea, but apparently she's not too ill to be on the phone. On several occasions, as before, I picked up only to realize that they were alert for any interference. Each time I apologized rather gruffly, saying I expected calls. Frankly, I'm not at all sure my wife was convinced, but of course she's in no position to question me. I'll be blunt, Mademoiselle. There is unspoken friction building up between us, and beneath the surface it is violent. May God give me strength.'

'I can only ask you to remember the objective,' broke in Marie. 'Remember your son.'

'Yes,' said the old man quietly. 'My son. And the whore who claims to revere his memory . . . I'm sorry.'

'It's all right. I'll convey what you've told me to our friend. He'll be calling within the hour.'

'*Please,*' interrupted Villiers. 'There's more. It's the reason I had to reach you. Twice while my wife was on the telephone the voices held meaning for me. The second I recognized; a face came to mind instantly. He's on a switchboard in Saint-Honoré.'

'We know his name. What about the first?'

'It was strange. I did not know the voice, there was no face to go with it, but I understood why it was there. It was an odd voice, half whisper, half command, an echo of itself. It was the command that struck me. You see, that voice was not having a conversation with my wife; it had issued an order. It was altered the instant I got on the line, of course; a pre-arranged signal for a swift good-bye, but the residue remained. That residue, even the tone, is well known to any soldier; it is his means of emphasis. Am I being clear?'

'I think so,' said Marie gently, aware that if the old man was implying what she thought he was, the strain on him had to be unbearable.

'Be assured of it, Mademoiselle,' said the general, 'it was the killer *pig*.' Villiers stopped, his breathing audible, the next words drawn out, a strong man close to weeping. 'He was . . . *instructing* . . . *my* . . . *wife*.' The old soldier's voice cracked. 'Forgive me the unforgivable. I have no right to burden you.'

'You have every right,' said Marie, suddenly alarmed. 'What's happening has to be terribly painful for you, made worse because you have no one to talk to.'

'I am talking to you, Mademoiselle. I shouldn't, but I am.'

'I wish we could keep talking. I wish one of us could be with you. But that's not possible and I know you understand that. Please try to hold on. It's terribly important that no connection be made between you and our friend. It could cost you your life.'

'I think perhaps I have lost it.'

'*C'est ridicule!*' said Marie sharply, an intended slap in the old soldier's face. '*Vous êtes soldat! Arrêtez!*'

'*Ahh, une institutrice parle à l'élève en retard. Vous avez raison.*'

'*On dit que vous êtes un géant. Je le crois.*' There was silence on the line; Marie held her breath. When Villiers spoke she breathed again.

'Our mutual friend is very fortunate. You are a remarkable woman.'

'Not at all. I just want my friend to come back to me. There's nothing remarkable about that.'

'Perhaps not. But I should also like to be your friend. You reminded a very old man of who and what he is. Or who and what he once was, and must try to be again. I thank you for a second time.'

'You're welcome . . . my friend.' Marie hung up, profoundly moved and equally disturbed. She was not convinced Villiers could face the next twenty-four hours and, if he could not, the assassin would know how deeply his apparatus had been penetrated. He would order every contact at Les Classiques to run from Paris and disappear. Or there would be a bloodbath in Saint-Honoré achieving the same result.

If either happened, there would be no answers, no address in New York, no message deciphered nor the sender found. The man she loved would be returned to his labyrinth. And he would leave her.

28

Bourne saw her at the corner, walking under the spill of the streetlight towards the small hotel that was her home. Monique Brielle, Jacqueline Lavier's number one girl, was a harder, more sinewy version of Janine Dolbert, he remembered seeing her at the shop. There was an assurance about her, her stride the stride of a confident woman, secure in the knowledge of her expertise. Very unflappable. Jason could understand why she was Lavier's number one. Their confrontation would be brief, the impact of the message startling, the threat inherent. It was time for the start of the second shock wave. He remained motionless and let her pass on the pavement, her heels clicking martially on the pavement. The street was not crowded, but neither was it deserted; there were perhaps a half dozen people on the block. It would be necessary to isolate her, then steer her out of earshot of any who might overhear the words, for they were words that no messenger would risk being heard. He caught up with her no more than thirty feet from the entrance to the small hotel, he slowed his pace to hers, staying at her side.

'Get in touch with Lavier right away,' he said in French, staring straight ahead.

'Pardon? What did you say? Who are you, Monsieur?'

'Don't stop! Keep walking. Past the entrance.'

'You know where I *live*?'

'There's very little we don't know.'

'And if I go straight inside? There's a doorman . . .'

'There's also Lavier,' interrupted Bourne. 'You'll lose your job and you won't be able to find another in Saint-Honoré. And I'm afraid that will be the least of your problems.'

'Who *are* you?'

'Not your enemy.' Jason looked at her. 'Don't make me one.'

'*You.* The American! Janine . . . Claude Oréale!'

'Carlos,' completed Bourne.

'*Carlos?* What is this *madness*? All afternoon, nothing but Carlos! And numbers! Everyone has a number no one's ever heard of! And talk of traps and men with guns! It's *crazy*!'

'It's happening. Keep walking. Please! For your own sake.'

She did, her stride less sure, her body stiffened, a rigid marionette uncertain of its strings. 'Jacqueline *spoke* to us,' she said, her voice intense. 'She told us it was all insane, that it – *you* – were out to ruin Les Classiques. That one of the other houses must have paid you to ruin us!'

'What did you expect her to say?'

'You are a hired *provocateur*'. She told us the truth!'

'Did she also tell you to keep your mouth shut? Not to say a word about any of this to anyone?'

'Of *course*!'

'Above all,' ran on Jason as if he had not heard her, 'not to contact the police, which under the circumstances would be the most logical thing in the world to do. In some ways, the *only* thing to do.'

'Yes, naturally . . .'

'Not naturally,' contradicted Bourne. 'Look, I'm just a relay, probably not much higher than you. I'm not here to convince you, I'm here to deliver a message. We ran a test on Dolbert; we fed her false information.'

'Janine? . . .' Monique Brielle's perplexity was compounded by mounting confusion. 'The things she said were incredible! As incredible as Claude's hysterical screaming – the things *he* said. But what *she* said was the opposite of what *he* said.'

'We know, it was done intentionally. She's been talking to Azur.'

'The House of Azur?'

'Check her out tomorrow. Confront her.'

'About what?'

'Just do it. It could be tied in.'

'With what?'

'The trap. Azur could be working with Interpol.'

'*Interpol? Traps?* This is the same craziness! Nobody knows what you're talking about!'

'Lavier knows. Get in touch with her right away.' They approached the end of the block; Jason touched her arm. 'I'll leave you here at the corner. Go back to your hotel and call Jacqueline. Tell her it's far more serious than we thought. Everything's falling apart. Worst of all, someone has turned. Not Dolbert, not one of the sales people but someone more highly placed. Someone who knows everything.'

'Turned? What does that mean?'

'There's a traitor in Les Classiques. Tell her to be careful. Of everyone. If she isn't, it could be the end for all of us.' Bourne released her arm, then stepped off the kerb and crossed the street. On the other side, he spotted a recessed doorway and quickly stepped inside.

He inched his face to the edge, and peered out, looking back at the corner. Monique Brielle was halfway down the block, rushing towards the entrance of the small hotel. The first panic of the second shock wave had begun. It was time to call Marie.

'I'm worried, Jason. It's tearing him apart. He nearly broke down on the phone. What happens when he looks at her? What must he be feeling, thinking?'

'He'll handle it,' said Bourne, watching the traffic on the Champs Élysées from inside the glass telephone box, wishing he felt more confident about André Villiers. 'If he doesn't, I've killed him. I don't want it on my head, but that's what I'll have done. I should have shut my goodamn mouth and taken her myself.'

'You couldn't have done that. You saw d'Anjou on the steps; you couldn't have gone inside.'

'I could have thought of something. As we've agreed, I'm resourceful – more than I like to think about.'

'But you are doing something! You're creating panic, forcing those who carry out Carlos's orders to show themselves. Someone's got to stop the panic, and even you said you didn't think Jacqueline Lavier was high enough. Jason, you'll see someone and you'll know. You'll get him! You will!'

'I hope so; *Christ*, I hope so! I know exactly what I'm doing, but every now and then . . .' Bourne stopped. He hated saying it, but he had to – he had to say it to her. 'I get confused. It's as if I'm split down the goddamn middle, one part of me saying "Save yourself", the other part . . . God help me . . . telling me to "Get Carlos".'

'It's what you've been doing from the beginning, isn't it?' said Marie softly.

'I don't *care* about Carlos!' shouted Jason, wiping away the sweat that had broken out on his hairline, aware, too, that he was cold. 'It's driving me crazy,' he added, not sure whether he had said the words out loud or to himself.

'Darling, come back.'

'What?' Bourne looked at the telephone, again not sure whether he had heard spoken words. or whether he had wanted to hear them, and so they were there. *It was happening again. Things were and they were not. The sky was dark outside, outside a telephone box on the Champs Élysées. It had once been bright, so bright, so blinding. And hot, not cold. With screeching birds and screaming streaks of metal* . . .

'Jason!'

'What?'

'Come back. Darling, *please* come back.'

'Why?'

'You're tired. You need rest.'

'I have to reach Trignon. Pierre Trignon. He's the book-keeper.'

'Do it tomorrow. It can wait until tomorrow.'

'No. Tomorrow's for the captains.' *What was he saying? Captains. Troops. Figures colliding in panic. But it was the way, the only way. The chameleon was a . . . provocateur.*

'Listen to me,' said Marie, her voice insistent. 'Something's happening to you. It's happened before; we both know that, my darling. And when it does, you have got to stop, we know that, too. Come back to the hotel. *Please.*'

Bourne closed his eyes, the sweat was drying and the sounds of the traffic outside the box replaced the screeching in his ears. He could see the stars in the cold night sky, no more blinding sunlight, no more unbearable heat. It had passed, whatever it was.

'I'm all right. Really, I'm okay now. A couple of bad moments, that's all.'

'Jason?' Marie spoke slowly, forcing him to listen. 'What caused them?'

'I don't know.'

'You just saw the Brielle woman. Did she say something to you? Something that made you think of something else?'

'I'm not sure. I was too busy figuring out what to say myself.'

'*Think*, darling!'

Bourne closed his eyes, trying to remember. Had there been something? Something spoken casually or so rapidly that it was lost at the moment. 'She called me a *provocateur*,' said Jason, not understanding why the word came back to him. 'But then, that's what I am, aren't I? That's what I'm doing.'

'Yes,' agreed Marie.

'I've got to get going,' continued Bourne. 'Trignon's place is only a couple of blocks from here. I want to reach him before ten.'

'Be careful.' Marie spoke as if her thoughts were elsewhere.

'I will. I love you.'

'I believe in you,' said Marie St Jacques.

The street was quiet, the block, that odd mixture of shops and flats indigenous to the centre of Paris, bustling with activity during the day, deserted at night.

Jason reached the small apartment house listed in the telephone directory as Pierre Trignon's residence. He climbed the steps and walked into the neat, dimly lit foyer. A row of brass letterboxes was on the right, each one above a small spoked circle through which a caller raised his voice loud enough to identify himself. Jason ran his finger along the printed names below the slots. *M. Pierre Trignon, App. 42*. He pushed the tiny black button twice; ten seconds later there was a crackling of static.

'*Oui?*'

'*Monsieur Trignon, s'il vous plaît?*'

'*Ici.*'

'*Télégramme, monsieur. Je ne laisse pas ma bicyclette.*'

'*Télégramme? Pour moi?*'

Pierre Trignon was not a man who often received telegrams; it was in his astonished tone. The rest of his words were barely distinguishable, but a female voice in the background registered shock, equating a telegram with all manner of horrendous disasters.

Bourne waited outside the frosted glass door that led to the apartment house interior. In seconds he heard the rapid clatter of footsteps growing louder as someone – obviously Trignon – came rushing down the staircase. The door swung open, concealing Jason, a balding, heavyset man, unnecessary braces creasing the flesh beneath a bulging white shirt, walked to the row of letterboxes, stopping at number 42.

'Monsieur Trignon?'

The heavyset man spun round, his cherubic face set in an expression of helplessness. 'A telegram! I have a telegram,' he cried. 'Did you bring me a telegram?'

'I apologize for the ruse, Trignon, but it was for your own benefit. I didn't think you wanted to be questioned in front of your wife and family.'

'*Questioned?*' exclaimed the bookkeeper, his thick, protruding lips curled, his eyes frightened. '*Me?* What about? What is this? Why are you here at my home? I'm a law-abiding citizen!'

'You work in Saint-Honoré? For a firm called Les Classiques?'

'I do. Who are you?'

'If you prefer, we can go down to my office,' said Bourne.

'Who *are* you?'

'I'm a special investigator for the Bureau of Taxation and Records, Division of Fraud and Conspiracy. Come along, my official car is outside.'

'*Outside? Come along?* . . . I have no jacket, no coat! My wife. She's upstairs expecting me to bring back a telegram. A telegram!'

'You can send her one, if you like. Come along now. I've been at this all day and I want to get it over with.'

'Please, Monsieur,' protested Trignon. 'I do not insist on going anywhere! You said you had questions. Ask your questions and let me go back upstairs. I have no wish to go to your office.'

'It might take a few minutes,' said Jason.

'I'll ring through to my wife and tell her it's a mistake. The telegram's for old Gravet; he lives here on the first floor and can barely read. She will understand.'

Madame Trignon did not understand, but her shrill objections were stilled by a shriller Monsieur Trignon. 'There, you see,' said the bookkeeper, coming away from the letterbox, the strings of hair on his bald scalp matted with sweat. 'There's no reason to go anywhere. What's a few minutes of a man's life? The television shows will be repeated in a month or two . . . Now, what in God's name *is* this, Monsieur? My books are immaculate, totally immaculate! Of course, I cannot be responsible for the accountant's work. That's a separate firm, *he's* a separate firm. Frankly, I've never liked him; he swears a great deal, if you know what I mean. But then, who am I to say?' Trignon's hands were held out palms up, his face pinched in an obsequious smile.

'To begin with,' said Bourne, dismissing the protestations, 'do not leave the city limits of Paris. If for any reason, personal or professional, you are called upon to do so, notify us. Frankly, it will not be permitted.'

'Surely you're joking, Monsieur!'

'Surely I'm not.'

'I have *no* reason to leave Paris – nor the money to do so – but to say such a thing to me is unbelievable. What have I done?'

'The Bureau will sequester your books in the morning. Be prepared.'

'*Sequester* . . . For what cause? Prepared for what?'

'Payments to so-called suppliers whose invoices are fraudulent. The merchandise was never received – was never meant to be received – the payments, instead, routed to a bank in Zürich.'

'Zürich? I don't know what you're talking about! I've prepared no cheques for Zürich.'

'Not directly, we know that. But how easy it was for you to prepare them for nonexistent firms, the monies paid, then wired to Zürich.'

'Every invoice is initialled by Madame Lavier! I pay *nothing* on my own!'

Jason paused, frowning. 'Now it's you who are joking,' he said.

'On my word! It's the house policy. Ask anyone! Les Classiques does not pay a *sou* unless authorized by *Madame*.'

'What you're saying, then, is that you take your orders directly from her.'

'But naturally!'

'Whom does she take orders from?'

Trignon grinned. 'It is said from God, when not the other way round. Of course, that's a joke, Monsieur.'

'I trust you can be more serious. Who are the specific owners of Les Classiques?'

'It is a partnership, Monsieur, Madame Lavier has many wealthy friends; they have invested in her abilities. And, of course, the talents of René Bergeron.'

'Do these investors meet frequently? Do they suggest policy? Perhaps advocate firms with which to do business?'

'I wouldn't know, Monsieur. Naturally, everyone has friends.'

'We may have concentrated on the wrong people,' interrupted Bourne. 'It's quite possible that you and Madame Lavier – as the two directly involved with day-to-day finances – are being used.'

'Used for what?'

'To funnel money into Zürich. To the account of one of the most vicious killers in Europe.'

Trignon convulsed, his large stomach quivering as he fell back against the wall. 'In the name of God, what are you *saying*?'

'Prepare yourselves. Especially you. You prepared the cheques, no one else.'

'Only upon approval!'

'Did you ever check the merchandise against the invoices?'

'It's not my job!'

'So, in essence you issued payments for supplies you never saw.'

'I never see anything! Only invoices that have been initialled. I pay only on those!'

'You'd better find every one. You and Madame Lavier had better start digging up every authorization in your files. Because the two of you – especially you – will face the charges.'

'Charges? What charges?'

'For lack of a specific writ, let's call it accessory to multiple homicide.'

'Multiple . . . ?'

'Assassination. The account in Zürich belongs to the assassin known as Carlos. You, Pierre Trignon, and your current employer, Madame Jacqueline Lavier, are directly implicated in financing the most sought-after killer in Europe. Ilich Ramirez Sanchez. Alias Carlos.'

'Aughhhh! . . .' Trignon slid down to the foyer floor, his eyes in shock, his puffed features twisted out of shape. 'All afternoon . . .' be whispered. 'People running around, hysterical meetings in the aisles, looking at me strangely, passing my cubicle and turning their heads. Oh, my *God*.'

'If I were you, I wouldn't waste a moment. Morning will be here soon, and with it possibly the most difficult day of your life.' Jason walked to the outside door and stopped, his hand on the knob. 'It's not my place to advise you, but, if I were you, I'd reach Madame Lavier at once. Start preparing your joint defence, it may be all you have. A public execution is not out of the question.'

The chameleon opened the door and stepped outside, the cold night air whipping across his face.

Get Carlos. Trap Carlos. Cain is for Charlie and Delta is for Cain.

False!

Find a number in New York. Find Treadstone. Find the meaning of a message. Find the sender.

Find Jason Bourne.

Sunlight burst through the stained-glass windows as the clean-shaven old man in the dated suit rushed down the aisle of the church in Neuilly-sur-Seine. The tall priest standing by the rack of novena candles watched him, struck by a feeling of familiarity. For a moment the cleric thought he had seen the man before, but could not place him. There had been a dishevelled beggar yesterday, about the same size, the same . . . No, this old man's shoes were shiny, his white hair combed neatly, and the clothes, although from another decade, were of good quality.

'Angelus Domini,' said the old man as he parted the curtains of the confessional booth.

'Enough!' whispered the silhouetted figure behind the scrim. 'What have you learned in Saint-Honoré?'

'Little of substance, but respect for his methods.'

'Is there a pattern?'

'Random, it would appear. He selects people who know absolutely nothing and instigates chaos through them. I would suggest no further activity at Les Classiques.'

'Naturally,' agreed the silhouette. 'But what's his purpose?'

'Beyond the chaos?' asked the old man. 'I'd say it was to spread distrust among those who do know something. The Brielle woman used the words. She said the American told her to tell Lavier there was "a traitor" inside, a patently false statement. Which of them would dare? Last night was insane, as you know. The bookkeeper, Trignon, went crazy. Waiting until two in the morning outside Lavier's house, literally assaulting her when she returned from Brielle's hotel, screaming and crying in the street.'

'Lavier herself did not behave much better. She was barely in control when she called Parc Monceau: she was told not to call again. No one is to call there . . . ever again. *Ever.*'

'We received the word. The few of us who know the number have forgotten it.'

'Be sure you have.' The silhouette moved suddenly: there was a ripple in the curtain. 'Of *course* to spread distrust! It follows chaos. There's no question about it now. He'll pick up the contacts, try to force information from them and, when one fails, throw him to the Americans and go on to the next. But he'll make the approaches alone; it's part of his ego. He *is* a madman. And obsessed.'

'He may be both,' countered the old man, 'but he's also a professional. He'll make sure the names are delivered to his superiors in the event he does fail. So regardless of whether you take him or not, *they* will be taken.'

'They will be dead,' said the assassin. 'But not Bergeron. He's far too valuable. Tell him to head for Athens; he'll know where.'

'Am I to assume I'm taking the place of Parc Monceau?'

'*That* would be impossible. But for the time being you will relay my decisions to whomever they concern.'

'And the first person I reach is Bergeron. To Athens.'

'Yes.'

'So Lavier and the colonial, d'Anjou, are marked, then?'

'They are marked. Bait rarely survives, and they will not. You may also relay another message, to the two teams covering Lavier and d'Anjou. Tell them I'll be watching them – all the time. There can be no mistakes.'

It was the old man's turn to pause, to bid silently for attention. 'I've saved the best for last, Carlos. The Renault was found an hour and a half ago in a garage in Montmartre. It was brought in last night.'

In the stillness the old man could hear the slow, deliberate breathing of the figure beyond the cloth. 'I assume you've taken measures to have it watched – even now at this moment – and followed – even now at this moment.'

The one-time beggar laughed softly. 'In accordance with your last instructions, I took the liberty of hiring a friend, a friend with a sound car. He in turn has employed three acquaintances, and together they are on four six-hour shifts on the street outside the garage. They know nothing, of course, except that they are to follow the Renault at any hour of day or night.'

'You do not disappoint me.'

'I can't afford to . . . And since Parc Monceau was eliminated, I had no telephone number to give them but my own, which as you know, is a run-down café in the Quarter. The owner and I were friends in the old days, the better days. I could contact him every five minutes for messages and he would never object. I know where he got the money to pay for his business, and who he had to kill to get it.'

'You've behaved well, you have value.'

'I also have a problem, Carlos. As none of us are to call Parc Monceau, how can I reach you? In the event I must. Say, for instance, the Renault.'

'Yes, I'm aware of the problem. Are you aware of the burden you ask for?'

'I would much prefer not to have it. My only hope is that when this is over and Cain is dead you will remember my contributions and, rather than killing me, change the number.'

'You *do* anticipate.'

'In the old days, it was my means of survival.'

The assassin whispered seven figures. 'You are the only man alive who has this number. Naturally, it is untraceable.'

'Naturally. Who would expect an old beggar to have it?'

'Every hour brings you closer to a better standard of living. The net is closing; every hour brings him nearer to one of several traps. Cain will be caught, and an impostor's body will be thrown back to the bewildered strategists who created him. They counted on a monstrous ego and he gave it to them. At the end, he was only a puppet, an expendable puppet. Everyone knew it but him.'

Bourne picked up the telephone. 'Yes?'

'Room Four-twenty?'

'Go ahead, General.'

'The telephone calls have stopped. She's no longer being contacted, not at least by telephone.'

'What do you mean?'

'Our couple was out and the phone rang twice. Both times she asked me to answer it. She really wasn't up to talking.'

'Who called?'

'The chemist about a prescription and a journalist requesting an interview. She couldn't have known either.'

'Did you get the impression she was trying to put you off by asking you to take the calls?'

Villiers paused, his reply laced with anger. 'It was there, the effect less than subtle in so far as she mentioned she might be having lunch out. She said she had a reservation at the Georges Cinq, and I could reach her there if she decides to go.'

'If she does, I want to get there first.'

'I'll let you know.'

'You said she's not being contacted by phone. "Not at least by telephone," I think you said. Did you mean something by that?'

'Yes. Thirty minutes ago a woman came to the house. My wife was reluctant to see her but, nevertheless, did so. I only saw her face for a moment in the parlour, but it was enough. The woman was in panic.'

'Describe her.'

Villiers did.

'Jacqueline Lavier,' said Jason.

'I thought it might be. From the look of her, the wolfpack was eminently successful; it was obvious she had not slept. Before taking her into the library, my wife told me she was an old friend in a marriage crisis. A fatuous lie; at her age there are no crises left in marriage, only acceptance and extraction.'

'I can't understand her going to your house. It's too much of a risk. It doesn't make sense . . . Unless she did it on her own, knowing that no further calls were to be made.'

'These things occurred to me,' said the soldier. 'So I felt the need of a little air, a stroll around the block. My aide accompanied me – a doddering old man taking his limited constitutional under the watchful eye of an escort. But my eyes, too, were watchful. Lavier was followed. Two men were seated in a car four houses away, the vehicle equipped with a radio. Those men did not belong to the street. It was in their faces, in the way they watched my house.'

'How do you know she didn't come with them?'

'We live on a quiet street. When Lavier arrived, I was in the sitting-room having coffee and heard her running up the steps. I went to the window in time to see a taxi drive away. She came in a taxi; she was followed.'

'When did she leave?'

'She hasn't. And the men are still outside.'

'What kind of car are they in?'

'Citroën. Grey. The first three letters of the licence plate are *NYR*.'

'Birds in the air, following a contact. Where do the birds come from?'

'I beg your pardon. What did you say?'

Jason shook his head. 'I'm not sure. Never mind . . . I'm going to try to get to your house before Lavier leaves. Do what you can to help me. Interrupt your wife, say you have to speak to her for a few minutes. Insist her "old friend" stay; say anything, just make sure she doesn't leave.'

'I will do my best.'

Bourne hung up and looked at Marie, standing by the window across the room. 'It's working. They're starting to distrust each other. Lavier went to Parc Monceau and she was followed. They're beginning to suspect their own.'

' "Birds in the air," ' said Marie. 'What did you mean?'

'I don't know; it's not important. There isn't time.'

'I think it is important, Jason.'

'Not now,' Bourne walked to the chair where he had dropped his overcoat and hat. He put them on quickly and went to the bureau, opened the drawer and took out the gun. He looked at it for a moment, remembering. The images were there, the past that was his whole yet not his whole at all, Zürich. The Bahnhofstrasse and the Carillon du Lac; the Drei Alpenhäuser and the Löwenstrasse; a filthy boarding house on Steppdeckstrasse and the Guisan Quai. The gun symbolized them all, for it had once nearly taken his life in Zürich.

But this was Paris. And everything started in Zürich was in motion.

Find Carlos. Trap Carlos. Cain is for Charlie and Delta is for Cain.

False! Goddamn you, false!

Find Treadstone! Find a message! Find a man!

29

Jason remained in the far corner of the back seat as the taxi entered Villiers's block in Parc Monceau. He scanned the cars lining the kerb; there was no grey Citroën, no licence plate with the letters *NYR*.

But there was *Villiers*. The old soldier was standing alone on the pavement, four doors away from his house.

Two men . . . in a car four houses away.

Villiers was standing now where that car had stood; it was a signal.

'*Arrêtez, s'il vous plaît*,' said Bourne to the driver. '*Le vieux homme. Je demande à lui.*' He rolled down the window and leaned forward. '*Monsieur?*'

'In English,' replied Villiers, walking towards the taxi, an old man summoned by a stranger.

'What happened?' asked Jason.

'I could not detain them.'

'Them?'

'My wife left with the Lavier woman. I was adamant, however. I told her to expect my call at the Georges Cinq. It was a matter of the utmost importance and I required her council.'

'What did she say?'

'That she wasn't sure she'd be at the Georges Cinq. That her friend insisted on seeing a priest in Neuilly-sur-Seine, at the Church of the Blessed Sacrament. She said she felt obliged to accompany her.'

'Did you object?'

'Strenuously. And for the first time in our life together, she stated the thoughts in my own mind. She said, "If it's your desire to check up on me. André, why not call the parish? I'm sure someone might recognize me and bring me to a telephone." Was she testing me?'

Bourne tried to think. 'Perhaps. Someone would see her there, she'd make sure of it. But bringing her to a phone might be something else again. When did they leave?'

'Less than five minutes ago. The two men in the Citroën followed them.'

'Were they in your car?'

'No. My wife called a taxi.

'I'm going out there,' said Jason.

'I thought you might,' said Villiers. 'I looked up the address of the church.'

Bourne dropped a fifty-franc note over the back of the front seat. The driver grabbed it. 'It's important to me to reach Neuilly-sur-Seine as fast as possible,' said Jason, 'to the Church of the Blessed Sacrament. Do you know where it is?'

'But of course, Monsieur. It is the most beautiful church in the district.'

'Get there quickly and there'll be another fifty francs.'

'We shall fly on the wings of blessed angels, Monsieur!'

They flew, the flight plan jeopardizing most of the traffic in their path.

'There are the spires of the Blessed Sacrament, Monsieur,' said the victorious driver twelve minutes later, pointing at three soaring towers of stone through the windscreen. 'Another minute, perhaps two if the idiots who should be taken off the streets will permit . . .'

'Slow down,' interrupted Bourne, his attention not on the spires of the church but on a car several vehicles ahead. They had taken a corner and he had seen it during the turn; it was a grey Citroën, two men in the front seat.

They came to a traffic light; the cars stopped. Jason dropped a second fifty-franc note over the seat and opened the door. 'I'll be right back. If the light changes, drive forward slowly and I'll jump in.'

Bourne got out, keeping his body low, and rushed between the cars until he saw the letters. *NYR*; the numbers following 768, but for the moment they were inconsequential. The taxi driver had earned his money.

The light changed and the row of vehicles turched forward like an elongated insect pulling its shelled parts together. The taxi drew alongside; Jason opened the door and climbed in. 'You do good work,' he said to the driver.

'I'm not sure I know the work I am doing.'

'An affair of the heart. One must catch the betrayer in the act.'

'In *church*, Monsieur? The world moves too swiftly for me.'

'Not in traffic,' said Bourne. They approached the final corner before the Church of the Blessed Sacrament. The Citroën made the turn, a single car between it and a taxi, the passengers indistinguishable. Something bothered Jason. The surveillance on the part of the two men was too open, far too obvious. It was as if Carlos's soldiers wanted someone in that taxi to know they were there.

Of course! Madame Villiers was in that cab. With Jacqueline Lavier. And the two men in the Citroën wanted Villiers's wife to *know* they were behind her.

'There is the Blessed Sacrament,' said the driver, entering the street where the church rose in minor medieval splendour in the centre of a manicured lawn criss-crossed by stone paths and dotted with statuary. 'What shall I do, Monsieur?'

'Pull into that space,' ordered Jason, gesturing at a break in the line of parked cars. The taxi with Villiers's wife and the Lavier woman stopped in front of a path guarded by a concrete saint. Villiers's stunning wife got out first, extending her hand for Jacqueline Lavier, who emerged ashen on the pavement. She wore large, orange-rimmed sunglasses and carried a white bag, but she was no longer elegant. Her crown of silverstreaked hair fell in straight, disassociated lines down the sides of her death-white mask of a face, and her stockings were torn. She was at least three hundred feet away but Bourne felt he could hear the erratic gasping for breath that accompanied the hesitant movements of the once-regal figure stepping forward in the sunlight.

The grey Citroën had proceeded beyond the taxi and was now pulling to the kerb. Neither man got out, but a thin metal rod, reflecting the glare of the sun, began rising out of the boot. The radio antenna was being activated, codes sent over a guarded frequency. Jason was mesmerized, not by the sight and the knowledge of what was being done, but by something else. Words came to him, from where he did not know but they were there.

Delta to Almanac, Delta to Almanac. We will not respond. Repeat, negative, brother.

Almanac to Delta. You will respond as ordered. Abandon, abandon. That is final.

Delta to Almanac. You're final, brother. Go fuck yourself. Delta out, equipment damaged.

Suddenly the darkness was all around him, the sunlight gone. There were no soaring towers of a church reaching for the sky; instead there were black shapes of irregular foliage shivering beneath the light of iridescent clouds. Everything was moving. *everything was moving,* he had to *move* with the *movement.* To remain immobile was to die! *Move!* For Christ's sake, *move*!

And take them *out.* One by *one.* Crawl in closer; overcome the fear – the *terrible* fear – and reduce the numbers. That was all there was to it! *Reduce the numbers!* The Monk had made that clear! Knife, wire, knee, thumb; you *know* the points of damage. Of death.

Death is a statistic for the computers. For you it is survival.

The Monk.

The *Monk*?

The sunlight came again, blinding him for a moment, his foot on the pavement, his gaze on the grey Citroën a hundred yards away. But it was difficult to see; why was it so difficult? Haze, mist . . . not darkness now but impenetrable mist. He was hot; no, he was cold. Cold! He jerked his head up, suddenly aware of where he was and what he was doing. His face had been pressed against the window; his breath had fogged the glass.

'I'm getting out for a few minutes,' said Bourne. 'Stay here.'

'All day, if you wish, Monsieur.'

Jason pulled up the lapels of his overcoat, pushed his hat forward and put on the tortoise-shell glasses. He walked alongside a couple towards a religious pavement stall, breaking away to stand behind a mother and child at the counter. He had a clear view of the grey Citroën, the taxi which had been summoned to Parc Monceau was no longer there, dismissed by Villiers's wife. It was a curious decision on her part, thought Bourne; cabs were not that readily available.

Three minutes later, the reason was clear . . . and disturbing. Villiers's wife came striding out of the church, walking rapidly, her tall statuesque figure drawing admiring glances from passers-by. She went directly to the Citroën, spoke directly to the men in front, then opened the rear door.

The bag. A *white* bag! Villiers's wife was carrying the bag that only minutes ago had been clutched in the hands of Jacqueline Lavier. She climbed into the Citroën's back seat and pulled the door shut. The car's engine was switched on and gunned, the prelude to a quick and sudden departure. As the vehicle rolled away, the shiny metal rod that was the vehicle's antenna became shorter and shorter, retracting into its base.

Where was Jacqueline Lavier? Why had she given her bag to Villiers's wife? Bourne started to move, then stopped, instinct warning him. A trap? If Lavier was followed, those following her might also be trailed – and not by him.

He looked up and down the street, studying the pedestrians on the pavement, then each car, each driver and passenger, watching for a face that did not belong, as Villiers had said the two men in the Citroën had not belonged in Parc Monceau.

There were no breaks in the parade, no darting eyes or hands concealed in outsized pockets. He was being over-cautious; Neuilly-sur-Seine was not a trap for him. He moved away from the stall and started for the church.

He stopped, his feet suddenly clamped to the pavement. A priest was coming out of the church, a priest in a black suit, a starched white collar and a black hat that partially covered his face. He had seen him before. Not long ago, not in a forgotten past, but recently. Very recently. Weeks, days . . . hours, perhaps. Where was it? *Where?* He knew him! It was in the walk, in the tilt of his head, in the wide shoulders that seemed to glide in place above the fluid movement of his body. He was a man with a gun! Where *was* it?

Zürich? The Carillon du Lac? Two men breaking through the crowds, converging, brokering death. One wore gold-rimmed glasses; it was not he. That man was dead. Was it that *other* man in the Carillon du Lac? Or on the Guisan Quai? An animal, grunting, wild-eyed in rape. Was it he? Or someone else. A dark-coated man in the corridor at the Auberge du Coin where the lights had shorted, the spill from the staircase illuminating the trap. A reverse trap where that man had fired his weapon in darkness at shapes he thought were human. Was it *that* man?

Bourne did not know, he only knew that he had seen the priest before, but not as a priest. As a man with a gun.

The killer in the priestly dark suit reached the end of the stone path and turned right at the base of a concrete saint, his face briefly caught in the sunlight. Jason froze; the *skin.* The killer's skin was dark, not tanned by the sun but by birth. A Latin skin, its hue tempered generations ago when ancestors lived beside the Mediterranean. Forebears who migrated across the globe . . . across the seas.

Bourne stood paralysed by the shock of his own certainty. He was looking at Ilich Ramirez Sanchez.

Get Carlos. Trap Carlos. Cain is for Charlie and Delta is for Cain.

Jason tore at the front of his coat, his right hand grasping the handle of the gun in his belt. He started running on the pavement, colliding with the backs and chests of strollers, shouldering a pavement vendor out of his way, lurching past a beggar digging into a wire rubbish . . . The *beggar*! The beggar's hand surged into his pocket: Bourne spun in time to see the barrel of an automatic emerge from the threadbare coat, the sun's rays bouncing off the metal. The beggar had a gun! His gaunt hand raised it, weapon and eyes steady. Jason lunged into the street, careening off the side of a small car. He heard the spits of the bullets above him and around him, piercing the air with sickening finality. Screams, shrill and in pain, came from unseen people on the pavement. Bourne ducked between two cars and raced through the traffic to the other side of the street. The beggar was running away; an old man with eyes of steel was racing into the crowds, into oblivion.

Get Carlos. Trap Carlos. Cain is . . . !

Jason spun again and lurched again, propelling himself forward, throwing everything in his path out of his path, racing in the direction of the assassin. He stopped, breathless, confusion and anger welling in his chest, sharp bolts of pain returning to his temples. Where *was* he? Where was *Carlos*? And then he saw him; the killer had climbed behind the wheel of a large black saloon. Bourne ran back into the traffic, slamming bonnets and boots as he threaded his way insanely towards the assassin. Suddenly he was blocked by two cars that had collided. He spread his hands on a glistening chrome grille and leaped sideways over the impacted bumpers. He stopped again, his eyes searing with pain, knowing it was pointless to go on. He was too late. The large black car had found a break in the traffic and Ilich Ramirez Sanchez sped away.

Jason crossed back to the far pavement as the shrieking of police whistles turned heads everywhere. Pedestrians had been grazed or wounded or killed; a beggar with a gun had shot them.

Lavier! Bourne broke into a run again, now back towards the Church of the Blessed Sacrament. He reached the stone path under the eye of the concrete saint and spun left, racing towards the arched, sculptured doors and the marble steps. He ran up and entered the Gothic church, facing racks of flickering candles, fused rays of coloured light streaming down from the stained-glass windows high in the dark stone walls. He walked down the centre aisle, staring at the worshippers, looking for streaked silver hair and a mask of a face laminated in white.

The Lavier woman was nowhere to be seen, yet she had not left; she was somewhere in the church. Jason turned, glancing up the aisle; there was a tall priest walking casually past the rack of candles. Bourne sidestepped his way through a cushioned row, emerged on the far right aisle and intercepted him.

'Excuse me, Father.' he said. 'I'm afraid I've lost someone.'

'No one is lost in the house of God, sir,' replied the cleric, smiling.

'She may not be in spirit, but if I don't find the rest of her, she'll be very upset. There's an emergency at her place of business. Have you been here long. Father?'

'I greet those of our flock who seek assistance, yes. I've been here for the better part of an hour.'

'Two women came in a few minutes ago. One was extremely tall, quite striking, wearing a light-coloured coat, and I think a dark kerchief over her hair. The other was an older lady, not so tall, and obviously not in good health. Did you by any chance see them?'

The priest nodded. 'Yes. There was sorrow in the older woman's face; she was pale and grieving.'

'Do you know where she went? I gather her younger friend left.'

'A devoted friend, may I say. She escorted the poor dear to confession, helping her inside the booth. The cleansing of the soul gives us all strength during the desperate times.'

'To confession?'

'Yes, the second booth from the right. She has a compassionate father confessor, I might add. A visiting priest from the archdiocese of Barcelona. A remarkable man, too; I'm sorry to say this is his last day. He returns to Spain . . .' The tall priest frowned. 'Isn't that odd? A few moments ago I thought I saw Father Manuel leave. I imagine he was replaced for a while. No matter, the dear lady is in good hands.'

'I'm sure of it,' said Bourne. 'Thank you, Father. I'll wait for her.' Jason walked down the aisle towards the row of confessional booths, his eyes on the second, where a small strip of white fabric proclaimed occupancy; a soul was being cleansed. He sat down in the front row, then knelt forward, angling his head slowly round so he could see the rear of the church. The tall priest stood at the entrance, his attention on the disturbance in the street. Outside, sirens could be heard wailing in the distance, drawing closer.

Bourne got up and walked to the second booth. He parted the curtain and looked inside, seeing what he expected to see. Only the method had remained in question.

Jacqueline Lavier was dead, her body slumped forward, rolled to the side, supported by the prayer stall, her mask of a face upturned, her eyes wide, staring in death at the ceiling. Her coat was open, the cloth of her dress drenched in blood. The weapon was a long, thin letter opener, plunged in above her left breast. Her fingers were curled around the handle, her lacquered nails the colour of her blood.

At her feet was a bag – not the white one she had clutched in her hands ten minutes ago, but a fashionable Yves St Laurent, the precocious initials stamped on the fabric an escutcheon of *haute couture*. The reason for it was clear to Jason. Inside were papers identifying this tragic suicide, this overwrought woman so burdened with grief she took her own life while seeking absolution in the eyes of God. Carlos was thorough, brilliantly thorough.

Bourne closed the curtain and stepped away from the booth. From somewhere high in a tower, the bells of the morning Angelus rang splendidly.

The taxi wandered aimlessly through the streets of Neuilly-sur-Seine, Jason in the back seat, his mind racing.

It was pointless to wait, perhaps deadly to do so. Strategies changed as conditions changed, and they had taken a deadly turn. Jacqueline Lavier had been followed, her death inevitable but out of sequence. Too soon; she was still valuable. Then Bourne understood. She had not been killed because she had been disloyal to Carlos, rather because she had disobeyed him. She had gone to Parc Monceau, that was her indefensible error.

There was another known relay at Les Classiques, a grey-haired switchboard operator named Philippe d'Anjou, whose face evoked images of violence and darkness and shattering flashes of light and sound. He had been in Bourne's past, of that Jason was certain, and because of that, the hunted had to be cautious; he could not know what that man meant to him. But he was a relay, and he, too, would be watched, as Lavier had been watched, additional bait for another trap, dispatch demanded when the trap closed.

Were these the only two? Were there others? An obscure, faceless clerk, perhaps, who was not a clerk at all but someone else? A supplier who spent hours in Saint-Honoré legitimately pursuing the cause of *haute couture*, but with another cause far more vital to him. Or her. Or the muscular designer, René Bergeron, whose movements were so quick and . . . *fluid.*

Bourne suddenly stiffened, his neck pressed back against the seat, a recent memory triggered. *Bergeron.* The darkly-tanned skin, the wide shoulders accentuated by tightly rolled up sleeves . . . shoulders that floated in place above a tapered waist, beneath which strong legs moved swiftly, like an animal's, a cat's.

Was it possible? Were the other conjectures merely phantoms, compounded fragments of familiar images he had convinced himself might be Carlos? Was the assassin – unknown to his relays – deep inside his own apparatus, controlling and shaping every move? Was it Bergeron?

He had to get to a telephone right away. *Right* away! Every minute he lost was a minute removed from the answer, and too many meant there would be no answer at all. But he could not make the call himself; the sequence of events had been too rapid, he had to hold back, store his own information.

'The first telephone box you see, pull over,' he said to the driver, who was still shaken by the chaos at the Church of the Blessed Sacrament.

'As you wish, Monsieur. But if Monsieur will please try to understand, it is past the time when I should report to the fleet garage. Way past the time!'

'I understand.'

'There's a telephone!'

'Good. Pull over.'

The red telephone box, its quaint panes of glass glistening in the sunlight, looked like a large doll's house from the outside and smelled of urine on the inside. Bourne dialled the Terrasse, inserted the coins and asked for room Four-twenty. Marie answered.

'What happened?'

'I haven't time to explain. I want you to call Les Classiques and ask for René Bergeron. D'Anjou will probably be on the switchboard, make up a name and tell him you've been trying to reach Bergeron on Lavier's private line for the past hour or so. Say it's urgent, you've got to talk to him.'

'When he comes on, what do I say?'

'I don't think he will, but if he does, just hang up. And if d'Anjou comes on the line again, ask him when Bergeron's expected. I'll call you back in three minutes.'

'Darling, are you all right?'

'I've had a profound religious experience. I'll tell you about it later.'

Jason kept his eyes on his watch, the infinitesimal jumps of the thin, delicate sweep hand too agonizingly slow. He began his own personal count down at thirty seconds, calculating the heartbeat that echoed in his throat as somewhere around two and a half per second. He started dialling at ten seconds, inserted the coins at four, and spoke to the Terrasse's switchboard at minus-five. Marie picked up the phone the instant it began to ring.

'What happened?' he asked. 'I thought you might still be talking.'

'It was a very short conversation. I think d'Anjou was wary. He may have a list of names of those who've been given the private number. I don't know. But he sounded withdrawn, hesitant.'

'What did he say?'

'Monsieur Bergeron is on a fabric search in the Mediterranean. He left this morning and isn't expected back for several weeks.'

'It's possible I may have just seen him eight hundred miles from the Mediterranean.'

'Where?'

'In church. If it *was* Bergeron, he gave absolution with the point of a very sharp instrument.'

'What are you talking about?'

'Lavier's dead.'

'Oh, my God! What are you going to do?'

'Talk to a man I think I knew. If he's got a brain in his head, he'll listen. He's marked for extinction.'

30

'D'Anjou.'

'*Delta?* I wondered when . . . I think I'd know your voice anywhere.'

He had said it! The name had been spoken! The name that meant nothing to him, and yet somehow, everything. D'Anjou knew. Philippe d'Anjou was part of the unremembered past! Delta. Cain is for Charlie and Delta is for Cain! Delta. Delta. Delta! He had known this man and this man had the answer! Alpha, Bravo, Cain, Delta, Echo, Foxtrot . . .

Medusa!

'Medusa,' he said softly, repeating the name that was a silent scream in his ears.

'Paris is not Tam Quan, Delta. There are no debts between us any longer. Don't look for payment. We work for different employers now.'

'Jacqueline Lavier's dead. Carlos killed her in Neuilly-sur-Seine less than thirty minutes ago.'

'Don't even try. As of two hours ago Jacqueline was on her way out of France. She called me herself from Orly Airport. She's joining Monsieur Bergeron . . .'

'On a fabric search in the Mediterranean?' interrupted Jason.

D'Anjou paused. 'The woman on the line asking for René . . . I thought as much. It changes nothing. I spoke with her; she called from Orly.'

'She was told to tell you that. Did she sound in control of herself?'

'She was upset and no one knows why better than you. You've done a remarkable job down here, Delta. Or Cain. Or whatever you call yourself now. Of course she wasn't herself. It's why she's going away for a while.'

'It's why she's dead. You're next.'

'The last twenty-four hours were worthy of you. This isn't.'

'She was followed, you're being followed. Watched every moment.'

'If I am it's for my own protection.'

'Then why is Lavier dead?'

'I don't believe she is.'

'Would she commit suicide?'

'Never.'

'Call the rectory at the Church of the Blessed Sacrament in Neuilly-sur-Seine. Ask about the woman who killed herself while making confession. What have you got to lose? I'll call you back.'

Bourne hung up and left the box. He stepped off the kerb, looking for a cab.

The next call to Philippe d'Anjou would be made a minimum of ten blocks away. The man from Medusa would not be convinced easily and, until he was, Jason would not risk electronic scanners picking up even the general location of the call.

Delta? I think I'd know your voice anywhere . . . Paris is not Tam Quan. Tam Quan . . . Tam Quan, Tam Quan! Cain is for Charlie and Delta is for Cain, Medusa!

Stop it! Do not think of things that . . . you cannot think about. Concentrate on what *is*. Now. *You*. Not what others say you are – not even what you may think you are. Only the now. And the now is a man who can give you answers.

We work for different employers . . .

That was the key.

Tell me! For Christ's sake, tell me! Who is it? Who is my employer, d'Anjou?

A taxi swerved to a stop perilously close to his kneecaps. Jason opened the door and climbed in. 'Place Vendôme,' he said, knowing it was near Saint-Honoré. He must be as close as possible to put in motion the strategy that was rapidly coming into focus. He had the advantage; it was a matter of using it for a dual purpose. D'Anjou had to be convinced that those following him were his executioners. But what those men could not know was that another would be following *them*.

The Vendôme was crowded as usual, the traffic wild as usual. Bourne saw a telephone box on the corner and got out of the taxi. He went inside and dialled Les Classiques; it had been fourteen minutes since he had called from Neuilly-sur-Seine.

'D'Anjou?'

'A woman took her own life while at confession, that's all I know.'

'Come on, you wouldn't settle for that . . . Medusa wouldn't settle for that.'

'Give me a moment to put the board on hold.' The line went dead for roughly four seconds. D'Anjou returned. 'A middle-aged woman with silver and white hair, expensive clothing, and a St Laurent bag. I've just described ten thousand women in Paris. How do I know you didn't take one, kill her, make her the basis of this call?'

'Oh, sure, I carried her into the church like a *pietà*, blood dripping in the aisles from her open stigmata. Be reasonable, d'Anjou. Let's start with the obvious. The bag wasn't hers; she carried a white leather handbag. She'd hardly be likely to advertise a competing house.'

'Lending credence to my belief. It was *not* Jacqueline Lavier.'

'Lends more to mine. The papers in that bag identified her as someone else. The body will be claimed quickly; no one touches Les Classiques.'

'Because you say so?'

'No. Because it's the method used by Carlos in five kills I can name.' *He could. That was the frightening thing.* 'A man is taken out, the police believing he's one person, the death an enigma, killers unknown. Then they find out he's someone else, by which time Carlos is in another country, another contract fulfilled. Lavier was a variation of that method, that's all.'

'Words, Delta. You never said much, but when you did, the words were there.'

'And if you were in Saint-Honoré three or four weeks from now – which you won't be – you'd see how it ends. A plane crash, or a boat lost in the Mediterranean. Bodies charred beyond recognition, or simply gone. The identities of the dead, however, clearly established. Lavier and Bergeron. But only one is really dead, Mme Lavier. Monsieur Bergeron is privileged – more than you ever knew. Bergeron is back in business. And as for you, you're a statistic in the Paris morgue.'

'And you?'

'According to the plan I'm dead too. They expect to take me through you.'

'Logical. We're both from Medusa, they know that – Carlos knows that. It's to be assumed you recognized me.'

'And you me?'

D'Anjou paused. 'Yes,' he said. 'As I told you, we work for different employers now.'

'That's what I want to talk about.'

'No talking. Delta. But for old times' sake – for what you did for us all in Tam Quan – take the advice of a Medusan. Get out of Paris, or you're that dead man you just mentioned.'

'I can't do that.'

'You should. If I have the opportunity, I'll pull the trigger myself and be well paid for it.'

'Then I'll give you that opportunity.'

'Forgive me if I find that ludicrous.'

'You don't know what I want, or how much I'm willing to risk to get it.'

'Whatever you want you'll take risks for it. But the real danger will be your enemy's. I know you, Delta. And I must get back to the switchboard. I'd wish you good hunting but . . .'

It was the moment to use the only weapon he had left, the sole threat that might keep d'Anjou on the line. 'Whom do you call for instructions now that Parc Monceau is out?'

The tension was accentuated by d'Anjou's silence. When he replied, his voice was a whisper. 'What did you say?'

'It's why she was killed, you know. Why you'll be killed, too. She went to Parc Monceau and she died for it. You've *been* to Parc Monceau and you'll die for it, too. Carlos can't afford you any longer; you simply know too much. Why should he jeopardize such an arrangement? He'll use you to trap me, then kill you, and set up another Les Classiques. As one Medusan to another, can you doubt it?'

The silence was longer now, more intense than before. It was apparent that the older man from Medusa was asking himself several hard questions. 'What do you *want* from me? Except me. You should know hostages are meaningless. Yet you provoke me, astonish me with what you've learned. I'm no good to you dead or alive; so what is it you *want*?'

'Information. If you have it, I'll get out of Paris tonight and neither Carlos nor you will ever hear from me again.'

'What information?'

'You'll lie if I ask for it now. I would. But when I see you, you'll tell me the truth.'

'With a wire around my throat?'

'In the middle of a crowd?'

'A crowd? Daylight?'

'An hour from now. Outside the Louvre. Near the steps. At the taxi stand.'

'The Louvre? Crowds? Information you think I have that will send you away? . . . You can't reasonably expect me to discuss my employer.'

'Not yours. Mine.'

'Treadstone?

He knew! Philippe d'Anjou had the answer! Remain calm. Don't let your anxiety show.

'Seventy-one,' completed Jason. 'Just a simple question and I'll disappear. And when you give me the answer – the truth – I'll give you something in exchange.'

'What could I possibly want from you? Except you?'

'Information that may let you live. It's no guarantee, but believe me when I tell you, you won't live without it. *Parc Monceau,* d'Anjou.'

Silence again. Bourne could picture the grey-haired former Medusan staring at his switchboard, the name of the wealthy Paris district echoing louder and louder in his mind. There was death from Parc Monceau and d'Anjou knew it as surely as he knew the dead woman in Neuilly-sur-Seine was Jacqueline Lavier.

'What might that information be?' asked d'Anjou.

'The identity of your employer. A name and sufficient proof to have sealed in an envelope and given to a lawyer, to be held throughout your natural life. But if your life were to end unnaturally, even accidentally, he'd be instructed to open the envelope and reveal the contents. It's protection, d'Anjou.'

'I see,' said the Medusan softly. 'But you say men watch me, follow me.'

'Cover yourself,' said Jason. 'Tell them the truth. You've got a number to call, haven't you?'

'Yes, there's a number, a man.' The older man's voice rose slightly in astonishment.

'Reach him, tell him exactly what I said . . . except for the exchange, of course. Say I contacted you, want a meeting with you. It's to be outside the Louvre in an hour. The truth.'

'You're insane.'

'I know what I'm doing.'

'You usually did . . . You're creating your own trap, mounting your own execution.'

'In which event you may be amply rewarded.'

'Or executed myself, if what you say is so.'

'Let's find out if it is. I'll make contact with you one way or another, take my word for it. They have my photographs; they'll know it when I do. Better a controlled situation than one in which there's no control at all.'

'Now I hear Delta,' said d'Anjou. 'He doesn't create his own trap; he doesn't walk in front of a firing squad and ask for a blindfold.'

'No, he doesn't,' agreed Bourne. 'You don't have a choice, d'Anjou. One hour. Outside the Louvre.'

The success of any trap lies in its fundamental simplicity. The reverse trap by the nature of its single complication must be swift and simpler still.

The words came to him as he waited in the taxi in Saint-Honoré, down the street from Les Classiques. He had asked the driver to take him round the block twice, an American tourist whose wife was shopping in the strip of *haute couture.* Sooner or later she would emerge from one of the stores and he would find her.

What he found was Carlos's surveillance. The rubber-capped antenna on the black saloon was both the proof and the danger signal. He would feel more secure if that radio transmitter were shorted out, but there was no way to do it. The alternative was misinformation. Some time during the next forty-five minutes Jason would do his best to make sure the wrong message was sent over that radio. From his concealed position in the back seat, he studied the two men in the car across the way. If there was anything that set them apart from a hundred other men like them in Saint-Honoré, it was the fact that they did not talk.

Philippe d'Anjou walked out onto the pavement, a grey Homburg covering his grey hair. His glances swept the street, telling Bourne that the former Medusan had covered himself. He had called a number; he had relayed his startling information, he knew there were men in a car prepared to follow him.

A taxi, apparently ordered by phone, pulled up to the kerb. D'Anjou spoke to the driver and climbed inside. Across the street an antenna rose ominously out of its cradle; the hunt was on.

The saloon pulled out after d'Anjou's taxi; it was the confirmation Jason needed. He leaned forward and spoke to the driver. 'I forgot,' he said irritably. 'She said it was the Louvre this morning, shopping this afternoon. Christ, I'm a half an hour late. Take me to the Louvre, will you please?'

'*Mais oui, monsieur, le Louvre.*'

Twice during the short ride to the monumental façade that overlooked the Seine, Jason's taxi passed the black saloon, only to be subsequently passed by it. The proximity gave Bourne the opportunity to see exactly what he needed to see. The man beside the driver spoke repeatedly into the hand-held radio microphone. Carlos was making sure the trap had no loose spikes; others were closing in on the execution ground.

They came to the enormous entrance of the Louvre. 'Pull in behind those other taxis,' said Jason.

'But they wait for fares, Monsieur. I have a fare; *you* are my fare. I will take you to the . . .'

'Just do as I say,' said Bourne dropping fifty francs over the seat.

The driver swerved into the line. The black saloon was twenty yards away on the right; the man on the radio had turned in the seat and was looking out of the left rear window. Jason followed his gaze and saw what he thought he might see. Several hundred feet to the west in the huge square was a grey car, the car that had followed Jacqueline Lavier and Villiers's wife to the Church of the Blessed Sacrament, and sped the latter away from Neuilly-sur-Seine after she had escorted Lavier to her final confession. Its antenna could be seen retracting down into its base. Over on the right, Carlos's soldier no longer held the microphone. The black saloon's antenna was also receding; contact had been made, visual sighting confirmed. Four men. These were Carlos's executioners.

Bourne concentrated on the crowds in front of the Louvre entrance, spotting the elegantly-dressed d'Anjou instantly. He was pacing slowly, cautiously, back and forth by the large block of white granite that flanked the marble steps on the left.

Now. It was time to send the misinformation.

'Pull out,' ordered Jason.

'*What*, Monsieur?'

'Two hundred francs if you do exactly what I tell you. Pull out and go to the front of the line, then make two left turns, heading back to the next aisle.'

'I don't understand, Monsieur!'

'You don't have to. Three hundred francs.'

The driver swung right and proceeded to the head of the line, where he spun the wheel, sending the taxi to the left towards the row of parked cars. Bourne pulled the automatic from his belt, keeping it between his knees, and checked the silencer, twisting the cylinder taut.

'Where do you wish to go, Monsieur?' asked the bewildered driver as they entered the aisle leading back towards the entrance to the Louvre.

'Slow down!' said Jason. 'That large grey car up ahead, the one pointing to the Seine exit. Do you see it?'

'But, of course.'

'Go around it slowly, to the right.' Bourne slid over to the left side of the seat and rolled down the window, keeping his head and the weapon concealed. He would show both in a matter of seconds.

The taxi approached the saloon's boot, the driver spinning the wheel again. They were parallel. Jason thrust his head and his gun into view. He aimed for the grey car's right rear window and fired, five spits coming one after another, shattering the glass, stunning the two men who screamed at each other, lurching below the window frames to the floor of the front seat. But they had *seen* him. That was the misinformation.

'Get *out* of here!' yelled Bourne to the terrified driver, as he threw three hundred francs over the seat and wedged his soft felt hat into the well of the rear window. The taxi shot ahead towards the stone gates of the Louvre.

Now.

Jason slid back across the seat, opened the door, and rolled out on to the cobblestone pavement, shouting his last instructions to the driver. 'If you want to stay alive, get out of here.'

The taxi exploded forward, engine gunning, driver screaming. Bourne dived between two parked cars, now hidden from the grey saloon, and got up slowly, peering between the windows. Carlos's men were quick, professional, losing no moment in the pursuit. They had the taxi in view, the cab no match for the powerful saloon, and in that taxi was the target. The man behind the wheel pulled the car into gear and raced ahead as his companion held the microphone, the antenna rising from its recess. Orders were being shouted to another sedan nearer the great stone steps. The speeding taxi swerved out into the street by the River Seine, the large grey car directly behind it. As they passed within feet of Jason, the expressions on the two men's faces said it all. They had Cain in their sights, the trap had closed, and they would earn their pay in a matter of minutes.

The reverse trap by the nature of its single complication must be swift and simpler still . . .

A matter of minutes . . . He had only a matter of moments if everything he believed was so. D'Anjou! The contact had played his role – his minor role – and was expendable – as Jacqueline Lavier had been expendable.

Bourne ran out from between the two cars towards the black saloon; it was no more than fifty yards ahead. He could see the two men; they were converging on Philippe d'Anjou, who was still pacing in front of the marble steps. One accurate shot from either man and d'Anjou would be dead, Treadstone Seventy-one gone with him. Jason ran faster, his hand inside his coat, gripping the heavy automatic.

Carlos's soldiers were only yards away, now hurrying themselves, the execution to be quick, the condemned man cut down before he understood what was happening.

'*Medusa!*' roared Bourne, not knowing why he shouted the name rather than d'Anjou's own. 'Medusa, *Medusa*!'

D'Anjou's head snapped up, shock on his face. The driver of the black saloon had spun round, his weapon levelled at Jason, while his companion moved towards d'Anjou, his gun aimed at the former Medusan. Bourne dived to his right, the automatic extended, steadied by his left hand. He fired in mid-air, his aim accurate; the man closing in on d'Anjou arched backwards as his stiffened legs were caught in an instant of paralysis; he collapsed on the cobblestones. Two spits exploded over Jason's head, the bullets impacting into metal behind him. He rolled to his left, his gun again steady, directed at the second man. He pulled the trigger twice; the driver screamed, an eruption of blood spreading across his face as he fell.

Hysteria swept through the crowds. Men and women screamed, parents threw themselves over children, others ran up the steps through the great doors of the Louvre as guards tried to get outside. Bourne rose to his feet, looking for d'Anjou. The older man had lunged behind the block of white granite, his great figure now crawling awkwardly in terror out of his sanctuary. Jason raced through the panicked crowd, shoving the automatic into his belt, separating the bysterical bodies that stood between himself and the man who could give him the answers. Treadstone! *Treadstone!*

He reached the grey-haired Medusan. 'Get up!' he ordered. 'Let's get out of here!'

'Delta! . . . It was Carlos's man! I know him, I've *used* him! He was going to kill me!'

'I know. Come on! Quickly! Others'll be coming back; they'll be looking for us. Come *on*!'

A patch of black fell across Bourne's eyes, at the corner of his eyes. He spun around, instinctively shoving d'Anjou down as four rapid shots came from a gun held by a dark figure standing by the line of taxis. Fragments of granite and marble exploded all around them. It was *him*! The wide, heavy shoulders that floated in space, the tapered waist outlined by a form-fitting black suit . . . the dark-skinned face encased in a white silk scarf below the narrow-brimmed black hat. Carlos!

Get Carlos! Trap Carlos! Cain is for Charlie and Delta is for Cain!

False!

Find Treadstone! Find a message; find a man! Find Jason Bourne!

He was going mad! Blurred images from the past converged with the terrible reality of the present, driving him insane. The doors of his mind opened and closed, crashing open, crashing shut; light streaming out one moment, darkness the next. The pain returned to his temples with sharp, jarring notes of deafening thunder. He started after the man in the black suit with the white silk scarf wrapped around his face. Then he saw the eyes and the barrel of the gun, three dark orbs zeroed in on him like black laser beams. Bergeron? . . . Was it Bergeron? *Was* it? Or Zürich . . . or . . . No *time*!

He feigned to his left then dived to the right, out of the line of fire. Bullets splattered into stone, the screeches of ricochets following each explosion. Jason spun under a stationary car, he could see the figure in black racing away between the wheels. The pain remained, but the thunder stopped. He crawled out on the cobblestones, rose to his feet and ran back towards the steps of the Louvre.

What had he done? D'Anjou was gone! How had it happened? The reverse trap was no trap at all! His own strategy had been used against him, permitting the only man who could give him the answers to escape. He had followed Carlos's soldiers, but Carlos had followed *him*! Since Saint-Honoré. It was all for nothing, a sickening hollowness spread through him.

And then he heard the words, spoken from behind a nearby car. Philippe d'Anjou came cautiously into view.

'Tam Quan's never far away it seems. Where shall we go, Delta? We can't stay here.'

They sat inside a curtained booth in a crowded café on the rue Visage, a back street that was hardly more than an alley in Montmartre. D'Anjou sipped his double brandy, his voice low, pensive.

'I shall return to Asia,' he said. 'To Singapore or Hong Kong or even the Seychelles, perhaps. France was never very good for me; now it's deadly.'

'You may not have to,' said Bourne, swallowing the whisky, the warm liquid spreading quickly, inducing a brief, spatial calm. 'I meant what I said. You tell me what I want to know. I'll give you . . .' He stopped, the doubts sweeping over him; no, he would say it. 'I'll give you Carlos's identity.'

'I'm not remotely interested,' replied the former Medusan, watching Jason closely. 'I'll tell you whatever I can. Why should I withhold anything?

Obviously, I won't go to the authorities, but if I have information that could help you take Carlos, the world would be a safer place for me, wouldn't it? Personally, however, I wish no involvement.'

'You're not even curious?'

'Academically, perhaps, for your expression tells me I'll be shocked. So ask your questions, and then astonish me.'

'You'll be shocked.'

Without warning d'Anjou said the name quietly. 'Bergeron?'

Jason did not move; speechless, he stared at the older man. D'Anjou continued.

'I've thought about it over and over again. Whenever we talk I look at him and wonder. Each time, however, I reject the idea.'

'Why?' Bourne interrupted, refusing to acknowledge the Medusan's accuracy.

'Mind you, I'm not sure, I just feel it's wrong. Perhaps because I've learned more about Carlos from René Bergeron than anyone else. He's obsessed by Carlos; he's worked for him for years, takes enormous pride in the confidence. My problem is that he talks *too* much about him.'

'The ego speaking through the assumed second party?'

'It's possible, I suppose, but inconsistent with the extraordinary precautions Carlos takes, the literally impenetrable wall of secrecy he's built around himself. I'm not certain, of course, but I doubt it's Bergeron.'

'You said the name. I didn't.'

D'Anjou smiled. 'You have nothing to be concerned about, Delta. Ask your questions.'

'I thought it *was* Bergeron. I'm sorry.'

'Don't be, for he may be. I told you, it doesn't matter to me. In a few days, I'll be back in Asia, following the franc, or the dollar, or the yen. We Medusans were always resourceful, weren't we?'

Jason was not sure why, but the haggard face of André Villiers came to his mind's eye. He had promised himself to learn what he could for the old soldier. He would not get the opportunity again.

'Where does Villiers's wife fit in?'

D'Anjou's eyebrows arched. 'Angélique?' he asked. 'But of course, you said Parc Monceau, didn't you? How? . . .'

'The details aren't important now.'

'Certainly not to me,' agreed the Medusan.

'What about her?' pressed Bourne.

'Have you looked at her closely?' asked d'Anjou. 'The skin?'

'I've been close enough. She's tanned. Very tall and very tanned.'

'She keeps her skin that way. The Riviera, the Greek Isles, Costa del Sol, Gstaad; she is never without a sun-drenched skin.'

'It's very becoming.'

'It's also a successful device. It covers what she is. For her there is no autumn or winter pallor, no lack of colour in her face or arms or very long legs. The attractive hue of her skin is always there, because it would be there in any event. With or without St Tropez or the Costa Brava or the Alps.'

'What are you talking about?'

'Although the stunning Angélique Villiers is presumed to be Parisian, she's not. She's Hispanic. Venezuelan, to be precise.'

'Sanchez,' whispered Bourne. 'Ilich Ramirez Sanchez.'

'Yes. Among the very few who speak of such things, it is said she is Carlos's first cousin, his lover since the age of fourteen. It is rumoured – among those very few people – that beyond himself she is the only person on earth he cares about.'

'And Villiers is the unwitting drone?'

'Words from Medusa, Delta?' d'Anjou nodded. 'Yes, Villiers is the drone. Carlos's brilliantly conceived wire into many of the most sensitive departments of the French government, including the files on Carlos himself.'

'Brilliantly conceived,' said Jason, remembering. 'Because it's unthinkable.'

'Totally.'

Bourne leaned forward, the interruption abrupt. 'Treadstone,' he said, both hands gripping the glass in front of him. 'Tell me about Treadstone Seventy-one.'

'What can *I* tell *you*?'

'Everything they know. Everything Carlos knows.'

'I don't think I'm capable of doing that. I hear things, piece things together, but except where Medusa's concerned, I'm hardly a consultant, much less a confidant.'

It was all Jason could do to control himself, curb himself from asking about Medusa, about Delta and Tam Quan, the winds in the night sky and the darkness and the explosions of light that blinded him whenever he heard the words. He could not; certain things had to be assumed, his own loss passed over, no indication given. The priorities. Treadstone. Treadstone Seventy-one!

'What have you heard? What have you pieced together?'

'What I heard and what I pieced together were not always compatible. Still, obvious facts were apparent to me.'

'Such as?'

'When I saw it was you, I knew. Delta had made a lucrative agreement with the Americans. Another lucrative agreement, a different kind than before, perhaps.'

'Spell that out, please.'

'Ten years ago, the rumours from Saigon were that the ice-cold Delta was the highest paid Medusan of us all. Surely, you were the most capable *I* knew, so I assumed you drove a hard bargain. You must have driven an infinitely harder one to do what you're doing now.'

'Which is? From what you've heard.'

'What we know. It was confirmed in New York. The Monk confirmed it before he died, that much I was told. It was consistent with the pattern since the beginning.'

Bourne held the glass, avoiding d'Anjou's eyes. The Monk. *The Monk. Do not ask. The Monk is dead, whoever and whatever he was. He is not pertinent now.* 'I repeat,' said Jason, 'what is it they think they know I'm doing?'

'Come, Delta, I'm the one who's leaving. It's pointless to . . .'

'*Please,*' interrupted Bourne.

'Very well. You agreed to become this Cain. This mythical killer with an unending list of contracts that never existed, each created out of whole cloth, given substance by all manner of reliable sources. Purpose. To challenge Carlos – "eroding his stature at every turn" was the way Bergeron phrased it – to undercut his prices, spread the word of his deficiencies, your own superiority. In essence, to draw out Carlos and take him. This was your agreement with the Americans.'

Rays of his own personal sunlight burst into the dark corners of Jason's mind. In the distance, doors were opening, but they were still too far away and opened only partially. But there was light where before there was only darkness.

'Then the Americans are . . .' Bourne did not finish the statement, hoping in brief torment that d'Anjou would finish it for him.

'Yes,' said the Medusan. 'Treadstone Seventy-one. The most controlled unit of American intelligence since the State Department's Consular Operations Created by the same man who built Medusa. David Abbott.'

'The Monk,' said Jason softly, instinctively, another door in the distance partially open.

'Of course. Who else would he approach to play the role of Cain but the man from Medusa known as Delta? As I say, the instant I saw you, I knew it.'

'A role . . .' Bourne stopped, the sunlight growing brighter, warm not blinding.

D'Anjou leaned forward. 'It's here, of course, that what I heard and what I pieced together were incompatible. It was said that Jason Bourne accepted the assignment for reasons I knew were not true. I was there, they were not; they could not know.'

'What did they say? What did you hear?'

'That you were an American intelligence officer, possibly military. Can you imagine? *You,* Delta! The man filled with contempt for so much, not the least of which was for most things American. I told Bergeron it was impossible, but I'm not sure he believed me.'

'What did you tell him?'

'What I believed. What I still believe. It wasn't money – no amount of money could have made you do it – it had to be something else. I think you did it for the same reason so many others agreed to Medusa ten years ago. To clean a slate somewhere, to be able to return to something you had before that was barred to you. I don't know, of course, and I don't expect you to confirm it, but that's what I think.'

'It's possible you're right,' said Jason, holding his breath, the cool winds of release blowing into the mists. *It made sense. A message was sent. This could be it. Find the message! Find the sender! Treadstone!*

'Which leads us back,' continued d'Anjou, 'to the stories about Delta. Who was he? What was he? This educated, oddly quiet man who could transform himself into a lethal weapon in the jungles. Who stretched himself and others beyond endurance for no cause at all. We never understood.'

'It was never required. Is there anything else you can tell me? . . . Do they know the precise location of Treadstone?'

'Certainly. I learned it from Bergeron. A residence in New York City, on East Seventy-first Street. Number One-forty. Isn't that correct?'

'Possibly . . . Anything else?'

'Only what you obviously know, the strategy of which I admit eludes me.'

'Which is?'

'That the Americans think you turned. Better phrased, they want Carlos to believe they think you turned.'

'Why?' *He was closer. It was here!*

'The story is a long period of silence, six months to be exact. Coinciding with Cain's inactivity. Plus stolen funds, but mainly the silence.'

That was it. The message. The silence. The months in Port Noir. The madness in Zürich, the insanity in Paris. No one could possibly know what had happened. He was being told to come in. To surface. You were right, Marie, my love, my dearest love. You were right from the beginning!

'Nothing else, then?' asked Bourne, trying to control the impatience in his voice, anxious now beyond any anxiety he had known to get back to Marie.

'It's all I know, but please understand, I was never told that much. I was brought in because of my knowledge of Medusa – and it was established that Cain was from Medusa – but I was never part of Carlos's inner circle.'

'You were close enough. Thank you.' Jason put several notes on the table and started to slide across the booth.

'There's one thing,' said d'Anjou. 'I'm not sure it's relevant now, but they know your name is not Jason Bourne.'

'What?'

'March twenty-fifth. Don't you remember, Delta? It's only two days from now, and the date's very important to Carlos. Word has been spread. He wants your corpse on the twenty-fifth. He wants to deliver it to the Americans on that day.'

'What are you trying to say?'

'On 25 March 1968, Jason Bourne was executed at Tam Quan. You executed him.'

31

She opened the door and for a moment he stood looking at her, seeing the large brown eyes that roamed his face, eyes that were afraid yet curious. She knew. Not the answer, but that there *was* an answer, and he had come back to tell her what it was. He walked into the room; she closed the door.

'It happened,' she said.

'It happened,' Bourne turned and reached for her. She came to him and they held each other, the silence of the embrace saying more than any spoken words. 'You were right,' he whispered finally, his lips against her soft hair. 'There's a great deal I don't know – may never know – but you were right. I'm not Cain because there is no Cain, there never was. Not the Cain they talk about; he never existed. He's a myth invented to draw out Carlos. I'm that creation. A man from Medusa called Delta agreed to become a lie named Cain. I'm that man.'

She pulled back, still holding him. '"Cain is for Charlie . . ."' She said the words quietly.

'"And Delta is for Cain",' completed Jason. 'You've heard me say it?'

Marie nodded. 'Yes. One night in the room in Switzerland, you shouted it in your sleep. You never mentioned Carlos; just Cain . . . Delta. I said something to you in the morning about it, but you didn't answer me. You just looked out of the window.'

'Because I didn't understand. I still don't, but I accept it. It explains so many things.'

She nodded again. 'The *provocateur.* The code words you use, the strange phrases, the perceptions. But why? Why *you*?'

'"To clean a slate somewhere." That's what he said.'

'Who said?'

'D'Anjou.'

'The man on the steps in Parc Monceau? The switchboard operator?'

'The man from Medusa. I knew him in Medusa.'

'What did he say?'

Bourne told her. And as he did, he could see in her the relief he had felt in himself. There was a light in her eyes, and a muted throbbing in her neck, sheer joy bursting from her throat. It was almost as if she could barely wait for him to finish so she could hold him again.

'*Jason!*' she cried, taking his face in her hands. 'Darling, my darling! My friend has come *back* to me! It's everything we knew, everything we *felt*!'

'Not quite everything,' he said, touching her cheek. 'I'm Jason to you, Bourne to me, because that's the name I was given, and have to use it because I don't have any other. But it's not mine.'

'An invention?'

'No, he was real. They say I killed him in a place called Tam Quan.'

She took her hands away from his face, sliding them to his shoulders, not letting him go. 'There must have been a reason.'

'I hope so. I don't know. Maybe it's the slate I'm trying to clean.'

'It doesn't *matter*,' she said, releasing him. 'It's in the past, ten *years* ago. All that matters now is that you reach the men at Treadstone, because they're trying to reach *you*.'

'D'Anjou said word was out that the Americans think I've turned. No word from me in over six months, millions taken out of Zürich. They must think I'm the most expensive miscalculation on record.'

'You can explain what happened. You haven't knowingly broken your agreement; on the other hand you can't go on. It's impossible. All the training you received means nothing to you. It's there only in fragments – images and phrases that you can't relate to anything. People you're supposed to know, you don't know. They're faces without names, without reasons for being where they are, or what they are.'

Bourne took off his coat and pulled the automatic from his belt. He studied the cylinder – the ugly, perforated extension of the barrel that guaranteed to reduce the decibel count of a gunshot to a spit. It sickened him. He walked to the bureau, put the weapon inside and pushed the drawer shut. He held onto the knobs for a moment, his eyes straying to the mirror, to the face in the glass that had no name.

'What do I say to them?' he asked. 'This is Jason Bourne calling. Of course, I know that's not my name because *I* killed a man named Jason Bourne, but it's the one you gave me . . . I'm sorry, gentlemen, but something happened to me on the way to Marseilles. I lost something – nothing you can put a price on – just my memory. Now, I gather we've got an agreement, but I don't remember what it is, except for crazy phrases like "Get Carlos!" and "Trap Carlos!" and something about Delta being Cain and Cain is supposed to replace Charlie and Charlie is really Carlos. Things like that, which may lead you to think I do remember. You might even say to yourselves "we've got one prime bastard here. Let's put him away for a couple of decades in a very tight stockade. He not only took us, but worse, he could prove to be one hell of an embarrassment." ' Bourne turned from the mirror and looked at Marie. 'I'm not kidding. What do I say?'

'The truth,' she answered. 'They'll accept it. They've sent you a message; they're trying to reach you. As far as the six months is concerned, wire Washburn in Port Noir. He kept records – extensive, detailed records.'

'He may not answer. We had our own agreement. For putting me back together he was to receive a third of Zürich, untraceable to him. I sent him over a million American dollars.'

'Do you think that would stop him from helping you?'

Jason paused. 'He may not be able to help himself. He's got a problem; he's a drunk. Not a drinker. A drunk. The worst kind; he knows it and likes it. How long can he live with a million dollars? More to the point, how long do you think those waterfront pirates will let him live once they find out?'

'You can still prove you were there. For six months you were ill, isolated. You weren't in contact with *anyone.*'

'How can the men at Treadstone be sure? From their view I'm a walking encyclopaedia of official secrets. I *had* to be to do what I've done. How can they be certain I haven't talked to the wrong people?'

'Tell them to send a team to Port Noir.'

'It'll be greeted with blank stares and silence. I left that island in the middle of the night with half the waterfront after me with hooks. If anyone down there made any money out of Washburn, he'll see the connection and walk the other way.'

'Jason, I don't know what you're *driving* at! You've got your answer, the answer you've been looking for since you woke up that morning in Port Noir. What more do you want?'

'I want to be careful, that's all!' said Bourne abrasively. 'I want to "look before I leap" and make damn sure the "stable door is shut" and "Jack be nimble, Jack be quick, Jack jump over the candle stick – but for Christ's sake don't fall into the fire!" How's that for *remembering*!' He was shouting; he stopped.

Marie walked across the room and stood in front of him. 'It's very good. But that's not it, is it? Being careful I mean.'

Jason shook his head. 'No, it isn't,' he said. 'With each step I've been afraid, afraid of the things I've learned. Now, at the end, I'm more frightened than ever. If I'm not Jason Bourne, who am I really? What have I left back there? Has that occurred to you?'

'In all its ramifications, my darling. In a way, I'm far more afraid than you. But I don't think that can stop us. I wish to God it could, but I know it can't.'

The attaché at the American Embassy on the Avenue Gabriel walked into the office of the First Secretary and closed the door. The man at the desk looked up.

'You're sure it's him?'

'I'm only sure he used the key words,' said the attaché, crossing to the desk, a red-bordered index card in his hand. 'Here's the flag,' he continued, handing the card to the First Secretary. 'I've checked off the words he used, and if that flag's accurate, I'd say he's genuine.'

The man behind the desk studied the card. 'When did he use the name Treadstone?'

'Only after I convinced him that he wasn't going to talk with anyone in US Intelligence unless or until he gave me a damn good reason. I think he thought it'd blow my mind when he said he was Jason Bourne. When I simply asked him what I could do for him, he seemed stuck, almost as if he might hang up on me.'

'Didn't he say there was a flag out for him?'

'I was waiting for it but he never said it. According to that eight-word sketch

– "Experienced field officer. Possible defection or enemy detention" – he could have just said the word "flag" and he would have been in sync. He didn't.'

'Then maybe he's not genuine.'

'The rest fits, though. He *did* say DC's been looking for him for more than six months. That was when he used the name Treadstone. He was from Treadstone; that's supposed to be the explosive. He also told me to relay the code words "Delta", "Cain", and "Medusa". The first two are on the flag, I checked them off . . . I don't know what "Medusa" means.'

'I don't know what *any* of this means,' said the First Secretary. 'Except that my orders are to high-tail it down to communications, clear all scrambler traffic to Langley, and get a sterile patch to a spook named Conklin. Him I've heard of: a mean son of a bitch who got his foot blown off ten or twelve years ago in 'Nam. He pushes very strange buttons over at the Company. Also he survived the purges, which leads me to think he's one man they don't want roaming the streets looking for a job. Or a publisher.'

'Who do you think this Bourne is?' asked the attaché. 'I've never seen such a concentrated but formless hunt for a person in my whole eight years away from the States.'

'Someone they want very badly.' The First Secretary got up from the desk. 'Thanks for this. I'll tell DC how well you handled it. What's the schedule? I don't suppose he gave you a telephone number.'

'No way. He wanted to call back in fifteen minutes, but I played the harried bureaucrat. I told him to call me in an hour or so. That'd make it past five o'clock, so we could gain another or two by my being out to dinner.'

'I don't know. We can't risk losing him. I'll let Conklin set up the game plan. He's the control on this. No one makes a move on Bourne unless it's authorized by him.'

Alexander Conklin sat behind the desk in his white-walled office in Langley, Virginia, and listened to the embassy man in Paris. He was convinced; it *was* Delta. The reference to Medusa was the proof, for it was a name no one would know *but* Delta. The *bastard*! He was playing the stranded agent, his controls at the Treadstone telephone not responding to the proper code words – whatever they were – because the dead could not talk. He was using the omission to get himself off the meathook! The sheer nerve of the *bastard* was awesome. Bastard, *bastard*!

Kill the controls and use the kills to call off the hunt. Any kind of hunt. How many men had done it before, thought Alexander Conklin. He had. There had been a source-control in the hills of Huong Khe, a maniac issuing maniacal orders, certain death for a dozen teams of Medusans on a maniacal hunt. A young intelligence officer named Conklin had crept back into Base Camp Kilo with a North Vietnamese rifle, Russian calibre, and had fired two bullets into the head of a maniac. There had been grieving and harsher security measures put in force . . . but the hunt was called off.

There had been prints on fragments of glass found in the jungle paths of Base Camp Kilo, however. Fragments with fingerprints that irrefutably identified the sniper as an occidental recruit from Medusa itself. There were such fragments found on Seventy-first Street, but the killer did not know it – Delta did not know it.

'At one point, we seriously questioned whether he was genuine,' said the embassy's First Secretary, rambling on as if to fill the abrupt silence from Washington. 'An experienced field officer would have told the attaché to check for a flag, but the subject didn't.'

'An oversight,' replied Conklin, pulling his mind back to the brutal enigma that was Delta-Cain. 'What are the arrangements?'

'Initially Bourne insisted on calling back in fifteen minutes, but I instructed lower-level to stall. For instance, we could use the dinner hour . . .' The embassy man was making sure a Company executive in Washington realized the perspicacity of his contributions. It would go on for the better part of a minute; Conklin had heard too many variations before.

Delta. Why had he turned? The madness must have eaten his head away, leaving only the instincts for survival. He had been around too long; he knew that sooner or later they would find him, kill him. There was never any alternative; he understood that from the moment he turned or broke – or whatever it was. There was nowhere to hide any longer; he was a target all over the globe. He could never know who might step out of the shadows and bring his life to an end. It was something they all lived with, the single most persuasive argument against turning. So another solution had to be found; survival. The biblical Cain was the first to commit fratricide. Had the mythical name triggered the obscene decision, the strategy itself? Was it as simple as that? God knew it was the perfect solution. Kill them *all*, kill your *brother*!

Webb gone, the Monk gone, the Yachtsman and his wife . . . who could deny the instructions Delta received, since these four *alone* relayed instructions to him? He had removed the millions and distributed them as ordered. Blind recipients he had assumed were intrinsic to the Monk's strategy. Who was Delta to question the Monk? The creator of Medusa, the genius who had recruited and created him. Cain.

The perfect solution. To be utterly convincing, all that was required was the death of a brother, the proper grief to follow. The official judgment would be rendered. Carlos had infiltrated and broken Treadstone. The assassin had won, Treadstone abandoned. The *bastard*!

'. . . so basically I felt the game plan should come from you.' The First Secretary in Paris had finished. He was an ass but Conklin needed him; one tune had to be heard while another was being played.

'You did the right thing,' said a respectful executive in Langley. 'I'll let our people over here know how well you handled it. You were absolutely right; we need time, but Bourne doesn't realize it. We can't tell him, either, which makes it tough . . . We're on sterile so may I speak accordingly?'

'Of course.'

'Bourne's under pressure. He's been . . . detained . . . for a long period of time. Am I clear?'

'The Soviets?'

'Right up to the Lubyanka. His run was made by means of a double entry. Are you familiar with the term?'

'Yes, I am. Moscow thinks he's working for them now.'

'That's what they think.' Conklin paused. 'And we're not sure. Crazy things happen in the Lubyanka.'

The First Secretary whistled softly. 'That's a basket. How are you going to make a determination?'

'With your help. But the classification priority is so high it's above embassy, even ambassadorial level. You're on the scene; you were reached. You can accept the condition or not, that's up to you. If you do, I think a commendation might come right out of the Oval office.'

Conklin could hear the slow intake of breath from Paris.

'I'll do whatever I can, of course. Name it.'

'You already did. We want him stalled. When he calls back, talk to him yourself . . .'

'Naturally,' interrupted the embassy man.

'Tell him you relayed the codes. Tell him Washington is flying over an officer-of-record from Treadstone by military transport. Say DC wants him to keep out of sight and away from the embassy: every route is being watched. Then ask him if he wants protection, and if he does, find out where he wants to pick it up. But don't send anyone; when you talk to me again I'll have been in touch with someone over there. I'll give you a name then and an eye-spot you can give to him.'

'Eye-spot?'

'Visual identification. Something or someone he can recognize.'

'One of your men?'

'Yes, we think it's best that way. Beyond you, there's no point in involving the embassy. As a matter of fact, it's vital we don't, so whatever conversations you have shouldn't be logged.'

'I can take care of that,' said the First Secretary. 'But how is the one conversation I'm going to have with him going to help you determine whether he's a double entry?'

'Because it won't be one; it'll be closer to ten.'

'Ten?'

'That's right. Your instructions to Bourne – from us through you – are that he's to check in on your phone every hour to confirm the fact that he's in safe territory. Until the last time when you tell him the Treadstone officer has arrived in Paris and will meet with him.'

'What will that accomplish?' asked the embassy man.

'He'll keep moving . . . if he's not ours. There are half a dozen known deep-cover Soviet agents in Paris, all with tripped phones. If he's working with Moscow, the chances are he'll use at least one of them. We'll be watching. And if that's the way it turns out, I think you'll remember the time you spent all night at the embassy for the rest of your life. Presidential commendations have a way of raising a career man's grade level. Of course, you don't have too much higher to go . . .'

'There's higher, Mr Conklin,' interrupted the First Secretary.

The conversation was over; the embassy man would call back after hearing from Bourne. Conklin got up from the chair and limped across the room to a grey filing cabinet against the wall. He unlocked the top panel. Inside was a stapled folder containing a sealed envelope bearing the names and locations of men who could be called upon in emergencies. They had once been good men, loyal men, who for one reason or another could no longer be on a Washington payroll. In all cases it had been necessary to remove them from the official scene, relocate them with new identities – those fluent in other languages frequently given citizenship by co-operating foreign governments. They had simply disappeared.

They were the outcasts, men who had gone beyond the laws in the service of their country, who often killed in the interests of their country. But their country could not tolerate their official existence; their covers had been exposed, their actions made known. Still, they could be called upon. Monies were constantly funnelled to accounts beyond official scrutiny, certain understandings intrinsic to the payments.

Conklin carried the envelope back to his desk and tore the marked tape from the flap: it would be resealed, re-marked. There was a man in Paris, a dedicated man, who had come up through the officer corps of Army Intelligence, a lieutenant-colonel by the time he was thirty-five. He could be counted on; he understood national priorities. He had killed a left-wing cameraman in a village near Hue a dozen years ago.

Three minutes later he had the man on the line, the call unlogged, unrecorded. The former officer was given a name and a brief sketch of defection, including a covert trip to the United States during which the defector in question on special assignment had eliminated those controlling the strategy.

'A double entry?' asked the man in Paris. 'Moscow?'

'No, not the Soviets,' replied Conklin, aware that if Delta requested protection there would be conversations between the two men.

'It was a long-range deep cover to snare Carlos.'

'The assassin?'

'That's right.'

'You may *say* it's not Moscow, but you won't convince *me.* Carlos was trained in Novgorod and as far as I'm concerned he's still a dirty gun for the KGB.'

'Perhaps. The details aren't for briefing, but suffice it to say we're convinced our man was bought off; he's made a few million and wants an unencumbered passport.'

'So he took out the controls and the finger's pointed at Carlos, which doesn't mean a damn thing but give him another kill.'

'That's it. We want to play it out, let him think he's home free. Best, we'd like an admission, whatever information we can get, which is why I'm on my way over. But it's definitely secondary to taking him out. Too many people in too many places were compromised to put him where he is. Can you help? There'll be a bonus.'

'My pleasure. And keep the bonus, I hate fuckers like him. They blow whole networks.'

'It's got to be airtight; he's one of the best. I'd suggest support, at least one.'

'I've got a man from the St-Gervais worth five. He's for hire.'

'Hire him. Here are the particulars. The control in Paris is an embassy blind; he knows nothing, but he's in communication with Bourne and may request protection for him.'

'I'll play it,' said the former intelligence officer. 'Go ahead.'

'There's not much more for the moment. I'll take a jet out of Andrews. My ETA in Paris will be anywhere between ten and one your time. I want to see Bourne within an hour or so after that, and be back here in Washington by tomorrow. It's tight, but that's the way it's got to be.'

'That's the way it'll be, then.'

'The blind at the embassy is the First Secretary. His name is . . .'

Conklin gave the remaining specifics and the two men worked out basic ciphers for their initial contact in Paris. Code words that would tell the man from the Central Intelligence Agency whether or not any problems existed when they spoke Conklin hung up. Everything was in motion exactly the way Delta would expect it to be in motion. The inheritors of Treadstone would go by the book, and the book was specific where collapsed strategies and strategists were concerned. They were to be dissolved, cut off, no official connection or acknowledgment permitted. Failed strategies and strategists were an embarrassment to Washington. And from its manipulative beginnings. Treadstone 71 had used, abused, and manoeuvred every major unit in the United States Intelligence community and not a few foreign governments. Very long poles would be held when touching any survivors.

Delta knew all this, and because he himself had destroyed Treadstone, he would appreciate the precautions, anticipate them, be alarmed if they were not there. And when confronted he would react in false fury and artificial anguish over the violence that had taken place in Seventy-first Street. Alexander Conklin would listen with all his concentration, trying to discern a genuine note, or even the outlines of a reasonable explanation, but he knew he would hear neither. Irregular fragments of glass could not beam themselves across the Atlantic only to be concealed beneath a heavy curtain in a Manhattan brownstone, and fingerprints were more accurate proof of a man having been at a scene than any photograph. There was no way they could be doctored.

Conklin would give Delta the benefit of two minutes to say whatever came to his facile tongue. He would listen, and then he would pull the trigger.

32

'Why are they doing it?' said Jason, sitting down next to Marie in the packed café. He had made the fifth telephone call, five hours after having reached the embassy. 'They want me to keep running. They're forcing me to run, and I don't know why.'

'You're forcing yourself,' said Marie. 'You could have made the calls from the room.'

'No, I couldn't. For some reason, they want me to know that. Each time I call, that son of a bitch asks me where I am now, am I in "safe territory"? Silly goddamn phrase, "safe territory". But he's saying something else. He's telling me that every contact must be made from a different location, so that no one outside *or* inside could trace me to a single phone, a single address. They don't want me in custody, but they want me on a string. They want me, but they're afraid of me; it doesn't make sense!'

'Isn't it possible you're imagining these things? No one said anything remotely like that.'

'They didn't have to. It's in what they didn't say. Why didn't they just tell me to come right over to the embassy. *Order* me. No one could touch me there, it's US territory. They didn't.'

'The streets are being watched; you were told that.'

'You know, I accepted that – blindly – until about thirty seconds ago when it struck me. By whom? *Who's* watching the streets?'

'Carlos, obviously. His men.'

'You know that and I know that – at least we can assume it – but *they* don't know that. I may not know who the hell I am or where I came from, but I know what's happened to me during the past twenty-four hours. *They* don't.'

'They could assume too, couldn't they? They might have spotted strange men in cars, or standing around too long, too obviously.'

'Carlos is brighter than that. And there are lots of ways a specific vehicle could get quickly inside an embassy's gates. Marine contingents everywhere are trained for things like that.'

'I believe you.'

'But they didn't do that; they didn't even suggest it. Instead, they're stalling me, making me play games, Goddamn it, *why*?'

'You said it yourself, Jason. They haven't heard from you in six months. They're being very careful.'

'Why *this* way? They get me inside those gates, they can do whatever they want. They control me. They can throw me a party or throw me into a cell. Instead, they don't want to touch me, but they don't want to lose me, either.'

'They're waiting for the man flying over from Washington.'

'What better place to wait for him than in the embassy?' Bourne pushed back his chair. 'Something's wrong. Let's get out of here.'

It had taken Alexander Conklin, inheritor of Treadstone, exactly six hours and twelve minutes to cross the Atlantic. To go back he would take the first Concorde flight out of Paris in the morning, reach Dulles by 7:30 Washington time and be at Langley at 9:00. If anyone tried to phone him or asked where he had spent the night, an accommodating major from the Pentagon would supply a false answer. And a First Secretary at the embassy in Paris would be told that if he ever mentioned having had a single conversation with the man from Langley, he'd be descaled to the lowest attaché on the ladder and shipped to a new post in Tierra del Fuego. It was guaranteed.

Conklin went directly to a row of pay phones against the wall and called the embassy. The First Secretary was filled with a sense of accomplishment.

'Everything's according to schedule, Conklin,' said the embassy man, the absence of the previously employed Mister a sign of equality. The Company executive was in Paris now, and turf was turf. 'Bourne's edgy. During our last communication, he repeatedly asked why he wasn't being told to come in.'

'He did?' At first, Conklin was surprised; then he understood. Delta was feigning the reactions of a man who knew nothing of the events on Seventy-first Street. If he had been told to come to the embassy, he would have bolted. He knew better; there could be no official connection. Treadstone was an anathema, a discredited strategy, a major embarrassment. 'Did you reiterate that the streets were being watched?'

'Naturally. Then he asked me who was watching them. Can you imagine?'

'I can. What did you say?'

'That he knew as well as I did, and all things considered I thought it was counter-productive to discuss such matters over the telephone.'

'Very good.'

'I rather thought so.'

'What did he say to that? Did he settle for it?'

'In an odd way, yes. He said, "I see," that's all.'

'Did he change his mind and ask for protection?'

'He's continued to refuse it. Even when I insisted.' The First Secretary paused briefly. 'He doesn't want to be watched, does he?' he said confidentially.

'No, he doesn't. When do you expect his next call?'

'In about fifteen minutes.'

'Tell him the Treadstone officer has arrived,' Conklin took the map from his pocket, it was folded to the area, the route marked in blue ink. 'Say the rendezvous has been set for one-thirty on the road between Chevreuse and Rambouillet, seven miles south of Versailles at the Cimetiére de Noblesse.'

'One-thirty, road between Chevreuse and Rambouillet . . . the cemetery. Will he know how to get there?'

'He's been there before. If he says he's going by taxi, tell him to take the normal precautions and dismiss it.'

'Won't that appear strange? To the driver, I mean. It's an odd hour for mourning.'

'I said you're to "tell him" that. Obviously, he won't take a taxi.'

'Obviously,' said the First Secretary quickly, recovering by volunteering the unnecessary. 'Since I haven't called your man here, shall I call him now and tell him you've arrived?'

'I'll take care of that. You've still got his number?'

'Yes, of course.'

'Burn it,' ordered Conklin. 'Before it burns you. I'll call you back in twenty minutes.'

A train thundered by in the lower level of the Métro, the vibrations felt throughout the platform. Bourne hung up the pay phone on the concrete wall and stared for a moment at the mouthpiece. Another door had partially opened somewhere in the distance of his mind, the light too far away, too dim to see inside. Still, there were images. On the road to Rambouillet . . . through an archway of iron latticework . . . a gently sloping hill with white marble. Crosses – large, larger, mausoleums . . . and statuary everywhere. La Cimetière de Noblesse. A cemetery, but far more than a resting place for the dead. A drop, but even more than that. A place where conversations took place . . . amid burials and the lowering of caskets. Two men dressed sombrely as the crowds were dressed sombrely, moving between the mourners until they met among the mourners and exchanged the words they had to say to each other.

There was a face, but it was blurred, out of focus; he saw only the eyes. And that unfocused face and those eyes had a name. David . . . Abbott. The Monk. The man he knew but did not know. Creator of Medusa and Cain. And now himself dead, part of a cemetery somewhere.

Jason blinked several times and shook his head as if to shake the sudden mists away. He glanced over at Marie who was fifteen feet to his left against the wall, supposedly scanning the crowds on the platform, watching for someone possibly watching him. She was not; she was looking at him herself, a frown of concern across her face. He nodded, reassuring her; it was not a bad moment for him. Instead, images had come to him. He had been to that cemetery; somehow he would know it. He walked towards Marie; she turned and fell in step beside him as they headed for the exit.

'He's here,' said Bourne. 'Treadstone's arrived. I'm to meet him near Rambouillet. At a cemetery.'

'That's a ghoulish touch. Why a cemetery?'

'It's supposed to reassure me.'

'Good God, how?'

'I've been there before. I've met people there . . . a man there. By naming it as the rendezvous – an unusual rendezvous – Treadstone's telling me he's genuine.'

She took his arm as they climbed the steps towards the street. 'I want to go with you.'

'Sorry.'

'You can't exclude me!'

'I have to, because I don't know what I'm going to find there. And if it's not what I expect, I'll want someone on my side.'

'Darling, that doesn't make sense! I'm being hunted by the police. If they find me, they'll send me back to Zürich on the next plane; you said so yourself. What good would I be to you in Zürich?'

'Not you. Villiers. He trusts us, he trusts you. You can reach him if I'm not back by daybreak, or haven't called explaining why. He can make a lot of noise, and God knows he's ready to. He's the one back-up we've got, the only one. To be more specific, his wife is – through him.'

Marie nodded, accepting his logic. 'He's ready,' she agreed. 'How will you get to Rambouillet?'

'We have a car, remember? I'll take you to the hotel, then head over to the garage.'

He stepped inside the lift of the garage complex in Montmartre and pressed the button for the third floor. His mind was on a cemetery somewhere between Chevreuse and Rambouillet, on a road he had driven over but had no idea when or for what purpose.

Which was why he wanted to drive there now, not wait until his arrival corresponded more closely to the time of rendezvous. If the images that came to his mind were not completely distorted, it was an enormous cemetery. Where precisely within those acres of graves and statuary was the meeting ground? He would get there by 1:00, leaving a half hour to walk up and down the paths looking for a pair of headlights or a signal. Other things would come to him.

The lift door scraped open. The floor was three-quarters filled with cars, deserted otherwise. Jason tried to recall where he had parked the Renault; it was in a far corner, he remembered that, but was it on the right or the left? He started tentatively to the left; the lift had been on his left when he had driven the car up several days ago. He stopped, logic abruptly orienting him. The lift had been on his left when he had *entered*, not after he had parked the car; it had been diagonally to his right then. He turned, his movement rapid, his thoughts on a road between Chevreuse and Rambouillet.

Whether it was the sudden, unexpected reversal of direction or an inexperienced surveillance, Bourne neither knew or cared to dwell upon. Whichever, the moment saved his life, of that he was certain. A man's head ducked below the bonnet of a car in the second aisle on his right; that man had been watching him. An experienced surveillance would have stood up, holding a ring of keys he had presumably picked up from the floor, or checked a windscreen wiper then walked away. The one thing he would not do was what this man did; risk being seen by ducking out of sight.

Jason maintained his pace, his thoughts concerned with this new development. Who was this man? How had he been found? And then both answers were so clear, so obvious he felt like a fool. The clerk at the Auberge du Coin!

Carlos had been thorough – as he was always thorough – every detail of failure examined. And one of those details was a clerk on duty during a failure. Such a man bore scrutiny, then questioning; it would not be difficult. The show of a knife or a gun would be more than sufficient. Information would pour from the night clerk's trembling lips, and Carlos's army ordered to spread throughout the city, each district divided into sectors, hunting for a specific black Renault. A painstaking search, but not impossible, made easier by a driver who had not bothered to switch licence plates. For how many unbroken hours had the garage been watched? How many men were there? Inside, outside? How soon would others arrive? Would Carlos arrive?

The questions were secondary. He had to get out. He could do without the car, perhaps, but the resulting dependency on unknown arrangements might cripple him; he needed transportation and he needed it now. No taxi would drive a stranger to a cemetery on the outskirts of Rambouillet at one o'clock in the morning, and it was no time to rely on the possibility of stealing a car in the streets.

He stopped, taking cigarettes and matches from his pockets; then, striking a match, he cupped his hands and angled his head to protect the flame. In the corner of his eye, he could see a shadow – square-shaped, stocky; the man had once more lowered himself, now behind the boot of a nearer car.

Jason dropped to a crouch, spun to his left, and lunged out of the aisle between two adjacent cars, breaking his fall with the palms of his hands, the manoeuvre made in silence. He crawled around the rear wheels of the vehicle on his right, arms and legs working rapidly, quietly down the narrow alley of cars, a spider scurrying across a web. He was behind the man now; he crept forward towards the aisle and got to his knees, inching his face along smooth metal and peered beyond a headlight. The heavy-set man was in full view, standing erect. He was evidently bewildered, for he moved hesitantly closer towards the Renault, his body low again, squinting to see beyond the windscreen. What he saw frightened him further; there was nothing, no one. He gasped the audible intake of breath a prelude to running. He had been tricked; he knew it and was not about to wait around for the consequences – which told Bourne something else. The man had been briefed on the driver of the Renault, the danger explained. He began to race towards the exit ramp.

Now. Jason sprang up and ran straight ahead across the aisle, between the cars to the second aisle, catching up with the running man, hurling himself at the man's back and throwing him to the concrete floor. He hammer-locked the man's thick neck, crashing the outsized skull into the pavement, the fingers of his left hand pressed into the man's eye sockets.

'You have exactly five seconds to tell me who's outside,' he said in French, remembering the grimacing face of another Frenchman in a lift in Zürich. There had been men outside then, men who wanted to kill him then, on the Bahnhofstrasse. 'Tell me! *Now*!'

'A man, one man, that's all!'

Bourne relocked the neck, digging his fingers deeper into the eyes. 'Where?'

'In a car,' spat out the man. 'Parked across the street. My *God*, you're choking me! You're blinding me.'

'Not yet. You'll know it when and if I do both. What kind of car?'

'Foreign. I don't know. Italian, I think. Or American. I don't *know. Please!* My eyes!'

'Colour!'

'Dark! Green, blue, very dark. Oh my *God*!'

'You're Carlos's man, aren't you?'

'Who?'

Jason yanked again, pressed again. 'You heard me! You're from Carlos!'

'I don't know any Carlos. We call a man; there is a number. That's all we do.'

'Has he been called?' The man did not reply; Bourne dug his fingers deeper. '*Tell* me!'

'Yes. I *had* to.'

'When?'

'A few minutes ago. The coin telephone on the second ramp. My *God!* I can't see.'

'Yes, you can. Get up!' Jason released the man, pulling him to his feet. 'Get over to the car. *Quickly!*' Bourne pushed the man back between the stationary vehicles to the Renault's aisle. The man turned, protesting, helpless. 'You heard me. Hurry!' shouted Jason.

'I'm only earning a few francs.'

'Now you can drive for it.' Bourne shoved him again towards the Renault.

Moments later the small black vehicle careened down an exit ramp towards a glass booth with a single attendant and the cash register. Jason was in the back seat, his gun pressed against the man's bruised neck. Bourne shoved a note and his dated ticket out of the window; the attendant took both.

'Drive!' said Bourne. 'Do exactly what I told you to do!'

The man pressed the accelerator and the Renault sped out through the exit. The man made a screeching U-turn in the street, coming to a sudden stop in front of a dark green American Chevrolet. A car door opened behind them; running footsteps followed.

'*Jules! Qu'est-ce que c'est que ça? Vous conduisez?*' A figure loomed in the open window.

Bourne raised his automatic, pointing the barrel at the man's face. 'Take two steps back,' he said in French. 'No more, just two. And then stand still.' He tapped the head of the man named Jules. 'Get out. Slowly.'

'We were only to follow you!' protested Jules, stepping out into the street. 'Follow you and report your whereabouts!'

'You'll do better than that,' said Bourne, getting out of the Renault, taking his map of Paris with him. 'You're going to drive me. For a while. Get in your car, both of you!'

Five miles outside Paris on the road to Chevreuse, the two men were ordered out of the car. It was a dark, poorly lighted, third-grade highway. There had been no shops, buildings, houses or telephones for the past three miles.

'What was the number you were told to call?' demanded Jason. 'Don't lie. You'd be in worse trouble.'

Jules gave it to him. Bourne nodded and climbed into the seat behind the wheel of the Chevrolet.

The old man in the threadbare overcoat sat huddled in the shadows of the empty booth by the telephone. The small restaurant was closed, his presence there an accommodation made by a friend from the old days, the better days. He kept looking at the instrument on the wall, wondering when it would ring. It was only a question of time, and when it did he would in turn make a call and the better days would return permanently. He would be the one man in Paris who was the link to Carlos. It would be whispered among the other old men, and respect would be his again.

The high-pitched sound of the bell burst from the telephone, echoing off the walls of the deserted restaurant. The beggar climbed out of the booth and rushed to the phone, his heart pounding with anticipation. It was the signal. Cain was cornered! The days of patient waiting merely a preface to the fine life. He lifted the phone from its curved recess.

'Yes?'

'It's Jules!' cried the breathless voice.

The old man's face turned ashen, the pounding in his chest growing so loud he could barely bear the terrible things being said. But he had heard enough.

He was a dead man.

White hot explosions joined the vibrations that took hold of his body. There was no air, only white light and deafening eruptions surging up from his chest to his head.

The beggar sank to the floor, the cord stretched taut, the phone still in his hand. He stared up at the horrible instrument that carried the terrible words. What could he do? What in the name of God could he *do*?

Bourne walked down the path between the graves, forcing himself to let his mind fall free as Washburn had commanded a lifetime ago in Port Noir. If ever he had to be a sponge, it was now; the man from Treadstone had to understand. He was trying with all his concentration to make sense out of the unremembered, to find meaning in the images that came to him without warning. He had not broken whatever agreement they had; he had not turned, or run . . . He was a cripple; it was as simple as that.

He had to find the man from Treadstone. Where inside those fenced acres of silence would he be? Where did he expect *him* to be? Jason had reached the cemetery wall before 1:00, the Chevrolet a faster car than the broken-down Renault. He had passed the gates, driven several hundred yards down the road, pulled off on to the shoulder and parked the car reasonably out of sight. On his way back to the gates it had started to rain. It was a cold rain, a March rain, but a quiet rain, little intrusions upon the silence.

He passed a cluster of graves within a plot bordered by a low iron railing, the centrepiece an alabaster cross rising eight feet out of the ground. He stood for a moment before it. Had he been here before? Was another door opening for him in the distance? Or was he trying too desperately to find one? And then it came to him. It was not this particular grouping of gravestones, not the tall alabaster cross, nor the low iron railing. It was the rain! *A sudden rain. Crowds of mourners gathered in black around a burial site, the snapping of umbrellas. And two men coming together, umbrellas touching, brief, quiet apologies muttered, as a long brown envelope exchanged hands, pocket to pocket, unnoticed by the mourners.*

There was something else. An image triggered by an image, feeding upon itself, seen only minutes ago. Rain cascading down white marble; not a cold, light rain, but a downpour, pounding against the wall of a glistening white surface . . . and columns . . . rows of columns on all sides, a miniature replica of an ancient treasure.

On the other side of the hill! Near the gates! A white mausoleum, someone's scaled-down version of the Parthenon. He had passed it less than five minutes before, looking at it but not seeing it. *That* was where the sudden rain had taken place, where two umbrellas had touched and an envelope been delivered. He squinted at the radium dial of his watch. It was fourteen minutes past one; he started running back up the path. He was still early; there was time left to see a car's headlights, or the striking of a match or . . .

The beam of a torch. It was there at the bottom of the hill and it was moving up and down, intermittently swinging back at the gates as though the holder was concerned that someone might appear. Bourne had an almost uncontrollable urge to race down between the rows of graves and statuary, shouting at the top of his voice. *I'm here! It's me. I understand your message. I've come back! I have so much to tell you . . . and there is so much you must tell me!*

But he did not shout and he did not run. Above all else, he had to show control, for what afflicted him was so uncontrollable. He had to appear completely lucid – sane within the boundaries of his memory. He began walking down the hill in the cold light rain, wishing his sense of urgency had allowed him to remember a torch.

The torch. Something was odd about the beam of light five hundred feet below. It was moving in short vertical strokes, as if in emphasis . . . as if the man holding it was speaking emphatically to another.

He was. Jason crouched, peering through the rain, his eyes struck by a sharp, darting reflection of light that shot out whenever the beam hit the object in front of it. He crept forward, his body close to the ground, covering well over a hundred feet in seconds, his gaze still on the beam and the strange reflection. He could see more clearly now; he stopped and concentrated. There were two men, one holding the torch, the other a short-barrelled rifle, the thick steel of the gun known only too well to Bourne. At distances of up to thirty feet it could blow a man six feet into the air. It was a very odd weapon for an officer-of-record sent by Washington to have at his command.

The beam of light shot over to the side of the white mausoleum; the figure holding the powerful, short-barrelled rifle retreated quickly, slipping behind a column no more than twenty feet away from the man holding the torch.

Jason did not have to think; he knew what he had to do. If there was an explanation for the deadly weapon, so be it, but it would not be used on him.

Kneeling, he judged the distance and looked for points of sanctuary, both for concealment and protection. He started out, wiping the rain from his face, feeling the gun in his belt that he knew he could not use.

He scrambled from gravestone to gravestone, statue to statue, heading to his right, then angling gradually to his left until the semi-circle was nearly complete. He was within fifteen feet of the mausoleum; the man with the murderous weapon was standing by the left corner column, under the short portico to avoid the rain. He was fondling his gun as though it were a sexual object, cracking the breech, unable to resist peering inside. He ran his palm over the inserted shells, the gesture obscene.

Now. Bourne crept out from behind the gravestone, hands and knees propelling him over the wet grass until he was within six feet of the man. He sprang up, a silent, lethal panther hurling dirt in front of him, one hand surging for the barrel of the rifle, the other for the man's head. He reached both, grabbed both, clasping the barrel in the fingers of his left hand, the man's hair in his right. The head snapped back, throat stretched, sound muted. He smashed the head into the white marble with such force that the expulsion of breath that followed signified a severe concussion. The man went limp, Jason supporting him against the wall, permitting the unconscious body to slip silently to the ground between the columns. He searched the man, removing a .357 Magnum automatic from a leather case sewn into his jacket, a razor-sharp scaling knife from a scabbard on his belt and a small .22 revolver from an ankle holster. Nothing remotely government issue; this was a hired killer, an arsenal on foot.

Break his fingers. The words came back to Bourne; they had been spoken by a man in gold-rimmed glasses in a large saloon car racing out of the Steppdeckstrasse. There was reason behind the violence. Jason grabbed the man's right hand and bent the fingers back until he heard the cracks; he did the same with the left, the man's mouth blocked, Bourne's elbow jammed between the teeth. No sound emerged above the sound of the rain, and neither hand could be used for a weapon or as a weapon, the weapons themselves placed out of reach in the shadows.

Jason stood up and edged his face around the column. The Treadstone officer now angled the light directly into the earth in front of him. It was the stationary signal, the beam a lost bird was to home into; it might be other things also, the next few minutes would tell. The man turned towards the gate taking a tentative step as though he might have heard something and for the first time Bourne saw the cane, observed the limp. The officer-of-record from Treadstone Seventy-one was a cripple . . . as he was a cripple.

Jason dashed back to the first gravestone, spun behind it and peered around the marble edge. The man from Treadstone still had his attention on the gates. Bourne glanced at his watch, it was 1:27. Time remained. He pushed himself away from the grave, hugging the ground until he was out of sight, then stood up and ran, retracing the arch back to the top of the hill. He stood for a moment, letting his breathing and his heartbeat resume a semblance of normality, then reached into his pocket for a book of matches. Protecting it from the rain, he tore off a match and struck it.

'Treadstone?' he said loud enough to be heard from below.

'Delta!'

Cain is for Charlie and Delta is for Cain. Why did the man from Treadstone use the name Delta rather than Cain? Delta was no part of Treadstone; he had disappeared with Medusa. Jason started down the hill, the cold rain whipping his face, his hand instinctively reaching beneath his jacket, pressing the automatic in his belt.

He walked onto the stretch of lawn in front of the white mausoleum. The man from Treadstone limped towards him, then stopped, raising his flash-light, the harsh beam causing Bourne to squint and turn his head away.

'It's been a long time,' said the crippled officer, lowering the light. 'The name's Conklin, in case you've forgotten.'

'Thank you. I had. It's only one of the things.'

'One of what things?'

'That I've forgotten.'

'You remembered this place, though. I guessed you would, I read Abbott's logs; it was here you last met, last made a delivery. During a state burial for some minister or other, wasn't it?'

'I don't know. That's what we have to talk about first. You haven't heard from me in over six months. There's an explanation.'

'Really? Let's hear it.'

'The simplest way to put it is that I was wounded, shot, the effects of the wounds causing a severe . . . dislocation. Disorientation is a better word, I guess.'

'Sounds good. What does it mean?'

'I suffered a memory loss. Total, I spent over five months on an island in the Mediterranean – south of Marseilles – not knowing who I was or where I came from. There's a doctor, an Englishman named Washburn, who kept medical records. He can verify what I'm telling you.'

'I'm sure he can,' said Conklin, nodding. 'And I'll bet those records are massive. Christ, you paid enough.'

'What do you mean?'

'We've got a record, too. A bank officer in Zürich who thought he was being tested by Treadstone transferred three million Swiss francs to Marseilles for an untraceable collection. Thanks for giving us the name.'

'That's part of what you have to understand. I didn't know. He'd saved my life, put me back together. I was damn near a corpse when I was brought to him.'

'So you decided a million-odd dollars was a pretty fair ball-park figure, is that is? Courtesy of the Treadstone budget.'

'I told you, I didn't *know*. Treadstone didn't exist for me; in many ways it still doesn't.'

'I forgot. You lost your memory. What was the word? Disorientation?'

'Yes, but it's not strong enough. The word is amnesia.'

'Let's stick to disorientation. Because it seems you oriented yourself straight into Zürich, right to the Gemeinschaft.'

'There was a negative surgically implanted near my hip.'

'There certainly was; you insisted on it. A few of us understood why. It's the best insurance you can have.'

'I don't know what you're talking about. Can't you understand *that*?'

'Sure. You found the negative with only a number on it and right away you assumed the name of Jason Bourne.'

'It didn't *happen* that way! Each day it seemed I learned something, one step at a time, one revelation at a time. A hotel clerk called me Bourne; I didn't learn the name Jason until I went to the bank.'

'Where you knew exactly what to do,' interrupted Conklin. 'No hesitation at all. In and out, four million gone.'

'Washburn told me what to do!'

'Then a woman came along who just happened to be a financial whizz kid to tell you how to squirrel away the rest! And before that you took out Chernak in the Löwenstrasse, and three men *we* didn't know but figured they sure as hell knew you. And here in Paris, another shot in a bank transfer truck. Another *associate*? You covered every track, every goddamned track. Until there was only one thing left to do. And you – you son of a bitch – you did it.'

'Will you *listen* to me! Those men tried to kill me; they've been hunting me since Marseilles. Beyond that, I honestly *don't* know what you're talking about! . . . Things come to me at times. Faces, streets, buildings; sometimes just images I can't place, but know they mean something, only I can't relate to them. And names – there are names, but then no faces. Goddamn you! I'm an *amnesiac*! That's the truth!'

'One of those names wouldn't be Carlos, would it?'

'Yes, and you know it! That's the *point*; you know much more about it than *I* do! I can recite a thousand facts about Carlos, but *I* don't know why. I was told I had an agreement with Treadstone by a man who's halfway back to Asia by now, a man who worked for Carlos. He said Carlos knows. That Carlos was closing in on me, that you put out the word that I'd turned. He couldn't understand the strategy, and I couldn't *tell* him. You thought I'd turned because you didn't hear from me, and I couldn't reach you because I didn't know who you were; I *still* don't know who you *are*!'

'Or the Monk, I suppose.'

'Yes, yes . . . the Monk. His name was Abbott.'

'Very good. And the Yachtsman? You remember the Yachtsman, don't you? And his wife?'

'Names. They're there, yes. No faces.'

'Elliot Stevens?'

'Nothing.'

'Or . . . Gordon Webb.' Conklin said the name quietly.

'What?' Bourne felt the jolt in his chest, then a stinging, searing pain that drove through his temples to his eyes. *His eyes were on fire! Fire! Explosions and darkness, high winds and pain . . . Almanac to Delta! Abandon, abandon! You will respond as ordered. Abandon!* 'Gordon . . .' Jason heard his own voice, but it was far away in a faraway wind. He closed his eyes, the eyes that burned so, and tried to push the mists away. Then he opened his eyes and was not at all surprised to see Conklin's gun aimed at his head.

'I don't know how you did it, but you did. The only thing left to do and you did it! You got back to New York and blew them all away. You butchered them, you son of a bitch. I wish to *Christ* I could bring you back and see you strapped into an electric chair, but I can't, so I'll do the next best thing. I'll take you myself.'

'I haven't been in New York for the past six months. Before then, I don't know, but not in the last six months.'

'Liar! Why didn't you do it *really* right? Why didn't you time your goddamn stunt so you could get to the funerals? The Monk's was just the other day; you would have seen a lot of old friends! And your *brother's*! Jesus God *Almighty*! You could have escorted his wife down the aisle of the church; maybe delivered the eulogy, that'd be the kicker! At least, speak well of the brother you killed!'

'Brother? . . . *Stop* it! For Christ's sake, stop it!'

'Why should I? Cain alive! We *made* him and he came to *life*!'

'I'm not *Cain*. He never *was*! *I* never was!'

'So you *do* know! *Liar! Bastard!*'

'Put that gun away. I'm telling you, put it down.'

'No chance. I swore to myself I'd give you two minutes because I wanted to hear what you'd come up with. Well, I've heard it and it smells. Who gave *you* the right? We all lose things; it goes with the job, and if you don't like the goddamned job you get out! If there's no accommodation you fade; that's what I thought you did and I was willing to pass on you, to persuade the others to *let* you fade! But no, you came back and turned your gun on us!'

'I didn't turn my gun on you.'

'Tell that to the laboratory techs who have eight fragments of glass that spell out two prints. Third and index fingers, right hand. You were there and you butchered five people! *You* – one of *them* – took out your guns – plural – and blew them away! Perfect set-up. Discredited strategy. Varied shells, multiple bullets, *infiltration.* Treadstone's aborted and you walk out free!'

'No, you're wrong! It was Carlos! Not me, *Carlos.* If what you're saying took place on Seventy-first Street, it was him! He knows! They know! A residence on Seventy-first Street. Number One hundred and forty. They know about it!'

Conklin nodded, his eyes clouded, the loathing in them seen in the dim light, through the rain. 'So perfect,' he said slowly. 'The prime mover of the strategy blows it apart by making a deal with the target. What's your take beside the four million plus? Carlos gave you immunity from his own particular brand of persecution? You two make a lovely couple!'

'That's *crazy*!'

'And accurate,' completed the man from Treadstone. 'Only eight people knew that address before seven-thirty last Friday night. Three of them were killed, and we're two of the other five. If Carlos found it, there's only one person who could have told him. *You!*'

'How *could* I? I didn't know it! I *don't* know it!'

'You just said it.' Conklin's left hand gripped the cane; it was a prelude to firing, steadying a crippled foot.

'*Don't*,' shouted Bourne, knowing the plea was useless, spinning to his left as he shouted, his right foot lashing out at the wrist that held the gun. *Che-sah*! was the unknown word that was the silent scream in his head. Conklin fell back firing wildly in the air, tripping over his cane. Jason spun around and down, now hammering his left foot at the weapon; it flew out of the hand that held it.

Conklin rolled on the ground, his eyes on the far columns of the mausoleum, expecting an explosion from the gun that would blow his attacker into the air. *No!* The man from Treadstone rolled again! Now to the *right*, his features in shock, his wild eyes focused on . . . *There was someone else!*

Bourne crouched, diving diagonally backwards as four gunshots came in rapid succession, three screeching ricochets spinning off beyond sound. Jason rolled over and over and over, pulling the automatic from his belt. He saw the man in the rain; a silhouetted figure rising above a gravestone. He fired twice; the man collapsed.

Ten feet away Conklin was thrashing on the wet grass, both hands spreading frantically over the ground, feeling for the steel of a gun. Bourne sprang up and raced over; he knelt beside the Treadstone man, one hand grabbing the wet hair, the other holding his automatic, its barrel pressed into Conklin's skull. From the far columns of the mausoleum came a prolonged, shattering scream. It grew steadily, eerily in volume, then stopped.

'That's your hired shotgun,' said Jason, yanking Conklin's head to the side. 'Treadstone's taken on some very strange employees. Who was the other man? What death row did you spring him from?'

'He was a better man than you ever were,' replied Conklin, his voice strained, the rain glistening on his face, caught in the beam of the fallen torch six feet away on the ground. 'They all are. They've all lost as much as you lost, but they never turned. We can count on them.'

'No matter what I say, you won't believe me. You don't want to believe me!'

'Because I know what you are, what you *did*! You just confirmed the whole damn thing! You can kill me, but they'll get you. You're the worst kind. You think you're special! You always did! I saw you after Phnom-Penh – *everybody* lost out there, but that didn't count with you! It was only you, just *you*! Then in Medusa! No rules for Delta! The animal just wanted to kill. And that's the kind that turns! Well, I lost, too, but I never turned. Go *on*! Kill me! Then you can go back to Carlos. But when I don't come back, they'll know! They'll come after you and they won't stop until they get you. Go on! Shoot!'

Conklin was shouting, but Bourne could hardly hear him. Instead, he had heard two words and the jolts of pain hammered at his temples. *Phnom-Penh! Phnom-Penh. Death in the skies, from the skies. Death of the young and the very young. Screeching birds and screaming machines and the deathlike stench of the jungle . . . and a river. He was blinded again, on fire again.*

Beneath him the man from Treadstone had broken away. His crippled figure was crawling in panic, lunging, his hands surging through the wet grass. Jason blinked, trying to force his mind to come back to him. Then instantly he knew he had to point the automatic and fire. Conklin had found his gun and was raising it! But Bourne could not pull the trigger.

He dived to his right, rolling on the ground, scrambling towards the marble columns of the mausoleum. Conklin's gunshots were wild, the crippled man unable to steady his leg or his aim. Then the firing stopped and Jason got to his feet, his face against the smooth wet stone. He looked out, his automatic raised; he had to kill this man for this man would kill him, kill Marie, link them both to Carlos.

Conklin was hobbling pathetically towards the gates, turning constantly, the gun extended, his destination a car outside in the road. Bourne raised his automatic, the crippled figure in his gunsight. A split half second and it would be over, his enemy from Treadstone dead, hope found with that death, for there were reasonable men in Washington.

He could not do it; he could not pull the trigger. He lowered the gun, standing helpless by the marble column as Conklin climbed into his car.

The *car*. He had to get back to Paris. There was a way. It had been there all along. *She* had been there!

He rapped on the door, his mind racing, facts analysed, absorbed and discarded as rapidly as they came to him, a strategy evolving. Marie recognized the knock, she opened the door.

'Dear God, *look* at you! What happened?'

'No time,' he said, rushing towards the telephone across the room. 'It was a trap. They're convinced I turned, sold out to Carlos.'

'*What*?'

'They say I flew into New York last week, last Friday. That I killed five people . . . among them a brother.' Jason closed his eyes briefly. 'There was a brother – *is* a brother. I don't know, I can't think about it now.'

'You never left Paris! You can prove it!'

'How? Eight, ten hours, that's all I'd need. And eight or ten hours unaccounted for is all *they* need now. Who's going to come forward?'

'*I* will. You've been with me!'

'They think you're part of it,' said Bourne, picking up the telephone and dialling. 'The theft, the turning, Port Noir, the whole damn thing. They've locked you into me. Carlos engineered this down to the last fragment of a fingerprint. Christ! Did he put it together!'

'What are you doing? Who are you calling?'

'Our back-up, remember? The only one we've got. Villiers. Villiers's *wife*. She's the one. We're going to take her, break her, put her on a hundred racks if we have to. But we won't have to; she won't fight because she can't win . . . Goddamn it. Why doesn't he *answer*?'

'The private phone's in his office. It's three in the morning. He's probably . . .'

'He's on! General? Is that you?' Jason had to ask; the voice on the line was oddly quiet, but not the quiet of interrupted sleep.

'Yes, it is I, my young friend. I apologize for the delay. I've been upstairs with my wife.'

'That's who I'm calling about. We've got to move. *Now*. Alert French Intelligence, Interpol and the American Embassy, but tell them not to interfere until I've seen her, talked to her. We have to talk.'

'I don't think so, Mr Bourne . . . Yes, I know your name, my friend. As for your talking to my wife, however, I'm afraid that's not possible. You see, I've killed her.'

33

Jason stared at the hotel room wall, at the flock paper with the faded designs that spiralled into one another in meaningless contortions of worn fabric. 'Why?' he said quietly into the phone. 'I thought you understood.'

'I tried, my friend,' said Villiers, his voice beyond anger or sorrow. 'The saints know I tried, but I could not help myself. I kept looking at her . . . seeing the son she did not bear behind her, killed by the pig animal that was her mentor. My whore was someone else's whore . . . the animal's whore. It could not be otherwise and, as I learned, it was not. I think she saw the outrage in my eyes, heaven knows it was there.' The general paused, the memory painful now. 'She not only saw the outrage, but the truth. She saw that I knew. What she was, what she had been during the years we'd spent together. At the end, I gave her the chance I told you I would give her.'

'To kill you?'

'Yes. It wasn't difficult. Between our beds is a night stand with a weapon in the drawer. She lay on her bed, Goya's Maja, splendid in her arrogance, dismissing me with her private thoughts as I was consumed by my own. I opened the drawer for a book of matches and walked back to my chair and my pipe, leaving the drawer open, the handle of the gun very much in evidence.

'It was my silence. I imagine, and the fact that I could not take my eyes off her that forced her to acknowledge me, then concentrate on me. The tension between us had grown to the point where very little had to be said to burst the floodgates, and – God help me – I said it. I heard myself asking. 'Why did you do it?' Then the accusation became complete. I called her my whore, the whore that killed my son.

'She stared at me for several moments, her eyes breaking away once to glance at the open drawer and the gun . . . and the telephone. I stood up, the embers in my pipe glowing, loose . . . *chauffé au rouge.* She spun her legs off the bed, put both hands into that open drawer, and took out the gun. I did not stop her, instead I had to hear the words from her own lips, hear my own indictment of myself as well as hers . . . What I heard will go to my grave with me, for there will be honour left my person and the person of my son. We will not be scorned by those who've given less than we. *Never.*'

'General . . .' Bourne shook his head, unable to think clearly, knowing he had to find the seconds in order to find his thoughts. 'General, what happened? She gave you my name. *How?* You've got to tell me that. *Please.*'

'Willingly. She said you were an insignificant gunman who wished to step into the shoes of a giant. That you were a thief from Zürich, a man your own people disowned.'

'Did she say who those people were?'

'If she did I didn't hear. I was blind, deaf, my rage uncontrolled. But you have nothing to fear from me. The chapter is closed, my life over with a telephone call.'

'*No!*' Jason shouted. 'Don't do that! Not now.'

'I must.'

'Please! Don't settle for Carlos's whore. Get Carlos! Trap Carlos!'

'Reaping scorn on my name from lying with that whore? Manipulated by the animal's slut?'

'*Goddamn* you, what about your *son*? Five sticks of dynamite on rue du Bac!'

'Leave him in peace. Leave me in peace. It's over.'

'It's *not* over! Listen to me! Give a moment, that's all I ask.' The images in Jason's mind raced furiously across his eyes, clashing, supplanting one another. But these images had meaning. Purpose. He could feel Marie's hand on his arm, gripping him firmly, somehow anchoring his body to a mooring of reality. 'Did anyone hear the gunshot?'

'There was no gunshot. The *coup de gras* is misunderstood in these times. I prefer its original intent. To still the suffering of a wounded comrade or a respected enemy. It is not used for a whore.'

'What do you mean? You said you killed her.'

'I strangled her, forcing her eyes to look into mine as the breath went out of her body.'

'She had your gun . . .'

'Ineffective when one's eyes are burning from the loose embers of a pipe. It's immaterial now, she might have won.'

'She *did* win if you let it stop here! Can't you *see* that? Carlos wins! She *broke* you! And you didn't have the brains to do anything but choke her to death! You talk about *scorn*? You're buying it all; there's nothing left but scorn!'

'Why do you persist, Monsieur Bourne?' asked Villiers wearily. 'I expect no charity from you, nor from anyone. Simply leave me alone. I accept what is. You accomplish nothing.'

'I will if I can get you to listen to me! Get Carlos, trap *Carlos*! How many times do I have to say it? He's the one you want! He squares it all for you! And he's the one I need! Without him I'm dead. *We're* dead. For God's sake, *listen to me*!'

'I would like to help you, but there's no way I can. Or will, if you like.'

'There *is*.' The images came into focus! He knew where he was, where he was going! The meaning and the purpose came together. 'Reverse the trap! Walk away from it untouched, with everything you've got in place!'

'I don't understand. How is that possible?'

'You didn't kill your wife. *I* did!'

'*Jason!*' Marie screamed, clutching his arm.

'I know what I'm doing,' said Bourne. 'For the first time, I really know what I'm doing. It's funny, but I think I've known it from the beginning.'

*

Parc Monceau was quiet, the street deserted, a few porch lights shimmering in the cold, mistlike rain, all the windows along the row of neat, expensive houses dark, except for the residence of André François Villiers, legend of St Cyr and Normandy, member of France's National Assembly . . . wife killer. The front windows above and to the left of the porch glowed dimly. It was the bedroom wherein the master of the house had killed the mistress of the house, where a memory-ridden old soldier had choked the life out of an assassin's whore.

Villiers had agreed to nothing; he had been too stunned to answer. But Jason had driven home his theme, hammered the message with such repeated emphasis that the words had echoed over the telephone. Get Carlos! Don't settle for the killer's whore! Get the man who killed your son! Who put five sticks of dynamite in a car on rue du Bac and took the last of the Villiers line. He's the one you want! Get him!

Get Carlos. Trap Carlos; Cain is for Charlie and Delta is for Cain. It was so clear to him. There was no other way. At the end, it was the beginning – as the beginning had been revealed to him. To survive he had to bring in the assassin; if he failed, he was a dead man. And there would be no life for Marie St Jacques. She would be destroyed, imprisoned, perhaps killed, for an act of faith that became an act of love. Cain's mark was on her, embarrassment avoided with her removal. She was a phial of nitroglycerine balanced on a high wire in the centre of an unknown ammunition depot. Use a net. Remove her. A bullet in the head neutralizes the explosives in her mind. She cannot be heard!

There was so much Villiers had to understand, and so little time to explain, the explanation itself limited both by a memory that did not exist and the current state of the old soldier's mind. A delicate balance had to be found in the telling, parameters established as to time and the general's immediate contributions. Jason understood; he was asking a man who held his honour above all things to lie to the world. For Villiers to do that, the objective had to be monumentally honourable.

Get Carlos!

There was a second, ground-floor entrance to the general's home, to the right of the steps, beyond a gate, where deliveries were made to the downstairs kitchen. Villiers had agreed to leave the gate and the door unlatched. Bourne had not bothered to tell the old soldier that it did not matter; that he would get inside in any event, a degree of damage intrinsic to his strategy. But first there was the risk that Villiers's house was being watched, there being good reasons for Carlos to do so, and equally good reasons not to do so. All things considered, the assassin might decide to stay as far away from Angélique Villiers as possible, taking no chance that one of his men could be picked up, thus proving his connection, the Parc Monceau connection. On the other hand, the dead Angélique was his cousin and lover . . . *the only person on earth he cares about.* Philippe d'Anjou.

D'Anjou! Of course there'd be someone watching – or two or ten! If d'Anjou had got out of France, Carlos could assume the worst; if the man from Medusa had not, the assassin would know the worst. The colonial would be broken, every word exchanged with Cain revealed. Where? Where were

Carlos's men? Strangely enough, thought Jason, if there was no one posted in Parc Monceau on this particular night, his entire strategy was worthless.

It was not; they were there. In a saloon car – the *same* car that had raced through the gates of the Louvre twelve hours ago, the same two men – killers who were the backups of killers. The car was fifty feet down the street on the left-hand side, with a clear view of Villiers's house. But were those two men slumped down in the seat, their eyes awake and alert, all that were there? Bourne could not tell; vehicles lined the kerbs on both sides of the street. He crouched in the shadows of the corner building, diagonally across from the two men in the stationary saloon. He knew what had to be done, but he was not sure how to do it. He needed a diversion, alarming enough to attract Carlos's soldiers, visible enough to flush out any others who might be concealed in the street or on a rooftop or behind a darkened window.

Fire. Out of nowhere. Sudden, away from Villiers's house, yet close enough and startling enough to send vibrations throughout the quiet, deserted, tree-lined street. Vibrations . . . *sirens*; explosive . . . explosions. It *could* be done. It was merely a question of equipment.

Bourne crept back behind the corner building into the intersecting street and ran silently to the nearest doorway, where he stopped and removed his jacket and overcoat. Then he took off his shirt, ripping the cloth from collar to waist; he put both coats on again, pulling up the lapels, buttoning the overcoat, the shirt under his arm. He peered into the night rain, scanning the cars in the street. He needed petrol, but this was Paris and most fuel tanks would be locked. Most, but not all; there had to be an unsecured top among the line of cars at the kerb.

And then he saw what he wanted to see directly ahead on the pavement, chained to an iron gate. It was a motorbike, its petrol tank a metal bubble between handlebars and seat. The top would have a chain attached, but it was unlikely to have a lock. Nine litres of fuel was not forty; the risk of any theft had to be balanced against the proceeds, and two gallons of fuel was hardly worth a five-hundred franc fine.

Jason approached the bike. He looked up and down the street; there was no one, no sound other than the quiet spattering of the rain. He put his hand on the tank top and turned it; it unscrewed easily. Better yet, the opening was relatively wide, the petrol level nearly full. He replaced the top; he was not yet ready to douse his shirt. Another piece of equipment was needed.

He found it at the next corner, by a sewer drain. A partially dislodged cobblestone, forced from its recess by a decade of careless drivers jumping the kerb. He pried it loose by kicking his heel into the slice that separated it from its jagged wall. He picked it up along with a smaller fragment and started back towards the motorbike, the fragment in his pocket, the large brick in his hand. He tested its weight . . . tested his arm. It would do; both would do.

Three minutes later he pulled the drenched shirt slowly out of the tank, the fumes mingling with the rain, the residue of oil covering his hands. He wrapped the cloth around the cobblestone, twisting and crisscrossing the sleeves, tying them firmly together, holding his missile in place. He was ready.

He crept back to the edge of the building at the corner of Villiers's street.

The two men in the saloon were still low in the front seat, their concentration still on Villiers's house. Behind their car were three others, a small Mercedes, a dark brown limousine and a Bentley. Directly across from Jason, beyond the Bentley, was a white stone building, its windows outlined in black enamel. An inside hall light spilled over to the casement bay windows on either side of the staircase, the left was obviously a dining-room; he could see chairs and a long table in the additional light of a rococo sideboard mirror. The windows of that dining-room with their splendid view of the quaint, rich Parisian street would do.

Bourne reached into his pocket and pulled out the stone; it was barely a quarter the size of the petrol-soaked brick, but it would serve the purpose. He inched around the corner of the building, cocked his arm, and threw the stone as far as he could above and beyond the saloon.

The crash echoed through the quiet street, it was followed by a series of cracks as the rock clattered across the bonnet of a car and dropped to the pavement. The two men in the saloon bolted up. The man next to the driver opened his door, his foot plunging down to the pavement, a gun in his hand. The driver lowered the window, then switched on the headlights. The beams shot forward, bouncing back in blinding reflection off the metal and chrome of the car in front. It was a patently stupid act serving only to point up the fear of the men stationed in Parc Monceau.

Now. Jason raced across the street, his attention on the two men whose hands were covering their eyes, trying to see through the glare of the reflected light. He reached the boot of the Bentley, the cobblestone brick under his arm, a match book in his left hand, a cluster of torn-off matches in his right. He crouched, struck the matches, lowered the brick to the ground, then picked it up by an extended sleeve. He held the burning matches beneath the petrol-soaked cloth; it burst instantly into flame.

He rose quickly, swinging the brick by the sleeve, and dashed over the kerb, hurling his missile towards the bulging framework of the casement window with all his strength, racing beyond the edge of the building as impact was made.

The crash of shattering glass was a sudden intrusion on the rain-soaked stillness of the street. Bourne raced to his left across the narrow avenue, then back towards Villiers's block, again finding the shadows he needed. The fire spread, fanned by the wind from the broken window, leaping up into the willowy backing of the drapes. Within thirty seconds the room was a flaming oven, the fire magnified by the huge sideboard mirror. Shouts erupted, windows lighted up nearby, then further down the street; a minute passed and the chaos grew. The door of the flaming house was yanked open and figures appeared – an elderly man in a nightshirt, a woman in a negligee and one slipper – both in panic.

Other doors opened, other figures emerged, adjusting from sleep to chaos, some racing towards the fire-swept residence – a neighbour was in trouble. Jason ran diagonally across the intersection, one more running figure in the rapidly gathering crowd; he stopped where he had started only minutes before, by the edge of the corner building, and stood motionless, trying to spot Carlos's soldiers.

He had been right; the two men were not the only guards posted in Parc Monceau. There were four men now, huddling by the saloon, talking rapidly, quietly. No, *five.* Another walked swiftly up the pavement, joining the four.

He heard sirens. Growing louder, drawing nearer. The five men were alarmed. Decisions had to be made; they could not all remain where they were. Perhaps there were police records to consider.

Agreement. One man would stay, the fifth man. He nodded and walked rapidly across the street to Villiers's side. The others climbed into the saloon, and, as a fire engine careened up the street, it curved out of its parking place and sped past the red behemoth racing in the opposite direction.

One obstacle remained; the fifth man. Jason rounded the building, spotting him halfway between the corner and Villiers's house. It was now a question of timing and shock. Bourne broke into a loping run, similar to that used by the people heading towards the fire, his head angled back towards the corner, running partially backwards, a figure melting into the surrounding pattern, only the direction in conflict. He passed the man; he had not been noticed – but he *would* be noticed if he continued to the downstairs gate of Villiers's house and opened it. The man was glancing back and forth, concerned, bewildered, perhaps frightened by the fact that now he was the only patrol in the street. He was standing in front of a low railing; another gate, another downstairs entrance to another expensive house in Parc Monceau.

Jason stopped, taking two rapid sidesteps towards the man, then pivoted, his balance on his left foot, his right lashing out at the fifth man's midsection, pummelling him backwards over the iron rail. The man shouted as he fell down into the narrow concrete corridor. Bourne leaped over the railing, the knuckles of his right hand rigid, the heels of both feet pushed forward. He landed on the man's chest, the impact breaking the ribs beneath him, his knuckles smashing into the man's throat. Carlos's soldier went limp. He would regain consciousness long after someone removed him to a hospital. Jason searched the man; there was a single gun strapped to his chest. Bourne took it out and put it into his overcoat pocket. He would give it to Villiers.

Villiers. The way was clear.

He climbed the staircase to the second floor. Halfway up the steps he could see a line of light at the bottom of the bedroom door; beyond that door was an old man who was his only hope. If ever in his life – remembered and unremembered – he had to be convincing, it was now. And his conviction was real – there was no room for the chameleon now. Everything he believed was based on one fact. Carlos had to come after him. It was the truth. It was the trap.

He reached the landing and turned to his left towards the bedroom door. He paused for a moment trying to dismiss the echo in his chest; it was growing louder, the pounding more rapid. *Part of the truth, not all of it.* No invention, simply omission.

An agreement . . . a contract . . . with a group of men – honourable men – who were after Carlos. That was all Villiers had to know; it was what he had to accept. He could not be told he was dealing with an amnesiac, for in that loss of memory might be found a man of dishonour. The legend of St Cyr, Algeria and Normandy would not accept that; not now, here, at the end of his life.

Oh, God, the balance was tenuous! The line between belief and disbelief so thin . . . as thin as it was for the man-corpse whose name was not Jason Bourne.

He opened the door and stepped inside, into an old man's private hell. Outside, beyond curtained windows, the sirens raged and the crowds shouted. Spectators in an unseen arena, jeering the unknown, oblivious to its unfathomable cause.

Jason closed the door and stood motionless. The large room was filled with shadows, the only light a bedside table lamp. His eyes greeted by a sight he wished he did not have to see. Villiers had dragged a high-backed desk chair across the room and was sitting on it at the foot of the bed, staring at the dead woman sprawled over the covers. Angélique Villiers's bronzed head was resting on the pillow, her eyes wide, bulging out of their sockets. Her throat was swollen, the flesh a reddish purple, the massive bruise having spread throughout her neck. Her body was still twisted, in contrast to the upright head, contorted in furious struggle, her long bare legs stretched out, her hips turned, the negligée torn, her breasts bursting out of the silk – even in death, sensual. There had been no attempt to conceal the whore.

The old soldier sat like a bewildered child, punished for an insignificant act, the meaningful crime having escaped his tormentor's reasoning and perhaps his own. He pulled his eyes away from the dead woman and looked at Bourne.

'What happened outside?' he asked in a monotone.

'Men were watching your house. Carlos's men, five of them. I started a fire up the street; no one was hurt. All but one man left; I took him out.'

'You're resourceful, Monsieur Bourne.'

'I'm resourceful,' agreed Jason. 'But they'll be back. The fire'll be out and they'll come back; before then, if Carlos puts it together, and I think he will. If he does, he'll send someone in here. He won't come himself, of course, but one of his guns will be here. When that man finds you . . . and her . . . he'll kill you. Carlos loses her, but he still wins. He wins a second time; he's used you through her and at the end he kills you. He walks away and you're dead. People can draw whatever conclusions they like, but I don't think they'll be flattering.'

'You're very precise. Assured of your judgment.'

'I know what I'm talking about. I'd prefer not to say what I'm going to say, but there's no time for your feelings.'

'I have none left. Say what you will.'

'Your wife told you she was French, didn't she?'

'Yes. From the south. Her family was from Loures Barouse, near the Spanish border. She came to Paris years ago. Lived with an aunt. What of it?'

'Did you ever meet her family?'

'No.'

'They didn't come up for your marriage?'

'All things considered, we thought it would be best not to ask them. The disparity of our ages would have disturbed them.'

'What about the aunt here in Paris?'

'She died before I met Angélique. What's the point of all this?'

'Your wife wasn't French. I doubt there was even an aunt in Paris, and her family didn't come from Loures Barouse, although the Spanish border has a certain relevance. It could cover a lot, explain a lot.'

'What do you mean?'

'She was Venezuelan. Carlos's first cousin, his lover since she was fourteen. They were a team, had been for years. I was told she was the only person on earth he cared about.'

'A whore.'

'An assassin's instrument. I wonder how many targets she set up. How many valuable men are dead because of her.'

'I cannot kill her twice.'

'You can use her. Use her death.'

'The insanity you spoke of?'

'The only insanity is if you throw your life away. Carlos wins it all; he goes on using his gun . . . and sticks of dynamite . . . and you're one more statistic. Another kill added to a long list of distinguished corpses. *That's* insane.'

'And you're the reasonable man? You assume the guilt for a crime you did not commit? For the death of a whore? Hunted for a killing that was not yours?'

'That's part of it. The essential part, actually.'

'Don't talk to me of insanity, young man. I beg you, leave. What you've told me gives me the courage to face Almighty God. If ever a death was justified, it was hers by my hand. I will look into the eyes of Christ and swear it.'

'You've written yourself out, then,' said Jason, noticing for the first time the bulge of a weapon in the old man's jacket pocket.

'I will not stand trial, if that's what you mean.'

'Oh, that's perfect, General! Carlos himself couldn't have come up with anything better! Not a wasted motion on his part; he doesn't even have to use his own gun. But those who count will know he did it; he caused it.'

'Those who *count* will know nothing. *Raisons du cœur. Maladie.* I am not concerned with the tongues of killers and thieves.'

'And if I told the truth? Told why you killed her!'

'Who would listen? Even should you live to speak. I'm not a fool, Monsieur Bourne. You are running from more than Carlos. You are hunted by many, not just one. You as much as told me so. You would not tell me your name . . . for my own safety, you claimed. When and if this was over, you said, it was *I* who might not care to be seen with *you*. Those are not the words of a man in whom much trust is placed.'

'You trusted me.'

'I told you why,' said Villiers, glancing away, staring at his dead wife. 'It was in your eyes.'

'The truth?'

'The truth.'

'Then look at me now! The truth is still there. On that road to Nanterre, you told me you'd listen to what I had to say because I gave you your life. I'm trying to give it to you again! You can walk away free, untouched, go on standing for the things you say are important to you, were important to your son. You can *win*! . . . Don't mistake me, I'm not being noble. Your staying alive and doing what I ask is the only way I can stay alive, the only way I'll ever be free.'

The old soldier looked up. 'Why?'

'I told you I wanted Carlos because something was taken from me – something very necessary to my life, my sanity – and he was the cause of it. That's the truth – I believe it's the truth – but it's not the whole truth. There are other people involved, some decent, some not, and my agreement with them was to get Carlos, trap Carlos. They want what you want. But something happened that I can't explain – I won't try to explain – and those people think I betrayed them. They think I made a pact with Carlos, that I stole millions from them, and killed others who were my links to them. They have men everywhere, and the orders are to execute me on sight. You were right. I'm running from more than Carlos. I'm hunted by men I don't know and can't see. For all the wrong reasons . . . I didn't do the things they say I did, but no one wants to listen. I have no pact with Carlos; *you know* I don't!'

'I believe you. There's nothing to prevent me from making a call on your behalf. I owe you that.'

'*How?* What are you going to say? "The man known to me as Jason Bourne has no pact with Carlos. I know this because he exposed Carlos's mistress to me, and that woman was my wife, the wife I choked to death so as not to bring dishonour to my name! I'm about to call the Sûreté and confess my crime – although, of course, I won't tell them why I killed her. Or why I'm going to kill myself." . . . Is that it, General? Is that what you're going to say?'

The old man stared silently at Bourne, the fundamental contradiction clear to him. 'I cannot help you then.'

'Good. *Fine!* Carlos wins it *all*! She wins! You *lose*. Your *son* loses. Go on! Call the police, then put the barrel of the gun in your goddamn mouth and blow your goddamn head off! Go *on*! That's what you want! Take yourself out, lie down and *die*! You're not good for anything else any more! You're a self-pitying old, *old man*! God knows you're no match for Carlos! No match for the man who placed five sticks of dynamite in rue du Bac and killed your son!'

Villiers's hands shook; the trembling spread to his head. 'Do not do this. I'm telling you, do not *do* this.'

' "Telling" me? You mean you're giving me an *order*? The little old man with the big brass buttons is issuing a *command*? Well, forget it! I don't take orders from men like you! You're *frauds*! You're worse than all the people you attack; at least they have the stomachs to do what they say they're going to do! You *don't*. All you've got is wind. Words and wind and self-serving bromides. Lie down and *die*, old man! But don't give me an order!'

Villiers unclasped his hands and shot out of the chair, his racked body now trembling. 'I told you. No *more*!'

'I'm not interested in what you tell me. I was right the first time I saw you. You belong to Carlos. You were his lackey alive, and you'll be his lackey dead.'

The old soldier's face grimaced in pain. He pulled out his gun, the gesture pathetic, the threat, however, real. 'I've killed many men in my time. In my profession it was unavoidable, often disturbing. I don't want to kill you now, but I will if you disregard my wishes. Leave me. Leave this house.'

'That's terrific. You must be wired into Carlos's head. You kill me, he sweeps the board!' Jason took a step forward, aware of the fact that it was the first movement he had made since entering the room. He saw Villiers's eyes widen; the gun shook, its oscillating shadow cast against the wall. A single half ounce of pressure and the hammer would plunge forward, the bullet finding its mark. For in spite of the madness of the moment, the hand that held that weapon had spent a lifetime gripping steel; it would be steady when the instant came. If it came. That was the risk Bourne had to take. Without Villiers, there was nothing; the old man had to understand. Jason suddenly shouted. "Go *on! Fire. Kill* me. Take your orders from *Carlos*! You're a soldier! You've got your orders. Carry them out!'

The trembling in Villiers's hand increased, the knuckles white as the gun rose higher, its barrel now levelled at Bourne's head. And then Jason heard the whisper from an old man's throat.

' "*Vous êtes soldat . . . arrêtez . . . Arrêtez!*" '

'What?'

'I am a soldier. Someone said that to me recently, someone very dear to you.' Villiers spoke quietly. 'She shamed an old warrior into remembering who he was . . . who he had been. "*On dit que vous êtes un géant. Je le crois.*" She had the grace, the kindness to say that to me also. She had been told I was a giant, and she believed it. She was wrong – Almighty God, she was wrong – but I shall try.' André Villiers lowered the gun; there was dignity in the submission. A soldier's dignity. A giant. 'What would you have me do?'

Jason breathed again. 'Force Carlos into coming after me. But not here, not in Paris. Not even in France.'

'Where then?'

Jason held his place. 'Can you get me out of the country? I should tell you, I'm wanted. My name and description by now are on every immigration desk and border check in Europe.'

'For the wrong reasons?'

'For the wrong reasons.'

'I believe you. There are ways. The Brevet has ways and will do as I ask.'

'With an identity that's false? Without telling them why?'

'My word is enough. I've earned it.'

'Another question. That aide of yours you talked about. Do you trust him, *really* trust him?'

'With my life. Above all men.'

'With another's life? One you correctly said was very dear to me.'

'Of course. Why? You'll travel alone?'

'I have to. She'd never let me go.'

'You'll have to tell her something.'

'I will. That I'm underground here in Paris, or Brussels, or Amsterdam. Cities where Carlos operates. But that she had to get away; our car was found in Montmartre. Carlos's men are searching every street, every flat, every hotel.

You're working with me now; your aide will take her into the country where she'll be safe. I'll tell her that.'

'I must ask the questions now. What happens if you don't come back?'

Bourne tried to keep the plea out of his voice. 'I'll have time on the plane. I'll write out everything that's happened, everything that I . . . remember. I'll send it to you and you will make the decisions. With her. She called you a giant. Make the right decisions. Protect her.'

'"*Vous êtes soldat . . . Arrêtez!*" You have my word. She'll not be harmed.'

'That's all I can ask.'

Villiers threw the gun on the bed. It landed between the twisted bare legs of the dead woman; the old soldier coughed abruptly, contemptuously, his posture returning. 'To practicalities, my young wolfpack,' he said, authority coming back to him awkwardly, but with definition. 'What's this strategy of yours?'

'To begin with, you're in a state of collapse, beyond shock. You're an automaton walking around in the dark, following instructions you can't understand but have to obey.'

'Not very different from reality, wouldn't you say?' interrupted Villiers. 'Before a young man with truth in his eyes forced me to listen to him. But how is this perceived state brought about? And why?'

'All you know – all you remember – is that a man broke into your house during the fire and smashed his gun into your head; you fell unconscious. When you woke up you found your wife dead, strangled, a note by her body. It's what's in the note that's driven you out of your mind.'

'What would that be?' asked the old soldier cautiously.

'The truth,' said Jason. 'The truth you can't ever permit anyone to know. What she was to Carlos, what he was to her. The killer who wrote the note left a telephone number, telling you that you could confirm what he's written. Once you were satisfied, you could destroy the note and report the murder any way you like. But for telling you the truth – for killing the whore who was so much a part of your son's death – he wants you to deliver a written message.'

'To Carlos?'

'No. He'll send a relay.'

'Thank God for that. I'm not sure I could go through with it, knowing it was him.'

'The message will reach him.'

'What is it?'

'I'll write it out for you; you can give it to the man he sends. It's got to be exact, both in what it says and what it doesn't say.' Bourne looked over at the dead woman, at the swelling in her throat. 'Do you have any alcohol?'

'A drink?'

'No. Rubbing alcohol. Perfume will do.'

'I'm sure there's rubbing alcohol in the medicine cabinet.'

'Would you mind getting it for me? Also a towel, please.'

'What are you going to do?'

'Put my hands where your hands were. Just in case, although I don't think anyone will question you. While I'm doing that, call whoever you have to call to get me out. The timing's important. I have to be on my way before you call Carlos's relay, long before you call the police. They'd have the airports watched.'

'I can delay until daybreak, I imagine. An old man's state of shock, as you put it. Not much longer than that. Where will you go?'

'New York. Can you do it? I have a passport identifying me as a man named George Washburn. It's a good job.'

'Making mine far easier. You'll have diplomatic status. Preclearance on both sides of the Atlantic.'

'As an Englishman? The passport's British.'

'On a NATO accommodation. Brevet channels; you are part of an Anglo-American team engaged in military negotiations. We favour your swift return to the United States for further instructions. It's not unusual, and sufficient to get you rapidly past both immigration points.'

'Good. I've checked the schedules. There's a seven a.m. flight, Air France to Kennedy.'

'You'll be on it.' The old man paused, he had not finished. He took a step towards Jason. 'Why New York? What makes you so certain Carlos will follow you to New York?'

'Two questions with different answers,' said Bourne. 'I have to deliver him where he marked me for killing four men and a woman I didn't know . . . one of those men very close to me, very much a part of me, I think.'

'I don't understand you.'

'I'm not sure I do, either. There's no time. It'll all be in what I write down for you on the plane. I have to prove *Carlos knew.* A building in New York. Where it all took place; they've got to understand. He *knew* about it. Trust me.'

'I do. The second question, then. Why will he come after you?'

Jason looked again at the dead woman on the bed. 'Instinct, maybe. I've killed the one person on earth he cares about. It she were someone else and Carlos killed her, I'd follow him across the world until I found him.'

'He may be more practical. I think that was your point to me.'

'There's something else,' replied Jason, taking his eyes away from Angélique Villiers. 'He has nothing to lose, everything to gain. No one knows what he looks like, but he knows me by sight. Still, he doesn't know my state of mind. He's cut me off, isolated me, turned me into someone I was never meant to be. Maybe he was too successful; maybe I'm mad, insane. God knows killing *her* was insane. My threats are irrational. How much more irrational am I? An irrational man, an insane man, is a panicked man. He can be taken out.'

'Is your threat irrational? Can you be taken out?'

'I'm not sure. I only know I don't have a choice.'

He did not. At the end it was as the beginning. Get Carlos. Trap Carlos. Cain is for Charlie and Delta is for Cain. The man and the myth were finally one, images and reality fused. There was no other way.

Ten minutes had passed since he had called Marie, lied to Marie, and heard the quiet acceptance in her voice, knowing it meant she needed time to think. She had not believed him, but she believed *in* him; she, too, had no choice. And he could not ease her pain; there had been no time, there *was* no time. Everything was in motion now, Villiers downstairs calling an emergency number at France's Brevet Militaire, arranging for a man with a false passport to fly out of Paris with diplomatic status. In less than three hours a man would be over the Atlantic approaching the anniversary of his own execution. It was the key; it was the trap. It was the last irrational act, insanity the order of that date.

Bourne stood by the desk; he put down the pen and studied the words he had written on a dead woman's stationery. They were the words a broken, bewildered old man was to repeat over the telephone to an unknown relay who would demand the paper and give it to Ilich Ramirez Sanchez.

I killed your bitch whore and I'll come back for you. There are seventy-one streets in the jungle. A jungle as dense as Tam Quan, but there was a path you missed, a vault in the cellars you did not know about – just as you never knew about me on the day of my execution ten years ago. One other man knew and you killed him. It doesn't matter. In that vault are documents that will set me free. Did you think I'd become Cain without that final protection? Washington won't dare touch me! It seems right that on the date of Bourne's death, Cain picks up the papers that guarantee him a very long life. You marked Cain. Now I mark you. I'll come back and you can join the whore.

Delta

Jason dropped the note on the desk and walked over to the dead woman. The alcohol was dry, the swollen throat prepared. He bent down and spread his fingers, placing his hands where another's had been placed.

Madness.

34

Early light broke over the spires of the church in Levallois-Perret in north-west Paris, the March morning cold, the night rain replaced by mist. A few old women, returning to their flats from all-night cleaning shifts in the city proper, trudged in and out of the bronze doors, holding railings and prayer books, devotions about to begin or finished with, precious sleep to follow before the drudgery of surviving the daylight hours. Along with the old women were shabbily-dressed men – most also old, others pathetically young – holding overcoats together, seeking the warmth of the church, these clutching bottles in their pockets, precious oblivion extended, another day to survive.

One old man, however, did not float with the trance-like movements of the others. He was an old man in a hurry. There was reluctance – even fear, perhaps – in his lined, sallow face, but no hesitation in his progress up the steps and through the doors, past the flickering candles and down the far left aisle of the church. It was an odd hour for a worshipper to seek confession; nevertheless the old beggar went directly to the first booth, parted the curtain and slipped inside.

'Angelus Domini . . .'

'Did you *bring* it?' the whisper demanded, the priestly silhouette behind the curtain trembling with rage.

'Yes. He thrust it in my hand like a man in a stupor, weeping, telling me to get out. He's burned Cain's note to him and says he'll deny everything if a single word is ever mentioned.' The old man shoved the pages of writing paper under the curtain.

'He used her stationery . . .' The assassin's whisper broke, a silhouetted hand brought to a silhouetted head, a muted cry of anguish now heard behind the curtain.

'I urge you to remember, Carlos,' pleaded the beggar. 'The messenger is not responsible for the news he bears. I could have refused to hear it, refused to bring it to you.'

'How? *Why?* . . .'

'Lavier. He followed her to Parc Monceau, then both of them to the church. I saw him in Neuilly-sur-Seine when I was your point. I told you that.'

'I know. But *why*? He could have used her in a hundred different ways! Against me! Why *this*?'

'It's in his note. He's gone mad. He was pushed too far, Carlos. It happens; I've seen it happen. A man on a double entry, his source-controls taken out; he has no one to confirm his initial assignment. Both sides want his corpse. He's stretched to the point where he may not even know who he is any longer.'

'He *knows*.' The whisper was drawn out in quiet fury. 'By signing the name Delta, he's telling me he knows. We both know where it comes from, where *he* comes from!'

The beggar paused. 'If that's true, then he's still dangerous to you. He's right. Washington won't touch him. It may not want to acknowledge him, but it will call off its hangmen. It may even be forced to grant him a privilege or two in return for his silence.'

'The papers he spoke of?' asked the assassin.

'Yes. In the old days – in Berlin. Prague, Vienna – they were called "final payments". Bourne uses "final protection", a minor variance. They were papers drawn up between a primary source-control and the infiltrator, to be used in the event the strategy collapsed, the primary killed, no other avenues open to the agent. It was not something you would have studied in Novgorod; the Soviets had no such accommodations. Soviet defectors, however, insisted upon them.'

'They were incriminating, then?'

'They had to be to some degree. Generally in the area of who was manipulated. Embarrassment is always to be avoided; careers are destroyed by embarrassment. But then, I don't have to tell you that. You've used the technique brilliantly.'

'"Seventy-one streets in the jungle . . ."' said Carlos, reading from the paper in his hand, an ice-like calm imposed on his whisper. '"A jungle as dense as Tam Quan." . . . This time the execution will take place as scheduled. Jason Bourne will not leave *this* Tam Quan alive. By any other name, Cain will be dead, and Delta will die for what he's done. *Angélique*! You have my *word*!' The incantation stopped, the assassin's mind racing to the practical. 'Did Villiers have any idea when Bourne left his house?'

'He didn't know. I told you, he was barely lucid, in as much a state of shock as with his telephone call.'

'It doesn't matter. The first flights to the United States began within the past hour. He'll be on one. I'll be in New York with him, and I won't miss this time . . . My knife will be waiting, its blade a razor. I'll peel his face away; the Americans will have their Cain without a face! They can give this Bourne, this Delta, whatever name they care to.'

The blue-striped telephone rang on Alexander Conklin's desk. Its bell was quiet, the understated sound lending an eerie emphasis. The blue-striped telephone was Conklin's direct line to the computer rooms and data banks. There was no one in the office to take the call.

The Central Intelligence executive suddenly rushed limping through the door, unused to the cane provided him by G-Two, SHAPE, Brussels last night, when he had commandeered a military transport to Andrews Field, Virginia. He threw the cane angrily across the room as he lurched for the phone. His eyes were bloodshot from lack of sleep, his breath short: the man responsible for the dissolution of Treadstone was exhausted. He had been in scrambler-communication with a dozen branches of clandestine operations – in Washington and overseas – trying to undo the insanity of the past twenty-four hours. He had spread every scrap of information he could cull from the files to every post in Europe, placed agents in the Paris–London–Amsterdam axis on alert. Bourne was alive and dangerous; he had tried to kill his DC control; he could be anywhere within ten hours of Paris. All airports and train stations were to be covered, all underground networks activated. Find him! *Kill him!*

'Yes?' Conklin braced himself against the desk and picked up the phone.

'This is Computer Dock Twelve,' said the male voice efficiently. 'We may have something. At least, State doesn't have any listing on it.'

'*What*, for Christ's sake?'

'The name you gave us four hours ago. Washburn.'

'What about it?'

'A George P. Washburn was pre-cleared out of Paris and into New York on an Air France flight this morning. Washburn's a fairly common name; he could be just a businessman with connections, but it was flagged on the readout, and since the status was NATO-diplomatic, we checked with State. They never heard of him. There's no one named Washburn involved with any ongoing NATO negotiations with the French government from any member nation.'

'Then how the hell was he pre-cleared? Who gave him the diplomatic?'

'We checked back through Paris; it wasn't easy. Apparently it was an accommodation of the Brevet Militaire. They're a quiet bunch.'

'The Brevet? Where do they get off clearing *our* people?'

'It doesn't have to be "our" people or "their" people: it can be anybody. Just a courtesy from the host country and that was a French carrier. It's one way to get a decent seat on an overbooked plane. Incidentally, Washburn's passport wasn't even US. It was British.'

There's a doctor, an Englishman named Washburn . . . It *was* him! It was Delta, and France's Brevet had co-operated with him! But why New York? What was in *New York* for *him*? And who placed so high in Paris would accommodate Delta? What had he told them? Oh, Christ! How *much* had he told them?

'When did the flight get in?' asked Conklin.

'Ten thirty-seven this morning. A little over an hour ago.'

'All right,' said the man whose foot had been blown off in Medusa, as he slid painfully around the desk into his seat. 'You've delivered, and now I want this scratched from the reels. Delete it. Everything you gave me. Is that clear?'

'Understood, sir, Deleted, sir.'

Conklin hung up. New York. *New York?* Not Washington but New York! There was nothing in New York any longer. Delta knew that. If he was after someone in Treadstone – if he was after *him* – he would have taken a flight directly to Dulles. What was in New York?

And why had Delta deliberately used the name Washburn? It was the same as telegraphing a strategy; he knew the name would be picked up sooner or later . . . Later . . . *After* he was inside the gates! Delta was telling whatever was left of Treadstone that he was dealing from strength. He was in a position to expose not only the Treadstone operation, but could go God knows how much further. Whole networks he had used as Cain, listening posts and ersatz consulates that were no more than electronic espionage stations . . . even the bloody spectre of Medusa. His connection inside the Brevet was his proof to Treadstone how high he had travelled. His signal that if he could reach within so rarefied a group of strategists, nothing could stop him. Goddamn it, stop him from *what*? What was the point? He had the millions; he could have *faded*!

Conklin shook his head, remembering. There had been a time when he would have let Delta fade, he had told him so twelve hours ago in a cemetery outside of Paris. A man could take only so much, and no one knew that better than Alexander Conklin, once among the finest covert field officers in the intelligence community. Only so much; the sanctimonious bromides about still being alive grew stale and bitter with time. It depended on what you were before, what you became with your deformity. Only so much . . . But Delta did *not* fade! He came back with insane statements, insane demands . . . crazy tactics no experienced intelligence officer would even contemplate. For no matter how much explosive information he possessed, no matter how high he penetrated, no sane man walked back into a minefield surrounded by his enemies. And all the blackmail in the world could not bring you back . . .

No sane man. No *sane* man. Conklin sat slowly forward in his chair.

I'm not Cain. He never was. I never was! I wasn't in New York . . . It was Carlos! Not me, Carlos! If what you're saying took place on Seventy-first Street, it was him! He knows!

But Delta *had* been at the brownstone on Seventy-first Street. Prints – third and index fingers, right hand. And the method of transport was now explained. Air France, Brevet cover . . . Fact: Carlos could not have known.

Things come to me . . . faces, streets, buildings. Images I can't place . . . I know a thousand facts about Carlos, but I don't know why!

Conklin closed his eyes. There was a phrase, a simple code phrase that had been used at the beginning of Treadstone. What was it? It came from Medusa . . . *Cain is for Charlie and Delta is for Cain.* That was it. Cain for *Carlos.* Delta-Bourne became the Cain that was the decoy for Carlos.

Conklin opened his eyes. Jason Bourne was to replace Ilich Ramirez Sanchez. That was the entire strategy of Treadstone Seventy-one. It was the keystone to the whole structure of deception, the parallax that would draw Carlos out of position into their sights.

Bourne. Jason Bourne. The totally unknown man, a name buried for a decade, a piece of human debris left in a jungle ten years ago. But he *had* existed; that, too, was part of the strategy.

Conklin separated the folders on his desk until he found the one he was looking for. It had no title, only an initial and two numbers followed by a black *X*, signifying that it was the only folder containing the origins of Treadstone.

T-71 X. The birth of Treadstone 71.

He opened it, almost afraid to see what he knew was there.

Date of execution. Tam Quan Sector. 25 March . . .

Conklin's eyes moved to the calendar on his desk.

24 March.

'Oh, my God,' he whispered, reaching for the telephone.

Dr Morris Panov walked through the double doors of the psychiatric ward on the third floor of Bethesda's Naval Annex and approached the nurses' counter. He smiled at the uniformed aide shuffling index cards under the stern gaze of the Head Floor Nurse standing beside her. Apparently the young trainee had misplaced a patient's file – if not a patient – and her superior was not going to let it happen again.

'Don't let Annie's whip fool you,' said Panov to the flustered girl. 'Underneath those cold, inhuman eyes is a heart of sheer granite. Actually, she escaped from the fifth floor two weeks ago but we're all afraid to tell anybody.'

The aide giggled: the nurse shook her head in exasperation. The phone rang on the desk behind the counter.

'Will you get that, please, dear,' said Annie to the young girl. The aide nodded and retreated to the desk. The nurse turned to Panov. 'Dr Mo, how am I ever going to get anything through their heads with you around?'

'With love, dear Annie. With love. But don't lose your bicycle chains.'

'You're incorrigible. Tell me, how's your patient in Five-A? I know you're worried about him.'

'I'm still worried.'

'I hear you stayed up all night.'

'There was a three a.m. movie on television I wanted to see.'

'Don't do it, Mo,' said the matronly nurse. 'You're too young to end up in there.'

'And maybe too old to avoid it, Annie. But thanks . . .'

Suddenly Panov and the nurse were aware that he was being paged, the wide-eyed trainee at the desk speaking into the microphone.

'Dr Panov, please. Telephone for . . .'

'I'm Dr Panov,' said the psychiatrist in a *sotto voce* whisper to the girl. 'We don't want anyone to know. Annie Donovan here's really my mother from Poland. Who is it?'

The trainee stared at Panov's ID card on his white coat; she blinked and replied. 'A Mr Alexander Conklin, sir.'

'Oh?' Panov was startled. Alex Conklin had been a patient on and off for five years, until they had both agreed he'd adjusted as well as he was ever going to adjust – which was not a hell of a lot. There were so many, and so little they could do for them. Whatever Conklin wanted had to be relatively serious for him to call Bethesda rather than the office. 'Where can I take this, Annie?'

'Room One,' said the nurse, pointing across the hall. 'It's empty. I'll have the call transferred.'

Panov walked towards the door, an uneasy feeling spreading through him.

'I need some very fast answers, Mo,' said Conklin, his voice strained.

'I'm not very good at fast answers, Alex. Why not come in and see me this afternoon?'

'It's not me. It's someone else. Possibly.'

'No games, please. I thought we'd gone beyond that.'

'No games. This is a Four-Zero emergency, and I need help.'

'Four-Zero? Call in one of your staff men. I've never requested that kind of clearance.'

'I can't. That's how tight it is.'

'Then you'd better whisper to God.'

'Mo, *please*! I only have to confirm possibilities, the rest I can put together myself. And I don't have five seconds to waste. A man may be running around ready to blow away ghosts, anyone he thinks is a ghost. He's already killed very real, very important people and I'm not sure he knows it. Help me, help *him*!'

'If I can. Go ahead.'

'A man is placed in a highly volatile, maximum stress situation for a long period of time, the entire period in deep cover. The cover itself is a decoy – very visible, very negative, constant pressure applied to maintain that visibility. The purpose is to draw out a target similar to the decoy by persuading the target that the decoy's a threat, forcing the target into the open . . . Are you with me so far?'

'So far,' said Panov. 'You say there's been constant pressure on the decoy to maintain a negative, highly visible profile. What's his environment been?'

'As brutal as you can imagine.'

'For how long a period of time?'

'Three years.'

'Good God,' said the psychiatrist. 'No breaks?'

'None at all. Twenty-four hours a day, three hundred and sixty-five days a year. Three years. Someone not himself.'

'When will you damn fools learn? Even prisoners in the worst camps could be themselves, talk to others who were themselves.' Panov stopped, catching his own words, and Conklin's meaning. 'That's your point, isn't it?'

'I'm not sure,' answered the intelligence officer. 'It's hazy, confusing, even contradictory. What I want to ask is this. Could such a man under these circumstances begin to . . . believe he's the decoy, assume the characteristics, absorb the mocked dossier to the point where he believes it's him?'

'The answer to that's so obvious I'm surprised you ask it. Of course he could. Probably would. It's an unendurably prolonged performance that can't be sustained unless the belief becomes a part of his everyday reality. The actor never off the stage in a play that never ends. Day after day, night after night.' The doctor stopped again, then continued carefully. 'But that's not really your question, is it?'

'No,' replied Conklin. 'I go one step further. Beyond the decoy. I have to; it's the only thing that makes sense.'

'Wait a minute,' interrupted Panov sharply. 'You'd better stop there, because I'm not confirming any blind diagnosis. Not for what you're leading up to. No way, Charlie. That's giving you a licence I won't be responsible for – with or without a consultation fee.'

'"No way . . . *Charlie*." Why did you say that, Mo?'

'What do you mean, why did I say it? It's a phrase. I hear it all the time. Kids in dirty blue jeans on the corner; hookers in my favourite saloons.'

'How do you know what I'm leading up to?' said the CIA man.

'Because I had to read the books and you're not very subtle. You're about to describe a classic case of paranoid schizophrenia with multiple personalities. It's not just your man assuming the role of the *decoy*, but the decoy himself transferring his identity to the one he's after. The *target.* That's what you're driving at, Alex. You're telling me your man is three people: himself, decoy and target. And I repeat. No way, Charlie. I'm not confirming anything remotely like that without an extensive examination. That's giving you rights you can't have: three reasons for dispatch. No way!'

'I'm not asking you to confirm anything! *I* just want to know if it's *possible.* For Christ's sake, Mo, there's a lethally experienced man running around with a gun, killing people he claims he didn't know, but whom he worked with for three years! He denies being at a specific place at a specific time when his own fingerprints prove he was *there*! He says images come to him – faces he can't place, names he's heard but doesn't know from where. He claims he was never the decoy, it was never *him*! But it *was*! It *is*! Is it *possible*? That's all I want to know! Could the stress and time and the everyday pressures break him like this? Into *three*?'

Panov held his breath for a moment. 'It's possible,' he said softly. 'If your facts are accurate, it's possible. That's all I'll say, because there are too many other possibilities.'

'Thank you.' Conklin paused. 'A last question. Say there was a date – a month and a day – that was significant to the mocked dossier, the decoy's dossier.'

'You'd have to be more specific.'

'I will. It was the date when the man whose identity was taken for decoy was killed.'

'Then obviously not part of the working dossier, but known to your man. Am I following you?'

'Yes, he knew it. Let's say he was there. Would he remember it?'

'Not as the decoy.'

'But as one of the other two?'

'Assuming the target was also aware of it, or that he'd communicated it through his transference, yes.'

'There's also a place where the strategy was conceived, where the decoy was created. If our man was in the vicinity of that place and the date of death was close at hand, would he be drawn to it? Would it surface and become important to him?'

'If it was associated with the original place of death because the decoy was born there, it's possible. It would depend on who he was at the moment.'

'Suppose he was the target?'

'And knew the location?'

'Yes, because another part of him had to.'

'Then he'd be drawn to it. It would be a subconscious compulsion.'

'Why?'

'To kill the decoy. He'd kill everything in sight, but the main objective would be the decoy. Himself.'

Alexander Conklin replaced the phone, his non-existent foot throbbing, his thoughts so convoluted he had to close his eyes again to find a consistent strain. He had been wrong in Paris . . . in a cemetery outside Paris. He had wanted to kill a man for the wrong reasons, the right ones beyond his comprehension. He *was* dealing with a madman. Someone whose afflictions were not explained in twenty years of training, but were understandable if one thought about the pains and the losses, the unending waves of violence . . . all ending in futility. No one knew anything really. Nothing made sense. A Carlos was trapped, killed today, and another would take his place. Why did we do it . . . David?

David. I say your name finally. We were friends once, David . . . Delta. I knew your wife and your children. We drank together and had a few dinners together in far-off posts in Asia. You were the best foreign service officer in the Orient and everyone knew it. You were going to be the key to the new policy, the one that was around the corner. And then it happened. Death from the skies in the Mekong . . . You turned, David. We all lost, but only one of us became Delta. In Medusa. I did not know you that well – drinks and a dinner or two do not a close companion make – but few of us become animals. You did, Delta.

And now you must die. Nobody can afford you any longer. None of us.

'Leave us, please,' said General Villiers to his aide as he sat down opposite Marie St Jacques in the Montmartre café. The aide nodded and walked to a table ten feet from the booth; he would leave but he was still on guard. The exhausted old soldier looked at Marie. 'Why did you insist on my coming here? He wanted you out of Paris. I gave him my word.'

'Out of Paris, out of the race,' said Marie, touched by the sight of the old man's haggard face. 'I'm sorry. I don't want to be another burden for you. I heard the reports on the radio.'

'Insanity,' said Villiers, picking up the brandy his aide had ordered for him. 'Three hours with the police living a terrible lie, condemning a man for a crime that was mine alone.'

'The description was accurate, uncannily accurate. No one could miss him.'

'He gave it to me himself. He sat in front of my wife's mirror and told me what to say, looking at his own face in the strangest manner. He saw it was the only way. Carlos could only be convinced by my going to the police, creating a manhunt. He was right, of course.'

'He was right,' agreed Marie, 'but he's not in Paris, or Brussels, or Amsterdam.'

'I beg your pardon?'

'I want you to tell me where he's gone.'

'He told you himself.'

'He lied to me.'

'How can you be certain?'

'Because I know when he tells me the truth. You see, we both listen for it.'

'You both . . . ? I'm afraid I don't understand.'

'I didn't think you would. I was sure he hadn't told you. When he lied to me on the phone, saying the things he said so hesitantly, knowing I knew they were lies. I couldn't understand. I didn't piece it together until I heard the radio reports. Yours and another. That description . . . so complete, so total, even to the scar on his left temple. Then I knew. He wasn't planning to stay in Paris, or within five hundred miles of Paris. He was going far away – where that description wouldn't mean very much – where Carlos could be led, delivered to the people Jason had his agreement with. Am I right?'

Villiers put down the glass. 'I've given my word. You're to be taken to safety in the country. I don't understand the things you're saying.'

'Then I'll try to be clearer,' said Marie, learning forward. 'There was another report on the radio, one you obviously didn't hear because you were with the police or in seclusion. Two men were found shot to death in a cemetery near Rambouillet this morning. One was a known killer from St-Gervais. The other was identified as a former American Intelligence officer living in Paris, a highly controversial man who was given the choice of retiring from the army or facing a court martial.'

'Are you saying the incidents are related?' asked the old man.

'Jason was instructed by the American Embassy to go to that cemetery last night to meet a man flying over from Washington.'

'*Washington?*'

'Yes. His agreement was with a small group of men from American Intelligence. They tried to kill him last night; they think they have to kill him.'

'Good God, why?'

'Because they can't trust him. They don't know what he's done or where he's been for a long period of time and he can't tell them.' Marie paused, closing her eyes briefly. 'He doesn't know who he is. He doesn't know who they are; and the man from Washington hired other men to kill him last night. That man wouldn't listen, they think he's betrayed them, stolen millions from them, killed men he's never heard of. He hasn't. But he doesn't have any clear answers either. He's a man with only fragments of a memory, each fragment condemning him. He's a near total amnesiac.'

Villiers's lined face was locked in astonishment, his eyes pained in recollection. '"For all the wrong reasons . . ." He said that to me. "They have men everywhere . . . the orders are to execute me on sight. I'm hunted by men I don't know and can't see. For all the wrong reasons."'

'For *all* the wrong reasons,' emphasized Marie, reaching across the narrow table and touching the old man's arm. 'And they do have men everywhere, men ordered to kill him on sight. Wherever he goes, they'll be waiting.'

'How will they know where he's gone?'

'He'll tell them. It's part of his strategy. And when he does, they'll kill him. He's walking into his own trap.'

For several moments Villiers was silent, his guilt overwhelming. Finally he spoke in a whisper. 'Almighty God, what have I done?'

'What you thought was right. What he persuaded you was right. You can't blame yourself. Or him, really.'

'He said he was going to write out everything that had happened to him, everything that he remembered . . . How painful that statement must have been for him. I can't wait for that letter, Mademoiselle. We can't wait. I must know everything you can tell me. Now.'

'What can you do?'

'Go to the American Embassy. To the ambassador. Now. *Everything.*'

Marie St Jacques withdrew her hand slowly as she leaned back in the booth, her dark red hair against the banquette. Her eyes were far away, clouded with the mist of tears. 'He told me his life began for him on a small island in the Mediterranean called Île de Port Noir . . .'

The Secretary of State walked angrily into the office of the director of Consular Operations, the department's section dealing with clandestine activities. He strode across the room to the desk of the astonished director, who rose at the sight of this powerful man, his expression a mixture of shock and bewilderment.

'Mr Secretary? . . . I didn't receive any message from your office, sir. I would have come upstairs right away.'

The Secretary of State slapped a yellow legal pad down on the director's desk. On the top page was a column of six names written with the broad strokes of a felt-tipped pen.

Bourne
Delta
Medusa
Cain
Carlos
Treadstone

'What is this?' asked the Secretary. 'What the hell *is* this?'

The director of Cons-Op leaned over the desk. 'I don't know, sir. They're names, of course. A code for the alphabet – the letter D – and a reference to Medusa; that's still classified, but I've heard of it. And I suppose the "Carlos" refers to the assassin; I wish we knew more about him. But I've never heard of "Bourne" or "Cain" or "Treadstone".'

'Then come up to my office and listen to a tape of a telephone conversation that I've just had with Paris and you'll learn all about them!' exploded the Secretary of State. 'There are extraordinary things on that tape, including killings in Ottawa and Paris and some very strange dealings our First Secretary in the Montaigne had with a CIA man. There's also outright lying to the authorities of foreign governments, to our *own* intelligence units and to the European newspapers – with neither the knowledge or the consent of the Department of State! There's been a global deception that's spread misinformation throughout more countries than I want to think about. We're flying over under a deep-diplomatic a Canadian woman, an economist for the government in Ottawa who's wanted for murder in Zürich. We're being *forced* to grant asylum to a fugitive, to subvert the laws, because if that woman's telling the truth we've got our ass in a sling! I want to know what's been going on. Cancel everything on your calendar, and I mean *everything.* You're spending the rest of the day and all night if you have to digging this damn thing out of the ground. There's a man walking around who doesn't know who he is, but with more classified information in his head than ten sterile computers!'

It was past midnight when the exhausted director of Consular Operations made the connection; he had nearly missed it. The First Secretary at the embassy in Paris, under threat of instant dismissal, had given him Alexander Conklin's name. But Conklin was nowhere to be found. He had returned to Washington from Brussels on a military jet in the morning; but had signed out of Langley at 1.22 in the afternoon, leaving no telephone number – not even an emergency number – where he could be reached. And from what the director had learned about Conklin, that omission was extraordinary. The CIA man was what was commonly referred to as a shark-killer; he directed individual strategies throughout the world where defection and treason were suspected. There were too many men in too many stations who might need his approval or disapproval at any given moment. It was not logical for him to sever that cord for twelve hours. What was also unusual was the fact that his telephone logs had been scratched; there were none for the past two days and the Central Intelligence Agency had very specific regulations concerning those logs. Traceable accountability was the new order of the new regime. However, the director of Cons-Op had learned one fact: Conklin had been attached to Medusa.

Using the threat of State Department retaliation, the director had requested a closed circuit readout of Conklin's logs for the past five weeks. Reluctantly, the agency beamed them over and the director sat in front of a screen for two hours, instructing the operators at Langley to keep the tape repeating until he told them to stop.

Eighty-six logicals had been called, the word Treadstone mentioned; none had responded. Then the director went back to the possible; there was an Army man he had not considered because of his well-known antipathy to the CIA. But Conklin had telephoned him twice during the space of twelve minutes a week ago. The director called his sources at the Pentagon and found what he was looking for: Medusa.

Brigadier-General Irwin Arthur Crawford, current ranking officer in charge of Army Intelligence data banks, former commander Saigon, attached to convert operations – still classified. *Medusa.*

The director picked up the conference room phone; it bypassed the switchboard. He dialled the Brigadier's home in Fairfax and, on the fourth ring. Crawford answered. The State Department man identified himself and asked if the General cared to return a call to State and be put through for verification.

'Why would I want to do that?'

'It concerns a matter that comes under the heading of Treadstone.'

'I'll call you back.'

He did so in eighteen seconds, and within the next two minutes the director had delivered the outlines of the State's information.

'There's nothing there we don't know about,' said the Brigadier. 'There's been a control committee on this from the beginning; the Oval office were given a preliminary summation within a week of the inauguration. Our objective warranted the procedures, you may be assured of that.'

'I'm willing to be convinced,' replied the man from State. 'Is this related to that business in New York a week ago? Elliot Stevens, that Major Webb and David Abbott? Where the circumstances were, shall we say, considerably altered?'

'You were aware of the alterations?'

'I'm the head of Cons-Op, General.'

'Yes, you would be . . . Stevens wasn't married; the rest understood. Robbery and homicide were preferable. The answer is affirmative.'

'I see . . . Your man Bourne flew into New York yesterday morning.'

'I know. We know – that is Conklin and myself. We're the inheritors.'

'You've been in touch with Conklin?'

'I last spoke to him around one o'clock in the afternoon. Unlogged. He insisted on it, frankly.'

'He's checked out of Langley. There's no number where he can be reached.'

'I know that, too. Don't try . . . With all due respect, tell the Secretary to back away. You back away. Don't get involved.'

'We are involved, General. We're flying over the Canadian woman by diplomatic.'

'For God's sake, *why*?'

'We were forced to; she forced us to.'

'Then keep her in isolation. You've *got* to! She's *our* resolve, we'll be responsible.'

'I think you'd better explain.'

'We're dealing with an *insane* man. A multiple schizophrenic. He's a walking firing squad; he could kill a dozen innocent people with one outburst, one explosion in his own head, and he wouldn't know *why*.'

'How do you know?'

'Because he's already killed. That massacre in New York last week – it was *him*. He killed Stevens, the Monk, Webb – above all, Webb – and two others you never heard of . . . We understand now. He *wasn't* responsible, but that can't change anything. Leave him to us. To Conklin.'

'Last week? Bourne?'

'Yes. We have proof. Prints. They were confirmed by the bureau. It was him.'

'Your man would leave prints?'

'He did.'

'He couldn't have,' said the man from State.

'What?'

'Tell me, where did you come up with the conclusion of insanity? This multiple schizophrenia, or whatever the hell you call it.'

'Conklin spoke to a psychiatrist – one of the best – an authority on stress-breakdowns. Alex described the history and it was brutal. The doctor confirmed our suspicions, Conklin's suspicions.'

'He *confirmed* them?' asked the director, stunned.

'Yes.'

'Based on what Conklin said? On what he *thought* he knew?'

'There's no other explanation. Leave him to us. He's our problem.'

'You're a damn fool. General. You should have stuck to your data banks, or maybe more primitive artillery.'

'I resent that.'

'Resent it all you like. If you've done what *I* think you've done you may not have anything left but resentment.'

'Explain that,' said Crawford harshly.

'You're not dealing with a madman, or with insanity, or with any goddamned multiple schizophrenia, which I doubt you know any more about than I do. You're dealing with an *amnesiac*, a man who's been trying for six months to find out who he is and where he comes from. And from a telephone tape we've got over here, we gather he tried to tell you – tried to tell Conklin, but Conklin wouldn't listen. None of you would *listen* . . . You sent a man out in deep cover for three years – three *years* – to pull in Carlos, and when the strategy broke, you assumed the worst.'

'Amnesia? . . . No, you're wrong! I spoke to Conklin; he *did* listen. You don't understand; we both knew . . .'

'I *don't* want to hear his name!' broke in the director of Consular Operations.

The general paused. 'We both knew . . . Bourne . . . years ago. I think you know from where; you read the name to me. He was the strangest man I ever met, as close to being paranoid as anyone in that outfit. He undertook missions – risks – no same man would accept. Yet he never asked for anything. He was filled with so much hate.'

'And that made him a candidate for a psychiatric ward ten years later?'

'Seven years,' corrected Crawford. 'I tried to prevent his selection in Treadstone. But the Monk said he was the best. I couldn't argue with that, not in terms of expertise. But I made my objections known. He was psychologically a borderline case; we knew why. I was proved right. I stand on that.'

'You're not going to stand on anything, General. You're going to fall right on your iron ass. Because the Monk was right. Your man is the best, with or without a memory. He's bringing in Carlos, delivering him right to your goddamn front door. That is, he's bringing him in unless you kill Bourne first.' Crawford's low, sharp intake of breath was precisely what the director was afraid he might hear. He continued. 'You can't reach Conklin, can you?' he asked.

'No.'

'He's gone under, hasn't he? Made his own arrangements, payments funnelled through third and fourth parties unknown to each other, the source untraceable, all connections to the agency and Treadstone obliterated. And by now there are photographs in the hands of men Conklin doesn't know, wouldn't recognize if they held him up. Don't talk to me about firing squads. Yours is in place but you can't see it, you don't know where it is. But it's prepared, a half a dozen rifles ready to fire when the condemned man comes into view. Am I reading the scenario?'

'You don't expect me to answer that,' said Crawford.

'You don't have to. This is Consular Operations; I've been there before. But you were right about one thing. This *is* your problem; it's right back in your court. We're not going to be touched by you. That's my recommendation to the Secretary. The State Department can't afford to know who you are. Consider this call unlogged.'

'Understood.'

'I'm sorry,' said the director, meaning it, hearing the futility in the general's voice. 'It all blows up sometimes.'

'Yes. We learned that in Medusa. What are you going to do with the girl?'

'We don't even know what we're going to do with you yet.'

'That's easy. Eisenhower at the summit. What U-Twos? We'll go along; no preliminary summation. Nothing . . . We can get the girl off the Zürich books.'

'We'll tell her. It may help. We'll be making apologies all over the place; with her we'll try for a very substantial settlement.'

'Are you *sure*?' interrupted Crawford.

'About the settlement?'

'No. The *amnesia.* Are you positive?'

'I've listened to that tape at least twenty times, heard her voice. I've never been so sure of anything in my life. Incidentally, she got in several hours ago. She's at the Pierre Hotel under guard. We'll bring her down to Washington in the morning after we work out what we're going to do.'

'Wait a minute.' The general's voice rose. 'Not tomorrow! She's *here* . . . ? Can you get me clearance to see her?'

'Don't dig that grave of yours any deeper, General. The fewer names she knows, the better. She was with Bourne when he was calling the embassy; she's aware of the First Secretary, probably Conklin by now. He may have to take the fall himself. Stay out of it.'

'You just told me to *play* it out.'

'Not this way. You're a decent man; so am I. We're professionals.'

'You don't understand! We have photographs, yes, but they may be useless. They're three years old, and Bourne's changed, changed drastically. It's why Conklin's on the scene – where I don't know – but he's there. He's the only one who's seen him, but it was night, raining. She may be our only chance. She's been with him – living with him for weeks, she *knows* him. It's possible that she'd recognize him before anyone else.'

'I don't understand.'

'I'll spell it out. Among Bourne's many, many talents is the ability to change his appearance, melt into a crowd or a field or a cluster of trees – be where you can't see him. If what you say is so, he wouldn't remember, but we used to have a word for him in Medusa. His men used to call him . . . a chameleon.'

'That's your Cain, General.'

'It was our Delta. There was no one like him . . . And that's why the girl can help. *Now.* Clear me! Let me see her, talk to her.'

'By clearing you, we acknowledge you. I don't think we can do that.'

'For God's sake, you just said we were decent men! *Are* we? We can save his life! *Maybe.* If she's with me and we find him, we can get him out of there!'

'*There?* Are you telling me you know exactly where he's going to be?'

'Yes.'

'*How?*'

'Because he wouldn't go anywhere else.'

'And the *time span*?' asked the incredulous director of Consular Operations. 'You know *when* he's going to be there?'

'Yes Today. It's the date of his own execution.'

35

Rock music blared from the transistor radio with tin-like vibrations as the long-haired driver of the Yellow Cab slapped his hand against the rim of the steering wheel and jolted his jaw with the beat. The taxi edged east on Seventy-first Street, locked into the line of cars that began at the exit on the East River Drive. Tempers flared as engines roared in place and cars lurched forward only to slam to sudden stops, inches away from bumpers in front. It was 8.45 in the morning, New York's rush hour traffic as usual a contradiction in syntax.

Bourne wedged himself into the corner of the back seat and stared at the tree-lined street beneath the rim of his hat and through the dark lenses of his sun glasses. He had *been* there; it was all indelible. He had walked the pavements, seen the doorways and the shopfronts and the walls covered with ivy – so out of place in the city, yet so right for this street. He had glanced up before and had noticed the roof gardens before, relating them to a gracious garden several blocks away towards the park, beyond a pair of elegant French doors at the far end of a large . . . complicated . . . room. That room was inside a tall, narrow building of brown, jagged stone, with a column of wide, lead-paned windows rising three storeys above the pavement. Windows made of thick glass that refracted light both inside and out in subtle flashes of purple and blue. Antique glass, perhaps, ornamental glass . . . bullet-proof glass. A brownstone residence with a set of thick outside steps. They were odd steps, unusual steps, each level criss-crossed with black ridges that protruded above the surface, protecting the descender from the elements. Shoes going down would not slip on ice or snow . . . and the weight of anyone climbing up would trigger electronic devices inside.

Jason knew that house, knew they were coming closer to it. The echo in his chest accelerated and became louder as they entered the block. He would see it any moment, and as he held his wrist he knew why Parc Monceau had struck such chords in his mind's eye. That small part of Paris was so much like this short stretch of the upper east side. Except for an isolated intrusion of an unkempt stoop or an ill-conceived white-washed facade, they could be identical blocks.

He thought of André Villiers. He had written down everything he could remember since a memory had been given him in the pages of a notebook bastily purchased at Orly Airport, From the first moment when a living, bullet-ridden man had opened his eyes in a humid, dingy room on Île de Port Noir through the frightening revelations of Marseilles, Zürich and Paris – especially

Paris, where the specture of an assassin's mantle had fallen over his shoulders, the expertise of a killer proven to be his. By any standards, it was a confession, as damning in what it could not explain as in what it described. But it was the truth as he knew the truth, infinitely more exculpatory after his death than before. In the hands of André Villiers it would be used well; the right decisions would be made for Marie St Jacques. That knowledge gave him the freedom he needed now. He had sealed the pages in an envelope and mailed it to Parc Monceau from Kennedy Airport. By the time it reached Paris he would be alive or he would be dead; he would kill Carlos or Carlos would kill him. Somewhere on that street – so like a street thousands of miles away – a man whose shoulders floated rigidly above a tapered waist would come after him. It was the only thing he was absolutely sure of; he would do the same. Somewhere on that street . . .

There it was! It was *there*, the morning sun bouncing off the black enamelled door and the shiny brass, penetrating the thick, lead-paned windows that rose like a wide column of glistening, purplish blue, emphasizing the ornamental splendour of the glass, but not its resistance to the impacts of high-powered rifles and heavy calibred automatic weapons. He was *here*, and for reasons – emotions he could not define, his eyes began to tear and there was a swelling in his throat. He had the incredible feeling that he had come back to a place that was as much a part of him as his body or what was left of his mind. Not a home; there was no comfort, no serenity in looking at that elegant east-side residence. But there was something else – an overpowering sensation of – *return*. He was back at the beginning, *the* beginning, at both departure and creation, black night and bursting dawn. Something was happening to him; he gripped his wrist harder, desperately trying to control the almost uncontrollable impulse to jump out of the taxi and race across the street to that monstrous, silent structure of jagged stone and deep blue glass. He wanted to leap up the steps and hammer his fist against the heavy black door.

Let me in! I am here! You must let me in! Can't you understand?

I AM INSIDE!

Images welled up in front of his eyes; jarring sounds assaulted his ears. A jolting, throbbing pain kept exploding at his temples. He was inside a dark room – *that* room – staring at a screen, at other, inner images that kept flashing on and off in rapid, blinding succession.

Who is he? Quickly. You're too late! You're a dead man. Where is this street? What does it mean to you? Who did you meet there? What? Good. Keep it simple; say as little as possible. Here's a list: eight names. Which are contacts? Quickly! Here's another. Methods of matching kills. Which are yours? . . . No, no, no! Delta might do that, not Cain! You are not Delta, you are not you! You are Cain. You are a man named Bourne. Jason Bourne! You slipped back. Try again. Concentrate! Obliterate everything else. Wipe away the past. It does not exist for you. You are only what you are here, became here!

Oh, God. Marie had said it.

Maybe you just know what you've been told . . . Over and and over and over again. Until there was nothing else . . . Things you've been told . . . but you can't re-live . . . because they're not you.

The sweat rolled down his face, stinging his eyes, as he dug his fingers into his wrist, trying to push the pain and the sounds and the flashes of light out of his mind. He had written to Carlos that he was coming back for hidden documents that were his . . . 'final protection.' At that time, the phrase had struck him as weak; he had nearly crossed it out, wanting a stronger reason for flying to New York. Yet instinct had told him to let it stand; it was a part of his past . . . somehow. Now he understood. His identity was inside that house. His *identity.* And whether Carlos came after him or not, he had to find it. He *had* to!

It was suddenly insane! He shook his head violently back and forth, trying to suppress the compulsion, to still the screams that were all around him – screams that were his screams, his voice. *Forget Carlos. Forget the trap. Get inside that house! It was there; it was the beginning!*

Stop it!

The irony was macabre. There was no final protection in that house, only a final explanation for himself. And it was meaningless without Carlos. Those who hunted him knew it and disregarded it; they wanted him dead because of it. But he was so close . . . he had to find it. It was there.

Bourne glanced up; the long-haired driver was watching him in the rear-view mirror. 'Migraine,' said Jason curtly. 'Drive around the block. To this block again. I'm early for my appointment. I'll tell you where to let me off.'

'It's your wallet, Mister.'

The brownstone was behind them now, passed quickly in a sudden, brief break in the traffic. Bourne swung around in the seat and looked at it through the rear window. The seizure was receding, the sights and sounds of personal panic fading; only the pain remained, but it too would diminish, he knew that. It had been an extraordinary few minutes. Priorities had become twisted; compulsion had replaced reason, the pull of the unknown had been so strong that for a moment or two he had nearly lost control. He could not let it happen again; the trap itself was everything. He had to see that house again; he had to study it again. He had all day to work, to refine his strategy, his tactics for the night, but a second, calmer appraisal was in order now. Others would come during the day, closer appraisals. The chameleon in him would be put to work.

Sixteen minutes later it was obvious that whatever he intended to study no longer mattered. Suddenly, everything was different, everything had changed. The line of traffic in the block slower, another hazard added to the street. A removal van had parked in front of the brownstone house; men in overalls stood smoking cigarettes and drinking coffee, putting off that moment when work was to commence. The heavy black door was open and a man in a green jacket, the moving company's emblem above the left pocket, stood in the foyer, a clipboard in his hand. Treadstone was being dismantled! In a few hours it could be gutted, a shell! It couldn't be. They had to stop!

Jason leaned forward, money in his hand, the pain gone from his head; all was movement now. He had to reach Conklin in Washington. Not later – not when the chess pieces were in place – but right now! Conklin had to tell them to stop! His entire strategy was based on darkness . . . *always darkness.* The beam of a torch shooting out of first one alleyway then another, then against dark walls and up at darkened windows. Orchestrated properly, swiftly, darting from one position to another. An assassin would be drawn to a stone building at night. At *night.* It would happen at night! Not now!

'Hey, Mister!' yelled the driver through the open window. Jason bent down. 'What is it?'

'I just wanted to say thanks. This makes my . . .'

A *spit.* Over his shoulder! Followed by a cough that was the start of a scream. Bourne stared at the driver, at the stream of blood that had erupted over the man's left ear. The man was dead, killed by a bullet meant for his fare, fired from a window somewhere in that street.

Jason dropped to the ground; then sprang to his left, spinning towards the kerb. Two more spits came in rapid succession, the first embedded in the side of the taxi, the second exploding the asphalt. It was unbelievable! He was marked before the hunt had begun! Carlos was *there.* In position! He or one of his men had taken the high ground, a window or a rooftop from which the entire street could be observed. Yet the possibility of indiscriminate death caused by a killer in a window or on a rooftop was crazy; the police would come, the street blocked off, even a reverse trap aborted. And Carlos was *not* crazy! It did not make sense. Nor did Bourne have the time to speculate; he had to get out of the trap . . . the reverse trap. *He had to get to that phone.* Carlos was here! At the doors of Treadstone! He had brought him back. He had actually brought him back! It was his proof!

He got to his feet and began running, weaving in and out of the groups of pedestrians. He reached the corner and turned right, the box was twenty feet away, but it was also a target. He could not use it.

Across the street was a delicatessen, a small rectangular sign above the door. *Telephone.* He stepped off the kerb and started running again, dodging the lurching cars. One of them might do the job Carlos had reserved for himself. That irony, too, was macabre.

'The Central Intelligence Agency, sir, is fundamentally a fact-finding organization,' said the man on the line condescendingly. 'The sort of activities you describe are the rarest part of our work, and frankly blown out of proportion by films and misinformed writers.'

'Goddamn it, *listen* to me!' said Jason, cupping the mouthpiece in the crowded delicatessen. 'Just tell me where Conklin is. It's an emergency!'

'His office already told you, sir. Mr Conklin left yesterday afternoon and is expected back at the end of the week. Since you say you know Mr Conklin, you're aware of his service-related injury. He often goes for physical therapy . . .'

'Will you *stop* it! I saw him in Paris – outside Paris – two nights ago. He flew over from Washington to meet me.'

'As to that,' interrupted the man in Langley, 'when you were transferred to this office, we'd already checked. There's no record of Mr Conklin having left the country in over a year.'

Then it's buried! He was there!

'You're looking for codes,' said Bourne desperately. 'I don't have them. But someone working with Conklin will recognize the words. Medusa, Delta, Cain . . . Treadstone! Someone *has* to!'

'No one does. You were told that.'

'By someone who doesn't. There are those who do. *Believe* me!'

'I'm sorry. I really . . .'

'Don't hang up!' There was another way; one he did not care to use but there was nothing else. 'Five or six minutes ago I got out of a taxi on Seventy-first Street. I was spotted and someone tried to take me out.'

'Take . . . you out?'

'Yes. The driver spoke to me and I bent down to listen. That movement saved my life, but the driver's dead, a bullet in his skull. That's the truth and I know you have ways of checking. There are probably half a dozen police cars on the scene by now. Check it out. That's the strongest advice I can give you.'

There was a brief silence from Washington. 'Since you asked for Mr Conklin – at least used his name – I'll follow this up. Where can I reach you?'

'I'll stay on. This call's on an international credit card. French issue, name of Chambord.'

'Chambord? You said . . .'

'*Please.*'

'I'll be back.'

The waiting was intolerable, made worse by a stern Hassidim glaring at him, fingering coins in one hand, a roll in another, and crumbs in his stringy, unkempt beard. A minute later the man in Langley was on the line, anger replacing compromise.

'I think this conversation has come to an end, Mr Bourne or Chambord, or whatever you call yourself. The New York police were reached; there's no such incident as you described on Seventy-first Street. And you were right. We do have ways of checking. I advise you that there are laws about such calls as this, strict penalties involved. Good day, sir.'

There was a click; the line went dead. Bourne stared at the dial in disbelief. For six months the men in Washington had searched for him, wanted to kill him for the silence they could not understand. Now, when he presented himself – presented them with the sole objective of his three-year agreement – he was dismissed. They still would not listen! . . . But that man *had* listened. And he had come back on the line denying a death that had taken place only minutes ago. It could not be . . . it was *insane*. It had *happened*!

Jason put the phone back on the hook, tempted to bolt from the crowded delicatessen. Instead, he walked calmly towards the door excusing himself through the rows of people lined up at the counter, his eyes on the glass front, scanning the crowds on the pavement. Outside he removed his overcoat, carrying it over his arm, and replaced the sunglasses with his tortoise-shells. Minor alterations, but he would not be where he was going long enough for them to be a major mistake. He hurried across the intersection towards Seventy-first Street.

At the far corner he fell in with a group of pedestrians waiting for the light. He turned his head to the left, his chin pressed down into his collar bone. The traffic was moving but the taxi was gone. It had been removed from the scene with surgical precision, a diseased, ugly organ cut from the body, the vital functions in normal process. It showed the precision of a master assassin, who knew precisely when to go in swiftly with a knife.

Bourne turned quickly, reversing his direction, and began walking south. He had to find a shop; he had to change his outer skin. The chameleon could not wait.

Marie St Jacques was angry as she held her place across the room from Brigadier-General Irwin Arthur Crawford in the suite at the Pierre Hotel. 'You wouldn't listen!' she accused. 'None of you would listen. Have you any idea what you've *done* to him?'

'All too well,' replied the officer, the apology in his acknowledgment not his voice. 'I can only repeat what I've told you. We didn't know what to listen *for*. The difference between the appearance and the reality were beyond our understanding, obviously beyond his own. And if beyond his, why not ours?'

'He's been trying to reconcile the appearance and reality, as you call it, for six months! And all you could do was send out men to kill him! He tried to *tell* you. What kind of people *are* you?'

'Flawed, Miss St Jacques. Flawed but decent, I think. It's why I'm here. The time span's begun and I want to save him if I can, if *we* can.'

'God, you make me sick!' Marie stopped, she shook her head and continued softly. 'I'll do whatever you ask, you know that. Can you reach this Conklin?'

'I'm sure I can. I'll stand on the steps of that house until he has no choice but to reach *me*. He may not be our concern, however.'

'Carlos?'

'Perhaps others.'

'What do you mean?'

'I'll explain on the way. Our main concern now – our *only* concern now – is to reach Delta.'

'Jason?'

'Yes. The man you call Jason Bourne.'

'And he's been one of you from the beginning,' said Marie. 'There were no slates to clean, no payments or pardons bargained for?'

'None. You'll be told everything in time, but this is *not* the time. I've made arrangements for you to be in an unmarked government car diagonally across from the house. We have binoculars for you; you know him better than anyone now. Perhaps you'll spot him. I pray to God you do.'

Marie went quickly to the cupboard and got her coat. 'He said one night that he was a chameleon . . .'

'He remembered?' interrupted Crawford.

'Remembered what?'

'Nothing. He had a talent for moving in and out of difficult situations without being seen. That's all I meant.'

'Wait a minute.' Marie approached the army man, her eyes suddenly riveted on his again. 'You say we have to reach Jason, but there's a better way. Let him come to us! To *me*. Put me on the steps of that house! He'll see *me*, get word to me!'

'Giving whoever's out there two targets?'

'You don't know your own man, General. I said "get word to me". He'll send someone, pay a man or a woman on the street to give me a message. I know him. He'll do it! It's the surest way!'

'I can't permit it.'

'Why not? You've done everything else stupidly! Blindly! Do one thing intelligently!'

'I can't. It might even solve problems you're not aware of, but I can't do it.'

'Give me a reason!'

'If Delta's right, if Carlos has come after him and is in the street, the risk is too great. Carlos knows you by sight. He'll kill you.'

'I'm willing to take that risk.'

'I'm not. I'd like to think I'm speaking for my government when I say that.'

'I don't think you are, frankly.'

'Leave it to others. May we go, please?'

'General Services Administration,' intoned a disinterested switchboard operator.

'Mr J. Petrocelli, please,' said Alexander Conklin, his voice tense, his fingers wiping the sweat from his forehead as he stood by the window, the telephone in his hand. 'Quickly, please!'

'Everybody's in a hurry . . .' The words were shorted out, replaced by the hum of a ring.

'Petrocelli, Reclamation Invoice Division.'

'What are you people *doing*?' exploded the CIA man, the shock calculated, a weapon.

The pause was brief. 'Right now, listening to some nut ask a stupid question.'

'Well, listen further. My name's Conklin, Central Intelligence Agency, Four-Zero clearance. You *do* know what that means?'

'I haven't understood anything you people've said in the past ten years.'

'You'd better understand this. It took me damn near an hour, but I just reached the dispatcher for a removal company up here in New York. He said he had an invoice signed by you to remove all the furniture from a brownstone on Seventy-first Street. One-Forty, to be exact.'

'Yeah, I remember that one. What about it?'

'Who gave you the order? That's *our* territory. We removed our equipment last week, but we did not – repeat, did *not* – request any further activity.'

'Just hold it,' said the bureaucrat. 'I saw that invoice. I mean I read it before I signed it; you guys make me curious. The order came directly from Langley on a priority sheet.'

'*Who* in Langley?'

'Give me a moment and I'll tell you. I've got a copy in my out file; it's here on my desk.' The crackling of paper could be heard on the line. It stopped and Petrocelli returned. 'Here it is, Conklin. Take up your beef with your own people in Administrative Controls.'

'They didn't know what they were doing. Cancel the order. Call up the removal company and tell them to clear out! *Now*!'

'Blow smoke, spook.'

'What?'

'Get a written priority requisition on my desk before three o'clock this afternoon, and it may – just may – get processed tomorrow. Then we'll put everything back.'

'Put everything *back*?'

'That's right. You tell us to take it out, we take it out. You tell us to put it back, we put it back. We have methods and procedures to follow just like you.'

'That equipment – everything – was on *loan*! It wasn't, *isn't* an agency operation.'

'Then why are you calling me? What have you got to do with it?'

'I don't have time to explain. Just get those people out of there. Call New York and get them out! Those are Four-Zero orders.'

'Make them a hundred and four and you can still blow smoke . . . Look, Conklin, we both know you can get what you want if I get what I need. Do it right. Make it legitimate.'

'I can't *involve* the agency!'

'You're not going to involve me, either.'

'Those people have got to get out! I'm telling you . . .' Conklin stopped, his eyes on the brownstone below and across the street, his thoughts suddenly paralysed. A tall man in a black overcoat had walked up the concrete steps; he turned and stood motionless in front of the open door. It was *Crawford.* What was he doing? What was he doing *here*? He had lost his senses; he was out of his mind! He was a stationary target; he could break the trap!

'Conklin? Conklin . . . ?' The voice floated up out of the phone as the CIA man hung up.

Conklin turned to a stocky man six feet away at an adjacent window. In the man's large hand was a rifle, a telescopic sight secured to the barrel. Alex did not know the man's name and he did not want to know it; he had paid enough not to be burdened.

'Do you see that man down there in the black overcoat standing by the door?' he asked.

'I see him. He's not the one we're looking for. He's too old.'

'Get over there and tell him there's a cripple across the street who wants to see him.'

Bourne walked out of the second-hand clothing shop on Third Avenue, pausing in front of the filthy glass window to appraise what he saw. It would do; everything was co-ordinated. The black woollen hat covered his head to the middle of his forehead, the wrinkled, patched army field jacket was several sizes too large; the red checked flannel shirt, the wide bulging khaki trousers and the heavy work shoes with thick rubber soles and huge rounded toes were all of a piece. He only had to find a walk to match the clothing. The walk of a strong, slow-witted man whose body had begun to show the effects of a lifetime of physical strain, whose mind accepted the daily inevitability of hard labour, reward found in a pack of beer at the end of the drudgery.

He would find that walk; he had used it before. Somewhere. But before he searched his imagination, there was a phone call to make; he saw a telephone box up the block, a mangled directory hanging from a chain beneath the metal shelf. He started walking, his legs automatically more rigid, his feet pressing weight on the pavement, his arms heavy in their sockets, the fingers of his hands slightly spaced, curved from years of abuse. A set, dull expression on his face would come later. Not now.

'Belkins Moving and Storage,' announced an operator somewhere in the Bronx.

'My name is Johnson,' said Jason impatiently but kindly. 'I'm afraid I have a problem, and I hope you might be able to help me.'

'I'll try, sir. What is it?'

'I was on my way over to a friend's house on Seventy-first Street – a friend who died recently, I'm sorry to say – to pick up something I'd lent him. When I got there your van was in front of the house. It's most embarrassing, but I think your men may remove my property. Is there someone I might speak to?'

'That would be a dispatcher, sir.'

'Might I have his name, please?'

'What?'

'His name.'

'Sure. Murray. Murray Schumach. I'll connect you.'

Two clicks preceded a long hum over the line.

'Schumach.'

'Mr Schumach?'

'That's right.'

Bourne repeated his embarrassing tale. 'Of course, I can easily obtain a letter from my attorney, but the item in question has little or no value . . .'

'What is it?'

'A fishing rod. Not an expensive one, but with an old fashioned casting reel, the kind that doesn't get tangled every five minutes.'

'Yeah, I know what you mean. I fish out of Sheepshead Bay. They don't make them reels like they used to. I think it's the alloys.'

'I think you're right, Mr Schumach. I know exactly in which closet he kept it.'

'Oh, what the hell, a fishing rod. Go up and see a guy named Dugan, he's the supervisor on the job. Tell him I said you could have it, but you'll have to sign for it. If he gives you static, tell him to go outside and call me; the phone's disconnected down there.'

'A Mr Dugan. Thank you very much, Mr Schumach.'

'Christ, that place is a ball-breaker today.'

'I beg your pardon?'

'Nothing. Some whacko called telling us to get out of there. And the job's firm, cash guaranteed. Can you believe it?'

Carlos. Jason could believe it.

'It's difficult, Mr Schumach.'

'Good fishing,' said the Belkins man.

Bourne walked west on Seventieth Street to Lexington Avenue. Three blocks south he found what he was looking for: an army-navy surplus store. He went inside.

Eight minutes later he came out carrying four brown padded blankets and six wide canvas straps with metal buckles. In the pockets of his field jacket were two ordinary road flares. They had been there on the counter looking like something they were not, triggering images beyond memory, back to a moment when there had been meaning and purpose. And anger. He slung the equipment over his left shoulder and trudged up towards Seventy-first. The chameleon was heading into the jungle, a jungle as dense as the unremembered Tam Quan.

It was 10:48 when he reached the corner of the tree-lined block that held the secrets of Treadstone Seventy-one. He was going back to the beginning – his beginning – and the fear that he felt was not the fear of physical harm. He was prepared for that, every sinew taut, every muscle ready; his knees and feet, hands and elbows, weapons, his eyes trip-wire alarms that would send instant signals to those weapons. His fear was far more profound. He was about to enter the place of his birth and he was terrified at what he might find there – remember there.

Stop it! The trap is everything. Cain is for Charlie and Delta is for Cain!

The traffic had diminished considerably, the rush hour over, the street in the doldrums of mid-morning quiescence. Pedestrians strolled now, they did not hasten; cars swung leisurely around the removal van, angry horns replaced by brief grimaces of irritation. Jason crossed with the light to the Treadstone side, the tall, narrow structure of brown, jagged stone and thick blue glass was fifty yards down the block. Blankets and straps in place, an already weary, slow-witted labourer walked behind a well-dressed couple towards it.

He reached the concrete steps as two muscular men, one black one white, were carrying a covered harp out of the door. Bourne stopped and called out, his words halting, his dialect coarse.

'Hey! Where's Doogan?'

'Where the hell d'you t'ink?' replied the white, angling his head around. 'Sittin' in a fuckin' chair.'

'He ain't gonna lift nothin' heavier than that clipboard, man,' added the black. 'He's an *executive*, ain't that right, Joey?'

'He's a crumb ball, is what he is. Watcha got there?'

'Schumach sent me,' said Jason. 'He wanted another man down here and figured you needed this stuff. Told me to bring it.'

'Murray the menace!' laughed the black. 'You new, man? I ain't seen you before. You come from shape-up?'

'Yeah.'

'Take that shit up to the executive,' grunted Joey, starting down the steps. 'He can *allocate* it, how about that, Pete? *Allocate*, you like it?'

'I love it, Joey. You a regular dictionary.'

Bourne walked up the reddish brown steps past the descending movers to the door. He stepped inside and saw the winding staircase on the right, and the long narrow corridor in front of him that led to another door thirty feet away. He had climbed those steps a thousand times, walked up and down that corridor thousands more. He had come back, and an overpowering sense of dread swept through him. He started down the dark narrow corridor; he could see shafts of sunlight bursting through a pair of French windows in the distance. He was approaching the room where Cain was born. *That* room. He gripped the straps on his shoulder and tried to stop the trembling.

Marie leaned forward in the back seat of the armour-plated government car, the binoculars in place. Something had happened; she was not sure what it was but she could guess. A short stocky man had passed by the steps of the brownstone house a few minutes ago, slowing his pace as he approached the general, obviously saying something to him. The man had then continued down the block and seconds later Crawford had followed him.

Conklin had been found.

It was a small step if what the general said was true. Hired gunmen, unknown to their employer, he unknown to them. Hired to kill a man . . . for all the wrong reasons! Oh, *God*, she loathed them all! Mindless, stupid men! Playing with the lives of *other* men, knowing so little, thinking they knew so much.

They had not listened! They never listened until it was too late, and then only with stern forbearance and strong reminders of what might have been – had things been as they were perceived to be, which they were not. The corruption came from blindness, the lies from obstinacy and embarrassment. Do not embarrass the powerful, the napalm said it all.

Marie focused the binoculars. A Belkins man was approaching the steps, blankets and straps over his shoulder, walking behind an elderly couple, obviously residents of the block out for a stroll. The man in the field jacket and the black knit hat stopped: he began talking to two other movers carrying a triangular-shaped object out of the door.

What was it? There was something . . . something odd. She could not see the man's face; it was hidden from view, but there was something about the neck, the angle of the head . . . what was it? The man started up the steps, a blunt man, weary of his day before it had begun . . . a slovenly man. Marie removed the binoculars; she was too anxious, too ready to see things that were not there.

Oh, God, my love, my Jason. Where are you? Come to me. Let me find you. Do not leave me for these blind, mindless men. Do not let them take you from me.

Where was Crawford? He had promised to keep her informed of every move, everything. She had been blunt. She did not trust him, any of them, she did not trust their intelligence, that word spelled with a lower case *i.* He had promised . . . where *was* he?

She spoke to the driver. 'Will you put down the window, please. It's stifling in here.'

'Sorry, Miss,' replied the civilian-clothed army man. 'I'll turn on the air-conditioning for you, though.'

The windows and doors were controlled by buttons only the driver could reach. She was in a glass and metal tomb in a sun-drenched, tree-lined street.

'I don't believe a word of it!' said Conklin, limping angrily across the room back to the window. He leaned against the sill looking out, his left hand pulled up to his face, his teeth against the knuckle of his index finger. 'Not a goddamned word!'

'You don't want to believe it, Alex,' countered Crawford. 'The solution is so much easier. It's in place, and so much simpler.'

'You didn't hear that tape. You didn't hear Villiers!'

'I've heard the woman; she's all I have to hear. She said we didn't listen . . . you didn't listen.'

'Then she's lying!' Awkwardly Conklin spun around. 'Christ, of *course* she's lying! Why wouldn't she? She's his woman. She'll do anything to get him off the meathook!'

'You're wrong and you know it. The fact that he's here proves you're wrong, proves I was wrong to accept what you said.'

Conklin was breathing heavily, his right hand trembling as he gripped his cane. 'Maybe . . . maybe we, maybe . . .' He did not finish; instead he looked at Crawford helplessly.

'. . . ought to let the solution stand?' asked the officer quietly. 'You're tired, Alex. You haven't slept for several days; you're exhausted. I don't think I heard that.'

'No.' The CIA man shook his head, his eyes closed, his face reflecting his disgust. 'No, you didn't hear it and I didn't say it. I just wish I knew where the hell to begin.'

'I do,' said Crawford going to the door and opening it. 'Come in, please.'

The stocky man walked in, his eyes darting to the rifle leaning against the wall. He looked at the two men, appraisal in his expression. 'What *is* it?'

'The exercise has been called off,' Crawford said. 'I think you must have gathered that.'

'What exercise? I was hired to protect him.' The gunman looked at Alex. 'You mean you don't need protection any more, sir?'

'You know exactly what we mean,' broke in Conklin. 'All signals are off, all stipulations.'

'What stipulations? I don't know about any stipulations. The terms of my employment are very clear. I'm protecting you, sir.'

'Good, fine,' said Crawford. 'Now what we have to know is who else out there is protecting him.'

'Who else where?'

'Outside this room, this apartment. In other rooms, on the street, in cars, perhaps. We have to *know*.'

The stocky man walked over to the rifle and picked it up. 'I'm afraid you gentlemen have misunderstood. I was hired on an individual basis. If others were employed, I'm not aware of them.'

'You *do* know them!' shouted Conklin. 'Who *are* they? *Where* are they?'

'I haven't any idea . . . sir.' The courteous gunman held the rifle in his right arm, the barrel angled down towards the floor. He raised it perhaps two inches, no more than six, the movement barely perceptible. 'If my services are no longer required, I'll be leaving.'

'Can you *reach* them?' interrupted the brigadier. 'We'll pay generously.'

'I've already been paid generously, sir. It would be wrong to accept money for a service I can't perform. And pointless for this to continue.'

'A man's life is at stake out there!' shouted Conklin.

'So's mine,' said the gunman, walking to the door, the weapon raised higher. 'Good-bye, gentlemen.' He let himself out.

'*Jesus!*' roared. Alex, swinging back to the window, his cane clattering against a radiator. 'What do we *do?*'

'To start with, get rid of that removal company. I don't know what part it played in your strategy, but it's only a complication now.'

'I can't. I tried. I didn't have anything to do with it. Agency Controls picked up our sheets when we had the equipment taken out. They saw that a store was being closed up and told GSA to get us the hell out of there.'

'With all deliberate speed,' said Crawford, nodding. 'The Monk covered that equipment by signature; his statement absolves the agency. It's in his files.'

'That'd be fine if we had twenty-four hours. We don't even know if we've got twenty-four minutes.'

'We'll still need it. There'll be a senate inquiry. Closed, I hope . . . Rope off the street.'

'What?'

'You heard me, rope off the street. Call in the police, tell them to rope everything off!'

'Through the agency? This is domestic!'

'Then *I* will. Through the Pentagon, from the Joint Chiefs if I have to. We're standing around making excuses, when it's right in front of our eyes! Clear the street, rope it off, bring in a truck with a public address system. Put *her* in it, put her on a *microphone*! Let her say anything she likes, let her scream her head off. She was *right.* He'll come to *her*!'

'Do you know what you're saying?' asked Conklin. 'There'll be questions. Newspapers, television, radio. Everything will be exposed. Publicly.'

'I'm aware of that,' said the brigadier. 'I'm also aware what she'll do for us if this goes down. She may do it anyway, no matter what happens, but I'd rather try to save a man I didn't like, didn't approve of. But I respected him once, and I think I respect him more now.'

'What about another man? If Carlos is really out there, you're opening the gates for him. You're handing him his escape.'

'We didn't create Carlos. We created Cain, and we abused him. We took away his mind and his memory. We owe him. Go down and get the woman. I'll use the phone.'

Bourne walked into the large library with the sunlight streaming through the wide, elegant French windows at the far end of the room. Beyond the panes of glass were the high walls of the garden . . . all around him objects too painful to look at; he knew them and did not know them. They were fragments of dreams – solid, to be touched, to be felt, to be used – not ephemeral at all. A long table where whisky was poured, leather armchairs where men sat and talked, bookshelves that housed books and other things – concealed things – that appeared with the touch of buttons. It was a room where a myth was born, a myth that had raced through South-east Asia and exploded in Europe.

He saw the long, tubular bulge in the ceiling and the darkness came, followed by flashes of light and images on a screen and voices shouting in his ears.

Who is he? Quick. You're too late! You're a dead man! Where is this street? What does it mean to you? Who did you meet there? . . . Methods of kills. Which are yours? No! . . . You are not Delta, you are not you! . . . You are only what you are here, became here!

'Hey! Who the hell are *you*?' The question was shouted by a large, red-faced man seated in an armchair by the door, a clipboard on his knees. Jason had walked right past him.

'You D*oo*gan?' Bourne asked.

'Yeah.'

'Schumach sent me. Said you needed another man.'

'What *for*? I got five awready, and this fuckin' place has hallways so tight you can't hardly get through 'em. They're climbing asses now.'

'I don't know. Schumach sent me, that's all I know. He told me to bring this stuff.' Bourne let the blankets and the straps fall to the floor.

'Murray sends new junk? I mean, that's new.'

'I don't . . .'

'I know, I *know*! Schumach sent you. Ask Schumach.'

'You can't. He said to tell you he was heading out to Sheepshead. Be back this afternoon.'

'Oh, that's great! He goes fishing and leaves me with the shit . . . You're new. You a crumb ball from the shape-up?'

'Yeah.'

'That Murray's a beaut. All I need's another crumb ball. Two wise-ass stiffs and now four crumb balls.'

'You want me to start in here? I can start in here.'

'No, asshole! Crumb balls start at the top, you ain't heard? It's further away, *capice*?'

'Yeah, I *capice*.' Jason bent down for the blankets and the straps.

'Leave that junk here, you don't need it. Get upstairs, top floor, and start with the single wood units. As heavy as you can carry, and don't give me no union bullshit.'

Bourne circled the landing on the first floor and climbed the narrow staircase to the second, as if drawn by a magnetic force beyond his understanding. He was being pulled to another room high up in the brownstone, a room that held both the comfort of solitude and the frustration of loneliness. The landing above was dark, no lights on, no sunlight bursting through windows anywhere. He reached the top and stood for a moment in silence. Which room was it? There were three doors, two on the left side of the hallway, one on the right. He started walking slowly towards the second door on the left, barely seen in the shadows. That was it; it was where thoughts came in the darkness . . . memories that haunted him, pained him. Sunlight and the stench of the river and the jungle . . . screaming machines in the sky, screaming down from the sky. *Oh, God, it hurt!*

He put his hand on the knob, twisted it, and opened the door. Darkness, but not complete. There was a small window at the far end of the room, a black blind pulled down, covering it, but not completely. He could see a thin line of sunlight, so narrow it barely broke through, where the blind met the sill. He walked towards it, towards that thin, tiny shaft of sunlight.

A scratch! A scratch in the darkness! He spun, terrified at the tricks being played on his mind. But it was not a trick! There was a diamond-like flash in the air, light bouncing off steel.

A knife was slashing up at his face.

'I would willingly see you die for what you've done,' said Marie, staring at Conklin. 'And that realization revolts me.'

'Then there's nothing I can say to you,' replied the CIA man, limping across the room towards the general. 'Other decisions could have been made – by him and by you.'

'Could they? Where was he to start? When that man tried to kill him in Marseilles? In the rue Saracin? When they hunted him in Zürich? When they shot at him in Paris? And all the while, he didn't know why. What was he to do?'

'Come out! Goddamn it, come *out*!'

'He did. And when he did, you tried to kill him.'

'*You* were there! You were with him. You had a *memory*.'

'Assuming I knew who to go to, would you have listened to me?'

Conklin returned her gaze. 'I don't know,' he answered, breaking the contact between them and turning to Crawford. 'What's happening?'

'Washington's calling me back within ten minutes.'

'But what's *happening*?'

'I'm not sure you want to hear it. Federal encroachment on state and municipal law-enforcement statutes. Clearances have to be obtained.'

'Jesus!'

'Look!' The army man suddenly bent down to the window. 'The truck's leaving.'

'Someone got through,' said Conklin.

'Who?'

'I'll find out.' The CIA man limped to the phone; there were scraps of paper on the table, telephone numbers written hastily. He selected one and dialled. 'Give me Schumach . . . please . . . Schumach? This is Conklin, Central Intelligence. Who gave you the word?'

The dispatcher's voice on the line could be heard halfway across the room. 'What word? Get off my back! We're on that job and we're going to finish it! Frankly, I think you're a whacko . . .'

Conklin slammed down the phone. 'Christ . . . oh, *Christ*!' His hand trembled as he gripped the instrument. He picked it up and dialled again, his eyes on another scrap of paper. 'Petrocelli. Reclamations,' he commanded. 'Petrocelli? Conklin again.'

'You faded out. What happened?'

'No time. Level with me. That priority invoice from Agency Controls. Who signed it?'

'What do you mean, who signed it? The topcat who always signs them. McGivern.'

Conklin's face turned white. 'That's what I was afraid of,' he whispered as he lowered the phone. He turned to Crawford, his head quivering as he spoke. 'The order to General Services was signed by a man who retired two weeks ago.'

'Carlos . . .'

'Oh, *God*!' screamed Marie. 'The man carrying the blankets, the straps! The way he held his head, his neck. Angled to the right. It was *him*! When his head hurts, he favours the right, It was *Jason*! He went *inside*.'

Alexander Conklin turned back to the window, his eyes focused on the black enamelled door across the way. It was closed.

The hand! The skin . . . the dark eyes in the thin shaft of light. *Carlos!*

Bourne whipped his head back as the razor-like edge of the blade sliced the flesh under his chin, the eruption of blood streaming across the hand that held the knife. He lashed his right foot out, catching his unseen attacker in the kneecap, then pivoted and plunged his left heel into the man's groin. Carlos spun and again the blade came out of the darkness, now surging towards him, the line of assault directly at his stomach. Jason sprang back off the ground, crossing his wrists, slashing downward, blocking the dark arm that was an extension of the handle. He twisted his fingers inward, yanking his hands together, vicing the forearm beneath his blood-soaked neck and wrenched the arm diagonally up. The knife creased the cloth of his field jacket and, once above his chest, Bourne spiralled the arm downward, twisting the wrist now in his grip, crashing his shoulder into the assassin's body, yanking again as Carlos plunged sideways off balance, his arm pulled half out of its socket.

Jason heard the clatter of the knife on the floor; he lurched towards the sound, at the same time reaching into his belt for his gun. It caught on the cloth; he rolled on the floor, but not quickly enough. The steel toe of a shoe crashed into the side of his head – his *temple* – and shock waves bolted through him. He rolled again, faster, faster, until he smashed into the wall; coiling upward on his knee, trying to focus through the weaving, obscure shadows in the near total darkness. The flesh of a hand was caught in the thin line of light from the window; he lunged at it, his own hands now claws, his arms battering rams. He gripped the hand, snapping it back, breaking the wrist. A scream filled the room.

A scream and the hollow, lethal spit of a gunshot. An ice-like incision had been made in Bourne's upper left chest, the bullet lodged somewhere near his shoulder blade. In agony, he crouched and sprang again, pummelling the killer with a gun into the wall above a sharp-edged piece of furniture; Carlos lunged away as two more muted shots were fired wildly. Jason dived to his left, freeing his gun, levelling it at the sounds in the darkness. He fired, the explosion deafening, useless. He heard the door crash shut; the killer had raced out into the hallway.

Trying to fill his lungs with air, Bourne crawled towards the door. As he reached it, instinct commanded him to stay at the side and smash his fist into the wood at the bottom. What followed was the core of a terrifying nightmare. There was a short burst of automatic gunfire as the panelled wood splintered, fragments flying across the room. The instant it stopped, Jason raised his own weapon and fired diagonally through the door; the burst was repeated. Bourne spun away, pressing his back against the well; the eruption stopped and he fired again. There were now two men inches from each other, wanting above all to kill each other. *Cain is for Charlie and Delta is for Cain. Get Carlos. Trap Carlos. Kill Carlos!*

And then they were not inches from each other. Jason heard racing footsteps, then the sounds of a railing being broken as a figure lurched down the staircase. Carlos was racing below; the pig-animal wanted support; he was hurt. Bourne wiped the blood from his face, from his throat, and moved in front of what was left of the door. He pulled it open and stepped out into the narrow corridor, his gun levelled in front of him. Painfully he made his way towards the top of the dark staircase. Suddenly he heard shouts below.

'What the hell *you doin', man? Pete! Pete!*'

Two spits filled the air.

'Joey! *Joey!*'

A single spit was heard; bodies crashed to a floor somewhere below.

'Jesus! *Jesus,* Mother of . . . !'

Two spits again, followed by a guttural cry of death. A third man was killed.

What had that third man said? *Two wise-ass stiffs and four crumb balls now.* The moving van was a Carlos operation! The assassin had brought two soldiers with him – the first three crumb balls from the shape up. Three men with weapons, and he was one with a single gun. Cornered on the top floor of the brownstone. Still Carlos was inside. *Inside.* If he could get out, it would be Carlos who was cornered! If he could get out. *Out!*

There was a window at the front end of the hall, obscured by a black blind. Jason veered towards it, stumbling, holding his neck, creasing his shoulder to blunt the pain in his chest. He ripped the blind from its spindle; the window was small, the glass here, too, thick, prismatic blocks of purple and blue light shooting through it. It was unbreakable, the frame riveted in place; there was no way he could smash a single pane. And then his eyes were drawn below to Seventy-first Street. The removal van was gone! Someone must have driven it away . . . one of Carlos's soldiers! That left two. *Two* men, not three. And he was on the high ground; there were always advantages on the high ground.

Grimacing, bent partially over, Bourne made his way to the first door on the left; it was parallel to the top of the staircase. He opened it and stepped inside. From what he could see it was an ordinary bedroom, lamps, heavy furniture, pictures on the walls. He grabbed the nearest lamp, ripped the cord from the wall and carried it out to the railing. He raised it above his head and hurled it down, stepping back as metal and glass crashed below. There was another burst of gunfire, the bullets shredding the ceiling, cutting a path in the plaster. Jason screamed, letting the scream fade into a cry, the cry into a prolonged desperate wail, and then silence; he edged his way to the rear of the railing. He waited. Silence.

It happened. He could hear the slow, cautious footsteps; the killer had been on the first-floor landing. The footsteps came closer, became louder; a faint shadow appeared on the dark wall. *Now.* Bourne sprang out of his recess and fired four shots in rapid succession at the figure on the staircase; a line of bullet holes and eruptions of blood appeared diagonally across the man's collar. The killer spun, roaring in anger and pain as his neck arched back and his body plummeted down the steps until it was still, sprawled face-up across the bottom three steps. In his hands was a deadly automatic field machine-gun with a rod and brace for a stock.

Now. Jason ran over to the top of the staircase and raced down, holding the railing, trying to keep whatever was left of his balance. He could not waste a moment, he might not find another. If he was going to reach the first floor it was now, in the immediate aftermath of the soldier's death. And as he leaped over the dead body, Bourne knew it was a soldier; it was *not* Carlos. The man was tall, and his skin was white, very white, his features Nordic, or northern European, in no way Latin.

Jason ran into the hallway of the first floor, seeking the shadows, hugging the wall. He stopped, listening. There was a sharp scrape in the distance, a brief scratch from below. He knew what he had to do now. The assassin was on the ground floor. And the sound had not been deliberate; it had not been loud enough or prolonged enough to signify a trap. Carlos was injured – a smashed kneecap or a broken wrist could disorient him to the point where he might collide with a piece of furniture or brush against a wall with a weapon in his hand, briefly losing his balance as Bourne was losing his. It was what he needed to know.

Jason dropped to a crouch and crept back to the staircase, to the dead body sprawled across the steps. He had to pause for a moment; he was losing strength, too much blood. He tried to squeeze the flesh at the top of his throat and press the wound in his chest, anything to stem the bleeding. It was futile; to stay alive he had to get out of the brownstone house, away from the place where Cain was born. Jason Bourne . . . there was no humour in the word association. He found his breath again, reached out and pried the automatic weapon from the dead man's hands. He was ready.

He was dying and he was ready. *Get Carlos. Trap Carlos . . . Kill Carlos!* He could not get out; he knew that. Time was not on his side. The blood would drain out of him before it happened. The end was the beginning: Cain was for Carlos and Delta was for Cain. Only one agonizing question remained: who was Delta? It did not matter. It was behind him now; soon there would be the darkness, not violent but peaceful . . . freedom from that question.

And with his death Marie would be free, his love would be free. Decent men would see to it, led by a decent man in Paris whose son had been killed on the rue du Bac, whose life had been destroyed by an assassin's whore. Within the next few minutes, thought Jason, silently checking the clip in the automatic weapon, he would fulfil his promise to that man, carry out the agreement he had with men he did not know. By doing both, the proof was his. Jason Bourne had died once on this day; he would die again but would take Carlos with him. He was ready.

He lowered himself to a prone position and crept, hands over elbows, towards the top of the staircase. He could smell the blood beneath him, the sweet, bland odour penetrating his nostrils, informing him of a practicality. Time was running out. He reached the top step, pulling his legs up under him, digging into his pocket for one of the road flares he had purchased at the army-navy store on Lexington Avenue. He knew now why he had felt the compulsion to buy them. He was back in the unremembered Tam Quan, forgotten except for brilliant, blinding flashes of light. The flares had reminded him of that fragment of memory; they would light up a jungle now.

He uncoiled the waxed fuse from the small round recess in the flare head, brought it to his teeth and bit through the cord, shortening the fuse to less than an inch. He reached into his other pocket and took out a plastic lighter; he pressed it against the flare, gripping both in his left hand. Then he angled the rod and brace of the weapon into his right shoulder, shoving the curved strip of metal into the cloth of his blood-soaked field jacket; it was secure. He stretched out his legs and, snake-like, started down the final flight of steps, head below, feet above, his back scraping the wall.

He reached the mid-point of the staircase. Silence, darkness, all the lights had been extinguished . . . Lights? *Lights?* Where were the rays of sunlight he had seen in that hallway only minutes ago? It had streamed through a pair of French windows at the far end of the room – that room – beyond the corridor, but he could see only darkness now. The door had been shut; the door beneath him, the only other door in that hallway, was also closed, marked only by a thin shaft of light. Carlos was making him choose. Behind which door? Or was the assassin using a better strategy? Was he in the darkness of the narrow hall itself?

Bourne felt a stabbing jolt of pain in his shoulder blade, then an eruption of blood that drenched the flannel shirt beneath his field jacket. Another warning: there was very little time.

He braced himself against the wall, the weapon levelled at the thin posts of the railing, aimed down into the darkness of the corridor. *Now!* He pulled the trigger. The staccato explosions tore the posts apart as the railing fell, the bullets shattering the walls and the door beneath him. He released the trigger, slipping his hand under the scalding barrel, grabbing the plastic lighter with his right hand, the flare in his left. He spun the flint; the wick took fire and he put it to the short fuse. He pulled his hand back to the weapon and squeezed the trigger again, blowing away everything below. A glass chandelier crashed to a floor somewhere; singing whines of ricochets filled the darkness. And then – *light*! Blinding light as the flare ignited, firing the jungle, lighting up the trees and the walls, the hidden paths and the mahogany corridors. The stench of death and the jungle was everywhere, and he was there.

Almanac to Delta. Almanac to Delta! Abandon, abandon!

Never. Not now. Not at the end. Cain is for Carlos and Delta is for Cain. Trap Carlos. Kill Carlos!

Bourne rose to his feet, his back pressed against the wall, the flare in his left hand, the exploding weapon in his right. He plunged down into the carpeted underbrush, kicking the door in front of him open, shattering silver frames and trophies that flew off tables and shelves into the air. Into the trees. He stopped; there was no one in that quiet, sound-proof elegant room. No one in the jungle path.

He spun around and lurched back into the hall, puncturing the walls with a prolonged burst of gunfire. No one.

The door at the end of the narrow, dark corridor. Beyond was the room where Cain was born. Where Cain would die, but not alone.

He held his fire, shifting the flare to his right hand beneath the weapon, reaching into his pocket for the second flare. He pulled it out, and again uncoiled the fuse and brought it to his teeth, severing the cord, now millimetres from its point of contact with the gelatinous incendiary. He shoved the first flare to it; the explosion of light was so bright it pained his eyes. Awkwardly, he held both flares in his left hand and, squinting, his legs and arms losing the battle for balance, approached the door.

It was open, the narrow crack extending from top to bottom on the lock side. The assassin was accommodating, but as he looked at that door, Jason instinctively knew one thing about it that Carlos did not know. It was a part of his past, a part of the room where Cain was born. He reached down with his right hand, bracing the weapon between his forearm and his hip, and gripped the knob.

Now. He sboved the door open six inches and hurled the flares inside. A long staccato burst from a Sten gun echoed throughout the room, throughout the entire house, a thousand dead sounds forming a running chord beneath as sprays of bullets embedded in a lead shield backed by a steel plate in the door.

The firing stopped, a final clip expended. *Now.* Bourne whipped his hand back to the trigger, crashed his shoulder into the door, and lunged inside, firing in circles as he rolled on the floor, swinging his legs counterclockwise. Gunshots were returned wildly as Jason honed his weapon towards the source. A roar of fury burst from blindness across the room; it accompanied Bourne's realization that the curtains had been drawn, blocking out the sunlight from the French windows. Then why was there so much light . . . magnified light beyond the sizzling blindness of the flares? It was overpowering, causing explosions in his head, sharp bolts of agony at his temples.

The *screen*! The huge screen was pulled down from its bulging recess in the ceiling, drawn taut to the floor, the wide expanse of glistening silver a white-hot shield of ice-cold fire. He plunged behind the large table to the protection of a copper corner bar; he rose and jammed the trigger back, in another burst – a *final* burst. The last clip had run out. He hurled the weapon by its rod-stock across the room at the figure in white overalls and a white silk scarf that had fallen below his face.

The *face*! He knew it! He had seen it before! Where . . . where? Was it Marseilles? Yes . . . no! Zürich? Paris? Yes and no! Then it struck him at that instant in the blinding vibrating light, that the face across the room was known to many, not just him. But from where? *Where?* As so much else, he knew it and did not know it. But he *did* know it! It was only the name he could not find?

He spiralled back off his feet, behind the heavy copper bar. Gunshots came, two . . . three, the second bullet tearing the flesh of his left forearm. He pulled his automatic from his belt; he had three shots left. One of them had to find its mark, Carlos. There was a debt to pay in Paris, and a contract to fulfil, his love far safer with the assassin's death. He took the plastic lighter from his pocket, ignited it, and held it beneath a cloth suspended from a hook. The cloth caught fire, he grabbed it and threw it to his right as he dived to his left. Carlos fired at the flaming rag as Bourne spun to his knees, levelling his gun, pulling the trigger twice.

The figure buckled but did not fall. Instead, he crouched, then sprang like a white panther diagonally forward, his hands outstretched. What was he *doing*? Then Jason knew. The assassin gripped the edge of the huge, silver screen, ripping it from its metal bracket in the ceiling, pulling it downwards with all his weight and strength.

It floated down above Bourne, filling his vision, blocking everything else from his mind. He screamed as the shimmering silver descended over him, suddenly more frightened of it than of Carlos, or of any other human being on the earth. It terrified him, infuriated him, splitting his mind in fragments; images flashed across his eyes and angry voices shouted in his ears. He aimed his gun and fired at the terrible shroud. As he slashed his hand against it wildly, pushing the rough, silver cloth away, he understood. He had fired his last shot, his *last*. Like a legend named Cain Carlos knew by sight and by sound every weapon on earth, he had counted the gunshots.

The assassin loomed above him, the automatic in his hand aimed at Jason's head. 'Your execution, Delta. On the day scheduled. For everything you've done.'

Bourne arched his back, rolling furiously to his right; at least he would die in motion! Gunshots filled the shimmering room, hot needles slicing across his neck, piercing his legs, cutting up to his waist. Roll, *roll*!

Suddenly the gunshots stopped, and in the distance he could hear repeated sounds of hammering, the smashing of wood and steel, growing louder, more insistent. There was a final deafening crash from the dark corridor outside the library, followed by men shouting, running and, beyond them somewhere in the unseen, outside world, the insistent whine of sirens.

'In here! He's in *here*!' screamed Carlos.

It was *insane*! The assassin was directing the invaders directly towards him, *to* him! Reason was madness, nothing on earth made sense!

The door was crashed open by a tall man in a black overcoat; someone was with him, but Jason could not see. The mists were filling his eyes, shapes and sounds becoming obscured, blurred. He was rolling in space. Away . . . away.

But then he saw the one thing he did not want to see. Rigid shoulders that floated above a tapered waist raced out of the room and down the dimly-lit corridor. *Carlos*. His screams had sprung the trap open! He had *reversed* it! In the chaos, he had trapped the *stalker*. He was *escaping*!

'Carlos . . .' Bourne knew he could not be heard; what emerged from his bleeding throat was a whisper. He tried again, forcing the sound from his stomach. 'It's *him*. It's . . . *Carlos!*'

There was confusion, commands shouted futilely, orders swallowed in consternation. And then a figure came into focus. A man was limping towards him, a cripple who had tried to kill him in a cemetery outside Paris. There was nothing *left*! Jason lurched, crawling towards the sizzling, blinding flare. He grabbed it and held it as though it were a weapon, aiming it at the killer with a cane.

'Come on! Come *on*! Closer, you *bastard*! I'll burn your eyes out! You think you'll kill me, you won't! I'll kill you! I'll burn your eyes!'

'You don't understand,' said the trembling voice of the limping killer. 'It's me, Delta. It's Conklin. I was wrong.'

The flare singed his hands, his eyes! . . . *Madness. The explosions were all around him now, blinding, deafening, punctuated by ear-splitting screeches from the jungle that erupted with each detonation.*

The jungle! Tam Quan! The wet, hot stench was everywhere, but they had reached it! The base camp was theirs!

An explosion to his left; he could see it! High above the ground, suspended between two trees, the spikes of a bamboo cage. The figure inside was moving. He was alive! Get to him, reach him!

A cry came from his right. Breathing, coughing in the smoke, a man was limping towards the dense underbrush, a rifle in his hand. It was him, the blond hair caught in the light, a fool broken from a parachute jump. The bastard! A piece of filth who had trained with them, studied the maps with them, flown north with them . . . all the time springing a trap on them! A traitor with a radio who told the enemy exactly where to look in that impenetrable jungle that was Tam Quan.

It was Bourne! Jason Bourne. Traitor, garbage!

Get him! Don't let him reach the others! Kill him! Kill Jason Bourne! He is your enemy! Fire!

He did not fall! The head that had been blown apart was still there. Coming towards him! What was happening? Madness. Tam Quan . . .

'Come with us,' said the limping figure, walking out of the jungle into what remained of an elegant room. *That* room. 'We're not your enemies. Come with us.'

'Get *away* from me!' Bourne lunged again, now back to the fallen screen. It was his sanctuary, his shroud of death, the blanket thrown over a man at birth, a lining for his coffin. 'You are my enemy! I'll take you all! I don't care, it doesn't *matter*! Can't you understand!? I'm *Delta*! Cain is for Charlie and Delta is for Cain! What more do you *want from me*? I was and I *was* not! I am and I *am* not! Bastards, *bastards!* Come on! *Closer!*'

Another voice was heard, a deeper voice, calmer, less insistent. 'Get her. Bring her in.'

Somewhere in the distance the sirens reached a crescendo, and then they stopped. Darkness came and the waves carried Jason up to the night sky, only to hurl him down again, crashing him into an abyss of watery violence. He was entering an eternity of weightless . . . memory. An explosion filled the night sky now, a fiery diadem rose above black waters. And then he heard the words, spoken from the clouds, filling the earth.

'Jason, my love. My only love. Take my hand. Hold it. Tightly, Jason. Tightly, my darling.'

Peace came with the darkness.

Epilogue

Brigadier-General Crawford put the folder down on the couch beside him. 'I don't need this,' he said to Marie St Jacques, who sat opposite him in a straight-backed chair. 'I've gone over it and over it, trying to find out where we went wrong.'

'You presumed where no one should,' said the only other person in the hotel suite. He was Dr Morris Panov, psychiatrist; he stood by the window, the morning sun streaming in, putting his expressionless face in shadow. 'I allowed you to presume, and I'll live with it for the rest of my life.'

'It's nearly two weeks now,' said Marie impatiently. 'I'd like some details. I think I'm entitled to them.'

'You are. It was an insanity called clearance.'

'Insanity,' agreed Panov.

'Protection, also,' added Crawford. 'I subscribe to that part. It has to continue for a very long time.'

'Protection?' Marie frowned.

'We'll get to it,' said the general, glancing at Panov. 'From everyone's point of view, it's vital. I trust we all accept that.'

'*Please!* Jason. Who is he?'

'His name is David Webb. He was a career foreign service officer, a specialist in Far Eastern affairs, until his separation from the government five years ago.'

'Separation?'

'Resignation by mutual agreement. His work in Medusa precluded any sustained career in the State Department. "Delta" was infamous and too many knew he was Webb. Such men are rarely welcome at the diplomatic conference tables. I'm not sure they should be, visceral wounds are reopened too easily with their presence.'

'He was everything they say? In Medusa?'

'Yes, I was there. He was everything they say.'

'It's hard to believe,' said Marie.

'He'd lost something very special to him and couldn't come to grips with it. He could only strike out.'

'What was that?'

'His family. His wife was a Thai; they had two children, a boy and a girl. He was stationed in Phnom-Penh, his house near the Mekong River. One Sunday afternoon while his wife and children were down at their dock, a stray aircraft circled and dived, dropping two bombs and strafing the area. By the time he reached the river the dock was blown away, his wife and children floating in the water, their bodies riddled.'

'Oh, God,' whispered Marie. 'Who did the plane belong to?'

'It was never identified. Hanoi disclaimed it; Saigon said it wasn't ours. Remember, Cambodia was neutral; no one wanted to be responsible. Webb had to strike out; he headed for Saigon and trained for Medusa. He brought a specialist's intellect to a very brutal operation. He became Delta.'

'Was that when he met d'Anjou?'

'Later on, yes. Delta was notorious by then. North Vietnamese intelligence had put an extraordinary price on his head, and it's no secret that among our own people a number hoped they'd succeed. Then Hanoi found out that Webb's younger brother was an army officer in Saigon and, having studied Delta – knowing knowing the brothers were close – decided to mount a trap; they had nothing to lose. They kidnapped Lieutenant Gordon Webb and took him north, sending back a Cong informant with word that he was being held in the Tam Quan sector. Delta bit; along with the informer – a double agent – he formed a team of Medusans who knew the area and picked a night when no aircraft should have left the ground to fly north. D'Anjou was in the unit. So was another man Webb didn't know about; a white man who'd been bought by Hanoi, an expert in communications who could assemble the electronic components of a high frequency radio in the dark. Which is exactly what he did, betraying his unit's position. Webb broke through the trap and found his brother. He also found the double agent and the white man. The Vietnamese escaped in the jungle; the white man didn't. Delta executed him on the spot.'

'And that man?' Marie's eyes were riveted on Crawford.

'Jason Bourne. A Medusan from Sydney, Australia, a runner of guns, narcotics and slaves throughout all South-east Asia; a violent man with a criminal record, who was nevertheless highly effective – if the price were high enough. It was in Medusa's interests to bury the circumstances of his death; he became an MIA from a specialized unit. Years later, when Treadstone was being formed and Webb called back, it was Webb himself who took the name of Bourne. It fitted the requirements of authenticity, traceability. He took the name of the man who'd betrayed him, the man he had killed in Tam Quan.'

'Where was he when he was called back for Treadstone?' asked Marie. 'What was he doing?'

'Teaching in a small college in New Hampshire. Living an isolated life, some said destructive. For him.' Crawford picked up the folder. 'Those are the essential facts, Miss St Jacques. Other areas will be covered by Dr Panov, who's made it clear that my presence is not required. There is, however, one remaining detail which must be thoroughly understood. It's a direct order from the White House.'

'The protection,' said Marie, her words a statement.

'Yes. Wherever he goes, regardless of the identity he assumes, or the success of his cover, he'll be guarded around the clock. For as long as it takes – even if it never happens.'

'Please explain that.'

'He's the only man alive who's ever seen Carlos. *As* Carlos. He knows his identity but it's locked away in his mind, part of an unremembered past. We understand from what he says that Carlos is someone known to many people – a visible figure in a government somewhere, or in the media, or international banking or society. It fits a prevalent theory. The point is that one day that identity may come into focus for Webb . . . We realize you've had several discussions with Dr Panov. I believe he'll confirm what I've said.'

Marie turned to the psychiatrist. 'Is it true, Mo?'

'It's possible,' said Panov.

Crawford left and Marie poured coffee for the two of them. Panov went to the couch where the brigadier had been sitting.

'It's still warm,' he said smiling. 'Crawford was sweating right down to his famous backside. He has every right to, they all do.'

'What's going to happen?'

'Nothing. Absolutely nothing until I tell them they can go ahead. And that may not be for months, a couple of years for all I know. Not until he's ready.'

'For what?'

'The questions. And photographs, volumes of them. They're compiling a photographic encyclopaedia based on the loose description he gave them. Don't get me wrong; one day he'll have to begin. He'll want to; we'll all want him to. Carlos has to be caught, and it's not my intention to blackmail them into doing nothing. Too many people have given too much; he's given too much. But right now, he comes first. His head comes first.'

'That's what I mean. What's going to happen to him?'

Panov put down his coffee. 'I'm not sure yet. I've too much respect for the human mind to deal you chicken soup psychology; there's too damn much of it floating around in the wrong hands. I've been in on all the conferences – I insisted upon that – and I've talked to the other shrinks and the neurosurgeons. It's true we can go in with a knife and reach the storm centres, reduce the anxieties, bring a kind of peace to him. Even bring him back to what he was, perhaps. But it's not the kind of peace he wants . . . and there's a far more dangerous risk. We might wipe away too much, take away the things he has found, will *continue* to find. With care. With time.'

'Time?'

'I believe it, yes. Because the pattern's been established. There's growth, the pain of recognition and the excitement of discovery. Does that tell you something?'

Marie looked into Panov's dark, weary eyes; there was a light in them. 'All of us,' she said.

'That's right. In a way, he's a functioning microcosm of us all. I mean, we're all trying to find out who the hell we are, aren't we?'

Marie went to the front window in the cottage on the water-front, with the rising dunes behind it, the fenced-off grounds surrounding it. And guards. Every fifty feet a man with a gun. She could see him several hundred yards down the beach; he was skipping shells over the water, watching them bounce across the waves that gently lapped into the shore. The months had been good to him, for him. His body was scarred but whole again, firm again. The nightmares were still there, and moments of anguish kept coming back during the daylight hours, but somehow it was all less terrifying. He was beginning to cope; he was beginning to laugh again. Panov had been right. Things were happening to him; images were becoming clearer, meaning found where there had been no meaning before.

Something had happened *now*! Oh, *God*, what *was* it? He had thrown himself into the water and was thrashing around, shouting. Then suddenly, he sprang out, leaping over the waves onto the beach. In the distance, by the barbed wire fence, a guard spun around, a rifle whipped up under an arm, a hand-held radio from a belt.

He began racing across the wet sand towards the house, his body lurching, swaying, his feet digging furiously into the soft surface, sending up sprays of water and sand behind him. *What was it?*

Marie froze, prepared for the moment they knew might come one day, prepared for the sound of gunfire.

He burst through the door, chest heaving, gasping for breath. He stared at her, his eyes as clear as she had ever seen them. He spoke softly, so softly she could barely hear him. But she did hear him.

'My name is David . . .'

She walked slowly towards him.

'Hello, David,' she said.

The Bourne Supremacy

For Shannon Paige Ludlum
Welcome, my dear
Have a great life

1

Kowloon. The teeming final extension of China that is no part of the north except in spirit – but the spirit runs deep and descends into the caverns of men's souls without regard for the harsh, irrelevant practicalities of political borders. The land and the water are one, and it is the will of the spirit that determines how man will use the land and the water – again without regard for such abstractions as useless freedom or escapable confinement. The concern is only with empty stomachs, with women's stomachs, children's stomachs. Survival. There is nothing else. All the rest is dung to be spread over the infertile fields.

It was sundown, and both in Kowloon and across Victoria Harbour on the island of Hong Kong an unseen blanket was gradually being lowered over the territory's daylight chaos. The screeching *Aiyas!* of the street merchants were muted with the shadows, and quiet negotiations in the upper regions of the cold, majestic structures of glass and steel that marked the colony's skyline were ending with nods and shrugs and brief smiles of silent accommodation. Night was coming, proclaimed by a blinding orange sun piercing an immense, jagged, fragmented wall of clouds in the west – sharply defined shafts of uncompromising energy about to plunge over the horizon, unwilling to let this part of the world forget the light.

Soon darkness would spread across the sky, but not below. Below, the blazing lights of human invention would garishly illuminate the earth – this part of the earth where the land and the water are anxious avenues of access and conflict. And with the never-ending, ever-strident nocturnal carnival, other games would begin, games the human race should have abandoned with the first light of Creation. But there was no human life then – so who recorded it? Who knew? Who cared? Death was not a commodity.

A small motorboat, its powerful engine belying its shabby exterior, sped through the Lamma Channel, heading around the coastline toward the harbour. To a disinterested observer it was merely one more *xiao wanju*, a legacy to a first son from a once unworthy fisherman who had struck minor riches – a crazy night of mah-jongg, hashish from the Triangle, smuggled jewels out of Macao – who cared how? The son could cast his nets or run his merchandise more efficiently by using a fast propeller rather than the slow sail of a junk or the sluggish engine of a sampan. Even the Chinese border guards and the marine patrols on and off the shores of the Shenzen Wan did not fire on such insignificant transgressors; they were unimportant, and who knew what families beyond the New Territories on the Mainland might benefit? It could be one of their own. The sweet herbs from the hills still brought full stomachs – perhaps filling one of their own. Who cared? Let them come. Let them go.

The small craft with its Bimini canvas enveloping both sides of the forward cockpit cut its speed and cautiously zigzagged through the scattered flotilla of junks and sampans returning to their crowded berths in Aberdeen. One after another the boat people shrieked angry curses at the intruder, at its impudent engine and its more impudent wake. Then each became strangely silent as the rude interloper passed; something under the canvas quieted their sudden bursts of fury.

The boat raced into the harbour's corridor, a dark, watery path now bordered by the blazing lights of the island of Hong Kong on the right, Kowloon on the left. Three minutes later the outboard motor audibly sank into its lowest register as the hull swerved slowly past two filthy barges docked at the godown, and slid into an empty space on the west side of the Tsim Sha Tsui, Kowloon's crowded, dollar-conscious waterfront. The strident hordes of merchants, setting up their nightly tourist traps on the wharf, paid no attention; it was merely one more *jigi* coming in from the catch. Who cared?

Then, like the boat people out in the channel, the stalls on the waterfront nearest the insignificant intruder began to quiet down. Excited voices were silenced amid screeching commands and countercommands as eyes were drawn to a figure climbing up the black, oil-soaked ladder to the pier.

He was a holy man. His shrouded figure was draped in a pure white caftan that accentuated his tall slender body – very tall for a *Zhongguo ren*, nearly six feet in height, perhaps. Little could be seen of his face, however, as the cloth was loose and the breezes kept pressing the white fabric across his dark features, drawing out the whiteness of his eyes – determined eyes, zealous eyes. This was no ordinary priest, anyone could see that. He was a *heshang*, a chosen one selected by elders steeped in wisdom who could perceive the inner spiritual knowledge of a young monk destined for higher things. And it did not hurt that such a monk was tall and slender and had eyes of fire. Such holy men drew attention to themselves, to their personages – to their eyes – and generous contributions followed, both in fear and in awe; mostly fear. Perhaps this *heshang* came from one of the mystic sects that wandered through the hills and forests of the Guangze, or from a religious brotherhood in the mountains of far-off Qing Gaoyuan – descendants, it was said, of a people in the distant Himalayas – they were always quite ostentatious and generally to be feared the most, for few understood their obscure teachings. Teachings that were couched in gentleness, but with subtle hints of indescribable agony should their lessons go unheeded. There was too much agony on the land and the water – who needed more? So give to the spirits, to the eyes of fire. Perhaps it would be recorded. Somewhere.

The white-robed figure walked slowly through the parting crowds on the wharf, past the congested Star Ferry pier, and disappeared into the growing pandemonium of the Tsim Sha Tsui. The moment had passed; the stalls returned to their hysteria.

The priest headed east on Salisbury Road until he reached the Peninsula

Hotel, whose subdued elegance was losing the battle with its surroundings. He then turned north into Nathan Road, to the base of the glittering Golden Mile, that strip of strips where opposing multitudes shrieked for attention. Both natives and tourists alike took notice of the stately holy man as he passed crowded storefronts and alleys bulging with merchandise, three-story discos and topless cafés where huge, amateurish billboards hawked Oriental charms above stalls offering the steamed delicacies of the noonday *dim sum*. He walked for nearly ten minutes through the garish carnival, now and then acknowledging glances with a slight bow of his head, and twice shaking it while issuing commands to the same short, muscular *Zhongguo ren*, who alternately followed him, then passed him with quick, dancelike steps, turning to search the intense eyes for a sign.

The sign came – two abrupt nods – as the priest turned and walked through the beaded entrance of a raucous cabaret. The *Zhongguo ren* remained outside, his hand unobtrusively under his loose tunic, his own eyes darting about the crazy street; a thoroughfare he could not understand. It was *insane!* Outrageous! But he was the *tudi*; he would protect the holy man with his life, no matter the assault on his own sensibilities.

Inside the cabaret the heavy layers of smoke were slashed by roving coloured lights, most whirling in circles and directed toward a platform stage where a rock group ululated in deafening frenzy, a frantic admixture of punk and Far East. Shiny black, tight-fitting, ill-fitting trousers quivered maniacally on spindly legs below black leather jackets over soiled white silk shirts open to the waist, while each head was shaved around its skull at the temple line, each face grotesque, heavily made up to accentuate its essentially passive Oriental character. And as if to emphasize the conflict between East and West, the jarring music would occasionally, startlingly, come to a stop, as the plaintive strains of a simple Chinese melody emerged from a single instrument, while the figures remained rigid under the swirling bombardment of the spotlights.

The priest stood still for a moment surveying the huge crowded room. A number of customers in varying stages of drunkenness looked up at him from the tables. Several rolled coins in his direction before they turned away, while a few got out of their chairs, dropped Hong Kong dollars beside their drinks, and headed for the door. The *heshang* was having an effect, but not the effect desired by the obese, tuxedoed man who approached him.

'May I be of assistance, Holy One?' asked the cabaret's manager.

The priest leaned forward and spoke into the man's ear, whispering a name. The manager's eyes widened, then he bowed and gestured toward a small table by the wall. The priest nodded back in appreciation and walked behind the man to his chair as adjacent customers took uncomfortable notice.

The manager leaned down and spoke with a reverence he did not feel. 'Would you care for refreshment, Holy One?'

'Goat's milk, if it is by chance available. If not, plain water will be more than sufficient. And I thank you.'

'It is the privilege of the establishment,' said the tuxedoed man, bowing and moving away, trying to place the slow, softly spoken dialect he could not recognize. It did not matter. This tall, white-robed priest had business with the *laoban*, and that was all that mattered. He had actually used the *laoban*'s name, a name seldom spoken in the Golden Mile, and on this particular evening the powerful taipan was on the premises – in a room he would not publicly acknowledge knowing. But it was not the province of the manager to tell the *laoban* that the priest had arrived; the berobed one had made that clear. All was privacy this night, he had insisted. When the august taipan wished to see him, a man would come out to find him. So be it; it was the way of the secretive *laoban*, one of the wealthiest and most illustrious taipans in Hong Kong.

'Send a kitchen stick down the street for some fuck-fuck mother goat's milk,' said the manager harshly to a head boy on the floor. 'And tell him to be damn-damn quick. The existence of his stinking offspring will depend upon it.'

The holy man sat passively at the table, his zealous eyes now gentler, observing the foolish activity, apparently neither condemning nor accepting but merely taking it all in with the compassion of a father watching errant children.

Abruptly through the whirling lights there was an intrusion. Several tables away a bright camper's match was struck and quickly extinguished. Then another, and finally a third, this last held under a long black cigarette. The brief series of flashes drew the attention of the priest. He moved his shrouded head slowly toward the flame and the lone, unshaven, coarsely dressed Chinese drawing in the smoke. Their eyes met; the holy man's nod was almost imperceptible, barely a motion, and was acknowledged by an equally obscure movement as the match went out.

Seconds later the crudely dressed smoker's table was suddenly in flames. Fire shot up from the surface, spreading quickly to all the articles of paper on the surface – napkins, menus, *dim sum* baskets, isolated eruptions of potential disaster. The dishevelled Chinese screamed and, with a shattering crash, overturned the table as waiters raced, shrieking, toward the flames. Customers on all sides leaped from their chairs as the fire on the floor – narrow strands of pulsing blue flame – inexplicably spread in rivulets around excited, stamping feet. The pandemonium grew as people rapidly slapped out the small fires with tablecloths and aprons. The manager and his head boys gestured wildly, shouting that all was under control; the danger had passed. The rock group played with even greater intensity, attempting to draw the crowd back into its frenzied orbit and away from the area of diminishing panic.

Suddenly, there was a greater disturbance, a more violent eruption. Two head boys had collided with the shabbily dressed *Zhongguo ren* whose carelessness and outsized matches had caused the conflagration. He responded with rapid *Wing Chun* chops – rigid hands crashing into shoulder blades and throats – as his feet hammered up into abdomens, sending the two *shi-ji* reeling back into the surrounding customers. The physical abuse compounded the panic, the chaos. The heavyset manager, now roaring, intervened and he, too, fell away, stunned by a well-placed kick to his rib cage. The unshaven *Zhongguo ren* then picked up a chair and hurled it at the screaming figures near the fallen man as three other waiters rushed into the melee in defence of their *Zongguan*. Men and women who only seconds ago were merely screaming now began thrashing their arms about, pummelling anyone and everyone near them. The rock group gyrated to its outer limits, frantic dissonance worthy of the scene. The riot had taken hold, and the burly peasant glanced across the room at the single table next to the wall. The priest was gone.

The unshaven *Zhongguo ren* picked up a second chair and smashed it down across a nearby table, splintering the wooden frame and swinging a broken leg into the crowd. Only moments to go, but those moments were everything.

The priest stepped through the door far back in the wall near the entrance of the cabaret. He closed it quickly, adjusting his eyes to the dim light of the long, narrow hallway. His right arm was stiff beneath the folds of his white caftan, his left diagonally across his waist, also under the sheer white fabric. Down the corridor, no more than twenty-five feet away a startled man sprang from the wall, his right hand plunging beneath his jacket to yank a large, heavy-calibre revolver from an unseen shoulder holster. The holy man nodded slowly, impassively, repeatedly, as he moved forward with graceful steps appropriate to a religious procession.

'*Amita-fo, Amita-fo*,' he said softly, over and over again as he approached the man. 'Everything is peaceful, all is in peace, the spirits will it.'

'*Jou matyeh*?' The guard was beside a door; he shoved the ugly weapon forward and continued in a guttural Cantonese bred in the northern settlements. 'Are you lost, priest? What are you doing here? Get out! This is no place for you!'

'*Amita-fo, Amita-fo* . . .'

'Get *out! Now!*'

The guard had no chance. Swiftly the priest pulled a razor-thin, double-edged knife from the folds at his waist. He slashed the man's wrist, half severing the hand with the gun from the guard's arm, then arced the blade surgically across the man's throat; air and blood erupted as the head snapped back in a mass of shining red; he fell to the floor, a corpse.

Without hesitation, the killer-priest slid the blemished knife into the cloth of his caftan where it held, and from under the right side of his robe he withdrew a thin-framed Uzi machine gun, its curved magazine holding more ammunition than he would need. He raised his foot and crashed it into the door with the strength of a mountain cat, racing inside to find what he knew he would find.

Five men – *Zhongguo ren* – were sitting around a table with pots of tea and short glasses of potent whisky near each; there were no written papers anywhere in sight, no notes or memoranda, only ears and watchful eyes. And as each pair of eyes looked up in shock the faces were contorted with panic. Two well-dressed negotiators plunged their hands inside their well-tailored jackets while they spun out of the chairs; another lunged under the table as the remaining two sprang up screaming and raced futilely into silk-covered walls, spinning around in desperation, seeking pardons yet knowing none would be forthcoming. A shattering fusillade of bullets ripped into the *Zhongguo ren*. Blood gushed from fatal wounds as skulls were pierced and eyes were punctured, mouths torn apart, bright red in muted screams of death. The walls and the floor and the polished table glistened sickeningly with the bloody evidence of death. Everywhere. It was over.

The killer surveyed his work. Satisfied, he knelt down by a large, stagnant pool of blood and moved his index finger through it. He then pulled out a square of dark cloth from his left sleeve and spread it over his handiwork. He rose to his feet and rushed out of the room, unbuttoning the white caftan as he ran down the dim hallway; the robe was open by the time he reached the door to the cabaret. He removed the razorlike knife from the cloth and shoved it into a scabbard on his belt. Then, holding the folds of cloth together, his hood in place, the lethal weapon secure at his side, he pulled the door back and walked inside, into the brawling chaos that showed no sign of lessening. But then why should it be different? He had left it barely thirty seconds ago and his man was well trained.

'*Faai-di!*' The shout came from the burly, unshaven peasant from Canton; he was ten feet away, overturning another table and striking a match, dropping it on the floor. 'The police will be here any moment! The bartender just reached a phone, I saw him!'

The killer-priest ripped the caftan away from his body and the hood from his head. In the wild revolving lights his face looked as macabre as any in the frenzied rock group. Heavy makeup outlined his eyes, white lines defining the shape of each, and his face was an unnatural brown. 'Go in front of me!' he commanded the peasant. He dropped his costume and the Uzi on the floor next to the door while removing a pair of thin surgical gloves; he shoved them into his flannel trousers.

For a cabaret in the Golden Mile to summon the police was not a decision easily arrived at. There were heavy fines for poor management, stiff penalties for endangering tourists. The police knew these risks and responded quickly when they were taken. The killer ran behind the peasant from Canton who joined the panicked crowd at the entrance screaming to get out. The coarsely dressed brawler was a bull; bodies in front of him fell away under the force of his blows. Guard and killer burst through the door and into the street, where another crowd had gathered shrieking questions and epithets and cries of bad joss – misfortune for the establishment. They threaded their way through the excited onlookers and were joined by the short, muscular Chinese who had waited outside. He grabbed the arm of his defrocked charge and pulled his priest into the narrowest of alleys, where he took out two towels from under his tunic. One was soft and dry, the other encased in plastic – it was warm and wet and perfumed.

The assassin gripped the wet towel and began rubbing it over his face, sinking it around and into the sockets of his eyes and across the exposed flesh of his neck. He reversed the cloth and repeated the process with even greater pressure, scrubbing his temples and his hairline until his white skin was apparent. He then dried himself with the second towel, smoothed his dark hair, and straightened the regimental tie that fell on the cream-coloured shirt under his dark blue blazer. '*Jau!*' he ordered his two companions. They ran and disappeared in the crowds.

And a lone, well-dressed Occidental walked out into the strip of Oriental pleasures.

Inside the cabaret the excited manager was berating the bartender who had called the *jing cha*; the fines would be on his fuck-fuck head! For the riot had inexplicably subsided, leaving the customers bewildered. Head boys and waiters were mollifying the patrons, patting shoulders and clearing away the debris, while straightening tables and producing new chairs and dispensing free glasses of whisky. The rock group concentrated on the current favourites, and as swiftly as the order of the evening had been disrupted it was restored. With luck, through the tuxedoed manager, the explanation that an impetuous bartender had mistaken a belligerent drunk for something far more serious would be acceptable to the police.

Suddenly, all thoughts of fines and official harassment were swept away as his eyes were drawn to a clump of white fabric on the floor across the room – in front of the door to the inner offices. White cloth, pure white – the priest? The *door!* The *laoban!* The *conference!* His breath short, his face drenched with sweat, the obese manager raced between the tables to the discarded caftan. He knelt down, his eyes wide, his breathing now suspended, as he saw the dark barrel of a strange weapon protruding from beneath the folds of white. And what made him choke on his barely formed terror was the sight of tiny specks and thin streaks of shiny, undried blood soiling the cloth.

'*Go hai matyeh?*' The question was asked by a second man in a tuxedo, but without the status conferred by a cummerbund – in truth the manager's brother and first assistant. 'Oh, damn the Christian *Jesus!*' he swore under his breath as his brother gathered up the odd-looking gun in the spotted caftan.

'*Come!*' ordered the manager, getting to his feet and heading for the door.

'The police!' objected the brother. 'One of us should speak to them, calm them, do what we can.'

'It may be that we can do *nothing* but give them our heads! *Quickly!*'

Inside the dimly lit corridor the proof was there. The slain guard lay in a river of his own blood, his weapon gripped by a hand barely attached to his wrist. Within the conference room itself, the proof was complete. Five bloodied corpses were in spastic disarray, one specifically, shockingly, the focus of the manager's horrified interest. He approached the body and the punctured skull. With his handkerchief he wiped away the blood and stared at the face.

'We are dead,' he whispered. 'Kowloon is dead, Hong Kong dead. All is dead.'

'*What?*'

'This man is the Vice-Premier of the People's Republic, successor to the Chairman himself.'

'Here! *Look!*' The first-assistant brother lunged toward the body of the dead *laoban.* Alongside the riddled, bleeding corpse was a black bandanna. It was lying flat, the fabric with the curlicues of white discoloured by blotches of red. The brother picked it up and gasped at the writing in the circle of blood underneath: *JASON BOURNE.*

The manager sprang across the floor. 'Great Christian Jesus!' he uttered, his whole body trembling. 'He's come back. The assassin has come back to Asia! *Jason Bourne!* He's come *back!*'

2

The sun fell behind the Sangre de Cristo Mountains in central Colorado as the Cobra helicopter roared out of the blazing light – a giant fluttering silhouette – and stutered its way down toward the threshold on the edge of the timberline. The concrete landing pad was several hundred feet from a large rectangular house of heavy wood and thick bevelled glass. Aside from generators and camouflaged communications discs, no other structures were in sight. Tall trees formed a dense wall, concealing the house from all outsiders. The pilots of these highly manoeuvrable aircraft were recruited from the senior officer corps of the Cheyenne complex in Colorado Springs. None was lower than a full colonel and each had been cleared by the National Security Council in Washington. They never spoke about their trips to the mountain retreat; the destination was always obscured on flight plans. Headings were issued by radio when the choppers were airborne. The location was not on any public map and its communications were beyond the scrutiny of allies and enemies alike. The security was total; it had to be. This was a place for strategists whose work was so sensitive and frequently entailed such delicate global implications that the planners could not be seen together outside government buildings or in the buildings themselves, and certainly never inside adjacent offices known to have connecting doors. There were hostile, inquisitive eyes everywhere – allies and enemies alike – who knew of the work these men did, and if they were observed together, alarms would surely go out. The enemy was vigilant and allies jealously guarded their own intelligence fiefdoms.

The doors of the Cobra opened. A frame of steel steps snapped to the ground as an obviously bewildered man climbed down into the floodlights. He was escorted by a major general in uniform. The civilian was slender, middle-aged, and of medium height, and was dressed in a pin-striped suit, white shirt and paisley tie. Even under the harsh, decelerating wash of the rotor blades his careful grooming remained intact, as though it were important to him and not to be abused. He followed the officer and together they walked up a concrete path to a door at the side of the house. The door opened as both men approached. However, only the civilian went inside; the general nodded, giving one of those informal salutes veteran soldiers reserve for the non-military and officers of their own rank.

'Nice to have met you, Mr McAllister,' said the general. 'Someone else will take you back.'

'You're not coming in?' asked the civilian.

'I've never *been* in,' replied the officer, smiling. 'I just make sure it's you, and get you from Point B to Point C.'

'Sounds like a waste of rank, General.'

'It probably isn't,' observed the soldier without further comment. 'But then I have other duties. Goodbye.'

McAllister walked inside, into a long panelled corridor, his escort now a pleasant-faced, well-dressed husky man who had all the outward signs of Internal Security about him – physically quick and capable, and anonymous in a crowd.

'Did you have a pleasant flight, sir?' asked the younger man.

'Does anybody, in one of those things?'

The guard laughed. 'This way, sir.'

They went down the corridor, passing several doors along both walls, until they reached the end where there was a pair of larger double doors with two red lights in the upper left and right corners. They were cameras on separate circuits. Edward McAllister had not seen devices like those since he left Hong Kong two years ago, and then only because he had been briefly assigned to British Intelligence MI6, Special Branch, for consultations. To him the British had seemed paranoid where security was concerned. He had never understood those people, especially after they awarded him a citation for doing minimal work for them in affairs they should have been on top of to begin with. The guard rapped on the door; there was a quiet click and he opened the right panel.

'Your other guest, sir,' said the husky man.

'Thank you so *very* much,' replied a voice. The astonished McAllister instantly recognized it from scores of radio and television newscasts over the years, its inflections learned in an expensive prep school and several prestigious universities, with a postgraduate career in the British Isles. There was, however, no time to adjust. The grey-haired, impeccably dressed man with a lined, elongated face that bespoke his seventy-plus years got up from a large desk and walked gingerly across the room, his hand extended. 'Mr Undersecretary, how good of you to come. May I introduce myself. I'm Raymond Havilland.'

'I'm certainly aware of who you are, Mr Ambassador. It's a privilege, sir.'

'Ambassador without portfolio, McAllister, which means there's very little privilege left. But there's still work.'

'I can't imagine any President of the United States within the past twenty years surviving without you.'

'Some muddled through, Mr Undersecretary, but with your experience at State, I suspect you know that better than I do.' The diplomat turned his head. 'I'd like you to meet John Reilly. Jack's one of those highly knowledgeable associates we're never supposed to know about over at the National Security Council. He's not so terrifying, is he?'

'I hope not,' said McAllister, crossing to shake hands with Reilly, who had got up from one of the two leather chairs facing the desk. 'Nice to meet you, Mr Reilly.'

'Mr Undersecretary,' said the somewhat obese man with red hair that matched a freckled forehead. The eyes behind the steel-rimmed glasses did not convey geniality; they were sharp and cold.

'Mr Reilly is here,' continued Havilland, crossing behind the desk and indicating the vacant chair on the right for McAllister, 'to make sure I stay in line. As I understand it, that means there are some things I can say, others I can't say, and certain things that only *he* can say.' The ambassador sat down. 'If that appears enigmatic to you, Mr Undersecretary, I'm afraid it's all I can offer you at this juncture.'

'Everything that's happened during the past five hours since I was ordered to Andrews Air Force Base has been an enigma, Ambassador Havilland. I have no idea why I was brought here.'

'Then let me tell you in general terms,' said the diplomat, glancing at Reilly and leaning forward on the desk. 'You are in a position to be of extraordinary service to your country – and to interests far beyond this country – exceeding anything you may have considered during your long and distinguished career.'

McAllister studied the ambassador's austere face, uncertain how to reply. 'My career at the Department of State has been fulfilling, and, I trust, professional, but it can hardly be called distinguished in the broadest sense. Quite frankly, the opportunities never presented themselves.'

'One has presented itself to you now,' interrupted Havilland. 'And you are uniquely qualified to carry it out.'

'In what way? Why?'

'The Far East,' said the diplomat with an odd inflection in his voice, as though the reply might itself be a question. 'You've been with the State Department for over twenty years since you received your doctorate in Far Eastern Studies at Harvard. You've served your government commendably with many years of outstanding foreign service in Asia, and since your return from your last post your judgments have proved to be extremely valuable in formulating policy in that troubled part of the world. You're considered a brilliant analyst.'

'I appreciate what you say, but there were others in Asia. Many others who attained equal and higher ratings than I did.'

'Accidents of events and posting, Mr Undersecretary. Let's be frank, you've done well.'

'But what separates me from the others? Why am I more qualified for this opportunity than they?'

'Because no one else compares with you as a specialist in the internal affairs of the People's Republic of China – I believe you played a pivotal role in the trade conferences between Washington and Peking. Also, none of the others spent seven years in Hong Kong.' Here Raymond Havilland paused, then added. 'Finally, no one else in our Asian posts was ever assigned to or accepted by the British government's MI-Six, Special Branch, in the territory.'

'I see,' said McAllister, recognizing that the last qualification, which seemed the least important to him, had a certain significance for the diplomat. 'My work in Intelligence was minimal, Mr Ambassador. The Special Branch's acceptance of me was based more on its own – disinformation, I think is the word, than any unique talents of mine. Those people simply believed the wrong sets of facts and the sums didn't total. It didn't take long to find the "correct figures," as I remember they put it.'

'They *trusted* you, McAllister. They still trust you.'

'I assume that trust is intrinsic to this opportunity, whatever it is?'

'Very much so. It's vital.'

'Then may I hear what the opportunity is?'

'You may.' Havilland looked over at the third participant, the man from the National Security Council. 'If you care to,' he added.

'My turn,' said Reilly, not unpleasantly. He shifted his heavy torso in the chair and gazed at McAllister, with eyes still rigid but without the coldness they had displayed previously, as though he was now asking for understanding. 'At the moment our voices are being taped – it's your constitutional right to know that – but it's a two-sided right. You must swear to absolute secrecy concerning the information imparted to you here, not only in the interests of national security but in the further and conceivably greater interests of specific world conditions. I know that sounds like a come-on to whet your appetite, but it's not meant to be. We're deadly serious. Will you agree to the condition? You can be prosecuted in a closed trial under the national security nondisclosure statutes if you violate the oath.'

'How can I agree to a condition like that when I have no idea what the information is?'

'Because I can give you a quick overview and it'll be enough for you to say yes or no. If it's no, you'll be escorted out of here and flown back to Washington. No one will be the loser.'

'Go ahead.'

'All right.' Reilly spoke calmly. 'You'll be discussing certain events that took place in the past – not ancient history, but not current by any means. The actions themselves were disavowed – buried, to be more accurate. Does that sound familiar, Mr Undersecretary?'

'I'm from the State Department. We bury the past when it serves no purpose to reveal it. Circumstances change; judgements made in good faith yesterday are often a problem tomorrow. We can't control these changes any more than the Soviets or the Chinese can.'

'Well put!' said Havilland.

'Not yet it isn't,' objected Reilly, raising a palm to the ambassador. 'The undersecretary is evidently an experienced diplomat. He didn't say yes and he didn't say no.' The man from the NSC again looked at McAllister; the eyes behind the steel-rimmed glasses were once again sharp and cold. 'What is it, Mr Undersecretary? You want to sign on, or do you want to leave?'

'One part of me wants to get up and leave as quickly as I can,' said McAllister, looking alternately at both men. 'The other part says "Stay."' He paused, his gaze settling on Reilly, and added, 'Whether you intended it or not, my appetite is whetted.'

'It's a hell of a price to pay for being hungry,' replied the Irishman.

'It's more than that.' The undersecretary of State spoke softly. 'I'm a professional, and if I am the man you want, I really don't have a choice, do I?'

'I'm afraid I'll have to hear the words,' said Reilly. 'Do you want me to repeat them?'

'It won't be necessary.' McAllister frowned in thought, then spoke. 'I, Edward Newington McAllister, fully understand that whatever is said during this conference—' He stopped and looked at Reilly. 'I assume you'll fill in the particulars, such as time and location and those present?'

'Date, place, hour and minute of entry and identifications – it's all been done and logged.'

'Thank you. I'll want a copy before I leave.'

'Of course.' Without raising his voice, Reilly looked straight ahead and quietly issued an order. 'Please note. Have a copy of this tape available for the subject upon his departure. Also equipment for him to verify its contents on the premises. I'll initial the copy. . . . Go ahead, Mr McAllister.'

'I appreciate that . . . With regard to whatever is said at this conference, I accept the condition of nondisclosure. I will speak to no one about any aspect of the discussion unless instructed to do so personally by Ambassador Havilland. I further understand that I may be prosecuted at a closed trial should I violate this agreement. However, should such a trial ever take place, I reserve the right to confront my accusers, not their affidavits or depositions. I add this, for I cannot conceive of any circumstances where I would or could violate the oath I've just taken.'

'There *are* circumstances, you know,' said Reilly gently.

'Not in my book.'

'Extreme physical abuse, chemicals, being tricked by men and women far more experienced than you. There are ways, Mr Undersecretary.'

'I repeat. Should a case ever be brought against me – and such things have happened to others – I reserve the right to face any and all accusers.'

'That's good enough for us.' Again Reilly looked straight ahead and spoke. 'Terminate this tape and pull the plugs. Confirm.'

'*Confirmed*,' said a voice eerily from a speaker somewhere overhead. '*You are now . . . out*.'

'Proceed, Mr Ambassador,' said the red-haired man. 'I'll interrupt only when I feel it's necessary.'

'I'm sure you will, Jack.' Havilland turned to McAllister. 'I take back my previous statement; he really is a terror. After forty-odd years of service, I'm told by a redheaded whippersnapper who should go on a diet when to shut up.'

The three men smiled; the ageing diplomat knew the moment and the method to reduce tension. Reilly shook his head and genially spread his hands. 'I would never do that, sir. Certainly, I hope not so obviously.'

'What say, McAllister? Let's defect to Moscow and say he was the recruiter. The Russkies would probably give us both dachas and he'd be in Leavenworth.'

'*You'd* get the dacha, Mr Ambassador. I'd share a flat with twelve Siberians. No thank you, sir. He's not interrupting me.'

'*Very* good. I'm surprised none of those well-intentioned meddlers in the Oval Office ever tapped you for his staff, or at least sent you to the UN.'

'They didn't know I existed.'

'That status will change,' said Havilland, abruptly serious. He paused, staring at the undersecretary, then lowered his voice. 'Have you ever heard the name Jason Bourne?'

'How could anyone posted in Asia not have heard it?' answered McAllister. 'Thirty-five to forty murders, the assassin for hire who eluded every trap ever set for him. A pathological killer whose only morality was the price of the kill. They say he was an American – *is* an American; I don't know, he faded from sight – and that he was a defrocked priest and an importer who'd stolen millions and a deserter from the French Foreign Legion and God knows how many other stories. The only thing I *do* know is that he was never caught, and our failure to catch him was a burden on our diplomacy throughout the Far East.'

'Was there any pattern to his victims?'

'None. They were random, across the board. Two bankers here, three attachés there – meaning CIA; a minister of state from Delhi, an industrialist from Singapore, and numerous – far too numerous – politicians, generally decent men. Their cars were bombed in the streets, their flats blown up. Then there were unfaithful husbands and wives and lovers of various persuasions in various scandals; he offered final solutions for bruised egos. There was no one he wouldn't kill, no method too brutal or demeaning for him . . . No, there wasn't a pattern, just money. The highest bidder. He was a monster – *is* a monster, if he's still alive.'

Once more Havilland leaned forward, his eyes steady on the undersecretary of State. 'You say he faded from sight. Just like that? You never picked up anything, any rumours or backstairs gossip from our Asian embassies or consulates?'

'There was talk, yes, but none of it was ever confirmed. The story I heard most often came from the Macao police, where Bourne was last known to be. They said he wasn't dead, or retired, but instead had gone to Europe looking for wealthier clients. If it's true, it might be only half the story. The police also claimed informants told them that several contracts had gone sour for Bourne, that in one instance he killed the wrong man, a leading figure in the Malaysian underworld, and in another, it was said he raped a client's wife. Perhaps the circle was closing in on him – and perhaps not.'

'What do you mean?'

'Most of us bought the first half of the story, not the second. Bourne wouldn't kill the wrong man, especially someone like that; he didn't make those kinds of mistakes. And if he raped a client's wife – which is doubtful – he would have done so out of hatred or revenge. He would have forced a bound husband to watch and then killed them both. No, most of us subscribed to the first story. He went to Europe, where there were bigger fish to fry – and murder.'

'You were meant to accept that version,' said Havilland, leaning back in his chair.

'I beg your pardon?'

'The only man Jason Bourne ever killed in post-Vietnam Asia was an enraged conduit who tried to kill him.'

Stunned, McAllister stared at the diplomat. 'I don't understand.'

'The Jason Bourne you've just described never existed. He was a myth.'

'You can't be serious.'

'Never more so. Those were turbulent times in the Far East. The drug networks operating out of the Golden Triangle were fighting a disorganized, unpublicized war. Consuls, vice-consuls, police, politicians, criminal gangs, border patrols – the highest and the lowest social orders – all were affected. Money in unimaginable amounts was the mother's milk of corruption. Whenever and wherever a well-publicized killing took place – regardless of the circumstances or those accused – Bourne was on the scene and took credit for the kill.'

'He *was* the killer,' insisted a confused McAllister. 'There were the signs, *his* signs. Everyone knew it!'

'Everyone *assumed* it, Mr Undersecretary. A mocking telephone call to the police, a small article of clothing sent in the mails, a black bandanna found in the bushes a day later. They were all part of the strategy.'

'The strategy? What are you talking about?'

'Jason Bourne – the original Jason Bourne – was a convicted murderer, a fugitive whose life ended with a bullet in his head in a place called Tam Quan during the last months of the Vietnam war. It was a jungle execution. The man was a traitor. His corpse was left to rot – he simply disappeared. Several years later, the man who executed him took on his identity for one of our projects, a project that nearly succeeded, *should* have succeeded, but went off the wire.'

'Off the what?'

'Out of control. That man – that very brave man – who went underground for us, using the name Jason Bourne for three years, was injured, and the result of those injuries was amnesia. He lost his memory; he neither knew who he was nor who he was meant to be.'

'Good *Lord* . . .'

'He was between a rock and a hard place. With the help of an alcoholic doctor on a Mediterranean island he tried to trace his life, his identity, and here, I'm afraid, he failed. *He* failed but the woman who befriended him did not fail; she's now his wife. Her instincts were accurate; she knew he wasn't a killer. She purposely forced him to examine his words, his abilities, ultimately to make the contacts that would lead him back to us. But we, with the most sophisticated Intelligence apparatus in the world, did not listen to the human quotient. We set a trap to kill him—'

'I must interrupt, Mr Ambassador,' said Reilly.

'Why?' asked Havilland. 'It's what we did and we're not on tape.'

'An individual made the determination, not the United States government. That should be clear, sir.'

'All right,' agreed the diplomat, nodding. 'His name was Conklin, but it's irrelevant, Jack. Government personnel went along. It happened.'

'Government personnel were also instrumental in saving his life.'

'Somewhat after the fact,' muttered Havilland.

'But *why?*' asked McAllister; he now leaned forward, mesmerized by the bizarre story. 'He was one of us. Why would anyone want to kill him?'

'His loss of memory was taken for something else. It was erroneously believed that he had turned, that he had killed three of his controls and disappeared with a great deal of money – government funds totalling over five million dollars.'

'Five *million* . . . ?' Astonished, the undersecretary of State slowly sank back into the chair. 'Funds of that magnitude were available to him *personally?*'

'Yes,' said the ambassador. 'They, too, were part of the strategy, part of the project.'

'I assume this is where silence is necessary. The project, I mean.'

'It's imperative,' answered Reilly. 'Not because of the project – in spite of what happened we make no apology for that operation – but because of the man we recruited to become Jason Bourne and where he came from.'

'That's cryptic.'

'It'll become clear.'

'The project, please.'

Reilly looked at Raymond Havilland; the diplomat nodded and spoke. 'We created a killer to draw out and trap the most deadly assassin in Europe.'

'*Carlos?*'

'You're quick, Mr Undersecretary.'

'Who else *was* there? In Asia, Bourne and the Jackal were constantly being compared.'

'Those comparisons were encouraged,' said Havilland. 'Often magnified and spread by the strategists of the project, a group known as Treadstone Seventy-one. The name was derived from a sterile house on New York's Seventy-first Street where the resurrected Jason Bourne was trained. It was the command post and a name you should be aware of.'

'I see,' said McAllister pensively. 'Then those comparisons, growing as they did with Bourne's reputation, served as a challenge to Carlos. That's when Bourne moved to Europe – to bring the challenge directly to the Jackal. To force him to come out and confront his challenger.'

'*Very* quick, Mr Undersecretary. In a nutshell, that was the strategy.'

'It's extraordinary. Brilliant, actually, and one doesn't have to be an expert to see that. God knows I'm not.'

'You may become one—'

'And you say this man who became Bourne, the mythical assassin, spent three years playing the role and then was injured—'

'Shot,' interrupted Havilland. 'Membranes of his skull were blown away.'

'And he lost his *memory?*'

'Totally.'

'My God!'

'Yet despite everything that happened to him, and with the woman's help – she was an economist for the Canadian government, incidentally – he came within moments of pulling the whole damn thing off. A remarkable story, isn't it?'

'It's incredible. But what kind of man would do this, *could* do it?'

The redheaded John Reilly coughed softly; the ambassador deferred with a glance. 'We're now reaching ground zero,' said the watchguard, again shifting his bulk to look at McAllister. 'If you've got any doubts I can still let you go.'

'I try not to repeat myself. You have your tape.'

'It's your appetite.'

'I suppose that's another way you people have of saying there might not even be a trial.'

'I'd never say that.'

McAllister swallowed, his eyes meeting the calm gaze of the man from the NSC. He turned to Havilland. 'Please go on, Mr Ambassador. Who is this man? Where *did* he come from?'

'His name is David Webb. He's currently an associate professor of Oriental Studies at a small university in Maine and married to the Canadian woman who literally guided him out of his labyrinth. Without her he would have been killed – but then without *him* she would have ended up a corpse in Zurich.'

'Remarkable,' said McAllister, barely audible.

'The point is, she's his second wife. His first marriage ended in a tragic act of wanton slaughter – that's when his story began for us. A number of years ago Webb was a young foreign service officer stationed in Phnom Penh, a brilliant Far East scholar, fluent in several Oriental languages, and married to a girl from Thailand he'd met in graduate school. They lived in a house on a riverbank and had two children. It was an ideal life for such a man. It combined the expertise Washington needed in the area with the opportunity to live in his own museum. Then the Vietnam action escalated and one morning a lone jet fighter – no one really knows from which side, but no one ever told Webb that – swooped down at low altitude and strafed his wife and children while they were playing in the water. Their bodies were riddled. They floated into the riverbank as Webb was trying to reach them; he gathered them in his arms, screaming helplessly at the disappearing plane above.'

'How *horrible*,' whispered McAllister.

'At that moment, Webb turned. He became someone he never was, never dreamed he could be. He became a guerrilla fighter known as Delta.'

'Delta?' said the undersecretary of State. 'A guerrilla . . . ? I'm afraid I don't understand.'

'There's no way you could.' Havilland looked over at Reilly, then back at McAllister. 'As Jack made clear a moment ago, we're now at ground zero. Webb fled to Saigon consumed with range, and, ironically, through the efforts of the CIA officer named Conklin, who years later tried to kill him, he joined a clandestine operations outfit called Medusa. No names were ever used by the people in Medusa, just the Greek letters of the alphabet – Webb became Delta One.'

'*Medusa?* I've never heard of it.'

'Ground zero,' said Reilly. 'The Medusa file is still classified, but we've permitted limited declassification in this instance. The Medusa units were a collection of internationals who knew the Vietnam territories, north and south. Frankly, most of them were criminals – smugglers of narcotics, gold, guns, jewels, all kinds of contraband. Also convicted murderers, fugitives who'd been sentenced to death in absentia . . . and a smattering of colonials whose businesses were confiscated – again by both sides. They banked on us – Big Uncle – to take care of all their problems if they infiltrated hostile areas, killing suspected Viet Cong collaborators and village chiefs thought to be leaning toward Charlie, as well as expediting prisoner-of-war escapes where they could. They were assassination teams – death squads, if you will – and that says it as well as it can be said, but of course we'll never say it. Mistakes were made, millions stolen, and the majority of those personnel wouldn't be allowed in any civilized army, Webb among them.'

'With his background, his academic credentials, he willingly became part of such a group?'

'He had an overpowering motive,' said Havilland. 'As far as he was concerned, that plane in Phnom Penh was North Vietnamese.'

'Some said he was a madman,' continued Reilly. 'Others claimed he was an extraordinary tactician, the supreme guerrilla who understood the Oriental mind and led the most aggressive teams in Medusa, feared as much by Command Saigon as he was by the enemy. He was uncontrollable; the only rules he followed were his own. It was as if he had mounted his own personal hunt, tracking down the man who had flown that plane and destroyed his life. It became his war, his rage; the more violent it became, the more satisfying it was for him – or perhaps closer to his own death wish.'

'Death . . .?' The undersecretary of State left the word hanging.

'It was the prevalent theory at the time,' interrupted the ambassador.

'The war ended,' said Reilly, 'as disastrously for Webb – or Delta – as it did for the rest of us. Perhaps worse; there was nothing left for him. No more purpose, nothing to strike out at, to kill. Until we approached him and gave him a reason to go on living. Or perhaps a reason to go on trying to die.'

'By becoming Bourne and going after Carlos the Jackal,' completed McAllister.

'Yes,' agreed the Intelligence officer. A brief silence ensued.

'We need him back,' said Havilland. The soft-spoken words fell like an axe on hard wood.

'Carlos has surfaced?'

The diplomat shook his head. 'Not Europe. We need him back in Asia and we can't waste a minute.'

'Someone else? Another .. target?' McAllister swallowed involuntarily. 'Have you spoken to him?'

'We can't approach him. Not directly.'

'Why not?'

'He wouldn't let us through the door. He doesn't trust anything or anyone out of Washington, and it's difficult to fault him for that. For days, for weeks, he cried out for help and we didn't listen. Instead, we tried to kill him.'

'Again I must object,' broke in Reilly. 'It wasn't us. It was an individual operating on erroneous information. And the government currently spends in excess of four hundred thousand dollars a year in a protection programme for Webb.'

'Which he scoffs at. He believes it's no more than a backup trap for Carlos in the event the Jackal unearths him. He's convinced you don't give a damn about him, and I'm not sure he's far off the mark. He *saw* Carlos and the fact that the face has not yet come back into focus for him isn't something Carlos knows. The Jackal has every reason to go after Webb. And if he does, you'll have your second chance.'

'The *chances* of Carlos finding him are so remote as to be practically nil. The Treadstone records are buried, and even if they weren't, they don't contain any current information as to where Webb is or what he does.'

'Come, Mr Reilly,' said Havilland testily. 'Only his background and qualifications. How difficult would it be? He's got academia written all over him.'

'I'm not opposing you, Mr Ambassador,' replied a somewhat subdued Reilly. 'I just want everything clear. Let's be frank, Webb has to be handled very delicately. He's recovered a large portion of his memory but certainly not all of it. However, he's recalled enough about Medusa to be a considerable threat to the country's interests.'

'In what way?' asked McAllister. 'Perhaps it wasn't the best and it probably wasn't the worst, but basically it was a military strategy in time of war.'

'A strategy that was unsanctioned, unlogged and unacknowledged. There's no official slate.'

'How is that possible? It was *funded*, and when funds are expended—'

'Don't read me the book,' interrupted the obese Intelligence officer. 'We're not on tape, but I've got yours.'

'Is that your answer?'

'No, this is: there's no statute of limitation on war crimes and murder, Mr Undersecretary, and murder and other violent crimes were committed against our own forces, as well as Allied personnel. In the main they were committed by killers and thieves in the process of stealing, looting, raping, and killing. Most of them were pathological criminals. As effective as the Medusa was in many ways, it was a tragic mistake, born of anger and frustration in a no-win situation. What possible good would it do to open all the old wounds? Quite apart from the claims against us, we would become a pariah in the eyes of much of the civilized world.'

'As I mentioned,' said McAllister softly, reluctantly. 'At State we don't believe in opening wounds.' He turned to the ambassador. 'I'm beginning to understand. You want me to reach this David Webb and persuade him to return to Asia. For another project, another target – although I've never used the word in that context in my life before this evening. And I assume it's because there are distinct parallels in our early careers – we're Asia men. We presumably have insights where the Far East is concerned, and you think he'll listen to me.'

'Essentially, yes.'

'Yet you say he won't touch us. That's where my understanding fades. How can I do it?'

'We'll do it together. As he once made the rules for himself, we'll make them now. It's imperative.'

'Because of a man you want killed?'

'"Neutralized" will suffice. It has to be done.'

'And Webb can do it?'

'No. *Jason Bourne* can. We sent him out alone for three years under extraordinary stress – suddenly his memory was taken from him and he was hunted like an animal. Still he retained the ability to infiltrate and kill. I'm being blunt.'

'I understand that. Since we're not on tape – and on the chance that we still are—' The undersecretary glanced disapprovingly at Reilly, who shook his head and shrugged. 'May I be permitted to know who the target is?'

'You may, and I want you to commit this name to memory, Mr Undersecretary. He's a Chinese minister of state, Sheng Chou Yang.'

McAllister flushed angrily. 'I don't *have* to commit it, and I think you *know* that. He was a fixture in the PRC's economics group and we were both assigned to the trade conferences in Peking in the late seventies. I read up on him, analysed him. Sheng was my counterpart and I could do no less – a fact I suspect you also know.'

'Oh?' The grey-haired ambassador arched his dark eyebrows, and dismissed the rebuke. 'And what did your reading tell you? What did you learn about him?'

'He was considered very bright, very ambitious – but then his rise in Peking's hierarchy tells us that. He was spotted by scouts sent out from the Central Committee some years ago at the Fudan University in Shanghai. Initially because he took to the English language so well and had a firm, even sophisticated, grasp of Western economics.'

'What else?'

'He was considered promising material, and after in-depth indoctrination was sent to the London School of Economics for graduate study. It took.'

'How do you mean?'

'Sheng's an avowed Marxist where the centralized state is concerned, but he has a healthy respect for capitalistic profits.'

'I see,' said Havilland. 'Then he accepts the failure of the Soviet system?'

'He's ascribed that failure to the Russian penchant for corruption and mindless conformity in the higher ranks, and alcohol in the lower ones. To his credit he's stamped out a fair share of those abuses in the industrial centres.'

'Sounds like he was trained at IBM, doesn't it?'

'He's been responsible for many of the PRC's new trade policies. He's made China a lot of money.' Again the undersecretary of State leaned forward in his chair, his eyes intense, his expression bewildered – stunned was perhaps more accurate. 'My *God*, why would *anyone* in the West want Sheng *dead?* It's *absurd!* He's our economic ally, a politically stabilizing factor in the largest nation on earth that's ideologically opposed to us! Through him and men like him we've reached accommodations. Without him, whatever the course, there's the risk of disaster. I'm a professional China analyst, Mr Ambassador, and, I repeat, what you suggest is absurd. A man of your accomplishments should recognize that before any of us.'

The aging diplomat looked hard at his accuser, and when he spoke he did so slowly, choosing his words carefully. 'A few moments ago we were at ground zero. A former foreign service officer named David Webb became Jason

Bourne for a purpose. Conversely, Sheng Chou Yang is not the man you know, not the man you studied as your counterpart. He *became* that man for a purpose.'

'What are you talking about?' shot back McAllister defensively. 'Everything I've said about him is on record – *records*, official – most top secret and eyes-only.'

'*Eyes*-only?' The former ambassador asked wearily. '*Ears*-only, tongues-only – wagging as busily as tails wag tigers. Because an official stamp is placed on recorded observations observed by men who have no idea where those records came from – they are there, and that's enough. No, Mr Undersecretary, it's not enough, it never is.'

'You obviously have other information I don't have,' said the State Department man coldly. 'If it *is* information and not disinformation. The man I described – the man I knew – is Sheng Chou Yang.'

'Just as the David Webb we described to you was Jason Bourne? . . . No, please, don't be angry, I'm not playing games. It's important that you understand. Sheng is not the man you knew. He never was.'

'Then whom *did* I know? Who *was* the man at those conferences?'

'He's a traitor, Mr Undersecretary. Sheng Chou Yang is a traitor to his country, and when his treachery is exposed – as it surely will be – Peking will hold the Free World responsible. The consequences of that inevitable error are unthinkable. However, there's no doubt as to his purpose.'

'*Sheng . . . a traitor?* I don't *believe* you! He's worshipped in Peking! One day he'll be chairman!'

'Then China will be ruled by a Nationalist zealot whose ideological roots are in Taiwan.'

'You're crazy – you're absolutely *crazy!* Wait a minute, you said he had a purpose – "no doubt as to his purpose," you said.'

'He and his people intend to take over Hong Kong. He's mounting a hidden economic blitzkrieg, putting all trade, all of the territory's financial institutions under the control of a "neutral" commission, a clearinghouse approved by Peking – which means approved by him. The instrument of record will be the British treaty that expires in 1997, his commission a supposedly reasonable prelude to annexation and control. It will happen when the road is clear for Sheng, when there are no more obstacles in his path. When his word is the only word that counts in economic matters. It could be in a month, or two months. Or next week.'

'You think Peking has *agreed* to this?' protested McAllister. 'You're wrong! It's – it's just *crazy!* The People's Republic will never substantively *touch* Hong Kong! It brokers sixty percent of its entire economy through the territory. The China Accords guarantee fifty years of a Free Economic Zone status and Sheng is a signatory, the most vital one!'

'But Sheng is not Sheng – not as you know him.'

'Then who the hell *is* he?'

'Prepare yourself, Mr Undersecretary. Sheng Chou Yang is the first son of a Shanghai industrialist who made his fortune in the corrupt world of the old China, Chiang Kai-shek's Kuomintang. When it was obvious that Mao's revolution would succeed, the family fled, as so many of the landlords and the warlords did, with whatever they could transfer. The old man is now one of the most powerful taipans in Hong Kong – but which one we don't know. The colony will become his and the family's mandate, courtesy of a minister in Peking, his most treasured son. It's the ultimate irony, the patriarch's final vengeance – Hong Kong will be controlled by the very men who corrupted Nationalist China. For years they bled their country without conscience, profiting from the labours of a starving, disenfranchised people, paving the way for Mao's revolution. And if that sounds like Communist bilge, I'm afraid for the most part it's embarrassingly accurate. Now a handful of zealots, boardroom thugs led by a maniac, want back what no international court in history would ever grant them.' Havilland paused, then spat out the single word '*Maniacs!*'

'But if you don't know who this taipan is, how do you know it's true, *any* of it?'

'The sources are maximum-classified,' interrupted Reilly, 'but they've been confirmed. The story was first picked up in Taiwan. Our original informer was a member of the Nationalist cabinet who thought it was a disastrous course that could only lead to a bloodbath for the entire Far East. He pleaded with us to stop it. He was found dead the next morning, three bullets in his head and his throat cut – in Chinese that means a dead traitor. Since then five other people have been murdered, their bodies similarly mutilated. It's true. The conspiracy is alive and well and coming from Hong Kong.'

'It's *insane!*'

'More to the point,' said Havilland, 'it will never work. If it had a prayer, we might look the other way and even say Godspeed, but it can't. It'll blow apart, as Lin Biao's conspiracy against Mao Zedong blew apart in '72, and when it does, Peking will blame American and Taiwanese money in complicity with the British – as well as the silent acquiescence of the world's leading financial institutions. Eight years of economic progress will be shot to hell because a group of fanatics want vengeance. In your words, Mr Undersecretary, the People's Republic is a suspicious turbulent nation – and if I may add a few of my own from those accomplishments you ascribe to me – a government quick to become paranoid, obsessed with betrayal both from within and without. China will believe that the world is out to isolate her economically, choke her off from world markets, and bring her to her knees while the Russians grin across the northern borders. She will strike fast and furiously, impound everything, absorb everything. Her troops will occupy Kowloon, the island, and all of the burgeoning New Territories. Investments in the trillions will be lost. Without the colony's expertise trade will be stymied, a labour force in the millions will be in chaos – hunger and disease will be rampant. The Far East will be in flames, and the result could touch off a war none of us wants to think about.'

'Jesus Christ,' McAllister whispered. 'It can't happen.'

'No, it can't,' agreed the diplomat.

'But why *Webb?*'

'Not Webb,' corrected Havilland. 'Jason Bourne.'

'All right! Why Bourne?'

'Because word out of Kowloon is that he's already there.'

'*What?*'

'And we know he's not.'

'*What* did you say?'

'He's struck. He's killed. He's back in Asia.'

'*Webb?*'

'No, Bourne. The myth.'

'You're not making one *goddamned* bit of sense!'

'I can assure you Sheng Chou Yang is making a lot of sense.'

'*How?*'

'He's brought him back. Jason Bourne's skills are once more for hire, and, as always, his client is beyond unearthing – in the present case the most unlikely client imaginable. A leading spokesman for the People's Republic who must eliminate his opposition both in Hong Kong and in Peking. During the past six months a number of powerful voices in Peking's Central Committee have been strangely silent. According to official government announcements, several died, and considering their ages it's understandable. Two others were supposedly killed in accidents – one in a plane crash, one by, of all things, a cerebral haemorrhage while hiking in the Shaoguan mountains – if it's not true, at least it's imaginative. Then another was "removed" – a euphemism for disgrace. Lastly, and most extraordinary, the PRC's Vice-Premier was murdered in Kowloon when no one in Peking knew he was there. It was a gruesome episode, five men massacred in the Tsim Sha Tsui with the killer leaving his calling card. The name Jason Bourne was etched in blood on the floor. An impostor's ego demanded that he be given credit for his kills.'

McAllister blinked repeatedly, his eyes darting aimlessly. 'This is all so far beyond me,' he said helplessly. Then, becoming the professional once again, he looked steadily at Havilland. 'Is there linkage?' he asked.

The diplomat nodded. 'Our Intelligence reports are specific. All of these men opposed Sheng's policies – some some openly, some guardedly. The Vice-Premier, an old revolutionary and veteran of Mao's Long March, was especially vocal. He couldn't stand the upstart Sheng. Yet what was he doing secretly in Kowloon in the company of bankers? Peking can't answer, so "face" mercifully required that the killing never happened. With his cremation he became a non-person.'

'And with the killer's "calling card" – the name written in blood – the second linkage is to Sheng,' said the undersecretary of State, his voice close to trembling, as he nervously massaged his forehead. 'Why would he do it? Leave his *name*, I mean!'

'He's in business and it was a spectacular kill. Now do you begin to understand?'

'I'm not sure what you mean.'

'For us this new Bourne is our direct route to Sheng Chou Yang. He's our trap. An impostor is posing as the myth, but if the original myth tracks down and takes out the impostor, he's in the position to reach Sheng. It's really very simple. The Jason Bourne *we* created will replace this new killer using his name. Once in place, *our* Jason Bourne sends out an urgent alarm – something drastic has happened that threatens Sheng's entire strategy – and Sheng has to respond. He can't afford not to, for his security must be absolute, his hands clean. He'll be forced to show himself, if only to kill his hired gun, to remove any association. When he does, this time we won't fail.'

'It's a circle,' said McAllister, his words barely above a whisper, as he stared at the diplomat. 'And from everything you've told me, Webb won't walk near it, much less into it.'

'Then we must provide him with an overpowering reason to do so,' said Havilland softly. 'In my profession – frankly, it was always my profession – we look for patterns, patterns that will trigger a man.' Frowning, his eyes hollow and empty, the ageing ambassador leaned back in his chair; certainly he was not at peace with himself. 'Sometimes they are ugly realizations – repugnant, actually – but one must weigh the greater good, the greater benefits. For everyone.'

'That doesn't tell me anything.'

'David Webb became Jason Bourne for essentially one reason – the same reason that propelled him into the Medusa. A wife was taken from him; his children and the mother of his children were killed.'

'Oh, my *God* . . .'

'This is where I leave,' said Reilly, getting out of his chair.

3

Marie! Oh, Christ, Marie, it happened again! A floodgate opened and I couldn't handle it. I tried to, my darling, I tried so hard but I got totalled – I got washed away and I was drowning! I know what you'll say if I tell you, which is why I won't tell you even though I know you'll see it in my eyes, hear it in my voice – somehow, as only you know how. You'll say I should have come home to you, to talk to you, be with you, and we could work it out together. Together! My God! How much can you take? How unfair can I be, how long can it go on this way? I love you so much, in so many ways, that there are times I have to do it myself. If only to let you off the goddamned hook for a while, to let you breathe for a while without having your nerves scraped to their roots while you take care of me. But, you see, my love, I can do it! I did it tonight and I'm all right. I've calmed down now, I'm all right now. And now I'll come home to you better than I was. I have to, because without you there isn't anything left.

His face drenched with sweat, his track suit clinging to his body, David Webb ran breathlessly across the cold grass of the dark field, past the bleachers, and up the cement path toward the university gym. The autumn sun had disappeared behind the stone buildings of the campus, its glow firing the early evening sky as it hovered over the distant Maine woods. The autumn chill was penetrating; he shivered. It was not what his doctors had had in mind.

Regardless, he had followed medical advice; it had been one of those days. The government doctors had told him that if there were times – and there *would* be times – when sudden, disturbing images or fragments of memory broke into his mind, the best way to handle them was with strenuous exercise. His EKG charts indicated a healthy heart, his lungs were decent, though he was foolish enough to smoke, and since his body could take the punishment, it was the best way to relieve his mind. What he needed during such times was equanimity.

'What's wrong with a few drinks and cigarettes?' he had said to the doctors, stating his genuine preference. 'The heart beats faster, the body doesn't suffer, and the mind is certainly far more relieved.'

'They're depressants' had been the reply from the only man he listened to. 'Artificial stimulants that lead only to further depression and increased anxiety. Run, or swim, or make love to your wife – or anybody else, for that matter. Don't be a goddamned fool and come back here a basket case . . . Forget about you, think of *me.* I worked too hard on you, you ingrate. Get out of here, Webb. Take up your life – what you can remember of it – and enjoy.

You've got it better than most people, and don't you forget that, or I'll cancel our controlled monthly blowouts at the saloons of our choosing and you can go to hell. And hell for you notwithstanding, I'd miss them . . . Go, David. It's time for you to go.'

Morris Panov was the only person besides Marie who could reach him. It was ironic, in a way, for initially Mo had not been one of the government doctors; the psychiatrist had neither sought nor been offered security clearance to hear the classified details of David Webb's background where the lie of Jason Bourne was buried. Nevertheless, Panov had forcefully inserted himself, threatening all manner of embarrassing disclosures if he was not given clearance and a voice in the subsequent therapy. His reasoning was simple, for when David had come within moments of being blown off the face of the earth by misinformed men who were convinced he had to die, that misinformation had been unwittingly furnished by Panov and the way it had happened infuriated him. He had been approached in panic by someone not given to panic, and asked 'hypothetical' questions pertaining to a possibly deranged deep-cover agent in a potentially explosive situation. His answers were restrained and equivocal; he could not and would not diagnose a patient he had never seen – but yes, this was possible and that not unheard of, but, of course, nothing could be considered remotely material without physical and psychiatric examination. The key word was *nothing*; he should have *said* nothing! he later claimed. For his words in the ears of amateurs had sealed the order for Webb's execution – 'Jason Bourne's' death sentence – an act that was aborted only at the last instant through David's own doing, while the squad of executioners were still in their unseen positions.

Not only had Morris Panov come on board at the Walter Reed Hospital and later at the Virginia medical complex, but he literally ran the show – Webb's show. *The son of a bitch has amnesia, you goddamned fools! He's been trying to tell you that for weeks in perfectly lucid English – I suspect too lucid for your convoluted mentality.*

They had worked together for months, as patient and doctor – and finally as friends. It helped that Marie adored Mo – good Lord, she needed an ally! The burden David had been to his wife was beyond telling, from those first days in Switzerland when she began to understand the pain within the man who had taken her captive, to the moment when she made the commitment – violently against his wishes – to help him, never believing what he himself believed, telling him over and over again that he was not the killer he thought he was, not the assassin others called him. Her belief became an anchor in his own crashing seas, her love the core of his emerging sanity. Without Marie he was a loveless, discarded dead man, and without Mo Panov he was little more than a vegetable. But with both of them behind him, he was brushing away the swirling clouds and finding the sun again.

Which was why he had opted for an hour of running around the deserted, cold track rather than heading home after his late-afternoon seminar. His weekly seminars often continued far beyond the hour when they were scheduled to end, so Marie never planned dinner, knowing they would go out to eat, their two unobtrusive guards somewhere in the darkness behind them – as one was walking across the barely visible field behind him now, the other no doubt inside the gym. *Insanity!* Or was it?

What had driven him to Panov's 'strenuous exercise' was an image that had suddenly appeared in his mind while he had been grading papers several hours ago in his office. It was a face – a face he knew and remembered, and loved very much. A boy's face that aged in front of his inner screen, coming to full portrait in uniform, blurred, imperfect, but a part of him. As silent tears rolled down his cheeks he knew it was the dead brother they had told him about, the prisoner of war he had rescued in the jungles of Tam Quan years ago amid shattering explosions and a traitor he had executed by the name of Jason Bourne. He could not handle the violent, fragmented pictures; he had barely got through the shortened seminar, pleading a severe headache. He had to relieve the pressures, accept or reject the peeling layers of memory with the help of reason, which told him to go to the gym and run against the wind, any strong wind. He could not burden Marie every time a floodgate burst; he loved her too much for that. When he could handle it himself, he had to. It was his contract with himself.

He opened the heavy door, briefly wondering why every gymnasium entrance was designed with the weight of a portcullis. He went inside and walked across the stone floor through an archway and down a white-walled corridor until he reached the door of the faculty locker room. He was thankful that the room was empty; he was in no frame of mind to respond to small talk, and if required to do so, he would undoubtedly appear sullen, if not strange. He could also do without the stares he would probably provoke. He was too close to the edge; he had to pull back gradually, slowly, first within himself, then with Marie. Christ, when would it all *stop*? How much could he ask of her? But then he never had to ask – she gave without being asked.

Webb reached the row of lockers. His own was toward the end. He walked between the long wooden bench and the connecting metal cabinets when his eyes were suddenly rivetted on an object up ahead. He rushed forward; a folded note had been taped to his locker. He ripped it off and opened it: *Your wife phoned. She wants you to call her as soon as you can. Says it's urgent. Ralph.*

The gym custodian might have had the brains to go outside and shout to him! thought David angrily as he spun the combination and opened the locker. After rummaging through his limp trousers for change, he ran to a pay telephone on the wall; he inserted a coin, disturbed that his hand trembled. Then he knew why. Marie never used the word 'urgent.' She avoided such words.

'Hello?'

'What is it?'

'I thought you might be there,' said his wife. 'Mo's panacea, the one he guarantees will cure you if it doesn't give you cardiac arrest.'

'What *is* it?'

'David, come home. There's someone here you must see. Quickly, darling.'

Undersecretary of State Edward McAllister kept his own introduction to a minimum, but by including certain facts let Webb know he was not from the lower ranks of the Department. On the other hand, he did not embellish his importance; he was the secure bureaucrat, confident that whatever expertise he possessed could weather changes in administrations.

'If you'd like, Mr Webb, our business can wait until you get into something more comfortable.'

David was still in his sweat-stained shorts and T-shirt, having grabbed his clothes from the locker and raced to his car from the gym. 'I don't think so,' he said. 'I don't think your business can wait – not where you come from, Mr McAllister.'

'Sit down, David.' Marie St Jacques Webb walked into the living room, two towels in her hands. 'You, too, Mr McAllister.' She handed Webb a towel as both men sat down facing each other in front of an unlit fireplace. Marie moved behind her husband and began blotting his neck and shoulders with the second towel, the light of a table lamp heightening the reddish tint of her auburn hair, her lovely features in shadows, her eyes on the man from the State Department. 'Please, go ahead,' she continued. 'As we've agreed, I'm cleared by the government for anything you might say.'

'Was there a *question?*' asked David, glancing up at her and then at the visitor, making no attempt to disguise his hostility.

'None whatsoever,' replied McAllister, smiling wanly yet sincerely. 'No one who's read of your wife's contributions would dare exclude her. Where others failed she succeeded.'

'That says it,' agreed Webb. 'Without saying anything, of course.'

'Hey, come on, David, loosen up.'

'Sorry. She's right.' Webb tried to smile; the attempt was not successfull. 'I'm prejudging, and I shouldn't do that, should I?'

'I'd say you have every right to,' said the undersecretary. 'I know I would, if I were you. In spite of the fact that our backgrounds are very much alike – I was posted in the Far East for a number of years – no one would have considered me for the assignment you undertook. What you went through is light years beyond me.'

'Beyond me, too. Obviously.'

'Not from where I stand. The failure wasn't yours, God knows.'

'Now you're being kind. No offence, but too much kindness – from where you stand – makes me nervous.'

'Then let's get to the business at hand, all right?'

'Please.'

'And I hope you haven't prejudged me too harshly. I'm not your enemy, Mr Webb. I want to be your friend. I can press buttons that can help you, protect you.'

'From what?'

'From something nobody ever expected.'

'Let's hear it.'

'As of thirty minutes from now your security will be doubled,' said McAllister, his eyes locked with David's. 'That's my decision, and I'll quadruple it if I think it's necessary. Every arrival on this campus will be scrutinized, the grounds checked hourly. The rotating guards will no longer be part of the scenery, keeping you merely in sight, but in effect will be very much in sight themselves. Very obvious, and, I hope, threatening.'

'Jesus!' Webb sprang forward in the chair. 'It's *Carlos!*'

'We don't think so,' said the man from State, shaking his head. 'We can't rule Carlos out, but it's too remote, too unlikely.'

'Oh?' David nodded. 'It must be. If it *was* the Jackal, your men would be all over the place and *out* of sight. You'd let him come after me and take him, and if I'm killed, the cost is acceptable.'

'Not to me. You don't have to believe that, but I mean it.'

'Thank you, but then what are we talking about?'

'Your file was broken – that is, the Treadstone file was invaded.'

'Invaded? Unauthorized disclosure?'

'Not at first. There was authorization, all right, because there was a crisis – and in a sense we had no choice. Then everything went off the wire and now we're concerned. For you.'

'Back up, please. Who got the file?'

'A man on the inside, high inside. His credentials were the best, no one could question them.'

'Who was he?'

'A British MI-Six operating out of Hong Kong, a man the CIA has relied on for years. He flew into Washington, and went directly to his primary liaison at the Agency, asking to be given everything there was on Jason Bourne. He claimed there was a crisis in the territory that was a direct result of the Treadstone project. He also made it clear that if sensitive information was to be exchanged between British and American Intelligence – *continued* to be exchanged – he thought it best that his request be granted forthwith.'

'He had to give a damn good reason.'

'He did.' McAllister paused nervously, blinking his eyes and rubbing his forehead with extended fingers.

'*Well?*'

'Jason Bourne is back,' said McAllister quietly. 'He's killed again. In Kowloon.'

Marie gasped; she clutched her husband's right shoulder, her large brown eyes angry, frightened. She stared in silence at the man from State. Webb did not move. Instead he studied McAllister, as a man might watch a cobra.

'What the *hell* are you talking about?' he whispered, then raised his voice. 'Jason Bourne – *that* Jason Bourne – doesn't exist anymore. He never *did!*'

'You know that and we know that, but in Asia his legend is very much alive. You created it, Mr Webb – brilliantly, in my judgement.'

'I'm not interested in your judgement, Mr McAllister,' said David, removing his wife's hand and getting out of the chair. 'What's this MI-Six agent working on? How old is he? What's his stability factor, his record? You must have run an up-to-date trace on him.'

'Of course we did and there was nothing irregular. London confirmed his outstanding service record, his current status, as well as the information he brought us. As chief of post for MI-Six, he was called in by the Kowloon–Hong

Kong police because of the potentially explosive nature of events. The Foreign Office itself stood behind him.'

'*Wrong!*' shouted Webb, shaking his head, then lowered his voice. 'He was turned, Mr McAllister! Someone offered him a small fortune to get that file. He used the only lie that would work and all of you swallowed it!'

'I'm afraid it's not a lie – not as he knew it. He believed the evidence, and London believes it. *A* Jason Bourne is back in Asia.'

'And what if I told you it wouldn't be the first time central control was fed a lie so an overworked, over-*risked, underpaid* man can turn! All the years, all the dangers, and nothing to show for it. He decides on one opportunity that gives him an annuity for life. In this case that *file!*'

'If that is the case, it won't do him much good. He's dead.'

'He's what . . . ?'

'He was shot to death two nights ago in Kowloon, in his office, an hour after he'd flown into Hong Kong.'

'Goddamn it, it doesn't *happen!*' cried David, bewildered. 'A man who turns backs himself up. He builds a case against his benefactor before the act, letting him know it'll get to the right people if anything ugly happens. It's his insurance, his *only* insurance.'

'He was clean,' insisted the State Department man.

'Or stupid,' rejoined Webb.

'No one thinks that.'

'What *do* they think?'

'That he was pursuing an extraordinary development, one that could erupt into widespread violence throughout the underworlds of Hong Kong and Macao. Organized crime becomes suddenly very disorganized, not unlike the tong wars of the twenties and thirties. The killings pile up. Rival gangs instigate riots; waterfronts become battlegrounds; warehouses, even cargo ships are blown up for revenge, or to wipe out competitors. Sometimes all it takes is several powerful warring factions – and a Jason Bourne in the background.'

'But since there is no Jason Bourne, it's *police* work! Not MI-Six.'

'Mr McAllister just said the man was called *in* by the Hong Kong police,' broke in Marie, looking hard at the undersecretary of State. 'MI-Six obviously agreed with the decision. Why was that?'

'It's the wrong ballpark!' David was adamant, his breath short.

'Jason Bourne wasn't the creation of the police authorities,' said Marie, going to her husband's side. 'He was created by US Intelligence by way of the State Department. But I suspect MI-Six inserted itself for a far more pressing reason than to find a killer posing as Jason Bourne. Am I right, Mr McAllister?'

'You're right, Mrs Webb. *Far* more. In our discussions these last two days, several members of our section thought you'd understand more clearly than we did. Let's call it an economic problem that could lead to serious political turmoil, not only in Hong Kong but throughout the world. You were a highly regarded economist for the Canadian government. You advised Canadian ambassadors and delegations all over the world.'

'Would you both mind explaining to the man who balances the chequebook around here?'

'These aren't the times to permit disruptions in Hong Kong's marketplace, Mr Webb, even – perhaps especially – its illegal marketplace. Disruptions accompanied by violence give the impression of government instability, if not far deeper instability. This isn't the time to give the expansionists in Red China any more ammunition than they have already.'

'Come again, please?'

'The treaty of 1997,' answered Marie quietly. 'The lease runs out in barely a decade, which is why the new Accords were negotiated with Peking. Still, everybody's nervous, everything's shaky and no one had better rock the boat. Calm stability is the name of the game.'

David looked at her, then back at McAllister. He nodded his head. 'I see. I've read the papers and the magazines . . . but it's just not a subject that I know a hell of a lot about.'

'My husband's interests lie elsewhere,' explained Marie to McAllister. 'In the study of people, their civilizations.'

'All right,' Webb agreed. '*So?*'

'Mine are with money and the constant exchange of money – the expansion of it, the markets and their fluctuations – the stability, or the lack of it. And if Hong Kong is nothing else, it's money. That's more or less its only commodity; it has little other reason for being. Its industries would die without it; without priming, the pump runs dry.'

'And if you take away the stability you have chaos,' added McAllister. 'It's the excuse for the old warlords in China. The People's Republic marches in to contain the chaos, suppress the agitators, and suddenly there's nothing left but an awkward giant fumbling with the entire colony as well as the New Territories. The cooler heads in Beijing are ignored in favour of more aggressive elements who want to save face through military control. Banks collapse, Far East trade is stymied. Chaos.'

'The PRC would *do* that?'

'Hong Kong, Kowloon, Macao and all the territories are part of their "great nation under heaven" – even the China Accords make that clear. It's one entity, and the Oriental won't tolerate a disobedient child, you know that.'

'Are you telling me that one man pretending to be Jason Bourne can do this – can bring about this kind of crisis? I don't *believe* you!'

'It's an extreme scenario, but yes, it could happen. You see, the myth rides with him, that's the hypnotic factor. Multiple killings are ascribed to him, if only to distance the real killers from the scenes – conspirators from the politically fanatic right and left using Bourne's lethal image as their own. When you think about it, it's precisely the way the myth itself was created, wasn't it? Whenever anyone of importance anywhere in the South China area was assassinated, you, as Jason Bourne, made sure the kill was credited to you. At the end of two years you were notorious, yet in fact you killed only one man, a drunken informer in Macao who tried to garrote you.'

'I don't remember that,' said David.

The man from State nodded sympathetically. 'Yes, I was told. But don't you see, if the men killed are perceived as political and powerful figures – let's say the Crown governor, or a PRC negotiator, or anyone like that is assassinated, the whole colony is in an uproar.' McAllister paused, shaking his head in weary dismissal. 'However, this is our concern, not yours, and I can tell you we have the best men in the Intelligence community working on it. Your concern is yourself, Mr Webb. And right now, as a matter of conscience, it's mine. You have to be protected.'

'That file,' said Marie coldly, 'should never have been given to *anyone*.'

'We had no choice. We work closely with the British; we had to prove that Treadstone was over, finished. That your husband was thousands of miles away from Hong Kong.'

'You told them where he *was?*' shouted Webb's wife. 'How *dare* you?'

'We had no choice,' repeated McAllister, again rubbing his forehead. 'We have to cooperate when certain crises arise. Surely you can understand that.'

'What I can't understand is why there ever *was* a file on my husband!' said Marie, furious. 'It was deep, *deep cover!*'

'Congressional funding of Intelligence operations demanded it. It's the law.'

'Get off it!' said David angrily. 'Since you're so up on me, you know where I come from. Tell me, where are all those records on Medusa?'

'I can't answer that,' replied McAllister.

'You just did,' said Webb.

'Dr Panov pleaded with you people to destroy *all* the Treadstone records,' insisted Marie. 'Or at the very least to use false names, but you wouldn't even do that. What kind of men are you?'

'*I* would have agreed to *both!*' said McAllister with sudden, surprising force. 'I'm sorry, Mrs Webb. Forgive me. It was before my time . . . Like you, I'm offended. You may be right, perhaps there never should have been a file. There are ways—'

'Bullshit,' broke in David, his voice hollow. 'It's part of another strategy, another trap. You want Carlos, and you don't care how you get him.'

'*I* care, Mr Webb, and you don't have to believe that, either. What's the Jackal to *me* – or the Far East Section? He's a *European* problem.'

'Are you telling me I spent three years of my life hunting a man who didn't *mean* a goddamned thing?'

'No, of course not. Times change, perspectives change. It's all so futile sometimes.'

'Jesus *Christ!*'

'Loosen up, David,' said Marie, her attention briefly on the man from State, who sat pale in his chair, his hands gripping the arms. 'Let's all loosen up.' Then she held her husband's eyes with her own. 'Something happened this afternoon, didn't it?'

'I'll tell you later.'

'Of course.' Marie looked at McAllister as David returned to the chair, his face lined and tired, older than it had been only minutes ago. 'Everything you've told us is leading up to something, isn't it?' she said to the man from State. 'There's something else you want us to know, isn't there?'

'Yes, and it's not easy for me. Please bear in mind that I've only recently been assigned, with full clearance, to Mr Webb's classified dossier.'

'Including his wife and children in Cambodia?'

'Yes.'

'Then say what you have to say, please.'

McAllister once again extended his thin fingers and nervously massaged his forehead. 'From what we've learned – what London confirmed five hours ago – it's possible that your husband is a target. A man wants him killed.'

'But not Carlos, *not* the Jackal,' said Webb, sitting forward.

'No. At least we can't see a connection.'

'What *do* you see?' asked Marie, sitting on the arm of David's chair. 'What have you learned?'

'The MI-Six officer in Kowloon had a great many sensitive papers in his office, any number of which would have brought high prices in Hong Kong. However, only the Treadstone file – the file on Jason Bourne – was taken. That was the confirmation London gave us. It's as though a signal was sent: He's the man we want, only Jason Bourne.'

'But *why?*' cried Marie, her hand gripping David's wrist.

'Because someone was killed,' answered Webb quietly. 'And someone else wants the account settled.'

'That's what we've been working on,' agreed McAllister, nodding. 'We've made some progress.'

'Who was killed?' asked the former Jason Bourne.

'Before I answer, you should know that all we've got is what our people in Hong Kong could dig up by themselves. By and large it's speculation; there's no proof.'

'What do you mean "by themselves"? Where the hell were the British? You *gave* them the Treadstone file!'

'Because they gave us proof that a man has killed in the name of Treadstone's creation, *our* creation – *you.* They weren't about to identify MI-Six's sources any more than we would turn over our contacts to them. Our people have worked around the clock, probing every possibility, trying to find out who the dead Sixer's main sources were on the assumption that one of them was responsible for his death. They ran down a rumour in Macao – only, it turned out to be more than a rumour.'

'I repeat,' said Webb, 'who was killed?'

'A woman,' answered the man from State. 'The wife of a Hong Kong banker named Yao Ming, a taipan whose bank is only a fraction of his wealth. His holdings are so extensive he's been re-welcomed in Beijing as an investor and consultant. He's influential, powerful, beyond reach.'

'Circumstances?'

'Ugly but not unusual. His wife was a minor actress who appeared in a number of films for the Shaw brothers, and quite a bit younger than her husband. She was also about as faithful as a mink in season, if you'll excuse—'

'Please,' said Marie, 'go on.'

'Nevertheless, he looked the other way; she was his young, beautiful trophy. She was also part of the colony's jet set, which has its share of unsavoury characters. One weekend it's gambling for extraordinary stakes in Macao, next the races in Singapore, or flying over to the Pescadores for the pistol games in backwater opium houses, betting thousands on who will be killed as men face one another across tables, spinning chambers and aiming at each other. And, of course, there's a widespread use of drugs. Her last lover was a distributor. His suppliers were in Guangzhou, his routes up to the Deep Bay waterways east of the Lok Ma Chau border.'

'According to reports, it's a wide avenue with lots of traffic,' interrupted Webb. 'Why did your people concentrate on him – on his operation?'

'Because his operation, as you so aptly term it, was rapidly becoming the only one in town, or on that avenue. He was systematically cutting out his competitors, bribing the Chinese marine patrols to sink their boats and dispose of the crews. Apparently they were effective; a great many bodies riddled with bullets ended up floating onto the mud flats and into the riverbanks. The factions were at war and the distributor – the young wife's lover – was marked for execution.'

'Under the circumstances, he had to have been aware of the possibility. He must have surrounded himself with a dozen bodyguards.'

'Right again. And that kind of security calls for the talents of a legend. His enemies hired that legend.'

'*Bourne*,' whispered David, shaking his head and closing his eyes.

'Yes,' concurred McAllister. 'Two weeks ago the drug dealer and Yao Ming's wife were shot in their bed at the Lisboa Hotel in Macao. It wasn't a pleasant kill; their bodies were barely recognizable. The weapon was an Uzi machine gun. The incident was covered up; the police and government officials were bribed with a great deal of money – a taipan's money.'

'And let me guess,' said Webb in a monotone. 'The Uzi. It was the same weapon used in a previous killing credited to this Bourne.'

'That specific weapon was left outside a conference room in a cabaret in Kowloon's Tsim Sha Tsui. There were five corpses in that room, three of the victims among the colony's wealthier businessmen. The British won't elaborate; they merely showed us several very graphic photographs.'

'This taipan, Yao Ming,' said David. 'The actress's husband. He's the connection your people found, isn't he?'

'They learned that he was one of MI-Six's sources. His connections in Beijing made him an important contributor to Intelligence. He was invaluable.'

'Then, of course, his wife was killed, his beloved young wife—'

'I'd say his beloved trophy,' interrupted McAllister. 'His *trophy* was taken.'

'All right,' said Webb. 'The trophy is far more important than the wife.'

'I've spent years in the Far East. There's a phrase for it – in Mandarin, I think, but I can't remember how it goes.'

'*Ren you jiaqian*,' said David. 'The price of a man's image, as it were.'

'Yes, I guess that's it.'

'It'll do. So the man from MI-Six is approached by his distraught contact, the taipan, and told to get the file on this Jason Bourne, the assassin who killed his wife – his trophy – or in short words, there might be no more information coming from his sources in Beijing to British Intelligence.'

'That's the way our people read it. And for his trouble the Sixer is killed because Yao Ming can't afford to have the slightest association with Bourne. The taipan has to remain unreachable, untouchable. He wants his revenge, but not with any possibility of exposure.'

'What do the British say?' asked Marie.

'In no uncertain terms to stay away from the entire situation. London was blunt. We made a mess of Treadstone, and they don't want our ineptitude in Hong Kong during these sensitive times.'

'Have they confronted Yao Ming?' Webb watched the undersecretary closely.

'When I brought up the name, they said it was out of the question. In truth, they were startled, but that didn't change their stand. If anything, they were angrier.'

'Untouchable,' said David.

'They probably want to continue using him.'

'In spite of what he *did?*' Marie broke in. 'What he *may* have done, and what he might do to my *husband!*'

'It's a different world,' said McAllister softly.

'You cooperated with them—'

'We had to,' interrupted the man from State.

'Then insist they cooperate with you. *Demand* it!'

'Then they could demand other things from us. We can't do that.'

'*Liars!*' Marie turned her head in disgust.

'I haven't lied to you, Mrs Webb.'

'Why don't I trust you, Mr McAllister?' asked David.

'Probably because you can't trust your government, Mr Webb, and you have very little reason to. I can only tell you that I'm a man of conscience. You can accept that or not – accept *me* or not – but in the meantime I'll make sure you're safe.'

'You look at me so strangely – why is that?'

'I've never been in this position, that's why.'

The chimes of the doorbell rang, and Marie, shaking her head to their sound, rose and walked rapidly across the room and into the foyer. She opened the door. For a moment she stopped breathing, and stared helplessly. Two men stood side by side, both holding up black plastic identification cases, each with a glistening silver badge attached to the top, each embossed eagle reflecting the light of the carriage lamps on the porch. Beyond, at the kerb, was a second dark sedan; inside could be seen the silhouettes of other men, and the glow of a lighted cigarette – other men, other guards. She wanted to scream, but she did not.

Edward McAllister climbed into the passenger seat of his own State Department car and looked through the closed window at the figure standing in the doorway. The former Jason Jason Bourne stood motionless, his eyes fixed rigidly on his departing visitor.

'Let's get out of here,' said McAllister to the driver, a man about his own age and balding, with tortoiseshell glasses.

The car started forward, the driver cautious on the strange, narrow, tree-lined street a block from the rocky beach in the small Maine town. For several minutes neither man spoke; finally the driver asked, 'How did everything go?'

'Go?' replied the man from State. 'As the ambassador might say, "All the pieces are in place." The foundation's there, the logic there; the missionary work is done.'

'I'm glad to hear it.'

'Are you? Then I'm glad too.' McAllister raised his trembling right hand; his thin fingers massaging his right temple. 'No, I'm *not!*' he said suddenly. 'I'm goddamned sick!'

'I'm sorry—'

'And speaking of missionary work, I *am a Christian.* I mean I *believe* – nothing so chic as being zealous, or born again, or teaching Sunday school, or prostrating myself in the aisle, but I *do* believe. My wife and I go to the Episcopal church at least twice a month, my two sons are acolytes. I'm generous because I *want* to be. Can you understand that?'

'Sure. I don't have quite those feelings, but I understand.'

'But I just walked out of that man's *house!*'

'Hey, easy. What's the matter?'

McAllister stared straight ahead, the oncoming headlights creating shadows rushing across his face. 'May God have mercy on my soul,' he whispered.

4

Screams suddenly filled the darkness, an approaching, growing cacophony of roaring voices. Then surging bodies were all around them, racing ahead, shouting, faces contorted in frenzy. Webb fell to his knees, covering his face and neck with both hands as best he could, swinging his shoulders violently back and forth, creating a shifting target within the circle of attack. His dark clothes were a plus in the shadows but would be no help if an indiscriminate burst of gunfire erupted, taking at least one of the guards with him. Yet bullets were not always a killer's choice. There were darts – lethal missiles of poison delivered by air-compressed weapons, puncturing exposed flesh, bringing death in a matter of minutes. Or seconds.

A hand gripped his shoulder! He spun around, arcing his arm up, dislodging the hand as he sidestepped to his left, crouching like an animal.

'You okay, Professor?' asked the guard on his right, grinning in the wash of his flashlight.

'What? What *happened?*'

'Isn't it great!' cried the guard on his left, approaching, as David got to his feet.

'*What?*'

'Kids with that kind of spirit. It really makes you feel good to see it!'

It was over. The campus quad was silent again, and in the distance between the stone buildings that fronted the playing fields and the college stadium, the pulsing flames of a bonfire could be seen through the empty bleachers. A football rally was reaching its climax, and his guards were laughing.

'How about you, Professor?' continued the man on his left. 'Do you feel better about things now, what with us here and all?'

It was over. The self-inflicted madness was over. Or was it? Why was his chest pounding so? Why was he so bewildered, so frightened? Something was wrong.

'Why does this whole parade bother me?' said David over morning coffee in the breakfast alcove of their old rented Victorian house.

'You miss your walks on the beach,' said Marie, ladling her husband's single poached egg over the single slice of toast. 'Eat that before you have a cigarette.'

'No, really. It bothers me. For the past week I've been a duck in a superficially protected gallery. It occurred to me yesterday afternoon.'

'What do you mean?' Marie poured out the water and placed the pan in the kitchen sink, her eyes on Webb. 'Six men are around you, four on your "flanks," as you said, and two peering into everything in front of you and behind you.'

'A parade.'

'Why do you call it that?'

'I don't know. Everyone in his place, marching to a drumbeat. I don't know.'

'But you feel something?'

'I guess so.'

'Tell me. Those feelings of yours once saved my life on the Guisan Quai in Zurich. I'd like to hear it – well, maybe I wouldn't, but I damn well better.'

Webb broke the yolk of his egg on the toast. 'Do you know how easy it would be for someone – someone who looked young enough to be a student – to walk by me on a path and shoot an air dart into me? He could cover the sound with a cough, or a laugh, and I'd have a hundred c.c.'s of strychnine in my blood.'

'You know far more about that sort of thing than I do.'

'Of course. Because that's the way I'd do it.'

'*No.* That's the way Jason Bourne might do it. Not *you.*'

'All right, I'm projecting. It doesn't invalidate the thought.'

'What happened yesterday afternoon?'

Webb toyed with the egg and toast on his plate. 'The seminar ran late as usual. It was getting dark, and my guards fell in and we walked across the quad toward the parking lot. There was a football rally – our insignificant team against another insignificant team but very large for us. The crowd passed the four of us – kids racing to a bonfire behind the bleachers, screaming and shouting and singing fight songs, working themselves up. And I thought to myself, this is *it.* This is when it's going to happen if it *is* going to happen. Believe me, for those few moments I *was* Bourne. I crouched and sidestepped and watched everyone I could see – I was close to panic.'

'*And?*' said Marie, disturbed by her husband's abrupt silence.

'My so-called guards were looking around and laughing, the two in front having a ball, enjoying the whole thing.'

'That disturbed you?'

'Instinctively. I was a vulnerable target in the centre of an excited crowd. My nerves told me that; my mind didn't have to.'

'Who's talking now?'

'I'm not sure. I just know that during those few moments nothing made sense to me. Then, only seconds later, as if to pinpoint the feelings I hadn't verbalized, the man behind me on my left came up and said something like "Isn't it great to see kids with that kind of spirit? Makes you feel good, doesn't it?" . . . I mumbled something inane, and then he said – and these are his exact words – "How about you, Professor? Do you feel better about things now, what with us here and all?"' David looked up at his wife. 'Did *I* feel better . . . *now? Me.*'

'He knew what their job was,' interrupted Marie. 'To protect you. I'm sure he meant if you felt safer.'

'Did he? Do they? That crowd of screaming kids, the dim light, the shadowy bodies, obscure faces . . . and he's joining in and laughing – they're *all* laughing. Are they really here to protect me?'

'What else?'

'I don't know. Maybe I've simply been where they haven't. Maybe I'm just thinking too much, thinking about McAllister and those eyes of his. Except for the blinking they belonged to a dead fish. You could read into them anything you wanted to – depending upon how you felt.'

'What he told you was a shock,' said Marie, leaning against the sink, her arms folded across her breasts, watching her husband closely. 'It had to have had a terrible effect on you. It certainly did on me.'

'That's probably it,' agreed Webb, nodding. 'It's ironic, but as much as there are so many things I want to remember, there's an awful lot I'd like to forget.'

'Why don't you call McAllister and tell him what you feel, what you think? You've got a direct line to him, both at his office and his home. Mo Panov would tell you to do that.'

'Yes, Mo would.' David ate his egg halfheartedly. ' "If there's a way to get rid of a specific anxiety, do it as fast as you can," that's what he'd say.'

'Then do it.'

Webb smiled, about as enthusiastically as he ate his egg. 'Maybe I will, maybe I won't. I'd rather not announce a latent, or passive, or recurrent paranoia, or whatever the hell they call it. Mo would fly up here and beat my brains out.'

'If he doesn't, I might.'

'*Ni shi nuhaizi*,' said David, using the paper napkin, as he got out of his chair and went to her.

'And what does that mean, my inscrutable husband and number eighty-seven lover?'

'Bitch goddess. It means, freely translated, that you are a little girl – and not so little – and I can still take you three out of five on the bed where there are other things to do with you instead of beating you up.'

'All that in such a short phrase?'

'We don't waste words, we paint pictures . . . I've got to leave. The class this morning deals with Siam's Rama the Second, and his claims on the Malay states in the early nineteenth century. It's a pain in the ass but important. What's worse is there's an exchange student from Moulmein, Burma, who I think knows more than I do.'

'Siam?' asked Marie, holding him. 'That's Thailand.'

'Yes. It's Thailand now.'

'Your wife, your children? Does it hurt, David?'

He looked at her, loving her so. 'I can't be that hurt where I can't see that clearly. Sometimes I hope I never do.'

'I don't think that way at all. I want you to see them and hear them and feel them. And to know that I love them too.'

'Oh, *Christ!*' He held her, their bodies together in a warmth that was theirs alone.

*

The line was busy for the second time, so Webb replaced the phone and returned to W F Vella's *Siam under Rama III* to see if the Burmese exchange student had been right about Rama II's conflict with the sultan of Kedah over the disposition of the island of Penang. It was confrontation time in the rarefied groves of academe; the Moulmein pagodas of Kipling's poetry had been replaced by a smart-ass postgraduate student who had no respect for his betters – Kipling would understand that, and torpedo it.

There was a brief knock on his office door, which opened before David could ask the caller in. It was one of his guards, the man who had spoken to him yesterday afternoon during the pre-game rally – among the crowds, amid the noise, in the middle of his fears.

'Hello there, Professor?'

'Hello. It's Jim, isn't it?'

'No, Johnny. It doesn't matter; you're not expected to get our names straight.'

'Is anything the matter?'

'Just the opposite, sir. I dropped in to say good-bye – for all of us, the whole contingent. Everything's clean and you're back to normal. We've been ordered to report to B-One-L.'

'To what?'

'Sounds kind of silly, doesn't it? Instead of saying 'Come on back to headquarters,' they call it B-One-L, as if anyone couldn't figure it out.'

'*I* can't figure it out.'

'Base-One-Langley. We're CIA, all six of us, but I guess you know that.'

'You're leaving? *All* of you?'

'That's about it.'

'But I thought . . . I thought there was a crisis *here*.'

'Everything's clean.'

'I haven't heard from anybody. I haven't heard from *McAllister*.'

'Sorry, don't know him. We just have our orders.'

'You can't simply come in here and say you're *leaving* without some explanation! I was told I was a target! That a man in Hong Kong wanted me *killed!*'

'Well, I don't know whether you were told that, or whether you told yourself that, but I do know we've got an A-one legitimate problem in Newport News. We have to get briefed and get on it.'

'A-one legitimate . . . ? What about *me?*'

'Get a lot of rest, Professor. We were told you need it.' The man from the CIA abruptly turned, went through the door, and closed it.

Well, I don't know whether you were told that, or whether you told yourself that . . . How about you, Professor? Do you feel better about things now, what with us here and all?

Parade? . . . *Charade!*

Where was McAllister's number? Where *was* it? Goddamnit, he had two copies, one at home and one in his desk drawer – no, his wallet! He found it, his whole body trembling in fear and in anger as he dialled.

'Mr McAllister's office,' said a female voice.

'I thought this was his private line. That's what I was told!'

'Mr McAllister is away from Washington, sir. In these cases we're instructed to pick up and log the calls.'

'Log the *calls?* Where *is* he?'

'I don't know, sir. I'm from the secretarial pool. He phones in every other day or so. Who shall I say called?'

'That's not good enough! My name is Webb. Jason Webb . . . *No, David* Webb! I have to talk to him right away! *Immediately!*'

'I'll connect you with the department handling his urgent calls . . .'

Webb slammed down the phone. He had the number for McAllister's home; he dialled it.

'Hello?' The voice of another woman.

'Mr McAllister, please.'

'I'm afraid he's not here. If you care to leave your name and a number, I'll give it to him.'

'When?'

'Well, he should be calling tomorrow or the next day. He always does.'

'You've got to give me the number where he is *now*, Mrs McAllister! – I assume this is Mrs McAllister.'

'I should hope so. Eighteen years' worth. Who are you?'

'Webb. *David* Webb.'

'Oh, of course! Edward rarely discusses business – and he certainly didn't in your case – but he did tell me what terribly nice people you and your lovely wife are. As a matter of fact, our older boy, who's in prep school, is, naturally, *very* interested in the university where you teach. Now, in the last year or so his marks dropped just a touch, and his SAT's weren't the highest, but he has such a wonderful, enthusiastic outlook on life, I'm sure he'd be an asset . . .'

'Mrs McAllister!' broke in Webb. 'I have to reach your husband! *Now!*'

'Oh, I'm terribly sorry, but I don't think that's possible. He's in the Far East, and, of course, I don't have a number where I can reach him there. In emergencies we always call the State Department.'

David hung up the phone. He had to alert – *phone* – Marie. The line had to be free by now; it had been busy for nearly an hour, and there was no one his wife could talk with on the telephone for an hour, not even her father, her mother, or her two brothers in Canada. There was great affection between them all, but she was the ranch-Ontario maverick. She was not the Francophile her father was, not a homebody like her mother, and although she adored her brothers, not the rustic, plain-spoken *lassos* they were. She had found another life in the stratified layers of higher economics, with a doctorate, and gainful employment with the Canadian government. And, at last, she had married an American.

Quel dommage.

The line was *still* busy! *Goddamnit*, Marie!

Then Webb froze, his whole body for an instant a block of searing hot ice. He could barely move, but he did move, and then he raced out of his small office and down the corridor with such speed that he pummelled three students and a colleague out of his path, sending two into walls, the others buckling under him; he was a man suddenly possessed.

Reaching his house, he slammed on the brakes; the car screeched to a stop as he leaped out of the seat and ran up the path to the door. He stopped, staring, his breath suddenly no longer in him. The door was open and on the angled, indented panel was a hand print stamped in red – *blood.*

Webb ran inside, throwing everything out of his way. Furniture crashed and lamps were smashed as he searched the ground floor. Then he went upstairs, his hands two thin slabs of granite, his every nerve primed for a sound, a weight, his killer instinct as clear as the red stains he had seen below on the outside door. For these moments he knew and accepted the fact that he was the assassin – the lethal animal – that Jason Bourne had been. If his wife was above, he would kill whoever tried to harm her – or who had harmed her already.

Prone on the floor, he pushed the door of their bedroom open.

The explosion blew apart the upper hallway wall. He rolled under the blast to the opposite side; he had no weapon, but he had a cigarette lighter. He reached into his trousers pockets for the scribbled notes all teachers gather, bunched them together, spun to his left and snapped the lighter; the flame was immediate. He threw the fired wad far into the bedroom as he pressed his back against the wall and rose from the floor, his head whipping toward the other two closed doors on the narrow second floor. Suddenly he lashed out with his feet, one crash after another, as he lunged back onto the floor and rolled into the shadows.

Nothing. The two rooms were empty. If there was an enemy he was in the bedroom. But by now the bedspread was on fire. The flames were gradually leaping toward the ceiling. Only seconds now.

Now!

He plunged into the room, and grabbing the flaming bedspread he swung it in a circle as he crouched and rolled on the floor until the spread was ashes, all the while expecting an ice-cold hit in his shoulder or his arm, but knowing he could overcome it and take his enemy. *Jesus!* He *was* Jason Bourne again!

There was nothing. His Marie was not there; there was nothing but a primitive string device that had triggered a shotgun, angled for a certain kill when he pushed the door open. He stamped out the flames, lurched for a table lamp and turned it on.

Marie! *Marie!*

Then he saw it. A note lying on the pillow on her side of the bed: '*A wife for a wife, Jason Bourne. She is wounded but not dead, as mine is dead. You know where to find me, and her, if you are circumspect and fortunate. Perhaps we can do business, for I have enemies, too. If not, what is the death of one more daughter?*'

Webb screamed, falling onto the pillows, trying to mute the outrage and the horror that came from his throat, pushing back the pain that swept through his temples. Then he turned over and stared at the ceiling, a terrible, brute passivity coming over him. Things unremembered suddenly came back to him – things he had never revealed even to Morris Panov. Of bodies collapsing under his knife, falling under his gun – these were not imagined killings, they were real. They had made him what he was not, but they had done the job too well. He had become the image, the man that was not supposed to be. He'd *had* to. He'd had to *survive* – without knowing who he was.

And now he knew the two men within him that made up his whole being. He would always remember the one because it was the man he wanted to be, but for the time being he had to be the other – the man he despised.

Jason Bourne rose from the bed and went to the walk-in closet where there was a locked drawer, the third in his built-in bureau. He reached up and pulled the tape from a key attached to the closeted ceiling. He inserted it in the lock and opened the drawer. Inside were two dismantled automatics, four strings of thin wire attached to spools that he could conceal in his palms, three valid passports in three different names, and six *plastique* explosive charges that could blow apart whole rooms. He would use one or all. David Webb would find his wife. Or Jason Bourne would become the terrorist no one ever dreamed of in his wildest nightmares. He did not care – too much had been taken from him. He would endure no more.

Bourne cracked the various parts in place and snapped the magazine of the second automatic. Both were ready. He was ready. He went back to the bed and lay down, staring again at the ceiling. The logistics would fall into place, he knew that. Then the hunt would begin. He would find her – dead or alive – and if she was dead, he would kill, kill and *kill again!*

Whoever it was would never get away from him. Not from Jason Bourne.

5

Barely in control of himself, he knew that calm was out of the question. His hand gripped the automatic while his mind cracked with surreal, rapid bursts of gunfire as one option after another slammed into his head. Above all, he could not stay still; he had to keep in motion. He had to get up and *move!*

The State Department. The men at State he had known during his last months in the remote, classified Virginia medical complex – those insistent, obsessed men who questioned him relentlessly, showing him photographs by the dozens until Mo Panov would order them to stop. He had learned their names and written them down, thinking that one day he might want to know who they were – no reason other than visceral distrust; such men had tried to kill him only months before. Yet he had never asked for their names, nor were they offered, except as Harry, Bill, or Sam, presumably on the theory that actual identities would simply add to his confusion. Instead, he had unobtrusively read their identification tags and, after they left, wrote the names down and placed the pieces of paper with his personal belongings in the bureau drawer. When Marie came to see him, which was every day, he gave her those names and told her to hide them in the house – hide them well.

Later, Marie admitted that although she had done as he instructed, she thought his suspicions were excessive, a case of overkill. But then one morning, only minutes after a heated session with the men from Washington, David pleaded with her to leave the medical complex immediately, run to the car, drive to the bank where they had a safety deposit box, and do the following: Insert a short strand of her hair in the bottom left border of the deposit box, lock it, get out of the bank, and return two hours later to see if it was still there.

It was not. She had securely fixed the strand of hair in place; it could not have fallen away unless the deposit box had been opened. She found it on the tiled floor of the bank vault.

'How did you *know?*' she had asked him.

'One of my friendly interrogators got hot and tried to provoke me. Mo was out of the room for a couple of minutes and he damn near accused me of faking, of hiding things. I knew you were coming, and so I played it out. I wanted to see for myself how far they would go – how far they *could* go.'

Nothing had been sacred then, and nothing was sacred now. It was all too symmetrical. The guards had been pulled, his own reactions condescendingly questioned, as if he were the one who had asked for the additional protection and not on the insistence of one Edward McAllister. Then within hours Marie was taken, according to a scenario that had been detailed far too accurately by a nervous man with dead eyes. And now this same McAllister was suddenly fifteen thousand miles away from his own, self-determined ground zero. Had the undersecretary turned? Had he been bought in Hong Kong? Had he betrayed Washington as well as the man he had sworn to protect? What was *happening?* Whatever it was, among the unholy secrets was code name Medusa. It had never been mentioned during the questioning, never referred to. Its absence was startling. It was as if the unacknowledged battalion of psychotics and killers had never existed; its history had been wiped off the books. But that history could be reinstated. This was where he would start.

Webb walked rapidly out of the bedroom and down the steps to his study, once a small library off the hallway in the old Victorian house. He sat at his desk, opened the bottom drawer, and removed several notebooks and various papers. He then inserted a brass letter opener and pried up the false bottom; lying on the second layer of wood were other papers. They were a vague, mostly bewildering assortment of fragmented recollections, images that had come to him at odd hours of the day and night. There were torn scraps and pages from small notebooks and scissored pieces of stationery on which he had jotted down the pictures and words that exploded in his head. It was a mass of painful evocations, many so tortured that he could not share them with Marie, fearing the hurt would be too great, the revelations of Jason Bourne too brutal for his wife to confront. And among these secrets were the names of the experts in clandestine operations who had come down to question him so intensely in Virginia.

David's eyes suddenly focused on the ugly heavy-calibre weapon on the edge of the desk. Without realizing it, he had gripped it in his hand and carried it down from the bedroom; he stared at it for a moment, then picked up the phone. It was the beginning of the most agonizing, infuriating hour of his life, as each moment Marie drifted farther away.

The first two calls were taken by wives or lovers; the men he was trying to reach were suddenly not there when he identified himself. He was still out of sanction! They would not touch him without authorization and that authorization was being withheld. *Christ,* he should have known!

'Hello?'

'Is this the Lanier residence?'

'Yes, it is.'

'William Lanier, please. Tell him it's urgent, a Sixteen Hundred alert. My name is Thompson, State Department.'

'Just one minute,' said the woman, concerned.

'*Who* is this?' asked a man's voice.

'It's David Webb. You remember Jason Bourne, don't you?'

'*Webb?*' A pause followed, filled with Lanier's breathing. 'Why did you say your name was Thompson? That it was a White House alert?'

'I had an idea you might not talk to me. Among the things I remember is that you don't make contact with certain people without authorization. They're out of bounds. You simply report the contact attempt.'

'Then I assume you also remember that it's highly irregular to call someone like me on a domestic phone.'

'*Domestic* phone? Does the domestic prohibitive now include where you live?'

'You know what I'm talking about.'

'I said it was an emergency.'

'It can't have anything to do with me,' protested Lanier. 'You're a dead file in my office—'

'Colour me deep-dead?' interrupted David.

'I didn't say that,' shot back the man from covert operations. 'All I meant was that you're not on my schedule and it's policy not to interfere with others.'

'What others?' asked Webb sharply.

'How the hell do I know?'

'Are you telling me that you're not interested in what I have to tell you?'

'Whether I'm interested or not hasn't anything to do with it. You're not on any list of mine, and that's all I have to know. If you have something to say, call your authorized contact.'

'I tried to. His wife said he was in the Far East.'

'Try his office. Someone there will process you.'

'I know that, and I don't care to be *processed*. I want to talk to someone I know, and I know you, Bill. Remember? It was "Bill" in Virginia, that's what you told me to call you. You were interested to hell and back in what I had to say then.'

'That was then, not now. Look, Webb, I can't help you because I can't advise you. No matter what you tell me, I can't respond. I'm not current on your status – I haven't been for almost a year. Your contact is – He can be reached. Call State back. I'm hanging up.'

'Medusa,' whispered David. 'Did you hear me, Lanier? *Medusa!*'

'Medusa what? Are you trying to tell me something?'

'I'll blow it all apart, do you read me? I'll expose the whole obscene mess unless I get some *answers!*'

'Why don't you get yourself processed instead?' said the man from covert operations coldly. 'Or check yourself into a hospital.' There was an abrupt click, and David, perspiring, hung up the phone.

Lanier did *not* know about Medusa. If he had known, he would have stayed on the phone, learning whatever he could, for Medusa crossed the lines of 'policy' and being 'current.' But Lanier was one of the younger interrogators, no more than thirty-three or thirty-four; he was very bright, but not a long-term veteran. Someone a few years older would probably have been given clearance, told about the renegade battalion that was still held in deep cover. Webb looked at the names on his list and at the corresponding telephone numbers. He picked up the phone.

'Hello?' A male voice.

'Is this Samuel Teasdale?'

'Yeah, that's right. Who are you?'

'I'm glad you answered the phone and not your wife.'

'The wife's standard where possible,' said Teasdale, suddenly cautious.

'Mine's no longer available. She's sailing somewhere in the Caribbean with someone I never knew about. Now that you know my life's story, who the hell are you?'

'Jason Bourne, remember?'

'*Webb?*'

'I vaguely remember that name,' said David.

'Why are you calling me?'

'You were friendly. Down in Virginia you told me to call you Sam.'

'Okay, okay, David, you're right. I told you to call me Sam – that's what I am to my friends, Sam . . .' Teasdale was bewildered, upset, searching for words. 'But that was almost a year ago, Davey, and you know the rules. You're given a person to talk to, either on the scene or over at State. That's the one you should reach – that's the person who's up to date on everything.'

'Aren't you up to date, Sam?'

'Not about you, no. I remember the directive; it was dropped on our desks a couple of weeks after you left Virginia. All inquiries regarding "said subject, et cetera" were to be bumped up to Section whatever-the-hell-it-was, "said subject" having full access and in direct touch with deputies on the scene and in the Department.'

'The deputies – if that's what they were – were pulled out, and my direct-access contact has disappeared.'

'Come on,' objected Teasdale quietly, suspiciously. 'That's crazy. It couldn't happen.'

'It *happened!*' yelled Webb. 'My *wife* happened!'

'What about your wife? What are you talking about?'

'She's *gone*, you bastard – all of you, *bastards!* You *let* it happen!' Webb grabbed his wrist, gripping it with all his strength to stop the trembling. 'I want answers, Sam. I want to know who cleared the way, who *turned?* I've got an idea who it is, but I need answers to nail him – nail *all* of you, if I have to.'

'Hold it right there!' broke in Teasdale angrily. 'If you're trying to compromise me, you're doing a rotten fucking job of it! This boy's not for neutering, *wacko.* Go sing to your head doctors, not to me! I don't have to talk to you, all I have to do is report the fact that you called me, which I'll do the second I cut you loose. I'll also add that I got hit with a bucket of wacko-time bullshit! Take care of that head of yours – !'

'*Medusa!*' cried Webb. 'No one wants to talk about code name Medusa, do they? Even today it's way down deep in the vaults, isn't it?'

There was no click on the line this time. Teasdale did not hang up. Instead, he spoke flatly, no comment in his voice. 'Rumours,' he said. 'Like Hoover's raw files – raw meat – good for stories over a few belts, but not worth a hell of a lot.'

'I'm not a rumour, Sam. I live, I breathe, I go to the toilet and I sweat – like I'm sweating now. That's not a rumour.'

'You've had your problems, Davey.'

'I was there! I fought with Medusa! Some people said I was the best, *or* the worst. It's why I was chosen, why I became Jason Bourne.'

'I wouldn't know about that. We never discussed it, so I wouldn't know. Did we ever discuss it, Davey?'

'Stop using that goddamned name. I'm not *Davey*.'

'We were "Sam" and "Davey" in Virginia, don't you remember?'

'That doesn't matter! We all played games. Morris Panov was our referee, until one day you decided to get rough.'

'I apologized,' said Teasdale gently. 'We all have bad days. I told you about my wife.'

'I'm not interested in *your* wife! I'm interested in *mine!* And I'll rip open Medusa unless I get some answers, some *help!*'

'I'm sure you can get whatever help you think you need if you'll just call your contact at State.'

'He's not there! He's *gone!*'

'Then ask for his backup. You'll be processed.'

'*Processed?* Jesus, what are you, a *robot?*'

'Just a man trying to do his job, Mr Webb, and I'm afraid I can't do anything more for you. Good night.' The click came and Teasdale was off the phone.

There was another man, thought David at fever pitch as he stared at the list, squinting as the sweat filled his eye sockets. An easygoing man, less abrasive than the others, a Southerner, whose slow drawl was either a cover for a quick mind or the halting resistance to a job in which he felt himself uncomfortable. There was no time for invention.

'Is this the Babcock residence?'

'Surely is,' replied a woman's voice imbued with magnolia. 'Not our home, of course, as I always point out, but we surely do reside here.'

'May I speak with Harry Babcock, please?'

'May *Ah* ask who's callin', please? He may be out in the garden with the kids, but on the other hand he may have taken them over to the park. It's so well lit these days – not like before – and you just don't fear for your life as long as you stay . . .'.

A cover for quick minds, both Mr and Mrs Harry Babcock.

'My name is Reardon, State Department. There's an urgent message for Mr Babcock. My instructions are to reach him as soon as possible. It's an emergency.'

There was the bouncing echo of a phone being covered, muffled sounds beyond. Harry Babcock got on the line, his speech slow and deliberate.

'I don't know a Mr Reardon, Mr Reardon. All *mah* relays come from a particular switchboard that identifies itself. Are you a switchboard, sir?'

'Well, *I* don't know if I've ever heard of someone coming in from a garden, or from across the street in a park so quickly, Mr Babcock.'

'Remarkable, isn't it? I should be runnin' in the Olympics, perhaps. However, I do know your voice. I just can't place the name.'

'How about Jason Bourne?'

The pause was brief – *a very quick mind.* 'Now, that name goes back quite a while, doesn't it? Just about a year, I'd say. It *is* you, isn't it, David.' There was no question implied.

'Yes, Harry. I've got to talk to you.'

'No, David, you should speak with others, not me.'

'Are you telling me I'm cut off?'

'Good heavens, that's so abrupt, so discourteous. I'd be more than *delighted* to hear how you and the lovely Mrs Webb are doing in your new life. Massachusetts, isn't it?'

'Maine.'

'Of course. Forgive me. Is everything well? As I'm sure you realize, my colleagues and I are involved with so many problems we haven't been able to stay in touch with your file.'

'Someone else said you couldn't get your hands on it.'

'*Ah* don't think anybody tried to.'

'I want to talk, Babcock,' said David harshly.

'I don't,' replied Harry Babcock flatly, his voice nearly glacial. 'I follow regulations, and to be frank, you *are* cut off from men like me. I don't question why – things change, they always change.'

'Medusa!' said David. 'We won't talk about me, let's talk about *Medusa!*'

The pause was longer than before. And when Babcock spoke, his words were frozen. 'This phone is sterile, Webb, so I'll say what I want to say. You were nearly taken out a year ago, and it would have been a mistake. We would have sincerely mourned you. But if you break the threads, there'll be no mournin' tomorrow. Except, of course, your wife.'

'You *son of a bitch!* She's *gone!* She was *taken!* You bastards let it *happen!*'

'I don't know what you're talking about.'

'My *guards!* They were pulled, every goddamned one of them, and she was *taken!* I want answers, Babcock, or I blow everything apart! Now, you do exactly as I tell you to do, or there'll be mournings you never *dreamed* of – *all* of you, *your* wives, orphaned children – try everything on for size! I'm Jason Bourne, remember!'

'You're a maniac, *that's* what I remember. With threats like those we'll send a team to find you. *Medusa* style. Try *that* on for size, boy!'

Suddenly a furious hum broke into the line; it was deafening, high-pitched, causing David to thrust the phone away from his ear. And then the calm voice of an operator was heard: 'We are breaking in for an emergency. Go ahead, Colorado.'

Webb slowly brought the phone back to his ear.

'Is this Jason Bourne?' asked a man in a mid-Atlantic accent, the voice refined, aristocratic.

'I'm David Webb.'

'Of course you are. But you are also Jason Bourne.'

'*Was*,' said David, mesmerized by something he could not define.

'The conflicting lines of identity get blurred, Mr Webb. Especially for one who has been through so much.'

'Who the hell *are* you?'

'A friend, be assured of that. And a friend cautions one he calls a friend. You've made outrageous accusations against some of our country's most dedicated servants, men who will never be permitted an unaccountable five million dollars – to this day unaccounted for.'

'Do you want to search me?'

'No more than I'd care to trace the labyrinthine ways your most accomplished wife buried the funds in a dozen European—'

'She's *gone!* Did your dedicated men tell you *that?*'

'You were described as being overwrought – "raving" was the word that was used – and making astonishing accusations relative to your wife, yes.'

'Relative to – *Goddamn* you, she was taken from our house! Someone's holding her because they want *me!*'

'Are you sure?'

'Ask that dead fish McAllister. It's his scenario, right down to the note. And suddenly he's on the other side of the world!'

'A note?' asked the cultured voice.

'Very clear. Very specific. It's McAllister's story, and he let it *happen! You* let it happen!'

'Perhaps you should examine the note further.'

'Why?'

'No matter. It may all become clearer to you with help – psychiatric help.'

'*What?*'

'We want to do all we can for you, believe that. You've given so much – more than any man should – and your extraordinary contribution cannot be disregarded even if it comes to a court of law. We placed you in the situation and we will stand by you – even if it means bending the laws, coercing the courts.'

'What are you *talking* about?' screamed David.

'A respected army doctor tragically killed his wife several years ago, it was in all the papers. The stress became too much. The stresses on you were tenfold.'

'I don't *believe* this!'

'Let's put it another way, Mr Bourne.'

'I'm not *Bourne!*'

'All right, Mr Webb, I'll be frank with you.'

'*That's* a step up!'

'You're not a well man. You've gone through eight months of psychiatric therapy – there's still a great deal of your own life you can't remember; you didn't even know your name. It's all in the medical records, meticulous records that make clear the advanced state of your mental illness, your compulsion for violence and your obsessive rejection of your own identity. In your torment you fantasize, you pretend to be people you are not; you seem to have a compulsion to be someone other than yourself.'

'That's crazy and you know it! *Lies!*'

'"Crazy" is a harsh word, Mr Webb, and the lies are not mine. However, it's my job to protect our government from vilification, unfounded accusations that could severely damage the country.'

'Such *as?*'

'Your secondary fantasy concerning an unknown organization you call Medusa. Now, I'm sure your wife will come back to you – if she can, Mr

Webb. But if you persist with this fantasy, with this figment of your tortured mind that you call Medusa, we'll label you a paranoid schizophrenic, a pathological liar prone to uncontrollable violence and self-deception. If such a man claims his wife is missing, who knows where that pathological trip could lead? Do I make myself clear?'

David closed his eyes, the sweat rolling down his face. 'Crystal clear,' he said quietly, hanging up the phone.

Paranoid . . . pathological. *Bastards!* He opened his eyes wanting to spend his rage by hurling himself against something, anything! Then he stopped and stood motionless as another thought struck him, the *obvious* thought. Morris Panov! Mo Panov would label the three monsters for what he knew they were. Incompetents and liars, manipulators and self-serving protectors of corrupt bureaucracies – and conceivably worse, *far* worse. He reached for the phone and, trembling, dialled the number that so often in the past had brought forth a calming, rational voice that provided a sense of worth when Webb felt there was very little of value left in him.

'David, how good to hear from you,' said Panov with genuine warmth.

'I'm afraid it's not, Mo. It's the worst call I've ever made to you.'

'Come on, David, that's pretty dramatic. We've been through a lot—'

'*Listen to me!*' yelled Webb. 'She's *gone!* They've *taken* her!' The words poured forth, sequences lacking order, the times confused.

'*Stop* it, David!' commanded Panov. 'Go back. I want to hear it from the beginning. When this man came to see you – after your . . . the memories of your brother.'

'*What* man?'

'From the State Department.'

'Yes! All right, yes. McAllister, that was his name.'

'Go from there. Names, titles, positions. And spell out the name of that banker in Hong Kong. And for Christ's sake, slow *down!*'

Webb again grabbed his wrist as he gripped the phone. He started again, imposing a false control on his speech; it became strident, tight, involuntarily gathering speed. Finally he managed to get everything out, everything he could recall, knowing in horror that he had not remembered everything. Unknown blank spaces filled him with pain. They were coming back, the terrible blank spaces. He had said all he could say for the moment; there was nothing left.

'David,' began Mo Panov firmly. 'I want you to do something for me. *Now.*'

'What?'

'It may sound foolish to you, even a little bit crazy, but I suggest you go down the street to the beach and take a walk along the shore. A half hour, forty-five minutes, that's all. Listen to the surf and the waves crashing against the rocks.'

'You can't be *serious!*' protested Webb.

'I'm very serious,' insisted Mo. 'Remember we agreed once that there were times when people should put their heads on hold – God knows, I do it more than a reasonably respected psychiatrist should. Things can overwhelm us, and before we can get our act together we have to get rid of part of the confusion.

Do as I ask, David. I'll get back to you as soon as I can, no more than an hour, I'd guess. And I want you calmer than you are now.'

It *was* crazy, but as with so much of what Panov quietly, often casually, suggested, there was truth in his words. Webb walked along the cold, rocky beach, never for an instant forgetting what had happened, but whether it was the change of scene, or the wind, or the incessant, repetitive sounds of the pounding ocean, he found himself breathing more steadily – every bit as deeply, as tremulously, as before, but without the higher registers of hysteria. He looked at his watch, at the luminous dial aided by the moonlight. He had walked back and forth for thirty-two minutes; it was all the indulgence he could bear. He climbed the path through the dune of wild grass to the street and headed for the house, his pace quickening with every step.

He sat in his chair at the desk, his eyes rigid on the phone. It rang; he picked it up before the bell had stopped. '*Mo?*'

'Yes.'

'It was damned cold out there. Thank you.'

'Thank *you.*'

'What have you learned?'

And then the extension of the nightmare began.

'How long has Marie been gone, David?'

'I don't know. An hour, two hours, maybe more. What's that got to do with anything?'

'Could she be shopping? Or did you two have a fight and perhaps she wanted to be by herself for a while? We agreed that things are sometimes very difficult for her – you made the point yourself.'

'What the *hell* are you talking about? There's a note spelling it out! Blood, *a hand print!*'

'Yes, you mentioned them before, but they're so incriminating. Why would anyone do that?'

'How do *I* know! It was *done* – *they* were done. It's all *here!*'

'Did you call the police?'

'Christ, *no!* It's not for the police! It's for us, for *me!* Can't you *understand* that? . . . What did you find out? Why are you *talking* like this?'

'Because I have to. In all the sessions, in all the months we talked we never said anything but the truth to each other because the truth is what you have to know.'

'*Mo!* For God's sake, it's *Marie!*'

'Please, David, let me finish. If they're lying – and they've lied before – I'll know it and I'll expose them. I couldn't do anything less. But I'm going to tell you exactly what they told me, what the number two man in the Far East Section made specifically clear, and what the chief of security for the State Department read to me, as the events were officially logged.'

'Officially logged . . . ?'

'Yes. He said *you* called security control a little over a week ago, and according to the log, you were in a highly agitated state—'

'*I* called *them?*'

'That's right, that's what he said. According to the logs, you claimed you had received threats; your speech was "incoherent" – that was the word they used – and you demanded additional security immediately. Because of the classified flag on your file, the request was bounced upstairs and the upper levels said, "Give him what he wants. Cool him." '

'I can't *believe* this!'

'It's only the middle, David. Hear me out, because I'm listening to you.'

'Okay. Go on.'

'That's it. Easy. Stay cool – no, strike that word "cool." '

'Please do.'

'Once the patrols were in place – again according to the logs – you called twice more complaining that your guards weren't doing their job. You said they were drinking in their cars in front of your house, that they laughed at you when they accompanied you on the campus, that they – and here I quote – "They're making a mockery of what they're supposed to be doing." I underlined that phrase.'

'A "*mockery*" . . .?'

'Easy, David. Here's the end of it, the end of the logs. You made a last call stating emphatically that you wanted everyone taken away – that your guards were your enemy, *they* were the men who wanted to kill you. In essence, you had transformed those who were trying to protect you into enemies who would attack you.'

'And I'm sure that fits snugly into one of those bullshit psychiatric conclusions that had me converting – or perverting – my anxieties into paranoia.'

'Very snugly,' said Panov. 'Too snugly.'

'What did the number two in Far East tell you?'

Panov was silent for a moment. 'It's not what you want to hear, David, but he was adamant. They never heard of a banker or any influential taipan named Yao Ming. He said the way things were in Hong Kong these days, if there was such a person he'd have the dossier memorized.'

'Does he think I made it all *up*? The name, the wife, the drug connection, the places, the circumstances – the British reaction! For Christ's sake, I couldn't invent those things if I *wanted* to!'

'It'd be a stretch for you,' agreed the psychiatrist softly. 'Then everything I've just told you you're hearing for the first time and none of it makes sense. It's not the way you recall things.'

'Mo, it's all a lie! I never called State. McAllister came to the house and told us both everything I've told you, including the Yao Ming story! And now she's *gone*, and I've been given a lead to follow. *Why?* For *Christ's* sake, what are they *doing* to us?'

'I asked about McAllister,' said Panov, his tone suddenly angry. 'The Far East deputy checked with State posting and called me back. They say McAllister flew into Hong Kong two weeks ago, that according to his very precise calendar he couldn't have been at your house in Maine.'

'He was *here!*'

'I think I believe you.'

'What does that mean?'

'Among other things, I can hear the truth in your voice, sometimes when you can't. Also that phrase "making a mockery" of something isn't generally in the vocabulary of a psychotic in a highly agitated state – certainly not in yours at your wildest.'

'I'm not with you.'

'Someone saw where you worked and what you did for a living and thought he'd add a little upgraded verbiage. Local colour, in your case.' Then Panov exploded. 'My God, what are they *doing*?'

'Locking me into a starting gate,' said Webb softly. 'They're forcing me to go after whatever it is they want.'

'Sons of *bitches!*'

'It's called recruitment.' David stared at the wall. 'Stay away, Mo, there's nothing you can do. They've got all their pieces in place. I'm recruited.' He hung up.

Dazed, Webb walked out of his small office and stood in the Victorian hallway surveying the upturned furniture and the broken lamps, china and glass strewn across the floor of the living room beyond. Then words spoken by Panov earlier in the terrible conversation came to him: 'They're so incriminating.'

Only vaguely realizing where his steps were taking him, he approached the front door and opened it. He forced himself to look at the hand print in the centre of the upper panel, the dried blood dull and dark in the light of the carriage lamps. Then he drew closer and examined it.

It was the imprint of a hand but not a hand print. There was the outline of a hand – the impression, the palm and the extended fingers – but no breaks in the bloody form, no creases or indentations that a bleeding hand pressed against hard wood would reveal, no identifying marks, no isolated parts of the flesh held in place so as to stamp its own particular characteristics. It was like a flat, coloured shadow from a piece of stained glass, no planes other than the single impression. A glove? A rubber glove?

David drew his eyes away, and slowly turned to the staircase in the middle of the hallway, his thoughts haltingly centring on other words spoken by another man. A strange man with a mesmerizing voice.

Perhaps you should examine the note further . . . It may all become clearer to you with help – psychiatric help.

Webb suddenly screamed, the terror within him growing, as he ran to the staircase and raced up the steps to the bedroom, where he stared at the typewritten note on the bed. He picked it up with sickening fear and carried it to his wife's dressing table. He turned on the lamp and studied the print under the light.

If the heart within him could have burst, it would have blown apart. Instead, Jason Bourne coldly examined the note before him.

The slightly bent, irregular *r's* were there, as well as the *d's*, the upper staffs incomplete, breaking off at the halfway mark.

Bastards!

The note had been written on his own typewriter.

Recruitment.

6

He sat on the rocks above the beach, knowing he had to think clearly. He had to define what was before him and what was expected of him and then how to outthink whoever was manipulating him. Above all, he knew he could not give in to panic, even the perception of panic – a panicked man was dangerous, a risk to be eliminated. If he went over the edge, he would only ensure the death of Marie and himself; it was that simple. Everything was so delicate – violently delicate.

David Webb was out of the question. Jason Bourne had to assume control. Jesus! It was *crazy!* Mo Panov had told him to walk on the beach – as Webb – and now he had to sit there as Bourne, thinking things out as Bourne would think them out – he had to deny one part of himself and accept the opposite.

Strangely, it was not impossible, nor even intolerable, for Marie was out there. His love, his only love – *Don't think that way.* Jason Bourne spoke: She is a valuable possession taken from you! Get her *back.* David Webb spoke: No, not a possession, my life!

Jason Bourne: *Then break all the rules! Find her! Bring her back to you!*

David Webb: *I don't know how. Help me!*

Use me! Use what you've learned from me. You've got the tools you've had them for years. You were the best in Medusa. Above all, there was control. You preached that, you lived that. And you stayed alive.

Control.

Such a simple word. Such an incredible demand.

Webb climbed off the rocks and once again went up the path through the wild grass to the street, and started back toward the old Victorian house, loathing its sudden, frightening, unfair emptiness. As he walked a name flashed across his thoughts; then it returned and remained fixed. Slowly the face belonging to that name came into focus – very slowly, for the man aroused hatred in David that was no less acute for the sadness he also evoked.

Alexander Conklin had tried to kill him – twice – and each time he had nearly succeeded. And Alex Conklin – according according to his deposition, as well as his own numerous psychiatric sessions with Mo Panov and what vague memories David could provide – had been a close friend of Foreign Service Officer Webb and his Thai wife and their children in Cambodia a lifetime ago. When death had struck from the skies, filling the river with circles of blood, David had fled blindly to Saigon, his rage uncontrollable, and it was his friend in the Central Intelligence Agency, Alex Conklin, who found a place for him in the illegitimate battalion they called Medusa.

If you can survive the jungle training, you'll be a man they want. But watch them – every goddamned one of them, every goddamned minute. They'll cut your arm off for a watch. Those were the words Webb recalled, and he specifically recalled that they had been spoken by the voice of Alexander Conklin.

He had survived the brutal training and become Delta. No other name, just a progression in the alphabet. Delta One. Then after the war, Delta became Cain. *Cain is for Delta and Carlos is for Cain. That was the challenge hurled at Carlos the assassin. Created by Treadstone 71, a killer named Cain would catch the Jackal.*

It was as Cain, a name the underworld of Europe knew in reality was Asia's Jason Bourne, that Webb had been betrayed by Conklin. A simple act of faith on Alex's part could have made all the difference, but Alex could not find it within himself to provide it; his own bitterness precluded that particular charity. He believed the worst of his former friend because his own sense of martyrdom made him want to believe it. It raised his own broken self-esteem, convincing him that he was better than his former friend. In his work with Medusa, Conklin's foot had been shattered by a land mine, and his brilliant career as a field strategist was cut short. A crippled man could not stay in the field where a growing reputation might take him up the ladders scaled by such men as Allen Dulles and James Angleton, and Conklin did not possess the skills for the bureaucratic infighting demanded at Langley. He withered, a once extraordinary tactician left to watch inferior talents pass him by, his expertise sought only in secrecy, the head of Medusa always in the background, dangerous, someone to be kept at arm's length.

Two years of imposed castration, until a man known as the Monk – a Rasputin of cover operations – sought him out because one David Webb had been selected for an extraordinary assignment and Conklin had known Webb for years. Treadstone 71 was created, Jason Bourne became its product and Carlos the Jackal its target. And for thirty-two months Conklin monitored this most secret of classified operations, until the scenario fell apart with Jason Bourne's disappearance and the withdrawal of over five million dollars from Treadstone's Zurich account.

With no evidence to the contrary, Conklin presumed the worst. The legendary Bourne had turned; life in the nether world had become too much for him and the temptation to come in from the cold with over five million dollars had been too alluring to resist. Especially for one known as the chameleon, a multilingual deep-cover specialist who could change appearances and life-styles with so little effort that he could literally vanish. A trap for an assassin had been baited and then the bait had vanished, revealing a scheming thief. For the crippled Alexander Conklin this was not only the act of a traitor but intolerable treachery. Considering everything that had been done to *him*, his foot now no more than a painfully awkward dead weight surgically encased in stolen flesh, a once brilliant career a shambles, his personal life filled with a loneliness that only a total commitment to the

Agency could bring about – a devotion not reciprocated – what right had anyone *else* to turn? What other man had given what he had given?

So his once close friend, David Webb, became the enemy, Jason Bourne. Not merely the enemy, but an obsession. He had helped create the myth; he would destroy it. His first attempt was with two hired killers on the outskirts of Paris.

David shuddered at the memory, still seeing a defeated Conklin limp away, his crippled figure in Webb's gunsight.

The second try was blurred for David. Perhaps he would never recall it completely. It had taken place at the Treadstone sterile house on New York's Seventy-first Street, an ingenious trap mounted by Conklin, which was aborted by Webb's hysterical efforts to survive and, oddly enough, the presence of Carlos the Jackal.

Later, when the truth was known, that the 'traitor' had no treason in him, but instead a mental aberration called amnesia, Conklin fell apart. During David's agonizing months of convalescence in Virginia, Alex tried repeatedly to see his once close friend, to explain, to tell his part of the bloody story – to apologize with every fibre of his being.

David, however, had no forgiveness in his soul.

'If he walks through that door, I'll kill him' had been his words.

That would change now, thought Webb, as he quickened his pace down the street toward the house. Whatever Conklin's faults and duplicities, few men in the Intelligence community had the insights and the sources he had developed over a lifetime of commitment. David had not thought about Alex in months; he thought about him now, suddenly remembering the last time his name came up in conversation. Mo Panov had rendered his verdict. 'I can't help him because he doesn't want to be helped. He'll carry his last bottle of sour mash up to that great big black operations room in the sky bombed out of his mercifully dead skull. If he lasts to his retirement at the end of the year, I'll be astonished. On the other hand, if he stays pickled they may put him in a strait-jacket, and that'll keep him out of traffic. I swear I don't know how he gets to work every day. That pension is one hell of a survival therapy – better than anything Freud ever left us.' Panov had spoken those words more than five months ago. Conklin was still in place.

I'm sorry, Mo. His survival one way or the other doesn't concern me. So far as I'm concerned, his status is dead.

It was not dead now, thought David, as he ran up the steps of the oversized Victorian porch. Alex Conklin was very much alive, whether drunk or not, and even if he was preserved in bourbon, he had his sources, those contacts he had cultivated during a lifetime of devotion to the shadow world that ultimately rejected him. Within that world debts were owed, and they were paid out of fear.

Alexander Conklin. Number one on Jason Bourne's hit list.

He opened the door and once again stood in the hallway, but his eyes did not see the wreckage. Instead, the logician in him ordered him to go back into his study and begin the procedures; there was nothing but confusion without imposed order, and confusion led to questions – he he could not afford them.

Everything had to be precise within the reality he was creating so as to divert the curious from the reality that was.

He sat down at the desk and tried to focus his thoughts. There was the ever-present spiral notebook from the College Shop in front of him. He opened the thick cover to the first lined page and reached for a pencil . . . He could not pick it up! His hand shook so much that his whole body trembled. He held his breath and made a fist, clenching it until his fingernails cut into flesh. He closed his eyes, then opened them, forcing his hand to return to the pencil, commanding it to do its job. Slowly, awkwardly, his fingers gripped the thin, yellow shaft and moved the pencil into position. The words were barely legible, but they were there.

The university – phone president and dean of studies. Family crisis, not Canada – can be traced. Invent – a brother in Europe, perhaps. Yes, Europe. Leave of absence – brief leave of absence. Right away. Will stay in touch.

House – call rental agent, same story. Ask Jack to check periodically. He has key. Turn thermostat to 60°.

Mail – fill out form at post office. Hold all mail.

Newspapers – cancel.

The little things, the goddamned *little* things – the unimportant daily trivia became so terribly important and had to be taken care of so that there would be no sign whatsoever of an abrupt departure without a planned return. That was vital; he had to remember it with every word he spoke. Questions had to be kept to a minimum, the inevitable speculations reduced to manageable proportions, which meant he had to confront the obvious conclusion that his recent bodyguards somehow led to his leave of absence. To defuse the connection, the most plausible way was to emphasize the short duration of that absence and to face the issue with a straightforward dismissal, such as 'Incidentally, if you're wondering whether this has anything to do with my concern for personal safety, well, don't. That's a closed book; it didn't have much merit anyway.' He would know better how to respond while talking to both the university's president and the dean; their own reactions would guide him. If anything could guide him. If he was capable of thinking! Don't slide back – keep going. Move that pencil! Fill out the page with things to do – then another page, and *another!* Passports, initials on wallets or billfolds or shirts to correspond with the names being used; airline reservations – connecting flights, no direct routes – Oh, *God!* To *where?* Marie! Where *are* you?

Stop it! Control yourself. You are capable, you *must* be capable. You have no choice, so be what you once were. Feel ice, Be ice.

Without warning, the shell he was building around himself was shattered by the earsplitting sound of the telephone inches from his hand on the desk. He looked at it, swallowing, wondering if he was capable of sounding remotely normal. It rang again, a terrible insistence in its ring. *You have no choice.*

He picked it up, gripping the receiver with such force that his knuckles turned white. He managed to get out the single word 'Yes?'

'This is the mobile-air operator, satellite transmission—'

'Who? What did you say?'

'I have a midflight radio call for a Mr Webb. Are you Mr Webb, sir?'

'Yes.'

And then the world he knew blew up in a thousand jagged mirrors, each an image of screaming torment.

'David!'

'*Marie?*'

'Don't panic, darling! Do you hear me, *don't panic!*' Her voice came through the static; she was trying not to shout but could not help herself.

'Are you all right? The note said you were hurt – wounded!'

'I'm all right. A few scratches, that's all.'

'Where *are* you?'

'Over the ocean, I'm sure they'll tell you that much. I don't know; I was sedated.'

'Oh, *Jesus!* I can't stand it! They took you away!'

'Pull yourself together, David. I know what this is doing to you, but *they don't.* Do you understand what I'm saying? They *don't!*'

She was sending him a coded message; it was not hard to decipher. *He had to be the man he hated. He had to be Jason Bourne, and the assassin was alive and well and residing in the body of David Webb.*

'All right. Yes, all right. I've been going out of my mind!'

'Your voice is being amplified—'

'Naturally.'

'They're letting me speak to you so you'll know I'm alive.'

'Have they *hurt* you?'

'Not intentionally.'

'What the hell are "scratches"?'

'I struggled. I fought. And I was brought up on a ranch.'

'Oh, my *God*—'

'David, *please!* Don't let them do this to you!'

'To me? It's *you!*'

'I *know*, darling. I think they're testing you, can you understand that?'

Again the message. Be Jason Bourne for both their sakes – for both their lives. 'All right. Yes, all right.' He lessened the intensity of his voice, trying to control himself. 'When did it happen?' he asked.

'This morning, about an hour after you left.'

'This *morning?* Christ, all *day!* How?'

'They came to the door. Two men—'

'*Who?*'

'I'm permitted to say they're from the Far East. Actually, I don't know any more than that. They asked me to accompany them and I refused. I ran into the kitchen and saw a knife. I stabbed one of them in the hand.'

'The hand print on the door . . .'

'I don't understand.'

'It doesn't matter.'

'A man wants to talk to you, David. Listen to him, but not in anger – not in a rage – can you *understand* that?'

'All right. Yes, all right. I understand.'

The man's voice came on the line. It was hesitant but precise, almost British in its delivery, someone who had been taught English by an Englishman, or by someone who had lived in the UK Nevertheless, it was identifiably Oriental; the accent was southern China, the pitch, the short vowels and sharp consonants sounding Cantonese.

'We do not care to harm your wife, Mr Webb, but if it is necessary, it will be unavoidable.'

'I wouldn't, if I were you,' said David coldly.

'Jason Bourne speaks?'

'He speaks.'

'The acknowledgment is the first step in our understanding.'

'What understanding?'

'You took something of great value from a man.'

'You've taken something of great value from me.'

'She is alive.'

'She'd better stay that way.'

'Another is dead. You killed her.'

'Are you sure about that?' *Bourne would not agree readily unless it served his purpose to do so.*

'We are very sure.'

'What's your proof?'

'You were seen. A tall man who stayed in the shadows and raced through the hotel corridors and across fire escapes with the movements of a mountain cat.'

'Then I wasn't really *seen*, was I? Nor could. I have been. I was thousands of miles away.' *Bourne would always give himself an option.*

'In these times of fast aircraft, what is distance?' The Oriental paused, then added sharply, 'You cancelled your duties for a period of five days two and a half weeks ago.'

'And if I told you I attended a symposium on the Sung and Yuan dynasties down in Boston – which was very much in line with my duties—'

'I am startled,' interrupted the man courteously, 'that Jason Bourne would employ such a lamentably feeble excuse.'

He had not wanted to go to Boston. That symposium was light years away from his lectures, but he had been officially asked to attend. The request came from Washington, from the Cultural Exchange Programme and filtered through the university's Department of Oriental Studies. Christ! Every pawn was in place!

'Excuse for what?'

'For being where he was not. Large crowds mingling among the exhibits, certain people paid to swear you were there.'

'That's ridiculous, not to say patently amateurish. I don't pay.'

'*You* were paid.'

'I was? How?'

'Through the same bank you used before. In Zurich. The Gemeinschaft in Zurich – on the Bahnhofstrasse, of course.'

'Odd I haven't received a statement,' said David, listening carefully.

'When you were Jason Bourne in Europe, you never needed one, for yours was a three-zero account – the most secret, which is very secret indeed in Switzerland. However, we found a draft transfer made out to the Gemeinschaft among the papers of a man – a dead man, of course.'

'Of course. But not the man I supposedly killed.'

'Certainly not. But one who ordered that man killed, along with a treasured prize of my employer.'

'A prize is a trophy, isn't it?'

'Both are won, Mr Bourne. Enough. You are you. Get to the Regent Hotel in Kowloon. Register under any name you wish, but ask for Suite six-nine-zero – say you believe arrangements were made to reserve it.'

'How convenient. My own rooms.'

'It will save time.'

'It'll also take me time to make arrangements here.'

'We are certain you will not raise alarms and will move as rapidly as you can. Be there by the end of the week.'

'Count on both. Put my wife back on the line.'

'I regret I cannot do that.'

'For Christ's sake, you can hear everything we say!'

'You will speak with her in Kowloon.'

There was an echoing click, and he could hear nothing on the line but static. He replaced the phone, his grip so intense a cramp had formed between his thumb and forefinger. He managed to remove his clenched hand and shook it violently. He was grateful that the pain allowed him to reenter reality more gradually. He grabbed his right hand with his left, held it steady, and pressed his left thumb into the cramp, and as he watched his fingers spread free he knew what he had to do – do without wasting an hour on the all-important unimportant trivia. He had to reach Conklin in Washington, the gutter rat who had tried to kill him in broad daylight on New York's Seventy-first Street. Alex, drunk or sober, made no distinction between the hours of day and night, nor did the operations he knew so well, for there was no night and day where his work was concerned. There was only the flat light of fluorescent tubes in offices that never closed. If he had to, he would press Alexander Conklin until the blood rolled out of the gutter rat's eyes; he would learn what he had to know, knowing that Conklin could get the information.

Webb rose unsteadily from the chair, walked out of his study and into the kitchen, where he poured himself a drink, grateful again that although his hand still trembled, it did so less than before.

He could delegate certain things. Jason Bourne never delegated anything, but he was still David Webb and there were several people on campus he could trust – certainly not with the truth but with a useful lie. By the time he returned to his study and the telephone he had chosen his conduit. *Conduit*, for God's sake! A word from the past he thought he had been free to forget. But the young man would do what he asked; the graduate student's master's thesis would ultimately be graded by his adviser, one David Webb. *Use the advantage, whether it's total darkness or blinding sunlight, but use it to frighten or use it with compassion, whatever worked.*

'Hello, James? It's David Webb.'

'Hi, Mr Webb. Where'd I screw up?'

'You haven't, Jim. Things have screwed up for me and I could use a little extracurricular help. Would you be interested? It'll take a little time.'

'This weekend? The game?'

'No, just tomorrow morning. Maybe an hour or so, if that. Then a little bonus in terms of your curriculum vitae, if that doesn't sound too horse-shit.'

'Name it.'

'Well, confidentially – and I'd appreciate the confidentiality – I have to be away for a week, perhaps two, and I'm about to call the powers that be and suggest that you sit in for me. It's no problem for you; it's the Manchu overthrow and the Sino-Russian agreements that sound very familiar today.'

'1900 to around 1912,' said the master's candidate with confidence.

'You can refine it, and don't overlook the Japanese and Port Arthur and old Teddy Roosevelt. Line it up and draw parallels; that's what I've been doing.'

'Can do. *Will* do. I'll hit the sources. What about tomorrow?'

'I have to leave tonight, Jim; my wife's already on her way. Have you got a pencil?'

'Yes, sir.'

'You know what they say about piling up newspapers and the mail, so I want you to call the newspaper delivery and go down to the post office and tell them both to hold everything – sign whatever you have to sign. Then call the Scully Agency here in town and speak to Jack or Adele and tell them to . . .'

The master's candidate was recruited. The next call was far easier than David expected, as the president of the university was at a dinner party in his honour at the president's residence and was far more interested in his upcoming speech than in an obscure – if unusual – associate-professor's leave of absence. 'Please reach the dean of studies, Mr – Wedd. I'm raising money, damn it.'

The dean of studies was not so easily handled. 'David, has this anything to do with those people who were walking around with you last week? I mean, after all, old boy, I'm one of the few people here who know that you were involved with some very hush-hush things in Washington.'

'Nothing whatsoever, Doug. That was nonsense from the beginning; this isn't. My brother was seriously injured, his car completely totalled. I've got to get over to Paris for a few days, maybe a week, that's all.'

'I was in Paris two years ago. The drivers are absolute maniacs.'

'No worse than Boston, Doug, and a hell of a lot better than Cairo.'

'Well, I suppose I can make arrangements. A week isn't that long, and Johnson was out for nearly a month with pneumonia—'

'I've already made arrangements – with your approval, of course. Jim Crowther, a master's candidate, will fill in for me. It's material he knows and he'll do a good job.'

'Oh, yes, Crowther, a bright young man, in spite of his beard. Never did trust beards, but then I was here in the sixties.'

'Try growing one. It may set you free.'

'I'll let that go by. Are you *sure* this hasn't anything to do with those people from the State Department? I really must have the facts, David. What's your brother's name? What Paris hospital is he in?'

'I don't know the hospital, but Marie probably does; she left this morning. Good-bye, Doug. I'll call you tomorrow or the next day. I have to get down to Logan Airport in Boston.'

'David?'

'Yes?'

'Why do I feel you're not being entirely truthful with me?'

Webb remembered. 'Because I've never been in this position before,' he said. 'Asking a favour from a friend because of someone I'd rather not think about.'

David hung up the phone.

The flight from Boston to Washington was maddening because of a fossilized professor of pedantry – David never did get the course – who had the seat next to his. The man's voice was as irritatingly authentic as the ponderous tones of the accomplished actor on television who assumed the role of the learned elder of a brokerage house and insisted, 'They *earn* it!' The phrase kept repeating itself over and over again in Webb's mind regardless of what the professor said, and he kept saying a great deal. It was only when they landed at National Airport that the pedant admitted the truth. 'I've been a bore, but do forgive me. I'm terrified of flying, so I just keep chattering. Silly, isn't it?'

'Not at all, but why didn't you say so? It's hardly a crime.'

'Fear of peer pressure, or scoffing condemnation, I imagine.'

'I'll remember that the next time I'm sitting next to someone like you.' Webb smiled briefly. 'Maybe I could help.'

'That's kind of you. And very honest. Thank you. Thank you so much.'

'You're welcome.'

David retrieved his suitcase from the luggage belt and went outside for a taxi, annoyed that the cabs were not taking single fares but insisting on two or more passengers going in the same direction. His backseat companion was a woman, an attractive woman who used body language in concert with imploring eyes. It made no sense to him, so he made no sense of her, but thanked her for dropping him off first.

He registered at the Jefferson Hotel on Sixteenth Street under a false name invented at the moment. The hotel, however, was carefully chosen; it was a block and a half from Conklin's apartment, the same apartment the CIA officer had lived in for nearly twenty years when he was not in the field. It was an address David made sure to get before he left Virginia – again instinct, visceral distrust. He had a telephone number as well, but knew it was useless; he could not phone Conklin. The once deep-cover strategist would mount defences, more mental than physical, and Webb wanted to confront an unprepared man. There would be no warning, only a presence demanding a debt that was owed and must now be paid.

David glanced at his watch; it was ten minutes to midnight, as good a time as any and better than most. He washed, changed his shirt, and finally dug out one of the two dismantled guns from his suitcase, removing it from the thick, foil-lined bag. He snapped the parts in place, tested the firing mechanism, and shoved the clip into the receiving chamber. He held the weapon out and studied his hand, satisfied that there was no tremor. It felt clean and unremarkable. Eight hours ago he would not have believed he could hold a gun in his hand for fear he might fire it. That was eight hours ago, not now. Now it was comfortable, a part of him, an extension of Jason Bourne.

He left the Jefferson and walked down Sixteenth Street, turning right at the corner and noting the descending numbers of the old apartments – very old apartments, reminding him of the brownstones on the Upper East Side of New York. There was a curious logic in the observation, considering Conklin's role in the Treadstone project, he thought. Treadstone 71's sterile house in Manhattan had been a brownstone, an odd, bulging structure with upper windows of tinted blue glass. He could see it so clearly, hear the voices so clearly, without really understanding – the incubating factory for Jason Bourne.

Do it again!

Who is the face?

What's his background? His method of kill?

Wrong! You're wrong! Do it again!

Who's this? What's the connection to Carlos?

Damn it, think! There can be no mistakes!

A brownstone. Where his other self was created, the man he needed so much now.

There it was, Conklin's apartment. He was on the second floor, facing front. The lights were on; Alex was home and awake. Webb crossed the street, aware that a misty drizzle had suddenly filled the air, diffusing the glare of the streetlamps, halos beneath the orbs of rippled glass. He walked up the steps and opened the door to the short foyer; he stepped inside and studied the names under the mailboxes of the six flats. Each had a webbed circle under the name into which a caller announced himself.

There was no time for complicated invention. If Panov's verdict was accurate, his voice would be sufficient. He pressed Conklin's button and waited for a response; it came after the better part of a minute.

'Yes? Who's there?'

'Harry Babcock *heah*,' said David, the accent exaggerated. 'I've got to see you, Alex.'

'*Harry?* What the hell . . . ? Sure, sure, come on up!' The buzzer droned, broke off once – a finger momentarily displaced.

David went inside and ran up the narrow staircase to the second floor, hoping to be outside Conklin's door when he opened it. He arrived less than a second before Alex, who, with his eyes only partially focused, pulled back the door and began to scream. Webb lunged, clamping his hand across Conklin's face, twisting the CIA man around in a hammerlock, and kicking the door shut.

He had not physically attacked a person for as long as he could remember with any accuracy. It should have been strange, even awkward, but it was neither. It was perfectly natural. *Oh, Christ!*

'I'm going to take my hand away, Alex, but if you raise your voice it goes back. And you won't survive if it does, is that clear?' David removed his hand, yanking Conklin's head back as he did so.

'You're one hell of a surprise,' said the CIA man, coughing, and lurching into a limp as he was released. 'You also call for a drink.'

'I gather it's a pretty steady diet.'

'We are what we are,' answered Conklin, awkwardly reaching down for an empty glass on the coffee table in front of a large, well-worn couch. He carried it over to a copper-plated dry bar against the wall where identical bottles of bourbon stood in a single row. There were no mixers, no water, just an ice bucket; it was not a bar for guests. It was for the host in residence, its gleaming metal proclaiming it to be an extravagance the resident permitted himself. The rest of the living room was not in its class. Somehow that copper bar was a statement.

'To what,' continued Conklin, pouring himself a drink, 'do I owe this dubious pleasure? You refused to see me in Virginia – said you'd kill me, and that's a fact. That's what you said. You'd kill me if I walked through the door, you said that.'

'You're drunk.'

'Probably. But then I usually am around this time. Do you want to start out with a lecture? It won't do a hell of a lot of good, but give it the old college try if you want to.'

'You're sick.'

'No, I'm drunk, that's what you said. Am I repeating myself?'

'Ad nauseam.'

'Sorry about that.' Conklin replaced the bottle, took several swallows from his glass and looked at Webb. 'I didn't walk through your door, you came through mine, but I suppose that's immaterial. Did you come here to finally carry out your threat, to fulfill the prophecy, to put past wrongs to rights or whatever you call it? That rather obvious flat bulge under your jacket I doubt is a pint of whisky.'

'I have no overriding urge to see you dead any longer, but yes, I may kill you. You could provoke that urge very easily.'

'Fascinating. How could I do that?'

'By not providing me with what I need – and you *can* provide it.'

'You must know something I don't.'

'I know you've got twenty years in grey to black operations and that you wrote the book on most of them.'

'History,' muttered the CIA man, drinking.

'It's revivable. Unlike mine, your memory's intact. Mine's limited, but not yours. I need information, I need answers.'

'To what? For what?'

'They took my wife away,' said David simply, ice in that simplicity. 'They took Marie away from me.'

Conklin's eyes blinked through his fixed stare. 'Say that again. I don't think I heard you right.'

'You heard! And you *bastards* are somewhere deep down in the rotten scenario!'

'Not *me!* I wouldn't – I *couldn't!* What the hell are you saying? Marie's *gone?*'

'She's in a plane over the Pacific. I'm to follow. I'm to fly to Kowloon.'

'You're crazy! You're out of your mind!'

'You listen to me, Alex. You listen carefully to everything I tell you . . .' Again the words poured forth, but now with a control he had not been able to summon with Morris Panov. Conklin drunk had sharper perceptions than most sober men in the Intelligence community, and he had to understand. Webb could not allow any lapses in the narrative; it had to be clear from the beginning – from that moment when he spoke to Marie over the gymnasium phone and heard her say, 'David, come home. There's someone here you must see. Quickly, darling.'

As he talked, Conklin limped unsteadily across the room to the couch and sat down, his eyes never once leaving Webb's face. When David had finished describing the hotel around the corner, Alex shook his head and reached for his drink.

'It's eerie,' he said after a period of silence, of intense concentration fighting the clouds of alcohol, and put the glass down. 'It's as though a strategy was mounted and went off the wire.'

'Off the wire?'

'Out of control.'

'*How?*'

'I don't know,' went on the former tactician, weaving slightly, trying not to slur his words. 'You're given a script that may or may not be accurate, then the targets change – your wife for you – and it's played out. You react predictably, but when you mention Medusa, you're told in no uncertain terms that you'll be burned if you persist.'

'That's predictable.'

'It's no way to prime a subject. Suddenly your wife's on a back burner, and Medusa's the overriding danger. Someone miscalculated. Something's off a wire, something happened.'

'You've got what's left of tonight and tomorrow to get me some answers. I'm on the seven p.m. flight to Hong Kong.'

Conklin sat forward, shaking his head slowly and, with his right hand trembling, again reached for his bourbon. 'You're in the wrong part of town,' he said, swallowing. 'I thought you knew; you made a tight little allusion to the sauce. I'm useless to you. I'm off limits, a basket case. No one tells me anything, and why should they? I'm a relic, Webb. Nobody wants to have a goddamned thing to do with me. I'm washed out and up and one more step I'll be beyond-salvage – which I believe is a phrase locked in that crazy head of yours.'

'Yes, it is. "Kill him. He knows too much." '

'Maybe you want to put me there, is that it? Feed him, wake up the sleeping Medusa, and make sure he gets it from his own. That would balance.'

'You put *me* there,' said David, taking the gun out of the holster under his jacket.

'Yes, I did,' agreed Conklin, nodding his head, and gazing at the weapon.

'Because I knew *Delta*, and as far as I was concerned, anything was possible – I'd seen you in the field. My God, you blew a man's head off – one of your *own* men – in Tam Quan because you believed – you didn't know, you *believed* – he was radioing a platoon on the Ho Chi Minh! No charges, no defence, just another swift execution in the jungle. It turned out you were right, but you might have been *wrong!* You could have brought him in; we might have learned things, but no, not Delta! He made up his own rules. *Sure*, you could have turned in Zurich!'

'I don't have the specifics about Tam Quan, but others did,' said David in quiet anger. 'I had to get nine men out of there – there wasn't room for a tenth who could have slowed us down or bolted, giving away our position.'

'*Good! Your* rules. You're inventive, so find a parallel here and for Christ's sake pull the trigger like you did with him – our bona fide Jason Bourne! I told you in Paris to do it!' Breathing hard, Conklin paused and levelled his bloodshot eyes at Webb; he spoke in a plaintive whisper. 'I told you then and I tell you now. Put me out of it. I don't have the guts to.'

'We were *friends*, Alex!' shouted David. 'You came to our house! You ate with us and played with the kids! You swam with them in the river . . .' *Oh my God! It was all coming back. The images, the faces . . . Oh, Christ, the faces . . . The bodies floating in circles of water and blood . . . Control yourself! Reject them! Reject! Only now. Now!*

'That was in another country, David. And besides – I don't think you want me to complete the line.'

' "Besides the wench is dead." No, I'd prefer you didn't repeat the line.'

'No matter what,' said Conklin hoarsely, swallowing most of his whisky. 'We were both erudite, weren't we? . . . I can't help you.'

'Yes, you can. You *will*.'

'Get off it, soldier. There's no way.'

'Debts are owed you. Call them in. I'm calling yours.'

'Sorry. You can pull that trigger anytime you want, but if you don't, I'm not putting myself beyond-salvage or blowing everything that's coming to me – legitimately coming to me. If I'm allowed to go to pasture, I intend to graze well. They took enough. I want some back.' The CIA officer got up from the couch and awkwardly walked across the room toward the copper bar. His limp was more pronounced than Webb remembered it, his right foot no more serviceable than an encased stump dragged at an angle across the floor, the effort painfully obvious.

'The leg's worse, isn't it?' asked David curtly.

'I'll live with it.'

'You'll die with it too,' said Webb, raising his automatic. 'Because I can't live without my wife and you don't give a goddamn. Do you know what that makes you, Alex? After everything you did to us, all the lies, the traps, the scum you used to nail us with—'

'*You!*' interrupted Conklin, filling his glass, and staring at the gun. 'Not her.'

'Kill one of us, you kill us both, but you wouldn't understand that.'

'I never had the luxury.'

'Your lousy self-pity wouldn't let you! You just want to wallow in it all by yourself and let the booze do the thinking. "There but for a fucking land mine goes the Director, or the Monk or the Gray Fox – the Angleton of the eighties." You're pathetic. You've got your life, your mind—'

'Jesus, take them away! *Shoot!* Pull the goddamn trigger but leave me *something!*' Conklin suddenly swallowed his entire drink; an extended, rolling, retching cough followed. After the spasm, he looked at David, his eyes watery, the red veins pronounced. 'You think I wouldn't try to help if I could, you son of a bitch?' he whispered huskily. 'You think I like all that "*thinking*" I indulge myself in? You're the one who's dense, the one who's stubborn, David. You don't understand, do you?' The CIA man held the glass in front of him with two fingers and let it drop to the hardwood floor; it shattered, fragments flying in all directions. Then he spoke, his voice a high-pitched singsong, as below the rheumy eyes a sad smile crept across his lips. 'I can't stand another *failure*, old friend. And I'd fail, believe me. I'd kill you both and I just don't think I could live with that.'

Webb lowered the gun. 'Not with what you've got in your head, not with what you've learned. Anyway, I'll take my chances; my options are limited, and I choose you. To be honest, I don't know anyone else. Also, I've several ideas, maybe even a plan, but it's got to be set up at high speed.'

'Oh?' Conklin held on to the bar to steady himself.

'May I make some coffee, Alex?'

7

Black coffee had a sobering effect on Conklin but nowhere near the effect of David's confidence in him. The former Jason Bourne respected the talents of his past, most deadly enemy and let him know it. They talked until four o'clock in the morning, refining the blurred outlines of a strategy, basing it on reality but carrying it much further. And as the alcohol diminished, Conklin began to function. He began to give shape to what David had formulated only vaguely. He perceived the basic soundness of Webb's approach and found the words.

'You're describing a spreading crisis-situation mounted in the fact of Marie's abduction, then sending it off the wire with lies. But as you said, it's got to be set off at high speed, hitting them hard and fast, with no letup.'

'Use the complete truth first,' interrupted Webb, speaking rapidly. 'I broke in here threatening to kill you. I made accusations based on everything that's happened – from McAllister's scenario to Babcock's statement that they'd send out an execution team to find me . . . to that Anglicized voice of dry ice who told me to cease and desist with Medusa or they'd call me insane and put me back in a mental stockade. None of it can be denied. It *did* happen and I'm threatening to expose everything, including Medusa.'

'Then we spiral off into the big lie,' said Conklin, pouring more coffee. 'A breakaway so out of sight that it throws everything and everybody into a corkscrew turn.'

'Such as?'

'I don't know yet. We'll have to think about it. It's got to be something totally unexpected, something that will unbalance the strategists, whoever they are – because every instinct tells me that somewhere they lost control. If I'm right, one of them will have to make contact.'

'Then get out your notebooks,' insisted David. 'Start going back and reach five or six people who are logical contenders.'

'That could take hours, even days,' objected the CIA officer. 'The barricades are up and I'd have to get around them. We don't have the time – *you* don't have the time.'

'There has to be time! Start *moving*.'

'There's a better way,' countered Alex. 'Panov gave it to you.'

'Mo?'

'Yes. The logs at State, the official logs.'

'The *logs* . . . ?' Webb had momentarily forgotten; Conklin had not. 'In what way?'

'It's where they started to build the new file on you. I'll reach Internal Security with another version, at least a variation that will call for answers from someone – if I'm right, if it's gone off the wire. Those logs are only an instrument, they record, they don't confirm accuracy. But the security personnel responsible for them will send up rockets if they think the system's been tampered with. They'll do our work for us . . . Still, we need the lie.'

'Alex,' said David, leaning forward in his chair opposite the long, worn couch. 'A few moments ago you used the term "breakaway"—'

'It simply means a disruption in the scenario, a break in the pattern.'

'I know what it means, but how about using it here literally. Not breakaway, but "broke *away*." They're calling me pathological, a schizophrenic – that means I fantasize, I sometimes tell the truth and sometimes not, and I'm not supposed to be able to tell the difference.'

'It's what they're saying,' agreed Conklin. 'Some of them may even believe it. So?'

'Why don't we take this way up, really out of sight? We'll say that Marie *broke away*. She reached me and I'm on my way to meet her.'

Alex frowned, then gradually widened his eyes, the creases disappearing. 'It's perfect,' he said quietly. 'My God, it's *perfect!* The confusion will spread like a brushfire. In any operation this deep only two or three men know all the details. The others are kept in the dark. *Jesus*, can you imagine? An officially sanctioned kidnapping! A few at the core might actually panic and collide with each other trying to save their asses. *Very* good, Mr Bourne.'

Oddly enough, Webb did not resent the remark, he merely accepted it without thinking. 'Listen,' he said, getting to his feet. 'We're both exhausted. We know where we're heading, so let's get a couple of hours' sleep and go over everything in the morning. You and I learned years ago the difference between a scratch of sleep and none at all.'

'Are you going back to the hotel?' asked Conklin.

'No way,' replied David, looking down at the pale, drawn face of the CIA man. 'Just get me a blanket. I'm staying right here in front of the bar.'

'You also should have learned when not to worry about some things,' said Alex, rising from the couch and limping toward a closet near the small foyer. 'If this is going to be my last hurrah – one way or another – I'll give it my best. It might even sort things out for me.' Conklin turned, having taken a blanket and a pillow from the closet shelf. 'I guess you could call it some kind of weird precognition, but do you know what I did last night after work?'

'Sure, I do. Among other clues there's a broken glass on the floor.'

'No, I mean before that.'

'What?'

'I stopped off at the supermarket and bought a ton of food. Steak, eggs, milk – even that glue they call oatmeal. I mean, I never do that.'

'You were ready for a ton of food. It happens.'

'When it does, I go to a restaurant.'

'What's your point?'

'You sleep; the couch is big enough. I'm going to eat. I want to think some more. I'm going to cook a steak, maybe some eggs, too.'

'You need sleep.'

'Two, two and a half hours'll be fine. Then I'll probably have some of that goddamned oatmeal.'

Alexander Conklin walked down the corridor of the State Department's fourth floor, his limp lessened through sheer determination, the pain greater because of it. He knew what was happening to him: there was a job facing him that he wanted very much to do well – even brilliantly, if that term had any relevance for him any longer. Alex realized that months of abusing the blood and the body could not be overcome in a matter of hours, but something within him could be summoned. It was a sense of authority, laced with righteous anger. *Jesus*, the irony! A year ago he had wanted to destroy the man they called Jason Bourne; now it was a sudden, growing obsession to help David Webb – because he had wrongfully tried to kill Jason Bourne. It could place him beyond-salvage, he understood that, but it was right that the risk was his. Perhaps conscience did not always produce cowards. Sometimes it made a man feel better about himself.

And look better, he considered. He had forced himself to walk many more blocks than he should have, letting the cold autumn wind in the streets bring a colour to his face that had not been there in years. Combined with a clean shave and a pressed pin-striped suit he had not worn in months, he bore little resemblance to the man Webb found last night. The rest was performance, he knew that, too, as he approached the sacrosanct double doors of the State Department's Chief of Internal Security.

Little time was spent on formalities, even less on informal conversation. At Conklin's request – read Agency demand – an aide left the room, and he faced the rugged former brigadier general from the Army's G-2 who now headed State's Internal Security. Alex intended to take command with his first words.

'I'm not here on an interagency diplomatic mission, General – it *is* General, isn't it?'

'I'm still called that, yes.'

'So I don't give a damn about being diplomatic, do you understand me?'

'I'm beginning not to like you, I understand that.'

'*That*,' said Conklin, 'is the least of my concerns. What does concern me, however, is a man named David Webb.'

'What about him?'

'*Him?* The fact that you recognize the name so readily isn't very reassuring. What's going *on*, *General*?'

'Do you want a megaphone, spook?' said the ex-soldier curtly.

'I want answers, *Corporal* – that's what you and this office are to us.'

'Back off, Conklin! When you called me with your so-called emergency and switchboard verification, I did a little verifying myself. That big reputation of yours is a little wobbly these days, and I use the term on good advice. You're a lush, spook, and no secret's been made about it. So you've got less than a minute to say what you want to say before I throw you out. Take your choice – the elevator or the window.'

Alex had calculated the probability that his drinking would be telegraphed. He stared at the chief of Internal Security and spoke evenly, even sympathetically. 'General, I will answer that accusation with one sentence, and if it ever reaches anyone else, I'll know where it came from and so will the Agency.' Conklin paused, his eyes clear and penetrating. 'Our profiles are often what we want them to be for reasons we can't talk about. I'm sure you understand what I mean.'

The State Department man received Alex's gaze with a reluctantly sympathetic one of his own. 'Oh, *Christ*,' he said softly. 'We used to give dishonourables to men we were sending out in Berlin.'

'Often at our suggestion,' agreed Conklin, nodding. 'And it's all we'll say on the subject.'

'Okay, okay. I was out of line, but I can tell you the profile's working. I was told by one of your deputy directors that I'd pass out at your breath with you halfway across the room.'

'I don't even want to know who he is, General, because I might laugh in his face. As it happens, I don't drink.' Alex had a childhood compulsion to cross his fingers somewhere out of sight, or his legs, or his toes, but no method came to him. 'Let's get back to David Webb,' he added sharply, no quarter in his voice.

'What's your beef?'

'My *beef*? My goddamned *life*, soldier. Something's going on and I want to know what it is! That son of a bitch broke into my apartment last night and threatened to *kill* me. He made some pretty wild accusations naming men on your payroll like Harry Babcock and Samuel Teasdale and William Lanier. We checked; they're in your covert division and still practising. What the hell did they *do?* One made it plain you'd send out an *execution* team after him! What kind of language is *that?* Another told him to go back to a hospital – he's been in *two* hospitals *and* our combined, very private clinic in Virginia – we *all* put him there – and he's got a clean bill! He's also got some secrets in his head none of us wants out. But that man is ready to explode because of something you idiots did, or let happen, or closed your fucking eyes to! He claims to have *proof* that you walked back into his life and turned it around, that you set him up and took a hell of a lot more than a pound of flesh!'

'*What* proof?' asked the stunned general.

'He spoke to his wife,' said Conklin in a sudden monotone.

'So?'

'She was taken from their home by two men who sedated her and put her on a private jet. She was flown to the West Coast.'

'You mean she was *kidnapped?*'

'You've got it. And what should make you swallow hard is that she overheard the two of them talking to the pilot, and gathered that the whole dirty business had something to do with the State Department – for reasons unknown – but the name *McAllister* was mentioned. For your enlightenment he's one of your undersecretaries from the Far East Section.'

'This is *nuts!*'

'I'll tell you what's more than nuts – mine and yours in a crushed salad. She got away during a refuelling stop in San Francisco. That's when she reached Webb back in Maine. He's on his way to meet her – God knows where – but you'd better have some solid answers, unless you can establish the fact that he's a lunatic who may have *killed* his wife – which I hope you can – and that there was no abduction – which I sincerely hope there wasn't.'

'He's *certifiable!*' cried the chief of State's Internal Security. 'I *read* those logs! I had to – someone else called about this Webb last night. Don't ask me who, I can't tell you.'

'What the *hell* is going on?' demanded Conklin, leaning across the desk, his hands on the edge, as much for support as for effect.

'He's *paranoid*, what can I say? He makes things up and believes them!'

'That's not what the government doctors determined,' said Conklin icily. 'I happen to know something about that.'

'I *don't*, damn it!'

'You probably never will,' agreed Alex. 'But as a surviving member of the Treadstone operation, you reach someone who can say the right words to me and put my mind at ease. Somebody over here has opened up a can of worms we intend to keep a tight lid on.' Conklin took out a small notebook and a ballpoint pen; he wrote down a number, tore off the page and dropped it on the desk. 'That's a sterile phone; a trace would only give you a false address,' he continued, his eyes hard, his voice firm, the slight tremble even ominous. 'It's to be used between three and four this afternoon, no other time. Have someone reach me then. I don't care who it is or how you do it. Maybe you'll have to call one of your celebrated policy conferences, but I want answers – *we* want answers!'

'You could be all wet, you know!'

'I hope I am. But if I'm not, you people over here are going to get strung up – *hard* – because you've crossed over into off-limits territory.'

David was grateful that there were so many things to do, for without them he might plummet into a mental limbo and become paralyzed by the strain of knowing both too much and too little. After Conklin left for Langley, he had returned to the hotel and started his inevitable list. Lists calmed him; they were preliminaries to necessary activity and forced him to concentrate on specific items rather than on the reasons for selecting them. Brooding over the reasons would cripple his mind as severely as a land mine had crippled Conklin's right foot. He could not think about Alex either – there were too many possibilities and impossibilities. Nor could he phone his once and former enemy. Conklin was thorough; he *was* the best. The ex-strategist projected each action and its subsequent reaction, and his first determination was that within minutes after he telephoned the State Department's chief of Internal Security, other telephones would be used, and two specific phones undoubtedly tapped. Both his. In his apartment and at Langley. Therefore, to avoid any interruptions or interceptions he did not intend to return to his office. He would meet David at the airport later, thirty minutes before Webb's flight to Hong Kong.

'You think you got here without someone following you?' he had said to Webb. 'I'm not certain of that. They're programming you, and when someone punches a keyboard he keeps his eye on the constant number.'

'Will you please speak English? Or Mandarin? I can handle those but not that horseshit.'

'They could have a microphone under your bed. I trust you're not a closet something-or-other.'

There would be no contact until they met at the lounge at Dulles Airport, which was why David now stood at a cashier's counter in a luggage store on Wyoming Avenue. He was buying an outsized flight bag to replace his suitcase; he had discarded much of his clothing. *Things* – precautions – were coming back to him, among them the unwarranted risk of waiting in an airport's luggage area, and since he wanted the greater anonymity of economy class, a carry on two-suiter might be disallowed. He would buy whatever he needed wherever he was, and that meant he had to have a great deal of money for any number of contingencies. This fact determined his next stop, a bank on Fourteenth Street.

A year ago while the government probers were examining what was left of his memory, Marie had quietly, rapidly withdrawn the funds David had left in Zurich's Gemeinschaft Bank as well as those he had transferred to Paris as Jason Bourne. She had wired the money to the Cayman Islands, where she knew a Canadian banker, and established an appropriately confidential account. Considering what Washington had done to her husband – the damage to his mind, the physical suffering and near loss of life because men refused to hear his cries for help – she was letting the government off lightly. If David had decided to sue, and in spite of everything, it was not out of the question, any astute attorney would go into court seeking damages upwards of $10 million, not roughly five-plus.

She had speculated aloud about her thoughts regarding legal redress with an extremely nervous deputy director of the Central Intelligence Agency. She did not discuss the missing funds other than to say that with her financial training she was appalled to learn that so little protection had been given the American taxpayers' hard-earned dollars. She had delivered this criticism in a shocked if gentle voice, but her eyes were saying something else. The lady was a highly intelligent, highly motivated tiger, and her message got through. So wiser and more cautious men saw the logic of her speculations and let the matter drop. The funds were buried under top-secret, eyes-only contingency appropriations.

Whenever additional money was needed – a trip, a car, the house – Marie or David would call their banker in the Caymans and he would credit the funds by wire to any of five dozen reciprocating banks in Europe, the United States, the Pacific Islands, and the Far East, exclusive of the Philippines.

From a pay phone on Wyoming Avenue, Webb placed a collect call, mildly astonishing his friendly banker by the amount of money he needed immediately, and the funds he wanted available in Hong Kong. The collect call came to less than eight dollars, the money to over half a million dollars.

'I assume that my dear friend, the wise and glorious Marie, approves, David?'

'She told me to call you. She said she can't be bothered with trifles.'

'How like her! The banks you will use are . . .'

Webb walked through the thick glass doors of the bank on Fourteenth Street, spent twenty irritating minutes with a vice president who tried too hard to be an instant chum, and walked out with $50,000, forty in $500 bills, the rest a mix.

He then hailed a cab and was driven to an apartment in DC North West, where a man he had known in his days as Jason Bourne lived, a man who had done extraordinary work for the State Department's Treadstone 71. The man was a silver-haired black who had been a taxi driver until one day a passenger left a Hasselblad camera in his car and never put in a claim. That was years ago, and for several years the cabbie had experimented, and had found his true vocation. Quite simply, he was a genius at 'alteration' – his speciality being passports and driver's licences with photographs and ID cards for those who had come in conflict with the law, in the main with felony arrests. David had not remembered the man, but under Panov's hypnosis he had said the name – improbably, the name was Cactus – and Mo had brought the photographer to Virginia to help jar a part of Webb's memory. There had been warmth and concern in the old black man's eyes on his first visit, and although it was an inconvenience, he had requested permission from Panov to visit David once a week.

'Why, Cactus?'

'He's troubled, sir. I saw that through the lens a couple of years ago. There's somethin' missin' in him, but for all that he's a good man. I can talk to him. I like him, sir.'

'Come whenever you like, Cactus, and please cancel that "sir" stuff. Reserve the privilege for me . . . sir.'

'My, how times change. I call one of my grandchildren a good nigger, he wants to stomp on my head.'

'He should . . . *sir.*'

Webb got out of the taxi, asking the driver to wait, but he refused. David left a minimum tip and walked up the overgrown flagstone path to the old house. In some ways it reminded him of the house in Maine, too large, too fragile and too much in need of repair. He and Marie had decided to buy on the beach as soon as a year was up; it was unseemly for a newly appointed associate professor to move into the high-rent district upon arrival. He rang the bell.

The door opened, and Cactus, squinting under a green eye shade, greeted him as casually as if they had seen each other several days ago.

'You got hubcaps on your car, David?'

'No car and no taxi; it wouldn't stay.'

'Must'a' heard all those unfounded rumours circulated by the fascist press. Me. I got three machine guns in the windows. Come on in, I've *missed* you. Why didn't you call this old boy?'

'Your number's not listed, Cactus.'

'Must'a' been an oversight.'

They chatted for several minutes in Cactus's kitchen, long enough for the photographer-specialist to realize Webb was in a hurry. The old man led David into his studio, placed Webb's three passports under an angled lamp for close inspection and instructed his client to sit in front of an open-lense camera.

'We'll make the hair light ash, but not as blond as you were after Paris. That ash tone varies with the lighting and we can use the same picture on each of these li'l dears with considerable differences – still retaining the face. Leave the eyebrows alone, I'll mess with them here.'

'What about the eyes?' asked David.

'No time for those fancy contacts they got you before, but we can handle it. They're regular glasses with just the right tinted prisms in the right places. You got blue eyes or brown eyes or Spanish-armada black, if you want 'em.'

'Get all three,' said Webb.

'They're expensive, David, and cash only.'

'I've got it on me.'

'Don't let it get around.'

'Now, the hair. Who?'

'Down the street. An associate of mine who had her own beauty shop until the gendarmes checked the upstairs rooms. She does fine work. Come on, I'll take you over.'

An hour later Webb ducked out from under a hair dryer in the small well-lighted cubicle and surveyed the results in the large mirror. The beautician-owner of the odd salon, a short black lady with neat grey hair and an appraiser's eye, stood alongside him.

'It's you, but it ain't you,' she said, first nodding her head, then shaking it. 'A fine job, I've got to say it.'

It was, thought David, looking at himself. His dark hair not only was far, far lighter, but matched the skin tones of his face. Too, the hair itself seemed lighter in texture, a groomed but a much more casual look – windblown, as the advertisements phrased it. The man he was staring at was both himself and someone else who bore a striking resemblance – but not him.

'I agree,' said Webb. 'It's *very* good. How much?'

'Three hundred dollars,' replied the woman simply. 'Of course, that includes five packets of custom-made rinse powder with instructions, and the tightest lips in Washington. The first will hold you for a couple of months, the second for the rest of your life.'

'You're all heart.' David reached into his pocket for his leather money clip, counted out the bills and gave them to her. 'Cactus said you'd call him when we were finished.'

'No need to; he's got his timing down. He's in the parlour.'

'The parlour?'

'Oh, I guess it's a hallway with a settee and a floor lamp, but I do so like to call it a parlour. Sounds nice, don't it?'

The photo session went swiftly, interrupted by Cactus's reshaping his eyebrows with a toothbrush and a spray for the three separate shots, and changing shirts and jackets – Cactus had a wardrobe worthy of a costume supply house – and finally wearing two pairs of glasses, tortoiseshell and steel-rimmed, which altered his hazel eyes respectively to blue and brown for two of the passports. The specialist then surgically proceeded to insert the photos in place, and under a large, powerful magnifying glass skillfully stamped out the original State Department perforations with a tool of his own design. When he finished, he handed the three passports to David for his approval.

'Ain't no customs jockey gonna' pick on them,' said Cactus confidently.

'They look more authentic than they did before.'

'I cleaned 'em up, which is to say I gave 'em a few creases and some ageing.'

'It's terrific work, old friend – older than I can remember, I know that. What do I owe you?'

'Oh, hell, I don't know. It was such a little job and it's been such a big year what with all the hasslin' goin' on—'

'How *much*, Cactus?'

'What's comfortable? I don't figure you're on Uncle's payroll.'

'I'm doing very nicely, thanks.'

'Five hundred's fine.'

'Call me a cab, will you?'

'Takes too long, and that's if you can get one out here. My grandson's waiting for you; he'll drive you wherever you want to go. He's like me, he don't ask questions. And you're in a hurry, David, I can sense that. Come on, I'll see you to the door.'

'Thanks. I'll leave the cash here on the counter.'

'Fine.'

Removing the money from his pocket, his back to Cactus, Webb counted out six $500 bills and left them in the darkest area of the studio counter. At $1,000 apiece the passports were a gift, but to leave more might offend his old friend.

He returned to the hotel, getting out of the car several blocks away in the middle of a busy intersection so that Cactus's grandson could not be compromised where an address was concerned. The young man, as it happened, was a senior at American University, and although he obviously adored his grandfather, he was just as obviously apprehensive about being any part of the old man's endeavours.

'I'll get out here,' said David in the stalled traffic.

'Thanks,' responded the young black, his voice pleasantly calm, his intelligent eyes showing relief. 'I appreciate it.'

Webb looked at him. 'Why did you do it? I mean, for someone who's going to be a lawyer, I'd think your antenna would work overtime around Cactus.'

'It does, constantly. But he's a great old guy who's done a lot for me. Also, he said something to me. He said it would be a privilege for me to meet you, that maybe years from now he'd tell me who the stranger was in my car.'

'I hope I can come back a lot sooner and tell you myself. I'm no privilege, but there's a story to tell that could end up in the law books. Good-bye.'

Back in his hotel room, David faced a final list that needed no items written out; he knew them. He had to select the few clothes he would take in the large flight bag and get rid of the rest of his possessions, including the two weapons he had brought down from Maine in his outrage. It was one thing to dismantle and wrap in foil the parts of a gun to be placed in a suitcase, and quite another to carry weapons through a security gate. They would be picked up; he would be picked up. He had to wipe them clean, destroy the firing pins and trigger housings and drop them into a sewer. He would buy a weapon in Hong Kong; it was not a difficult purchase.

There was a last thing he had to do, and it was difficult and painful. He had to force himself to sit down and rethink everything that had been said by Edward McAllister that early evening in Maine – everything they all had said, in particular Marie's words. Something was buried somewhere in that highly charged hour of revelation and confrontation, and David knew he had missed it – *was* missing it.

He looked at his watch. It was 3:37; the day was passing quickly, nervously. *He had to hold on!* Oh, God, *Marie! Where are you?*

Conklin put down his glass of flat ginger ale on the scratched, soiled bar of the seedy establishment on Ninth Street. He was a regular patron for the simple reason that no one in his professional circle – and what was left of his social one – would ever walk through the filthy glass doors. There was a certain freedom in that knowledge, and the other patrons accepted him, the 'gimp' who always took off his tie the moment he entered, limping his way to a stool by the pinball machine at the end of the bar. And whenever he did, the rocks-glass filled with bourbon was waiting for him. Also, the owner-bartender had no objections to Alex receiving calls at the still-standing antiquated booth against the wall. It was his 'sterile phone,' and it was ringing now.

Conklin trudged across the floor, entered the old booth, and closed the door. He picked up the phone. 'Yes?' he said.

'Is this Treadstone?' asked an odd-sounding male voice.

'I was there. Were you?'

'No, I wasn't, but I'm cleared for the file, for the whole mess.'

The *voice!* thought Alex. How had Webb described it? Anglicized? Mid-Atlantic, refined, certainly not ordinary. It was the same man. The gnomes had been working; they had made progress. Someone was afraid.

'Then I'm sure your memory corresponds with everything I've written down because I *was* there and I *have* written it down – written it all down. Facts, names, events, substantiations, backups . . . everything, including the story Webb told me last night.'

'Then I can assume that if anything ugly happened, your voluminous reportage will find its way to a Senate subcommittee or a pack of congressional watchdogs. Am I right?'

'I'm glad we understand each other.'

'It wouldn't do any good,' said the man condescendingly.

'If anything ugly happened, I wouldn't care, would I?'

'You're about to retire. You drink a great deal.'

'I didn't always. There's usually a reason for both of those things for a man of my age and competence. Could they be admittedly tied into a certain file?'

'Forget it. Let's talk.'

'Not before you say something a little closer. Treadstone was bandied about here and there; it's not that substantive.'

'All right. Medusa.'

'Stronger,' said Alex. 'But not strong enough.'

'Very well. The creation of Jason Bourne. The Monk.'

'Warmer.'

'Missing funds – unaccounted for and never recovered – estimated to be around five million dollars. Zurich, Paris, and points west.'

'There were rumours. I need a capstone.'

'I'll give it to you. The execution of Jason Bourne. The date was May twenty-third in Tam Quan . . . and the same day in New York years later. On Seventy-first Street. Treadstone Seventy-one.'

Conklin closed his eyes and breathed deeply, feeling the hollowness in his throat. 'All right,' he said quietly. 'You're in the circle.'

'I can't give you my name.'

'What are you going to give me?'

'Two words: Back off.'

'You think I'll accept that?'

'You have to,' said the voice, his words precise. 'Bourne is needed where he's going.'

'*Bourne?*' Alex stared at the phone.

'Yes, Jason Bourne. He can't be recruited in any normal way, we both know that.'

'So you steal his *wife* from him? Goddamned *animals!*'

'She won't be harmed.'

'You can't guarantee that! You don't have the controls. You've got to be using second and third parties right now, and if I know my business – and I *do* – they're probably paid blinds so you can't be traced; you don't even know who they are . . . My *God*, you wouldn't have called me if you *did!* If you could reach them and get the verifications you want, you wouldn't be talking to me!'

The cultured voice paused. 'Then we both lied, didn't we, Mr Conklin? There was no escape on the woman's part, no call to Webb. Nothing. You went fishing, and so did I, and we both came up with nothing.'

'You're a barracuda, Mr No-name.'

'You've been where I am, Mr Conklin. Right down to David Webb . . . Now, what can *you* tell *me?*'

Alex again felt the hollowness in his throat, now joined with a sharp pain in his chest. 'You've lost them, haven't you?' he whispered. 'You've lost *her.*'

'Forty-eight hours isn't permanent,' said the voice guardedly.

'But you've been trying like hell to make contact!' accused Conklin. 'You've called in your conduits, the people who hired the blinds, and suddenly they're not there – you can't find them. *Jesus*, you *have* lost control! It *did* go off the wire! Someone walked in on your strategy and you have no idea who it is. He played your scenario and took it away from you!'

'Our safeguards are spread out,' objected the man without the conviction he had displayed during the past moments. 'The best men in the field are working every district.'

'Including *McAllister?* In Kowloon? Hong Kong?'

'You know that?'

'I know.'

'McAllister's a damn fool, but he's good at what he does. And, yes, he's there. We're not panicked. We'll recover.'

'Recover *what?*' asked Alex, filled with anger. 'The merchandise? Your strategy's aborted! Someone else is in charge. Why would he give you back the merchandise? You've killed Webb's wife, Mr No-name! What the *hell* did you think you were *doing?*'

'We just wanted to get him over there,' replied the voice defensively. 'Explain things, show him. We *need* him.' Then the man resumed his calm delivery. 'And for all we know, everything's still *on* the wire. Communications are notoriously bad in that part of the world.'

'The *ex-culpa* for everything in this business.'

'In most businesses, Mr Conklin . . . How do you read it? Now I'm the one who's asking – very sincerely. You have a certain reputation.'

'*Had*, No-name.'

'Reputations can't be taken away or contradicted, only added to, positively or negatively, of course.'

'You're a fount of unwarranted information, you know that?'

'I'm also right. It's said you were one of the best. How *do* you read it?'

Alex shook his head in the booth; the air was close, the noise outside his 'sterile' phone growing louder in the seedy bar on Ninth Street. 'What I said before. Someone found out what you people were planning – mounting for Webb – and decided to take over.'

'For God's sake, *why?*'

'Because whoever it is wants Jason Bourne more than you do,' Alex said and hung up.

It was 6:28 when Conklin walked into the lounge at Dulles Airport. He had waited in a taxi down the street from Webb's hotel and had followed David, giving the driver precise instructions. He had been right, but there was no point in burdening Webb with the knowledge. Two grey Plymouths had picked up David's cab and alternately exchanged positions during the surveillance. So be it. One Alexander Conklin might be hanged and then again, he might not. People at State were behaving stupidly, he had thought as he wrote down the licence numbers. He spotted Webb in a darkened back booth.

'It is you, isn't it?' said Alex, dragging his dead foot into the banquette. 'Do blonds really have more fun?'

'It worked in Paris. What did you find?'

'I found slugs under rocks who can't find their way up out of the ground. But then they wouldn't know what to do with the sunlight, would they?'

'Sunlight's illuminating; you're not. Cut the crap, Alex. I have to get to the gate in a few minutes.'

'In short words, they worked out a strategy to get you over to Kowloon. It was based on a previous experience—'

'You can skip that,' said David. '*Why?*'

'The man said they needed you. Not you – Webb, they needed Bourne.'

'Because they say Bourne's already there. I told you what McAllister said. Did he go into it?'

'No, he wasn't going to give me that much, but maybe I can use it to press them. However, he told me something else, David, and you have to know it. They can't find their conduits, so they don't know who the blinds are or what's happening. They think it's temporary, but they've lost Marie. Somebody else wants you out there and he's taken over.'

Webb brought his hand to his forehead, his eyes closed, and suddenly, in silence, the tears fell down his cheeks. 'I'm *back*, Alex. Back into so much I can't remember. I love her so, I *need* her so!'

'Cut it *out!*' ordered Conklin. 'You made it clear to me last night that I still had a mind, if not much of a body. You have *both.* Make them *sweat!*'

'*How?*'

'Be what they want you to be – be the chameleon! *Be* Jason Bourne.'

'It's been so long . . .'

'You can still do it. Play the scenario they've given you.'

'I don't have any choice, do I?'

Over the loudspeakers came the last call for Flight 26 to Hong Kong.

The grey-haired Havilland replaced the phone in its cradle, leaned back in his chair and looked across the room at McAllister. The undersecretary of State was standing next to a huge revolving globe of the world that was perched on an ornamental tripod in front of a bookcase. His index finger was on the southernmost part of China, but his eyes were on the ambassador.

'It's done,' said the diplomat. 'He's on the plane to Kowloon.'

'It's God-awful,' replied McAllister.

'I'm sure it appears that way to you, but before you render judgement, weigh the advantages. We're free now. We are no longer responsible for the events that take place. They are being manipulated by an unknown party.'

'Which is *us!* I repeat, it's God-awful!'

'Has your God considered the consequences if we fail?'

'We're given free will. Only our ethics restrict us.'

'A banality, Mr Undersecretary. There's the greater good.'

'There's also a human being, a man we're manipulating, driving him back into his nightmares. Do we have that right?'

'We have no choice. He can do what no one else can do – if we give him a reason to do it.'

McAllister spun the globe; it whirled around as he walked toward the desk. 'Perhaps I shouldn't say it, but I will,' he said, standing in front of Raymond Havilland. 'I think you're the most immoral man I've ever met.'

'Appearances, Mr Undersecretary. I have one saving grace which supersedes all the sins I have committed. I will go to any lengths, indulge in all venalities, to stop this planet from blowing itself up. And that includes the life of one David Webb – known where I want him as Jason Bourne.'

8

The mists rose like layers of diaphanous scarves above Victoria Harbour as the huge jet circled for the final approach into Kai-tak Airport. The early morning haze was dense, the promise of a humid day in the colony. Below on the water the junks and the sampans bobbed beside the outlying freighters, the squat barges, the chugging multitiered ferries, and the occasional marine patrols that swept through the harbour. As the plane descended into the Kowloon airport, the serried ranks of skyscrapers on the island of Hong Kong took on the appearance of alabaster giants, reaching up through the mists and reflecting the first penetrating light of the morning sun.

Webb studied the scene below, both as a man under a horrible strain and as one consumed by an eerily detached curiosity. Down there somewhere in the seething, vastly overpopulated territory was Marie – that was uppermost in his thoughts and the most agonizing to think about. Yet another part of him was like a scientist filled with a cold anxiety as he peered into the clouded lens of a microscope trying to discern what his eye and his mind could understand. The familiar and the unfamiliar were joined, and the result was bewilderment and fear. During Panov's sessions in Virginia, David had read and reread hundreds of travel folders and illustrated brochures describing all the places the mythical Jason Bourne was known to have been; it was a continuous, often painful exercise in self-probing. Fragments would come to him in flashes of recognition; many were all too brief and confusing, others prolonged, his sudden memories astonishingly accurate, the descriptions his own, not those of travel agents' manuals. As he looked down now, he saw much that he knew he knew but could not specifically remember. So he looked away and concentrated on the day ahead.

He had wired the Regent Hotel in Kowloon from Dulles Airport requesting a room for a week in the name of one *Howard Cruett*, the identity on Cactus's refined, blue-eyed passport. He had added: 'I believe arrangements were made for our firm with respect to Suite six-nine-zero, if it is available. Arrival day is firm, flight is not.'

The suite would be available. What he had to find out was who had made it available. It was the first step toward Marie. And either before or after or during the process there were items to purchase – some would be simple to buy, others not, but even finding the more inaccessible would not be impossible. This was Hong Kong, the colony of survival and the tools of survival. It was also the one civilized place on earth where religions flourished but the only commonly acknowledged god of believers and nonbelievers alike was money. As Marie had put it: 'It has no other reason for being.'

The tepid morning reeked with the odours of a crowded, rushing humanity, the smells strangely not unpleasant. Kerbsides were being hosed ferociously, steam rising from pavements drying in the sun, and the fragrance of herbs boiling in oil wafted through the narrow streets from carts and concessions screeching for attention. The noises accumulated; they became a series of constant crescendos demanding acceptance and a sale or at least a negotiation. Hong Kong was the essence of survival; one worked furiously or one did not survive. Adam Smith was outdone and outdated; he could never have conceived of such a world. It mocked the disciplines he projected for a free economy; it was madness. It was Hong Kong.

David held up his hand for a taxi, knowing that he had done so before, knowing the exit doors he had headed for after the prolonged drudgery of customs, knowing he knew the streets through which the driver took him – not really remembering, but somehow knowing. It was both comforting and profoundly terrifying. He knew and he did not know. He was a marionette being manipulated on the stage of his own sideshow, and he did not know who was the puppet or who the puppeteer.

'It was an error,' said David to the clerk behind the oval marble counter in the centre of the Regent's lobby. 'I don't want a suite. I'd prefer something smaller; a single or a double room will do.'

'But the arrangements have been made, Mr Cruett,' replied the bewildered clerk, using the name on Webb's false passport.

'Who made them?'

The youthful Oriental peered down at a signature on the computer printout reservation. 'It was authorized by the assistant manager, Mr Liang.'

'Then in courtesy I should speak with Mr Liang, shouldn't I?'

'I'm afraid it will be necessary. I'm not sure there's anything else available.'

'I understand. I'll find another hotel.'

'You are considered a most important guest, sir. I will go back and speak with Mr Liang.'

Webb nodded, as the clerk, reservation in hand, ducked under the counter on the far left and walked rapidly across the crowded floor to a door behind the concierge's desk. David looked around at the opulent lobby, which in a sense started outside in the immense circular courtyard with its tall, gushing fountains, and extended through the bank of elegant glass doors and across the marble floor to a semicircle of enormously high tinted windows that looked out over Victoria Harbour. The ever-moving tableau beyond was a hypnotic addition to the *mise en scène* of the open curving lounge in front of the wall of soft-coloured glass. There were dozens of small tables and leather settees, mostly occupied, with uniformed waiters and waitresses scurrying about. It was an arena from which tourists and negotiators alike could view the panorama of the harbour's commerce, played out in front of the rising skyline of the island of Hong Kong in the distance. The watery view outside was familiar to Webb, but nothing else. He had never been inside the extravagant hotel before; at least nothing of what he saw aroused any flashes of recognition.

Suddenly his eyes were drawn to the sight of the clerk rushing across the lobby several steps ahead of a middle-aged Oriental, obviously the Regent's assistant manager, Mr Liang. Again the younger man ducked under the counter and quickly resumed his position in front of David, his accommodating eyes as wide as they could be in anticipation. Seconds later the hotel executive approached, bowing slightly from the waist, as befitted his professional station.

'This is Mr Liang, sir,' announced the clerk.

'May I be of service?' said the assistant manager. 'And may I say it is a pleasure to welcome you as our guest?'

Webb smiled and shook his head politely. 'It may have to be another time, I'm afraid.'

'You are displeased with the accommodations, Mr Cruett?'

'Not at all, I'd probably like them very much. But, as I told your young man, I prefer smaller quarters, a single or even a double room, but not a suite. However, I understand there may not be anything available.'

'Your wire specifically mentioned Suite six-ninety, sir.'

'I realize that and I apologize. It was the work of an overzealous sales representative.' Webb frowned in a friendly, quizzical manner and asked courteously, 'Incidentally, who did make those arrangements? I certainly didn't.'

'Your representative, perhaps,' offered Liang, his eyes noncommittal.

'In sales? He wouldn't have the authority. No, he said it was one of the companies over here. We can't accept, of course, but I'd like to know who made such a generous offer. Surely, Mr Liang, since you personally authorized the reservation, you can tell me.'

The noncommittal eyes became more distant, then blinked; it was enough for David, but the charade had to be played out. 'I believe one of our staff – our very large staff – came to me with the request, sir. There are so many reservations, we are so busy, I really can't recall.'

'Certainly there are billing instructions.'

'We have many honoured clients whose word on a telephone is sufficient.'

'Hong Kong has changed.'

'And always changing, Mr Cruett. It is possible your host wishes to tell you himself. It would not be proper to intrude on such wishes.'

'Your sense of trust is admirable.'

'Backed by a billing code in the cashier's computer, naturally.' Liang attempted a smile; it was false.

'Well, since you have nothing else, I'll strike out on my own. I have friends at the Pen across the street,' said Webb, referring to the revered Peninsula Hotel.

'That will not be necessary. Further arrangements can be made.'

'But your clerk said—'

'He is not the assistant manager of the Regent, sir.' Liang briefly glared at the young man behind the counter.

'My screen shows nothing to be available,' protested the clerk in defence.

'Be quiet!' Liang instantly smiled, as falsely as before, aware that he had undoubtedly lost the charade with his command. 'He is so young – they are all so young and inexperienced – but very intelligent, very willing . . . We keep several rooms in reserve for misunderstood occasions.' Again he looked at the clerk and spoke harshly while smiling. '*Ting, ruan-ji!*' He continued rapidly in Chinese, every word understood by an expressionless Webb. 'Listen to me, you boneless chicken! Do not offer information in my presence unless I ask you! You will be spit from the garbage shoot if you do it again. Now assign this fool Room two-zero-two. It is listed as Hold; remove the listing and proceed.' The assistant manager, his waxen smile even more pronounced turned back to David. 'It is a very pleasant room with a splendid view of the harbour, Mr Cruett.'

The charade was over, and the winner minimized his victory with persuasive appreciation. 'I'm most grateful,' said David, his eyes boring into those of the suddenly insecure Liang. 'It will save me the trouble of phoning all over the city telling people where I'm staying.' He stopped, his right hand partially raised, a man about to continue. David Webb was acting on one of several instincts, instincts developed by Jason Bourne. He knew it was the moment to instill fear. 'When you say a room with a splendid view, I assume you mean "*you hao jingse de fang jian*." Am I right? Or is my Chinese too foolish?'

The hotel man stared at the American. 'I could not have phrased it better,' he said softly. 'The clerk will see to everything. Enjoy your stay with us, Mr Cruett.'

'Enjoyment must be measured by accomplishment, Mr Liang. That's either a very old or very new Chinese proverb, I don't know which.'

'I suspect it's new, Mr Cruett. It's too active for passive reflection, which is the soul of Confucius, as I'm sure you do know.'

'Isn't that accomplishment?'

'You are too swift for me, sir.' Liang bowed. 'If there's anything you need, don't hesitate to reach me.'

'I hardly think that will be necessary, but thank you. Frankly, it was a long and dreadful flight, so I'll ask the switchboard to hold all calls until dinner-time.'

'Oh?' Liang's insecurity became something far more pronounced; he was a man afraid. 'But surely if an emergency arises—'

'There's nothing that can't wait. And since I'm not in Suite six-ninety, the hotel can simply say I'm expected later. That's plausible, isn't it? I'm terribly tired. Thank you, Mr Liang.'

'Thank *you*, Mr Cruett.' The assistant manager bowed again, searching Webb's eyes for a last sign. He found none and turned quickly, nervously, and headed back to his office.

Do the unexpected. Confuse the enemy, throw him off-balance. – Jason Bourne. Or was it Alexander Conklin?

'It is a *most* desirable room, sir!' exclaimed the relieved clerk. 'You will be *most* pleased.'

'Mr Liang is very accommodating,' said David. 'I should show my appreciation, as, indeed, I will, for your help.' Webb took out his leather money clip and unobtrusively removed an American $20 bill. He extended a handshake, the bill concealed. 'When does Mr Liang leave for the day?'

The bewildered but overjoyed young man glanced to his right and left, speaking as he did so in disjointed phrases. 'Yes! You are most kind, sir. It is not necessary, sir, but thank you, sir. Mr Liang leaves his office every afternoon at five o'clock. I, too, leave at that hour. I would stay, of course, if our management requested, for I try very hard to do the best I can for the honour of the hotel.'

'I'm sure you do,' said Webb. 'And most capably. My key, please. My luggage will arrive later due to a switch in flights.'

'Of course, sir!'

David sat in the chair by the tinted window looking across the harbour at the island of Hong Kong. Names came to him accompanied by images – Causeway Bay, Wanchai, Repulse Bay, Aberdeen, the Mandarin, and finally, so clear in the distance, Victoria Peak with its awesome view of the entire colony. Then he saw in his mind's eye the masses of humanity meshing through the jammed, colourful, frequently filthy streets, and the crowded hotel lobbies and lounges with their softly lit chandeliers of gold filigree where the well-dressed remnants of the empire reluctantly mingled with the emerging Chinese entrepreneurs – the old crown and the new money had to find accommodation . . . Alleyways . . . For some reason thronged and run-down alleyways came into focus. Figures raced through the narrow thoroughfares, crashing into cages of small screeching birds and writhing snakes of various sizes – wares of peddlers on the lowest rungs of the territory's ladder of commerce. Men and women of all ages, from children to ancients, were dressed in rags, and pungent, heavy smoke curled slowly upward, filling the space between the decaying buildings, diffusing the light, heightening the gloom of the dark stone walls blackened by use and misuse. He saw it all and it all had meaning for him, but he did not understand. Specifics eluded him; he had no points of reference and it was maddening.

Marie was out there! He had to find her! He sprang up from the chair in frustration, wanting to pound his head to clear the confusion, but he knew it would not help – nothing helped, except time, and he could not stand the strain of time. He had to find her, hold her, protect her, as she had once protected him by believing in him when he had not believed in himself. He passed the mirror above the bureau and looked at his haggard, pale face. One thing was clear. He had to plan and act quickly, but not as the man he saw in the glass. He had to bring into play everything he had learned and forgotten as Jason Bourne. From somewhere within him he had to summon the elusive past and trust unremembered instincts.

He had taken the first step; the connection was solid, he knew that. One way or another, Liang would provide him with something, probably the lowest level of information, but it would be a beginning – a name, a place, or a drop, an initial contact that would lead to another and still another. What he had to do was to move quickly with whatever he was given, not giving his enemy time to manoeuvre, backing whomever he reached into positions of deliver-and-survive or be-silent-and-die – and mean it. But to accomplish anything he had to be prepared. Items had to be purchased, and a tour of the colony arranged. He wanted an hour or so of observing from the backseat of an automobile, dredging up whatever he could from his damaged memory.

He picked up a large red-leather hotel directory, sat on the edge of the bed and opened it, thumbing through the pages rapidly. *The New World Shopping Centre, a magnificent 5 storeyed open complex bringing under one roof the finest goods from the 4 corners of the earth* . . . Hyperbole notwithstanding, the 'complex' was adjacent to the hotel; it would do for his purposes. *Limousines available. From our fleet of Daimler motor cars arrangements can be made by the hour or the day for business or sightseeing. Please contact the Concierge. Dial 62.* Limousines also meant experienced chauffeurs knowledgeable in the ways of the confusing streets, back streets, roads, and traffic patterns of Hong Kong, Kowloon, and the New Territories, and knowledgeable in other ways, too. Such men knew the ins and outs and lower depths of the cities they served. Unless he was mistaken, and instinct told him he was not, an additional need would be covered. He had to have a gun. Finally, there was a bank in Hong Kong's Central District that had certain arrangements with a sister institution thousands of miles away in the Cayman Islands. He had to walk into that bank, sign whatever was required of him, and walk out with more money than any sane man would carry on his person in Hong Kong – or anywhere else, for the matter. He would find someplace to conceal it but not in a bank where business hours restricted its availability. Jason Bourne knew: Promise a man his life and he will usually cooperate; promise him his life and a great deal of money and the cumulative effect will lead to total submission.

David reached for the message pad and pencil next to the phone on the bedside table; he started another list. The little things loomed larger with every hour that passed, and he did not have that many hours left. It was almost eleven o'clock. The harbour now glistened in the near-noon sun. He had so many things to do before 4:30, when he intended to station himself unobtrusively somewhere near the employees' exit, or down inside the hotel garage, or wherever he learned he could follow and trap the waxen-faced Liang, his first connection.

Three minutes later his list was complete. He tore off the page, got up from the bed and reached for his jacket on the desk chair. Suddenly the telephone rang, piercing the quiet of the hotel room. He had to close his eyes, clenching every muscle in his arms and stomach so as not to leap for it, hoping beyond hope for the sound of Marie's voice, even as a captive. He must not pick up the phone. *Instinct. Jason Bourne.* He has no controls. If he answered the phone, *he* would be the one controlled. He let it ring as he walked in anguish across the room and went out the door.

It was ten minutes past noon when he returned carrying a number of thin plastic bags from various stores in the Shopping Centre. He dropped them on the bed and began removing his purchases. Among the articles were a dark, lightweight raincoat and a dark canvas hat, a pair of grey tennis sneakers, black trousers and a sweater, also black; these were the clothes he would wear at night. Then there were other items: a spool of 75-pound-test fishing line with two palm-sized eyehooks through which a three-foot section of line would be looped and secured at both ends, a 20-ounce paperweight in the shape of a miniature brass barbell, one ice pick, and a sheathed, highly sharpened, double-edged hunting knife with a narrow 4-inch blade. These were the silent weapons he would carry both night and day. One more item remained to be found; he would find it.

As he examined his purchases, his concentration narrowing down to the eyehooks and the fishing line, he became aware of a tiny, subtle blinking of light. Start, stop . . . start, stop. It was annoying because he could not find the source, and, as happened so often, he had to wonder if there actually was a source or whether the intrusion was simply an aberration of his mind. Then his eyes were drawn to the bedside table; sunlight streamed in the harbour windows, washing over the telephone, but the pulsating light was there in the lower left-hand corner of the instrument – barely visible, but there. It was the message signal, a small red dot that shone for a second, went dark for a second, and then resumed its signalling at those intervals. A *message* was not a call, he reflected. He went to the table, studied the instructions on the plastic card, and picked up the phone; he pressed the appropriate button.

'Yes, Mr Cruett?' said the operator at her computerized switchboard.

'There's a message for me?' he asked.

'Yes, sir. Mr Liang has been trying to reach you—'

'I thought my instructions were clear,' interrupted Webb. 'There were to be no calls until I told the switchboard otherwise.'

'Yes, sir, but Mr Liang is the assistant manager – the senior manager when his superior is not here, which is the case this morning . . . this afternoon. He tells us it is most urgent. He has been calling you every few minutes for the past hour. I am ringing him now, sir.'

David hung up the phone. He was not ready for Liang, or more properly put, Liang was not yet ready for him – at least, not the way David wanted him. Liang was stretched, possibly on the edge of panic, for he was the first and lowliest contact and he had failed to place the subject where he was meant to be – in a wired suite where the enemy could overhear every word. But the edge of panic was not good enough. David wanted Liang over the edge. The quickest way to provoke that state was to permit no contact, no discussion, no exculpating explanations aimed at enlisting the subject to get the offender off the hook.

Webb grabbed the clothes off the bed and put them into two bureau drawers along with the things he had taken out of his flight bag; he stuffed the eyehooks and the fishing line between the layers of fabric. He then placed the paperweight on top of a room service menu on the desk and shoved the hunting knife into his jacket pocket. He looked down at the ice pick and was suddenly struck by a thought again born of a strange instinct: a man consumed with anxiety would overreact when stunned by the unexpected sight of something terrifying. The grim image would shock him, deepening his fears. David pulled out a handkerchief from his breast pocket, reached down for the ice pick and wiped the handle clean. Gripping the lethal instrument in the cloth, he walked rapidly to the small foyer, estimated the eye level, and plunged the pick into the white wall opposite the door. The telephone rang, then rang again steadily, as if in a frenzy. Webb let himself out and ran down the hallway toward the bank of elevators; he slipped into the next angled corridor and watched.

He had not miscalculated. The gleaming metal panels slid apart and Liang raced out of the middle elevator into Webb's hallway. David spun around the corner and dashed to the elevators, then rapidly, quietly, walked to the corner of his own corridor. He could see the nervous Liang ringing his bell repeatedly, finally knocking on the door with increasing persistence.

Another elevator opened and two couples emerged, laughing. One of the men looked quizzically at Webb, then shrugged as the party turned left. David returned his attention to Liang. The assistant manager was now frantic, ringing the bell and pounding the door. Then he stopped and put his ear to the wood; satisfied, he reached into his pocket and withdrew a ring of keys. Webb snapped his head back out of sight as the assistant manager turned to look up and down the corridor while inserting a key. David did not have to see; he wanted only to hear.

He had not long to wait. A suppressed, guttural shriek was followed by the loud crash of the door. The ice pick had had its effect. Webb ran back to his sanctuary beyond the last elevator, again inching his body to the edge of the wall; he watched. Liang was visibly shaken, breathing erratically, deeply, as he repeatedly pressed his finger against the elevator button. Finally a bell pinged, and the metal panels of the second elevator opened. The assistant manager rushed inside.

David had no specific plan, but he knew vaguely what he had to do, for there was no other way of doing it. He walked down the corridor rapidly past the elevators, and ran the remaining distance to his room. He let himself inside and picked up the bedside telephone, pressing the digits he had committed to memory.

'Concierge's desk,' said a pleasant voice which did not sound Oriental; it was probably Indian.

'Am I speaking to the concierge?' asked Webb.

'You are, sir.'

'Not one of his assistants?'

'I'm afraid not. Is there a specific assistant you wished to speak with? Someone resolving a problem, perhaps?'

'No, I want to talk to you,' said David quietly. 'I have a situation that must be handled in the strictest confidence. May I count on yours? I can be generous.'

'You are a guest in the hotel?'

'I am a guest.'

'And there is nothing untoward involved, of course. Nothing that would damage the establishment.'

'Only enhance its reputation for aiding cautious businessmen who wish to bring trade to the territory. A great deal of trade.'

'I am at your service, sir.'

It was arranged that a Daimler limousine with the most experienced driver available would pick him up in ten minutes at the ramped courtyard drive on Salisbury Road. The concierge would be standing by the car and for his confidence would receive $200 American, roughly $1,500 Hong Kong. There would be no individual's name assigned to the rental – which was to be paid in cash for twenty-four hours – only the name of a firm picked at random. And 'Mr Cruett,' escorted by a floor boy, could use a service elevator to the Regent's lower level, where there was an exit that led to the New World Centre with its direct access to the pickup on Salisbury Road.

The amenities and the cash disposed of, David climbed into the backseat of the Daimler, and confronted the lined, tired face of a uniformed middle-aged driver whose weary expression was only partially leavened by a strained attempt to be pleasant.

'Welcome, sir! My name is Pak-fei, and I shall endeavour to be of excellent service to you! You tell me where, and I take you. I know everything!'

'I was counting on that,' said Webb softly.

'I beg your words, sir?'

'*Wo bushi luke*,' said David, stating that he was not a tourist. 'But as I haven't been here in years,' he continued in Chinese, 'I want to reacquaint myself. How about the normal, boring tour of the island and then a quick trip through Kowloon? I have to be back in a couple of hours or so . . . And from here on, let's speak English.'

'*Ahh!* Your Chinese is very good – very high class, but I understand everything you say. Yet only two *zhongtou*—'

'Hours,' interrupted Webb. 'We're speaking English, remember, and I don't want to be misunderstood. But these two hours and your tip, and the remaining twenty-two hours and *that* tip, will depend on how well we get along, won't it?'

'Yes, *yes!*' cried Pak-fei, the driver, as he gunned the Daimler's motor and authoritatively careened out into the intolerable traffic of Salisbury Road. 'I shall endeavour to provide *very* excellent service!'

He did, and the names and images that had come to David in the hotel room were reinforced by their actual counterparts. He knew the streets of the Central District, recognized the Mandarin hotel, and the Hong Kong Club, and Chater Square with the colony's Supreme Court opposite the banking giants of Hong Kong. He had walked through the crowded pedestrian lanes to the wild confusion that was the Star Ferry, the island's continuous link to Kowloon. Queen's Road, Hillier, Possession Street . . . the garish Wanchai – it all came back to him, in the sense that he had been there, been to those places, knew them, knew the streets, even the shortcuts to take going from one place to another. He recognized the winding road to Aberdeen, anticipated the sight of the gaudy floating restaurants and, beyond, the unbelievable congestion of junks and sampans of the boat people, a massive, floating community of the perpetually dispossessed; he could even hear the clatter and slaps and shrieks of the mah-jongg players, hotly contesting their bets under the dim glow of swaying lanterns at night. He had met men and women – contacts and conduits, he reflected – on the beaches of Shek O and Big Wave, and he had swum in the crowded waters of Repulse Bay, with its huge ersatz statuary and the decaying elegance of the old Colonial Hotel. He had seen it all, he knew it all, yet he could relate it all to nothing.

He looked at his watch; they had been driving for nearly two hours. There was a last stop to make on the island, and then he would put Pak-fei to the test. 'Head back to Chater Square,' he said. 'I have business at one of the banks. You can wait for me.'

Money was not only a social and industrial lubricant; in large enough amounts it was a passport to maneuverability. Without it, men running were stymied, their options limited, and those in pursuit frequently frustrated by lacking the means to sustain the hunt. And the greater the amount, the more facile its release; witness the struggle of the man whose resources permit him to apply for no more than a $500 loan as compared with the relative ease another has with a line of credit of $500,000. So it was for David at the bank in Chater Square. Accommodation was swift and professional; an attaché case was provided without comment for the transport of the funds, and the offer of a guard to accompany him to his hotel was made should he feel more comfortable with one. He declined, signed the release papers and no further questions were asked. He returned to the car in the busy street.

He leaned forward, resting his left hand on the soft fabric of the front seat inches from the driver's head. He held an American $100 bill between his thumb and index finger. 'Pak-fei,' he said, 'I need a gun.'

Slowly the driver's head turned. He gazed at the bill, then turned further to look at Webb. Gone was the forced ebullience, the overweening desire to please. Instead, the expression on his lined face was passive, his sloped eyes distant. 'Kowloon,' he answered. 'In the Mongkok.' He took the hundred dollars.

9

The Daimler limousine crawled through the congested street in Mongkok, an urban mass that had the unenviable distinction of being the most densely populated city district in the history of mankind. Populated, it must be recorded, almost exclusively by Chinese. A Western face was so much a rarity that it drew curious glances, at once hostile and amused. No white man or woman was ever encouraged to go to Mongkok after dark; no Oriental Cotton Club existed here. It was not a matter of racism but the recognition of reality. There was too little space for their own – and they guarded their own as all Chinese had done from the earliest dynasties. The family was all, it was everything, and too many families lived not so much in squalor but within the confines of a single room with a single bed and mats on coarse, clean floors. Everywhere the multitude of small balconies attested to the demands of cleanliness, as no one ever appeared on them except to hang continuous lines of laundry. The tiers of these open balconies filled the sides of adjacent apartment houses and seemed to be in constant agitation as the breezes blew against the immense walls of fabric, causing garments of all descriptions to dance in place by the tens of thousands, further proof of the extraordinary numbers that inhabited the area.

Nor was the Mongkok poor. Lavishly manufactured colour was everywhere, with bright red the predominant magnet. Enormous and elaborate signs could be seen wherever the eye roamed above the crowds; advertisements that successively rose three stories high lined the streets and the alleyways, the Chinese characters emphatic in their attempts to seduce consumers. There was money in Mongkok, quiet money, as well as hysterical money, but not always legitimate money. What there was not was excess space, and what there was of it belonged to their own, not outsiders, unless an outsider – brought in by one of their own – also brought in money to feed the insatiable machine that produced a vast array of worldly goods, and some not so much worldly as other-worldly. It was a question of knowing where to look and having the price. Pak-fei, the driver, knew where to look, and Jason Bourne had the price.

'I will stop and make a phone call,' said Pak-fei, pulling behind a double-parked truck. 'I will lock you in and be quick.'

'Is that necessary?' asked Webb.

'It is your briefcase, sir, not mine.'

Good Lord, thought David, he was a *fool!* He had not considered the attaché case. He was carrying over $300,000 into the heart of Mongkok as if it were his lunch. He gripped the handle, pulling the case to his lap, and checked the hasps; they were secure, but if both buttons were jolted even slightly, the lid would snap up. He yelled at the driver, who had climbed out of the car. 'Get me some *tape!* Adhesive tape!'

It was too late. The sounds of the street were deafening, the crowds nothing less than a weaving human blanket, and they were everywhere. And suddenly a hundred pairs of eyes peered in from all sides as contorted faces pressed against the glass – on all sides – and Webb was the core of a newly erupted street volcano. He could hear the questioning shrieks of *Bin go ah?* and *Chong man tui*, roughly the English equivalent of 'Who is it?' and 'A mouth that's full,' or as combined, 'Who's the big shot?' He felt like a caged animal being studied by a horde of beasts of another species, perhaps vicious. He held on to the case, staring straight ahead, and as two hands started clawing at the slight space in the upper window on his right, he reached slowly down into his pocket for the hunting knife. The fingers broke through.

'*Jau!*' screamed Pak-fei, thrashing his way through the crowd. 'This is a most important taipan and the police up the street will pour boiling oil on your genitals if you disturb him! Get away, *away!*' He unlocked the door, jumped in behind the wheel, and yanked the door shut amid furious curses. He started the engine, gunned it, then pressed his hand on the powerful horn and held it there, raising the cacophony to unbearable proportions, as the sea of bodies, slowly, reluctantly parted. The Daimler lurched in fits and starts down the narrow street.

'Where are we going?' shouted Webb. 'I thought we were there!'

'The merchant you will deal with has moved his place of business, sir, which is good, for this is not a savoury district of the Mongkok.'

'You should have called first. That wasn't very pleasant back there.'

'If I may correct the impression of imperfect service, sir,' said Pak-fei, glancing at David in the rearview mirror. 'We now know that you are not being followed. As a consequence *I* am not being followed to where I drive you.'

'What are you talking about?'

'You go with your hands free into a large bank on Chater Square and you come out with your hands not free. You carry a briefcase.'

'So?' Webb watched the driver's eyes as they kept darting up at him.

'No guard accompanied you, and there are bad people who watch for such men as yourself – often signals are sent from other bad people inside. These are uncertain times, so it was better to be certain in this instance.'

'And you're certain . . . now.'

'Oh, yes, sir!' Pak-fei smiled. 'An automobile following us on a back street in the Mongkok is easily seen.'

'So there was no phone call.'

'Oh, indeed there *was*, sir. One must always call first. But it was *very* quick, and I then walked back on the pavement, without my cap, of course, for many metres. There were no angry men in automobiles, and none climbed out to run in the street. I will now take you to the merchant much relieved.'

'I'm relieved, too,' said David, wondering why Jason Bourne had temporarily deserted him. 'And I didn't even know I should have been worried. Not about being followed.'

The dense crowds of the Mongkok thinned out as the buildings became lower and Webb could see the waters of Victoria Harbour behind high, chain link fences. Beyond the forbidding barricades were clusters of warehouses fronting piers where merchant ships were docked and heavy machinery crawled and groaned, lifting huge boxcars into holds. Pak-fei turned into the entrance of an isolated one-storey warehouse; it appeared deserted, asphalt everywhere and only two cars in sight. The gate was closed; a guard walked out of a small, glass-enclosed office toward the Daimler, a clipboard in his hand.

'You won't find my name on a list,' said Pak-fei in Chinese and with singular authority as the guard approached. 'Inform Mr Wu Song that Regent Number Five is here and brings him a taipan as worthy as himself. He expects us.' The guard nodded, squinting in the afternoon sunlight to catch a glimpse of the important passenger. '*Aiya!*' screamed Pak-fei at the man's impertinence. Then he turned and looked at Webb. 'You must not misunderstand, sir,' he said as the guard ran back to his telephone. 'My use of the name of my fine hotel has nothing to do with my fine hotel. In truth, if Mr Liang, or anyone else, knew I mentioned its name in such business as this, I would be relieved of my job. It is merely that I was born on the fifth day of the fifth month in the year of our Christian Lord, 1935.'

'I'll never tell,' said David, smiling to himself, thinking that Jason Bourne had not deserted him after all. The myth that he once had been knew the avenues that led to the right contacts – knew them blindly – and that man was there inside David Webb.

The curtained whitewashed room of the warehouse, lined with locked, horizontal display cases, was not unlike a museum displaying such artifacts from past civilizations as primitive tools, fossilized insects, mystic carvings of religions past. The difference here was in the objects. These were exploding weapons that ran the gamut, from the lowest-calibre handguns and rifles to the most sophisticated weapons of modern warfare – thousand-round automatic machine guns with spiralling clips on near-weightless frames to laser-guided rockets to be fired from the shoulder, an arsenal for terrorists. Two men in business suits stood guard, one outside the entrance to the room, the other inside. As was to be expected, the former bowed his apology and moved an electronic scanner up and down the clothes of Webb and his driver. Then the man reached for the attaché case. David pulled it away, shaking his head and gesturing at the wandlike scanner. The guard had waved it over the surface of the case, checking his dials as he did so.

'Private papers,' Webb said in Chinese to the startled guard as he walked into the room.

It took David nearly a full minute to absorb what he saw, to shake off his disbelief. He looked at the bold – emblazoned – No Smoking signs in English, French, and Chinese that were all over the walls and wondered why they were there. Nothing was exposed. He walked over the small-arms display and examined the wares. He clutched the attaché case in his hand as though it were a lifeline to sanity in a world gone mad with instruments of violence.

'*Huanying!*' cried a voice, followed by the appearance of a youngish-looking man. He came out of a panelled door in one of those tight-fitting European suits that exaggerate the shoulders and hug the waist, the rear panels of the jacket flowing like a peacock's tail – the product of designers determined to be chic at the price of neutering the male image.

'This is Mr Wu Song, sir,' said Pak-fei, bowing first to the merchant and then to Webb. 'It is not necessary for you to give your name, sir.'

'*Bu!*' spat out the young merchant, pointing at David's attaché case. '*Bu jing ya!*'

'Your client, Mr Song, speaks fluent Chinese.' The driver turned to David. 'As you heard, sir, Mr Song objects to the presence of your briefcase.'

'It doesn't leave my hand,' said Webb.

'Then there can be no serious discussion of business,' rejoined Wu Song in flawless English.

'Why not? Your man checked it. There are no weapons inside, and even if there were and I tried to open it, I have an idea I'd be on the floor before the lid was up.'

'Plastic?' asked Wu Song. 'Plastic microphones leading to recording devices where the metal content is so low as to be dismissed even by sophisticated machinery?'

'You're paranoid.'

'As they say in your country, it goes with the territory.'

'Your idiom's as good as your English.'

'Columbia University, '73.'

'Did you major in armaments?'

'No, marketing.'

'*Aiya!*' shrieked Pak-fei, but he was too late. The rapid colloquy had covered the movement of the guards; they had walked across the room, at the last instant lunging at Webb and the driver.

Jason Bourne spun around, dislodging his attacker's arm from his shoulder, clamping it under his own and, twisting it, forced the man down and smashed the attaché case into the Oriental's face. *The moves were coming back to him. The violence was returning as it had to a bewildered amnesiac on a fishing boat beyond the shoals of a Mediterranean island. So much forgotten, so much unexplained, but remembered.* The man fell to the floor, stunned, as his partner turned in fury to Webb after pummelling Pak-fei, the driver, to the ground. He rushed forward, his hands held up in a diagonal thrust, his wide chest and shoulders the base of his dual battering rams. David dropped the attaché case, lurched to his right, then spun again, again to his right, his left foot lashing up from the floor, catching the Chinese in the groin with such force that the man doubled over, screaming. Webb instantly kicked out with his right foot, his toe digging into the attacker's throat directly under his jaw; the man rolled on the floor, gasping for air, one hand on his groin, the other gripping his neck. The first guard started to rise; Bourne stepped forward and smashed his knee into the man's chest, sending him halfway across the room where he fell unconscious beneath a display case.

The young arms merchant was stunned. He was witnessing the unthinkable, expecting any moment that what he saw would be reversed, his guards the victors. Then suddenly, emphatically, he knew it was not going to happen; he ran in panic to the paneled door, reaching it as Webb reached him. David gripped the padded shoulders, spinning the merchant back across the floor. Wu Song tripped over his twisting feet and fell; he held up his hands, pleading. 'No, please! *Stop!* I cannot *stand* physical confrontation! Take what you will!'

'You can't stand *what?*'

'You heard me, I get *ill!*'

'What the hell do you think all *this* is about?' yelled David, sweeping his arm around the room.

'I service a demand, that is all. Take whatever you want, but don't touch me. *Please!*'

Disgusted, Webb crossed to the fallen driver, who was getting to his knees, blood trickling from the corner of his mouth. 'What I take I pay for,' he said to the arms merchant as he grabbed the driver's arm and helped him to his feet. 'Are you all right?'

'You ask for great trouble, sir,' replied Pak-fei, his hands trembling, fear in his eyes.

'It had nothing to do with you. Wu Song knows that, don't you, Wu?'

'I brought you here!' insisted the driver.

'To make a purchase,' added David quickly. 'So let's get it over with. But first tie up those two goons. Use the curtains. Rip them down.'

Pak-fei looked imploringly at the young merchant.

'Great Christian *Jesus*, do as he *says!*' yelled Wu Song. 'He will strike me! Take the curtains! Tie them, you *imbecile!*'

Three minutes later Webb held in his hand an odd-looking gun, bulky but not large. It was an advanced weapon; the perforated cylinder that was the silencer was pneumatically snapped on, reducing the decibel count of a gunshot to a loud spit – but no more than a spit – the accuracy unaffected at close range. It held nine rounds, clips released and inserted at the base of the handle in a matter of seconds; there were three in reserve – thirty-six shells with the firepower of a .357 Magnum available instantly in a gun half the size and weight of a Colt .45.

'Remarkable,' said Webb, glancing at the bound guards and a quaking Pak-fei. 'Who designed it?' *So much expertise was coming back to him. So much recognition. From where?*

'As an American, it may offend you,' answered Wu Song, 'But he is a man in Bristol, Connecticut, who realized that the company he works for – designs for – would never recompense him adequately for his invention. Through intermediaries he went on the closed international market and sold to the highest bidder.'

'You?'

'I do not invest. I market.'

'That's right, I forgot. You service a demand.'

'Precisely.'

'Whom do you pay?'

'A numbered account in Singapore, I know nothing else. I'm protected, of course. Everything's on consignment.'

'I see. How much for this?'

'Take it. My gift to you.'

'You smell. I don't take gifts from people who smell. How much?'

Wu Song swallowed. 'The list price is eight hundred American dollars.'

Webb reached into his left pocket and pulled out the denominations he had placed there. He counted out eight $100 bills and gave them to the arms merchant. 'Paid in full,' he said.

'Paid,' agreed the Chinese.

'Tie him up,' said David, turning to the apprehensive Pak-fei. 'No, don't worry about it. Tie him up!'

'Do as he says, you *idiot!*'

'Then take the three of them outside. Along the side of the building by the car. And stay out of sight of the gate.'

'*Quickly!*' yelled Song. 'He is angry!'

'You can count on it,' agreed Webb.

Four minutes later the two guards and Wu Song walked awkwardly through the outside door into the blazing afternoon sunlight, made harsher by the dancing reflections off the waters of Victoria Harbour. Their knees and arms were tied in the ripped cloth of the curtains, so their movements were hesitant and uncertain. Silence was guaranteed by wads of fabric in the mouths of the guards. No such precautions were needed for the young merchant; he was petrified.

Alone, David put his retrieved attaché case on the floor and walked rapidly around the room studying the displays in the cases until he found what he wanted. He smashed the glass with the handle of his gun, and picked around the shards for the weapons he would use – weapons coveted by terrorists everywhere – timer grenades, each with the impact of a 20-pound bomb. *How did he know? Where did the knowledge come from?*

He removed six grenades and checked each battery charge. *How could he do that? How did he know where to look, what to press? No matter. He knew.* He looked at his watch.

He set the timers of each and ran along the display cases, crashing the handle of his weapon into the glass tops and dropping into each a grenade. He had one left and two cases to go; he looked up at the trilingual No Smoking signs and made another decision. He ran to the panelled door, opened it, and saw what he thought he might see. He threw in the final grenade.

Webb checked his watch, picked up the attaché case and went outside, making a point of being very much in control. He approached the Daimler at the side of the warehouse where Pak-fei seemed to be apologizing to his prisoners, perspiring as he did so. The driver was being alternately berated and consoled by Wu Song, who wanted nothing more than to be spared any further violence.

'Take them over to the breakwater,' ordered David, pointing to the stone wall that rose above the waters of the harbour.

Wu Song started at Webb. 'Who *are* you?' he asked.

The moment had come. It was now.

Webb again looked at his watch as he walked over to the arms merchant. He gripped Wu Song's elbow and shoved the frightened Chinese farther along the side of the building where soft-spoken words would not be overheard by the others. 'My name is Jason Bourne,' said David simply.

'*Jason Bou – !*' The Oriental gasped, reacting as though a stiletto had punctured his throat, his own eyes witnessing the final, violent act of his own death.

'And if you have any ideas about restoring a bruised ego by punishing someone – say, my driver – get rid of them. I'll know where to find you.' Webb paused for a single beat, then continued. 'You're a privileged man, Wu, but with that privilege goes a responsibility. For certain reasons you may be questioned, and I don't expect you to lie – I doubt that you're very good at lying anyway – so we met, I'll accept that. I even stole from you, if you like. But if you give an accurate description of me, you'd better be on the other side of the world – and dead. It would be less painful for you.'

The Columbia graduate froze, his lower lip trembling as he stared at Webb. David returned the look in silence, nodding his head once. He released Wu Song's arm and walked back to Pak-fei and the two bound guards, leaving the panicked merchant to his racing thoughts.

'Do as I told you, Pak-fei,' he said, once more looking at his watch. 'Get them over to the wall and tell them to lie down. Explain that I'm covering them with my gun, and will be covering them until we drive through the gate. I think their employer will attest to the fact that I'm a reasonably proficient marksman.'

The driver reluctantly barked the orders in Chinese, bowing to the arms merchant, as Wu Song started ahead of the others, awkwardly manoeuvring himself toward the breakwater some seventy-odd yards away. Webb looked inside the Daimler.

'Throw me the keys!' he shouted to Pak-fei. 'And hurry up!'

David snatched the keys from the air and climbed into the driver's seat. He started the engine, slipped the Daimler into gear, and followed the odd-looking parade across the asphalt directly behind the warehouse.

Wu Song and his two guards lay prostrate on the ground. Webb leaped out of the car, the motor running, and raced around the trunk to the other side, his newly purchased weapon in his hand, the silencer affixed. 'Get in and drive!' he shouted to Pak-fei. '*Quickly!*'

The driver jumped in, bewildered. David fired three shots – spits that blew up the asphalt several feet in front of each captive's face. It was enough; all three rolled in panic into the wall. Webb got into the front seat of the car. 'Let's go!' he said, for a final time looking at his watch, his gun out the window aimed in the vicinity of the three prostrate figures. '*Now!*'

The gate swung back for the august taipan in the august limousine. The Daimler raced through and turned right into the speeding traffic on the dual-lane highway to Mongkok.

'Slow down!' ordered David. 'Pull over to the side, on the dirt.'

'These drivers are madmen, sir. They speed because they know that in minutes they will barely move. It will be difficult to get back on the road.'

'Somehow I don't think so.'

It happened. The explosions came one after another – three, four, five . . . *six*. The isolated one-storey warehouse blew to the skies, flames and deep black smoke filling the air above the land and the harbour, causing automobiles and trucks and buses to come to screeching stops on the highway.

'*You?*' shrieked Pak-fei, his mouth gaping, his bulging eyes on Webb.

'I was there.'

'*We* were there, sir! I am dead! *Aiya!*'

'No, Pak-fei, you're not,' said David. 'You're protected, take my word for that. You'll never hear from Mr Wu Song again. I suspect he'll be on the other side of the world, probably in Iran, teaching marketing to the mullahs. I don't know who else would accept him.'

'But why? *How*, sir?'

'He's finished. He dealt in what's called "consignments," which means he pays as his merchandise is sold. Are you following me?'

'I think so, sir.'

'He has no more merchandise, but it wasn't sold. It just went away.'

'Sir?'

'He kept wired rolls of dynamite and cases of explosive plastic in the back room. They were too primitive to put in the display cases. Also too bulky.'

'*Sir?*'

'I couldn't have a cigarette . . . Weave around the traffic, Pak-fei. I have to get back to Kowloon.'

As they entered the Tsim Sha Tsui, the movements of Pak-fei's constantly turning head intruded on Webb's thoughts. The driver kept looking at him. 'What is it?' he asked.

'I am not certain, sir. I am frightened, of course.'

'You didn't believe what I told you? That you've got nothing to be afraid of?'

'That is not it, sir. I think I must believe you, for I saw what you did, and I saw Wu Song's face when you spoke with him. I think it is you I am frightened of, but I also think this may be wrong, for you did protect me. It was in Wu Song's eyes. I cannot explain.'

'Don't bother,' said David, reaching into his pocket for money. 'Are you married, Pak-fei? Or have a girlfriend, or a boyfriend? It doesn't matter.'

'Married, sir. I have two grown children who have not-bad jobs. They contribute; my joss is good.'

'Now it'll be better. Go home and pick up your wife – and children, if you like – and drive, Pak-fei. Drive up into the New Territories for many miles. Stop and have a fine meal in Tuen Mun or Yuen Long and then drive some more. Let them enjoy this fine automobile.'

'Sir?'

'A *xiao xin*,' went on Webb, the money in his hand. 'What we call in English a little white lie that doesn't hurt anybody. You see, I want the mileage on this car to approximate where you've driven me today – and tonight.'

'Where is that?'

'You drove Mr Cruett first up to Lo Wu and then across the base of the mountain range to Lok Ma Chau.'

'Those are checkpoints into the People's Republic.'

'Yes, they are,' agreed David, removing two $100 bills, and then a third. 'Do you think you can remember that and make the mileage right?'

'Most certainly, sir.'

'And do you think,' added Webb, his finger on a fourth $100 bill, 'that you could say I left the car at Lok Ma Chau and wandered up in the hills for an hour or so.'

'Ten hours, if you like, sir. I need no sleep.'

'One hour is fine.' David held out the $400 in front of the driver's startled eyes. 'And I'll know if you don't live up to our agreement.'

'You have no concerns, sir!' cried Pak-fei, one hand on the wheel, the other grasping the bills. 'I shall pick up my wife, my children, her parents, and my own as well. This animal I drive is big enough for twelve. I thank you, sir! I thank you!'

'Drop me off around ten streets from Salisbury Road and get out of the area. I don't want this car seen in Kowloon.'

'No, sir, it is not possible. We will be in Lo Wu, in Lok Ma Chau!'

'As far as tomorrow morning goes, say whatever you like. I won't be here, I'm leaving tonight. You won't see me again.'

'Yes, sir.'

'Our contract's concluded, Pak-fei,' said Jason Bourne, his thoughts returning to a strategy that became clearer with each move he made. And each move brought him closer to Marie. All was colder now. There was a certain freedom in being what he was not.

Play the scenario as it was given to you . . . Be everywhere at once. Make them sweat.

At 5:02 an obviously disturbed Liang walked rapidly out the glass doors of the Regent. He looked anxiously around at the arriving and departing guests, then turned to his left and hurried down the pavement toward the ramp leading to the street. David watched him through the spraying fountains on the opposite side of the courtyard. Using the fountains as his cover, Webb ran across the busy area, dodging cars and taxis; he reached the ramp and followed Liang down toward Salisbury Road.

He stopped midway to the street and turned, angling his body and his face to the left. The assistant manager had come to an abrupt halt, his body lurching forward, as an anxious person in a hurry will do when he has suddenly remembered something or changes his mind. It had to be the latter, thought David, as he cautiously shifted his head and saw Liang rushing across the entrance drive toward the crowded pavement of the New World Shopping Centre. Webb knew he would lose him in the crowds if he did not hurry, so he held up both hands, stopping the traffic, and raced diagonally down the ramp as horns bellowed and angry shrieks came from drivers. He reached the pavement, sweating, anxious. He could not see Liang! Where was he? The sea of Oriental faces became a blur, so much the same, yet not the same. Where *was* he? David rushed ahead, muttering excuses as he collided with bodies and startled faces; he saw him! He was sure it was Liang – but *not* sure, not really. He had seen a dark-suited figure turn into the entrance of the harbour walkway, a long stretch of concrete above the water where people fished and strolled and performed their *tai chi* exercises in the early mornings. Yet he had seen only the back of a man; if it was not Liang he would leave the street and lose him completely. *Instinct. Not yours but Bourne's – the eyes of Jason Bourne.*

Webb broke into a run, heading for the arched entrance of the walkway. The skyline of Hong Kong sparkled in the sunlit distance, the traffic in the harbour bobbing furiously, winding up the day's labours on the water. He slowed down as he passed under the arch; there was no way back to Salisbury Road but through the entrance. The walkway was a dead-end intrusion on the waterfront, and that raised a question, as well as supplying an answer to another. Why had Liang – if it was Liang – boxed himself into a dead end? What drew him to it? A contact, a drop, a relay? Whatever it was, it meant that the Chinese had not considered the possibility that he was being followed; that was the immediate answer David needed. It told him what he had to know. His prey was in panic; the unexpected could only propel him into further panic.

Jason Bourne's eyes had not lied. It *was* Liang, but the first question remained unanswered, even compounded by what Webb saw. Of the thousands upon thousands of public telephones in Kowloon – tucked away in crowded arcades and in recessed corners of darkened lobbies – Liang had chosen to use a pay phone on the inner wall of the walkway. It was exposed, in the open, in the centre of a wide thoroughfare that was in itself a dead end. It made no sense; even the rankest amateur had basic protective instincts. When in panic he sought cover.

Liang reached into his pocket for change, and suddenly, as if commanded by an inner voice, David knew that he could not permit that call to be made. When it was made, *he* had to make it. It was part of his strategy, a part that would bring him closer to Marie! The control had to be in *his* hands, not others'!

He began running, heading straight toward the white plastic shell of the pay phone, wanting to shout but knowing he had to get closer to be heard over the sounds of the windblown waterfront. The assistant manager had just finished dialing. Somewhere a telephone was ringing.

'*Liang!*' roared Webb. 'Get off that phone! If you want to live, hang up and get *out* of there!'

The Chinese spun around, his face a rigid mask of terror. '*You!*' he shouted hysterically, pressing his body back into the shell of white plastic. 'No . . . *no!* Not now! Not *here!*'

Gunfire suddenly filled the winds off the water, staccato bursts that joined the myriad sounds of the harbour. Pandemonium swept over the walkway, as people screamed and shrieked, dropping to the ground or racing in all directions away from the terror of instant death.

10

'*Aiya!*' roared Liang, diving to the side of the telephone shell as bullets ripped into the wall of the walkway and cracked in the air overhead. Webb lunged toward the Chinese, crawling beside the hotel man, his hunting knife out of its scabbard. 'Do *not!* What are you *doing?*' Liang screamed as David, lying sideways, gripped him by the front of his shirt and shoved the blade up into the manager's chin, breaking the skin, drawing blood. '*Ahhee!*' The hysterical cry was lost in the pandemonium of the walkway.

'Give me the number! *Now!*'

'Don't do this to me! I swear to you I did not know it was a *trap!*'

'It's not a trap for me, Liang,' said Webb breathlessly, the sweat rolling down his face. 'It's for you!'

'*Me?* You're mad! Why *me?*'

'Because they know I'm here now, and you've seen me, you've talked to me. You made your phone call and they can't afford you any longer.'

'But *why?*'

'You were given a telephone number. You did your job and they can't allow any traces.'

'That explains *nothing!*'

'Maybe my name will. It's Jason Bourne.'

'Oh, my *God . . . !*' whispered Liang, his face pale and lips parted, as he stared at David.

'You're a trace,' said Webb. 'You're dead.'

'No, *no!*' The Chinese shook his head. 'It can't *be!* I don't *know* anyone, only the number! It is a deserted office in the New World Centre, a temporary telephone installed. *Please!* The number is three-four, four, zero, one! Do not *kill* me, Mr Bourne! For the love of our Christian God, do not *do* it!'

'If I thought the trap was for me, there'd be blood all over your throat, not your chin . . . Three-four, four, zero, one?'

'Yes, exactly!'

The gunfire stopped as suddenly and as startlingly as it had begun.

'The New World Centre's right above us, isn't it? One of those windows up there.'

'Exactly!' Liang shuddered, unable to take his eyes off David's face. Then he shut them tight, tears dripping beneath his lids as he shook his head violently. 'I have never *seen* you! I swear on the cross of holy Jesus!'

'Sometimes I wonder if I'm in Hong Kong or the Vatican.' Webb raised his head and looked around. All along the walkway terrified people were hesitantly beginning to rise. Mothers clutched children; men held women, and men, women, and children got to their knees, then their feet, and suddenly formed a mass stampede toward the Salisbury arch. 'You were told to make your call from here, weren't you?' said David rapidly, turning to the frightened hotel man.

'Yes, sir.'

'*Why?* Did they give you a reason?'

'Yes, sir.'

'For Christ's sake, open your eyes!'

'Yes, sir.' Liang did so, looking away as he spoke. 'They said they did not trust the guest who asked for Suite six-nine-zero. He was a man who might force another to convey lies. Therefore they wanted to observe me when I spoke to them . . . Mr Bourne – *no*, I did not *say* that! Mr *Cruett* – I tried all day to reach you, Mr *Cruett!* I wanted you to know I was being pressed repeatedly, Mr *Cruett*. They kept phoning me, wanting to know when I would place my call to them – from *here*. I kept saying you had not arrived! What else could I *do?* By trying to reach you so constantly, you can see I was trying to warn you, sir! It is obvious, is it *not?*'

'What's obvious is that you're a damn fool.'

'I am not equipped for this work.'

'Why did you do it?'

'Money, sir! I was with Chiang, with the Kuomintang. I have a wife and five children – two sons and three daughters. I have to get out! They search backgrounds; they give us incontestable labels with no appeals. I am a learned man, sir! Fudan University, second in my class – I owned my own hotel in Shanghai. But all that is meaningless now. When Beijing takes over, I am dead, my family is dead. And now you say I am dead as of this moment. What am I to *do?*'

'Peking – Beijing – won't touch the colony, they won't change anything,' said David, remembering the words Marie had said to him that terrible evening after McAllister had left their house. 'Unless the crazies take over.'

'They are *all* crazy, sir. Believe nothing else. You don't *know* them!'

'Maybe not. But I know a few of you. And, frankly, I'd rather not.'

'"Let who is without sin among you cast the first stone," sir.'

'Stones, but not bags of silver from Chiang's corruption, right?'

'Sir?'

'What are your three daughter's names? *Quickly!*'

'They are . . . they are . . . Wang . . . Wang Sho—'

'Forget it!' yelled David, glancing down at the Salisbury arch. '*Ni bushi ren!* You're not a man, you're a *pig!* Stay well, Liang of the Kuomintang. Stay well as long as they let you. Frankly, I couldn't care less.'

Webb got to his feet, prepared to throw himself down again at the first irregular flash of light from a window above on his left. The eyes of Jason Bourne were accurate: there was nothing. David joined the stampede at the arch and slithered his way through the crowds to Salisbury Road.

*

He placed the call from a phone in a congested, noisy arcade off Nathan Road. He put his index finger in his right ear to hear more clearly.

'*Wei?*' said a male voice.

'It's Bourne, and I'll speak English. Where is my wife?'

'*Wode tian ah!* It is said you speak our language in numerous dialects.'

'It's been a long time and I want everything clearly understood. I asked you about my *wife!*'

'Liang *gave* you this number?'

'He didn't have a choice.'

'He is also dead.'

'I don't care what you do, but if I were you, I'd have second thoughts about killing him.'

'Why? He is lower than a worm.'

'Because you picked a damn fool – worse, an hysterical one. He talked to too many people. A switchboard operator told me he was calling me every few minutes—'

'Calling *you?*'

'I flew in this morning, Where is my *wife*—'

'Liang the *liar!*'

'You didn't expect me to stay in that suite, did you? I had him switch me to another room. We were seen talking together – arguing – with half a dozen clerks watching us. You kill him, there'll be more rumours than any of us want. The police will be looking for a rich American who disappeared.'

'His trousers are soiled,' said the Chinese. 'Perhaps it is enough.'

'It's enough. Now, what about my *wife!*'

'I heard you. I am not privileged with such information.'

'Then put on someone who is. *Now!*'

'You will meet with others more knowledgeable.'

'*When?*'

'We will get back to you. What room are you in?'

'I'll call *you.* You've got fifteen minutes.'

'You are giving *me* orders?'

'I know where you are, which window, which office – you're sloppy with your rifle. You should have corked the barrel; sunlight reflects off metal, that's basic. In thirty seconds I'll be a hundred feet from your door, but you won't know where I am and you can't leave that phone.'

'I don't believe you!'

'Try me. You're not watching *me* now, I'm watching *you.* You've got fifteen minutes, and when I call you back I want to talk to my wife.'

'She's not here!'

'If I thought she were, you'd be dead, your head knifed from the rest of you and thrown out the window to join the other garbage in the harbour. If you think I'm exaggerating, check around. Ask people who've dealt with me. Ask your taipan, the Yao Ming who doesn't exist.'

'I cannot make your wife *appear,* Jason Bourne!' shouted the frightened minion.

'Get me a number where I can reach her. Either I hear her voice – *talking* to me – or there's nothing. Except for your headless corpse and a black bandanna across your bleeding neck. *Fifteen minutes!*'

David hung up the phone and wiped the sweat from his face. He had done it. The mind and the words were Jason Bourne's – he had gone back in only vaguely remembered time and instinctively knew what to do, what to say, what to threaten. There was a lesson somewhere. Appearance far outdistanced reality. Or was there a reality within him crying to come out, wanting control, telling David Webb to trust the man inside him?

He left the oppressively crowded arcade and turned right on the equally congested pavement. The Golden Mile of the Tsim Sha Tsui was preparing for its nightly games, and so would he. He could return to the hotel now; the assistant manager would be miles away, conceivably booking a flight to Taiwan, if there was any truth at all in his hysterical statements. Webb would use the freight elevator to reach his room in case others were awaiting him in the lobby, although he doubted it. The shooting gallery that was a deserted office in the New World Centre was not a command post, and the marksman was not a commander but a relay, now frightened for his life.

With each step David took down Nathan Road, the shorter his breath became, the louder his chest pounded. Twelve minutes from now he would hear Marie's voice. Oh God, he *wanted* to hear it so! He *had* to! It was all that would keep him sane, all that mattered.

'Your fifteen minutes are over,' said Webb, sitting on the edge of the bed, trying to control his heartbeat, wondering if the rapid echo could be heard as he heard it, hoping it caused no tremor in his voice.

'Call five-two, six, five, three.'

'Five?' David recognized the exchange. 'She's over in Hong Kong, not Kowloon.'

'She will be moved immediately.'

'I'll call you back after I've spoken to her.'

'There is no need, Jason Bourne. Knowledgeable men are there and they will speak with you. My business is finished and you have never seen me.'

'I don't have to see you. A photograph will be taken when you leave that office, but you won't know from where or by whom. You'll probably see a number of people – in the hallway, or in an elevator or the lobby – but you won't know which one has a camera with a lens that looks like a button on his jacket, or an emblem on her purse. Stay well, minion. Think nice thoughts.'

Webb depressed the telephone bar, disconnecting the line; he waited three seconds, released it, heard the dial tone, and touched the buttons. He could hear the ring. *Christ*, he couldn't *stand* it!

'*Wei?*'

'This is Bourne. Put my wife on the line.'

'As you wish.'

'*David?*'

'Are you all *right?*' shouted Webb on the edge of hysteria.

'Yes, just tired, that's all, my darling. Are *you* all right—'

'Have they hurt you – have they *touched* you?'

'No, David, they've been quite kind, actually. But you know how tired I get sometimes. Remember that week in Zurich when you wanted to see the Fraumünster and the museums and go out sailing on the Limmat, and I said I just wasn't up to it?'

There'd been no week in Zurich. Only the nightmare of a single night when both of them nearly lost their lives. He running the gauntlet of his would-be executioners in the Steppdeckstrasse, she nearly raped, sentenced to death on a deserted riverfront in the Guisan Quai. What was she trying to tell him?

'Yes, I remember.'

'So you mustn't worry about me, darling. Thank *God* you're here! We'll be together soon, they've promised me that. It'll be like Paris, David. Remember Paris, when I thought I'd lost you? But you came to me and we both knew where to go. That lovely street with the dark green trees and the—'

'That will be all, Mrs Webb,' broke in a male voice. 'Or should I say Mrs Bourne,' the man added, speaking directly into the phone.

'*Think*, David, and be *careful!*' yelled Marie in the background. 'And don't worry, darling! That lovely street with the row of green trees, my *favourite* tree—'

'*Ting zhi!*' cried the male voice, issuing an order in Chinese. 'Take her away! She's giving him information! Quickly. Don't let her speak!'

'You harm her in any way, you'll regret it for the rest of your short life,' said Webb icily. 'I swear to *Christ* I'll find you.'

'There has been no cause for unpleasantness up to this moment,' replied the man slowly, his tone sincere. 'You heard your wife. She has been treated well. She has no complaints.'

'Something's wrong with her! What the hell have you done that she can't *tell* me?'

'It is only the tension, Mr Bourne. And she *was* telling you something, no doubt in her anxiety trying to describe this location – erroneously, I should add – but even if it were accurate, it would be as useless to you as the telephone phone number. She is on her way to another apartment, one of millions in Hong Kong. Why would we harm her in any way? It would be counterproductive. A great taipan wants to meet with you.'

'Yao Ming?'

'Like you, he goes by several names. Perhaps you can reach an accommodation.'

'Either we do or he's dead. And so are you.'

'I believe what you say, Jason Bourne. You killed a close blood relative of mine who was beyond your reach, in his own island fortress on Lantau. I'm sure you recall.'

'I don't keep records. Yao Ming. *When?*'

'Tonight.'

'Where?'

'You must understand, he's very recognizable, so it must be a most unusual place.'

'Suppose I choose it?'

'Unacceptable, of course. Do not insist. We have your wife.'

David tensed; he was losing the control he desperately needed. 'Name it,' he said.

'The Walled City. We assume you know it.'

'*Of* it,' corrected Webb, trying to focus what memory he had. 'The filthiest slum on the face of the earth, if I remember.'

'What else would it be? It is the only legal possession of the People's Republic in all of the colony. Even the detestable Mao Zedong gave permission for our police to purge it. But civil servants are not paid that much. It remains essentially the same.'

'What time tonight?'

'After dark, but before the bazaar closes. Between nine-thirty and not later than fifteen minutes to ten.'

'How do I find this Yao Ming – who isn't Yao Ming?'

'There is a woman in the first block of the open market who sells snake entrails as aphrodisiacs, predominantly cobra. Go up to her and ask her where a great one is. She will tell you the descending steps to use, which alley to take. You will be met.'

'I might never get there. The colour of my skin isn't welcome down there.'

'No one will harm you. However, I suggest you not wear garish clothing or display expensive jewellery.'

'Jewellery?'

'If you own a high-priced watch, do not wear it.'

They'd cut your arm off for a watch. Medusa. So be it.

'Thanks for the advice.'

'One last thing. Do not think of involving the authorities or your consulate in a reckless attempt to compromise the taipan. If you do, your wife will die.'

'That wasn't necessary.'

'With Jason Bourne everything is necessary. You will be watched.'

'Nine-thirty to nine-forty-five,' said Webb, replacing the phone and getting up from the bed. He went to the window and stared out at the harbour. What *was* it? What was Marie trying to tell him?

. . . you know how tired I get sometimes.

No, he did not know that. His wife was a strong Ontario ranch girl who never complained of being tired.

. . . you mustn't worry about me, darling.

A foolish plea, and she must have realized it. Marie did not waste precious moments being foolish. Unless . . . was she rambling incoherently?

. . . It'll be like Paris, David . . . we both knew where to go . . . that lovely street with the dark green trees.

No, not rambling, only the appearance of rambling; there *was* a message. But what? *What* lovely street with 'dark green trees'? Nothing came to him and it was driving him out of his mind! He was failing her. She was sending a signal and it eluded him.

. . . Think, David, and be careful! . . . don't worry, darling! That lovely street with the row of green trees, my favourite tree –

What lovely street? What goddamned row of trees, what *favourite* tree?

Nothing made sense to him and it should make sense! He should be able to respond, not stare out a window, his memory blank. Help me, *help me!* he cried silently to no one.

An inner voice told him not to dwell on what he could not understand. There were things to do; he could not willingly walk into the meeting ground of the enemy's choosing without some foreknowledge, some cards of his own to play . . . *I suggest you do not wear garish clothing* . . . It would not have been garish in any event, thought Webb, but now it would be something quite opposite – and unexpected.

During the months in which he had peeled away the layers of Jason Bourne one theme kept repeating itself. Change, change, change. Bourne was a practitioner of change; they called him 'the chameleon,' a man who could melt into different surroundings with ease. Not as a grotesque, a cartoon with fright wigs and nose putty, but as one who could adapt the essentials of his appearance to his immediate environment so that those who had met the 'assassin' – rarely, however, in full light or standing close to him – gave widely varying descriptions of the man hunted throughout Asia and Europe. The details were always in conflict: the hair was dark or light; the eyes brown, blue, or speckled; the skin pale, or tanned, or blotched; the clothes well made and subdued if the rendezvous took place in a dimly lit expensive café, or rumpled and ill-fitting if the meeting was held on the waterfront or in the lower depths of a city. Change. Effortlessly, with the minimum of artifice. David Webb would trust the chameleon within him. Free fall. Go where Jason Bourne directed.

After the harrowing phone call, he went over to the Peninsula Hotel and, with a large, unseen tip, got a room, depositing his attaché case in the hotel vault. He had the presence of mind to register under the name of Cactus's third false passport. If men were looking for him, they would flash the name he used at the Regent; it was all they had.

He again went back across Salisbury Road, used the service elevator, walked rapidly to his room and packed what few clothes he needed in the flight bag. But he did not check out of the Regent. If men were looking for him, he wanted them to look where he was not.

Once settled in the Peninsula, he had time for something to eat, and to forage in several shops until nightfall. By the time darkness came he would be in the Walled City – before nine-thirty. Jason Bourne was giving the commands and David Webb obeyed them.

The Walled City of Kowloon has no visible wall around it, but it is as clearly defined as if there were one made of hard, high steel. It is instantly sensed in the congested open market that runs along the street in front of the row of dark run-down flats – shacks haphazardly perched on top of one another giving the impression that at any moment the entire blighted complex would collapse under its own weight, leaving nothing but rubble where elevated rubble had stood. But there is deceptive strength found as one walks down the short flight of steps into the interior of the sprawling slum. Below ground level, cobblestoned alleyways that are in most cases tunnels traverse beneath the ramshackle structures. In squalid corridors crippled beggars vie with half-dressed prostitutes and drug peddlers in the eerie wash of naked bulbs that hang from exposed wires along the stone walls. A putrid dampness abounds; all is decay and rot, but the strength of time has hardened this decomposition, petrifying it.

Within the foul alleyways in no particular order or balance are narrow, barely lit staircases leading to the vertical series of broken-down flats, the average rising three storeys, two of which are above ground. Inside the small, dilapidated rooms the widest varieties of narcotics and sex are sold; all is beyond the reach of the police – silently agreed to by all parties – for few of the colony's authorities care to venture into the bowels of the Walled City. It is its own self-contained hell. Let it be.

Outside in the open market that fills the garbage-strewn street where no traffic is permitted, soiled tables piled high with rejected and/or stolen merchandise are sandwiched between grimy stalls where pockets of vapour rise from huge vats of boiling oil in which questionable pieces of meat, fowl, and snake are continuously plunged, then ladled out and placed on newspapers for immediate sale. The crowds move under the weak light of dull streetlamps from one vendor to the next, haggling in high-pitched voices, shrieking back and forth, buying and selling. Then there are the kerb people, bedraggled men and women without stalls or tables, whose merchandise is spread out on the pavement. They squat behind displays of trinkets and cheap jewellery, much of it stolen from the docks, and woven cages filled with crawling beetles and fluttering tiny birds.

Near the mouth of the strange, fetid bazaar a lone, muscular female sat on a low wooden stool, her thick legs parted, skinning snakes and removing their entrails, her dark eyes seemingly obsessed with each thrashing serpent in her hands. On either side were writhing burlap bags, every now and then convulsing as the doomed reptiles struck out in hissing fury at one another, enraged by their captivity. Clamped under the heavyset woman's bare right foot was a king cobra, its jet-black body immobile and erect, its head flat, its small eyes steady, hypnotized by the constantly moving crowds. The squalor of the open market was a fitting barricade for the wall-less Walled City beyond.

Rounding the corner at the opposite end of the long bazaar, a dishevelled figure turned into the overflowing avenue. The man was dressed in a cheap, loose-fitting brown suit, the trousers too bulky, the coat too large, yet tight around the hunched shoulders. A soft, widebrimmed hat, black and unmistakably Oriental, threw a constant shadow across his face. His gait was slow, as befitted a man pausing in front of various stalls and tables examining the merchandise, but only once did he reach tentatively into his pocket to make a single purchase. Then, too, there was a stooped quality in his posture, the frame of a man that had been bent from years of hard labour in the field or on the waterfront, his diet never sufficient for a body from which so much was extracted. There was a sadness as well in this man, a futility born of too little, too late, and too costly for the mind and the body. It was the recognition of impotence, of pride abandoned, for there was nothing to be proud of; the price of survival had been too much. And this man, this stooped figure who haltingly bought a newspaper cone of fried questionable fish, was not unlike many of the males in the marketplace – in fact, one could say he was indistinguishable from them. He approached the muscular woman who was tearing the intestines from a still-writhing snake.

'Where is the great one?' asked Jason Bourne in Chinese, his eyes fixed on the immobile cobra, the grease from the newspaper rolling over his left hand.

'You are early,' replied the woman without expression. 'It is dark, but you are early.'

'I was summoned quickly. Do you question the taipan's instructions?'

'He is fuck-fuck cheap for a taipan!' she spat out in guttural Cantonese. 'What do I care? Go down the steps behind me and take the first alleyway to the left. A whore will be standing fifteen, twenty metres down. She waits for the white man and will lead him to the taipan . . . Are you the white man? I cannot tell in this light and your Chinese is good – but you do not look like a white man, you do not wear a white man's clothes.'

'If you were me, would you make a heavenly point of looking like a white man, dressing like a white man, if you were told to come down here?'

'I would make the point of a thousand devils that I was from the Qing Gaoyan!' said the woman, laughing through half-gone teeth. 'Especially if you carry money. Do you carry money . . . our *Zhongguo ren?*'

'You flatter me, but no.'

'You lie. White people lie with heavenly words about money.'

'Very well, I lie. I trust your snake will not attack me for it.'

'Fool! He is old and has no fangs, no poison. But he is the heavenly image of a man's organ. He brings me money. Will *you* give me money?'

'For a service, yes.'

'*Aiya!* You want this old body, you must have an axe in your trousers! Chop up the whore, not me!'

'No axe, just words,' said Bourne, his right hand slipping into his trousers pocket. He withdrew a US $100 bill and palmed it in front of the snake seller's face, keeping it out of sight of the surrounding bargain hunters.

'*Aiya – aiya!*' whispered the woman as Jason pulled it away from her grasping fingers; the dead snake dropped between her thick legs.

'The service,' Bourne repeated. 'Since you thought I was one of you, I expect others will think so, too. All I want you to do is to tell anyone who asks you that the white man never showed up. Is that fair?'

'*Fair!* Give me the money!'

'The *service?*'

'You bought snakes! Snakes! What do I know of a white man. He never appeared! Here. Here is your snake. Make love!' The woman took the bill, bunched the entrails in her hand and shoved them into a plastic bag on which there was a designer's signature. It read *Christian Dior.*

Remaining stooped, Bourne bowed rapidly twice and backed his way out of the crowd, dropping the snake entrails in the kerb far enough away from a streetlight so as not to be noticed. Holding the dripping cone of foul-smelling fish, he repeatedly mimed reaching for mouthfuls as he slowly made his way to the steps and descended into the steaming bowels of the Walled City. He looked at his watch, spilling fish as he did so. It was 9:15; the taipan's patrols would be moving into place.

He had to know the extent of the banker's security. He wanted the lie that he had told a marksman in a deserted office above the harbour walkway to be the truth. Instead of being watched, he wanted to be the one watching. He would memorize each face, each role in the command structure, the rapidity with which each guard made a decision under pressure, the communications equipment, and, above all, discover where the weaknesses were in the taipan's security. David understood that Jason Bourne was taking over; there was a point in what *he* was doing. The banker's note had started with the words: *A wife for a wife . . .* Only one word had to be changed. *A taipan for a wife.*

Bourne turned into the alleyway on his left and walked several hundred feet past sights he scrupulously ignored; a resident of the Walled City would do no less. On a darkened staircase a woman on her knees performed the act for which she was being paid, the man above her holding money in his hand over her head; a young couple, two obvious addicts in near frenzy, were pleading with a man in an expensive black leather jacket; a small boy, smoking a marijuana cigarette, urinated against the stone wall; a beggar without legs clattered on his wheeled board over the cobblestones chanting '*Bong ngo, bong ngo!*' – a plea for alms; and on another dimly lit staircase a well-dressed pimp was threatening one of his whores with facial disfigurement if she did not produce more money. David Webb mused that he was not in Disneyland. Jason Bourne studied the alley as if it were a combat zone behind enemy lines, 9:24. The soldiers would be going to their posts. The outer and the inner man turned around and started back.

The banker's whore was walking into position, her bright red blouse unbuttoned, barely covering her small breasts; the traditional slit in her black skirt reached her thigh. She was a caricature. The 'white man' was not to make a mistake. Point one: Accentuate the obvious. Something to remember; subtlety was not a strong suit. Several yards behind her a man spoke into a hand-held radio; he caught up with the woman, shook his head and rushed forward toward the end of the alley and the steps. Bourne stopped, his posture sagging, and turned into the wall. The footsteps were behind him, hurrying, emphatic, the pace quickening. A second Chinese approached and passed him, a small middle-aged man in a dark business suit, tie, and shoes polished to a high gloss. He was no citizen of the Walled City; his expression was a mixture of apprehension and disgust. Ignoring the whore, he glanced at his watch and raced ahead. He had the look and demeanour of an executive ordered to assume duties he found distasteful. A company man, precise, orderly, the bottom line his motive, for the figures did not lie. A banker?

Jason studied the irregular row of staircases; the man had to come from one of them. The sound of the footsteps had been abrupt and recent, and judging by the pace, they had begun no more than sixty or seventy feet away. On the third staircase on the left or the fourth on the right. In one of the flats above either staircase a taipan was waiting for his visitor. Bourne had to find out which and on what level. The taipan had to be surprised, even shocked. He had to understand whom he was dealing with and what his actions would cost him.

Jason started up again, now assuming a drunken walk; the words of an old Mandarin folk tune came to him. '*Me li hua cherng zhang liu yue*,' he sang softly, bouncing gently off the wall as he approached the whore. 'I have money,' he said pleasantly, his words in Chinese imprecise. 'And you, beautiful woman, have what I need. Where do we go?'

'Nowhere, fancy drunk. Get away from here.'

'*Bong ngo! Cheng bong ngo!*' screeched the legless beggar clattering down the alley, careening into the wall as he screamed. '*Cheng bong ngo!*'

'*Jau!*' yelled the woman. 'Get out of here before I kick your useless body off your board, Loo Mi! I've told you not to interfere with business!'

'This cheap drunk is *business?* I'll get you something better!'

'He's not my business, darling. He's an annoyance. I'm waiting for someone.'

'Then I'll chop his feet!' shouted the grotesque figure, pulling a cleaver from his board.

'What the hell are you *doing?*' roared Bourne in English, shoving his foot into the beggar's chest, sending the half-man and his board into the opposite wall.

'There are *laws!*' shrieked the beggar. 'You attacked a cripple! You are robbing a cripple!'

'Sue me,' said Jason, turning to the woman, as the beggar clattered away down the alley.

'You talk . . . English.' The whore stared at him.

'So do you,' said Bourne.

'You speak Chinese, but you are not Chinese.'

'In spirit, perhaps. I've been looking for you.'

'You are the *man?*'

'I am.'

'I will take you to the taipan.'

'No. Just tell me which staircase, which level.'

'Those are not my instructions.'

'They're new instructions, given by the taipan. Do you question his new instructions?'

'They must be delivered by his head-head man.'

'The small *Zhongguo ren* in a dark suit?'

'He tells us everything. He pays us for the taipan.'

'Whom does he pay?'

'Ask him yourself.'

'The taipan wants to know.' Bourne reached into his pocket and pulled out a stack of folded bills. 'He told me to give you extra money if you cooperated with me. He thinks his head man may be cheating him.'

The woman backed into the wall looking alternately at the money and at Bourne's face. 'If you are lying—'

'Why would I lie? The taipan wants to see me, you know that. You're to bring me to him. He told me to dress like this, to behave this way, to find you and watch his men. How would I know about you if he hadn't told me?'

'Up in the market. You are to see someone.'

'I haven't been there. I came directly down here.' Jason removed several bills. 'We're both working for the taipan. Here, he wants you to take this and leave, but you're not to go up in the street.' He held out the money.

'The taipan is generous,' said the whore, reaching for the bills.

'Which staircase?' asked Bourne, pulling the money back. 'Which level? The taipan didn't know.'

'Over there,' replied the woman, pointing to the far wall. 'The third steps, the second level. The money.'

'Who's on the head man's payroll? Quickly.'

'In the market there is the snake bitch, and the old thief selling bad gold chains from the north, and the wok man with his dirty fish and meat.'

'That's all?'

'We talk. That is all.'

'The taipan's right, he's being cheated. He'll thank you.' Bourne unfolded another bill. 'But I want to be fair. Besides the one with the radio, how many others work for the head man?'

'Three others, also with radios,' said the whore, her eyes fixed on the money, her hand inching forward.

'Here, take it and leave. Head that way and don't go up on the street.'

The woman grabbed the bills and ran down the alley, her high heels clicking, her figure disappearing in the dim light. Bourne watched until she was out of sight, then turned and walked rapidly out of the filthy passageway to the steps. He again assumed a stooped appearance and climbed up into the street. Three guards and a head-head man. He knew what he had to do, and it had to be done quickly. It was 9:36. *A taipan for a wife.*

He found the first guard talking to the fishmonger, talking anxiously with sharp, stabbing gestures. The noise of the crowd was an impediment. The vendor kept shaking his head. Bourne chose a heavyset man near the guard; he rushed forward shoving the unsuspecting onlooker into the guard and side-stepped as the taipan's man recoiled. In the brief melee that erupted, Jason pulled the bewildered guard aside, hammered his knuckles into the base of the man's throat, twisted him as he began to fall, and slashed his rigid hand across the back of the guard's neck at the top of the spine. He dragged the unconscious man across the pavement, apologizing to the crowd in Chinese for his drunken friend. He dropped the guard in the remains of a storefront, took the radio and smashed it.

The taipan's second man required no such tactics. He was off to the side of the crowd by himself, shouting into his radio. Bourne approached, his sorry figure presenting no threat, and he held out his hand, as if he were a beggar. The guard waved him away; it was the last gesture he would remember, for Bourne gripped his wrist, twisted it, and broke the man's arm. Fourteen seconds later the taipan's second guard lay in the shadows of a mound of garbage, his radio thrown into the debris.

The third guard was in conference with the 'snake bitch.' To Bourne's satisfaction, she, too, kept shaking her head as the fishmonger had done; there was a certain loyalty in the Walled City where bribes were concerned. The man pulled out his radio, but had no chance to use it. Jason ran up to him, grabbed the ancient, toothless cobra and thrust its flat head into the man's face. The horrified gasp, followed by a scream, was all the reaction Jason Bourne needed. The nerves in the throat are a magnificent network of immobilizing, cordlike fibres connecting the body organs to the central nervous system. Bourne played upon them swiftly, and once again dragged his victim through the crowd, apologizing profusely, as he left the unconscious guard on a dark patch of concrete. He held the radio up to his ear; there was nothing on the receiver. It was 9:40. One head-head man remained.

The small, middle-aged Chinese in the expensive suit and polished shoes all but held his nose as he raced from one point to another trying to spot his men, reluctant to make the slightest physical contact with the hordes gathered around the vendors' stalls and tables. His lack of height made it hard for him to see. Bourne watched where he was heading, ran ahead of him, then quickly turned around and sent his fist crashing into the executive's lower abdomen. As the Chinese buckled over, Jason reached around the man's waist with his left arm, picked him up and carried the limp figure to a section of the kerb where two men sat, weaving, passing a bottle back and forth. He placed a *Wushu* chop across the banker's neck and dropped him between the two men. Even through their haze the drunken men would make sure their new companion stayed unconscious for a considerable length of time. There were pockets to ransack, clothes and a pair of shoes to be removed. All would bring a price; whatever cash there was would be a bonus for their labours. *9:43.*

Bourne no longer stooped, gone was the chameleon. He rushed across the street overflowing with humanity and raced down the steps and into the alley. He had *done* it! He had removed the Praetorian Guard. *A taipan for a wife!* He reached the staircase – the third staircase in the right wall – and yanked out the remarkable weapon he had purchased from an arms merchant in the Mongkok. As quietly as he could manage, testing each step with a foot, he climbed to the second level. He braced himself outside the door, balanced his weight, lifted his left leg and smashed it into the thin wood.

The door crashed open. He sprang through and crouched, the weapon extended.

Three men faced him, forming a semicircle, each with a gun aimed at his head. Behind them, dressed in a white silk suit, a huge Chinese sat in a chair. The man nodded to his guards.

He had lost. Bourne had miscalculated and David Webb would die. Far more excruciating, he knew Marie's death would soon follow. Let them fire, thought David. Pull the triggers that would mercifully put him out of it! He had killed the only thing that mattered in his life.

'Shoot, goddamn you! *Shoot!*'

11

'Welcome, Mr Bourne,' said the large man in the white silk suit, waving his guards aside. 'I assume you see the logic of putting your gun on the floor and pushing it away from you. There's really no alternative, you know.'

Webb looked at the three Chinese; the man in the centre cracked the hammer back on his automatic. David lowered the gun and shoved it forward. 'You expected me, didn't you?' he asked quietly, getting to his feet, as the guard on his right picked up the weapon.

'We didn't know what to expect – except the unexpected. How did you do it? Are my people dead?'

'No. They're bruised and unconscious, not dead.'

'Remarkable. You thought I was alone here?'

'I was told you travelled with your head man and three others, not six. I thought it was logical. Any more, it seemed to me, would be conspicuous.'

'That's why these men came early to make arrangements and have not left this hole since they arrived. So you thought you could take me, exchange me for your wife.'

'It's obvious that she didn't have a damn thing to do with it. Let her go; she can't hurt you. Kill me but let her go.'

'*Pi ge!*' said the banker, ordering two of the guards out of the flat; they bowed and left quickly. 'This man will remain,' he continued, turning back to Webb. 'Outside of the immense loyalty he has for me, he doesn't speak or understand a word of English.'

'I see you trust your people.'

'I trust no one.' The financier gestured at a dilapidated wooden chair across the shabby room, revealing as he did so a gold Rolex on his wrist, diamonds encrusted around its dial, matching his bejeweled gold cuff links. 'Sit down,' he ordered. 'I've gone to great lengths and spent much money to bring about this conference.'

'Your head man – I assume it was your head man—' said Bourne aimlessly, studying every detail of the room as he walked over to the chair, 'told me not to wear an expensive watch down here. I guess you didn't listen to him.'

'I arrived in a soiled, filthy caftan with sleeves wide enough to conceal it. As I look at your clothes, I'm certain the Chameleon understands.'

'You're Yao Ming.' Webb sat down.

'It is a name I've used, you surely understand. that. The Chameleon goes by many shapes and colours.'

'I didn't kill your wife – or the man who happened to be with her.'

'I know that, Mr Webb.'

'You *what?*' David shot up from the chair and the guard took a rapid step forward, his gun levelled.

'Sit down,' repeated the banker. 'Don't alarm my devoted friend or we both may regret it, you far more than me.'

'You *knew* it wasn't me and still you've *done* this to us!'

'Sit quickly, please.'

'I want an *answer!*' said Webb, sitting down.

'Because you are the true Jason Bourne. That is why you are here, why your wife remains in my custody, and will remain so until you accomplish what I ask of you.'

'I talked to her.'

'I know you did. I permitted it.'

'She didn't sound like herself – even considering the circumstances. She's strong, stronger than I was during those lousy weeks in Switzerland and Paris. Something's *wrong* with her! Is she drugged?'

'Certainly not.'

'Is she *hurt?*'

'In spirit, perhaps, but not in any other way. However, she will be hurt and she *will* die, if you refuse me. Can I be clearer?'

'You're dead, taipan.'

'The true Bourne speaks. That's very good. It's what I need.'

'Spell it out.'

'I am being hounded by someone in your name,' began the taipan, his voice hard, his intensity mounting. 'Far more severely – may the spirits forgive me – than the loss of a young wife. From all sides in all areas, the terrorist, this *new* Jason Bourne, attacks! He kills my people, blows up shipments of valuable merchandise, threatens other taipans with death if they do business with me! His exorbitant fees come from my enemies here in Hong Kong and Macao, and up the Deep Bay water routes, north into the provinces *themselves!*'

'You have a lot of enemies.'

'My interests are extensive.'

'So, I was told, were those of the man I didn't kill in Macao.'

'Oddly enough,' said the banker, breathing hard and gripping the arm of his chair in an effort to control himself. 'He and I were not enemies. In certain areas our interests converged. It's how he met my wife.'

'How convenient. Shared assets, as it were.'

'You are offensive.'

'They're not my rules,' replied Bourne, his eyes cold, levelled at the Oriental. 'Get to the point. My wife's alive and I want her back without a mark on her or a voice raised against her. If she's harmed in any way whatsoever, you and your *Zhongguo ren* won't be any match for what I'll mount against you.'

'You are not in a position to make threats, Mr Webb.'

'Webb isn't,' agreed the once most hunted man in Asia and Europe. 'Bourne is.'

The Oriental looked hard at Jason, then nodded twice as his eyes dropped below Webb's gaze. 'Your audacity matches your arrogance. To the point. It's very simple, very clear-cut.' The taipan suddenly clenched his right hand into a fist, then raised it and crashed it down on the fragile arm of the decrepit chair. 'I want *proof* against my enemies!' he shouted, his angry eyes peering out behind two partially closed walls of swollen flesh. 'The only way I'll get it is for you to bring me this all too credible impostor who takes your place! I want him facing me, *watching* me as he feels his life leaving him in agony until he tells me everything I must know. *Bring* him to me, Jason Bourne!' The banker breathed deeply, then added quietly, 'Then, and only then, will you be reunited with your wife.'

Webb stared at the taipan in silence. 'What makes you think I can do it?' he said finally.

'Who better to trap a pretender than the original?'

'Words,' said Webb. 'Meaningless.'

'He's *studied* you! He's analyzed your methods, your techniques. He could not pass himself off as you if he had not. *Find* him! Trap him with the tactics you yourself created.'

'Just like that?'

'You'll have help. Several names and descriptions, men I am convinced are involved with this new killer who uses an old name.'

'Over in Macao?'

'*Never!* It must *not* be Macao! There's to be no mention, no reference whatsoever to the incident at the Lisboa Hotel. It is closed, finished; you know nothing about it. In no way can my person be associated with what you are doing. You have nothing to do with me! If you surface, you are hunting a man who has assumed your mantle. You are protecting yourself, defending yourself. A perfectly natural thing to do under the circumstances.'

'I thought you wanted proof—'

'It will come when you bring me the *impostor!*' shouted the taipan.

'If not Macao, where then?'

'Here in Kowloon. In the Tsim Sha Tsui. Five men were slain in the back room of a cabaret, among them a banker – like myself, a taipan, my associate from time to time and no less influential – as well as three others whose identities were concealed; apparently it was a government decision. I've never found out who they were.'

'But you know who the fifth man was,' said Bourne.

'He worked for me. He took my place at that meeting. Had I been there myself, your namesake would have killed me. This is where you will start, here in Kowloon, in the Tsim Sha Tsui. I will give you the names of the two known dead and the identities of many men who were the enemies of both, now my enemies. Move quickly. Find the man who kills in your name and bring him to me. And a last warning, Mr Bourne. Should you try to find out who I am, the order will be swift, the execution swifter. Your wife will die.'

'Then so will you. Give me the names.'

'They're on this paper,' said the man who used the name Yao Ming, reaching into the pocket of his white silk vest. 'They were typed by a public stenographer at the Mandarin. There would be no point in trying to trace a specific typewriter.'

'A waste of time,' said Bourne, taking the sheet of paper. 'There must be twenty million typewriters in Hong Kong.'

'But not so many taipans of my size and girth, eh?'

'That I'll remember.'

'I'm sure you will.'

'How do I reach you?'

'You don't. Ever. This meeting never took place.'

'Then why *did* it? Why did everything that's happened take place? Say I manage to find and take this cretin who calls himself Bourne – and it's a damn big *if* – what do I do with him? Leave him on the steps outside here in the Walled City?'

'It could be a splendid idea. Drugged, no one would pay the slightest attention beyond rifling his pockets.'

'*I'd* pay a lot of attention. A prize for a prize, taipan. I want an ironclad guarantee. I want my wife back.'

'What would you consider such a guarantee?'

'First her voice on the phone convincing me she's unharmed, and then I want to see her – say, walking up and down a street under her own power with no one near her.'

'Jason Bourne speaks?'

'He speaks.'

'Very well. We've developed a high-technology industry here in Hong Kong, ask anyone in the electronics business in your country. On the bottom of that page is a telephone number. When and if – and *only* when and if – the impostor is in your hands, call that number and repeat the words "snake lady" several times—'

'*Medusa*,' whispered Jason, interrupting. 'Airborne.'

The taipan arched his brows, his expression noncommittal. 'Naturally, I was referring to the woman in the bazaar.'

'Like hell you were. Go on.'

'As I say, repeat the words several times until you hear a series of clicks—'

'Triggering another number, or numbers,' broke in Bourne again.

'Something to do with the sounds of the phrase, I believe,' agreed the taipan. 'The sibilant *s*, followed by a flat vowel and hard consonants. Ingenious, wouldn't you say?'

'It's called aurally receptive programming, instruments activated by a voice print.'

'Since you're not impressed, do let me emphasize the condition under which the call may be made. For your wife's sake, I hope *it* impresses you. The call is to be placed only when you are prepared to deliver the impostor within a matter of minutes. Should you or anyone else use the number and the code words without that guarantee, I'll know a trace is being put out over the lines. In that event, your wife will be killed, and a dead, disfigured white woman without identification dropped into the waters of the out islands. Do I make myself clear?'

Swallowing, suppressing his fury despite the sickening fear, Bourne spoke icily. 'The condition is understood. Now you understand mine. When and if I make that call, I'll want to speak to my wife – not within minutes but within seconds. If I don't, whoever's on the line will hear the gunshot and you'll know that your assassin, the prize you say you've got to have, has just had his head blown away. You'll have thirty seconds.'

'Your condition is understood and will be met. I'd say the conference is over, Jason Bourne.'

'I want my weapon. One of the guards who left has it.'

'It will be given to you on your way out.'

'He'll take my word for it?'

'He doesn't have to. If you walked out of here, he was to give it to you. A corpse has no need of a gun.'

What remain of the stately homes from Hong Kong's extravagant colonial era are high in the hills above the city in an area known as Victoria Peak, named for the island's mountain summit, the crown of all the territory. Here graceful gardens complement rose-bordered paths that lead to gazebos and verandas from which the wealthy observe the splendours of the harbour below and the out islands in the distance. The residences with the most enviable views are subdued versions of the great houses of Jamaica. They are high-ceilinged and intricate; rooms flow into one another at odd angles to take advantage of summer breezes during that long and oppressive season, and everywhere there is polished carved wood surrounding and reinforcing windows made to withstand the winds and the rains of the mountain winter. Strength and comfort are joined in these minor mansions, the designs dictated by climate.

One such house in the Peak district, however, differed from the others. Not in size or strength or elegance, nor in the beauty of its gardens, which were rather more extensive than many of its neighbours', nor in the impressiveness of its front gate and the height of the stone wall bordering the grounds. Part of what made it seem different was the sense of isolation that surrounded it, especially at night when only a few lights burned in the numerous rooms and no sounds came from the windows or the gardens. It was as if the house were barely inhabited; certainly there was no sign of frivolity. But what dramatically set it apart were the men at the gate and others like them who could be seen from the road patrolling the grounds beyond the wall. They were armed and in fatigue uniforms. They were American marines.

The property was leased by the United States Consulate at the direction of the National Security Council. To any inquiries, the consulate was to comment only that during the next month numerous representatives of the American government and American industry would be flying into the colony at various undetermined times, and security as well as the efficacy of accommodations warranted the lease. It was all the consulate knew. However, selected personnel in British MI6, Special Branch, were given somewhat more information, as their cooperation was deemed necessary and had been authorized by London. However, again, it was limited to an immediate-need-to-know basis, also firmly agreed to by London. Those on the highest levels of both governments, including the closest advisers to the President and the Prime Minister, came to the same conclusion: any disclosures regarding the true nature of the property in Victoria Peak could have catastrophic consequences for the Far East and the world. It was a sterile house, the headquarters of a covert operation so sensitive that even the President and the Prime Minister knew few of the details, only the objectives.

A small sedan drove up to the gate. Instantly, powerful floodlights were tripped, blinding the driver, who brought his arm up to shield his eyes. Two marine guards approached on either side of the vehicle, their weapons drawn.

'You should know the car by now, lads,' said the large Oriental in the white silk suit squinting through the open window.

'We know the car, Major Lin,' replied the lance corporal on the left. 'We just have to make sure of the driver.'

'Who could impersonate me?' joked the huge major.

'Man Mountain Dean, sir,' answered the marine on the right.

'Oh, yes, I recall. An American wrestler.'

'My granddad used to talk about him.'

'Thank you, son. You might have at least said your father. May I proceed or am I impounded?'

'We'll turn off the lights and open the gate, sir,' said the first marine. 'By the way, Major, thanks for the name of that restaurant in the Wanchai. It's a class act and doesn't bust the bankroll.'

'But, alas, you found no Suzie Wong.'

'Who, sir?'

'Never mind. The gate, if you please, lads.'

Inside the house, in the library, which had been converted into an office, Undersecretary of State Edward Newington McAllister sat behind a desk, studying the pages of a dossier under the glare of a lamp, making checkmarks in the margins beside certain paragraphs and certain lines. He was consumed, his attention riveted. The intercom buzzed, and he had to force his eyes and his hand to the telephone. 'Yes?' He listened and replied. 'Send him in, of course.' McAllister hung up and returned to the dossier in front of him, the pencil in his hand. On the top of the page he was reading were the words repeated in the same position on each page: *Ultra Maximum Classified. PRC Internal. Sheng Chou Yang.*

The door opened and the immense Major Lin Wenzu of British Intelligence, MI6, Special Branch, Hong Kong, walked in, closed the door, and smiled at McAllister, who remained absorbed in the dossier.

'It's still the same, isn't it, Edward? Buried in the words there's a pattern, a line to follow.'

'I wish I could find it,' answered the undersecretary of State, reading feverishly.

'You will, my friend. Whatever it is.'

'I'll be with you in a moment.'

'Take your time,' said the major, removing the gold Rolex wristwatch and the cuff links. He placed them on the desk, and spoke quietly. 'Such a pity to give these back. They add a certain presence to my presence. You will, however, pay for the suit, Edward. It's not basic to my wardrobe, but as ever in Hong Kong, it was reasonable, even for one of my size.'

'Yes, of course,' agreed the undersecretary, preoccupied.

Major Lin sat down in the black leather chair in front of the desk, remaining silent for the better part of a minute. It was obvious that he could remain silent no longer. 'Is that anything I might help you with, Edward? Or more to the point, is it anything that pertains to the job at hand? Something you can tell me about?'

'I'm afraid it isn't, Lin. On all counts.'

'You will have to tell us sooner or later. Our superiors in London will have to tell us. "Do what he asks," they say. "Keep records of all conversations and directives, but follow his orders and advise him." *Advise* him? There *is* no advice but tactics. A man in an unoccupied office firing four bullets into the wall of the harbour walk, six into the water, and the rest blanks – thank *God* there were no cardiac arrests – and we've created the situation you want. Now, *that* we can understand—'

'I gather everything went very well.'

'There was a riot, if that's what you mean by "very well." '

'It's what I mean.' McAllister leaned back in his chair, the slender fingers of his right hand massaging his temples.

'Score one, my friend. The authentic Jason Bourne was convinced and he made his moves. Incidentally, you will pay for the hospitalization of one man with a broken arm, and two others who claim they are still in shock with extremely painful necks. The fourth is too embarrassed to say anything.'

'Bourne's very good at what he does – what he did.'

'He's *lethal*, Edward!'

'You handled him, I gather.'

'Thinking every second he'd make another move and blow that filthy room apart! I was petrified. The man's a maniac. Incidentally, why is he to stay out of Macao? It's an odd restriction.'

'There's nothing he can't do from here. The killings took place here. The impostor's clients are obviously here in Hong Kong, not Macao.'

'As usual, that is no answer.'

'Let's put it another way, and this much I can tell you. Actually you already know it, since you played the role tonight. The lie about our mythical taipan's young wife and lover having been murdered in Macao: Any thoughts on it?'

'An ingenious device,' said Lin, frowning. 'Few acts of vengeance are as readily understood as an "eye for an eye." In a sense, it's the basis of your strategy – what I know of it.'

'What do you think Webb would do if he found out it *was* a lie?'

'He couldn't. You made it clear the killings were covered up.'

'You underestimate him. Once in Macao, he'd turn over every piece of garbage to learn who this taipan is. He'd question every bellhop, every maid – probably threaten or bribe a dozen hotel personnel at the Lisboa and most of the police until he learned the truth.'

'But we have his wife, and that is not a lie. He will act accordingly.'

'Yes, but in a different dimension. Whatever he thinks now – and certainly he must have suspicions – he can't know, know for certain. If he digs in Macao, however, and learns the truth, he will have proof that he's been deceived by his government.'

'How, specifically?'

'Because the lie was delivered to him by a senior official of the State Department – namely, me. And by his lights at best, he was betrayed before.'

'That much we do know.'

'I want a man at all times at immigration in Macao – around the clock. Hire people you can trust, and give them photographs but no information. Offer a bonus for anyone who spots him and calls you.'

'It can be done, but he wouldn't risk it. He believes the odds are against him. One informer in the hotel or at police headquarters and his wife dies. He wouldn't take the chance.'

'And we can't take *that* chance, however remote. If he found out that he's being used again – betrayed again – he might come unhinged, do things and say things that would have unthinkable consequences for us all. Frankly, if he heads for Macao, he could become a terrible liability rather than the asset we think we've created.'

'Termination?' asked the major simply.

'I can't use that word.'

'I don't think you'll have to. I was very convincing. I slammed my hand on the chair and raised my voice most effectively. "Your wife will die!" I yelled. He believed me. I should have trained for the opera.'

'You did well.'

'It was a performance worthy of Akim Tamiroff.'

'Who?'

'Please. I went through this at the gate.'

'I beg your pardon?'

'Forget it. In Cambridge they said I'd meet people like you. I had a don in Oriental History who said you can't let go, any of you. You insist on keeping secrets because the *Zhongguo ren* are inferior; they cannot comprehend. Is that the case here, *yang quizi*?'

'Good Lord, no.'

'Then what are we *doing*? The obvious I understand. We recruit a man who's in the unique position of hunting a killer because the killer is impersonating him – impersonating the man he was. But to go to such lengths – kidnapping his wife, involving *us*, these elaborate and, frankly, dangerous games we play. Truthfully, Edward, when you gave me the scenario, I myself questioned London. "Follow orders," they repeated. "Above all, keep silent." Well, as you said a moment ago, it's *not* good enough. We should be told more. Without knowledge, how can Special Branch assume responsibility?'

'For the moment, the responsibility's ours, the decisions ours. London's agreed to that, and they wouldn't have agreed if they weren't convinced it was the best way to go. Everything must be contained; there's no room whatsoever for leakage or miscalculation. Incidentally, those were London's words.' McAllister leaned forward, clasping his hands together, his knuckles white from the grip. 'I'll tell you this much, Lin. I wish to God it *wasn't* our responsibility, especially with me near the centre. Not that I make the final decisions, but I'd rather not make any. I'm not qualified.'

'I wouldn't say that, Edward. You're one of the most thorough men I've ever met, you proved that two years ago. You're a brilliant analyst. You don't have to possess the expertise yourself as long as you take your orders from someone who does. All you need is understanding and conviction – and conviction is written all over your troubled face. You will do the right thing if it is given to you to execute.'

'Thank you, I guess.'

'What you wanted was accomplished tonight, so you'll soon know if your resurrected hunter retains his old skills. During the coming days we can monitor events, but that's all we can do. They're out of our hands. This Bourne begins his dangerous journey.'

'He has the names, then?'

'The *authentic* names, Edward. Among the most vicious members of the Hong Kong-Macao underworld – upper-level soldiers who carry out orders, captains who initiate deals and arrange contracts, violent ones. If there are any in the territory who have knowledge of this impostor-killer, they'll be found on that list.'

'We start phase two. Good.' McAllister unclasped his hands and looked at his watch. 'Good heavens, I had no idea of the time. It's been a long day for you. You certainly didn't have to return the watch and the cuff links tonight.'

'I certainly knew that.'

'Then why?'

'I don't wish to burden you further, but we may have an unforeseen problem. At least one we hadn't considered, perhaps foolishly.'

'What is it?'

'The woman may be ill. Her husband sensed it when he talked with her.'

'You mean *seriously*?'

'We can't rule it out – the doctor can't rule it out.'

'The *doctor?*'

'There was no point in alarming you. I called in one of our medical staff several days ago – he's completely reliable. She wasn't eating and complained of nausea. The doctor thought it might be anxiety or depression, or even a virus, so he gave her antibiotics and mild tranquilizers. She has not improved. In fact, her condition has rapidly deteriorated. She's become listless; she has trembling seizures and her mind appears to wander. None of this is like that woman, I can assure you.'

'It certainly isn't!' said the undersecretary of State as he blinked his eyes rapidly, his lips pursed. 'What can we do?'

'The doctor thinks she should be admitted to the hospital immediately for tests.'

'She *can't* be! Good *Christ*, it's out of the question!'

The Chinese Intelligence officer rose from the chair and approached the desk slowly. 'Edward,' he began calmly. 'I don't know the ramifications of this operation, but I can obviously piece together several basic objectives, especially one. I'm afraid I must ask you: What happens to David Webb if his wife is seriously ill? What happens to your Jason Bourne if she dies?'

12

'I need her medical history, and I want it just as fast as you can provide it, Major. That's an order, sir, from a former lieutenant in Her Majesty's Medical Corps.'

He's the English doctor who examined me. He's very civil, but cold, and, I suspect, a terribly good physician. He's bewildered. That's fine.

'We'll get it for you; there are ways. You say she couldn't tell you the name of her doctor back in the United States?'

That's the huge Chinese who's always polite – unctuous, actually, but rather sincere. He's been nice to me, as his men have been nice to me. He's following orders – they're all following orders – but they don't know why.

'Even in her lucid moments she draws a blank, which is not encouraging. It could be a defence mechanism indicating that she was aware of a progressive illness she wants to block out.'

'She's not that sort, Doctor. She's a strong woman.'

'Psychological strength is relative, Major. Often the strongest among us are loath to accept mortality. The ego refuses it. Get me her history. I *must* have it.'

'A man will call Washington, and people there will make other calls. They know where she lives, her circumstances, and within minutes they'll know her neighbours. Someone will tell us. We'll find her doctor.'

'I want everything on a satellite computer printout. We have the equipment.'

'Any transmission of information must be received at our offices.'

'Then I'll go with you. Give me a few minutes.'

'You're frightened, aren't you, Doctor?'

'If it's a neurological disorder, that's always frightening, Major. If your people can work quickly, perhaps I can talk to her doctor myself. That would be optimum.'

'You found nothing in your examination?'

'Only possibilities, nothing concrete. There *is* pain here, and there *isn't* pain there. I've ordered a CAT scan in the morning.'

'You *are* frightened.'

'Shitless, Major.'

Oh, you're all doing exactly what I wanted you to do. Good God, I'm hungry! I'll eat for five straight hours when I get out of here – and I will get out! David, did you understand? Did you understand what I was telling you? The dark trees are maple trees; they're so common, darling, so identifiable. The single leaf is Canada. The embassy! Here in Hong Kong it's the consulate! That's what we did in Paris, my darling! It was terrible then, but it won't be terrible here. I'll know someone. Back in Ottawa I instructed so many who were being posted all over the world. Your memory is clouded, my love, but mine isn't . . . And you must understand, David, that the people I dealt with then are not so different from the people who are holding me now. In some ways, of course, they're robots, but they're also individuals who think and question and wonder why they are asked to do certain things. But they follow a regimen, darling, because if they don't, they get poor service reports, which is tantamount to a fate worse than dismissal – which rarely happens – because it means no advancement, limbo. They've actually been kind to me – gentle, really – as if they're embarrassed by what they've been ordered to do but must carry out their assignments. They think I'm ill and they're concerned for me, genuinely concerned. They're not criminals or killers, my sweet David. They're bureaucrats in search of direction! They're bureaucrats, David! This whole incredible thing has GOVERNMENT *written all over it. I know! These are the sort of people I worked with for years. I was one of them!*

Marie opened her eyes. The door was closed, the room empty, but she knew a guard was outside – she had heard the Chinese major giving instructions. No one was permitted in her room but the English doctor and two specific nurses the guard had met and who would be on duty until morning. She knew the rules, and with that knowledge she could break them.

She sat up – *Jesus, I'm hungry!* – and was darkly amused at the thought of their neighbours in Maine being questioned about her doctor. She barely knew her neighbours and there *was* no doctor. They had been in the university town less than three months, starting with the late summer session for David's preparations, and with all the problems of renting a house and learning what the new wife of a new associate professor should do, or be, and finding the stores and the laundry and the bedding and the linens – the thousand and ten things a woman does to make a home – there simply had been no time to think about a doctor. Good Lord, they had lived with doctors for eight months, and except for Mo Panov she would have been content never to see another one.

Above all, there was David, fighting his way out of his personal tunnels, as he called them, trying so hard not to show the pain, so grateful when there was light and memory. *God,* how he attacked the books, overjoyed when whole stretches of history came back to him, but the joy was balanced by the anguish of realizing it was only segments of his own life that eluded him. And so often at night she would feel the mattress ripple and know he was getting out of bed to be by himself with his half-thoughts and haunting images. She would wait a few minutes, and then go out into the hallway and sit on the steps, listening. And once in a great while it happened: the quiet sobbing of a strong, proud man in agony. She would go to him and he would turn away; the embarrassment and the hurt were too much. She would say, 'You're not fighting this yourself, darling. We're fighting it together. Just as we fought before.' He would talk then, reluctantly at first, then expanding, the words coming faster and faster until the floodgates burst and he would find things, discover things.

Trees, David! My favourite tree, the maple tree. The maple leaf, David! The consulate, my darling! She had work to do. She reached for the cord and pressed the button for the nurse.

Two minutes later the door opened and a Chinese woman in her mid-forties entered, her nurse's uniform starched and immaculate. 'What can I do for you, my dear?' she said pleasantly, in pleasantly accented English.

'I'm dreadfully tired, but I'm having a terrible time getting to sleep. May I have a pill that might help me?'

'I'll check with your doctor; he's still here. I'm sure it will be all right.' The nurse left and Marie got out of bed. She went to the door, the ill-fitting hospital gown slipping down over her left shoulder, and with the air conditioning, the slit in the back bringing a chill. She opened the door, startling the muscular young guard who sat in a chair on the right.

'Yes, Mrs . . . ?' The guard jumped up.

'*Shhh!*' ordered Marie, her index finger at her lips. 'Come in here! *Quickly!*'

Bewildered, the young Chinese followed her into the room. She walked rapidly to the bed and climbed on it but did not pull up the covers. She sloped her right shoulder; the gown slipped off, held barely in place by the swell of her breast.

'Come here!' she whispered. 'I don't want anyone to hear me.'

'What is it, lady?' asked the guard, his gaze avoiding Marie's exposed flesh and focusing instead on her face and her long auburn hair. He took several steps forward, but still kept his distance. 'The door is closed. No one can hear you.'

'I want you to—' Her whisper fell below an audible level.

'Even I can't hear you, Mrs . . .' The man moved closer.

'You're the nicest of my guards. You've been very kind to me.'

'There was no reason to be otherwise, lady.'

'Do you know why I'm being held?'

'For your own safety,' the guard lied, his expression noncommittal.

'I see.' Marie heard the footsteps outside drawing nearer. She shifted her body; the gown travelled down, baring her legs. The door opened and the nurse entered.

'*Oh?*' The Chinese woman was startled. It was obvious that her eyes appraised a distasteful scene. She looked at the embarrassed guard as Marie covered herself. 'I wondered why you were not outside.'

'The lady asked to speak with me,' replied the man, stepping back.

The nurse glanced quickly at Marie. 'Yes?'

'If that's what he says.'

'This is foolish,' said the muscular guard, going to the door and opening it. 'The lady's not well,' he added. 'Her mind strays. She says foolish things.' He went out the door and closed it firmly behind him.

Again the nurse looked at Marie, her eyes now questioning. 'Do you feel all right?' she asked.

'My mind does not stray, and I'm not the one who says foolish things. But I do as I'm told.' Marie paused, then continued. 'When that giant of a major leaves the hospital, please come and see me. I have something to tell you.'

'I'm sorry, I cannot do that. You must rest. Here, I have a sedative for you. I see you have water.'

'You're a *woman*,' said Marie, staring hard at the nurse.

'Yes,' agreed the Oriental flatly. She placed a tiny paper cup with a pill in it on Marie's bedside table and returned to the door. She took a last, questioning look at her patient and left.

Marie got off the bed and walked silently to the door. She put her ear to the metal panel; outside in the corridor she heard the muffled sounds of a rapid exchange, obviously in Chinese. Whatever was said and however the brief, excited conversation was resolved, she had planted the seed. *Work on the visual*, Jason Bourne had emphasized and reemphasized during the hell they had gone through in Europe. *It's more effective than anything else. People will draw the conclusions you want on the basis of what they see far more than from the most convincing lies you can tell them.*

She went to the clothes closet and opened it. They had left the few things they had bought for her in Hong Kong at the apartment, but the slacks, blouse, and shoes she had worn the day they brought her to the hospital were hanging up; it had not occurred to anyone to remove them. Why should they have? They could see for themselves that she was a very sick woman. The trembling and spasms had convinced them; they saw it all. Jason Bourne would understand. She glanced at the small white telephone on the bedside table. It was a flat, self-contained unit, the panel of touch buttons built into the instrument. She wondered, although there was no one she could think of calling. She went to the table and picked it up. It was dead, as she expected it would be. There was the signal for the nurse; it was all she needed and all she was permitted.

She walked to the window and raised the white shade, only to greet the night. The dazzling, coloured lights of Hong Kong lit up the sky, and she was closer to the sky than to the ground. As David would say – or rather, Jason: *So be it. The door. The corridor.*

So be it.

She crossed to the washbasin. The hospital-supplied toothbrush and toothpaste were still encased in plastic; the soap was also virginal, wrapped in the manufacturer's jacket, the words guaranteeing purity beyond the breath of angels.

Next there was the bathroom; nothing much different except a dispenser of sanitary napkins and a small sign in four languages explaining what not to do with them. She walked back into the room. What was she looking for? Whatever it was she had not found it.

Study everything. You'll find something you can use. Jason's words, not David's. Then she saw it.

On certain hospital beds – and this was one of them – there is a handle beneath the baseboard that when turned one way or the other raises or lowers the bed. This handle can be removed – and often is – when a patient is being fed intravenously, or if a physician wants him to remain in a given position – for example, in traction. A nurse can unlock and remove this handle by pressing in, turning to the left, and yanking it out as the cog lock is released. This is frequently done during visiting hours, when visitors might succumb to a patient's wishes to change position against the doctor's wishes. Marie knew this bed and she knew this handle. When David was recovering from the wounds he received at Treadstone 71, he was kept alive by intravenous feedings; she had watched the nurses. Her soon-to-be husband's pain was more than she could bear, and the nurses were obviously aware that in her desire to make things easier for him, she might disrupt the medical treatment. She knew how to remove the handle, and once removed, it was nothing less than a wieldy angle iron.

She removed it and climbed back into the bed, the handle beneath the covers. She waited, thinking how different her two men were – in one man. Her lover, Jason, could be so cold and patient, waiting for the moment to spring, to shock, to rely for survival upon violence. And her husband, David, so giving, so willing to listen – the scholar – avoiding violence at all costs because he had been there and he hated the pain and the anxiety – above all, the necessity to eliminate one's feelings to become a mere animal. And now he was called upon to be the man he detested. David, my *David!* Hold on to your *sanity!* I love you so.

Noises in the corridor. Marie looked at the clock on the bedside table. Sixteen minutes had passed. She placed both her hands above the covers as the nurse entered, lowering her eyelids as though she were drowsy.

'All right, my dear,' said the woman, taking several steps from the door. 'You have touched me, I will not deny that. But I have my orders – very specific instructions about you. The major and your doctor have left. Now, what is it you wanted to tell me?'

'Not . . . now,' whispered Marie, her head sinking into her chin, her face more asleep than awake, 'I'm so tired. I took . . . the pill.'

'Is it the guard outside?'

'He's sick . . . He never touches me – I don't care. He gets me things . . . I'm *so* tired.'

'What do you mean, "sick"?'

'He . . . likes to look at women . . . He doesn't . . . bother me when I'm . . . asleep.' Marie's eyes closed.

'*Zang!*' said the nurse under her breath. 'Dirty, *dirty!*' She spun on her heels, walked out the door, closed it, and addressed the guard. 'The woman is asleep! Do you understand me!'

'That is most heavenly fortunate.'

'She says you never touch her!'

'I never even thought about it.'

'Don't think about it now!'

'I do not need lectures from you, hag nurse. I have a job to do.'

'See that you do it! I will speak to Major Lin Wenzu in the morning!' The woman glared at the man and walked down the corridor, her pace and her posture aggressive.

'*You!*' The harsh whisper came from Marie's door, which was slightly ajar. She opened it an inch further and spoke. 'That *nurse!* Who is she?'

'I thought you were asleep, Mrs . . .' said the bewildered guard.

'She told me she was going to tell you that.'

'What?'

'She's coming *back* for me! She says there are connecting doors to the other rooms. Who *is* she?'

'She *what?*'

'Don't talk! Don't look at me! She'll *see* you!'

'She went down the hallway to the right.'

'You never can tell. Better a devil you know than one you don't! You know what I mean?'

'I do not know what *anybody* means!' pleaded the guard, talking softly, emphatically, to the opposite wall. 'I do not know what *she* means and I do not know what *you* mean, lady!'

'Come inside. *Quickly!* I think she's a Communist! From Peking!'

'*Beijing?*'

'I won't *go* with her!' Marie pulled back the door, then spun behind it.

The guard rushed in as the door slammed shut. The room was dark; only the light in the bathroom was on, its glow diminished by the bathroom door, which was nearly closed. The man could be seen, but he could not see. 'Where are you, Mrs . . . ? Be calm. She will not take you anywhere—'

The guard was not capable of saying anything further. Marie had crashed the iron handle across the base of his skull with the strength of an Ontario ranch girl quite used to the bullwhip in a cattle drive. The guard collapsed; she knelt down and worked quickly.

The Chinese was muscular but not large, not tall. Marie was not large, but she was tall for a woman. With a hitch here and a tuck there, the guard's clothes and shoes fit reasonably well for a fast exit, but her hair was the problem. She looked around the room. *Study everything. You'll find something you can use.* She found it. Hanging from a chrome bar on the bedside table was a hand towel. She pulled it off, piled her hair on top of her head and wrapped the towel around it, tucking the cloth within itself. It undoubtedly looked foolish and could hardly bear close scrutiny, but it *was* a turban of sorts.

Stripped to his undershorts and socks, the guard moaned and began to raise himself, then collapsed back into unconsciousness. Marie ran to the closet, grabbed her own clothes, and went to the door, opening it cautiously, no more than an inch. Two nurses – one Oriental, the other European – were talking quietly in the hallway. The Chinese was not the woman who had returned to hear her complaint about the guard. Another nurse appeared, nodded to the two, and went directly to a door across the hall. It was a linen supply closet. A telephone rang at the floor desk fifty feet down the hallway; before the circular desk was a bisecting corridor. An EXIT sign hung from the ceiling, the arrow pointing to the right. The two conversing nurses turned and started toward the desk; the third left the linen closet carrying a handful of sheets. *The cleanest escape is one done in stages, using whatever confusion there is.*

Marie slipped out of the room and ran across the hall to the linen closet. She went inside and closed the door. Suddenly, a woman's roar of protest filled the hallway, petrifying her. She could hear heavy racing footsteps, coming closer; then more footsteps.

'The guard!' yelled the Chinese nurse in English. 'Where is that dirty guard?'

Marie opened the closet door less than an inch. Three excited nurses were in front of her hospital room; they burst inside.

'You! You took off your clothes! *Zangsile* dirty man! Look in the bathroom!'

'You!' yelled the guard unsteadily. 'You let her get *away!* I will hold you for my superiors.'

'Let me go, filthy man! You lie!'

'You are a *Communist!* From *Beijing!*'

Marie slipped out of the linen closet, a stack of towels over her shoulder, and ran to the bisecting corridor and the EXIT sign.

'*Call Major Lin! I've caught a Communist infiltrator!*'

'*Call the police! He is a pervert!*'

Out on the hospital grounds, Marie ran into the parking lot, into the darkest area, and sat breathless in the shadows between two cars. She had to think; she had to appraise the situation. She could not make any mistakes. She dropped the towels and her clothes and began going through the guard's pockets, looking for a wallet or a billfold. She found it, opened it, and counted the money in the dim light. There was slightly more than $600 Hong Kong, which was slightly less than $100 American. It was barely enough for a hotel room; then she saw a credit card issued by a Kowloon bank. *Don't leave home without it.* If she had to, she would present the card – if she had to – and if she could find a hotel room. She removed the money and the plastic card, put the wallet back into the pocket, and began the awkward process of changing clothes while studying the streets beyond the hospital grounds. To her relief, they were crowded, and those crowds were her immediate security.

A car suddenly raced into the parking lot, its tires screeching, as it careened in front of the EMERGENCY door. Marie rose and looked through the automobile windows. The heavyset Chinese major and the cold, precise doctor leaped out of the car and raced toward the entrance. As they disappeared through the doors, Marie ran out of the parking lot and into the street.

She walked for hours, stopping to gorge herself at a fast-food restaurant until she could not stand the sight of another hamburger. She went to the ladies' room and looked at herself in the mirror. She had lost weight and there were dark circles under her eyes, yet withal, she was herself. But the damned *hair!* They would be scouring Hong Kong for her, and the first items of any description would be her height and her hair. She could do little about the former, but she could drastically modify the latter. She stopped at a pharmacy and bought bobby pins and several clasps. Then remembering what Jason had asked her to do in Paris when her photograph appeared in the newspapers, she pulled her hair back, securing it into a bun, and pinned both sides close to her head. The result was a much harsher face, heightened by the loss of weight and no makeup. It was the effect Jason – *David* – had wanted in Paris . . . No, she reflected, it was not David in Paris. It was Jason Bourne. And it was night, as it had been in Paris.

'Why you do that, miss?' asked a clerk standing near the mirror at the cosmetics counter. 'You have such pretty hair, very beautiful.'

'Oh? I'm tired of brushing it, that's all.'

Marie left the pharmacy, bought flat sandals from a vendor on the street, and an imitation Gucci purse from another – the *G*'s were upside down. She had $45 American left and no idea where she would spend the night. It was both too late and too soon to go to the consulate. A Canadian arriving after midnight asking for a roster of personnel would send out alarms; also she had not had time to figure out how to make the request. Where could she go? She needed sleep. *Don't make your moves when you're tired or exhausted. The margin for error is too great. Rest is a weapon. Don't forget it.*

She passed an arcade that was closing up. A young American couple in blue jeans were bargaining with the owner of a T-shirt stand.

'Hey, come on, man,' said the youthful male. 'You want to make just *one* more sale tonight, don't you? I mean, so you cut your profit a bit, but it's still a few *dineros* in your pocket, right?'

'No *dineros*,' cried the merchant, smiling. 'Only dollars, and you offer too few! I have children. You take the precious food from their mouths!'

'He probably owns a restaurant,' said the girl.

'You want restaurant? Authentic-real Chinese food?'

'Jesus, you're right, Lacy!'

'My third cousin on my father's side has an exquisite stand two streets from here. Very near, very cheap, very good.'

'Forget it,' said the boy. 'Four bucks, US, for the six T's. Take it or leave it.'

'I take. Only because you are too strong for me.' The merchant grabbed the proffered bills and shoved the T-shirts into a paper bag.

'You're a wonder, Buzz.' The girl kissed him on the cheek and laughed. 'He's still working on a four hundred percent markup.'

'That's the trouble with you business majors! You don't consider the aesthetics. The smell of the hunt, the pleasure of the verbal conflict!'

'If we ever get married, I'll be supporting you for the rest of my miserable life, you great negotiator.'

Opportunities will present themselves. Recognize them, act on them. Marie approached the two students.

'Excuse me,' she said, speaking primarily to the girl. 'I overheard you talking—'

'Wasn't I *terrific?*' broke in the young man.

'Very agile,' replied Marie. 'But I suspect your friend has a point. Those T-shirts undoubtedly cost him less than twenty-five cents apiece.'

'Four hundred percent,' said the girl, nodding. 'Keystone should be so lucky.'

'Key *who?*'

'A jeweller's term,' explained Marie. 'It's one hundred percent.'

'I'm surrounded by philistines!' cried the young man. 'I'm an art history major. Someday I'll run the Metropolitan!'

'Just don't try to buy it,' said the girl, turning to Marie. 'I'm sorry, we're not flakes, we're just having fun. We interrupted you.'

'It's most embarrassing, really, but my plane was a day late and I missed my tour into China. The hotel is full and I wondered—'

'You need a place to crash?'interrupted the art history student.

'Yes, I do. Frankly, my funds are adequate but limited. I'm a schoolteacher from Maine – economics, I'm afraid.'

'Don't be,' said the girl, smiling.

'I'm joining my tour tomorrow, but I'm afraid that's tomorrow, not tonight.'

'We can help you, can't we, Lacy?'

'I'm sure we can. Our college has an arrangement with the Chinese University of Hong Kong.'

'It's not much on room service but the price is right,' said the young man. 'Three bucks, US, a night. But, holy roller, are they antediluvian!'

'He means there's a certain puritan code over here. The sexes are separated.'

'"Boys and girls together – "' sang the art history major. 'Like *hell* they are!' he added.

Marie sat on the cot in the huge room under a 50-foot ceiling; she assumed it was a gymnasium. All around her young women were asleep and not asleep. Most were silent, but a few snored, others lighted cigarettes, and there were sporadic lurchings toward the bathroom, where the fluorescent lights remained on. She was among children, and she wished she were a child now, free of the terrors that were everywhere. *David, I need you! You think I'm so strong, but, darling, I can't cope! What do I do? How do I do it!*

Study everything, you'll find something you can use – Jason Bourne.

13

The rain was torrential, pitting the sand, snapping into the floodlights that lit up the grotesque statuary of Repulse Bay – reproductions of enormous Chinese gods, angry myths of the Orient in furious poses, some rising as high as thirty feet. The dark beach was deserted, but there were crowds in the old hotel up by the road and the anachronistic hamburger shop across the way. They were strollers and drop-ins, tourists and islanders alike, who had come down to the bay for a late-night drink or something to eat and to look out at the forbidding statues repelling whatever malign spirits might at any moment emerge from the sea. The sudden downpour had forced the strollers inside; others waited for the storm to let up before heading home.

Drenched, Bourne crouched in the foliage twenty feet from the base of a fierce-looking idol halfway down on the beach. He wiped the rain from his face as he stared at the concrete steps that led to the entrance of the old Colonial Hotel. He was waiting for the third name on the taipan's list.

The first man had tried to trap him on the Star Ferry, the agreed-upon meeting ground, but Jason, wearing the same clothes he had worn at the Walled City, had spotted the man's two stalking patrols. It was not as easy as looking for men with radios, but it had not been difficult, either. By the third trip across the harbour, Bourne not having appeared at the appointed window on the starboard side, the same two men had passed by his contact twice, each speaking briefly, and each going to opposite positions, their eyes fixed on their superior. Jason had waited until the ferry approached the pier and the passengers started en masse toward the exit ramp in the bow. He had taken out the Chinese on the right with a blow to the kidneys as he passed him in the crowd, then struck the back of the man's head with the heavy brass paperweight; the passengers rushed by in the dim light. Bourne then walked through the emptying benches to the other side; he faced the second man, jammed his gun into the patrol's stomach and marched him to the stern. He arched the man above the railing and shoved him overboard as the ship's whistle blew in the night and the ferry pulled into the Kowloon pier. He then returned to his contact by the deserted window at midship.

'You kept your word,' Jason said. 'I'm afraid I'm late.'

'*You* are the one who called?' The contact's eyes had roamed over Bourne's shabby clothes.

'I'm the one.'

'You don't look like a man with the money you spoke of on the telephone.'

'You're entitled to that opinion.' Bourne withdrew a folded stack of American bills, $1,000 denominations visible when rolled open.

'You are the man.' The Chinese had glanced quickly over Jason's shoulders. 'What is it that you want?' the man asked anxiously.

'Information about someone for hire who calls himself Jason Bourne.'

'You have reached the wrong person.'

'I'll pay generously.'

'I have nothing to sell.'

'I think you do.' Bourne had put away the money and pulled out his weapon, moving closer to the man as the Kowloon passengers streamed on board. 'You'll either tell me what I want to know for a fee, or you'll be forced to tell me for your life.'

'I know only this,' the Chinese had protested. 'My people will not *touch* him!'

'Why not?'

'He's not the same man!'

'What did you say?' Jason held his breath, watching the man closely.

'He takes risks he would never have taken before.' The Chinese again looked beyond Bourne; sweat broke out on his hairline. 'He comes back after two years. Who knows what happened? Drink, narcotics, disease from whores, who knows?'

'What do you mean, "risks"?'

'That is *what* I mean! He walks into a cabaret in the Tsim Sha Tsui – there was a riot, the police were on their way. Still, he enters and kills five men! He could have been caught, his clients traced! He would not have done such a thing two years ago.'

'You may have your sequence backward,' said Jason Bourne. 'He may have gone in – as one man – and started the riot. He kills *as* that man, and leaves as another, escaping in the confusion.'

The Oriental stared briefly into Jason's eyes, suddenly more frightened than before as he again looked at the shabby, ill-fitting clothes in front of him. 'Yes, I imagine that is possible,' he said tremulously, now whipping his head first to one side, then the other.

'How can this Bourne be reached?'

'I don't know, I swear on the *spirits!* Why do you ask me these questions?'

'*How?*' repeated Jason, leaning into the man, their foreheads touching, the gun shoved into the Oriental's lower abdomen. 'If you won't touch him, you know where he *can* be touched, where he can be reached! Now, *where?*'

'Oh, Christian *Jesus.*'

'Goddamn it, not Him! *Bourne!*'

'*Macao!* It is whispered he works out of Macao, that is all I know, I *swear* it!' The man looked in panic to his right and left.

'If you're trying to find your two men, don't bother, I'll tell you,' said Jason. 'One's in a clump over there, and I hope the other can swim.'

'Those men are – Who *are* you?'

'I think you know,' Bourne had answered. 'Go to the back of the ferry and stay there. If you take one step forward before we dock, you'll never take another.'

'Oh, God, you *are*—'

'I wouldn't finish that if I were you.'

The second name was accompanied by an unlikely address, a restaurant in Causeway Bay that specialized in classic French food. According to Yao Ming's brief notes, the man acted as the manager, but was actually the owner, and a number of the waiters were as adept with guns as they were with trays. The contact's home address was not known; all his business was done at the restaurant, and it was suspected that he had no permanent residence. Bourne had returned to the Peninsula, discarded his jacket and hat, and walked rapidly through the crowded lobby to the elevator; a well-dressed couple had tried not to show their shock at his appearance. He had smiled and muttered apologetically.

'A company treasure hunt. It's kind of silly, isn't it.'

In his room, he had permitted himself a few moments to be David Webb again. It was a mistake; he could not stand the suspension of Bourne's train of thought. *I'm him again. I have to be. He knows what to do. I don't!* . . . He had showered off the filth of the Walled City and the oppressive humidity of the Star Ferry, shaved away the shadow on his face, and dressed for a late French dinner.

I'll find him, Marie! I swear to Christ I'll find him! It was David Webb's promise, but it was Jason Bourne who shouted in fury.

The restaurant looked more like an exquisite rococo dining palace on Paris's Avenue Montaigne than a one-storey structure in Hong Kong. Intricate chandeliers hung from the ceiling with the tiny bulbs dimmed; encased candles flickered on tables with the purest linen and the finest silver and crystal.

'I'm afraid we have no tables this evening, monsieur,' the maître d' said. He was the only Frenchman in evidence.

'I was told to ask for Jiang Yu and say it was urgent,' Bourne had replied, showing a \$100 bill, American. 'Do you think *he* might find something, if this finds him?'

'*I* will find it, monsieur.' The maître d' subtly shook Jason's hand, receiving the money. 'Jiang Yu is a fine member of our small community, but it is I who select. *Comprenez-vous?*'

'*Absolument.*'

'*Bien!* You have the face of an attractive, sophisticated man. This way, please, monsieur.'

The dinner was not to be had; events occurred too quickly. Within minutes after the arrival of his drink, a slender Chinese in a black suit had appeared at his table. If there was anything odd about him, thought David Webb, it was in the darker colour of his skin and the larger slope of his eyes. Malaysian was in his bloodline. *Stop it!* commanded Bourne. *That doesn't do us any good!*

'You asked for me?' said the manager, his eyes searching the face that looked up at him. 'How can I be of service?'

'By first sitting down.'

'It is most irregular to sit with guests, sir.'

'Not really. Not if you own the place. Please. Sit down.'

'Is this another tiresome intrusion by the Bureau of Taxation? If so, I hope you enjoy your dinner, which you will pay for. My records are quite clear and quite accurate.'

'If you think I'm British, you haven't listened to me. And if by "tiresome" you mean that half a million dollars is boring, then you can get the hell out of my sight and I'll enjoy my dinner.' Bourne leaned back in the booth and sipped his drink with his left hand. His right was hidden.

'Who *sent* you?' asked the Oriental of mixed blood, as he sat down.

'Move away from the edge. I want to talk very quietly.'

'Yes, of course.' Jiang Yu inched his way directly opposite Bourne. 'I must ask. Who sent you?'

'I must ask,' said Jason, 'do you like American movies? Especially our Westerns?'

'Of course. American films are beautiful, and I admire the movies of your old West most of all. So poetic in retribution, so righteously violent. Am I saying the correct words?'

'Yes, you are. Because right now you're in one.'

'I beg your pardon?'

'I have a very special gun under the table. It's aimed between your legs.' Within the space of a second, Jason held back the cloth, pulled up the weapon so the barrel could be seen, and immediately shoved the gun back into place. 'It has a silencer that reduces the sound of a forty-five to the pop of a champagne cork, but not the impact. *Liao jie ma?*'

'*Liao jie . . .*' said the Oriental, rigid, breathing deeply in fear. 'You are with Special Branch?'

'I'm with no one but myself.'

'There is no half million dollars, then?'

'There's whatever you consider your life is worth.'

'Why *me?*'

'You're on a list,' Bourne answered truthfully.

'For *execution?*' whispered the Chinese, gasping, his face contorted.

'That depends on you.'

'I must pay you not to *kill* me?'

'In a sense, yes.'

'I don't carry half a million dollars in my pockets! Nor here on the premises!'

'Then pay me something else.'

'*What?* How *much?* You confuse me!'

'Information instead of money.'

'What information?' asked the Chinese as his fear turned into panic. 'What information would *I* have? Why come to *me?*'

'Because you've had dealings with a man I want to find. The one for hire who calls himself Jason Bourne.'

'*No!* Never did it happen!'

The Oriental's hands began to tremble. The veins in his throat throbbed, and his eyes for the first time strayed from Jason's face. The man had lied.

'You're a liar,' said Bourne quietly, pushing his right arm further underneath the table as he leaned forward. 'You made the connection in Macao.'

'Macao, *yes!* But *no* connection. I swear on the graves of my family for generations!'

'You're very close to losing your stomach and your life. You were sent to Macao to reach him!'

'I was sent, but I did *not* reach him!'

'Prove it to me. How were you to make contact?'

'The *Frenchman.* I was to stand on the top steps of the burned-out Basilica of St Paul on the Calcada. I was to wear a black kerchief around my neck and when a man came up to me – a Frenchman – and remarked about the beauty of the ruins, I was to say the following words: "Cain is for Delta." If he replied, "And Carlos is for Cain," I was to accept him as the link to Jason Bourne. But I *swear* to you, he never—'

Bourne did not hear the remainder of the man's protestations. Staccato explosions erupted in his head; his mind was thrown back. Blinding white light filled his eyes, the crashing sounds were unbearable. *Cain is for Delta and Carlos is for Cain . . . Cain is for Delta! Delta One is Cain! Medusa moves; the snake sheds his skin. Cain is in Paris and Carlos will be his!* They were the words, the codes, the challenges hurled at the Jackal. *I am Cain and I am superior and I am here! Come find me, Jackal! I dare you to find Cain, for he kills better than you do. You'd better find me before I find you, Carlos. You're no match for Cain!*

Good God! Who halfway across the world would know those words – *could* know them? They were locked away in the deepest archives of covert operations! They were a direct connection to *Medusa!*

Bourne had nearly squeezed the trigger of the unseen automatic, so sudden was the shock of this incredible revelation. He removed his index finger, placing it around the trigger housing; he had come close to killing a man for revealing extraordinary information. But how could it have *happened?* Who was the conduit to the new 'Jason Bourne' that *knew* such things?

He had to come down, he knew that. His silence was betraying him, betraying his astonishment. The Chinese was staring at him; the man was inching his hand beyond the edge of the booth. 'Pull that back, or your balls and your stomach will be blown away.'

The Oriental's shoulder yanked up and his hand appeared on the table. 'What I have told you is true,' the man said. 'The Frenchman never came to me. If he had, I would tell you everything. So would you if you were me. I protect only myself.'

'Who sent you to make the contact? Who gave you the words to use?'

'That is honestly beyond me, you must believe that. All is done by telephone through second and third parties who know only the information they carry. The proof of integrity is in the arrival of the funds I am paid.'

'How do they arrive? Someone has to give them to you.'

'Someone who is a no one, who is hired himself. An unfamiliar host of an expensive dinner party will ask to see the manager. I will accept his compliments and during our conversation an envelope will be slipped to me. I will have ten thousand American dollars for reaching the Frenchman.'

'Then what? How do you reach him?'

'One goes to Macao, to the Kam Pek casino in the downtown area. It is mostly for the Chinese, for the games of *fan-tan* and *dai sui*. One goes to Table Five and leaves the telephone number of a Macao hotel – not a private telephone – and a name, any name, not one's own, naturally.'

'He calls you at that number?'

'He may or he may not. You stay twenty-four hours in Macao. If he has not called you by then, you have been turned down because the Frenchman has no time for you.'

'Those are the rules?'

'Yes. I was turned down twice, and the single time I was accepted he did not appear at the Calcada steps.'

'Why do you think you were turned down? Why do you think he didn't show up?'

'I have no idea. Perhaps he has too much business for his master killer. Perhaps I said the wrong things to him on the first two occasions. Perhaps on the third he thought he saw suspicious men on the Calcada, men he believed were with me and meant him no good. There were no such people, naturally, but there is no appeal.'

'Table Five. The dealers,' said Bourne.

'The croupiers change constantly. His arrangement is with the table. A blanket fee, I imagine. To be divided. And certainly he does not go to the Kam Pek himself – he undoubtedly hires a whore from the streets. He is very cautious, very professional.'

'Do you know anyone else who's tried to reach this Bourne?' asked Bourne. 'I'll know if you're lying.'

'I think you would. You are obsessed – which is not my business – and you trapped me in my first denial. No, I do not, sir. That is the truth, for I do not care to have my intestines blown away with the sound of a champagne cork.'

'You can't get much more basic than that. In the words of another man, I think I believe you.'

'*Believe*, sir. I am only a courier – an expensive one, perhaps – but a courier, nevertheless.'

'Your waiters are something else, I'm told.'

'They have not been noticeably observant.'

'You'll still accompany me to the door,' he had said.

And now there was the third name, a third man, in the downpour at Repulse Bay.

The contact had responded to the code: '*Écoutez, monsieur. "Cain is for Delta and Carlos is for Cain."*'

'We were to meet in Macao!' the man had shrieked over the telephone. 'Where *were* you?'

'Busy,' said Jason.

'You may be too late. My client has very little time and he is very knowledgeable. He hears that your man moves elsewhere. He is disturbed. You promised him, Frenchman!'

'Where does he think my man is going?'

'On another assignment, of course. He's heard the details!'

'He's wrong. The man is available if the price is met.'

'Call me back in several minutes. I will speak to my client and see if matters are to be pursued.'

Bourne had called five minutes later. Consent was given, the rendezvous set. Repulse Bay. One hour. The statue of the war god halfway down the beach on the left toward the pier. The contact would wear a black kerchief around his neck; the code was to remain the same.

Jason looked at his watch; it was twelve minutes past the hour. The contact was late, and the rain was not a problem – on the contrary, it was an advantage, a natural cover. Bourne had scouted every foot of the meeting ground, forty feet in every direction that had a sight line to the statue of the idol, and he had done so after the appointed time, using up minutes as he kept his eyes on the path to the statue. Nothing so far was irregular. There was no trap in the making.

The *Zhongguo ren* came into view, his shoulders hunched as he dashed down the steps in the downpour, as if the shape of his body would ward off the rain. He ran along the path toward the statue of the war god and stopped as he approached the huge, snarling idol. He skirted the wash of the floodlights, but what could briefly be seen of his face conveyed his anger at finding no one in sight.

'Frenchman, *Frenchman!*'

Bourne raced back through the foliage toward the steps, checking once more before rendezvous, reducing his vulnerability. He edged his way around the thick stone post that bordered the steps and peered through the rain at the upper path to the hotel. He saw what he hoped to God he would *not* see! A man in a raincoat and hat came out of the run-down Colonial Hotel and broke into a fast walk. Halfway to the steps he stopped, pulling something out of his pocket; he turned; there was a slight glow of light . . . returned instantly by a corresponding tiny flash at one of the windows of the crowded lobby. Penlights. Signals. A scout was on his way to a forward post, as his relay or his backup confirmed communications. Jason spun around and retraced the path he had made through the drenched foliage.

'*Frenchman*, where *are* you?'

'Over here!'

'Why did you not answer? *Where?*'

'Straight ahead. The bushes in front of you. *Hurry up!*'

The contact approached the foliage; he was an arm's length away. Bourne sprang up and grabbed him, spinning him around and pushing him further into the wet bushes, as he did so clamping his left hand over the man's mouth. 'If you want to live, don't make a sound!'

Thirty feet into the shoreline woods, Jason slammed the contact into the trunk of a tree. 'Who's with you?' he asked harshly, slowly removing his hand from the man's mouth.

'*With* me? *No* one is with me!'

'Don't *lie!*' Bourne pulled out his gun and placed it against the contact's throat. The Chinese crashed his head back into the tree, his eyes wide, his mouth gaping. 'I don't have time for traps!' continued Jason. 'I don't have *time!*'

'And there is no one *with* me! My word in these matters is my livelihood! Without it I have no profession!'

Bourne stared at the man. He put the gun back in his belt, gripped the contact's arm and propelled him to the right. 'Be quiet. Come with me.'

Ninety seconds later Jason and the contact had crawled through the soaking wet underbrush toward an area of the path some twenty-odd feet to the west of the massive idol. The downpour covered whatever noises might have been picked up on a dry night. Suddenly, Bourne grabbed the Oriental's shoulder, stopping him. Up ahead the scout could be seen, crouching, hugging the border of the path, a gun in his hand. For a moment he crossed through a wash of the statue's floodlight before he disappeared; it was only for an instant, but it was enough. Bourne looked at the contact.

The Chinese was stunned. He could not take his eyes off the spot in the light where the scout had crossed through. His thoughts were coming to him rapidly, the terror in him building; it was in his stare. '*Shi*,' he whispered. '*Jiagian!*'

'In short English words,' said Jason, speaking through the rain. 'That man's an executioner?'

'*Shi!* . . . Yes.'

'Tell me, what have you brought me?'

'Everything,' answered the contact, still in shock. 'The first money, the instructions . . . everything.'

'A client doesn't send money if he's going to kill the man he's hiring.'

'I know,' said the contact softly, nodding his head and closing his eyes. 'It is me they want to kill.'

His words to Liang on the harbour walk had been prophetic, thought Bourne. '*It's not a trap for me . . . It's for you . . . You did your job and they can't allow any traces . . . They can't afford you any longer.*'

'There's another up at the hotel. I saw them signalling each other with flashlights. It's why I couldn't answer you for several minutes.'

The Oriental turned and looked at Jason; there was no self-pity in his eyes. 'The risks of my profession,' he said simply. 'As my foolish people say, I will join my ancestors, and I hope they are not so foolish. Here.' The contact reached into his inside pocket and withdrew an envelope. 'Here is everything.'

'Have you checked it out?'

'Only the money. It's all there. I would not meet with the Frenchman with less than his demands, and the rest I do not care to know.' Suddenly the man looked hard at Bourne, blinking his eyes in the downpour. 'But you are *not* the Frenchman!'

'Easy,' said Jason. 'Things have come pretty fast for you tonight.'

'Who *are* you?'

'Someone who just showed you where you stood. How much money did you bring?'

'Thirty thousand American dollars.'

'If that's the first payment, the target must be someone impressive.'

'I assume he is.'

'Keep it.'

'*What?* What are you *saying?*'

'I'm not the Frenchman, remember?'

'I do not understand.'

'I don't even want the instructions. I'm sure someone of your professional calibre can turn them to your advantage. A man pays well for information that can help him; he pays a hell of a lot more for his life.'

'Why would you *do* this?'

'Because none of it concerns me. I have only one concern. I want the man who calls himself Bourne and I can't waste time. You've got what I just offered you plus a dividend – I'll get you out of here alive if I have to leave two corpses here in the Bay, I don't care. But you've got to give me what I asked for on the phone. You said your client told you the Frenchman's assassin was going someplace else. *Where?* Where is *Bourne?*'

'You talk so rapidly—'

'I told you, I haven't *time!* Tell me! If you refuse, I leave and your client kills you. Take your choice.'

'Shenzen,' said the contact, as if frightened at the name.

'*China?* There's a target in *Shenzen?*'

'One can assume that. My wealthy client has sources in Queen's Road.'

'What's that?'

'The consulate of the People's Republic. A very unusual visa was granted. Apparently it was cleared on the highest authority in Beijing. The source did not know why, and when he questioned the decision he was promptly removed from the section. He reported this to my client. For money, of course.'

'Why was the visa unusual?'

'Because there was no waiting period and the applicant did not appear at the consulate. Both are unheard of.'

'Still, it was just a visa.'

'In the People's Republic there is no such thing as "just a visa." Especially not for a white male travelling alone under a questionable passport issued in Macao.'

'Macao?'

'Yes.'

'What's the entry date?'

'Tomorrow. The Lo Wu border.'

Jason studied the contact. 'You said your client has sources in the consulate. Do you?'

'What you are thinking will cost a great deal of money, for the risk is very great.'

Bourne raised his head and looked through the sheets of rain at the floodlit idol beyond. There was movement; the scout was searching for his target. 'Wait here,' he said.

The early morning train from Kowloon to the Lo Wu border took barely over an hour. The realization that he was in China took less than ten seconds.

Long Live the People's Republic!

There was no need for the exclamation point, the border guards lived it. They were rigid, staring, and abusive, pummelling passports with their rubber stamps with the fury of hostile adolescents. There was, however, an ameliorating support system. Beyond the guards a phalanx of young women in uniform stood smiling behind several long tables stacked with pamphlets extolling the beauty and virtues of their land and its system. If there was hypocrisy in their postures, it did not show.

Bourne had paid the betrayed, marked contact the sum of $7,000 for the visa. It was good for five days. The purpose of the visit was listed as 'business investments in the Economic Zone,' and was renewable at Shenzen immigration with proof of investment along with the corroborating presence of a Chinese banker through whom the money was to be brokered. In gratitude, and for no additional charge, the contact had given him the name of a Shenzen banker who could easily steer 'Mr Cruett' to investment possibilities, the said Mr Cruett being still registered at the Regent Hotel in Hong Kong. Finally, there was a bonus from the man whose life he had saved in Repulse Bay: the description of the man traveling under a Macao passport across the Lo Wu border. He was '6′ 1″ tall, 185 lbs., white skin, light brown hair.' Jason had stared at the information, unconsciously recalling the data on his own government ID card. It had read: 'HT: 6′ 1″ WT: 187 lbs. White Male. Hair: Lt. Brn.' An odd sense of fear spread through him. Not the fear of confrontation; he wanted that, above all, for he wanted Marie back above everything. Instead, it was the horror that he was responsible for the creation of a monster. A stalker of death that came from a lethal virus he had perfected in the laboratory of his mind and body.

It had been the first train out of Kowloon, occupied in the main by skilled labour and the executive personnel permitted – enticed – into the Free Economic Zone of Shenzen by the People's Republic in hopes of attracting foreign investments. At each stop on the way to the border, as more and more passengers boarded, Bourne had walked through the cars, his eyes resting for an intense instant on each of the white males, of whom there was a total of only fourteen by the time they reached Lo Wu. None had even vaguely fit the description of the man from Macao – the description of himself. The new 'Jason Bourne' would be taking a later train. The original would wait on the other side of the border. He waited now.

During the four hours that passed he explained sixteen times to inquiring border personnel that he was waiting for a business associate; he had obviously misunderstood the schedule and had taken a far too early train. As with people in any foreign country, but especially in the Orient, the fact that a courteous American had gone to the trouble of making himself understood in their language was decidedly beneficial. He was offered four cups of coffee, seven hot teas, and two of the uniformed girls had giggled as they presented him with an overly sweet Chinese ice cream cone. He accepted all – to do otherwise would have been rude, and since most of the Gang of Four had lost not only their faces but their heads, rudeness was out, except for the border guards.

It was 11:10. The passengers emerged through the long, fenced open-air corridor after dealing with immigration – mostly tourists, mostly white, mostly bewildered and awed to be there. The majority were in small tour groups, accompanied by guides – one each from Hong Kong and the People's Republic – who spoke acceptable English, or German, or French and, reluctantly, Japanese for those particularly disliked visitors with more money than Marx or Confucius ever had. Jason studied each white male. The many that were over six feet in height were too young or too old or too portly or too slender or too obvious in their lime-green and lemon-yellow trousers to be the man from Macao.

Wait! Over *there!* An older man in a tan gabardine suit who appeared to be a medium-sized tourist with a limp was suddenly taller – and the limp was gone! He walked rapidly down the steps through the middle of the crowd and ran into the huge parking lot filled with buses and tour vans and a few taxis, each with a ZHAN – off-duty – posted in the front windows. Bourne raced after the man, dodging between the bodies in front of him, not caring whom he pushed aside. *It was the man – the man from Macao!*

'Hey, are you crazy? Ralph, he shoved me!'

'Shove back. What do you want from me?'

'*Do* something!'

'He's gone.'

The man in the gabardine suit jumped into the open door of a van, a dark green van with tinted windows that according to the Chinese characters belonged to a department called the Chutang Bird Sanctuary. The door slid shut and the vehicle instantly broke away from its parking space and careened around the other vehicles into the exit lane. Bourne was frantic; he could not let him go! An old taxi was on his right, the motor idling. He pulled the door open, to be greeted by a shout.

'*Zhan!*' screamed the driver.

'*Shi ma?*' roared Jason, pulling enough American money from his pocket to insure five years of luxury in the People's Republic.

'*Aiya!*'

'*Zou!*' ordered Bourne, leaping into the front seat and pointing to the van, which had swerved into the semicircle. 'Stay with him and you can start your own business in the zone,' he said in Cantonese. 'I *promise* you!'

Marie, I'm so close! I know it's him! I'll take him! He's mine now! He's our deliverance!

The van sped out of the exit road, heading south at the first intersection, avoiding the large square jammed with tour buses and crowds of sightseers cautiously avoiding the endless stream of bicycles in the streets. The taxi driver picked up the van on a primitive highway paved more with hard clay than asphalt. The dark-windowed vehicle could be seen up ahead entering a long curve in front of an open truck carrying heavy farm machinery. A tour bus waited at the end of the curve, swinging into the road behind the truck.

Bourne looked beyond the van; there were hills up ahead and the road began to rise. Then another tour bus appeared, this one behind them.

'*Shumchun*,' said the driver.

'*Bin do?*' asked Jason.

'The Shumchun water supply,' answered the driver in Chinese. 'A very beautiful reservoir, one of the finest lakes in all China. It sends its water south to Kowloon and Hong Kong. Very crowded with visitors this time of year. The autumn views are excellent.'

Suddenly the van accelerated, climbing the mountain road, pulling away from the truck and the tour bus. 'Can't you go faster? Get around the bus, that truck!'

'Many curves ahead.'

'Try it!'

The driver pressed his foot to the floor and swerved around the bus, missing its bulging front by inches as he was forced back in line by an approaching army half-track with two soldiers in the cabin. Both the soldiers and the tour guides yelled at them through open windows. 'Sleep with your ugly mothers!' screamed the driver, full of his moment of triumph, only to be faced with the wide truck filled with farm machinery blocking the way.

They were going into a sharp right curve. Bourne gripped the window and leaned out as far as he could for a clearer view. 'There's no one coming!' he yelled at the driver through the onrushing wind. 'Go ahead! You can get around. *Now!*'

The driver did so, pushing the old taxi to its limits, the tyres spinning on a stretch of hard clay, which made the cab sideslip dangerously in front of the truck. Another curve, now sharply to the left, and rising steeper. Ahead the road was straight, ascending a high hill. The van was nowhere to be seen; it had disappeared over the crest of the hill.

'*Kuai!*' shouted Bourne. 'Can't you make this damn thing go faster?'

'It has never been this fast! I think the fuck-fuck spirits will explode the motor! Then what will I do? It took me five years to buy this unholy machine, and many unholy bribes to drive in the Zone!'

Jason threw a handful of bills on the floor of the cab by the driver's feet. 'There's ten times more if we catch that van! Now, *go*.'

The taxi soared over the top of the hill, descending swiftly into an enormous glen at the edge of a vast lake that seemed to extend for miles. In the distance Bourne could see snow-capped mountains and green islands dotting the blue-green water as far as the eye could see. The taxi came to a halt beside a large red and gold pagoda reached by a long, polished concrete staircase. Its open balconies overlooked the lake. Refreshment stands and curio shops were scattered about on the borders of the parking lot, where four tour buses were standing with the dual guides shouting instructions and pleading with their charges not to get in the wrong vehicles at the end of their walks.

The dark-windowed van was nowhere to be seen. Bourne shifted his head swiftly, looking in all directions. Where *was* it? 'What's that road over there?' he asked the driver.

'Pump stations. No one is permitted down that road, it is patrolled by the army. Around the bend is a high fence and a guardhouse.'

'Wait here.' Jason climbed out of the cab and started walking toward the prohibited road, wishing he had a camera or a guidebook – something to mark him as a tourist. As it was, the best he could do was to assume the hesitant walk and wide-eyed expression of a sightseer. No object was too insignificant for his inspection. He approached the bend in the badly paved road; he saw the high fence and part of the guardhouse – then all of it. A long metal bar fell across the road, two soldiers were talking, their backs to him, looking the other way – looking at two vehicles parked side by side farther down by a square concrete structure painted brown. One of the vehicles was the dark-windowed van, the other the brown sedan. The van began to move. It was heading back to the gate!

Bourne's thoughts came rapidly. He had no weapon; it was pointless even to consider carrying one across the border. If he tried to stop the van and drag the killer out, the commotion would bring the guards, their rifle fire swift and accurate. Therefore he had to draw the man from Macao out – of *his* own volition. The rest Jason was primed for; he would take the impostor one way or another. Take him back to the border and crossing over – one way or another. No man was a match for him; no eyes, no throat, no groin safe from an assault, swift and agonizing. David Webb had never come to grips with that reality. Bourne lived it.

There *was* a way!

Jason ran back to the beginning of the deserted bend in the road, beyond the view of the gate and the soldiers. He reassumed the pose of the mesmerized sightseer and listened. The van's engine fell to idle; the creaking meant the gate was being lifted. Only moments now. Bourne held his position in the brush by the side of the road. The van rounded the turn as he timed his moves.

He was suddenly there, in front of the large vehicle, his expression terrified, as he spun to the side below the driver's window and slammed the flat of his hand into the door, uttering a cry of pain as if he had been struck, perhaps killed, by the van. He lay supine on the ground as the vehicle came to a stop; the driver leaped out, an innocent about to protest his innocence. He had no chance to do so. Jason's arm was extended; he yanked the man by the ankle, pulling him off his feet, and sending his head crashing back into the side of the van. The driver fell unconscious, and Bourne dragged him back to the rear of the van beneath the clouded windows. He saw a bulge in the man's jacket; it was a gun, predictably, considering his cargo. Jason removed it and waited for the man from Macao.

He did not appear. It was not logical.

Bourne scrambled to the front of the van, gripped the rubberized ledge to the driver's seat, and lunged up, his weapon at the ready, sweeping the rear seats from side to side.

No one. It was empty.

He climbed back out and went to the driver, spat in his face and slapped him into consciousness.

'*Nali?*' he whispered harshly. 'Where is the man who was in here?'

'Back there!' replied the driver, in Cantonese, shaking his head. 'In the official car with a man nobody knows. Spare my terrible life! I have seven children!'

'Get up in the seat,' said Bourne, pulling the man to his feet and pushing him to the open door. 'Drive out of here as fast as you can.'

No other advice was necessary. The van shot out of the Shumchun reservoir area, careening around the curve into the main exit at such speed that Jason thought it would go over the bank. *A man nobody knows.* What did that mean? No matter, the man from Macao was trapped. He was in a brown sedan inside the gate on the forbidden road. Bourne raced back to the taxi and climbed into the front seat; the scattered money had been removed from the floor.

'You are satisfied?' said the cabdriver. 'I will have ten times what you dropped on my unworthy feet?'

'Cut it, Charlie Chan! A car's going to come out of that road to the pump station and you're going to do exactly what I tell you. Do you understand me?'

'Do you understand ten times the amount you left in my ancient, undistinguished taxi?'

'I understand. It could be fifteen times if you do your job. Come on, *move.* Get over to the edge of the parking lot. I don't know how long we'll have to wait.'

'Time is money, sir.'

'Oh, shut up!'

The wait was roughly twenty minutes. The brown sedan appeared, and Bourne saw what he had not seen before. The windows were tinted darker than those of the van; whoever was inside was invisible. Then Jason heard the very last words he wanted to hear.

'Take your money back,' said the driver quietly. 'I will return you to Lo Wu. I have never seen you.'

'*Why?*'

'That is a government car – one of our government's official vehicles – and I will not be the one who follows it.'

'Wait a minute! Just – wait a minute. *Twenty* times what I gave you, with a bonus if it all comes out all right! Until I say otherwise you can stay way behind him. I'm just a tourist who wants to look around. No, wait! Here, I'll show you! My visa says I'm investing money. Investors are permitted to look around!'

'*Twenty* times?' said the driver, staring at Jason. 'What guarantee do I have that you will fulfill your promise?'

'I'll put it on the seat between us. You're driving; you could do a lot of things with this car I wouldn't be prepared for. I won't try to take it back.'

'*Good!* But I stay far behind. I know these roads. There are only certain places one can travel.'

Thirty-five minutes later, with the brown sedan still in sight but far ahead, the driver spoke again. 'They go to the airfield.'

'What airfield?'

'It is used by government officials and men with money from the south.'

'People investing in factories, industry?'

'This is the Economic Zone.'

'I'm an investor,' said Bourne. 'My visa says so. Hurry up! *Close* in!'

'There are five vehicles between us, and we agreed – I stay far behind.'

'Until I said otherwise! It's different now. I have money. I'm investing in China!'

'We will be stopped at the gate. Telephone calls will be made.'

'I've got the name of a banker in Shenzen!'

'Does he have your name, sir? And a list of the Chinese firms you are dealing with? If so, you may do the talking at the gate. But if this banker in Shenzen does not know you, you will be detained for giving false information. Your stay in China would be for as long as it took to thoroughly investigate you. Weeks, months.'

'I have to reach that car!'

'You approach that car, you will be shot.'

'*Goddamn it!*' shouted Jason in English, then instantly reverting to Chinese: 'Listen to me. I don't have time to explain, but I've got to *see* him!'

'This is not my business,' said the driver coldly, warily.

'Get in line and drive up to the gate,' ordered Bourne. 'I'm a fare you picked up in Lo Wu, that's all. I'll do the talking.'

'You ask too much! I will not be seen with someone like you.'

'Just do it,' said Jason, pulling the gun from his belt.

The pounding in his chest was unbearable as Bourne stood by a large window looking out on the airfield. The terminal was small and for privileged travellers. The incongruous sight of casual Western businessmen carrying attaché cases and tennis rackets unnerved Jason because of the stark contrast to the uniformed guards, standing about rigidly. Oil and water were apparently compatible.

Speaking English to the interpreter, who translated accurately for the officer of the guard, he had claimed to be a bewildered executive instructed by the consulate on Queen's Road in Hong Kong to come to the airport to meet an official flying in from Beijing. He had misplaced the official's name, but they had met briefly at the State Department in Washington and would recognize each other. He implied that the present meeting was looked upon with great favour by important men on the Central Committee. He was given a pass restricting him to the terminal, and lastly, he asked if the taxi could be permitted to remain in case transportation was needed later. The request was granted.

'If you want your money, you'll stay,' he had said to the driver in Cantonese as he picked up the folded bills between them.

'You have a gun and angry eyes. You will kill.'

Jason had stared at the driver. 'The last thing on earth I want to do is kill the man in that car. I would only kill to protect his life.'

The brown sedan with the dark, opaque windows was nowhere in the parking area. Bourne walked as rapidly as he thought acceptable into the terminal, to the window where he stood now, his temples exploding with anger and frustration, for outside on the field he saw the government car. It was parked on the tarmac not fifty feet away from him, but an impenetrable wall of glass separated him from it – and deliverance. Suddenly the sedan shot forward toward a medium-sized jet several hundred yards north on the runway. Bourne strained his eyes, wishing to Christ he had binoculars! Then he realized they would have been useless; the car swung around the tail of the plane and out of sight.

Goddamn it!

Within seconds the jet began rolling to the foot of the runway as the brown sedan swerved and raced back toward the parking area and the exit.

What could he *do? I can't be left this way! He's there! He's me and he's there! He's getting away!* Bourne ran to the first counter and assumed the attitude of a terribly distraught man.

'The plane that's about to take off! I'm supposed to be *on* it! It's going to Shanghai and the people in Beijing said I was to be *on* it! *Stop* it!'

The clerk behind the counter picked up her telephone. She dialled quickly, then exhaled through her tight lips in relief. 'That is not your plane, sir,' she said. 'It flies to Guangdong.'

'Where?'

'The Macao border, sir.'

'*Never! It must not be Macao!*' the taipan had screamed . . . '*The order will be swift, the execution swifter! Your wife will die!*'

Macao. Table Five. The Kam Pek casino.

'*If he heads for Macao,*' McAllister had said quietly, '*he could be a terrible liability . . .*'

'*Termination?*'

'*I can't use that word.*'

14

'You will *not*, you *cannot* tell me this!' shouted Edward Newington McAllister, leaping out of his chair. 'It's *unacceptable!* I can't handle it. I won't *hear* of it!'

'You'd better, Edward,' said Major Lin Wenzu. 'It happened.'

'It's my fault,' added the English doctor, standing in front of the desk in the Victoria Peak, facing the American. 'Every symptom she exhibited led to a prognosis of rapid, neurological deterioration. Loss of concentration and visual focus; no appetite and a commensurate drop in weight – most significantly, spasms when there was a complete lack of motor controls. I honestly thought the degenerative process had reached a negative crisis—'

'What the hell does *that* mean?'

'That she was dying. Oh, not in a matter of hours or even days or weeks, but that the course was irreversible.'

'Could you have been right?'

'I would like nothing better than to conclude that I was, that my diagnosis was at least reasonable, but I can't. Simply put, I was dragooned.'

'You were *hit?*'

'Figuratively, yes. Where it hurts the most, Mr Undersecretary. My professional pride. That bitch fooled me with a carnival act, and she probably doesn't know the difference between a femur and a fever. Everything she did was calculated, from her appeals to the nurse to clubbing and disrobing the guard. All her moves were planned and the only disorder was mine.'

'Christ, I've got to reach Havilland!'

'*Ambassador* Havilland?' asked Lin, his eyebrows arched.

McAllister looked at him. 'Forget you heard that.'

'I will not repeat it, but I can't forget. Things are clearer, London's clearer. You're talking General Staff and Overlord and a large part of Olympus.'

'Don't mention that name to anyone, Doctor,' said McAllister.

'I've quite forgotten it. I'm not sure I even know who he is.'

'What can I say? What are you *doing?*'

'Everything humanly possible,' answered the major. 'We've divided Hong Kong and Kowloon up into sections. We're questioning every hotel, thoroughly examining their registrations. We've alerted the police and the marine patrols; all personnel have copies of her description and have been instructed that finding her is the territory's priority concern—'

'My God, what did you *say?* How did you explain?'

'I was able to help here,' said the doctor. 'In light of my stupidity it was the least I could do. I issued a medical alert. By doing so, we were able to enlist the help of paramedic teams who've been sent out from all the hospitals, staying in radio contact for other emergencies, of course. They're scouring the streets.'

'What kind of medical alert?' asked McAllister sharply.

'Minimum information, but the sort that creates a stir. The woman was known to have visited an unnamed island in the Luzon Strait that is off limits to international travellers for reasons of a rampant disease transmitted by unclean eating utensils.'

'Categorizing it as such,' interrupted Lin, 'our good doctor removed any hesitation on the part of the teams to approach her and take her into custody. Not that they would, but every basket has its less than perfect fruit and we cannot afford any. I honestly believe we'll find her, Edward. We all know she stands out in a crowd. Tall, attractive, that hair of hers – and over a thousand people looking for her.'

'I hope to God you're right. But I worry. She received her first training from a chameleon,' said McAllister.

'I beg your pardon?'

'It's nothing, Doctor,' said the major. 'A technical term in our business.'

'Oh?'

'I've got to have the entire file, *all* of it!'

'What, Edward?'

'They were hunted together in Europe. Now they're apart, but still hunted. What did they do then? What will they do now?'

'A thread? A pattern?'

'It's always there,' said McAllister, rubbing his right temple. 'Excuse me, gentlemen, I must ask you to leave. I have a dreadful call to make.'

Marie bartered clothes and paid a few dollars for others. The result was acceptable: with her hair pulled back under a floppy wide-brimmed sun hat, she was a plainlooking woman in a pleated skirt and a nondescript grey blouse that concealed any outline of a figure. The flat sandals lowered her height and the ersatz Gucci purse marked her as a gullible tourist in Hong Kong, exactly what she was not. She called the Canadian consulate and was told how to get there by bus. The offices were in the Asian House, fourteenth floor, Hong Kong. She took the bus from the Chinese University through Kowloon and the tunnel over to the island; she watched the streets carefully and got off at her stop. She rode up in the elevator, satisfied that none of the men riding with her gave her a second glance; that was not the usual reaction. She had learned in Paris – taught by a chameleon – how to use the simple things to change herself. The lessons were coming back to her.

'I realize this will sound ridiculous,' she said in a casual, humorously bewildered voice to the receptionist, 'but a second cousin of mine on my mother's side is posted here and I promised to look him up.'

'That doesn't sound ridiculous to me.'

'It will when I tell you I've forgotten his name.' Both women laughed. 'Of course, we've never met and he'd probably like to keep it that way, but then I'd have to answer to the family back home.'

'Do you know what section he's in?'

'Something to do with economics, I believe.'

'That would be the Division of Trade most likely.' The receptionist opened a drawer and pulled out a narrow white booklet with the Canadian flag embossed on the cover. 'Here's our directory. Why don't you sit down and look through it?'

'Thanks very much,' said Marie, going to a leather armchair and sitting down. 'I have this terrible feeling of inadequacy,' she added, opening the directory. 'I mean I *should* know his name. I'm sure *you* know the name of your second cousin on your mother's side of the family.'

'Honey, I haven't the vaguest.' The receptionist's phone rang; she answered it.

Turning the pages, Marie read quickly, scanning down the columns looking for a name that would evoke a face. She found three, but the images were fuzzy, the features not clear. Then on the twelfth page, a face *and* a voice leaped up at her as she read the name. *Catherine Staples.*

'Cool' Catherine, 'Ice-cold' Catherine, 'Stick' Staples. The nicknames were unfair and did not give an accurate picture or appraisal of the woman. Marie had gotten to know Catherine Staples during her days with the Treasury Board in Ottawa when she and others in her section briefed the diplomatic corps prior to their overseas assignments. Staples had come through twice, once for a refresher course on the European Common Market . . . the second, *of course*, for Hong Kong! It was thirteen or fourteen months ago, and although their friendship could not be called deep – four or five lunches, a dinner that Catherine had prepared, and one reciprocated by Marie – she had learned quite a bit about the woman who did her job better than most men.

To begin with, her rapid advancement at the Department of External Affairs had cost her an early marriage. She had forsworn the marital state for the rest of her life, she declared, as the demands of travel and the insane hours of her job were unacceptable to any man worth having. In her mid-fifties, Staples was a slender, energetic woman of medium height, who dressed fashionably but simply. She was a no-nonsense professional with a sardonic wit that conveyed her dislike of cant, which she saw through swiftly, and self-serving excuses, which she would not tolerate. She could be kind, even gentle, with men and women unqualified for the work they were assigned through no fault of their own, but brutal with those who had issued such assignments, regardless of rank. If there was a phrase that summed up Senior Foreign Service Officer Catherine Staples, it was 'tough but fair'; also, she was frequently very amusing in a self-deprecating way. Marie hoped she would be fair in Hong Kong.

'There's nothing here that rings a bell,' said Marie, getting out of the chair and bringing the directory back to the receptionist. 'I feel so stupid.'

'Do you have any idea what he looks like?'

'I never thought to ask.'

'I'm sorry.'

'I'm sorrier. I'll have to place a very embarrassing call to Vancouver . . . Oh,

I did see one name. It has nothing to do with my cousin, but I think she's a friend of a friend. A woman named Staples.'

'"Catherine the Great"? She's here, all right, although a few of the staff wouldn't mind seeing her promoted to ambassador and sent to Eastern Europe. She makes them nervous. She's topflight.'

'Oh, you mean she's here now?'

'Not thirty feet away. You want to give me your friend's name and see if she has time to say hello?'

Marie was tempted, but the onus of officialdom prohibited the shortcut. If things were as Marie thought they were and alarms had been sent out to friendly consulates, Staples might feel compelled to cooperate. She probably would not, but she had the integrity of her office to uphold. Embassies and consulates constantly sought favors from one another. She needed time with Catherine, and not in an official setting. 'That's very nice of you,' Marie said to the receptionist. 'My friend would get a kick out of it . . . Wait a minute. Did you say "*Catherine*"?'

'Yes. Catherine Staples. Believe me, there's only one.'

'I'm sure there is, but my friend's friend is Christine. Oh, Lord, this isn't my day. You've been very kind, so I'll get out of your hair and leave you in peace.'

'You've been a pleasure, hon. You should see the ones who come in here thinking they bought a Cartier watch for a hell of a good price until it stops and a jeweller tells them the insides are two rubber bands and a miniature yo-yo.' The receptionist's eyes dropped to the Gucci purse with the inverted *G*'s. 'Oh, oh,' she said softly.

'What?'

'Nothing. Good luck with your phone call.'

Marie waited in the lobby of the Asian House for as long as she felt comfortable, then went outside and walked back and forth in front of the entrance for nearly an hour in the crowded street. It was shortly past noon, and she wondered if Catherine even bothered to have lunch – lunch would be a very good idea. Also, there was another possibility, an impossibility perhaps, but one she could pray for, if she still knew how to pray. David might appear, but it would not be as David, it would be as Jason Bourne, and that could be anyone. Her husband in the guises of Bourne would be far more clever; she had seen his inventiveness in Paris and it was from another world, a lethal world where a misstep could cost a person his life. Every move was premeditated in three or four dimensions. What if I . . . ? What if he . . . ? The intellect played a far greater role in the violent world than the nonviolent intellectuals would ever admit – their brains would be blown away in a world they scorned as barbarian because they could not think fast enough or deeply enough. *Cogito ergo* nothing. Why was she thinking these things? She belonged to the latter and so did David! And then the answer was very clear. They had been thrown back; they had to survive and find each other.

There she *was!* Catherine Staples walked – marched – out of the Asian House and turned right. She was roughly forty feet away; Marie started running, pummelling off bodies in her path as she tried to catch up. *Try never to run, it marks you.* I don't care! I must talk to her!

Staples cut across the pavement. There was a consulate car, with the maple-leaf insignia printed on the door, waiting for her at the curb. She was climbing inside.

'No! *Wait!*' shouted Marie, crashing through the crowd, grabbing the door as Catherine was about to close it.

'I *beg* your pardon?' cried Staples, as the chauffeur spun around in his seat, a gun appearing out of nowhere.

'*Please!* It's *me!* Ottawa. The briefings.'

'*Marie?* Is that *you?*'

'Yes. I'm in trouble and I need your help.'

'Get in,' said Catherine Staples, moving over on the seat. 'Put that silly thing away,' she ordered the driver. 'This is a friend of mine.'

Cancelling her scheduled lunch on the pretext of a summons from the British delegation – a common occurrence during the round-robin conferences with the People's Republic over the 1997 treaty – Foreign Service Officer Staples instructed the driver to drop them off at the beginning of Food Street in Causeway Bay. Food Street encompassed the crushing spectacle of some thirty restaurants within the stretch of two blocks. Traffic was prohibited on the street and even if it was not, there was no way motorized transport could make its way through the mass of humanity in search of some four thousand tables. Catherine led Marie to the service entrance of a restaurant. She rang the bell, and fifteen seconds later the door opened, followed by the wafting odours of a hundred Oriental dishes.

'Miss Staples, how good to see you,' said the Chinese dressed in the white apron of a chef – one of many chefs. 'Please-please. As always, there is a table for you.'

As they walked through the chaos of the large kitchen, Catherine turned to Marie. 'Thank God there are a few perks left in this miserably underpaid profession. The owner has relatives in Quebec – damn fine restaurant on St John Street – and I make sure his visa gets processed, as they say, "damn-damn quick."'

Catherine nodded at one of the few empty tables in the rear section; it was near the kitchen door. They were seated, literally concealed by the stream of waiters rushing in and out of the swinging doors, as well as by the continuous bustle taking place at the scores of tables throughout the crowded restaurant.

'Thank you for thinking of a place like this,' said Marie.

'My dear,' replied Staples in her throaty, adamant voice. 'Anyone with your looks who dresses the way you're dressed now, and makes up the way you're made up, doesn't care to draw attention to herself.'

'As they say, that's putting it mildly. Will your lunch date accept the British delegation story?'

'Without a thought to the contrary. The mother country is marshalling its most persuasive forces. Beijing buys enormous quantities of much needed wheat from us – but then you know that as well as I do, and probably a lot more in terms of dollars and cents.'

'I'm not very current these days.'

'Yes, I understand.' Staples nodded, looking sternly yet kindly at Marie, her eyes questioning. 'I was over here by then, but we heard the rumours and read the European papers. To say we were in shock can't describe the way those of us who knew you felt. In the weeks that followed we all tried to get answers, but we were told to let it alone, drop it – for *your* sake. "Don't pursue it," they kept saying. "It's in her best interests to stay away." . . . Of course, we finally heard that you were exonerated of all charges – *Christ*, what an insulting phrase after what you were put through! Then you just faded, and no one heard anything more about you.'

'They told you the truth, Catherine. It *was* in my interest – our interests – to stay away. For months we were kept hidden, and when we took up our civilized lives again it was in a fairly remote area and under a name few people knew. The guards, however, were still in place.'

'We?'

'I married the man you read about in the papers. Of course, he wasn't the man *described* in the papers; he was in deep cover for the American government. He gave up a great deal of his life for that awfully strange commitment.'

'And now you're in Hong Kong and you tell me you're in trouble.'

'I'm in Hong Kong and I'm in serious trouble.'

'May I assume that the events of the past year are related to your current difficulties?'

'I believe they are.'

'What can you tell me?'

'Everything I know because I want your help. I have no right to ask it unless you know everything I know.'

'I like succinct language. Not only for its clarity but because it usually defines the person delivering it. You're also saying that unless I know everything I probably can't do anything.'

'I hadn't thought of it that way, but you're probably right.'

'Good. I was testing you. In the *nouvelle diplomatie*, overt simplicity has become both a cover and a tool. It's frequently used to obscure duplicity, as well as to disarm an adversary. I refer you to the recent proclamations of your new country – new as a wife, of course.'

'I'm an economist, Catherine, not a diplomat.'

'Combine the talents that I know you have, and you could scale the heights in Washington as you would have in Ottawa. But then you wouldn't have the obscurity you so desire in your regained civilized life.'

'We *must* have that. It's all that matters. I don't.'

'Testing again. You were not without ambition. You love that husband of yours.'

'Very much. I want to find him. I want him back.'

Staples's head snapped as her eyes blinked. 'He's *here?*'

'Somewhere. It's part of the story.'

'Is it complicated?'

'Very.'

'Can you hold back – and I *mean* that, Marie – until we go someplace where it's quieter?'

'I was taught patience by a man whose life depended on it twenty-four hours a day for three years.'

'Good God. Are you hungry?'

'Famished. That's also part of the story. As long as you're here and listening to me, may we order?'

'Avoid the *dim sum*, it's oversteamed and overfried. The duck, however, is the best in Hong Kong . . . *Can* you wait, Marie? Would you rather leave?'

'I can wait, Catherine. My whole life's on hold. A half hour won't make any difference. And if I don't eat I won't be coherent.'

'I know. It's part of the story.'

They sat opposite each other in Staples's flat, a coffee table between them, sharing a pot of tea.

'I think,' said Catherine, 'that I've just heard what amounts to the most blatant misuse of office in thirty years of foreign service – on our side, of course. Unless there's a grave misinterpretation.'

'You're saying you don't believe me.'

'On the contrary, my dear, you couldn't have made it up. You're quite right. The whole damn thing's full of illogical logic.'

'I didn't say that.'

'You didn't have to, it's there. Your husband is primed, the possibilities implanted, and then he's shot up like a nuclear rocket. *Why?*'

'I told you. There's a man killing people who claims he's Jason Bourne – the role David played for three years.'

'A killer's a killer, no matter the name he assumes, whether it's Genghis Khan or Jack the Ripper, or, if you will, Carlos the Jackal – even the assassin Jason Bourne. Traps for such men are planned with the consent of the trappers.'

'I don't understand you, Catherine.'

'Then listen to me, my dear. This is an old-time mind speaking. Remember when I went to you for the Common Market refresher with the emphasis on Eastern trade?'

'Yes. We cooked dinners for each other. Yours was better than mine.'

'Yes, it was. But I was really there to learn how to convince my contacts in the Eastern block that I could use the fluctuating rates of exchange so that purchases made from us would be infinitely more profitable for them. I did it. Moscow was furious.'

'Catherine, what the hell has that got to do with me?'

Staples looked at Marie, her gentle demeanor again underlined with firmness. 'Let me be clearer. If you thought about it at all, you had to assume that I'd come to Ottawa to gain a firmer grasp of European economics so as to do my job better. In one sense that was true, but it wasn't the real reason. I was actually there to learn how to use the fluctuating rates of the various currencies and offer contracts of the greatest advantage to our potential clients. When the deutsche mark rose, we sold on the franc or the guilder or whatever. It was built into the contracts.'

'That was hardly self-serving.'

'We weren't looking for profits, we were opening markets that had been closed to us. The profits would come later. You were very clear about exchange rate speculation. You preached its evils, and I had to learn to be something of a devil – for a good cause, of course.'

'All right, you picked what brains I have for a purpose I didn't know about—'

'It had to be kept totally secret, obviously.'

'But what's it got to do with anything I've told you?'

'I smell a bad piece of meat, and this nose is experienced. Just as I had an ulterior motive to go to you in Ottawa, whoever is doing this to you has a deeper reason than the capture of your husband's impostor.'

'Why do you say that?'

'Your husband said it first. This is primarily and quite properly a police matter, even an international police matter for Interpol's highly respected Intelligence network. They're far more qualified for this sort of thing than State Departments or Foreign Offices, CIA's or MISix's. Overseas Intelligence branches don't concern themselves with nonpolitical criminals – everyday murderers – they can't afford to. My God, most of those asses would expose whatever covers they'd managed to build if they interfered with police work.'

'McAllister said otherwise. He claimed that the best people in US and UK Intelligence were working on it. He said the reason was that if this killer who's posing as my husband – what my husband was in people's eyes – murdered a high political figure on either side, or started an underworld war, Hong Kong's status would be in immediate jeopardy. Peking would move quickly and take over, using the pretext of the '97 treaty. "The Oriental doesn't tolerate a disobedient child" – those were his words.'

'Unacceptable and *unbelievable!*' retorted Catherine Staples. 'Either your undersecretary is a liar or he has the IQ of a fern! He gave you *every* reason for our Intelligence services to stay *out* of it, to stay absolutely *clean!* Even a hint of covert action would be disastrous. That *could* fire up the wild boys on the Central Committee. Regardless, I don't believe a word he said. London would never permit it, not even the mention of Special Branch's name.'

'Catherine, you're wrong. You weren't listening. The man who flew to Washington for the Treadstone file was British, and he *was* MI-Six. Good Lord, he was murdered for that file.'

'I heard you before. I simply don't believe it. Above all else, the Foreign Office would insist that this whole mess remain with the police and *only* the police. They wouldn't let MI-Six in the same restaurant with a detective third grade, even on Food Street. Believe me, my dear, I know what I'm talking about. These are very delicate times and *no* time for hanky-panky, especially the sort that has an official Intelligence organization messing around with an assassin. No, you were brought here and your husband was forced to follow for quite another reason.'

'For heaven's sake, *what?*' cried Marie, shooting forward in her chair.

'I don't know. There's someone else perhaps.'

'*Who?*'

'It's quite beyond me.'

Silence. Two highly intelligent minds were pondering the words each had spoken.

'Catherine,' said Marie finally. 'I accept the logic of everything you say, but you also said everything was rife with illogical logic. Suppose I'm right, that the men who held me were not killers or criminals, but bureaucrats following orders they didn't understand, that *government* was written all over their faces and in their evasive explanations, even in their concern for my comfort and well-being. I know you think that the McAllister I described to you is a liar or a fool, but suppose he's a liar and not a fool? Assuming these things – and I believe them to be true – we're talking about *two* governments acting in concert during these very delicate times. What then?'

'Then there's a disaster in the making,' said Senior Foreign Officer Staples quietly.

'And it revolves around my husband?'

'*If* you're right, yes.'

'It's possible, isn't it?'

'I don't even want to think about it.'

15

Forty miles southwest of Hong Kong, beyond the out islands in the South China Sea, is the peninsula of Macao, a Portuguese colony in ceremonial name only. Its historical origins are in Portugal, but its modern, freewheeling appeal to the international set, with its annual Grand Prix and its gambling and its yachts, is based on the luxuries and life-styles demanded by the wealthy of Europe. Regardless, make no mistake. It is Chinese. The controls are in Peking.

Never! It must not be Macao! The order will be swift, the execution swifter! Your wife will die!

But the assassin was in Macao, and a chameleon had to enter another jungle.

Scanning the faces and peering into the shadowed corners of the small, packed terminal, Bourne moved with the crowd out onto the pier of the Macao hydrofoil, a trip that took roughly an hour. The passengers were divided into three distinct categories: returning residents of the Portuguese colony – in the main Chinese and silent; professional gamblers – a racial mix talking quietly when they talked at all, continually glancing around to size up their competition; and late-night revelers – boisterous tourists, exclusively white, many of them drunk, in oddly shaped hats and loud tropical shirts.

He had left Shenzen and taken the three o'clock train from Lo Wu to Kowloon. The ride was exhausting, his reasoning stunned, his emotions were drained. The impostor-killer had been so close! If only he could have isolated the man from Macao for less than a minute, he could have gotten him out! There were ways. Both their visas were in order; a man doubled up in pain, his throat damaged to the point of speechlessness, could be passed off as a sick man, a diseased man perhaps, an unwelcome visitor whom they would gladly have let go. But it was not to be, not this time. If only he could have *seen* him!

And then there was the startling discovery that this new assassin, this myth that was no myth but a brutal killer, had a connection in the People's Republic. It was profoundly disturbing, for Chinese officials who acknowledged such a man would do so only to use him. It was a complication David did not want. It had nothing to do with Marie and himself, and the two of them were all he cared about. *All* he cared about! Jason Bourne: *Bring in the man from Macao!*

He had gone back to the Peninsula, stopping at the New World Centre to buy a dark, waist-length nylon jacket and a pair of navy blue sneakers with a heavy tread. David Webb's anxiety was overpowering. Jason Bourne planned without consciously having a plan. He ordered a light meal from room service and picked at it as he sat on the bed staring mindlessly at a television news program. Then David lay back on the pillow, briefly closing his eyes, wondering where the words came from: *Rest is a weapon. Don't forget it.* Bourne woke up fifteen minutes later.

Jason had purchased a ticket for the 8:30 run at a booth in the Mass Transit concourse in the Tsim Sha Tsui during the rush hour. To be certain he was not being followed – and he had to be *absolutely* certain – he had taken three separate taxis to within a quarter of a mile of the Macao Ferry pier an hour before departure and walked the rest of the way. He had then entered upon a ritual he had been trained to perform. The memory of that training was clouded, but not the practice. He had melted into the crowds in front of the terminal, dodging, weaving, going from one pocket to another, then abruptly standing motionless on the sidelines, concentrating on the patterns of movement behind him, looking for someone he had seen moments before, a face or a pair of anxious eyes directed at him. There had been no one. Yet Marie's life depended on the certainty, so he had repeated the ritual twice again, ending up inside the dimly lit terminal filled with benches that fronted the dock and the open water. He kept looking for a frantic face, for a head that kept turning, a person spinning in place, intent on finding someone. Again, there had been no one. He was free to leave for Macao. He was on his way there now.

He sat in a rear seat by the window and watched the lights of Hong Kong and Kowloon fade into a glow in the Asian sky. New lights appeared and disappeared as the hydrofoil gathered speed and passed the out islands, islands belonging to China. He imagined uniformed men peering through infrared telescopes and binoculars, not sure what they were looking for but ordered to observe everything. The mountains of the New Territories rose ominously, the moonlight glancing off their peaks and accentuating their beauty, but also saying: *This is where you stop. Beyond here, we are different.* It was not really so. People hawked their goods in the squares of Shenzen. Artisans prospered; farmers butchered their animals and lived as well as the educated classes in Beijing and Shanghai – usually with better housing. China was changing, not fast enough for the West, and certainly it was still a paranoid giant, but withal, thought David Webb, the distended stomachs of children, so prevalent in the China of years ago, were disappearing. Many at the top of the inscrutable political ladder were fat, but few in the fields were starving. There had been progress, mused David, whether much of the world approved of the methods or not.

The hydrofoil decelerated, its hull lowered into the water. It passed through a space between the boulders of a man-made reef illuminated by floodlights. They were in Macao, and Bourne knew what he had to do. He got up, excused himself past his seat companion, and walked up the aisle where a group of Americans, a few standing, the rest sitting, were huddled around their seats, singing an obviously rehearsed rendition of 'Mr Sandman.'

'Boom boom boom boom . . .
Mr Sandman, sing me a song
Boom boom boom boom
Oh, Mr Sandman . . .'

They were high, but not drunk, not obstreperous. Another group of tourists, by the sound of their speech German, encouraged the Americans, and at the end of the song applauded.

'*Gut!*'

'*Sehr gut!*'

'*Wunderbar!*'

'*Danke, meine Herren.*' The American standing nearest Jason bowed to the Germans. A brief, friendly conversation followed, the Germans speaking English and the American replying in German.

'That was a touch of home,' said Bourne to the American.

'Hey, a *Landsmann!* That song also dates you, pal. Some of those oldies are goldies, right? Say, are you with the group?'

'Which group is that?'

'Honeywell-Porter,' answered the man, naming a New York advertising agency Jason recognized as having branches worldwide.

'No, I'm afraid not.'

'I didn't think so. There're only about thirty of us, counting the Aussies, and I thought I pretty much knew everybody. Where are you from? My name's Ted Mather. I'm from HP's LA office.'

'My name's Howard Cruett. No office, I teach, but I'm from Boston.'

'Beanburg! Let me show you *your Landsmann*, or is it *Stadtsmann?* Howard, meet Beantown Bernie.' Mather bowed again, this time to a man slumped back in the seat by the window, his mouth open, his eyes closed. He was obviously drunk and wore a Red Sox baseball cap. 'Don't bother to speak, he can't hear. Bernard the Brain is from our Boston office. You should have seen him three hours ago. J. Press suit, striped tie, pointer in his hand and a dozen charts only he could understand. But I'll say this for him – he kept us awake. I think that's why we all had a few – him too many. What the hell, it's our last night.'

'Heading back tomorrow?'

'Late-evening flight. Gives us time to recover.'

'Why Macao?'

'A mass itch for the tables. You, too?'

'I thought I'd give them a whirl. Christ, that cap makes me homesick! The Red Sox may take the pennant, and until this trip I hadn't missed a game!'

'And Bernie won't miss his hat!' The advertising man laughed, leaning over and yanking the baseball cap off Bernard the Brain's head. 'Here, Howard, you wear it. You deserve it!'

The hydrofoil docked. Bourne got off and went through immigration with the boys from Honeywell-Porter as one of them. As they descended the steep cement staircase down into the poster-lined terminal, Jason – with the visor of his Red Sox cap angled down and his walk unsteady – spotted a man by the left wall studying the new arrivals. In the man's hand was a photograph, and Bourne knew the face on the photograph was his. He laughed at one of Ted Mather's remarks as he held on to the weaving Beantown Bernie's arm.

Opportunities will present themselves. Recognize them, act on them.

The streets of Macao are almost as garishly lit as those of Hong Kong; what is lacking is the sense of too much humanity in too little space. And what is different – different and anachronistic – are the many buildings on which are fixed blazing modern signs with pulsating Chinese characters. The architecture of these buildings is very old Spanish – Portuguese, to be accurate – but textbook Spanish, Mediterranean in character. It is as if an initial culture had surrendered to the sweeping incursion of another, but refused to yield its first imprimatur, proclaiming the strength of its stone over the gaudy impermanence of coloured tubes of glass. History is purposely denied; the empty churches and the ruins of a burnt-out cathedral exist in a strange harmony with overflowing casinos where the dealers and croupiers speak Cantonese and the descendants of the conquerors are rarely seen. It is all fascinating and not a little ominous. It is Macao.

Jason slipped away from the Honeywell-Porter group and found a taxi whose driver must have been trained by watching the annual Macao Grand Prix. He was taken to the Kam Pek casino – over the driver's objections.

'Lisboa for you, not Kam Pek! Kam Pek for Chinee! *Dai sui! Fan-tan!*'

'Kam Pek, *cheng nei*,' said Bourne, adding the Cantonese *please*, but saying no more.

The casino was dark. The air was humid and foul, and the curling smoke that spiralled around the shaded lights above the tables sweet and full and pungent. There was a bar set back away from the games; he went to it and sat down on a stool, lowering his body to lessen his height. He spoke in Chinese, the baseball cap throwing a shadow across his face, which was probably unnecessary, as he could barely read the labels of the bottles on the counter. He ordered a drink, and when it came he gave the bartender a generous tip in Hong Kong money.

'*Mgoi*,' said the aproned man, thanking him.

'*Hou*,' said Jason, waving his hand.

Establish a benign contact as soon as you can. Especially in an unfamiliar place where there could be hostility. That contact could give you the opportunity or the time you need. Was it Medusa or was it Treadstone? It did not matter that he could not remember.

He turned slowly on the stool and looked at the tables; he found the dangling placard with the Chinese character for 'five.' He turned back to the bar and took out his notebook and ballpoint pen. He then tore off a page and wrote out the telephone number of a Macao hotel he had memorized from the *Voyager* magazine provided to passengers on the hydrofoil. He printed a name he would recall only if it was necessary and added the following: *No friend of Carlos.*

He lowered his glass below the bar counter, spilled the drink, and held up his hand for another. With its appearance, he was more generous than before.

'*Mgoi saai*,' said the bartender, bowing.

'*Msa*,' said Bourne, again waving his hand, then suddenly holding it steady, a signal for the bartender to remain where he was. 'Would you do me a small favour?' he continued in the man's language. 'It would take you no more than ten seconds.'

'What is it, sir?'

'Give this note to the dealer at Table Five. He's an old friend, and I want him to know I'm here.' Jason folded the note and held it up. 'I'll pay you for the favour.'

'It is my heavenly privilege, sir.'

Bourne watched. The dealer took the note, opened it briefly as the bartender walked away, and shoved it beneath the table. The waiting began.

It was interminable, so long that the bartender was relieved for the night. The dealer was moved to another table, and two hours later he was also replaced. And two hours after that still another dealer took over Table Five. The floor beneath him now damp with whisky, Jason logically ordered coffee and settled for tea; it was ten minutes past two in the morning. Another hour and he would go to the hotel whose number he had written down and, if he had to buy shares in its stock, get a room. He was fading.

The fading stopped. It was happening! A Chinese woman in the slit-skirted dress of a prostitute walked up to Table Five. She sidestepped her way around the players to the right corner and spoke quickly to the dealer, who reached under the counter and unobtrusively gave her the folded note. She nodded and left, heading for the door of the casino.

He does not appear himself, of course. He uses whores from the street.

Bourne left the bar and followed the woman. Out in the dark street, which had a number of people in it but was deserted by Hong Kong standards, he stayed roughly fifty feet behind her, stopping every now and then to look into the lighted store windows, then hurrying ahead so as not to lose her.

Don't accept the first relay. They think as well as you do. The first could be an indigent looking for a few dollars and who knows nothing. Even the second or the third. You'll recognize the contact. He'll be different.

A stooped old man approached the whore. Their bodies brushed, and she shrieked at him while passing him the note. Jason feigned drunkenness and turned around, taking up the second relay.

It happened four blocks away, and the man *was* different. He was a small, well-dressed Chinese, his compact body with its broad shoulders and narrow waist exuding strength. The quickness of his gestures as he paid the seedy old man and began walking rapidly across the street was a warning to any adversary. For Bourne it was an irresistible invitation; this was a contact with authority, a link to the Frenchman.

Jason dashed to the other side; he was close to fifty yards behind the man and losing ground. There was no point in being subtle any longer; he broke into a run. Seconds later he was directly behind the contact, the soles of his sneakers having dulled the sound of his racing feet. Up ahead was an alleyway that cut between what looked like two office buildings; the windows were dark. He had to move quickly, but move in such a way that would not cause a commotion, not give the night strollers a reason to shout or call for the police. In this, the odds were with him; most of the people wandering around were more drunk or drugged than sober, the rest weary labourers, having finished their working hours, anxious to get home. The contact approached the opening of the alley. *Now.*

Bourne rushed ahead to the man's right side. 'The *Frenchman!*' he said in Chinese. 'I have news from the Frenchman! *Hurry!*' He spun into the alley, and the contact, stunned, his eyes bulging, had no choice but to walk like a bewildered zombie into the mouth of the alleyway. *Now!*

Lunging from the shadows, Jason grabbed the man's left ear, yanking it, twisting it, propelling the contact forward, bringing his knee up into the base of the man's spine, his other hand on the man's neck. He threw him down into the bowels of the dark alley, racing with him, crashing his sneaker into the back of the contact's knee; the man fell, spinning in the fall, and stared up at Bourne.

'*You!* It is *you!*' Then the contact winced in the dim light. 'No,' he said, suddenly calm, deliberate. 'You are *not* him.'

Without a warning move, the Chinese lashed his right leg out, shoving his body off the pavement like a speeding trajectory in reverse. He caught the muscles of Jason's left thigh, following the blow with his left foot, pummelling it into Bourne's abdomen as he leaped to his feet, hands extended and rigid, his muscular body moving fluidly, even gracefully, in a semicircle and in anticipation.

What followed was a battle of animals, two trained executioners, each move made in intense premeditation, each blow lethal if it landed with full impact. One fought for his life, the other for survival and deliverance – and the woman he could not live without, *would* not live without. Finally, height and weight and a motive beyond life itself made the difference, giving victory to one and defeat to the other.

Entwined against the wall, both sweating and bruised, blood trickling from mouths and eyes, Bourne hammerlocked the contact's neck from behind, his left knee jammed into the small of the man's back, his right leg wrapped around the contact's ankles, clamping them.

'You know what happens next!' he whispered breathlessly, spacing the Chinese words for final emphasis. 'One snap and your spine goes. It's not a pleasant way to die. And you don't *have* to die. You can live with more money than the Frenchman would ever pay you. Take my word for it, the Frenchman and his killer won't be around much longer. Take your choice. *Now!*' Jason strained; the veins in the man's throat were distended to the point of bursting.

'*Yes, yes!*' cried the contact. 'I live, not die!'

They sat in the dark alleyway, their backs against the wall, smoking cigarettes. It was established that the man spoke English fluently, which he had learned from the nuns in a Portuguese Catholic school.

'You're very good, you know,' said Bourne, wiping the blood from his lips.

'I am the champion of Macao. It is why the Frenchman pays me. But you bested me. I am dishonoured, no matter what happens.'

'No you're not. It's just that I know a few more dirty tricks than you do. They're not taught where you were trained, and they never should be. Besides, no one will ever know.'

'But I am young! You are old.'

'I wouldn't go that far. Besides, I stay in pretty good shape, thanks to a crazy doctor who tells me what to do. How old do you think I am?'

'You are over *thirty!*'

'Agreed.'

'*Old!*'

'Thanks.'

'You are also very strong, very heavy – but it is more than that. I am a sane man. You are *not!*'

'Perhaps.' Jason crushed out his cigarette on the pavement. 'Let's talk sensibly,' he said, pulling money from his pocket. 'I meant what I said, I'll pay you well . . . Where's the Frenchman?'

'Everything is not in balance.'

'What do you mean?'

'Balance is important.'

'I know that, but I don't understand you.'

'There is a lack of harmony, and the Frenchman is angry. How much will you pay me?'

'How much can you tell me?'

'Where the Frenchman and his assassin will be tomorrow night.'

'Ten thousand American dollars.'

'*Aiya!*'

'But only if you take me there.'

'It is across the *border!*'

'I have a visa for Shenzen. It's good for another three days.'

'It may help, but it is not legal for the Guangdong border.'

'Then you figure it out. Ten thousand dollars, American.'

'I will figure it out.' The contact paused, his eyes on the money held out by the American. 'May I have what I believe you call an instalment?'

'Five hundred dollars, that's all.'

'Negotiations at the border will cost much more.'

'Call me. I'll bring you the money.'

'Call you where?'

'Get me a hotel room here in Macao. I'll put my money in its vault.'

'The Lisboa.'

'No, not the Lisboa. I can't go there. Someplace else.'

'There is no problem. Help me to my feet . . . *No!* It would be better for my dignity if I did not need help.'

'So be it,' said Jason Bourne.

Catherine Staples sat at her desk, the disconnected telephone still in her hand; absently she looked at it and hung up. The conversation she had just concluded astonished her. As there was no Canadian Intelligence Force currently operating in Hong Kong, foreign service officers cultivated their own sources within the Hong Kong police for those times when accurate information was needed. These occasions were invariably in the interests of Canadian citizens residing in or traveling through the colony. The problems ranged from those arrested to those assaulted, from Canadians who were swindled to those doing the swindling. Then, too, there were deeper concerns, matters of security and espionage, the former covering visits of ranking government officials, the latter involving means of protection against electronic surveillance and the gaining of sensitive information through acts of blackmail against consulate personnel. It was quiet but common knowledge that agents from the Eastern bloc and fanatically religious Middle East regimes used drugs and prostitutes of both sexes for whatever the preferences of both sexes in a never-ending pursuit of a hostile government's classified data. Hong Kong was a needle and meat market. And it was in this area that Staples had done some of her best work in the territory. She had saved the careers of two attachés in her own consulate, as well as an American and three British. Photographs of personnel in compromising acts had been destroyed along with the corresponding negatives, the extortionists banished from the colony with threats not simply of exposure but of physical harm. In one instance, an Iranian consular official, yelling in high dudgeon from his quarters at the Gammon House, accused her of meddling in affairs far above her station. She had listened to the ass for as long as she could tolerate the nasal twang, then terminated the call with a short statement: 'Didn't you know? Khomeini likes little boys.'

All of this had been made possible through her relationship with a late-middle-aged English widower who had opted for retirement from Scotland Yard to become chief of Crown Colonial Affairs in Hong Kong. At sixty-seven, Ian Ballantyne had accepted the fact that his tenure at the Yard was over, but not the use of his professional skills. He was willingly posted to the Far East, where he shook up the Intelligence division of the colony's police, and in his quiet way shaped an aggressively efficient organization that knew more about Hong Kong's shadow world than did any of the other agencies in the territory, including MI6, Special Branch. Catherine and Ian had met at one of those bureaucratically dull dinners demanded by consular protocol, and after prolonged conversation laced with wit and appraisal of his table partner, Ballantyne had leaned over and said simply, 'Do you think we can still do it, old girl?'

'Let's try,' she had replied.

They had. They enjoyed it, and Ian became a fixture in Staples's life, no strings or commitments attached. They liked each other; that was enough.

And Ian Ballantyne had just given the lie to everything Undersecretary of State Edward McAllister told Marie Webb and her husband in Maine. There was no taipan in Hong Kong named Yao Ming, and his impeccable sources – read very well paid – in Macao assured him there had been no double murder involving a taipan's wife and a drug runner at the Lisboa Hotel. There had been no such killings since the departure of the Japanese occupation forces in 1945. There had been numerous stabbings and gunshot wounds around the tables in the casino, and quite a few deaths in the rooms attributed to overdoses of narcotics, but no such incident as described by Staples's informer.

'It's a fabric of lies, Cathy old girl,' Ian had said. 'For what purpose, I can't fathom.'

'My source is legitimate, old darling. What do you smell?'

'Rancid odours, my dear. Someone is taking a great risk for a sizeable objective. He's covering himself, of course – one can buy anything over here, including silence – but the whole damn thing's fiction. Do you want to tell me more?'

'Suppose I told you it's Washington-oriented, not UK?'

'I'd have to contradict you. To go this far London has to be involved.'

'It doesn't make sense!'

'From your viewpoint, Cathy. You don't know theirs. And I can tell you this – that maniac, Bourne, has us all in a sticky wicket. One of his victims is a man nobody will talk about. I won't even tell you, my girl.'

'Will you if I bring you more information?'

'Probably not, but do try.'

Staples sat at her desk filtering the words.

One of his victims is a man nobody will talk about.

What did Ballantyne mean? What was happening? And why was a former Canadian economist in the centre of the sudden storm?

Regardless, she was safe.

Ambassador Havilland, attaché case in hand, strode into the office in Victoria Peak as McAllister bounced out of the chair, prepared to vacate it for his superior.

'Stay where you are, Edward. What news?'

'Nothing, I'm afraid.'

'*Christ*, I don't want to hear that!'

'I'm sorry.'

'Where's the retarded son of a bitch who let this happen?'

McAllister blanched as Major Lin Wenzu, unseen by Havilland, rose from the couch against the back wall. 'I am the retarded son of a bitch, the Chinese who let it happen, Mr Ambassador.'

'I'll not apologize,' said Havilland, turning and speaking harshly. 'It's your necks we're trying to save, not ours. We'll survive. You won't.'

'I'm not privileged to understand you.'

'It's not his fault,' protested the undersecretary of State.

'Is it *yours*?' shouted the ambassador. 'Were you responsible for her custody?'

'I'm responsible for everything here.'

'That's very Christian of you, Mr McAllister, but at the moment we're not reading the Scriptures in Sunday school.'

'It was *my* responsibility,' broke in Lin. 'I accepted the assignment and I failed. Simply put, the woman outsmarted us.'

'You're Lin, Special Branch?'

'Yes, Mr Ambassador.'

'I've heard good things about you.'

'I'm sure my performance invalidates them.'

'I'm told she also outsmarted a very able doctor.'

'She did,' confirmed McAllister. 'One of the best internists in the territory.'

'An Englishman,' added Lin.

'That wasn't necessary, Major. Any more than your slipping in the word "Chinese" in reference to yourself. I'm not a racist. The world doesn't know it, but it hasn't time for that crap.' Havilland crossed to the desk; he placed the attaché case on top, opened it, and removed a thick manila envelope with black borders. 'You asked for the Treadstone file. Here it is. Needless to say, it cannot leave this room and when you're not reading it, lock it in the vault.'

'I want to start as soon as possible.'

'You think you'll find something there?'

'I don't know where else to look. Incidentally, I've moved to an office down the hall. The vault's in here.'

'Feel free to come and go,' said the diplomat. 'How much have you told the major?'

'Only what I was instructed to tell him.' McAllister looked at Lin Wenzu. 'He's complained frequently that he should be told more. Perhaps he's right.'

'I'm in no position to press my complaint, Edward. London was firm, Mr Ambassador. Naturally, I accept the conditions.'

'I don't want you to "accept" anything, Major. I want you more frightened than you've ever been in your life. We'll leave Mr McAllister to his reading and take a stroll. As I was driven in I saw a large attractive garden. Will you join me?'

'It would be a privilege, sir.'

'That's questionable, but it *is* necessary. You must thoroughly understand. You've *got* to find that woman!'

Marie stood at the window in Catherine Staples's flat looking down at the activity below. The streets were crowded, as always, and she had an overpowering urge to get out of the apartment and walk anonymously among those crowds, in those streets, walk around the Asian House in hopes of finding David. At least she would be moving, staring, hearing, hoping – not thinking in silence, half going crazy. But she could not leave; she had given her word to Catherine. She had promised to stay inside, admit no one, and answer the phone only if a second, immediate call was preceded by two previous rings. It would be Staples on the line.

Dear Catherine, capable Catherine – frightened Catherine. She tried to hide her fear, but it was in her probing questions, asked too quickly, too intensely, her reactions to answers too astonished, frequently accompanied by a shortness of breath, as her eyes strayed, her throughts obviously racing. Marie had not understood, but she did understand that Staples's knowledge of the dark world of the Far East was extensive, and when such a knowledgeable person tried to conceal her fear of what she heard, there was far more to the tale than the teller knew.

The telephone. Two rings. Silence. Then a third. Marie ran to the table by the couch and picked up the phone as the third bell began. '*Yes?*'

'Marie, when this liar, McAllister, spoke to you and your husband, he mentioned a cabaret in the Tsim Sha Tsui, if I recall. Am I right?'

'Yes, he did. He said that an Uzi – that's a gun—'

'I know what it is, my dear. The same weapon was supposedly used to kill the taipan's wife and her lover in Macao, wasn't that it?'

'That's it.'

'But did he say anything about the men who had been killed in the cabaret over in Kowloon? Anything at all?'

Marie thought back. 'No, I don't think so. His point was the weapon.'

'You're positive.'

'Yes, I am. I'd remember.'

'I'm sure you would,' agreed Staples.

'I've gone over that conversation a thousand times. Have you learned anything?'

'Yes. No such killing as McAllister described to you ever took place at the Lisboa Hotel in Macao.'

'It was covered up. The banker paid.'

'Nowhere near what my impeccable source has paid – in more than money. In the coveted, impeccable stamp of his office which can lead to far greater profits for a very long time. In exchange for information, of course.'

'Catherine, what are you *saying?*'

'This is either the clumsiest operation I've ever heard of, or a brilliantly conceived plan to involve your husband in ways he would never have considered, certainly never agreed to. I suspect it's the latter.'

'Why do you say that?'

'A man flew into Kai-tak Airport this afternoon, a statesman who's always been far more than a diplomat. We all know it but the world doesn't. His arrival was on all our printouts. He demurred when the media tried to interview him, claiming he was strictly on vacation in his beloved Hong Kong.'

'And?'

'He's never taken a vacation in his life.'

McAllister ran out into the walled garden with its trellises and white wrought-iron furniture and rows of roses and rock-filled ponds. He had put the Treadstone file in the vault, but the words were indelibly printed on his mind. Where *were* they? Where was *he?*

There they were! Sitting on two concrete benches beneath a cherry tree, Lin leaning forward, mesmerized. McAllister could not help it; he broke into a run, out of breath when he reached the tree, staring at the major from Special Branch, MI6.

'*Lin!* When Webb's wife took the call from her husband – the call you terminated – what *exactly* did she say?'

'She began talking about a street in Paris where there was a row of trees, her favourite trees, I think she said,' replied Lin, bewildered. 'She was obviously trying to tell him where she was, but she was totally wrong.'

'She was totally *right!* When I questioned you, you also said that she told

Webb that "things had been terrible" on that street in Paris, or something like that—'

'That's what she said,' interrupted the major.

'But that they'd be better over *here*.'

'That is what she said.'

'In Paris a man was killed at the embassy, a man who tried to help them both!'

'What are you trying to say, McAllister?' interrupted Havilland.

'The *row* of trees is insignificant, Mr Ambassador, but not her *favourite* tree. The maple tree, the maple *leaf*. Canada's symbol! There is no Canadian embassy in Hong Kong, but there *is* a consulate. That's their meeting ground. It's the pattern! It's Paris all over again!'

'You didn't alert friendly embassies – consulates?'

'*Goddamn* it!' exploded the undersecretary of State. 'What the hell was I going to say? I'm under an oath of silence, remember, *sir*?'

'You're quite right. The rebuke is deserved.'

'You cannot tie all our hands, Mr Ambassador,' said Lin. 'You are a person I respect greatly, but a few of us, too, must be given a measure of respect if we are to do our jobs. The same respect you just gave me in your telling me of this most frightening thing. Sheng Chou Yang. *Incredible!*'

'Discretion must be absolute.'

'It will be,' said the major.

'The Canadian consulate,' said Havilland. 'Get me the roster of its entire personnel.'

16

The call had come at five o'clock in the afternoon and Bourne was ready for it. No names were exchanged.

'It is arranged,' said the caller. 'We are to be at the border shortly before twenty-one hundred hours, when the guard changes shifts. Your Shenzen visa will be scrutinized and rubber stamps will fly, but none will touch it. Once inside you are on your own, but you did not come through Macao.'

'What about getting back out? If what you told me is true and things go right, there'll be someone with me.'

'It will not be me. I will see you over and to the location. After that, I leave you.'

'That doesn't answer my question.'

'It is not so difficult as getting in, unless you are searched and contraband is found.'

'There won't be any.'

'Then I would suggest drunkenness. It is not uncommon. There is an airfield outside of Shenzen used by special—'

'I know it.'

'You were on the wrong airplane, perhaps, that too is not uncommon. The schedules are very bad in China.'

'How much for tonight?'

'Four thousand, Hong Kong, and a new watch.'

'Agreed.'

Some ten miles north of the village of Gongbei the hills rise, soon becoming a minor range of densely forested small mountains. Jason and his former adversary from the alley in Macao walked along the dirt road. The Chinese stopped and looked up at the hills above.

'Another five or six kilometres and we will reach a field. We will cross it and head up into the second level of woods. We must be careful.'

'You're sure they'll be there?'

'I carried the message. If there is a campfire, they will be there.'

'What was the message?'

'A conference was demanded.'

'Why across the border?'

'It could *only* be across the border. That, too, was part of the message.'

'But you don't know why.'

'I am only the messenger. Things are not in balance.'

'You said that last night. Can't you explain what you mean?'

'I cannot explain it to myself.'

'Could it be because the conference had to take place over here? In China?'

'That is part of it, certainly.'

'There's more?'

'*Wen ti*,' said the guide. 'Questions that arise from feelings.'

'I think I understand.' And Jason did. He had the same questions, the same feelings, when it had become clear to him that the assassin who called himself Bourne was riding in an official vehicle of the People's Republic.

'You were too generous with the guard. The watch was too expensive.'

'I may need him.'

'He may not be in the same post.'

'I'll find him.'

'He'll sell the watch.'

'Good. I'll bring him another.'

Crouching, they ran through the tall grass of the field one section at a time, Bourne following the guide, his eyes constantly roving over their flanks and up ahead, finding shadows in the darkness – and yet not total darkness. Fast, low-flying clouds obscured the moon, filtering the light, but every now and then shafts streamed down for brief moments illuminating the landscape. They reached a rising stretch of tall trees and began making their way up. The Chinese stopped and turned, both hands raised.

'What is it?' whispered Jason.

'We must go slowly, make no noise.'

'Patrols?'

The guide shrugged. 'I do not know. There is no harmony.'

They crawled up through the tangled forest, stopping at every screech of a disturbed bird and the subsequent flutter of wings, letting the moments pass. The hum of the woods was pervasive; the crickets clicked their incessant symphony, a lone owl hooted, to be answered by another, and small ferretlike creatures scampered through the underbrush. Bourne and his guide came to the end of the tall trees; there was a second sloping field of high grass in front of them, and in the distance were the jagged dark outlines of another climbing forest.

There was also something else. A glow at the top of the next hill, at the summit of the woods. It was a campfire, *the* campfire! Bourne had to hold himself in check, stop himself from getting up and racing across the field and plunging into the woods, scrambling up to the fire. Patience was everything now, and he was in the dark environs he knew so well; vague memories told him to trust himself – told him that he was the best there was. Patience. He would get across the field and silently make his way to the top of the forest; he would find a spot in the woods with a clear view of the fire, of the meeting ground. He would wait, and watch; he would know when to make his move. He had done it so often before – the specifics eluded him, but not the pattern. A man would leave, and like a cat stalking silently through the forest he would follow that man until the moment came. Again, he would know that moment, and the man would be his.

Marie, I won't fail us this time. I can move with a kind of terrible purity now – that sounds crazy, I know, but then it's true . . . I can hate with purity – that's where I came from, I think. Three bleeding bodies floating into a riverbank taught me to hate. A bloody hand print on a door in Maine taught me to reinforce that hate, and never to let it happen again. I don't often disagree with you, my love, but you were wrong in Geneva, wrong in Paris. I am a killer.

'What is *wrong* with you?' whispered the guide, his head close to Jason's. 'You do not follow my signal!'

'I'm sorry. I was thinking.'

'So am I, *peng you!* For our lives!'

'You don't have to worry, you can leave now. I see the fire up there on the hill.' Bourne pulled money from his pocket. 'I'd rather go alone. One man has less chance of being spotted than two.'

'Suppose there are other men – patrols? You bested me in Macao, but I am not unworthy in this regard.'

'If there are such men, I intend to find one.'

'In the name of Jesus, *why?*'

'I want a gun. I couldn't risk bringing one across the border.'

'*Aiya!*'

Jason handed the guide the money. 'It's all there. Nine thousand five hundred. You want to go back in the woods and count it? I've got a small flashlight.'

'One does not question the man who has bested him. Dignity would not permit such impropriety.'

'Your words are terrific, but don't buy a diamond in Amsterdam. Go on, get out of here. It's my territory.'

'And this is my gun,' said the guide, taking a weapon from his belt and handing it to Bourne as he took the money. 'Use it if you must. The magazine is full – nine shells. There is no registry, no trace. The Frenchman taught me.'

'You took this across the *border?*'

'You brought the watch, I did not. I might have dropped it into a garbage bag but then I saw the guard's face. I will not need it now.'

'Thanks. But I should tell you, if you've lied to me, I'll find you. Count on it.'

'Then the lies would not be mine and the money would be returned.'

'You're too much.'

'You bested me. I must be honourable in all things.'

Bourne crawled slowly, ever so slowly, across the expanse of tall, starched grass filled with nettles, pulling the needles from his neck and forehead, grateful for the nylon jacket that repelled them. He instinctively knew something his guide did not know, why he did not want the Chinese to come with him. A field with high grass was the most logical place to have patrols; the reeds moved when hidden intruders crawled through them. Therefore one had to observe the swaying grass from the ground and go forward with the prevailing breezes and the sudden mountain winds.

He saw the start of the woods, trees rising at the edge of the grass. He began to raise himself to a crouching position, then suddenly, swiftly, lowered his body and remained motionless. Up ahead to his right, a man stood on the border of the field, a rifle in his hands, watching the grass in the intermittent moonlight, looking for a pattern of reeds that bent against the breezes. A gust of wind swirled down from the mountains. Bourne moved with it, coming to within ten feet of the guard. Half a foot by half a foot he crawled to the edge of the field; he was now parallel with the man whose concentration was focused in front of him, not on his flanks. Jason inched up so he could see through the reeds. The guard looked to his left. *Now!*

Bourne sprang out of the grass and, rushing forward, lunged at the man. In panic, the guard instinctively swung the butt of the rifle to ward off the sudden attack. Jason grabbed the barrel, twisting it over the man's head, and crashed it down on the exposed skull as he rammed his knee into the guard's rib cage. The patrol collapsed. Bourne quickly dragged him into the high grass, out of sight. With as few movements as possible, Jason removed the guard's jacket and ripped the shirt from his back, tearing the cloth into strips. Moments later the man was bound in such a way that with every move he tightened the improvised straps. His mouth was gagged, a torn sleeve wrapped around his head holding the gag in place.

Normally, as in previous times – Bourne instinctively knew it had been the normal course of similar events – he would have lost no time racing out of the field and starting up through the woods toward the fire. Instead, he studied the unconscious figure of the Oriental below; something disturbed him – something not in harmony. For openers, he had expected the guard would be in the uniform of the Chinese army, for he all too vividly recalled the sight of the government vehicle in Shenzen and knew who was inside. But it was not simply the absence of a uniform, it was the clothes this man wore. They were cheap and filthy, rancid with the smell of grease-laden food. He reached down and twisted the man's face, opening his mouth; there were few teeth, black with decay. What kind of guard was this, what kind of patrol? He was a thug – no doubt experienced – a brute criminal, contracted in the skid rows of the Orient where life was cheap and generally meaningless. Yet the men at this 'conference' dealt in tens of thousands of dollars. The price they paid for a life was very high. Something was *not* in balance.

Bourne grabbed the rifle and crawled out of the grass. Seeing nothing, hearing nothing but the murmurs of the forest before him, he got to his feet and raced into the woods. He climbed swiftly, silently, stopping as before with every screech of a bird, every flutter of wings, each abrupt cessation of the cricket symphony. He did not crawl now, he crept on bent legs, holding the barrel of the rifle, a club if the need arose. There could be no gunshots unless his life depended on them, no warning to his quarry. The trap was closing, it was simply a matter of patience now, patience and the final stalk when the jaws of the trap would snap shut. He reached the top of the forest, gliding noiselessly behind a boulder on the edge of the campsite. Silently he lowered the rifle to the ground, withdrew from his belt the gun that the guide had given him and peered around the huge rock.

What he had expected to find below in the field he now saw. A soldier, standing erect in his uniform, a sidearm strapped to his waist, was roughly twenty feet to the left of the fire. It was as if he wanted to be seen but not identified. Out of balance. The man looked at his watch; the waiting had begun.

It lasted the better part of an hour. The soldier had smoked five cigarettes; Jason had remained still, barely breathing. And then it happened, slowly, subtly, no heralding trumpets, an entrance devoid of drama. A second figure appeared; he walked casually out of the shadows, parting the final branches of the forest as he came into view. And, without warning, bolts of lightning streaked down from the night sky, burning, searing into David Webb's head, numbing the mind of Jason Bourne.

For as the man came into the light of the fire, Bourne gasped, gripping the barrel of the gun to keep from screaming – or from killing. He was looking at a ghost of himself, a haunting apparition from years ago come back to stalk him, no matter who was the hunter now. The face was at once his face yet not his face – perhaps the face as it might have been before the surgeons altered it for Jason Bourne. Like the lean, taut body, the face was younger – younger than the myth he was imitating – and in that youth was strength, the strength of a Delta from Medusa. It was *incredible.* Even the guarded, catlike walk, the long arms loose at the sides that were so obviously proficient in the deadly arts. It *was* Delta, the Delta he had been told about, the Delta who had become Cain and finally Jason Bourne. He was looking at himself but not himself, yet withal a killer. An assassin.

A crack in the distance intruded upon the sounds of the mountain forest. The assassin stopped, then spun away from the fire and dove to his right as the soldier dropped to the ground. A deafening, echoing, staccato burst of gunfire erupted from the woods; the killer rolled over and over on the campsite grass, bullets ripping up the earth as he reached the darkness of the trees. The Chinese soldier was on one knee, firing wildly in the assassin's direction.

Then the ear-shattering battle escalated, not from one level to the next but in three separate stages. The explosions were immense. A first grenade destroyed the campsite, followed by a second, uprooting trees, the dry, wind-blown branches catching fire, and finally a third, hurled high in the air, detonating with enormous force in the area of the woods from which the machine gun had been triggered. Suddenly flames were everywhere, and Bourne shielded his eyes, moving around the boulder, weapon in hand. A trap had been set for the killer and he had walked into it! The Chinese soldier was dead, his gun blown away, as well as most of his body. A figure suddenly raced from the left into the inferno that had been the campsite, then whipped around and ran through the flames, turning twice and, seeing Jason, firing at him. The assassin had doubled back in the woods, hoping to trap and kill those who would kill him. Spinning, Bourne leaped first to his right, then to his left, then fell to the ground, his eyes on the running man. He got to his feet and sprang forward. *He could not let him get away!* He raced through the raging fires; the figure ahead of him was weaving through the trees. It was the killer! The impostor who claimed to be the lethal myth that had enraged Asia, using that myth for his own purposes, destroying the original and the wife that man loved. Bourne ran as he had never run before, dodging trees and leaping over the underbrush with an agility that denied the years between Medusa and the present. He was *back* in Medusa! He *was* Medusa! And with every ten yards he closed the gap by five. He knew the forests, and every forest was a jungle and every jungle was his friend. He had survived in the jungles; without thinking – only feeling – he knew their curvatures, their vines, the sudden pits and the abrupt ravines. He was gaining, *gaining!* And then he was *there*, the killer only feet ahead of him!

With what seemed like the last breath in his body, Jason lunged – Bourne against Bourne! His hands were the claws of a mountain cat as he gripped the shoulders of the racing figure in front of him, his fingers digging into the hard flesh and bone as he whipped the killer back, his heels dug into the earth, his right knee crashing up into the man's spine. His rage was such that he consciously had to remind himself not to kill. *Stay alive!* You are my freedom, *our* freedom!

The assassin screamed as the true Jason Bourne hammerlocked his neck, wrenching the head to the right and forcing the pretender down. Both fell to the ground, Bourne's forearm jammed across the man's throat, his left hand clenched, repeatedly pounding the killer's lower abdomen, forcing the air out of the weakening body.

The face? The *face?* Where was the face that belonged to years ago? To an apparition that wanted to take him back into a hell that memory had blocked out. Where was the *face?* This was not *it!*

'*Delta!*' screamed the man beneath him.

'What did you *call me?*' shouted Bourne.

'*Delta!*' shrieked the writhing figure. 'Cain is for *Carlos, Delta is for Cain!*'

'God*damn* you! Who—'

'*D'Anjou!* I am *d'Anjou! Medusa!* Tam Quan! We have no names, only symbols! For God's sake, *Paris!* The Louvre! You saved my life in *Paris* – as you saved so many lives in *Medusa!* I am *d'Anjou!* I told you what you had to know in Paris! *You* are Jason Bourne! The madman who runs from us is but a *creation! My* creation!'

Webb stared at the contorted face below, at the perfectly groomed grey moustache and the silver hair that swept back over the aging head. The nightmare had returned . . . he was in the steaming infested jungles of Tam Quan with no way out and death all around them. Then suddenly he was in Paris, nearing the steps of the Louvre in the blinding afternoon sunlight. *Gunshots.* Cars screeching, crowds screaming. He had to save the face beneath him! Save the face from Medusa who could supply the missing pieces of the insane puzzle!

'*D'Anjou?*' whispered Jason. 'You're *d'Anjou?*'

'If you will give me back my throat,' choked the Frenchman, 'I will tell you a story. I'm sure you have one to tell me.'

*

Philippe d'Anjou surveyed the wreckage of the campsite, now a smoking ruin. He crossed himself as he searched the pockets of the dead 'soldier,' removing whatever valuables he found. 'We'll free the man below when we leave,' he said. 'There's no other access to this place. It's why I posted him there.'

'And told him to look for what?'

'Like you, I'm from Medusa. Fields of grass – poets and consumers notwithstanding – are both avenues and traps. Guerrillas know that. We knew that.'

'You couldn't have anticipated *me.*'

'Hardly. But I could and did anticipate every countermove my creation might consider. He was to arrive alone. The instructions were clear, but who could trust him, least of all me?'

'You're ahead of me.'

'It's part of my story. You'll hear it.'

They walked down through the woods, the elderly d'Anjou gripping the trunks of trees and saplings to ease the descent. They reached the field, hearing the muted screams of the bound guard as they walked into the tall grass. Bourne cut the cloth straps with his knife and the Frenchman paid him.

'*Zou ba!*' yelled d'Anjou. The man fled into the darkness. 'He is garbage. They are all garbage, but they kill willingly for a price and disappear.'

'You tried to kill *him* tonight, didn't you? It was a trap.'

'Yes. I thought he was wounded in the explosions. It's why I went after him.'

'I thought he'd doubled back to take you at the rear.'

'Yes, we would have done that in Medusa—'

'It's why I thought you were him.' Jason suddenly shouted in fury. 'What have you *done?*'

'It's part of the story.'

'I want to hear it. *Now!*'

'There's a flat stretch of ground several hundred yards, over there to the left,' said the Frenchman, pointing. 'It used to be a grazing field, but recently it's been used by helicopters flying in to meet with an assassin. Let's go to the far end and rest – and talk. Just in case what remains of the fire draws anyone from the village.'

'It's five miles away.'

'Still, this is China.'

The clouds had dispersed, blown away with the night winds; the moon was descending, yet was still high enough to wash the distant mountains with its light. The two men of Medusa sat on the ground. Bourne lit a cigarette as d'Anjou spoke. 'Do you remember back in Paris, that crowded café where we talked after the madness at the Louvre?'

'Sure. Carlos nearly killed us both that afternoon.'

'You nearly trapped the Jackal.'

'But I didn't. What about Paris, the café?'

'I told you then I was coming back to Asia. To Singapore or Hong Kong, perhaps the Seychelles, I think I said. France was never good for me – or to me. After Dienbienphu – everything I had was destroyed, blown up by our own troops – the talk of reparations was meaningless. Hollow babbling from hollow men. It's why I joined Medusa. The only possible way to get back my own was with an American victory.'

'I remember,' said Jason. 'What's that got to do with tonight?'

'As is obvious, I came back to Asia. Since the Jackal had seen me, the routing was circuitous, which left me time to think. I had to make a clear appraisal of my circumstances and the possibilities before me. As I was fleeing for my life, my assets were not extensive but neither were they pathetic. I took the risk of returning to the shop in St Honoré that afternoon and frankly stole every *sou* in and out of sight. I knew the combination of the safe, and fortunately it was well endowed. I could comfortably buy myself across the world, out of Carlos's reach, and live for many weeks without panic. But what was I to do with myself? The funds would run out, and my skills – so apparent in the civilized world – were not such that would permit me to live out the autumn of my life over here in the comfort that was stolen from me. Still, I had not been a snake in the head of Medusa for nothing. God knows I discovered and developed talents I never dreamed were within me – and found, frankly, that morality was not an issue. I had been wronged, and I could wrong others. And nameless, faceless strangers had tried to kill me countless times, so I could assume the responsibility for the death of nameless, faceless other strangers. You see the symmetry, don't you? At once removed, the equations became abstract.'

'I hear a lot of horseshit,' replied Bourne.

'Then you are not listening, Delta.'

'I'm not Delta.'

'Very well. Bourne.'

'I'm not – go on, perhaps I am.'

'*Comment?*'

'*Rien.* Go on.'

'It struck me that regardless of what happened to you in Paris – whether you won or lost, whether you were killed or spared – Jason Bourne was finished. And by all the holy saints, I knew Washington would never utter a word of acknowledgment or clarification; you would simply disappear. "Beyond-salvage," I believe is the term.'

'I'm aware of it,' said Jason. 'So I was finished.'

'*Naturellement.* But there would be no explanations, there could *not* be. *Mon Dieu,* the assassin they invented had gone mad – he had *killed!* No, there would be nothing. Strategists retreat into the darkest shadows when their plans go – "off the wire," I think is the phrase.'

'I'm aware of that one, too.'

'*Bien.* Then you can comprehend the solution I found for myself, for the last days of an older man.'

'I'm beginning to.'

'*Bien encore.* There was a void here in Asia. Jason Bourne was no longer, but his legend was still alive. And there are men who will pay for the services of such an extraordinary man. Therefore I knew what I had to do. It was simply a matter of finding the right contender—'

'Contender?'

'Very well, *pretender*, if you wish. And train him in the ways of Medusa, in the ways of the most vaunted member of that so unofficial, criminal fraternity. I went to Singapore and searched the caves of the outcasts, often fearing for my life, until I found the man. And I found him quickly, I might add. He was desperate; he had been running for his life for nearly three years, staying, as they say, only steps away from those hunting him. He is an Englishman, a former Royal Commando who got drunk one night and killed seven people in the London streets while in a rage. Because of his outstanding service record he was sent to a psychiatric hospital in Kent, from which he escaped and somehow – God *knows* how – made his way to Singapore. He had all the tools of the trade; they simply needed to be refined and guided.'

'He looks like me. Like I used to look.'

'Far more now than he did. The basic features were there, also the tall frame and the muscular body; they were assets. It was merely a question of altering a rather prominent nose and rounding a sharper chin than I remembered your having – as Delta, of course. You were different in Paris, but not so radically that I could not recognize you.'

'A commando,' said Jason quietly. 'It fits. Who is he?'

'He's a man without a name but not without a macabre story,' replied d'Anjou, gazing at the mountains in the distance.

'No name . . . ?'

'None he ever gave me that he would not contradict in the next breath – none remotely authentic. He guards that name as if it were the sole extension of his life, its revelation inevitably leading to his death. Of course, he's right; the present circumstances are a case in point. If I had a name, I could forward it through a blind to the British authorities in Hong Kong. Their computers would light up; specialists would be flown from London and a manhunt that I could never mount would be set in motion. They'd never take him alive – he wouldn't permit it and they wouldn't care to – and thus my purpose would be served.'

'Why do the British want him terminated?'

'Suffice it to say that Washington had its Mai Lais and its Medusa, while London has a far more recent military unit led by a homicidal psychotic who left hundreds slaughtered in his wake – few distinctions were made between the innocent and the guilty. He holds too many secrets, which, if exposed, could lead to violent eruptions of revenge throughout the Mideast and Africa. Practicality comes first, you know that. Or you should.'

'He *led?*' asked Bourne, as stunned as he was bewildered.

'No mere foot soldier he, Delta. He was a captain at twenty-two and a major at twenty-four when rank was next to impossible to obtain due to Whitehall's service economies. No doubt he'd be a brigadier or even a full general by now if his luck had held out.'

'That's what he told you?'

'In periodic drunken rages when ugly truths would surface – but never his name. They usually occurred once or twice a month, several days at a time when he'd block out his life in a drunken sea of self-loathing. Yet he was always coherent enough before the outbursts came, telling me to strap him down, confine him, protect him from himself . . . He would relive horrible events from his past, his voice hoarse, guttural, hollow. As the drink took over he would describe scenes of torture and mutilation, questioning prisoners with knives puncturing their eyes, and their wrists slit, ordering his captives to watch as their lives flowed out of their veins. So far as I could piece the fragments together, he commanded many of the most dangerous and savage raids against the fanatical uprisings of the late seventies and early eighties, from Yemen down to the bloodbaths in East Africa. In one moment of besotted jubilation he spoke of how Idi Amin himself would stop breathing at the mention of his name, so widespread was his reputation for matching – even surpassing – Amin's strategy of brutality.' D'Anjou paused, nodding his head slowly and arching his brows in the Gallic acceptance of the inexplicable. 'He was subhuman – *is* subhuman – but for all that a highly intelligent so-called officer and a gentleman. A complete paradox, a total contradiction of the civilized man . . . He'd laugh at the fact that his troops despised him and called him an animal yet none ever dared to raise an official complaint.'

'Why not?' asked Jason, stirred and pained at what he was hearing. 'Why didn't they report him?'

'Because he always brought them out – most of them out – when the order of battle seemed hopeless.'

'I see,' said Bourne, letting the remark ride with the mountain breezes. 'No, I *don't* see,' he cried angrily, as if suddenly, unexpectedly stung. 'Command structure is *better* than that. Why did his superiors put up with him? They had to *know!*'

'As I understood his rantings, he got the jobs done when others couldn't – or wouldn't. He learned the secret we in Medusa learned long ago. Play by the enemy's most ruthless conditions. Change the rules according to the culture. After all, human life to others is not what it is to the Judeo-Christian concept. How could it be? For so many, death is a liberation from intolerable human conditions.'

'Breathing is *breathing!*' insisted Jason harshly. 'Being is *being* and thinking is *thinking!*' added David Webb. 'He's a Neanderthal.'

'No more than Delta was at certain times. And you got *us* out of how many—'

'Don't *say* that!' protested the man from Medusa, cutting off the Frenchman. 'It wasn't the same.'

'But certainly a variation,' insisted d'Anjou. 'Ultimately the motives do not really matter, do they? Only the results. Or don't you care to accept the truth? You lived it once. Does Jason Bourne now live with lies?'

'At the moment I simply live – from day to day, from night to night – until it's over. One way or another.'

'You must be clearer.'

'When I want to or have to,' replied Bourne icily. 'He's good, then, isn't he? Your commando – major without a name. Good at what he does.'

'As good as Delta – perhaps better. You see, he has no conscience, none whatsoever. You, on the other hand, as violent as you were, showed flashes of compassion. Something inside you demanded it. "Spare this man," you would say. "He is a husband, a father, a brother. Incapacitate him, but let him live, let him function later" . . . My creation, your impostor, would never do that. He wants always the final solution – death in front of his eyes.'

'What happened to him? Why did he kill those people in London? Being drunk's not a good enough reason, not where he's been.'

'It is if it's a way of life you can't resign from.'

'You keep your weapon in place unless you're threatened. Otherwise you invite the threats.'

'He used no weapon. Only his hands that night in London.'

'*What?*'

'He stalked the streets looking for imagined enemies – that's what I gathered from his ravings. "It was in their eyes!" he'd scream. "It's always in the eyes! They know who I am, *what* I am." I tell you, Delta, it was both frightening and tedious, and I never got a name, never a specific reference other than Idi Amin, which any drunken soldier of fortune would use to further himself. To involve the British in Hong Kong would mean involving myself, and, after all, I certainly could not do that. The whole thing's so frustrating, so I went back to the ways of Medusa. Do it yourself. You taught us that, Delta. You constantly told us – ordered us – to use our imagination. That's what I did tonight. And I failed, as an old man might be expected to fail.'

'Answer my question,' pressed Bourne. 'Why did he kill those people in London?'

'For a reason as banal as it was pointless – and entirely too familiar. He'd been rejected, and his ego could not tolerate that rejection. I sincerely doubt that any other emotion was involved. As with all his indulgences, sexual activity is simply an animal release; no affection is involved, for he has no capacity for it. *Mon Dieu*, he was so *right!*'

'Again. What happened?'

'He had returned, wounded, from some particularly brutal duty in Uganda expecting to take up where he left off with a woman in London – someone, I gather, rather highborn, as the English say, a throwback to his earlier days, no doubt. But she refused to see him and hired armed guards to protect her house in Chelsea after he called her. Two of those men were among the seven he killed that night. You see, she claimed his temper was uncontrollable and his bouts of drinking made him murderous, which, of course, they did. But for me he was the perfect contender. In Singapore I followed him outside a disreputable bar and saw him corner two murderous thugs in an alleyway – *contrebandiers* who had made a great deal of money with a narcotics sale in that filthy waterfront cave – and watched as he backed them against the wall, slashing both their throats with a single sweep of his knife and removing the proceeds from their pockets. I knew then that he had it all. I had found my Jason Bourne. I approached him slowly, silently, my hand extended, holding more money than he had extracted from his victims. We talked. It was the beginning.'

'So Pygmalion created his Galatea, and the first contract you accepted became Aphrodite and gave it life. Bernard Shaw would love you, and I could kill you.'

'To what end? You came to find him tonight. I came to destroy him.'

'Which is part of your story,' said David Webb, looking away from the Frenchman at the fired mountains, thinking of Maine and the life with Marie that had been so violently disrupted. 'You *bastard!*' he suddenly shouted. 'I *could* kill you! Have you any idea what you've *done?*'

'That is your story, Delta. Let me finish mine.'

'Make it neat . . . *Echo.* That *was* your name, wasn't it? Echo?' *The memories came back.*

'Yes, it was. You once told Saigon that you would not travel without "old Echo." I had to be with your team because I could discern trouble with the tribes and the village chiefs that others could not – which had little to do with my alphabetical symbol. Of course, it was nothing mystic. I had lived in the colonies for ten years. I knew when the *Quan-si* were lying.'

'Finish your story,' ordered Bourne.

'Betrayal,' said d'Anjou, palms outstretched. 'Just as you were created, I created my own Jason Bourne. And just as you went mad, my creation did the same. He turned on me; he became the reality that was my invention. Dismiss Galatea, Delta, he became Frankenstein's monster with none of that creature's torment. He broke away from me and began to think for himself, *do* for himself. Once his desperation left him – with my inestimable help and a surgeon's knife – his sense of authority came back to him, as well as his arrogance, his ugliness. He considers me a trifle. That's what he called me, a "trifle"! An insignificant nonentity who *used* him! *I* who created him!'

'You mean he makes contracts on his own?'

'Perverted contracts, grotesque and extraordinarily dangerous.'

'But I traced him through you, through *your* arrangements at the Kam Pek casino. Table Five. The telephone number of a hotel in Macao and a name.'

'A method of contact he finds convenient to maintain. And why not? It's virtually security-proof and what can I do? Go to the authorities and say, "See here, gentlemen, there's this fellow I'm somewhat responsible for who insists on using arrangements I created so he can be paid for killing someone." He even uses my conduit.'

'The *Zhongguo ren* with the fast hands and faster feet?'

D'Anjou looked at Jason. 'So that's how you did it, how you found this place. Delta hasn't lost his touch, *n'est-ce pas?* Is the man alive?'

'He is, and ten thousand dollars richer.'

'He's a money-hungry *cochon.* But I can hardly criticize, I used him myself. I paid him five hundred to pick up and deliver a message.'

'That brought your creation here tonight so you could kill him? What made you so sure he'd come?'

'A Medusan's instinct, and skeletal knowledge of an extraordinary liaison he has made, a contact so profitable to him and so dangerous it could have all Hong Kong at war, the entire colony paralyzed.'

'I heard that theory before,' said Jason, recalling McAllister's words spoken that early evening in Maine, 'and I still don't believe it. When killers kill each other, they're the ones who usually lose. They blow themselves away and informers come out of the woodwork thinking they might be next.'

'If the victims are restricted to such a convenient pattern, certainly you are right. But not when they include a powerful political figure from a vast and aggressive nation.'

Bourne stared at d'Anjou. '*China?*' he asked softly.

The Frenchman nodded. 'Five men were killed in the Tsim Sha Tsui—'

'I know that.'

'Four of those corpses were meaningless. Not the fifth. He was the Vice-Premier of the People's Republic.'

'Good God!' Jason frowned, the image of a car coming to him. A car with its windows blacked out and an assassin inside. An official government vehicle of the Chinese government.

'My sources tell me that the wires burned between Government House and Beijing, practicality and face winning out – *this* time. After all, what was the Vice-Premier doing in Kowloon, to begin with? Was such an august leader of the Central Committee also one of the corrupted? But, as I say, that is this time. No, Delta, my creation must be destroyed before he accepts another contract that could plunge us all into an abyss.'

'Sorry, Echo. Not killed. Taken and brought to someone else.'

'That is your story, then?' asked d'Anjou.

'Part of it, yes.'

'Tell me.'

'Only what you have to know. My wife was kidnapped and brought to Hong Kong. To get her back – and I'll get her back, or every goddamned one of you will die – I have to deliver your son-of-a-bitch creation. And now I'm one step closer because you're going to help me, and I mean *really* help me. If you don't—'

'Threats are unnecessary, Delta,' interrupted the former Medusan. 'I know what you can do. I've seen you do it. You want him for your reasons and I want him for mine. The order of battle is joined.'

17

Catherine Staples insisted that her dinner guest have another vodka martini, demurring for herself, as her glass was still half full.

'It's also half empty,' said the thirty-two-year-old American attaché, smiling wanly and nervously, pushing his dark hair away from his forehead. 'That's stupid of me, Catherine,' he added. 'I'm sorry, but I can't forget that you saw the photographs – never mind that you saved my career and probably my life – it's those goddamned photographs.'

'No one else saw them except Inspector Ballantyne.'

'But *you* saw them.'

'I'm old enough to be your mother.'

'That compounds it. I look at you and feel so ashamed, so damned dirty.'

'My former husband, wherever he is, once said to me that there was absolutely nothing that could or should be considered dirty in sexual encounters. I suspect there was a motive for his making the statement, but I happen to think he was right. Look, John, put them out of your mind. I have.'

'I'll do my best.' A waiter approached; the drink was ordered by signal. 'Since your call this afternoon I've been a basket case. I thought more had surfaced. That was a twenty-four-hour period of pure outer space.'

'You were heavily and insidiously drugged. On that level you weren't responsible. And *I'm* sorry, I should have told you it had nothing to do with our previous business.'

'If you had, I might have earned my salary for the last five hours.'

'It was forgetful and cruel of me. I apologize.'

'Accepted. You're a great girl, Catherine.'

'I appeal to your infantile regressions.'

'Don't bet too much money on that.'

'Then don't you have a fifth martini.'

'It's only my second.'

'A *little* flattery never hurt anyone.'

They laughed quietly. The waiter returned with John Nelson's drink; he thanked the man and turned back to Staples. 'I have an idea that the prospect of flattery didn't get me a free meal at the Plume. This place is out of my range.'

'Mine, too, but not Ottawa's. You'll be listed as a terribly important person. In fact you are.'

'That's nice. No one ever told me. I'm in a pretty good job over here because

I learned Chinese. I figured that with all those Ivy League recruits, a boy from Upper Iowa College in old Fayette, Big I, ought to have an edge somewhere.'

'You have it, Johnny. The consulates like you. Our out-posted "Embassy Row" thinks very highly of you, and they should.'

'If they do, it's thanks to you and Ballantyne. And *only* you two.' Nelson paused, slipped his martini, and looked at Staples over the rim of the glass. He lowered his drink and spoke again. 'What is it, Catherine? Why am I important?'

'Because I need your help.'

'Anything. *Anything* I can do.'

'Not so fast, Johnny. It's deep-water time and I could be drowning myself.'

'If anyone deserves a lifeline from me, it's you. Outside of minor problems, our two countries live next door to each other and basically like each other – we're on the same side. What is it? How can I help you?'

'Marie St Jacques . . . Webb,' said Catherine, studying the attaché's face.

Nelson blinked, his eyes roving aimlessly in thought. 'Nothing,' he said. 'The name doesn't mean anything to me.'

'All right, let's try Raymond Havilland.'

'*Oh*, now that's another barrel of pickled herring.' The attaché widened his eyes and cocked his head. 'We've *all* been scuttlebutting about *him*. He hasn't come to the consulate, hasn't even called our head honcho, who wants to get his picture in the papers with him. After all, Havilland's a class act – kind of metaphysical in this business. He's been around since the loaves and the fishes, and he probably engineered the whole scam.'

'Then you're aware that over the years your aristocratic ambassador has been involved with more than diplomatic negotiations.'

'Nobody ever says it, but only the naïve accept his above-the-fray posture.'

'You *are* good, Johnny.'

'Merely observant. I do earn some of my pay. What's the connection between a name I *do* know and one that I don't?'

'I wish I knew. Do you have any idea why Havilland is over here? Any rumours you've picked up?'

'I've no idea why he's here, but I do know you won't find him at a hotel.'

'I assume he has wealthy friends—'

'I'm sure he does, but he's not staying with them, either.'

'Oh?'

'The consulate quietly leased a house in Victoria Peak, and a second marine contingent was flown over from Hawaii for guard duty. None of us in the upper-middle ranks knew about it until a few days ago when one of those dumb things happened. Two marines were having dinner in the Wanchai and one of them paid the bill with a temporary cheque drawn on a Hong Kong bank. Well, you know servicemen and cheques; the manager gave this corporal a hard time. The kid said neither he nor his buddy had had time to round up cash and that the cheque was perfectly good. Why didn't the manager call the consulate and talk to a military attaché?'

'Smart corporal,' broke in Staples.

'Unsmart consulate,' said Nelson. 'The military boys had gone for the day, and our hotshot security personnel in their limitless paranoia about secrecy hadn't rostered the Victoria Peak contingent. The manager said later that the corporal showed a couple of ID's and seemed like a nice kid, so he took a chance.'

'That was reasonable of him. He probably wouldn't have if the corporal had behaved otherwise. Again, smart marine.'

'He *did* behave otherwise. The next morning down at the consulate. He read the riot act in all but barracks language in a voice so loud even I heard him, and my office is at the end of the corridor from the reception room. He wanted to know who the hell we civvies thought they were up there on that mountain and how come they weren't rostered, since they'd been there for a week. He was one angry gyrene, let me tell you.'

'And suddenly the whole consulate knew there was a sterile house in the colony.'

'You said that, Catherine, I didn't. But I'll tell you exactly what the memorandum to all personnel instructed us to say – the memo arrived on our desks an hour after the corporal had left, having spent twenty minutes with some very embarrassed security clowns.'

'And what you were instructed to say is not what you believe.'

'No comment,' said Nelson. 'The house in Victoria was leased for the convenience and security of travelling government personnel as well as representatives of US corporations doing business in the territory.'

'Hogwash. Especially the latter. Since when does the American taxpayer pick up those kinds of tabs for General Motors and ITT?'

'Washington is actively encouraging an expansion of trade in line with our widening open-door policy with respect to the People's Republic. It's consistent. We want to make things easier, more accessible, and this place is crowded as hell. Try getting a decent reservation on two days' notice.'

'You sound like you rehearsed that.'

'No comment. I've told you only what I was instructed to tell you should you bring the matter up – which I'm sure you did.'

'Of course I did. I have friends in the Peak who think the neighbourhood's going to seed, what with all those corporal types hanging around.' Staples sipped her drink. 'Havilland's up there?' she asked, placing the glass back on the table.

'Almost guaranteed.'

'Almost?'

'Our information officer – her office is next to mine – wanted to get some PR mileage out of the ambassador. She asked the CG which hotel he was at, and she was told that he wasn't. Then whose residence? Same answer. "We'll have to wait until he calls us, if he does," said our boss. She cried on my shoulder, but the order was firm. No tracking him down.'

'He's up in the Peak,' concluded Staples quietly. 'He's built himself a sterile house and he's mounted an operation.'

'Which has something to do with this Webb, this Marie St Somebody Webb?'

'St Jacques. Yes.'

'Do you want to tell me about it?'

'Not now – for your sake as well as mine. If I'm right and anyone thought you'd been given information, you could be transferred to Reykjavik without a sweater.'

'But you said you didn't know what the connection was, that you wished you did.'

'In the sense that I can't understand the reasons for it if, indeed, it exists. I only know one side of the story and it's filled with holes. I could be wrong.' Catherine again drank a small portion of her whisky. 'Look, Johnny,' she continued. 'Only you can make the decision and if it's negative, I'll understand. I have to know if Havilland's being over here has anything to do with a man named David Webb and his wife, Marie St Jacques. She was an economist in Ottawa before her marriage.'

'She's Canadian?'

'Yes. Let me tell you why I have to know without telling you so much you could get into trouble. If the connection's there, I have to go one way; if it's not, I can turn a hundred and eighty degrees and take another route. If it's the latter, I can go public. I can use the newspapers, radio, television, anything that can spread the word and pull her husband in.'

'Which means he's out in the cold,' broke in the attaché. 'And you know where she is, but others don't.'

'As I said before, you're very quick.'

'But if it's the former – if there *is* a connection to Havilland, which you believe there is—'

'No comment. If I answered you, I'd be telling you more than you should know.'

'I see. It's touchy. Let me think.' Nelson picked up his martini, but instead of drinking he put it down. 'How about an anonymous phone call that I got?'

'Such as?'

'A distraught Canadian woman looking for information about her missing American husband.'

'Why would she have called you? She's experienced in government circles. Why not the consul general himself?'

'He wasn't in. I was.'

'I don't want to disabuse you of your dreams of glory, Johnny, but you're not next in line.'

'You're right. And anyone could check the switchboard and find out I never got the call.'

Staples frowned, then leaned forward. 'There is a way if you're willing to lie a bit further. It's based on reality. It happened, and no one could say that it didn't.'

'What is it?'

'A woman stopped you in Garden Road when you were leaving the consulate. She didn't tell you very much but enough to alarm you, and she wouldn't go inside because she was frightened. She's the distraught woman looking for her missing American husband. You could even describe her.'

'Start with her description,' said Nelson.

Sitting in front of McAllister's desk, Lin Wenzu read from his notebook as the undersecretary of State listened. 'Although the description differs, the differences are minor and easily achieved. Hair pulled back and covered by a hat, no makeup, flat shoes to reduce her height but not that much – it is she.'

'And she claimed not to recognize the name of anyone in the directory who could be her so-called cousin?'

'A second cousin on her mother's side. Just farfetched yet specific enough to be credible. According to the receptionist she was quite awkward, even flustered. She also carried a purse that was so obviously a Gucci imitation that the receptionist took her for a backwoods hick. Pleasant but gullible.'

'She recognized someone's name,' said McAllister.

'If she did, why didn't she ask to see him? She wouldn't waste time under the circumstances.'

'She probably assumed that we'd sent out an alert, that she couldn't take the chance of being recognized, not on the premises.'

'I don't think that would concern her, Edward. With what she knows, what she's been through, she could be extremely convincing.'

'With what she *thinks* she knows, Lin. She can't be sure of anything. She'll be very cautious, afraid to make a wrong move. That's her husband out there, and take my word for it – I saw them together – she's extremely protective of him. My God, she stole over five million dollars for the simple reason that she thought quite correctly he'd been wronged by his own people. By her lights he deserved it – *they* deserved it – and let Washington go to hell in a basket.'

'She did that?'

'Havilland cleared you for everything. She did that and got away with it. Who was going to raise his voice? She had clandestine Washington just the way she wanted it. Frightened and embarrassed, both to the teeth.'

'The more I learn, the more I admire her.'

'Admire her all you like, just *find* her.'

'Speaking of the ambassador, where is he?'

'Having a quiet lunch with the Canadian High Commissioner.'

'He's going to tell him everything?'

'No, he's going to ask for blind cooperation with a telephone at his table so he can reach London. London will instruct the commissioner to do whatever Havilland asks him to do. It's all been arranged.'

'He moves and shakes, doesn't he?'

'There's no one like him. He should be back any minute now – actually, he's late.' The telephone rang and McAllister picked it up. 'Yes? . . . No, he's not here. *Who?* . . . Yes, of course, I'll talk to him.' The undersecretary covered the mouthpiece and spoke to the major. 'It's our consul general. I mean American.'

'Something's happened,' said Lin, nervously getting out of his chair.

'Yes, Mr Lewis, this is McAllister. I want you to know how much we appreciate everything, sir. The consulate's been most cooperative.'

Suddenly, the door opened and Havilland walked into the room.'

'It's the American consul general, Mr Ambassador,' said Lin. 'I believe he was asking for you.'

'This is no time for one of his damned dinner parties!'

'Just a minute, Mr Lewis. The ambassador just arrived. I'm sure you want to speak with him.' McAllister extended the phone to Havilland, who walked rapidly to the desk.

'Yes, Jonathan, what is it?' His tall, slender body rigid, his eyes fixed on an unseen spot in the garden beyond the large bay window, the ambassador stood in silence, listening. Finally, he spoke. 'Thank you, Jonathan, you did the right thing. Say absolutely *nothing* to anyone and I'll take it from here.' Havilland hung up and looked alternately at McAllister and Lin. 'Our breakthrough, if it is a breakthrough, just came from the wrong direction. Not the Canadian but the *American* consulate.'

'It's not consistent,' said McAllister. 'It's not Paris, not the street with her favourite tree, the maple tree, the maple *leaf*. That's the *Canadian* consulate, *not* the American.'

'And with that analysis are we to disregard it?'

'Of course not. What happened?'

'An attaché named Nelson was stopped in Garden Road by a Canadian woman trying to find her American husband. This Nelson offered to help her, to accompany her to the police but she was adamant. She wouldn't go to the police, and neither would she go back with him to his office.'

'Did she give any reasons?' asked Lin. 'She appeals for help and then refuses it.'

'Just that it was personal. Nelson described her as high-strung, overwrought. She identified herself as Marie Webb and said that perhaps her husband had come to the consulate looking for her. Could Nelson ask around and she'd call him back.'

'That's *not* what she said before,' protested McAllister. 'She was clearly referring to what had happened to them in Paris, and that meant reaching an official of her own government, her own country. Canada.'

'Why do you persist?' asked Havilland. 'That's not a criticism, I simply want to know why.'

'I'm not sure. Something's not right. Among other things, the major here established the fact that she did go to the Canadian consulate.'

'Oh?' The ambassador looked at the man from Special Branch.

'The receptionist confirmed it. The description was close enough, especially for someone trained by a chameleon. Her story was that she had promised her family she would look up a distant cousin whose last name she had forgotten. The receptionist gave her a directory and she went through it.'

'She found someone she knew,' interrupted the undersecretary of State. 'She made contact.'

'Then there's your answer,' said Havilland firmly. 'She learned that her husband had *not* gone to a street with a row of maple trees, so she took the next best course of action. The American consulate.'

'And identifies herself when she has to know people are looking for her all over Hong Kong?'

'Giving a false name would serve no purpose,' the ambassador replied.

'They both speak French. She could have used a French word – *toile*, for instance. It means web.'

'I know what it means, but I think you're reaching.'

'Her husband would have understood. She would have done something less obvious.'

'Mr Ambassador,' interrupted Lin Wenzu, slowly taking his eyes off McAllister. 'Hearing your words to the American consul general, that he should say absolutely nothing to anyone, and now fully understanding your concerns for secrecy, I assume Mr Lewis has not been apprised of the situation.'

'Correct, Major.'

'Then how did he know to call you? People frequently get lost here in Hong Kong. A missing husband or a missing wife is not so uncommon.'

For an instant Havilland's expression was creased with self-doubt. 'Jonathan Lewis and I go back a long time,' he said, his voice lacking its usual authority. 'He may be something of a bon vivant, but he's no fool – he wouldn't be here if he were. And the circumstances under which the woman stopped his attaché – well, Lewis knows me and he drew certain conclusions.' The diplomat turned to McAllister; when he continued, his authority gradually returned. 'Call Lewis back, Edward. Tell him to instruct this Nelson to stand by for a call from you. I'd prefer a less direct approach, but there isn't time. I want you to question him, question him on anything and everything you can think of. I'll be listening on the line in your office.'

'You agree, then,' said the undersecretary. 'Something's wrong.'

'Yes,' answered Havilland, looking at Lin. 'The major saw it and I didn't. I'd phrase it somewhat differently, but it's essentially what disturbs him. The question is not why Lewis called me, it's why an attaché went to *him*. After all, a highly agitated woman says her husband's missing but she won't go to the police, won't enter the consulate. Normally such a person would be dismissed as a crank. Certainly on the surface it's not a matter to bring to the attention of an overworked CG. Call Lewis.'

'Of course. But, first, did things go smoothly with the Canadian commissioner? Will he cooperate?'

'The answer to your first question is no, things did not go smoothly. As to the second, he has no choice.'

'I don't understand.'

Havilland exhaled in weary irritation. 'Through Ottawa he'll provide us with a list of everyone on his staff who's had any dealings whatsoever with Marie St Jacques – reluctantly. That's the cooperation he's been instructed to deliver, but he was damned testy about it. To begin with, he himself went through a two-day seminar with her four years ago, and he ventured that probably a quarter of the consulate had done the same. Not that she'd remember them, but they certainly would remember her. She was "outstanding," was the way he put it. She's also a Canadian who was thoroughly messed up by a group of American assholes – mind you, he had no compunction at all using the word – in some kind of mentally deranged black operation – yes, that was the phrase he used, "mentally deranged" – an *idiotic* operation mounted by these same assholes – indeed, he repeated it – that has never been satisfactorily explained.' The ambassador stopped briefly, smiling briefly, as he coughed a short laugh. 'It was all very refreshing. He didn't pull a single punch, and I haven't been talked to like that since my dear wife died. I need more of it.'

'But you *did* tell him it was for her own good, didn't you? That we've *got* to find her before any harm's done to her.'

'I got the distinct impression that our Canadian friend had serious doubts about my mental faculties. Call Lewis. God knows when we'll get that list. Our maple leaf will probably have it sent by train from Ottawa to Vancouver, and then on a slow freighter to Hong Kong, where it'll get lost in the mailroom. In the meantime, we've got an attaché who behaves very strangely. He leaps over fences when no such jumps are required.'

'I've met John Nelson, sir,' said Lin. 'He's a bright lad and speaks a fair Chinese. He's quite popular with the consulate crowd.'

'He's also something else, Major.'

Nelson hung up the phone. Beads of perspiration had broken out on his forehead; he wiped them off with the back of his hand, satisfied that he had handled himself as well as he did, all things considered. He was especially pleased that he had turned the thrust of McAllister's questions against the questioner, albeit diplomatically.

Why did you feel compelled to go to the consul general?

Your call would seem to answer that, Mr McAllister. I sensed that something out of the ordinary had happened. I thought the consul should be told.

But the woman refused to go to the police; she even refused to come inside the consulate.

As I said, it was out of the ordinary, sir. She was nervous and tense, but she wasn't a ding-dong.

A what?

She was perfectly lucid, you could even say controlled, in spite of her anxiety.

I see.

I wonder if you do, sir. I have no idea what the consul general told you, but I did suggest to him that what with the house in Victoria Peak, the marine guards, and then the arrival of Ambassador Havilland, he might consider calling someone up there.

You suggested it?

Yes, I did.

Why?

I don't think it would serve any purpose for me to speculate on these matters, Mr McAllister. They don't concern me.

Yes, of course, you're right. I mean – yes, all right. But we must find that woman, Mr Nelson. I've been instructed to tell you that if you can help us it would be greatly to your advantage.

I want to help in any event, sir. If she reaches me, I'll try to set up a meeting somewhere and call you. I knew I was right to do what I did, to say what I did.

We'll wait for your call.

Catherine was on target, thought John Nelson, there was one hell of a connection. So much of a connection that he did not dare use his consulate phone to reach Staples. But when he did reach her, he would ask her some very hard questions. He trusted Catherine, but the photographs and their consequences not withstanding, he was not for sale. He got up from his desk and headed for the door of his office. A suddenly remembered dental appointment would suffice. As he walked down the corridor toward the reception room his thoughts returned to Catherine Staples. Catherine was one of the strongest people he had ever met, but the look in her eyes last night had conveyed not strength, but a kind of desperate fear. It was a Catherine he had never seen before.

'He diverted your questions to his own ends,' said Havilland, coming through the door, the immense Lin Wenzu behind him. 'Do you agree, Major?'

'Yes, and that means he anticipated the questions. He was primed for them.'

'Which means someone primed him!'

'We never should have called him,' said McAllister quietly, sitting behind the desk, his nervous fingers once again massaging his right temple. 'Nearly everything he brought up was meant to provoke a response from me.'

'We had to call him,' insisted Havilland, 'if only to learn that.'

'He stayed in control. I lost it.'

'You could not have behaved differently, Edward,' said Lin. 'To react other than you did would have been to question his motives. In essence, you would have threatened him.'

'And at the moment, we don't want him to feel threatened,' agreed Havilland. 'He's getting information for someone, and we've got to find out who it is.'

'And that means Webb's wife *did* reach someone she knew and told that person everything.' McAllister leaned forward, his elbows on the desk, his hands tightly clasped.

'You were right, after all,' said the ambassador, looking down at the under-secretary of State. 'A street with her favourite maple trees. Paris. The inevitable repetition. It's quite clear. Nelson is working for someone in the Canadian consulate – and whoever it is, is in touch with Webb's wife.'

McAllister looked up. 'Then Nelson's either a damn fool or a bigger damn fool. By his own admission he knows – at least, he assumes – that he's dealing with highly sensitive information involving an adviser to presidents. Dismissal aside, he could be sent to prison for conspiring against the government.'

'He's not a fool, I can assure you,' said Lin.

'Then either someone is forcing him to do this against his will – blackmail most likely – or he's being paid to find out if there's a connection between Marie St Jacques and this house in Victoria Peak. It can't be anything else.' Frowning, Havilland sat down in the chair in front of the desk.

'Give me a day,' continued the major from MI6. 'Perhaps I can find out. If I can, we'll pick up whoever it is in the consulate.'

'No,' said the diplomat whose expertise lay in covert operations. 'You have until eight o'clock tonight. We can't afford *that*, but if we can avoid a confrontation and any possible fallout, we must try. Containment is everything. Try, Lin. For God's sake, *try*.'

'And after eight o'clock, Mr Ambassador? What then?'

'Then, Major, we pull in our clever and evasive attaché and break him. I'd much prefer to use him without his knowing it, without risking alarms, but the woman comes first. Eight o'clock, Major Lin.'

'I'll do everything I can.'

'And if we're wrong,' went on Havilland, as if Lin Wenzu had not spoken, 'if this Nelson has been set up as a blind and knows nothing, I want all the rules broken. I don't care how you do it or how much it costs in bribes or the garbage you have to employ to get it done. I want cameras, telephone taps, electronic surveillance – whatever you can manage – on every single person in that consulate. Someone there knows where she is. Someone there is hiding her.'

'Catherine, it's John,' said Nelson into the pay phone on Albert Road.

'How good of you to call,' answered Staples quickly. 'It's been a trying afternoon, but do let's have drinks one of these days. It'll be so good to see you after all these months, and you can tell me about Canberra. But do tell me one thing now. Was I right in what I told *you*?'

'I have to see you, Catherine.'

'Not even a hint?'

'I have to see you. Are you free?'

'I have a meeting in forty-five minutes.'

'Then later, around five. There's a place called the Monkey Tree in the Wanchai, on Gloucester—'

'I know it. I'll be there.'

John Nelson hung up. There was nothing else to do but go back to the office. He could not stay away for three hours, not after his conversation with Undersecretary of State Edward McAllister; appearances precluded such an absence. He had heard about McAllister; the undersecretary had spent seven years in Hong Kong, leaving only months before Nelson had arrived. Why had he returned? Why was there a sterile house in Victoria Peak with Ambassador Havilland suddenly in residence? Above all, why was Catherine Staples so frightened? He owed Catherine his life, but he had to have a few answers. He had a decision to make.

Lin Wenzu had all but exhausted his sources. Only one gave him pause for thought. Inspector Ian Ballantyne, as he usually did, answered questions with other questions, rather than delivering concise answers himself. It was maddening, for one never knew whether or not the vaunted transfer from Scotland Yard knew something about a given subject, in this case an American attaché named John Nelson.

'Met the chap several times,' Ballantyne had said. 'Bright sort. Speaks your lingo, did you know that?'

'My "lingo," Inspector?'

'Well, damn few of us did, even during the Opium War. Interesting period of history, wasn't it, Major?'

'The Opium War? I was talking about the attaché John Nelson.'

'Oh, is there a connection?'

'With what, Inspector?'

'The Opium War.'

'If there is, he's a hundred and fifty years old and his dossier says thirty-two.'

'Really? That young, eh?'

But Ballantyne had employed several pauses too many to satisfy Lin. Regardless, if the old war-horse did know something, he was not going to reveal it. Everyone else – from the Hong Kong and Kowloon police to the 'specialists' who worked the American consulate gathering information for payment – gave Nelson as clean a bill of health as was respectable in the territory. If Nelson had a vulnerable side, it was in his extensive and not too discriminating search for sex, but insofar as it was heterosexual, and he was single, it was to be applauded, not condemned. One 'specialist' told Lin that he heard Nelson had been warned to have himself medically checked on a fairly regular basis. No crime; the attaché was a cocksman – ask him to dinner.

The telephone rang; Lin grabbed it. 'Yes?'

'Our subject walked to the Peak Tram and took a taxi to the Wanchai. He is in a café called the Monkey Tree. I am with him. I can see him.'

'It's out of the way and very crowded,' said the major. 'Has anyone joined him?'

'No, but he asked for a table for two.'

'I'll be there as soon as I can. If you have to leave, I'll contact you by radio. You're driving Vehicle Seven, are you not?'

'Vehicle Seven, sir . . . *Wait!* A woman is walking toward his table. He's getting up.'

'Do you recognize her?'

'It's too dark here. No.'

'Pay the waiter. Disrupt the service. But not obviously, only for a few minutes. I'll use our ambulance and the siren until I'm a block away.'

'Catherine, I owe you so much, and I want to help you in any way I can, but I have to know more than what you've told me.'

'There's a connection, isn't there? Havilland and Marie St Jacques.'

'I won't confirm that – I *can't* confirm it – because I haven't spoken to Havilland. I did, however, speak to another man, a man I've heard a lot about who used to be stationed here – one hell of a brain – and he sounded as desperate as you did last night.'

'I seemed that way to you last night?' said Staples, smoothing her grey-streaked hair. 'I wasn't aware of it.'

'Hey, come on. Not in your words, maybe, but in the way you talked. The stridency was just below the surface. You sounded like *me* when you gave me the photographs. Believe me, I can identify.'

'Johnny, believe *me.* We may be dealing with something neither one of us should get near, something way up in the clouds that we – *I* – don't have the knowledge to make a proper decision.'

'I have to make a decision, Catherine.' Nelson looked up for the waiter. 'Where are those goddamned drinks?'

'I'm not panting.'

'I am. I owe you everything and I like you and I know you wouldn't use the photographs against me, which makes it all worse—'

'I gave you all there were, and we burned the negatives together.'

'So my debt's *real*, don't you see that? *Jesus*, the kid was what – twelve years *old?*'

'You didn't know that. You were drugged.'

'My passport to oblivion. No secretary of State in my future, only secretary of kiddie-porn. One hell of a trip!'

'It's over and you're being melodramatic. I just want you to tell me if there's a connection between Havilland and Marie St Jacques – which I think you can do. Why is that so difficult? I *will* know what to do then.'

'Because if I do, I have to tell Havilland that I told you.'

'Then give me an hour.'

'Why?'

'Because I *do* have several photographs in my vault at the consulate,' lied Catherine Staples.

Nelson shot back in his chair, stunned. 'Oh, *God.* I don't *believe* this!'

'Try to understand, Johnny. We all play hardball now and then because it's in the best interests of our employers – our individual countries, if you like. Marie St Jacques was a friend of mine – *is* a friend of mine – and her life became nothing in the eyes of self-important men who ran a covert operation that didn't give a holy damn about her and her husband. They used them both and then tried to *kill* them both! Let me tell you something, Johnny. I detest your Central Intelligence Agency and your State Department's so grandly named Consular Operations. It's not that they're bastards, it's that they're such *stupid* bastards. And if I sense that an operation is being mounted, again using these two people who've been through so much pain, I intend to find out why and act accordingly. But no more blank cheques with their lives. I'm experienced and they're not, and I'm angry enough – no, *furious* enough – to demand answers.'

'Oh, *Christ*—'

The waiter arrived with their drinks, and as Staples looked up to signify thanks, her eyes were drawn to a man by a telephone booth in the crowded outside corridor watching them. She looked away.

'What's it going to be, Johnny?' she continued. 'Confirm or deny?'

'Confirmed,' whispered Nelson, reaching for his glass.

'The house in Victoria Peak?'

'Yes.'

'Who was the man you spoke with, the one who had been stationed here?'

'McAllister. Undersecretary of State McAllister.'

'Good *Lord!*'

There was excessive movement in the outside corridor. Catherine shielded her eyes and turned her head slightly, which widened her peripheral vision. A large man entered and walked toward the telephone against the wall. There was only one man like him in all of Hong Kong. It was *Lin Wenzu*, MI6, Special Branch! The Americans had enlisted the best, but it could be the worst for Marie and her husband.

'You've done nothing wrong, Johnny,' said Staples, rising from her chair. 'We'll talk further, but right now I'm going to the ladies' room.'

'Catherine?'

'What?'

'Hardball?'

'Very hard, my darling.'

Staples walked past a shrinking Lin, who turned away. She went into the ladies' room, waited several seconds, then walked out with two other women and broke away, continuing down the corridor and into the Monkey Tree's kitchen. Without saying a word to the startled waiters and cooks, she found the exit and went outside. She ran up the alley into Gloucester Road; she turned left, her stride quickening until she found a phone booth. Inserting a coin, she dialled.

'Hello?'

'*Marie*, get out of the flat! My car's in a garage a block to your right as you leave the building. It's called Ming's; the sign's in red. Get there as quickly as you can! I'll meet you. *Hurry!*'

Catherine Staples hailed a taxi.

'The woman's name is Staples, Catherine *Staples!*' said Lin Wenzu sharply into the phone on the corridor wall of the Monkey Tree, raising his voice to be heard over the din. 'Insert the consulate disk and search it through the computer. *Quickly!* I want her address and make damn-damn sure it's current!' The muscles of the major's jaw worked furiously as he waited, listening. The answer was delivered, and he issued another order: 'If one of our team's vehicles is in the area, get on the radio and tell him to head over there. If not, dispatch one immediately.' Lin paused, again listening. 'The American woman,' he said quietly into the phone. 'They're to watch for her. If she's spotted, close in and take her. We're on our way.'

'Vehicle Five, *respond!*' repeated the radio operator, speaking into a microphone, his hand on a switch in the lower right-hand corner of the console in front of him. The room was white and without windows, the hum of the air conditioning low but constant, the whir of the filtering system even quieter. On three walls there were banks of sophisticated radio and computer equipment above spotless white counters made of the smoothest Formica. There was an antiseptic quality about the room; hardness was everywhere. It might have been an electronics laboratory in a well-endowed medical centre, but it was not. It was another kind of centre. The communications centre of MI6, Special Branch, Hong Kong.

'Vehicle Five *responding!*' shouted an out-of-breath voice over the speaker.

'I received your signal, but I was a street away covering the Thai. We were right. Drugs.'

'Go on scrambler!' ordered the operator, throwing the switch. There was a whistling sound that stopped as abruptly as it had started. 'You're off the Thai,' continued the radioman. 'You're nearest. Get over to Arbuthnot Road; the Botanical Garden entrance is the quickest way.' He gave the address of Catherine Staples's building and ended with a final command. 'The American woman. Watch for her. Take her.'

'*Aiya*,' whispered the breathless agent from Special Branch.

Marie tried not to panic, imposing a control over herself she did not feel. The situation was ludicrous. It was also deadly serious. She was dressed in Catherine's ill-fitting robe, having taken a long hot bath and, far worse, having washed her clothes in Staples's kitchen sink. They were hanging over the plastic chairs on Catherine's small balcony and were still wet. It had seemed so natural, so logical, to wash away the heat and the dirt of Hong Kong from herself as well as from strangers' clothes. And the cheap sandals had raised blisters on the soles of her feet; she had broken an ugly one with a needle and walking was difficult. But she dared not walk, she had to run.

What had happened? Catherine was not the sort of person to issue peremptory commands. Any more than she herself was, especially with David. People like Catherine avoided the imperative approach because it only clouded a victim's thinking – and her friend Marie St Jacques was a victim now, not to the degree that poor David was, but a victim nevertheless. *Move!* How often had Jason said that in Zurich and Paris? So frequently she still tensed at the word.

She dressed, the wet clothes clinging to her body, and rummaged through Staples's closet for a pair of slippers. They were uncomfortable but softer than the sandals. She could run; she *had* to run.

Her hair! Oh, *Christ*, the hair! She ran to the bathroom, where Catherine kept a porcelain jar filled with hairpins and clasps. In seconds, she secured her hair on the top of her head, walked rapidly back into the flat's tiny living room, found her foolish hat and jammed it on.

The wait for the elevator was interminable! According to the lighted numbers above the panels, both elevators jogged between floors one, three, and seven, neither venturing above to the ninth floor. Preceding residents going out for the evening had programmed the vertical monsters, delaying her descent.

Avoid elevators whenever you can. They're traps. Jason Bourne. Zurich.

Marie looked up and down the hallway. She saw the fire-exit staircase door and ran to it.

Out of breath, she lunged into the short lobby, composing herself as best she could to deflect the glances directed at her by five or six tenants, some entering, some leaving. She did not count; she could barely see; she had to get out!

My car's in a garage a block to your right as you leave the building. It's called Ming's. Was it to the right? Or was it *left?* Out on the pavement she hesitated.

Right or *left?* 'Right' meant so many things, 'left' was more specific. She tried to think. What had Catherine *said?* Right! She had to go right; it was the first thing that came to her mind. She had to trust that.

Your first reflections are the best, the most accurate, because the impressions are stored in your head, like information in a data bank. That's what your head is. Jason Bourne. Paris.

She started running. Her left slipper fell off; she stopped, stooping down to retrieve it. Suddenly a car came careening around the gates of the Botanical Gardens across the wide street, and, like an angry heat-searching missile, whipped to its left and zeroed in on her. The automobile swerved in a semicircle, screeching as it spun in the road. A man leaped out and raced toward her.

18

There was nothing else to do. She was cornered, trapped. Marie screamed, and screamed again, and again, as the Chinese agent approached, her hysteria mounting as the man politely but firmly took her by the arm. She recognized him – he was one of *them*, one of the bureaucrats! Her screams reached a crescendo. People stopped and turned in the street. Women gasped as startled men stepped hesitantly forward or looked around frantically for the police, several shouting for them.

'*Please, Mrs* . . . !' cried the Oriental, trying to keep his voice controlled. 'No harm will come to you. Allow me to escort you to my vehicle. It is for your own protection.'

'*Help me!*' shrieked Marie as the astonished twilight strollers gathered into a crowd. 'This man's a *thief!* He stole my purse, my money! He's trying to take my jewellery!'

'See here, chap!' shouted an elderly Englishman, hobbling forward, raising his walking stick. 'I've sent a lad for the police, but until they arrive, by God, I'll *thrash* you!'

'Please, sir,' insisted the man from Special Branch quietly. 'This is a matter for the authorities, and I am with the authorities. Permit me to show you my identification.'

'*Easy, myte!*' roared a voice with an Australian accent as a man rushed forward, gently pushing the elderly Britisher aside and lowering his cane. 'You're a grand fair dinkum, old man, but don't half bother yourself! These punks call for a younger type.' The strapping Australian stood in front of the Chinese agent. 'Tyke yer hands off the lady, punkhead! And I'd be goddamned quick about it, if I were you.'

'Please, sir, this is a serious misunderstanding. The lady is in danger and she is wanted for questioning by the authorities.'

'I don't see you in no uniform!'

'Permit me to show you my credentials.'

'*That's* what he said an hour ago when he attacked me in Garden Road!' shouted Marie hysterically. 'People tried to help me then! He lied to everyone! Then he stole my purse! He's been *following* me!' Marie knew that none of the things she kept screaming made sense. She could only hope for confusion, something that Jason had taught her to use.

'I'm not saying it *agyne*, myte!' yelled the Australian, stepping forward. 'Tyke yer bloody hands off the lady!'

'Please, sir. I cannot do that. Other officials are on their way.'

'Oh, they are, are they? You punkheads travel in gangs, do you? Well, you'll be a pitiful sight for their eyes when they get here!' The Australian grabbed the Oriental by the shoulder, spinning him to his left. But as the man from Special Branch spun, his right foot – the toe of his leather shoe extended like a knife point – whipped around, crashing up into the Australian's abdomen. The good Samaritan from Down Under doubled over, falling to his knees.

'I'll ask you again not to *interfere*, sir!'

'Do you, now? You slope-eyed *son of a bitch!*' The furious Australian lunged up, hurling his body at the Oriental, his fists pounding the man from Special Branch. The crowd roared its approval, its collective voice filling the street – and Marie's arm was *free!* Then other sounds joined the melee. Sirens, followed by three racing automobiles, among them an ambulance. All three swerved in their sudden turns, as tires screeched and the vehicles came to jolting stops.

Marie plunged through the crowd and reached the inner pavement; she started running toward the red sign a half block away. The slippers had fallen off her feet; the swollen, shredded blisters burned, sending shafts of pain up her legs. She could not allow herself to think about pain. She had to run, *run, get away!* Then the booming voice surged over and through the noises in the street, and she pictured a large man roaring. It was the huge Chinese they called the major.

'Mrs *Webb!* Mrs Webb, I *beg you! Stop!* We mean you no harm! You'll be told *everything!* For God's sake, *stop!*'

Told everything! thought Marie. Told lies and *more lies!* Suddenly people were rushing toward her. What were they *doing? Why* . . . ? Then they raced past, mostly men, but not all men, and she understood. There was a panic in the street – perhaps an accident, mutilation, death. *Let's go see. Let's watch!* From a distance, mind you.

Opportunities will present themselves. Recognize them, act on them.

Marie suddenly whipped around, crouching, lunging through the still-onrushing crowd to the kerb, keeping her body as low as possible, and ran back to where she had come so close to recapture. She kept turning her head to her left – watching, hoping. She *saw* him through the racing bodies! The huge major ran past in the other direction; with him was another man, another well-dressed man, another bureaucrat.

The crowd was cautious, as the ghoulish are always cautious, inching forward but not so far as to get involved. What they saw was not flattering to the Chinese onlookers or to those who held the martial arts of the Orient in mystical esteem. The lithe, strapping Australian, his language magnificently obscene, was pummelling three separate assailants out of his personal boxing ring. Suddenly, to the astonishment of everyone, the Australian picked up one of his fallen adversaries and let out a roar as loud as the immense major's. 'Fer *Christ's syke!* Will you cryzies cut this out? Yer not punkheads, even I can tell *that!* We was *both* snookered!'

Marie ran across the wide street to the entrance of the Botanical Gardens. She stood under a tree by the gate with a direct line of sight to Ming's Parking

Palace. The major had passed the garage, pausing at several alleyways that intersected Arbuthnot Road, sending his subordinate down several of them, constantly looking around for his support troops. They were not there; Marie saw that for herself as the crowd dispersed. All three were breathing hard and leaning against the ambulance, led there by the Australian.

A taxi drove up to Ming's. No one, at first, got out, then the driver emerged. He walked into the open garage and spoke to someone behind a glass both. He bowed in thanks, returned to the cab, and spoke to his passenger. Cautiously his fare opened the door and stepped into the kerb. It was Catherine! She, too, walked into the wide opening, far more rapidly than the driver, and spoke into the glass booth, shaking her head, indicating that she had been told what she did not want to hear.

Suddenly Lin appeared. He was retracing his steps, obviously angered by the men who were supposed to be tracing *his* steps. He was about to cross the open garage; he would see Catherine!

'*Carlos!*' screamed Marie, assuming the worst, knowing it would tell her everything. '*Delta!*'

The major spun around, his eyes wide in shock. Marie raced into the Botanical Gardens; it was the *key! Cain is for Delta and Carlos will be killed by Cain* . . . or whatever the codes were that had been spread through Paris! They *were* using David again! It wasn't a probability anymore, it was the reality! They – *it* – the United States government – was sending her husband out to play the role that had nearly killed him, killed by his own people! What kind of bastards *were* they? . . . Or, conversely, what kind of ends justified the means supposedly sane men would use to reach them?

Now more than ever she had to find David, find him before he took risks others should be taking! He had given so much and now they asked for more, demanded more in the cruellest way possible. But to find him she had to reach Catherine, who was no more than a hundred yards away. She had to draw out the enemy and get back across the street without the enemy seeing her. *Jason*, what can I *do?*

She hid behind a cluster of bushes, inching farther inside, as the major ran through the Garden's gates. The immense Oriental stopped and looked around with his squinting, penetrating gaze, then turned and shouted for his subordinate, who had apparently emerged from an alley on Arbuthnot Road. The second man had difficulty getting across the street; the traffic was heavier and slower because of the stationary ambulance and two additional vehicles blocking the normal flow near the entrance to the Botanical Gardens. The major suddenly grew furious as he saw and understood the reasons for the growing traffic.

'Get those fools to move the cars!' he roared. 'And send them over here . . . *No!* Send one to the gates on Albany Road. The rest of you come back here! *Hurry!*'

The early-evening strollers became more numerous. Men loosened the ties they had worn all day at their offices, while women carried high-heeled shoes in casual bags, supplanting them with sandals. Wives wheeling baby carriages were joined by husbands; lovers embraced and walked arm in arm among the rows of exploding flowers. The laughter of racing children pealed across the Gardens, and the major held his place by the entrance gate. Marie swallowed, the panic in her growing. The ambulance and the two automobiles were being moved; the traffic began to flow normally.

A crash! Near the ambulance an impatient driver had rammed the car in front of him. The major could not help himself; the proximity of the accident so close to his official vehicle forced him to move forward, obviously to ascertain whether or not his men were involved. *Opportunities will present themselves . . . use them.* Now!

Marie raced around the far end of the bushes, then dashed across the grass to join a foursome on the gravel path that led out of the Gardens. She glanced to her right, afraid of what she might see but knowing she had to know. Her worst fears were borne out; the huge major had sensed – or seen – the figure of a woman running behind him. He paused for a moment, uncertain, unsure, then broke into a rapid stride toward the gate.

A horn blew – four short, quick blasts. It was Catherine, waving at her through the open window of a small Japanese car as Marie raced into the street.

'Get in!' shouted Staples.

'He saw me!'

'*Hurry!*'

Marie jumped into the front seat as Catherine gunned the small car and swerved out of line, half on the side-walk, then swung back with a break in the accelerating traffic. She turned into a side street and drove swiftly down it to an intersection where there was a sign with a red arrow pointing right. *Central. Business District.* Staples turned right.

'Catherine!' shouted Marie. 'He *saw* me!'

'Worse,' said Staples. 'He saw the car.'

'A two-door green Mitsubishi!' shouted Lin Wenzu into his hand-held radio. 'The licence number is AOR-five, three, five, zero – the zero could be a six, but I don't think so. It doesn't matter, the first three letters will be enough. I want it flashed on all points, emergency status using the police telephone banks! The driver and the passenger are to be taken into custody and there are to be no conversations with either party. It is a Government House matter and no explanations will be given. Get on this! *Now!*'

Staples turned into a parking garage on Ice House Street. The newly lighted, bright red sign of the Mandarin could be seen barely a block away. 'We'll rent a car,' said Catherine as she accepted her ticket from the man in the booth. 'I know several head boys at the hotel.'

'*We* park? You park?' The grinning attendant obviously hoped for the former.

'You park,' replied Staples, withdrawing several Hong Kong dollars from her purse. 'Let's go,' she said, turning to Marie. 'And stay on my right, in the shadows, close to the buildings. How are your feet?'

'I'd rather not say.'

'Then don't. There's no time to do anything about them now. Bear up, old girl.'

'Catherine, stop sounding like C. Aubrey Smith in drag.'

'Who's that?'

'Forget it. I like old movies. Let's go.'

Marie hobbling, the two women walked down the street to a side entrance of the Mandarin. They climbed the hotel steps and went inside. 'There's a ladies' room to the right, past the line of shops,' said Catherine.

'I see the sign.'

'Wait there. I'll be with you as soon as I can make arrangements.'

'Is there a drugstore here?'

'I don't want you walking around. There'll be descriptions out everywhere.'

'I understand that, but can *you* walk around? Just a bit.'

'Bad time of the month?'

'*No*, my *feet!* Vaseline, skin lotion, sandals – no, *not* sandals. Rubber thongs, perhaps, and peroxide.'

'I'll do what I can, but time is everything.'

'It's been that way for the past year. A terrible tread-mill. Will it stop, Catherine?'

'I'm doing my damnedest to see to it. You're a friend and a countryman, my dear. And I'm a very *angry* woman – and speaking of such – how many women did you encounter in the hallowed halls of the CIA or its bumbling counterpart at the State Department, Consular Operations?'

Marie blinked, trying to remember. 'None, actually.'

'Then *fuck* 'em!'

'There was a woman in Paris—'

'There always *is*, dear. Go to the ladies' room.'

'An automobile is a hindrance in Hong Kong,' said Lin, looking at the clock on the wall of his office in the headquarters of MI6, Special Branch. It read 6:34. 'Therefore we must assume she intends driving Webb's wife some distance, hiding her, and will not risk taxi records. Our eight o'clock deadline has been rescinded, the chase now takes its place. We must intercept her. Is there anything we haven't considered?'

'Putting the Australian in jail,' suggested the short, well-dressed subordinate firmly. 'We suffered casualties in the Walled City, but *his* were a public embarrassment. We know where he's staying. We can pick him up.'

'On what charge?'

'Obstruction.'

'To what end?'

The subordinate shrugged angrily. 'Satisfaction, that's all.'

'You've just answered your own question. Your pride is inconsequential. Stick to the woman – the women.'

'You're right, of course.'

'Every garage, the car rental agencies here on the island and in Kowloon all have been reached by the police, correct?'

'Yes, sir. But I must point out that the Staples woman could easily call upon one of her friends – her Canadian friends – and she would have an automobile we could not track.'

'We operate on what we can control, not what we can't. Besides, from what I knew before and what I have subsequently learned about Foreign Service Officer Staples, I would say she's acting alone, certainly not under official sanction. She won't involve anyone else for the time being.'

'How can you be sure?'

Lin looked at his subordinate; he had to choose his words carefully. 'Just a guess.'

'Your guesses have a reputation for accuracy.'

'An inflated judgement. Common sense is my ally.' The telephone rang. The major's hand shot out. 'Yes?'

'Police Central Four,' droned a male voice.

'We appreciate your cooperation, Central Four.'

'A Ming's Parking Palace responded to our inquiry. The Mitsubishi AOR has a space there leased on a monthly basis. The owner's name is Staples. Catherine Staples, a Canadian. The car was taken out roughly thirty-five minutes ago.'

'You've been most helpful, Central Four,' said Lin. 'Thank you.' He hung up and looked at his anxious subordinate. 'We now have three new pieces of information. The first is that the inquiry we sent out through the police was definitely sent out. The second is that at least one garage wrote down the information, and thirdly, Mrs Staples leases her parking space by the month.'

'It's a start, sir.'

'There are three major and perhaps a dozen minor rental agencies, not counting the hotels, which we've covered separately. Those are manageable statistics, but, of course, the garages are not.'

'Why not?' questioned the subordinate. 'At most there are, perhaps, a hundred. Who cares to build a garage in Hong Kong when he could house a dozen shops – businesses? At maximum, the police telephone banks are twenty to thirty operators. They can reach them all.'

'It's not the numbers, old friend. It's the mentality of the employees, for the jobs are not enviable. Those who can write are too lazy or too hostile to bother, and those who can't flee from any association with the police.'

'One garage responded.'

'A true Cantonese. It was the owner.'

'The owner should be told!' cried the parking boy in shrill Chinese to the booth attendant at the garage on Ice House Street.

'Why?'

'I explained it to you! I wrote it *down* for you—'

'Because you go to school and write somewhat better than I do does not make you boss-boss here.'

'You cannot write at all! You were shit-shit afraid! You called for me when the man on the telephone said it was a police emergency. You illiterates always run from the police. That was the *car*, the green Mitsubishi I parked on Level Two! If you won't call the police, you must call the owner.'

'There are things they don't teach you in school, boy with small organ.'

'They teach us not to go against the police. It is bad joss.'

'I *will* call the police – or, better, you may be their hero.'

'Good!'

'*After* the two women return, and I have a short talk with the driver.'

'What?'

'She thought she was giving me – us – two dollars, but it was eleven. One of the bills was ten-dollar note. She was very nervous, very upset. She is frightened. She did not watch her money.'

'You said it *was* two dollars!'

'And now I'm being honest. Would I be honest with you if I did not have both our interests in my heart?'

'In what way?'

'I will tell this rich, frightened American – she spoke American – that you and I have not called back the police on *her* behalf. She will reward us on the spot – very, *very* generously – for she will understand that she may not retrieve her car without doing so. You may watch me from inside the garage by the other telephone. After she pays, I will send another boy for her car, which he will have great trouble finding, for I will give him the wrong location, and you will call the police. The police will arrive, we will have done our heavenly duty, and had a night of money like few other nights in this miserable job.'

The parking boy squinted, shaking his head. 'You're right,' he said. 'They don't teach such things in school. And I suppose I do not have a choice.'

'Oh, but you do,' said the attendant, pulling a long knife from his belt. 'You can say no, and I will cut out your talk-talk tongue.'

Catherine approached the concierge's desk in the Mandarin lobby, annoyed that she did not know either of the two clerks behind the counter. She needed a favour quickly, and in Hong Kong that meant dealing with a person one knew. Then to her relief she spotted the evening shift's Number one concierge. He was in the middle of the lobby trying to mollify an excited guest. She moved to the right and waited, hoping to catch Lee Teng's eye. She had cultivated Teng, sending numerous Canadians to him when problems of convenience had seemed insurmountable. He had always been paid handsomely.

'Yes, may I be of help, Mrs . . . ?' said the young Chinese clerk, moving in front of Staples.

'I'll wait for Mr Teng, if you please.'

'Mr Teng is very busy, Mrs . . . A very bad time for Mr Teng. You are a guest of the Mandarin, Mrs . . .?'

'I'm a resident of the territory and an old friend of Mr Teng. Where possible I bring my business here so the desk gets the credit.'

'*Ohh* . . . ?' The clerk responded to Catherine's non-tourist status. He leaned forward, speaking confidentially. 'Lee Teng has terrible joss tonight. The lady goes to the grand ball at Government House but her clothes go to Bangkok. She must think Mr Teng has wings under his jacket and jet engines in his armpits, yes?'

'An interesting concept. The lady just flew in?'

'Yes, Mrs . . . But she had many pieces of luggage. She did not miss the one she misses now. She blames first her husband and now Lee Teng.'

'Where's her husband?'

'In the bar. He offered to take the next plane to Bangkok, but his kindness only made his wife angrier. He will not leave the bar, and he will not get to Government House in a way that will make him pleased with himself in the morning. Bad joss all around . . . Perhaps I can be of assistance to you while Mr Teng does his best to calm everybody.'

'I want to rent a car and I need one as fast as you can get it for me.'

'*Aiya*,' said the clerk. 'It is seven o'clock at night, and the rental offices do little leasing in the evening hours. Most are closed.'

'I'm sure there are exceptions.'

'Perhaps a hotel car with a chauffeur?'

'Only if there's nothing else available. As I mentioned, I'm not a guest here and, frankly, I'm not made of money.'

' "Who among us"?' asked the clerk enigmatically. 'As the good Christian Book says – somewhere, I think.'

'Sounds right,' agreed Staples. 'Please, get on the phone and do your best.'

The young man reached beneath the counter and pulled out a plastic-bound list of car rental agencies. He went to a telephone several feet to his right, picked it up, and started dialling. Catherine looked over at Lee Teng; he had steered his irate lady to the wall by a miniature palm in an obvious attempt to keep her from alarming the other guests who sat around the ornate lobby greeting friends and ordering cocktails. He was speaking rapidly, softly, and by God, throught Staples, he was actually getting her attention. Whatever her legitimate complaints, mused Catherine, the woman was an ass. She wore a chinchilla stole in just about the worst climate on earth for such delicate fur. Not that she, Foreign Service Officer Staples, ever had to consider such a problem. She might have if she had chucked the FSO status and stuck with Owen Staples. The son of a bitch owned at least four banks in Toronto now. Not a bad sort, really, and to add to her sense of guilt, Owen had never remarried. Not *fair*, Owen! She had run across him three years ago, after her stint in Europe, while attending the Brit-organized conference in Toronto. They had had drinks at the Mayfair Club in the King Edward Hotel, not so unlike the Mandarin, actually.

'Come on, Owen. Your looks, your *money* – and you had the looks before your money – why not? There are a thousand beautiful girls within a five-block radius who'd grab you.'

'Once was enough, Cathy. You taught me that.'

'I don't know, but you make me feel – oh, I don't know – somehow so guilty. I left you, Owen, but not because I wasn't fond of you.'

' "Fond" of me?'

'You know what I mean.'

'Yes, I think so.' Owen had laughed. 'You left me for all the right reasons, and I accepted your leaving without animus for like-minded reasons. If you had waited five minutes longer, I think I would have thrown you out. I'd paid the rent that month.'

'You bastard!'

'Not at all, neither of us. You had your ambitions and I had mine. They simply weren't compatible.'

'But that doesn't explain why you never remarried.'

'I just told you. You taught me, my dear.'

'Taught you what? That *all* ambitions are incompatible?'

'Where they existed in our extremes, yes. You see, I learned that I wasn't interested on any permanent basis in anyone who *didn't* have what I suppose you'd call a passionate "drive," or an overriding ambition, but I couldn't live with such a person day in and day out. And those without ambitions left something wanting in our relationship. No permanency there.'

'But what about a family? Children?'

'I have two children,' Owen had said quietly. 'Of whom I'm immensely – fond. I love them very much, and their very ambitious mothers have been terribly kind. Even *their* subsequent respective husbands have been understanding. While they were growing up I saw my children constantly. So, in a sense, I had three families. Quite civilized, if frequently confusing.'

'*You?* The paragon of the community, the banker's *banker!* The man they said took a shower in a Dickens' *nightshirt!* A deacon of the church!'

'I gave *that* up when you left. At any rate, it was simply statecraft on my part. You practise it every day.'

'*Owen*, you never *told* me.'

'You never asked, Cathy. You had your ambitions and I had mine. But I will tell you my one regret, if you want to hear it.'

'I do.'

'I'm genuinely sorry that we never had a child together. Judging by the two I have, he or she would have been quite marvellous.'

'You bastard, I'm going to cry.'

'Please don't. Let's be honest, neither of us has any regrets.'

Catherine's reverie was suddenly interrupted. The clerk lurched back from the telephone, his hands triumphantly on the counter. 'You have good *joss*, Mrs . . . !' he cried. 'The dispatcher at the Apex agency on Bonham Strand East was still there, and he has cars available but nobody to drive one here.'

'I'll take a taxi. Write out the address.' Staples looked around for the hotel drugstore. There were too many people in the lobby, too much confusion. 'Where can I buy some – skin lotion or Vaseline, sandals or thongs?' she asked, turning to the clerk.

'There is a newspaper stand down the hallway to the right, Mrs . . . They have many of the items you describe. But, may I please have money, as you must present a receipt to the dispatcher? It is one thousand dollars, Hong Kong, whatever remains to be returned or additional monies to be added—'

'I don't have that much on me. I'll have to use a card.'

'So much the better.'

Catherine opened her purse and pulled out a credit card from an inside pocket. 'I'll be right back,' she said, placing it on the counter, as she started for the hallway on the right. For no reason in particular, she glanced over at Lee Teng and his distraught lady. To her brief amusement, the overdressed woman in the foolish fur was nodding appreciatively as Teng pointed to the line of overpriced shops one reached by climbing a staircase above the lobby. Lee Teng was a true diplomat. Without question, he had explained to the overwrought guest that she had an option that would both serve her needs and her nerves and hit her errant husband in his financial solar plexus. This was Hong Kong, and she could purchase the best and the most glittering, and for a price everything would be ready in time for the grand ball at Government House. Staples continued toward the hallway.

'*Catherine!*' The name was so sharply spoken Staples froze. '*Please,* Mrs *Catherine!*'

Rigid, Staples turned. It was Lee Teng, who had broken away from his now mollified guest. 'What is it?' she asked, frightened as the middle-aged Teng approached, his face lined with concern, sweat evident on his balding skull.

'I saw you only moments ago. I had a problem.'

'I know all about it.'

'So do you, Catherine.'

'I beg your pardon?'

Teng glanced at the counter – oddly enough, not at the young man who had helped her, but at the other clerk, who was at the opposite end of the desk. The man was by himself, with no guests in front of him, and he was looking at his associate. 'Damn bad joss!' exclaimed Teng under his breath.

'What are you talking about?' asked Staples.

'Come over here,' said the Number one concierge of the night shift as he pulled Catherine to the side, away from the sight of the counter. He reached into his pocket and removed a perforated half-page of paper on which there was a computer printout. 'Four copies of this were sent down from upstairs. I managed to obtain three, but the fourth is under the counter.'

Emergency. Government control. A Canadian woman by the name of Mrs Catherine Staples may attempt to lease an automobile for personal use. She is fifty-seven years of age, with partially grey hair, of medium height, and a slender figure. Delay all proceedings and contact Police Central Four.'

Lin Wenzu had drawn a conclusion based on an observation, thought Catherine, along with the knowledge that anyone who willingly drove a car in Hong Kong was either crazy or had a peculiar reason for doing so. He was covering his bases quickly and completely. 'The young man just got me a car over in Bonham Strand East. He obviously hasn't read this.'

'He found you a rental at this hour?'

'He's writing up the credit charge now. Do you think he'll see this?'

'It is not him that I worry about. He is in training and I can tell him anything and he will accept what I say. The other one not so; he wants my job badly. Wait here. Stay out of sight.'

Teng walked to the counter as the clerk was anxiously looking around, the layered credit card slips in his hand. Lee Teng took the charges and put them in his pocket. 'That won't be necessary,' he said. 'Our customer has changed her mind. She found a friend in the lobby who will drive her.'

'Oh? Then I should tell our associate not to bother. As the amount is over the limit, he is clearing it for me. I am still somewhat unsure and he offered—'

Teng waved him quiet as he crossed to the second clerk on the telephone at the other end of the counter. 'You may give me the card and forget the call. There are too many distressed ladies tonight for me! This one has found other means of transportation.'

'Certainly, Mr Teng,' said the second clerk obsequiously. He handed over the credit card, apologized quickly to the operator on the line, and hung up the telephone.

'A bad night.' Teng shrugged, turning, and heading back into the crowded lobby-lounge. He approached Catherine, pulling out his billfold as he did so. 'If you are short of money. I will cover it, Don't use this.'

'I'm not short at home or at the bank, but I don't carry so much with me. It's one of the unwritten rules.'

'One of the better ones,' said Teng, nodding.

Staples took the bills in Teng's hand and looked up at the Chinese. 'Do you want an explanation?' she asked.

'It's not required, Catherine. Whatever Central Four says, I know you are a good person, and if you are not and you run away and I never see my money again, I am still many thousands, Hong Kong, to the better.'

'I shan't run anywhere, Teng.'

'You will not walk, either. One of the chauffeurs owes me a good turn, and he's in the garage now. He will drive you to your car in Bonham Strand. Come, I'll take you down there.'

'There's someone else with me. I'm taking her out of Hong Kong. She's in the ladies' room.'

'I'll wait in the hallway. Do hurry.'

'Sometimes I think the time passes more quickly when we are flooded with problems,' said the second, somewhat older clerk to his younger associate-in-training as he removed the half-page computer printout from beneath the counter and unobtrusively shoved it into his pocket.

'If you are right, Mr Teng has barely experienced fifteen minutes since we came on duty two hours ago. He's very good, isn't he?'

'His lack of head hair helps him. People look upon him as having wisdom even when he has no wise words to offer.'

'Still, he has a way with people. I wish to be very much like him one day.'

'Lose some hair,' said the second clerk. 'In the meantime, since there is no one bothering us, I have to go to the toilet. By the way, just in case I ever need to know a rental agency open at this hour, it *was* the Apex on Bonham Strand East, wasn't it?'

'Oh, yes.'

'That was very diligent of you.'

'I simply went by the list. It was near the end.'

'Some of us would have stopped before then. You are to be commended.'

'You are too kind to an unworthy trainee.'

'I want only the best for you,' said the older clerk. 'Always remember that.'

The older man left the counter. He cautiously went past the potted palms until he saw Lee Teng. The night concierge was standing at the foot of the hallway to the right; it was enough. He was waiting for the woman. The clerk turned quickly and walked up the staircase to the line of shops with less dignity than was proper. He was in a hurry and entered the first boutique at the top of the steps.

'Hotel business,' he said to the bored saleswoman as he grabbed the phone off the wall behind a glass counter displaying glistening precious stones. He dialled.

'Police Central Four.'

'Your directive, sir, regarding the Canadian woman, Mrs Staples—'

'Do you have information?'

'I believe so, sir, but it is somewhat embarrassing for me to relay it.'

'Why is that? This is an emergency, a government matter!'

'Please understand, Officer, I am only a minor employee, and it is quite possible the night concierge did not recall your directive. He is a very busy man.'

'What are you trying to say?'

'Well, Officer – sir – the woman I overheard asking for the concierge bore a striking resemblance to the description in the government directive. But it would be most embarrassing for me if it was learned that I called you.'

'You will be protected. You may remain anonymous. What is the information?'

'Well, sir, I overheard . . .' With cautious ambivalence, the first assistant clerk did his best for himself and consequently the worst for his superior, Lee Teng. His final statements, however, were concise and without equivocation. 'It is the Apex Car Rental Agency in Bonham Strand East. I suggest you hurry, as she is on her way there now.'

The early-evening traffic was less dense than the rush hour, but still formidable. It was the reason why Catherine and Marie looked uneasily at each other in the backseat of the Mandarin's limousine; the chauffeur, rather than accelerating into the sudden wide space in front of him, swung the enormous automobile into an empty section of the kerb in Bonham Strand East. There was no sign of a rental agency on either side of the street.

'Why are we stopping?' asked Staples sharply.

'Mr Teng's instructions, Mrs . . .' answered the chauffeur turning around in the seat. 'I will lock the car with the alarm on. No one will bother you, as the lights flash beneath all four door handles.'

'That's very comforting, but I'd like to know why you're not taking us to the car.'

'I will bring the car to you, Mrs . . .'

'I beg your pardon?'

'Mr Teng's instructions. He was very firm, and he is making the proper phone call to the Apex garage. It is in the next street, Mrs . . . I shall be back presently.' The chauffeur removed his hat and his jacket, placed both on the seat, switched on the alarm and climbed out.

'What do you make of it?' asked Marie, putting her right leg over her knee and holding tissues she had taken from the ladies' room against the sole of her foot. 'Do you trust this Teng?'

'Yes, I do,' replied Catherine, her expression bewildered. 'I can't understand it. He's obviously being extra cautious – but they're extra risks for himself – and I don't know why. As I told you back at the Mandarin, that computerized missive about me said "Government Control." Those two words are not taken lightly in Hong Kong. What in the world is he doing? And why?'

'Obviously, I can't answer you,' said Marie. 'But I can make an observation.'

'What is it?'

'I saw the way he looked at you. I'm not sure you did.'

'What?'

'I'd say he's very fond of you.'

'Fond . . . of me?'

'It's one way to put it. There are stronger ways, of course.'

Staples turned away and looked out the window. 'Oh, my *God*,' she whispered.

'What's the matter?'

'A little while ago, back at the Mandarin, and for reasons too unreasonable to analyse – it started with a foolish woman in a chinchilla stole – I thought about Owen.'

'Owen?'

'My former husband.'

'Owen Staples? The *banker*, Owen Staples?'

'That's my name and that's my boy – *was* my boy. In those days one stayed with the acquired name.'

'You never told me your husband was Owen Staples.'

'You never asked me, my dear.'

'You're not making sense, Catherine.'

'I suppose not,' agreed Staples, shaking her head. 'But I was thinking about the time Owen and I met a couple of years ago in Toronto. We had drinks at the Mayfair Club and I learned things about him I never would have believed before. I was genuinely happy for him despite the fact that the bastard nearly made me cry.'

'Catherine, for heaven's sake what's that got to do with right *now?*'

'It's got to do with Teng. We also had drinks one evening, not at the Mandarin, of course, but at a café on the waterfront in Kowloon. He said it wouldn't be good joss for me to be seen with him here on the island.'

'Why not?'

'That's what I said. You see, he was protecting me then just as he's protecting me now. And I may have misunderstood him. I assumed he was simply looking after an additional source of income, but I may have been terribly wrong.'

'In what way?'

'He said a strange thing that night. He said he wished things were different, that the differences between people were not so obvious and those differences not so disturbing to other people. Of course, I accepted his banalities as a rather amateurish attempt at . . . at statecraft, as my former husband phrased it. Perhaps it was something else.'

Marie laughed quietly as their eyes locked. 'Dear, *dear* Catherine. The man's in love with you.'

'Christ in *Calgary*, I don't need this!'

Lin Wenzu sat in the front seat of the MI6 Vehicle Two, his patient gaze on the entrance of the Apex agency on Bonham Strand East. Everything was in order; both women would be in his custody within a matter of minutes. One of his men had gone inside and spoken to the dispatcher. The agent had proffered his government identification and was shown the evening's records by the frightened employee. The dispatcher, indeed, *had* a reservation for a Mrs Catherine Staples but it had been cancelled, the car in question assigned to another name, the name of a chauffeur from the hotel. And since Mrs Catherine Staples was no longer leasing a car, the dispatcher saw no reason to call Police Control Four. What was there to say? And no, certainly not, no one else could pick up the car, as it was reserved by the Mandarin.

Everything was in order, thought Lin. Victoria Peak would feel an enormous sweep of relief the moment he reached the sterile house with his news. The major knew the exact words he would say: 'The women are taken – the *woman* is taken.'

Across the street a man in shirt sleeves entered the agency door. He appeared hesitant to Lin and there was something . . . A taxi suddenly drove up and the major bolted forward, reaching for the door handle – the hesitant man was forgotten.

'Be alert, lads,' said Lin into the microphone attached to the dashboard radio. 'We must be as quick and as unobtrusive as possible. No Arbuthnot Road can be tolerated here. And no weapons, of course. *Ready*, now!'

But there was nothing to be ready for; the taxi drove away without disgorging anyone.

'Vehicle *Three!*' said the major curtly. 'Get that licence and call the cab company! I want them in radio contact. Find out exactly what their taxi was doing here! Better yet, Follow it and do as I tell you. It could be the women.'

'I believe there was only a man in the backseat, sir,' said the driver.

'They could have ducked below the seat! Damned eyes. A man, you say?'

'Yes, sir.'

'I smell a rotten squid.'

'Why, Major?'

'If I knew, the stench would not be so strong.'

The waiting continued, and the immense Lin Wenzu began to perspire. The dying sun cast both a blinding orange light through the windshield and pockets of dark shadows along Bonham Strand East.

'It's too long,' whispered the major to himself.

Static erupted from the radio. 'We have the report from the cab company, sir.'

'Go on!'

'The taxi in question is trying to find an import house on Bonham Strand

East, but the driver told his fare that the address must be on Bonham Strand *West.* Apparently, his passenger is very angry. He got out and threw money into the window only moments ago.'

'Break away and return here,' ordered Lin as he watched the garage doors opening across the street at the Apex agency. A car emerged, turning left, driven by the shirt-sleeved man.

The sweat now rolled down the major's face. Something was *not* in order; another order was being superimposed. What was it that bothered him? What *was* it?'

'*Him!*' shouted Lin to his startled driver.

'Sir?'

'A wrinkled white shirt, but trousers creased like steel. A uniform! A *chauffeur!* Swing around! *Follow* him!'

The driver held his hand on the horn, breaking the line of traffic, as he made a U-turn while the major issued instructions to the backups, ordering one to stay at the Apex agency, the others to take up the new chase.

'*Aiya!*' screamed the driver, jamming on his breakes, screeching to a stop, as a huge brown limousine roared out of a side street blocking their way. Only the slightest contact had been made, the government car barely touching the left rear door of the large automobile.

'*Feng zi!*' yelled the limousine's chauffeur, calling Lin's driver a crazy dog, as he jumped out of his outsized sedan to see if any damage had been done to his vehicle.

'*Lai! Lai!*' shrieked the major's driver, leaping out, ready for combat.

'*Stop* it!' roared Wenzu. 'Just get him *out* of here!'

'It is *he* who does not move, sir!'

'Tell him he must *do* so! Show him your identification!'

All traffic came to a stop; horns blared, people in automobiles and in the streets yelled angrily. The major closed his eyes and shook his head in frustration. There was nothing he could do but get out of the car.

As another did from the limousine. A middle-aged Chinese with a balding head. 'I gather we have a problem,' said Lee Teng.

'I *know* you!' shouted Lin. 'The Mandarin!'

'Many who have the taste to frequent our fine hotel know me, sir. I'm afraid I cannot reciprocate. Have you been a guest, sir?'

'What are you *doing* here?'

'It is a confidential errand for a gentleman at the Mandarin, and I have no intention of saying anything further.'

'Damn-*damn!* A government directive was sent out! A Canadian woman named Staples! One of your people called us!'

'I have no idea what you're talking about. For the last hour I have been trying to solve a problem for a guest who's attending the ball at Government House tonight. I'd be happy to furnish you with her name – if your position warrants it.'

'My position *warrants* it! I repeat! Why have you stopped us?'

'I believe it was your man who sped across the changing light.'

'Not *so!*' screamed Lin's driver.

'Then it is a matter for the courts,' said Lee Teng. 'May we proceed?'

'*Not* yet,' replied the major, approaching the Mandarin's concierge. 'I repeat again. A government directive was received at your hotel. It stated clearly that a woman named Staples might try to lease a car and you were to report the attempt to Police Central Four.'

'Then *I* repeat, sir. I have not been near my desk for well over an hour, nor have I seen any such directive as you describe. However, in cooperation with your unseen credentials. I will tell you that all car rental arrangements would have to be made through my first assistant, a man, quite frankly, I have found quite compromising in many areas.'

'But *you* are *here!*'

'How many guests at the Mandarin have late business in Bonham Strand East, sir? Accept the coincidence.'

'Your eyes smile at me, *Zhongguo ren.*'

'Without laughter, sir. I will proceed. The damage is minor.'

'I don't give a damn if you and your people have to stay there all *night,*' said Ambassador Havilland. 'It's the only crack we've *got.* The way you've described it she'll return the car and then pick up her own. *Goddamn* it, there's a Canadian-American strategy conference at four o'clock tomorrow afternoon. She *has* to be back! Stay *with* it! Stay with all the *posts!* Just bring her in to me!'

'She will claim harassment. We will be breaking the laws of international diplomacy.'

'Then *break* them! Just get her here, in Cleopatra's carpet, if you have to! I haven't any time to waste – not a *minute!*'

Held firmly in check by two agents, a furious Catherine Staples was led into the room in the house on Victoria Peak. Lin Wenzu had opened the door; he now closed it as Staples faced Ambassador Raymond Havilland and Undersecretary of State Edward McAllister. It was 11:35 in the morning, the sun streaming through the large bay window overlooking the garden.

'You've gone too far, Havilland,' said Catherine, her throaty voice ice-like in its flat delivery.

'I haven't gone far enough where you're concerned, Mrs Staples. You actively compromised a member of the American legation. You engaged in extortion to the grave disservice of my government.'

'You can't prove that because there's no evidence, no photographs—'

'I don't have to prove it. At precisely seven o'clock last night the young man drove up here and told us everything. A sordid little chapter, isn't it?'

'Damn *fool!* He's blameless, but *you're* not! And since you bring up the word "sordid," there's nothing he's done that could match the filth of your own actions.' Without missing a verbal beat, Catherine looked at the undersecretary of State. 'I presume this is the liar called McAllister.'

'You're very trying,' said the undersecretary.

'And you're an unprincipled lackey who does another man's dirty work. I've heard it all and it's all disgusting! But every thread was woven' – Staples snapped her head toward Havilland – 'by an *expert.* Who gave *you* the right to play *God? Any* of you? Do you know what you've done to those two people out there? Do you know what you've *asked* of them?'

'We know,' said the ambassador simply. 'I know.'

'She knows, too, in spite of the fact that I didn't have the heart to give her the final confirmation. *You,* McAllister! When I learned it was you up here, I wasn't sure she could handle it. Not at the moment. But I intend to tell her. You and your lies! A taipan's wife murdered in Macao – oh, the symmetry of it all, what an excuse to take another man's wife! *Lies!* I have my sources and it never *happened!* Well, get this straight. I'm bringing her in to the consulate under the full protection of my government. And if I were you, Havilland, I'd be damned careful about throwing around alleged illegalities. You and your goddamned people have lied to and manipulated a Canadian citizen into a life-threatening operation – whatever the hell it is *this* time. Your arrogance is simply beyond belief! But I assure you it's coming to a stop. Whether my government likes it or not, I'm going to expose you, *all* of you! You're no better than the barbarians in the KGB. Well, the American juggernaut of covert operations is going to be handed a bloody setback! I'm sick of you, the *world* is sick of you!'

'My dear woman!' shouted the ambassador, losing the last vestiges of control in his sudden anger. 'Make all the threats you like, but you *will* hear me out! And if after you've heard what I have to say you wish to declare *war,* you go right ahead! As the song says, *my* days are dwindling down, but not millions of others'! I'd like to do what I can to prolong those other lives. But you may disagree, so declare your war, dear lady! And, by Christ, *you* live with the consequences!'

19

Leaning forward in the chair, Bourne snapped the trigger housing out of its recess and checked the weapon's bore under the light of the floor lamp above him. It was a repetitive, pointless exercise; the bore was spotless. During the past four hours he had cleaned d'Anjou's gun three times, dismantling it three times and each time oiling each mechanism until each part of the dark metal glistened. The process occupied his time. He had studied d'Anjou's arsenal of weapons and explosives, but since most of the equipment was in sealed boxes, conceivably tripped against theft, he let them be and concentrated on the single gun. There was only so much pacing one could do in the Frenchman's flat on the Rua das Lorchas overlooking Macao's Porto Interior – or Inner Harbour – and they had agreed he was not to go outside in daylight. Inside, he was as safe as he could be anywhere in Macao. D'Anjou, who changed residences at will and whim, had rented the waterfront apartment less than two weeks ago using a false name and a lawyer he had never met, who in turn employed a 'rentor' to sign the lease, which the attorney sent by messenger to his unknown client by way of the checkroom at the crowded Floating Casino. Such were the ways of Philippe d'Anjou, formerly Echo of Medusa.

Jason reassembled the weapon, depressed the shells in the magazine, and cracked it up through the handle. He got out of the chair and walked to the window, the gun in his hand. Across the expanse of water was the People's Republic, so accessible for anyone who knew the procedures arising from simple human greed. There was nothing new under the sun since the time of the pharaohs where borders were concerned. They were erected to be crossed – one way or another.

He looked at his watch. It was close to five o'clock; the afternoon sun was descending. D'Anjou had called him from Hong Kong at noon. The Frenchman had gone to the Peninsula with Bourne's room key, packed his suitcase without checking out, and was taking the one o'clock jetfoil back to Macao. Where was he? The trip took barely an hour, and from the Macao pier to the Rua das Lorchas was no more than ten minutes by cab. But then predictability was not Echo's strong suit.

Fragments of the Medusa memories came back to Jason, triggered by the presence of d'Anjou. Although painful and frightening, certain impressions provided a certain comfort, again thanks to the Frenchman. Not only was d'Anjou a consummate liar when it counted most and an opportunist of the first rank, but he was extraordinarily resourceful. Above all, the Frenchman was a pragmatist. He had proven that in Paris, and those memories were clear. If he was delayed, there was a good reason. If he did not appear, he was dead. And this last was unacceptable to Bourne. D'Anjou was in a position to do something Jason wanted above all to do himself but dared not risk Marie's life in doing it. It was risk enough that the trail of the impostor-assassin had brought him to Macao in the first place, but as long as he stayed away from the Lisboa Hotel he trusted his instincts. He would remain hidden from those looking for him – looking for someone who even vaguely resembled him in height, or build, or colouring. Someone asking questions in the Lisboa Hotel.

One call from the Lisboa to the taipan in Hong Kong and Marie was dead. The taipan had not merely threatened – threats were too often a meaningless ploy – he had used a far more lethal expedient. After shouting and crashing his large hand on the arm of the fragile chair, he had quietly given his word: Marie would die. It was a promise made by a man who kept his promises, kept his word.

Yet for all that, David Webb sensed something he could not define. There was about the huge taipan something a bit larger than life, too operatic, that had nothing to do with his size. It was if he had used his immense girth to advantage in a way that large men rarely do, preferring to let only their sheer size do the impressing. Who *was* the taipan? The answer was at the Lisboa Hotel, and since he dared not go there himself, d'Anjou's skills could serve him. He had told the Frenchman very little; he would tell him more now. He would describe a brutal double killing, the weapon an Uzi, and say that one of the victims was a powerful taipan's wife. D'Anjou would ask the questions he could not ask, and if there were answers he would take another step toward Marie.

Play the scenario. – Alexander Conklin.

Whose scenario? – David Webb.

You're wasting time! – Jason Bourne. *Find the impostor. Take him!*

Quiet footsteps in the outside hallway. Jason spun away from the window and raced silently to the wall, pressing his back against it, the gun levelled at the door, where the swinging panel would conceal him. A key was cautiously, quietly inserted. The door swung slowly open.

Bourne crashed it back into the intruder, spinning around and grabbing the stunned figure in the frame. He yanked him inside and kicked the door shut, the weapon aimed at the head of the fallen man, who had dropped a suitcase and a very large package. It was d'Anjou.

'That's one way to get your head blown off, Echo!'

'*Sacre-bleu!* It is also the last time I will ever be considerate of you! You don't see yourself, Delta. You look as you did in Tam Quan, without sleep for days. I thought you might be resting.'

Another memory, briefly flashed. 'In Tam Quan,' said Jason, 'you told me I had to sleep, didn't you? We hid in the brush and you formed a circle around me and damn near gave me an order to get some rest.'

'It was purely a self-serving request. *We* couldn't get ourselves out of there, only *you* could.'

'You said something to me then. What was it? I listened.'

'I explained that rest was as much a weapon as any blunt instrument or firing mechanism man had ever devised.'

'I used a variation later. It became an axiom for me.'

'I'm so glad you had the intelligence to listen to your elders. May I please rise? Will you *please* lower that damned gun?'

'Oh, sorry.'

'We have no time,' said d'Anjou, getting up and leaving the suitcase on the floor. He tore the brown paper off the large package. Inside were pressed khaki clothes, two belted holsters and two visored hats; he threw them all on a chair. 'These are uniforms. I have the proper identifications in my pocket. I am afraid I outrank you, Delta, but then age has its privileges.'

'They're uniforms of the Hong Kong police.'

'Kowloon, to be precise. We may have our *chance*, Delta! It's why I was so long getting back. Kai-tak Airport! The security is enormous, just what the impostor wants in order to show he's better than you ever were! There's no guarantee, of course, but I'd stake my life on it – it's the classic challenge for an obsessed maniac. "Mount your forces, I'll break through them!" With one kill like that he reestablishes the legend of his utter invincibility. It's him, I'm sure of it!'

'Start from the beginning,' ordered Bourne.

'As we dress, yes,' agreed the Frenchman, removing his shirt and unbuckling his trousers. '*Hurry!* I have a motor launch across the road. Four hundred horse-power. We can be in Kowloon in forty-five minutes. Here! This is yours! *Mon Dieu*, the money I've spent makes me want to vomit!'

'The PRC patrols,' said Jason, peeling off his clothes and reaching for the uniform. 'They'll shoot us out of the water!'

'Idiot, certain known boats are negotiated with by radio in code. There is, after all, honour among us. How do you think we run our merchandise? How do you think we survive? We meet in coves at the Chinese islands of Teh Sa Wei and payments are made. *Hurry!*'

'What about the airport? Why are you so sure it's him?'

'The Crown governor. Assassination.'

'*What?*' shouted Bourne, stunned.

'I walked from the Peninsula to the Star Ferry with your suitcase. It's only a short distance, and the ferry is far quicker than a taxi through the tunnel. As I passed the Kowloon Police Hill on Salisbury Road I saw seven patrol cars drive out at emergency speed, one behind the other, all turning left, which is not to the godown. It struck me as odd – yes, two or three for a local eruption, but *seven?* It was good joss, as these people say. I called my contact on the Hill and he was cooperative – it was also not much of an internal secret any longer. He said if I stayed around I'd see another ten cars, twenty vans, all heading out to Kai-tak within the next two hours. Those I saw were the advance search teams. They had received word through their underground sources that an attempt was to be made on the Crown governor's life.'

'Specifics!' commanded Bourne harshly, buckling his trousers and reaching for the long khaki shirt that served as a jacket under the bullet-laden holster belt.

'The governor is flying in from Beijing tonight with his own entourage from the Foreign Office, as well as another Chinese negotiating delegation. There will be newspaper people, television crews, everyone. Both governments want full coverage. There is to be a joint meeting tomorrow between all the negotiators and leaders of the financial sector.'

'The '97 treaty?'

'Yet another round in the endless verbosity about the Accords. But, for all our sakes, just pray they keep talking pleasantly.'

'The *scenario*,' said Jason softly, stopping all movement.

'What scenario?'

'The one you yourself brought up, the scenario that had the wires burning between Peking and Government House. Kill a Crown governor for the murder of a vice-premier? Then perhaps a foreign secretary for a ranking member of the Central Committee – a prime minister for a chairman? How far does it go? How many selected killings before the breaking point is reached? How long before the parent refuses to tolerate a disobedient child and marches into Hong Kong? Christ, it *could* happen. Someone *wants* it to happen!'

D'Anjou stood motionless, holding the wide belt of the holster with its ominous strand of brass-capped shells. 'What I suggested was no more than speculation based on the random violence caused by an obsessed killer who accepts his contracts without discrimination. There's enough greed and political corruption on both sides to justify that speculation. But what you're suggesting, Delta, is quite different. You're saying it's a plan, an organized plan to disrupt Hong Kong to the point that the Mainland takes over.'

'The scenario,' repeated Jason Bourne. 'The more complicated it gets, the simpler it appears.'

The rooftops of Kai-tak Airport were swarming with police, as were the gates and the tunnels, the immigration counters and the luggage areas. Outside, on the immense field of black tarmac, powerful floodlights were joined by roving, sharper searchlights probing every moving vehicle, every inch of visible ground. Television crews uncoiled cables under watching eyes, while interviewers standing behind sound trucks practised pronunciation in a dozen languages. Reporters and photographers were kept beyond the gates as airport personnel shouted through the amplifiers that roped-off sections on the field would soon be available for all legitimate journalists with proper passes issued by the Kai-tak management. It was madness. And then the totally unexpected happened as a sudden rainstorm swept over the colony from the darkness of the western horizon. It was yet another autumn deluge.

'The impostor has good luck – good joss – as they say, doesn't he?' said d'Anjou as he and Bourne in their uniforms marched with a phalanx of police through a covered walkway made of corrugated tin to one of the huge repair hangars. The hammering of the rain was deafening.

'Luck had nothing to do with it,' replied Jason. 'He studied the weather reports from as far away as Sichuan. Every airport has them. He spotted it yesterday, if not two days ago. Weather's a weapon, too, Echo.'

'Still, he could not dictate the arrival of the Crown governor on a Chinese aircraft. They are often hours late, *usually* hours late.'

'But not days, *not* usually. When did the Kowloon police get word of the attempt?'

'I asked specifically,' said the Frenchman. 'Around eleven-thirty this morning.'

'And the plane from Peking was scheduled to arrive sometime this evening?'

'Yes, I told you that. The newspaper and the television people were ordered to be here by nine o'clock.'

'He studied the weather reports. Opportunities present themselves. You grab them.'

'And this is what *you* must do, Delta! *Think* like him, *be* him! It is our chance!'

'What do you think I'm doing? . . . When we get to the hangar, I want to break away. Can your ersatz identification make it possible?'

'I am a British Sector commander from the Mongkok Divisional Police.'

'What does *that* mean?'

'I really don't know, but it was the best I could do.'

'You don't sound British.'

'Who would know that out here at Kai-tak, old *chap?*'

'The British.'

'I'll avoid them. My Chinese is better than yours. The *Zhongguo ren* will respect it. You'll be free to roam.'

'I have to be,' said Jason Bourne. 'If it's your commando, I want him before anyone else spots him! Here. *Now!*' Roped stanchions were moved out of the high-domed hangar by maintenance personnel in glossy yellow rain slickers. Then a truckload of the yellow coats arrived for the police contingents; men caught them as they were thrown out of the rear of the van. Putting them on, the police then formed several groups to receive instructions from their superiors. Order was rapidly emerging from the confusion compounded by the newly arrived, bewildered troops and the problems caused by the sudden downpour. It was the sort of order Bourne distrusted. It was too smooth, too conventional for the job they faced. Ranks of brightly dressed soldiers marching forward were in the wrong place with the wrong tactics when seeking out guerrillas – even one man trained in guerrilla warfare. Each policeman in his yellow slicker was both a warning and a target – and he was also something else. A pawn. Each could be replaced by another dressed the same way, by a killer who knew how to assume the look of his enemy.

Yet the strategy of infiltration for the purpose of a kill was suicidal, and Jason knew there was no such commitment on the part of his impostor. Unless . . . unless the weapon to be used had a sound level so low, the rain would eliminate it . . . but even then the target's reaction could not be instantaneous. A cordon would immediately be erected around the killing ground at the first sign of the Crown governor's collapse, every exit blocked, everyone in the vicinity ordered under guns to remain in place. A delayed reaction? A tiny air dart whose impact was no greater than a pinprick, a minor annoyance to be swatted away like a bothersome fly, as the lethal drop of poison entered the bloodstream to cause death slowly but inevitably, time not a consideration. It was a possibility, but again there were too many obstacles to surmount, too much accuracy demanded beyond the limits of an air-compressed weapon. The Crown governor would undoubtedly be wearing a protective vest, and targeting the face was out. Facial nerves exaggerated pain, and any foreign object making contact so close to the eyes would produce an immediate and dramatic reaction. That left the hands and the throat: the first were too small and conceivably could be moving too fast; the second was simply too limited an area. A high-powered rifle on a rooftop? A rifle of unquestioned accuracy with an infrared telescopic sight? Another possibility – an all too familiar yellow slicker replaced by one worn by an assassin. But again, it was suicidal, for such a weapon would produce an isolated explosion, and to mount a silencer would reduce the accuracy of the rifle to the point where it could not be trusted. The odds were against a killer on a rooftop. The kill would be too obvious.

And the kill was everything. Bourne understood that, especially under the circumstances. D'Anjou was right. All the factors were in place for a spectacular assassination. Carlos the Jackal could not ask for more – nor could Jason Bourne, reflected David Webb. To pull it off in spite of the extraordinary security would crown the new 'Bourne' king of his sickening profession. Then *how?* Which option would he *use?* And after the decision was made, what avenue of escape would be most effective, most possible?

One of the television trucks with their complicated equipment was too obvious a means for an escape. The incoming aircraft's maintenance crews were checked and double-and triple-checked; an outsider would be spotted instantly. All the journalists would pass through electronic gates that picked up an excess of ten milligrams of metal. And the rooftops were out. *How*, then?

'You're cleared!' said d'Anjou, suddenly appearing at his side, holding a piece of paper in his hand. 'This is signed by the prefect of the Kai-tak police.'

'What did you tell him?'

'That you are a Jew trained by the Mossad in antiterrorist activities and posted to us in an exchange programme. The word will be spread.'

'Good God, I don't speak *Hebrew!*'

'Who here does? Shrug and continue in your tolerable French – which *is* spoken here but very badly. You'll get away with it.'

'You're impossible, you know that, don't you?'

'I know that Delta, when he was our leader in Medusa, told Command Saigon that he would not go out in the field without "old Echo."'

'I must have been out of my mind.'

'You were less in command of it then, I'll grant you that.'

'Thanks a lot, Echo. Wish me luck.'

'You don't need luck,' said the Frenchman. 'You are Delta. You will always be Delta.'

Removing the bright yellow rain slicker and the visored hat, Bourne walked outside and showed his clearance to the guards by the hangar doors. In the distance, the press was being herded through the electronic gates toward the roped stanchions. Microphones had been placed on the edge of the runway, and police vans were joined by motorcycle patrols forming a tight semicircle around the press conference area. The preparations were about complete, all the security forces in place, the media equipment in working order. The plane from Peking had obviously begun its descent in the downpour. It would land in a matter of minutes, minutes Jason wished could be extended. There were so many things to look for and so little time to search. *Where? What?* Everything was both possible and impossible. Which option would the killer use? What vantage point would he zero in on for the perfect kill? And how would he most logically escape from the killing ground alive?

Bourne had considered every option he could think of and ruled each out. *Think again!* And *again!* Only minutes left. Walk around and start at the beginning . . . the beginning. The premise: the assassination of the Crown governor. Conditions: seemingly airtight, with security police training guns from rooftops, blocking every entrance, every exit, every staircase and escalator, all in radio contact. The odds were overwhelmingly against. Suicide . . . Yet it was these same heavily negative odds that the impostor-killer found irresistible. D'Anjou had been right again: with one spectacular kill under these conditions an assassin's supremacy would be established – or reestablished. What had the Frenchman said? *With one kill like that he reestablishes the legend of his invincibility.*

Who? Where? How? Think! *Look!*

The downpour drenched his Kowloon police uniform. He continuously wiped the water from his face as he moved about peering at everyone and everything. *Nothing!* And then the muted roar of the jet engines could be heard in the distance. The jet from Peking was making its final approach at the far end of the runway. It was landing.

Jason studied the crowd standing inside the roped stanchions. An accommodating Hong Kong government, in deference to Peking and in the desire for 'full coverage,' had supplied ponchos and squares of canvas and cheap pocket raincoats for all who wanted them. The Kai-tak personnel countered the media's demands for an inside conference by stating simply – and wisely without explanation – that it was not in the interests of security. The statements would be short, an aggregate of no more than five or six minutes. Certainly the fine members of the journalistic establishment could tolerate a little rain for such an important event.

The photographers? *Metal!* Cameras were passed through the gates but not all 'cameras' took pictures. A relatively simple device could be inserted and locked into a mount, a powerful firing mechanism that released a bullet – or a dart – with the assistance of a telescopic view-finder. Was that the way? Had the assassin taken *that* option, expecting to smash the 'camera' under his feet and take another from his pocket as he moved swiftly to the outskirts of the crowd, his credentials as authentic as those of d'Anjou and the 'antiterrorist' from the Mossad? It was possible.

The huge jet dropped onto the runway, and Bourne walked quickly into the roped-off area, approaching every photographer he could see, looking – looking for a man who looked like himself. There must have been two dozen men with cameras; he became frantic as the plane from Peking taxied toward the crowd, the flood- and searchlights now centred on the space around the microphones and the television crews. He went from one photographer to the next, rapidly ascertaining that the man could not be the killer, then looking again to see if postures were erect, faces cosmeticized. Again *nothing!* No one! He had to *find* him, *take* him! Before anyone else found him. The assassination was beside the point, it was irrelevant to him! Nothing mattered except Marie!

Go back to the beginning! Target – the Crown governor. Conditions – highly negative for a kill, the target under maximum security, undoubtedly protected by personal armour, the whole security corps orderly, disciplined, the officers in tight command . . . The *beginning?* Something was missing. Go over it again. The Crown governor – the target, a single kill. Method of the kill: suicide ruled out everything but a delayed-reaction device – an air dart, a pellet – yet the demands of accuracy made such a weapon illogical, and the loud report of a conventional gun would instantly activate the entire security force. *Delay?* Delayed *action*, not *re*action! The beginning, the first assumption, was *wrong!* The target was not just the Crown governor. *Not* a single kill but multiple killings, indiscriminate killings! How much more spectacular! How much more effective for a maniac who wanted to throw Hong Kong into chaos! And the chaos would begin instantly with the security forces. *Dis*order, escape!

Bourne's mind was racing as he roamed through the crowd in the downpour, his eyes darting everywhere. He tried to recall every weapon he had ever known. A weapon that could be fired or released silently, unobtrusively from a restricted, densely populated area, its effect delayed long enough for the killer to reposition himself and make a clean escape. The only device that came to mind was a grenade, but he immediately dismissed it. Then the thought of time-fused dynamite or *plastique* struck him. The latter was far more manageable in terms of delays and concealment. The plastic explosives could be set in time spans of minutes and fractions of minutes rather than a few seconds only; they could be hidden in small boxes or in wrapped packages, even narrow briefcases – or thicker cases supposedly filled with photographic equipment, not necessarily carried by a photographer. He started again, going back into the crowd of reporters and photographers, his eyes scanning the black tarmac below trousers and skirts, looking for an isolated container that remained stationary on the hard asphalt. Logic made him concentrate on the rows of men and women nearest the roped-off runway. In his mind the 'package' would be no more than twelve inches in length if it was thick, twenty if it was an attaché case. A smaller charge would not kill the negotiators of both governments. The airfield lights were strong, but they created myriad shadows, darker pockets within the darkness. He wished he had had the sense to carry a flashlight – he had *always* carried one, if only a penlight, for it, too, was a weapon! Why had he *forgotten?* Then to his astonishment he saw flashlight beams crisscrossing the black floor of the airfield, darting between the same trousers and skirts he had been peering beyond. The security police had arrived at the same theory, and why shouldn't they? La Guardia Airport, 1972; Lod Airport, Tel Aviv, 1974; Rue de Bac, Paris, 1975; Harrods, London,

1982. And a half-dozen embassies from Teheran to Beirut, why *shouldn't* they? They were current, he was not. His thinking was slow – and he could not allow that!

Who? Where?

The enormous 747 starship of the People's Republic came into view like a great silver bird, its jet engines roaring through the deluge, whirring down as it was manoeuvred into position on alien ground. The doors opened and the parade began. The two leaders of the British and the Chinese delegations emerged together. They waved and walked in unison down the metal staircase, one in the impeccable clothes of Whitehall, the other in the drab, rankless uniform of the People's army. They were followed by two lines of aides and adjutants, Occidentals and Orientals doing their best to appear congenial with one another for the cameras. The leaders approached the microphones, and as the voices droned over the loudspeakers and through the rain the next minutes were a blur for Jason. A part of his mind was on the ceremony that was taking place under the floodlights, the larger part on the final search – for it *would* be final. If the impostor was there, he had to *find* him – *before* the kill, before the *chaos!* But, goddamn it, *where?* Bourne moved out beyond the ropes on the far right to get a better view of the proceedings. A guard objected; Jason showed the man his clearance and remained motionless, studying the television crews, their looks, their eyes, their equipment. If the assassin was among them, which one *was* he?

'We are jointly pleased to announce that further progress has been made with regard to the Accords. We of the United Kingdom . . .'

'We of the People's Republic of China – the only true China on the face of the earth – express a desire to find a close communion with those who wish . . .'

The speeches were interrupted by each leader giving support to his counterpart, yet letting the world know there was still much to negotiate. There was tension beneath the civility, the verbal placebos, and the plastic smiles. And Jason found nothing he could focus on, *nothing*, so he wiped the rain from his face and nodded to the guard as he ducked under the rope and moved once again back through the crowd behind the stanchions. He threaded his way to the left side of the press conference.

Suddenly, Bourne's eyes were drawn to a series of headlights in the downpour that curved into the runway at the far end of the field and rapidly accelerated toward the stationary aircraft. Then, as if on cue, there was a swelling of applause. The brief ceremony was over, signified by the arrival of the official limousines, each with a motorcycle escort driving up between the delegations and the roped-off crowd of journalists and photographers. Police surrounded the television trucks, ordering all but two preselected cameramen to get inside their vehicles.

It was the moment. If anything was going to happen, it would happen now. If an instrument of death was about to be placed, its charges to be exploded within the time span of a minute or less, it would have to be placed *now!*

Several feet to his left, he saw an officer of a police contingent, a tall man whose eyes were moving as rapidly as his own. Jason leaned toward the man and spoke in Chinese while holding out his clearance, shielding it from the rain with his hand. 'I'm the man from the Mossad!' he yelled, trying to be heard through the applause.

'Yes, I know about you!' shouted the officer. 'I was told. We're grateful you're here!'

'Do you have a flashlight – a torch?'

'Yes, of course. Do you want it?'

'Very much.'

'Here.'

'Clear me!' ordered Bourne, lifting the rope, gesturing for the officer to follow. 'I haven't time to show papers!'

'Certainly!' The Chinese followed, reaching out and intercepting a guard who was about to stop Jason – by shooting him if it was necessary. 'Let him be! He's one of us! He's trained in this sort of thing!'

'The Jew from the Mossad?'

'It is he.'

'We were told. Thank you, sir . . . But, of course, he can't understand me.'

'Oddly enough, he does. He speaks *Guangdong hua*.'

'In Food Street there is what they call a Kosur restaurant that serves our dishes—'

Bourne was now between the row of limousines and the roped stanchions. As he walked down the line of rope, his flashlight directed below on the black tarmac, he gave orders in Chinese and English – shouting yet not shouting; the commands of a reasonable man looking, perhaps, for a lost object. One by one the men and women of the press moved back, explaining to those behind them. He approached the lead limousine; the flags of both Great Britain and the People's Republic were displayed respectively on the right and left, indicating that England was the host, China the guest. The representatives rode together. Jason concentrated on the ground; the exalted passengers were about to enter the elongated vehicle with their most trusted aides amid sustained applause.

It *happened*, but Bourne was not sure what it was! His left shoulder touched another shoulder and the contact was electric. The man he had grazed first lurched forward and then had swung back with such ferocity that Jason was shoved off balance. He turned and looked at the man on the police escort motorcycle, then raised his flashlight to see through the dark plastic oval of the helmet.

Lightning struck, sharp, jagged bolts crashing into his skull, his eyes riveted as he tried to adjust to the incredible. He was staring at *himself* – from only years ago! The dark features behind the opaque bubble were *his!* It was the *commando!* The *impostor!* The *assassin!*

The eyes that stared back at him also showed panic, but they were quicker than Webb's. A flattened, rigid hand lashed out, crashing into Jason's throat, cutting off all speech and thought. Bourne fell back, unable to scream, grabbing his neck, as the assassin lurched off his motorcycle. He rushed past Jason and ducked under the rope.

Get him! Take him! . . . *Marie!* The words were absent – only hysterical thoughts screamed silently in Bourne's mind. He retched, exploding the chop in his throat, and leaped over the rope, plunging into the crowd, following the path of fallen-away bodies that had been pummelled by the killer in his race to escape.

'Stop . . . *him!*' Only the last word emerged from Jason's throat; it was a hoarse whisper. 'Let *me through!*' Two words were audible, but no one was listening. From somewhere near the terminal a band was playing in the downpour.

The path was closed! There were only people, people, *people!* Find him! Take him! *Marie!* He's gone! He's *disappeared!* 'Let me through!' he screamed, the words now clear but heeded by no one. He yanked and pulled and bucked his way to the edge of the crowd, another crowd facing him behind the glass doors of the terminal.

Nothing! No one! The killer was gone!

Killer? The *kill!*

It was the limousine, the *lead* limousine with the flags of both countries! *That* was the target! Somewhere in that car or beneath that car was the timed mechanism that would blow it to the skies, killing the leaders of both delegations. Result – the scenario . . . chaos. *Takeover!*

Bourne spun around, frantically looking for someone in authority. Twenty yards beyond the rope, standing at attention as the British anthem was being played, was an officer of the Kowloon police. Clipped to his belt was a radio. A *chance!* The limousines had started their stately procession toward an unseen gate in the airfield.

Jason yanked the rope, pulling it up, toppling a stanchion, and started running toward the short, erect Chinese officer. '*Xun su!*' he roared.

'*Shemma?*' replied the startled man, instinctively reaching for his holstered gun.

'*Stop* them! The cars, the *limousines!* The one in *front!*'

'What are you talking about? Who are you?'

Bourne nearly struck the man in frustration. '*Mossad!*' he screamed.

'You are the one from Israel? I've heard—'

'*Listen* to me! Get on that radio and tell them to stop! Get everyone out of that car! It's going to blow! *Now!*'

Through the rain the officer looked up into Jason's eyes, then nodded once and pulled the radio from his belt. 'This is an emergency! Clear the channel and patch me to Red Star One. *Immediately.*'

'*All* the cars!' interrupted Bourne. 'Tell them to peel away!'

'*Change!*' cried the police officer. 'Alert all vehicles. Put me through!' And with his voice tense but controlled, the Chinese spoke clearly; emphasizing each word. 'This is Colony Five and we have an emergency. With me is the man from the Mossad and I relay his instructions. They are to be complied with at once. Red Star One is to stop instantly and order everyone out of the vehicle, instructing them to run for cover. All other cars are to turn to the left toward the centre of the field, away from Red Star One. Execute *immediately!*'

Stunned, the crowds watched as in the distance the engines roared in unison. Five limousines swung out of position, racing into the outer darkness of the airport. The first car screeched to a stop; the doors opened and men leaped out, running in all directions.

Eight seconds later it happened. The limousine called Red Star One exploded forty feet from an open gate. Flaming metal and shattered glass spiralled up into the downpour as the band music halted in midbreath.

Peking. 11:25 P.M.

Above the northern suburbs of Peking is a vast compound rarely spoken of, and certainly not for public inspection. The major reason is security, but there is also an element of embarrassment in this egalitarian society. For inside this sprawling, forested enclave in the hills are the villas of China's most powerful figures. The compound is shrouded in secrecy, as befits a complex enclosed by a high wall of grey stone, the entrances guarded by seasoned army veterans, the dense woods within continuously patrolled by attack dogs. And if one were to speculate on the social or political relationships cultivated there, it should be noted that no villa can be seen from another, for each structure is surrounded by its own inner wall, and all personal guards are personally selected after years of obedience and trust. The name, when it is spoken, is Jade Tower Mountain, which refers not to a geological mountain, but to an immense hill that rises above the others. At one time or another, with the ebb and flow of political fortunes, such men as Mao Zedong, Liu Shaoqi, Lin Biao, and Zhou Enlai lived here. Among the residents now was a man shaping the economic destiny of the People's Republic. The world press referred to him simply as Sheng, and the name was immediately recognizable. His full name was Sheng Chou Yang.

A brown sedan sped down the road fronting the imposing grey wall. It approached Gate Number Six, and as though preoccupied, the driver suddenly applied the brakes and the car sideslipped into the entrance, stopping inches from the bright orange barrier that reflected the beams of the headlights. A guard approached.

'Who is it you come to see and what is your name? I will need your official identification.'

'Minister Sheng,' said the driver. 'And my name is not important, nor are my papers required. Please inform the minister's residence that his emissary from Kowloon is here.'

The soldier shrugged. Such replies were standard at Jade Tower Mountain, and to press further might result in a conceivable transfer from this heavenly duty where the leftover food was beyond one's imagination and even foreign beer was given for obedient and cooperative service. Still, the guard used the telephone. The visitor had to be admitted properly. To do otherwise could bring one to kneel in a field and be shot in the back of the head. The guard returned to the gatehouse and dialled the villa of Sheng Chou Yang.

'Admit him. *Quickly!*'

Without going back to the sedan, the guard pressed a button and the orange bar was raised. The car raced in, far too quickly over the gravel, thought the guard. The emissary was in a great hurry.

'Minister Sheng is in the garden,' said the army officer at the door, looking beyond the visitor, his eyes, darting about, peering into the darkness. 'Go to him.'

The emissary rushed through the front room filled with red lacquered furniture to an archway beyond which was a walled garden complete with four connecting lily ponds subtly lit with yellow lights beneath the water. Two intersecting paths of white gravel formed an X between the ponds, and low black wicker chairs and tables were placed at the far end of each path within an oval setting. Seated alone at the end of the eastern leg by the brick wall was a slender man of medium height, with close-cropped, prematurely grey hair and gaunt features. If there was anything about him that might startle someone meeting him for the first time, it was his eyes, for they were the dark eyes of a dead man, the lids never blinking even for an instant. Contrarily, they were also the eyes of a zealot whose blind dedication to a cause was the core of his strength; white heat was in the pupils, lightning in the orbs. These were the eyes of Sheng Chou Yang, and at the moment they were on fire.

'*Tell* me!' he roared, both hands gripping the black arms of the wicker chair. 'Who *does* this?'

'It's all a *lie*, Minister! We have checked with our people in Tel Aviv. There is no such man as was described. There is no agent from the Mossad in Kowloon! A *lie!*'

'What action did you take?'

'It is most confusing—'

'What *action?*'

'We are tracing an Englishman in the Mongkok whom no one seems to know about.'

'Fools and *idiots!* Idiots and *fools!* Whom have you spoken with?'

'Our key man in the Kowloon police. He is bewildered, and I'm sorry to say I think he is frightened. He made several references to Macao, and I did not like his voice.'

'He is dead.'

'I will transmit your instructions.'

'I'm afraid you cannot.' Sheng gestured with his left hand, his right in shadows, reaching beneath the low table. 'Come pay your obedience to the Kuomintang,' he commanded.

The emissary approached the minister. He bowed low and reached for the great man's left hand. Sheng lifted his right hand. In it was a gun.

An explosion followed, blowing the emissary's head away. Fragments of skull and tissue seared into the lily ponds. The army officer appeared in the archway as the corpse sprang back from the impact with the white gravel.

'Dispose of him,' ordered Sheng. 'He heard too much, learned too much . . . presumed too much.'

'Certainly, Minister.'

'And reach the man in Macao. I have instructions for him and they are to be implemented immediately, while the fires in Kowloon still light up the sky. I want him here.'

As the officer approached the dead courier, Sheng suddenly rose from the chair, and walked slowly to the edge of the nearest pond, his face illuminated by the lights beneath the water. He spoke once again, his voice flat but filled with purpose.

'Soon all of Hong Kong and the territories,' he said, staring at a lily pad. 'Soon thereafter, all of China.'

'You lead, Minister,' said the officer, watching Sheng, his eyes glowing with devotion. 'We follow. The march you promised has begun. We return to our Mother and the land will be ours again.'

'Yes, it will,' agreed Sheng Chou Yang. 'We cannot be denied. *I* cannot be denied.'

20

By noon of that paralysing day when Kai-tak was merely an airport and not an assassination field, Ambassador Havilland had described to a stunned Catherine Staples the broad outlines of the Sheng conspiracy with its roots in the Kuomintang. Objective: a consortium of taipans with a central leader, whose son Sheng was, taking over Hong Kong, and turning the colony into the conspirators' own financial empire. Inevitable result: the conspiracy would fail, and the raging giant that was the People's Republic would strike out, marching into Hong Kong, destroying the Accords and throwing the Far East into chaos. In utter disbelief Catherine had demanded substantiation, and by 2:15 had twice read the State Department's lengthy and top secret dossier on Sheng Chou Yang, but she continued to strenuously object, as the accuracy of authorship could not be verified. At 3:30 she had been taken to the radio room and by satellite-scrambler transmission was presented with an array of 'facts' by a man named Reilly of the National Security Council in Washington.

'You're only a voice, Mr Reilly,' Staples had said. 'How do I know you're not down at the bottom of the Peak in the Wanchai?'

There was at that moment a pronounced click on the line and a voice Catherine and the world knew very well was speaking to her. 'This is the President of the United States, Mrs Staples. If you doubt that, I suggest you call your consulate. Ask them to reach the White House by diplomatic phone and request a confirmation of our transmission. I'll hang on. You'll receive it. At the moment I have nothing better to do – *nothing* more vital.'

Shaking her head and briefly closing her eyes, Catherine had answered quietly, 'I believe you, Mr President.'

'Forget about me, believe what you've heard. It's the truth.'

'It's just so unbelievable – *inconceivable.*'

'I'm no expert, Mrs Staples, and I never claimed to be, but then neither was the Trojan Horse very believable. Now, that may be legend and Menelaus' wife may have been a figment of a campfire storyteller's imagination, but the concept is valid – it's become a symbol of an enemy destroying his adversary from within.'

'Menelaus . . . ?'

'Don't believe the media, I've read a book or two. But do believe our people, Mrs Staples. We need you. I'll call your Prime Minister if it will help, but, in all honesty, I'd rather not. He might feel it necessary to confer with others.'

'No, Mr President. Containment *is* everything. I'm beginning to understand Ambassador Havilland.'

'You're one up on me. I don't always understand him.'

'Perhaps it's better that way, sir.'

At 3:58 there was an emergency call – highest priority – to the sterile house in Victoria Peak, but it was not for either the Ambassador or Undersecretary of State McAllister. It was for Major Lin Wenzu, and when it came, a frightening vigil began that lasted four hours. The scant information was so electrifying that all concentration was rivetted on the crisis, and Catherine Staples telephoned her consulate telling the High Commissioner that she was not well and would not attend the strategy conference with the Americans that afternoon. Her presence in the sterile house was welcome. Ambassador Havilland wanted the foreign service officer to see and understand for herself how close the Far East was to upheaval. How an inevitable error on either Sheng's or his assassin's part could bring about an explosion so drastic that troops from the People's Republic could move into Hong Kong within hours, bringing not only the colony's world trade to a halt, but with it widespread human suffering – savage rioting everywhere, death squads from the left and the right exploiting resentments going back forty years, racial and provincial factions pitted against one another and the military. Blood would flow in the streets and the harbour, and as nations everywhere had to be affected, global war was a very real possibility. He said these things to her as Lin worked furiously on the telephone, giving commands, coordinating his people with the colony's police and the airport's security.

It all had started with the major from MI6 cupping the phone and speaking in a quiet voice in that Victorian room in Victoria Peak: 'Kai-tak tonight. The Sino-British delegations. Assassination. The target is the Crown governor. They believe it's Jason Bourne.'

'I can't *understand* it!' protested McAllister, leaping from the couch. 'It's premature. Sheng isn't ready! We'd have gotten an inkling of it if he was – an official statement from his ministry alluding to a proposed commission of some sort. It's *wrong!*'

'Miscalculation?' asked the ambassador coldly.

'Possibly. Or something else. A strategy we haven't considered.'

'Go to work, Major,' said Havilland.

After issuing his last orders, Lin received a final order himself from Havilland before heading for the airport. 'Stay out of sight, Major,' said the ambassador. 'I mean that.'

'Impossible,' replied Lin. 'With respect, sir, I must be with my men *on* the scene. These are experienced eyes.'

'With equal respect,' continued Havilland. 'I must make it a condition of your getting through the outside gate.'

'*Why*, Mr Ambassador?'

'With your perspicacity, I'm surprised you ask.'

'I have to! I don't understand.'

'Then perhaps it's my fault, Major. I thought I'd made it clear why we went to such extremes to bring *our* Jason Bourne over here. Accept the fact that he's extraordinary, his record proves it. He has his ears not only to the ground, but they're also locked into the four winds. We must presume, if the medical prognosis is accurate and portions of his memory continue to come back to him, that he has contacts all over this part of the world in nooks and crannies we know nothing about. Suppose – just suppose, Major – that one of those contacts informs him that an emergency alert has been sent out for Kai-tak Airport tonight, that a large security force has been gathered to protect the Crown governor. What do you think he'd do?'

'Be there,' answered Lin Wenzu softly, reluctantly. 'Somewhere.'

'And suppose again that *our* Bourne saw *you*? Forgive me, but you are not easily overlooked. The discipline of his logical mind – logic, discipline, and imagination were always his means of survival – would force him to find out precisely who you are. Need I say more?'

'I don't think so,' said the major.

'The connection is made,' said Havilland, overriding Lin's words. 'There is no taipan with a murdered young wife in Macao. Instead there is a highly regarded field officer of British Intelligence posing as a fictitious taipan, having fed him yet another lie, echoing a previous lie. He will know that once again he has been manipulated by government forces, manipulated in the most brutal fashion possible – the abduction of his wife. The mind, Major, is a delicate instrument, his more delicate than most. There's only so much stress it can take. I don't even want to think about what he might do – what *we* might be forced to do.'

'It was always the weakest aspect of the scenario, and yet it was the core,' said Lin.

'"An ingenious device,"' interrupted McAllister, obviously quoting. '"Few acts of vengeance are as readily understood as an eye for an eye." Your words, Lin.'

'If so, you should *not* have chosen me to play your taipan!' insisted the major. 'There's a crisis here in Hong Kong and you've crippled me!'

'It's the same crisis facing all of us,' said Havilland gently. 'Only this time we have a warning. Also, who else could we have chosen? What other Chinese but the proven chief of Special Branch would have been cleared by London for what you were initially told, to say nothing of what you know now? Set up your command post inside the airport's tower. The glass is dark.'

In silence the huge major turned angrily and left the room. 'Is it wise to let him go?' asked McAllister as he, the ambassador and Catherine Staples watched Lin leave.

'Certainly,' answered the diplomat of covert operations.

'I spent several weeks here with MI-Six,' continued the undersecretary rapidly. 'He's been known to disobey in the past.'

'Only when the orders were given by posturing British officers with less experience than himself. He was never reprimanded; he was right. Just as he knows I'm right.'

'How can you be sure?'

'Why do you think he said we've crippled him? He doesn't like it, but he accepts it.' Havilland walked behind the desk and turned to Catherine. 'Please sit down, Mrs Staples. And, Edward, I should like to ask a favour of you, and it has nothing to do with confidentiality. You know as much as I do and you're probably more current, and I'll no doubt call for you if I need information. However, I'd like to talk with Mrs Staples alone.'

'By all means,' said the undersecretary, gathering up papers on the desk as Catherine sat down in a chair facing the diplomat. 'I've a great deal of thinking to do. If this Kai-tak thing isn't a hoax – if it's a direct order from Sheng – then he's conceived of a strategy we really *haven't* considered, and that's dangerous. From every avenue, every direction I've explored, he has to offer up his clearinghouse, his damned economic commission, under *stable* conditions, not *unstable.* He could blow everything apart – but he's not stupid, he's brilliant. What's he *doing?*'

'Consider, if you will,' broke in the ambassador, frowning as he sat down, 'the reverse of our approach, Edward. Instead of implanting his financial clearing-house of assorted taipans during a period of stability, he does so in *instability* – but with sympathy – the point being to restore order quickly. No raging giant but rather a protective father, caring for his emotionally disturbed offspring, wanting to calm it down.'

'To what advantage?'

'It takes place rapidly, that's all. Who would so closely examine a group of respected financiers from the colony put in place during a crisis? After all, they *represent* stability. It's something to think about.'

McAllister held the papers in his hands and looked at Havilland. 'It's too much of a gamble for him,' he said. 'Sheng risks losing control of the expansionists in the Central Committee, the old military revolutionaries who are looking for any excuse to move into the colony. A crisis based on violence would play right into their hands. That's the scenario we gave Webb, and it's a realistic one.'

'Unless Sheng's own position is now strong enough to suppress them. As you said yourself, Sheng Chou Yang has made China a great deal of money, and if there ever was a basically capitalistic people, it's the Chinese. They have more than a healthy respect for money, it's an obsession.'

'They also have respect for the old men of the Long March, and it, too, is obsessive. Without those early Maoists most of China's younger leadership would be illiterate peasants breaking their backs in the field. They revere those old soldiers. Sheng wouldn't risk a confrontation.'

'Then there's an alternative theory that could be a combination of what we're both saying. We did *not* tell Webb that a number of the more vocal leaders of Peking's old guard haven't been heard from in months. And in several instances, when the word was officially released, this one or that one had died of natural causes, or a tragic accident, and in one case was removed in disgrace. Now, if our assumption is right, that at least some of these silenced men are victims of Sheng's hired gun—'

'Then he's solidified his position by elimination,' broke in McAllister. 'Westerners are all over Peking; the hotels are filled to capacity. What's one more – especially an assassin who could be anyone – an attaché, a business executive . . . a chameleon.'

'And who better than the manipulative Sheng to set up secret meetings between *his* Jason Bourne and selected victims? Any number of pretexts would do, but primarily military high-tech espionage. The targets would leap at it.'

'If any of this is near the truth, Sheng's much further along than we thought.'

'Take your papers. Request anything you need from our Intelligence people and MI-Six. Study everything, but find us a pattern, Edward. If we lose a Crown governor tonight, we may be on our way to losing Hong Kong in a matter of days. For all the wrong reasons.'

'He'll be protected,' muttered McAllister, heading for the door, his face troubled.

'I'm counting on it,' said the ambassador, as the undersecretary left the room. Havilland turned to Catherine Staples. 'Are you *really* begining to understand me?' he asked.

'The words and their implications, yes, but not certain specifics,' replied Catherine, looking oddly at the door the undersecretary of State had just closed. 'He's a strange man, isn't he?'

'McAllister?'

'Yes.'

'Does he bother you?'

'On the contrary. He lends a certain credibility to everything that's been said to me. By you, by that man Reilly – even by your President, I'm afraid.' Staples turned back to the ambassador. 'I'm being honest.'

'I want you to be. And I understand the wavelength you're on. McAllister's one of the best analytical minds in the State Department, a brilliant bureaucrat who will never rise to the level of his own worth.'

'Why not?'

'I think you know, but if you don't, you sense it. He's a thoroughly moral man and that morality has stood in the way of his advancement. Had I been cursed with his sense of moral outrage, I never would have become the man I am – and in my defence, I never would have accomplished what I have. But I think you know that too. You said as much when you came in here.'

'Now you're the one being honest. I appreciate it.'

'I'm glad. I want the air cleared between us because I want your help.'

'Marie?'

'And beyond,' said Havilland. 'What specifics disturb you? What can I clarify?'

'This clearinghouse, this commission of bankers and taipans Sheng will propose to oversee the colony's financial policies—'

'Let me anticipate,' interrupted the diplomat. 'On the surface they will be disparate in character and position and eminently acceptable. As I said to McAllister when we first met, if we thought the whole insane scheme had a prayer, we'd look the other way and wish them great success, but it doesn't have a chance. All powerful men have enemies; there'll be sceptics here in Hong Kong and in Peking – jealous factions who've been excluded – and they'll dig deeper than Sheng expects. I think you know what they'll find.'

'That all roads, above and below ground, lead to Rome. Rome here being this taipan, Sheng's father, whose name your highly selective documents never mention. He's the spider whose webs reach out to every member of that clearinghouse. He controls them. For God's sake, who the hell *is* he?'

'I wish we knew,' said Havilland, his voice flat.

'You really *don't?*' asked Catherine Staples, astonished.

'If we did, life would be far simpler, and I would have told you. I'm not playing games with you, we've never learned who he is. How many taipans are there in Hong Kong? How many zealots wanting to strike back at Peking in any way they can in the cause of the Kuomintang? By their lights China was stolen from them. Their motherland, the graves of their ancestors, their possessions – everything. Many were decent people, Mrs Staples, but many others were not. The political leaders, the warlords, the landlords, the immensely rich – they were a privileged society that gorged themselves on the sweat and suppression of millions. And if that sounds like a crock of today's Communist propaganda, it was a classic case of yesterday's provocation that gave rise to such bilge. We're dealing with a handful of obsessed expatriates who want their own back. They forget the corruption that led to their own collapse.'

'Have you thought of confronting Sheng himself? Privately?'

'Of course, and his reaction is all too predictable. He would feign outrage and tell us bluntly that if we pursue such despicable fantasies in an attempt to discredit him, he'll void the China Accords, claiming duplicity, and move Hong Kong into Peking's economic orbit immediately. He'd claim that many of the old-line Marxists on the Central Committee would applaud such a move, and he'd be right. Then he would look at us and probably say, "Gentlemen, you have your choice. Good day." '

'And if you made Sheng's conspiracy public the same thing would happen, and he knows *you know* it,' said Staples, frowning. 'Peking *would* pull out of the Accords blaming Taiwan and the West for messing around. Their face is beet-red with internal capitalistic corruption, so the territory marches to a Marxist drum – actually they wouldn't have a choice. And what follows is economic collapse.'

'That's the way we read it,' agreed Havilland.

'The solution?'

'There's only one. Sheng.'

Staples nodded her head. 'Hardball,' she said.

'The most extreme act, if that's what you mean.'

'That's obviously what I mean,' said Catherine. 'And Marie's husband, this Webb, is intrinsic to the solution?'

'Jason Bourne is intrinsic to it, yes.'

'Because this impostor, this assassin who calls himself Bourne, can be trapped by the extraordinary man he emulates – as McAllister put it, but not in that context. He takes his place and pulls out Sheng where he can implement the solution, the extreme solution . . . Hell, he kills him.'

'Yes. Somewhere in China, of course.'

'In China . . . "of course"?'

'Yes, making it appear as internal fratricide with no external connections.

Peking can't blame anyone but unknown enemies of Sheng within its own hierarchy. Regardless, at that juncture, if it happens, it's probably going to be irrelevant. The world won't officially hear of Sheng's death for weeks, and when the announcement *is* made, his "sudden demise" will undoubtedly be attributed to a massive coronary or a cerebral haemorrhage, certainly not to murder. The giant does not parade its aberrations, it conceals them.'

'Which is precisely what you want.'

'Naturally. The world goes on, the taipans are cut off from their source, Sheng's clearinghouse collapses like a house of cards, and reasonable men go forward honouring the Accords for everyone's benefit . . . But we're a long way from there, Mrs Staples. To begin with, there's today, tonight. Kai-tak. It could be the beginning of the end, for we have no immediate countermeasures to put in place. If I appear calm, it's an illusion born of years of concealing tension. My two consolations at this moment are that the colony's security forces are among the best on earth, and second – the tragedy of death notwithstanding – is that Peking has been alerted to the situation. Hong Kong's concealing nothing, nor does it care to. So, in a sense, it becomes both a joint risk and a joint venture to protect the Crown governor.'

'How does that help if the worst happens?'

'For what it's worth, psychologically. It may avert the appearance if not the fact of instability, for the emergency has been labelled beforehand as an isolated act of premeditated violence, not symptomatic of the colony's unrest. Above all, it's been shared. Both delegations have their own military escorts; they'll be put to use.'

'So on such subtle points of protocol a crisis can be contained?'

'From what I've been told, you don't need any lessons in containing crises, or precipitating them, either. Besides, everything can go off the wire with one development that throws subtleties into the garbage heap. Despite everything I've said, I'm frightened to death. There's so much room for error and miscalculation – they're our enemies, Mrs Staples. All we can do is wait, and waiting is the hardest part, the most draining.'

'I have other questions,' said Catherine.

'By all means, ask as many as you like. Make me think, make me sweat, if you can. It may help us both take our minds off the waiting.'

'You just referred to my questionable abilities in the area of containing crises. But you added – I think more confidently – that I could also precipitate them.'

'I'm sorry, I couldn't resist. It's a bad habit.'

'I assume you meant the attaché, John Nelson.'

'Who? . . . Oh, yes, the young man from the consulate. What he lacks in judgement he makes up in courage.'

'You're wrong.'

'About the judgement?' asked Havilland, his thick eyebrows arched in mild astonishment. 'Really?'

'I'm not excusing his weaknesses, but he's one of the finest people you've got. His professional judgement is superior to that of most of your more experienced personnel. Ask anyone in the consulates who's been in conferences with him. He's also one of the few who speak a damn good Cantonese.'

'He also compromised what he knew was a highly classified operation,' said the diplomat curtly.

'If he hadn't, you wouldn't have found me. You wouldn't have come within arm's reach of Marie St Jacques, which is where you are now. An arm's reach.'

'An "arm's *reach*" . . . ?' Havilland leaned forward, his eyes angry, questioning. 'Surely, you won't continue to *hide* her.'

'Probably not. I haven't decided.'

'My *God*, woman, after everything you've been *told!* She's got to *be* here! Without her we've lost, we've *all* lost! If Webb found out she wasn't with us, that she'd disappeared, he'd go mad! You've *got* to deliver her!'

'That's the point. I can deliver her anytime. It doesn't have to be when you say.'

'*No!*' thundered the ambassador. 'When and *if* our Jason Bourne completes his assignment, a series of telephone calls will be placed putting him in direct contact with his wife!'

'I won't give you a telephone number,' said Staples matter-of-factly. 'I might as well give you an address.'

'You don't know what you're doing! What do I have to say to *convince* you?'

'Simple. Reprimand John Nelson verbally. Suggest counselling, if you wish, but keep everything off the record and keep him here in Hong Kong, where his chances for recognition are the best.'

'Jesus *Christ!*' exploded Havilland. 'He's a drug addict!'

'That's ludicrous but typical of the primitive reaction of an American "moralist" given a few key words.'

'*Please*, Mrs Staples—'

'He was drugged; he doesn't *take* drugs. His limit is three vodka martinis, and he likes girls. Of course, a few of your male attachés prefer boys, and their limit is nearer six martinis, but who's counting? Frankly, I personally don't give a damn what adults do within the four walls of a bedroom – I don't really believe that whatever it is affects what they do *outside* the bedroom – but Washington has this peculiar preoccupation with—'

'All *right*, Mrs Staples! Nelson is reprimanded – by me – and the consul general will not be informed and nothing goes into his record. Are you *satisfied*?'

'We're getting there. Call him this afternoon and tell him that. Also tell him to get his extracurricular act together for his own benefit.'

'That will be a pleasure. Is there anything *else*?'

'Yes, and I'm afraid I don't know how to put it without insulting you.'

'That hasn't fazed you.'

'It fazes me now because I know far more than I did three hours ago.'

'Then insult me, dear lady.'

Catherine paused, and when she spoke her voice was a cry for understanding. It was hollow yet vibrant and filled the room. '*Why*? Why did you *do* it? Wasn't there *another* way?'

'I presume you mean Mrs Webb.'

'Of course I mean Mrs Webb, and no less her husband! I asked you before, have you any idea what you've *done* to them? It's *barbaric* and I mean that in the full ugliness of the word. You've put both of them on some kind of medieval rack, literally pulling their minds and their bodies apart, making them live with the knowledge that they may never see each other again, each believing that with a wrong decision one can cause the other's death. An American lawyer once asked a question in a Senate hearing, and I'm afraid I must ask it of you . . . Have you no sense of decency, Mr Ambassador?'

Havilland looked wearily at Staples. 'I have a sense of duty,' he said, his voice tired, his face drawn. 'I had to develop a situation rapidly that would provoke an immediate response, a total commitment to act instantly. It was based on an incident in Webb's past, a terrible thing that turned a civilized young scholar into – the phrase used to describe him was the "supreme guerrilla." I needed that man, that hunter, for all the reasons you've heard. He's here, he's hunting, and I assume his wife is unharmed and we obviously never intended anything else for her.'

'The incident in Webb's past. That was his first wife? In Cambodia?'

'You know, then?'

'Marie told me. His wife and two children were killed by a lone jet fighter sweeping down along a river, strafing the water where they were playing.'

'He became another man,' said Havilland, nodding. 'His mind snapped, and it became *his* war despite the fact that he had little or no regard for Saigon. He was venting his outrage in the only way he knew how, fighting an enemy who had stolen his life from him. He would usually take on only the most complex and dangerous assignments where the objectives were major, the targets within the framework of command personnel. One doctor said that in his mental warp Webb was killing the killers who sent out other mindless killers. I suppose it makes sense.'

'And by taking his second wife in Maine you raised the spectre of his first loss. The incident that turned him into this "supreme guerrilla," then later as Jason Bourne, hunter of Carlos the Jackal.'

'Yes, Mrs Staples, *hunter*,' interjected the diplomat quietly. 'I wanted that hunter on the scene immediately. I couldn't waste any time – not a minute – and I didn't know any other way to get immediate results.'

'He's an Oriental *scholar!*' cried Catherine. 'He understands the dynamics of the Orient a hell of a lot better than any of us, the so-called experts. Couldn't you have *appealed* to him, appealed to his sense of history, pointing out the consequences of what could *happen?*'

'He may be a scholar, but he's first a man who believes – with certain justification – that he was betrayed by his government. He asked for help and a trap was set to kill him. No appeals of mine would have broken through that barrier.'

'You could have *tried!*'

'And risk delay when every hour counted? In a way, I'm sorry you've never been put in my position. Then, perhaps, you might really understand me.'

'Question,' said Catherine, holding up her hand defiantly. 'What makes you think that David Webb will go into China after Sheng if he *does* find and take the impostor? As I understand it, the agreement is for him to deliver the man who calls himself Jason Bourne and Marie is returned to him.'

'At that point, if it occurs, it doesn't really matter. *That's* when we'll tell him why we did what we did. That's when we'll appeal to his Far East expertise and the global consequences of Sheng's and the taipans' machinations. If he walks away, we have several experienced field agents who can take his place. They're not men you'd care to bring home to meet your mother, but they're available and they can do it.'

'*How?*'

'Codes, Mrs Staples. The original Jason Bourne's methods always included codes between himself and his clients. That was the structured myth, and the impostor has studied every aspect of the original. Once this new Bourne is in our hands we'll get the information we need one way or another – confirmed by chemicals, of course. We'll know how to reach Sheng, and that's all we have to know. One meeting in the countryside outside Jade Tower Mountain. One kill and the world goes on. I'm not capable of coming up with any other solution. Are you?'

'No,' said Catherine softly, slowly shaking her head. 'It's hardball.'

'Give us Mrs Webb.'

'Yes, of course, but not tonight. She can't go anywhere, and you've got enough to worry about with Kaitak. I took her to a flat in Tuen Mun in the New Territories. It belongs to a friend of mine. I also brought her to a doctor who bandaged her feet – she bruised them badly running from your Lin Wenzu – and he gave her a sedative. My God, she's a wreck; she hasn't slept in days, and the pills didn't do much for her last night; she was too tense, still too frightened. I stayed with her and she talked until dawn. Let her rest. I'll pick her up in the morning.'

'How will you manage it? What will you say?'

'I'm not sure. I'll call her later and try to keep her calm. I'll tell her I'm making progress – more, perhaps, than I thought I would. I just want to give her hope, to ease the tension. I'll tell her to stay near the phone, get as much rest as she can, and I'll drive up in the morning, I think with good news.'

'I'd like to send a backup with you,' said Havilland. 'Including McAllister. He knows her, and I honestly believe his moral suasion will be communicated. It will bolster your case.'

'It might,' agreed Catherine, nodding. 'As you said, I sensed it. All right, but they're to stay away until I've talked to her, and that could take a couple of hours. She has a finely honed distrust of Washington, and I've got a lot of convincing to do. That's her husband out there and she loves him very much. I can't and I won't tell her that I approve of what you did, but I can say that in light of the extraordinary circumstances – not excluding the conceivable economic collapse of Hong Kong – I understand why you did it. What *she* has to understand – if nothing else – is that she's closer to her husband being *with* you than being away from you. Of course, she may try to kill you, but that's your problem. She's a very feminine, good-looking woman, more than attractive, quite striking actually, but remember she's a ranch girl from Calgary. I wouldn't advise being alone with her in a room. I'm sure she's wrestled calves to the ground far stronger than you.'

'I'll bring in a squad of marines.'

'Don't. She'd turn them against you. She's one of the most persuasive people I've ever met.'

'She has to be,' replied the ambassador, leaning back in his chair. 'She forced a man with no identity, with overwhelming feelings of guilt, to look into himself and walk out of the tunnels of his own confusion. No easy task . . . Tell me about her – not the dry facts of a dossier, but the *person*.'

Catherine did, telling what she knew from observation and instinct. Time passed; the minutes and the half hours punctuated with repeated phone calls apprising Havilland of the conditions at Kai-tak Airport. The sun descended beyond the walls of the garden outside. A light supper was provided by the staff.

'Would you ask Mr McAllister to join us?' said Havilland to a steward.

'I asked Mr McAllister if I could bring him something, sir, and he was pretty firm about it. He told me to get out and leave him alone.'

'Then never mind, thank you.'

The phone calls kept coming; the subject of Marie St Jacques was exhausted, and the conversation now turned exclusively on the developments at Kai-tak. Staples watched the diplomat in amazement, for the more intense the crisis became, the slower and more controlled was his speech.

'Tell me about yourself, Mrs Staples. Only what you care to professionally, of course.'

Catherine studied Raymond Havilland and began quietly. 'I sprang from an ear of Ontario corn . . .'

'Yes, of course,' said the ambassador with utter sincerity, glancing at the phone.

Staples now understood. This celebrated statesman was carrying on an innocuous conversation while his mind was riveted on an entirely different subject. Kai-tak. His eyes kept straying to the telephone; his wrist turned constantly so that he could look at his watch, and yet he never missed the breaks in their dialogue where he was expected to voice a response.

'My former husband sells shoes—'

Havilland's head snapped up from looking at his watch. He would not have been thought capable of an embarrassed smile, but he showed one at that moment. 'You've caught me,' he said.

'A long time ago,' said Catherine.

'There's a reason. I know Owen Staples quite well.'

'It figures. I imagine you move in the same circles.'

'I saw him last year at the Queens Plate race in Toronto. I think one of his horses ran respectably well. He looked quite grand in his cutaway, but then he was one of the Queen Mother's escorts.'

'When we were married, he couldn't afford a suit off the rack.'

'You know,' said Havilland, 'when I read up on you and learned about Owen, I had a fleeting temptation to call him. Not to *say* anything, obviously, but to ask him about you. Then I thought, My God, in this age of post-marital civility, suppose they still talk with each other. I'd be tipping my hand.'

'We're still talking, and you tipped your hand when you flew into Hong Kong.'

'For you, perhaps. But only after Webb's wife reached you. Tell me, what did you think when you first heard I was here?'

'That the UK had called you in for consultation on the Accords.'

'You flatter me—'

The telephone rang, and Havilland's hand flew out for it. The caller was Lin Wenzu, reporting the progress being made at Kai-tak, or more substantively, as was apparent, the lack of progress.

'Why don't they simply call the whole damn thing off?' asked the ambassador angrily. 'Pile them into their cars and get the hell out of there!' Whatever reply the major offered only served to further exasperate Havilland. 'That's ridiculous! This isn't a show of gamesmanship, it's a potential assassination! No one's image or honour is involved under the circumstances, and believe me, the world isn't hanging by its collective teeth waiting for that damned press conference. Most of it's asleep, for God's sake!' Again the diplomat listened. Lin's remarks not only astonished him, they infuriated him. 'The *Chinese* said that? It's *preposterous!* Peking has no right to make such a demand! It's—' Havilland glanced at Staples. 'It's *barbaric!* Someone should tell them it's not their Asian faces that are being saved; it's the Anglo Crown governor's, and *his* face is attached to his head, which could be blown *off!*' Silence; the ambassador's eyes blinked in angry resignation. 'I know, I know. The heavenly red star must continue to shine in a heavenly blackout. There's nothing you can do, so do your best, Major. Keep calling. As one of my grandchildren puts it, I'm "eating bananas," whatever the hell that means.' Havilland hung up and looked over at Catherine. 'Orders from Peking. The delegations are not to run in the *face* of Western terrorism. Protect all concerned, but carry on.'

'London would probably approve. The "Carry on" has a familiar ring.'

'Orders from Peking . . .' said the diplomat softly, not hearing Staples. 'Orders from *Sheng*!'

'Are you quite sure of that?'

'It's *his* ballgame! He calls the shots. My God, he *is* ready!'

The tension grew geometrically with each quarter hour, until the air was filled with electricity. The rains came, pounding the bay window with a relentless tattoo. A television set was rolled in and turned on, the American ambassador-at-large and the Canadian foreign service officer watching in fear and in silence. The huge jet taxied in the downpour to its appointed rendezvous with the crowds of reporters and camera crews. The English and the Chinese honour guards emerged first, simultaneously from both sides of the open door. Their appearance was startling, for instead of a stately processional expected of such military escorts, these squads moved rapidly into flanking positions down the metal steps, elbows bent skyward, sidearms gripped, guns at the ready. The leaders then filed out waving to the onlookers; they started down the staircase followed by two lines of awkwardly grinning subordinates.

The strange 'press conference' began, and Undersecretary of State Edward McAllister burst into the room, the heavy door crashing into the wall as he flung it open.

'I *have* it!' he cried, a page of paper in his hand. 'I'm *sure* I have it!'

'Calm *down*, Edward! Speak sensibly.'

'The Chinese delegation!' shouted McAllister out of breath, racing to the diplomat and thrusting the paper at him. 'It's headed by a man named Lao Sing! The second in command is a general named Yunshen! They're powerful, and they've opposed Sheng Chou Yang for years, objecting to his policies openly on the Central Committee! Their inclusion in the negotiating teams was Sheng's apparent willingness to have a balance – which made him look fair in the eyes of the old guard.'

'For God's sake, what are you trying to *say?*'

'It's *not* the Crown governor! Not *just* him! It's *all* of them! With one action he removes his two strongest opponents in Peking and clears the path for himself. Then, as you put it, he implants his clearinghouse – his taipans – during a period of *instability*, now shared by *both* governments!'

Havilland yanked the telephone out of its cradle. 'Get me Lin at Kai-tak,' he ordered the switchboard. '*Quickly!* . . . Major Lin, please. At *once!* . . . What do you mean, he's not there? Where *is* he? . . . Who's this? . . . Yes, I know who you are. Listen to me and listen carefully! The target is *not* the Crown governor alone, it's worse. It includes two members of the Chinese delegation. Separate all parties – You *know that?* . . . A man from the *Mossad?* What the hell . . . ? There's no such arrangement, there *couldn't* be! . . . Yes, of course, I'll get off the line.' Breathing rapidly, his lined face pale, the diplomat looked at the wall and spoke in a barely audible voice. 'They found out, from God knows where, and are talking immediate countermeasures . . . *Who?* For Christ's sake, who *was* it?'

'*Our* Jason Bourne,' said McAllister quietly. 'He's there.'

On the television screen a distant limousine jolted to a stop while others peeled away into the darkness. Figures fled from the stationary car in panic, and seconds later the screen was filled with a blinding explosion.

'He's there,' repeated McAllister, whispering. 'He's *there!*'

21

The motor launch pitched violently in the darkness and the torrential rains. The crew of two bailed out the water that continuously swept back over the gunwales as the grizzled Chinese-Portuguese captain, squinting through the cabin's large windows, inched his way forward toward the black outlines of the island. Bourne and d'Anjou flanked the boat's owner; the Frenchman spoke, raising his voice over the downpour. 'How far do you judge it to the beach?'

'Two hundred metres, plus or minus ten or twenty,' said the captain.'

'It's time for the light. Where is it?'

'In the locker beneath you. On the right. Another seventy-five metres and I hold. Any farther, the rocks can be dangerous in this weather.'

'We have to get into the beach!' cried the Frenchman. 'It's imperative, I *told* you that!'

'Yes, but you forgot to tell me there would be this rain, these swells. Ninety metres, and you can use the little boat. The engine is strong, you'll get there.'

'*Merde!*' spat out d'Anjou, opening the locker and pulling out a casement light. 'That could leave a hundred-plus metres!'

'In any event it would not be less than fifty, I told *you* that.'

'And between the two is deep water!'

'Shall I turn around and head for Macao?'

'And get us blown up by the patrols? You make payment when it is due or you do not make your destination! You *know* that!'

'One hundred metres, no more.'

D'Anjou nodded testily while holding the casement light up to his chest. He pressed a button, immediately releasing it, and for a brief moment an eerie, dark blue flash illuminated the pilot's window. Seconds later a corresponding blue signal was seen through the mottled glass from the island's shoreline. 'You see, *mon capitaine*, had we not come in for the rendezvous this miserable scow would have been blown out of the water.'

'You were fond enough of her this afternoon!' said the helmsman, working furiously at the wheel.

'That was *yesterday* afternoon. It is now one-thirty the next morning and I have come to know your thieving ways.' D'Anjou replaced the light in the locker and glanced at Bourne, who was looking at him. Each was doing what he had done many times in the days of Medusa – checking out a partner's apparel and equipment. Both men had rolled their clothing in canvas bags –

trousers, sweaters and thin rubber skullcaps, all black. The only equipment other than Jason's automatic and the Frenchman's small .22 calibre pistol were scabbarded knives – all unseen. 'Get in as close as you can,' said d'Anjou to the captain. 'And remember, you won't receive the final payment if you're not here when we return.'

'Suppose they take your money and *kill* you?' cried the pilot, spinning the wheel. 'Then I'm *out!*'

'I'm touched,' said Bourne.

'Have no fear of that,' answered the Frenchman, glaring at the Chinese-Portuguese. 'I've dealt with this man many times over many months. Like you, he is the pilot of a fast boat and every bit the thief you are. I line his Marxist pockets so that his mistresses live like concubines of the Central Committee. Also, he suspects I keep records. We are in God's hands, perhaps better.'

'Then take the light,' muttered the captain grudgingly. 'You may need it, and you're no good to me stranded or ripped up on the rocks.'

'Your concern overwhelms me,' said d'Anjou, retrieving the light and nodding at Jason. 'We'll familiarize ourselves with the skiff and its motor.'

'The motor's under thick canvas. Don't start it until you're in the water!'

'How do we know it *will* start?' asked Bourne.

'Because I want my money, Silent One.'

The ride into the beach drenched them both, both bracing themselves against the panels of the small boat, Jason gripping the sides and d'Anjou the rudder and the stern so as to keep from pitching overboard. They grazed a shoal. Metal ground against the rocks as the Frenchman swerved the rudder to starboard, pushing the throttle to maximum.

The strange, dark blue flash came once again from the beach. They had strayed in the wet darkness; d'Anjou angled the boat toward the signal and within minutes the bow struck sand. The Frenchman swung the stick down, elevating the motor, as Bourne leaped overboard, grabbing the rope and pulling the small craft up on the beach.

He gasped, startled by the figure of a man suddenly next to him, gripping the line in front of him. 'Four hands are better than two,' shouted the stranger, an Oriental, in perfectly fluent English – English with an American accent.

'You're the *contact?*' yelled Jason, bewildered, wondering if the rain and the waves had distorted his hearing.

'That's such a foolish term!' replied the man, shouting back. 'I'm simply a friend!'

Five minutes later, having beached the small boat, the three men walked through the thick, shorefront foliage, which was suddenly replaced by scrubby trees. The 'friend' had constructed a primitive lean-to out of a ship's tarpaulin; a small fire faced the dense woods in front, unseen from the sides and the rear, concealed by the tarp. The warmth was welcome; the winds and the drenching rain had chilled Bourne and d'Anjou. They sat cross-legged around the fire and the Frenchman spoke to the uniformed Chinese.

'This was hardly necessary, Gamma—'

'*Gamma?*' erupted Jason.

'I've implemented certain traditions of our past, Delta. Actually, I could have used *Tango* or *Fox Trot* – it wasn't *all* Greek, you know. The Greek was reserved for the leaders.'

'This is a bullshit conversation. I want to know why we're here. Why you haven't paid him and we get the hell out?'

'*Man . . . !*' said the Chinese, drawing out the word, purposely emphasizing the American idiom. 'This cat's uptight! What's his beef?'

'My beef, *man*, is that I want to get back to that boat. I really don't have time for tea!'

'How about Scotch?' said the officer of the People's Republic, reaching behind him, pulling his arm forward, and displaying a bottle of perfectly acceptable whisky. 'We'll have to share the cork, as it were, but I don't think we're infectious people. We bathe, we brush our teeth, we sleep with clean whores – at least *my* heavenly government makes sure they're clean.'

'Who the hell *are* you?' asked Jason Bourne.

'"Gamma" will do, Echo's convinced me of that. As to *what* I am, I leave that to your imagination. You might try USC – that's the University of Southern California – with graduate studies in Berkeley – all those protests in the sixties, surely you remember them.'

'You were a part of that crowd?'

'Certainly not! I was a staunch conservative, a member of the John Birch Society who wanted them all *shot!* Screeching freaks with no regard for their nation's moral commitments.'

'This *is* a bullshit conversation.'

'My friend Gamma,' interrupted d'Anjou, 'is the perfect intermediary. He is an educated double or triple or conceivably a quadruple agent working all sides for the benefit of his own interests. He is the totally amoral man, and I respect him for that.'

'You came back to China? To the People's Republic?'

'It's where the money was,' admitted the officer. 'Any repressive society offers vast opportunities for those willing to take minor risks on behalf of the repressed. Ask the commissars in Moscow and the Eastern bloc. Of course, one must have contacts in the West and possess certain talents that can also serve the regimental leaders. Fortunately, I'm an exceptional sailor, courtesy of friends in the Bay Area who owned yachts and small motor craft. I'll return one day. I really do like San Francisco.'

'Don't try to fathom his Swiss accounts,' said d'Anjou. 'Instead, let's concentrate on why Gamma has made us such a pleasant retreat in the rainstorm.' The Frenchman took the bottle and drank.

'It will cost you, Echo,' said the Chinese.

'With you, what doesn't? What is it?' D'Anjou passed the bottle to Jason.

'I may speak in front of your companion?'

'Anything.'

'You'll want the information. I guarantee it. The price is one thousand American.'

'That's it?'

'It should be enough,' said the Chinese officer, taking the bottle of Scotch from Bourne. 'There are two of you, and my patrol boat is half a mile away in the south cove. My crew thinks I'm holding a secret meeting with our undercover people in the colony.'

'I'll "want the information," and you'll "guarantee it." For those words I'm to produce a thousand dollars without a struggle when it's entirely possible you have a dozen *Zhongguo ren* outside in the bush.'

'Some things must be taken on faith.'

'Not my money,' countered the Frenchman. 'You don't get a *sou* until I have an idea what you're selling.'

'You are Gallic to the core,' said Gamma, shaking his head. 'Very well. It concerns your disciple, the one who no longer follows his master, but instead picks up his thirty pieces of silver and a great deal more.'

'The *assassin?*'

'*Pay* him!' ordered Bourne, rigid, staring at the Chinese officer.

D'Anjou looked at Jason and the man called Gamma, then pulled up his sweater and unbuckled his soaking wet trousers. He reached below his waist and forced up an oilcloth money belt; he unzipped the centre pocket, slipped out the bills one after another with his fingers and held them out for the Chinese officer. 'Three thousand for tonight and one for this new information. The rest is counterfeit. I always carry an extra thousand for contingencies, but only a thousand—'

'The *information*,' broke in Jason Bourne.

'He paid for it,' replied Gamma. 'I shall address him.'

'Address whomever the hell you like, just talk.'

'Our mutual friend in Guangzhou,' began the officer speaking to d'Anjou. 'The radioman at Headquarters One.'

'We've done business,' said the Frenchman guardedly.

'Knowing I'd be meeting you here at this hour, I refuelled at the pumps in Zhuhai Shi shortly after ten-thirty. There was a message for me to reach him – we have a safe relay. He told me there was a call rerouted through Beijing with an unidentified Jade Tower priority code. It was for Soo Jiang—'

D'Anjou bolted forward, both hands on the ground. 'The *pig!*'

'Who is he?' asked Bourne quickly.

'Supposedly chief of Intelligence for Macao operations,' replied the Frenchman, 'but he would sell his mother to a brothel if the price was right. At the moment he is the conduit to my once and former disciple. My *Judas!*'

'Who's suddenly been summoned to Beijing,' interrupted the man called Gamma.

'You're *sure* of that?' said Jason.

'Our mutual friend is sure,' answered the Chinese, still looking at d'Anjou. 'An aide to Soo came to Headquarters One and checked all of tomorrow's flights from Kai-tak to Beijing. Under his department's authorization he reserved space – a single space – on every one. In several cases it meant that the original passengers were reduced to stand-by status. When an officer at Headquarters One asked for Soo's personal confirmation, the aide said he had left for Macao on urgent business. Who has business in Macao at midnight? Everything's closed.'

'Except the casinos,' volunteered Bourne. 'Table Five. The Kam Pek. Totally controlled circumstances.'

'Which, in light of the reserved space,' said the Frenchman, 'means that Soo isn't sure when he will reach the assassin.'

'But he *is* sure he'll reach him. Whatever message he's carrying is nothing short of an order that has to be complied with.' Jason looked at the Chinese officer. 'Get us into Beijing,' he said. 'The airport, the earliest flight. You'll be rich, I guarantee it.'

'Delta, you're *mad!*' cried d'Anjou. 'Peking is out of the question!'

'Why? No one's looking for us and there are French, English, Italians, Americans – God knows who else – all over the city. We've both got passports that'll get us through.'

'Be reasonable!' pleaded Echo. 'We'll be in their nets. Knowing what we know, if we're spotted in the vaguest questionable circumstances we'll be killed on the spot! He'll show up again down here, most likely in a matter of days.'

'I don't have days,' said Bourne coldly. 'I've lost your creation twice. I'm not going to lose him a third time.'

'You think you can possibly take him in *China?*'

'Where else would he least expect a trap?'

'*Madness!* You *are* mad!'

'Make the arrangements,' Jason ordered the Chinese officer. 'The first flight out of Kai-tak. When I've got the tickets, I'll hand over fifty thousand dollars American to whoever gives them to me. Send someone you can trust.'

'Fifty *thousand* . . . ?' The man called Gamma stared at Bourne.

The skies over Peking were hazy, the dust travelling on the winds from the North China plains creating pockets of vapid yellow and dull browns in the sunlight. The airport, like all other internationals, was immense, the runways a crisscrossing patchwork of black avenues, several over two miles in length. If there was a difference between Peking airport and its Western counterparts, it was in the huge dome-shaped terminal with its adjacent hotel and various freeways leading into the complex. Although contemporary in design, there was an underlying sense of functionalism and an absence of eye-pleasing touches. It was an airport to be used and admired for its efficiency, not for its beauty.

Bourne and d'Anjou went through customs with a minimum of effort, the way eased for them by their fluent Chinese. The guards were actually pleasant, barely glancing at their minimal luggage, more curious about their linguistic ability than their possessions. The chief official accepted without question the story of two Oriental scholars on a holiday where pleasant travels would no doubt find their way into the lecture halls. They converted a thousand dollars each into *renminbi* – literally, the People's Money – and were given nearly two thousand *yuan* apiece in return. And Bourne took off the glasses he had purchased in Washington from his friend Cactus.

'One thing bewilders me,' said the Frenchman as they stood in front of an electronic sign showing the next three hours of arrivals and departures. 'Why would he be flown in on a commercial plane? Certainly, whoever is paying him has government or military aircraft at his disposal.'

'Like ours, those aircraft have to be signed out and accounted for,' answered Jason. 'And whoever it is has to keep his distance from your assassin. He has to come in as a tourist or a businessman and then the convoluted process of making contact begins. At least that's what I'm counting on.'

'*Madness!* Tell me, Delta, if you *do* take him – and I add that it's a significant "if" because he's extraordinarily capable – have you any idea how to get him out?'

'I've got money, American money, large bills, more than you can imagine. It's in the lining of my jacket.'

'That's why we stopped at the Peninsula, isn't it? Why you told me not to check you out yesterday. Your money's there.'

'It was. In the hotel safe. I'll get him out.'

'On the wings of Pegasus?'

'No, probably a Pan Am flight with the two of us helping a very sick friend. Actually, somewhere along the line I think you gave me the idea.'

'Then I am a mental case!'

'Stay by the window,' said Bourne. 'There's another twelve minutes before the next plane is due from Kai-tak, but then that could mean two minutes or twelve hours. I'm going to buy us both a present.'

'Madness,' mumbled the Frenchman, too tired to do more than shake his head.

Jason returned, directing d'Anjou into a corner within sight of the immigration doors, which were kept closed except for those passengers emerging from customs. Bourne reached into his inside jacket pocket and pulled out a long, thin, brightly covered box with the sort of gaudy wrapping found in souvenir shops the world over. He removed the top; inside on ersatz felt was a narrow brass letter-opener, with Chinese characters along the handle. The point was obviously honed and sharp. 'Take it,' said Jason. 'Put it in your belt.'

'How's the balance?' asked Medusa's Echo as he slid the blade under his trousers.

'Not bad. It's about halfway to the base of the handle and brass gives it weight. The thrust should be decent.'

'Yes, I recall,' said d'Anjou. 'One of the first rules was never to throw a knife, but one evening at dusk you watched a Gurkha take out a scout ten feet away without firing a shot or risking hand-to-hand combat. His carbine bayonet spun through the air like a whirling missile, right into the scout's chest. The next morning you ordered the Gurkha to teach us – some did better than others.'

'How did you do?'

'Reasonably well. I was older than all of you, and whatever defences I could learn that did not take great physical exertion I felt drawn to. Also I kept practising. You saw me; you commented on it frequently.'

Jason looked at the Frenchman. 'It's funny, but I don't remember any of that.'

'I just naturally thought . . . I'm sorry, Delta.'

'Forget it. I'm learning to trust things I don't understand.'

The vigil continued, reminding Bourne of his wait in Lo Wu as one trainload after another crossed the border, no one revealed until a short, elderly man with a limp became someone else in the distance. The 11:30 plane was over two hours late. Customs would take an additional fifty minutes.

'*That* one!' cried d'Anjou, pointing to a figure walking out of the immigration doors.

'With a cane?' asked Jason. 'With a limp?'

'His shabby clothes cannot conceal his shoulders!' exclaimed Echo. 'The grey hair is too new; he hasn't brushed it sufficiently, and the dark glasses too wide. Like us, he is tired. You were right. The summons to Beijing had to be complied with, and he is careless.'

'Because "rest is a weapon" and he disregarded it?'

'Yes. Last night Kai-tak had to have taken its toll on him, but, more important, he had to obey. *Merde!* His fees must be in the hundreds of thousands!'

'He's heading for the hotel,' said Bourne. 'Stay back here, I'll follow him – at a distance. If he spotted you, he'd run and we could lose him.'

'He could spot *you!*'

'Not likely. I invented the game. Also, I'll be behind him. Stay here, I'll come back for you.'

Carrying his flight bag, his gait showing the weariness of jet lag, Jason fell in line with the disembarked passengers heading into the hotel, his eyes on the grey-haired man up ahead. Twice the former British commando stopped and turned around, and twice, with each brief movement of the shoulders, Bourne also turned and bent down, as if brushing an insect from his leg or adjusting the strap of his flight bag, his body and face out of sight. The crowd at the registration counter grew and Jason was eight people behind the killer in the second line, making himself as inconspicuous as possible, continually stooping to kick his flight bag ahead. The commando reached the female clerk; he showed his papers, signed the register, and limped with his cane toward a bank of brown elevators on the right. Six minutes later Bourne faced the same clerk. He spoke in Mandarin.

'*Ni neng bang-zhu wo ma?*' he began, asking for help. 'It was a sudden trip and I've no place to stay. Just for the night.'

'You speak our language very well,' said the clerk, her almond-shaped eyes wide in appreciation. 'You do us honour,' she added politely.

'I hope to do much better during my stay here. I'm on a scholarly trip.'

'It is the best kind. There are many treasures in Beijing, and elsewhere, of course, but this is the heavenly city. You have no reservation?'

'I'm afraid not. Everything was last-minute, if you know what I mean.'

'As I speak both languages, I can tell you that you said it correctly in ours. Everything is rush-rush. I'll see what I can do. It will not be terribly grand, of course.'

'I can't afford terribly grand,' said Jason shyly. 'But I have a roommate – we can share the same bed, if necessary.'

'I'm certain it will be on such short notice.' The clerk's fingers leafed through the file cards. '*Here*,' she said. 'A single back room on the second floor. I think it may fit your economics—'

'We'll take it,' agreed Bourne. 'By the way, a few minutes ago I saw a man in this line whom I'm sure I know. He's getting on now, but I think he was an old professor of mine when I studied in England. Grey-haired, with a cane . . . I'm certain it's he. I'd like to call him.'

'Oh, yes, I remember.' The clerk now separated the most recent registration cards in front of her. 'The name is Wadsworth, Joseph Wadsworth. He's in three-twenty-five. But you may be wrong. His occupation is listed as an off-shore oil consultant from Great Britain.'

'You're right, wrong man,' said Jason, shaking his head in embarrassment. He took the key to the room.

'We can take him! *Now!*' Bourne gripped d'Anjou's arm, pulling the Frenchman away from the deserted corner of the terminal.

'Now? So easily? So quickly? It is incredible!'

'The opposite,' said Jason, leading d'Anjou toward the crowded row of glass doors that was the entrance to the hotel. 'It's completely credible. Your man's mind is on a dozen different things right now. He's got to stay out of sight. He can't place a call through a switchboard, so he'll remain in his room waiting for a call to *him* giving him his instructions.' They walked through a glass door, looked around and headed to the left of the long counter. Bourne continued, speaking rapidly. 'Kai-tak didn't work last night, so he has to consider another possibility. His own elimination on the basis that whoever discovered the explosives under the car saw him and identified him – which is the truth. He has to insist that his client be alone at the arranged rendezvous so he can reach him one on one. It's his ultimate protection.' They found a staircase and started climbing. 'And his clothes,' went on Medusa's Delta, 'he'll change them. He can't appear as he *was* and he can't appear as he *is*. He has to be someone else.' They reached the third floor, and Jason, his hand on the knob, turned to d'Anjou. 'Take my word for it, Echo, your boy's involved. He's got exercises going on in his head that would challenge a Russian chess player.'

'Is this the academic speaking or the man they once called Jason Bourne?'

'Bourne,' said David Webb, his eyes cold, his voice ice. 'If it ever was, it's now.'

The flight bag strapped over his shoulder, Jason slowly opened the staircase door, inching his body into the frame. Two men in dark pin-striped suits walked up the hallway toward him complaining at the apparent lack of room service; their speech was British. They opened the door to their room and went inside. Bourne pulled the staircase door back and pushed d'Anjou through; they walked down the corridor. The room numbers were in Chinese and English.

341, 339, 337 – they were in the right hallway, the room was along the left wall. Three Indian couples suddently emerged from a brown elevator, the women in their saris, the men in tight-fitting trousers; they passed Jason and d'Anjou chattering, looking for their rooms, the husbands obviously annoyed to be carrying their own luggage.

335, 333, 331 –

'This is the *end!*' screamed a female voice as an obese woman in hair curlers strode martially out of a door on the right wearing a bathrobe. The nightgown underneath trailed below, twice snarling her feet. She yanked it up, revealing a pair of legs worthy of a rhinoceros. 'The toilet doesn't work and you can *forget* the phone!'

'Isabel, I told you!' shouted a man in red pajamas peering through the open door. 'It's the jet lag. Get some sleep and remember this isn't Short Hills! Don't nitpick. Expand yourself!'

'Since I can't use the bathroom, I have no choice! I'll find *some* slant-eyed bastard and yell like hell! Where are the stairs? I wouldn't walk *into* one of those goddamned elevators. If they move at all, it's probably sideways and right through the walls into a seven forty-seven!'

The distraught woman swept by on her way to the staircase exit. Two of the three Indian couples had difficulty with their keys, finally managing to negotiate the locks with loud, well-placed kicks, and the man in the red pajamas slammed the door of his room after shouting to his wife in high dudgeon. 'It's like that class reunion at the club! You're so *embarrassing*, Isabel!'

329, 327 . . . *325*. The room. The hallway was deserted.

They could hear the strains of Oriental music from behind the door. The radio was turned up, the volume loud, to be made louder with the first ring of a telephone bell. Jason pulled d'Anjou back and spoke quietly against the wall. 'I don't remember any Gurkhas or any scouts—'

'A part of you did, Delta,' interrupted Echo.

'Maybe, but that's beside the point. This is the beginning of the end of the road. We'll leave our bags out here. I'll go for the door and you follow hard. Keep your blade ready. But I want you to understand something, and there *can't* be a mistake – don't throw it unless you absolutely *have* to. If you do, go for his legs. Nothing above the waist.'

'You put more faith in an older man's accuracy than I do.'

'I'm hoping I won't have to call on it. These doors are made of hollow plywood and your assassin's got a lot on his mind. He's thinking about strategy, not about us. How could we know he's here, and even if we did, how could we get across the border on such short notice? And I *want* him! I'm *taking* him! Ready?'

'As I ever will be,' said the Frenchman, lowering his small suitcase and pulling the brass letter-opener from his belt. He held the blade in his hand, his fingers spread, seeking the balance.

Bourne slipped the flight bag off his shoulder to the floor and quietly positioned himself in front of Room 325. He looked at d'Anjou. Echo nodded, and Jason sprang toward the door, his left foot a battering ram, crashing into the space below the lock. The door plunged inward, as though blown apart; wood shattered, hinges were torn from their bolts. Bourne lunged inside, rolling over and over on the floor, his eyes spinning in all directions.

'*Arrêtez!*' roared d'Anjou.

A figure came through an inner doorway – the grey-haired man, the *assassin!* Jason sprang to his feet, hurling himself at his quarry, grabbing the man's hair, yanking him to the left, then to the right, crashing him back into the doorframe. Suddenly the Frenchman screamed as the brass blade of the letter-opener flashed through the air, embedding itself in the wall, the handle quivering. It was off the mark, a warning.

'Delta! *No!*'

Bourne stopped all movement, his quarry pinned, helpless under his weight and grip.

'*Look!*' cried d'Anjou.

Jason slowly moved back, his arms rigid, caging the figure in front of him. He stared into the gaunt, wrinkled face of a very old man with thinning grey hair.

22

Marie lay on the narrow bed staring up at the ceiling. The rays of the noonday sun streamed through the shadeless windows, filling the small room with blinding light and too much heat. Sweat matted her face, and her torn blouse clung to her moist skin. Her feet ached from the midmorning madness that had begun as a walk down an unfinished coastal road to a rocky beach below – a stupid thing to do, but at the time the only thing she *could* do; she had been going out of her mind.

The sounds of the street floated up, a strange cacophony of high-pitched voices, sudden shrieks and bicycle bells and the blaring horns of trucks and public buses. It was as if a crowded, bustling, hustling section of Hong Kong had been ripped out of the island and set down in some faraway place where a wide river and endless fields and distant mountains replaced Victoria Harbour and the countless rows of ascending tall buildings made of glass and stone. In a sense the transplant had happened, she reflected. The miniature city of Tuen Mun was one of those space-oriented phenomena that had sprung up north of Kowloon in the New Territories. One year it had been an arid river plain, the next a rapidly developing metropolis of paved roads and factories, shopping districts, and spreading apartment buildings, all beckoning those from the south with the promise of housing and jobs in the thousands, and those who heeded the call brought with them the unmistakable hysteria of Hong Kong's commerce. Without it they would be filled with innocuous anxieties too placid to contend with; these were the descendants of Guangzhou – the province of Canton – not world-weary Shanghai.

Marie had awakened with the first light, what sleep she had managed had been wracked with nightmares – and knew that she faced another suspension of time until Catherine called her. Staples had telephoned late last night, dragging her out of a sleep induced by total exhaustion, only to tell her cryptically that several unusual things had happened that could lead to favourable news. She was meeting a man who had taken an interest, a remarkable man who could help. Marie was to stay in the flat by the telephone in case there were new developments. Since Catherine had instructed her not to use names or specifics on the phone, Marie had not questioned the brevity of the call. 'I'll phone you first thing in the morning, my dear.' Staples had abruptly hung up.

She had not called by 8:30 or by 9:00, and by 9:36 Marie could stand it no longer. She reasoned that names were unnecessary, each knew the other's voice, and Catherine had to understand that David Webb's wife was entitled to *something* 'first thing in the morning.' Marie had dialled Staples's flat in Hong Kong; there was no answer, so she dialled again to make sure she had spun the correct numbers. Nothing. In frustration and without caring, she had called the consulate.

'Foreign Service Officer Staples, please. I'm a friend from the Treasury Board in Ottawa. I'd like to surprise her.'

'The connection's very good, honey.'

'I'm not *in* Ottawa, I'm here,' said Marie, picturing the face of the talkative receptionist only too well.

'Sorry, hon, Mrs Staples is off-premises with no instructions. To tell you the truth, the High Commish is looking for her too. Why don't you give me a number—'

Marie lowered the phone into its cradle, panic rising in her. It was nearly 10:00, and Catherine was an early riser. 'First thing in the morning' might be anytime between 7:30 and 9:30, most likely splitting the difference, but not ten o'clock, *not* under the circumstances. And then twelve minutes later the phone had rung. It was the beginning of a far less subtle panic.

'Marie?'

'*Catherine*, are you all *right?*'

'Yes, of course.'

'You said "first thing in the morning"! Why didn't you call before? I've been going out of my mind! Can you talk?'

'Yes, I'm in a public booth—'

'What's happened? What's *happening?* Who's the man you met with?'

There had been a brief pause on the line from Hong Kong. For an instant it seemed awkward and Marie had not known why. 'I want you to stay calm, my dear,' said Staples. 'I didn't call before because you need all the rest you can get. I may have the answers that you want, that you need. Things are not as terrible as you think, and you *must* stay calm.'

'Damn it, I *am* calm, at least I'm reasonably sensible! What the hell are you talking about?'

'I can tell you that your husband's alive.'

'And I can tell you that he's very good at what he does – what he *did*. You're not telling me anything!'

'I'm driving out to see you in a few minutes. The traffic's rotten, as usual, made worse by all the security surrounding the Sino-British delegations, tying up the streets and the tunnel, but it shouldn't take me more than an hour and a half, perhaps two.'

'Catherine, I want *answers!*'

'I'm bringing them to you, a few at least. Rest, Marie, try to relax. Everything's going to be all right. I'll be there soon.'

'This *man*,' asked David Webb's wife, pleading. 'Will he be with you?'

'No, I'll be alone, no one with me. I want to talk. You'll see him later.'

'All right.'

Had it been Staples's tone of voice? Marie had wondered after hanging up. Or that Catherine had literally told her nothing after admitting she could talk freely over a public phone? The Staples she knew would try to allay the fears of a terrified friend if she had concrete facts to offer in comfort, even a single piece of vital information, if the fabric of the whole was too complex. *Something.* David Webb's wife deserved *something!* Instead there had been a diplomat's talk, the allusion to but not the substance of reality. Something was wrong, but it was beyond her understanding. Catherine had protected her, taken enormous risks for her both professionally, in terms of not seeking guidance from her consulate, and personally, in confronting acute physical danger. Marie knew that she should feel gratitude, overwhelming gratitude, but instead she felt a growing sense of doubt. *Say it again, Catherine,* she had screamed inside herself, *say everything will be all right! I can't think anymore. I can't think in here! I've got to get out . . . I've got to have air!*

She had lurched about unsteadily for the clothes they had bought for her when they had reached Tuen Mun last night, clothes purchased after Staples had taken her to a doctor who ministered to her feet, applying cushioned gauze, giving her hospital slippers and prescribing thick-soled sneakers if she had to do any extended walking during the next several days. Actually, Catherine had picked out the clothes while Marie waited in the car, and considering the tension Staples was under, her selections were both functional and attractive. A light green, sheer cotton skirt was complemented by a white cotton blouse and a small white-shell purse. Also a pair of dark green slacks – shorts were inappropriate – and a second, casual blouse. All were successful counterfeits of well-known designers, the labels correctly spelled.

'They're very nice, Catherine. Thank you.'

'They go with your hair,' Staples had said. 'Not that anyone in Tuen Mun will notice – I want you to stay in the flat – but we'll have to leave here sometime. Also, in case I get stuck at the office and you need anything, I've put some money in the purse.'

'I thought I wasn't supposed to leave the flat, that we were going to pick up a few things at a market.'

'I don't know what's back in Hong Kong any more than you do. Lin could be so furious he might dig up an old colonial law and put me under house arrest . . . There's a shoe store in Blossom Soon Street. You'll have to go inside and try on the sneakers yourself. I'll come with you, of course.'

Several moments had passed and Marie spoke. 'Catherine, how do you know so much about this place? I've yet to see another Occidental in the streets. Whose flat is it?'

'A friend's,' said Staples without further elaboration. 'There's no one using it a great deal of the time, so I come up here to get away from it all.' Catherine had said no more; the subject was not to be explored. Even when they had talked for most of the night, no amount of prodding had brought forth any more information from Staples. It was a topic she simply would not discuss.

Marie had put on the slacks and the blouse and struggled with the outsized sneakers. Cautiously she had walked down the stairs and into the busy street, instantly aware of the stares she attracted, wondering whether she should turn around and go back inside. She could not; she was finding a few minutes of freedom from the stifling confines of the small apartment and they were like a tonic. She strolled slowly, painfully, down the pavement, mesmerized by the colour and the hectic movement and the unending, staccato chatter all around her. As in Hong Kong, garish signs rose everywhere above the buildings, and everywhere people haggled with one another alongside stands and in store-front doorways. It *was* as if a slice of the colony had been uprooted and set down on a vast frontier.

She had found an unfinished road at the end of a back street, the work apparently abandoned but only temporarily, as levelling machinery – unused and rusting – stood on the borders. Two signs in Chinese were on either side of the road at the top of a slope. Taking each step carefully, she made her way down the steep decline to the deserted shoreline and sat on a cluster of rocks; the minutes of freedom were opening up precious moments of peace. She looked out and watched the boats sailing from the docks of Tuen Mun, as well as those heading in from the People's Republic. From what she could see, the first were fishing craft, nets draped over bows and gunwales, while those from the Chinese Mainland were mostly small cargo ships, their decks bulging with crates of produce. There were also the sleek, grey navy patrol boats flying the colours of the People's Republic. Ominous black guns were mounted on all sides of the various craft, uniformed men standing motionless next to them, peering through binoculars. Every now and then a naval vessel would pull alongside a fishing boat, provoking wildly excited gestures from the fishermen. Stoic responses were the replies as the powerful patrols would slowly spin and slip away. It was all a game, thought Marie. The North was quietly asserting its total control while the South was left to protest the disturbance of its fishing grounds. The former had the strength of hard steel and a disciplined chain of command, the latter soft nets and perseverance. No one was the victor except those opposing sisters, Boredom and Anxiety.

'*Jing-cha!*' shouted a male voice from behind in the distance.

'*Shei!*' shrieked a second. '*Ni zai zher gan shemma?*'

Marie spun around. Two men up on the road had broken into a run; they were racing down the unfinished access toward her, their screams directed at her, commanding her. Awkwardly she got to her feet, steadying herself on the rocks as they ran up to her. Both men were dressed in some sort of para-military clothing, and as she looked at them she realized they were young – late teenagers, twenty at most.

'*Bu xing!*' barked the taller boy, looking back up the hill, and gesturing for his companion to grab her. Whatever it was, it was to be done quickly. The second boy pinned her arms from behind.

'*Stop* this!' cried Marie, struggling. 'Who *are* you?'

'Lady speaks English,' observed the first young man. '*I* speak English,' he added proudly, unctuously. 'I worked for a jeweller in Kowloon.' Again he glanced up at the unfinished road.

'Then tell your friend to take his hands off me!'

'The lady does not tell me what to do. I tell the lady.' The postadolescent came closer, his eyes fixed on the swell of Marie's breasts under the blouse. 'This is forbidden road, a forbidden part of the shore. The lady did not see the signs?'

'I don't read Chinese. I'm sorry, I'll leave. Just tell him to let go of me.' Suddenly Marie felt the body of the young man behind her pressing against her own. '*Stop* it!' she yelled, hearing quiet laughter in her ear, feeling a warm breath on her neck.

'Is the lady to meet a boat with criminals from the People's Republic? Does she signal men on the water?' The taller Chinese raised both his hands to Marie's blouse, his fingers on the top buttons. 'Is she concealing a radio perhaps, a signalling device? It is our duty to learn these things. The police expect it of us.'

'*Goddamn you*, take your *hands* off me!' Marie twisted violently, kicking out in front of her. The man behind pulled her back off her feet as the taller boy grabbed her legs, straddling them with his own and scissoring them. She could not move; her body was stretched taut diagonally up from the rocky beach, held firmly in place. The first Chinese ripped off her blouse and then her brassiere, and cupped her breasts with both hands. She screamed and thrashed and screamed again until she was slapped and two fingers pincered her throat, cutting off all sound but throated coughs. The nightmare of Zurich came back to her – rape and death on the Guisan Quai.

They carried her to a stretch of tall grass, the boy behind clamping his hand over her mouth, then replacing it quickly with his right arm, cutting off air and any screams she might have managed as he yanked her forward. She was thrown to the ground, one of her attackers now covering her face with his bare stomach as the other began pulling off her slacks and thrusting his hands between her legs. It *was* Zurich, and instead of writhing in the cold Swiss darkness there was the wet heat of the Orient; instead of the Limmat, another river, far wider, far more deserted; instead of one animal there were two. She could feel the body of the tall Chinese on top of her, thrusting in his panic, furious that he was not able to enter her, her thrashing repelling his assault. For an instant the boy across her face reached under his trousers to his groin – there was a brief moment of space and for Marie the world went mad! She sank her teeth into the flesh above her, drawing blood, feeling the sickening flesh in her mouth.

Screams followed; her arms were released. She kicked as the young Oriental rolled away clutching his stomach; she crashed her knee up into the exposed organ above her waist, then clawed at the wild-eyed, sweating face of the taller man, now screaming herself – yelling, pleading, shouting as she had never shouted in her life before. Holding his testicles beneath his shorts, the infuriated boy threw himself down on her, but rape was no longer a consideration, he wanted only to keep her quiet. Suffocating, the darkness had begun to close in on Marie – and then she had heard other voices in the distance, excited voices closing that distance, and she knew she had to send up a final cry for help. In a desperate surge, she dug her nails into the contorted face above her, for an instant freeing her mouth from the grip.

'*Here!* Down *here! Over here!*'

Bodies were suddenly swarming around her; she could hear slaps and kicks and furious screams, but none of the madness was directed at her. Then the darkness had come, her last thoughts only partly about herself. *David! David, for God's sake where are you? Stay alive, my dearest! Don't let them take your mind again. Above all, don't allow that! They want mine and I won't give it to them! Why are they doing this to us? Oh, my God, why?*

She had awakened on a cot in a small room with no windows, a young Chinese woman wiping her forehead with a cool, perfumed cloth. '*Where* . . . ?' whispered Marie. 'Where is this? Where *am* I?'

The girl smiled sweetly and shrugged, nodding at a man on the other side of the cot, a Chinese Marie judged to be in his thirties, dressed in tropical clothes, a white guayabera instead of a shirt. 'Permit me to introduce myself,' said the man in accented but clear English. 'My name is Jitai, and I am with the Tuen Mun branch of the Hang Chow Bank. You are in the back room of a fabric shop belonging to a friend and client, Mr Chang. They brought you here and called for me. You were attacked by two hoodlums of the Di-di Jing Cha, which can be translated as the Young People's Auxiliary Police. It is one of those well-meant social programmes that have many benefits, but on occasion also have their very rotten apples, as you Americans say.'

'Why do you think I'm American?'

'Your speech. While you were unconscious you spoke about a man named David. A dear friend, no doubt. You wish to find him.'

'What else did I say?'

'Nothing, really. You were not very coherent.'

'I don't know anyone named David,' said Marie firmly. 'Not in that way. It must have been one of those deliriums that go back to the first grade.'

'It is immaterial. It is your well-being that matters. We are filled with shame and sorrow at what happened.'

'Where are those two punks, those *bastards*?'

'They are caught and will be punished.'

'I hope they spend ten years in jail.'

The Chinese frowned. 'To bring that about will mean involving the police – a formal complaint, a hearing before a magistrate, so many legalities.' Marie stared at the banker. 'Now, if you wish, I will accompany you to the police and act as your interpreter, but it was our opinion that we should first hear your desires in this regard. You have been through so much – and you are alone here in Tuen Mun for reasons only you know.'

'No, Mr Jitai,' said Marie quietly. 'I'd rather not press charges. I'm all right, and vengeance isn't a high priority with me.'

'It is with us, madame.'

'What do you mean?'

'Your attackers will carry our shame to their wedding beds, where their performances will be less than expected.'

'I see. They *are* young—'

'This morning, as we have learned, is not their first offence. They are filth, and lessons must be taught.'

'This morning? Oh, my God, what *time* is it? How long have I been here?'

The banker looked at his watch. 'Nearly an hour.'

'I've got to get back to the apartment – the flat – right away. It's important.'

'The ladies wish to mend your clothing. They're excellent seamstresses and it will not take long. However, they believed you should not wake up without your clothes.'

'I haven't time. I have to get back now. Oh, Christ! I don't know where it is and I don't have an address!'

'We know the building, madame. A tall, attractive white woman alone in Tuen Mun is noticed. Word spreads. We'll take you there at once.' The banker turned and spoke in rapid Chinese, addressing a half-opened door behind him, as Marie sat up. She was suddenly aware of the crowd of people peering inside. She got to her feet – her painful feet – and stood for a moment, weaving but slowly finding her balance, holding the ripped folds of her blouse together.

The door was pulled back and two old women entered, each carrying an article of brightly coloured silk. The first was a kimonolike garment, which was gently lowered over her head to cover her torn blouse and much of her soiled green slacks. The second was a long, wide sash, which was wrapped around her waist and tied, also gently. Tense as she was, Marie saw that each article was exquisite.

'Come, madame,' said the banker, touching her elbow. 'I will escort you.' They walked out into the fabric shop, Marie nodding and trying to smile as the crowd of Chinese men and women bowed to her, their dark eyes filled with sadness.

She had returned to the small apartment, removed the beautiful sash and garment, and lay down on the bed trying to make sense where no reason was to be found. She buried her face in the pillow, trying to push the horrible images of the morning out of her head, but the ugliness was beyond purging. Instead, it made the sweat pour out of her, and the tighter she closed her eyes, the more violent the images became, interweaving the terrible memories of Zurich on the Guisan Quai when a man named Jason Bourne had saved her life.

She stifled a scream and leaped off the bed, standing there, trembling. She walked into the tiny kitchen and turned on the faucet, reaching for a glass. The stream of water was weak and thin and she watched vacantly as the glass filled, her mind elsewhere.

There are times when people should put their heads on hold – God knows I do it more than a reasonably respected psychiatrist should . . . Things overwhelm us . . . we have to get our acts together. Morris Panov, friend to Jason Bourne.

She shut off the faucet, drank the lukewarm water, and went back toward the confining room that served the triple functions of sleeping, sitting, and pacing. She stood in the doorframe and looked around, knowing what she found so grotesque about her sanctuary. It was a cell, as surely as if it were in some remote prison. Worse, it was a very real form of solitary confinement. She was again isolated with her thoughts, with her terrors. She walked to a window as a prisoner might, and peered at the world outside. What she saw was an extension of her cell; she was not free down in that teeming street below either. It was not a world she knew, and it did not welcome her. Quite aside from the obscene madness of the morning on the beach, she was an intruder who could neither understand nor be understood. She was alone, and that loneliness was driving her crazy.

Numbly Marie gazed at the street. The *street?* There she was! Catherine! She was standing with a man by a grey car, their heads turned, watching three *other* men ten yards behind them by a second car. All five were glaringly apparent, for they were like no other people in the street. They were Occidentals in a sea of Chinese, strangers in an unfamiliar place. They were obviously excited, concerned about something, as they kept nodding their heads and looking in all directions, especially across the street. At the apartment house. Three of the men had close-cropped hair – military cuts . . . marines. *American marines!*

Catherine's companion, a civilian to judge by his hair, was talking rapidly, his index finger jabbing the air . . . Marie *knew* him! It was the man from the State Department, the one who had come to see them in Maine! The undersecretary with the dead eyes, who kept rubbing his temples and barely protested when David told him he did not trust him. It was *McAllister!* He was the man Catherine said she was to meet.

Suddenly, abstract and terrible pieces of the horrible puzzle fell into place as Marie watched the scene below. The two marines by the second car crossed the street and separated. The one standing with Catherine talked briefly with McAllister, then ran to his right, pulling a small hand-held radio from his pocket. Staples spoke to the undersecretary of State and glanced up at the apartment house. Marie spun away from the window.

I'll be alone, no one with me.

All right.

It was a trap! Catherine Staples had been reached. She was not a friend; she was the *enemy!* Marie knew she had to run. *For God's sake, get away!* She grabbed the white-shell purse with the money, and for a split second stared at the silks from the fabric shop. She picked them up and ran out of the flat.

There were two hallways, one running the width of the building along the front with a staircase on the right leading down to the street, the other hallway bisecting the first to form an inverted T, and leading to a door in the rear. It was a second staircase used for carrying garbage to the bins in the back alley. Catherine had casually pointed it out when they arrived, explaining that there was an ordinance forbidding refuse in the street, which was the main thoroughfare of Tuen Mun. Marie raced down the bisecting hall to the rear door and opened it. She gasped, suddenly confronted by the stooped figure of an old man with a straw broom in his hand. He squinted at her for a moment, then shook his head, his expression one of intense curiosity. She stepped out into the dark landing as the Chinese went inside; she held the door slightly open, waiting for the sight of Staples emerging from the front stairs. If Catherine, finding the flat empty, quickly returned to the staircase so as to rush down into the street to McAllister and the marine contingent, Marie could slip back into the apartment and pick up the clothes Staples had bought for her. In her panic she had only fleetingly thought about them, grabbing the silks instead, not daring to lose precious moments rummaging through the closet where Catherine had hung them, stuffed among various other clothing. She thought about them now. She could not walk, much less run through the streets in a torn blouse and filthy slacks. Something was *wrong*. It was the old man! He just stood there staring at the crack in the doorframe.

'Go *away!*' whispered Marie.

Footsteps. The clacking of high-heeled shoes walking rapidly up the metal staircase in the front of the building. If it was Staples, she would pass the bisecting hallway on her way to the flat.

'*Deng yi deng!*' yelped the old Chinese, still standing motionless with his broom, still staring at her. Marie closed the door further, watching through barely a half inch of space.

Staples came into view, glancing briefly, curiously at the old man, apparently having heard his sharp, high-pitched angry voice. Without breaking stride she continued down the hall, intent only on reaching the flat. Marie waited; the pounding in her chest seemed to echo throughout the dark stairwell. Then the words came, pleas shouted in hysteria. '*No! Marie!* Marie, where *are* you?' The footsteps hammered now, racing on the cement. Catherine rounded the corner and began running toward the old Chinese and the door – toward *her.* 'Marie, it's not what you *think!* For *God's* sake, *stop!*'

Marie Webb spun and ran down the dark steps. Suddenly, a shaft of bright yellow sunlight spread up the staircase, and just as suddenly was no more. The ground-floor door three storeys below had been opened; a figure in a dark suit had entered swiftly, a marine taking up his post. The man raced up the steps; Marie crouched in the corner of the second landing. The marine reached the top step, about to round the turn, steadying himself on the railing. Marie lunged out, her hand – the hand with the bunched silks – crashing into the astonished soldier's face, catching him off balance; she slammed her shoulder into the marine's chest, sending him reeling backwards down the staircase. Marie passed his tumbling body on the steps as she heard the screams from above. 'Marie! *Marie!* I know it's you! For Christ's sake, *listen* to me!'

She lurched out into the alley, and another nightmare began its dreadful course, played out in the blinding sunlight of Tuen Mun. Running through the connecting thoroughfare behind the row of apartment buildings, her feet now bleeding inside the sneakers, Marie threw the kimonolike garment over her head and stopped by a row of garbage cans, where she removed her green slacks and threw them inside the nearest one. She then draped the wide sash over her head, covering her hair, and ran into the next alleyway that led to the main street. She reached it and seconds later walked into the mass of humanity that was a slice of Hong Kong in the new frontier of the colony. She crossed the street.

'*There!*' shouted a male voice. 'The tall one!'

The chase began again, but abruptly, without any indication, it was different. A man raced down the pavement after her, suddenly stopped by a wheeled stand blocking his way; he tried to shove it aside, only to put his hands into recessed pots of boiling fat. He screamed, overturning the cart, and was now met with shrieks by the proprietor obviously demanding payment, as he and others surrounded the marine, forcing him back into the kerb.

'There's the *bitch!*'

As Marie heard the words she was confronted by a phalanx of women shoppers. She spun to her right and ran into another alley off the street, an alley she suddenly discovered was a dead end, ending with the wall of a Chinese temple. It happened again! Five young men – teenagers in paramilitary outfits – suddenly appeared from a doorway and gestured for her to pass.

'Yankee *criminal!* Yankee *thief!*' The shouts were in the cadence of a rehearsed foreign language.The young men locked arms and without violence intercepted the man with close-cropped hair, crowding him against a wall.

'Get out of my way, you pricks!' shouted the marine. 'Get out of my way or I'll take every one of you brats!'

'You raise your arms . . . or a weapon—' cried a voice in the background.

'I never said anything about a weapon!' broke in the soldier from Victoria Peak.

'But if you do either,' continued the voice, 'they will release their arms, and five Di-di Jing Cha – so many trained by our American friends – will certainly contain one man.'

'Goddamn it, *sir!* I'm only trying to do my *job!* It's none of your business!'

'I'm afraid it is, sir. For reasons you do not know.'

'*Shit!*' The marine leaned against the wall, out of breath, and looked at the smiling young faces in front of him.

'*Lai!*' said a woman to Marie, pointing to a wide, oddly shaped door with no visible handle on what appeared to be a thick, impenetrable exterior. '*Xiao xin.* Kaa-fill.'

'*Careful?* I understand.' An aproned figure opened the door and Marie rushed inside, instantly feeling the harsh blasts of cold air. She was standing in a large walk-in refrigerator where carcasses of meat hung eerily on hooks under the glow of mesh-encased light bulbs. The man in the apron waited a full minute, his ear at the door. Marie wrapped the wide silk sash around her neck and clutched her arms to ward off the sudden, bitter cold made worse by the contrasting oppressive heat outside. Finally, the clerk gestured for her to follow him; she did so, threading her way around the carcasses until they reached the huge refrigerator's entrance. The Chinese yanked a metal lever and pushed the heavy door open, nodding for Marie, who was shivering, to walk through. She now found herself in a long, narrow deserted butcher shop, the bamboo blinds on the front windows filtering the intense noonday sunlight. A white-haired man stood behind the counter by the far-right window, peering through the slats at the street outside. He beckoned for Marie to join him quickly. Again she did as she was instructed, and noticed an oddly shaped floral wreath behind the glass of the front door, which appeared to be locked.

The older man indicated that Marie should look through the window. She parted two curved bamboo slats and gasped, astonished at the scene outside. The search was at its frenzied peak. The marine with scalded hands kept waving them in the air as he went from store to store across the street. She saw Catherine Staples and McAllister in a heated conversation with a crowd of Chinese who obviously were objecting to the foreigners disturbing the peaceful if hectic way of life in Tuen Mun. McAllister in his panic apparently had shouted something offensive and was challenged by a man twice his age, and ancient in an Oriental gown, who had to be restrained by younger, cooler heads. The undersecretary of State backed away, his arms raised, pleading innocence, as Staples shouted to no avail in her efforts to extricate them both from the angry mob.

Suddenly, the marine with the wounded hands came crashing out of a doorway across the street; shattered glass flew in all directions as he rolled on the pavement, yelling in pain as his hands touched the cement. He was pursued by a young Chinese dressed in the white tunic, sash, and knee-length trousers of a martial-arts instructor. The marine sprang to his feet, and as his Oriental adversary ran up to him he pounded a low left hook into the young man's kidney, and followed it with a well-aimed right fist into the Oriental face, pummelling his assailant back into the storefront while screaming in agony at the pain both blows caused his scalded hands.

A last marine from Victoria Peak came running down the street, one leg limping, his shoulders sagging as if damaged from a fall – a fall down a flight of stairs, thought Marie, as she watched in amazement. He came to the aid of his anguished comrade and was very effective. The amateurish attempts at combat by the berobed students of the unconscious martial-arts instructor were met by a flurry of slashing legs, crashing chops, and the whirling manoeuvres of a judo expert.

Suddenly again, with no warning whatsoever, the cacophonic strains of Oriental music swelled in the street, the cymbals and the primitive wood instruments reaching abrupt crescendos with each stride of the ragtag band that marched down the street, its followers carrying placards mounted with flowers. The fighting stopped as arms were restrained everywhere. Silence spread along the main avenue of commerce of Tuen Mun. The Americans were confused; Catherine Staples choked back her frustration and Edward McAllister threw up his hands in exasperation.

Marie watched, literally hypnotized by the change outside. Everything came to a stop, as if a halt had been ordered by an announcement from some sepulchral presence not to be denied. She shifted her angle of sight between the bamboo blinds and looked at the ragged group approaching. It was led by the banker Jitai! It was heading for the butcher shop!

Her eyes darting, Marie saw Catherine Staples and McAllister race past the odd gathering in front of the shop. Then across the street the two marines once again took up the chase. They all disappeared in the blinding sunlight.

There was a knock on the front door of the butcher shop. The old man with white hair removed the wreath and opened it. The banker, Jitai, walked in and bowed to Marie.

'Did you enjoy the parade, madame?' he asked.

'I wasn't sure what it was.'

'A funeral march for the dead. In this instance, no doubt, for the slain animals in Mr Woo's cold storage.'

'*You . . . ?* This was all *planned?*'

'In a state of readiness, you might say,' explained Jitai. 'Frequently our cousins from the north manage to get across the border – not the thieves but family members wishing to join their own – and the soldiers want only to capture them and send them back. We must be prepared to protect our own.'

'But *me . . . ?* You *knew?*'

'We watched; we waited. You were in hiding, running from someone, that much we did know. You told us that when you said you did not care to go before the magistrate, to "press charges," as you put it. You were directed into the alley outside.'

'The line of women with the shopping bags—'

'Yes. They crossed the street when you did. We must help you.'

Marie glanced at the anxious faces of the crowd beyond the bamboo slats, then looked at the banker. 'How do you know I'm not a criminal?'

'It doesn't matter. The outrage against you resulting from two of our people is what matters. Also, madame, you do not look or speak like a fugitive from justice.'

'I'm not. And I do need help. I have to get back to Hong Kong, to a hotel where they won't find me, where there's a telephone I can use. I don't really know who, but I have to reach people who can help me . . . help us.' Marie paused, her eyes locked with Jitai's. 'The man named David is my husband.'

'I can understand,' said the banker. 'But first you have to see a doctor.'

'What?'

'Your feet are bleeding.'

Marie looked down. Blood had seeped through the bandages, penetrating the canvas of her sneakers. They were a sickening mess. 'I guess you're right,' she agreed.

'Then there will be clothes, transportation – I myself will find you a hotel under any name you wish. And there is the matter of money. Do you have funds?'

'I don't know,' said Marie, putting the silks on the counter and opening the white-shell purse. 'That is, I haven't looked. A friend – someone that I thought was a friend – left me money.' She pulled out the bills Staples had placed in the purse.

'We are not wealthy here in Tuen Mun, but perhaps we can help. There was talk of taking up a collection.'

'I'm not a poor woman, Mr Jitai,' interrupted Marie. 'If that is necessary and, frankly, if I'm alive, every cent will be returned with interest far in excess of the prime rate.'

'As you wish. I am a banker. But what would such a lovely lady like yourself know of interests and prime rates?' Jitai smiled.

'You're a banker and I'm an economist. What do bankers know about the impacts on floating currencies caused by inflated interests, especially in the prime rates?' Marie smiled for the first time in a very long time.

She had over an hour to think in the countryside quiet as she sat in the taxi that drove her down to Kowloon. It would be another forty-five minutes once they reached the less quiet outskirts, particularly a congested district called Mongkok. The contrite people of Tuen Mun had been not only generous and protective, but inventive as well. The banker, Jitai, apparently had confirmed that the hoodlums' victim was indeed a white woman in hiding and running for her life, and therefore, as she was in the process of reaching people who might help her, perhaps her appearance might be altered. Western clothes were brought from several shops, clothes that struck Marie as odd; they seemed drab and utilitarian, neat but dreary. Not cheap, but the kind of clothes that would be selected by a woman who had either no sense of design or felt herself above it. Then after an hour in the back room of a beauty shop she understood why such a costume had been chosen. The women fussed over her; her hair was washed and blown dry, and when the process was over she had looked in the mirror, barely breathing as she did so. Her face – drawn; pale and tired – was framed by a shell of hair no longer a striking auburn but mouse-grey with subtle tinges of white. She had aged more than a decade; it was an extension of what she had attempted after escaping from the hospital but far bolder, far more complete. She was the Chinese image of the upper-middle-class, serious, no-nonsense tourist – probably a widow – who peremptorily issued instructions, counted her money, and never went anywhere without a guidebook, which she continuously checked off with each site visited on her well-organized itinerary. The people of Tuen Mun knew such tourists well and their portrait was accurate. Jason Bourne would approve.

There were other thoughts, however, that occupied her on the ride to Kowloon, desperate thoughts that she tried to control and keep in perspective, pushing away the panic that could so easily engulf her, causing her to do the wrong thing, make a wrong move that could harm David – kill David. *Oh, God, where are you? How can I find you? How?*

She searched her memory for anyone who could help her, constantly rejecting every name and every face that came to her because in one way or another each had been a part of that horrible strategy so ominously termed *beyond-salvage* – the death of an individual the only acceptable solution. Except, of course, Morris Panov, but Mo was a pariah in the eyes of the government; he had called the official killers by their rightful names: incompetents and murderers. He would get nowhere, and conceivably bring about a second order for beyond-salvage.

Beyond-salvage . . . A face came to her, a face with tears running down his cheeks, muted cries for mercy in his tremulous voice, a once-close friend of a young foreign service officer and his wife and children in a remote outpost called Phnom Penh. *Conklin!* His name was *Alexander Conklin!* Throughout David's long convalescence he had tried repeatedly to see her husband, but David would not permit it, saying that he would kill the CIA man if he walked through the door. The crippled Conklin had wrongfully, stupidly made accusations against David, not listening to the pleas of an amnesiac, instead assuming treachery and 'turning' – to the point where he had tried to kill David himself outside of Paris. And, finally, he had mounted a last attempt on New York's Seventy-first Street, at a sterile house called Treadstone 71, that nearly succeeded. When the truth about David was known, Conklin had been consumed with guilt, shattered by what he had done. She had actually felt sorry for him; his anguish was so genuine, his guilt so devastating to him. She had talked with Alex over coffee on the porch, but David would never see him. He was the only one she could think of that made sense – any sense at *all!*

The hotel was called the Empress, on Chatham Road in Kowloon. It was a small hotel in the crowded Tsim Sha Tsui frequented by a mix of cultures, neither rich nor poor, by and large salesmen from the East and West who had business to do without the largesse of executive expense accounts. The banker, Jitai, had done his job; a single room had been reserved for a Mrs Austin, Penelope Austin. The 'Penelope' had been Jitai's idea, for he had read many English novels, and Penelope seemed 'so right.' So *be it*, as Jason Bourne would have said, thought Marie.

She sat on the edge of the bed and reached for the telephone, unsure of what to say but knowing she had to say it. 'I need the number of a person in Washington, DC, in the United States,' she said to the operator. 'It's an emergency.'

'There is a charge for overseas information—'

'Charge it,' broke in Marie. 'It's urgent. I'll stay on the line.'

'*Yes?*' said the voice filled with sleep. '*Hello?*'

'Alex, it's Marie Webb.'

'*Goddamn* you, where *are* you? Where are *both* of you? He *found* you!'

'I don't know what you're talking about. I haven't found him and he hasn't found me. You *know* about all this?'

'Who the hell do you think almost broke my *neck* last week when he flew into Washington? *David!* I've got relays on every phone that can reach me! Mo Panov's got the same! Where *are* you?'

'Hong Kong – Kowloon, I guess. The Empress Hotel, under the name of Austin. David *reached* you?'

'And Mo! He and I have turned every trick in the deck to find out what the hell is going on and we've been *stonewalled!* No, I take it back – not stonewalled – no one else knows what's going on either! I'd know if they did! Good *Christ*, Marie, I haven't had a drink since last Thursday!'

'I didn't know you missed it.'

'I miss it! What's *happening?*'

Marie told him, including the unmistakable stamp of government bureaucracy on the part of her captors, and her escape, and the help given by Catherine Staples that turned into a trap, engineered by a man named McAllister, whom she had seen on the street with Staples.

'*McAllister?*' You *saw* him?'

'He's here, Alex. He wants to take me back. With me he controls *David*, and he'll *kill* him! They tried before!'

There was a pause on the line, a pause filled with anguish. '*We* tried before,' said Conklin softly. 'But that was then, not now.'

'What can I *do?*'

'Stay where you are,' ordered Alex. 'I'll be on the earliest plane to Hong Kong. Don't go out of your room. Don't make any more calls. They're searching for you, they have to be.'

'David's *out* there, Alex! Whatever they've forced him to do because of me, I'm frightened to death!'

'Delta was the best man ever developed in Medusa. No one better ever walked into that field. I know. I saw.'

'That's one aspect, and I've taught myself to live with it. But not the *other*, Alex! His *mind!* What will happen to his *mind?*'

Conklin paused again, and when he spoke his voice was pensive. 'I'll bring a friend with me, a friend to all of us. Mo won't refuse. Stay put, Marie. It's time for a showdown. And, by *Christ*, there's going to be one!'

23

'Who *are you?*' screamed Bourne in a frenzy, gripping the old man by the throat and pressing him into the wall.

'Delta, *stop it!*' commanded d'Anjou. 'Your voice! People will hear you. They'll think you're killing him. They'll call the desk.'

'I *may* kill him and the phones don't work!' Jason released the impostor's impostor, released his throat but gripped the front of his shirt, ripping it as he swung the man down into a chair.

'The *door*,' continued d'Anjou steadily, angrily. 'Put it in place as best you can, for God's sake. I want to get out of Beijing alive, and every second with you diminishes my prospects. The *door!*'

Half crazed, Bourne whipped around, picked up the shattered door and shoved it into the frame, adjusting the sides and kicking them into place. The old man massaged his throat and suddenly tried to spring out of the chair.

'*Non, mon ami!*' said the Frenchman, blocking him. 'Stay where you are. Do not concern yourself with me, only with him. You see, he really might kill you. In his rage he has no respect for the golden years, but since I'm nearly there, I do.'

'Rage'? This is an *outrage!*' sputtered the old man, coughing his words. 'I fought at El Alamein and, by Christ, I'll fight *now!*' Again the old man struggled out of the chair, and again d'Anjou pushed him back as Jason returned.

'Oh, the stoically heroic British,' observed the Frenchman. 'At least you had the grace not to say Agincourt.'

'Cut the crap!' shouted Bourne, pushing d'Anjou aside and leaning over the chair, his hands on both arms, crowding the old a man back into the seat. 'You tell me where he is and you tell me quickly, or you may wish you never got out of El Alamein!'

'Where *who* is, you maniac?'

'You're not the man downstairs! You're not Joseph Wadsworth going up to Room three-twenty-five!'

'This *is* Room three-twenty-five and I *am* Joseph Wadsworth! Brigadier, retired, Royal Engineers!'

'When did you check in?'

'Actually, I was spared that drudgery,' replied Wadsworth haughtily. 'As a professional guest of the government, certain courtesies are extended. I was escorted through customs and brought directly here. I must say the room service is hardly up to snuff – God knows, it's not the Connaught – and the damned telephone's mostly on the fritz.'

'I asked you *when!*'

'Last night, but since the plane was six hours late, I suppose I should say this morning.'

'What were your instructions?'

'I'm not sure it's any of your business.'

Bourne whipped out the brass letter-opener from his belt and held the sharp point against the old man's throat. 'It is, if you want to get out of that chair alive.'

'Good God, you *are* a maniac.'

'You're right, I haven't much time for sanity. In fact, none at all. The *instructions!*'

'They're harmless enough. I was to be picked up sometime around twelve noon, and as it's now after three, one can assume that the People's government is not run by the clock any more than its airline.'

D'Anjou touched Bourne's arm. 'The eleven-thirty plane,' said the Frenchman quietly. 'He's the decoy and knows nothing.'

'Then your Judas is here in another room,' replied Jason over his shoulder. 'He *has* to be!'

'Don't say any more, he'll be questioned.' With sudden and unexpected authority, d'Anjou edged Bourne away from the chair and spoke in the impatient tones of a superior officer. 'See here, Brigadier, we apologize for the inconvenience, it's a damned nuisance, I know. This is the third room we've broken into – we learned the name of each occupant for the purposes of shock interrogation.'

'Shock *what?* I don't understand.'

'One of four people on this floor has smuggled in over five million dollars' worth of narcotics. Since it wasn't the three of you, we have our man. I suggest you do as the others are doing. Say your room was broken into by a raging drunk, furious over the accommodations – that's what they're saying. There's a lot of that going around, and it's best not to be put under suspicion, even by mistaken association. The government here often overreacts.'

'Wouldn't want that,' sputtered Wadsworth, formerly of the Royal Engineers. 'Damned pension's little enough to get by on. This is a bloody feather from the goose's ass.'

'The door, Major,' ordered d'Anjou, addressing Jason. 'Easy, now. Try to keep it upright.' The Frenchman turned to the Englishman. 'Stand by and hold it, Brigadier. Just lean it back and give us twenty minutes to get our man, then do whatever you like. Remember, a raging drunk. For your own sake.'

'Yes, yes, of course. A drunk. Raging.'

'Come, Major!'

Out in the hallway they picked up their bags and started rapidly toward the staircase. 'Hurry *up!*' said Bourne. 'There's still time. He has to make his change – *I'd* have to make it! We'll check the street entrances, the taxi stands, try to pick two logical ones, or, goddamn it, *illogical* ones. We'll each take one and work out signals.'

'First there are two doors,' broke in d'Anjou breathlessly. 'In this hallway. Pick any two you wish, but do it quickly. Kick them in and yell abusive language, slurring your words, of course.'

'You were *serious?*'

'Never more so, Delta. As we saw for ourselves, the explanation is entirely plausible, and embarrassment will restrict any formal investigation. The management will no doubt persuade our brigadier to keep his mouth shut. They could lose their comfortable jobs. Quickly now! Take your choice and do the job!'

Jason stopped at the next door on the right. He braced himself, then rushed toward it, crashing his shoulder into the middle of the flimsy upper panel. The door flew open.

'*Madad demaa!*' screamed a woman in Hindi, half out of her sari, which was draped around her feet.

'*Kyaa baat hai?*' shrieked a naked man racing out of the bathroom, hastily covering his genitals.

Both stood gaping at the mad intruder, who lurched about with unfocused eyes as he swept articles off the nearest bureau, yelling in a coarse, drunken voice. 'Rotten hotel! *Toilets* don't work, phones don't work! Nothing – *Jesus*, this isn't my *room!* Shhorry . . .'

Bourne weaved out, slamming the door shut behind him.

'That was fine!' said d'Anjou. 'They had trouble with the lock. *Hurry.* One more. *That* one!' The Frenchman pointed to a door on the left. 'I heard laughter inside. Two voices.'

Again Jason crashed into a door, smashing it open, roaring his drunken complaints. However, instead of being met by two startled guests, he faced a young couple, both bare to the waist, each drawing on a pinched cigarette, inhaling deeply, their eyes glazed.

'Welcome, neighbour,' said the young American male, his voice floating, his diction precise, if at quarter speed. 'Don't let things trouble you so. The phones don't work, but our can does. Use it, share it. Don't get so uptight.'

'What the *hell* are you doing in my *room?*' yelled Jason even more drunkenly, his slur now obscuring his words.

'If this is your room, macho boy,' interrupted the girl, swaying in her chair, 'you were privy to private things and we're not like that.' She giggled.

'Christ, you're *stoned!*'

'And without taking the Lord's name in vain,' countered the young man, 'you're very drunk.'

'We don't believe in alcohol,' added the spaced-out girl. 'It produces hostility. It rises to the surface like Lucifer's demons.'

'Get yourself detoxified, neighbour,' continued the young American liltingly. 'Then get healthy with grass. I will lead you into the fields where you will find your soul again—'

Bourne raced out of the room slamming the door, and grabbed d'Anjou's arm. 'Let's *go,*' he said, adding as they approached the staircase, 'If that story you gave the brigadier gets around, those two will spend twenty years deballing sheep in Outer Mongolia.'

The Chinese proclivity for close observation and intense security dictated that the airport hotel have a single large entrance in the front for guests, and a second for employees at the side of the building. The latter was replete with uniformed guards who scrutinized everyone's working papers and searched all purses and bags and bulging pockets when the employees left for the day. The lack of familiarity between guards and workers suggested that the former were changed frequently, putting space between potential bribes and bribers.

'He won't chance the guards,' said Jason as they passed the employees' exit after hastily checking their two suitcases, pleading lateness for a meeting due to the delayed plane. 'They look as if they get Brownie points for picking up anyone who steals a chicken wing or a bar of soap.'

'They also intensely dislike those who work here,' agreed d'Anjou. 'But why are you so certain he's still in the hotel? He knows Beijing. He could have taken a taxi to another hotel, another room.'

'Not looking the way he did on the plane, I told you that. He wouldn't allow it. *I* wouldn't. He wants the freedom to move around without being spotted or followed. He's got to have it for his own protection.'

'If that's the case, they could be watching his room right now. Same results. They'll know what he looks like.'

'If it were me – and that's all I've got to go on – he's not there. He's made arrangements for another room.'

'You contradict yourself!' objected the Frenchman as they approached the crowded entrance of the airport hotel. 'You said he'd be receiving his instructions by phone. Whoever calls will ask for the room they assigned him, certainly not the decoy's, not Wadsworth's.'

'If the phones are working – a condition that's a plus for your Judas, incidentally – it's a simple matter to have calls transferred from one room to another. A plug is inserted in the switchboard if it's primitive, or programmed if it's computerized. It's not a big deal. A business conference, old friends on the plane – read that any way you like – or no explanation at all, which is probably best.'

'Fallacy!' proclaimed d'Anjou. 'His client here in Beijing will alert the hotel operators. He'll be wired into the switchboard.'

'That's the one thing he won't do,' said Bourne, pushing the Frenchman through a revolving door out onto the pavement, which was crawling with confused tourists and businessmen trying to arrange transportation. 'It's a gamble he can't afford to take,' continued Jason as they walked past a line of small, shabby buses and well-aged taxis at the kerb. 'Your commando's client has to keep maximum distance between the two of them. There can't be the slightest possibility that a connection could be traced, so that means everything's restricted to a very tight, very elite circle, with no runs on a switchboard, no calling attention to anyone, especially your commando. They won't risk wandering around the hotel either. They'll stay away from him, let him make the moves. There are too many secret police here; someone in that elite circle could be recognized.'

'The phones, Delta. From all we've heard, they're *not* working. What does he do then?'

Jason frowned while walking, as if trying to recall the unremembered. 'Time's on his side, that's the plus. He'll have backup instructions to follow in case he's not reached within a given period of time after his arrival – for whatever reasons – and there could be any number considering the precautions they have to take.'

'In that event they'd still be watching for him, wouldn't they? They'd wait somewhere outside and try to pick him up, no?'

'Of course, and he knows that. He has to get by them and reach his position without being seen. It's the only way he retains control. It's his first job.'

D'Anjou gripped Bourne's elbow. 'Then I think I've just spotted one of the spotters.'

'What?' Jason turned, looking down at the Frenchman and slowing his pace.

'Keep walking,' ordered d'Anjou. 'Head over to that truck, the one half out on the street with the man on the extension ladder.'

'It follows,' said Bourne. 'It's the telephone repair service.' Remaining anonymous in the crowds, they reached the truck.

'Look up. Look interested. Then look to your left. The van quite far ahead of the first bus. Do you see it?'

Jason did, and instantly he knew the Frenchman was right. The van was white and fairly new and had tinted glass windows. Except for the colour it could be the van that had picked up the assassin in Shenzen, at the Lo Wu border. Bourne started to read the Chinese characters on the door panel. '*Niao Jing Shan* . . . My God, it's the same! The name doesn't matter – it belongs to a *bird sanctuary*, the Jing Shan *Bird* Sanctuary! In Shenzen it was Chutang, here something else. How did you notice it?'

'The man in the open window, the last window on this side. You can't see him too clearly from here, but he's looking back at the entrance. He's also somewhat of a contradiction – for an employee of a bird sanctuary, that is.'

'Why?'

'He's an army officer, and by the cut of his tunic and the obviously superior fabric, one of high rank. Is the glorious People's Army now conscripting egrets for its assault troops? Or is he an anxious man waiting for someone he's been ordered to pick up and follow, using a rather acceptable cover flawed by an angle of sight that demands an open window?'

'Can't go anywhere without Echo,' said Jason Bourne, once Delta, the scourge of Medusa. 'Bird sanctuaries – Christ, it's *beautiful*. What a smoke screen. So removed, so peaceful. It's one *hell* of a cover.'

'It's so Chinese, Delta. The righteous mask conceals the unrighteous face. The Confucian parables warn of it.'

'That's not what I'm talking about. Back in Shenzen, at Lo Wu, where I missed your boy the first time, he was picked up by a van then – a van with tinted windows – and it also belonged to a government bird sanctuary.'

'As you say, an excellent cover.'

'It's more than that, Echo. It's some kind of mark or identification.'

'Birds have been revered in China for centuries,' said d'Anjou, looking at Jason, his expression puzzled. 'They've always been depicted in their great art, the great silks. They're considered delicacies for both the eye and the palate.'

'In this case they could be a means to something much simpler, much more practical.'

'Such as?'

'Bird sanctuaries are large preserves. They're open to the public but subject to government regulations, as they are everywhere.'

'Your point, Delta?'

'In a country where any ten people opposed to the official line are afraid to be seen together, what better place than a nature preserve that usually stretches for miles? No offices or houses or apartments being watched, no telephone taps or electronic surveillance. Just innocent bird-watchers in a nation of bird lovers, each holding an official pass that permits him entry when the sanctuary is officially closed – day or night.'

'From Shenzen to Peking? You're implying a situation larger than we had considered.'

'Whatever it is,' said Jason, glancing around. 'It doesn't concern us. Only *he* does . . . We've got to separate but stay in sight. I'll head over—'

'No need!' broke in the Frenchman. 'There he is!'

'*Where?*'

'Move back! Closer to the truck. In its shadow.'

'Which one *is* he?'

'The priest patting the child, the little girl,' answered d'Anjou, his back to the truck, staring into the crowd in front of the hotel's entrance. 'A man of the cloth,' continued the Frenchman bitterly. 'One of the guises I taught him to use. He had a priestly black suit made for him in Hong Kong complete with an Anglican benediction sewn into the collar under the name of a Savile Row tailor. It was the suit I recognized first. I paid for it.'

'You come from a wealthy diocese,' said Bourne, studying the man he wanted more than his life to race over and take, to subdue and force up into a hotel room and start on the road back to Marie. The assassin's cover was good – more than good – and Jason tried to analyze that judgement. Grey sideburns protruded below the killer's dark hat; thin steel-rimmed glasses were perched low on the nose of his pale, colourless face. His eyes wide and his brows arched, he showed joy and wonder at what he saw in this unfamiliar place. All were God's works and God's children, signified by the act of being drawn to a little Chinese girl and patting her head lovingly, smiling and nodding graciously to the mother. That was it, thought Jason, in grudging respect. The son of a bitch exuded *love*. It was in his every gesture, every hesitant movement, every glance of his gentle eyes. He *was* a compassionate man of the cloth, a shepherd of his flock. And as such, in a crowd he might be glanced at but instantly dismissed by eyes seeking out a killer.

Bourne remembered. *Carlos!* The Jackal had been dressed in the clothes of a priest, his dark Latin features above the starched white collar, walking out of the church in Neuilly-sur-Seine in Paris. Jason had *seen* him! They had seen each other, their eyes locking, each knowing who the other was without words being spoken. *Get Carlos. Trap Carlos. Cain is for Charlie and Carlos is for*

Cain! The codes had exploded in his head as he raced after the Jackal in the streets of Paris . . . only to lose him in the traffic, as an old beggar, squatting on the pavement, smiled obscenely.

This was not Paris, thought Bourne. There was no army of dying old men protecting this assassin. He would take this jackal in Peking.

'Be ready to move!' said d'Anjou, breaking into Jason's memories. 'He's nearing the bus.'

'It's full.'

'That's the point. He'll be the last one on. Who refuses a pleading priest in a hurry? One of my lessons, of course.'

Again the Frenchman was right. The door of the small, packed shabby bus began to close, stopped by the inserted arm of the priest, who wedged his shoulder inside and obviously begged to be released, as he had been caught. The door snapped open; the killer pressed himself inside and the door closed.

'It's the express to Tian An Men Square,' said d'Anjou. 'I have the number.'

'We have to find a taxi. Come on!'

'It will not be easy, Delta.'

'I've perfected a technique,' replied Bourne, walking out of the shadow of the telephone truck as the bus passed by, the Frenchman at his heels. They weaved through the crowd in front of the airport hotel and proceeded down the line of taxis until they reached the end. A last cab rounded the circle, about to join the line, when Jason rushed into the street, holding up the palms of his hands unobtrusively. The taxi came to a stop as the driver pushed his head out the window.

'*Shemma?*'

'*Wei!*' cried Bourne, running to the driver and holding up fifty American dollars' worth of unmetered yuan. '*Bi yao bang zhu*,' he said, telling the man he needed help badly and would pay for it.

'*Hao!*' exclaimed the driver as he grabbed the money. '*Bingle ba!*' he added, justifying his action on behalf of a tourist who was suddenly ill.

Jason and d'Anjou climbed in, the driver vocally annoyed that there was a second fare entering the kerbside door. Bourne dropped another twenty yuan over the seat, and the man was mollified. He swung his cab around, away from the line of taxis, and retraced his path out of the airport complex.

'Up ahead there is a bus,' said d'Anjou, leaning forward in the seat, addressing the driver in an awkward attempt at Mandarin. 'Can you understand me?'

'Your tongue is Guangzhou, but I understand.'

'It is on the way to Tian An Men Square.'

'Which gate?' asked the driver. 'Which bridge?'

'I don't know. I know only the number on the front of the bus. It is seven-four-two-one.'

'Number one ending,' said the driver. 'Tian Gate, second bridge. Imperial city entrance.'

'Is there a parking section for the buses?'

'There will be a line of many bus-vehicles. All are filled. They are very crowded. Tian An Men is very crowded this angle of the sun.'

'We should pass the bus I speak of on the road, which is favorable to us for we wish to be at Tian An Men before it arrives. Can you do this?'

'Without difficulty,' answered the driver, grinning. 'Bus-vehicles are old and often break down. We may get there several days before it reaches the heavenly north gate.'

'I hope you're not serious,' interrupted Bourne.

'Oh, no, generous tourist. All the drivers are superior mechanics – when they have the good fortune to locate their engines.' The driver laughed contemptuously and pressed his foot on the accelerator.

Three minutes later they passed the 'bus-vehicle' carrying the killer. Forty-six minutes after that they reached the sculptured white marble bridge over the flowing waters of a man-made moat that fronted the massive Gate of Heavenly Peace, where the leaders of China displayed themselves on the wide platform above, approving the paraded instruments of war and death. Inside the misnomered gate is one of the most extraordinary human achievements on earth. Tian An Men Square. The electrifying vortex of Beijing.

The majesty of its sheer vastness first catches the visitor's eye, then the architectural immensity of the Great Hall of the People on the right, where reception areas accommodate as many as three thousand people. The single banquet hall seats over five thousand, the major 'conference room' ten thousand with space to spare. On the opposite side of the Gate, reaching toward the clouds, is a four-sided shaft of stone, an obelisk mounted on a two-story terrace of balustraded marble, all glistening in the sunlight, while in the shadows below on the huge base of the structure are carved the struggles and triumphs of Mao's revolution. It is the Monument to the People's Heroes, Mao first in the pantheon. There are other building, other structures – memorials, museums, gates and libraries – as far as the eye can see. But, above all, the eye is struck by the compelling vastness of open space. Space and people . . . and for the ear something else, totally unexpected. A dozen of the world's great stadiums, all dwarfing Rome's Colosseum, could be placed within Tian An Men Square and not exhaust the acreage; people in the hundreds of thousands can wander about the open areas and still leave room for hundreds of thousands more. But there is an absence of an element whose lack would never have been found in Rome's bloody arena, much less tolerated in the contemporary great stadiums of the world. Sound; it is barely there, only decibels above silence, interrupted by the soft rippling notes of bicycle bells. The quiet is at first peaceful, and then frightening. It is as though an enormous, transparent geodesic dome had been lowered over a hundred acres, as an unspoken, but understood, command from a nether kingdom repeatedly informs those below that they are in a cathedral. It is unnatural, unreal, and yet there is no hostility toward the unheard voice, only acceptance – and that is more frightening. Especially when the children are quiet.

Jason observed these things quickly and dispassionately. He paid the driver the sum based on the odometer reading and shifted his concentration to the purpose and the problems facing him and d'Anjou. For whatever reason, whether a phone call had reached him or whether he had opted for back-up instructions, the commando was on his way to Tian An Men Square. The pavane would begin with his arrival, the slow steps of the cautious dance bringing the killer closer and closer to his client's representative, the assumption being that the client would remain out of sight. But no contact would be made until the impostor was convinced the rendezvous was clean. Therefore the 'priest' would mount his own surveillance, circling the appointed coordinates of the meeting ground, searching out whatever armed minions were in place. He would take one, perhaps two, pressing them at the point of a knife or jamming a silenced gun into their ribs to elicit the information he needed; a false look in the eyes would tell him that the conference was a prelude to execution. Finally, if the landscape seemed clear, he would propel a minion under a gun to approach the client's representative and give his ultimatum: the client himself must show up and walk into the net of the assassin's making. Anything else was unacceptable; the central figure, the client, had to be the deadly balance. A second meeting ground would be established. The client would arrive first, and at the first sign of deception he would be blown away. That was the way of Jason Bourne. It would be the commando's if he had half a brain in his head.

Bus number 7421 rolled lethargically into place at the end of the line of vehicles disgorging tourists. The assassin in priestly garb emerged, helping an elderly woman down to the pavement, patting her hand as he nodded his gentle good-byes. He turned away, walked rapidly to the rear of the bus, and disappeared around it.

'Stay a good thirty feet behind and watch me,' said Jason. 'Do as I do. When I stop, you stop; when I turn, you turn. Be in a crowd; go from one group to another, but make sure there are always people around you.'

'Be careful, Delta. He is not an amateur.'

'Neither am I.' Bourne ran to the end of the bus, stopped, and edged his way around the hot, foul-smelling louvres of the rear engine. His priest was about fifty yards ahead, his black suit a dark beacon in the hazy sunlight. Crowds or no crowds, he was easy to follow. The commando's cover was acceptable, his playing of it even more so, but like most covers there was always the glaring but unrecognized liability. It was in limiting those liabilities that the best distinguished themselves from the merely better. Professionally, Jason approved the clerical status, not the clerical colour. A Roman priest might be wedded to black, but not an Anglican vicar; a solid grey was perfectly acceptable under the collar. Grey faded in the sunlight, black did not.

Suddenly, the assassin broke away from the crowd and walked up behind a Chinese soldier taking pictures, the camera at eye level, the soldier's head moving constantly. Bourne understood. This was no insignificant enlisted man on leave in Beijing; he was too mature, his uniform too well tailored – as d'Anjou had remarked about the army officer in the truck. The camera was a transparent device to scan the crowds; the initial meeting ground was not far away. The commando, now playing his role to the fullest, clasped a fatherly right hand on the military man's left shoulder. His left was unseen, but his black coat filled the space between them – a gun had been jammed into the officer's ribs. The soldier froze, his expression stoic even in his panic. He moved with the assassin, the commando now gripping his arm and issuing orders. The soldier abruptly, out of character, bent over, holding his left side, recovering quickly and shaking his head; the weapon had been rammed again into his rib cage. He would follow orders, or he would die in Tian An Men Square. There was no compromise.

Bourne spun around, lowering his body and tying a perfectly firm shoelace, apologizing to those behind him. The assassin had checked his rear flank; the evasive action was demanded. Jason stood up. Where *was* he? Where was the *impostor? There!* Bourne was bewildered; the commando had let the soldier go! *Why?* The army officer was suddenly running through the crowds, screaming, his gestures wildly spastic, then in a frenzy he collapsed, and chattering, excited people gathered around his unconscious body.

Diversion! *Watch* him. Jason raced ahead, feeling the time was right. It had been not a gun but a needle – not jammed but puncturing the soldier's rib cage. The assassin had taken out one protector; he would look for another, and perhaps another after that. The scenario Bourne had predicted was being played out. And as the killer's concentration was solely on his search for his next victim, the time was right! *Now!* Jason knew he could take out anyone on earth with a paralyzing blow to the kidneys, especially a man whose least concern was an attack on himself – for the quarry was attacking and his concentration was absolute. Bourne closed the gap between himself and the impostor. Fifty feet, forty, thirty-five, thirty . . . he broke away from one crowd into another . . . the black-suited 'priest' was within reach. He could *take* him! *Marie!*

A soldier. Another soldier! But now, instead of an assault there was communication. The army man nodded and gestured to his left. Jason looked over, bewildered. A short Chinese in civilian clothing and carrying a government briefcase was standing at the foot of a wide stone staircase that led up to the entrance of an immense building with granite pillars everywhere supporting twin sloping pagoda roofs. It was directly behind the Heroes' Monument, the carved calligraphy over the huge doors proclaiming it to be the Chairman Mao Memorial Hall. Two lines were moving up the steps, guards separating the individual groups. The civilian was between the two lines, the briefcase a symbol of authority; he was left alone. Suddenly, without any indication that he would make such a move, the tall assassin gripped the soldier's arm, propelling the smaller army man in front of him. The officer's back arched, his shoulders snapping upright; a weapon had been shoved into his spine, the commands specific.

As the excitement mounted and the crowds and the police kept running to the collapsed first soldier, the assassin and his captive walked steadily toward the civilian at the steps of the Mao Memorial. The man was afraid to move, and again Bourne understood. These men were known to the killer; they were at the core of the tight, elite circle that led to the assassin's client, and that client was nearby. They were no mere minions; once they appeared the lesser figures took on lesser importance, for these men rarely exposed themselves. The diversion, which was now reduced to a mild disturbance as the police swiftly controlled the crowds and carried the body away, had given the impostor the seconds he needed to control the chain that led to the client.

The soldier in his grip was dead if he disobeyed, and with a single shot any reasonably competent marksman could kill the man by the steps. The meeting was in two stages, and as long as the assassin controlled the second stage he was perfectly willing to proceed. The client was obviously somewhere inside the vast mausoleum and could not know what was happening outside, nor would a mere minion dare follow his superiors up into the conference area.

There was no more time for analysing, Jason knew. He had to act. *Quickly.* He had to get inside Mao Zedong's monument and watch, wait for the meeting to conclude one way or another – and the repugnant possibility that he might have to protect the assassin crossed his mind. Yet it was within the realm of reality and the only plus for him was the fact that the impostor had followed a scenario he himself might have created. And if the conference was peaceful, it was simply a matter of following the assassin, by then inevitably buoyed by the success of his tactics as well as by whatever the client delivered – and taking an unsuspecting supreme egotist in Tian An Men Square.

Bourne turned, looking for d'Anjou. The Frenchman was on the edge of a controlled tourist group; he nodded, as if he had read Delta's thoughts. He pointed to the ground beneath him, then made a circle with his index finger. It was a silent signal from their days in Medusa. It meant he would remain where he was, but if he had to move he would stay in sight of that specific location. It was enough. Jason crossed behind the assassin and his prisoner, and walked diagonally through the crowd, rapidly negotiating the open space to the line on the right half of the staircase and up to the guard. He spoke pleadingly in polite Mandarin: 'High Officer, I'm most embarrassed! I was so taken by the calligraphy on the People's Monument that I lost my group, which passed through here only minutes ago.'

'You speak our language very well,' said the astonished guard, apparently used to the strange accents of tongues he neither knew nor cared to know. 'You are most courteous.'

'I'm simply an underpaid teacher from the West who has an enduring love of your great nation, High Officer.'

The guard laughed. 'I'm not so high, but our nation is great. My daughter wears blue jeans in the street.'

'I beg your pardon?'

'It's nothing. Where is your tour-group identification?'

'My what?'

'The name tag to be worn on all outer clothing.'

'It kept falling off,' said Bourne, shaking his head helplessly. 'It wouldn't stay pinned. I must have lost it.'

'When you catch up, see your guide and get another. Go ahead. Get in back of the line on the steps. Something is going on. The next group may have to wait. You'll miss your tour.'

'Oh? Is there a problem?'

'I don't know. The official with the government briefcase gives us our orders. I believe he counts the yuan that could be made here, thinking this holy place should be like Beijing's underground train.'

'You've been most kind.'

'Hurry, sir.'

Bourne rushed up the steps, bending down behind the crowd, once again tightening a secure shoelace, his head angled to watch the assassin's progress. The imposter talked quietly to the civilian with the soldier still in his grip – but something was odd. The short Chinese in the dark suit nodded, but his eyes were not on the impostor; they were focused beyond the commando. Or were they? Jason's angle of vision was not the best. No matter, the scenario was being followed, the client reached on the assassin's terms.

He walked through the doors into the semidarkness, as awed as everyone in front of him by the sudden appearance of the enormous white marble sculpture of a seated Mao, rising so high and so majestically that one nearly gasped in its presence. Too, theatricality was not omitted. The shafts of light that played on the exquisite, seemingly translucent marble created an ethereal effect that isolated the gigantic sitting figure from the velvet tapestry behind it and the outer darkness around it. The massive statue with its searching eyes seemed alive and aware.

Jason pulled his own eyes away and looked for doorways and corridors. There were none. It *was* a mausoleum, a hall dedicated to a nation's saint. But there were pillars, wide high shafts of marble that provided areas of seclusion. In the shadows behind any one of them could be the meeting ground. He would wait. He would stay in other shadows and watch.

His group entered the second great hall, and it was, if anything, more electrifying than the first. Facing them was a crystal glass coffin encasing the body of Chairman Mao Zedong, draped in the Red flag, the waxen corpse in peaceful repose – the closed eyes, however, any second likely to open wide and glare in fiery disapproval. There were flowers surrounding the raised sarcophagus, and two rows of dark green pine trees in huge ceramic pots lined the opposing walls. Again shafts of light played a dramatic symphony of colour, pockets of darkness pierced by intersecting beams that washed over the brilliant yellows and reds and blues of the banks of flowers.

A commotion somewhere in the first hall briefly intruded on the awed silence of the crowd, but was arrested as rapidly as it had begun. As the last tourist in line, Bourne broke away without being noticed by the others. He slipped behind a pillar, concealed in the shadows, and peered around the glistening white marble.

What he saw paralysed him as a dozen thoughts clashed in his head – above all, the single word *trap!* There was no group following his own! It was the last admitted – *he* was the last *person* admitted – before the heavy doors were closed. That was the sound he had heard – the shutting of the doors and the disappointed groans from those outside waiting to be admitted.

Something is going on . . . The next group may have to wait . . . A kindly guard on the steps.

My God, from the beginning it was a *trap!* Every move, every appearance had been calculated! From the *beginning!* The information paid for on a rain-soaked island, the nearly unobtainable airline tickets, the first sight of the assassin at the airport – a professional killer capable of a far better disguise, his hair too obvious, his clothes inadequate to cover his frame. Then the complication with an old man, a retired brigadier from the Royal Engineers – so illogically logical! So right, the scent of deception so accurate, so irresistible! A soldier in a truck's window, not looking for *him* but for *them!* The priestly black suit – a dark beacon in the sunlight, paid for by the impostor's creator – so easily spotted, so easily followed. *Christ*, from the *beginning!* Finally, the scenario played out in the immense square, a scenario that could have been written by Bourne himself – again irresistible to the pursuer. A reverse trap: Catch the hunter as he stalks his quarry!

Frantically Jason looked around. Ahead in the distance was a steady shaft of sunlight. The exit doors were at the other end of the mausoleum; they would be watched, each tourist studied as he left.

Footsteps. Over his right shoulder. Bourne spun to his left, pulling the brass letter-opener from his belt. A figure in a grey Mao suit, the cut military, cautiously passed by the wide pillar in the dim outer light of the pine trees. He was no more than five feet away. In his hand was a gun, the bulging cylinder on the barrel a guarantee that a detonation would be reduced to the sound of a spit. Jason made his lethal calculations in a way David Webb would never understand. The blade had to be inserted in such a way as to cause instant death. No noise could come from his enemy's mouth as the body was pulled back into darkness.

He lunged, the rigid fingers of his left hand clamped vice-like over the man's face as he plunged the letter-opener into the soldier's neck, the blade rushing through sinew and fragile cartilage, severing the windpipe. In one motion, Bourne dropped his left hand, clutching the large weapon still in his enemy's grip, and swung the corpse around, dropping with it under the branches of the row of pine trees lined up along the right wall. He slid the body out of sight into the dark shadows between two large ceramic pots holding the roots of two trees. He crawled over the corpse, the weapon in front of his face, and made his way back against the wall toward the first hall, to where he could see without being seen.

A second uniformed man crossed through the shaft of light that lit up the darkness of the entrance to the second hall. He stood in front of Mao's crystal coffin, awash in the eerie beams, and looked around. He raised a hand-held radio to his face and spoke, listening; five seconds later his expression changed to one of concern. He began walking rapidly to his right, tracing the assigned path of the first man. Jason scrambled back toward the corpse, hands and knees silently pounding the marble floor, and moved out toward the edge of the low-slung branches.

The soldier approached, walking more slowly, studying the last people in the line up ahead. *Now!* Bourne sprang up as the man passed, hammerlocking his neck, choking off all sound as he pulled him back down under the branches, the gun pressed far up in the flesh of the soldier's stomach. He pulled the trigger; the muffled report was like a burst of air, no more. The man expunged a last violent breath and went limp.

He had to get *out!* If he was trapped and killed in the awesome silence of the mausoleum, the assassin would roam free and Marie's death would be assured. His enemies were closing the reverse trap. He had to reverse the reversal and somehow survive! *The cleanest escape is made in stages, using whatever confusion there is or can be created.*

Stages One and Two were accomplished. A certain confusion already existed if other men were whispering into radios. What had to be brought about was a focal point of disruption so violent and unexpected that those hunting him in the shadows would themselves become the subjects of a sudden, hysterical search.

There was only one way and Jason felt no obscure heroic feelings of I-may-die-trying. He *had* to do it! He had to make it work. Survival was everything, for reasons beyond himself. The professional was at his apex, calm and deliberate.

Bourne stood up and walked through branches, crossing the open space to the pillar in front of him. He then ran to the one behind, and then the one behind that, the first pillar in the second hall, thirty feet from the dramatically lit coffin. He edged his body around the marble and waited, his eyes on the entrance door.

It happened. *They* happened. The officer who was the assassin's 'captive' emerged with the short civilian carrying his government briefcase. The soldier held a radio at his side; he brought it up to speak and listen, then shook his head, placing the radio in his right-hand pocket and removing the gun from his holster. The civilian nodded once, reached under his jacket and pulled out a short-barrelled revolver. Each walked forward toward the glass coffin containing the remains of Mao Zedong, then looked at each other and began to separate, one to the left, one to the right.

Now! Jason raised his weapon, took rapid aim and fired. *Once!* A hair to the right. *Twice!* The spits were like coughs in shadows as both men fell into the sarcophagus. Grabbing the edges of his coat, Bourne gripped the hot cylinder on the barrel of his pistol and spun it off. There were five shells left. He squeezed the trigger in rapid succession. The explosions filled the mausoleum, echoing off the marble walls, shattering the crystal glass of the coffin, the bullets embedding themselves in the spastically jerked corpse of Mao Zedong, one penetrating a bloodless forehead, another blowing out an eye.

Sirens erupted; clamouring bells split the air and deafened the ear, as soldiers, appearing at once from everywhere, raced in panic toward the scene of the horrible outrage. The two lines of tourists, feeling trapped in the eerie light of the house of death, exploded into hysteria. En masse, the crowds rushed toward the doors and the sunlight, trampling those in their paths. Jason Bourne joined them, crashing his way into the centre of an inside column. Reaching the blinding light of Tian An Men Square, he raced down the steps.

D'Anjou! Jason ran to his right, rounding the stone corner, and ran down the side of the pillared structure until he reached the front. Guards were doing their best to calm the agitated crowds while trying to find out what had happened. A riot was in the making.

Bourne studied the place where he had last seen d'Anjou, then moved his eyes over a grid area within which the Frenchman might logically be seen. Nothing, no one even vaguely resembling him.

Suddenly, there was the screeching of tyres far off on a thoroughfare to

Jason's left. He whipped around and looked. A van with tinted windows had circled the stanchioned pavement and was speeding toward the south gate of Tian An Men Square.

They had taken d'Anjou. Echo was gone.

24

'*Qu'est-ce qu'il y a?*

'*Des coups de feu! Les gardes sont paniqués!*'

Bourne heard the shouts and, running, joined the group of French tourists led by a guide whose concentration was riveted on the chaos taking place on the steps of the mausoleum. He buttoned his jacket, covering the gun in his belt, and slipped the perforated silencer into his pocket. Glancing around, he moved quickly back through the crowd next to a man taller than himself, a well-dressed man with a disdainful expression on his face. Jason was grateful that there were several others of nearly equal height in front of them; with luck and in the excitement he might remain inconspicuous. Above, at the top of the mausoleum's stairs, the doors had been partially opened. Uniformed men were racing back and forth along the stairs. Obviously the leadership was a shambles, and Bourne knew why. It had fled, had simply disappeared, wanting no part of the terrible events. All that concerned Jason now was the assassin. Would he come out? Or had he found d'Anjou, capturing his creator himself and leaving with Echo in the van, convinced that the original Jason Bourne was trapped, a second unlikely corpse in the desecrated mausoleum.

'*Qu'est-ce que c'est?*' asked Jason, addressing the tall, well-dressed Frenchman beside him.

'Another ungodly delay, no doubt,' replied the man in a somewhat effeminate Parisian accent. 'This place is a madhouse, and my tolerance is at an end! I'm going back to the hotel.'

'Can you do that?' Bourne upgraded his French from middle-class to a decent *université*. It meant so much to a Parisien. 'I mean, are we permitted to leave our tour? We hear constantly that we must stay together.'

'I'm a businessman, not a tourist. This "tour," as you call it, was not part of my agenda. Frankly, I had the afternoon off – these people linger endlessly over decisions – and thought I'd take in a few sights, but there wasn't a French-speaking driver available. The concierge assigned me – mind you, *assigned* me – to this group. The guide, you know, is a student of French literature and speaks as though she had been born in the seventeenth century. I haven't a clue what this so-called tour is all about.'

'It's the five-hour excursion,' explained Jason accurately, reading the Chinese characters printed on the identification tag affixed to the man's lapel. 'After Tian An Men Square we visit the Ming tombs, then drive out to watch the sunset from the Great Wall.'

'Now, really, I've *seen* the Great Wall! My God, it was the first place all twelve of those bureaucrats from the Trade Commission took me, prattling incessantly through the interpreter that it was a sign of their permanence. Shit! If the labour wasn't so unbelievably cheap and the profits so extraordinary—'

'I, too, am in business, but for a few days also a tourist. My line is wicker imports. What's yours, if I may ask?'

'Fabrics, what else? Unless you consider electronics, or oil, or coal, or perfume – even wicker.' The businessman allowed himself a superior and knowing smile. 'I tell you, these people are sitting on the wealth of the world and they haven't the vaguest idea what to *do* with it.'

Bourne looked closely at the tall Frenchman. He thought of Medusa's Echo and a Gallic aphorism that proclaimed that the more things changed the more they remained the same. *Opportunities will present themselves. Recognize them, act on them.* 'As I said,' continued Jason while staring up at the chaos on the staircase, 'I, too, am a businessman, who is taking a short sabbatical – courtesy of our government's tax incentives for those of us who plough the foreign fields – but I've travelled a great deal here in China and have learned a good deal of the language.'

'Wicker has come up in the world,' said the Parisien sardonically.

'Our quality product is a white-enameled staple of the Côte d'Azur, as well as points north and south. The family Grimaldi has been a client for years.' Bourne kept his eyes on the staircase.

'I stand corrected, my business friend . . . in the foreign fields.' For the first time the Frenchman actually looked at Jason.

'And I can tell you now,' said Bourne, 'that no more visitors will be permitted into Mao's tomb, and that everyone on every tour in the vicinity will be cordoned off and possibly detained.'

'My God, *why?*'

'Apparently something terrible happened inside and the guards are shouting about foreign gangsters . . . Did you say you were *assigned* to this tour but not really a part of it?'

'Essentially, yes.'

'Grounds for at least speculation, no? Detention, almost certainly.'

'*Inconceivable!*'

'This is China—'

'It cannot be! Millions upon millions of francs are hanging in the balance! I'm only here on this horrid tour because—'

'I suggest you leave, my business friend. Say you were out for a stroll. Give me your identification tag and I'll get rid of it for you—'

'Is *that* what it is?'

'Your country of origin and passport number are on it. It's how they control your movements while you're on a guided tour.'

'I'm *forever* in your debt!' cried the businessman, ripping the plastic tag off his lapel. 'If you're ever in Paris—'

'I spend most of the time with the prince and his family in—'

'But of *course!* Again, my thanks!' The Frenchman, so different and yet so much like Echo, left in a hurry, his well-dressed figure conspicuous in the hazy, greyish-yellow sunlight as he headed toward the Heavenly Gate – as obvious as the false quarry who had led a hunter into a trap.

Bourne pinned the plastic tag to his own lapel and now became part of an official tour; it was his way out of the gates of Tian An Men Square. After the group had been hastily diverted from the mausoleum to the Great Hall, the bus passed through the northern gate, and Jason saw through the window the apoplectic French businessman pleading with the Beijing police to let him pass. Fragments of reports of the outrage had been fitted together. The word was spreading. A white foreigner had horribly defiled the coffin and the hallowed body of Chairman Mao. A white terrorist from a tour without the proper identification on his outer clothing. A guard on the steps had reported such a man.

'I do recalleth,' said the tour guide in obsolete French. She was standing by the statue of an angry lion on that extraordinary Avenue of Animals, where huge stone replicas of large cats, horses, elephants, and ferocious mythical beasts lined the road, guarding the final way to the tombs of the Ming Dynasty. 'But my memory faileth where your usage of our language concerns my immediate reflections. And I do feel without reflected doubt that you just performed that indulgence.'

A student of French literature and speaks as though she were in the seventeenth century . . . an indignant businessman, now undoubtedly far more indignant.

'I didn't before,' replied Bourne in Mandarin, 'because you were with others and I didn't care to stand out. But let's speak your language now.'

'You do so very well.'

'I thank you. Then you do recall that I was added to your tour at the last minute?'

'The manager of the Beijing Hotel actually spoke to my superior, but, yes, I do recall.' The woman smiled and shrugged. 'In truth, as it is such a large group, I only recall giving a tall man his tour-group emblem, and it is in front of my face right now. You will have to pay additional yuan on your hotel bill. I am sorry, but then you are not part of the tourist programme.'

'No, I'm not, because I'm a businessman negotiating with your government.'

'May you do well,' said the guide with her piquant smile. 'Some do, some do not.'

'My point is that I may not be able to do *anything*,' said Jason, smiling back. 'My Chinese speech is far better than my Chinese reading. A few minutes ago several words fell into place for me and I realized I'm to be at the Beijing Hotel in about a half hour from now for a meeting. How can I do that?'

'It is a question of finding transportation. I will write out what you need and you can present it to the guards at the Dahongmen—'

'The Great Red Gate?' interrupted Bourne. 'The one with the arches?'

'Yes. There are bus-vehicles that will take you back to Beijing. You may be late, but then it is customary, I understand, for government people to be late also.' She took out a notebook from the pocket of her Mao jacket and then a reedlike ballpoint pen.

'I won't be stopped?'

'If you are, ask those who stop you to call the government people,' said the guide, writing out instructions in Chinese and tearing off the page.

'This is not your tour group!' barked the operator of the bus in lower-class Mandarin, shaking his head and stabbing his finger at Jason's lapel. The man obviously expected his words to have no effect whatsoever on the tourist, so he compensated with exaggerated gestures and a strident voice. It was also apparent that he hoped that one of his superiors under the arches of the Great Red Gate would take notice of his alertness. One did.

'What's the problem?' asked a well-spoken soldier, walking rapidly up to the door of the bus, parting his way through the tourists behind Bourne.

Opportunities will present themselves . . .

'There's no problem,' said Jason curtly, even arrogantly, in Chinese, as he withdrew the guide's note, thrusting it into the hand of the young officer. 'Unless you wish to be responsible for my missing an urgent meeting with a delegation from the Trade Commission, whose military procurements chief is a General Liang-Somebody-or-other.'

'You speak the Chinese language.' Startled, the soldier pulled his eyes away from the note.

'I'd say that's obvious. So does General Liang.'

'I do not understand your anger.'

'Perhaps you'll understand General Liang's,' interrupted Bourne.

'I do not know a General Liang, sir, but then there are so many generals. You are upset with the tour?'

'I'm upset with the fools who told me it was a three-hour excursion when it turns out to be *five* hours! If I miss this meeting because of incompetence there'll be several *very* upset commissioners, including a powerful general of the People's army who's anxious to conclude certain purchases from France.' Jason paused, holding up his hand, then continued quickly in a softer voice. 'If, however, I get there on time I'll certainly commend – by name – anyone who might help me.'

'*I* will help you, sir!' said the young officer, his eyes bright with dedication. 'This sick whale of a bus could take you well over an hour, and that is only if this miserable driver stays on the road. I have at my disposal a much faster vehicle and a fine driver who will escort you. I would do so myself, but it would not be proper to leave my post.'

'I'll also mention your commitment to duty to the general.'

'It's my natural instinct, sir. My name is—'

'Yes, do let me have your name. Write it on that slip of paper.'

Bourne sat in the bustling lobby of the Beijing Hotel's east wing, a half-folded newspaper covering his face, the left edge off-centre so he could see the line of doors that was the entrance. He was waiting, watching for the sight of Jean-Louis Ardisson of Paris. It had not been difficult for Jason to learn his name. Twenty minutes ago he had walked up to the guided-tour travel desk and said to the female clerk in his best Mandarin, 'I'm sorry to bother you, but I'm first interpreter for all French delegations having business with government industry, and I'm afraid I've lost one of my confused sheep.'

'You must be a fine interpreter. You speak excellent Chinese. What happened to your . . . bewildered sheep?' The woman permitted herself a slight giggle at the phrase.

'I'm not sure. We were having coffee in the cafeteria, about to go over his schedule, when he looked at his watch and said he would call me later. He was going on one of the five-hour tours and apparently was late. It was an inconvenience for me, but I know what happens when visitors first arrive in Peking. They're overwhelmed.'

'I believe they are,' agreed the clerk. 'But what can we do for you?'

'I need to know the correct spelling of his name, and whether he has a middle name or what's called a baptismal name – the specifics that must be included on the government papers that I'll fill out for him.'

'But how can we help?'

'He left this behind in the cafeteria.' Jason held up the French businessman's identification tag. 'I don't know how he even got on the tour.'

The woman laughed casually as she reached under the counter for the day's tour ledger. 'He was told the departure area and the guide understood; each carries a list. Those things fall off all the time, and she no doubt gave him a temporary ticket.' The clerk took the tag and began turning pages as she continued, 'I tell you, the idiots who make these are not worth the small yuan they are paid. We have all these precise regulations, these strict rules, and we are made to look foolish at the beginning. *Who is who?*' The woman stopped, her finger on an entry in the ledger. 'Oh, bad-luck spirits,' she said softly, looking up at Bourne. 'I do not know if your sheep is bewildered, but I can tell you he bleats a great deal. He believes himself very grand and was himself very disagreeable. When he was told there was no chauffeur who spoke French, he took it as an insult to his nation's honour as well as his own – which was more important to him. Here, you read the name. I cannot pronounce it.'

'Thank you so much,' said Jason, reading.

He had then gone to a house phone marked 'English' and asked the operator for Mr Ardisson's room.

'You may *dial* it, sir,' said the male operator, a note of triumph in his voice – this was high technology. 'It is Room one-seven-four-three. Very fine accommodations. Very fine view of the Forbidden City.'

'Thank you.' Bourne had dialled. There was no answer. Monsieur Ardisson had not yet returned, and under the circumstances he might not return for quite a while. Still, a sheep that was known for bleating a great deal would not stay silent if his dignity was affronted or his business was in jeopardy. Jason decided to wait. The outlines of a plan were coming into focus. It was a desperate strategy based on probabilities, but it was all he had left. He bought a month-old French magazine at the newsstand and sat down, feeling suddenly drained and helpless.

The face of Marie intruded on David Webb's inner screen, and then the sound of her voice filled the close air around him, echoing in his ears, suspending thought and creating a terrible pain at the centre of his forehead. Jason Bourne removed the intrusion with the force of a sledgehammer. The screen went dark, its last flickering light rejected by harsh commands spoken by an ice-cold authority: *Stop it! There is no time. Concentrate on what we must think about. Nothing else!*

Jason's eyes strayed intermittently, constantly returning to the entrance. The clientele of the east-wing lobby was international, a mix of languages, of clothing from Fifth and Madison avenues, Savile Row, St Honoré, and the Via Condotti, as well as the more sombre apparel of both Germanys and the Scandinavian countries. The guests wandered in and out of the brightly lighted shops, amused and intrigued by the pharmacy selling only Chinese medicines, and flocking into the crafts shop next to a large relief map of the world on the wall. Every now and then someone with an entourage came through the doors; also, obsequious interpreters bowing and translating between uniformed government officials trying to appear casual and weary executives from across the globe whose eyes were dazed from jet lag and the need for sleep, to be preceded, perhaps, by whisky. This might be Red China, but negotiations were older than capitalism, and the capitalists, aware of their fatigue, would not discuss business until they could think straight. Bravo Adam Smith and David Hume.

There he was! Jean-Louis Ardisson was being escorted through the doors by no fewer than four Chinese bureaucrats, all of whom were doing their best to mollify him. One rushed ahead to the lobby liquor store as the others detained him by the elevator, chattering continuously through the interpreter. The buyer returned carrying a plastic bag, the bottom stretched and sagging under the weight of several bottles. There were smiles and bows as the elevator doors opened. Jean-Louis Ardisson accepted his booty and walked inside, nodding once as the doors closed.

Bourne remained seated watching the lights as the elevator ascended. *Fifteen, sixteen, seventeen.* It had reached the top floor, Ardisson's floor. Jason got up and walked back to the bank of telephones. He looked at the sweep hand of his watch; he could only guess at the timing, but a man in an agitated state would not stroll slowly to his room once he left the elevator. The room signified a measure of peace, even the relief of solitude after several hours of tension and panic. To be held for questioning by the police in a foreign country was frightening for anyone, but it became terrifying when an incomprehensible language and radically different faces were added to the knowledge that the prisoner was in a country where people frequently disappeared without explanation. After such an ordeal a man would enter his room and in no particular order would collapse, trembling in fear and exhaustion; light one cigarette after another, forgetting where he left the last one; take several strong drinks, swallowing rapidly for a faster effect; and grab the telephone to share his dreadful experience, unconsciously hoping to minimize the aftereffects of his terror by sharing them. Bourne could allow Ardisson's collapsing, and as much wine or liquor as the man could handle, but he could not permit the telephone. There could be no sharing, no lessening of the terror. Rather, Ardisson's terror had to be extended, amplified to the point where he would be paralysed, fearing for his life if he left his room. Forty-seven seconds had elapsed; it was time to call.

'*Allo?*' The voice was strained, breathless.

'I'll speak quickly,' said Jason quietly in French. 'Stay where you are and do not use the telephone. In precisely eight minutes I'll knock on your door, twice rapidly, then once. Admit me, but no one else before me. Especially a maid or a housekeeper.'

'Who *are* you?'

'A countryman who must speak to you. For your own safety. Eight minutes.' Bourne hung up and returned to the chair, counting off the minutes and calculating the time it took an elevator with the usual number of passengers to go from one floor to the next. Once on a specific floor, thirty seconds were enough to reach any room. Six minutes went by, and Jason walked to an elevator where the lightened numbers indicated it would be the next to reach the lobby. Eight minutes were ideal for priming a subject; five were too few, not long enough for the right degree of tension. Six were better but passed too quickly. Eight, however, while still within an urgent time span, provided those additional moments of anxiety that wore down a subject's resistance. The plan was not yet clear in Bourne's mind. The objective, however, was crystallized, absolute. It was all he had left, and every instinct in his Medusan body told him to go after it. Delta One knew the Oriental mind. In one respect it had not varied for centuries. Secrecy was worth ten thousand tigers, if not a kingdom.

He stood outside the door of 1743, looking at his watch. Eight minutes precisely. He knocked twice, paused, then knocked once again. The door opened and a shocked Ardisson stared at him.

'*C'est vous!*' cried the businessman, bringing his hand to his lips.

'*Soyez tranquille,*' said Jason, stepping inside and closing the door. 'We have to talk,' he continued in French. 'I must know what happened.'

'*You!* You were next to me in that horrid place. We *spoke*. You took my *identification!* You were the cause of *everything!*'

'Did you mention me?'

'I didn't *dare*. It would have looked as if I had done something illegal – giving my pass to someone else. Who *are* you? Why are you here? You've caused me enough trouble for one day! I think you should leave, monsieur.'

'Not until you tell me exactly what happened.' Bourne walked across the room and sat down in a chair next to a red lacquered table. 'It's urgent that I know.'

'Well, it's not urgent that I tell you. You have no right to walk in here, make yourself comfortable, and give me orders.'

'I'm afraid I do have that right. Ours was a private tour and you intruded.'

'I was *assigned* to that damn tour!'

'On whose orders?'

'The concierge, or whatever you call that idiot downstairs.'

'Not him. Above him. Who was it?'

'How would *I* know? I haven't the vaguest idea what you're talking about.'

'You left.'

'My God, it was *you* who *told* me to leave!'

'I was testing you.'

'Testing . . . ? This is unbelievable!'

'Believe,' said Jason. 'If you're telling the truth, no harm will come to you.'

'*Harm?*'

'We do not kill the innocent, only the enemy.'

'*Kill* . . . the *enemy?*'

Bourne reached under his jacket, took the gun from his belt, and placed it on the table. 'Now, convince me you're not the enemy. What happened after you left us?'

Stunned, Ardisson staggered back into the wall, his wide, frightened eyes riveted on the weapon. 'I swear by all the saints you are talking to the wrong man,' he whispered.

'Convince me.'

'Of *what?*'

'Your innocence. What happened?'

'I . . . Down in the square,' began the terrified businessman, 'I thought about the things *you* said, that something terrible had happened inside Mao's tomb and that the Chinese guards were shouting about foreign gangsters and how people were going to be cordoned off and detained – especially someone like me who was not really part of the tour group . . . So I started to run – my God, I couldn't *possibly* be placed in such a situation! Millions of francs are involved, half the cost of Singapore, profits on a scale unheard of in the high-fashion industry! I'm no mere bargainer, I represent a *consortium!*'

'So you began running and they stopped you,' interrupted Jason, anxious to get the nonessentials out of the way.

'*Yes!* They spoke so rapidly I didn't understand a word anyone was saying, and it was an hour before they found an official who spoke French!'

'Why didn't you simply tell them the truth? That you were with our tour.'

'Because I was running away from that damned tour and I had given *you* my damned identification card! How would *that* look to these barbarians who see a fascist *criminal* in every white face?'

'The Chinese people are not barbarians, monsieur,' said Bourne gently. Then suddenly he shouted. 'It is only their government's political philosophy that's *barbaric!* Without the grace of *Almighty God*, with only Satan's benediction!'

'I beg your pardon?'

'Later, perhaps,' replied Jason, his voice abruptly calm again. 'So an official who spoke French arrived. What happened then?'

'I told him I was out for a stroll – *your* suggestion, monsieur. And that I suddenly remembered I was expecting a call from Paris and was hurrying back to the hotel, which accounted for my running.'

'Quite plausible.'

'Not for the official, monsieur. He began abusing me, making the most insulating remarks and insinuating the most dreadful things. I wonder what in the name of God happened in that tomb?'

'It was a beautiful piece of work, monsieur,' answered Bourne, his eyes wide.

'I beg your pardon?'

'Later perhaps. So the official was abusive?'

'Entirely! But he went too far when he attacked Paris fashions as a decadent bourgeois industry! I mean, after all, we *are* paying money for their damned fabrics – they certainly don't have to know the margins, of course.'

'So what did you do?'

'I carry a list of the names with whom I'm negotiating – some are rather important, I understand, as they should be, considering the money. I insisted the official contact them, and I refused – and I *did* refuse – to answer any more questions until at least several of them arrived. Well, after another *two* hours they did, and let me tell you, *that* changed things! I was brought back here in a Chinese version of a limousine – damned cramped for a man of my size – and four escorts. And far worse, they told me that our final conference is postponed yet again. It will not take place tomorrow morning but instead in the evening. What kind of hour is that to do *business?*' Ardisson pushed himself away from the wall, breathing hard, his eyes now pleading. 'That's all there is to tell you, monsieur. You really *do* have the wrong man. I am not involved in anything over here but my consortium.'

'You *should* be!' cried Jason accusingly, raising his voice again. 'To do business with the godless is to debase the work of the *Lord!*'

'I beg your pardon?'

'You have satisfied me,' said the chameleon. 'You are simply a mistake.'

'A what?'

'I will *tell* you what happened inside the tomb of Mao Zedong. *We* did it. We shot up the crystal coffin as well as the body of the infamous unbeliever!'

'You *what?*'

'And we will continue to destroy the enemies of Christ wherever we find them! We will bring His message of love back into the world if we have to kill every diseased animal who thinks otherwise! It will be a *Christian* globe or no globe at *all!*'

'Surely there is room for negotiation. Think of the money, the *contributions.*'

'Not from Satan!' Bourne rose from the chair, picked up the gun and shoved it under his belt, then buttoned his jacket and tugged at the cloth as though it were a military tunic. He approached the distraught businessman. 'You are not the enemy, but you're close, monsieur. Your billfold, please, and your trade papers, including the names of those with whom you negotiate.'

'Money . . . ?'

'We do not accept contributions. We have no need of them.'

'Then *why?*'

'For your protection as well as ours. Our cells here must check out individuals to see whether or not you're being used as a dupe. There is evidence we may have been infiltrated. Everything will be returned to you tomorrow.'

'I really must protest—'

'Don't,' broke in the chameleon, reaching under his jacket, his hand remaining there. 'You asked who I was, no? Suffice it to say that as our enemies employ the services of such as the PLO and the Red Armies, the

Ayatollah's fanatics and Baader-Meinhof, we have mounted our own brigades. We neither seek nor offer any quarter. It is a struggle unto death.'

'My God!'

'We fight in His name. Do not leave this room. Order your meals from room service. Do not call your colleagues or your counterparts here in Beijing. In other words, stay out of sight and pray for the best. In truth, I must tell you that if I myself was followed and it is known that I came to your room, you will simply disappear.'

'*Unbelievable . . . !*' His eyes suddenly unfocused, Ardisson's whole body began to tremble.

'Your billfold and your papers, please.'

Showing the full array of Ardisson's papers, including the Frenchman's list of government negotiators. Jason hired a car under the name of Ardisson's consortium. He made it plain to a relieved dispatcher at the China International Travel Service on Chaoyangmen Street that he both read and spoke Mandarin, and as the rented car would be driven by one of the Chinese officials, no driver was required. The dispatcher told him the car would be at the hotel by 7:00 P.M. If everything fell into place, he would have twenty-four hours to move as freely as a Westerner could in Beijing. The first ten of those hours would tell him whether or not a strategy conceived in desperation would lead him out of the darkness or plunge both Maric and David Webb into an abyss. But Delta One knew the Oriental mind. For a score of centuries it had not varied in one respect. Secrecy was worth ten thousand tigers, if not a kingdom.

Bourne walked back to the hotel, stopping in the crowded shopping district of Wang Fu Jing, around the corner of the hotel's east wing. At number 255 was the Main Department Store, where he made the necessary purchases of clothing and hardware. At number 261 he found a shop named Tuzhang Menshibu, translated as the Seal Engraving Store, where he selected the most official-looking stationery he could find. (To his amazement and delight, Ardisson's list included not one but two generals, and why not? The French produced the Exocet, and although hardly high-fashion, it was high on the list of high-tech military.) Finally, at the Arts Store, numbered 265 on the Wang Fu Jing, he bought a calligraphy pen and a map of Beijing and its environs, as well as a second map showing the roads leading from Beijing to the southern cities.

Carrying his purchases back to the hotel, he went to a desk in the lobby and began his preparations. First, he wrote a note in Chinese relieving the driver of the rented car of all responsibility in turning the automobile over to the foreigner. It was signed by a general and amounted to an order. Second, he spread out the map and circled a small green area on the outskirts of northwest Beijing.

The Jing Shan Bird Sanctuary.

Secrecy was worth ten thousand tigers, if not a kingdom.

25

Marie leaped out of the chair at the shrill, jangling bell of the telephone. She ran, limping and wincing, across the room and picked it up. 'Yes?'

'Mrs Austin, I presume.'

'*Mo?* . . . Mo Panov! Thank *God.*' Marie closed her eyes in gratitude and relief. It had been nearly thirty hours since she had spoken to Alexander Conklin, and the waiting and the tension – above all, the helplessness – had driven her to the edge of panic. 'Alex said he was going to ask you to come with him. He thought you would.'

'Thought? Was there a doubt? How are you feeling, Marie? And I don't expect an answer from Pollyanna.'

'Going mad, Mo. I'm trying not to, but I'm going *mad!*'

'As long as you haven't completed the journey I'd say you were remarkable, and the fact that you're fighting every step of the way even more so. But then you don't need any chicken-soup psychology from me. I just wanted an excuse to hear your voice again.'

'To find out whether I was a babbling wreck,' said Marie gently, making a statement.

'We've been through too much together for such a third-rate subterfuge – I'd never get away with it with you. Which I just didn't.'

'Where's Alex?'

'Talking into the pay phone next to me; he asked me to call you. Apparently he wants to speak with you while whoever it is he's talking to is still on the line . . . Wait a second. He's nodding. The next voice you hear, et cetera, et cetera.'

'Marie?'

'*Alex?* Thank you. *Thank* you for coming—'

'As your husband would say, "No time for that." What were you wearing when they last saw you?'

'Wearing?'

'When you got away from them.'

'I got away twice. The second time was in Tuen Mun.'

'Not then,' interrupted Conklin. 'The contingent was small and there was too much confusion – if I remember what you told me. A couple of marines actually saw you but nobody else did. *Here.* Here in Hong Kong. That'd be the description they'd start with, the one that would stick in their minds. What were you wearing then?'

'Let me think. At the hospital—'

'Later,' broke in Alex. 'You said something to me about swapping clothes and buying a few things. The Canadian consulate, Staples's apartment. Can you remember?'

'Good Lord, how can *you* remember?'

'No mystery, I make notes. It's one of the by-products of alcohol. Hurry, Marie. Just generally, what were you wearing?'

'A pleated skirt – yes, a grey pleated skirt, that was it. And a kind of bluish blouse with a high collar—'

'You'd probably change that.'

'What?'

'Never mind. What else?'

'Oh, a hat, a fairly wide-brimmed hat to cover my face.'

'*Good!*'

'And a fake Gucci purse I bought in the street. Oh, and sandals to make me shorter.'

'I want the height. We'll stick to heels. That's fine, that's all I need.'

'For *what*, Alex? What are you doing?'

'Playing Simon Says. I know perfectly well the State Department passport computers picked me up, and with my smooth, athletic walk even State's warthogs could spot me in customs. They won't know a damn thing, but someone's giving them orders and I want to know who else shows up.'

'I'm not sure I understand.'

'I'll explain later. Stay where you are. We'll get there as soon as we can make a clean break. But it has to be *very* clean – sterile, in fact – so it may take an hour or so.'

'What about Mo?'

'He has to stay with me. If we separate now, at the least they'll follow him, at worst they'll take him in.'

'What about you?'

'They won't touch me beyond a tight surveillance.'

'You're confident.'

'I'm angry. They can't know what I've left behind or with whom or what my instructions are if there's a break in any prearranged phone calls. For them, right now I'm a walking – limping – megabomb that could blow apart their entire operation, whatever the *hell* it is.'

'I know you say there's no time, Alex, but I've got to tell you something. I'm not sure why, but I have to. I think one of the things about you that so hurt and enraged David was the fact that he thought you were the best at what you did. Every once in a while, when he'd have a few drinks or his mind wandered – opening a door or two for him – he'd shake his head sadly or pound his fist furiously and ask himself, *Why?* "Why?" he'd say. "He was better than that . . . he was the best." '

'I was no match for Delta. No one was. Ever.'

'You sound awfully good to me.'

'Because I'm not coming in from the cold, I'm going out. With a better reason than I've ever had in my life before.'

'Be careful, Alex.'

'Tell *them* to be careful.' Conklin hung up the phone, and Marie felt the tears rolling slowly down her cheeks.

Morris Panov and Alex left the gift shop in the Kowloon railroad station and headed for the escalator that led to the lower level, Tracks 5 and 6. Mo, the friend, was perfectly willing to follow his former patient's instructions. But, Panov, the psychiatrist, could not resist offering his professional opinion.

'No wonder you people are all fucked up,' he said, carrying a stuffed panda under his arm and a brightly coloured magazine in his hand. 'Let me get this straight. When we go downstairs, I walk to the right, which is Track six, and then proceed to my left toward the rear of the train, which we assume will arrive within minutes. Correct, so far?'

'Correct,' answered Conklin, beads of sweat on his forehead as he limped beside the doctor.

'I then wait by the last pillar, holding this foul-smelling stuffed animal under my arm while glancing through the pages of this extremely pornographic magazine, until a woman approaches me.'

'Correct again,' said Alex as they stepped down into the escalator. 'The panda's a perfectly normal gift; it's a favourite with Westerners. Think of it as a present to her kid. The porno magazine simply completes the recognition signal. Pandas and dirty pictures with naked women don't usually go together.'

'On the contrary, the combination could be positively Freudian.'

'Score one for the funny farm. Just do as I say.'

'Say? You never told me *what* I was to say to the woman.'

'Try "Nice to meet you," or "How's the kid?" It doesn't matter. Give her the panda and get back to this escalator as fast as you can without running.' They reached the lower platform, and Conklin touched Panov's elbow, angling the doctor to the right. 'You'll do fine, Coach. Just do as I say and come back here. Everything's going to be all right.'

'That's easier said from where I usually sit.'

Panov walked down to the end of the platform as the train from Lo Wu thundered into the station. He stood by the last pillar, and as passengers by the hundreds poured out the doors the doctor awkwardly held the black-and-white panda under his arm and raised the magazine in front of his face. And when it happened, he nearly collapsed.

'You must be Harold!' exclaimed the loud falsetto voice as a tall figure, heavily made up under a soft, widebrimmed hat and dressed in a grey pleated skirt, slapped his shoulder. 'I'd know you *anywhere*, darling!'

'Nice to meet you. How's the kid?' Morris could barely speak.

'How's *Alex?*' countered the suddenly bass male voice quietly. 'I owe him and I pay my debts, but this is crazy! Has he still got both his oars in the water?'

'I'm not sure any of you do,' said the astonished psychiatrist.

'*Quickly*,' said the strange figure. 'They're closing in. Give me the panda, and when I start running, fade into the crowd and get out of here! *Give* it to me!'

Panov did as he was told, aware that several men were breaking through the straggling groups of passengers and converging on them. Suddenly, the heavily rouged man in women's clothes ran behind the thick pillar and emerged on the other side. He kicked off his high heels, circled the pillar again, and like a broken-field football back raced into the crowd nearest the train, passing a Chinese who tried to grab him, dodging through pummelled bodies and startled faces. Behind him other men took up the chase, thwarted by the increasingly hostile passengers who began using suitcases and knapsacks toward off the bewildering assaults. Somehow in the near riot the panda was put in the hands of a tall Occidental female who was also holding an unfolded train schedule. The woman was grabbed by two well-dressed Chinese; she screamed; they looked at her, yelled at each other, and plunged ahead.

Morris Panov again did as he had been instructed to do: he quickly mingled with the departing crowd on the opposite side of the platform and walked rapidly along the edge of Track 5 back to the escalator, where a line had formed. There was a line but no Alex Conklin! Suppressing his panic, Mo slowed his pace but kept walking, looking around, scanning the crowds, as well as those riding up on the escalator. What had *happened?* Where was the CIA man?

'*Mo!*'

Panov spun to his left, the brief shout both a relief and a warning. Conklin had edged his way partially around a pillar thirty feet beyond the escalator. From his quick, rapid gestures he made it clear that he had to stay where he was, and for Mo to reach him, but slowly, cautiously. Panov assumed the air of a man annoyed with the line, a man who would wait for the crowd to thin out before attempting to get on the escalator. He wished he smoked or at least had not thrown the pornographic magazine down onto the tracks; either would have given him something to do. Instead, he clasped his hands behind his back and strolled casually along the deserted area of the platform, glancing around twice, frowning at the line. He reached the pillar, slid behind it, and gasped.

At Conklin's feet lay a stunned, middle-aged man in a raincoat, with Conklin's clubbed foot in the centre of his back. 'I'd like you to meet Matthew Richards, Doctor. Matt's an old Far East hand going back to the early Saigon days when we first knew each other. Of course, he was younger then and a lot more agile. But then, again, weren't we all.'

'For Christ's sake, Alex, let me up!' pleaded the man named Richards, shaking his head as best he could in his supine position. 'My head hurts like hell! What did you hit me with, a *crowbar?*'

'No, Matt. The shoe belonging to my nonexistent foot. Heavy, isn't it? But then it has to take a lot of abuse. As to letting you up, you know I can't do that until you answer my questions.'

'Goddamn it, I *have* answered them! I'm a lousy case officer, not the station chief. We picked you up from a DC directive that said to put you under surveillance. Then State moved in with another "direct," which I *didn't* see!'

'I told you, I find that hard to believe. You've got a tight unit here;

everybody sees everything. Be reasonable, Matt, we go back a long time. What did the State directive say?'

'I don't *know*. It was eyes-only for the SC!'

'That's "station chief," Doctor,' said Conklin, looking over at Panov. 'It's the oldest cop-out we have. We use it all the time when we get in rhubarbs with other government agencies. "What do *I* know? Ask the SC." That way our noses are clean because no one wants to hassle a station chief. You see, SC's have a direct line to Langley, and depending on the Oval Yo-Yo, Langley has a direct line to the White House. It's very politicized, let me tell you, and has very little to do with gathering intelligence.'

'Very enlightening,' said Panov, staring at the supine man, not knowing what else to say, grateful that the platform was now practically deserted, and the pillar at the rear was in shadows.

'*No* cop-out!' yelled Richards, struggling under the pressing weight of Conklin's heavy boot. '*Jesus*, I'm telling you the truth! I get out next February! Why would I want any trouble from you or anybody *else* at headquarters?'

'Oh, Matt, poor Matt, you never were the best or the brightest. You just answered your own question. You can taste that pension just like me, and you don't want any waves. I'm listed as a pickup, a tight surveillance, and you don't want to louse up a directive where you're concerned. Okay, pal, I'll wire back an evaluation report that'll get you transferred to Central American demolitions until your time's up – if you last that long.'

'Cut it out!'

'Imagine, being skunk-trapped behind a pillar in a crowded train station by a lousy cripple. They'll probably let you mine a few harbours all by yourself.'

'I don't *know* anything!'

'Who are the Chinese?'

'I don't—'

'They're not the police, so who *are* they?'

'Government.'

'What branch? They had to tell you that – the SC had to tell you. He couldn't expect you to work blind.'

'That's just it, we *are!* The only thing he told us was that they were cleared by DC on the top floors. He swore that was all *he* knew! What the hell were we supposed to do? Ask to see their driver's licences?'

'So no one's accountable because no one knows anything. It'd turn out nice if they were Chin-Comms picking up a defector, wouldn't it?'

'The SC's accountable. We lay it on *him*.'

'Oh, the higher morality of it all. "We just follow orders, *Herr General*."' Conklin employed the hard German *G* for the rank. 'And, naturally, *Herr General* doesn't know anything either because he's following *his* orders.' Alex paused, squinting. 'There was one man, a big fellow who looked like a Chinese Paul Bunyan.' Conklin stopped. Richards's head suddenly twitched, as did his body. 'Who is he, Matt?'

'I don't know . . . for sure.'

'*Who?*'

'I've seen him, that's all. He's hard to miss.'

'That isn't all. Because he is hard to miss *and* considering the places where you've seen him, you asked questions. What did you learn?'

'Come on, Alex! It's just gossip, nothing set in concrete.'

'I love gossip. Tattle, Matt, or this ugly, heavy thing on my leg may just have to pound your face. You see, I can't control it; it's got a mind of its own and it doesn't like you. It can be very hostile, even to me.' With effort, Conklin suddenly raised his club foot and pounded it down between Richards's shoulder blades.

'*Christ!* You're breaking my back!'

'No, I think it wants to break your face. Who *is* he, Matt?' Again, grimacing, Alex raised his false foot and lowered it now on the base of the CIA man's skull.

'All *right!* As I said, it's not gospel, but I've heard he's high up in Crown CI.'

'Crown CI,' explained Conklin to Morris Panov, 'means British Counter Intelligence here in Hong Kong, which means a branch of MI-Six, which means they take their orders from London.'

'Very enlightening,' said the psychiatrist, as bewildered as he was appalled.

'*Very,*' agreed Alex. 'May I have your necktie, Doctor?' asked Conklin as he began removing his own. 'I'll replace it out of contingency funds because we now have a new wrinkle. I'm officially at work. Langley is apparently funding – by way of Matthew's salary and time – something involving an ally's Intelligence operation. As a civil servant under a like classification I should put my shoulder to the wheel. I need your necktie, too, Matt.'

Two minutes later, Case Officer Richards lay behind the pillar, his feet and hands tied and his mouth drawn taut, all accomplished with three neckties.

'We're sterile,' said Alex, studying what remained of the crowd beyond the pillar. 'They've all gone after our decoy, who's probably halfway to Malaysia by now.'

'Who was she – *he?* I mean, he certainly wasn't a woman.'

'No sexism intended, but a woman probably couldn't have made it out of here. He did, taking the others with him – after him. He jumped over the escalator railing and worked his way up. Let's go. We're clear.'

'But who *is* he?' pressed Panov, as they walked around the pillar toward the escalator and the few stragglers forming a short line.

'We've used him occasionally over here, mainly as a pair of eyes for out-of-the-way border installations, which he knows something about, since he has to get past them with his merchandise.'

'Narcotics?'

'He wouldn't touch them; he's a top-notch jock. He runs stolen gold and jewels, operating between Hong Kong, Macao, and Singapore. I think it has something to do with what happened to him a number of years ago. They took away his medals for conduct unbecoming just about everything. He posed for some raunchy photographs when he was in college and needed the money. Later, through the good offices of a sleazy publisher with the ethics of an alley cat, they surfaced and he was crucified, ruined.'

'That magazine I carried!' exclaimed Mo as they both stepped onto the escalator.

'Something like it, I guess.'

'What medals?'

'1976 Olympics. Track and field. The high hurdles were his specialty.'

Speechless, Panov stared at Alexander Conklin as they rose on the escalator, nearing the entrance to the terminal. A platoon of sweepers carrying wide brooms over their shoulders appeared on the opposite escalator heading down to the platform. Alex jerked his head toward them, snapped the fingers of his right hand, and with the thumb extended, jabbed the air in the direction of the terminal's exit doors above. The message was clear. Within moments a bound CIA agent would be found behind a pillar.

'That'd be the one they call the major,' said Marie, sitting in a chair opposite Conklin while Morris Panov knelt beside her, examining her left foot. '*Ouch!*' she cried, pulling back her crossed leg. 'I'm sorry, Mo.'

'Don't be,' said the doctor. 'It's a nasty bruise spread over the second and third metatarsals. You must have taken quite a spill.'

'Several. You know about feet?'

'Right now I feel more secure with podiatry than psychiatry. You people live in a world that would drive my profession back to the Middle Ages – not that most of us aren't still there; the words are just cuter.' Panov looked up at Marie, his eyes straying to her severely styled grey-streaked hair. 'You had fine medical treatment, dark-redhead-that-was. Except the hair. It's atrocious.'

'It's brilliant,' corrected Conklin.

'What do you know? You were a patient of mine.' Mo returned to the foot. 'They're both healing nicely – the cuts and the blisters, that is – the bruise will take longer. I'll pick up some things later and change the dressings.' Panov got up and pulled a straight-backed chair away from the small writing table.

'You're staying here then?' asked Marie.

'Down the hall,' said Alex. 'I couldn't get either of the rooms next door.'

'How did you even manage that?'

'Money. This is Hong Kong, and reservations are always getting lost by somebody who isn't around . . . Back to the major.'

'His name is Lin Wenzu. Catherine Staples told me he was with British Intelligence, speaks English with UK accent.'

'She was *sure?*'

'Very. She said he was considered the best Intelligence officer in Hong Kong, and that included everyone from the KGB to the CIA.'

'It's not hard to understand. His name is Wenzu, not Ivanovitch or Joe Smith. A talented native is sent to England, educated and trained, and brought back to assume a responsible position in government. Standard colonial policy, especially in the area of law enforcement and territorial security.'

'Certainly from a psychological viewpoint,' added Panov, sitting down. 'There are fewer resentments that way, and another bridge is built to the governed foreign community.'

'I understand that,' said Alex, nodding, 'but something's missing; the pieces don't fit. It's one thing for London to give a green light for an undercover DC operation – which everything we've learned tells us this is, only more bizarre than most – but it's another for MI-Six to lend us their local people in a colony the UK is still running.'

'Why?' asked Panov.

'Several reasons. First, they don't trust us – oh, not that they mistrust our intentions, just our brains. In some ways they're right, in others they're dead wrong, but that's their judgement. Second, why risk exposing their personnel for the sake of decisions made by an American bureaucrat with no expertise in on-the-scene deep-cover administration? That's the sticking point, and London would reject it out of hand.'

'I assume you're referring to McAllister,' said Marie.

'Till the cows come home from a field of new alfalfa.' Conklin shook his head, exhaling as he did so. 'I've done my research, and I can tell you he's either the strongest or the weakest factor in this whole damned scenario. I suspect the latter. He's pure, cold brains, like McNamara before his conversion to doubt.'

'Knock off the bullshit,' said Mo Panov. 'What do you mean in straight talk, not chicken soup? Leave that to me.'

'I mean, *Doctor*, that Edward Newington McAllister is a rabbit. His ears spring up at the first sign of conflict or off-the-wire lapses, and he scampers off. He's an analyst and one of the best, but he is *not* qualified to be a case officer, to say nothing of a station chief, and don't even consider his being the strategist behind a major covert operation. He'd be laughed off the scene, believe me.'

'He was terribly convincing with David and me.' broke in Marie.

'He was given that script: "Prime the subject," he was told. Stick to the convoluted narrative that would become clearer to the subject in stages once he made his first moves, which he had to make because you were gone.'

'Who wrote the script?' asked Panov.

'I wish I knew. No one I reached in Washington knows, and that includes a number of people who should know. They weren't lying; after all these years I can spot a swallow in a voice. It's so damn deep and filled with so many contradictions it makes Treadstone Seventy-one look like an amateur effort – which it wasn't.'

'Catherine said something to me,' interrupted Marie.

'I don't know whether it will help or not, but it stuck in my mind. She said a man flew into Hong Kong, a "statesman," she called him, someone who was "far more than a diplomat," or something like that. She thought there might be a connection with everything that's happened.'

'What was his name?'

'She never told me. Later, when I saw McAllister down in the street with her, I assumed it was he. But maybe not. The analyst you just described and the nervous man who spoke to David and me is hardly a diplomat, much less a statesman. It had to be someone else.'

'When did she say this to you?' asked Conklin.

'Three days ago, when she was hiding me in her apartment in Hong Kong.'

'*Before* she drove you up to Tuen Mun?' Alex leaned forward in the chair.

'Yes.'

'She never mentioned him again?'

'No, and when I asked her, she said there was no point in either of us getting our hopes up. She had more digging to do, was the way she put it.'

'You *settled* for that?'

'Yes, I did, because at the time I thought I understood. I had no reason to question her then. She was taking a personal and professional risk helping me – accepting my word on her own without asking for consular advice, which others might have done simply to protect themselves. You mentioned the word "bizarre," Alex. Well, let's face it, what I told her was so bizarre it was outrageous – including a fabric of lies from the US State Department, vanishing guards from the Central Intelligence Agency, suspicions that led to the higher levels of your government. A lesser person might have backed away and covered herself.'

'Gratitude notwithstanding,' said Conklin gently, 'she was withholding information you had a right to know. *Christ,* after everything you and David have been through—'

'You're wrong, Alex,' interrupted Marie softly. 'I told you I thought I understood her, but I didn't finish. The cruellest thing you can do to a person who's living every hour in panic is to offer him or her a hope that turns out false. When the crash comes it's intolerable. Believe me, I've spent over a year with a man desperately looking for answers. He's found quite a few, but those he followed only to find them wrong nearly broke him. Dashed hopes are no fun for the one hoping.'

'She's right,' said Panov, nodding his head and looking at Conklin. 'And I think you know it, don't you?'

'It happened,' replied Alex, shrugging and looking at his watch. 'At any rate, it's time for Catherine Staples.'

'She'll be watched, *guarded!*' It was Marie who now sat forward in her chair, her expression concerned, her eyes questioning. 'They'll assume you both came over here because of me, and that you reached me and I told you about her. They'll expect you to go after her. They'll be waiting for you. If they could do what they've done so far, they could kill you!'

'No, they couldn't,' said Conklin, getting up and limping toward the bedside telephone. 'They're not good enough,' he added simply.

'You're a goddamned basket case!' whispered Matthew Richards from behind the wheel of the small car parked across the street from Catherine Staples's apartment.

'You're not very grateful, Matt,' said Alex, sitting in the shadows next to the CIA man. 'Not only did I not send in that evaluation report, but I also let you get me back under surveillance. Thank me, don't insult me.'

'Shit!'

'What did you tell them back at the office?'

'What else? I was mugged, for Christ's sake.'

'By how many?'

'At least five teenaged punks. *Zhongguo ren.*'

'And if you fought back, making a lot of ruckus, I might have spotted you.'

'That's the story board,' agreed Richards quietly.

'And when I called you, naturally it was one of the street people you've cultivated who saw a white man with a limp.'

'Bingo.'

'You might even get a promotion.'

'I just want to get out.'

'You'll make it.'

'Not this way.'

'So it was old Havilland himself who blew into town.'

'You didn't get that from me! It was in the papers.'

'The sterile house in Victoria Peak wasn't in the papers, Matt.'

'Hey, come *on*, that was a trade-off! You're nice to me. I'm nice to you. No lousy report about me getting clobbered by a shoe with no foot in it and you get an address. Anyway, I'd deny it. You got it from Garden Road. It's all over the consulate, thanks to a pissed-off marine.'

'Havilland,' mused Alex out loud. 'It fits. He's tightass with the British, even talks like them . . . My God, I should have recognized the voice!'

'The voice?' asked a perplexed Richards.

'Over the phone. Another page in the scenario. It was *Havilland!* He wouldn't let anyone else do it! "We've *lost* her." Oh, *Jesus*, and I was sucked right in!'

'Into what?'

'Forget it.'

'Gladly.'

An automobile slowed down and stopped across the street in front of Staples's apartment house. A woman got out of the rear kerbside door, and seeing her in the wash of the streetlights, Conklin knew who it was. Catherine Staples. She nodded to the driver, turned around and walked across the pavement to the thick glass doors of the entrance.

Suddenly, an engine roaring at high pitch filled the quiet street by the park. A long black sedan swerved out of a space somewhere behind them and screeched to a stop beside Staples's car. Staccato explosions thundered from the second vehicle. Glass was shattered both in the street and across the pavement as the windows of the parked automobile were blown away, along with the driver's head, and the doors of the apartment house riddled, collapsing in bloody fragments, as the body of Catherine Staples was nailed into the frame under the fusillade of bullets.

Tires spinning, the black sedan raced away in the dark street, leaving the carnage behind, blood and torn flesh everywhere.

'Jesus *Christ!*' roared the CIA man.

'Get out of here,' ordered Conklin.

'*Where?* For Christ's sake, *where?*'

'Victoria Peak.'

'Are you out of your *mind?*'

'No, but somebody else is. One blue-blooded son of a bitch has been taken. He's been *had.* And he's going to hear it first from me. *Move!*'

26

Bourne stopped the black Shanghai sedan on the dark, tree-lined, deserted stretch of road. According to the map, he had passed the Eastern Gate of the Summer Palace – actually once a series of ancient royal villas set down on acres of sculptured countryside dominated by a lake known as Kunming. He had followed the shoreline north until the coloured lights of the vast pleasure ground of emperors past faded, giving way to the darkness of the country road. He extinguished the headlights, got out, and carried his purchases, now in a waterproof knapsack, to the wall of trees lining the road, and dug his heel into the ground. The earth was soft, making his task easier, for the possibility that his rented car might be searched was real. He reached inside the knapsack, pulled out a pair of workman's gloves and a long-bladed hunting knife. He knelt down and dug a hole deep enough to conceal the sack; he left the top of it open, picked up the knife and cut a notch in the trunk of the nearest tree to expose the white wood beneath the bark. He replaced the knife and gloves in the knapsack, pressed it down into the earth and covered it with dirt. He returned to the car, checked the odometer, and started the engine. If the map was as accurate about distances as it was in detailing those areas in and around Beijing where it was prohibited to drive, the entrance to the Jing Shan Sanctuary was no more than three-quarters of a mile away around a long curve up ahead.

The map was accurate. Two floodlights converged on the high green metal gate beneath huge panels depicting brightly coloured birds; the gate was closed. In a small glass-enclosed structure on the right sat a single guard. At the sight of Jason's approaching headlights he sprang up and ran out. It was difficult to tell whether the man's jacket and trousers were a uniform or not; there was no evidence of a weapon.

Bourne drove the sedan up to within feet of the gate, climbed out, and approached the Chinese behind it, surprised to see that the man was in his late fifties or early sixties.

'*Bei tong, bei tong!*' began Jason before the guard could speak, apologizing for disturbing him. 'I've had a terrible time,' he continued rapidly, pulling out the list of the French-assigned negotiators from his inside pocket. 'I was to be here three and a half *hours* ago, but the car didn't arrive and I couldn't reach Minister—' He picked out the name of a textile minister from the list. '—Wang Xu, and I'm sure he's as upset as I am!'

'You speak our language,' said the bewildered guard. 'You have a car with no driver.'

'The minister cleared it. I've been to Beijing many, many times. We were going to have dinner together.'

'We are closed, and there is no restaurant here.'

'Did he leave a note for me, perhaps?'

'No one leaves anything here but lost articles. I have very nice Japanese binoculars I could sell you cheap.'

It happened. Beyond the gate, about thirty yards down the dirt road, Bourne saw a man in the shadows of a tall tree, a man wearing a long tunic – four buttons – an *officer.* Around his waist was a thick holster belt. A weapon.

'I'm sorry, I have no use for binoculars.'

'A present, perhaps?'

'I have few friends and my children are thieves.'

'You are a sad man. There is nothing but children and friends – and the spirits, of course.'

'Now, really, I simply want to find the *minister.* We are discussing *renminbi* in the millions!'

'The binoculars are but a few yuan.'

'All *right!* How much?'

'Fifty.'

'Get them for me,' said the chameleon impatiently, reaching into his pocket, his gaze casually straying beyond the green fence as the guard rushed back to the gatehouse. The Chinese officer had retreated farther into the shadows but was still watching the gate. The pounding in Jason's chest once again felt like kettledrums – as it so often had in the days of Medusa. He had turned a trick, exposed a strategy. Delta knew the Oriental mind. *Secrecy.* The lone figure did not, of course, confirm it, but he did not deny it, either.

'Look how grand they are!' cried the guard, running back to the fence and holding out the binoculars. 'One hundred yuan.'

'You said fifty!'

'I didn't notice the lenses. Far superior. Give me the money and I'll throw them over the gate.'

'Very well,' said Bourne, about to push the money through the crisscrossing mesh of the fence. 'But under one condition, *thief.* If by any chance you are questioned about me, I choose not to be embarrassed.'

'Questioned? That's foolish. There's no one here but me.'

Delta was right.

'But in case you are, I insist you tell the truth! I am a French businessman urgently seeking this minister of textiles because my car was unpardonably delayed. I will *not* be embarrassed!'

'As you wish. The money, please.'

Jason shoved the yuan bills through the fence; the guard clutched them and threw the binoculars over the gate. Bourne caught them and looked pleadingly at the Chinese. 'Have you any idea where the minister might have gone?'

'Yes, and I was about to tell you without additional money. Men so grand as you and he would no doubt go to the dining house named Ting Li Guan. It is a favourite of rich foreigners and powerful men of our heavenly government.'

'Where is it?'

'In the Summer Palace. You passed it on this road. Go back fifteen, twenty kilometres, and you will see the great Dong An Men gate. Enter it, and the guides will direct you, but show your papers, sir. You travel in a very unusual way.'

'Thank you!' yelled Jason, running to the car. '*Vive la France!*'

'How beautiful,' said the guard, shrugging, heading back to his post and counting his money.

The officer walked quietly up to the gatehouse and tapped on the glass. Astonished, the night watchman leaped out of his chair and opened the door.

'Oh, sir, you startled me! I see you were locked inside. Perhaps you fell asleep in one of our beautiful resting places. How unfortunate. I will open the gate at once!'

'Who was that man?' asked the officer calmly.

'A foreigner, sir. A French businessman who has had much misfortune. As I understood him, he was to meet the minister of textiles here hours ago and then proceed to dinner, but his automobile was delayed. He's very upset. He does not wish to be embarrassed.'

'What minister of textiles?'

'Minister Wang Xu, I believe he said.'

'Wait outside, please.'

'Certainly, sir. The gate?'

'In a few minutes.' The soldier picked up the telephone on the small counter and dialled. Seconds later he spoke again. 'May I have the number of a minister of textiles named Wang Xu? . . . Thank you.' The officer pressed down the centre bar, released it, and dialled again. 'Minister Wang Xu, please?'

'I am he,' said a somewhat disagreeable voice at the other end of the line. 'Who is this?'

'A clerk at the Trade Council Office, sir. We're doing a routine check on a French businessman who has you listed as a reference—'

'Great Christian *Jesus*, not that idiot *Ardisson!* What's he done now?'

'You know him, sir?'

'I wish I didn't! Special this, special that! He thinks that when he defecates, the odour of lilacs fills the stalls.'

'Were you to have dinner with him tonight, sir?'

'Dinner? I might have said *anything* to keep him quiet this afternoon! Of course, he hears only what he wants to hear and his Chinese is terrible. On the other hand, it's perfectly possible that he would use my name to obtain a reservation when he didn't have one. I told you, special this, special that! Give him whatever he wants. He's a lunatic but harmless enough. We'd send him back to Paris on the next plane if the fools he represents weren't paying so much for such third-rate material. He's cleared for the best illegal whores in Beijing! Just don't bother me, I'm entertaining.' The minister abruptly hung up.

His mind at ease, the army officer replaced the phone and walked outside to the night watchman. 'You were accurate,' he said.

'The foreigner was most agitated, sir. And very confused.'

'I'm told both conditions are normal for him.' The army man paused for a moment, then added, 'You may open the gate now.'

'Certainly, sir.' The guard reached into his pocket and pulled out a ring of keys. He stopped, looking over at the officer. 'I see no automobile, sir. It is many kilometres to any transportation. The Summer Palace would be the first—'

'I've telephoned for a car. It should be here in ten or fifteen minutes.'

'I'm afraid *I* will not be here then, sir. I can see the light of my relief's bicycle down the road now. I am off duty in five minutes.'

'Perhaps I'll wait here,' said the officer, dismissing the watchman's words. 'There are clouds drifting down from the north. If they bring rain, I could use the gate-house for shelter until my car arrives.'

'I see no clouds, sir.'

'Your eyes are not what they once were.'

'Too true.' The repeated ringing of a bicycle bell broke the outer silence. The relief guard approached the fence as the watchman started to unlock the gate. 'These young ones announce themselves as though they were descending spirits from heaven.'

'I should like to say something to you,' said the officer sharply, stopping the watchman in his tracks. 'Like the foreigner, I, too, do not wish to be embarrassed for catching an hour of much needed sleep in a beautiful resting place. Do you like your job?'

'Very much, sir.'

'And the opportunity to sell such things as Japanese binoculars turned over to you for safekeeping?'

'Sir?'

'My hearing's acute and your shrill voice is loud.'

'*Sir?*'

'Say nothing about me and I will say nothing about your unethical activities, which would undoubtedly send you into a field with a pistol put to your head. Your behaviour is reprehensible.'

'I have never *seen* you, sir! I swear on the spirits in my soul!'

'We in the party reject such thoughts.'

'Then on anything you *like!*'

'Open the gate and get out of here.'

'First my bicycle, sir!' The watchman ran to the far edge of the fence, wheeled out his bicycle and unlocked the gate. He swung it back, nodding with relief as he literally threw the new man the ring of keys. Mounting the saddle of his bicycle, he spend off down the road.

The second guard walked casually through the gate holding his bicycle by the handlebars. 'Can you imagine?' he said to the officer. 'The son of a Kuomintang warlord taking the place of a feeble-minded peasant who would have served us in the kitchens.'

Bourne spotted the white notch in the tree trunk and drove the sedan off the road between two pine trees. He turned off the lights and got out. Rapidly he broke numerous branches to camouflage the car in the darkness. Instinctively, he worked quickly – he would have done so in any event – but to his alarm, within seconds after he finished concealing the sedan, headlights appeared far down on the road to Beijing. He bent down, kneeling in the underbrush and watched the automobile pass by, fascinated by the sight of a bicycle strapped to its roof, then concerned when moments later the noise of the engine was abruptly cut off; the car had stopped around the bend up ahead. Wary that some part of his own car had been seen by an experienced field man who would park out of sight and return on foot, Jason raced across the road into the tangled brush beyond the trees. He ran in spurts to his right, from pine to pine, to the midpoint of the curve where again he knelt in the shadowed greenery, waiting, studying every foot of the thoroughfare's borders, listening for any sound that did not belong to the hum of the deserted country road.

Nothing. Then finally something, and when he saw what it was, it simply did not make sense. Or did it? The man on the bicycle with a friction light on the front fender was pedalling up the road as if his life depended on a speed he could not possibly attain. As he drew closer Bourne saw that it was the watchman . . . on a bicycle . . . and a bicycle had been strapped to the roof of the car that had stopped around the bend. Had it been for the watchman? Of course not; the car would have proceeded to the gate . . . A second bicycle? A second watchman – arriving on a bicycle? *Of course.* If what he believed was true, the guard at the gate would be changed, a conspirator put in his place.

Jason waited until the watchman's light was barely a speck in the distant darkness, then ran in the road back to his car and the tree with the notch in the bark. He now dug up the knapsack and began sorting out the articles of his trade. He removed his jacket and white shirt and put on a black turtleneck sweater; he secured the sheath of the hunting knife to the belt of his dark trousers and shoved the automatic with a single shell in it on the other side. He picked up two spools connected by a three-foot strand of thin wire, and thought that the lethal instrument was far better than the one he had fashioned in Hong Kong. Why not? He was much closer to his objective, if anything he had learned in that distant Medusa had any value. He rolled the wire into both spools equally, and carefully pushed them down inside his trousers' right back pocket, then picked up a small penlight and clipped it to the lower edge of his right front pocket. He placed a long, double strand of outsized Chinese firecrackers, which was folded and held in place by an elastic band, in his left front pocket along with three books of matches and a small wax candle. The most awkward item was a hand-held medium-gauge wire cutter, the size of a pair of pliers. He inserted it head down into his left back pocket, then sprang the release so that the two short handles were pressed against the cloth, thus locking the instrument in its shell. Finally, he reached for a wrapped pile of clothing that was coiled so tight its dimensions were no more than that of a rolling pin. He centred it on his spine, pulled the elastic band around his waist, and snapped the clips into place. He might never use the clothes but then he could leave nothing to chance – he was too close!

I'll take him, Marie! I swear I'll take him and we'll have our life again. It's David and I love you so! I need you so!

Stop it! There are no people, only objectives. No emotions, only targets and kills and men to be eliminated who stand in the way. I have no use for you, Webb. You're soft and I despise you. Listen to Delta – listen to Jason Bourne!

The killer who was a killer by necessity buried the knapsack with his white shirt and tweed jacket and stood up between the pine trees. His lungs swelled at the thought of what was before him, one part of him frightened and uncertain, the other furious, ice-cold.

Jason started walking north into the curve, going from tree to tree as he had done before. He reached the car that had passed him with the bicycle strapped to its roof; parked on the side of the road, it had a large sign taped under the front window. He edged closer and read the Chinese characters, smiling to himself as he did so:

This is a disabled official vehicle of the government. Tampering with any part of the mechanism is a serious crime. Theft of this vehicle will result in the swift execution of the offender.

In the lower left-hand corner there was a column in small print:

People's Printing Plant Number 72. Shanghai.

Bourne wondered how many hundreds of thousands of such signs had been made by Printing Plant 72. Perhaps they took the place of a warranty, two with each vehicle.

He backed into the shadows and continued around the bend until he reached the open space in front of the floodlit gate. His eyes followed the line of the green fence. On the left it disappeared into the forest darkness. On the right it extended perhaps two hundred feet beyond the gatehouse, running the length of a parking lot with numbered areas for tour buses and taxis, where it angled sharply south. As he expected, a bird sanctuary in China would be enclosed, a deterrent for poachers. As d'Anjou had phrased it: 'Birds have been revered in China for centuries. They're considered delicacies for the eyes and the palate.' Echo. Echo was gone. He wondered if d'Anjou had suffered . . . *No time.*

Voices! Bourne snapped his head back toward the gate as he lurched into the nearest foliage. The Chinese army officer and a new, much younger watchman – no, now definitely a guard – walked out from behind the gatehouse. The guard was wheeling a bicycle while the officer held a small radio to his ear.

'They'll start arriving shortly after nine o'clock,' said the army man, lowering the radio and shoving down the antenna. 'Seven vehicles each three minutes apart.'

'The truck?'

'It will be the last.'

The guard looked at his watch. 'Perhaps you should get the car, then. If there's a telephone check, I know the routine.'

'A good thought,' agreed the officer, clamping the radio to his belt and taking the bicycle's right handlebar. 'I have no patience with those bureaucratic females who bark like chows.'

'But you must have,' insisted the guard, laughing. 'And you must take out the lonely ones, the ugly ones, and perform at your best between their legs. Suppose you received a poor report? You could lose this heavenly job.'

'You mean that feeble-minded peasant you relieved—'

'No, no,' broke in the guard, releasing the bicycle. 'They seek out the younger ones, the handsome ones, like me. From our photographs, of course. He's different; he pays them yuan from his sales of lost items. I sometimes wonder if he makes a profit.'

'I have trouble understanding you civilians.'

'Correction, if I may, Colonel. In the true China I am a captain in the Kuomintang.'

Jason was stunned by the younger man's remark. What he had heard was incredible! *In the true China I am a captain in the Kuomintang.* The *true* China? *Taiwan?* Good God, had it *started?* The war of the two Chinas? Was that what these men were about? *Madness!* Wholesale slaughter! The Far East would be blown off the face of the earth! Christ! In his hunt for an assassin had he stumbled on the *unthinkable?*

It was too much to absorb, too frightening, too cataclysmic. He had to move quickly, putting all thought on hold, concentrating only on movement. He read the radium dial of his watch. It was 8:54, and he had very little time to do what had to be done. He waited until the army officer bicycled past, then made his way cautiously, silently through the foliage until he saw the fence. He approached it, taking out the penlight from his pocket, flashing it twice to judge the dimensions. They were extraordinary. Its height was no less than twelve feet, and the top angled outward like the inner barricade of a prison fence with coils of barbed wire strung along the parallel strands of steel. He reached into his back pocket, squeezed the handles together and removed the wire cutter. He then probed with his left hand in the darkness, and when he found the criss-crossing wires closest to the ground, he placed the head of the cutter to the lowest.

Had David Webb not been desperate, and Jason Bourne not furious, the job would not have been accomplished. The fence was no ordinary fence. The gauge of the metal was far, far stronger than that of any barricade enclosing the most violent criminals on earth. Each strand took all the strength Jason had as he manipulated the cutter back and forth until the metal snapped free. And each snap came, but only with the passing of precious minutes.

Again Bourne looked at the glowing dial of his watch. *9:06.* Using his shoulder, his feet digging into the ground, he bent the barely two-foot vertical rectangle inward through the fence. He crawled inside, sweat drenching his body everywhere, and lay on the ground breathing heavily. *No time. 9:08.*

He rose unsteadily to his knees, shook his head to clear it and started to his right, holding the fence for support until he came to the corner that fronted the parking area. The floodlit gate was two hundred feet to his left.

Suddenly, the first vehicle arrived. It was a Russian Zia limousine, vintage late sixties. It circled into the parking lot and took the first position on the right beside the gatehouse. Six men got out and walked in martial unison toward what was apparently the main path of the bird sanctuary. They disappeared in the dark, the beams of flashlights illuminating their way. Jason watched closely; he would be taking that path.

Three minutes later, precisely on schedule, a second car drove through the gate and parked alongside the Zia. Three men got out of the back while the driver and the front-seat passenger talked. Seconds later the two men emerged, and it was all Bourne could do to control himself when his stare centred in on the passenger, the tall, slender passenger who moved like a cat as he walked to the rear of the automobile to join the driver. It was the assassin! The chaos at Kai-tak Airport had demanded the elaborate trap in Beijing. Whoever was stalking this assassin had to be caught quickly and silenced. Information had to be leaked, reaching the assassin's creator – for who else knew the hired killer's tactics better than the one who had taught them to him? Who else wanted revenge more than the Frenchman? Who else was capable of unearthing the other Jason Bourne? D'Anjou was the key, and the impostor's client knew it.

And Jason Bourne's instincts – born of the gradually, painfully remembered Medusa – were accurate. When the trap had so disastrously collapsed inside Mao's tomb, a desecration that would shake the republic, the elite circle of conspirators had to regroup swiftly, secretly, beyond the scrutiny of their peers. An unparalleled crisis faced them; there was no time to lose in determining their next moves.

Paramount, however, was secrecy. Wherever they met, secrecy was their most crucial weapon. *In the true China I am a captain in the Kuomintang.* Christ! Was it *possible?*

Secrecy. For a lost kingdom? Where better could it be found than in the wild acreages of idyllic government bird sanctuaries, official parks controlled by powerful moles from the Kuomintang in Taiwan? A strategy that came out of desperation had led Bourne to the core of an incredible revelation. *No time! It's not your business! Only he is!*

Eighteen minutes later the six automobiles were in place, the passengers dispersed, joining their colleagues somewhere within the dark forest of the sanctuary. Finally, twenty-one minutes after the arrival of the Russian limousine, a canvas-covered truck lumbered through the gate, making a wide circle and parking next to the last entry, no more than thirty feet from Jason. Shocked, he watched as bound and gagged men and women with gaping mouths held in place by strands of cloth were pushed out of the van; without exception they fell, rolling on the ground, moaning in protest and in pain. Then just within the covered opening a man was struggling, twisting his short, thin body and kicking at the two guards, who held him off and finally threw him down on the gravelled parking lot. It was a white man . . . Bourne *froze.* It was *d'Anjou!* In the glow of the distant floodlights he could see that Echo's face was battered, his eyes swollen. When the Frenchman pulled himself to his feet, his left leg kept bending and collapsing, yet he would not give into his captors' taunting; he remained defiantly on his feet.

Move! Do something! What? *Medusa – we had signals.* What were they? Oh

God, what *were* they? Stones, sticks, rocks . . . *gravel!* Throw something to make a sound, a small distracting sound that could be anything – away from an area, ahead, as *far* ahead as possible! Then follow it up quickly. *Quickly!*

Jason dropped to his knees in the shadows of the right-angled fence. He reached down and grabbed a small handful of gravel and threw it in the air over the heads of prisoners struggling to their feet. The brief clatter on the roofs of several cars was by and large lost amid the stifled cries of the bound captives. Bourne repeated the action, now with a few more stones. The guard standing next to d'Anjou glanced over in the direction of the splattering gravel, then dismissed the sound when his attention was suddenly drawn to a woman who had gotten to her feet and had started to run toward the gate. He raced over, grabbed her by the hair, and threw her back into the group. Again Jason reached for more stones.

He stopped all movement. D'Anjou had fallen to the ground, his weight on his right knee, his bound hands supporting him on the gravel. He watched the distracted guard, then slowly he turned in Bourne's direction. Medusa was never far away from Echo – *he had remembered.* Swiftly, Jason shoved the palm of his hand out, once, *twice.* The dim reflected light off his flesh was enough; the Frenchman's gaze was drawn to it. Bourne moved his head forward in the shadows. Echo saw him! Their eyes made contact. D'Anjou nodded, then turned away, and awkwardly, painfully rose to his feet as the guard returned.

Jason counted the prisoners. There were two women and five men, including Echo. They were herded by the guards, both of whom had removed heavy night sticks from their belts and used them as prods, driving the group toward the path outside the parking lot. D'Anjou fell. He collapsed on his left leg, twisting his body as he dropped to the ground. Bourne watched closely; there was something strange about the fall. Then he understood. The fingers of the Frenchman's hands, which were tied together in front, were spread apart. Covering the movement with his body, Echo scooped up two fistfuls of gravel, and as a guard approached, pulling him to his feet, d'Anjou again started briefly in Jason's direction. It was a signal. Echo would drop the tiny stones as long as they lasted so that his fellow Medusan would have a path to follow.

The prisoners were directed to the right, out of the gravelled area, as the young guard, the 'captain in the Kuomintang,' locked the gate. Jason ran out of the shadows of the fence into the shadows of the truck, pulling the hunting knife from its sheath as he crouched by the hood, looking at the gatehouse. The guard was just outside the door, speaking into the hand-held radio that connected him to the meeting ground. The radio would have to be taken out. So would the man.

Tie him up. Use his clothes to gag him.

Kill him! There can't be any additional risks. Listen to me!

Bourne dropped to the ground, plunging the hunting knife into the truck's left front tyre, and as it deflated he ran to the rear and did the same. Rounding the back of the truck, he raced into the space between it and the adjacent automobile. Pivoting back and forth as he moved forward, he slashed the remaining tyres of the truck and those on the left side of the car. He repeated the tactic down the line of vehicles until he had slashed all the tyres except those of the Russian Zia, only ten-odd yards away from the gatehouse. It was time for the guard.

Tie him –

Kill him! Each step has to be covered, and each step leads back to your wife!

Silently, Jason opened the door of the Russian automobile, reached inside and released the hand brake. Closing the door as quietly as he had opened it, he judged the distance from the hood to the fence; it was approximately eight feet. Gripping the window frame, he pressed his full weight forward, grimacing as the huge car began to roll. Giving the vehicle a final, surging shove, he dashed in front of the car next to the Zia as the limousine crashed into the fence. He lowered himself out of sight and reached into his right back pocket.

Hearing the crash, the startled guard ran around the gatehouse and into the parking lot, shifting his eyes in all directions, then staring at the stationary Zia. He shook his head, as if accepting a vehicle's unexplained malfunction, and walked over to the door.

Bourne sprang out of the darkness, the spools in both hands, the wire arcing over the guard's head. It was over in less than three seconds, no sound emitted other than a sickening expulsion of air. The garrote was lethal; the captain from the Kuomintang was dead.

Removing the radio from the man's belt, Jason searched the clothes. There was always the possibility that something might be found, something of value. There was – *were!* The first was a weapon – not surprisingly, an automatic. The same calibre as the one he had taken from another conspirator in Mao's tomb. Special guns for special people, another recognition factor, the armaments consistent. Instead of one shell, he now had the full complement of nine, in addition to a silencer that precluded disturbing the revered dead in a revered mausoleum. The second was a billfold that contained money and an official document proclaiming the bearer to be a member of the People's Security Forces. The conspirators had colleagues in high places. Bourne rolled the corpse under the limousine, slashed the left tyres and raced around the car, plunging his hunting knife into those on the right. The huge automobile settled into the ground. The captain from the Kuomintang was provided a secure, concealed resting place.

Jason ran to the gatehouse, debating whether or not to shoot out the floodlights, and he decided against it. If he survived he would need the illumination of the landmark. If – *if?* He *had* to survive! *Marie!* He went inside and, kneeling below the window, removed the shells from the guard's automatic, inserting them into his own. He then looked around for schedules or instructions; there was a roster tacked to the wall next to the ring of keys hanging on a nail. He grabbed the keys.

A telephone rang! The earsplitting bell reverberated off the glass walls of the small gatehouse. *If there's a telephone check, I know the routine. A captain from the Kuomintang.* Bourne rose, picked up the phone from the counter and crouched again, spreading his fingers over the mouthpiece.

'*Jing Shan,*' he said hoarsely. 'Yes?'

'Hello, my thrusting butterfly,' answered a female voice in what Jason determined to be decidedly uncultured Mandarin. 'How are all your birds tonight?'

'They're fine but I'm not.'

'You don't sound like yourself. This is Wo, isn't it?'

'With a terrible cold and vomiting and running back to the stalls every two minutes. Nothing stays down or inside.'

'Will you be all right in the morning? I don't wish to be contaminated.'

Take out the lonely ones, the ugly ones . . .

'I wouldn't want to miss our date—'

'You'll be too weak. I'll call you tomorrow night.'

'My heart withers like the dying flower.'

'Cow dung!' The woman hung up.

As he talked Jason's eyes strayed to a pile of heavy coiled chain in the corner of the gatehouse, and he understood. In China, where so many mechanical things failed, the chain was a backup should the lock in the centre of the gate refuse to close. On top of the coiled chain was an ordinary steel padlock. One of the keys on the ring should fit it, he thought, as he inserted several until the lock sprang open. He gathered up the chain and started outside, then stopped, turned around, and ripped the telephone out of the wall. One more piece of malfunctioning equipment.

At the gate he uncoiled the chain and wound the entire length around the midpoint of the two centre posts until there was a bulging mass of coiled steel. He pressed four links of the chain together so that the open spaces were clear, inserted the curved bar, and secured the lock. Everything was stretched taut, and contrary to generally accepted belief, firing a bullet into the mass of hard metal would not blow it apart, only heighten the possibility that a deflected bullet might kill the one firing and endanger the lives of anyone else in the area. He turned and started down the centre path, once more staying in the shadows of the border.

The path was dark. The glow from the floodlit gate was blocked by the dense woods of the bird sanctuary, but the light was still visible in the sky. Cupping his penlight in the palm of his left hand, his arm stretched downward toward the ground, he could see every six or seven feet a small piece of gravel. Once he saw the first two or three he knew what to look for: tiny discolourations on the dark earth, the distance relatively consistent between them. D'Anjou had squeezed up each stone, probably between his thumb and forefinger, rubbing it as hard as he could to remove the grime of the parking lot and impart the oils of his flesh so that each might stand out. The battered Echo had not lost his presence of mind.

Suddenly, there were two stones, not one, and only inches apart. Jason looked up, squinting in the tiny glow of the concealed penlight. The two stones were no accident, but another signal. The main path continued straight ahead, but the one taken by the herded prisoners veered sharply to the right. Two stones meant a turn.

Then, abruptly, there was a change in the relative distances between the pebbles. They were farther and farther apart, and just when Bourne thought there were no more, he saw another. Suddenly, there were two on the ground, marking another intersecting path. D'Anjou knew he was running out of stones and so had begun a second strategy, a tactic that quickly became clear to Jason. As long as the prisoners remained on a single path, there would be no stones, but when they turned into other paths, two pieces of gravel indicated the direction.

He skirted the edges of marshes, and went deep into fields and out of them, everywhere hearing the sudden fluttering of wings and the screeches of disturbed birds as they winged off into the moonlit sky. Finally there was only one narrow path and it led down into a glen of sorts –

He stopped, instantly extinguishing the cupped penlight. Below, about a hundred feet down the narrow path he saw the glow of a cigarette. It moved slowly, casually up and down, an unconcerned man smoking, but still a man placed where he was for a reason. Then Jason studied the darkness beyond – because it was a different darkness; specks of light flickered now and then through the dense woods of the descending glen. Torches, perhaps, for there was nothing constant about the barely discernible light. Of course, torches. He had reached it. Below in the distant glen, beyond the guard with his cigarette, was the meeting ground.

Bourne lurched into the tangled brush on the right side of the path. He started down only to find that the serpentine reeds were like fishnets, stalks woven together by years of erratic winds. To rip them apart or to break them would create noise inconsistent with the normal sounds of the sanctuary. Snaps and zipperlike scratchings were not the sudden fluttering of wings or the screeches of disturbed inhabitants. They were man-made and signified a different intrusion. He reached for his knife, wishing the blade were longer, and began a journey that had he remained on the path would have taken him no more than thirty seconds. It took him now nearly twenty minutes to slice his way silently to within sight of the guard.

'My *God!*' Jason held his breath, suppressing the cry in his throat. He had slipped; the slithering, hissing creature beneath his left foot was at least a yard and a half in length. It coiled around his leg, and in panic he clutched a part of the body, pulling it away from his flesh, and severing it in midair with his knife. The snake thrashed violently about for several seconds, then the spasms stopped; it was dead, uncoiled at his foot. He closed his eyes and shivered, letting the moment pass. Again he crouched and crept closer to the guard, who was now lighting another cigarette or trying to light it with one match after another that failed to ignite. The guard seemed furious with his government-subsidized book of matches.

'*Ma de shizi, shizi!*' he said under his breath, the cigarette in his mouth.

Bourne crawled forward, slicing the last few reeds of thick grass until he was six feet from the man. He sheathed the hunting knife, and again reached into his right back pocket for the garrote. There could be no misplaced blade that permitted a scream; there could only be utter silence broken by an unheard expulsion of air.

He's a human being! A son, a brother, a father!

He is the enemy. He's our target. That's all we have to know. Marie is yours, not theirs.

Jason Bourne lunged out of the grass as the guard inhaled his first draft of tobacco. The smoke exploded from his gaping mouth. The garrote was arced in place, the trachea severed as the patrol fell back in the underbrush, his body limp, his life over.

Whipping out the bloody wire, Jason shook it in the grass, then rolled the spools together and shoved them back into his pocket. He pulled the corpse deeper into the foliage, away from the path, and began searching the pockets. He first found what felt like a thick wad of folded toilet tissue, not at all uncommon in China where such paper was continuously in short supply. He unsnapped his penlight, cupped it and looked at his find, astonished. The paper was folded and soft but it was not tissue. It was *renminbi*, thousands of yuan, more than several years' income for most Chinese. The guard at the gate, the 'captain of the Kuomintang,' had money – somewhat more than Jason thought usual – but nowhere near this amount. A billfold was next. There were photographs of children, which Bourne quickly replaced, a driving permit, a housing allocation certificate, and an official document proclaiming the bearer to be . . . a member of the *People's Security Forces!* Jason pulled out the paper he had taken from the first guard's billfold and placed both side by side on the ground. They were identical. He folded both and put them into his pocket. A last item was as puzzling as it was interesting. It was a pass allowing the bearer access to Friendship Stores, those shops that serve foreign travellers and are all but prohibited to the Chinese except for the highest government officials. Whoever the men were below, thought Bourne, they were a strange and rarefied group. Subordinate guards carried enormous sums of money, enjoyed official privileges light years beyond their positions, and bore documents identifying themselves as members of the government's secret police. If they *were* conspirators – and everything he had seen and heard from Shenzen to Tian An Men Square to this wildlife preserve would seem to confirm it – the conspiracy reached into the hierarchy of Beijing. *No time! It's not your concern!*

The weapon strapped to the man's waist was, as he expected, similar to the one in his belt, as well as the gun he had thrown into the woods at the Jing Shan gate. It was a superior weapon, and weapons were symbols. A sophisticated weapon was no less a mark of status than an expensive watch, which might have many imitators, but those who had a schooled eye for the merchandise would know the genuine article. One might merely show it to confirm one's status, or deny it as government issue from an army that bought its weapons from every available source in the world. It was a subtle point of recognition – only one superior kind allocated to one elite circle. *No time! It's no concern of yours! Move!*

Jason extracted the shells, put them in his pocket, and threw the gun into the forest. He crawled out to the path and started slowly, silently, down toward the flickering light beyond the wall of high trees below.

It was more than a glen, it was a huge well dug out of prehistoric earth, a rupture dating from the Ice Age that had not healed. Birds flapped above, in fear and curiosity; owls hooted in angry dissonance. Bourne stood at the edge of the precipice looking down through the trees at the gathering below. A pulsating circle of torches illuminated the meeting ground. David Webb gasped, wanting to vomit, but the ice-cold command dictated otherwise: *Stop it. Watch. Know what we're dealing with.*

Suspended from the limb of a tree by a rope attached to his bound wrists, his arms stretched out above him, his feet barely inches off the ground, a male prisoner writhed in panic, muted cries coming from his throat, his eyes wild and pleading above his gagged mouth.

A slender, middle-aged man dressed in a Mao jacket and trousers stood in front of the violently twisting body. His right hand was extended, clasping the jewelled hilt of an upended sword, its blade long and thin, its point resting in the earth. David Webb recognized the weapon – weapon and not a weapon. It was a ceremonial sword of a fourteenth-century warlord belonging to a ruthless class of militarists who destroyed villages and towns and whole countrysides, and were even suspected of opposing the will of the Yuan emperors – Mongols who left nothing but fire and death and the screams of children in their wake. The sword was also used for ceremonies far less symbolic, far more brutal than rites performed at the dynasty's courts. David felt a wave of nausea and apprehension gripping him as he watched the scene below.

'*Listen to me!*' shouted the slender man in front of the prisoner as he turned to address his audience. His voice was high-pitched but deliberate, instructive. Bourne did not know him, but his was a face that would be hard to forget. The close-cropped grey hair, the gaunt, pale features – above all, the stare. Jason could not see the eyes clearly, but it was enough that the fires of the torches danced off them. They, too, were on fire.

'The nights of the great blade *begin!*' screamed the slender man suddenly. 'And they will continue *night* after *night* until all those who would betray us are sent to *hell!* Each of these poisonous insects have committed crimes against our holy cause, crimes we are aware of, all of which could lead to the great crime demanding the great blade.' The speaker turned to the suspended prisoner. '*You!* Indicate the truth and *only* the truth! Do you know the Occidental?'

The prisoner shook his head, throated moans accompanying the wild movement.

'*Liar!*' shrieked a voice from the crowd. 'He was in the Tian An Men this afternoon!'

Again the prisoner shook his head spastically in panic.

'He spoke against the true China!' shouted another. 'I heard him in the Hua Gong Park among the young people!'

'And in the coffee house on the Xidan Bei!'

The prisoner convulsed, his wide, stunned eyes fixed in shock on the crowd. Bourne began to understand. The man was hearing lies and he did not know why, but Jason knew. The star-chamber inquisition was in session; a trouble-maker, or a man with doubts, was being eliminated in the name of a greater crime. And on the outside possibility that he might have committed it. *The nights of the great blade begin – night after night!* It was a reign of terror inside a small, bloody kingdom within a vast land where centuries of bloodstained warlords had prevailed.

'He did these things?' shouted the gaunt-faced orator. 'He *said* these things?'

A frenzied chorus of affirmatives filled the glen.

'In the Tian An Men . . . !'

'He talked to the Occidental . . . !'

'He betrayed us all . . . !'

'He caused the trouble at the hated Mao's tomb . . . !'

'He would see us dead, our cause lost . . . !'

'He speaks against our leaders and wants them killed . . . !'

'To oppose our leaders,' said the orator, his voice calm but rising, 'is to *vilify* them, and, by so doing, to remove the care one must accord the precious gift called life. When these things occur, the gift must be taken away.'

The suspended man writhed more furiously, his cries growing louder and matching the moans of the other prisoners who were forced to kneel in front of the speaker in full view of the imminent execution. Only one kept refusing, continuously trying to rise in disobedience and disrespect, and continuously beaten down by the guard nearest him. It was Philippe d'Anjou. Echo was sending another message to Delta, but Jason Bourne could not understand it.

'. . . this diseased, ungrateful hypocrite, this teacher of the young, who was welcomed like a brother into our dedicated ranks because we believed the words he spoke – so courageously, we thought – in opposition to our motherland's tormentors, is no more than a *traitor*. His words are *hollow*. He is a sworn companion of the treacherous winds and they would take him to our enemies, the tormentors of Mother China! In his death may he find purification!' The now shrill-voiced orator pulled the sword out of the ground. He raised it above his head.

And so that his seed may not be spread, recited the scholar David Webb to himself, recalling the words of the ancient incantation and wanting to close his eyes, but unable to, ordered by his other self not to. *We destroy the well from which the seed springs, praying to the spirits to destroy all it has entered here on earth.*

The sword arced vertically down, hacking into the groin and genitalia of the screaming, twisting body.

And so that his thoughts may not be spread, diseasing the innocent and the weak, we pray to the spirits to destroy them wherever they may be, as we here destroy the well from which they spring.

The sword was now swung horizontally, slashing through the prisoner's neck. The writhing body fell to the ground under a shower of blood from the severed head, which the slender man with the eyes of fire continued to abuse with the blade until there was no recognition of a human face.

The rest of the terrified prisoners filled the glen with wails of horror as they groveled on the ground, soiling themselves, begging for mercy. Except one. D'Anjou rose to his feet and stared in silence at the messianic man with the sword. The guard approached. Hearing him, the Frenchman turned and spat in his face. The guard, mesmerized, perhaps sickened by what he had seen, backed away. What was Echo *doing? What was his message?*

Bourne then looked over at the executioner with the gaunt face and the close-cropped grey hair. He was wiping the long blade of the sword with a white silk scarf as aides removed the body and what was left of the prisoner's skull. He pointed to a striking, attractive woman who was being dragged by the two guards over to the rope. Her posture was erect, defiant. Delta studied the executioner's face. Beneath the maniacal eyes, the man's thin mouth was stretched into a slit. He was smiling.

He was dead. Sometime. Somewhere. Perhaps tonight. A butcher, a blood-stained, blind fanatic who would plunge the Far East into an unthinkable war – China against China, the rest of the world to follow.

Tonight!

27

'This woman is a courier, one of those to whom we gave our *trust*,' went on the orator, gradually escalating his voice like a fundamentalist minister, preaching the gospel of love while his eye is on the work of the devil. 'The trust was not earned but given in *faith*, for she is the wife of one of our own, a brave soldier, a first son of an illustrious family of the true China. A man who as I speak now risks his life infiltrating our enemies in the south. He, too, gave her his trust . . . and she *betrayed* that trust, she *betrayed* that gallant husband, she betrayed us *all!* She is no more than a *whore* who sleeps with the *enemy!* And while her lust is satiated how many secrets has she revealed, how much *deeper* is her betrayal? Is she the Occidental's contact here in Beijing? Is she the one who informs on us, who tells our enemies what to look for, what to expect? How else could this terrible day have happened? Our most experienced, dedicated men set a trap for our enemies that would have cut them down, ridding ourselves of Western criminals who see only riches by groveling in front of China's tormentors. It is related that she was at the airport this morning. The *airport!* Where the trap was in *progress!* Did she give her wanton body to a dedicated man, drugging him, perhaps? Did her lover tell her what to do, what to say to our *enemies?* What has this harlot *done?*'

The scene was set, thought Bourne. A case so flagrantly leapfrogging over facts and 'related' facts that even a court in Moscow would send a puppet prosecutor back to the drawing board. The reign of terror within the warlord tribe continued. *Weed out the misfits among the misfits. Find the traitor. Kill anyone who might be he or she.*

A subdued but angry chorus of 'Whore!' and 'Traitor!' came from the audience, as the bound woman struggled with the two guards. The orator held up his hands for silence. It was immediate.

'Her lover was a despicable journalist for the Xinhua News Agency, that lying, discredited organ of the despicable regime. I say "was," for as of an hour ago the loathsome creature is dead, shot through the head, his throat cut, for all to know that he, too, was a traitor! I have spoken myself to this whore's husband, for I accord him honour. He instructed me to do as our ancestral spirits demand. He wants nothing further to do with her—'

'*Aiyaaa!*' With extraordinary strength and fury the woman ripped the tightly bound cloth from her mouth. '*Liar!*' she screamed. 'Killer of *killers!* You killed a decent man and I have betrayed *no one!* It is *I* who have been betrayed! I was not at the airport, and you know it! I have never seen this

Occidental and you know that, too! I knew nothing of this trap for Western criminals and you can see the truth in my face! How *could* I?'

'By whoring with a dedicated servant of the cause and corrupting him, *drugging* him! By offering him your breasts and misused tunnel-of-corruption, withholding, withdrawing, until the herbs make him *mad!*'

'*You're* mad! You say these things, these *lies*, because you sent my husband south and came to me for many days, first with promises and then with threats. I was to *service* you. It was my duty, you said! You lay with me and I learned things—'

'Woman, you are *contemptible!* I came to you pleading with you to leave honour to your husband, to the cause! To abandon your lover and seek forgiveness.'

'A *lie!* Men came to you, taipans from the south sent by my husband, men who could not be seen near your high offices. They came secretly to the shops below my flat, the flat of a so-called honourable widow – another lie you left for me and my child!'

'*Whore!*' shrieked the wild-eyed man with the sword.

'Liar to the depths of the northern lakes!' shouted the woman in reply. 'Like you, my husband has many women and cares nothing for me! He beats me and you tell me it is his right, for he is a great son of the true China! I carry messages from one city to another, which if found on me would bring me torture and death, and I receive only scorn, never paid for my railroad fares, or the yuan withheld from my place of work, for you tell me it is my *duty!* How is my girl child to eat? The child your great son of China barely recognizes, for he wanted only sons!'

'The spirits would not grant you sons, for they would be *women*, disgracing a great house of China! *You* are the traitor! You went to the airport and reached our enemies permitting a great criminal to escape! You would enslave us for a thousand years—'

'You would make us your cattle for *ten* thousand!'

'You don't know what freedom is, woman.'

'*Freedom?* From your mouth? You tell me – you tell *us* – you will give us back the freedoms our elders had in the true China but *what* freedoms, *liar?* The freedom that demands blind obedience, that takes the rice from my child, a child dismissed by a father who believes only in *lords* – war*lords*, land*lords*, *lords* of the earth! *Aiya!*' The woman turned to the crowd, rushing forward, away from the orator. '*You!*' she cried. '*All* of you! I have not betrayed you, nor our cause, but I have learned many things. All was not as this great liar says! There *is* much pain and restriction, which we all know, but there was pain *before*, *restriction* before! . . . My lover was no evil man, no blind follower of the regime, but a literate man, a gentle man, and a believer in *eternal* China! He wanted the things *we* want! He asked only for time to correct the evils that had infected the old men in the committees that lead us. There will be changes, he told me. Some are showing the way. *Now!* . . . Do not permit the liar to do this to me! Do not permit him to do it to *you!*'

'*Whore! Traitor!*' The blade came slashing through the air, decapitating the woman. Her headless body lurched to the left, her head to the right, both spouting geysers of blood. The messianic orator then swung the sword down, slicing into her remains, but the silence that had fallen on the crowd was heavy, awesome. He stopped; he had lost the moment. He regained it swiftly. 'May the sacred ancestral spirits grant her peace and purification!' he shouted, his eyes roving, stopping, staring at each member of his congregation. 'For it is not in hatred that I end her life, but in compassion for her weakness. She will find peace and forgiveness. The spirits will understand – but *we* must understand here in the *motherland!* We cannot deviate from our *cause* – we must be *strong!* We must—'

Bourne had had enough of this maniac. He was hatred incarnate. And he was dead. Sometime. Somewhere. Perhaps tonight – if possible, *tonight!*

Delta unsheathed his knife and started to his right, crawling through the dense Medusan woods, his pulse strangely quiet, a furious core of certainty growing within him – David Webb had vanished. There were so many things he could not remember from those clouded, faraway days, but there was much, too, that came back to him. The specifics were unclear but not his instincts. Impulses directed him, and he was at one with the darkness of the forest. The jungle was not an adversary; instead it was his ally, for it had protected him before, saved him before in those distant, disordered memories. The trees and the vines and the underbrush were his friends; he moved through and around them like a wild cat, surefooted and silent.

He turned to his left above the ancient glen and began his descent while focusing on the tree where the assassin stood so casually. The orator had once again altered his strategy in dealing with his congregation. He was cutting his losses in place of cutting up another woman – a sight the sons of mothers found borderline madness, regardless of any earthly cause. The impassioned pleas of a dead, mutilated female prisoner had to be put out of mind. A master of his craft – his art – the orator knew when to revert to the gospel of love, momentarily omitting Lucifer. Aides had swiftly removed the evidence of violent death, and the remaining woman was summoned with a gesture of the ceremonial sword. She was no more than eighteen, if that, and a pretty girl, weeping and vomiting, as she was dragged forward.

'Your tears and your illness are not called for, child,' said the orator in his most paternal voice. 'It was always our intent to spare you, for you were asked to perform duties beyond your competence at your age, privileged to learn secrets beyond your understanding. Youth frequently speaks when it should be silent . . . You were seen in the company of two Hong Kong brothers – but not *our* brothers. Men who work for the disgraced English Crown, that enfeebled, decadent government that sold out the motherland to our tormentors. They gave you trinkets, pretty jewellery and lip rouge and French perfume from Kowloon. Now, child, what did you give *them*?'

The young girl, hysterically coughing vomit through her gag, shook her head furiously, the tears streaming down her face.

'Her hand was beneath a table, between a man's legs, in a café on the Guangquem!' shouted an accuser.

'It was one of the pigs who work for the British!' added another.

'*Youth* is subject to arousal,' said the orator, looking up at those who had spoken, his eyes glaring, as if commanding silence. 'There is forgiveness in our hearts for such young exuberance – as long as betrayal is no part of that arousal, that exuberance.'

'She was at the Qian Men Gate . . . !'

'She was *not* in the Tian An Men. I, *myself*, have determined it!' shouted the man with the sword. 'Your information is wrong. The only question that remains is a simple one. *Child!* Did you *speak* of us? Could your words have been conveyed to our enemies here or in the south?'

The girl writhed on the ground, her whole body swaying frantically back and forth, denying the implied accusation.

'I accept your innocence, as a father would, but not your foolishness, child. You are too free with your associations, your love of trinkets. When these do not serve us, they can be dangerous.'

The young woman was put in the custody of a smug, obese middle-aged member of the chorus for 'instruction and reflective meditation.' From the expression on the man's face it was clear that his mandate would be far more inclusive than that prescribed by the orator. And when he was finished with her, a child-siren who had elicited secrets from the Beijing hierarchy that demanded young girls – believing that such liaisons, as Mao had decreed, extended their life spans – would disappear.

Two of the three remaining Chinese men were literally put on trial. The initial charge was trafficking in drugs, their network the Shanghai-Beijing axis. Their crime, however, was not distributing narcotics, but constantly skimming off the profits, depositing huge sums of money into personal accounts in numerous Hong Kong banks. Several in the audience stepped forward to corroborate the damning evidence, stating that as subordinate distributors they had given the two 'bosses' great sums of cash never recorded in the organization's secret books. That was the initial charge, but not the major one. It came with the high-pitched singsong voice of the orator. 'You travel south to Kowloon. Once, twice, often *three* times a month. The Kai-tak Airport . . . *You!*' screamed the zealot with the sword, pointing to the prisoner on his left. 'You flew back this afternoon. You were in Kowloon last night. Last *night!* The Kai-tak! We were *betrayed* last night at the *Kai-tak!*' The orator walked ominously out of the light of the torches to the two petrified men kneeling in front. 'Your devotion to money transcends your devotion to our cause,' he intoned like a sorrowful but angry patriarch. 'Brothers in blood and brothers in thievery. We've known for many weeks now, known because there was so much anxiety in your greed. Your money had to multiply like rodents in putrid sewers, so you went to the criminal triads in Hong Kong. How enterprising, industrious, and how grossly stupid! You think certain triads are unknown to us or we to them? You think there are not areas where our interests might converge? You think they have less *loathing* for traitors than *we* do?'

The two bound brothers grovelled in the dirt, rising to their knees in supplication, shaking their heads in denial. Their muted cries were pleas to be heard, to be allowed to speak. The orator approached the prisoner on his left and yanked the gag downward, the rope scraping the man's flesh.

'We betrayed *no one*, great sir!' he shrieked. '*I* betrayed no one! I was at the Kai-tak, *yes*, but only in the crowds. To *observe*, sir! To be filled with joy!'

'To whom did you speak?'

'No one, great sir! Oh, yes, the clerk. To confirm my flight for the next morning, sir, that was all, I swear on the spirits of our ancestors. My young brother's and mine, sir.'

'The money. What about the money you *stole?*'

'Not stole, great sir. I *swear* it! We believed in our proud hearts – hearts made proud by our cause – that we could use the money to advantage for the true China! Every yuan of profit was to be returned to the *cause!*'

The crowd thundered its response. Derisive catcalls were hurled at the prisoners; dual thematic fugues of treachery and theft filled the glen. The orator raised his arms for silence. The voices trailed off.

'Let the word be spread,' he said slowly with gathering force. 'Those of our growing band who might harbour thoughts of betrayal be *warned.* There is no mercy in us, for none was shown us. Our cause is righteous and pure and even thoughts of treachery are an abomination. Spread the word. You don't know who we are or where we are – whether a bureaucrat in a ministry or a member of the security police. We are nowhere and we are everywhere. Those who waver and doubt are dead . . . The trial of these poisonous dogs is over. It's up to you, my children.'

The verdict was swift and unanimous: guilty on the first count, probable on the second. The sentence: one brother would die, the other would live, to be escorted south to Hong Kong, where the money would be retrieved. The choice was to be decided by the age-old ritual of *yi zang li*, literally 'one funeral.' Each man was given an identical knife with blades that were serrated and razor-sharp. The area of combat was a circle, the diameter ten paces. The two brothers faced each other and the savage ritual began as one made a desperate lunge and the other sidestepped away from the attack, his blade lacerating the attacker's face.

The duel within the deadly circle, as well as the audience's primitive reactions to it, covered whatever noise Bourne made in his decision to move quickly. He raced down through the underbrush, snapping branches and slashing away the webbed reeds of high grass, until he was twenty feet behind the tree where the assassin was standing. He would return and move closer, but first there was d'Anjou. Echo had to know he was *there.*

The Frenchman and the last male Chinese prisoner were off to the right of the circle, the guards flanking them. Jason crept forward as the crowd roared insults and encouragement at the gladiators. One of the combatants, both now covered with blood, had delivered a near-fatal blow with his knife, but the life he wanted to end would not surrender. Bourne was no more than eight or nine feet from d'Anjou; he felt around the ground and picked up a fallen branch. With another roar from the crazed audience he snapped it twice. From the three sections he held in his hand he stripped the foliage and reduced the bits of wood into manageable sticks. He took aim and hurled the first end over end, keeping the trajectory low. It fell short of the Frenchman's legs. He threw the second; it struck the back of Echo's knees! D'Anjou nodded his head twice to acknowledge Delta's presence. Then the Frenchman did a strange thing. He began moving his head slowly back and forth. Echo was trying to tell him something. Suddenly, d'Anjou's left leg collapsed and he fell to the ground. He was yanked up harshly by the guard on his right, but the man's concentration was on the bloody battle taking place within the one-funeral circle.

Again Echo shook his head slowly, deliberately, finally holding it steady and staring to his left, his gaze on the assassin who had moved away from the tree to watch the deadly combat. And then he turned his head once more, now directing his stare at the maniac with the sword.

D'Anjou collapsed again, this time struggling to his feet before the guard could touch him. As he rose he moved his thin shoulders back and forth. And breathing deeply, Bourne closed his eyes in the only brief moment of grief he could permit himself. The message was clear. Echo was taking himself out, telling Delta to go after the assassin – and while doing so, to kill the evangelical butcher. D'Anjou knew he was too battered, too weak to be any part of an escape. He would only be an impediment, and the impostor came first . . . Marie came first. Echo's life was over. But he would have his bonus in the maniacal butcher's death, the zealot who would surely take his life.

A deafening scream filled the glen; the crowd was abruptly silent. Bourne snapped his head to the left, where he could see beyond the edge of the row of onlookers. What he saw was as sickening as what he had seen during the past violent minutes. The messianic orator had sunk his ceremonial sword in the neck of a combatant; he pulled it out as the bloodied corpse rattled in death and sprawled on the ground. The minister of killing raised his head and spoke. '*Surgeon!*'

'Yes, sir?' said a voice from the crowd.

'Tend to the survivor. Mend him as best you can for his imminent journey south. If I'd let this continue, both would be dead and our money gone. These close-knit families bring years of hostility to the *yi zang li.* Take his brother away and throw him into the swamps with the others. All will be sweet carrion for the more aggressive birds.'

'Yes, sir.' A man with a black medicine bag stepped forward into the dirt-ringed circle as the dead body was hauled away and a stretcher appeared out of the darkness from the far end of the crowd. Everything had been planned, everything considered. The doctor administered a hypodermic into the arm of the moaning, blood-covered brother, who was carried out of the circle of brotherly death. Wiping his sword with a fresh silk cloth, the orator nodded his head in the direction of the two remaining prisoners.

Stunned, Bourne watched as the Chinese beside d'Anjou calmly undid his bound wrists and reached up to the back of his neck, untying the supposedly strangling strip of cloth and rope that supposedly kept his gaping mouth incapable of any sound but throated moans. The man walked over to the orator and spoke in a raised voice, addressing both his leader and the crowd of followers. 'He says nothing and he reveals nothing, yet his Chinese is fluent and he had every opportunity to speak to me before we boarded the truck and the gags were in place. Even then I communicated with him by loosening my own, offering to do the same for him. He refused. He is obstinate and corruptly brave, but I am sure he knows what he will not tell us.'

'*Tong ku, tong ku!*' Wild shouts came from the crowd, demanding torture. To these were added instructions narrowing the area for pain to be inflicted to the testicles of the Occidental.

'He is old and frail and will collapse into unconsciousness, as he has done before,' insisted the false prisoner. 'Therefore I suggest the following, with our leader's permission.'

'If there's a chance of success, whatever you wish,' said the orator.

'We have offered him his freedom in exchange for the information, but he does not trust us. He's been dealing with the Marxists too long. I propose taking our reluctant ally to the Beijing airport and using my position to secure him passage on the next plane to Kai-tak. I will clear him through immigration, and all he must do before boarding with his ticket is give me the information. Where is there a greater show of trust? We will be in the midst of our enemies, and if his conscience is so offended, all he has to do is raise his voice. He has seen and heard more than any person who ever walked away from us alive. We might in time become true allies, but first there must be trust.'

The orator studied the provocateur's face, then shifted his gaze to d'Anjou, who stood erect, peering out of his swollen eyes, listening without expression. Then the man with the bloodstained sword turned and addressed the assassin by the tree, suddenly speaking in English. 'We have offered to spare this insignificant manipulator if he tells us where his comrade can be found. Do you agree?'

'The Frenchman will lie to you!' said the killer in a clipped British accent, stepping forward.

'To what purpose?' asked the orator. 'He has his life, his freedom. He has little or no regard for others, his entire dossier is proof of that.'

'I'm not sure,' said the Englishman. 'They worked together in an outfit called Medusa. He talked about it all the time. There were rules – codes, you might call them. He'll lie.'

'The infamous Medusa was made up of human refuse, men who would kill their brothers in the field if it could save their own lives.'

The assassin shrugged. 'You asked for my opinion,' he said. 'That's it.'

'Let us ask the one to whom we are prepared to offer mercy.' The orator reverted to Mandarin, issuing orders, as the assassin returned to the tree and lit a cigarette. D'Anjou was brought forward. 'Untie his hands; he's not going anywhere. And remove the rope from his mouth. Let him be heard. Show him we can extend . . . trust, as well as less attractive aspects of our nature.'

D'Anjou shook his hands at his sides, then raised his right and massaged his mouth. 'Your trust is as compassionate and convincing as your treatment of prisoners,' he said in English.

'I forgot.' The orator raised his eyebrows. 'You understand us, don't you?'

'Somewhat more than you think,' replied Echo.

'Good. I prefer speaking English. In a sense, this is between us, isn't it?'

'There's nothing between us. I try never to deal with madmen, they're so unpredictable.' D'Anjou glanced over at the assassin by the tree. 'I've made mistakes, of course. But somehow I think one will be rectified.'

'You can live,' said the orator.

'For how long?'

'Longer than tonight. The remainder is up to you, your health and your abilities.'

'No, it's not. It's all ended when I walk off that plane in Kai-tak. You won't miss as you did last evening. There'll be no security forces, no bulletproof limousines, just one man walking in or out of the terminal, and another with a silenced pistol or a knife. As your rather unconvincing fellow "prisoner" of mine put it, I've been here tonight. I've seen, I've heard, and what I've seen and heard marks me for death . . . Incidentally, if he wonders why I didn't confide in him, tell him he was far too obvious, too anxious, And that suddenly loosened mouthpiece. Really! He could never become a pupil of mine. Like you, he has unctuous words, but he's fundamentally stupid.'

'Like *me!*'

'Yes, and there's no excuse for you. You're a well-educated man, a world traveller – it's in your speech. Where did you matriculate? Was it Oxford? Cambridge?'

'The London School of Economics,' said Sheng Chou Yang, unable to stop himself.

'Well put – the old school tie, as the English say. Yet for all of that you're hollow. A clown. You're not a scholar, not even a student, only a zealot with no sense of reality. You're a fool.'

'You *dare* say this to me?'

'*Fengzi*,' said Echo, turning to the crowd. '*Shenjing bing!*' he added, laughing, explaining that he was conversing with a crazy corkscrew.

'*Stop* that!'

'*Wei shemme?*' continued the enfeebled Frenchman, asking *Why?* – including the crowd as he spoke in Chinese. 'You're taking these people to their oblivion because of your lunatic theories of changing lead into gold! Piss into wine! But as that unfortunate woman said – *whose* gold, whose *wine? Yours or theirs?*' D'Anjou swept his hand toward the crowd.

'I *warn* you!' cried Sheng in English.

'You *see!*' shouted Echo hoarsely, weakly in Mandarin. 'He will not talk with me in your language! He *hides* from you! This spindly-legged little man with the big sword – is it to make up for what he lacks else where? Does he hack women with his blade because he has no other equipment and can do nothing else with them? And look at that balloon head with the foolish flat top—'

'*Enough!*'

'—and the eyes of a screeching, disobedient, *ugly* child! As I say, he's nothing more than a crazy corkscrew. Why give him your time? He'll give you only piss in return, no wine at all!'

'I'd stop it if I were you,' said Sheng, stepping forward with his sword. 'They'll kill you before I do.'

'Somehow I doubt that,' answered d'Anjou in English. 'Your anger clouds your hearing, Monsieur Windbag. Did you not detect a snicker or two? I did.'

'*Gou le!*' roared Sheng Chou Yang, ordering Echo to be silent. 'You will give us the information we must have,' he continued, his shrill Chinese the bark of a man accustomed to being obeyed. 'The games are finished and we will not tolerate you any longer! Where is the killer you brought from Macao?'

'Over there,' said d'Anjou casually, gesturing his head toward the assassin.

'Not *him!* The one who came *before.* This madman you called back from the grave to avenge you! Where is your rendezvous? Where do you meet? Your base here in Beijing, where *is* it?'

'There is no rendezvous,' answered Echo, reverting to English. 'No base of operations, no plans to meet.'

'There *were* plans! You people always concern yourselves with contingencies, *emergencies.* It's how you survive!'

'Survived. Past tense, I fear me.'

Sheng raised his sword. 'You tell us or you die – unpleasantly, monsieur.'

'I'll tell you this much. If he could hear my voice, I would explain to him that *you* are the one he must kill. For you are the man who will bring all Asia to its knees with millions drowning in oceans of their brothers' blood. He must tend to his own business, I understand that, but I would tell him with my last breath that *you* must be *part* of that business! I would tell him to *move. Quickly!*'

Mesmerized by d'Anjou's performance, Bourne winced as if struck. Echo was sending a final signal! *Move! Now!* Jason reached into his left front pocket and pulled out the contents as he crawled swiftly through the woods beyond the staging area of the savage rituals. He found a large rock rising several feet out of the ground. The air was still behind it and its size more than enough to conceal his work. As he started he could hear d'Anjou's voice; it was weak and tremulous, but nevertheless defiant. Echo was finding resources within himself not only to face his final moments but also to buy Delta the precious few he needed.

'. . . Don't be hasty, *mon général* Genghis Khan, or whoever you are. I am an old man and your minions have done their work. As you observed, I'm not going anywhere. On the other hand, I'm not sure I care for where you intend to send me . . . We were not clever enough to perceive the trap you set for us. If we had been, we would never have walked into it, so why so you think we were clever enough to agree on a rendezvous?'

'Because you *did* walk into it,' said Sheng Chou Yang calmly. 'You followed – *he* followed – the man from Macao into the mausoleum. The madman expected to come out. Your contingencies would include both chaos and a rendezvous.'

'On the surface your logic might appear unassailable—'

'*Where?*' shouted Sheng.

'My inducement?'

'Your *life!*'

'Oh, yes, you mentioned that.'

'Your time runs short.'

'I shall *know* my time, monsieur!' *A last message. Delta understood.*

Bourne struck a match, cupping the flame, and lit the thin wax candle, the fuse embedded an eighth of an inch below the top. He quickly crawled deeper into the woods, unravelling the string attached to the succeeding double rolls of fireworks. He reached the end and started back toward the tree.

'. . . What guarantee do I have for my life?' persisted Echo, perversely enjoying himself, a master of chess plotting his own inevitable death.

'The truth,' replied Sheng. 'It's all you need.'

'But my former pupil tells you that I'll lie – as you have lied so consistently this evening.' D'Anjou paused and repeated his statement in Mandarin. '*Liao jie?*' he said to the onlookers, asking if they understood.

'*Stop* that!'

'You repeat yourself incessantly. You really must learn to control it. It's such a tiresome habit.'

'And my patience is at an end! *Where* is your *madman?*'

'In your line of work, *mon général*, patience is not only a virtue but a necessity.'

'*Hold it!*' shouted the assassin, springing away from the tree, astonishing everyone. 'He's stalling you! He's *playing* with you. I *know* him!'

'For what reason?' asked Sheng, his sword poised.

'I don't know,' said the British commando. 'I just don't like it, and that's reason enough for me!'

Ten feet behind the tree, Delta looked at the radium dial of his watch, concentrating on the second hand. He had timed the burning candle in the car, and the time was now. Closing his eyes, pleading with something he could not understand, he grabbed a handful of earth and hurled it high to the right of the tree, arcing it farther to the right of d'Anjou. When he heard the first drops of the shower, Echo raised his voice to the loudest roar he could command.

'*Deal with you?*' he screamed. 'I would as soon deal with the archangel of *darkness!* I may yet have to, but then again I may not, for a merciful God will know that you have committed sins beyond any I have approached, and I leave this earth wanting only to take you *with* me! Your obscene brutality aside, *mon général*, you are a fatuous, hollow *bore*, a cruel joke on your people! Come *die* with me, General *Dung!*'

With his final words, d'Anjou flung himself at Sheng Chou Yang, clawing at his face, spitting into the wide, astonished eyes. Sheng leaped back, swinging the ceremonial sword, slashing the blade into the Frenchman's head. Mercifully quick, it was over for Echo.

It *began!* A staccato burst of fireworks filled the glen, resounding through the woods, swelling in intensity as the stunned crowd reacted in shock. Men threw themselves to the ground, others scrambled behind trees and into the underbrush, yelling in panic, frightened for their lives.

The assassin lurched behind the tree trunk, crouching, a weapon in his hand. Bourne, with the silencer affixed to his gun, strode up to the killer and stood over him. He took aim and fired, blowing the weapon out of the assassin's hand, the flesh between the commando's thumb and forefinger erupting in blood. The killer spun around, his eyes wide, his mouth gaping in shock. Jason fired again, now creasing the assassin's cheekbone.

'Turn around!' ordered Bourne, shoving the barrel of his gun into the commando's left eye. 'Now, grab the tree! *Grab* it! Both arms, tight, *tighter!*' Jason rammed the weapon into the back of the killer's neck as he peered around the trunk. Several of the torches that were stuck in the ground had been ripped up, their flames extinguished.

Another series of explosions came from deeper within the woods. Panicked men began to fire their guns in the direction of sounds. The assassin's leg moved! Then his right hand! Bourne fired two shots directly into the tree; the bullets seared the wood, shattering the bark less than an inch from the commando's skull. He gripped the trunk, his body still, rigid.

'Keep your head to the left!' said Jason harshly. 'You move once more and it's blown away!' *Where was he? Where was the killer maniac with the sword? Delta owed that much to Echo. Where . . . there!* The man with the fanatical eyes was rising from the ground, looking everywhere at once, shouting orders to those near him and demanding a weapon. Jason stepped away from the tree and raised his gun. The zealot's head stopped moving. Their eyes met. Bourne fired just as Sheng pulled a guard in front of him. The soldier arched backward, his neck snapping under the impact of the bullets. Sheng held on to the body, using it as a shield, as Jason fired twice more, jolting the guard's corpse. He could not do it! Whoever the maniac was, he was covered by a dead soldier's body! Delta could not do what Echo had told him to do! General *Dung* would survive! I'm *sorry*, Echo! *No time! Move! Echo was gone . . . Marie!*

The assassin shifted his head, trying to see. Bourne squeezed the trigger. Bark exploded in the killer's face and he whipped his hands up to his eyes, then shook his head, blinking to regain his vision.

'Get up!' ordered Jason, gripping the assassin's throat and pivoting the commando toward the path he had broken through the underbrush as he raced down into the glen. 'You're coming with me!'

A third series of fireworks, deeper still in the woods, exploded in rapid, overlapping bursts. Sheng Chou Yang screamed hysterically, commanding his followers to go in two directions – toward the vicinity of the tree and after the detonating sounds. The explosions stopped as Bourne propelled his prisoner into the brush, ordering the killer to lie prone, Jason's foot on the back of his neck. Bourne crouched, feeling the ground; he picked up three rocks and threw them in the air one after another past the men searching the area around the tree, each rock thrown farther away. The diversion had its effect.

'*Nali!*'

'*Shu ner!*'

'*Bu! Caodi ner!*'

They began moving forward, weapons at the ready. Several rushed ahead, plunging into the overgrowth. Others joined them as the fourth and last cannonade of fireworks burst forth. In spite of the distance the reports were as loud or louder than the previous explosions. It was the final stage, the climax of the display, longer and more booming than the explosions preceding it.

Delta knew that time was now measured in minutes, and if ever a forest was a friend, this one had to be now. In moments, perhaps seconds, men would find the hollow shells of exploded fireworks strewn on the ground and the tactical distraction would be exposed. A massive, hysterical race for the gate would follow.

'*Move!*' ordered Bourne, grabbing the assassin's hair, pulling him to his feet, and shoving him forward. 'Remember, you *bastard*, there isn't a trick you've learned I haven't perfected, and that makes up for a certain difference in our ages! You *look* the wrong way, you've got two bullet holes for eye sockets. Move *out!*'

As they raced up the broken path through the wooded glen, Bourne reached into his pocket and pulled out a handful of shells. While the assassin ran in front of him, breathlessly rubbing his eyes and wiping away the blood from his cheek, Jason removed the clip from his automatic, replaced his full complement of bullets, and cracked the magazine back into place. Hearing the sound of a weapon being dismantled, the commando whipped his head around but realized he was too late; the gun was already reassembled. Bourne fired, grazing the killer's ear. 'I warned you,' he said, breathing loud but steadily. 'Where do you want it? In the centre of your forehead?' He levelled the automatic in front of him.

'Good *Christ*, that butcher was right!' cried the British commando holding his ear. 'You *are* a madman!'

'And you're dead unless you move. *Faster!*'

They reached the corpse of the guard who had been posted on the narrow path leading down to the deep glen. 'Go to the right!' ordered Jason.

'*Where*, for Christ's sake? I can't *see!*'

'There's a path. You'll feel the space. *Move!*'

Once on the bird sanctuary's series of dirt thoroughfares, Bourne kept jamming his automatic into the assassin's spine, forcing the killer to run faster, *faster!* For a moment David Webb returned, and a grateful Delta acknowledged him. Webb was a runner, a ferocious runner, for reasons that went back in time and tortured memories past Jason Bourne to the infamous Medusa. Racing feet and sweat and the wind against his face made living each day easier for David, and at the moment Jason Bourne was breathing hard but nowhere near as breathlessly as the younger, stronger assassin.

Delta saw the glow of light in the sky – the gate was at the end of a field and past three dark, twisting paths. No more than half a mile! He fired a shot between the commando's churning legs. 'I want you to run *faster!*' he said, imposing control on his voice, making it seem that the strenuous movement had minor effect on him.

'*Jesus*, I *can't!* I've got no *wind* left!'

'Find it,' commanded Jason.

Suddenly, in the distance behind them they heard the hysterical shouts of men ordered by their maniacal leader back to the gate, told to find and kill an intruder so dangerous that their very lives and fortunes were hanging in the balance. The jagged, paper remnants of fireworks had been found; a radio had been activated with no response from a gatehouse. *Find him! Stop him! Kill him!*

'If you have any ideas, Major, forget them!' yelled Bourne.

'*Major?*' said the commando, barely able to speak, as he kept running.

'You're an open book to me, and what I've read makes me sick! You watched d'Anjou die like a slaughtered pig. You grinned, you *bastard*.'

'He *wanted* to die! He wanted to *kill* me!'

'*I'll* kill you if you stop running. But before I do, I'll slice you up from your balls to your throat so slowly you'll wish you'd gone with the man who created you.'

'Where's my choice? You'll kill me anyway!'

'Maybe I won't. Ponder it. Maybe I'm saving your life. Think about it!'

The assassin ran faster. They raced through the final dark path, running into the open space of the floodlit gate.

'The parking lot!' shouted Jason. 'The far right end!' Bourne stopped. '*Hold it!*' The bewildered assassin stood still in his tracks. Jason took out his penlight, then aimed his automatic. As he walked up to the killer's back he fired five shots, missing with one. The floodlights exploded; the gate fell into darkness and Bourne rammed the gun into the base of the commando's skull. He turned on the penlight, shining it into the side of the assassin's face. 'The situation is in hand, Major,' he said. 'The operation proceeds. *Move*, you son of a *bitch!*'

Racing across the darkened parking lot, the killer stumbled, sprawling prone on the gravel. Jason fired twice in the glow of the penlight; the bullets ricocheted away from the commando's head. He got to his feet and continued running past the cars and the truck to the end of the lot.

'The fence!' cried Bourne in a loud whisper. 'Head over to it.' At the edge of the gravel he gave another order. 'Get on your hands and knees – look *straight ahead!* You turn around, I'm the last thing you'll see. Now, crawl!' The assassin reached the broken opening in the fence. 'Start through it,' said Jason, once more reaching into his pocket for shells and quietly removing the automatic's magazine. '*Stop!*' he whispered when the psychotic former commando was halfway through. He replaced the expended bullets in the darkness and cracked the magazine into its chamber. 'Just in case you were counting,' he said. 'Now get through there and crawl two lengths away from the fence. *Hurry up!*'

As the assassin scrambled under the bent wire, Bourne crouched and surged through the opening inches behind him. Expecting otherwise, the commando whipped around, rising to his knees. He was met by the beam of the penlight, the glow illuminating the weapon levelled at his head. 'I'd have done the same,' said Jason, getting to his feet. 'I'd have thought the same. Now go back to the fence, reach under, and yank that section back into place. *Quickly!*'

The killer did as he was told, straining as he pulled the thick wire mesh down. At the three-quarter mark Bourne spoke. 'That's enough. Get up and walk past me with your hands behind your back. Go straight ahead, shouldering your way through the branches. My light's on your hands. If you unclasp them I'll kill you. Am I clear?'

'You think I'd snap a limb back in your face?'

'*I* would.'

'You're clear.'

They reached the road in front of the eerily dark gate. The distant shouts were clearer now, the advance party was nearer. 'Down the road,' said Jason. '*Run!*' Three minutes later he snapped on the penlight. '*Stop!*' he shouted. 'That pile of green over there, can you see it?'

'Where?' asked the breathless assassin.

'My beam's on it.'

'They're branches, parts of the pine trees.'

'Pull them away. *Hurry up!*'

The commando began throwing the branches aside, in moments revealing the black Shanghai sedan. It was time for the knapsack. Bourne spoke. 'Follow my light, to the left of the hood.'

'To what?'

'The tree with the white notch on the trunk. See it?'

'Yes.'

'Under it, about eighteen inches in front, there's loose dirt. Beneath there's a knapsack. Dig it out for me.'

'Fucking technician, aren't you.'

'Aren't *you?*'

Without replying, the sullen killer dug through the dirt and pulled the knapsack out of the ground. With the straps in his right hand, he stepped forward as if to hand the bag to his captor. Then suddenly he swung the knapsack, sweeping it diagonally up toward Jason's weapon and the penlight as he lunged forward, the fingers of his hands spread like the extended claws of a furious cat.

Bourne was prepared. It was the precise moment *he* would have used to gain the advantage, however transient, for it would have given him the seconds he needed to race away into the darkness. He stepped back, smashing the automatic into the assassin's head as the lunging figure passed him.

He crashed his knee down into the back of the splayed-out commando, grabbing the assassin's right arm while clenching the penlight between his teeth.

'I *warned* you,' said Jason, yanking the killer up by his right arm. 'But I also *need* you. So instead of your life, we'll do a little bullet surgery.' He put the barrel of his automatic laterally against the flesh of the assassin's arm muscle and pulled the trigger.

'*Jesus!*' screamed the killer as the spit echoed and blood erupted.

'No bone was broken,' said Delta. 'Only muscle tissue, and now you can forget about using your arm. You're fortunate that I'm a merciful man. In that knapsack is gauze and tape and disinfectant. You can repair yourself, Major. Then you're going to drive. You'll be my chauffeur in the People's Republic. You see, I'll be in the backseat with my gun at your head, and I have a map. If I were you, I wouldn't make a wrong turn.'

Twelve of Sheng Chou Yang's men raced to the gate, with only four flashlights among them.

'*Wei shemme? Cuo wu!*'

'*Mafan! Feng Kuang!*'

'*You mao bing!*'

'*Wei fan!*'

A dozen screaming voices were raised against the unlit floodlights, blaming everything and everyone from inefficiency to treachery. The gatehouse was checked; the electric switches and the telephone were found to be inoperative, the guard was nowhere in evidence. Several studied the coiled chain around the gate's lock and issued orders to the others. Since none could get out, they reasoned, the offenders had to be inside the sanctuary.

'*Biao!*' shouted the infiltrator who had been d'Anjou's false prisoner. '*Quan bu zai zheli!*' he shrieked, telling the others to share the lights and search the parking lot, the surrounding woods, and the swamps beyond. The hunters spread out with guns extended, racing across the parking area in different directions. Seven additional men arrived, only one carrying a flashlight. The false prisoner demanded it and proceeded to explain the situation so as to form another search party. He was countered by objections that one light among them was insufficient for the darkness. In frustration the organizer roared a series of profanities, ascribing incredible stupidity to everyone but himself.

The dancing flames of torches grew brighter as the last of the conspirators arrived from the glen, led by the striding figure of Sheng Chou Yang, the ceremonial sword swinging at his side in its belted scabbard. He was shown the coiled chain and apprised of the circumstances by the infiltrator.

'You're not thinking correctly,' said Sheng, exasperated. 'Your approach is wrong! That chain was not placed there by one of our people to keep the criminal or criminals inside. Instead, it was put there by the offender or the offenders to delay us, to keep *us* inside!'

'But there are too many obstacles—'

'Studied and considered!' shouted Sheng Chou Yang. 'Must I repeat myself? These people are survivors. They stayed alive in that criminal battalion called Medusa because they considered everything! They *climbed* out!'

'Impossible,' protested the younger man. 'The top pipe and the extended panel of barbed wire are electrified, sir. Any weight in excess of thirty pounds activates them. That way the birds and animals are not electrocuted.'

'Then they found the source of the current and shut it off!'

'The switches are *inside*, and at least seventy-five metres from the gate concealed in the ground. Even I'm not sure where they are.'

'Send someone up,' ordered Sheng.

The subordinate looked around. Twenty feet away two men were talking quietly, rapidly, to each other, and it was doubtful either had heard the heated conversation. 'You!' said the young leader, pointing to the man on the left.

'Sir?'

'Scale the fence!'

'Yes, sir!' The lesser subordinate ran to the fence and leaped up, his hands gripping the open, crisscrossing squares of wire mesh, as his feet worked furiously below. He reached the top pipe and started over the angled panel of coiled barbed wire. '*Aiyaaa!*'

A shattering cascade of static was accompanied by blinding, blue-white bolts of fired electricity. His body rigid, his hair and eyebrows singed to their roots, the climber fell backward, hitting the earth with the impact of a heavy flat rock. Flashlight beams converged. The man was dead.

'The *truck!*' screamed Sheng. 'This is *idiocy!* Bring out the truck and break through! Do as I say! *Instantly!*'

Two men raced into the parking lot and within seconds the roar of the truck's powerful engine filled the night. The gears whined as the reverse was found. The heavy truck lurched backward, its whole chassis shaking violently until it came to a sudden, leaden stop. The deflated tyres spun, smoke curling up from the burning rubber. Sheng Chou Yang stared in growing apprehension and fury.

'The *others!*' he shrieked. 'Start the others! *All* of them!'

One by one the vehicles were started, and one after another each lurched in reverse only to rattle and groan, sinking into the gravel, unable to move. In a frenzy, Sheng ran up to the gate, pulled out a gun, and fired twice into the coiled chain. A man on his right screamed, holding his bleeding forehead, as he fell to the ground. Sheng raised his face to the dark sky and screamed a primeval roar of protest. He yanked out his ceremonial sword and began crashing it repeatedly down on the chained lock of the gate. It was an exercise in futility.

The blade broke.

28

'There's the house, the one with the high stone wall,' said CIA Case Officer Matthew Richards as he drove the car up the hill in Victoria Peak. 'According to our information, there are marines all over the place, and it won't do me any goddamned good being seen with *you*.'

'I gather you want to owe me a few more dollars,' said Alex Conklin, leaning forward and peering through the windshield. 'It's negotiable.'

'I just don't want to be *involved*, for Christ's sake! And dollars I haven't got.'

'Poor Matt, sad Matt. You take things too literally.'

'I don't know what you're talking about.'

'I'm not sure I do, either, but drive by the house as if you were going to somebody else's place. I'll tell you when to stop and let me out.'

'You will?'

'Under conditions. Those are the dollars.'

'Oh, shit.'

'They're not hard to take and I may not even call them in. The way I see it now, I'll want to stay on ice and out of sight. In other words, I want a man inside. I'll call you several times a day asking you if our lunch or dinner dates are still on, or whether I'll see you at the Happy Valley Race—'

'Not *there*,' interrupted Richards.

'All right, the Wax Museum – anything that comes to mind, except the track. If you say "No, I'm busy," I'll know I'm not being closed in on. If you say "Yes," I'll get out.'

'I don't even know where the hell you're staying! You told me to pick you up on the corner of Granville and Carnarvon.'

'My guess is that your unit will be called in to keep the lines straight and the responsibility where it belongs. The British will insist on it. They're not going to take a solo fall if DC blows it. These are touchy times for the Brits over here, so they'll cover their colonial asses.'

They passed the gate. Conklin shifted his gaze and studied the large Victorian entrance.

'I swear, Alex, I don't know what you're talking about.'

'That's better yet. Do you agree? Are you my guru inside?'

'Hell, yes. I can do without the marines.'

'Fine. Stop here. I'll get out and walk back. As far as anyone's concerned I took the tram to the Peak, got a cab to the wrong house, and made my way to the right address only a couple of hundred feet down the road. Are you happy, Matt?'

'Ecstatic,' said the case officer, scowling, as he braked the car.

'Get a good night's sleep. It's been a long time since Saigon, and we all need more rest as we get older.'

'I heard you were a lush. It's not true, is it?'

'You heard what we wanted you to hear,' replied Conklin flatly. This time, however, he was able to cross the fingers of both hands before he climbed awkwardly out of the car.

A brief knock and the door was flung open. Startled, Havilland looked up as Edward McAllister, his face ashen, walked rapidly into the room. 'Conklin's at the gate,' said the undersecretary. 'He's demanding to see you and says he'll stay there all night if he has to. He also says if it gets chilly, he'll build a fire in the road to keep warm.'

'Crippled or not, he hasn't lost his panache,' said the ambassador.

'This is totally unexpected,' continued McAllister, massaging his right temple. 'We're not prepared for a confrontation.'

'It seems we haven't a choice. That's a public road out there, and it's the province of the colony's Fire Department in the event our neighbours become alarmed.'

'Surely, he wouldn't—'

'Surely, he would,' broke in Havilland. 'Let him in. This isn't only unexpected, it's extraordinary. He hasn't had time to assemble his facts or organize an attack that would give him leverage. He's openly exposing his involvement, and given his background in covert to black operations, he wouldn't do that lightly. It's far too dangerous. He, himself, once gave the order for beyond-salvage.'

'We can presume he's in touch with the *woman*,' protested the undersecretary, heading for the telephone on the ambassador's desk. 'That gives him all the facts he needs!'

'No, it doesn't. She hasn't got them.'

'And you,' said McAllister, his hand on the phone. 'How does he know to come to *you*?'

Havilland smiled grimly. 'All he'd have to hear is that I'm in Hong Kong. Besides, we spoke, and I'm sure he's put it all together.'

'But this *house*?'

'He'll never tell us. Conklin's an old Far East hand, Mr Undersecretary, and he has contacts we can't presume to know about. And we won't know what brings him here unless he's admitted, will we?'

'No, we won't.' McAllister picked up the phone; he dialled three digits. 'Officer of the Guard? . . . Let Mr Conklin through the gate, search him for a weapon, and escort him yourself to the East Wing office . . . He *what*? . . . Admit him quickly and put the damn thing out!'

'What happened?' asked Havilland as the undersecretary hung up the phone.

'He started a fire on the other side of the road.'

*

Alexander Conklin limped into the ornate Victorian room as the marine officer closed the door. Havilland rose from the chair and came around the desk, his hand extended.

'Mr Conklin?'

'Keep your hand, Mr Ambassador. I don't want to get infected.'

'I see. Anger precludes civility?'

'No, I really don't want to catch anything. As they say over here, you're rotten joss. You're carrying something. A disease, I think.'

'And what might that be?'

'Death.'

'So melodramatic? Come, Mr Conklin, you can do better than that.'

'No, I mean it. Less than twenty minutes ago I saw someone killed, cut down in the street with forty or fifty bullets in her. She was blown into the glass doors of her apartment house, her driver shot up in the car. I tell you the place is a mess, blood and glass all over the pavement—'

Havilland's eyes were wide with shock, but it was the hysterical voice of McAllister that stopped the CIA man. 'Her? *She?* Was it the *woman?*'

'*A* woman,' said Conklin, turning to the undersecretary, whose presence he had not yet acknowledged. 'You McAllister?'

'Yes.'

'I don't want to shake your hand either. She was involved with both of you.'

'Webb's wife is *dead?*' yelled the undersecretary, his whole body paralysed.

'No, but thanks for the confirmation.'

'Good God!' cried the long-standing ambassador of the State Department's clandestine activities. 'It was Staples. Catherine *Staples!*'

'Give the man an exploding cigar. And thanks again for the second confirmation. Are you planning to have dinner with the Canadian consulate's High Commissioner soon? I'd love to be there – just to watch the renowned Ambassador Havilland at work. Gosh and golly, I betcha us low-level types could learn an awful lot.'

'*Shut up*, you *goddamned fool!*' shouted Havilland, crossing behind the desk and plummetting into his chair; he leaned back, his eyes closed.

'That's the one thing I'm *not* going to do,' said Conklin, stepping forward, his clubbed foot pounding the floor. 'You are *accountable . . . sir!*' The CIA man leaned over, gripping the edge of the desk. 'Just as you're accountable for what's happened to David and Marie Webb! Who the *fuck* do you think you are? And if my language offends you, *sir*, look up the derivation of the offending word. It comes from a term in the Middle Ages meaning to plant a seed in the ground, and in a way that's your specialty! Only in your case they're rotten seeds – you dig in clean dirt and turn it into filth. Your seeds are lies and deception. They grow inside of *people*, turning them into angry and frightened puppets, dancing on *your* strings to *your* goddamned scenarios! I repeat, you aristocratic son of a bitch, who the fuck do you think you are?'

Havilland half opened his lidded eyes and leaned forward. His expression was that of an old man willing to die, if only to remove the pain. But those same eyes were alive with a cold fury that saw things others could not see. 'Would it serve your argument if I said to you that Catherine Staples said essentially the same thing to me?'

'Serves it and completes it!'

'Yet she was killed because she joined forces with us. She didn't like doing that, but in her judgement there was no alternative.'

'Another *puppet*?'

'No. A human being with a first-rate mind and a wealth of experience who understood what faced us. I mourn her loss – and the manner of her death – more than you can imagine.'

'Is it her loss, *sir* or is it the fact that your holy operation was *penetrated*?'

'How *dare* you?' Havilland, his voice low and cold, rose from the chair and stared at the CIA man. 'It's a little late for you to be moralizing, Mr Conklin. Your lapses have been all too apparent in the areas of deception and ethics. If you'd had your way, there'd be no David Webb, no Jason Bourne. *You* put him beyond-salvage, no one else did. You planned his execution and nearly succeeded.'

'I've paid for that lapse. *Christ*, how I've paid for it!'

'And I suspect you're still paying for it, or you wouldn't be in Hong Kong now,' said the ambassador, nodding his head slowly, the coldness leaving his voice. 'Lower your cannons, Mr Conklin, and I'll do the same. Catherine Staples really *did* understand, and if there's any meaning in her death, let's try to find it.'

'I haven't the vaguest idea where to start looking.'

'You'll be given chapter and verse . . . just as Staples was.'

'Maybe I shouldn't hear it.'

'I have no choice but to insist that you do.'

'I guess you weren't listening. You've been penetrated! The Staples woman was killed because it was assumed she had information that called for her to be taken out. In short, the mole who's bored his way in here saw her in a meeting or meetings with both of you. The Canadian connection was made, the order given, and you let her walk around without protection!'

'Are you afraid for your life?' asked the ambassador.

'Constantly,' replied the CIA man. 'And right now I'm also concerned with someone else's.'

'Webb's?'

Conklin paused, studying the old diplomat's face. 'If what I believe is true,' he said quietly. 'There's nothing I can do for Delta that he can't do better for himself. But if he doesn't make it, I know what he'd ask me to do. Protect Marie. And I can do that best by fighting you, not listening to you.'

'And how do you propose fighting me?'

'The only way I know how. Down and very dirty. I'll spread the word in all those dark corners in Washington that this time you've gone too far, you've lost your grip, maybe at your age even looney. I've got Marie's story, Mo Panov's—'

'*Morris* Panov?' interrupted Havilland cautiously. 'Webb's psychiatrist?'

'You get another cigar. And, last of all, my own contribution. Incidentally, to jog your memory, I'm the only one who talked to David before he came over here. All together, including the slaughter of a Canadian foreign service officer, they'd make interesting reading – as affidavits, carefully circulated, of course.'

'By so doing you'd jeopardize *everything*.'

'Your problem, not mine.'

'Then, again, I'd have no choice,' said the ambassador, ice once more in his eyes and in his voice. 'As you issued an order for beyond-salvage, I'd be forced to do the same. You wouldn't leave here alive.'

'Oh, my *God!*' whispered McAllister from across the room.

'That'd be the dumbest thing you could do,' said Conklin, his eyes locked with Havilland's. 'You don't know what I've left behind or with whom. Or what's released if I don't make contact by a certain time with certain people and so on. Don't underestimate me.'

'We thought you might resort to that kind of tactic,' said the diplomat, walking away from the CIA man as if dismissing him, and returning to his chair. 'You also left something else behind, Mr Conklin. To put it kindly, perhaps accurately, you were known to have a chronic illness called alcoholism. In anticipation of your imminent retirement, and in recognition of your long-past accomplishments, no disciplinary measures were taken, but neither were you given any responsibility. You were merely tolerated, a useless relic about to go to pasture, a drunk whose paranoid outbursts were the talk and concern of your colleagues. Whatever might surface from whatever source would be categorized and substantiated as the incoherent ramblings of a crippled, psychopathic alcoholic.' The ambassador leaned back in the chair, his elbow resting on the arm, the long fingers of his right hand touching his chin. 'You are to be pitied, Mr Conklin, not censured. The dovetailing of events might be dramatized by your suicide—'

'*Havilland!*' cried McAllister, stunned.

'Rest easy, Mr Undersecretary,' said the diplomat. 'Mr Conklin and I know where we're coming from. We've both been there before.'

'There's a difference,' objected Conklin, his gaze never wavering from Havilland's eyes. 'I never took any pleasure from the game.'

'You think *I* do?' The telephone rang. Havilland shot forward, grabbing it. 'Yes?' The ambassador listened, frowning, staring at the darkened bay window. 'If I don't sound shocked, Major, it's because the news reached me a few minutes ago . . . No, not the police but a man I want you to meet tonight. Say, in two hours, is that convenient? . . . Yes, he's one of us now.' Havilland raised his eyes to Conklin. 'There are those who say he's better than most of us, and I daresay his past service record might bear that out . . . Yes, it's he . . . Yes, I'll tell him . . . What? *What* did you say?' The diplomat again looked at the bay window, the frown returning. 'They covered themselves quickly, didn't they? Two hours, Major.' Havilland hung up the phone, both elbows on the table, his hands clasped. He took a deep breath, an exhausted old man gathering his thoughts, about to speak.

'His name is Lin Wenzu,' said Conklin, startling both Havilland and McAllister. 'He's Crown CI which means MI-Six-oriented, probably Special

Branch. He's Chinese and UK-educated and considered about the best Intelligence officer in the territory. Only his size works against him. He's easily spotted.'

'*Where – ?*' McAllister took a step toward the CIA man.

'A little bird, Cock Robin,' said Conklin.

'A redheaded cardinal, I presume,' said the diplomat.

'Actually, not anymore,' replied Alex.

'I see.' Havilland unclasped his hands, lowering his arms on the desk. 'He knows who you are, too.'

'He should. He was part of the detail at the Kowloon station.'

'He told me to congratulate you, to tell you that your Olympian outraced them. He got away.'

'He's sharp.'

'He knows where to find him but won't waste the time.'

'Sharper still. Waste is waste. He told you something else, too, and since I overheard your flattering assessment of my past, would you care to tell me what it was?'

'Then you'll listen to me?'

'Or be carried out in a box? Or boxes? Where's the option?'

'Yes, quite true,' said the diplomat. 'I'd have to go through with it, you know.'

'I know *you* know, *Herr General.*'

'That's offensive.'

'So are you. What did the major tell you?'

'A terrorist tong from Macao telephoned the South China New Agency claiming responsibility for the killings. Only, they said the woman was incidental, the driver was the target. As a native member of the hated British secret security arm, he had shot to death one of their leaders on the Wanchai waterfront two weeks ago. The information was correct. He was the protection we assigned to Catherine Staples.'

'It's a lie!' shouted Conklin. '*She* was the target!'

'Lin says it's a waste of time to pursue a false source.'

'Then he knows?'

'That we've been penetrated?'

'What the hell *else?*' said the exasperated CIA man.

'He's a proud *Zhongguo ren* and has a brilliant mind. He doesn't like failure in any form, especially now. I suspect he's started his hunt . . . Sit down, Mr Conklin. We have things to talk about.'

'I don't *believe* this!' cried McAllister in a deeply emotional whisper. 'You talk of *killings*, of *targets*, of "beyond-*salvage*" . . . of a mocked-up *suicide* – the victim *here*, talking about his own *death* – as if you were discussing the Dow-Jones or a restaurant menu! What kind of people *are* you?'

'I've told you, Mr Undersecretary,' said Havilland gently. 'Men who do what others won't, or can't, or shouldn't. There's no mystique, no diabolical universities where we were trained, no driving compulsion to destroy. We drifted into these areas because there were voids to fill and the candidates were few. It's all rather accidental, I suppose. And with repetition you find that either you do or you don't have the stomach for it – because somebody has to. Would you agree, Mr Conklin?'

'This is a waste of time.'

'No, it's not,' corrected the diplomat. 'Explain to Mr McAllister. Believe me, he's valuable and we need him. He has to understand us.'

Conklin looked at the undersecretary of State, his expression without charity. 'He doesn't need any explanations from me, he's an analyst. He sees it all as clearly as we do, if not clearer. He knows what the hell is going on down in the tunnels, he just doesn't want to admit it, and the easiest way to remove himself is to pretend to be shocked. Beware the sanctimonious intellect in any phase of this business. What he gives in brains he takes away with phony recriminations. He's the deacon in a whore-house gathering material for a sermon he'll write when he goes home and plays with himself.'

'You were right before,' said McAllister, turning toward the door. 'This is a waste of time.'

'Edward?' Havilland, clearly angry with the crippled CIA man, called out sympathetically to the undersecretary. 'We can't always choose the people we deal with, which is obviously the case now.'

'I understand,' said McAllister coldly.

'Study everyone on Lin's staff,' went on the ambassador. 'There can't be more than ten or twelve who know anything about us. Help him. He's your friend.'

'Yes, he is,' said the undersecretary, going out the door.

'Was that *necessary?*' snapped Havilland when he and Conklin were alone.

'Yes, it was. If you can convince me that what you've done was the only route you could take – which I doubt – or if I can't come up with an option that'll get Marie and David out with their lives, if not their sanity, then I'll have to work with you. The alternative of beyond-salvage is unacceptable on several grounds, basically personal, but also because I owe the Webbs. Do we agree so far?'

'We work together, one way or another. Checkmate.'

'Given the reality, I want that son of a bitch, McAllister, that *rabbit*, to know where *I'm* coming from. He's in as deep as any of us, and that intellect of his had better go down into the filth and come up with every plausibility and every possibility. I want to know whom we should kill – even those marginally important – to cut our losses and get the Webbs out. I want him to know that the only way he can save his soul is to bury it with accomplishment. If we fail, *he* fails, and he can't go back teaching Sunday school anymore.'

'You're too harsh on him. He's an analyst, not an executioner.'

'Where do you think the executioners get their input? Where do *we* get our input? From whom? The paladins of congressional oversight?'

'Checkmate, again. You're as good as they say you were. He's come up with the breakthroughs. It's why he's here.'

'Talk to me, *sir*,' said Conklin, sitting in the chair, his back straight, his club foot awkwardly at an angle. 'I want to hear your story.'

'First the woman. Webb's wife. She's all right? She's safe?'

'The answer to your first question is so obvious I wonder how you can ask it. No, she's not all right. Her husband's missing and she doesn't know whether he's alive or dead. As to the second, yes, she's safe. With me, not with you. I can move us around and I know my way around. You have to stay here.'

'We're *desperate*,' pleaded the diplomat. 'We need her!'

'You've also been penetrated, that doesn't seem to sink in. I won't expose her to that.'

'This house is a fortress!'

'All it takes is one rotten cook in the kitchen. One lunatic on a staircase.'

'Conklin, *listen* to me! We picked up a passport check – everything fits. It's him, we know it. Webb's in Peking. *Now!* He wouldn't have gone in if he wasn't after the target – the *only* target. If somehow, God knows how, your Delta comes out with the merchandise and his wife isn't in place, he'll kill the one connection we *must have!* Without it we're lost. We're all lost.'

'So that was the scenario from the beginning. *Reductio ad absurdum.* Jason Bourne hunts Jason Bourne.'

'Yes. Painfully simple, but without the escalating complications he never would have agreed. He'd still be in that old house in Maine, poring over his scholarly papers. We wouldn't have our hunter.'

'You really *are* a bastard,' said Conklin slowly, softly, a certain admiration in his voice. 'And you were convinced he could still do it? Still handle this kind of Asia the way he did years ago as Delta?'

'He has physical checkups every three months, it's part of the government protection programme. He's in superb condition – something to do with his obsessive running, I understand.'

'Start at the beginning.' The CIA man settled into the chair. 'I want to hear it step by step because I think the rumours are true. I'm in the presence of a master bastard.'

'Hardly, Mr Conklin,' said Havilland. 'We're all groping. I'll want your comments, of course.'

'You'll get them. Go ahead.'

'All right. I'll begin with a name I'm sure you'll recognize. Sheng Chou Yang. Any comment?'

'He's a tough negotiator, and I suspect that underneath his benevolent exterior there's a ramrod. Still, he's one of the most reasonable men in Peking. There should be a thousand like him.'

'If there were, the chances of a Far East holocaust would be a thousand times greater.'

Lin Wenzu slammed his fist down on the desk, jarring the nine photographs in front of him and making the attached summaries of their dossiers leap off the surface. *Which?* Which *one?* Each had been certified through London, each background checked and rechecked and triple-checked; there was no room for error. These were not simply well-schooled *Zhongguo ren* selected by bureaucratic elimination but the products of an intensive search for the brightest minds in government – and in several cases outside of government – who might be recruited into this most sensitive of services. It had been Lin's contention that the writing was on the wall – the Great Wall, perhaps – and that a superior special Intelligence force manned by the colony's own could well be its first line of defence prior to 1997, and, in the event of a takeover, its first line of cohesive resistance afterwards. The British *had* to relinquish leadership in the area of secret Intelligence operations for reasons that were as clear as they were unpalatable to London: the Occidental could never fully understand the peculiar subtleties of the Oriental mind, and these were not the times to render misleading or poorly evaluated information. London had to know – the West had to know – exactly where things stood . . . for Hong Kong's sake, for the sake of the entire Far East.

Not that Lin believed that his growing task force of Intelligence gatherers was pivotal to policy decisions; he did not. But he believed thoroughly, intensely, that if the colony was to have a Special Branch it should be staffed and run by those who could do the job best, and that did not include veterans, however brilliant, of the European-oriented British secret services. For starters, they all looked alike and were not compatible with either the environment or the language. And after years of work and proven worth, Lin Wenzu had been summoned to London and for three days grilled by unsmiling Far East Intelligence specialists. On the morning of the fourth day, however, the smiles had appeared along with the recommendation that the major be given command of the Hong Kong branch with wide powers of authority. And for a number of years thereafter he had lived up to the commission's confidence, he knew that. He also knew that now, in the single most vital operation of his professional and personal life, he had failed. There were thirty-eight Special Branch officers in his command, and he had selected nine – hand-picked *nine* – to be part of this extraordinary, *insane* operation. Insane until he had heard the ambassador's extraordinary explanation. The nine were the most exceptional of the thirty-eight-man task force, each capable of assuming command if their leader was taken out; he had written as much in their evaluation reports. And he had failed. One of the hand-picked nine was a traitor.

It was pointless to restudy the dossiers. Whatever inconsistencies he might find would take too long to unearth, for they – or *it* – had eluded his own experienced eyes as well as London's. There was no time for intricate analyses, the painfully slow exploration of nine individual lives. He had only one choice. A frontal assault on each man, and the word 'front' was intrinsic to his plan. If he could play the role of a taipan, he could play the part of a traitor. He realized that his plan was not without risk – a risk neither London nor the American, Havilland, would tolerate, but it had to be taken. If he failed, Sheng Chou Yang would be alerted to the secret war against him and his countermoves could be disastrous, but Lin Wenzu did not intend to fail. If failure was written on the northern winds, nothing else would matter, least of all his life.

The major reached for his telephone. He pushed the button on his console for the radio operator in the computerized communication centre of MI6, Special Branch.

'Yes, sir?' said the voice from the white, sterile room.

'Who in Dragonfly is still on duty?' asked Lin, naming the elite unit of nine who reported in but never gave explanations.

'Two, sir. In vehicles three and seven, but I can reach the rest in a few minutes. Five have checked in – they're at home – and the remaining two have left numbers. One is at the Pagoda Cinema until eleven-thirty, when he'll return to his flat, but he can be reached by beeper until then. The other is at the Yacht Club in Aberdeen with his wife and her family. She's English, you know.'

Lin laughed softly. 'No doubt charging the British family's bill to our woefully inadequate budget from London.'

'Is that possible, Major? If so, would you consider me for Dragonfly, whatever it is?'

'Don't be impertinent.'

'I'm sorry, sir—'

'I'm joking, young man. Next week I'll take you to a fine dinner myself. You do excellent work and I rely on you.'

'Thank you, sir!'

'The thanks are mine.'

'Shall I contact Dragonfly and put out an alert?'

'You may contact each and every one, but quite the opposite of an alert. They've all been overworked, without a clean day off in several weeks. Tell each that, of course, I want any changes of locations to be reported, but unless informed otherwise we're secure for the next twenty-four hours, and the men in vehicles three and seven may drive them home but not up into the Territories for drinks. Tell them I said they should all get a good night's sleep, or however they wish to pass the time.'

'Yes, sir. They'll appreciate that, sir.'

'I myself will be wandering around in vehicle four. You may hear from me. Stay awake.'

'Of course, Major.'

'You've got a dinner coming, young man.'

'If I may, sir,' said the enthusiastic radio operator, 'and I know I speak for all of us. We wouldn't care to work for anyone but you.'

'Perhaps two dinners.'

Parked in front of an apartment house on Yun Ping Road, Lin lifted the microphone out of its cradle below the dashboard. 'Radio, it's Dragonfly Zero.'

'Yes, sir?'

'Switch me to a direct telephone line with a scrambler. I'll know we're on scrambler when I hear the echo on my part of the call, won't I?'

'Naturally, sir.'

The faint echo pulsated over the line, with the dial tone. The major punched in the numbers; the ringing began and a female voice answered.

'Yes?'

'Mr Zhou. *Kuai!*' said Lin, his words rushed, telling the woman to hurry.

'Certainly,' she replied in Cantonese.

'Zhou here,' said the man.

'*Xun su! Xiao Xi!*' Lin spoke in a throated whisper; it was the sound of a desperate man pleading to be heard. 'Sheng! Contact instantly! Sapphire is gone!'

'*What?* Who *is* this?'

The major pressed down the bar and pushed a button to the right of the microphone. The radio operator spoke instantly.

'Yes, Dragonfly?'

'Patch into my private line, also on scrambler, and reroute all calls here. Right *away!* This will be standard procedure until I instruct otherwise. *Understood?*'

'Yes, sir,' said a subdued radioman.

The mobile phone buzzed and Lin picked it up, speaking casually. 'Yes?' he answered, feigning a yawn.

'Major, this is Zhou! I just had a very strange call. A man phoned me – he sounded badly hurt – and told me to contact someone named Sheng. I was to say that Sapphire was *gone.*'

'*Sapphire?*' said the major, suddenly alert. 'Say nothing to anyone, Zhou! Damned computers – I don't know how it happened, but that call was meant for me. This is beyond Dragonfly. I repeat, say nothing to anyone!'

'Understood, sir.'

Lin started the car and drove several blocks west to Tanlung Street. He repeated the exercise, and again the call came over his private line.

'*Major?*'

'Yes?'

'I just got off the phone with someone who sounded like he was *dying!* He wanted me to . . .'

The explanation was the same: a dangerous error had been made, beyond the purview of Dragonfly. Nothing was to be repeated. The order was understood.

Lin called three more numbers, each time from in front of each recipient's apartment or boardinghouse. All were negative; each man reached him within moments after a call with his startling news and none had raced outside to a random sterile pay phone. The major knew only one thing for certain. Whoever the infiltrator was, he would not use his home phone to make contact. Telephone bills recorded all numbers dialled, and all bills were submitted for departmental audit. It was a routine containment procedure that was welcomed by the agents. Excess charges were picked up by Special Branch as if they were related to business.

The two men in vehicles three and seven, having been relieved of duty, had checked in with headquarters by the fifth telephone call. One was at a girlfriend's house and made it plain that he had no intention of leaving for the next twenty-four hours. He pleaded with the radioman to take all 'emergency calls from clients,' telling everyone who tried to reach him that his superiors had sent him to the Antarctic. *Negative. It was not the way of a double agent, including the humour. He neither cut himself off nor revealed the whereabouts or the identity of a drop.* The second man was, if possible, more negative. He informed headquarters-communications that he was available for any and all problems, major or minor, related or unrelated to Dragonfly, even to answering the phones. His wife had recently given birth to triplets, and he confided in a voice that bordered on panic – according to the radioman – he got more rest on the job than at home. *Negative.*

Seven down and seven negative. That left one man at the Pagoda Cinema for another forty minutes, and the other at the Yacht Club in Aberdeen.

His mobile phone hummed – emphatically, it seemed, or was it his own anxiety? 'Yes?'

'I just received a message for you, sir,' said the radio operator. '"Eagle to Dragonfly Zero. Urgent. Respond."'

'Thank you.' Lin looked at the clock in the centre of the dashboard. He was thirty-five minutes late for his appointment with Havilland and the legendary crippled agent from years past, Alexander Conklin. 'Young man?' said the major, bringing the microphone back to his lips.

'Yes, sir?'

'I have no time for the anxious if somewhat irrelevant "Eagle," but I don't wish to offend him. He'll call again when I don't respond, and I want you to explain that you've been unable to reach me. Of course, when you do, you'll give me the message immediately.'

'It will be a delight, Major.'

'I beg your pardon?'

'The "Eagle" who called was very disagreeable. He shouted about appointments that should be kept when they were confirmed and that . . .'

Lin listened to the secondhand diatribe and made a mental note that if he survived the night he would talk to Edward McAllister about telephone etiquette, especially during emergencies. Sugar brought gentle expressions, salt only grimaces. 'Yes, yes, I understand, young man. As our ancestors might say, "May the eagle's beak be caught in its elimination canal." Just do as I say, and in the meantime – in fifteen minutes from now – raise our man at the Pagoda Cinema. When he calls in, give him my unlisted fourth-level number and patch it into this frequency, scrambler continuing, of course.'

'Of course, sir.'

Lin sped east on Hennessy Road past Southorn Park to Fleming, where he turned south into Johnston and east again on Burrows Street and the Pagoda Cinema. He swerved into the parking lot, taking the spot reserved for the assistant manager. He stuck a police card in the front window, got out, and ran up to the entrance. There were only a few people at the window for the midnight showing of *Lust in the Orient*, an odd choice for the agent inside. Nevertheless, to avoid calling attention to himself, since he had six minutes to go, he stood behind three men who were waiting in front of the booth. Ninety seconds later he had paid for and received his ticket. He went inside, gave it to the taker, and adjusted his eyes to the darkness and to the pornographic motion picture on the distant screen. It *was* an odd choice of entertainment for the man he was testing, but he had vowed to himself he would permit no prejudgements, no balancing of one suspect against another.

It was admittedly difficult in this case, however. Not that he particularly liked the man who was somewhere in that darkened theatre, watching along with the feverishly attentive audience the sexual gymnastics of the wooden 'actors.' In truth he did *not* like the man; he simply recognized the fact that he was among the best in his command. The agent was arrogant and unpleasant, but he was also a brave soul whose defection from Beijing was eighteen months in the making, his every hour in the Communist capital a threat to his life. He had been a high-ranking officer in the Security Forces, with access to invaluable Intelligence information. And in a heartrending gesture of sacrifice he had left behind a beloved wife and girl child when he escaped south, protecting them with a charred, bullet-ridden corpse that he made sure was identified as himself – a hero of China shot and then burned by a roving band of hoodlums in the recent crime wave that had swept through the Mainland. Mother and daughter were secure, pensioned by the government, and like all high-level defectors, he was subjected to the most rigorous examinations designed to trap potential infiltrators. Here his arrogance had actually helped him. He had made no attempt to ingratiate himself; he was what he was and he had done what he had done for the good of Mother China. Either the authorities could accept him with all he had to offer or he would look elsewhere. Everything checked, except the well-being of his wife and child. They were not being taken care of in the manner the defector had expected. Therefore money was filtered through to her place of work without explanation. She could be told nothing; if there was the slightest suspicion that her husband was alive, she could be tortured for information she did not possess. The in-depth profile of such a man was not the profile of a double agent, regardless of his taste in films.

That left the man in Aberdeen, and he was something of a puzzle to Lin. The agent was older than the others, a small man who always dressed impeccably, a logician and former accountant who professed such loyalty that once Lin had almost made him a confidant, but had pulled himself up short when he was close to revealing things he should not reveal. Perhaps because the man was nearer his own age he felt a stronger kinship . . . On the other hand, what an extraordinary cover for a mole from Beijing. Married to an Englishwoman, and a member of the rich and social Yacht Club by way of marriage. Everything was in place for him; he was respectability itself. It seemed incredible to Lin that his closest colleague, the man who had imposed such order on his personal life but still wanted to arrest an Australian brawler for causing Dragonfly to lose face, could have been reached by Sheng Chou Yang and corrupted . . . No, *impossible!* Perhaps, thought the major, he should go back and examine further a comical off-duty agent who wanted all clients to be told he was in the Antarctic, or the overworked father of triplets who was willing to answer phones to escape his domestic chores.

These speculations were not in order! Lin Wenzu shook his head as if ridding his mind of such thoughts. *Now. Here. Concentrate!* His sudden decision to move came from the sight of a stairway. He walked over to it and climbed the steps to the balcony; the projection room was directly in front of him. He knocked once on the door and went inside, the weight of his body breaking the cheap, thin bolt on the door.

'*Ting zhi!*' yelled the projectionist; a woman was on his lap, his hand under her skirt. The young woman leaped away from her perch and turned to the wall.

'Crown Police,' said the major, showing his identification. 'And I mean no harm to either of you, please believe that.'

'You shouldn't!' replied the projectionist. 'This isn't exactly a place of worship.'

'That might be disputed, but it certainly isn't a church.'

'We operate with a fully paid licence—'

'You have no argument from me, sir,' interrupted Lin. 'The Crown simply needs a favour, and it could hardly be against your interests to provide it.'

'What is it?' asked the man, getting up, angrily watching the woman slip through the door.

'Stop the film for, say, thirty seconds and turn up the lights. Announce to the audience that there was a break and that it will be repaired quickly.'

The projectionist winced. 'It's almost over! There'll be screaming!'

'As long as there are lights. *Do it!*'

The projector ground down with a whir; the lights came up, and the announcement was made over the loudspeaker. The projectionist was right. Catcalls echoed throughout the motion picture house, accompanied by waving arms and numerous extended third fingers. Lin's eyes scanned the audience – back and forth, row by row.

There was his man . . . *Two* men – the agent was leaning forward talking to someone Lin Wenzu had never seen before. The major looked at his watch, then turned to the projectionist. 'Is there a public phone downstairs?'

'When it works, there is. When it isn't broken.'

'Is it working now?'

'I don't know.'

'Where is it?'

'Below the staircase.'

'Thank you. Start the film again in sixty seconds.'

'You said thirty!'

'I've changed my mind. And you do enjoy the privileges of a good job because of a licence, don't you?'

'They're *animals* down there!'

'Put a chair against the door,' said Lin, going outside. 'The lock's broken.'

In the lobby beneath the staircase the major passed the exposed pay phone. Barely pausing, he yanked the spiral cord out of the box, and proceeded outside to his car, stopping at the sight of a phone booth across the road. He raced over and read the number, instantly memorizing it, and ran back to the car. He climbed into the seat and looked at his watch; he backed up the automobile, drove out into the street, and double-parked several hundred feet beyond the theatre's marquee. He turned his headlights off and watched the entrance.

A minute and fifteen seconds later the defector from Beijing emerged, looking first to his right, then to his left, obviously agitated. He then looked straight ahead, seeing what he wanted to see, what Lin expected him to see, since the telephone in the theatre was not working. It was the phone booth on the other side of the road. Lin dialled as his subordinate ran over to it, spinning into the plastic shell that faced the street. It rang before the man could insert his coins.

'*Xun su! Xiao Xi!*' Lin coughed as he whispered. 'I knew you would find the phone! *Sheng!* Contact instantly! Sapphire is *gone!*' He replaced the microphone, but left his hand on the instrument, expecting to remove it with the agent's incoming call on his private line.

It did not come. He turned in his seat and looked back at the open, plastic shell of the pay phone across the road. The agent had dialled another number, but the defector was not speaking to him. There was no need to drive to Aberdeen.

The major silently got out of the car, walked across the street into the shadows of the far pavement, and started toward the pay phone. He stayed in the relative darkness, moving slowly, calling as little attention to his bulk as he could, cursing, as he often did, the genes that had produced his outsized figure. Remaining well back in the shadows, he approached the phone. The defector was eight feet away, his back to Lin, talking excitedly, exasperation in every sentence.

'Who is *Sapphire?* Why this *telephone?* Why would he reach *me?* . . . No, I *told* you, he used the leader's name! . . . Yes, that's right, his *name!* No code, no symbol! It was *insane!*'

Lin Wenzu heard all he had to hear. He pulled out his service automatic and walked rapidly out of the darkness.

'The film broke and they turned up the lights! My contact and I were—'

'Hang up the phone!' ordered the major.

The defector spun around. '*You!*' he screamed.

Lin rushed the man, his immense body crushing the double agent into the plastic shell as he grabbed the phone, smashing it into the metal box. '*Enough!*' he roared.

Suddenly, he felt the blade slicing with ice-cold heat into his abdomen. The defector crouched, the knife in his left hand, and Lin squeezed the trigger. The sound of the explosion filled the quiet street as the traitor dropped to the pavement, his throat ripped open by the bullet, blood streaming down his clothes, staining the concrete below.

'*Ni made!*' screamed a voice on the major's left, cursing him. It was the second man, the contact who had been inside the theatre talking with the defector. He raised a gun and fired as the major lunged, and Lin's huge bleeding torso fell into the man like a wall. Flesh blew apart in Lin's upper right chest, but the killer's balance was shaken. The major fired his automatic; the man fell clutching his right eye. He was dead.

Across the street, the pornographic film had ended and the crowd began to emerge on the street, sullen, angry, ungratified. And with what remained of his enormous strength, the badly wounded Lin picked up the bodies of the two dead conspirators and half dragged, half carried them back to his car. A number of people from the Pagoda's audience watched him with glazed or disinterested stares. What they saw was a reality they could not contend with or comprehend. It was beyond the narrow confines of their fantasies.

Alex Conklin rose from the chair and limped awkwardly, noisily to the darkened bay window. 'What the *hell* do you want me to say?' he asked, turning and looking at the ambassador.

'That given the circumstances I took the only road open to me, the only one that would have recruited Jason Bourne.' Havilland held up his hand. 'Before you answer, I should tell you in all fairness that Catherine Staples did not agree with me. She felt I should have appealed to David Webb directly. He was, after all, a Far East scholar, an expert who would understand stakes, the tragedy that could follow.'

'She was nuts,' said Alex. 'He would have told you to shove it.'

'Thank you for that.' The diplomat nodded his head.

'Just hold it,' Conklin broke in. 'He would have said that to you not because he thought you were wrong, but because he didn't think he could *do* it. What you did – by taking Marie away from him – was to make him go back and be someone he wanted to forget.'

'Oh?'

'You really *are* one son of a bitch, you son of a bitch.'

Sirens suddenly erupted, ringing throughout the enormous house and the grounds, as searchlights began spinning through the windows. Gunfire accompanied the sound of smashing metal as tyres screeched outside. The ambassador and the CIA man lurched to the floor; in seconds it was all over. Both men got to their feet as the door was crashed open. His chest and stomach drenched in blood, Lin Wenzu staggered in, carrying two dead bodies under his arms.

'Here is your traitor, sir,' said the major, dropping both corpses. 'And a colleague. With these two, I believe we've cut off Dragonfly from Sheng—' Wenzu's eyes rolled upward until the sockets were white. He gasped and fell to the floor.

'Call an *ambulance!*' shouted Havilland to the people who had gathered at the door.

'Get gauze, tape, towels, antiseptic – for Christ's sake, anything you can *find!*' yelled Conklin, limping, racing over to the fallen Chinese. 'Stop the goddamned *bleeding!*'

29

Bourne sat in the racing shadows of the backseat, the intermittent moonlight bright, creating brief explosions of light and dark inside the automobile. At sudden, irregular, unexpected moments he leaned forward and pressed the barrel of his gun into the back of his prisoner's neck. 'Try crashing off the road and there's a bullet in your head. Do you understand me?'

And always there was the same reply, or a variation of it, spoken in a clipped British accent. 'I'm not a fool. You're behind me and you've got a weapon and I can't see you.'

Jason had ripped the rearview mirror from its bracket, the bolt having cracked easily in his hand. 'Then I'm your eyes back here, remember that. I'm also the end of your life.'

'Understood,' the former officer in the Royal Commandos repeated without expression.

The government road map spread out on his lap, the penlight cupped in his left hand, the automatic in his right, Bourne studied the roads heading south. As each half hour passed and landmarks were spotted, Jason understood that time was his enemy. Although the assassin's right arm was effectively immobilized, Bourne knew he was no match for the younger, stronger man in sheer stamina. The concentrated violence of the last three days had taken its toll physically, mentally, and – whether he cared to acknowledge it or not – emotionally, and while Jason Bourne did not have to acknowledge it, David Webb proclaimed it with every fibre of his emotional being. The scholar had to be kept at bay, deep down inside, his voice stilled.

Leave me alone! You're worthless to me!

Every now and then Jason felt the dead weight of his lids closing over his eyes. He would snap them open and abuse some part of his body, pinching hard the soft sensitive flesh of his inner thigh or digging his nails into his lids, to create instant pain so as to dispel the exhaustion. He recognized his condition – only a suicidal fool would not – and there was no time or place to remedy it with an axiom he had stolen from Medusa's Echo. *Rest is a weapon, never forget it.* Forget it, Echo . . . brave Echo . . . there's no time for rest, no place to find it.

And while he accepted his own assessment of himself, he also had to accept his evaluation of his prisoner. The killer was totally alert; his sharpness was in his skill at the wheel, for Jason demanded speed over the strange, unfamiliar roads. It was in his constantly moving head, and it was in his eyes whenever

Bourne saw them, and he saw them frequently whenever he directed the assassin to slow down and watch for an off-shooting road on the right or the left. The imposter would turn in the seat – the sight of his so-familiar features always a shock to Jason – and ask whether the road ahead was the one his '*eyes*' wanted. The questions were superfluous; the former commando was continuously making his own assessment of his captor's physical and mental condition. He was a trained killer, a lethal machine who knew that survival depended on gaining the advantage over his enemy. He was waiting, watching, anticipating the moment when his adversary's eyelids might close for that brief instant or when the weapon might suddenly drop to the floor, or his enemy's head might recline for a second into the comfort of the backseat. These were the signs he was waiting for, the lapses he could capitalize on to violently alter the circumstances. Bourne's defence, therefore, depended upon his mind, in doing the unexpected so that the psychological balance remained in his favour. How long could it last – could *he* last?

Time was his enemy, the assassin in front of him a secondary problem. In his past – that vaguely remembered past – he had handled killers before, manipulated them before, because they were human beings subject to the wiles of his imagination. *Christ*, it came down to that! So simple, so logical – and he was so tired . . . His *mind*. There was nothing else left! He had to keep thinking, had to keep prodding his imagination and make it do its work. Balance, *balance!* He had to keep it on *his* side! *Think. Act.* Do the *unexpected!*

He removed the silencer from his weapon, levelled the gun at the closed right-front window, and pulled the trigger. The explosion was ear-shattering, reverberating throughout the enclosed car, as the glass splintered, blowing out into the rushing night air.

'What the hell was *that* for?' screamed the impostor-assassin, clutching the wheel, holding an involuntary swerve in control.

'To teach you about balance,' answered Jason. 'You should understand that I'm unbalanced. The next shot could blow your head away.'

'You're a fucking *lunatic*, that's what you are!'

'I'm glad you understand.'

The map. One of the more civilized things about a PRC road map – and consistent with the quality of its vehicles – was the starred indicators of garages which were open twenty-four hours a day along the major routes. One had only to think of the confusion that might result from military and official transports breaking down to understand the necessity; it was heaven-sent for Bourne.

'There's a gas station about four miles down this road,' he said to the assassin – to *Jason Bourne*, he reflected. 'Stop and refill and don't say a word – which would be foolish if you tried, because you obviously can't speak the language. You must memorize the few pathetic words you need.'

'You *do* speak it?'

'It's why I'm the original and you're the fake.'

'You can bloody well *have* it, Mr *Original!*'

Jason fired the gun again, blowing the rest of the window away. 'The *fake!*' he yelled, raising his voice over the sound of the wind. 'Remember that.'

Time was the enemy.

He took a mental inventory of what he had, and it was not much. Money was his primary ammunition; he had more than a hundred Chinese could make in a hundred lifetimes, but money in itself was not the answer. Only time was the answer. If he had a prayer to get out of the vast land of China, it had to be by air, not on the ground. He would not last that long. Again, he studied the map. It would take thirteen to fifteen hours to reach Shanghai – *if* the car held up and if *he* held up, and if *they* could get by the provincial checkpoints where he knew there would be alarms out for a Westerner, or two Westerners, attempting to pass through. He would be taken – *they* would be taken. And even if they reached Shanghai, with its relatively lax airport, how many complications might arise?

There was an option – there were always options. It was crazy and outrageous, but it was the only thing left.

Time was the enemy. Do it. There is no other choice.

He circled a small symbol on the outskirts of the city of Jinan. An airport.

Dawn. Wetness everywhere. The ground, the tall grass, and the metal fence glistened with morning dew. The single runway beyond was a shining black shaft cutting across the close-cropped field, half green with today's moisture, half dullish brown from the pounding of yesterday's broiling sun. The Shanghai sedan was far off the airport road, as far off as the assassin could drive it, again concealed by foliage. The impostor was once more immobilized, now by the thumbs. Pressing the gun into his right temple, Jason had ordered the assassin to wind the spools of wire into double slipknots around each thumb, and then he had snapped the spools away with his cutter, run the wire back and coiled the two remaining strands tightly around the killer's wrists. As the commando discovered, with any slight pressure, such as twisting or separating his hands, the wire dug deeper into his flesh.

'If I were you,' said Bourne, 'I'd be careful. Can you imagine what it would be like having no thumbs? Or if your wrists were cut?'

'Fucking technician!'

'Believe it.'

Across the airfield a light was turned on in a one-story building with a row of small windows along the side. It was a barracks of sorts, simple in design and functional. Then there were other lights – naked bulbs, the glows more like glares. A barracks. Jason reached for the coiled roll of clothing he had removed from the small of his back; he undid the straps, unfurled the garments over the grass and separated them. There was a large Mao jacket, a pair of rumpled outsized trousers, and a visored cloth hat that was standard for the clothes. He put on the hat and the jacket, buttoning the latter over his dark sweater, then stood up and pulled the large trousers over his own. A webbed cloth belt held them in place. He smoothed the drab, bulky jacket over the trousers, and turned to the assassin, who was watching him with astonishment and curiosity.

'Get over to the fence,' said Jason, bending down and digging into his knapsack. 'Get on your knees and lean into it,' he continued, pulling out a five-foot length of thin nylon rope. 'Press your face into the links. Eyes front! Hurry *up!*'

The killer did as he was told, his bound hands awkwardly, painfully in front of him between his body and the fence, his head pressed into the wire mesh. Bourne walked rapidly over and quickly threaded the rope through the fence on the right side of the assassin's neck, and with his fingers reaching through the open squares he swung the line across the commando's face and pulled the rope back through. He yanked it taut and knotted it at the base of the assassin's skull. He had worked so swiftly and so unexpectedly that the former officer could barely get out the words before he realized what had happened. 'What the *hell* are you – oh, *Christ!*'

'As that maniac remarked about d'Anjou before he hacked into his head, you're not going anywhere, Major.'

'You're going to *leave* me here?' asked the killer, stunned.

'Don't be foolish. We're on the buddy system. Where I go, you go. Actually, you're going first.'

'*Where?*'

'Through the fence,' said Jason, taking the wire cutter from the knapsack. He began cutting a pattern around the assassin's torso, relieved that the wire links were nowhere near as thick as those at the bird sanctuary. The outline complete, Bourne stepped back and raised his right foot, placing it between the impostor's shoulder blades. He shoved his leg forward. Killer and fence fell collapsing onto the grass on the other side.

'*Jesus!*' cried the commando in pain. 'Pretty fucking funny, aren't you?'

'I don't feel remotely amusing,' replied Jason. 'Every move I make is very unfunny, very serious. Get up and keep your voice down.'

'For Christ's sake, I'm tied to the damn fence!'

'It's free. Get up and turn around.' Awkwardly the assassin staggered to his feet. Bourne surveyed his work; the sight of the outline of wire mesh attached to the killer's upper body, as though held in place by a protruding nose, *was* funny. But the reason for its being there was not funny at all. Only with the assassin secure in front of his eyes was all risk eliminated. Jason could not control what he could not see, and what he could not see could cost him his life . . . Far more important, the life of David Webb's wife – even David Webb. *Stay away from me! Don't interfere! We're too close!*

Bourne reached over and yanked the bowknot free, holding on to one end of the line. The fence fell away, and before the assassin could adjust, Jason whipped the rope around the commando's head, raising it so that the line was caught in the killer's mouth. He pulled it tight, *tighter*, stretching the assassin's jaw open until it was a gaping dark hole surrounded by a border of white teeth, the flesh creased in place, unintelligible sounds emerging from the commando's throat.

'I can't take credit for this, Major,' said Bourne, knotting the thin nylon rope, the remaining thirty-odd inches hanging loose. 'I watched d'Anjou and the others. They couldn't talk, they could only gag on their own vomit. You saw them, too, and you grinned. How does it feel, Major? . . . Oh, I forgot, you can't answer, can you?' He shoved the assassin forward, then gripped his shoulder, sending him to the left. 'We'll skirt the end of the runway,' he said. '*Move!*'

As they rounded the airfield grass, staying in the darkness of the borders, Jason studied the relatively primitive airport. Beyond the barracks was a small circular building with a profusion of glass but no lights shining except a single glare in a small square structure set in the centre of the roof. The building was Jinan's terminal, he thought, the barely lit square on top the control tower. To the left of the barracks, at least two hundred feet to the west, was a dark, open, high-ceilinged maintenance hangar with huge wheeled ladders near the wide doors reflecting the early light. It was apparently deserted, with the crews still in their quarters. Down in the southern perimeter of the field, on both sides of the runway and barely discernible, were five aircraft, all props and none imposing. The Jinan Airport was a secondary, even tertiary, landing field, undoubtedly being upgraded, as were so many airports in China in the cause of foreign investment, but it was a long way from international status. Then, again, the air corridors were channels in the sky and not subject to the cosmetic or technological whims of airports. One simply had to enter those channels and, stay on course. The sky acknowledged no borders; only earth-bound men and machines did. Combined, they were another problem.

'We're going into the hangar,' whispered Jason, jabbing the commando's back. 'Remember, if you make any noise, I won't have to kill you – they will. And I'll have my chance to get away because you'll be giving it to me. Don't doubt it. Get *down!*'

Thirty yards away a guard walked out of the cavernous structure, a rifle slung over his shoulder, his arms stretching as his chest swelled with a yawn. Bourne knew it was the moment to act; a better one might not present itself. The assassin was prone, his wire-bound hands beneath him, his gaping mouth pressed into the earth. Grabbing the loose nylon rope, Jason gripped the killer's hair, yanking up his head, and looped the line twice around the commando's neck. 'You move, you *choke*,' whispered Bourne, getting to his feet.

He ran silently to the hangar's wall, then quickly walked to the corner and peered around the edge. The guard had barely moved. Then Jason understood – the man was urinating. Perfectly natural and perfectly perfect. Bourne stepped away from the building, dug his right foot into the grass and rushed forward, his weapon a rigid right hand preceded by an arcing left foot striking the base of the guard's spine. The man collapsed, unconscious. Jason dragged him back to the corner of the hangar, then across the grass to where the assassin lay immobile, afraid to move.

'You're learning, Major,' said Bourne, again grabbing the commando's hair and pulling the nylon rope from around his neck. The fact that the looped rope would not have choked the impostor, any more than a loose clothes-line wound around a person's neck would, told Delta something. His prisoner could not think geometrically; stresses were not a strong point in the killer's imagination, only the spoken threat of death. It was something to bear in mind. 'Get up,' ordered Jason. The assassin did so, his gaping mouth swallowing air, his eyes full of hatred. 'Think about Echo,' said Bourne, his own eyes returning the killer's loathing. 'Excuse me, I mean d'Anjou. The man who gave you your life back – *a* life, at any rate, and one you apparently took to. Your Pygmalion, *old chap!* . . . Now, hear me, and hear me well. Would you like the rope removed?'

'*Auggh!*' grunted the assassin, nodding his head, his eyes reduced from hatred to pleading.

'And your thumbs released?'

'*Auggh, auggh!*'

'You're not a guerrilla, you're a gorilla,' said Jason, pulling the automatic from his belt. 'But as we used to say in the old days – before your time, *chap* – there are "conditions." You see, either we both get out of here alive, or we disappear, our mortal remains consigned to a Chinese fire, no past, no present – certainly no retrospective regarding our subzero contributions to society . . . I see I'm boring you. Sorry, I'll forget the whole thing.'

'*Auggh!*'

'Okay, if you insist. Naturally, I won't give you a weapon, and if I see you trying to grab one, you're dead. But if you behave, we might – just *might* – get away. What I'm really saying to you, Mr *Bourne*, is that whoever your client is over here can't allow you to live any more than he can *me*. Understand? Dig? *Capisce?*'

'*Auggh!*'

'One thing more,' added Jason, tugging at the rope that fell over the commando's shoulder. 'This is nylon, or polyurethane, or whatever the hell they call it. When it's burned, it just swells up like a marshmallow; there's no way you can untie it. It'll be attached to both your ankles, both knots curled up into cement. You'll have a step-span of approximately five feet – only because I'm a technician. Do I make myself clear?'

The assassin nodded, and as he did so Bourne sprang to his right, kicking the back of the commando's knees, sending the impostor to the ground, his bound thumbs bleeding. Jason knelt down, the gun in his left hand pressed into the killer's mouth, the fingers of his right undoing the bowknot behind the commando's head.

'Christ *Almighty!*' cried the assassin as the rope fell away.

'I'm glad you're of a religious persuasion,' said Bourne, dropping the weapon and rapidly lashing the rope around the commando's ankles, forming a square knot on each; he ignited his lighter and fired the ends. 'You may need it.' He picked up the gun, held it against the killer's forehead, and uncoiled the wire around his prisoner's wrists. 'Take off the rest,' he ordered. 'Be careful with the thumbs, they're damaged.'

'My right arm's no piece of cake, either!' said the Englishman, struggling to remove the slipknots. His hands freed, the assassin shook them, then sucked the blood from his wounds. 'You got your magic box, Mr *Bourne?*' he asked.

'Always an arm's length away, Mr Bourne,' replied Jason. 'What do you need?'

'Tape. Fingers bleed. It's called gravity.'

'You're well schooled.' Bourne reached behind him for the knapsack and pulled it forward, dropping it in front of the commando, his gun levelled at the killer's head. 'Feel around. It's a spool near the top.'

'Got it,' said the assassin, removing the tape and rapidly winding it around his thumbs. 'This is one rotten fucking thing to do to anybody,' he added when he had finished.

'Think of d'Anjou,' said Jason flatly.

'He *wanted* to die, for Christ's sake! What the hell was *I* supposed to do?'

'Nothing. Because you are nothing.'

'Well then, that kind of puts me on *your* level, doesn't it, sport? He made me into *you!*'

'You don't have the talent,' said Jason Bourne. 'You're lacking. You can't think geometrically.'

'What does *that* mean?'

'Ponder it.' Delta rose to his feet. 'Get up,' he commanded.

'Tell me,' said the assassin, pushing himself off the ground and staring at the weapon aimed at his head. 'Why *me?* Why did you ever get out of the business?'

'Because I was never in it.'

Suddenly, floodlights – one after another – began to wash over the field, and with a single brilliant illumination, yellow marker lights appeared along the entire length of the runway. Men ran out of the barracks, a number toward the hangar, others behind their quarters where the engines of unseen vehicles abruptly roared. The lights of the terminal were turned on; activity was at once everywhere.

'Take his jacket off and the hat,' ordered Bourne, pointing the gun at the unconscious guard. 'Put them on.'

'They won't fit!'

'You can have them altered in Savile Row. *Move!*'

The impostor did as he was told, his right arm so much a problem that Jason had to hold the sleeve for him. With Bourne prodding the commando with the gun, both men ran to the wall of the hangar, then moved cautiously toward the end of the building.

'Do we agree?' asked Bourne, whispering, looking at the face that was so like his own years ago. 'We get out or we die?'

'Understood,' answered the commando. 'That screaming bastard with his bloody fancy sword is a fucking lunatic. I want out!'

'That reaction wasn't on your face.'

'If it had been, the maniac might have turned on me!'

'Who is he?'

'Never got a name. Only a series of connections to reach him. The first was a man at the Guangdong garrison named Soo Jiang—'

'I've heard the name. They call him the Pig.'

'It's probably accurate, I don't know.'

'Then what?'

'A number is left at Table Five at the casino in—'

'The Kam Pek, Macao,' interrupted Jason. 'What then?'

'I call the number and speak French. This Soo Jiang is one of the few slants who speak the language. He sets the time of the meet; it's always the same place. I go across the border to a field up in the hills where a chopper comes in and someone gives me the name of the target. And half the money for the kill . . . *Look!* Here it comes! He's circling into his approach.'

'My gun's at your head.'

'Understood.'

'Did your training include flying one of those things?'

'No. Only jumping out of them.'

'That won't do us any good.'

The incoming plane, its red lights blinking on the wings, swept down, out of the brightening sky toward the runway. The jet landed smoothly. It taxied to the end of the asphalt, swung to the right, and headed back to the terminal.

'*Kai guan qi you!*' shouted a voice from in front of the hangar, the man pointing at three fuel trucks off to the side, explaining which one was to be used.

'They're gassing up,' said Jason. 'The plane's taking off again. Let's get on it.'

The assassin turned, his face – that *face* – pleading. 'For Christ's sake, give me a knife, *something!*'

'Nothing.'

'I can *help!*'

'This is my show, Major, not yours. With a knife you'd slice my stomach apart. No way, *chap.*'

'*Da long xia!*' cried the same voice from in front of the hangar, describing government officials in terms of large crayfish. '*Fang song,*' he continued, telling everyone to relax, that the plane would taxi away from the terminal and the first of the three fuel trucks should be driven out to meet it.

The officials disembarked; the plane circled in place and began charging back over the runway while the tower instructed the pilot where he would refuel. The truck raced out; men leaped from the carriage and began pulling the hoses from their recesses.

'It'll take about ten minutes,' said the assassin. 'It's a Chinese version of an upgraded DC-Three.'

The aircraft came to a stop, the engines cut, as rolling ladders were pushed to the wings and men scaled them. The fuel tanks were opened, the nozzles inserted amid constant chatter between the maintenance crews. Suddenly the hatch door in the centre of the fuselage was reopened, the metal steps slapping down to the ground. Two men in uniform walked out.

'The pilot and his flight officer,' said Bourne, 'and they're not stretching their legs. They're checking every damn thing those people are doing. We'll time this very carefully, Major, and when I say "Move," you *move.*'

'Straight to the hatch,' agreed the assassin. 'When the second bloke hits the first step.'

'That's about it.'

'Diversion?'

'In what way?'

'You had a pretty fancy one last night. You had your own Yank Fourth of July, you did.'

'Wrong way. Besides, I used them all up . . . Wait a minute. The fuel truck.'

'You blow it, there goes the plane. Also, you couldn't time it to the blokes getting back on board.'

'Not *that* truck,' said Jason, shaking his head and staring beyond the commando. 'The one over there.' Bourne gestured at the nearer of the two red trucks directly in front of them, about a hundred feet away. 'If it went up, the first order of business would be to get the plane out of there.'

'And we'd be a lot closer than we are now. Let's do it.'

'No,' corrected Jason. 'You'll do it. Exactly the way I tell you with my gun inches from your head. *Move!*'

The assassin in front, they raced out to the truck, covered by the dim light and the commotion around the plane. The pilot and his flight officer were shining flashlights over the engines and barking impatient orders to the maintenance crews. Bourne ordered the commando to crouch down in front of him as he knelt over the open knapsack and withdrew the roll of gauze. He removed the hunting knife from his belt, pulled a coiled hose off its rack, dropping it to the ground, and slid his left hand to the base where it entered the tank.

'*Check* them,' he told the commando. 'How much longer? And move slowly, Major. I'm watching you.'

'I said I wanted *out*. I'm not going to screw up!'

'Sure, you want out, but I've got a hunch you'd rather go it alone.'

'The thought never occurred to me.'

'Then you're not my man.'

'Thanks a lot.'

'No, I meant it. The thought would have occurred to *me* . . . How much longer?'

'Between two and three minutes, as I judge.'

'How good is your judgement?'

'Twenty-odd missions in Oman, Yemen, and points south. Aircraft similar in structure and mechanism. I know it all, sport. It's old hat. Two to three minutes, no more than that.'

'Good. Get back here.' Jason pricked the hose with his knife and made a small incision, enough to permit a steady stream of gasoline to flow out, but little enough so that the pump barely operated. He rose to his feet, covering the assassin with his gun as he handed him the roll of gauze. 'Pull out about six feet and drench it with the fuel that's leaking down there.' The killer knelt down and followed Bourne's instructions. 'Now,' continued Jason, 'stuff the end into the slit where I've cut the hose. Farther – *farther*. Use your thumb!'

'My arm's not what it used to be!'

'Your left hand is! Press *harder!*' Bourne looked quickly over at the refuelling – refuelled – aircraft. The commando's judgement had been accurate. Men were climbing off the wings and winding the hoses back into the fuel truck. Suddenly, the pilot and the flight officer were making their final check. They would head for the hatch door in less than a minute! Jason reached into his pocket for matches and threw them down in front of the assassin, his weapon levelled at the killer's head. 'Light it. *Now!*'

'It'll go up like a goddamned stick of nitro! It'll blow us both into the sky, especially *me!*'

'Not if you do it right! Lay the gauze on the grass, it's wet—'

'Retarding the fire – ?'

'Hurry up! *Do* it!'

'*Done!*' The flame leaped up from the end of the cloth strip, then instantly fell back and began its gradual march up the gauze. 'Bloody technician,' said the commando under his breath as he rose to his feet.

'Get in front of me,' ordered Bourne as he strung the knapsack to his belt. 'Start walking straight forward. Lower your height and shrink your shoulders like you did in Lo Wu.'

'Jesus Christ! *You* were – ?'

'*Move!*'

The fuel truck began backing away from the plane, then circled forward, swinging around the rolling ladders, heading to its left beyond where the first red truck was parked . . . and circling again, now to the right behind *both* stationary trucks to take up its position next to the one with the lighted gauze heading into its fuel tank. Jason whipped his head around, his eyes riveted on the fired tape. It had burst into its final flame! One spark entering the leaking petcock and the exploding tank would send hot metal into its sister trucks' vulnerable shells. Any second!

The pilot gestured to his flight officer. They marched together toward the hatch door.

'*Faster!*' yelled Bourne. 'Be ready to run!'

'*When?*'

'You'll know. Keep your shoulders low! Bend your spine, goddamn it!' They turned right toward the plane, passing through an oncoming crowd of maintenance personnel heading back to the hangar. '*Gongju ne?*' cried Jason, admonishing a colleague for having left behind a valuable set of tools by the aircraft.

'*Gong ju?*' shouted a man at the end of the crowd, grabbing Bourne's arm and holding up a toolbox. Their eyes met and the crewman was stunned, his face contorted in shock. '*Tian a!*' he screamed.

It happened. The fuel truck exploded, sending erratic pillows of fire pulsating into the sky as deadly shards of twisted metal pierced the space above and to the sides of the flaming vehicle. The crews screamed en masse; men raced in all directions, most to the protection of the hangar.

'*Run!*' shouted Jason. The assassin did not have to be told; both men raced to the plane and the hatch door, where the pilot, who had climbed inside, was peering out in astonishment while the flight officer remained frozen on the ladder. '*Kuai!*' yelled Bourne, keeping his face in the shadows and forcing the commando's head down on the metal steps. '*Jiu feiji . . . !*' he added, screaming, telling the pilot to get out of the fire zone for the safety of the plane – that he was maintenance and would secure the hatchway.

A second truck blew up, the opposing walls of explosives forming a volcanic eruption of fire and spewing metal.

'You're right!' shouted the pilot in Chinese, grabbing his officer co-pilot by the shirt and pulling him inside; both raced up the short aisle to the flight deck.

It was the moment, thought Jason. *He wondered.* 'Get in!' he ordered the commando as the third fuel truck blasted over the field and into the early light.

'*Right!*' yelled the assassin, raising his head and straightening his body for the leap up the steps. Then suddenly, as another deafening explosion took place and the plane's engines roared, the killer spun around on the ladder, his right foot plunging toward Bourne's groin, his hand lashing out to deflect the weapon.

Jason was ready. He crashed the barrel of his gun into the commando's ankle, then swung it up, smashing it across the assassin's temple; blood flowed as the killer fell back into the fuselage. Bourne leaped up the steps, kicking the unconscious body of the impostor back across the metal floor. He yanked the hatchway into place, slamming the latches down and securing the door. The plane began to taxi, instantly swerving to the left away from the flaming centre of danger. Jason ripped the knapsack from his belt, pulled out a second length of nylon rope and tied the assassin's wrists to two widely separated seat clamps. There was no way the commando could free himself – none that Bourne could think of – but just in case he was mistaken, Jason cut the rope attached to the assassin's ankles, separated his legs and tied each foot to the opposite clamps across the aisle.

He got up and started toward the flight deck. The aircraft was now on the runway, racing down the blacktop; suddenly the engines were cut. The plane was stopping in front of the terminal, where the group of government officials was gathered, watching the ever-growing conflagrations taking place less than a quarter of a mile away to the north.

'*Kai ba!*' said Bourne, placing the barrel of his automatic against the back of the pilot's head. The co-pilot whirled around in his seat. Jason spoke in clear Mandarin as he shifted his arm. 'Watch your dials, and prepare for takeoff, then give me your maps.'

'They will not clear us!' yelled the pilot. 'We are to pick up five outgoing commissioners!'

'To where?'

'Baoding.'

'That's north,' said Bourne.

'Northwest,' insisted the co-pilot.

'Good. Head south.'

'It will not be permitted!' shouted the pilot.

'Your first duty is to save the aircraft. You don't know what's going on out there. It could be sabotage, a revolt, an uprising. Do as I tell you, or you're both dead. I really don't care.'

The pilot snapped his head around and looked at Jason. 'You are a Westerner! You speak Chinese but you are a *Westerner!* What are you *doing?*'

'Commandeering this aircraft. You've got plenty of runway left. *Take off! South!* And give me the maps.'

The memories came back. Distant sounds, distant sights, distant thunder.

'*Snake Lady, Snake Lady! Respond! What are your sector coordinates?*'

They were heading into Tam Quan and Delta would not break silence. He *knew where they were and that was all that mattered. Command Saigon could go to hell, he wasn't about to give the North Viet monitoring posts an inkling as to where they were going.*

'*If you won't or can't respond, Snake Lady, stay below six hundred feet! This is a friend talking, you assholes! You don't have many down here! Their radar will pick you up over six-fifty.*'

I know that, Saigon, and my pilot knows it, even if he doesn't like it, and I still won't break silence.

'*Snake Lady, we've completely lost you! Can any retard on that mission read an air map?*'

Yes, I can read one very well, Saigon. Do you think I'd go up with my team trusting any of you? Goddamnit, that's my brother down there! I'm not important to you but he *is!*

'You're crazy, Western man!' yelled the pilot. 'In the name of the spirits, this is a heavy aircraft and we're barely over the treetops!'

'Keep your nose up,' said Bourne, studying a map. 'Dip and grab altitude, that's all.'

'That is also foolishness!' shouted the co-pilot. 'One downdraught at this level and we are into the forests! We are *gone!*'

'The weather reports on your radio say there's no turbulence anticipated—'

'That is *above*,' screamed the pilot. 'You don't understand the risks! Not down *here!*'

'What was the last report out of Jinan?' asked Jason, knowing full well what it was.

'They have been trying to track this flight to Baoding,' said the officer. 'They have been unable to do so for the past three hours. They are now searching the Hengshui mountains . . . Great spirits, why am I telling *you?* You heard the reports yourself! You speak better than my parents, and they were educated!'

'Two points for the Republic's Air Force . . . Okay, take a hundred-and-sixty-degree turn in two and a half minutes and climb to an altitude of a thousand feet. We'll be over water.'

'We'll be in range of the Japanese! They'll shoot us *down!*'

'Put out a white flag – or better still, I'll get on the radio. I'll think of something. They may even escort us to Kowloon.'

'*Kowloon!*' shrieked the flight officer. 'We'll be *shot!*'

'Entirely possible,' agreed Bourne. 'But not by me,' he added. 'You see, in the final analysis, I have to get there without you. As a matter of fact, you can't even be a part of my scene. I can't allow that.'

'You're making positively *no* sense!' said the exasperated pilot.

'You just make a hundred-and-sixty-degree turn when I tell you.' Jason studied the airspeed, calibrating the knots on the map, and calculated the estimated distance he wanted. Below, through the window, he saw the coast of China fall behind them. He looked at his watch; ninety seconds had passed. 'Make your turn, Captain,' he said.

'I would have made it anyway!' cried the pilot. 'I am not of the divine wind of the Kamikaze. I do not fly into my own death.'

'Not even for your heavenly government?'

'Least of all.'

'Times change,' said Bourne, his concentration once more on the air map. 'Things change.'

'*Snake Lady, Snake Lady! Abort! If you can hear me, get out of there and return to base camp. It's a no-win! Do you read me? Abort!*'

'*What do you want to do, Delta?*'

'*Keep flying, mister. In three more minutes you can get out of here.*'

'*That's me. What about you and your people?*'

'*We'll make it.*'

'*You're suicidal, Delta.*'

'*Tell me about it . . . All right, everyone check your chutes and prepare for cast-off. Someone help Echo, put his hand on the cord.*'

'*Déraisonnable!*'

The airspeed held steady at close to 370 miles per hour. The route Jason chose, flying at low altitude through the Formosa Strait – past Longhai and Shantou on the Chinese coast, and Hsinchu and Fengshan on Taiwan – was something over 1,435 miles. Therefore the estimate of four hours, plus or minus minutes, was reasonable. The out islands north of Hong Kong would be visible in less than half an hour.

Twice during the flight they had been challenged by radio, once from the Nationalist garrison on Quemoy, the other from a patrol plane out of Raoping. Each time Bourne took over communications, explaining in the first instance that they were on a search mission for a disabled ship bringing Taiwanese goods into the Mainland, for the second a somewhat more ominous declaration that as part of the People's Security Forces they were scouting the coast for contraband vessels that had undoubtedly eluded the Raoping patrols. For this last communication, he not only was unpleasantly arrogant but also used the name and the official – highly classified – identification number of a dead conspirator who lay underneath a Russian limousine in the Jing Shan Bird Sanctuary. Whether either interrogator believed him or not was, as he expected, irrelevant. Neither cared to disturb the *status quo ante.* Life was complicated enough. *Let things be, let them go. Where was the threat?*

'Where's your equipment?' asked Jason, addressing the pilot.

'I'm *flying* it!' replied the man, studying his instruments, visibly shaking at each eruption of static from the radio, each reporting communication from commercial aircraft. 'As you may or may not know, I have no flight plan. We could be on a collision course with a dozen different planes!'

'We're too low,' said Bourne, 'and the visibility's fine. I'll trust your eyes not to bump into anybody.'

'You're *insane!*' shouted the co-pilot.

'On the contrary. I'm about to walk back into sanity. Where's your emergency equipment? The way you people build things, I can't imagine that you don't have any.'

'Such as?' asked the pilot.

'Life rafts, signaling devices – parachutes.'

'Great *spirits!*'

'Where?'

'The compartment in the rear of the plane, the door to the right of the gallery.'

'It's all for the officials,' added the co-pilot dourly. 'If there are problems, *they* are supplied.'

'That's reasonable,' said Bourne. 'How else would you attend to business?'

'Madness.'

'I'm going aft, gentlemen, but my gun will be pointed right back here. Keep on course, Captain. I'm very experienced and very sensitive. I can feel the slightest variation in the air, and if I do, we're all dead. Understood?'

'*Maniac!*'

'Tell me about it.' Jason got up from the deck and walked back through the fuselage, stepping over his roped-up, splayed-out prisoner, who had given up the struggle to free himself, the layers of dried blood covering the wound at his left temple. 'How are things, Major?'

'I made a mistake. What else do you want?'

'Your warm body in Kowloon, that's what I want.'

'So some son of a bitch can put me in front of a firing squad?'

'That's up to you. Since I'm beginning to put things together, some son of a bitch might even give you a medal if you play your cards the way you should play them.'

'You're very big with the cryptics, Bourne. What does *that* mean?'

'With luck, you'll find out.'

'Thanks a lot!' shouted the Englishman.

'No thanks to me. You gave me the idea, *sport.* I asked you if, in your training, you'd learned how to fly one of these things. Do you remember what you told me?'

'What?'

'You said you only knew how to jump out of them.'

'Holy *shit!*'

The commando, the parachute securely strapped to his back, was bound upright between two seats, legs and hands tied together, his right hand lashed to the release cord.

'You look crucified, Major, except that the arms should be extended.'

'For God's sake, will you make *sense?*'

'Forgive me. My other self keeps trying to express himself. Don't do anything stupid, you bastard, because you're going out that hatch! Hear me? *Understood?*'

'Understood.'

Jason walked to the flight deck, sat on the deck, picked up the map, and spoke to the flight officer. 'What's the check?' he asked.

'Hong Kong in six minutes if we don't "*bump* into anybody".'

'I have every confidence in you, but defection notwithstanding, we can't land at Kai-tak. Head north into the New Territories.'

'*Aiya!*' screamed the pilot. 'We cross *radar!* The mad Gurkhas will fire on anything remotely Mainland!'

'Not if they don't pick you up, Captain. Stay below six hundred feet up to the border, then climb over the mountains at Lo Wu. You can make radio contact with Shenzen.'

'And what in the name of the spirits do I *say?*'

'You were hijacked, that's all. You see, I can't allow you to be a part of me. We can't land in the colony. You'd draw attention to a very shy man – and his companion.'

The parachutes snapped open above them, the sixty-foot rope connecting them by their waists stretched in the winds, as the aircraft sped north toward Shenzen.

They landed in the waters of a fish hatchery south of Lok Ma Chau. Bourne hauled in the rope, pulling the bound assassin toward him, as the owners of the hatchery screamed on the banks of their squared-off pond. Jason held up money – more money than the husband and wife could earn in a year.

'We are *defectors!*' he cried. '*Rich* defectors! Who *cares?*'

No one cared, least of all the owners of the hatchery. '*Mgoi! Mgoisaai!*' they kept repeating, thanking the strange pink creatures who fell from the sky, as Bourne dragged the assassin out of the water.

The Chinese garments discarded and the commando's wrists lashed behind his back, Bourne and his captive reached the road that headed south into Kowloon. Their drenched clothes were drying rapidly under the heat of the sun, but their appearance would not attract what few vehicles there were on the road and the fewer still that might be willing to pick up hitchhikers. It was a problem that had to be solved. Solved quickly, accurately. Jason was exhausted; he could barely walk and his concentration was fading. One misstep and he could lose – but he could *not* lose! Not *now!*

Peasants, mainly old women, trudged along the borders of the pavement, their outsized, wide-brimmed black hats shielding withered faces from the sun, yokes spread across ancient shoulders supporting baskets of produce. A few looked curiously at the dishevelled Westerners, but only briefly; their world did not invite surprises. It was enough to survive; their memories were strong.

Memories. *Study everything. You'll find something you can use.*

'Get down,' said Bourne to the assassin. 'On the side of the road.'

'What? *Why?*'

'Because if you don't, you won't see three more seconds of daylight.'

'I thought you wanted my warm body in Kowloon!'

'I'll take a cold body if I have to. *Down!* On your *back!* Incidentally, you can shout as loud as you want, no one will understand you. You might even be helping me.'

'Christ, *how?*'

'You're in trauma.'

'*What?*'

'Down! *Now!*'

The killer lowered himself to the pavement, rolled over on his back, and stared into the bright sunlight, his chest heaving with awkward gulps of breath. 'I heard the pilot,' he said. 'You *are* a fucking maniac!'

'To each his own interpretation, Major.' Suddenly, Jason turned in the road and began shouting to the peasant women. '*Jiu ming!*' he screamed. '*Qing bangmang!*' He pleaded with the ancient survivors to help his hurt companion, who had either a broken back or crushed ribs. He reached into his knapsack and pulled out money, explaining that every minute counted, that medical help was required as soon as possible. If they could give assistance, he would pay a great deal for their kindness.

As one, the peasants rushed forward, their eyes not on the patient but on the money, their hats flying in the wind, their yokes forgotten.

'*Na gunzi lai!*' yelled Bourne, asking for splints or sticks of wood that would hold the damaged man rigid.

The women ran into the fields, returning with long bamboo stalks, slicing away the fibres that would give the poor man in pain a measure of relief when he was strapped in place. And having done so amid much vociferous expressions of sympathy and in spite of the patient's protestations in English, they accepted Bourne's money and went on their way.

Except one. She spotted a truck coming down from the north.

'*Duo shao qian?*' she said, leaning into Jason's ear, asking him how much he would pay.

'*Ni shuo ne,*' answered Bourne, telling her to name a price.

She did and Delta accepted. With her arms outstretched, the woman walked out onto the road, and the truck stopped. A second negotiation was made with the driver, and the assassin was loaded onto the van, supine, strapped to the bamboo. Jason climbed on behind him.

'How are you doing, Major?'

'This thing is filled with lousy, fucking ducks!' screamed the commando, staring around at the banks of wooden cages on all sides, the odour overpowering, sickening.

A particular fowl, in its infinite wisdom, chose the moment to squirt a stream of excrement into the assassin's face.

'Next stop, Kowloon,' said Jason Bourne, closing his eyes.

30

The telephone rang. Marie spun around in the chair – stopped by Mo Panov's raised hand. The doctor walked across the hotel room, picked up the bedside phone and spoke. 'Yes?' he said quietly. He frowned as he listened, then as if he realized that his expression might alarm the patient, he looked over at Marie and shook his head, his hand now dismissing whatever urgency she might have attached to the call. 'All right,' he continued after nearly a minute. 'We'll stay put until we hear from you, but I have to ask you, Alex, and forgive my directness. Did anyone feed you drinks?' Panov winced as he pulled the phone briefly away from his ear. 'My only response is that I'm entirely too kind and experienced to speculate on *your* antecedents. Talk to you later.' He hung up.

'What's *happened?*' asked Marie, half out of the chair.

'Far more than he could go into, but it was enough.' The psychiatrist paused, looking down at Marie. 'Catherine Staples is dead. She was shot down in front of her apartment house several hours ago—'

'Oh, my *God*,' whispered Marie.

'That huge Intelligence officer,' continued Panov. 'The one we saw in the Kowloon station whom you called the major and Staples identified as a man named Lin Wenzu—'

'What about him?'

'He's severely wounded and in critical condition at the hospital. That's where Conklin called from, a pay phone in the hospital.'

Marie studied Panov's face. 'There's a connection between Catherine's death and Lin Wenzu, isn't there?'

'Yes. When Staples was killed, it was apparent that the operation had been penetrated—'

'*What* operation? By *whom?*'

'Alex said that'll all come later. In any event, things are coming to a boil and this Lin may have given his life to rip out the penetration – "neutralizing it," was the way Conklin put it.'

'Oh, God,' cried Marie, her eyes wide, her voice on the edge of hysteria. '*Operations! Penetrations . . . neutralizing*, Lin, even *Catherine* – a friend who turned on me – I don't *care* about those things! What about *David?*'

'They say he went into China.'

'Good Christ, they've *killed* him!' screamed Marie, leaping out of the chair.

Panov rushed forward and grabbed her by the shoulders. He gripped her harder, forcing her spastically shaking head to stop its movement, insisting in silence that she look at him. 'Let me tell you what Alex said to me . . . *Listen* to me!'

Slowly, breathlessly, as if trying to find a moment of clarity in her confusion and exhaustion, Marie stood still, staring at her friend. 'What?' she whispered.

'He said that in a way he was glad David was up there – or out there – because in his judgement he had a better chance to survive.'

'You *believe* that?' screamed David Webb's wife, tears filling her eyes.

'Perhaps,' said Panov, nodding, and speaking softly. 'Conklin pointed out that here in Hong Kong David could be shot or stabbed in a crowded street – crowds, he said, were both an enemy and a friend. Don't ask me where these people find their metaphors, I don't know.'

'What the *hell* are you trying to tell me?'

'What Alex told me. He said they made him go back, made him be someone he wanted to forget. Then he said there never was anyone like "Delta." "Delta" was the best there ever was . . . David Webb *was* "Delta," Marie. No matter what he wanted to put out of his mind, he *was* "Delta," Jason Bourne was an afterthought, an extension of the pain he had to inflict on himself, but his skills were honed as "*Delta.*" . . . In some respects I know your husband as well as you do.'

'In those respects, far better, I'm sure,' said Marie, resting her head against the comforting chest of Morris Panov. 'There were so many things he wouldn't talk about. He was too frightened, or too ashamed . . . Oh, God, Mo! Will he come *back* to me?'

'Alex thinks "Delta" will come back.'

Marie leaned away from the psychiatrist and looked into his eyes; through the tears her stare was rigid. 'What about *David?*' she asked in a plaintive whisper. 'Will *he* come back?'

'I can't answer that. I wish I could, but I can't.'

'I see.' Marie released Panov and walked to a window, and looked down at the crowds below in the congested, garishly lighted streets. 'You asked Alex if he'd been drinking. Why did you do that, Mo?'

'The moment the words came out I regretted them.'

'Because you offended him?' asked Marie, turning back to the psychiatrist.

'No. Because I knew you'd heard them and you'd want an explanation. I couldn't refuse you that.'

'Well?'

'It was the last thing he said to me – two things, actually. He said you were wrong about Staples—'

'*Wrong?* I was *there.* I *saw.* I heard her *lies!*'

'She was trying to protect you without sending you into panic.'

'*More* lies! What was the other?'

Panov held his place and spoke simply, his eyes locked with Marie's. 'Alex said that as crazy as things seemed, they weren't really so crazy, after all.'

'My God, they've turned *him!*'

'Not all the way. He won't tell them where you are – where we are. He told me we should be ready to move within minutes after his next call. He can't take the chance of coming back here. He's afraid he'll be followed.'

'So we're running again – with nowhere to go but back into hiding. And all of a sudden there's a rotten growth in our collective armour. Our crippled St George who slays dragons now wants to lie with them.'

'That's not fair, Marie. That's not what he said, not what I said.'

'*Bullshit*, Doctor! That's my husband out there, or *up* there! They're using him, *killing* him, without telling us why! Oh, he may – just *may* – survive because he's so terribly good at what he does – *did* – which was everything he despised, but what's going to be left of the man and his *mind?* You're the expert, *Doctor!* What's going to be left when all the memories come back? And they damn well better come back, or he *won't* survive!'

'I told you, I can't answer that.'

'Oh, you're *terrific*, Mo! All you've got is carefully qualified positions and no *answers*, not even well-couched projections. You're *hiding!* You should have been an economist! You missed your calling!'

'I miss a lot of things. Almost including the plane to Hong Kong.'

Marie stood motionless, as if struck. She burst into a new wave of tears as she ran to Panov, embracing him. 'Oh, God, I'm sorry, Mo! Forgive me, *forgive* me!'

'I'm the one who should apologize,' said the psychiatrist. 'It was a cheap shot.' He tilted her head back, gently stroking the grey hair streaked with white. 'Lord, I can't stand that wig.'

'It's not a wig, Doctor.'

'My degrees, by way of Sears Roebuck, never included cosmetology.'

'Only taking care of feet.'

'They're easier than heads, take my word for it.'

The telephone rang. Marie gasped and Panov stopped breathing. He slowly turned his head toward the hateful ringing.

'You try that again or anything like it and you're *dead!*' roared Bourne, gripping the back of his hand where the flesh was darkening from the force of the blow. The assassin, his wrists tied in front of him beneath the sleeves of his jacket, had lunged against the door of the cheap hotel, jamming Jason's left hand into the doorframe.

'What the hell do you *expect* me to do?' the former British commando yelled. 'Walk gently into that good night smiling at my own firing squad?'

'So you're a closet reader, too,' said Bourne, watching the killer clutch his rib cage, where Jason's right foot had landed an agonizing blow. 'Maybe it's time I asked you why you're in the business I was never actually a part of. *Why*, Major?'

'Are you really interested, Mr Original?' grunted the assassin, falling into a worn-out armchair against the wall. 'Then it's my turn to ask why.'

'Perhaps because I never understood myself,' said David Webb. 'I'm quite rational about that.'

'Oh, I know all about *you!* It was part of the Frenchman's training. The great Delta was bonkers! His wife and kiddies were blown up in the water in a place called Phnom Penh by a stray jet. This oh-so-civilized *scholar* went crazy, and it's a fact nobody could control him and nobody gave a damn because he and the teams he led did more damage than most of the search-and-destroys put together. Saigon said you were suicidal, and from its point of view, the more so the better. They wanted you and the garbage you commanded to buy it. They never *wanted* you back. You were an embarrassment!'

Snake Lady, Snake Lady . . . this is a friend talking, you assholes. You don't have many down here . . . Abort! It's a no-win!

'I know, or I think I know that part of it,' said Webb. 'I asked about you.'

The assassin's eyes grew wide as he stared at his bound wrists. When he spoke, it was barely above a whisper, the voice that emerged an echo of itself, and unreal. 'Because I'm *psycho*, you son of a *bitch!* I've known it since I was a kid. The nasty dark thoughts, the knives into animals just to watch their eyes and their mouths. Raping a neighbour's daughter, a vicar's kid, because I knew she couldn't say anything, and then catching up with her on the street afterwards and walking her to school. I was eleven years old. And later, at Oxford, during club hazing, holding a lad under water, just below the surface, until he drowned – to watch *his* eyes, *his* mouth. Then going back to classes and excelling in that nonsense any damn fool could do who had the wits to get out of a thundershower. *There* I was the right sort of fellow, as befitted the son of the father.'

'You never sought help?'

'*Help?* With a name like Allcott-Price?'

'*Allcott – ?*' Stunned, Bourne stared at his prisoner. '*General* Allcott-Price? Montgomery's boy genius in World War Two? "Slaughter Allcott," the man who led the flank attack on Tobruk, and later barrelled through Italy and Germany? England's *Patton?*'

'I wasn't alive then, for Christ's sake! I was a product of his third wife – perhaps his fourth, for all I know. He was very large in that department – women, I mean.'

'D'Anjou said you never told him your real name.'

'He was bloody well right! The *general*, swilling his brandy in his oh-so-superior club in St James's, has passed the word. "*Kill* him! Kill the rotten *seed* and never let the name out. He's no *part* of me, the woman was a whore!" But I *am* part of him and he knows it. He knows where I get my kicks from, the sadistic bastard, and we both have a slew of citations for doing what we like doing best.'

'He knew, then? About your sickness?'

'He knew . . . he knows. He kept me out of Sandhurst – our West Point, in case you don't know – because he didn't want me anywhere near his precious army. He figured they'd find me out and it'd dim his precious image. He damn near had apoplexy when I joined up. He won't have a decent night's sleep until he's told quietly that I'm out – dead out with all the traces buried.'

'Why are you telling *me* who you are?'

'Simple,' replied the former commando, his eyes boring into Jason's. 'The way I read it, whichever way it goes, only one of us is going to make it through. I'll do my damnedest to see that it's me, I told you that. But it may not be – you're no slouch – and if it isn't, you'll have a name you can shock the goddamn world with, probably make a bloody fortune in the bargain, what with literary and cinema rights, that sort of thing.'

'Then the general will spend the rest of his life sleeping peacefully.'

'*Sleep?* He'll probably blow his brains out! You weren't listening. I said he'd be told quietly, all the traces buried, no name surfacing. But this way *nothing's* buried. It's all hanging out like Maggie's drawers, the whole sick sordid mess with no apologies on my part, chap. I *know* what I am, I accept it. Some of us are just plain different. Let's say we're antisocial, to put it one way; hard-core violent is another; rotten, still another. The only difference with my being different is that I'm bright enough to know it.'

'And accept it,' said Bourne quietly.

'Wallow in it! Positively intoxicated by the highs! And let's look at it this way. If I lose and the story blows, how many practising antisocials might be fired up by it? How many other *different* men are out there who'd be only too happy to take my place, as I took yours? This bloody world is crawling with Jason Bournes. Give them direction, give them an idea, and they'll flock to the source and be off and running. That was the Frenchman's essential genius, can't you see?'

'I see garbage, that's all I see.'

'Your eyesight's not too shabby. That's what the general will see – a reflection of himself – and he'll have to live with the exposure, choke with it.'

'If he wouldn't help you, you should have helped yourself, committed yourself. You're bright enough to know that.'

'And cut off all the fun, all the highs? Unthinkable, sport! You go your way and find the most expendable outfit in the service, hoping the accident will happen that will put an end to it before they peg you for what you are. I found the outfit, but the accident never happened. Unfortunately, competition brings out the best in all of us, doesn't it? We survive because somebody else doesn't want us to . . . And then, of course, there's drink. It gives us confidence, even the courage to do the things we're not sure we can do.'

'Not when you're working.'

'Of course not, but the memories are there. The whisky bravado that tells you you *can* do it.'

'False,' said Jason Bourne.

'Not entirely,' countered the assassin. 'You draw strength from what you can.'

'There are two people,' said Jason. 'One you know, the other you don't – or you don't want to.'

'False!' repeated the commando. 'He wouldn't *be* there unless I wanted my kicks, don't kid yourself. And don't delude yourself, either, Mr Original. You'd be better off putting a bullet in my head, because I'll take you if I can. I'll kill you if I can.'

'You're asking me to destroy what you can't live with.'

'*Cut* the crap, Bourne! I don't know about you, but I *get* my kicks! I *want* them! I don't want to live *without* them!'

'You just asked me again.'

'*Stow* it, you fucker!'

'And again.'

'*Stop* it!' The assassin lurched out of the chair. Jason took two steps forward, his right foot again lashing out, again pounding the killer's ribs, sending him back into the chair. Allcott-Price screamed in pain.

'I won't kill you, Major,' said Bourne quietly. 'But I'll make you wish you were dead.'

'Grant me a last wish,' coughed the killer, holding his chest with his bound hands. 'Even I've done that for targets . . . I can take the unexpected bullet, but I can't take the Hong Kong garrison. They'd hang me late at night when no one's around, just to make it official, according to the regs. They'd put a thick rope around my neck and make me stand on a platform. I *can't take that!*'

Delta knew when to switch gears. 'I told you before,' he said calmly. 'That may not be in store for you. I'm not dealing with the British in Hong Kong.'

'You're not *what?*'

'You assumed it, but I never said it.'

'You're *lying!*'

'Then you're less talented than I thought, which wasn't much to begin with.'

'I *know*. I can't think *geometrically!*'

'You certainly can't.'

'Then you're a premium man – what you Americans call a bounty hunter – but you're working privately.'

'In a sense, yes. And I have an idea that the man who sent me after you may want to hire you, not kill you.'

'Jesus *Christ*—'

'And my price was heavy. Very heavy.'

'Then you are in the business.'

'Only this once. I couldn't refuse the reward. Lie down on the bed.'

'What?'

'You heard me.'

'I have to go to the loo.'

'Be my guest,' replied Jason, walking to the bathroom door and opening it. 'It's not one of my favourite sports, but I'll be watching you.' The assassin relieved himself with Bourne's gun trained on him. Finished, he walked out into the small, shabby room in the cheap hotel south of the Mongkok. 'The bed,' said Bourne again, gesturing with his weapon. 'Get prone and spread your legs.'

'That fairy behind the desk downstairs would love to hear *this* conversation.'

'You can phone him later on your own time. Down. *Quickly!*'

'You're always in a hurry—'

'More than you'll ever understand.' Jason lifted his knapsack from the floor and put it on the bed, pulling out the nylon cords, as the deranged killer crawled on top of the soiled spread. Ninety seconds later the commando's ankles were lashed to the bed's rear metal springs, his neck circled with the thin white line, the rope stretched and knotted to the springs in front. Finally, Bourne slipped off the pillowcase and tied it around the major's head, covering his eyes and ears, leaving his mouth free to breathe. His wrists bound beneath him, the assassin was again immobilized. But now his head began to twitch in sudden jerks and his mouth stretched with each spasm. Extreme anxiety had overcome former Major Allcott-Price. Jason recognized the signs dispassionately.

The squalid hotel he had managed to find had no such conveniences as a telephone. The only communication with the outside world was a knock on the door, which meant either the police or a wary desk clerk informing the guest that if the room was to be occupied another hour, an additional day's rent was required. Bourne crossed to the door, slipped silently out into the dingy corridor, and headed for the pay phone he had been told was at the far end of the hallway.

He had committed the telephone number to memory, waiting – praying, if it were possible – for the moment when he would dial it. He inserted a coin and did so now, his breath short, the blood racing to his head. '*Snake Lady!*' he said into the phone, drawing out the two words in harsh, flat emphasis. '*Snake Lady*, Snake – !'

'*Qing, qing*,' broke in an impersonal voice over the line, speaking rapidly in Chinese. 'We are experiencing a temporary disruption of service for many telephones on this exchange. Service should be resumed shortly. This is a recording . . . *Qing, qing*—'

Jason replaced the phone; a thousand fragmented thoughts, like broken mirrors, collided in his mind. He walked rapidly back down the dimly lit corridor, passing a whore in a doorway counting money. She smiled at him, raising her hands to her blouse; he shook his head and ran to the room. He waited fifteen minutes, standing quietly by the window, hearing the guttural sounds that emerged from his prisoner's throat. He returned to the door and once more stepped outside noiselessly. He walked to the phone, again inserted money and dialled.

'*Qing*—' He slammed the telephone down, his hands trembling, the muscles of his jaw working furiously, as he thought about the prostrate 'merchandise' he had brought back to exchange for his wife. He picked up the phone for a third time and, using his last coin, dialled *O*. 'Operator,' he began in Chinese, 'this is an emergency! It's most urgent I reach the following number.' He gave it to her, his voice rising in barely controlled panic. 'A recording explained that there was difficulty on the line, but this *is* an *emergency*—'

'One minute, please. I will attempt to be of assistance.' Silence followed, every second filled with a growing echo in his chest, reverberating like an accelerating kettledrum. His temples throbbed; his mouth was dry, his throat parched – burning, as a new fever spread through him.

'The line is temporarily in disuse, sir,' said a second female voice.

'The *line? That* line?'

'Yes, sir.'

'Not "many telephones" on the exchange?'

'You asked the operator about a specific number, sir. I would not know about other numbers. If you have them, I will gladly check for you.'

'The recording specifically said *many* telephones, yet you're saying *one line!* Are you telling me you can't confirm a . . . a multiple malfunction?'

'A what?'

'Whether a whole lot of phones aren't *working!* You've got computers. They spell out trouble spots. I told the other operator this is an *emergency!*'

'If it is medical, I will gladly summon an ambulance. If you will give me your address—'

'I want to know whether a lot of phones are out or whether it's just *one!* I *have* to *know* that!'

'It will take me some time to gather such information, sir. It's past nine o'clock in the evening and the repair stations are on reduced crews—'

'But they can tell you if there's an area problem, *goddamn* it!'

'Please, sir, I am not paid to be abused.'

'Sorry, I'm *sorry!* . . . Address? Yes, the address! What's the address of the number I gave you?'

'It is unpublished, sir.'

'But you *have* it!'

'Actually, I do not, sir. The laws of confidentiality are most strict in Hong Kong. My screen shows only the word "unpublished." '

'I repeat! This really *is* a matter of life and death!'

'Then let me reach a hospital . . . Oh, sir, please wait. You were correct, sir. My screen now shows that the last three digits of the number you gave me are electronically crossing over into one another, so the repair station is attempting to correct the problem.'

'What's the geographical location?'

'The prefix is "five," therefore it is on the island of Hong Kong.'

'*Narrower!* Whereabouts on the island?'

'Digits on telephone numbers have nothing to do with specific streets or locations. I'm afraid I cannot help you any further, sir. Unless you care to give me your address so that I might send an ambulance.'

'My address . . . ?' said Jason bewildered, exhausted, on the edge of panic. 'No,' he continued, 'I don't think I'll do that.'

Edward Newington McAllister bent over the desk as the woman replaced the phone. She was visibly shaken, her Oriental face pale from the strain of the call. The under-secretary of State hung up a separate phone on the other side of the desk, a pencil in his right hand, an address on a notepad before him. 'You were absolutely wonderful,' he said, patting the woman's arm. 'We have it. We've *got* him. You kept him on long enough – longer than he would have permitted in the old days – the trace is confirmed. At least the building, and that's enough. A hotel.'

'He speaks very fine Chinese. The dialect is rather Northern, but he adjusts to *Guangdong hua.* He also did not trust me.'

'It doesn't matter. We'll put people around the hotel. Every entrance and exit. It's on a street called Shek Lung.'

'Below the Mongkok, in the Yau Ma Ti, actually,' said the woman interpreter. 'There's probably only one entrance, through which the garbage is taken every morning, no doubt.'

'I have to reach Havilland at the hospital. He shouldn't have *gone* there!'

'He appeared to be most anxious,' offered the interpreter.

'Last statements,' said McAllister, dialling. 'Vital information from a dying man. It's permitted.'

'I don't understand any of you.' The woman got up from the desk as the undersecretary moved around and sat in the chair. 'I can follow instructions, but I don't understand you.'

'Good Lord, I forgot. You have to leave now. What I'm discussing is highly classified . . . We're extremely appreciative and I can assure you have our gratitude and, I'm quite certain, a bonus, but I'm afraid I must ask you to leave.'

'Gladly, sir,' said the interpreter. 'And you may forget the gratitude, but please include the bonus. I learned that much in Economics Eight at the University of Arizona.' The woman left.

'*Emergency*, police facilities!' McAllister fairly shouted into the phone. 'The ambassador, please. It's urgent! No, no names are required, thank you, and bring him to a telephone where we can talk privately.' The under-secretary massaged his left temple, digging deeper and deeper into his scalp until Havilland got on the line.

'Yes, Edward?'

'He *called*. It *worked*. We know where he *is!* A hotel in the Yau Ma Ti.'

'Surround it, but don't make any moves! Conklin has got to understand. If he smells what he thinks is rotten bait, he'll pull back. And if we don't have the wife, we don't have our assassin. For God's sake, don't *blow* this, Edward! Everything must be tight – and very, *very* delicate! Beyond-salvage could well be the next order of business.'

'Those aren't words I'm used to, Mr Ambassador.'

There was a pause on the line; when Havilland spoke his voice was cold. 'Oh, yes, they are, Edward. You protest too much. Conklin was right about that. You could have said no at the beginning, at Sangre de Cristo in Colorado. You could have walked away but you didn't, you couldn't. In some ways you're like me – without my accidental advantages, of course. We think and outthink; we take sustenance from our manipulations. We swell with pride with every progressive move in the human chess game – where every move can have terrible consequences for someone – because we believe in something. It all becomes a narcotic, and the sirens' songs are really an appeal to our egos. We have our minor powers because of our major intellects. Admit it, Edward – I have. And if it makes you feel any better, I'll say what I said before. Someone has to do it.'

'Nor do I care for out-of-context lectures,' said McAllister.

'You'll receive no more from me. Just do as I tell you. Cover all the exits at that hotel, but inform every man that no overt moves are to be made. If Bourne goes anywhere, he's to be discreetly followed, not touched under any circumstances. We *must* have the woman before contact is made.'

Morris Panov picked up the phone. 'Yes?'

'Something's happened.' Conklin spoke rapidly, quietly. 'Havilland left the waiting room to take an emergency call. Is anything going on over there?'

'No, nothing. We've just been talking.'

'I'm worried. Havilland's men could have found you.'

'Good Lord, *how?*'

'Checking every hotel in the colony for a white man with a limp, that's how.'

'You paid the clerk not to say anything to anyone. You said it was a confidential business conference – perfectly normal.'

'They can pay, too, and say it's a confidential government matter that brings generous rewards or equally generous harassment. Guess who takes precedence?'

'I think you're overreacting,' protested the psychiatrist.

'I don't care what you think, Doctor, just get out of there. Now. Forget Marie's luggage – if she has any. Leave as quickly as you can.'

'Where should we go?'

'Where it's crowded, but where I can find you.'

'A restaurant?'

'It's been too many years and they change names every twenty minutes over here. Hotels are out; they're too easily covered.'

'If you're right, Alex, you're taking too much time—'

'I'm *thinking!* . . . All right. Take a cab to the foot of Nathan Road at Salisbury – have you got that? *Nathan* and *Salisbury*. You'll see the Peninsula Hotel, but don't go inside. The strip heading north is called the Golden Mile. Walk up and down on the right side, the *east* side, but stay within the first four blocks. I'll find you, as soon as I can.'

'All right,' said Panov. 'Nathan and Salisbury, the first four blocks north on the right . . . Alex, you're quite certain you're right, aren't you?'

'On two counts,' answered Conklin. 'For starters, Havilland didn't ask me to go with him to find out what the "emergency" was – that's not our arrangement. And if the emergency isn't you and Marie, it means Webb's made contact. If that's the case, I'm not trading away my only bargaining chip, which is Marie. Not without on-sight guarantees. Not with Ambassador Raymond Havilland. Now, get *out* of there!'

Something was wrong! What was it? Bourne had returned to the filthy hotel room and stood at the foot of the bed watching his prisoner, whose twitch was more pronounced now, his stretched body spastically reacting to each nervous movement. What *was* it? Why did the conversation with the Hong Kong operator bother him so? She was courteous and helpful; she even tolerated his abuse. Then what *was* it? . . . Suddenly, words from a long-forgotten past came to him. Words spoken years ago to an unknown operator without a face, with only an irritable voice.

I asked you for the number of the Iranian consulate.

It is in the telephone book. Our switchboards are full and we have no time for such inquiries. Click. Line dead.

That was *it!* The operators in Hong Kong – with justification – were among the most peremptory in the world. They wasted no time, no matter how persistent the customer. The workload in this congested, frenetic financial megalopolis would not permit it. Yet the second operator had been the soul of tolerance . . . *I would not know about other numbers. If you have them, I will gladly check for you . . . If you will give me your address . . . Unless you care to give me your address . . .* The address! And without really considering the question, he had instinctively answered. *No, I don't think I'll do that.* From deep within him an alarm had gone off.

A *trace!* They had bounced him around, keeping him on the line long enough to put an electronic trace on his call! Pay phones were the most difficult to track down. The vicinity was determined first; next the location or premises, and finally the specific instrument, but it was only a matter of minutes or fractions of minutes between the first step and the last. Had he stayed on long enough? And if so, to what degree of progress? The vicinity? The hotel? The pay phone itself? Jason tried to reconstruct his conversation with the operator – the second operator – when the trace would have begun. Maddeningly, frantically, but with all the precision he could summon, he tried to recapture the rhythm of their words, their voices, realizing that when he had accelerated she had slowed down. *It will take me some time . . . Actually, I do not, sir. The laws of confidentiality are most strict in Hong Kong* – a lecture! *Oh, sir, please wait. You were correct . . . my screen now shows* – a mollifying explanation, taking up time. *Time!* How could he have *allowed* it? How *long . . . ?*

Ninety seconds – two minutes at the outside. Timing was an instinct for him, rhythms remembered. Say two minutes. Enough to determine a vicinity, conceivably to pinpoint a location, but, given the hundreds of thousands of miles of trunk lines, probably inadequate to pick up a specific phone. For some elusive reason images of Paris came to him, then the blurred outlines of telephone booths as he and Marie raced from one to another through the blinding Paris streets, making blind, untraceable calls, hoping to unravel the enigma that was Jason Bourne. *Four minutes. It takes that long, but we have to get out of the area! They've got that by now!*

The taipan's men – if there *was* a huge, obese taipan, to begin with – might have traced the hotel, but it was unlikely they would have tracked the pay phone or the floor. And there was another time span to be considered, one that could work for him if he in turn worked quickly. If the trace had been made and the hotel unearthed, it would take the hunters some time to reach the southern Mongkok, presuming they were in Hong Kong, which the telephone prefix indicated. The key at the moment was speed. *Quickly.*

'The blindfold stays, Major, but you're moving,' he said to the assassin as he swiftly undid the gag and the knots on the mattress springs, coiling the three nylon ropes and stuffing them into the commando's jacket.

'*What?* What did you say?'

Bourne raised his voice. 'Get up. We're going for a walk.' Jason grabbed his knapsack, opened the door and checked the hallway. A drunk staggered into a room on the left and slammed the door. The right corridor was clear, all the way up to the pay phone and the fire exit beyond it. '*Move*,' ordered Bourne, shoving his prisoner.

The fire escape would have been rejected by underwriters at a glance. The metal was corroded and the railings bent under pressure. If one was escaping a fire, a smoke-filled staircase might have been preferable. Still, if it descended in the darkness without collapsing, that was all that mattered. Jason grabbed the commando's lapel, leading him down the creaking metal steps until they reached the first landing. Beneath there was a broken ladder extended in its track halfway to the alley below. The drop to the pavement was no more than six or seven feet, easily negotiated going down and – more important – coming back up.

'Sleep well,' said Bourne, taking aim in the dim light and crashing his knuckles into the base of the commando's skull. The assassin collapsed on the staircase as Bourne whipped out the cords and secured the killer to the steps and the railing, at the last yanking down the pillowcase, covering the impostor's mouth and tying the cloth tighter. The nocturnal sounds of Hong Kong's Yau Ma Ti and the nearby Mongkok would easily cover whatever cries Allcott-Price might manage – if he awoke before Jason awakened him, which was doubtful.

Bourne climbed down the ladder, dropping into the narrow alleyway only seconds before three young men appeared, running around the corner from the busy street. Out of breath, they huddled in the shadows of a doorway as Jason remained on his knees – he hoped out of sight. Beyond the alley's entrance another group of youths raced by in pursuit, shouting angrily. The three young men lurched from the darkened doorway and ran out, heading in the opposite direction, away from their pursuers. Bourne got up and walked quickly to the mouth of the alley, looking back up at the fire escape. The assassin could not be seen.

He collided simultaneously with two running bodies. Bouncing off them and into the wall, he could only assume that the young men were part of the crowd chasing the previous three who had hidden in the doorway. One of these, however, held a knife menacingly in his hand. Jason did not *need* this confrontation, he could not permit it! Before the youth realized what had happened, Bourne lashed out and gripped the young man's wrist, twisting it clockwise until the blade fell from the youngster's hand while he screamed in pain.

'Get *out* of here!' shouted Jason in harsh Cantonese. 'Your gang is no match for your elders and betters! If we see any of you around here, your mothers will get corpses for their labours. Get out!'

'*Aiya!*'

'We look for thieves! For eye-eyes from the north! They steal, they—'

'*Out!*'

The young men fled from the alleyway, disappearing into the semicrowded street in the Yau Ma Ti. Bourne shook his hand, the hand the assassin had tried to crush in the hotel doorframe. In his anxiety he had forgotten about the pain; it was the best way to tolerate it.

He looked up at the sound – *sounds.* Two dark sedans came racing down Shek Lung Street and stopped in front of the hotel. Both vehicles had *official* written all over them. Jason watched in anguish as men climbed out of each car, two from the first, three from the one behind it.

Oh, God, Marie! We're going to lose! I've killed us – oh, Christ, I've killed us!

He fully expected the five men to rush into the hotel, question the desk clerk, take up positions and make their moves. They would learn that the occupants of Room 301 had not been seen leaving the premises; therefore presumably they were still upstairs. The room would be broken into in less than a minute, the fire escape discovered seconds later! Could he *do* it? Could he climb back up, cut loose the killer, get him down into the alley and *escape?* He *had* to! He took a last look before racing back to the ladder.

Then he stopped. Something was wrong – something unexpected, *totally* unexpected. The first man from the lead car had removed his suit coat – his official dress coat – and loosened his tie. He ran his hand through his hair, dishevelling it, and walked – unsteadily? – toward the entrance of the run-down hotel. His four companions were spreading out away from the cars, looking up at the windows, two over to the right, two to the left, toward the alleyway – toward *him.* What was *happening?* These men were not acting *officially.* They were behaving like criminals, like mafiosi closing in on a kill they could not be associated with – a trap laid for others, not themselves. Good God, had Alex Conklin been *wrong* back at Dulles Airport in Washington?

Play the scenario. It's deep down and it's there. Play it out. You can do it, Delta!

No time. There was no time to think any longer. There were no precious instants to lose thinking about the existence or the nonexistence of a huge, obese taipan, too operatic to be real. The two men heading toward him had spotted the alleyway. They began running – toward the alley, toward the 'merchandise,' toward the destruction and death of everything Jason held dear in this rotten world he would gladly leave but for Marie.

The seconds were ticked off in milliseconds of premeditated violence, at once accepted and at once reviled. David Webb was silenced as Jason Bourne again assumed complete command. Get *away from me! This is all we've got left!*

The first man fell, his rib cage shattered, his voice stilled by the force of a blow to his throat. The second man was accorded preferential treatment. It was vital that he be cognisant, even alert, for what followed. He dragged both men into the deepest shadows of the alley, ripping their clothes with his knife, binding their feet, their arms and their mouths with strips of their own clothing.

His arms pinned beneath Jason's knees, the blade of the knife breaking the flesh around the socket of his left eye, Bourne gave his ultimatum to the second man. 'My *wife!* Where is she? Tell me *now!* Or lose your eye, then the other one! I'll carve you up, *Zhongguo ren,* believe me!' He ripped the gag from the man's mouth.

'We are not your enemy, *Zhangfu!*' cried the Oriental in English, using the Cantonese word for husband. 'We have been trying to find her! We hunt everywhere!'

Jason stared down at the man, the knife trembling in his hand, his temples throbbing, his personal galaxy about to explode, the heavens to rain down fire and pain beyond his imagination. '*Marie!*' he screamed in agony. 'What have you done with her? I was given a *guarantee!* I bring out the merchandise and my wife is returned to me! I was to hear her voice on the phone but the phone doesn't *work!* Instead, a trace is put on me and suddenly *you're* here but my wife *isn't!* Where *is* she?'

'If we knew, she would be here with us.'

'*Liar!*' cried Bourne, drawing out the word.

'I'm not lying to you, sir, nor should I be killed for not lying to you. She escaped from the hospital—'

'The *hospital?*'

'She was ill. The doctor insisted. I was *there*, outside her room, watching over her! She was weak, but she got away—'

'Oh, Christ! Sick? *Weak?* Alone in *Hong Kong?* My God, you've killed her.'

'No, sir! Our orders were to see to her comforts—'

'*Your* orders,' said Jason Bourne, his voice flat and cold. 'But not your taipan's. He followed other orders, orders given before in Zurich and Paris and on Seventy-first Street in New York. I've been there – *we've* been there. And now you've killed her. You used me, as you used me before, and when you thought it was over, you took her away from me. What's the "death of one more daughter"? Silence is everything.' Jason suddenly gripped the man's face with his left hand, the knife poised in his right. 'Who's the fat man? Tell me, or the blade goes in! Who's the *taipan?*'

'He's not a taipan! He is British-schooled and trained, an officer much respected in the territory. He works with your countrymen, the Americans. He's with the Intelligence Service.'

'I'm sure he is . . . From the beginning it was the same. Only this time it wasn't the Jackal but *me.* I was moved around the chessboard until I had no choice but to hunt myself – an extension of myself, a man called Bourne. When he brings him in, kill him. Kill her. They know too much.'

'*No!*' cried the Oriental, perspiring, his eyes wide, staring at the blade pressing into his flesh. 'We are told very little, but I have heard *nothing* like that!'

'What are you doing here, then?' asked Jason harshly.

'Surveillance, I *swear* it! That's all!'

'Until the *guns* move in?' said Bourne icily. 'So your three-piece suits can stay clean, no blood on your shirts, no traces back to those nameless, faceless people you work for.'

'You're *wrong!* We are *not* like that, our superiors are not like that!'

'I told you, I've been there. You're like that, believe me . . . Now you're going to tell *me* something. Whatever this is, it's down and dirty and totally secure. Nobody runs an operation like that without a camouflaged base. Where is it?'

'I don't understand you.'

'Headquarters or Base Camp One, or a sterile house, or a coded Command Centre – whatever the hell you want to call it. Where *is* it?'

'Please, I cannot—'

'You *can.* You *will.* If you don't, you're blind, your eyes cut out of your head. *Now!*'

'I have a wife, *children!*'

'So did I. Both counts. I'm losing patience.' Jason stopped, only slightly reducing the pressure of the blade. 'Besides, if you're so sure you're right – that your superiors aren't what I say they are, where's the harm? Accommodations can be reached.'

'*Yes!*' yelled the frightened man. 'Accommodations! They are good men. They won't harm you!'

'They won't have a chance,' whispered Bourne.

'What, sir?'

'Nothing. Where *is* it? Where's this oh-so-quiet headquarters? *Now!*'

'Victoria Peak!' said the petrified Intelligence subordinate. 'The twelfth house down on the right, with high walls . . .'

Bourne listened to the description of a sterile house, a quiet, patrolled estate among other estates in a wealthy district. He heard what he had to hear; there was nothing else he needed. He smashed the heavy bone handle of the knife into the man's skull, replaced the gag, and rose to his feet. He looked up at the fire escape, at the barely discernible outline of the assassin's body.

They wanted Jason Bourne and were willing to kill for him. They would get two Jason Bournes and die for their lies.

31

Ambassador Havilland confronted Conklin in the hospital corridor outside the police emergency room. The diplomat's decision to speak with the CIA man in the busy white-walled hallway was predicated on the fact that it *was* busy – nurses and attendants, doctors and interns, roamed the halls conferring and answering phones that seemed to ring continuously. Under the circumstances Conklin would be unlikely to indulge in a loud, heated argument. Their discussion might be charged, but it would be quiet; the ambassador could make his case better under those conditions.

'Bourne's made contact,' said Havilland.

'Let's go outside,' said Conklin.

'We can't,' replied the diplomat. 'Lin may be about to die any minute or we may be able to see him any minute. We can't miss that opportunity and the doctor knows we're here.'

'Then let's go back inside.'

'There are five other people in the emergency room. You don't want them overhearing us any more than I do.'

'*Christ*, you cover your ass, don't you?'

'I have to think of all of us. Not one or two or three of us, but *all* of us.'

'What do you want from me?'

'The woman, of course. You know that.'

'I know that – of course. What are you prepared to offer?'

'My God, *Jason Bourne!*'

'I want David Webb. I want Marie's husband. I want to know that he's alive and well in Hong Kong. I want to see him with my own eyes.'

'That's impossible.'

'Then you'd better tell me why.'

'Before he shows himself he expects to speak with his wife within thirty seconds of contact. That's the agreement.'

'But you just said he *made* contact!'

'He did. We didn't. We couldn't afford to without having Marie Webb near the phone.'

'You've lost me!' said Conklin angrily.

'He had his own conditions, not unlike yours, which is certainly understandable. You were both—'

'What *were* they?' broke in the CIA man.

'If he made the call, it meant that he had the impostor – it was the bilateral agreement.'

'Jesus! "*Bilateral*"?'

'Both sides agreed to it.'

'I know what it *means!* You just send me into space, that's all.'

'Keep your voice down . . . *His* condition was that if we did not produce his wife within thirty seconds, whoever was on the phone would hear a gunshot, meaning that the assassin was dead, that Bourne had killed him.'

'Good old Delta.' Conklin's lips formed a thin half-smile. 'He never missed a trick. And I suspect he had a follow-up, right?'

'Yes,' said Havilland grimly. 'A point of exchange is to be mutually agreed upon—'

'Not bilaterally?'

'Shut up! . . . He'll be able to see his wife walking alone, under her own power. When he's satisfied, he'll come out with his prisoner – under a gun, we presume – and the exchange will be made. From the initial contact to the switch, everything is to take place in a matter of minutes, certainly no more than half an hour.'

'Double time with no one orchestrating any extraneous moves.' Conklin nodded. 'But if you didn't respond, how do you know he made contact?'

'Lin put a flag on the telephone number with a second relay to Victoria Peak. Bourne was told that the line was temporarily out of service, and when he tried to get a verification – which under the circumstances he had to do – he was relayed to the Peak. We kept him on the line long enough to trace the location of the pay phone he was using. We know where he is. Our people are on the way there now with orders to stay out of sight. If he smells or sees anything, he'll kill our man.'

'A trace?' Alex studied the diplomat's face, not kindly. 'He let you keep him talking long enough for *that?*'

'He's in a state of extreme anxiety, we counted on it.'

'Webb, maybe,' said Conklin. 'Not Delta. Not when he thinks about it.'

'He'll keep calling,' insisted Havilland. 'He has no choice.'

'Maybe, maybe not. How long has it been since his last call?'

'Twelve minutes,' answered the ambassador, looking at his watch.

'And the first one?'

'About a half hour.'

'And every time he calls you know about it?'

'Yes. The information's relayed to McAllister.'

'Phone him and see if Bourne's tried again.'

'Why?'

'Because, as you put it, he's in a state of extreme anxiety and will keep calling. He can't help himself.'

'What are you trying to say?'

'That you may have made a mistake.'

'Where? How?'

'I don't know, but I *do* know Delta.'

'What could he do without reaching us?'

'Kill,' said Alex simply.

Havilland turned, looked down the busy hallway, and started walking toward the floor's reception desk. He spoke briefly to a nurse; she nodded and he picked up a telephone. He talked for a moment and hung up. Frowning, he returned to Conklin. 'It's odd,' he remarked. 'McAllister feels the way you do. Edward expected Bourne to call every five minutes, if he waited *that* long.'

'Oh?'

'He was led to believe that telephone service might be restored at any moment.' The ambassador shook his head, as if dismissing the improbable. 'We're all too tense. There could be a number of explanations starting with coins for a pay phone to unsettled bowels.'

The emergency-room door opened and the British doctor appeared. 'Mr Ambassador?'

'Lin?'

'A remarkable man. What he's been through would kill a horse, but then they're about the same size and a horse can't manifest a will to live.'

'Can we see him?'

'There'd be no point, he's still unconscious – stirring now and then but nowhere near coherent. Every minute he rests without a reversal is encouraging.'

'You understand how urgent it is that we talk to him, don't you?'

'Yes, Mr Havilland, I do. Perhaps more than you realize. You know that I was the one responsible for the woman's escape—'

'I do know,' said the diplomat. 'I was also told that if she could fool you she could probably fool the best internist at the Mayo Clinic.'

'That's dubious, but I like to think I'm competent. Instead, I feel like an idiot. I'll do everything in my power to help you and my good friend Major Lin. The judgement was medical and mine, the error mine, not his. If he makes it through the next hour or so, I believe he has a chance to live. If that happens, I'll bring him to and you can question him as long as you keep your questions brief and simple. If I think a reversal is too severe and that he's slipping away, I'll also call you.'

'That's fair, Doctor. Thank you.'

'I could do no less. It's what Lin would want. I'll go back to him now.'

The waiting began. Havilland and Alex Conklin reached their own bilateral agreement. When Bourne next tried to reach the number for Snake Lady, he was to be told that the line would be clear in twenty minutes. During that time Conklin would be driven to the sterile house on Victoria Peak, prepared to take the call. He would set up the exchange, telling David that Marie was safe and with Morris Panov. The two men returned to the police emergency room and sat in opposite chairs, each silent minute compounding the strain.

The minutes, however, stretched into quarter hours and these into over an hour. Three times the ambassador called the Peak to ask if there was any word from Jason Bourne. There was none. Twice the English doctor came out to report on Lin's condition. It was unchanged, a fact that allowed for hope rather than diminishing it. Once the emergency-room telephone rang and both Havilland and Conklin snapped their heads toward it, their eyes riveted on the nurse who calmly answered. The call was not for the ambassador. The tension mounted between the two men as every now and then they would look at each other with the same message in their eyes. *Something was wrong. Something had gone off the wire.* A Chinese doctor came out and approached two people in the back of the room, a young woman and a priest; he spoke quietly. The woman screamed, then sobbed and fell into the enveloping arms of the priest. A new police widow had been created. She was led away to say a last good-bye to her husband.

Silence.

The telephone rang again, and again the diplomat and the CIA man stared at the counter.

'Mr Ambassador,' said the nurse, 'it's for you. The gentleman says it's most urgent.' Havilland got up and hurried to the desk, nodding his thanks, as he took the phone.

Whatever it was, it had happened. Conklin watched, never thinking he would see what he saw now. The consummate diplomat's face became suddenly ashen; his thin, usually tight lips were now parted, his dark brows arched, his eyes wide and hollow. He turned and spoke to Alex, his voice barely audible; it was the whisper of fear.

'Bourne's gone. The impostor's gone. Two of the men were found bound and severely injured.' He returned to the phone, his eyes narrowing as he listened. 'Oh, my *God!*' he cried, turning back to Conklin.

The CIA man was not there.

David Webb had disappeared, only Jason Bourne remained. Yet he was both more and less than the hunter of Carlos the Jackal. He was Delta the predator, the animal wanting only vengeance for a priceless part of his life that had been taken from him once again. And as an avenging predator, he went through the motions – the instinctive logistics – in a trancelike state, each decision precise, each movement deadly. His eye was on the kill, and his human brain had become animal.

He wandered the squalid streets of the Yau Ma Ti, his prisoner in tow, wrists still in traction, finding what he wanted to find, paying thousands of dollars for items worth a fraction of the amounts paid. Word spread up into the Mongkok about the strange man and his even stranger silent companion, who was bound and feared for his life. Other doors were opened to him, doors reserved for the runners of contraband – drugs, exported whores, jewels, gold, and materials of destruction, deception, death – and exaggerated warnings accompanied the word about this obsessed man carrying thousands on his person.

He is a maniac and he is white and he will kill quickly. It is said two throats were slit by those dishonest to him. It is heard that a Zhongguo ren *was shot to death because he cheated on a delivery. He is mad. Give him what he wants. He pays hard cash. Who cares? It is not our problem. Let him come. Let him go. Just take his money.*

By midnight Delta had the tools of his lethal trade. And success was uppermost in the Medusan's mind. He *had* to succeed. The kill was everything.

Where was Echo? He needed Echo. Old Echo was his good luck charm!

Echo was dead, slain by a madman with a ceremonial sword in a peaceful forest of birds. Memories.

Echo.

Marie.

I'll kill them for what they did to you!

He stopped a dilapidated taxi in the Mongkok and, showing money, asked the driver to step outside.

'Yes, what is, sir?' asked the man in broken English.

'What's your car worth?' said Delta.

'I do not understand.'

'How *much? Money?* For your *car!*'

'You *feng kuang!*'

'*Bu!*' shouted Delta, telling the driver he was not unbalanced. 'How much will you take for your car?' he continued in Chinese. 'Tomorrow morning you can say it was stolen. The police will find it.'

'It's my only source of livelihood and I have a large family! You are crazy!'

'How's four thousand, American?'

'*Aiya.* Take it!'

'*Kuai!*' said Jason, telling the man to hurry. 'Help me with this diseased one. He has the shaking sickness and must be tied down so he can't hurt himself.'

The owner of the taxi, his eyes on the large bills in Bourne's hand, helped Jason throw the assassin into the back seat, holding the killer down as the man from Medusa whipped the nylon ropes around the commando's ankles, knees and elbows, once again gagging and blindfolding him with the strips of cloth ripped from the cheap hotel's pillowcase. Unable to understand what was being said – shouted in Chinese – the prisoner could only passively resist. It was not merely the punishment inflicted on his wrists with each protesting movement, it was something he saw as he stared at his captor. There was a change in the original Jason Bourne; he had gone into another world, a far darker world. The kill was in the Medusan's extended periods of silence. It was in his eyes.

As he drove through the congested tunnel from Kowloon to the island of Hong Kong, Delta primed himself for the assault, imagining the obstacles that would face him, conjuring up the countermeasures he would employ. All were overdrawn and excessive, thus preparing himself for the worst.

He had done the same in the jungles of Tam Quan. There was nothing he had not considered, and he had brought them out – all but one. A piece of garbage, a man who had no soul but the want for gold, a traitor who would sell the lives of his comrades for small advantage. It was where it had all begun. In the jungles of Tam Quan. Delta had executed the piece of garbage, blown his temple out with a bullet, as this garbage was on a radio relaying their position to the Cong. The garbage was a man from Medusa named Jason Bourne, left to rot in the jungles of Tam Quan. He was the beginning of the madness. Yet Delta had brought out all the others, including a brother he could not remember. He had brought them out through two hundred miles of enemy territory because he had studied the probabilities and imagined the improbabilities – the latter far more important to their escape, for they had happened, and his mind was prepared for the unexpected. It was the same now. There was nothing a sterile house in Victoria Peak could mount that he could not surmount. Death would be answered with death.

He saw the high walls of the estate and drove casually past them – slowly, as a guest or a tourist might, unsure of his way down the stately road. He spotted the glass of the concealed searchlights, noted the barbed wire coiled above the wall. He zeroed in on the two guards in back of the enormous gate. They were in shadows, but the cloth of their marine field jackets reflected what light there was – a mistake, the cloth should have been dulled or replaced by less military apparel. The high wall ended in front; it was the corner; the stone stretched to the right as far as the eye could see. The sterile house was obvious to the trained eye. To the innocent it was clearly the residence of an important diplomat, an ambassador, perhaps, who required protection because of the dangerous times. Terrorism was everywhere; hostages were prized, deterrents the order of the day. Cocktails were served at sundown amid the quiet laughter of the elite who moved governments, but outside the guns were ready, cocked with the darkness, ready to fire. Delta understood. It was why he carried his bulging knapsack.

He drove the battered car off the side of the road. There was no need to conceal it; he would not be coming back. He did not care to come back. Marie was gone and it was over. Whatever lives he had led were finished. David Webb. Delta. Jason Bourne. They were the past. He wanted only peace. The pain had exceeded the limits of his endurance. Peace. But first he must kill. His enemies, Marie's enemies, all the enemies of the men and women everywhere who were driven by the nameless, faceless manipulators would be taught a lesson. A minor lesson, of course, for sanitized explanations would come from the experts, made plausible by complicated words and distorted half-truths. Lies. *Stave off doubts, eliminate the questions, be as outraged as the people themselves and march to the drums of consensus. The objective is everything, the insignificant players nothing but necessary digits in the deadly equations. Use them, drain them, kill them if you must, just get the jobs done because we say so. We see things others cannot see. Do not question us. You have no access to our knowledge.*

Jason climbed out of the car, opened the rear door, and with his knife sliced the ropes away from the assassin's ankles and knees. He then removed the blindfold, keeping the gag in place. He grabbed his prisoner by the shoulder and –

The blow was paralysing! The killer spun in place, crashing his right knee up into Bourne's left kidney, swinging his clasped bound hands up into Jason's throat as Delta buckled over. A second knee caught Bourne's rib cage; he fell to the ground as the commando raced into the road. *No. It can't happen! I need his gun, his firepower. It's part of the strategy!*

Delta rose to his feet, his chest and side bursting with pain, and plunged after the running figure in the road. In seconds the killer would be enveloped in darkness! The man from Medusa ran faster, the pain forgotten, concentrating only on the assassin in the part of his mind that still functioned. Faster, *faster!* Suddenly headlights shot up from the bottom of the hill, catching the assassin in their beams. The commando lurched to the side of the road to avoid the light. Bourne stayed on the right side of the pavement until the last instant, knowing he was gaining precious yards as the car raced past. His arms useless, the killer stumbled on the soft shoulder of the road; he crawled quickly, awkwardly back to the asphalt, and, getting to his feet, began to run again. It was too late. Delta hurled his shoulder into the base of his prisoner's spine; both men went down. The commando's guttural roars were the sounds of an animal in fury. Jason turned the assassin over and jammed his knee brutally into his prisoner's stomach.

'You listen to me, *scum!*' he said breathlessly, the sweat rolling down his face. 'Whether you die or not makes no difference to me. A few minutes from now you won't concern me any longer, but until then you're part of the plan, *my* plan! And whether or not you die then will be up to you, *not* me. I'm giving you a chance, which is more than you ever did for a target. Now, *get* up! Do everything I tell you or your one chance will be blown away with your head – which is exactly what I promised them.'

They stopped back at the car. Delta picked up his knapsack and, removing a gun he had taken in Beijing, showed it to the commando. 'You begged me for a weapon at the airport in Jinan, remember?' The assassin nodded, his eyes wide, his mouth stretched under the tension of the cloth gag. 'It's yours,' continued Jason Bourne, his voice flat, without emotion. 'Once we're over that wall up there – you in front of me – I'll hand it to you.' The killer frowned, his eyes narrowing. 'I forgot,' said Delta. 'You couldn't see it. There's a sterile house about five hundred feet up the road. We're going in. I'm staying, taking out everyone I can. You? You've got nine shells and I'll give you a bonus. One "bubble." ' The Medusan lifted a packet of *plastique* from the Mongkok out of the knapsack and showed it to his prisoner. 'As I read it, you'd never get back over the wall; they'd cut you down. So your only way out is through the gate; it'll be somewhere diagonally to the right. To get there you'll have to kill your way through. The timer on the plastic can be set as low as ten seconds. Handle it any way you like, I don't care. *Capisce?*'

The assassin raised his bound hands, then gestured at the gag. The sounds from his throat indicated that Jason should free his arms and remove the cloth.

'At the wall,' said Delta. 'When I'm ready, I'll cut the ropes. But when I do, if you try to take the gag off before I tell you, there goes your chance.' The killer stared at him and nodded once.

Jason Bourne and the lethal pretender walked up the road on Victoria Peak toward the sterile house.

Conklin limped down the hospital steps as rapidly as he could, holding on to the centre rail, looking frantically for a taxi in the drive below. There was none; instead a uniformed nurse stood alone reading the *South China Times* in the glow of the outdoor lights. Every now and then she glanced up toward the parking-lot entrance.

'*Excuse* me, miss,' said Alex, out of breath. 'Do you speak English?'

'A little,' replied the woman, obviously noticing his limp and his agitated voice. 'You are with difficulty?'

'Much difficulty. I have to find a taxi. I have to reach someone right away and I can't do it by phone.'

'They will call one for you at the desk. They call for me every night when I leave.'

'You're waiting . . . ?'

'Here it comes,' said the woman as approaching headlights shone through the parking-lot entrance.

'*Miss!*' cried Conklin. 'This is urgent. A man is dying and another may die if I don't reach him! *Please.* May I—'

'*Bie zhaoji,*' exclaimed the nurse, telling him to calm down. 'You have urgency, I have none. Take my taxi. I will ask for another.'

'Thank you,' said Alex as the cab pulled up to the kerb. '*Thank* you!' he added, opening the door and climbing inside. The woman nodded pleasantly and shrugged as she turned and started back up the steps. The glass doors above crashed open and Conklin watched through the rear window as the nurse nearly collided into two of Lin's men. One stopped her and spoke; the other reached the kerb and squinted, peering out of the light into the receding darkness beyond. 'Hurry!' said Alex to the driver as they passed through the gate. '*Kuai diar*, if that's right.'

'It will do,' answered the driver wearily in fluent English. '"Hurry" is better, however.'

The base of Nathan Road was the galactic entrance to the luminescent world of the Golden Mile. The blazing coloured lights, the dancing, flickering, shimmering lights, were the walls of this congested, urban valley of humanity where seekers sought and sellers shrieked for attention. It was the bazaar of bazaars, a dozen tongues and dialects vying for the ears and the eyes of the ever-shifting crowds. It was here, in this gauntlet of freewheeling commercial chaos, that Alex Conklin got out of the cab. Walking painfully, his limp pronounced, the veins of his footless leg swelling, he hurried up the east side of the street, his eyes roving like those of an angry wildcat seeking its young in the territory of hyenas.

He reached the end of the fourth block, the *last* block. Where were they? Where was the slender, compact Panov and the tall, striking, auburn-haired Marie? His instructions had been clear, *absolute.* The first four blocks north on the right side, the *east* side. Mo Panov had recited them back to him . . . Oh, *Christ!* He had been looking for two people, one whose physical appearance could belong to hundreds of men in those four crowded blocks. But his *eyes* had been searching for the tall, dark-redheaded woman – which she was *no longer!* Her hair had been dyed *grey* with streaks of *white!* Alex started back down toward Salisbury Road, his eyes now attuned to what he should look for, not what his painful memories told him he would find.

There they *were!* On the outskirts of a crowd surrounding a street vendor whose cart was piled high with silks of all descriptions and labels – the silks relatively genuine, the labels as ersatz as the distorted signatures.

'Come on with me!' said Conklin, his hands on both their elbows.

'*Alex!*' cried Marie.

'Are you all right?' asked Panov.

'No,' said the CIA man. 'None of us is.'

'It's *David*, isn't it?' Marie grabbed Conklin's arm, gripping it.

'Not now. Hurry up. We have to get out of here.'

'They're *here?*' Marie gasped, her grey-haired head turning right and left, fear in her eyes.

'Who?'

'I don't *know!*' she shouted over the din of the crowds.

'No, *they're* not here,' said Conklin. 'Come on. I've got a taxi holding down by the Pen.'

'What pen?' asked Panov.

'I told you. The Peninsula Hotel.'

'Oh, yes, I forgot.' All three started walking down Nathan Road, Alex – as was obvious to Marie and Morris Panov – with difficulty. 'We can slow down, can't we?' asked the psychiatrist.

'No, we *can't!*'

'You're in pain,' said Marie.

'Knock it off! *Both* of you. I don't need your horseshit.'

'Then tell us what's *happened!*' yelled Marie as they crossed a street filled with carts they had to dodge, and buyers and sellers and tourist-voyeurs who made for the exotic congestion of the Golden Mile.

'There's the taxi,' said Conklin as they approached Salisbury Road. 'Hurry up. The driver knows where to go.'

Inside the cab, Panov between Marie and Alex, she once again reached out, clutching Conklin's arm. 'It *is* David, isn't it?'

'Yes. He's back. He's here in Hong Kong.'

'Thank *God!*'

'You hope. We hope.'

'What does that mean?' asked the psychiatrist sharply.

'Something's gone wrong. The scenario's off the wire.'

'For Christ's sake!' exploded Panov. 'Will you speak *English!*'

'He means,' said Marie, staring at the CIA man, 'that David either did something he wasn't supposed to do, or *didn't* do something he was expected to do.'

'That's about it.' Conklin's eyes drifted toward the lights of Victoria Harbour and the island of Hong Kong beyond. 'I used to be able to read Delta's moves, usually before he made them. Then later, when he was Bourne, I was able to track him when others couldn't, because I understood his options and knew which ones he would take. That is, until things happened to him, and no one could predict anything because he'd lost touch with the Delta inside him. But Delta's back now, and as happened so often so long ago, his enemies have underestimated him. I hope I'm wrong – *Jesus*, I hope I'm *wrong!*'

*

His gun against the back of the assassin's neck, Delta moved silently through the underbrush in front of the high wall of the sterile house. The killer balked; they were within ten feet of the darkened entrance. Delta jammed the weapon into the commando's flesh and whispered, 'There aren't any trip lights in the wall or on the ground. They'd be set off by tree rats every thirty seconds. Keep going! I'll tell you when to stop.'

The order came four feet from the gate. Delta grabbed his prisoner by the collar and swung him around, the barrel of the gun still touching the assassin's neck. The man from Medusa then reached into his pocket, pulled out a globule of *plastique* and stretched his arm out as far as he could toward the gate. He pressed the adhesive side of the packet against the wall; he had pre-set the small digital timer in the soft centre of the explosive for seven minutes, the number chosen both for luck and to give him time to get the killer and himself in place several hundred feet away. '*Move!*' he whispered.

They rounded the corner of the wall and proceeded along the side to the midpoint, from where the end of the stone was visible in the moonlight. 'Wait here,' said Delta, reaching into his knapsack, which was strapped across his chest like a bandolier, the bag on his right side. He pulled out a square black box, five inches wide, three high, and two deep. At its side was a coiled forty-foot line of thin, black plastic tubing. It was a battery-amplified speaker; he placed it on top of the wall and snapped a switch in the back; a red light glowed. He uncoiled the thin tubing as he shoved the killer forward. 'Another twenty or thirty feet,' he said. They reached the spot acceptable to the Medusan. The branches of a cascading willow tree were spread out above the wall, arcing downward. Concealment. 'Here!' he whispered harshly, and stopped the commando by gripping his shoulder. He removed the wire cutters from the knapsack and pushed the assassin against the wall; they faced each other. 'I'm cutting you loose now, but not free. Do you understand that?' The commando nodded, and Delta snipped the ropes between his prisoner's wrists and elbows while levelling his gun at the assassin's head. He stepped back and bent his right leg forward in front of the killer as he handed him the wire cutters. 'Stand on my leg and cut the coils. You can reach them if you jump a bit and slide your hand under for a grip. Don't try anything. You haven't got a gun yet, but I have, and as I'm sure you've gathered, I don't care anymore.'

The prisoner did as he was told. The leap from Delta's leg was minimal; the assassin's left arm expertly slithered between the coils, his hand gripping the opposite side of the top of the wall. He severed the coiled wire noiselessly, holding the cutters against the metal on one side to reduce the sound of snapping tension. The open space above was now five feet wide. 'Climb up there,' said Delta.

The killer did so, and as his left leg swung over the wall, Delta leaped up to grab the assassin's trousers and pulled himself up against the stone, swinging his own left leg over the top. He straddled the wall simultaneously with the commando.

'Nicely done, Major Allcott-Price,' he said, a small circular microphone in his hand, his weapon again aimed at the assassin's head. 'Not much longer now. If I were you, I'd study the grounds.'

*

Under Conklin's urgent pleas to the driver, the taxi sped up the road in Victoria Peak. They passed a broken-down car of the side of the road; it seemed out of place in the elegant surroundings, and Alex swallowed as he saw it, wondering in dread if it was really disabled. 'There's the house!' cried the CIA man. 'For God's sake, *hurry!* Go up to the—'

He did not – could not – finish. Up ahead a shattering explosion filled the road and the night. Fire and stone flew in all directions, as first a large part of the wall collapsed and then the huge iron gates fell forward in eerie slow motion beyond the flames.

'Oh, my God, I was right,' said Alexander Conklin softly to himself. 'Delta's come back. He wants to die. He *will* die.'

32

'*Not yet!*' roared Jason Bourne as the wall blew apart beyond the stately gardens filled with rows of lilacs and roses. 'I'll tell you when,' he added quietly, holding the small circular microphone in his free hand.

The assassin grunted, his instincts roused to their primeval limits, his desire to kill equal to his desire to survive, the one dependent upon the other. He was on the edge of madness; only the barrel of Delta's gun stopped him from an insane assault. He was still human, and it was better to try to live than to accept death through default. But when, *when?* The nervous tic returned to Allcott-Price's face; his lower lip twitched as screams and shouts and the sound of men running in panic filled the gardens. The killer's hands trembled as he stared at Delta in the dim, pulsating light of the distant flames.

'Don't even think about it,' said the man from Medusa. 'You're dead if you make a move. You've studied me, so you know there's no reprieve. You make it, you make it on your own. Swing your leg over the wall and be ready to jump when I tell you. Not before.' Without warning, Bourne suddenly brought the microphone to his lips and snapped a switch. When he spoke, his amplified words echoed eerily throughout the grounds, a haunting, reverberating sound that matched the thunder of the explosion, made more ominous by its calm simplicity, its frigidity.

'You *marines.* Take cover and stay out of this. It's not your fight. Don't die for the men who brought you here. To them you're garbage. You're expendable – as I was expendable. There's no legitimacy here, no territory to be defended, no honour of your country in question. You're here for the sole purpose of protecting killers. The only difference between you and me is the fact that they used me, too, but now they want to kill me because I know what they've done. Don't die for these men, they're not worth it. I give you my word I won't fire on you unless you shoot at me, and then I'll have no choice. But there's another man here who isn't going to make any deals—'

A fusillade of gunfire erupted, shattering the source of the sound, blasting the unseen speaker randomly off the wall. Delta was ready; it was bound to happen. One of the faceless, nameless manipulators had given an order and it was carried out. He reached into the knapsack, removing a fifteen-inch pre-set tear gas launcher, the canister in place. It could smash heavy glass at fifty yards; he aimed and pulled the trigger. A hundred feet away a bay window was shattered and the fog of gas billowed throught the room inside. He could see figures running beyond the fragmented glass. Lamps and chandeliers were extinguished, supplanted by a startling array of floodlights positioned in the eaves of the great house and the trunks of the surrounding trees. Suddenly the grounds were awash with blinding white light. The branches of the overhanging tree would be a magnet for darting eyes and levelled weapons, and he understood that no appeal of his would countermand the orders. He had delivered that appeal both as an honest warning and as a salve for what conscience remained to a barely thinking, barely feeling robot avenger. In the shadows of the mind he had left he did not want to take the lives of youngsters called to serve the paranoid egos of manipulators – he had seen too much of that in Saigon years ago. He wanted only the lives of those inside the sterile house, and he intended to have them. Jason Bourne would not be denied. They had taken everything from him, and his personal account was now going to be settled. For the man from Medusa the decision was made – he was a puppet on the strings of his own rage, and apart from that rage his life was over.

'*Jump!*' whispered Delta, swinging his right leg over the wall, pummelling the assassin down to the ground. He followed while the commando was in midair and grabbed the assassin's shoulder as the startled killer – arms extended on his knees – righted himself on the grass. Bourne dragged him out of sight into a latticed arbour with a profusion of bougainvillaea that reached nearly six feet high. 'Here's your gun, Major,' said the original Jason Bourne. 'Mine's on *you*, and don't you forget it.'

The assassin simultaneously grabbed the weapon and tore the cloth from his mouth, coughing and spitting out saliva, as a savage burst of gunfire tore leaves and branches all along the wall. 'Your little lecture didn't do much fucking good, *did* it?'

'I didn't expect it to. The truth of the matter is that they want you, not me. You see, I'm *really* expendable now. That was their plan from the beginning. I bring you out and I'm dead. My wife's dead. We know too much. She because she learned who they were – she had to, she was the bait – me because they knew I'd put some figures together in Peking. You're messed up with a bloodbath, Major. A megabomb that can blow the whole Far East apart, and will if saner heads in Taiwan don't isolate and rip out those lunatic clients of yours. Only, I don't give a shit anymore. Play your goddamned games and blow yourselves up. I just want to get inside that house.'

A squad of marines assaulted the wall, running alongside the stone, rifles poised, ready to fire. Delta pulled a second *plastique* from his knapsack, set the miniaturized digital timer for ten seconds, and threw the packet as far as he could toward the rear garden wall, away from the guards. 'Come on!' he ordered the commando, ramming his weapon into the killer's spine. 'You in front! Down this path. Nearer the house.'

'Give me one of those! Give me a plastic!'

'I don't think so.'

'*Christ*, you gave me your word!'

'Then either I lied or I changed my mind.'

'*Why?* What do *you* care?'

'I care. I didn't know there were so many kids. Too many kids. You could take out ten of them with one of these, maim a lot more.'

'It's a little late for you to become such a fucking Christian!'

'The club's not that exclusive; it never was. I know who I want and who I don't want and I don't want kids in pressed GI pajamas. I want the men inside that—'

The explosion came some forty yards away at the rear of the grounds. Trees and dirt, bushes and whole beds of flowers flamed into the air – a panorama of greens and browns and speckled dots of colour within the billowing grey smoke illuminated by the hot, white floodlinghts. '*Move!*' whispered Delta. 'To the end of the row. It's about sixty feet from the house and there's a pair of doors—' Bourne closed his eyes in angry futility as a series of seemingly unending spurts of rifle fire filled the rear gardens. *They were children. They fired blindly out of fear, killing imaginary demons but no targets. And they would not listen.*

Another group of marines, these obviously led by an experienced officer, took up equidistant positions in front of the great house and circled it, legs bent, feet dug in for recoils, weapons angled forward. The manipulators had called for their Practorian guard. So be it. Delta again reached into his knapsack, felt around his arsenal, and removed one of the two manual firebombs he had purchased in the Mongkok. It was similar to a grenade at the top – circular but covered with a shield of heavy plastic. The base, however, was a handle, five inches long, so that the thrower could hurl the explosive farther and with greater accuracy. The trick was in the throwing, the accuracy, and the timing. For once the plastic was removed, the shell of the bomb itself would adhere to any surface by an instant steel-like adhesive activated by air, and with the explosion of a chemical would shoot out in all directions, prolonging the flames, embedding itself in all porous surfaces, seeping and burning. From the removal of the plastic covering to the explosion took fifteen seconds. The sides of the great house, the sterile house, were the standard Victorian clapboard above an imposing lower border of stone. Delta shoved the assassin into a cluster of roses, stripped off the plastic, and heaved the firebomb into the clapboard far above and to the left of the French doors thirty-odd feet away. It stuck to the wood, the rest was waiting for the seconds to pass while the rifle fire – hesitant now, diminishing – ceased altogether.

The wall of the house blew apart. A gaping hole revealed a formal Victorian bedroom, complete with a canopied bed and delicate English furniture. The flames spread instantly, shooting spokes of fire from a central hub, spewing along the clapboard and spitting inside the house.

An order was given, and again there was an eruption of rifle fire, bullets spraying the flower beds away from the rear garden wall and the contingent of marines who had raced in the direction of the previous explosion. Commands and countercommands were shouted in anger and frustration as two officers appeared, sidearms in their hands. One rounded the circle of protecting guards, checking their positions and their weapons, peering in front of each. The other headed for the side wall and began retracing the route of the first squad, his eyes constantly shifting to his inner flanks, to the succeeding rows of flowers. He stopped beneath the willow tree and studied the wall, then the grass. He raised his head and looked over at the arbour of bougainvillaea. With his weapon, now steadied by both hands, he started toward the arbour.

Delta watched the soldier through the bushes, his own gun still pressed into the commando's back. He removed another *plastique*, set the timer, and threw it over the bushes far forward toward the side wall. 'Go through there!' ordered Bourne, pivoting the assassin by the shoulder and sending him into the row of bushes on the left. Jason plunged through after the commando, cracking the barrel of his automatic into the killer's head, stopping him as he lurched for the knapsack. 'Just a few more minutes, Major, then you're on your own.'

The fourth explosion tore away six feet of the side wall, and as though they expected enemy troops to pour through, the marine guards opened fire on the collapsing stone. In the distance, on the roads of Victoria Peak, two-note sirens wailed in counterpoint to the sounds of carnage taking place within the grounds of the sterile house. Delta pulled out his next to last plastic packet, set the timer for ninety seconds, and heaved it toward the corner of the rear wall where the grounds were deserted. It was the beginning of his final diversion, the rest would be cold mathematics. He removed the tear gas launcher, inserted a canister, and spoke to the commando. 'Turn around.' The assassin did so, the barrel of Bourne's gun in front of his eyes. 'Take this,' said Delta. 'You can hold it with one hand. When I tell you, fire it into the stone to the right of the French doors. The gas will spread, blinding most of those kids. They won't be able to shoot, so don't waste bullets, you haven't got that many.'

The killer did not at first reply. Instead, he raised his weapon level with Bourne's and aimed it at Jason's head. 'Now we're one-on-one, Mr Original,' said the commando. 'I told you I could take a bullet in the head, I've been waiting for it for years. But somehow I don't think you can take the idea of not getting inside that house.' There was a sudden roar of voices and yet another fusillade of gunfire as a squad of marines rushed the collapsed side wall. Delta watched, waiting for the instant when the assassin's concentration would break for that split second. The instant did not come. Instead the commando continued quietly, his voice tense but controlled, as he stared at Jason Bourne. 'They must be expecting an invasion, the silly geese. When in doubt attack, as long as your flanks are covered, isn't that right, Mr Original? . . . Empty your bag of tricks, Delta. It *was* "Delta," wasn't it?'

'There's nothing left.' Bourne cocked the hammer of his automatic. The assassin did the same.

'Then let's have a feel around,' said the commando, his left hand slowly reaching out, softly touching the knapsack strapped on Delta's right hip, their eyes locked. The killer felt the canvas, squeezing the harsh cloth in several places. Again slowly, he withdrew his hand. 'With all the shalt-nots in the bloody big Book, none ever mentions a lie, does it? Except false witness, of course, which isn't the same. I guess you took the lapse to heart, sport. There's a shell-framed automatic repeater in there and two or three clips, I judge by the curves, holding at least fifty rounds apiece.'

'Forty, to be exact.'

'That's a lot of firepower. That little beast could get me out of here. *Give!* Or one of us goes right here. Right now.'

The fifth *plastique* explosion shook the ground; the startled assassin blinked. It was enough. Bourne's hand shot up, deflecting the killer's gun, crashing his heavy automatic into the commando's left temple with the force of a hammer.

'Son of a *bitch!*' cried the assassin hoarsely as he fell to his left, Jason's knee on his wrist, the killer's gun wrenched free.

'You keep begging for a quick demise, Major,' said Bourne as pandemonium reached its height within the grounds of the Victorian sterile house. The squad of marines that had charged the collapsed side wall were ordered to assault the rear of the gardens. 'You really don't like yourself, do you? But you've got a good idea. I will empty my bag of tricks. It's almost time now.'

Bourne removed the straps and upturned his open knapsack. The contents fell on the grass, the flames from the ever-expanding fire on the second floor of the sterile house illuminating them. There was one firebomb and one *plastique* left, and, as was accurately described by the assassin, a hand-held repeating MAC-10 machine pistol that needed only its stock frame and a clip to be inserted in order to fire. He inserted the frame of the lethal weapon, cracked in one of the four clips, and shoved the remaining three into his belt. He then released the spring of the launcher, put the canister in place, and reset the mechanism. It was ready to go – *to save the lives of children, children called to die by the aging egos of manipulators.* The firebomb remained. He knew where to direct it. He lifted it up, tore off the shield, and threw it with all his strength toward the A-framed apex above the French doors. It clung to the wood. It was the moment. He pulled the trigger of the launcher, sending the canister of gas into the stone to the right of the French doors. It exploded, bouncing off the wall to the ground; the vapours spread instantly, clouds of gas swirling, choking men within its billowing periphery. Weapons were clung to, but free hands rubbed swollen, watery eyes and covered inflamed nostrils.

The second firebomb exploded, tearing away the elegant Victorian façade above the French doors, shattering the panes of glass, whole sections of the upper wall plummeting down into the tiled foyer beyond. Flames spread upward toward the eaves and inside, firing drapes and upholstery. The marine guards scrambled away from the thunderous explosion and the flames into the clouds of tear gas. A number now dropped their rifles, as all lurched in every direction, colliding with one another, trying to get away from the fumes, gagging, coughing, seeking relief.

Delta rose to a crouch, the machine pistol in his hand, yanking the assassin up beside him. It was time; the chaos was complete. The swirling gas in front of the shattered French doors was being sucked in by the heat of the flames; it would dissipate sufficiently for him to make headway. Once inside, his search would be quick, over in moments. The directors of a covert operation that required a sterile house in foreign territory would stay within the protective confines of the house itself for two reasons. The first was that the size and disposition of the attacking force could not be accurately estimated and the risk of capture or death outside was too great. The second was more practical:

papers had to be destroyed, burned, not shredded, as they had learned in Teheran. Directives, dossiers, operational progress reports, background materials, all had to go. The sirens in Victoria Peak were growing louder, nearer; the frantic race up the steep roads was nearly over.

'It's the countdown,' said Bourne, setting the timer on the last *plastique* explosive. 'I'm not giving this to you, but I'll use it to advantage – both yours and mine. Thirty seconds, Major Allcott-Price.' Jason arced the packet as far as he could toward the right front wall.

'My *weapon!* For Christ's sake, give me the gun!'

'It's on the ground. Under my foot.'

The assassin lurched down. 'Let go of it!'

'When I want to – and I *will* want to. But if you try to take it, the next thing you'll see is a cell in the Hong Kong garrison, and – according to you – a scaffold, a thick rope, and a hangman in your immediate future.'

The killer looked up in panic. 'You goddamned *liar!* You *lied!*'

'Frequently. Don't you?'

'You *said*—'

'I know what I said. I also know why you're here, and why instead of nine shells you you have three.'

'*What?*'

'You're my diversion, Major. When I let you free with the gun, you'll head for the gate or a blown-out section of the wall – whichever, it's your choice. They'll try to stop you. You'll fire back, naturally, and while they concentrate on you, I'll get inside.'

'You *bastard!*'

'My feelings are hurt, but then I don't have feelings any longer, so it doesn't matter. I simply have to get inside—'

The last explosion blew up a sculptured tree, its roots smashing into a weakened section of the wall, stones falling out of place, the wall itself half crumbling, splitting rocks forming a V at the centre of secondary impact. Marines from the gate contingent rushed forward.

'*Now!*' roared Delta, rising to his full height.

'Give me the *gun!* Let *go* of it!'

Jason Bourne suddenly froze. He could not move – except that by some instinct or other he crashed his knee up into the killer's throat, sending the assassin over on his side. A man had appeared beyond the shattered glass doors of the burning foyer. A handkerchief covered his face, but it could not cover his limp. His *limp!* With his clubbed foot the silhouetted figure kicked down the left frame of the French doors and awkwardly walked down the three steps to the short flagstone patio fronting the once stately gardens. He dragged himself forward and yelled as loud as he could, ordering the guards who could hear him to hold their fire. The figure did not have to lower his handkerchief, Delta knew the face. It was the face of his *enemy. It was Paris, a cemetery outside of Paris. Alexander Conklin had come to kill him. Beyond-salvage was the order from on high.*

'*David!* It's Alex! Don't do what you're *doing! Stop it!* It's *me*, David! I'm here to help you!'

'You're here to *kill* me! You came to kill me in Paris, you tried again in New York! *Treadstone Seventy-one!* You've got a short memory, you bastard!'

'You don't have *any* memory, *goddamn* you! You became *Delta*, that's what they wanted! I know the whole story, David. I flew over here because we put it together! Marie, Mo Panov, and I! We're all here. Marie's safe!'

'*Lies! Tricks!* All of you, you *killed* her! You would have killed her in Paris, but I wouldn't let you near her! I kept her *away* from you!'

'She's not dead, David! She's *alive!* I can bring her to you! *Now!*'

'More *lies!*' Delta crouched and pulled the trigger, spraying the patio, the bullets ricocheting up into the burning foyer, but for reasons unknown to him they did not cut down the man himself. 'You want to pull me out so you can give the order and I'm dead. Beyond-salvage carried out! *No* way, *executioner!* I'm going inside! I want the silent, secret men behind you! They're *there!* I *know* they're there!' Bourne grabbed the fallen assassin and pulled him to his feet, handing him the gun. 'You wanted a Jason Bourne, he's *yours!* I'm setting him loose among the roses. Kill him while I kill *you!*'

Half madman, half survivor, the commando lunged through the flowering bushes away from Bourne. He raced first down the path, then instantly returned, seeing that the marine guards were at the north and south areas of the wall. If he showed himself on the east border of the garden, he was caught between both contingents. He was dead if he moved.

'I haven't any more *time*, Conklin!' yelled Bourne. *Why couldn't he kill the man who had betrayed him? Squeeze the trigger! Kill the last of Treadstone Seventy-one! Kill. Kill! What stopped him?*

The assassin threw himself over the row of flowers, clutching the warm barrel of Bourne's machine gun, wrenching it downward, levelling and firing his own gun at Jason. The bullet grazed Bourne's forehead, and in fury, Jason yanked back the trigger of the repeating weapon. Bullets thundered into the ground, the vibrations within their small, deadly arena earth-shattering. He grabbed the Englishman's gun, twisting it counter-clockwise. The assassin's mutilated right arm was no match for the man from Medusa. The gun exploded as Bourne wrenched it free. The impostor fell back on the grass, his eyes glazed, within them the knowledge that he had lost.

'*David!* For God's sake, listen to me! You *have* to—'

'There is no *David* here!' screamed Jason, his knee rammed into the assassin's chest. 'My rightful name is *Bourne*, sprung from *Delta*, spawned by Medusa! The *Snake Lady! Remember?*'

'We have to talk!'

'We have to die! *You* have to die! The secret men inside are my contract with myself, with *Marie! They* have to die!' Bourne gripped the lapel of the assassin's jacket, pulling him up on his feet. 'I repeat! Here's your Jason Bourne! He's all yours!'

'Don't *shoot!* Hold your fire!' roared Conklin as bewildered segments of the three marine contingents began to close in and the deafening sirens of the Hong Kong police roared to a stop at the demolished gate.

The man from Medusa slammed his shoulder into the commando's back, propelling the killer out into the light of the roaring flames and the floodlights. 'There he *is!* That's the prize you *wanted!*'

There was a burst of rifle fire as the assassin reeled out, then dove to the ground, rolling over and over to avoid the bullets.

'Stop it! Not *him!* For Christ's sake, hold your fire. Don't *kill* him!' screamed Conklin.

'Not *him?*' roared Jason Bourne. '*Not him? Only me!* Isn't that right, you son of a bitch? Now, you *do* die! For *Marie*, for *Echo*, for *all* of us!'

He squeezed the trigger of the machine gun, but still the bullets would not hit their mark! He swung around and, swinging back and forth, aimed his deadly weapon at both converging squads of marines. Again, he fired several prolonged bursts, crouching, ducking, moving from place to place behind the roses. *Yet he angled the barrel above their heads! Why? The children could not stop him. But then the children in their pressed GI issue should not die for the manipulators.* He had to get inside the sterile house. Now! No moments were left. It was now!

'*David!*' A woman's voice. Oh Christ, a *woman's* voice! 'David, David, *David!*' A figure in a flowing skirt ran out of the sterile house. She grabbed Alexander Conklin and pushed him away. She stood alone on the patio. 'It's *me*, David! I'm *here!* I'm *safe!* Everything's all *right*, my darling!'

Another trick, another lie. It was an old woman with grey hair, white hair! 'Get out of my way, lady, or I'll kill you. You're just another lie, another *trick!*'

'David, it's *me!* Can't you *hear* me—'

'I can *see* you! A *trick!*'

'*No*, David!'

'My name's not *David.* I told your scum friend, there's no David here!'

'*Don't!*' screamed Marie, desperately shaking her head and running in front of several marines who had crawled out on the grass, away from the swirling, vanishing clouds of gas. They were on their knees with a clear view of Bourne, getting their bearings, levelling their rifles unsteadily at him. Marie positioned herself between the recovering guards and their target. 'Haven't you done *enough* to him? For God's sake, somebody *stop* them!'

'And get blown away by some son of a bitch *terrorist?*' yelled a youthful voice from the ranks by the front wall.

'He's not what you *think!* Whatever he is, the people inside *made* him that way! You heard him. He won't fire on you if you don't shoot!'

'He's already *fired*,' roared an officer.

'You're still *standing!*' yelled back Alex Conklin from the edge of the patio. 'And he's a better marksman with more weapons than any man here! Account for it! *I* can!'

'I don't *need* you!' thundered Jason Bourne, once again triggering a burst of machine-gun fire into the burning wall of the sterile house.

Suddenly the assassin was on his feet, crouching, then lunging for the marine nearest him, a hatless youngster still coughing from the gas. The killer grabbed the guard's rifle, kicking him in the head, and fired the weapon into the next nearest marine, who lurched backward grabbing his stomach. The killer spun around; he spotted an officer with a machine pistol not unlike

Bourne's; he shot him in the neck, and grabbed the weapon from the falling body. He paused for only a split second evaluating his chances, then whipped the machine pistol up under his left arm. Delta watched, instinctively knowing what the commando would do, knowing, too, that his diversion was about to take place.

The assassin did it. He fired again, one round after another, into the closed ranks of the young, inexperienced marines by the front wall, racing, dodging his way across the short stretch of grass into the shoulder-high row of flowers on Bourne's left. It was his only escape route, the least illuminated – the collapsed right rear wall.

'*Stop* him!' shouted Conklin, limping frantically across the patio. 'But don't *shoot!* Don't kill him! For Christ's sake, don't *kill* him!'

'*Bullshit!*' came the reply from someone in the squad of marines by the left rear wall. The assassin, twisting, turning, crouching, his rifle on repeat fire, quickly worked his way toward the broken wall, pinning the guards down by his rapid bursts. The rifle chamber ran out of shells; he threw the weapon down, swinging the murderous machine pistol into place, and started his last race toward the broken wall, spraying the prone contingent of marines. He was there! The darkness beyond was his escape!

'You *motherfucker!*' It was a teenager's cry, the voice immature, in torment, but nevertheless lethal. 'You killed my *buddy!* You blew his fucking face off! You're going to *buy* it, you *shithead!*'

A young black marine leaped away from his dead white companion and raced toward the wall as the assassin swung around, vaulting over the stone. Another burst from the killer caught the marine in the shoulder; he lunged to the ground, rolled over twice to his left, and fired four rounds of ammunition.

They were followed by an agonizing, hysterical scream of defiance. It was the scream of death; the assassin, his eyes wide in hatred, fell into the jagged rocks. Major Allcott-Price, formerly of the Royal Commandos, was gone.

Bourne started forward, his weapon raised. Marie ran to the border of the patio, the distance between them no more than a few feet. 'Don't *do* it, David!'

'I'm not *David*, lady! Ask your scum-ball friend, we go back a long time. Get out of my way!' *Why couldn't he kill her? One burst, and he was free to do what he had to do! Why?*

'All right!' screamed Marie, holding her place. 'There is no David, *all right?* You're Jason Bourne! You're *Delta!* You're anything you want to be, but you're also *mine!* You're my *husband!*' The revelation had the impact of a sudden bolt of lightning on the guards who heard it. The officers, their elbows bent, held up their hands – the universal command to hold fire – as they and the men stared in astonishment.

'I don't *know* you!'

'My voice is my own. You know it, Jason.'

'A *trick!* An actress, a *mimic!* A *lie!* It's been done before.'

'And if I look different, it's because of you, *Jason Bourne!*'

'Get out of my way or get *killed!*'

'You taught me in *Paris!* On the rue de Rivoli, the Hotel Meurice, the newsstand on the corner. Can you remember? The newspapers with the story out of Zurich, my photograph on all the front pages! And the small hotel in the Montparnasse when we were checking out, the concierge reading the paper, my picture in front of his face! You were so frightened you told me to run outside . . . The *taxi!* Do you remember the taxi? On the way to Issy-les-Moulineaux – I'll never forget that impossible name. "Change your hair," you said. "Pull it up or push it back!" You said you didn't care what I did so long as I *changed* it! You asked me if I had an eyebrow pencil – you told me to thicken my brows, make them longer! *Your* words, *Jason!* We were running for our lives and you wanted me to look *different*, to remove any likeness to the photograph that was all over *Europe!* I had to become a chameleon because Jason Bourne was a chameleon. He had to teach his lover, his *wife!* That's all I've *done*, Jason!'

'*No!*' cried Delta, drawing the word out into a scream, the mists of confusion enveloping him, sending his mind into the outer regions of panic. The images were there! Rue de Rivoli, the Montparnasse, the taxi. *Listen to me. I am a chameleon called Cain and I can teach you many things I do not care to teach you but I must. I can change my colour to accommodate the forest, I can shift with the wind by smelling it. I can find my way through natural and man-made jungles. Alpha, Bravo, Charlie, Delta . . . Delta is for Charlie and Charlie is for Cain. I am Cain. I am death. And I must tell you who I am and lose you.*

'You *do* remember!' shouted David Webb's wife.

'A trick! The chemicals – I said the words. They *gave* you the words! They have to *stop* me!'

'They gave me nothing! I want *nothing* from them. I only want my husband! I'm *Marie!*'

'You're a lie! They *killed* her!' Delta squeezed the trigger and the fusillade of bullets exploded the earth at Marie's feet. Rifles were quickly brought up to firing positions.

'Don't *do* it!' screamed Marie, whipping her head over at the marine guards, her eyes glaring, her voice a command. 'All right, Jason. If you don't know me, I don't want to live. I can't be plainer than that, my darling. It's why I understand what you're doing. You're throwing your life away because a part of you that's taken over thinks I'm gone and you don't want to live without me. I understand that very well because I don't want to live without you.' Marie took several steps across the grass and stood motionless.

Delta raised the machine gun, the snub-nosed sight on the barrel centring on the grey hair streaked with white. His index finger closed around the trigger. Suddenly, involuntarily, his right hand began to tremble, then his left. The murderous weapon began to waver, at first slowly, back and forth, then faster – in circles – as Bourne's head swayed in fitful jerks; the trembling spread; his neck began to lose control.

There was a commotion within the gathering crowd at the smouldering ruins of the gate and the guardhouse several hundred feet away. A man struggled; he was held by two marines. 'Let me go, you goddamned fools! I'm a doctor, *his* doctor!' With a surge of strength, Morris Panov broke away and raced across the lawn into the glare of the floodlights. He stopped twenty feet from Bourne.

Delta began to moan; the sound and the rhythm was barbaric. Jason Bourne dropped the weapon . . . and David Webb fell to his knees weeping. Marie started toward him.

'*No!*' commanded Panov, his voice quietly emphatic, stopping Webb's wife. 'He has come to you. He must.'

'He *needs* me!'

'Not that way. He has to recognize you. *David* has to recognize you and tell his other self to let him free. You can't do that for him. He has to do it for himself.'

Silence. Floodlights. Fire.

And like a cringing, beaten child, David Webb raised his head, the tears streaming down his cheeks. Slowly, painfully, he rose to his feet and ran into the arms of his wife.

33

They were in the sterile house, in the white-walled communications centre – in an antiseptic cell belonging to some futuristic laboratory complex. White-faced computers rose above the white counters on the left, dozens of thin, dark rectangular mouths sporadically indented, their teeth digital readouts forming luminescent green numbers that constantly changed with inviolate frequency alterations and less sophisticated, less secure means of sending and receiving information. On the right was a large white conference table above the white-tiled floor, the only deviation from colour conformity and asepsis being several black ashtrays. The players were in place around the table. The technicians had been dismissed, all systems put on hold, only the ominous Red-Alert, a three-by ten-inch panel in the central computer remained active; an operator was outside the closed door should the alarming red lights appear. Beyond this sacrosanct, isolated room the Hong Kong fire fighters were hosing down the last of the smouldering embers as the Hong Kong police were calming the panicked residents from the nearby estates on Victoria Peak – many of whom were convinced that Armageddon had arrived in the form of a Mainland onslaught – telling everyone that the terrible events were the work of a deranged criminal killed by government emergency units. The sceptical Peakers were not satisfied. The times were not on their side; their world was not as it should be and they wanted proof. So the corpse of the dead assassin was paraded on a stretcher past the curious onlookers, the punctured, blood-drenched body partially uncovered for all to see. The stately residents returned to their stately homes, having by this time contemplated all manner of insurance claims.

The players sat in white plastic chairs, living, breathing robots waiting for a signal to commence, none really possessing the courage or the energy to open the proceedings. Exhaustion, mingled with the fear of violent death, marked their faces – marked all but one face. His possessed the deep lines and dark shadows of extreme fatigue, but there was no hollow fear in his eyes, only passive, bewildered acceptance of things still beyond his understanding. Minutes ago death had held no fear for him; it was preferable to living. Now, in his confusion, with his wife gripping his hand, he could feel the swelling of distant anger, distant in the sense that it was far back in the recesses of his mind, relentlessly pushing forward like the faraway thunder over a lake in an approaching summer storm.

'Who did this to us?' said David Webb, his voice barely above a whisper.

'I did,' answered Havilland, at the end of the rectangular white table. The ambassador leaned slowly forward, returning Webb's deathlike stare. 'If I were in a court of law seeking mercy for an ignominious act, I would have to plead extenuating circumstances.'

'Which were?' asked David in a monotone.

'First, there is the crisis,' said the diplomat. 'Second, there was yourself.'

'Explain that,' interrupted Alex Conklin at the other end of the table, facing Havilland. Webb and Marie were on his left in front of the white wall, Morris Panov and Edward McAllister opposite them. 'And don't leave anything out,' added the rogue Intelligence officer.

'I don't intend to,' said the ambassador, his eyes remaining on David. 'The crisis is real, the catastrophe imminent. A cabal has been formed deep in Peking by a group of zealots led by a man so deeply entrenched in the hierarchy of his government, so revered as a philosopher-prince that he cannot be exposed. No one would believe it. Anyone who attempted to expose him would become a pariah. Worse, any attempt at exposure would risk a backlash so severe that Peking would cry insult and outrage, and revert to suspicion and intransigence. But if the conspiracy is not aborted, it will destroy the Hong Kong Accords and blow the colony apart. The result will be the immediate occupation by the People's Republic. I don't have to tell you what that would mean – economic chaos, violence, bloodshed and undoubtedly war in the Far East. How long could such hostilities be contained before other nations are forced to choose sides? The risk is unthinkable.'

Silence. Eyes locked with eyes.

'Fanatics from the Kuomintang,' said David, his voice flat and cold. 'China against China. It's been the war cry of maniacs for the past forty years.'

'But only a cry, Mr Webb. Words, talk, but no movement, no strikes, no ultimate strategy.' Havilland cupped his hands on the table, breathing deeply. 'There is now. The strategy's in place, a strategy so oblique and devious, so long in the making, they believe it can't fail. But of course it will, and when it does, the world will be faced with a crisis of intolerable proportions. It could well lead to the final crisis, the one we can't survive. Certainly the Far East won't.'

'You're not telling me anything I haven't seen for myself. They've gone down deep in high places, and they're probably spreading, but they're still fanatics, a lunatic fringe. And if the maniac I saw who was running the show is anything like the others, they'd all be hanged in Tian An Men Square. It'd be televised and approved by every group opposed to capital punishment. He was – *is* – a messianic sadist, a butcher. Butchers aren't statesmen. They're not taken seriously.'

'Herr Hitler was in 1933,' observed Havilland. 'The Ayatollah Khomeini only a few years ago. But then you obviously don't know who their true leader is. He'd never show himself under any circumstances where you might even remotely see *him*. However, I can assure you he's a statesman and taken very seriously. However, again, his objective is not Peking. It's Hong Kong.'

'I saw what I saw and heard what I heard, and it'll all be with me for a long time . . . You don't need me, you never *did! Isolate* them, spread the word in the Central Committee, call in Taiwan to disown them – they *will!* Times change. They don't want that war any more than Peking does.'

The ambassador studied the Medusan, obviously evaluating David's information, realizing that Webb had seen enough in Peking to draw conclusions of his own, but not enough to understand the essence of the Hong Kong conspiracy. 'It's too late,' said the diplomat. 'The forces have been set in motion. Treachery at the highest levels of China's government, treachery by the hands of the despised Nationalists, assumed to be in collusion with Western financial interests. Even the devoted followers of Deng Xiaoping could not accept that blow to Peking's pride, that loss of international face – the role of the duped cuckold. Neither would we if it was learned that General Motors, IBM, and the New York Stock Exchange were being run by American traitors, trained in the Soviet, diverting billions to projects not in our nation's interests.'

'The analogy is accurate,' broke in McAllister, his fingers at his right temple. 'Cumulatively, that's what Hong Kong will be to the People's Republic – that and a hundred thousand times more. But there's another element, and it's as alarming as anything else we've learned. I should like to bring it up now – in my position as an analyst, as someone who's supposed to calculate the reactions of adversaries and potential adversaries—'

'Make it short,' interrupted Webb. 'You talk too much and you keep rubbing your head too much and I don't like your eyes. They belong on a dead fish. You talked too much in Maine. You're a liar.'

'Yes. Yes, I understand what you're saying and why you're saying it. But I'm a decent man, Mr Webb. I believe in decency.'

'I don't. Not any longer. Go on. This is all very enlightening, and I don't understand a goddamned thing because nobody's said a goddamned thing that makes sense. What's your contribution, liar?'

'The organized crime factor.' McAllister swallowed at David's repeated insult, but still delivered the statement as if he expected everyone to understand. When faced with blank looks, he added. 'The *triads!*'

'Mafia-structured groups, Oriental style,' said Marie, her eyes on the undersecretary of State. 'Criminal brotherhoods.'

McAllister nodded. 'Narcotics, illegal immigration, gambling, prostitution, loan-sharking – all the usual pursuits.'

'And some not so usual,' added Marie. 'They're deep into their own form of economics. They own banks – indirectly, of course – throughout California, Oregon, the State of Washington, and up into my country, in British Columbia. They launder money in the millions every day by way of international transfers.'

'Which only serves to compound the crisis,' said McAllister emphatically.

'Why?' asked David. 'What's your point?'

'*Crime*, Mr Webb. The leaders of the People's Republic are obsessed with crime. Reports indicate that over a hundred thousand executions have taken place during the last three years with little distinction made between misdemeanors and felonies. It's consistent with the regime – the origins of the regime. All revolutions believe they are conceived in purity; the purity of the cause is everything. Peking will make ideological adjustments to benefit from the West's marketplace, but there'll be no accommodation for even the hint of organized crime.'

'You make them sound like a collection of paranoids,' interjected Panov.

'They are. They can't afford to be anything else.'

'Ideologically?' asked the psychiatrist skeptically.

'Sheer numbers, Doctor. The purity of the revolution is the cover, but it's the numbers that frighten them. A huge, immensely populated country with vast resources – my God, if organized crime moved in, and with a billion people inside its borders, don't think for a minute the overlords aren't champing at the bit – it could become a *nation* of triads. Villages, towns, whole cities could be divided into "family" terrains, all profiting from the influx of Western capital and technology. There'd be an explosion of illegal exports flooding the contraband markets across the world. Narcotics from uncountable hills and fields that could not possibly be patrolled, weapons from subsidiary factories set up through graft, textiles from hundreds of underground plants using stolen machinery and peasant labour crippling those industries in the West. *Crime.*'

'That's a "great leap forward" no one over here's been able to accomplish in the last forty years,' said Conklin.

'Who would dare try?' asked McAllister. 'If a person can be executed for stealing fifty yuan, who's going to go for a hundred thousand? It takes protection, organization, people in high places. This is what Peking fears, why it's paranoid. The leaders are terrified of corrupters in high places. The political infrastructure could be eroded. The leaders would lose control, and *that* they will not risk. Again, their fears *are* paranoid, but for them they're terribly real. Any hint that powerful criminal factions are in league with internal conspirators, all infiltrating their economy, would be enough for them to disown the Accords and send their troops down into Hong Kong.'

'Your conclusion's obvious,' said Marie. 'But where's the logic? How could it happen?'

'It's happening, Mrs Webb,' answered Ambassador Havilland. 'It's why we needed Jason Bourne.'

'Somebody had better start at the beginning,' said David.

The diplomat did. 'It began over thirty years ago when a brilliant young man was sent from Taiwan back to the land of his father's birth and given a new name, a new family. It was a long-range plan; its roots were in zealotry and revenge . . .'

Webb listened as the incredible story of Sheng Chou Yang unfolded, each block in place, each fact convincingly the truth, for there was no reason any longer for lies. Twenty-seven minutes later, when he had finished, Havilland picked up a black-bordered file folder. He lifted the cover, revealing a clasped sheaf of some seventy-odd pages, closed it, and reached over, placing it in front of David. 'This is everything we know, everything we've learned – the detailed specifics of everything I've told you. It can't leave this house except as ashes, but you're welcome to read it. If you have any doubts or questions, I swear to you I'll move every source in the United States government – from the Oval Office to the National Security Council – to satisfy you. I could do no less.' The diplomat paused, his eyes fixed on Webb's. 'Perhaps we have no right to ask it, but we need your help. We need all the information you can give us.'

'So you can send someone in to take out this Sheng Chou Yang.'

'Essentially, yes. But it's far more complex than that. Our hand must be invisible. It can't be seen or even remotely suspected. Sheng's covered himself brilliantly. Peking looks upon him as a visionary, a great patriot who works slavishly for Mother China – you might say, a saint. His security is absolute. The people around him, his aides, his guards, they're his protective shock troops, their allegiance is solely to him.'

'Which is why you wanted the impostor,' interrupted Marie. 'He was your link to Sheng.'

'We knew he had accepted contracts from him. Sheng had to – *has* to – eliminate his opposition, both those who oppose him ideologically and those he intends to exclude from his operations.'

'In this latter group,' McAllister broke in, 'are the leaders of rival triads that Sheng doesn't trust, that the fanatics of the Kuomintang don't trust. He knows that if they're around to see that they're being squeezed out; a destabilizing gangland war would erupt, which Sheng couldn't tolerate any more than the British can with Peking up the street. Within the past two months seven triad overlords have been killed, their organizations crippled.'

'The new Jason Bourne was Sheng's perfect solution,' continued the ambassador. 'The hired assassin with no political or national ties, for, above all, the killings could never be traced back to China.'

'But he went to *Peking*,' objected Webb. 'It's where I tracked him. Even if it started out as a trap for me, which it was—'

'A trap for *you?*' exclaimed Havilland. 'They *knew* about you?'

'I came face-to-face with my successor two nights ago at the airport. We each knew who the other was – it was impossible not to know. He wasn't going to keep it a secret and take the fall for a failed contract.'

'It *was* you,' interrupted McAllister. 'I *knew* it!'

'So did Sheng and his people. I was the new gun in town and had to be stopped, killed on a priority-one basis. They couldn't risk what I'd pieced together. The trap was conceived that night, set that night.'

'*Jesus!*' cried Conklin. 'I read about Kai-tak in Washington. The papers said it was assumed to be right-wing lunatics. Keep the Commies out of capitalism. Instead, it was *you?*'

'Both governments had to come up with something for the world press,' added the undersecretary. 'Just as we have to say something about tonight—'

'My *point* is,' said David, ignoring McAllister. 'This Sheng called for the commando, used him to mount a trap for me, and by doing so made him part of the inner circle. That's no way for a concealed client to keep his distance from a hired killer.'

'It is if he didn't expect him to walk out of that circle alive,' replied Havilland, glancing at the undersecretary of State. 'It's Edward's theory, and one to which I subscribe, that when the final contract was carried out, *or* when it was deemed that he knew too much and was therefore a liability, the impostor was to be killed collecting a payment – believing, of course, that he was being given another assignment. Everything untraceable, the slate clean. The events at Kai-tak no doubt sealed his death warrant.'

'He wasn't smart enough to see it,' said Jason Bourne. 'He couldn't think geometrically.'

'I beg your pardon?' asked the ambassador.

'Nothing,' answered Webb, again staring at the diplomat. 'So everything you told me was part truth, part lie. Hong Kong could blow apart, but not for the reasons you gave me.'

'The truth was our credibility; you had to accept that, accept our deep, frightening concerns. The lies were to recruit you.' Havilland leaned back in his chair. 'And I can't be any more honest than that.'

'*Bastards*,' said Webb, his voice low, ice-like.

'I'll grant you that,' agreed Havilland. 'But as I mentioned before, there were extenuating circumstances, specifically two. The crisis and yourself.'

'And?' said Marie.

'Let me ask you, Mr Webb . . . Mrs Webb. If we had come to you and stated our case, would you have joined forces with us? Would you willingly have become Jason Bourne again?'

Silence. All eyes were on David as his own strayed blankly over the surface of the table, then rested on the file folder. 'No,' he said softly. 'I don't trust you.'

'We knew that,' agreed Havilland, again nodding his head. 'But from our point of view we *had* to recruit you. You were able to do what no one else could do, and insofar as you did it, I submit that that judgement was correct. The cost was terrible, no one underestimates it, but we felt – I felt – that there was no other choice. Time and the consequences were against us – *are* against us.'

'As much as before,' said Webb. 'The commando's dead.'

'The commando?' McAllister leaned forward.

'Your assassin. The impostor. What you did to us was all for nothing.'

'Not necessarily,' objected Havilland. 'It will depend on what you can tell us. News of *a* death up here will be in tomorrow's headlines, we can't stop it, but Sheng can't know *whose* death. No photographs were taken, no press was here at the time, and those who've arrived since have been cordoned off several hundred yards away by the police. We can control the information by simply providing it.'

'What about the body?' asked Panov. 'There are medical procedures—'

'Overruled by MI-Six,' said the ambassador. 'This is still British territory, and communications between London, Washington, and Government House were swift. The impostor's face was too shattered for anyone who saw it to give a description, and his remains are in custody, beyond scrutiny. It was Edward's thinking, and he was damn quick about it.'

'There's still David and Marie,' persisted the psychiatrist. 'Too many people saw them, heard them.'

'Only several squads of marine guards were close enough to see and hear clearly,' said McAllister. 'The entire contingent is being flown back to Hawaii in an hour, including two dead and seven wounded. They've left the premises and are sequestered at the airport. There was a great deal of confusion and panic. The police and the firemen were occupied elsewhere; none were in the gardens. We can say anything we like.'

'That seems to be a habit with you,' commented Webb.

'You heard the ambassador,' said the undersecretary, avoiding David's gaze. 'We didn't feel we had a choice.'

'Be fair to yourself, Edward.' Again Havilland looked at Webb while addressing the undersecretary. '*I* didn't feel we had a choice. You strenuously objected.'

'I was *wrong*,' said McAllister firmly as the diplomat snapped his eyes over at him. 'But that's irrelevant,' continued the undersecretary quickly. 'We've got to decide what we're going to say. The consulate's been swamped by calls from the press—'

'The *consulate*?' broke in Conklin. 'Some sterile house!'

'There wasn't time for a proper leasing cover,' said the ambassador. 'It was kept as quiet as possible and we prepared a plausible story. So far as we know, there were no questions, but the police report had to list the owner and the lessee. How's Garden Road handling it, Edward?'

'Simply that the situation hasn't been clarified. They're waiting for us, but they can't stall much longer. It's better that we prepare something than leave the circumstances to speculation.'

'Infinitely,' agreed Havilland. 'I suspect that means you have something in mind.'

'It's stop-gap, but it could serve, if I heard Mr Webb correctly.'

'About what?'

'You've used the word "commando" several times, I assume not as a figure of speech. The assassin was a commando?'

'Former. An officer and a mental case. Homicidal, to be accurate.'

'Did you get an identity, learn his name?'

David looked hard at the analyst, recalling Allcott-Price's words, spoken in a warped sense of sick triumph . . . *If I lose and the story blows, how many practicing antisocials will be fired up by it? How many other 'different' men are out there who'd be only too happy to take my place, as I took yours? This bloody world is crawling with Jason Bournes. Give them direction, an idea – and they'll be off and running* . . . 'I never found out who he was,' said Webb simply.

'But nevertheless he *was* a commando.'

'That's right.'

'Not a Ranger or a Green Beret or Special Forces—'

'No.'

'I assume therefore that you mean he was British.'

'Yes.'

'Then we'll put out a story that implicitly denies those specifics. Not an Englishman, no military record – go in the opposite direction.'

'A white male American,' said Conklin quietly, with even a measure of respect, as he looked at the under-secretary of State. 'Give him a name and a history from a dead file. Preferably fourth-rate garbage, a psychopath with a hang-up so heavy he goes after someone up here.'

'Something like that, but perhaps not entirely,' said McAllister, awkwardly shifting his position in the chair, as if he did not care to disagree with the experienced CIA man. Or something else. 'White male, yes. American, yes. Certainly a man with an obsession so compelling that he's driven to wholesale slaughter, his fury directed at a target – as you say – up here.'

'Who?' asked David.

'Me,' replied McAllister, his eyes locked with Webb's.

'Which means *me*,' said David. 'I'm that *man*, that *obsessed* man.'

'Your name would not be used,' continued the under-secretary calmly, coldly. 'We could invent an American expatriate who several years ago was hunted by the authorities throughout the Far East for crimes ranging from multiple murders to running narcotics. We'll say I cooperated with the police in Hong Kong, Macao, Singapore, Japan, Malaysia, Sumatra, and the Philippines. Through my efforts his operations were effectively shut down and he lost millions. He learns I've returned and am posted here on Victoria Peak. He comes after me, the man who ruined him.' McAllister paused, turning to David. 'Since I spent a number of years here in Hong Kong, I can't imagine that Peking overlooked me. I'm sure there's an extensive dossier on an analyst who made a number of enemies during his tour of duty here. I *did* make enemies, Mr Webb. It was my job. We were trying to increase our influence in this part of the world, and wherever Americans were involved in criminal activities, I did my level best to help the authorities apprehend them, or, at the least, force them out of Asia. It was the best way to show our good intentions, going after our own. It was also the reason State recalled me to Washington. And by using my name we lend a certain authenticity for Sheng Chou Yang. You see, we knew each other. He'll speculate on a dozen possibilities – I hope the right one, but none remotely connected to a British commando.'

'The right speculation,' interrupted Conklin quietly, 'being the fact that no one over here has heard from the first Jason Bourne in a couple of years.'

'Exactly.'

'So *I'm* the corpse that's in custody,' said Webb, 'beyond scrutiny.'

'You could be, yes,' said McAllister. 'You see, we don't know what Sheng knows, how deep his penetration went. The only thing we want to establish is that the dead man is *not* his assassin.'

'Leaving the way open for another impostor to go back up and draw Sheng out for the kill,' added Conklin, respectfully. 'You're something, Mr Analyst. A son of a bitch, but something.'

'You'd be exposing yourself, Edward,' said Havilland, his gaze levelled at the undersecretary. 'I never asked that of you. You *do* have enemies.'

'I want to do it this way, Mr Ambassador. You employ me to render the best judgements that I can, and in my judgement this is the most productive course. There's got to be a convincing smoke screen. My name can provide it – for Sheng. The rest can be couched in ambiguous language, language that everyone we want to reach will understand.'

'So be it,' said Webb, suddenly closing his eyes, hearing the words Jason Bourne had spoken so often.

'David—' Marie touched his face.

'Sorry.' Webb fingered the file folder in front of him, then opened it. On the first page was a photograph with a name printed underneath. It was identified as the face of Sheng Chou Yang, but it was far more than that. It was *the face*. It was the face of the *butcher!* The madman who hacked women and men to death with his jewelled ceremonial sword, who forced brothers to fight with razor-sharp knives until one killed the other, who took a brave, tortured Echo's life with a slash to the head. Bourne stopped breathing, enraged by the unimaginable cruelty, as bloody images overcame him. As he stared at the photograph the sight of Echo, throwing his life away to save Delta, brought him back to that clearing in the forest. Delta knew that it was Echo's death that had made the assassin's capture possible. Echo had died defiantly, accepting his unbearably painful execution, so that a fellow Medusan could not only make good his escape, but obey a final gesture telling him that the madman with the sword must be killed!

'*This*,' whispered Jason Bourne, 'is the son of your unknown taipan?'

'Yes,' said Havilland.

'Your *revered* philosopher-prince? The Chinese saint no one can expose?'

'Again, yes.'

'You were *wrong!* He showed himself! *Christ*, did he show himself!'

Stunned, the ambassador shot forward. 'You're certain?'

'There's no way I could be more certain.'

'The circumstances must have been extraordinary,' said the astonished McAllister. 'And it certainly confirms that the impostor never would have gotten out of there alive. Still, the circumstances must have been *earth-shaking* for him!'

'Considering the fact that no one outside of China ever learned about them, they were. Mao's tomb became a shooting gallery. It was part of the trap, and they lost. Echo lost.'

'Who?' asked Marie, still gripping his hand.

'A friend.'

'Mao's *tomb?*' repeated Havilland. 'Extraordinary!'

'Not at all,' said Bourne. 'How bright. The last place in China a target would expect an attack. He goes in thinking he's the pursuer following his quarry, expecting to pick him up outside, on the other side. The lights are dim, his guard down. And all the while *he's* the quarry, hunted, isolated, set up for the kill. Very bright.'

'Very *dangerous* for the hunters,' said the ambassador. 'For Sheng's people. One misstep and they could have been taken. *Insanity!*'

'No missteps were possible. They would have killed their own if I hadn't killed them. I understand that now. When everything went off the wire, they simply disappeared. With Echo.'

'Back to Sheng, *please*, Mr Webb.' Havilland was himself obsessed, his eyes pleading. 'Tell us what you saw, what you know.'

'He's a monster,' said Jason quietly, his eyes glazed, staring at the photograph. 'He comes from hell, a Savonarola who tortures and kills – men, women, kids – with a smile on his face. He gives sermons like a prophet talking to children, but underneath he's a maniac who rules his gang of misfits by sheer terror. Those shock troops you mentioned aren't troops, they're goons, sadistic thugs who've learned their craft from a master. He's Auschwitz, Dachau, and Bergen-Belsen all rolled into one. God help us all if he runs anything over here.'

'He can, Mr Webb,' said Havilland quietly, his terrified gaze fixed on Jason Bourne. 'He will. You've just described a Sheng Chou Yang the world has never seen, and at this moment he is the most powerful man in China. As Adolf Hitler marched victoriously into the Reichstag, so Sheng will march into the Central Committee, making it his puppet. What you've told us is far more catastrophic than anything we've conceived of – China against China . . . Armageddon to follow. Oh, my God!'

'He's an animal,' whispered Jason hoarsely. 'He has to kill like a predator, but his only hunger is for killing – not for food but for the kill.'

'You're talking in *generalities.*' McAllister's interruption was cold but intense. 'We have to know more – *I* have to know more!'

'He called a conference.' Bourne spoke dreamily, his head swaying, his eyes again riveted on the photograph. 'It was the start of – the nights of the great blade, he said. There was a traitor, he said. The conference was something only a madman could create, torches everywhere, held in the countryside, an hour out of Peking, in a bird sanctuary – can you believe it? A *bird* sanctuary – and he really did what I say he did. He killed a man suspended by ropes, hacking his sword into the screaming body. Then a woman who tried to argue her innocence, cutting her head off – her *head!* In front of everyone! And then two brothers—'

'A *traitor?*' whispered McAllister, ever the analyst. 'Did he *find* one? Did anyone confess? Is there any kind of counterinsurgency?'

'*Stop* it!' cried Marie.

'*No,* Mrs Webb! He's going back. He's reliving it. Look at him. Can't you see? He's *there.*'

'I'm afraid our irritating colleague is right, Marie,' said Panov softly, watching Webb. 'He's in and out, trying to find his own reality. It's okay. Let him ride it. It could save us all a lot of time.'

'*Bullshit!*'

'Forever accurate, my dear, and forever debatable. Shut up.'

'. . . There was no traitor, no one who spoke, only the woman with doubts. He killed her and there was silence, an awful silence. He was warning everyone, telling everyone that they, the true China, were everywhere and at the same time they were invisible. In the ministries, in the security police, everywhere . . . And then he killed Echo, but Echo knew he had to die. He wanted to die quickly because he couldn't live much longer anyway. After they tortured him, he was in awful shape. Still, if he could give me time—'

'Who is Echo, David?' asked Morris Panov. 'Tell us, please.'

'Alpha, Bravo, Charlie, Delta, Echo . . . Foxtrot—'

'Medusa,' said the psychiatrist. 'It's Medusa, isn't it? Echo was in Medusa.'

'He was in Paris. The Louvre. He tried to save my life, but I saved his. That was okay, it was right. He saved mine before, years ago. "Rest is a weapon," he said. He put the others around me and made me sleep. And then we got out of the jungle.'

' "Rest is a weapon" . . .' Marie spoke quietly and closed her eyes, pressing her husband's hand, the tears falling down her cheeks. 'Oh, *Christ!*'

'. . . Echo saw me in the woods. We used the old signals we used before, years ago. He hadn't forgotten. None of us ever forget.'

'Are we in the countryside, in the bird sanctuary, David?' asked Panov, gripping McAllister's shoulder to stop him from intruding.

'Yes,' replied Jason Bourne, his eyes now floating, unfocused. 'We both know. He's going to die. So simple, so clear. Die. Death. No more. Just buy time, precious minutes. Then maybe I can do it.'

'Do what – *Delta?*' Panov drew out the name in quiet emphasis.

'Take out the son of a bitch. Take out the butcher. He doesn't deserve to live, he has no *right* to live! He kills too easily – with a smile on his face. Echo saw it. I saw it. Now it's *happening* – everything's happening at once. The explosions in the forest, everybody running, shouting. I can *do* it now! He's a clean kill . . . He *sees* me! He's *staring* at me! He knows I'm his enemy! I *am* your enemy, *butcher!* I'm the last face you'll *see!* . . . What's wrong? Something's *wrong!* He's shielding himself! He's pulling someone in front of him. I have to get out! I can't *do* it!'

'*Can't* or *won't?*' asked Panov, leaning forward. 'Are you Jason Bourne or are you David Webb? Who *are* you?'

'*Delta!*' screamed the victim, stunning everyone at the table by his outburst. 'I am *Delta!* I am *Bourne!* Cain is for *Delta* and Carlos is for *Cain!*' The victim, whoever he was, collapsed back in the chair, his head snapped down into his chest. He was silent. No one spoke.

It took several minutes – none knew how long, none counted – until the man who was unable to establish an identity for himself raised his head. His eyes were now half free, half prisoner of the agony he was experiencing. 'I'm sorry,' said David Webb. 'I don't know what happened to me. I'm sorry.'

'No apologies, David,' said Panov. 'You went back. It's understandable. It's okay.'

'Yes, I went back. Screwy, isn't it?'

'Not at all,' said the psychiatrist. 'It's perfectly natural.'

'I *have* to go back, that's understandable, too, isn't it, Mo?'

'*David!*' screamed Marie, reaching for him.

'I *have* to,' said Jason Bourne, gently holding her wrists. 'No one else can do it, it's as simple as that. I know the codes. I know the way . . . Echo traded in his life for mine, believing I'd do it, that I'd kill the butcher. I failed then. I won't fail now.'

'What about *us?*' Marie clutched him, her voice reverberating off the white walls. 'Don't *we* matter?'

'I'll come back, I promise you,' said David, removing her arms and looking into her eyes. 'But I have to go back, can't you understand?'

'For *these* people? These *liars!*'

'No, not for them. For someone who wanted to live – above everything. You didn't know him; he was a survivor. But he knew when his life wasn't worth the price of my death. I had to live and do what I had to do. I had to live and come back to you, he knew that, too. He faced the equation and made his decision. Somewhere along the line we all have to make that decision.' Bourne turned to McAllister. 'Is there anyone here who can take a picture of a corpse?'

'Whose?' asked the undersecretary of State.

'Mine,' said Jason Bourne.

34

The grisly photograph was taken on the white conference table by a sterile house technician under the reluctant supervision of Morris Panov. A bloodstained white sheet covered Webb's body; it was angled across his throat revealing a blood-streaked face, the eyes wide, the features clear.

'Develop the roll as fast as you can and bring me the contacts,' instructed Conklin.

'Twenty minutes,' said the technician, heading for the door, as McAllister entered the room.

'What's happening?' asked David, sitting up on the table. Marie, wincing, wiped his face with a warm, wet towel.

'The consulate press people called the media,' replied the undersecretary. 'They said they'd issue a statement in an hour or so, as soon as all the facts were in place. They're mocking one up now. I gave them the scenario with a go-ahead to use my name. They'll work it out with embassy obfuscation and read it to us before issuing it.'

'Any word on Lin?' asked the CIA man.

'A message from the doctor. He's still critical but holding on.'

'What about the press down the road?' asked Havilland. 'We've got to let them in here sooner or later. The longer we wait, the more they'll think it's a cover-up. We can't afford that, either.'

'We've still got some rope in that area,' said McAllister. 'I sent word that the police – at great risk to themselves – were sweeping the grounds for undetonated explosives. Reporters can be very patient under those conditions. Incidentally, in the scenario I gave the press people, I told them to stress the fact that the man who attacked the house was obviously an expert with demolitions.'

Jason Bourne, one of the most proficient demolitions men to come out of Medusa, looked at McAllister. The undersecretary looked away. 'I've got to get out of here,' Jason said. 'I've got to get to Macao as quickly as possible.'

'*David*, for God's sake!' Marie stood in front of her husband, staring at him, her voice low and intense.

'I wish it didn't have to be this way,' said Webb, getting off the table. 'I wish it didn't,' he repeated softly, 'but it *does.* I have to be in place. I have to start the sequence to reach Sheng before the story breaks in the morning papers, before that photograph appears confirming the message I'm sending through channels he's convinced no one knows about. He's got to believe I'm his assassin, the man he was going to kill, not the Jason Bourne from Medusa who tried to kill him in that forest glen. He has to get word from me – from who he thinks I am – before he's given any other information. Because the information I'm sending him is the last thing he wants to hear. Everything else will seem insignificant.'

'The bait,' said Alex Conklin. 'Feed him the critical information first and the cover falls in place because he's stunned, preoccupied, and accepts the printed official version, in particular the photograph in the newspapers.'

'What are you going to tell him?' asked the ambassador, his voice conveying the fact that he disliked the prospect of losing control of this blackest of operations.

'What you told me. Part truth, part lie.'

'Spell it out, Mr Webb,' said Havilland firmly. 'We owe you a great deal but—'

'You *owe* me what you can't *pay* me!' snapped Jason Bourne, interrupting. 'Unless you blow your brains out right here in front of me.'

'I understand your anger, but still I must insist. You'll do nothing to jeopardize the lives of five million people, or the vital interests of the United States government.'

'I'm glad you got the sequence right – for once. All right, Mr *Ambassador*, I'll tell you. It's what I would have told you before, if you'd had the decency, the *decency*, to come to me and "state your case." I'm surprised it never occurred to you – no, not surprised, shocked – but I guess I shouldn't be. You believe in your rarefied manipulations, in the trappings of your quiet power . . . you probably think you deserve it all because of your great intellect, or something like that. You're all the same. You relish complexity – and *your* explanations of it – so that you can't see when the simple route is a hell of a lot more effective.'

'I'm waiting to be instructed,' said Havilland coldly.

'So be it,' said Bourne. 'I listened very carefully during your ponderous explanation. You took pains to *explain* why no one could officially approach Sheng and tell him what you knew. You were right, too. He'd have laughed in your face, or spit in your eye, or told you to pound sand – whatever you like. Sure, he would've. He's got the leverage. You pursue your "outrageous" accusations, he pulls Peking out of the Hong Kong Accords. You lose. You try to go over his head, good luck. You lose again. You have no proof but the words of several dead men who've had their throats cut, members of the Kuomintang who'd say anything to discredit party officials in the People's Republic. He smiles and, without saying it, lets you know that you'd better go along with him. You figure you can't go along because the risks are too great – if the whistle blows on Sheng, the Far East blows. You were right about that, too – more for the reasons "*Edward*" gave us than you did. Peking might possibly overlook a corrupt commission as one of those temporary concessions to greed, but it won't permit a spreading Chinese Mafia to infiltrate its industry or its labour forces or its government. As "Edward" said, they could lose their jobs—'

'I'm still waiting, Mr Webb,' said the diplomat.

'Okay. You recruited me, but you forgot the lesson of Treadstone Seventy-one. Send out an assassin to catch an assassin.'

'That's the *one* thing we did not forget,' broke in the diplomat, now astonished. 'We based *everything* on it.'

'For the wrong reasons,' said Bourne sharply. 'There was a better way to reach Sheng and draw him out for the kill. *I* wasn't necessary. My *wife* wasn't necessary! But you couldn't see it. Your superior brain had to complicate everything.'

'What was it I couldn't see, Mr Webb?'

'Send in a conspirator to catch a conspirator. *Un*officially . . . It's too late for that now, but it's what I would have told you.'

'I'm not sure you've told me anything.'

'Part truth, part lie – your own strategy. A courier is sent to Sheng, preferably a half-senile old man who's been paid by a blind and fed the information over the phone. No traceable source. He carries a verbal message, ears only, Sheng's only, nothing on paper. The message contains enough of the truth to paralyze Sheng. Let's say that the man sending it is someone in Hong Kong who stands to lose millions if Sheng's scheme falls apart, a man smart enough and frightened enough not to use his name. The message could allude to leaks, or traitors in the boardrooms, or excluded triads banding together because they've been cut out – all the things you're certain will happen. The truth. Sheng has to follow up, he can't afford not to. Contacts are made and a meeting is arranged. The Hong Kong conspirator is every bit as anxious to protect himself as Sheng, and every bit as leery, demanding a neutral meeting ground. It's set. It's the trap.' Bourne paused, glancing at McAllister. 'Even a third-rate demolitions grunt could show you how to carry it off.'

'Very quick and very professional,' said the ambassador. 'And with a glaring flaw. Where do we find such a conspirator in Hong Kong?'

Jason Bourne studied the elder statesman, his expression bordering on contempt. 'You make him up,' he said. 'That's the lie.'

Havilland and Alex Conklin were alone in the white-walled room, each at either end of the conference table facing the other. McAllister and Morris Panov had gone to the undersecretary's office to listen on separate telephones to a mocked-up profile of an American killer created by the consulate for the benefit of the press. Panov had agreed to provide the appropriate psychiatric terminology with the correct Washington overtones. David Webb had asked to be alone with his wife until it was time to leave. They had been taken to a room upstairs; the fact that it was a bedroom had not occurred to anyone. It was merely a door to an empty room at the south side of the old Victorian house, away from the water-soaked men and ruins on the north side. Webb's departure had been estimated by McAllister to be in fifteen minutes or less. A car would drive Jason Bourne and the undersecretary to Kai-tak Airport. In the interests of speed and because the hydrofoils stopped running at 2100 hours, a medical helicopter would fly them to Macao, where all immigration permits would be cleared for the delivery of emergency supplies to the Kiang Wu Hospital on the Rua Coelho do Amaral.

'It wouldn't have worked, you know,' said Havilland, looking over at Conklin.

'What wouldn't have?' asked the man from Langley, his own thoughts broken off by the diplomat's statement. 'What David told you?'

'Sheng never would have agreed to a meeting with someone he didn't know, with someone who didn't identify himself.'

'It'd depend on how it was presented. That kind of thing always does. If the critical information is mind-blowing and the facts authentic, the subject doesn't have much of a choice. He can't question the messenger – he doesn't know anything – so he has to go after the source. As Webb put it, he can't afford not to.'

'Webb?' asked the ambassador flatly, his brows arched.

'Bourne, Delta. Who the hell knows? The strategy's sound.'

'There are too many possible miscalculations, too many chances for a misstep when one side invents a mythical party.'

'Tell that to Jason Bourne.'

'Different circumstances. Treadstone had a willing agent provocateur to go after the Jackal. An obsessed man who chose extreme risk because he was trained for it and had lived with violence too long to let go. He didn't want to let go. There was no place else for him.'

'It's academic,' said Conklin, 'but I don't think you're in a position to argue with him. You sent him out with all the odds against him and he comes back with the assassin in tow – and he finds *you.* If he said it could be done another way, he's probably right, and you can't say he isn't.'

'I can say, however,' said Havilland, resting his forearms on the table and fixing his eyes on the CIA man, 'that what we did really *did* work. We lost the assassin, but we gained a willing, even obsessed *provocateur.* From the beginning he was the optimum choice, but we never for a minute thought that he could be recruited to do the final job willingly by himself. Now he won't let anybody else do it; he's going back in, demanding his right to do it. So in the end we were right – I was right. One sets the forces in motion, on a collision course, always watching, ready to abort, to kill, if one has to, but knowing that as the complications mount and the closer they come to each other's throat, the nearer the solution is. Ultimately – in their hatreds, their suspicions, their passions – they create their own violence, and the job is done. You may lose your own people, but one has to weigh that loss against what it's worth to disrupt the enemy, to expose him.'

'You also risk exposing your own hand, the hand you insisted has to be kept out of sight.'

'How so?'

'Because it's not the end yet. Say Webb doesn't make it. Say he's caught, and you can bet your elegant ass the order will be to take him alive. When a man like Sheng sees that a trap is set to kill him, he'll want to know who's behind it. If pulling out a fingernail or ten doesn't do it – and it probably wouldn't – they'll needle him full of juice and find out where he comes from. He's heard everything you've told him—'

'Even down to the point where the United States government cannot be involved,' interrupted the diplomat.

'That's right, and he won't be able to help himself. The chemicals will bring it all out. Your hand's revealed. Washington *is* involved.'

'By whom?'

'By Webb, for Christ's sake! By Jason Bourne, if you like.'

'By a man with a history of mental illness, with a record of random aggression and self-deception? A paranoid schizophrenic whose logged telephone calls show a man disintegrating into dementia, making insane accusations, wild threats aimed at those trying to help him?' Havilland paused, then added quietly, 'Come now, Mr Conklin, such a man does not speak for the United States government. How could he? We've been searching for him everywhere. He's an irrational, fantasizing time bomb who finds conspiracies wherever his sick, tortured mind takes him. We want him back in therapy. We also suspect that because of his past activities he left the country with an illegal passport—'

'Therapy . . . ?' Alex broke in, stunned by the old man's words. 'Past *activities?*'

'Of course, Mr Conklin. If it's necessary, especially over a hot line – Sheng's hot line – we're willing to admit that he once worked for the government and was severely damaged by that work. But in no way is it possible he would have any official standing. Again, how could he? This tragic, violent man may have been responsible for the death of a wife he claims disappeared.'

'*Marie?* You'd use *Marie?*'

'We'd have to. She's in the logs, in the affidavits volunteered by men who knew Webb as a mental patient, who tried to help him.'

'Oh, *Jesus!*' whispered Alex, mesmerized by the cold, precise elder statesman of covert operations. 'You told him everything because you had your own backups. Even if he was taken, you could cover your ass with official logs, psychiatric evaluation – you could disassociate yourself! Oh, God, you *bastard.*'

'I told him the truth because he would have known it if I tried to lie to him again. McAllister, of course, went further, emphasizing the organized crime factor which is all too true but a sensitive issue I'd prefer not to bring up. Nobody does. But then I didn't tell Edward everything. He hasn't yet put enough distance between his ethics and the demands of his job. When he does, he may join me on the heights, but I don't think he's capable.'

'You told David everything in case he *was* taken,' went on Conklin, not listening to Havilland. 'If the kill doesn't happen, you *want* him taken. You're *counting* on the amphetamines and the scopolamine. The *drugs!* Then Sheng will get the message that his conspiracy's known to us and he'll get it *unofficially*, not from us but from an unsanctioned mental case. *Jesus!* It's a variation of what Webb *told* you!'

'Unofficially,' agreed the diplomat. 'So much is achieved that way. No confrontations, very smooth. Very cheap. No cost at all, really.'

'Except a man's *life!*' shouted Alex. 'He'll be *killed.* He *has* to be killed from everyone's point of view.'

'The price, Mr Conklin, if it must be paid.'

Alex waited, as if he expected Havilland to finish his statement. Nothing was forthcoming, only the strong, sad eyes gazing into his. 'That's all you've got to say? It's the price – if it has to be paid?'

'The stakes are far higher than we imagined – far higher. You know that as well as I do, so don't look so shocked.' The ambassador leaned back in his chair somewhat stiffly. 'You've made such decisions before, such calculations.'

'Not like this. *Never* like this! You send in your own and you know the risks, but you don't set up a field man sealing off his escape route! He was better off believing – *believing* – he was bringing in the assassin to get his wife back!'

'The objective is different. Infinitely more vital.'

'I *know* that. Then you don't *send* him! You get the codes and send someone *else!* Someone who isn't half dead from exhaustion!'

'Exhausted or not, he's the best man for the job and he insists on doing it.'

'Because he doesn't know what you've *done!* How you've boxed him in, made him the messenger who has to be killed!'

'I had no choice. As you say, he found me. I had to tell him the truth.'

'Then, I repeat, send in someone *else!* A hit team recruited on the outside by a blind, no connection to us, just payment for a professional kill, the target Sheng. Webb knows how to reach Sheng, he told you that. I'll convince him to give you the codes or the sequence or whatever the hell it is, and you buy a *hit* team!'

'You'd put us on a level with the Qaddafis of this world?'

'That's so puerile I can't find words to—'

'Forget it,' broke in Havilland. 'If it was ever traced back to us – and it *could* be – we'd have to launch against China before they dropped something on us. Unthinkable.'

'What you're *doing* here is unthinkable.'

'There are more important priorities than the survival of a single individual, Mr Conklin, and again you know that as well as I do. It's been your life's work – if you'll forgive me – but the present case is on a higher level than anything you ever experienced. Let's call it a geopolitical level.'

'Son of a bitch!'

'Your own guilt is showing now, Alex – if I may call you Alex – since you call in question my immediate family line. I never put Jason Bourne beyond-salvage. My most fervent hope is that he'll succeed, that the kill will take place. If that happens, he's free; the Far East is rid of a monster and the world will be spared an Oriental Sarajevo. That's *my* job, Alex.'

'At least *tell* him! *Warn* him!'

'I can't. Any more than you would in my position. You don't tell a *tueur à gages*—'

'Come again, elegant ass?'

'A man sent in to kill must have the confidence of his convictions. He can't, for a second, reflect on his motives or his reasons. He must have no doubts at all. None. The obsession must be intact. It's his only chance to succeed.'

'Suppose he doesn't succeed? Suppose he's killed?'

'Then we start again as quickly as possible putting someone else in his place. McAllister will be with him in Macao and learn the sequence codes to reach Sheng. Bourne's agreed to that. If the worst happens, we might even try his conspirator-for-a-conspirator theory. He says it's too late, but he could be wrong. You see, I'm not above learning, Alex.'

'You're not above *anything*,' Conklin said angrily, getting out of the chair. 'But you forgot something – you forgot what you said to David. There's a glaring flaw.'

'What's that?'

'I won't let you get away with it.' Alex limped toward the door. 'You can ask so much of a man, but there comes a point when you don't ask any more. You're *out*, elegant ass. Webb's going to be told the truth. The *whole* truth.'

Conklin opened the door. He faced the back of a tall marine, who, upon hearing the sound of the door opening, did a precise about-face, his rifle at port arms.

'Get out of my way, soldier,' said Alex.

'*Sorry*, sir!' barked the marine, his eyes distant, staring straight ahead.

Conklin turned back to the diplomat seated behind the desk. Havilland shrugged. 'Procedures,' he said.

'I thought these people were out of here. I thought they were sequestered at the airport.'

'The ones you saw are. These are a squad from the consulate contingent. Thanks to Downing Street's bending a few rules, this is officially US territory now. We are entitled to a military presence.'

'I want to see Webb!'

'You can't. He's leaving.'

'Who the *hell* do you think you are?'

'My name is Raymond Oliver Havilland. I am ambassador-at-large for the government of the United States of America. My decisions are to be carried out without debate during periods of crisis. This is a period of crisis. Fuck off, Alex.'

Conklin closed the door and walked awkwardly back to his chair. 'What's next, Mr *Ambassador?* Do the three of us get bullets in our heads or are we given lobotomies?'

'I'm sure we can all come to a mutual understanding.'

They held each other, Marie knowing that he was only partly there, only partly himself. It was Paris all over again, when she knew a desperate man named Jason Bourne, who was trying to stay alive, but not sure he would, or even should, his self-doubts in some ways as lethal to him as those who wanted him killed. But it was not Paris. There were no self-doubts now, no tactics feverishly improvised to elude pursuers, no race to trap the hunters. What reminded her of Paris was the distance she felt between them. David was trying to reach her – generous David, compassionate David – but Jason Bourne would not let him go. Jason was now the hunter, not the hunted, and this strengthened his will. It was summed up in a word he used with staccato regularity: *Move!*

'Why, David? *Why?*'

'I told you. Because I can. Because I have to. Because it has to be done.'

'That's not an answer, my darling.'

'All right.' Webb gently released his wife and held her by the shoulders, looking into her eyes. 'For us, then.'

'*Us?*'

'Yes. I'd see those images for the rest of my life. They'd keep coming back and they'd tear me apart because I'd know what I left behind and I wouldn't be able to handle it. I'd go into tailspins and take you with me because for all your brains you haven't the sense to bail out.'

'I'd rather go into senseless tailspins with you than without you. Read that as seeing you alive.'

'That's not an argument.'

'I think it's considerable.'

'I'll be calling the moves, not making them.'

'What the hell does that mean?'

'I want Sheng taken out, I mean that. He doesn't deserve to live, but I won't be doing the taking—'

'The *God* image doesn't suit you!' interrupted Marie sharply. 'Let others make that decision. Walk away from it. Stay safe.'

'You're not listening to me. I was there and I saw him – heard him. He *doesn't* deserve to live. In one of his diatribes he called life a precious gift. That may be debatable, depending on the life, but life doesn't mean a thing to him. He wants to kill – maybe he has to, I don't know, ask Panov – it's in his eyes. He's Hitler and Mengele and Genghis Khan . . . the chain-saw killer – whatever – but he has to go. And I have to make sure he goes.'

'But *why?*' pleaded Marie. 'You haven't *answered* me!'

'I did, but you didn't hear me. One way or another I'd see him every day, hear that voice. I'd be watching him toy with terrified people before killing them, *butchering* them. Try to understand. *I've* tried and I'm no expert, but I've learned a few things about myself. Only an idiot wouldn't. It's the images, Marie, the goddamned *pictures* that keep coming back, opening doors – memories I don't want to know about, but have to. The clearest and simplest way I can put it is that I can't take any more. I can't add to that collection of bad surprises. You see, I want to get better – not entirely cured, I can accept that, live with it – but I can't slide back, either. I *won't* slide back. For both our sakes.'

'And you think by engineering a man's death you'll get rid of those images?'

'I think it'll help, yes. Everything's relative, and I wouldn't be here if Echo hadn't thrown his life away so I could live. It's not always fashionable to say it, but like most people I have a conscience. Or maybe it's guilt because I survived. I simply have to do it because I can.'

'You've convinced yourself?'

'Yes, I have. I'm best equipped.'

'And you say you're calling the moves, not making them?'

'I wouldn't have it any other way. I'm coming back because I want a long life with you, lady.'

'What's my guarantee? Who's going to *make* the moves?'

'The whore who got us into this.'

'Havilland?'

'No, he's the pimp. McAllister's the whore, he always was. The man who believes in decency, who wears it on his sleeve until the power boys ask him to put out. He'll probably call in the pimp and that's fine. Between them they can do it.'

'But *how?*'

'There are men – and women – who will kill if the price is high enough. They may not have the egos of the mythical Jason Bourne or the very real Carlos the Jackal, but they're everywhere in that goddamned filthy shadow world. Edward, the whore, told us he made enemies throughout the Far East, from Hong Kong to the Philippines, from Singapore to Tokyo, all in the name of Washington, who wanted influence over here. If you make enemies, you know who they are, know the signals to send out to reach them. That's what the whore and the pimp are going to do. I'll set up the kill, but someone else will do the killing, and I don't care how many millions it costs them. I'll watch from a distance to make sure that the butcher's killed, that Echo gets what's coming to him, that the Far East is rid of a monster who can plunge it into a terrible war – but that's all I'll do. Watch. McAllister doesn't know it, but he's coming with me. We're extracting our pound of flesh.'

'Who's talking now?' asked Marie. 'David or Jason?'

The husband paused, his silent thoughts deep. 'Bourne,' he said finally. 'It has to be Bourne until I'm back.'

'You *know* that?'

'I accept it. I don't have a choice.'

There was a soft, rapid knocking at the bedroom door. 'Mr Webb. It's McAllister. It's time to leave.'

35

The Emergency Medical Service helicopter roared across Victoria Harbour past the out islands of the South China Sea toward Macao. The patrol boats of the People's Republic had been apprised by way of the naval station in Gongbei; there would be no firing at the low-flying aircraft on an errand of mercy. As McAllister's luck would have it, a visiting party official from Peking had been admitted to the Kiang Wu Hospital with a bleeding duodenal ulcer. He required RH-negative blood, which was continuously in short supply. *Let them come, let them go. If the official were a peasant from the hills of Zhuhai, he'd be given the blood of a goat and let him hope for the best.*

Bourne and the undersecretary of State wore the white, belted coveralls and caps of the Royal Medical Corps, with no rank of substance indicated on their sleeves; they were merely grousing subordinates ordered to carry blood to a *Zhongguo ren* belonging to a regime that was in the process of further dismantling the Empire. Everything was being done properly and efficiently in the new spirit of cooperation between the colony and its soon-to-be new masters. *Let them come, let them go. It's all a lifetime away and for us without meaning. We will not benefit. We never benefit. Not from them, not from those above.*

The hospital's rear parking area had been cleared of vehicles. Four searchlights outlined the threshold. The pilot shuttered the aircraft into vertical-hold, then began his descent, clammering down toward the concrete landing zone. The sight of the lights and the sound of the roaring helicopter had drawn crowds on the street beyond the hospital's gates on the Rua Coelho do Amaral. That was all to the good, thought Bourne, looking down from the open hatchway. He trusted that even more onlookers would be attracted for the chopper's departure in roughly five minutes as the slapping blades continued to rotate at slow speed, the searchlights remained on, and the cordon of police stayed in place – all signs of this most unusual activity. Crowds were the best that he and McAllister could hope for; in the confusion they could become part of the curious onlookers as two other men in the white coveralls of the Royal paramedics took their places by rushing to the aircraft, their bodies bent beneath the rotors, for the return trip to Hong Kong.

Grudgingly, Jason had to admire McAllister's ability to move his chess pieces. The analyst had the convictions of his connivance. He knew which buttons to press to shift his pawns. In the current crisis the pawn was a doctor at the Kiang Wu Hospital who several years ago had diverted IMF medical funds to his own clinic on the Almirante Sergio. Since Washington was a sponsor of the International Monetary Fund, and since McAllister had caught the doctor with his hands in the till, he was in a position to expose him and had threatened to do so. Yet the doctor had prevailed. The physician had asked McAllister how he expected to replace him – there was a dearth of competent doctors in Macao. Would it not be better for the American to overlook his indiscretion if his clinic serviced the indigent? With records of such service? The choirboy in McAllister had capitulated, but not without remembering the doctor's indiscretion – and his debt. It was being paid tonight.

'Come on!' yelled Bourne, rising and gripping one of the two canisters of blood. '*Move!*'

McAllister clung to a wall bar on the opposite side of the aircraft as the helicopter thump-crashed onto the cement. He was pale, his face frozen into a mask of itself. 'These things are an *abomination*,' he mumbled. 'Please wait till we're settled.'

'We're settled. It's your schedule, analyst. *Move.*'

Directed by the police, they raced across the parking area to a pair of double doors held open by two nurses. Inside, a white-jacketed Oriental doctor, the inevitable stethoscope hanging from a pocket, grabbed McAllister's arm.

'Good to see you again, sir,' he said in fluent but heavily accented English. 'Although it is under curious circumstances—'

'So were *yours* three years ago,' broke in the analyst sharply, breathlessly, peremptorily cutting off the once errant doctor. 'Where do we go?'

'Follow me to the blood laboratory. It is at the end of the corridor. The head nurse will check the seals and sign the receipts, after which you will also follow me into another room where the two men who will take your places are waiting. Give them the receipts, change clothes, and they will leave.'

'Who are they?' asked Bourne. 'Where did you find them?'

'Portuguese interns,' replied the doctor. 'Unmonied young doctors sent from Pedroso to complete their residencies out here.'

'Explanations?' pressed Jason as they started down the hallway.

'None, actually,' answered the Macaoan. 'What you call in English, "a trade." Perfectly legitimate. Two British medics who wish to spend a night over here and two overworked interns who deserve a night in Hong Kong. They will return on the hydrofoil in the morning. They'll know nothing, they'll suspect nothing. They will simply be pleased that an older doctor recognized their needs and deserts.'

'You found the right man, analyst.'

'He's a thief.'

'You're a whore.'

'I beg your pardon?'

'Nothing. Let's go.'

Once the canisters were delivered, the seals inspected, and the receipts signed, Bourne and McAllister followed the doctor into a locked adjacent office that held drug supplies and had its own door to the corridor, also locked. The two Portuguese interns were waiting in front of the glass cabinets; one was taller than the other and both were smiling. There were no introductions, just nods and a short statement by the doctor, addressing the undersecretary of State.

'On the basis of your descriptions – not that I needed yours – I'd say their sizes are about right, wouldn't you?'

'They'll do,' replied McAllister as he and Jason began removing the white coveralls. 'These are outsized. If they run fast enough and keep their heads down, they'll be okay. Tell them to leave the garments and the receipts with the pilot. He's to sign us in once he gets to Hong Kong.' Bourne and the analyst changed into dark, rumpled trousers and loose-fitting jackets. Each handed his counterpart his coveralls and cap. McAllister said, 'Tell them to hurry. Departure's scheduled for less than two minutes.'

The doctor spoke in broken Portuguese, then turned back to the undersecretary. 'The pilot can't go anywhere without them, sir.'

'Everything's timed and officially cleared down to the minute,' the analyst snapped, fear now in his voice. 'There's no room for someone to become any more curious than necessary. Everything has to be clockwork. *Hurry!*'

The interns dressed; the caps were low and in place and the receipts for the canisters of blood were in their pockets. The doctor issued his last instructions to the Americans as he handed them two orange hospital passes. 'We'll go out together; the door locks automatically I will immediately escort our young doctors, thanking them loudly and profusely past the police ranks until they can dash to the aircraft. You head to the right, then left into the front lobby and the entrance. I hope – I really do hope – that our association, as pleasant as it has been, is now finished.'

'What are these for?' asked McAllister, holding up his hospital pass.

'Probably – hopefully – nothing. But in case you are stopped they explain your presence and you will not be questioned.'

'Why? What do they say?' There was no fact, no fragment of data, that the analyst could leave unexplained.

'Quite simply,' said the doctor, looking calmly at McAllister, 'they describe you as indigent expatriates, totally without funds, whom I generously treat at my clinic without charge. For gonorrhea, to be precise. Naturally, there are the usual identifying features – height, approximate weight, hair and eye colouring, nationality. Yours are more complete, I'm afraid, as I had not met your friend. Naturally, again, there are duplicates in my files, and no one could mistake it was you, sir.'

'What?'

'Once you are out on the streets I believe my long-ago debt is cancelled. Wouldn't you agree?'

'*Gonorrhea?*'

'Please, sir, as you say, we must hurry. Everything clockwork.' The doctor opened the door, ushered out the four men and instantly headed to the left with the two interns toward the side entrance and the medical helicopter.

'Let's go,' whispered Bourne, touching McAllister's arm and starting to the right.

'Did you *hear* that man?'

'You said he was a thief.'

'He was. *Is!*'

'There are times when a person shouldn't take that bromide about stealing from a thief too literally.'

'What does *that* mean?'

'Simply this,' said Jason Bourne, looking down at the analyst at his side. 'He's got you on several counts. Collusion, corrupt practices, *and* gonorrhea.'

'Oh, my God.'

They stood at the rear of the crowds by the high fence watching the helicopter roar up from the landing zone and then soar off into the night sky. One by one the searchlights were turned off, and the parking lot was once again lit by its dim lamps. Most of the police climbed into a van; those remaining walked casually back to their previous posts while several of them lighted cigarettes, as if to announce the excitement was over. The crowds began to disperse amid questions hurled at anyone and everyone. *Who was it? Someone very important, no? What do you think happened? Do you think we'll ever be told? Who cares? We had our show, so let's have a drink, yes? Will you look at that woman? A first-class whore, I think, don't you agree? She's my first cousin, you bastard!*

The excitement was over.

'Let's go,' said Jason. 'We have to move.'

'You know, Mr Webb, you have two commands you use with irritating frequency. "Move" and "Let's go." '

'They work.' Both men started across the Amaral.

'I'm as aware as you are that we must move quickly, only you haven't explained where we're going.'

'I know I haven't,' said Bourne.

'I think it's time you did.' They kept walking, with Bourne setting the pace. 'You called me a whore,' continued the undersecretary.

'You are.'

'Because I agreed to do what I thought was right, what had to be done?'

'Because they used you. The boys in power used you and they'll throw you away without thinking twice. You saw limousines and high-level conferences in your future and you couldn't resist. You were willing to throw away my life without looking for an alternative – which is what you're paid to do. You were willing to risk the life of my wife because the pull was too great. Dinners with the Forty Committee, perhaps even becoming a member; quiet, confidential meetings in the Oval Office with the celebrated Ambassador Havilland. To me that's being a whore. Only, I repeat, they'll throw you out without a second thought.'

Silence. For nearly a long Macao block. 'You think I don't know that, Mr Bourne?'

'What?'

'That they'll throw me out.'

Again Jason looked down at the meticulous bureaucrat at his side. 'You know that?'

'Of course I do. I'm not in their league and they don't want me in it. Oh, I've got the credentials and the mind, but I don't have that extraordinary sense of performance that they have. I'm not prepossessing. I'd freeze in front of a television camera – although I watch idiots who do perform consistently make the most ridiculous errors. So, you see, I recognize my limitations. And since I can't do what these men can do, I have to do what's best for them and for the country. I have to think for them.'

'You thought for *Havilland?* You came to us in Maine and took my *wife* from me! There weren't any other options in that swollen brain of yours?'

'None that I could come up with. None that covered everything as thoroughly as Havilland's strategy. The assassin was the untraceable link to Sheng. If you could hunt him down and bring him in, it was the shortcut we needed to draw Sheng out.'

'You had a hell of a lot more confidence in me than I did.'

'We had confidence in Jason Bourne. In Cain – in the man from Medusa called Delta. You had the strongest motive possible: to get your wife back, the wife you love very much. And there would be no connection whatsoever to our government—'

'We smelled a covert scenario from the beginning!' exploded Bourne. '*I* smelled it, and so did Conklin.'

'Smelling isn't tasting,' protested the analyst, as they rushed down a dark cobblestoned alley. 'You knew nothing concrete that you could have divulged, no intermediary who pointed to Washington. You were obsessed with finding a killer who was posing as you so that an enraged taipan would return your wife to you – a man whose own wife had supposedly been murdered by the assassin who called himself Jason Bourne. At first I thought it was madness, but then I saw the serpentine logic of it all. Havilland was right. If there was one man alive who could bring in the assassin, and in that way neutralize Sheng, it was you. But you couldn't have any connection to Washington. Therefore you had to be manoeuvred within the framework of an extraordinary lie. Anything less, and you might have reacted more normally. You might have gone to the police, or to government authorities, people you knew in the past – what you could remember of the past, which was also to our advantage.'

'I did go to people I knew before.'

'And learned nothing except that the more you threatened to break silence, the more likely the government would put you back in therapy. After all, you came from Medusa and had a history of amnesia, even schizophrenia.'

'Conklin went to others—'

'And was initially told only enough for us to find out what he knew, what he'd pieced together. I gather he was once one of the best we had.'

'He was. He still is.'

'He put you beyond-salvage.'

'History. Under the circumstances, I might have done the same. He learned a lot more than I did in Washington.'

'He was led to believe exactly what he wanted to believe. It was one of Havilland's really more brilliant strokes and done at a moment's notice. Remember, Alexander Conklin is a burned-out, bitter man. He has no love for the world he spent his adult life in, nor for the people with whom he shared that life. He was told that a *possible* black operation *may* have gone off the wire, that the scenario *may* have been taken over by hostile elements.' McAllister paused as they emerged from the alley and rounded a corner in the late-night Macao crowds; coloured lights were flashing everywhere. 'It was back to the square-one lie, don't you see?' continued the analyst.'Conklin was convinced that someone else *had* moved in, that your situation was hopeless and so was your wife's unless you followed the *new* scenario run by the hostile elements that had taken over.'

'That's what he told me,' said Jason, frowning, remembering the lounge at Dulles Airport and the tears that had come to his eyes. 'He told me to play out the scenario.'

'He had no choice.' McAllister suddenly gripped Bourne's arm, nodding toward a darkened storefront up ahead on the right. 'We have to talk.'

'We *are* talking,' said the man from Medusa sharply. 'I know where we're going and there's no time to lose.'

'You have to *take* the time,' insisted the analyst. The desperation in his voice forced Bourne to stop and look at him, and then to follow him into the recessed storefront. 'Before you do *anything*, you have to understand.'

'What do I have to understand? The lies?'

'No, the truth.'

'You don't know what the truth is,' said jason.

'I know, perhaps better than *you* do. As you said, it's my job. Havilland's strategy would have proved sound had it not been for your wife. She escaped; she got away. She caused the strategy to fall apart.'

'I'm aware of that.'

'Then surely you're aware of the fact that whether or not he's identified her, Sheng knows about her and understands her importance.'

'I hadn't thought about it one way or the other.'

'Think about it now. Lin Wenzu's unit was penetrated when it and all of Hong Kong were searching for her. Catherine Staples was killed because she was linked to your wife and it was correctly perceived that through this mystery woman she either had learned too much or was closing in on some devastating truths. Sheng's orders obviously are to eliminate all opposition, even potential opposition. As you saw in Peking, he's a fanatic and sees substance where there are only shadows – enemies in every dark corner.'

'What's your point?' asked Bourne impatiently.

'He's also brilliant and his people are all over the colony.'

'So?'

'When the story breaks in the morning papers and on television, he'll make certain assumptions and have the house in Victoria Peak as well as MI-Six scrutinized every minute of every hour, even if he has to hold hostage the estate next door and once again infiltrate British Intelligence.'

'Goddamn it, what are you *driving* at?'

'He'll find Havilland and then he'll find your wife.'

'*And?*'

'Suppose you fail? Suppose you're killed? Sheng won't rest until he learns everything there is to learn. The key is undoubtedly the woman with Havilland, the tall woman everyone was looking for. She *has* to be because she's the enigma at the centre of the mystery and is connected to the ambassador. If anything happens to you, Havilland will be forced to let her go, and Sheng will have her picked up – at Kai-tak, or Honolulu or Los Angeles or New York. Believe me, Mr Webb, he won't stop until he's caught her. He has to know what's been mounted against him, and she *is* the key. There's no one else.'

'Again, your point?'

'Everything could happen all over again with far more horrible results.'

'The *scenario?*' asked Jason, bloody images of the glen in the bird sanctuary assaulting him.

'Yes,' said the analyst firmly. 'Only, this time your wife is taken for real, not simply as part of the strategy to recruit you. Sheng would make certain of it.'

'Not if he's dead!'

'Probably not. However, there's the very real risk of failure – that he'll remain alive.'

'You're trying to say something but you're not saying it!'

'All right, I'll say it now. As the assassin, you're the link to Sheng, the one to reach him, but I'm the one who can draw him out.'

'*You?*'

'It was the reason I told the embassy to use my name in the press release. You see, Sheng knows me, and I listened carefully when you outlined your conspirator-for-a-conspirator theory to Havilland. He didn't buy it and, frankly, I didn't either. Sheng wouldn't accept a conference with an unknown person, but he will with someone he knows.'

'Why with you?'

'Part truth, part lie,' said the analyst, repeating Bourne's words.

'Thanks for listening so carefully. Now, explain that.'

'The truth first, Mr Webb, or Bourne, or whatever you want to be called. Sheng is aware both of my contributions to my government and of my obvious lack of progress. I'm a bright but unseen, unknown bureaucrat who's been passed over because I lack those qualities that could elevate me, lead me to a degree of prominence, and to lucrative jobs in the private sector. In a way, I'm like Alexander Conklin without his drinking problem, but not without a degree of his bitterness. I was as good as Sheng and he knew it, but he made it and I didn't.'

'A touching confessional,' said Jason, impatiently again. 'But why would he meet with you? How could you draw him out – for a kill, Mr Analyst, and I trust you know what that means?'

'Because I want a piece of that Hong Kong pie of his. I was nearly killed last night. It was the final indignity, and now after all these years I want something for myself, for my family. That's the lie.'

'You're on tenth base. I can't find you.'

'Because you're not listening between the lines. That's what I'm paid to do, remember? . . . I've had it. I'm at the end of my professional rope. I was sent over here to trace down and analyse a rumour out of Taiwan. This rumour about an economic conspiracy in Peking seemed to me to have substance, and if it was true, there could be only one source in Peking: my old counterpart from the Sino-American trade conferences, the power behind China's new trade policies. Nothing like this could be done without him, not even contemplated. So I assumed there was at best enough substance for me to contact him, *not* to blow the whistle but officially to *dispose* of the rumour for a price. I could even go so far as to say I see nothing against my government's interests, and certainly not against mine. The main point is that he'd *have* to meet with me.'

'Then what?'

'Then you'd tell me what to do. You said a demolitions "grunt" could do it, so why can't I? Except not with explosives, I couldn't handle that. A weapon, instead.'

'You'd get killed.'

'I'll accept the risk.'

'Why?'

'Because it has to be done, Havilland's right about that. And the instant Sheng sees you're not the impostor, that you're the original assassin, the one who tried to kill him in that bird sanctuary, his guards would cut you down.'

'I never intended for him to see me,' said Bourne quietly. 'You were going to take care of that, but not this way.'

In the shadows of the dark storefront, McAllister stared at the Medusan. 'You're taking me with you, aren't you?' asked the analyst finally. 'Force me, if you have to.'

'Yes.'

'I thought so. You wouldn't have agreed so readily to my coming with you to Macao. You could have told me how to reach Sheng back at the airport and demanded that we give you a certain amount of time before we acted. We wouldn't have violated it; we're too frightened. Regardless, you can see now that you don't have to force me. I even brought along my diplomatic passport.' McAllister paused for a single beat, then added, 'And a second one that I removed from the technicians' file – it belongs to that tall fellow who took the picture of you on the table.'

'You *what?*'

'All State Department technical personnel dealing in classified matters must surrender their passports. It's a security measure and for their own protection—'

'I have *three* passports,' interrupted Jason. 'How the hell do you think I got around?'

'We knew you had at least two based on the Bourne records. You used one of the previous names flying into Peking, the one that said you had brown eyes, not hazel. How did you manage that?'

'I wore glasses – clear glass. By way of a friend who uses an odd name and is better than anyone you've got.'

'Oh, yes. A black photographer and ID specialist who calls himself Cactus. Actually, he worked secretly for Treadstone, but then you obviously remembered that, or the fact that he used to come and visit you in Virginia. According to the records, he had to be let go because he deals with criminal elements.'

'If you touch him, I'll blow you out of the bureaucratic waters.'

'There's no intention of doing so. Right now, however, we'll simply transfer one of the three photographs that best suits the features described in the technician's passport.'

'It's a waste of time.'

'Not at all. Diplomatic passports have considerable advantages, especially over here. They eliminate the time-consuming process of a temporary visa, and although I'm sure you have sources to buy one, this is easier. China wants our money, Mr Bourne, *and* our technology. We'll be passed through quickly and Sheng will be able to check immigration and ascertain that I am who I say I am. We'll also be provided with priority transportation if we want it, and that might be important, depending upon our sequential telephone conversations with Sheng and his aides.'

'Our sequential *what?*'

'You'll talk with his subordinates in whatever sequence is required. I'll tell you what to say, but when the final clearance is given, *I'll* speak with Sheng Chou Yang.'

'You're a *flake!*' yelled Jason, as much into the dark glass of the storefront as at McAllister. 'You're an *amateur* in this kind of thing!'

'In what you do, I am, indeed. But not in what I do.'

'Why didn't you tell Havilland about this grand plan of yours?'

'Because he wouldn't have permitted it. He would have placed me under house arrest because he thinks I'm inadequate. He'll always think so. I'm not a performer. I don't have those glib answers that ring with sincerity but are also woefully uninformed. This, however, is different, and the performers see it so clearly because it's all part of their global, macho theatrics. Economics aside, this is a conspiracy to undermine the leadership of a suspicious, authoritarian regime. And who's at the core of this conspiracy that *has* to fail? Who are these infiltrators whom Peking trusts as its own? China's most deeply committed enemies – their own brothers from the Kuomintang on Taiwan. Again, to use the vernacular, when the shit hits the fan – as it surely will – the performers on all sides will step up to the podiums and scream their screams of treason and righteous "internal revolt" because there's nothing else the performers can *do.* The embarrassment's total, complete, and on the world's stage, massive embarrassment leads to massive violence.'

It was Bourne's turn to stare at the analyst. As he did, Marie's words came to him, from a different context but not irrelevant in the present case. 'That's not an answer,' he said. 'It's a point of view, but it's not an answer. Why *you?* I hope it's not to prove your decency. That would be very foolish. Very dangerous.'

'Oddly enough,' said McAllister, frowning, briefly looking at the ground. 'Where you and your wife are concerned, I suppose that's part of it – a minor part.' The undersecretary of State raised his eyes and continued calmly, 'But the basic reason, Mr Bourne, is that I'm rather tired of being Edward Newington McAllister, maybe a brilliant but surely an inconsequential analyst. I'm the mind in the back room that's brought out when things get too complicated, and then sent back after he's rendered a judgement. You might say I'd like that chance for a moment in the sun – out of the back room, as it were.'

Jason studied the undersecretary in the shadows. 'A couple of moments ago you said there was the risk of my failing, and I'm experienced. You're not. Have you considered the consequences if *you* fail?'

'I don't think I will.'

'You don't think you will,' repeated Bourne flatly. 'May I ask why?'

'I've thought it out.'

'That's nice.'

'No, I mean it,' protested McAllister. 'The strategy is fundamentally simple: to get Sheng along with me. I can do that but you can't do it for me. And you certainly can't get him alone with you. All I need is a few seconds – and a weapon.'

'If I allowed it, I don't know which would frighten me more. Your succeeding or your failing. May I remind you that you're an undersecretary of State for the United States government? Suppose you're caught? It's goodbye, Charlie, for everyone.'

'I've considered that since the day I arrived back in Hong Kong.'

'You *what?*'

'For weeks I've thought that this might be the solution, that *I* might be the solution. The government's covered. It's all written down in my papers back on Victoria Peak, with a copy for Havilland and another set to be delivered to the Chinese consulate in Hong Kong in seventy-two hours. The ambassador may even have found his set by now. So, you see, there's no turning back.'

'What the hell have you *done!*'

'Described what amounts to a blood feud between Sheng and myself. Given my record and the time I spent over here, as well as Sheng's well-known penchant for secrecy, it's actually quite plausible. Certainly his enemies in the Central Committee will leap at it. If I'm killed or captured, so much attention will be focused on Sheng, so many questions regardless of his denials, he won't dare move – if he survives.'

'Good Christ, *save* me,' said Bourne, stunned.

'It's not necessary for you to know the particulars, but you'll recognize the main point of your conspirator-for-a-conspirator conspirator theory. In essence I accuse him of going back on his word, of cutting me out of his Hong Kong manipulations after I spent years secretly helping him develop the structure. He's cutting me out because he doesn't need me any longer and he knows I can't possibly say anything because I'd be ruined. I wrote that I was even frightened for my life.'

'*Forget* it!' shouted Jason. 'Forget the whole goddamned thing! It's *crazy!*'

'You're assuming I'll fail. Or be captured. I'm assuming neither – with your help, of course.'

Bourne took a deep breath and lowered his voice. 'I admire your courage, even your latent sense of decency, but there's a better way and you can provide it. You'll have your moment in the sun, Mr Analyst, but not this way.'

'What way, then?' asked the undersecretary of State, now bewildered.

'I've seen you operate, and Conklin was right. You may be a son of a bitch but you're *something.* You reach into the Foreign Office in London and know who can change the rules. You spent six years over here digging around the dirty-tricks business, tracking killers and thieves and the pimps of the Far East in the name of neighbourly government policy. You know which button to press and where the bodies are buried. You even remembered a squirrely doctor here in Macao who owed you a favour and you made him pay.'

'That's all second nature. One doesn't easily forget such people.'

'Find me others. Find me killers for a price. Between you and Havilland the two of you can do it. You're going to get on the phone to him and tell him these are my demands. He's to transfer a million – five million if he has to – over here to Macao in the morning, and by midafternoon I want a killer unit here ready to go up into China. I'll make the arrangements. I know a rendezvous that's been used before in the hills of Guangdong; there are fields that can easily be reached by helicopter, where Sheng or his lieutenants used to meet with the commando. Once he gets my message he'll make the trip, take my word for it. You just do your part. Dig around that head of yours and come up with three or four experienced scumbags. Tell them the risk is minimal and the price high. That's your moment in the sun, Mr Analyst. It should be irresistible. You'll have something on Havilland for the rest of his life. He'll make you his chief aide, probably Secretary of State, if you want it. He can't afford not to.'

'Impossible,' said McAllister quietly, his eyes locked with Jason's.

'Well, maybe Secretary of State's a bit much—'

'What you have just suggested is impossible,' broke in the undersecretary.

'Are you telling me there aren't such men, because if you are, you're lying again.'

'I'm sure there are. I might even know of several and I'm sure others are on that list of names Lin gave you when he was playing the role of the white-suited taipan in the Walled City. But I wouldn't touch them. Even if Havilland ordered me to, I'd refuse.'

'Then you don't want Sheng! Everything you said was just another lie. Liar!'

'You're wrong, I *do* want Sheng. But to use your words, not this way.'

'Why not?'

'Because I won't put my government, my country, in that kind of compromised position. Actually, I think Havilland would agree with me. Hiring killers is too traceable, the transferring of money too traceable. Someone gets angry or boastful or drunk; he talks and an assassination is laid at Washington's feet. I couldn't be a part of that. I refer you to the Kennedys' attempts on Castro's life using the Mafia. Insanity . . . No, Mr Bourne, I'm afraid you're stuck with me.'

'I'm not stuck with anyone! I can reach Sheng; you *can't!*'

'Complicated issues can usually be reduced to simple equations if certain facts are remembered.'

'What does that mean?'

'It means I insist we do things my way.'

'Why?'

'Because Havilland has your wife.'

'She's with *Conklin!* With Mo Panov! He wouldn't *dare*—'

'You don't know him,' McAllister interrupted. 'You insult him but you don't know him. He's like Sheng Chou Yang. He'll stop at nothing. If I'm right – and I'm sure I am – Mrs Webb, Mr Conklin, and Dr Panov are guests at the house in Victoria Peak for the duration.'

'Guests?'

'That house arrest I mentioned a few minutes ago.'

'Son of a *bitch!*' whispered Jason, the muscles in his face pulsating.

'Now, how do we reach Peking?'

With his eyes closed, Bourne answered. 'A man at the Guangdong garrison named Soo Jiang. I speak to him in French and he leaves a message for us here in Macao. At a table in a casino.'

'*Move!*' said McAllister.

36

The telephone rang, startling the naked woman who quickly sat up in the bed. The man lying next to her was suddenly wide awake; he was wary of any intrusion, especially one in the middle of the night, or, more accurately, the early hours of the morning. The expression on his soft, round Oriental face, however, showed that such intrusions were not infrequent, only unnerving. He reached for the phone on the bedside table.

'*Wei?*' he said softly.

'*Macao lai dianhua,*' replied the switchboard operator at headquarters, Guangdong garrison.

'Connect me on scrambler and remove all recording devices.'

'It is done, Colonel Soo.'

'I will conduct my own study of that,' said Soo Jiang, sitting up and reaching for a small, flat, rectangular object with a raised circle at one end.

'It's not necessary, sir.'

'I would hope not for your sake.' Soo placed the circle over the mouthpiece and pressed a button. Had there been an intercept on the line, the piercing whistle that suddenly erupted for one second would have continued pulsating until the listening device was removed or a listener's eardrum was punctured. There was only silence, magnified by the moonlight streaming through the window. 'Go ahead, Macao,' said the colonel.

'*Bon soir, mon ami,*' said the voice from Macao, the French instantly accepted as being spoken by the impostor. '*Comment ça va?*'

'*Vous?*' gasped Soo Jiang, stunned, swinging his short fat legs from under the sheet and planting them on the floor. '*Attendez!*' The colonel turned to the woman. 'You. Out. Get out of here,' he ordered in Cantonese. 'Take your clothes and put them on in the front room. Keep the door open so I can see you leave.'

'You owe me money!' whispered the woman stridently. 'For two times you owe me money, and double for what I did for you below!'

'Your payment is in the fact that I may not have your husband fired. Now get out! You have thirty seconds or you have a penniless husband.'

'They call you the Pig,' said the woman, grabbing her clothes and rushing to the bedroom door, where she turned, glaring at Soo. '*Pig!*'

'*Out.*'

Seconds later Soo returned to the phone, continuing in French. 'What *happened?* The reports from Beijing are incredible! No less so the news from the airfield in Shenzen. He took you prisoner!'

'He's dead,' said the voice from Macao.

'*Dead?*'

'Shot by his own people, at least fifty bullets in his body.'

'And *you?*'

'They accepted my story. I was an innocent hostage picked up in the streets and used as a shield as well as a decoy. They treated me well and, in fact, kept me from the press at my insistence. Of course, they're trying to minimize everything, but they won't have much success. The newspaper and television people were all over the place, so you'll read about it in the morning papers.'

'My God, where did it *happen?*'

'An estate on Victoria Peak. It's part of the consulate and damned secret. That's why I have to reach your leader-one. I learned things that he should know about.'

'Tell *me.*'

The 'assassin' laughed derisively. 'I sell this kind of information, I don't give it away – especially not to pigs.'

'You'll be well taken care of,' insisted Soo.

'Too well in my book.'

'What do you mean by "leader-one"?' asked the colonel dismissing the remark.

'Your head man, the chief, the big rooster – whatever you want to call him. He was the man in that forest preserve who did all the talking, wasn't he? The one who used his sword with such efficiency, the wild-eyed corkscrew with the short hair, the one I tried to warn about the Frenchman's delaying tactics—'

'You *dare* . . . ? You did that?'

'*Ask* him. I told him something was wrong, that the Frenchman was stalling him. Christ, I paid for his not listening to me! He should have hacked that French bastard when I told him to! Now you tell him I want to talk to him!'

'Even I do not talk to him,' said the colonel. 'I reach only subordinates by their code names. I don't know their real ones—'

'You mean the men who fly down to the hills in Guangdong to meet me and deliver the assignments?' interrupted Bourne.

'Yes.'

'I won't talk to any of them!' exploded Jason, now posing as his own impostor. 'I want to talk to the *man.* And he'd better want to talk to me.'

'You will speak with others first, but still, even for them, there must be very strong reasons. They do the summoning, others do not. You should know that by now.'

'All right, you can be the courier. I was with the Americans for almost three hours, mounting the best cover I ever mounted in my life. They questioned me at length and I answered them openly – I don't have to tell you that I have backups all over the territory, men and women who'll swear I'm a business associate, or that I was with them at a specific time, no matter who calls—'

'You don't have to tell me that,' Soo broke in. 'Please, just give me the message I'm to convey. You talked with the Americans. Then what?'

'I listened, too. The colonials have a stupid habit of talking too freely among themselves in the presence of strangers.'

'I hear a British voice now. The voice of superiority. We've all heard it before.'

'You're damned right. The wogs don't do that, and God knows you slants don't either.'

'Please, sir, continue.'

'The one who took me prisoner, the man who was killed by the Americans, was an American himself.'

'So?'

'I leave a signature with my kills. The name has a long history. It's Jason Bourne.'

'We know that. And?'

'He was the *original!* He was an American, and they've been hunting him for nearly two years.'

'*And?*'

'They think Beijing found him and hired him. *Someone* in Beijing who needed the most important kill of his life, who needed to kill a man in that house. Bourne's for sale to anybody, an equal-opportunity employee, as the Americans might say.'

'Your language is elusive. Please be clearer!'

'There were several others in that room with the Americans. Chinese from Taiwan who said outright that they oppose most of the leaders of the secret societies in the Kuomintang. They were angry. Frightened, too, I think.' Bourne stopped. Silence.

'Yes?' pressed the colonel apprehensively.

'They said a number of other things. They also kept mentioning the name of someone called Sheng.'

'*Aiya!*'

'That's the message you'll convey and I'll expect a response at the casino within three hours. I'll send someone to pick it up and don't try anything foolish. I have people there who can start a riot as easily as they can roll a seven. Any interference and your men are dead.'

'We remember the Tsim Sha Tsui a few weeks ago,' said Soo Jiang. 'Five of our enemies killed in a back room while a cabaret erupts in violence. There'll be no interference; we're not fools where you are concerned. We often wondered if the original Jason Bourne was as proficient as his successor.'

'He wasn't.' *Bring up the possibility of a riot at the casino in case Sheng's people try to trap you. Say their men will be killed. You don't have to elaborate. They'll understand . . . The analyst knew whereof he spoke.* 'A question,' said Jason, genuinely interested. 'When did you and the others decide I wasn't the original?'

'At first sight,' replied the colonel. 'The years leave their marks, don't they? The body may remain agile, even improve with care, but the face reflects time; it is inescapable. Your face could not possibly be the face of the man from Medusa. That was over fifteen years ago and you are, at best, a man in your early thirties. The Medusa did not recruit children. You were the reincarnation of the Frenchman.'

'The code word is "*crisis*" and you have *three hours,*' said Bourne, hanging up the phone.

'This is *crazy!*' Jason stepped out of the open glass booth in the all-night telephone complex and looked angrily at McAllister.

'You did it very well,' said the analyst, writing on a small notepad. 'I'll pay the bill.' The undersecretary started toward the raised platform where the operators accepted payments for international calls.

'You're missing the point,' continued Bourne at McAllister's side, his voice low, harsh. 'It can't work. It's too unorthodox, too obvious for anyone to buy it.'

'If you were demanding a meeting I'd agree with you, but you're not. You're only asking for a telephone conversation.'

'I'm asking him to acknowledge the core of his whole goddamned scam! That he *is* the core!'

'To quote you again,' said the analyst, picking up the bill on the counter and holding out money, 'he can't afford not to respond. He *has* to.'

'With preconditions that'll throw you out of the box.'

'I'll want your input in such matters, of course.' McAllister took his change, nodding thanks to the weary female operator, and started for the door, Jason beside him.

'I may not have any input to give.'

'Under the circumstances, you mean,' said the analyst, as they stepped out onto the crowded pavement.

'What?'

'It's not the strategy that upsets you, Mr Bourne, because it's basically *your* strategy. What makes you furious is that I'm the one implementing it, not you. Like Havilland, you don't think I'm capable.'

'I don't think this is the time or the occasion for you to prove you're Machine Gun *Kelly!* If you fail, your life's the last thing that concerns me. Somehow the Far East comes first, the world comes first.'

'There's no way I can fail. I told you, even if I fail, I don't. Sheng loses no matter whether he lives or not. In seventy-two hours the consulate in Hong Kong will make sure of it.'

'Premeditated self-sacrifice isn't something I approve of,' said Jason, as they started up the street. 'Self-deluding heroics always get in the way and screw things up. Besides, your so-called strategy reeks of a trap. They'll smell it!'

'They would if *you* negotiated with Sheng and not me. You tell me it's unorthodox, too obvious, the movements of an amateur. That's fine. When Sheng hears me on the phone, everything will fall into place for him. I *am* the embittered amateur, the man who's never been in the field, the first-rate bureaucrat who's been passed over by the system he's served so well. I know what I'm doing, Mr Bourne. You just get me a weapon.'

The request was not difficult to fulfill. Over in Macao's Porto Interior, on the Rua das Lorchas, was d'Anjou's flat, which was a minor arsenal of weapons, the tools of the Frenchman's trade. It was simply a matter of getting inside and selecting those arms most easily dismantled so as to cross the relatively lax border at Guangdong with diplomatic passports. But it took something over two hours, the process of selection being the most time-consuming as Jason put gun after gun in McAllister's hand, with Jason watching the analyst's grip and the expression on his face. The weapon finally chosen was the smallest, lowest calibrated pistol in d'Anjou's arsenal, a Charter Arms .22 with a silencer.

'Aim for the head, at least three bullets in the skull. Anything else would be a beesting.'

McAllister swallowed, staring at the gun, as Jason studied the weapons, deciding which had the greatest fire-power in the smallest package. He chose for himself three Interdynamic KG-9 machine pistols that used outsized clips holding thirty rounds of ammunition.

With their weapons concealed beneath their jackets, they entered the half-filled Kam Pek casino at 3:35 in the morning and walked to the end of the long mahogany bar. Bourne went to the seat he had occupied previously. The undersecretary sat four stools away. The bartender recognized the generous customer who had given him close to a week's salary less than a week ago. He greeted him like a patron with a long history of dispensing largesse.

'*Nei hou a!*'

'*Mchoh La. Mgoi,*' said Bourne, saying that he was fine, in good health.

'The English whisky, isn't it?' asked the bartender, sure of his memory, hoping it would produce a reward.

'I told friends at the casino in the Lisboa that they should talk to you. I think you're the best man behind a bar in Macao.'

'The *Lisboa?* That's where the true money is! I thank you, sir.' The bartender rushed to pour Jason a drink that would have crippled Caesar's legions. Bourne nodded without comment, and the man turned reluctantly to McAllister four chairs away. Jason noted that the analyst ordered white wine, paid with precision, and wrote the amount in his notebook. The bartender shrugged, performed the unpleasant service, and walked to the centre of the sparsely occupied bar, keeping his eyes on his favoured customer.

Step one.

He was *there!* The well-dressed Chinese in the tailored dark suit, the martial-arts veteran who did not know enough dirty moves, the man he had fought in an alley and who had led him up into the hills of Guangdong. Colonel Soo Jiang was taking no risks under the circumstances. He wanted only the most proven conduits working tonight. No impoverished old men, no whores.

The man walked slowly past several tables, as if studying the action, appraising the dealers and the players, trying to determine where he should test his luck. He arrived at Table Five and, after observing the play of the cards for nearly three minutes, casually sat down and withdrew a roll of bills from his pocket. Among them, thought Jason, was a message marked *Crisis.*

Twenty minutes later the impeccably dressed Chinese shook his head, put his money back in his pocket, and got up from the table. He was the *shortcut* to Sheng! He knew his way around both Macao and the border at Guangdong, and Bourne knew he had to reach this man, and reach him quickly! He glanced first at the bartender, who had gone to the end of the bar to prepare drinks for a waiter who was serving the tables, then over at McAllister.

'*Analyst!*' he whispered sharply. '*Stay* here!'

'What are you doing?'

'Saying hello to my mother, for Christ's sake!' Jason got off the stool and started for the door after the conduit. Passing the bartender, he said in Cantonese. 'I'll be right back.'

'It's no problem, sir.'

Out on the pavement, Bourne followed the well-dressed man for several blocks until he turned into a narrow, dimly lit side street and approached an empty parked car. He was meeting no one; he had delivered the message and was getting out of the area. Jason rushed forward, and as the conduit opened the car door he touched the man's shoulder. The conduit spun around, crouching, his experienced left foot lashing out viciously. Bourne jumped back, raising his hands in a gesture of peace.

'Let's not go through *this* again,' he said in English, for he remembered the man spoke English, taught him by Portuguese nuns. 'I still hurt from the beating you gave me a week ago.'

'*Aiya! You!*' The conduit raised his hands in a like gesture of noncombat. 'You do me honour when I do not deserve it. You bested me that night, and for that reason I have practised six hours a day to improve myself . . . You bested me, *then*. But not now.'

'Considering your age and then considering mine, take my word for it, you weren't bested. My bones ached far more than yours did, and I'm not about to check out your new training schedule. I'll pay you a lot of money, but I won't fight you. The word for it is cowardice.'

'Not you, sir,' said the Oriental, lowering his hands and grinning. 'You are very good.'

'Yes, *me*, sir,' replied Jason. 'You scare the hell out of me. And you did me a great favour.'

'You paid me well. Very well.'

'I'll pay you better now.'

'The message was for *you?*'

'Yes.'

'Then you have taken the Frenchman's place?'

'He's dead. Killed by the people who sent the message.'

The conduit looked bewildered, perhaps even sad. 'Why?' he asked. 'He serviced them well and he was an old man, older than you.'

'Thanks a lot.'

'Did he betray those he serviced?'

'No, he was betrayed.'

'The Communists?'

'Kuomintang,' said Bourne, shaking his head.

'*Dong wu!* They are no better than the Communists. What do you want from me?'

'If everything goes right, pretty much what you did before, but this time I want you to stay around. I want to hire a pair of eyes.'

'You go up into the hills in Guangdong?'

'Yes.'

'You need assistance crossing the border, then?'

'Not if you can find me someone who can shift a photograph from one passport to another.'

'It is done every day. The children can do it.'

'Good. Then we're down to my hiring your eyes. There's a degree of risk, but not much. There's also twenty thousand dollars, American. Last time I paid you ten, this time it's twenty.'

'*Aiya*, a *fortune!*' The conduit paused, studying Bourne's face. 'The risk must be great.'

'If there's trouble, I'll expect you to get out. We'll leave the money here in Macao, accessible only to you. Do you want the job, or do I look elsewhere?'

'These are the eyes of the hawk bird. Look no further.'

'Come back with me to the casino. Wait outside, down the street, and I'll have the message picked up.'

The bartender was only too pleased to do as Jason requested. He was confused by the odd word 'crisis' that was to be used until Bourne explained that it was the name of a race horse. He carried a 'special' drink to a bewildered player at Table Five and returned with the sealed envelope under his tray. Jason had scanned the nearby tables looking for turning heads and shifting eyes amid the spiralling clouds of smoke; he saw none. The sight of the maroon-jacketed bartender among the maroon-jacketed waiters was too common to draw attention. As instructed, the tray was placed between Bourne and McAllister. Jason shook a cigarette out of his pack and shoved a book of matches down the bar toward the non-smoking analyst. Before the perplexed undersecretary could understand, Bourne got off his stool and walked over to him. 'Have you got a light, mister?'

McAllister looked at the matches, quickly picked them up, tore one out and struck it, holding the flame up for the cigarette. When Jason returned to his seat, the sealed envelope was in his hand. He opened it, removed the paper inside and read the typewritten English script: *Telephone Macao – 32–61–443.*

He looked around for a pay phone and then realized that he had never used one in Macao, and even if there were instructions, he was not familiar with the Portuguese colony's coins. It was always the little things that loused up the bigger things. He signalled the bartender, who reached him before his hand was back on the bar.

'Yes, sir? Another whisky, sir?'

'Not for a week,' said Bourne, placing Hong Kong money in front of him. 'I have to make a phone call to someone here in Macao. Tell me where a pay phone is and let me have the proper coins, will you, please?'

'I could not permit so fine a gentleman as yourself to use a common telephone, sir. Between us, I believe many of the customers here may be diseased.' The bartender smiled. 'Allow me, sir. I have a telephone on my counter – for very special people.'

Before Jason could protest or give thanks, a telephone was put in front of him. He dialled as McAllister stared at him.

'*Wei?*' said a female voice.

'I was instructed to call this number,' replied Bourne in English. The dead impostor had not known Chinese.

'We will meet.'

'We *won't* meet.'

'We insist.'

'Then *de*sist. You know me better than that, or you should. I want to talk to the man, and only the *man*.'

'You are presumptuous.'

'You're less than an idiot. So's the skinny preacher with the big sword unless he talks to me.'

'You *dare*—'

'I've heard that once before tonight,' interrupted Jason sharply. 'The answer is yes, I *do* dare. He's got a hell of a lot more to lose than I do. He's only one client, and my list is growing. I don't need him, but right now I think he needs me.'

'Give me a reason that can be confirmed.'

'I don't give reasons to corporals. I was once a major, or didn't you know that?'

'There's no need for insults.'

'There's no need for this conversation. I'll call you back in thirty minutes. Offer me something better, offer me the *man*. And I'll know if it's himself because I'll ask a question or two that only he can answer. *Ciao*, lady.' Bourne hung up.

'What are you *doing?*' whispered an agitated McAllister four chairs away.

'Arranging your day in the sun, and I hope you've got some lotion. We're getting out of here. Give me five minutes, then follow me. Turn right out the door and keep walking. We'll pick you up.'

'*We?*'

'There's someone I want you to meet. An old friend – young friend – whom I think you'll approve of. He dresses like you do.'

'Someone *else?* Are you *insane?*'

'Don't blow your cool, analyst, we're not supposed to know each other. No, I'm not insane. I just hired a backup in case I'm outthought. Remember, you wanted my input in such matters.'

The introductions were short and no names were used, but it was evident that McAllister was impressed by the stocky, broad-shouldered, well-dressed Chinese.

'Are you an executive with one of the firms over here?' asked the analyst as they walked toward the side street where the conduit's car was parked.

'In a manner of speaking, yes, sir. My own firm, however. I run a courier service for very important people.'

'But how did *he* find you?'

'I'm sorry, sir, but I'm sure you can understand. Such information is confidential.'

'Good Lord,' muttered McAllister, glancing at the man from Medusa.

'Get me to a phone in twenty minutes,' said Jason in the front seat. The bewildered undersecretary sat in the back.

'They are using a relay, then?' asked the conduit. 'They did so many times with the Frenchman.'

'How did he handle them?' asked Bourne.

'With delays. He would say, "Let them sweat." May I suggest an hour?'

'You're on. Is there a restaurant open around here?'

'Over in the Rua Mercadores.'

'We need food, and the Frenchman was right – he was always right. Let them sweat.'

'He was a decent man to me,' said the conduit.

'At the end he was some kind of eloquent if perverted saint.'

'I do not understand, sir.'

'It's not necessary that you do. But I'm alive and he's not because he made a decision.'

'What kind of decision, sir?'

'That he should die so that I could live.'

'Like the Christian Scriptures. The nuns taught them to us.'

'Hardly,' said Jason, amused at the thought. 'If there'd been another way out we would have taken it. There wasn't. He simply accepted the fact that his death was *my* way out.'

'I liked him,' said the conduit.

'Take us to the restaurant.'

It was all Edward McAllister could do to contain himself. What he did not know and what Bourne would not discuss at the table was choking him with frustration. Twice he tried to broach the subject of relays and the current situation and twice Jason cut him off, admonishing the undersecretary with a stare, as the conduit, in gratitude, looked away. There were certain facts the Chinese knew about and there were other facts he did not care to know about for his own safety.

'Rest and food,' mused Bourne, finishing the last of his *tian-suan rou*. 'The Frenchman said they were weapons. He was right, of course.'

'I suggest he needed the first more than you did, sir,' said the conduit.

'Perhaps. Anyway, he was a student of military history. He claimed more battles were lost from fatigue than from inferior firepower.'

'This is all *very* interesting,' McAllister interrupted sharply, 'but we've been here for some time and I'm sure there are things we should be doing.'

'We will, Edward. If you're uptight, think what they're going through. The Frenchman also used to say that the enemy's exposed nerves were our best allies.'

'I'm becoming rather tired of your Frenchman,' said McAllister testily.

Jason looked at the analyst and spoke quietly. 'Don't ever say that to me again. You weren't there.' Bourne checked his watch. 'It's over an hour. Let's find a phone.' He turned to the conduit. 'I'll need your help,' he added. 'You just put in the money. I'll dial.'

'You said you'd call back in *thirty minutes!*' spat out the woman at the other end of the line.

'I had business to take care of. I have other clients and I'm not too crazy about your attitude. If this is going to be a waste of time, I've got other things to do and you can answer to the *man* when the typhoon comes.'

'How could that happen?'

'Come *on*, lady! Give me a trunk filled with more money than you've ever thought about and I might tell you. On the other hand, I probably wouldn't. I like to be owed favours by men in high places. You've got ten seconds and I hang up.'

'*Please.* You will meet a man who will take you to a house on the Guia Hill where there is highly sophisticated communications equipment—'

'And where a half-dozen of your goons will crack my skull and throw me into a room where a doctor fills me with juice and you get it all for *nothing!*' Bourne's anger was only partly feigned; Sheng's troops were the ones behaving like amateurs. 'I'll tell you about another piece of sophisticated equipment. It's called a telephone and I don't think there'd be *communications* from Macao to the Guangdong garrison if you didn't have scramblers. Of course, you bought them in Tokyo because if you made them yourselves they probably wouldn't work! *Use* one. I'm calling you just once more, lady. Have a number for me. The *man's* number.' Jason hung up.

'That's interesting,' said McAllister several feet away from the pay phone, glancing briefly at the Chinese conduit who had returned to the table. 'You used the stick when I would have used the carrot.'

'Used the what?'

'I would have emphasized what extraordinary information I had to reveal. Instead, you threatened, as if you were dismissing whoever it was.'

'Spare me,' answered Bourne, lighting a cigarette, grateful that his hand was not shaking. 'For your edification I did both. The threat emphasizes the revelation and the dismissal reinforces both.'

'Your input is showing,' said the undersecretary of State, a hint of a smile on his face. 'Thank you.'

The man from Medusa looked hard at the man from Washington. 'If this damn thing works, can you do it, analyst? Can you whip out the gun and pull the trigger? Because if you can't, we're both dead.'

'I can do it,' said McAllister calmly. 'For the Far East. For the world.'

'And for your day in the sun.' Jason started toward the table. 'Let's get out of here. I don't want to use this phone again.'

The serenity of Jade Tower Mountain was belied by the frantic activity inside the villa of Sheng Chou Yang. The turmoil was caused not by the number of people, for there were only five, but by the intensity of the players. The minister listened as his aides came and went from the garden bringing news of the latest developments and timidly offered advice, which was instantly withdrawn at the first sign of displeasure.

'Our people have confirmed the story, sir!' cried a uniformed middle-aged man rushing from the house. 'They've talked to the journalists. Everything was as the assassin described and a photograph of the dead man was distributed to the newspapers.'

'*Get* it,' ordered Sheng. 'Have it wired here at once. This whole thing is incredible.'

'It's being done,' said the soldier. 'The consulate sent an attaché to the *South China News.* It should be arriving within minutes.'

'Incredible,' repeated Sheng softly, his eyes straying to the lily pads in the nearest of the four man-made ponds. 'The symmetry is too perfect, the timing too perfect, and that means something is imperfect. Someone has imposed order.'

'The assassin?' asked another aide.

'For what purpose? He has no idea that he would have been a corpse before the night was over in the sanctuary. He thought he was privileged, but we were only using him to trap his predecessor, unearthed by our man in Special Branch.'

'Then who?' questioned another.

'That's the dilemma. *Who?* Everything is at once tempting yet clumsy. It's all too apparent, fraught with unprofessional ego. The assassin, if he's telling the truth, has to believe he has nothing to fear from me, but still he threatens, conceivably throwing over a most profitable client. Professionals don't do that, and that's what bothers me.'

'You are suggesting a third party, Minister?' asked the third aide.

'If so,' said Sheng, his eyes now rivetted on a single lily pad, 'someone with no experience or with the intelligence of an ox. It's a dilemma.'

'It's *here,* sir!' shouted a young man, racing into the garden, holding a teletyped photograph.

'Give it to me. *Quickly!'* Sheng grabbed the paper and angled it into the glare of a floodlight. 'It is *he!* I'll never forget that face as long as I *breathe!* Clear everything! Tell the woman in Macao to give our assassin the number and electronically sweep all conceivable interceptions. Failure is *death.*'

'Instantly, Minister!' The operator ran back to the house.

'My wife and my children,' said Sheng Chou Yang reflectively. 'They may be upset by all this disturbance. Will one of you please go inside and explain that affairs of state keep me from their beloved presence?'

'It is my honour, sir,' said an aide.

'They suffer so from the demands of my work. They are all angels. One day they will be rewarded.'

Bourne touched the conduit's shoulder, then pointed to the lightened marquee of a hotel on the right side of the street. 'We'll check in here, then head for a phone booth on the other side of the city. Okay?'

'It's wise,' said the Chinese. 'They are all over the telephone company.'

'And we've got to get some sleep. The Frenchman never stopped telling me that rest was also a weapon. Christ, why do I keep *repeating* myself?'

'Because you're obsessed,' said McAllister from the backseat.

'Tell me about it. No, don't.'

Jason dialled the number in Macao that tripped a relay in China into a swept telephone in Jade Tower Mountain. As he did so he looked at the analyst. 'Does Sheng speak French?' he asked quickly.

'Of course,' said the undersecretary. 'He deals with the Quai d'Orsay and speaks the language of everyone he negotiates with. It's one of his strengths. But why not use Mandarin? You know it.'

'The commando didn't, and if I speak English he might wonder where the British accent went. French'll cover it, as it did with Soo Jiang, and I'll also know whether or not it's Sheng.' Bourne stretched a handkerchief across the mouthpiece as he heard a second, echoing ring fifteen hundred miles away. The scramblers were in place.

'*Wei?*'

'*Comme le colonel, je préfère le français.*'

'*Shemma?*' cried the voice, bewildered.

'*Fawen,*' said Jason, the Mandarin for French.

'*Fawen? Wo buhui!*' replied the man excitedly, stating that he did not speak French. The call was expected. Another voice intruded; it was in the background and too low to be heard. And then it was there on the line.

'*Pourquoi vous parlez français?*' It was Sheng! No matter the language, Bourne would never forget the orator's singsong delivery. It was the zealous minister of an unmerciful God seducing an audience before assaulting it with fire and brimstone.

'Let's say I feel more comfortable.'

'Very well. What is this incredible story you bring? This madness during which a name was mentioned?'

'I was also told you speak French,' interrupted Jason.

There was a pause in which only Sheng's steady breathing could be heard. 'You know who I am?'

'I know a name that doesn't mean anything to me. It does to someone else, though. Someone you knew years ago. He wants to talk to you.'

'*What?*' screamed Sheng. '*Betrayal!*'

'Nothing of the sort, and if I were you, I'd listen to him. He saw right through everything I told them. The others didn't, but he did.' Bourne glanced at McAllister beside him; the analyst nodded his head, as if to say that Jason was convincingly using the words the undersecretary had given him. 'He took one look at me and put the figures together. But then the Frenchman's original boy was pretty well shot up; his head was a bloody cauliflower.'

'What have you *done?*'

'Probably the biggest favour you ever got, and I expect to be paid for it. Here's your friend. He'll use English.' Bourne handed the phone to the analyst, who spoke instantly.

'It's Edward McAllister, Sheng.'

'*Edward . . . ?*' The stunned Sheng Chou Yang could not complete the name.

'This conversation is off the record, with no official sanction. My whereabouts are unlogged and unknown. I'm speaking solely for my own benefit – and yours.'

'You . . . astonish me, my old friend,' said the minister slowly, fearfully collecting himself.

'You'll read about it in the morning papers and it's undoubtedly on all the newscasts from Hawai already. The consulate wanted me to disappear for a few days – the fewer questions the better – and I knew just whom I wanted to go with.'

'What happened, and *how* did you—'

'The similarity in their appearance was too obvious to be coincidental,' broke in the undersecretary of State. 'I suppose d'Anjou wanted to trade on the legend as totally as possible, and that included the physical characteristics for those who had seen Jason Bourne in the past. An unnecessary fillip, in my opinion, but it was effective. In the panic on Victoria Peak – and from the nearly unrecognizable face – no one else noticed that striking resemblance. But then none of the others knew Bourne. I did.'

'*You?*'

'I drove him out of Asia. I'm the one he came to kill, and consistent with his perverse sense of irony and revenge, he decided to do it by leaving the corpse of your assassin on Victoria Peak. Fortunately for me, his ego didn't permit him to evaluate your man's abilities correctly. Once the firing started, our now mutual associate overpowered him and threw him into the guns.'

'Edward, the information is coming too fast, I cannot assimilate it. Who brought Jason Bourne back?'

'Obviously the Frenchman. His pupil and immensely successful meal ticket had defected from him. He wanted revenge and knew where to find the one man who could give him that. His colleague from Medusa, the original Jason Bourne.'

'*Medusa!*' whispered Sheng with loathing.

'Despite their reputation, in certain units there were intense loyalties. You save a man's life, he doesn't forget.'

'What led you to the *preposterous* conclusion that I have anything to do with the man you call an assassin—'

'Please, Sheng,' interrupted the analyst. 'It's too late for protestations. We're *talking*. But I'll answer your question. It was in the pattern of several killings. It started with a vice-premier of China in the Tsim Sha Tsui and four other men. They all were your enemies. And at Kai-tak the other night, two of your most vocal critics in the Peking delegation – targets of a bomb. There were also rumours; there always are in the underworld. The whispers spoke of messages between Macao and Guangdong, of powerful men in Beijing – of *one* man with immense power. And finally there was the file . . . The figures added up. *You.*'

'The *file?* What is this, Edward?' asked Sheng, feigning strength. 'Why is this an unofficial, unreported communication between us?'

'I think you know.'

'You're a brilliant man. You know I would not ask if I did. We're above such pavanes.'

'A brilliant bureaucrat kept in the back room, wouldn't you also say?'

'In truth, I expected better things for you. You provided most of the words and the moves for your so-called negotiators during the trade conferences. And everyone knows you did exemplary work in Hong Kong. By the time you left, Washington had every major influence in the territory in its orbit.'

'I've decided to retire, Sheng. I've given twenty years of my life to my government, but I won't give it my death. I won't be ambushed and shot at or truck-bombed. I won't become a target for terrorists, whether it's here or in Iran or Beirut. It's time I got something for myself, for my family. Times change, people change, and living's expensive. My pension and my prospects are far less than I deserve.'

'I agree with you completely, Edward, but what has it got to do with *me?* We were compromisers together – adversaries, to be sure, as in a courtroom, but certainly not enemies in the arena of violence. And what in the name of heaven is this foolishness about my name being mentioned by jackals of the Kuomintang?'

'Spare me.' The analyst glanced over at Bourne. 'Whatever was said by our mutual associate, the words were provided by me; they weren't his. Your name was never mentioned in Victoria Peak, and there were no Taiwanese in our interrogation of your man. I gave him those words because there's a certain validity in them for you. As to your name, it's for a restricted few, their eyes only. It's in the file I mentioned, a file locked in my office in Hong Kong. It's marked "Ultra Maximum Security." There is only one copy of this file, and it's buried in a vault in Washington to be released or destroyed only by me. However, should the unexpected happen – say, a plane crash, or if I disappeared, or was killed – the file would be turned over to the National Security Council. The information in this file, in the wrong hands, could prove catastrophic for the entire Far East.'

'I am intrigued, Edward, by your candid, if incomplete, information.'

'Meet with me, Sheng. And bring money, a great deal of money – American money. Our mutual associate tells me there are hills in Guangdong where your people flew down to see him. Meet me there tomorrow, between ten o'clock and midnight.'

'I must protest, my adversarial friend. You have not provided me with an incentive.'

'I can destroy both copies of that file. I was sent over here to track down a story out of Taiwan, a story so detrimental to all our interests that a hint of its contents could start a chain of events that terrifies everyone. I believe there's considerable substance to the story, and if I'm right, it can be traced directly to my old counterpart during the Sino-American conferences. It couldn't be happening without him . . . It's my last assignment, Sheng, and a few words from me can remove that file from the face of the earth. I simply determine the information to be totally false and dangerously inflammatory, compiled by your enemies in Taiwan. The few who know about it want to believe that, take my word for it. The file is then sent to the shredder. So is the copy in Washington.'

'You still have not told me why I should *listen* to you!'

'The son of a Kuomintang taipan would know. The leader of a cabal in

Beijing would know. A man who could be disgraced and decapitated tomorrow morning *certainly* would know.'

The pause was long, the breathing erratic over the line. Finally, Sheng spoke. 'The hills in Guangdong. *He* knows where.'

'Only one helicopter,' said McAllister. 'You and the pilot, no one else.'

37

Darkness. The figure dressed in the uniform of a United States marine dropped down from the top of the wall at the rear of the grounds in the house on Victoria Peak. He crept to his left, passing a sheet of interwoven strands of barbed wire that filled a space where a section of the wall had been blown away, and proceeded around the edge of the property. Staying in the shadows, he raced across the lawn to the corner of the house. He peered around at the demolished bay windows of what had been a large Victorian study. In front of the shattered glass and the profusion of broken frames stood a marine guard, an M-16 rifle planted casually on the grass, the end of the barrel in his hand, a .45 automatic strapped to his belt. The addition of a rifle to the smaller weapon was a sign of max-alert – the intruder understood this, and smiled to see that the guard did not think it necessary to hold the M-16 in his hands. Marines and poised weapons were not welcome. The stock of a rifle would crash into a man's head before he knew it was into its whip. The intruder waited for the opportune moment; it came when the guard's chest swelled with a long yawn and his eyes briefly closed as he inhaled deeply. The intruder raced around the corner, springing off his feet, the wire of a garrote looping over the guard's head. It was over in seconds. There was barely a sound.

The killer left the body where it lay, as it was far darker in this area of the grounds than elsewhere. Many of the rear floodlights had been shattered by the explosions. He got to his feet and edged his way to the next corner, where he took out a cigarette, lighting it with the cupped flame from a butane lighter. He then stepped out into the glare of the floodlights and walked casually around the corner toward the huge, charred French doors where a second marine was at his post on the brick steps. The intruder held the cigarette in his left hand, which covered his face as he drew on it.

'Out for a smoke?' asked the guard.

'Yeah, I couldn't sleep,' said the man, with an American accent that was a product of the Southwest.

'Those fuckin' cots weren't made for sleeping. Just sit on one and you know it . . . Hey, *wait* a minute! Who the hell are *you?*'

The marine had no chance to level his rifle. The intruder lunged, thrusting his knife straight into the guard's throat with deadly accuracy, cutting off all sound, all life. The killer quickly dragged the corpse around the corner of the building and left it in the shadows. He wiped the blade off on the dead man's uniform, reinserted it beneath his tunic, and returned to the French doors. He entered the house.

He walked down the long, dimly lit corridor at the end of which stood a third marine in front of a wide, sculptured door. The guard angled his rifle downward and looked at his watch. 'You're early,' he said. 'I'm not due to be relieved for another hour and twenty minutes.'

'I'm not with this unit, buddy.'

'You with the Oahu group?'

'Yeah.'

'I thought they got you jokers out of here pronto and back to Hawaii. That's the scuttlebutt.'

'A few of us were ordered to stay behind. We're down at the consulate now. That guy, what's-his-name, McAllister, has been taking our testimonies all night.'

'I tell you, pal, this whole goddamned thing is *weird!*'

'You got it, triple weird. By the way, where's that fruit-cake's office? He sent me up here to bring him back his special pipe tobacco.'

'It figures. Mix some grass in it.'

'Which office?'

'Earlier I saw him and the doctor go in that first door on the right. Then later, before he left, he went in here.' The guard tilted his head to indicate the door behind him.

'Whose place is that?'

'I don't know his name, but he's the top banana. They call him the ambassador.'

The killer's eyes narrowed. 'The ambassador?'

'Yeah. The room's fractured. Half of it's blown apart by that fucking maniac, but the safe's intact, which is why I'm here and another guy outside in the tulips. Must be a couple of million in there for extracurricular activities.'

'Or something else,' said the intruder softly. 'The first door on the right, huh?' he added, turning and reaching under his tunic.

'*Hold* it,' said the marine. 'Why didn't the gate send word in here?' He reached for the hand-held radio strapped to his belt. 'Sorry, but I've got to check you out, buddy. It's standard—'

The killer threw his knife. As it plunged into the guard's chest he hurled himself on the marine, his thumbs centring in on the man's throat. Thirty seconds later he opened the door of Havilland's office and dragged the dead man inside.

They crossed the border in full darkness, business suits and regimental ties replacing the rumpled, nondescript clothes they had worn previously. Added to their attire were two proper attaché cases strapped with *diplomatique* tape, indicating government documents beyond the scrutiny of immigration points. In truth, the cases held their weapons, as well as several additional items Bourne had picked up in d'Anjou's flat after McAllister produced the sacrosanct plastic tape that was respected even by the People's Republic –

respected as long as China wanted the same courtesy extended to its own foreign service personnel. The conduit from Macao whose name was Wong – at least that was the name he offered – was impressed by the diplomatic passports, but for safety's sake, as well as for the $20,000 American for which he said he felt a moral obligation, decided to prepare the border-crossing his way.

'It's not as difficult as perhaps I led you to believe before, sir,' explained Wong. 'Two of the guards are cousins on my blessed mother's side – may she rest with the holy Jesus – and we help each other. I do more for them than they do for me, but then I am in a better position. Their stomachs are fuller than most in the city of Zhuhai Shi and both have television sets.'

'If they're cousins,' said Jason, 'why did you object to the watch I gave one of them before? You said it was too expensive.'

'Because he'll sell it, sir, and I don't care to see him spoiled. He'll expect too much from me.'

On such considerations, thought Bourne, were the tightest borders in the world patrolled. Regardless, they were directed by the Wong to enter the last gate on the right at precisely 8:55: he would cross separately a few minutes later. Their red-striped passports were studied, sent to an inside office, and amid many abrupt smiles on the part of a cousin, the honoured diplomats were rapidly passed through. They were instantly welcomed to China by the prefect of the Zhuhai Shi-Guangdong Province Control who returned their passports. She was a short, broad-shouldered, muscular woman. Her English was obscured by a thick accent but was understandable.

'You have government business in Zhuhai Shi?' She asked, her smile belied by her clouded, vaguely hostile eyes. 'The Guangdong garrison, perhaps? I can arrange auto transport, please?'

'*Bu xiexie*,' said the undersecretary of State, declining, and then for courtesy's sake reverting to English to show respect for his host's diligence in learning it. 'It's a minor conference, lasting for only a few hours, and we'll return to Macao later tonight. We'll be contacted here, so we'll have some coffee and wait.'

'In my office, please?'

'Thank you, but I think not. Your people will be looking for us in the . . . *kafie dian* – the café.'

'Over on the left-right, sir. On the street. Welcome again to the People's Republic.'

'Your courtesy will not be forgotten,' said McAllister, bowing.

'You are with thanks,' replied the heavyset woman, nodding and striding away.

'To use your words, analyst,' said Bourne, 'you did that very well. But I should tell you she's not on our side.'

'Of course not,' agreed the undersecretary. 'She's been instructed to call someone either here at the garrison in Bejing confirming that we've crossed over. That someone will reach Sheng, and he'll know it's me – and you. No one else.'

'He's airborne,' said Jason as they walked slowly toward the dimly lit coffee shop at the end of a dingy concrete walkway that emerged on the street. 'He's on his way here. Incidentally, we'll be followed, you know that, don't you?'

'No, I don't know that,' replied McAllister, looking briefly at Bourne. 'Sheng will be cautious. I've given him enough information to alarm him. If he thought there was only one file – which happens to be the truth – he might take chances, thinking he could buy it from me and kill me. But he thinks, or has to assume, that there's a copy in Washington. That's the one he wants destroyed. He won't do anything to upset me or to make me panic and run. Remember, I'm the amateur and I frighten easily. I know him. He's putting it all together now and is probably carrying more money to me than I've ever dreamed of. Of course, he expects to get it back once the files are destroyed and he *does* kill me. So, you see, I have a very strong reason not to fail – or not to succeed by failing.'

The man from Medusa again stared at the man from Washington. 'You've really thought this out, haven't you?'

'Thoroughly,' answered McAllister, looking straight ahead. 'For weeks. Every detail. Frankly, I didn't think you'd be a part of it because I thought you'd be dead, but I knew I could reach Sheng. Somehow – unofficially, of course. Any other way, including a confidential conference, would entail protocol, and even if I got him alone, without his aides, I couldn't touch him. It would look like a government-sanctioned assassination. I considered reaching him directly, for old times' sake, and using words that would trigger a response – pretty much what I did last night. As you said to Havilland, the simplest ways are usually the best. We tend to complicate things.'

'In your defence, you frequently have to. You can't be caught with a smoking gun.'

'That's such a trite expression,' said the analyst with a derisive laugh. 'What does it mean? That you were led or misled into an error of inconsequential consequence? Policy doesn't revolve around a single man's embarrassment, or it shouldn't. I'm constantly appalled by the people's cries for righteousness when they have no idea, no concept, of how we have to deal.'

'Maybe the people every now and then want a straight answer.'

'They can't *have* one,' said McAllister as they approached the door of the coffee shop, 'because they couldn't understand.'

Bourne stood in front of the door without opening it. 'You're blind,' he said, his eyes locked with the under-secretary's. 'I wasn't given a straight answer, either, much less an explanation. You've been in Washington too long. You should try a couple of weeks in Cleveland or Bangor, Maine. It might broaden that perspective of yours.'

'Don't lecture me, Mr Bourne. Less than forty-six percent of our population care enough to cast a ballot – which determines the directions we take. It's all left to us – the performers and the professional bureaucrats. We're all you've got . . . May we go inside, please? Your friend Mr Wong said we were to spend only a few minutes being seen having coffee and then go out on the street. He said he'd meet us there in exactly twenty-five minutes, and twelve have already elapsed.'

'Twelve? Not ten or fifteen, but twelve?'

'Precisely.'

'What do we do if he's two minutes late? Shoot him?'

'Very funny,' said the analyst, pushing the door open.

They walked out of the coffee shop and into the dark, bruised pavement of the run-down square fronting the Guangdong checkpoint. As it was a slow time at the gates, there were no more than a dozen people crossing the thoroughfare, disappearing into the darkness. Of the three streetlights in the immediate vicinity, only one was working, dimly. Visibility was poor. The twenty-five-minute mark passed, and was stretched to thirty, then approached thirty-eight. Bourne spoke.

'Something's wrong. He should have made contact by now.'

'Two minutes and we shoot him?' said McAllister, instantly disliking his own attempt at humour. 'I mean, I gathered that staying calm was everything.'

'For two minutes, not close to fifteen,' replied Jason. 'It's not normal,' he added softly, as if to himself. 'On the other hand, it could be normally *abnormal.* He wants us to make contact with *him.*'

'I don't understand—'

'You don't have to. Just walk alongside me, as if we were strolling, passing the time until we're met. If she sees us, the lady wrestler won't be surprised. Chinese officials are notoriously late for conferences; they feel it gives them the advantage.'

' "Let them sweat"?'

'Exactly. Only that's not who we're meeting now. Come on, let's go to the left; it's darker, away from the light. Be casual; talk about the weather, anything. Nod your head, shake it, shrug – just keep up steady, low-keyed movements.'

They walked for about fifty feet when it happened. '*Kam Pek!*' The name of the casino in Macao was whispered, shot out of the shadows beyond a deserted news-stand.

'*Wong?*'

'Stay where you are and make a show of conversation, but listen to me!'

'What's happened?'

'You're being followed.'

'Two points for a brilliant bureaucrat,' said Jason. 'Any comment, Mr Undersecretary?'

'It's unexpected but not illogical,' answered McAllister. 'A safeguard, perhaps. False passports abound over here, as we happen to know.'

'Queen Kong checked us out. Strike one.'

'Then, perhaps, to make sure we don't link up with the kind of people you suggested last night,' whispered the analyst, his words too low to be heard by the Chinese conduit.

'That's possible.' Bourne raised his voice slightly so that the conduit could hear him, his eyes on the border gate's entrance. There was no one. 'Who's following us?'

'The Pig.'

'*Soo Jiang?*'

'Ever so, sir. It is why I must stay out of sight.'

'Anyone else?'

'No one that I could see, but I don't know who is on the road to the hills.'

'I'll take him out,' said the man from Medusa called Delta.

'*No!*' objected McAllister. 'His orders from Sheng may include confirming that we *remain* alone, that we don't meet others. You just agreed it was possible.'

'The only way he could do that is to reach others himself. He can't do that – if he can't do that. And your old *friend* wouldn't permit a radio transmission while he's in a plane or a chopper. It could be picked up.'

'Suppose there are specific signals – a flare or a powerful flashlight beamed up, telling the pilot everything's clear?'

Jason looked at the analyst. 'You *do* think things out.'

'There is a way,' said Wong from the shadows, 'and it is a privilege I should like to reserve for myself, no additional charge.'

'What privilege?'

'I will kill the Pig. It will be done in such a way that cannot be compromised.'

'*What?*' Astonished, Bourne started to turn his head.

'*Please*, sir! Look straight ahead.'

'Sorry. But *why*?'

'He fornicates indiscriminately, threatening the women he favours with loss of employment for themselves and their husbands, even brothers and cousins. Over the past four years he has brought shame to many families, including mine on my blessed mother's side.'

'Why hasn't he been killed before now?'

'He travels with armed guards, even in Macao. Yet in spite of this, several attempts have been made by enraged men. They resulted in reprisals.'

'Reprisals?' asked McAllister quietly.

'People were chosen, again indiscriminately, and charged with stealing supplies and equipment from the garrison. The punishment for such crimes is death in the fields.'

'*Jesus*,' muttered Bourne. 'I won't ask questions. You've got reason enough. But how tonight?'

'His guards are not with him now. They may be waiting for him on the road to the hills, but they are not with him *now*. You start out, and if he follows you I will follow him. If he does not follow you, I will know that your journey will not be interrupted and I will catch up with you.'

'Catch up with us?' Bourne frowned.

'After I kill the Pig and leave his pig body in its proper and, for him, disgraceful place. The female toilet.'

'And if he *does* follow us?' asked Jason.

'My opportunity will come, even as I serve as your eyes. I will see his guards, but they will not see me. No matter what he does, the moment will be there when he separates himself, if only by a few feet in the darkness. It will be enough, and it will be assumed he has brought shame to one of his own men.'

'We'll get started.'

'You know the way, sir.'

'As if I had a road map.'

'I will meet you at the base of the first hill beyond the high grass. Do you remember it?'

'It'd be hard to forget. I nearly bought a grave in China there.'

'After seven kilometres, head into forest toward the fields.'

'I intend to, you taught me. Have a good hunt, Wong.'

'I will, sir. I have reason enough.'

The two Americans walked across the ravaged old square, away from the dim light into complete darkness. An obese figure in civilian clothes watched them from the shadows of the concrete walkway. He looked at his watch and nodded, half smiling to himself in satisfaction. Colonel Soo Jiang then turned and walked back through the man-made tunnel into the stark immigration complex with iron gates and wooden booths and barbed wire in the distance, all bathed in dull grey light. He was greeted by the prefect of the Zhuhai Shi–Guangdong Province Control, who strode purposefully, martially, enthusiastically, toward him.

'They must be very important men, Colonel,' said the prefect, her eyes not at all hostile, but instead with a look that bordered on blind worship. And fear.

'Oh, they are, they are,' agreed the colonel.

'Surely they have to be for such an illustrious officer as yourself to make sure of their requirements. I made the telephone call to the man in Guangzhou, as you requested, and he thanked me, but he did not get my name—'

'I will make sure he has it,' Soo broke in wearily.

'And I will keep only my best people on the gates to greet them when they return later tonight to Macao.'

Soo looked at the woman. 'That won't be necessary. They will be taken to Beijing for strictly confidential, highest-level conferences. My orders are to remove all records of their having crossed the Guangdong border.'

'*That* confidential?'

'Ever so, Madame Comrade. These are secret affairs of state and must be kept as such even from your most intimate associates. Your office, please.'

'At once,' said the broad-shouldered woman, turning with military precision. 'I have tea or coffee, and even the British whisky from Hong Kong.'

'Ah, yes, the British whisky. May I escort you, comrade? My work is finished.'

The two somewhat grotesquely Wagnerian figures marched in waddling lockstep toward the streaked glass door of the prefect's office.

'*Cigarettes!*' whispered Bourne, gripping McAllister's shoulder.

'*Where?*'

'Up ahead, off the road on the left. In the woods!'

'I didn't see them.'

'You weren't looking for them. They're being cupped but they're there. The barks of the trees get a touch of light one moment, then they're dark the next.

No rhythm, just erratic. Men smoking. Sometimes I think the Far East likes cigarettes more than sex.'

'What do we do?'

'Exactly what we're doing, only louder.'

'*What?*'

'Keep walking and say whatever comes to mind. They won't understand. I'm sure you know "Hiawatha" or "Horatio on the Bridge," or in your wild college days maybe *Aura Lee.* Don't sing, just say the words; it'll keep your mind off things.'

'But *why?*'

'Because this is what you predicted. Sheng is making sure that we don't link up with anyone who could be a threat to him. Let's give him that reassurance, okay?'

'Oh, my God! Suppose one of them speaks English?'

'It's highly unlikely, but if you'd rather, we'll just improvise a conversation.'

'No, I'm not good at that. I hate parties and dinners, I never know what to say.'

'That's why I suggested the doggerel. I'll interrupt whenever you pause. Go ahead now, speak casually but rapidly. This is no place for Chinese scholars who speak fast English . . . The cigarettes are out. They've spotted us! Go *on!*'

'Oh, Lord . . . very well. Ah, ah . . . "Sitting on O'Reilly's porch, telling tales of blood and slaughter—" '

'That's very appropriate!' said Jason, glaring at his pupil.

' "Suddenly it came to me, why not shag O'Reilly's daughter—" '

'Why, Edward, you constantly surprise me.'

'It's an old fraternity song,' whispered the analyst.

'*What?* I can't hear you, Edward. Speak up.'

' "Fiddilly-eye-*eee*, fiddilly-eye-*ohh*, fiddilly-eye-eee to the one ball Reilly—" '

'That's terrific!' interrupted Bourne as they passed the section of the woods where only seconds ago concealed cealed men had been smoking. 'I think you friend will appreciate your point of view. Any further thoughts?'

'I forgot the words.'

'Your thoughts, you mean. I'm sure they'll come to you.'

'Something about "old man Reilly." . . . Oh, yes, I remember. First there was "Shag, shag and shag some more, shag until the fun was over," and *then* came old Reilly . . . "Two horse pistols by his side, looking for the dog who shagged his daughter." I *did* remember.'

'You belong in a museum, if Ripley owns one . . . But look at it this way, you can research the entire project back in Macao.'

'What project? . . . There was another that was always great fun. "A hundred bottles of beer on the wall, a hundred bottles of beer; one fell down" – Oh, Lord, it's been so long. It was repetitious reduction – "ninety-nine bottles of beer on the wall—" '

'Forget it, they're out of earshot.'

'Oh? Earshot? Thank God!'

'You sounded fine. If any of those clowns understood a word of English, they're even more confused than I am. Well done, analyst. Come on, let's walk faster.'

McAllister looked at Jason. 'You did that on purpose, didn't you? You prodded me into remembering something – anything – knowing I'd concentrate and not panic.'

Bourne did not answer; he simply made a statement. 'Another hundred feet and you keep going by yourself.'

'*What?* You're *leaving* me?'

'For about ten, maybe fifteen, minutes. Here, keep walking and angle your arm up so I can put my briefcase on it and open the damn thing.'

'Where are you going?' asked the undersecretary as the attaché case rested awkwardly on his left arm. Jason opened it, took out a long-bladed knife, and closed the case. 'You can't leave me alone!'

'You'll be all right, nobody wants to stop you – us. If they did, it would have been done.'

'You mean that could have been an *ambush?*'

'I was counting on your analytical mind that it wasn't. Take the case.'

'But what are you—'

'I have to see what's back there. Keep walking.'

The man from Medusa spun off to his left and entered the woods at a turn in the road. Running rapidly, silently, instinctively avoiding the tangled underbrush at the first touch of resistance, he moved to his right in a wide semicircle. Minutes later he saw the glow of cigarettes, and, moving like a forest cat, crept closer and closer until he was within ten feet of the group of men. The intermittent moonlight, filtered through the massive trees, provided enough illumination for him to count the number. There were six, each armed with a lightweight machine gun strapped over his shoulders . . . And there was something else, something that was strikingly inconsistent. Each of the men wore the four-buttoned, tailored uniforms of high officers in the army of the People's Republic. And from the snatches of conversation he could hear, it was clear that they spoke Mandarin, not Cantonese, which was the normal dialect for soldiers, even officers, of the Guangdong Garrison. These men were not from Guangdong. Sheng had flown in his own elite guard.

Suddenly, one of the officers snapped his lighter and looked at his watch. Bourne studied the face above the flame. He knew it, and seeing it confirmed his judgement. It was the face of the man who had tried to trap Echo by posing as a prisoner on the truck that terrible night, the officer Sheng treated with a degree of deference. A thinking killer with a soft voice.

'*Xian zai,*' said the man, stating that the moment had come. He picked up a hand-held radio and spoke. '*Da li shi, da li shi!*' he barked, raising his party by the code name Marble. 'They are alone, there is no one else. We will proceed as instructed. Prepare for the signal.'

The six officers rose in unison, adjusted their weapons, and extinguished their cigarettes by grinding them under their boots. They started rapidly for the back country road.

Bourne scrambled around on his hands and knees, got to his feet and raced through the woods. He had to reach McAllister before Sheng's contingent closed in on him and saw through the sporadic moonlight that the analyst was alone. Should the guards become alarmed they might send a different 'signal': *Conference aborted.* He reached the turn in the road and ran faster, jumping over fallen branches other men would not see, slithering through vines and linked foliage others would not anticipate. In less than two minutes he sprang silently out of the woods at McAllister's side.

'Good *God!*' gasped the undersecretary of State.

'Be quiet!'

'You're a maniac!'

'Tell me about it.'

'It would take hours.' With trembling hands, McAllister handed Jason his attaché case. 'At least, this didn't explode.'

'I should have told you not to drop it or jar it too much.'

'Oh, Jesus! . . . Isn't it time to get off the road? Wong said—'

'Forget it. We're staying in plain view until we reach the field on the second hill, then you'll be more in view than me. Hurry up. Some kind of signal's going to be given, which means you were right again. A pilot's going to get clearance to land – no radio communication, just a light.'

'We're to meet Wong somewhere. At the base of the first hill, I think he said.'

'We'll give him a couple of minutes, but I think we can forget him, too. He'll see what I saw, and if it were me, I'd head back to Macao and twenty thousand, American, and say I lost my way.'

'What *did* you see?'

'Six men armed with enough firepower to defoliate one of the hills here.'

'Oh, my God, we'll never get *out!*'

'Don't give up yet. That's one of the things *I've* been thinking about.' Bourne turned to McAllister as he quickened their pace. 'On the other hand,' he added, his voice deadly serious. 'The risk was always there – doing things your way.'

'Yes, I know. I won't panic. I will *not* panic.' The woods were suddenly gone; the dirt road now cut a path throught fields of tall grass. 'What do you think those men are here for?' asked the analyst.

'Backups in case of a trap, which any low life in this business would think it was. I told you that, and you didn't want to believe me. But if something you said is accurate, and I think it is, they'll stay far out of sight – to make sure you won't panic and run. If that's the case, it'll be our way out.'

'How?'

'Head to the right, through the field,' replied Jason without answering the question. 'I'll give Wong five minutes, unless we spot a signal somewhere or hear a plane, but no more. And that long only because I really want the pair of eyes I paid for.'

'Could he get around those men without being seen?'

'He can if he's not on his way back to Macao.'

They reached the end of the field of high grass and the base of the first hill where trees rose out of the ascending ground. Bourne looked at his watch, then at McAllister. 'Let's get up there, out of sight,' he said, gesturing at the trees above them. 'I'll stay here; you go up farther, but don't walk out on that field, don't expose yourself, stay at the edge. If you see any lights or hear a plane, whistle. You *can* whistle, can't you?'

'Actually, not very well. When the children were younger and we had a dog, a golden retriever—'

'Oh, for Christ's sake! Throw rocks down through the trees, I'll hear them. Go *on!*'

'Yes, I understand. *Move.*'

Delta – for he *was* Delta now – began his vigil. The moonlight was constantly intercepted by the drifting, low-flying clouds and he kept straining his eyes, scanning the field of tall grass, looking for a break in the monotonous pattern, for bent reeds moving toward the base of the hill, toward *him.* There minutes passed, and he had nearly decided it was a waste of time when a man suddenly lurched out of the grass on his right and plunged into the foliage. Bourne lowered his attaché case and pulled the long knife from his belt.

'*Kam Pek!*' whispered the man.

'*Wong?*'

'Yes, sir,' said the conduit, walking around the trunks of trees, approaching Jason. 'I am greeted with a knife?'

'There are a few other people back there, and frankly, I didn't think you'd show up. I told you you could get out if the risks looked too great. I didn't think it'd happen so early on, but I would have accepted it. Those are impressive weapons they're carrying.'

'I might have taken advantage of the situation, but, added to the money, you afforded me an act of immense gratification. For many others as well. More people than you can imagine will give thanks.'

'Soo the Pig?'

'Yes, sir.'

'Wait a minute,' said Bourne, alarmed. 'Why are you so sure they'll think one of those men did it?'

'What men?'

'That patrol of machine guns back there! They're not from Guangdong, not from the garrison. They're from *Beijing!*'

'The act took place in Zhuhai Shi. At the gate.'

'*Goddamn* you! You've blown *everything!* They were *waiting* for him!'

'If they were, sir, he never would have arrived.'

'What?'

'He was getting drunk with the prefect of the gate. He went to relieve himself, which was where I confronted him. He is now next door, lying in a soiled female commode, his throat slit, his genitals removed.'

'Good *God* . . . Then he didn't follow us?'

'Nor did he show any indication of doing so.'

'I see – no, I don't see. He was cut out of tonight. It's strictly a Beijing operation. Yet he was the primary contact down here—'

'I would know nothing of such matters,' broke in Wong defensively.

'Oh, sorry. No, you wouldn't.'

'Here are the eyes you hired, sir. Where do you wish me to look and what do you want me to do?'

'Did you have any trouble getting by that patrol in the road?'

'None. I saw them, they did not see me. They are now sitting in the woods at the edge of the field. If it would be of help to you, the man with the radio instructed the one he reached to leave once the 'signal' was given. I don't know what that means, but I presume it concerns a helicopter.'

'You presume?'

'The Frenchman and I followed the English major here one night. It's how I knew where to take you before. A helicopter landed and men came out to meet the Englishman.'

'That's what he told me.'

'*Told* you, sir?'

'Never mind. Stay here. If that patrol across the field starts coming over, I want to know about it. I'll be up in the field before the second hill, on the right. The same field where you and Echo saw the helicopter.'

'Echo?'

'The Frenchman.' Delta paused, thinking quickly. 'You can't light a match, you can't draw attention to yourself—' Suddenly, there were the sharp if muted sounds of objects striking other objects. *Trees! Rocks!* McAllister was signalling him!

'Grab stones, pieces of wood or rocks, and keep throwing them into the woods on the right. I'll hear them.'

'I will fill my pockets with some now.'

'I have no right to ask you this,' said Delta, picking up the attaché case, 'but do you have a weapon?'

'A three-fifty-seven-calibre magnum with a beltful of ammunition, courtesy of my cousin on my mother's side, may she rest with the holy Jesus.'

'I hope I don't see you, and if I don't, good-bye, Wong. Another part of me may not approve of you, but you're a hell of a man. And believe me, you really did beat me last time.'

'No, sir, you bested me. But I would like to try again.'

'*Forget* it!' cried the man from Medusa, racing up the hill.

Like a giant, monstrous bird, its lower body pulsating with blinding light, the helicopter descended onto the field. As arranged, McAllister stood in full view, and, as expected, the chopper's searchlight zeroed in on him. Also, as arranged, Jason Bourne was forty-odd yards away, in the shadows of the woods – visible, but not clearly. The rotors wound down to a grinding, abrasive halt. The silence was emphatic. The door opened, the stairs sprang out, and the slender, grey-haired Sheng Chou Yang walked down the steps, carrying a briefcase.

'So good to see you after all these years, Edward,' called out a taipan's first son. 'Would you care to inspect the aircraft? As you requested, there is no one but myself and my most trusted pilot.'

'No, Sheng, you can do it for me!' yelled McAllister, several hundred feet away, pulling a canister from inside his jacket and throwing it toward the helicopter. 'Tell the pilot to step outside for a few minutes and spray the cabin. If there's anyone inside, he – or they – will come out quickly.'

'This is so unlike you, Edward. Men like us know when to trust one another. We're not fools.'

'*Do* it, Sheng!'

'Of course I will.' Under orders, the pilot stepped out of the aircraft. Sheng Chou Yang picked up the canister and sprayed the immobilizing fog into the helicopter. Several minutes elapsed; no one came out. 'Are you satisfied, or should I blow the damn thing up, which would serve neither of us. Come, my friend, we're beyond these games. We always were.'

'But you became what you are. I remained what I was.'

'We can correct that, Edward! I can demand your presence at all our conferences. I can elevate you to a position of prominence. You'll be a star in the foreign service firmament.'

'It's true, then, isn't it? Everything in the file. You're back. The Kuomintang is back in China—'

'Let's talk quietly together, Edward.' Sheng glanced at the presumed assassin in the shadows, then gestured to his right. 'This is a private matter.'

Bourne moved quickly; he raced to the aircraft while the two negotiators were standing with their backs to him. As the pilot climbed into the chopper and reached his seat, the man from Medusa was behind him.

'*An jing!*' whispered jason, ordering the man to keep silent, his KG-9 machine pistol reinforcing the command. Before the stunned pilot could react, Bourne whipped a strip of heavy cloth over the man's head, bridling it across the shocked, open mouth and yanked it taut. Then, pulling a long, thin nylon cord from his pocket, Jason lashed the man to the seat, pinning his arms. There would be no sudden lift-off.

Returning his weapon to the belt under his jacket, Bourne crawled out of the helicopter. The huge machine blocked his view of McAllister and Sheng Chou Yang, which meant that it blocked theirs of him. He walked rapidly back to his previous position, constantly turning his head, prepared to change direction if the two men emerged on either side of the aircraft; the chopper was his visual shield. He stopped; he was near enough; it was time to appear casual. He took out a cigarette and struck a match, lighting it. He then strolled aimlessly, to his left, to where he could just barely see the two figures on the other side of the helicopter. He wondered what was being said between the two enemies. He wondered what McAllister was waiting for.

Do it, analyst. Do it now! It's your maximum opportunity. Every moment you delay you give away time, and time holds complications! Goddamn it, do it!

Bourne froze. He heard the sound of a stone hitting a tree close to where he had walked out on the field. Then another much nearer and another quickly following. It was Wong's warning! Sheng's patrol was crossing the field below!

Analyst, you'll get us killed! If I run over and shoot, the sound will bring six men rushing us with more firepower than we can handle! For Christ's sake, do it!

The man from Medusa stared at Sheng and McAllister, his self-hatred rising, close to exploding. He never should have let it happen this way. Death by the hands of an amateur, an embittered bureaucrat who wanted his moment in the sun.

'*Kam Pek!*' It was Wong! He had crossed through the woods on the second level and was behind him, concealed in the trees.

'Yes? I heard the stones.'

'You will not like what you hear now, sir.'

'What is it?'

'The patrol crawls up the hill.'

'It's a protective action,' said Jason, his eyes rivetted on the two figures in the field. 'We may still be all right. They can't see a hell of a lot.'

'I am not sure that matters, sir. They prepare themselves. I heard them – they've locked their weapons into firing positions.'

Bourne swallowed, a sense of futility spreading over him. For reasons he could not fathom, it was a reverse trap. 'You'd better get out of here, Wong.'

'May I ask? Are these the people who killed the Frenchman?'

'Yes.'

'And for whom the Pig, Soo Jiang, has worked so obscenely these past four years?'

'Yes.'

'I believe I will stay, sir.'

Without saying a word, the man from Medusa walked back to his attaché case. He picked it up and threw it into the woods. 'Open it,' he said. 'If we get out of this, you can spend your days at the casino without picking up messages.'

'I do not gamble.'

'You're gambling now, Wong.'

'Did you really think that we, the great warlords of the most ancient and cultured empire the world has ever known, would leave it to unwashed peasants and their ill-born offspring, schooled in the discredited theories of egalitarianism?' Sheng stood in front of McAllister; he held his briefcase across his chest with both hands. 'They should be our slaves, not our rulers.'

'It was that kind of thinking that lost you the country – you, the leaders, not the people. They weren't consulted. If they were, there might have been accommodations, compromises, and you would still have it.'

'One does not compromise with Marxist animals – or with liars. As I will not compromise with you, Edward.'

'What was that?'

With his left hand Sheng snapped his briefcase open and pulled out the file stolen from Victoria Peak. 'Do you recognize it?' he asked calmly.

'I don't *believe* it!'

'Believe, my old adversary. A little ingenuity can produce anything.'

'It's *impossible!*'

'It's here. In my hand. And the opening page clearly states that there is only one copy, to be sent by military escort under Ultra Maximum Security wherever it goes. Quite correctly, in my judgement, for your appraisal was accurate when we spoke over the telephone. The contents would inflame the Far East – make war unavoidable. The right-wingers in Beijing would march on Hong Kong – right-wingers there, you'd call them left on your side of the world. Foolish, isn't it?'

'I had a copy made and sent to Washington,' broke in the undersecretary, quickly, quietly, firmly.

'I don't believe that,' said Sheng. 'All diplomatic transmissions, by telephone-computer or by pouch, must be cleared by the highest superior officer. The notorious Ambassador Havilland wouldn't permit it, and the consulate wouldn't touch it without his authorization.'

'I sent a copy to the *Chinese* consulate!' shouted McAllister. 'You're *finished*, Sheng!'

'Really? Who do you think receives *all* communications from *all* outside sources at our consulate in Hong Kong? Don't bother to answer, I'll do it for you. One of our people.' Sheng paused, his messianic eyes suddenly on fire. 'We are *everywhere*, Edward! We will not be *denied!* We will have our nation back, our *empire!*'

'You're *insane*. It can't work. You'll start a war!'

'Then it will be a *just* war! Governments across the world will have to choose. Individual rule or state rule. Freedom or tyranny!'

'Too few of you gave freedom and too many of you were tyrants.'

'We will prevail – one way or the other.'

'My God, that's what you *want!* You want to push the world to the brink, force it to choose between annihilation and survival! That's how you think you'll get what you want, that the choice of survival will win out! This economic commission, your whole Hong Kong strategy, is just a *beginning!* You want to spread your poison to the whole Far East! You're a zealot, you're *blind!* Can't you see the tragic consequences—'

'Our nation was *stolen* from us and we will have it *back!* We cannot be *stopped!* We *march!*'

'You *can* be stopped,' said McAllister quietly, his right hand edging to the fold in his jacket. '*I'll* stop you.'

Suddenly, Sheng dropped his briefcase, revealing a gun. He fired as McAllister instinctively recoiled in terror, grabbing his shoulder.

'*Dive!*' roared Bourne, racing in front of the aircraft in the wash of its lights, releasing a burst of gunfire from his machine pistol. 'Roll, *roll!* If you can move, roll *away!*'

'*You!*' Sheng screamed, firing two rapid shots down into the fallen undersecretary of State, then raising his weapon and repeatedly pulling the trigger, aiming at the zigzagging man from Medusa running toward him.

'For *Echo!*' shouted Bourne at the top of his lungs. 'For the people you hacked to death! For the teacher on a rope you butchered! For the woman that you couldn't stop – oh, *Christ!* For those two brothers, but mainly for *Echo*, you *bastard!*' A short burst exploded from the machine pistol – then no *more*, and no amount of pressure on the trigger could activate it! It was jammed! *Jammed!* Sheng knew it; he levelled his weapon carefully as Jason threw the gun down, pounding toward the killer. Sheng fired; Delta instinctively pivoted to his right, spinning in midair as he pulled his knife from his belt, then planted his foot on the ground, reversing direction, and abruptly lunged toward Sheng. The knife found its mark and the man from Medusa ripped open the fanatic's chest. The actual killer of hundreds and would-be killer of millions was dead.

His hearing had been suspended; it wasn't now. The patrol had raced out of the woods, bursts from machine guns filling the night and the field . . . Other bursts came from beyond the helicopter – Wong had opened the attaché case and found what he needed. Two soldiers of the patrol fell; the remaining four dropped to the ground; one crawled back into the woods – he was shouting. The *radio!* He was reaching other men, other backups! How far away were they? How *near?*

Priorities! Bourne raced behind the aircraft and over to Wong, who was crouched by a tree at the edge of the woods. 'There's another one of those in there!' he whispered. '*Give* it to me!'

'Conserve your ammunition,' said Wong. 'There's not much more.'

'I know that. Stay here and pin them down as best you can but keep your fire low to the ground.'

'Where are you going, sir?'

'Circling back through the trees.'

'That's what the Frenchman would have ordered me to do.'

'He was right. He was always right.' Jason dashed deeper into the woods with the bloody knife in his belt; his lungs were bursting, his legs straining, his eyes peering into the forest darkness. He threaded his way through the dense foliage as fast as he could, making as little noise as he could.

Two *snaps!* Thick twigs on the ground broken by having been stepped on! He saw the shrouded silhouette of a figure coming toward him and spun around the trunk of a tree. He knew who it was – the officer with the radio, the thoughtful, soft-spoken killer from the Beijing sanctuary, an experienced combat soldier: Take to the flanks and outflank. What he lacked was guerrilla training, and that lack would cost him his life. One did not step on thick objects in the forest.

The officer walked by, crouching. Jason sprang, his left arm encircling the man's neck, the gun in his hand slammed against the soldier's head, the knife once again doing its work. Bourne knelt down over the corpse, put his weapon in his belt, and took the officer's powerful machine gun. He found two additional clips of ammunition; the odds were better now. It was even possible they would get out alive. Was McAllister alive? Or had a frustrated bureaucrat's moment in the sun ended in perpetual darkness. *Priorities!*

He circled the field's curving border to the point where he had entered it. Wong's sporadic gunfire was keeping the three remaining men of Sheng's elite patrol where they were, afraid to move. Suddenly, something made him turn around – a hum in the distance, a bright fleck in his eye. It was *both!* The sound was that of a racing engine, the fleck a moving searchlight scanning the dark sky. Above the descending trees he could make out a vehicle – a truck – with a searchlight mounted on its van, operated by an experienced hand. The truck sped off the road, obscured now by the high grass; only the bright searchlight was visible, moving faster and faster toward the base of the hill barely two hundred yards below. Priorities. Move!

'*Hold fire!*' Bourne roared, lurching away from his position. The three officers spun around in place on the ground, their machine guns erupting, bullets spraying the space from which the voice had come.

The man from Medusa stepped out. It was over in seconds as the powerful weapon blew up the earth and those killers who would have killed him

'*Wong!*' he shouted, running into the field. 'Come on! With *me.*' Seconds later he reached the bodies of McAllister and Sheng – one still alive, one a corpse. Jason bent over the analyst, who was moving both arms, his right hand stretched out, trying desperately to reach something. 'Mac, can you *hear* me?'

'The *file!*' whispered the undersecretary of State. 'Get the *file!*'

'What – ?' Bourne looked over at the body of Sheng Chou Yang, and, in the dim wash of the moonlight, saw the last thing in the world he thought he would see. It was Sheng's black-bordered dossier, one of the most secret, most explosive documents on earth. 'Jesus *Christ!*' said Jason softly, reaching for it. 'Listen to me, analyst!' Bourne raised his voice as Wong joined them. 'We have to move you, and it may hurt, but we haven't a choice!' He glanced up at Wong and continued, 'There's another patrol on its way here and it's closing in. An emergency backup, and by my estimate they'll be here in less than two minutes. Grit your teeth, Mr Undersecretary. We *move!*'

Together Jason and Wong carried McAllister toward the helicopter. Suddenly, Bourne cried out. 'Christ, *wait* a minute! . . . *No*, go on – *you* carry him,' he shouted to the conduit. 'I have to go back!'

'*Why?*' whispered the undersecretary, in agony.

'What are you *doing*, sir?' cried Wong.

'Food for revisionist thought,' shouted Jason enigmatically as he raced back to the body of Sheng Chou Yang. When he reached it, he bent down and shoved a flat object under the dead man's tunic. He rose and ran back to the aircraft as Wong was carefully, gently, placing McAllister across two of the backseats. Bourne leaped in the front, took out his knife and slashed the nylon cord that bound the pilot, then cut the cloth that gagged him. The pilot had a spasm of coughing and gasping; even before it subsided, Jason gave his orders.

'*Kai feiji ba!*' he shouted.

'You may speak English,' the pilot gasped. 'I am fluent. It was a requirement.'

'*Airborne*, you son of a bitch! *Now!*'

The pilot snapped the switches and started the rotors as a swarm of soldiers, clearly visible in the helicopter's lights, broke into the field. The new patrol instantly saw the five dead men of Sheng's elite guard. The entire squad began firing at the slowly ascending aircraft.

'Get the hell *out* of here!' roared Jason.

'The armour on this equipment is Sheng's armour,' said the pilot calmly. 'Even the glass will withstand heavy fire. Where do we go?'

'Hong Kong!' shouted Bourne, astonished to see that the pilot, now ascending rapidly, powerfully, turned to him, smiling.

'Surely, the generous Americans or the benevolent British will grant me asylum, sir? It is a dream from the spirits!'

'I'll be goddamned,' said the man from Medusa as they reached the first layer of low-flying clouds.

'This was a most efficient idea, sir,' said Wong from the shadows at the rear of the helicopter. 'How did it occur to you?'

'It worked once before,' said Jason, lighting a cigarette. 'History – even recent history – usually repeats itself.'

'Mr Webb?' whispered McAllister.

'What is it, analyst? How are you feeling?'

'Never mind that. Why did you go back – back to Sheng?'

'To give him a farewell present. A bankbook. A confidential account in the Cayman Islands.'

'*What?*'

'It won't do anybody any good. The names and the account numbers have been scissored out. But it'll be intersting to see how Peking reacts to its existence, won't it?'

38

Edward Newington McAllister, on crutches, limped into the once impressive study of the old house on Victoria Peak, its huge bay windows now covered with heavy plastic, the carnage all too apparent. Ambassador Raymond Havilland watched as the undersecretary of State threw the Sheng file on his desk.

'I believe this is something you lost,' said the analyst, angling his crutches and settling down in the chair with difficulty.

'The doctors tell me that your wounds aren't critical,' said the diplomat. 'I'm pleased.'

'You're *pleased?*' Who the hell are *you* to be so royally pleased?'

'It's a manner of speaking – sounds arrogant, if you like – but I mean it. What you did was extraordinary, beyond anything I would have imagined.'

'I'm sure of that.' The undersecretary shifted his position, easing his wounded shoulder into the back of the chair. 'Actually, I didn't do it. *He* did.'

'You made it possible, Edward.'

'I was out of my element – my territory, as it were. These people do things the rest of us only dream about, or fantasize, or watch on a screen, disbelieving every moment because it's so outrageously implausible.'

'We wouldn't have such dreams, or fantasize, or stay mesmerized by invention, if the fundamentals weren't in the human experience. They do what they do best just as we do what we do best. To each his own territory, Mr Undersecretary.'

McAllister stared at Havilland, his look uncompromising. 'How did it happen? How did they get the *file?*'

'Another kind of territory. A professional. Three young men were killed, quite horribly. An impenetrable safe was penetrated.'

'Inexcusable!'

'Agreed,' said Havilland, leaning forward, suddenly raising his voice. 'Just as *your* actions were inexcusable! Who in God's name do you think you *are* to have done what you did? What *right* had you to take matters in your own hands – *inexperienced* hands? You've violated every oath you've ever taken in the service of your government! Dismissal is *inadequate!* Thirty years in prison would more suitably fit your crimes! Have you any idea what might have *happened?* A war that could plunge the Far East – the *world* – into *hell!*'

'I did what I did because I could do it. That's a lesson I learned from Jason Bourne, our Jason Bourne. Regardless, you have my resignation, Mr Ambassador. Effective immediately – unless you're pressing charges.'

'And let you *loose?*' Havilland collapsed back in his chair. 'Don't be ridiculous. I've talked with the President and he agrees. You're going to be chairman of the National Security Council.'

'Chairman – ? I can't *handle* it!'

'With your own limousine and all kinds of other crap.'

'I won't know what to say!'

'You know how to *think*, and I'll be at your side.'

'Oh, my *God!*'

'Relax. Just evaluate. And tell those of us who speak what to say. That's where the real power is you know. Not those who speak, but those who think.'

'It's all so sudden, so—'

'So *deserved*, Mr Undersecretary,' interrupted the diplomat. 'The mind is a marvellous thing. Let's never underestimate it. Incidentally, the doctor tells me Lin Wenzu will pull through. He's lost the use of his left arm, but he'll live. I'm sure you'll have a recommendation to forward to MI-Six, London. They'll respect it.'

'Mr and Mrs Webb? Where are they?'

'In Hawaii, by now. With Dr Panov and Mr Conklin, of course. They don't think much of me, I'm afraid.'

'Mr Ambassador, you didn't give them much reason to.'

'Perhaps not, but then that's not my job.'

'I think I understand. Now.'

'I hope your God has compassion for men like you and me, Edward. I should not care to meet Him if He doesn't.'

'There's always forgiveness.'

'Really? Then I should not care to know Him. He'd turn out to be a fraud.'

'Why?'

'Because He unleashed upon the world a race of unthinking, bloodthirsty wolves who care not one whit about the tribe's survival, only their own. That's hardly a perfect God, is it?'

'He *is* perfect. We're the imperfect ones.'

'Then it's only a game for Him. He puts His creations in place and for His own amusement watches them blow themselves up. He watches us blow ourselves up.'

'They're *our* explosives, Mr Ambassador. We have free will.'

'According to the Scriptures, however, it's all *His* will, isn't that so? Let *His* will be done.'

'It's a grey area.'

'Perfect! One day you might really be Secretary of State.'

'I don't think so.'

'Nor do I,' agreed Havilland. 'But in the meantime we do our jobs – keep the pieces in place, stop the world from destroying itself. Thank the spirits, as they say here in the East, for people like you and me, and Jason Bourne *and* David Webb. We push the hour of Armageddon always a day away. What happens when we're not here?'

Her long auburn hair fell over his face, her body pressed against his, her lips next to his lips. David opened his eyes and smiled. It was as though there had been no nightmare that had jarringly interrupted their lives, no outrage inflicted upon them that had brought them to the edge of an abyss that held horror and death. They were together, and the splendid comfort of that reality filled him with profound gratitude. It *was*, and that was enough – more than he ever thought possible.

He began to reconstruct the events of the past twenty-four hours and his smile widened, a brief laugh escaping from his throat. Things were never as they should be, never as one expected. He and Mo Panov had had far too much to drink on the flight from Hong Kong to Hawaii, while Alex Conklin had stayed with iced tea or club soda or whatever newly reformed drunks want others to know they're staying with – no lectures, just quiet martyrdom. Marie had held the eminent Dr Panov's head while the noted psychiatrist threw up in the British military aircraft's suffocatingly small toilet, and had covered Mo with a blanket when he fell into a dead sleep. She had then gently but firmly rejected her husband's amorous advances, but had made up for those rejections when she and a sobered mate reached the hotel in Kahala. A splendid, delirious night of making love that adolescents dream of, washing away the terrors of the nightmare.

Alex? Yes, he remembered. Conklin had taken the first commercial flight out of Oahu to Los Angeles and Washington. 'There are heads to break' was the way he had phrased it. 'And I intend to break them.' Alexander Conklin had a new mission in his fragmented life. It was called accountability.

Mo? Morris Panov? Scourge of the chicken-soup psychologists and the charlatans of his profession? He was next door in the adjoining room, no doubt nursing the most massive hangover of his life.

'You laughed,' whispered Marie, her eyes closed, nestling her face into his throat. 'What the hell is so funny?'

'You, me, us – everything.'

'Your sense of humour positively *escapes* me. On the other hand, I think I hear a man named David.'

'That's all you'll ever hear from now on.'

There was a knock on the door, not the door to the hallway but the one to the adjoining room. Panov. Webb got out of bed, walked rapidly to the bathroom and grabbed a towel, whipping it around his naked waist. 'Just a second, Mo!' he called out, going to the door.

Morris Panov, his face pale but composed, stood there with a suitcase in his hand. 'May I enter the Temple of Eros?'

'You're there, friend.'

'I should hope so . . . Good afternoon, my dear,' said the psychiatrist, addressing Marie in the bed, as he went to a chair by the glass door that led to the balcony overlooking the Hawaiian beach. 'Don't fuss, don't prepare a meal, and if you get out of bed, don't worry. I'm a doctor. I think.'

'How are you, Mo?' Marie sat up, pulling the sheet over her.

'Far better than I was three hours ago, but you wouldn't know anything about that. You're maddeningly sane.'

'You were stretched, you had to let loose.'

'If you charge a hundred dollars an hour, lovely lady, I'll mortgage my house and sign up for five years of therapy.'

'I'd like that defined,' said David, smiling and sitting down opposite Panov. 'Why the suitcase?'

'I'm leaving. I have patients back in Washington and I like to think they may need me.'

The silence was moving, as David and Marie looked at Morris Panov. 'What do we say, Mo?' asked Webb. 'How do we say it?'

'You don't say anything, I'll do the talking. Marie has been hurt, pained beyond normal endurance. But then her endurance is beyond normality and she can handle it. Perhaps outrageously, we expect as much from certain people. It's unfair, but that's the way it is.'

'I had to survive, Mo,' said Marie, looking at her husband. 'I had to get him back. That's the way it *was*.'

'You, David. You've gone through a traumatizing experience, one that only you can deal with and you don't need any chicken-soup crap from me to face it. You are *you* now, not anybody else. Jason Bourne is gone. He can't come back. Build your life as David Webb – concentrate on Marie and David – that's all there is and all there should be. And if at any moment the anxieties come back – they probably won't, but I'd appreciate your manufacturing a few – call me and I'll take the next plane up to Maine. I love you both, and Marie's beef stew is outstanding.'

Sundown, the brilliant orange circle settling on top of the western horizon, slowly disappearing into the Pacific. They walked along the beach, their hands gripped fiercely, their bodies touching – so natural, so right.

'What do you do when there's a part of you that you hate?' said Webb.

'Accept it,' answered Marie. 'We all have a dark side, David. We wish we could deny it, but we can't. It's there. Perhaps we can't exist without it. Yours is a legend called Jason Bourne, but that's all it is.'

'I loathe him.'

'He brought you back to me. That's all that matters.'

The Bourne Ultimatum

for Bobbi and Leonard Raichert,
two lovely people who have enriched
our lives – our thanks

Prologue

Darkness had descended on Manassas, Virginia, the countryside alive with nocturnal undercurrents, as Bourne crept through the woods bordering the estate of General Norman Swayne. Startled birds fluttered out of their black recesses; crows awoke in the trees and cawed their alarms, and then, as if calmed by a foraging co-conspirator, kept silent.

Manassas! The key was here! The key that would unlock the subterranean door that led to Carlos the Jackal, the assassin who wanted only to destroy David Webb and his family . . . Webb! *Get away from me, David!* screamed Jason Bourne in the silence of his mind. *Let me be the killer you cannot be!*

With each scissoring cut into the thick, high wire fence, he understood the inevitable, confirmed by his heavy breathing and the sweat that fell from his hairline. No matter how hard he tried to keep his body in reasonable shape, he was fifty years of age; he could not do with ease what he did thirteen years ago in Paris when, under orders, he had stalked the Jackal. It was something to think about, not dwell upon. There were Marie and his children now – David's wife, David's children – and there was *nothing* he could not do as long as he willed it! David Webb was disappearing from his psyche, only the predator Jason Bourne would remain.

He was *through*! He crawled inside and stood up, instinctively, rapidly checking his equipment with the fingers of both hands. Weapons: an automatic, as well as a CO_2 dart pistol; Zeiss-Ikon binoculars; a scabbarded hunting knife. They were all the predator needed, for he was now behind the lines in enemy territory, the enemy that would lead him to Carlos.

Medusa. The bastard battalion from Vietnam, the unlogged, unsanctioned, unacknowledged collection of killers and misfits who roamed the jungles of Southeast Asia directed by Command Saigon, the original death squads who brought Saigon more intelligence input than all the search-and-destroys put together. Jason Bourne had come out of Medusa with David Webb only a memory – a scholar who had another wife, other children, all slaughtered.

General Norman Swayne had been an elite member of Command Saigon, the sole supplier of the old Medusa. And now there was a *new* Medusa – different, massive, evil incarnate cloaked in contemporary respectability, searching out and destroying whole segments of global economies, all for the benefit of the few. All financed by the profits from a long-ago bastard battalion, unlogged, unacknowledged – non-history. This modern Medusa was the bridge to Carlos the Jackal. The assassin would find the principals irresistible as clients, and both camps would demand the death of Jason Bourne. *That* had to happen! And for it to happen, Bourne had to learn the secrets concealed within the grounds belonging to General Swayne, head of all procurements for the Pentagon, a panicked man with a small tattoo on his inner forearm. A Medusan.

Without sound or warning, a black Doberman crashed through the dense foliage, its frenzy in full force. Jason whipped the CO_2 pistol from its nylon holster as the salivating attack dog lunged into his stomach, its teeth bared. He fired into its head; the dart took effect in seconds. He cradled the animal's unconscious body to the ground.

Cut its throat! roared Jason Bourne in silence.

No, countered his other self, David Webb. *Blame the trainer, not the animal.*

Get away from me, David!

1

The cacophony spun out of control as the crowds swelled through the amusement park in the countryside on the outskirts of Baltimore. The summer night was hot and nearly everywhere faces and necks were drenched with sweat, except for those screaming as they plunged over the crests of a roller coaster, or shrieking as they plummeted down the narrow, twisting gullies of racing water in torpedo sleds. The garishly coloured, manically blinking lights along the central gangway were joined by the grating sounds of emphatic music metallically erupting out of an excess of loudspeakers – calliopes *presto*, marches *prestissimo*. Pitchmen yelled above the din, nasally hawking their wares in monotonic diatribes while erratic explosions in the sky lit up the darkness, sending sprays of myriad fireworks cascading over a small adjacent black lake. Roman candles bright, arching bursts of fire blinding.

A row of Hit-the-Gong machines drew contorted faces and thick necks bulging with veins as men sought furiously and frequently in frustration to prove their manhood, crashing heavy wooden mallets down on the deceitful planks that too often refused to send the little red balls up to the bells. Across the way, others shrieked with menacing enthusiasm as they crashed their Dodgem cars into the whirling, surrounding vehicles, each collision a triumph of superior aggression, each combatant a momentary movie star who overcomes all odds against him. *Gunfight at OK Corral* at 9:27 in the evening in a conflict that meant nothing.

Farther along was a minor monument to sudden death, a shooting gallery that bore little resemblance to the innocent minimum-calibre variety found in state fairs and rural carnivals. Instead, it was a microcosm of the most lethal equipment of modern weaponry. There were mocked-up versions of MAC-10 and Uzi machine pistols, steel-framed missile launchers and anti-tank bazookas, and, finally, a frightening replica of a flamethrower spewing out harsh, straight beams of light through billowing clouds of dark smoke. And again there were the perspiring faces, continuous beads of sweat rolling over maniacal eyes and down across stretched necks – husbands, wives and children – their features grotesque, twisted out of shape as if each were blasting away at hated enemies – wives, husbands, parents, and offspring. All were locked in a never-ending war without meaning – at 9:29 in the evening, in an amusement park whose theme was violence. Unmitigated and unwarranted, man against himself and all his hostilities, the worst, of course, being his fears.

A slender figure, a cane gripped in his right hand, limped past a booth where angry, excited customers were hurling sharp-pointed darts into balloons on which were stencilled the faces of public figures. As the rubber heads exploded, the bursts gave rise to fierce arguments for and against the sagging, pinched remnants of political icons and their dart-wielding executioners. The limping man continued down the gangway, peering ahead through the maze of strollers as if he were looking for a specific location in a hectic, crowded, unfamiliar part of town. He was dressed casually but neatly in a jacket and sport shirt as though the oppressive heat had no effect on him and the jacket was somehow a requirement. His face was the pleasant face of a middle-aged man, but worn and given to premature lines and deep shadows under the eyes, all of which resulted more from the life he had led than the years. His name was Alexander Conklin, and he was a retired covert operations officer in the Central Intelligence Agency. He was also at this moment apprehensive and consumed with anxiety. He did not wish to be in this place at this hour, and he could not imagine what catastrophic event had taken place that forced him to be there.

He approached the pandemonium of the shooting gallery and suddenly gasped, stopping all movement, his eyes locked on a tall, balding man about his own age with a seersucker jacket slung over his shoulder. *Morris Panov* was walking towards the thunderous counter of the shooting gallery from the opposite direction! *Why*? What had *happened*? Conklin snapped his head around in every direction, his eyes darting towards faces and bodies, instinctively knowing that he and the psychiatrist were being watched. It was too late to stop Panov from entering the inner circle of the meeting ground but perhaps *not* too late to get them both out! The retired intelligence officer reached under his jacket for the small Baretta automatic that was his constant companion, and lurched rapidly forward, limping and flailing his cane against the crowd, smashing kneecaps and prodding stomachs and breasts and kidneys until the stunned, angry strollers erupted in successive cries of shock, a near riot in the making. He then rushed forward, slamming his frail body into the bewildered doctor and shouting into Panov's face through the roars of the crowd.

'What the hell are *you* doing here?'

'The same thing I assume *you* are. David, or should I say *Jason*? That's what the telegram said.'

'It's a *trap*!'

There was a piercing scream overriding the surrounding melee. Both Conklin and Panov instantly looked over at the shooting gallery only yards away. An obese woman with a pinched face had been shot in the throat. The crowd went into a frenzy. Conklin spun around trying to see where the shot came from, but the panic was at full pitch; he saw nothing but rushing figures. He grabbed Panov and propelled him through the screaming, frantic bodies across the gangway and again through the strolling crowds to the base of the massive roller coaster at the end of the park where excited customers were edging towards the booth through the deafening noise.

'My *God*!' yelled Panov. 'Was that meant for one of *us*?'

'Maybe . . . maybe not,' replied the former intelligence officer breathlessly as sirens and whistles were heard in the distance.

'You said it was a *trap*!'

'Because we both got a crazy telegram from David using a name he hasn't used in five years – *Jason Bourne*! And if I'm not mistaken, your message also said that under *no* condition should we call his house.'

'That's right.'

'It's a trap . . . You move better than I do, Mo, so move those legs of yours. Get out of here – run like a son of a bitch and find a telephone. A *pay* phone, nothing traceable!'

'What?'

'Call his house! Tell David to pack up Marie and the kids and get out of there!'

'*What?*'

'Someone found us, Doctor! Someone looking for Jason Bourne – who's *been* looking for him for years and won't stop until he's got him in his gun sight . . . You were in charge of David's messed-up head, and I pulled every rotten string in Washington to get him and Marie out of Hong Kong alive . . . The rules were broken and we were found, Mo. *You* and *me*! The only officially recorded connections to Jason Bourne, address and occupation unknown.'

'Do you know what you're saying, Alex?'

'You're goddamned right I do . . . It's Carlos. Carlos the *Jackal*. Get out of here, Doctor. Reach your former patient and tell him to disappear!'

'Then what's he to do?'

'I don't have many friends, certainly no one I trust, but you do. Give him the name of somebody, say one of your medical buddies who gets urgent calls from his patients the way I used to call you. Tell David to reach him or her when he's secure. Give him a code.'

'A *code*?'

'Jesus, Mo, use your *head*! An alias, a Jones or a Smith—'

'They're rather common names—'

'Then Schickelgrubber or Moskowitz, whatever you *like*! Just tell him to let us know where he *is*.'

'I understand.'

'Now get out of here, and *don't go* home! . . . Take a room at the Brookshire in Baltimore under the name of – Morris, Phillip Morris. I'll meet you there later.'

'What are you going to do?'

'Something I hate . . . Without my cane I'm buying a ticket for this fucking roller coaster. Nobody'll look for a cripple on one of these things. It scares the hell out of me, but it's a logical exit even if I have to stay on the damn thing all night . . . Now get *out* of here! *Hurry!*'

The station wagon raced south down a backcountry road through the hills of New Hampshire towards the Massachusetts border, the driver a long-framed man, his sharp-featured face intense, the muscles of his jaw pulsating, his clear light-blue eyes furious. Beside him sat his strikingly attractive wife, the reddish glow of her auburn hair heightened by the dashboard lights. In her arms was an infant, a baby girl of eight months; in the first backseat was another child, a blond-haired boy of five, asleep under a blanket, a portable guardrail protecting him from sudden stops. The father was David Webb, professor of Oriental studies, but once part of the notorious, unspoken-of Medusa, twice the legend that was Jason Bourne – assassin.

'We knew it had to happen,' said Marie St Jacques Webb, Canadian by birth, economist by profession, saviour of David Webb by accident. 'It was merely a question of time.'

'It's *crazy*!' David whispered so as not to wake the children, his intensity in no way diminished by his whisper. 'Everything's buried, maximum archive security and all the rest of that crap! How did anyone *find* Alex and Mo?'

'We don't know but Alex will start looking. There's no one better than Alex, you said that yourself—'

'He's marked now – he's a dead man,' interrupted Webb grimly.

'That's premature, David. "He's the best there ever was," those were your words.'

'The only time he wasn't was thirteen years ago in Paris.'

'Because you were better—'

'No! Because I didn't know who I was, and he was operating on prior data that I didn't know a damn thing about. He assumed it was *me* out there, but *I* didn't know *me*, so I couldn't act according to his script . . . He's still the best. He saved both our lives in Hong Kong.'

'Then you're saying what I'm saying, aren't you? We're in good hands.'

'Alex's, yes. Not Mo's. That poor beautiful man is dead. They'll take him and break him!'

'He'd go to his grave before giving anyone information about us.'

'He won't have a choice. They'll shoot him up to the moon with Amytals and his whole life will be on tape. Then they'll kill him and come after me . . . after us, which is why you and the kids are heading south, *way* south. The Caribbean.'

'I'll send *them*, darling. Not me.'

'Will you *stop* it! We agreed when Jamie was born. It's why we got the place down there, why we damned near bought your kid brother's *soul* to look after it for us . . . Also, he's done pretty damn well. We now own half interest in a flourishing inn down a dirt road on an island nobody ever heard of until that Canadian hustler landed there in a seaplane.'

'Johnny was always the aggressive type. Dad once said he could sell a broken-down heifer as a prime steer and no one would check the parts.'

'The point is he loves you . . . and the kids. I'm also counting on that wild man's – Never mind, I trust Johnny.'

'While you're trusting so much in my younger brother, don't trust your sense of direction. You just passed the turn to the cabin.'

'Goddamn it!' cried Webb, braking the car and swerving around. '*Tomorrow!* You and Jamie and Alison are heading out of Logan Airport. To the island!'

'We'll discuss it, David.'

'There's nothing to discuss.' Webb breathed deeply, steadily, imposing a strange control. 'I've been here before,' he said quietly.

Marie looked at her husband, his suddenly passive face outlined in the dim wash of the dashboard lights. What she saw frightened her far more than the spectre of the Jackal. She was not looking at David Webb the soft-spoken scholar. She was staring at a man they both thought had disappeared from their lives forever.

2

Alexander Conklin gripped his cane as he limped into the conference room at the Central Intelligence Agency in Langley, Virginia. He stood facing a long impressive table, large enough to seat thirty people, but instead there were only three, the man at the head the grey-haired DCI, director of Central Intelligence. Neither he nor his two highest-ranking deputy directors appeared pleased to see Conklin. The greetings were perfunctory, and rather than taking his obviously assigned seat next to the CIA official on the DCI's left, Conklin pulled out the chair at the far end of the table, sat down, and with a sharp noise slapped his cane against the edge.

'Now that we've said hello, can we cut the crap, gentlemen?'

'That's hardly a courteous or an amiable way to begin, Mr Conklin,' observed the director.

'Neither courtesy nor amiability is on my mind just now, *sir*. I just want to know why airtight Four Zero regulations were ignored and maximum-classified information was released that endangers a number of lives, including mine!'

'That's *outrageous*, Alex!' interrupted one of the two associates.

'Totally inaccurate!' added the other. 'It couldn't happen and you know it!'

'I don't know it and it did happen and I'll tell you what's outrageously *accurate*,' said Conklin angrily. 'A man's out there with a wife and two children, a man this country and a large part of the world owe more to than anyone could ever repay, and he's running, hiding, frightened out of his mind that he and his family are targets. We gave that man our word, *all* of us, that no part of the official record would ever see the light of day until it was confirmed beyond *doubt* that Ilich Ramirez Sanchez, also known as Carlos the Jackal, was dead . . . All right, I've heard the same rumours you have, probably from the same or much better sources, that the Jackal was killed here or executed there, but no one – repeat *no one* – has come forward with indisputable proof . . . Yet a part of that file was leaked, a very vital part, and it concerns me deeply because my name is there . . . Mine and Dr Morris Panov, the chief psychiatrist of record. We were the only – repeat *only* – two individuals acknowledged to have been close associates of the unknown man who assumed the name of Jason Bourne, considered in more sectors than we can count to be the rival of Carlos in the killing game . . . But that information is buried in the vaults here in Langley. How did it get out? According to the rules, if anyone wants any part of that record – from the White House to the

State Department to the holy Joint Chiefs – he has to go through the offices of the director and his chief analysts right here at Langley. They have to be briefed on all the details of the request and even if they're satisfied as to the legitimacy, there's a final step. *Me.* Before a release is signed, *I'm* to be contacted, and in the event I'm not around any longer, Dr Panov is to be reached, either one of us legally empowered to turn the request down flat . . . That's the way it is, gentlemen, and no one knows the rules better than I do because I'm the one who *wrote* them – again right here at Langley, because this was the place I knew best. After twenty-eight years in this corkscrew business, it was my final contribution – with the full authority of the President of the United States and the consent of Congress through the select committees on intelligence in the House and the Senate.'

'That's heavy artillery, Mr Conklin,' commented the grey-haired director, sitting motionless, his voice flat, neutral.

'There were heavy reasons for pulling out the cannons.'

'So I gather. One of the sixteen-inchers reached me.'

'You're damned right he did. Now there's the question of accountability. I want to know how that information surfaced and most important, *who got* it.'

Both deputy directors began talking at once, as angrily as Alex, but they were stopped by the DCI, who touched their arms, a pipe in one hand, a lighter in his other. 'Slow down and back up, Mr Conklin,' said the director gently, lighting his pipe. 'It's obvious that you know my two associates, but you and I never met, have we?'

'No. I resigned four and a half years ago, and you were appointed a year after that.'

'Like many others – quite justifiably, I think – did you consider me a crony appointment?'

'You obviously were, but I had no trouble with that. You seemed qualified. As far as I could tell, you were an apolitical Annapolis admiral who ran naval intelligence and who just happened to work with an FMF marine colonel during the Vietnam war who became president. Others were passed over, but that happens. No sweat.'

'Thank you. But do you have any "sweat" with my two deputy directors?'

'It's history but I can't say either one of them was considered the best friend an agent in the field ever had. They were analysts, not field men.'

'Isn't that a natural aversion, a conventional hostility?'

'Of course it is. They analysed situations from thousands of miles away with computers we didn't know who programmed and with data we hadn't passed on. You're damned right it's a natural aversion. We dealt with human quotients; they didn't. They dealt with little green letters on a computer screen and made decisions they frequently shouldn't have made.'

'Because people like you had to be *controlled*,' interjected the deputy on the director's right. 'How many times, even today, do men and women like you lack the full picture? The *total* strategy, and not just *your* part of it?'

'Then we should be given a fuller picture going in, or at least an overview so we can try to figure out what makes sense and what doesn't.'

'Where does an overview stop, Alex?' asked the deputy on the DCI's left. 'At what point do we say, "We can't reveal this . . . for everyone's benefit"?'

'I don't know, you're the analysts, I'm not. On a case-by-case basis, I suppose, but certainly with better communication than I ever got when I was in the field . . . Wait a minute. *I'm* not the issue, *you* are.' Alex stared at the director. 'Very smooth, *sir*, but I'm not buying a change of subject. I'm here to find out who got what and how. If you'd rather, I'll take my credentials over to the White House or up to the Hill and watch a few heads roll. I want answers. I want to know what to *do*!'

'I wasn't trying to change the subject, Mr Conklin, only to divert it momentarily to make a point. You obviously objected to the methods and the compromises employed in the past by my colleagues, but did either of these men ever mislead you, lie to you?'

Alex looked briefly at the two deputy directors. 'Only when they had to lie to me, which had nothing to do with field operations.'

'That's a strange comment.'

'If they haven't told you, they should have . . . Five years ago I was an alcoholic – I'm still an alcoholic but I don't drink any more. I was riding out the time to my pension, so nobody told me anything and they damn well shouldn't have.'

'For your enlightenment, all my colleagues said to me was that you had been ill, that you hadn't been functioning at the level of your past accomplishments until the end of your service.'

Again Conklin studied both deputies, nodding to both as he spoke. 'Thanks, Casset, and you, too, Valentino, but you didn't have to do that. I was a drunk and it shouldn't be a secret whether it's me or anybody else. That's the dumbest thing you can do around here.'

'From what we heard about Hong Kong, you did a hell of a job, Alex,' said the man named Casset softly. 'We didn't want to detract from that.'

'You've been a pain in the ass for longer than I care to remember,' added Valentino. 'But we couldn't let you hang out as an accident of booze.'

'Forget it. Let's get back to Jason Bourne. That's why I'm here, why you damn well had to see me.'

'That's also why I momentarily sidetracked us, Mr Conklin. You have professional differences with my deputies, but I gather you don't question their integrity.'

'Others, yes. Not Casset or Val. As far as I was concerned, they did their jobs and I did mine; it was the system that was fouled up – it was buried in fog. But *this* isn't, *today* isn't. The rules are clear-cut and absolute, and since I wasn't reached, they were broken and I *was* misled, in a very real sense, *lied* to. I repeat. How did it happen and *who* got the information?'

'That's all I wanted to hear,' said the director, picking up the telephone on the table. 'Please call Mr DeSole down the hall and ask him to come to the conference room.' The DCI hung up and turned to Conklin. 'I assume you're aware of Steven DeSole.'

'DeSole the mute mole.' Alex nodded.

'I beg your pardon?'

'It's an old joke around here,' explained Casset to the director. 'Steve knows where the bodies are buried, but when the time comes he won't even tell God unless He shows him a Four Zero clearance.'

'I assume that means the three of you, especially Mr Conklin, consider Mr DeSole a thorough professional.'

'I'll answer that,' Alex said. 'He'll tell you anything you have to know but no more than that. Also, he won't lie. He'll keep his mouth shut, or tell you he can't tell you, but he won't lie to you.'

'That's another thing I wanted to hear.' There was a brief knock on the door and the DCI called out for the visitor to enter. A medium-sized, slightly overweight man with wide eyes magnified behind steel-rimmed glasses walked into the room, closing the door behind him. His casual second glance at the table revealed Alexander Conklin to him; he was obviously startled by the sight of the retired intelligence officer. Instantly, he changed his reaction to one of pleasant surprise, crossing to Conklin's chair, his hand extended.

'Good to see you, old boy. It's been two or three years now, hasn't it?'

'More like four, Steve,' replied Alex, shaking hands. 'How's the analysts' analyst and keeper of the keys?'

'Not much to analyse or to lock up these days. The White House is a sieve and the Congress isn't much better. I should get half pay, but don't tell anyone.'

'We still keep some things to ourselves, don't we?' interrupted the DCI, smiling. 'At least from past operations. Perhaps you earned double your pay then.'

'Oh, I suspect I did.' DeSole nodded his head humorously as he released Conklin's hand. 'However, the days of archive custodians and armed transfers to underground warehouses are over. Today it's all computerized photo scans entered by machines from on high. I don't get to go on those wonderful trips any longer with military escorts, pretending I'll be deliciously attacked by Mata Hari. I haven't had a briefcase chained to my wrist since I can't remember when.'

'A lot safer that way,' said Alex.

'But very little I can tell my grandchildren about, old boy . . "What did you do as a big spy, Grandpa?" . . . "Actually, in my last years, a great many crossword puzzles, young man." '

'Be careful, Mr DeSole,' said the DCI, chuckling. 'I shouldn't care to put in a recommendation to cut your pay . . . On the other hand, I couldn't, because I don't believe you for an instant.'

'Neither do I.' Conklin spoke quietly, angrily. 'This is a setup,' he added, staring at the overweight analyst.

'That's quite a statement, Alex,' countered DeSole. 'Would you mind explaining it?'

'You know why I'm here, don't you?'

'I didn't know you *were* here.'

'Oh, I see. It just happened to be convenient for you to be "down the hall" and ready to come in here.'

'My *office* is down the hall. Quite far down, I might add.'

Conklin looked at the DCI. 'Again, very smooth, *sir*. Bring in three people you figure I've had no major run-ins with outside of the system itself, three men you've determined I basically trust, so I'll believe whatever's said.'

'That's fundamentally accurate, Mr Conklin, because what you'll hear is the truth. Sit down, Mr DeSole . . . Perhaps at this end of the table so that our former colleague can study us as we explain to him. I understand it's a technique favoured by field officers.'

'I haven't a *damn* thing to explain,' said the analyst as he headed for the chair next to Casset. 'But in light of our former colleague's somewhat gross remarks, I'd like to study *him* . . . Are you *well*, Alex?'

'He's well,' answered the deputy director named Valentino. 'He's snarling at the wrong shadows but he's well.'

'That information couldn't have surfaced without the consent and cooperation of the people in this room!'

'What information?' asked DeSole, looking at the DCI, suddenly widening his large eyes behind his glasses. 'Oh, the max-classified thing you asked me about this morning?'

The director nodded, then looked at Conklin. 'Let's go back to this morning . . . Seven hours ago, shortly after nine o'clock, I received a call from Edward McAllister, formerly of the State Department and currently chairman of the National Security Agency. I'm told Mr McAllister was with you in Hong Kong, Mr Conklin, is that correct?'

'Mr McAllister was with us,' agreed Alex flatly. 'He flew undercover with Jason Bourne to Macao, where he was shot up so badly he damn near died. He's an intellectual oddball and one of the bravest men I've ever met.'

'He said nothing about the circumstances, only that he was there, and I was to shred my calendar, if need be, but to consider our meeting with you as Priority Red . . . Heavy artillery, Mr Conklin.'

'To repeat. There are heavy reasons for the cannons.'

'Apparently . . . Mr McAllister gave me the precise maximum-classified codes that would clarify the status of the file you're talking about – the record of the Hong Kong operation. I, in turn, gave the information to Mr DeSole, so I'll let him tell you what he learned.'

'It hasn't been touched, Alex,' said DeSole quietly, his eyes levelled on Conklin. 'As of nine-thirty this morning, it's been in a black hole for four years, five months, twenty-one days, eleven hours and forty-three minutes without penetration. And there's a very good reason why that status is pure, but I have no idea whether you're aware of it or not.'

'Where that file is concerned I'm aware of *everything*!'

'Perhaps, perhaps not,' said DeSole gently. 'You were known to have a problem, and Dr Panov is not that experienced where security matters are concerned.'

'What the hell are you driving at?'

'A third name was added to the clearance procedures for that official record on Hong Kong . . . Edward Newington McAllister, by his own insistence and with both presidential and congressional authority. He made sure of it.'

'Oh, my *God*,' said Conklin softly, hesitantly. 'When I called him last night from Baltimore he said it was *impossible.* Then he said I had to understand for myself, so he'd set up the conference . . . Jesus, what *happened*?'

'I'd say we'd have to look elsewhere,' said the DCI. 'But before we do that, Mr Conklin, you have to make a decision. You see, none of us at this table knows what's in that maximum-classified file . . . We've talked, of course, and as Mr Casset said, we understood that you did a hell of a job in Hong Kong, but we don't know what that job *was.* We heard the rumours out of our Far East stations which, frankly, most of us believed were exaggerated in the spreading, and paramount among them was your name and that of the assassin Jason Bourne. The scuttlebutt then was that you were responsible for the capture and execution of the killer we knew *as* Bourne, yet a few moments ago in your anger you used the phrase "the unknown man who *assumed* the name of Jason Bourne," stating that he was alive and in hiding. In terms of specifics, we're at a loss – at least *I* am, God knows.'

'You didn't pull the record out?'

'No,' answered DeSole. 'That was my decision. As you may or may not know, every invasion of a maximum-classified file is automatically marked with the date and hour of penetration . . . Since the director informed me that there was a large Security Agency flap over an illegal entry, I decided to leave well enough alone. Not penetrated in nearly five years, therefore not read or even known about and consequently not given to the evil people, whoever they are.'

'You were covering your ass right down to the last square inch of flesh.'

'Most assuredly, Alex. That data has a White House flag on it. Things are relatively stable around here now and it serves no one to ruffle feathers in the Oval Office. There's a new man at that desk, but the former President is still very much alive and opinionated. He'd be consulted, so why risk trouble?'

Conklin studied each face and spoke quietly. 'Then you really *don't* know the story, do you?'

'It's the truth, Alex,' said Deputy Director Casset.

'Nothing but, you pain,' agreed Valentino, permitting himself a slight smile.

'My word on it,' added Steven DeSole, his clear, wide eyes rigid on Conklin.

'And if you want our help, we should know something besides contradictory rumours,' continued the director, leaning back in his chair. 'I don't know if we *can* help, but I do know there's little we can do so completely in the dark.'

Again Alex looked at each man, the lines in his pained face more pronounced than ever, as if the decision was momentarily too difficult for him. 'I won't tell you his name because I've given my word – maybe later, not now. And it can't be found in the record, it's not there either; it's a cover – I gave my word on that, too. The rest I'll tell you because I do want your help and I want that record to remain in its black hole . . . Where do I begin?'

'With this meeting perhaps?' suggested the director. 'What prompted it?'

'All right, that'll be quick.' Conklin stared pensively at the surface of the table, absently gripping his cane, then raised his eyes. 'A woman was killed last night at an amusement park outside Baltimore—'

'I read about it in the *Post* this morning,' interrupted DeSole, nodding, his full cheeks jiggling. 'Good *Lord*, were you—'

'So did I,' broke in Casset, his steady brown eyes on Alex. 'It happened in front of a shooting gallery. They closed the guns down.'

'I saw the article and figured it was some kind of terrible accident.' Valentino shook his head slowly. 'I didn't actually read it.'

'I was given my usual thick sheaf of scissored newspaper stories, which is enough journalism for anyone in the morning,' said the director. 'I don't remember any such article.'

'*Were* you involved, old boy?'

'If I wasn't, it was a horrible waste of life . . . I should say if we weren't involved.'

'*We?*' Casset frowned in alarm.

'Morris Panov and I received identical telegrams from Jason Bourne asking us to be at the amusement park at nine-thirty last night. It was urgent, and we were to meet him in front of the shooting gallery, but we were not, under any condition, to call his house or anyone else . . . We both independently assumed that he didn't want to alarm his wife, that he had something to tell us individually that he didn't want her to know . . . We arrived at the same time, but I saw Panov first and figured it was a bad scene. From any point of view, especially Bourne's, we should have reached each other and talked before going up there; instead, we had been told not to. It smelled, so I did my best to get us out of there fast. The only way seemed to be a diversion.'

'You stampeded them,' said Casset, making a statement.

'It was the only thing I could think of, and one of the few things this goddamned cane is good for other than keeping me upright. I cracked every shin and kneecap I could see and lanced a few stomachs and tits. We got out of the circle, but that poor woman was killed.'

'How did you figure it – *do* you figure it?' asked Valentino.

'I just don't know, Val. It was a trap, no question about that, but what kind of trap? If what I thought then and what I think now are correct, how could a hired marksman miss at that distance? The shot came from my upper left – not that I necessarily heard it – but the position of the woman and the blood all over her throat indicated that she had turned and caught the bullet in her body swing. It couldn't have come from the gallery; those guns are chained and the massive haemorrhage in her neck was caused by a far larger calibre than any of the toys there. If the killer wanted to take out either Mo Panov or me, his telescopic cross hairs wouldn't be that far off the mark. Not if my thinking is right.'

'"Right," Mr Conklin,' interjected the DCI, 'meaning the assassin, Carlos the Jackal.'

'*Carlos?*' exclaimed DeSole. 'What in heaven's name has the Jackal to do with a killing in *Baltimore*?'

'Jason Bourne,' answered Casset.

'Yes, I gather that, but this is all terribly confusing! Bourne was a scum hit man out of Asia who moved to Europe to challenge Carlos and lost. As the director just said, he went back to the Far East and was killed four or five years ago, yet Alex talks as if he's still alive, that he and someone named Panov got telegrams from him . . . What in God's name does a dead scumball and the world's most elusive assassin have to do with last night?'

'You weren't here a few minutes ago, Steve,' again Casset answered quietly. 'Apparently they had a lot to do with last night.'

'I *beg* your pardon.'

'I think you should start at the beginning, Mr Conklin,' said the director. 'Who *is* Jason Bourne?'

'As the world knew him, a man who never existed,' replied the former intelligence officer.

3

'The original Jason Bourne was garbage, a paranoid drifter from Tasmania who found his way into the Vietnam war as part of an operation no one wants to acknowledge even today. It was a collection of killers, misfits, smugglers and thieves, mostly escaped criminals, many under death sentences, but they knew every inch of Southeast Asia and operated behind enemy lines – funded by us.'

'Medusa,' whispered Steven DeSole. 'It's all buried. They were animals, killing wantonly without reason or authorization and stealing millions. *Savages.*'

'Most, not all,' said Conklin. 'But the original Bourne fitted every rotten profile you could come up with, including the betrayal of his own men. The leader of a particularly hazardous mission – hazardous, *hell*, it was suicidal – found Bourne radioing their position to the North Vietnamese. He executed him on the spot, shoving the body into a swamp to rot in the jungles of Tam Quan. Jason Bourne disappeared from the face of the earth.'

'He obviously reappeared, Mr Conklin,' observed the director, leaning forward on the table.

'In another body,' agreed Alex, nodding. 'For another purpose. The man who executed Bourne in Tam Quan took his name and agreed to be trained for an operation that we called Treadstone Seventy-one, after a building on New York's Seventy-first Street, where he went through a brutal indoctrination programme. It was a brilliant strategy on paper, but ultimately failed because of something no one could predict, even consider. After nearly three years of living the role of the world's second most lethal assassin and moving into Europe – as Steve accurately described – to challenge the Jackal in his own territory, our man was wounded and lost his memory. He was found half dead in the Mediterranean and brought by a fisherman to the island of Port Noir. He had no idea who he was or what he was – only that he was a master of various martial arts, spoke several Oriental languages, and was obviously an extremely well-educated man. With the help of a British doctor, an alcoholic banished to Port Noir, our man started to piece his life – his identity – back together from fragments both mental and physical. It was a hell of a journey . . . and we who had mounted the operation, who invented the myth, were no help to him. Not knowing what had happened, we thought he had turned, had actually become the mythical assassin we'd created to trap Carlos. I, myself, tried to kill him in Paris, and when he might have blown my head off, he couldn't do it. He finally made his way back to us only through the extraordinary talents of a Canadian woman he met in Zurich who is now his wife. That lady had more guts and brains than any woman I've ever met. Now she and her husband and their two kids are back in the nightmare, running for their lives.'

Aristocratic mouth agape, his pipe in midair in front of his chest, the director spoke. 'Do you mean to sit there and tell us that the assassin we knew as Jason Bourne was an *invention*? That he *wasn't* the killer we all presumed he was?'

'He killed when he had to kill in order to survive, but he was no assassin. We created the myth as the ultimate challenge to Carlos, to draw the Jackal out.'

'Good *Christ*!' exclaimed Casset. '*How?*'

'Massive disinformation throughout the Far East. Whenever a killing of consequence took place, whether in Tokyo or Hong Kong, Macao or Korea – wherever – Bourne was flown there and took the credit, planting evidence, taunting the authorities, until he became a legend. For three years our man lived in a world of filth – drugs, warlords, crime, tunnelling his way in with only one objective: Get to Europe and bait Carlos, threaten his contracts, force the Jackal out into the open if only for a moment, just long enough to put a bullet in his head.'

The silence around the table was electric. DeSole broke it, his voice barely above a whisper. 'What kind of man would accept an assignment like that?'

Conklin looked at the analyst and answered in a monotone. 'A man who felt there wasn't much left to live for, someone who had a death wish, perhaps . . . a decent human being who was driven into an outfit like Medusa out of hatred and frustration.' The former intelligence officer stopped; his anguish was apparent.

'Come on, Alex,' said Valentino softly. 'You can't leave us with that.'

'No, of course not.' Conklin blinked several times, adjusting to the present. 'I was thinking how horrible it must be for him now – the memories, what he can remember. There's a lousy parallel I hadn't considered. The wife, the kids.'

'What's the parallel?' asked Casset, hunched forward, staring at Alex.

'Years ago, during Vietnam, our man was a young foreign service officer stationed in Phnom Penh, a scholar married to a Thai woman he'd met here in graduate school. They had two children and lived on the banks of a river . . . One morning while the wife and kids were swimming, a stray jet from Hanoi strafed the area killing the three of them. Our man went crazy; he chucked everything and made his way to Saigon and into Medusa. All he wanted to do was kill. He became Delta One – no names were ever used in Medusa – and he was considered the most effective guerrilla leader in the war, as often as not fighting Command Saigon over orders as he did the enemy with death squads.'

'Still, he obviously supported the war,' observed Valentino.

'Outside of having no use for Saigon and the ARVN, I don't think he gave a damn one way or another. He had his own private war and it was way behind enemy lines, the nearer Hanoi the better. I think in his mind he kept looking for the pilot who had killed his family . . . That's the parallel. Years ago there was a wife and two kids and they were butchered in front of his eyes. Now there's another wife and two children and the Jackal is closing in, hunting him down. That's got to be driving him close to the edge. *Goddamn* it!'

The four men at the opposite end of the table looked briefly at one another and let Conklin's sudden emotion pass. Again, the director spoke, again gently. 'Considering the time span,' he began, 'the operation mounted to trap Carlos had to have taken place well over a decade ago, yet the events in Hong Kong were much more recent. Were they related? Without giving us a name or names at this juncture, what do you feel you can tell us about Hong Kong?'

Alex gripped his cane and held it firmly, his knuckles white as he replied. 'Hong Kong was both the filthiest black operation ever conceived in this town and without question the most extraordinary I've ever heard of. And to my profound relief we here at Langley had nothing to do with the initial strategy, the plaudits can go to hell. I came in late and what I found turned my stomach. It sickened McAllister, too, for he *was* in at the beginning. It was why he was willing to risk his life, why he damn near ended up a corpse across the Chinese border in Macao. His intellectualized morality couldn't let a decent man be killed for the strategy.'

'That's a hell of an indictment,' offered Casset. 'What happened?'

'Our own people arranged to have Bourne's wife kidnapped, the woman who had led that man without a memory back to us. They left a trail that forced him to go after her – to Hong Kong.'

'Jesus, *why*?' cried Valentino.

'The strategy; it was perfect, and it was also abominable . . . I told you the "assassin" called Jason Bourne had become a legend in Asia. He disappeared in Europe, but he was no less a legend for that in the Far East. Then suddenly, out of nowhere, a new enterprising killer operating out of Macao revived that legend. He took the name of "Jason Bourne" and the killings for hire started all over again. A week rarely went by, often only days, when another hit was made, the same evidence planted, the same taunting of the police. A false Bourne was back in business, and he had studied every trick of the original.'

'So who better to track him down than the one who invented those tricks – the original, *your* original,' interjected the director. 'And what better way to force the original Bourne into the hunt than by taking his wife from him. But *why*? Why was Washington so consumed? There were no longer any ties to *us*.'

'There was something much worse. Among the new Jason Bourne's clients was a madman in Beijing, a Kuomintang traitor in the government who was about to turn the Far East into a fire storm. He was determined to destroy the Sino-British Hong Kong Accords, shutting down the colony, leaving the whole territory in chaos.'

'*War*,' said Casset quietly. 'Beijing would march into Hong Kong and take over. We'd all have to choose sides . . . *War*.'

'In the nuclear age,' added the director. 'How far had it all progressed, Mr Conklin?'

'A vice premier of the People's Republic was killed in a private massacre in Kowloon. The impostor left his calling card. "Jason Bourne." '

'Good God, he *had* to be stopped!' exploded the DCI, gripping his pipe.

'He was,' said Alex, releasing his cane. 'By the only man who could hunt him down. Our Jason Bourne . . . That's all I'll tell you for now except to repeat that man is back here with his wife and children, and Carlos is closing in. The Jackal won't rest until he knows the only person alive who can identify him is dead. So call in every debt that's owed to us in Paris, London, Rome, Madrid – especially *Paris*. Someone's got to know *something*. Where is Carlos *now*? Who are his points over *here*? He's got eyes here in Washington and whoever they are, they found Panov and me!' The former field officer again absently gripped his cane, staring at the window. 'Don't you see?' he added quietly, as if talking to himself. 'We can't let it happen. Oh, my *God*, we can't let it *happen*!'

Once more the emotional moment passed in silence as the men of the Central Intelligence Agency exchanged glances. It was as though a consensus had been reached among them without a word being said; three pairs of eyes fell on Casset. He nodded, accepting his selection as the one closest to Conklin, and spoke.

'Alex, I agree that everything points to Carlos, but before we start spinning our wheels in Europe, we have to be sure. We can't afford a false alarm because we'd be handing the Jackal a grail he'd have to go after, showing him how vulnerable we were where Jason Bourne is concerned. From what you've told us, Carlos would pick up on a long dormant operation known as Treadstone Seventy-one if only because none of our agents or subagents has been in his personal neighbourhood for over a decade.'

The retired Conklin studied Charles Casset's pensive, sharp-featured face. 'What you're saying is that if I'm wrong and it isn't the Jackal, we're ripping open a thirteen-year-old wound and presenting him with an irresistible kill.'

'I guess that's what I'm saying.'

'And I guess that's pretty good thinking, Charlie . . . I'm operating on externals, aren't I? They're triggering instincts but they're still externals.'

'I'd trust those instincts of yours far more than I would any polygraph—'

'So would I,' interrupted Valentino. 'You saved our personnel in five or six sector crises when all the indicators said you were wrong. However, Charlie's got a legitimate query. Suppose it isn't Carlos? We not only send the wrong message to Europe, but more important we've wasted time.'

'So stay out of Europe,' mused Alex softly, again as if to himself. 'At least for now . . . Go after the bastards *here*. Draw *them* out. Pull them in and break them. I'm the target, so let them come after me.'

'That would entail far looser protection than I envisage for you and Dr Panov, Mr Conklin,' said the director firmly.

'Then disenvisage, sir.' Alex looked back and forth at Casset and Valentino, suddenly raising his voice. 'We can *do* it if you two will listen to me and let me mount it!'

'We're in a grey area,' stated Casset. 'This thing may be foreign-oriented but it's domestic turf. The Bureau should be brought in—'

'No *way*,' exclaimed Conklin. '*Nobody's* brought in outside of this room!'

'Come on, Alex,' said Valentino kindly, slowly shaking his head. 'You're retired. You can't give orders here.'

'Good, *fine*!' shouted Conklin, awkwardly getting out of the chair and supporting himself on his cane. '*Next* stop the White House, to a certain chairman of the NSA named McAllister!'

'Sit *down*,' said the DCI firmly.

'I'm retired! You can't give orders to me.'

'I wouldn't dream of it, I'm simply concerned for your life. As I read the scenario, what you're suggesting is based on the questionable supposition that whoever fired at you last night intended to miss, not caring whom he hit, only determined to take you alive during the subsequent chaos.'

'That's a couple of leaps—'

'Based on a couple of dozen operations I've been involved with both here and at the Department of the Navy *and* in places you couldn't pronounce or know anything about.' The director's elbows were planted on the arms of his chair, his voice suddenly harsh, commanding. 'For your information, *Conklin*, I didn't suddenly bloom as a gold-braided admiral running naval intelligence. I was in the SEALs for a few years and made runs off submarines into Kaesong and later into Haiphong harbour. I *knew* a number of those Medusa pricks and I can't think of one that I didn't want to put a bullet in his head! Now *you* tell me there *was* one, and he became your "Jason Bourne" and you'll break your balls or bust open your heart to see that he stays alive and well and out of the Jackal's gun sights . . . So let's cut the crap, *Alex*. Do you want to work with me or not?'

Conklin slowly sank back in his chair, a smile gradually emerging on his lips. 'I told you I had no sweat with your appointment, *sir*. It was just intuition, but now I know why. You were a field man . . . I'll work with you.'

'Good, *fine*,' said the director. 'We'll work up a controlled surveillance and hope to Christ your theory that they want you alive is correct because there's no way we can cover every window or every rooftop. You'd better understand the risk.'

'I do. And since two chunks of bait are better than one in a tank of piranhas, I want to talk to Mo Panov.'

'You can't ask him to be a part of this,' countered Casset. 'He's not one of us, Alex. Why should he?'

'Because he *is* one of us and I'd *better* ask him. If I didn't he'd give me a flu shot filled with strychnine. You see, he was in Hong Kong, too – for reasons not much different from mine. Years ago I tried to kill my closest friend in Paris because I'd made a terrible mistake believing my friend had turned when the truth was that he had lost his memory. Only days later, Morris Panov, one of the leading psychiatrists in the country, a doctor who can't stand the chicken-shit psychobabble so popular these days, was presented with a "hypothetical" psychiatric profile that required his immediate reaction. It described a rogue deep-cover agent, a walking time bomb with a thousand secrets in his head, who had gone over the edge . . . On the basis of Mo's on-the-spot evaluation of that hypothetical profile – which he hours later suspected was no more hypothetical than Campbell's soup – an innocent amnesiac was nearly blown away in a government ambush on New York's Seventy-first Street. When what was left of that man survived, Panov demanded to be assigned as his *only* head doctor. He's never forgiven himself. If any of you were he, what would you do if I didn't talk to you about what we're talking about right now?'

'Tell you it's a flu shot and pump you full of strychnine, old boy,' concluded DeSole, nodding.

'Where is Panov now?' asked Casset.

'At the Brookshire Hotel in Baltimore under the name of Morris, Phillip Morris. He called off his appointments today – he has the flu.'

'Then let's go to work,' said the DCI, pulling a yellow legal pad in front of him. 'Incidentally, *Alex*, a competent field man doesn't concern himself with rank and won't trust a man who can't convincingly call him by his first name. As you well know, my name is Holland and my first name is Peter. From here on we're Alex and Peter, got it?'

'I've got it – Peter. You must have been one son of a bitch in the SEALs.'

'Insofar as I'm here – geographically, not in this chair – it can be assumed I was competent.'

'A field man,' mumbled Conklin in approval.

'Also, since we've dropped the diplomatic drivel expected of someone in this job, you should understand that I was a hard-nosed son of a bitch. I want pro input here, Alex, not emotional output. Is that clear?'

'I don't operate any other way, Peter. A commitment may be based in emotions and there's nothing wrong with that, but the execution of a strategy is ice-cold . . . I was never in the SEALs, you hard-nosed son of a bitch, but I'm also geographically here, limp and all, and that presumes I'm also competent.'

Holland grinned; it was a smile of youth belied by streaked grey hair, the grin of a professional momentarily freed of executive concerns so as to return to the world he knew best. 'We may even get along,' said the DCI. And then, as if to drop the last vestige of his directorial image, he placed his pipe on the table, reached into his pocket for a pack of cigarettes, popped one up to his mouth and snapped his lighter as he began to write on the legal pad. 'To hell with the Bureau,' he continued. 'We'll use only our men and we'll check every one out under a fast microscope.'

Charles Casset, the lean, bright heir apparent of the CIA's directorship, sat back in his chair and sighed. 'Why do I have the idea that I'm going to have to ride herd on both you gentlemen?'

'Because you're an analyst at heart, Charlie,' answered Holland.

The object of controlled surveillance is to expose those who shadow others so as to establish their identities or take them into custody, whichever suits the strategy. The aim in the present case was to trap the agents of the Jackal who had lured Conklin and Panov to the amusement park in Baltimore. Working through the night and most of the following day, the men of the Central Intelligence Agency formed a detail of eight experienced field personnel, defined and redefined the specific routes that Conklin and Panov were to take both individually and together for the next twenty-four hours – these routes covered by the armed professionals in swift progressive relays – and finally to design an irresistible rendezvous, unique in terms of time and location. The early morning hours at the Smithsonian Institution. It was the *Dionaea muscipula*, the Venus flytrap.

Conklin stood in the narrow, dimly lit lobby of his apartment house and looked at his watch, squinting to read the dial. It was precisely 2:35 in the morning; he opened the heavy door and limped out into the dark street, which was devoid of any signs of life. According to their plan he turned left, maintaining the pace agreed upon; he was to arrive at the corner as close to 2:38 as possible. Suddenly, he was alarmed; in a shadowed doorway on his right was the figure of a man. Unobtrusively Alex reached under his jacket for his Baretta automatic. There was nothing in the strategy that called for someone to be in a doorway on this section of the street! Then, as suddenly as he had been alarmed, he relaxed, feeling equal parts of guilt and relief at what he understood. The figure in shadows was an indigent, an old man in worn-out clothes, one of the homeless in a land of so much plenty. Alex kept going; he reached the corner and heard the low, single click of two fingers snapped apart. He crossed the avenue and proceeded down the pavement, passing an alleyway. The *alleyway.* Another *figure* . . . another old man in dishevelled clothing moving slowly out into the street and then back into the alley. Another derelict protecting his concrete cave. At any other time Conklin might have approached the unfortunate and given him a few dollars, but not now. He had a long way to go and a schedule to keep.

Morris Panov approached the intersection still bothered by the curious telephone conversation he had had ten minutes ago, still trying to recall each segment of the plan he was to follow, afraid to look at his watch to see if he had reached a specific place within a specific time span – he had been told *not* to look at his watch in the street . . . and why couldn't they say 'at approximately such and such' rather than the somewhat unnerving term 'time span', as if a military invasion of Washington were imminent. Regardless, he kept walking, crossing the streets he was told to cross, hoping some unseen clock kept him relatively in tune with the goddamned 'time spans' that had been determined by his striding back and forth between two pegs on some lawn behind a garden apartment in Vienna, Virginia . . . He would do anything for David Webb – good Christ, *anything*! – but this was insane . . . Yet, of course, it wasn't. They would not ask him to do what he was doing if it were.

What was *that*? A face in shadows peering at him, just like the other *two*! This one hunched over on a kerb, raising wine-soaked eyes up at him. Old men – weather-beaten, old, *old* men who could barely move – *staring* at him! Now, *he* was allowing his imagination to run away with him – the cities were filled with the homeless, with perfectly harmless people whose psychoses or poverty drove them into the streets. As much as he would like, there was nothing he could do but professionally badger an unresponsive Washington . . . There was *another*! In an indented space between two storefronts barricaded by iron gates – he, too, was *watching* him. *Stop* it! You're being irrational . . . Or was he? Of *course*, he was. Go *on*, keep to the schedule, that's what you're supposed to do . . . Good *God*! There's *another*. Across the street . . . keep *going*!

*

The vast moonlit grounds of the Smithsonian dwarfed the two figures as they converged from intersecting paths, joining each other and proceeding to a bench. Conklin lowered himself with the aid of his cane while Mo Panov looked around nervously, listening, as if he expected the unexpected. It was 3:28 in the predawn morning, the only noises the subdued rattle of crickets and mild summer breezes through the trees. Guardedly Panov sat down.

'Anything happen on the way here?' asked Conklin.

'I'm not sure,' replied the psychiatrist. 'I'm as lost as I was in Hong Kong, except that over there we knew where we were going, whom we expected to meet. You people *are* crazy.'

'You're contradicting yourself, Mo,' said Alex, smiling. 'You told me I was cured.'

'Oh, that? That was merely obsessive manic-depression bordering on dementia praecox. This is *nuts*! It's nearly four o'clock in the morning. People who aren't nuts do not play games at four o'clock in the morning.'

Alex watched Panov in the dim wash of a distant Smithsonian floodlight that illuminated the massive stone structure. 'You said you weren't sure. What does that mean?'

'I'm almost embarrassed to say – I've told too many patients that they invent uncomfortable images to rationalize their panic, justify their fears.'

'What the hell does *that* mean?'

'It's a form of transference—'

'Come on, Mo!' interrupted Conklin. 'What bothered you? What did you see?'

'Figures . . . some bent over, walking slowly, awkwardly – not like you, Alex, not incapacitated by injuries, but from age. Worn out and old and staying in the darkness of storefronts and side streets. It happened four or five times between my apartment house and here. Twice I almost stopped and called out for one of your men, and then I thought to myself, My God, *Doctor*, you're overreacting, mistaking a few pathetic homeless people for what they're not, seeing things that aren't there.'

'*Right* on!' Conklin whispered emphatically. 'You saw exactly what *was* there, Mo. Because I saw the same, the same kind of old people *you* saw, and they *were* pathetic, mostly in beat-up clothes and who moved slower than I move . . . What does it mean? What do *they* mean? Who are they?'

Footsteps. Slow, hesitant, and through the shadows of the deserted path walked two short men – old men. At first glance they, indeed, appeared to be part of the swelling army of indigent homeless, yet there was something different about them, a sense of purpose, perhaps. They stopped nearly twenty feet away from the bench, their faces in darkness. The old man on the left spoke, his voice thin, his accent strange. 'It is an odd hour and an unusual place for two such well-dressed gentlemen to meet. Is it fair for you to occupy a place of rest that should be for others not so well off as you?'

'There are a number of unoccupied benches,' said Alex pleasantly. 'Is this one reserved?'

'There are no reserved seats here,' replied the second old man, his English clear but not native to him. 'But why are *you* here?'

'What's it to you?' asked Conklin. 'This is a private meeting and none of your business.'

'Business at this hour and in this place?' The first aged intruder spoke while looking around.

'I repeat,' repeated Alex. 'It's none of your business and I really think you should leave us alone.'

'Business is business,' intoned the second old man.

'What in God's name is he *talking* about?' whispered the bewildered Panov to Conklin.

'Ground zero,' said Alex under his breath. 'Be quiet.' The retired field agent turned his head up to the two old men. 'Okay, fellas, why don't you go on your way?'

'Business is business,' again said the second tattered ancient, glancing at his colleague, both their faces still in shadows.

'You don't have any business with us—'

'You can't be sure of that,' interrupted the first old man, shaking his head back and forth. 'Suppose I were to tell you that we bring you a message from Macao?'

'*What?*' exclaimed Panov.

'Shut *up*!' whispered Conklin, addressing the psychiatrist but his eyes on the messenger. 'What does Macao mean to us?' he asked flatly.

'A great taipan wishes to meet with you. The greatest taipan in Hong Kong.'

'Why?'

'He will pay you great sums. For your services.'

'I'll say it again. *Why?*'

'We are to tell you that a killer has returned. He wants you to find him.'

'I've heard that story before; it doesn't wash. It's also repetitious.'

'That is between the great taipan and yourselves, sir. Not with us. He is waiting for you.'

'Where is he?'

'At a great hotel, sir.'

'Which one?'

'We are again to tell you that it has a great-sized lobby with always many people, and its name refers to this country's past.'

'There's only one like that. The Mayflower.' Conklin directed his words towards his left lapel, into a microphone sewn into the buttonhole.

'As you wish.'

'Under what name is he registered?'

'Registered?'

'Like in reserved benches, only rooms. Who do we ask for?'

'No one, sir. The taipan's secretary will approach you in the lobby.'

'Did that same secretary approach you also?'

'Sir?'

'Who hired you to follow us?'

'We are not at liberty to discuss such matters and we will not do so.'

'*That's it!* shouted Alexander Conklin, yelling over his shoulder as floodlights suddenly lit up the Smithsonian grounds around the deserted path, revealing the two startled old men to be Orientals. Nine personnel from the Central Intelligence Agency walked rapidly into the glare of light from all directions, their hands under their jackets. Since there was no apparent need for them, their weapons remained hidden.

Suddenly the need was there but the realization came too late. Two high-powered rifle shots exploded from the outer darkness, the bullets ripping open the throats of the two Oriental messengers. The CIA men lunged to the ground, rolling for cover as Conklin grabbed Panov, pulling him down to the path in front of the bench for protection. The unit from Langley lurched to their feet and, like the combat veterans they were, including the former commando Director Peter Holland, they started scrambling, zigzagging one after another towards the source of the gunfire, weapons extended, shadows sought. In moments, an angry cry split the silence.

'*Goddamn* it!' shouted Holland, the beam of his flashlight angled down between tree trunks. 'They made their break!'

'How can you tell?'

'The grass, son, the heel imprints. Those bastards were overqualified. They dug in for one shot apiece and got out – look at the slip marks on the lawn. Those shoes were running. Forget it! No use now. If they stopped for a second position, they'd blow us into the Smithsonian.'

'A *field* man,' said Alex, getting up with his cane, the frightened, bewildered Panov beside him. Then the doctor spun around, his eyes wide, rushing towards the two fallen Orientals.

'Oh, my God, they're *dead*,' he cried, kneeling beside the corpses, seeing their blown-apart throats. '*Jesus*, the amusement park! It's the *same*!'

'A message,' agreed Conklin, nodding, wincing. 'Put rock salt on the trail,' he added enigmatically.

'What do you mean?' asked the psychiatrist, snapping his head around at the former intelligence officer.

'We weren't careful enough.'

'*Alex!*' roared the grey-haired Holland, running to the bench. 'I heard you but this neuters the hotel,' he said breathlessly. 'You can't go there now. I won't let you.'

'It neuters – *fucks* up – more than the hotel. This isn't the Jackal! It's *Hong Kong*! The externals were right, but my instincts were wrong. *Wrong!*'

'Which way do you want to go?' asked the director softly.

'I don't know,' answered Conklin, a plaint in his voice. 'I was *wrong* . . . Reach our man, of course, as soon as possible.'

'I spoke to David – I spoke to *him* about an hour ago,' said Panov, instantly correcting himself.

'You *spoke* to him?' cried Alex. 'It's late and you were at home. *How?*'

'You know my answering machine,' said the doctor. 'If I picked up every crazy call after midnight, I'd never get to the office in the morning. So I let it ring and because I was getting ready to go out and meet you, I listened. All he said was "Reach me," and by the time I got to the phone, he'd hung up. So I called him back.'

'You called him *back*? On *your* phone?'

'Well . . . yes,' answered Panov hesitantly. 'He was very quick, very guarded. He just wanted us to know what was happening, that "M" – he called her "M" – was leaving with the children first thing in the morning. That was it; he hung up right away.'

'They've got your boy's name and address by now,' said Holland. 'Probably the message as well.'

'A location, yes; the message, maybe,' broke in Conklin, speaking quietly, rapidly. 'Not an address, not a name.'

'By morning they will have—'

'By morning he'll be on his way to Tierra del Fuego, if need be.'

'Christ, what have I *done*?' exclaimed the psychiatrist.

'Nothing anybody else in your place wouldn't do,' replied Alex. 'You get a message at two o'clock in the morning from someone you care about, someone in trouble, you call back as fast as you can. Now we have to reach him as fast as *we* can. So it's not Carlos, but somebody with a lot of firepower is still closing in, making breakthroughs we thought were impossible.'

'Use the phone in my car,' said Holland. 'I'll put it on override. There'll be no record, no log.'

'Let's go!' As quickly as possible, Conklin limped across the lawn towards the Agency vehicle.

'David, it's Alex.'

'Your timing's pretty scary, friend, we're on our way out the door. If Jamie hadn't had to hit the potty we'd be in the car by now.'

'At this hour?'

'Didn't Mo tell you? There was no answer at your place, so I called him.'

'Mo's a little shook up. Tell me yourself. What's happening?'

'Is this phone secure? I wasn't sure his was.'

'None more so.'

'I'm packing Marie and the kids off south – *way* south. She's screaming like hell but I chartered a Rockwell jet out of Logan Airport, everything precleared thanks to the arrangements you made four years ago. The computers spun and everyone cooperated. They take off at six o'clock, before it's light – I want them *out*.'

'And you, David? What about you?'

'Frankly, I thought I'd head to Washington and stay with you. If the Jackal's coming for me after all these years, I want to be in on what we're doing about it. I might even be able to help . . . I'll arrive by noon.'

'No, David. Not today and not here. Go with Marie and the children. Get out of the country. Stay with your family and Johnny St Jacques on the island.'

'I can't do that, Alex, and if you were me you couldn't, either. My *family*'s not going to be free – really *free* – until Carlos is out of our lives.'

'It's not Carlos,' said Conklin, interrupting.

'*What*? Yesterday you told me—'

'Forget what I told you, I was wrong. This is out of Hong Kong, out of Macao.'

'That doesn't make sense, Alex! Hong Kong's finished, *Macao*'s finished.

They're dead and forgotten and there's no one alive with a reason to come after me.'

'There is somewhere. A great taipan, "the greatest taipan in Hong Kong," according to the most recent and most recently dead source.'

'They're *gone.* That whole house of Kuomintang cards collapsed. There's no one left!'

'I repeat, there is somewhere.'

David Webb was briefly silent; then Jason Bourne spoke, his voice cold. 'Tell me everything you've learned, every detail. Something happened tonight. What was it?'

'All right, every detail,' said Conklin. The retired intelligence officer described the controlled surveillance engineered by the Central Intelligence Agency. He explained how he and Morris Panov spotted the old men who followed them, picking each up in sequence as they made their separate ways to the Smithsonian, none showing himself in the light until the confrontation on a deserted path on the Smithsonian grounds, where the messenger spoke of Macao and Hong Kong and a great taipan. Finally, Conklin described the shattering gunfire that silenced the two aged Orientals. 'It's out of Hong Kong, David. The reference to Macao confirms it. It was your impostor's base camp.'

Again there was silence on the line, only Jason Bourne's steady breathing audible. 'You're wrong, Alex,' he said at last, his voice pensive, floating. 'It's the Jackal – by way of Hong Kong and Macao, but it's still the Jackal.'

'David, now *you're* not making sense. Carlos hasn't anything to do with taipans or Hong Kong or messages from Macao. Those old men were *Chinese*, not French or Italian or German or whatever. This is out of Asia, *not* Europe.'

'The old men, they're the only ones he trusts,' continued David Webb, his voice still low and cold, the voice of Jason Bourne. '"The old men of Paris," that's what they were called. They were his network, his couriers throughout Europe. Who suspects decrepit old men, whether they're beggars or whether they're just holding on to the last remnants of mobility? Who would think of interrogating them, much less putting them on a rack? And even then they'd stay silent. Their deals were made – *are* made – and they move with impunity. For Carlos.'

For a moment, hearing the strange, hollow voice of his friend, the frightened Conklin stared at the dashboard, unsure of what to say. 'David, I don't understand you. I know you're upset – we're *all* upset – but please be clearer.'

'What? . . . Oh, I'm sorry, Alex, I was going back. To put it simply, Carlos scoured Paris looking for old men who were either dying or knew they hadn't long to live because of their age, all with police records and with little or nothing to show for their lives, their crimes. Most of us forget that these old men have loved ones and children, legitimate or not, that they care for. The Jackal would find them and swear to provide for the people his about-to-die couriers left behind if they swore the rest of their lives to him. In their places, with nothing to leave those who survive us but suspicion and poverty, which of us would do otherwise?'

'They *believed* him?'

'They had good reason to – they still have. Scores of bank cheques are delivered monthly from multiple unlisted Swiss accounts to inheritors from the Mediterranean to the Baltic. There's no way to trace those payments, but the people receiving them know who makes them possible and why . . . Forget your buried file, Alex. Carlos dug around Hong Kong, that's where his penetration was made, where he found you and Mo.'

'Then we'll do some penetrating ourselves. We'll infiltrate every Oriental neighbourhood, every Chinese bookie joint and restaurant, in every city within a fifty-mile radius of DC.'

'Don't do anything until I get there. You don't know what to look for, I do . . . It's kind of remarkable, really. The Jackal doesn't know that there's still a great deal I can't remember, but he just assumed that I'd forgotten about the old men of Paris.'

'Maybe he didn't, David. Maybe he's counting on the fact that you'd remember. Maybe this whole charade is a prelude to the real trap he's setting for you.'

'Then he made another mistake.'

'Oh?'

'I'm better than that. Jason Bourne's better than that.'

4

David Webb walked through the National Airport terminal and out the automatic doors onto the crowded platform. He studied the signs and proceeded across the walkway leading to the Short Term Parking area. According to plan, he was to go to the farthest aisle on the right, turn left, and continue down the row of parked cars until he saw a metallic grey 1986 Pontiac LeMans with an ornamental crucifix suspended from the rearview mirror. A man would be in the driver's seat wearing a white cap, the window lowered. Webb was to approach him and say, 'The flight was very smooth.' If the man removed his cap and started the engine, David was to climb in the backseat. Nothing more would be said.

Nothing more *was* said, not between Webb and the driver. However, the latter reached under the dashboard, removed a microphone and spoke quietly but clearly. 'Our cargo's on board. Please commence rotating vehicle cover.'

David thought that the exotic procedures bordered on the laughable, but since Alex Conklin had traced him to the Rockwell jet's departure area at Logan Airport, and, further, had reached him on Director Peter Holland's private override telephone, he assumed the two of them knew what they were doing. It crossed Webb's mind that it had something to do with Mo Panov's call to him nine hours ago. It was all but confirmed when Holland himself got on the phone insisting that he drive down to Hartford and take a commercial flight out of Bradley to Washington, adding enigmatically that he wanted no further telephone communication or private or government aircraft involved.

This particular government-oriented car, however, wasted no time getting out of National Airport. It seemed like only minutes when they were rushing through the countryside and, only minimally less rapidly, through the suburbs of Virginia. They swung up to the private gate of an expensive garden apartment complex, the sign reading VIENNA VILLAS, after the township in which it was located. The guard obviously recognized the driver and waved him through as the heavy bar across the entrance was raised. It was only then that the driver spoke directly to Webb.

'This place has five separate sections over as many acres, sir. Four of them are legitimate condominiums with regular owners, but the fifth, the one farthest from the gate, is an Agency proprietary with its own road and security. You couldn't be healthier, sir.'

'I didn't feel particularly sick.'

'You won't be. You're DCI cargo and your health is very important to him.'

'That's nice to know, but how do *you* know?'

'I'm part of the team, sir.'

'In that case, what's your name?'

The driver was silent for a moment, and when he answered, David had the uneasy feeling that he was being propelled back in time, to a time he knew he was re-entering. 'We don't have names, sir. You don't and I don't.'

Medusa.

'I understand,' said Webb.

'Here we are.' The driver swung the car around a circular drive and stopped in front of a two-storey attached Colonial structure that looked as though the fluted white pillars might have been made of Carrara marble. 'Excuse me, sir, I just noticed. You don't have any luggage.'

'No, I don't,' said David, opening the door.

'How do you like my temporary digs?' asked Alex, waving his hand around the tastefully appointed apartment.

'Too neat and too clean for a cantankerous old bachelor,' replied David. 'And since when did you go in for floral curtains with pink and yellow daisies?'

'Wait'll you see the wallpaper in my bedroom. It's got baby roses.'

'I'm not sure I care to.'

'Your room has hyacinths . . . Of course, I wouldn't know a hyacinth if it jumped up and choked me, but that's what the maid said.'

'The maid?'

'Late forties and black and built like a sumo wrestler. She also carries two popguns under her skirt and, rumour has it, several straight razors.'

'Some maid.'

'Some high-powered patrol. She doesn't let a bar of soap or a roll of toilet paper in here that doesn't come from Langley. You know, she's a pay grade *ten* and some of these clowns leave her tips.'

'Do they need any waiters?'

'That's good. Our scholar, Webb the waiter.'

'Jason Bourne's been one.'

Conklin paused, then spoke seriously. 'Let's get to him,' he said, limping to an armchair. 'By the way, you've had a rough day and it's not even noon, so if you want a drink there's a full bar behind those puce shutters next to the window . . . *Don't* look at me like that, our black Brünnhilde *said* they were puce.'

Webb laughed; it was a low, well-felt laugh as he looked at his friend. 'It doesn't bother you a bit, does it, Alex?'

'Hell, no, you know that. Have you ever hid any liquor from me when I visited you and Marie?'

'There was never any stress—'

'Stress is irrelevant,' Conklin broke in. 'I made a decision because there was only one other one to make. Have a drink, David. We have to talk and I want you calm. I look at your eyes and they tell me you're on fire.'

'You once told me that it's always in the eyes,' said Webb, opening the purplish shutters and reaching for a bottle. 'You can still see it, can't you?'

'I told you it was *behind* the eyes. Never accept the first level . . . How are Marie and the children? I assume they got off all right.'

'I went over the flight plan ad nauseam with the pilot and knew they were all right when he finally told me to get off his case or fly the run myself.' Webb poured a drink and walked back to the chair opposite the retired agent. 'Where are we, Alex?' he asked, sitting down.

'Right where we were last night. Nothing's moved and nothing's changed, except that Mo refuses to leave his patients. He was picked up this morning at his apartment, which is now as secure as Fort Knox, and driven to his office under guard. He'll be brought here later this afternoon with four changes of vehicles, all made in underground parking lots.'

'Then it's open protection, no one's hiding any longer?'

'That'd be pointless. We sprung a trap at the Smithsonian and our men were very obvious.'

'It's why it might work, isn't it? The unexpected? Backups behind a protection unit told to make mistakes.'

'The unexpected works. David, not the dumb.' Conklin quickly shook his head. 'I take that back. Bourne could turn the dumbs into smarts, but not an officially mounted surveillance detail. There are too many complications.'

'I don't understand.'

'As good as those men are, they're primarily concerned with guarding lives, may be saving them; they also have to coordinate with each other and make reports. They're career people, not one-shot, prepaid lowlifes with an assassin's knife at their throats if they screw up.'

'That sounds so melodramatic,' said Webb softly, leaning back in the chair and drinking. 'I guess I did operate like that, didn't I?'

'It was more image than reality, but it was real to the people you used.'

'Then I'll find those people again, use them again.' David shot forward, gripping his glass in both hands. 'He's forcing me *out*, Alex! The Jackal's calling my cards and I have to show.'

'Oh, shut up,' said Conklin irritably. 'Now you're the one who's being melodramatic. You sound like a Grade Z Western. You show yourself, Marie's a widow and the kids have no father. *That's* reality, David.'

'You're wrong.' Webb shook his head, staring at his glass. 'He's coming after me, so I have to go after him; he's trying to pull me out, so I have to pull him out first. It's the only way it can happen, the only way we'll get him out of our lives. In the final analysis it's Carlos against Bourne. We're back where we were thirteen years ago. "Alpha, Bravo, Cain, Delta . . . Cain is for Carlos and Delta is for Cain." '

'That was a crazy Paris code thirteen years ago!' interrupted Alex sharply. 'Medusa's *Delta* and his mighty challenge to the Jackal. But this *isn't* Paris and it's thirteen years *later*!'

'And in five more years it'll be eighteen, five years after that, twenty-three. What the hell do you want me to do? Live with the spectre of that son of a bitch over my family, frightened every time my wife or my children leave the house, living in fear for the rest of my life? . . . No, *you* shut up, field man! You know better than that. The analysts can come up with a dozen strategies and we'll use bits and pieces of may be six and be grateful, but when it gets down to the mud, it's between the Jackal and me . . . And I've got the advantage. I've got you on my side.'

Conklin swallowed while blinking. 'That's very flattering, David, maybe too flattering. I'm better in my own element, a couple of thousand miles away from Washington. It was always a little stifling for me here.'

'It wasn't when you saw me off on that plane to Hong Kong five years ago. You'd put together half the equation by then.'

'That was easier. It was a down-and-dirty DC operation that had the smell of rotten halibut, so rotten it offended my nostrils. This is different; this is Carlos.'

'That's my point, Alex. It *is* Carlos, not a voice over the telephone neither of us knew. We're dealing with a known quantity, someone predictable—'

'*Predictable?*' broke in Conklin, frowning. 'That's also crazy. In what way?'

'He's the hunter. He'll follow a scent.'

'He'll examine it first with a very experienced nose, then check the spoors under a microscope.'

'Then we'll have to be authentic, won't we?'

'I prefer foolproof. What did you have in mind?'

'In the gospel according to Saint Alex, it's written that in order to bait a trap one has to use a large part of the truth, even a dangerous amount.'

'That chapter and verse referred to a target's microscope. I think I just mentioned it. What's the relevance here?'

'Medusa,' said Webb quietly. 'I want to use Medusa.'

'Now you're *out* of your mind,' responded Conklin, no louder than David. 'That name is as off-limits as you are – let's be honest, a hell of a lot more so.'

'There were rumours, Alex, stories all over Southeast Asia that floated up the China Sea to Kowloon and Hong Kong, where most of those bastards ran with their money. Medusa wasn't exactly the secret evil you seem to think it was.'

'Rumours, yes, and stories, of course,' interrupted the retired intelligence officer. 'Which of those animals didn't put a gun or a knife to the heads of a dozen or two dozen or two *hundred* marks during their so-called "tours"? Ninety percent were killers and thieves, the original death squads. Peter Holland said that when he was a SEAL in the northern operations he never met a member of that outfit he didn't want to waste.'

'And without them, instead of fifty-eight thousand casualties, there could well have been sixty-plus. Give the animals their due, Alex. They knew every inch of the territories, every square foot of jungle in the triangle. They – *we* – sent back more functional intelligence than all the units sent out by Saigon put together.'

'My *point*, David, is that there can never be any connection between Medusa and the United States government. Our involvement was never logged, much less acknowledged; the name itself was concealed as much as possible. There's no statute of limitations on war crimes, and Medusa was officially determined to be a private organization, a collection of violent misfits who wanted the corrupt Southeast Asia back the way they knew it and used it. If it was ever established that Washington was behind Medusa, the reputation of some very important people in the White House and the State Department would be ruined. They're global power brokers now, but twenty years ago they were hotheaded junior staffers in Command Saigon . . . We can live with questionable tactics in time of war, but not with being accomplices in the slaughter of noncombatants and the diversion of funds totalling millions, both unknowingly paid for by the taxpayers. It's like those still-sealed archives that detail how so many of our fat-cat financiers bankrolled the Nazis. Some things we never want out of their black holes, and Medusa's one of them.'

Webb again leaned back in the chair – now, however, taut, his eyes steady on his old friend, who was once briefly his deadly enemy. 'If what memory I have left serves me, Bourne was identified as having come out of Medusa.'

'It was an entirely believable explanation and a perfect cover,' agreed Conklin, returning David's gaze. 'We went back to Tam Quan and "discovered" that Bourne was a paranoid Tasmanian adventurer who disappeared in the jungles of North Vietnam. Nowhere in that very creative dossier was there the slightest clue of a Washington connection.'

'But that's all a lie, isn't it, Alex? There was and is a Washington connection, and the Jackal *knows* it now. He knew it when he found you and Mo Panov in Hong Kong – found your names in the ruins of that sterile house on Victoria Peak where Jason Bourne was supposedly blown away. He confirmed it last night when his messengers approached you at the Smithsonian and – your words – "our men were very obvious". He knew finally that everything he's believed for thirteen years is true. The member of Medusa who was called Delta was Jason Bourne, and Jason Bourne was a creation of American intelligence – and he's still alive. Alive and in hiding and protected by his government.'

Conklin slammed his fist on the arm of his chair. 'How did he find us, find *me*? Everything, *everything*, was under a black drape. McAllister and I made sure of it!'

'I can think of several ways but that's a question we can postpone, we haven't time for it now. We have to move now on what we know Carlos knows . . . *Medusa*, Alex.'

'What? Move *how*?'

'If Bourne was plucked from Medusa, it has to follow that our covert operations were working with it – with them. Otherwise, how could the Bourne switch be created? What the Jackal doesn't know or hasn't put together yet is how far this government – especially certain people in this government – will go to keep Medusa in its black hole. As you pointed out, some very important men in the White House and the State Department could get burned, a lot of nasty labels branded on the foreheads of global power brokers, I think you called them.'

'And suddenly we've got a few Waldheims of our own.' Conklin nodded, frowning and looking down, his thoughts obviously racing.

'*Nuy Dap Ranh*,' said Webb, barely above a whisper. At the sound of the Oriental words, Alex's eyes snapped back up at David. 'That's the key, isn't it?' continued Webb. '*Nuy Dap Ranh* – Snake Lady.'

'You remembered.'

'Just this morning,' replied Jason Bourne, his eyes cold. 'When Marie and the kids were airborne, the plane disappeared into the mists over Boston harbour and suddenly I was there. In another plane, in another time, the words crackling out of a radio through the static. "Snake Lady. Snake Lady, abort . . . Snake Lady, do you read me? *Abort!*" I responded by turning the damn thing off and looked around at the men in the cabin, which seemed ready to break apart in the turbulence. I studied each man, wondering, I guess, whether this one or that one would come out alive, whether I'd come out alive, and if we didn't, how we would die . . . Then I saw two of the men rolling up their sleeves, comparing those small ugly tattoos on their forearms, those lousy little emblems that obsessed them—'

'*Nuy Dap Ranh*,' said Conklin flatly. 'A woman's face with snakes for strands of hair. Snake Lady. You refused to have one done on you—'

'I never considered it a mark of distinction,' interrupted Webb-Bourne, blinking. 'Somewhat the reverse, in fact.'

'Initially it was meant for identification, not a standard or a banner of any distinction one way or the other. An intricate tattoo on the underside of the forearm, the design and the colours produced by only one artist in Saigon. No one else could duplicate it.'

'That old man made a lot of money during those years; he was special.'

'Every officer in Command Headquarters who was connected to Medusa had one. They were like manic kids who'd found secret code rings in cereal boxes.'

'They weren't kids, Alex. Manic, you can bet your ass on it, but not kids. They were infected with a rotten virus called unaccountability, and more than a few millionaires were made in the ubiquitous Command Saigon. The real kids were being maimed and killed in the jungles while a lot of pressed khaki in the South had personal couriers routed through Switzerland and the banks on Zurich's Bahnhofstrasse.'

'Careful, David. You could be speaking of some very important people in our government.'

'Who are they?' asked Webb quietly, his glass poised in front of him.

'The ones I knew who were up to their necks in garbage I made damn sure faded after Saigon fell. But I was out of the field a couple of years before then, and nobody talks very much about those months and nothing at all about Snake Lady.'

'Still, you've got to have some ideas.'

'Sure, but nothing concrete, nothing even close to proof. Just possibilities based on life-styles, on real estate they shouldn't have or places they go they shouldn't be able to afford or the positions some hold or held in corporations justifying salaries and stock options when nothing in their backgrounds justified the jobs.'

'You're describing a network,' said David, his voice now tight, the voice of Jason Bourne.

'If it is, it's very tight,' agreed Conklin. 'Very exclusive.'

'Draw up a list, Alex.'

'It'd be filled with holes.'

'Then keep it at first to those important people in our government who were attached to Command Saigon. Maybe even further to the ones who have real estate they shouldn't have or who held high-paying jobs in the private sector they shouldn't have gotten.'

'I repeat, any such list could be worthless.'

'Not with your instincts.'

'David, what the *hell* has any of this to do with Carlos?'

'Part of the truth, Alex. A dangerous part, I grant you, but foolproof and irresistible to the Jackal.'

Stunned, the former field officer stared at his friend. 'In what way?'

'That's where your creative thinking comes in. Say you come up with fifteen or twenty names, you're bound to hit three or four targets we can confirm one way or another. Once we ascertain who they are, we apply pressure, squeezing them in different ways, delivering the same basic message: A former Medusan has gone over the edge, a man who's been in protective custody for years is about to blow the head off Snake Lady and he's got the ammunition – names, crimes, the locations of secret Swiss accounts, the whole Caesar salad. Then – and this'll test the talents of the old Saint Alex we all knew and revered – word is passed on that there's someone who wants this dangerous, disgruntled turncoat more than they do.'

'Ilich Ramirez Sanchez,' supplied Conklin softly. 'Carlos the Jackal. And what follows is equally impossible: Somehow – only God knows how – word gets out calling for a meeting between the two interested parties. That is to say, interested in a joint assassination, the parties of the first part unable to participate actively, due to the sensitive nature of their high official positions, is that about it?'

'Just about, except that these same powerful men in Washington can gain access to the identity and the whereabouts of this much desired corpse-to-be.'

'Naturally,' agreed Alex, nodding in disbelief. 'They simply wave a wand and all the restrictions applicable to maximum-classified files are lifted and they're given the information.'

'Exactly,' said David firmly. 'Because whoever meets with Carlos's emissaries has to be so high up, so authentic, that the Jackal has no choice but to accept him or them. He can't have any doubts, all thoughts of a trap gone with their coming forward.'

'Would you also like me to make baby roses bloom during a January blizzard in Montana?'

'Close to it. Everything's got to happen within the next day or two while Carlos is still stinging from what happened at the Smithsonian.'

'*Impossible!* . . . Oh, hell, I'll try. I'll set up shop here and have Langley send me what I need. Four Zero security, of course . . . I hate like hell to lose whoever it is at the Mayflower.'

'We may not,' said Webb. 'Whoever it is won't fold so fast. It's not like the Jackal to leave an obvious hole like that.'

'The Jackal? You think it's Carlos himself?'

'Not him, of course, but someone on his payroll, someone so unlikely he could carry a sign around his neck with the Jackal's name on it and we wouldn't believe him.'

'Chinese?'

'Maybe. He might play that out and then he might not. He's geometric; whatever he does is logical, even his logic seems illogical.'

'I hear a man from the past, a man who never was.'

'Oh, he *was*, Alex. He was indeed. And now he's back.'

Conklin looked towards the door of the apartment, David's words suddenly provoking another thought. 'Where's your suitcase?' he asked. 'You brought some clothes, didn't you?'

'No clothes, and these will be dropped in a Washington sewer once I have others. But first I have to see another old friend of mine, another genius who lives in the wrong section of town.'

'Let me guess,' said the retired agent. 'An elderly black man with the improbable name of Cactus, a genius where false papers such as passports and drivers' licences and credit cards are concerned.'

'That's about it. Him.'

'The Agency could do it all.'

'Not as well and too bureaucratically. I want nothing traceable, even with Four Zero security. This is solo.'

'Okay. Then what?'

'You get to work, field man. By tomorrow morning I want a lot of people in this town shaken up.'

'Tomorrow *morning* . . . ? That is *impossible*!'

'Not for you. Not for Saint Alex, the prince of dark operations?'

'Say whatever the hell you like, I'm not even in training.'

'It comes back quickly, like sex and riding a bicycle.'

'What about you? What are *you* going to do?'

'After I consult with Cactus, I'll get a room at the Mayflower hotel,' answered Jason Bourne.

Culver Parnell, hotel magnate from Atlanta whose twenty-year reign in the hostelry business had led to his appointment as chief of protocol for the White House, angrily hung up his office phone as he scribbled a sixth obscenity on a legal pad. With the election and now the turnover of White House personnel, he had replaced the previous administration's well-born female who knew nothing about the political ramifications of 1600's invitation list. Then, to his profound irritation, he found himself at war with his own first assistant, another middle-aged female, also from one of the ass-elegant Eastern colleges, and, to make it worse, a popular Washington socialite who contributed her salary to some la-di-da dance company whose members pranced around in their underwear when they wore any.

'*Hot damn!*' fumed Culver, running his hand through his fringed grey hair; he picked up the telephone and poked four digits on his console. 'Gimme the Redhead, you sweet thing,' he intoned, exaggerating his already pronounced Georgia accent.

'Yes, *sir*,' said the flattered secretary. 'He's on another line but I'll interrupt. Just hold on a sec, Mr Parnell.'

'You're the loveliest of the peaches, lovely child.'

'Oh, golly, *thank* you! Now just hold *on*.'

It never failed, mused Culver. A little soft oil from the magnolia worked a hell of a lot better than the bark of a gnarled oak. That bitch of a first assistant of his might take a lesson from her Southern superiors; she talked like some Yankee dentist had bonded her fucking teeth together with permanent cement.

'That you, Cull?' came the voice of Redhead over the line, intruding on Parnell's thoughts as he wrote a seventh obscenity on the legal pad.

'You're momma letchin' right, boy, and we got a *problem*! The fricassee bitch is doin' it again. I got our Wall Streeters inked in for a table at the reception on the twenty-fifth, the one for the new French ambassador and *she* says we gotta bump 'em for some core-dee-ballet fruitcakes – she says she and the *First Lady* feel mighty strong about it. *Shee-it!* Those money boys gotta lot of French interests goin' for them and this White House bash could put 'em on top. Every frog on the *Bourse* will think they got the ears of the whole town here!'

'Forget it, Cull,' broke in the anxious Redhead. 'We may have a bigger problem, and I don't know what it means.'

'What's that?'

'When we were back in Saigon, did you ever hear of something or someone called Snake Lady?'

'I heard a hell of a lot about snake eyes,' chuckled Parnell, 'but no Snake Lady. Why?'

'The fellow I was just talking to – he's going to call back in five minutes – sounded as though he was threatening me. I mean actually *threatening* me, Cull! He mentioned Saigon and implied that something terrible happened back then and repeated the name Snake Lady several times as if I should have run for cover.'

'You leave that son of a bitch to *me*!' roared Parnell, interrupting. 'I know *exactly* what that bastard's talking about! This is that snotty bitch first assistant of mine – *that's* the fuckin' Snake Lady! You give that slug worm my number and tell him I know all about his horseshit!'

'Will you please tell *me*, Cull?'

'What the hell, you were there, Redhead . . . So we had a few games going, even a few mini casinos, and some clowns lost a couple of shirts, but there was nothin' soldiers haven't done since they threw craps for Christ's *clothes*! . . . We just put it on a higher plane and maybe tossed in a few broads who'd have been walkin' the streets anyway . . . No, Redhead, that elegant-ass, so-called assistant, thinks she's got somethin' on me – that's why she's goin' through you,' cause everybody knows we're buddies . . . You tell that slime to call me and *I'll* settle his grits along with that bitch's twat! *Oh*, boy, she made a wrong move! My Wall Streeters are in and her pansies are *out*!'

'Okay, Cull, I'll simply refer him to you,' said the Redhead, otherwise known as the Vice President of the United States, as he hung up the phone.

It rang four minutes later and the words were spat out at Parnell. '*Snake Lady*, Culver, and we're all in trouble!'

'No, you listen to me, Divot Head, and I'll tell you who's in trouble! She's no lady, she's a *bitch*! One of her thirty or forty eunuch husbands may have thrown a few snake eyes in Saigon and lost some of her well-advertised come-and-take-me cash, but nobody gave a shit then and nobody gives a shit now. Especially a marine colonel who liked a sharp game of poker every once in a while, and that man is sitting in the Oval Office at this moment. And furthermore, you ball-less scrotum, when he learns that she's trying to further defame the brave boys who wanted only a little relaxation while fighting a thankless war—'

In Vienna, Virginia, Alexander Conklin replaced the phone. *Misfire One* and *Misfire Two* . . . and he had never heard of Culver Parnell.

The chairman of the Federal Trade Commission, Albert Armbruster, swore out loud as he turned off the shower at the sound of his wife's shrieking voice in the steam-filled bathroom. 'What the hell is it, Mamie? I can't take a shower without you *yammering*?'

'It could be the White House, Al! You know how they talk, so low and quiet and always saying it's urgent.'

'*Shit!*' yelled the chairman, opening the glass door and walking naked to the phone on the wall. 'This is Armbruster. What is it?'

'There's a crisis that requires your immediate attention.'

'Is this 1600?'

'No, and we hope it never goes up there.'

'Then who the hell *are* you?'

'Someone as concerned as you're going to be. After all these years – oh, *Christ*!'

'Concerned about *what*? What are you talking about?'

'Snake Lady, Mr Chairman.'

'Oh, my *God*!' Armbruster's hushed voice was a sudden involuntary cry of panic. Instantly, he controlled himself but it was too late. *Mark One.* 'I have no idea what you're talking about . . . What's a snake whatever-it-is? Never heard of it.'

'Well, hear it now, Mr *Medusa.* Somebody's got it all, everything. Dates, diversions of matériel, banks in Geneva and Zurich – even the names of a half-dozen couriers routed out of Saigon – and worse . . . Jesus, *the* worst! Other names – MIAs established as never having been in combat . . . eight investigating personnel from the inspector general's office. *Everything.*'

'You're not making sense! You're talking gibberish!'

'And you're on the list, Mr *Chairman.* That man must have spent fifteen years putting it together and now he wants payment for all those years of work or he blows it open – everything, *everyone.*'

'Who? Who *is* he, for Christ's sake?'

'We're centring in. All we know is that he's been in the protection programme for over a decade and no one gets rich in those circumstances. He must have been cut out of the action in Saigon and now he's making up for lost time. Stay tight. We'll be back in touch.' There was a click and the line went dead.

Despite the steam and the heat of the bathroom, the naked Albert

Armbruster, chairman of the Federal Trade Commission, shivered as the sweat rolled down his face. He hung up the phone, his eyes straying to the small, ugly tattoo on the underside of his forearm.

Over in Vienna, Virginia, Alex Conklin looked at the telephone.

Mark One.

General Norman Swayne, chief of Pentagon procurements, stepped back from the tee satisfied with his long straight drive down the fairway. The ball would roll to an optimum position for a decent five-iron approach shot to the seventeenth green. 'That ought to do it,' he said, turning to address his golfing partner.

'Certainly ought to, Norm,' replied the youngish senior vice president of Calco Technologies. 'You're taking my butt for a ride this afternoon. I'm going to end up owing you close to three hundred clams. At twenty a hole, I've only gotten four so far.'

'It's your hook, young fella. You ought to work on it.'

'That's certainly the truth, Norm,' agreed the Calco executive in charge of marketing as he approached the tee. Suddenly, there was the high granting sound of a golf cart's horn as a three-wheeled vehicle appeared over the incline from the sixteenth fairway going as fast as it could go. 'That's your driver, General,' said the armaments marketer, immediately wishing he had not used his partner's formal title.

'So it is. That's odd; he never interrupts my golf game.' Swayne walked towards the rapidly approaching cart, meeting it thirty feet away from the tee. 'What is it?' he asked a large, middle-aged beribboned master sergeant who had been his driver for over fifteen years.

'My guess is that it's rotten,' answered the noncommissioned officer gruffly while he gripped the wheel.

'That's pretty blunt—'

'So was the son of a bitch who called. I had to take it inside, on a *pay* phone. I told him I wouldn't break into your game, and he said I goddamned well better if I knew what was good for me. Naturally, I asked him who he was and what rank and all the rest of the bullshit but he cut me off, more scared than anything else. "Just tell the general I'm calling about Saigon and some reptiles crawling around the city damn near twenty years ago." Those were his exact words—'

'Jesus *Christ*!' cried Swayne, interrupting. '*Snake* . . . ?'

'He said he'd call back in a half hour – that's eighteen minutes now. Get in, Norman. I'm part of this, remember?'

Bewildered and frightened, the general mumbled. 'I . . . I have to make excuses. I can't just walk away, drive away.'

'Make it quick. And, *Norman*, you've got on a short-sleeved shirt, you goddamned idiot! Bend your arm.'

Swayne, his eyes wide, stared at the small tattoo on his flesh, instantly crooking his arm to his chest in British brigadier fashion as he walked unsteadily back to the tee, summoning a casualness he could not feel. 'Damn, young fella, the army calls.'

'Well, damn also, Norm, but I've got to pay you. I *insist*!'

The general, half in a daze, accepted the debt from his partner, not counting the bills, not realizing that it was several hundred dollars more than he was owed. Proffering confused thanks, Swayne walked swiftly back to the golf cart and climbed in beside his master sergeant.

'So much for my hook, soldier boy,' said the armaments executive to himself, addressing the tee and swinging his club, sending the little pocked white ball straight down the fairway far beyond the general's and with a much better lie. 'Four hundred million's worth, you brass-plated bastard.'

Mark Two.

'What in heaven's name are you *talking* about?' asked the senator, laughing as he spoke into the phone. 'Or should I say, what's Al Armbruster trying to pull? He doesn't need my support on the new bill and he wouldn't get it if he did. He was a jackass in Saigon and he's a jackass now, but he's got the majority vote.'

'We're not talking about votes, Senator. We're talking about *Snake Lady*!'

'The only snakes I knew in Saigon were jerks like Alby who crawled around the city pretending to know all the answers when there weren't any . . . Who the hell *are* you anyway?'

In Vienna, Virginia, Alex Conklin replaced the telephone.

Misfire Three.

Phillip Atkinson, ambassador to the Court of St James's, picked up his phone in London, assuming that the unnamed caller, code 'courier DC,' was bearing an exceptionally confidential instruction from the State Department and automatically, as was the order, Atkinson snapped the switch on his rarely used scrambler. It would create an eruption of static on British intelligence's intercepts and later he would smile benignly at good friends in the Connaught bar who asked him if there was anything new out of Washington, knowing that this one or that one had 'relatives' in MI5.

'Yes, Courier District?'

'Mr Ambassador, I assume we can't be picked up,' said the low, strained voice from Washington.

'Your assumption's correct unless they've come up with a new type of Enigma, which is unlikely.'

'Good . . . I want to take you back to Saigon, to a certain operation no one talks about—'

'Who *is* this?' broke in Atkinson, bolting forward in his chair.

'The men in that outfit never used names, Mr Ambassador, and we didn't exactly advertise our commitments, did we?'

'Goddamn you, who *are* you? I *know* you?'

'No way, Phil, although I'm surprised you don't recognize my voice.'

Atkinson's eyes widened as they roamed rapidly about his office, seeing nothing, only trying to remember, trying desperately to put a voice with a face. 'Is that you, Jack – *believe* me, we're on a scrambler!'

'Close, Phil—'

'The Sixth Fleet, Jack. A simple reverse Morse. Then bigger things, *much* bigger. It's *you*, isn't it?'

'Let's say it's a possible, but it's also irrelevant. The point is we're in heavy weather, *very* heavy—'

'It *is* you!'

'Shut up. Just listen. A bastard frigate got loose from its moorings and is crashing around, hitting too many shoals.'

'Jack, I was ground, not sea. I can't understand you.'

'Some swab-jockey must have been cut out of the action back in Saigon and from what I've learned he was put in protection for something or other and now he's got it all put together. He's got it *all*, Phil. *Everything*.'

'Holy Christ!'

'He's ready to launch—'

'*Stop* him!'

'That's the problem. We're not sure who he is. The whole thing's being kept very close over in Langley.'

'Good God, man, in your position you can give them the order to back off! Say it's a DOD dead file that was never completed – that it was designed to spread *disinformation*! It's all *false*!'

'That could be walking into a salvo—'

'Have you called Jimmy T over in Brussels?' interrupted the ambassador. 'He's tight with the top max at Langley.'

'At the moment I don't want anything to go any further. Not until I do some missionary work.'

'Whatever you say, Jack. You're running the show.'

'Keep your halyards taut, Phil.'

'If that means keep my mouth shut, don't you worry about it!' said Atkinson, crooking his elbow, wondering who in London could remove an ugly tattoo on his forearm.

Across the Atlantic in Vienna, Virginia, Alex Conklin hung up the telephone and leaned back in his chair a frightened man. He had been following his instincts as he had done in the field for over twenty years, words leading to other words, phrases to phrases, innuendos snatched out of the air to support suppositions, even conclusions. It was a chess game of instant invention and he knew he was a skilled professional – sometimes too skilled. There were things that should remain in their black holes, undetected cancers buried in history, and what he had just learned might well fit that category.

Marks Three, Four and Five.

Phillip Atkinson, ambassador to Great Britain. James Teagarten, supreme commander of NATO. Jonathan 'Jack' Burton, former admiral of the Sixth Fleet, currently chairman of the Joint Chiefs of Staff.

Snake Lady. Medusa.

A network.

5

It was as if nothing had changed, thought Jason Bourne, knowing that his other self, the self called David Webb, was receding. The taxi had brought him out to the once elegant, now run-down neighbourhood in northeast Washington and, as happened five years ago, the driver refused to wait. He walked up the overgrown flagstone path to the old house, thinking as he did the first time that it was too old and too fragile and too much in need of repair; he rang the bell, wondering if Cactus was even alive. He was; the old, thin black man with the gentle face and warm eyes stood in the doorframe exactly as he had stood five years before, squinting beneath a green eyeshade. Even Cactus's first words were a minor variation of those he had used five years ago.

'You got hubcaps on your car, Jason?'

'No car and no cab; it wouldn't stay.'

'Musta heard all those scurrilous rumours circulated by the fascist press. Me, I got howitzers in the windows just to impress this neighbourly turf of my friendly persuasion. Come on in, I think of you a lot. Why didn't you phone this old boy?'

'Your number's not listed, Cactus.'

'Musta been an oversight.' Bourne walked into the hallway as the old man closed the door. 'You got a few streaks of grey in your hair, Brer Rabbit,' added Cactus, studying his friend. 'Other than that you ain't changed much. Maybe a line or six in your face, but it adds character.'

'I've also got a wife and two kids, Uncle Remus. A boy and a girl.'

'I know that. Mo Panov keeps me up on things even though he can't tell me where you are – which I don't care to know, Jason.'

Bourne blinked while slowly shaking his head. 'I still forget things, Cactus. I'm sorry. I forgot you and Mo are friends.'

'Oh, the good doctor calls me at least once a month and says "Cactus, you rascal, put on your Pierre Cardin suit and your Gucci shoes and let's have lunch." So I say to him, "Where's this old nigger gonna get such threads?" and he says to me, "You probably own a shopping centre in the best part of town." . . . Now that's an exaggeration, s' help me. I do have bits and pieces of decent white real estate but I never go near them.'

As both men laughed, Jason stared at the dark face and warm black eyes in front of him. 'Something else I just remembered. Thirteen years ago in that hospital in Virginia . . . you came to see me. Outside of Marie and those government bastards you were the only one.'

'Panov understood, Brer Rabbit. When in my very unofficial status I worked on you for Europe, I told Morris that you don't study a man's face in a lens without learning things about that face, that man. I wanted you to talk about the things I found missing in that lens and Morris thought it might not be a bad idea . . . And now that confessional hour is over, I gotta say that it's really *good* to see you, Jason, but to tell you the truth I'm not *happy* to see you, if you catch my meaning.'

'I need your help, Cactus.'

'That's the root of my unhappiness. You've been through enough and you wouldn't be here unless you were itching for more, and in my professional, lens-peering opinion, that ain't healthy for the face I'm lookin' at.'

'You've got to help me.'

'Then you'd better have a damn good reason that passes muster for the good doctor. 'Cause I ain't gonna' mess around with anything that could mess you up further . . . I met your lovely lady with the dark red hair a few times in the hospital – she's somethin' special, Brer, and your kids have got to be outstanding, so you see I can't mess around with anything that might hurt them. Forgive me, but you're all like kinfolk from a distance, from a time we don't talk about, but it's on my mind.'

'They're why I need your help.'

'Be clearer, Jason.'

'The Jackal's closing in. He found us in Hong Kong and he's zeroing in on me and my family, on my wife and my children. Please, *help* me.'

The old man's eyes grew wide under the green shade, a moral fury in his expanded pupils. 'Does the good doctor know about this?'

'He's part of it. He may not approve of what I'm doing, but if he's honest with himself, he knows that the bottom line is the Jackal and me. *Help* me, Cactus.'

The aged negro studied his pleading client in the hallway, in the afternoon shadows. 'You in good shape, Brer Rabbit?' he asked. 'You still got juices?'

'I run six miles every morning and I press weights at least twice a week in the university gym—'

'I didn't hear that. I don't want to know anything about colleges or universities.'

'Then you didn't hear it.'

'Course I didn't You look in pretty fair condition, I'll say that.'

'It's deliberate, Cactus,' said Jason quietly. 'Sometimes it's just a telephone suddenly ringing, or Marie's late or out with the kids and I can't reach her . . . or someone I don't know stops me in the street to ask directions, and it comes back – *he* comes back. The Jackal. As long as there's a possibility that he's alive, I have to be ready for him because he won't stop looking for me. The awful irony is that his hunt is based on a supposition that may not be true. He thinks I can identify him but I'm not sure I could. Nothing's really in focus yet.'

'Have you considered sending that message to him?'

'With his assets maybe I'll take an ad out in the *Wall Street Journal*. "Dear Old Buddy Carlos: Boy, have I got news for *you*." '

'Don't chortle, Jason, it's not inconceivable. Your friend Alex could find a way. His gimp doesn't affect that head of his. I believe the fancy word is serpentine.'

'Which is why if he hasn't tried it there's a reason.'

'I guess I can't argue with that . . . So let's go to work, Brer Rabbit. What did you have in mind?' Cactus led the way through a wide archway towards a door at the rear of a worn-out living room replete with ancient furniture and yellowed antimacassars. 'My studio isn't as elegant as it was but all the equipment's there. You see, I'm sort of semi-retired. My financial planners worked out a hell of a retirement programme with great tax advantages so the pressure's not so great.'

'You're only incredible,' said Bourne.

'I imagine some people might say that, the ones not doin' time. What *did* you have in mind?'

'Pretty much myself. Not Europe or Hong Kong, of course. Just papers, actually.'

'So the Chameleon retreats to another disguise. Himself.'

Jason stopped as they approached the door. 'That was something else I forgot. They used to call me that, didn't they?'

'Chameleon? . . . They sure did and not without cause, as they say. Six people could come face-to-face with our boy Bourne and there'd be six different descriptions. Without a jar of make-up, incidentally.'

'It's all coming back, Cactus.'

'I wish to almighty God that it didn't have to, but if it does, you make damn *sure* it's all back . . . Come on into the magic room.'

Three hours and twenty minutes later the magic was completed. David Webb, Oriental scholar and for three years Jason Bourne, assassin, had two additional aliases with passports, driver's licences, and voter registration cards to confirm the identities. And since no cabs would travel out to Cactus's 'turf', an unemployed neighbour wearing several heavy gold chains around his neck and wrists drove Cactus's client into the heart of Washington in his new Cadillac Allanté.

Jason found a pay phone in Garfinkel's department store and called Alex in Virginia, giving him both aliases, and selecting one for the Mayflower hotel. Conklin would officially secure a room through the management in the event summer reservations were tight. Further, Langley would activate a Four Zero imperative and do its best to furnish Bourne with the material he needed, delivering it to his room as soon as possible. The estimate was a minimum of an additional three hours, no guarantees as to the time or authenticity. Regardless, thought Jason, as Alex reconfirmed the information on a second direct line to the CIA, he needed at least two of those three hours before going to the hotel. He had a small wardrobe to put together; the Chameleon was reverting to type.

'Steve DeSole tells me he'll start spinning the disks, cross-checking ours with the army data banks and naval intelligence,' said Conklin, returning to the line. 'Peter Holland can make it happen; he's the President's crony.'

'Crony? That's an odd word coming from you.'

'Like in crony appointment.'

'Oh? . . . Thanks, Alex. How about you? Any progress?'

Conklin paused, and when he answered his quiet voice conveyed his fear; it was controlled but the fear was there. 'Let's put it this way . . . I'm not equipped for what I've learned. I've been away too long. I'm afraid, Jason – sorry . . . David.'

'You're right the first time. Have you discussed—'

'*Nothing* by name,' broke in the retired intelligence officer quickly, firmly.

'I see.'

'You couldn't,' contradicted Alex. '*I* couldn't. I'll be in touch.' With these cryptic words Conklin abruptly hung up.

Slowly Bourne did the same, frowning in concern. Alex was the one now sounding melodramatic, and it was not like him to think that way or act that way. Control was his byword, understatement his persona. Whatever he had learned profoundly disturbed him . . . so much so as to make it seem to Bourne that he no longer trusted the procedures he himself had set up, or even the people he was working with. Otherwise he would have been clearer, more forthcoming; instead, for reasons Jason could not fathom, Alexander Conklin did not want to talk about Medusa or whatever he had learned in peeling away twenty years of deceit . . . Was it *possible*?

No time! No use, not now, considered Bourne, looking around the huge department store. Alex was not only as good as his word, he lived by it, as long as one was not an enemy. Ruefully, suppressing a short throated laugh, Jason remembered Paris thirteen years ago. He knew *that* side of Alex, too. But for the cover of gravestones in a cemetery on the outskirts of Rambouillet, his closest friend would have killed him. That was then, not now. Conklin said he'd 'be in touch'. He would. Until then the Chameleon had to build several covers. From the inside to the outside, from underwear to outerwear and everything in between. No chance of a laundry or a cleaning mark coming to light, no microscopic chemical evidence of a regionally distributed detergent or fluid – *nothing.* He had given too much. If he had to kill for David's family . . . oh, my *God*! For *my* family! . . . he refused to live with the consequences of that killing or those killings. Where he was going there were no rules; the innocent might well die in the crossfire. So be it. David Webb would violently object, but Jason Bourne didn't give a goddamn. He'd been there before; he knew the statistics, Webb knew nothing.

Marie, I'll *stop* him! I *promise* you I'll rip him out of your lives. I'll take the Jackal and leave a dead man. He'll never be able to touch you again – you'll be *free.*

Oh, *Christ,* who *am* I? Mo, help me! . . . No, Mo, *don't*! I am what I have to be. I am cold and I'm getting colder. Soon I'll be ice . . . clear, transparent ice, ice so cold and pure it can move anywhere without being seen. Can't you understand, Mo – you, too, Marie – I *have* to! David has to go. I can't have him around any longer.

Forgive me, Marie, and you forgive me, Doctor, but I'm thinking the truth. A truth that has to be faced right now. I'm not a fool, nor do I fool myself. You both want me to let Jason Bourne get out of my life, release him to some infinity, but the *reverse* is what I have to do now. David has to leave, at least for a while.

Don't bother me with such considerations! I have *work* to do.

Where the hell is the men's department? When he was finished making his purchases, all paid for in cash with as many different clerks as possible, he would find a men's room where he would replace every stitch of clothing on his body. After that he would walk the streets of Washington until he found a hidden sewer grate. The Chameleon, too, was back.

It was 7:35 in the evening when Bourne put down the single-edged razor blade. He had removed all the labels from the assortment of new clothes, hanging up each item in the closet when he had finished except for the shirts; these he steamed in the bathroom to remove the odour of newness. He crossed to the table, where room service had placed a bottle of Scotch whisky, club soda and a bucket of ice. As he passed the desk with the telephone he stopped; he wanted so terribly to call Marie on the island but knew he could not, not from the hotel room. That she and the children had arrived safely was all that mattered and they had; he had reached John St Jacques from another pay phone in Garfinkel's.

'Hey, Davey, they're bushed! They had to hang around the big island for damn near four hours until the weather cleared. I'll wake Sis if you want me to, but after she fed Alison she just crashed.'

'Never mind, I'll call later. Tell her I'm fine and take care of them, Johnny.'

'Will do, fella. Now you tell *me*. Are you okay?'

'I said I'm fine.'

'Sure, you can say it and she can say it, but Marie's not just my only sister, she's my favourite sister, and I know when that lady's shook up.'

'That's why you're going to take care of her.'

'I'm also going to have a talk with her.'

'Go easy, Johnny.'

For a few moments he had been David Webb again, mused Jason, pouring himself a drink. He did not like it; it felt wrong. An hour later, however, Jason Bourne was back. He had spoken to the clerk at the Mayflower about his reservation; the night manager had been summoned.

'Ah, yes, Mr *Simon*,' the man had greeted him enthusiastically. 'We understand you're here to argue against those terrible tax restrictions on business travel and entertainment. Godspeed, as they say. These politicians will ruin us all! . . . There were no double rooms, so we took the liberty of providing you with a suite, no additional charge, of course.'

All that had taken place over two hours ago, and since then he had removed the labels, steamed the shirts, and scuffed the rubber-soled shoes on the hotel's window ledge. Drink in hand, Bourne sat in a chair staring blankly at the wall; there was nothing to do but wait and think.

A quiet tapping at the door ended the waiting in a matter of minutes. Jason walked rapidly across the room, opened the door, and admitted the driver who had met him at the airport. The CIA man carried an attaché case; he handed it to Bourne.

'Everything's there, including a weapon and a box of shells.'

'Thanks.'

'Do you want to check it out?'

'I'll be doing that all night.'

'It's almost eight o'clock,' said the agent. 'Your control will reach you around eleven. That'll give you time to get started.'

'My control . . . ?'

'That's who he is, isn't he?'

'Yes, of course,' replied Jason softly. 'I'd forgotten. Thanks again.'

The man left and Bourne hurried to the desk with the attaché case. He opened it, removing first the automatic and the box of ammunition, then picking up what had to be several hundred computer printouts secured in file folders. Somewhere in those myriad pages was a name that linked a man or a woman to Carlos the Jackal. For these were the informational printouts of every guest currently at the hotel, including those who had checked out within the past twenty-four hours. Each printout was supplemented by whatever additional information was found in the data banks of the CIA, Army G-2, and naval intelligence. There could be a score of reasons why it might all be useless, but it was a place to start. The hunt had begun.

Five hundred miles north, in another hotel suite, this on the third floor of Boston's Ritz-Carlton, there was another tapping on another hotel door. Inside, an immensely tall man, whose tailored, pin-striped suit made him appear even larger than life than his nearly six feet five inches of height, came rushing out of the bedroom. His bald head, fringed by perfectly groomed grey hair above his temples, was like a crown of immaculate white skin capping the skull of an anointed éminence grise of some royal court where kings, princes and pretenders deferred to his wisdom – delivered no doubt with the eyes of an eagle and the soaring voice of a prophet. Although his rushing figure revealed a vulnerable anxiety, even it did not diminish his image. He was important and powerful and he knew it. All this was in contrast to the older man he admitted through the door. There was little that was distinguished about this short, gaunt, elderly visitor; instead, he conveyed the appearance of defeat.

'Come in. *Quickly!* Did you bring the information?'

'Oh, yes, yes, indeed,' answered the grey-faced man whose rumpled suit and ill-fitting collar had both seen better days perhaps a decade ago. 'How grand you look, Randolph,' he continued in a thin voice while studying his host and glancing around at the opulent suite. 'And how grand a place this is, so proper for such a distinguished professor.'

'The information, please,' insisted Dr Randolph Gates of Harvard, expert in antitrust law and highly paid consultant to numerous industries.

'Oh, give me a moment, my old friend. It's been a long time since I've been near a hotel suite, much less stayed in one . . . Oh, how things have changed for us over the years. I read about you frequently and I've watched you on television. You're so – erudite, Randolph, that's the word, but it's not enough. It's what I said before – "grand", that's what you are, grand and erudite. So tall and imperious.'

'You might have been in the same position, you know,' broke in the impatient Gates. 'Unfortunately, you looked for shortcuts where there weren't any.'

'Oh, there were lots of them. I just chose the wrong ones.'

'I gather things haven't gone well for you—'

'You don't "gather," Randy, you *know.* If your spies didn't inform you, certainly you can tell.'

'I was simply trying to find you.'

'Yes, that's what you said on the phone, what a number of people said to me in the street – people who had been asked a number of questions having nothing to do with my residence, such as it is.'

'I had to know if you were capable. You can't fault me for that.'

'Good heavens, no. Not considering what you had me do, what I *think* you had me do.'

'Merely act as a confidential messenger, that's all. You certainly can't object to the money.'

'Object?' said the visitor, with a high-pitched and tremulous laugh. 'Let me tell you something, Randy. You can be disbarred at thirty or thirty-five and still get by, but when you're disbarred at fifty and your trial is given national press along with a jail sentence, you'd be shocked at how your options disappear – even for a learned man. You become an untouchable, and I was never much good at selling anything but my wits. I proved that, too, over the last twenty-odd years, incidentally. Alger Hiss did better with greetings cards.'

'I haven't time to reminisce. The information, please.'

'Oh, yes, of course . . . Well, first the money was delivered to me on the corner of Commonwealth and Dartmouth, and naturally I wrote down the names and the specifics you gave me over the phone—'

'Wrote *down*?' asked Gates sharply.

'Burned as soon as I'd committed them to memory – I *did* learn a few things from my difficulties. I reached the engineer at the telephone company, who was overjoyed with your – excuse me – *my* largesse, and took his information to that repulsive private detective, a sleaze if I ever saw one, Randy, and considering his methods, someone who could really use my talents.'

'*Please*,' interrupted the renowned legal scholar. 'The facts, not your appraisals.'

'Appraisals often contain germane facts, Professor. Surely you understand that.'

'If I want to build a case, I'll ask for opinions. Not now. What did the man find out?'

'Based on what you told me, a lone woman with children – how many being undetermined – and on the data provided by an underpaid telephone company mechanic, namely, a narrowed-down location based on the area code and the first three digits of a number, the unethical sleaze went to work at an outrageous hourly rate. To my astonishment, he was productive. As a matter of fact, with what's left of my legal mind, we may form a quiet, unwritten partnership.'

'Damn you, what did he *learn*?'

'Well, as I say, his hourly rate was beyond belief, I mean it really invaded the corpus of my own well-deserved retainer, so I think we should discuss an adjustment, don't you?'

'Who the hell do you think you *are*? I sent you three thousand dollars! Five hundred for the telephone man and fifteen hundred for that miserable keyhole slime who calls himself a private detective—'

'Only because he's no longer on the public payroll of the police department, Randolph. Like me, he fell from grace, but he obviously does very good work. Do we negotiate or do I leave?'

In fury, the balding imperious professor of law stared at the grey-faced old disbarred and dishonoured attorney in front of him. 'How *dare* you?'

'Dear me, Randy, you really do believe your press, don't you? Very well, I'll tell why I dare, my arrogant old friend. I've read you, seen you, expounding on your esoteric interpretations of complex legal matters, assaulting every decent thing the courts of this country have decreed in the last thirty years, when you haven't the vaguest idea what it is to be poor, or hungry, or have an unwanted mass in your belly you neither anticipated nor can provide a life for. You're the darling of the royalists, my unprofound fellow, and you'd force the average citizen to live in a nation where privacy is obsolete, free thought suspended by censorship, the rich get richer, and for the poorest among us the beginnings of potential life itself may well have to be abandoned in order to survive. And you expound on these unoriginal, medieval concepts only to promote yourself as a brilliant maverick – of disaster. Do you want me to go on, *Doctor* Gates? Frankly, I think you chose the wrong loser to contact for your dirty work.'

'How . . . *dare* you?' repeated the perplexed professor, sputtering as he regally strode to the window. 'I don't have to listen to this!'

'No, you certainly don't, Randy. But when I was an associate at the law school and you were one of my kids – one of the best but not the brightest – you damn well had to listen. So I suggest you listen now.'

'What the hell do you *want*?' roared Gates, turning away from the window.

'It's what *you* want, isn't it? The information you underpaid me for. It's that important to you, isn't it?'

'I must have it.'

'You were always filled with anxiety before an exam—'

'*Stop* it! I *paid*. I demand the information.'

'Then I must demand more money. Whoever's paying you can afford it.'

'Not a dollar!'

'Then I'm leaving.'

'*Stop!* . . . Five hundred more, that's it.'

'Five thousand or I go.'

'*Ridiculous!*'

'See you in another twenty years—'

'All right . . . all *right*, five thousand.'

'Oh, Randy, you're so obvious. It's why you're not really one of the brightest, just someone who can use language to make yourself appear bright, and I think we've seen and heard enough of that these days . . . *Ten* thousand, Dr Gates, or I go to the raucous bar of my choice.'

'You can't *do* this.'

'Certainly I can. I'm now a confidential legal consultant. *Ten* thousand dollars. How do you want to pay it? I can't imagine you have it with you, so how will you honour the debt – for the information?'

'My word—'

'*Forget* it, Randy.'

'All right. I'll have it sent to the Boston Five in the morning. In your name. A bank cheque.'

'That's very endearing of you. But in case it occurs to your superiors to stop me from collecting, please advise them that an unknown person, an old friend of mine in the streets, has a letter detailing everything that's gone on between us. It is to be mailed to the Massachusetts Attorney General, Return Receipt Requested, in the event I have an accident.'

'That's absurd. The information, *please.*'

'Yes, well you should know that you've involved yourself in what appears to be an extremely sensitive government operation, that's the bottom line . . . On the assumption that anyone in an emergency leaving one place for another would do so with the fastest transportation possible, our rumbottom detective went to Logan Airport, under what guise I don't know. Nevertheless, he succeeded in obtaining the manifests of every plane leaving Boston yesterday morning from the first flight at six-thirty to ten o'clock. As you recall, that corresponds with the parameters of your statement to me – "leaving first thing in the morning".'

'*And?*'

'Patience, Randolph. You told me not to write anything down, so I must take this step by step. Where was I?'

'The *manifests.*'

'Oh, yes. Well, according to Detective Sleaze, there were eleven unaccompanied children booked on various flights, and eight women, two of them nuns, who had reservations with minors. Of these eight, including the nuns who were taking nine orphans to California, the remaining six were identified as follows.' The old man reached into his pocket and shakily took out a typewritten sheet of paper. 'Obviously, I did not write this. I don't own a typewriter because I can't type; it comes from Führer Sleaze.'

'Let me have it!' ordered Gates, rushing forward, his hand outstretched.

'Surely,' said the seventy-year-old disbarred attorney, giving the page to his former student. 'It won't do you much good, however,' he added. 'Our Sleaze checked them out, more to inflate his hours than for anything else. Not only are they all squeaky clean, but he performed that unnecessary service after the *real* information was uncovered.'

'What?' asked Gates, his attention diverted from the page. 'What information?'

'Information that neither Sleaze nor I would write down anywhere. The first hint of it came from the morning setup clerk for Pan American Airlines. He mentioned to our lowbrow detective that among his problems yesterday was a hotshot politician, or someone equally offensive, who needed diapers several minutes after our clerk went on duty at five forty-five. Did you know that diapers come in sizes and are locked away in an airline's contingency supplies?'

'What are you trying to tell me?'

'All the stores in the airport were closed. They open at seven o'clock.'

'So?'

'So someone in a hurry forgot something. A lone woman with a five-year-old child and an infant were leaving Boston on a private jet taking off on the runway nearest the Pan Am's shuttle counters. The clerk responded to the request and was personally thanked by the mother. You see, he's a young father and understood about diaper sizes. He brought three different packages—'

'For God's sake, will you get to the *point*, Judge?'

'Judge?' The grey-faced old man's eyes widened. 'Thank you, Randy. Except for my friends in various gin mills, I haven't been called that in years. It must be the aura I exude.'

'It was a throwback to that same *boring* circumlocution you used both on the bench and in the classroom!'

'Impatience was always your weak suit. I ascribed it to your annoyance with other people's points of view that interfered with your conclusions . . . Regardless, our Major Sleaze knew a rotten apple when the worm emerged and spat in his face, so he hied himself off to Logan's control tower, where he found a bribable off-duty traffic controller who checked yesterday morning's scheduless. The jet in question had a computer readout of Four Zero, which to our Captain Sleaze's astonishment he was told meant it was government-cleared and maximum-classified. No manifest, no names of anyone on board, only a routing to evade commercial aircraft and a destination.'

'Which *was*?'

'Blackburne, Montserrat.'

'What the hell is that?'

'The Blackburne Airport on the Caribbean island of Montserrat.'

'That's where they went? That's *it*?'

'Not necessarily. According to Corporal Sleaze, who I must say does his follow-ups, there are small flight connections to a dozen or so minor offshore islands.'

'*That's* it?'

'That's it, Professor. And considering the fact that the aircraft in question had a Four Zero government classification, which, incidentally, in my letter to the attorney general I so specified, I think I've earned my ten thousand dollars.'

'You drunken *scum*—'

'Again, you're wrong, Randy,' interrupted the judge. 'Alcoholic, certainly, drunk hardly ever. I stay on the edge of sobriety. It's my one reason for living. You see in my cognisance I'm always amused – by men like you, actually.'

'Get out of here,' said the professor ominously.

'You're not even going to offer me a drink to help support this dreadful habit of mine? . . . Good heavens, there must be half a dozen unopened bottles over there.'

'Take one and leave.'

'Thank you, I believe I will.' The old judge walked to a cherry-wood table against the wall where two silver trays held various whiskies and a brandy. 'Let's see,' he continued, picking up several white cloth napkins and wrapping them around two bottles, then a third. 'If I hold these tightly under my arm, they could be a pile of laundry I'm taking out for quick service.'

'Will you *hurry*!'

'Will you please open the door for me? I'd hate like hell dropping one of these while manipulating the knob. If it smashed it wouldn't do much for your image, either. You've never been known to have a drink, I believe.'

'Get *out*,' insisted Gates, opening the door for the old man.

'Thank you, Randy,' said the judge, walking out into the hallway and turning. 'Don't forget the bank cheque at the Boston Five in the morning. Fifteen thousand.'

'*Fifteen . . .?*'

'My word, can you imagine what the attorney general would say just knowing that you'd even consorted with me? Goodbye, Counsellor.'

Randolph Gates slammed the door and ran into the bedroom, to the bedside telephone. The smaller enclosure was reassuring, as it removed him from the exposure to scrutiny inherent in larger areas – the room was more private, more personal, less open to invasion. The call he had to make so unnerved him he could not understand the pull-out flap of instructions for overseas connections. Instead, in his anxiety, he dialled the operator.

'I want to place a call to Paris,' he said.

6

Bourne's eyes were tired, the strain painful as he studied the results of the computer printouts spread across the coffee table in front of the couch. Sitting forward, he had analysed them for nearly four hours, forgetting time, forgetting that his 'control' was to have reached him by then, concerned only with a link to the Jackal at the Mayflower hotel.

The first group, which he temporarily put aside, was the foreign nationals, a mix of British, Italian, Swedish, West German, Japanese and Taiwanese. Each of them had been extensively examined with respect to authentic credentials and fully substantiated business or personal reasons for entering the country. The State Department and the Central Intelligence Agency had done their homework. Each person was professionally and personally vouched for by a minimum of five reputable individuals or companies; all had long-standing communications with such people and firms in the Washington area; none had a false or questionable statement on record. If the Jackal's man was among them – and he might well be – it would take far more information than was to be found in the printouts before Jason could refine the list. It might be necessary to go back to this group, but for the moment he had to keep reading. There was so little time!

Of the remaining five hundred or so American guests at the hotel, two hundred and twelve had entries in one or more of the intelligence data banks, the majority because they had business with the government. However, seventy-eight had raw-file negative evaluations. Thirty-one were Internal Revenue Service matters which meant they were suspected of destroying or falsifying financial records and/or had tax havens in Swiss or Cayman Island accounts. They were zero, nothing, merely rich and not very bright thieves, and, further, the sort of 'messengers' Carlos would avoid like lepers.

That left forty-seven possibles. Men and women – in eleven cases ostensibly husbands and wives – with extensive connections in Europe, in the main with technological firms and related nuclear and aerospace industries, all under intelligence microscopes for possibly selling classified information to brokers of the Eastern bloc and therefore to Moscow. Of these forty-seven possibles, including two of the eleven couples, an even dozen had made recent trips to the Soviet Union – scratch *all* of them. The *Komitet Gosudarstvennoi Bezopasnosti*, otherwise known as the KGB, had less use for the Jackal than the Pope. Ilich Ramirez Sanchez, later Carlos the assassin, had been trained in the American compound of Novgorod, where the streets were lined with American gas stations and grocery stores, boutiques and Burger Kings, and everyone spoke American/English with diverse dialects – no Russian was allowed – and only those who passed the course were permitted to proceed to the next level of infiltrators. The Jackal had, indeed, passed, but when the *Komitet* discovered that the young Venezuelan revolutionary's solution for all things disagreeable was to eliminate them violently, it was too much for even the inheritors of the brutal OGPU. Sanchez was expelled and Carlos the Jackal was born. Forget about the twelve people who had travelled to the Soviet Union. The assassin would not touch them for there was a standing order in all branches of Russian intelligence that if Carlos was tracked he was to be shot. Novgorod was to be protected at all cost.

The possibles were thus narrowed to thirty-five, the hotel's register listing them as nine couples, four single women, and thirteen single men. The raw-file printouts from the data banks described in detail the facts and speculations that resulted in the negative evaluation of each individual. In truth, the speculations far outnumbered the facts and were too often based on hostile appraisal given by enemies or competitors, but each had to be studied, many with distaste, for among the information might be a word or phrase, a location or an act, that was the link to Carlos.

The telephone rang, breaking Jason's concentration. He blinked at the harsh, intrusive sound as if trying to locate the source, then he sprang from the couch and rushed to the desk, reaching the phone on the third ring.

'Yes?'

'It's Alex. I'm calling from down the street.'

'Are you coming up?'

'Not through that lobby, I'm not. I've made arrangements for the service entrance, with a temporary guard hired this afternoon.'

'You're covering all the bases, aren't you?'

'Nowhere near as many as I'd like to,' replied Conklin. 'This isn't your normal ball game. See you in a few minutes. I'll knock once.'

Bourne hung up the phone and returned to the couch and the printouts, separating three that had caught his attention, not that any of them contained anything that evoked the Jackal, for they did not. Instead, it was seemingly offhand data that might conceivably, link the three to each other when no apparent connection existed between them. According to their passports, these three Americans had flown in to Philadelphia's International Airport within six days of one another eight months ago. Two women and a man, the women from Marrakesh and Lisbon, the man from West Berlin. The first woman was an interior decorator on a collecting trip to the old Moroccan city, the second an executive for the Chase Bank, Foreign Department; the man was an aerospace engineer on loan to the Air Force from McDonnell-Douglas. Why would three such obviously different people, with such dissimilar professions, converge on the same city within a week of one another? Coincidence? Entirely possible, but considering the number of international airports in the country, including the most frequented – New York, Chicago, Los Angeles, Miami – the coincidence of Philadelphia seemed unlikely. Stranger still, and even more unlikely, was the fact that these same three people were staying at the same hotel at the same time in Washington eight months later. Jason wondered what Alex Conklin would say when he told him.

'I'm getting the book on each of them,' said Alex, sinking into an armchair across from the couch and the printouts.

'You *knew*?'

'It wasn't hard to put together. Of course, it was a hell of a lot easier with a computer doing the scanning.'

'You might have included a note! I've been poring over these things since eight o'clock.'

'I didn't find it – them – until after nine and I didn't want to call you from Virginia.'

'That's another story, isn't it?' said Bourne, sitting down on the couch, once again leaning forward anxiously.

'Yes, it is, and it's God-awful.'

'Medusa?'

'It's worse than I thought, and worse than that, I didn't think it could be.'

'That's a mouthful.'

'It's a bowelful,' countered the retired intelligence officer. 'Where do I start? . . . Pentagon procurements? The Federal Trade Commission? Our ambassador in London, or would you like the Supreme Commander of NATO?'

'My *God* . . .!'

'Oh, I can go one better. For size, try on the chairman of the Joint Chiefs.'

'Christ, what is it? Some kind of *cabal*?'

'That's so academic, Dr Scholar. Now try collusion, down deep and elusive and after all these years still breathing, still alive. They're in contact with each other in high places. Why?'

'What's the purpose? The objective?'

'I just said that, asked that, really.'

'There has to be a *reason*!'

'Try motive. I just said that, too, and it may be as simple as hiding past sins. Isn't that what we are looking for? A collection of former Medusans who'd run to the hills at the thought of the past coming to light?'

'Then that's it.'

'No, it's not, and this is Saint Alex's instincts searching for words. Their reactions were too immediate, too visceral, too loaded with today, not twenty years ago.'

'You've lost me.'

'I've lost myself. Something's different from what we expected, and I'm goddamned sick of making mistakes . . . But this isn't a mistake. You said this morning that it could be a network, and I thought you were way the hell off base. I thought that maybe we'd find a few high profiles who didn't want to be publicly drawn and quartered for things they did twenty years ago, or who legitimately didn't want to embarrass the government, and we could use them, force them in their collective fear to do things and say things we told them to do. But this is different. It's *today*, and I can't figure it out. It's more than fear, it's panic; they're frightened out of their minds . . . We've bumbled and stumbled onto something, Mr Bourne, and in your rich friend Cactus's old-time minstrel show language, "in the focus, it could be bigger than bo'fus".'

'In my considered opinion there's *nothing* bigger than the Jackal! Not for me. The rest can go to hell.'

'I'm on *your* side and I'll go to the wall shouting it. I just wanted you to know my thoughts . . . Except for a brief and pretty rotten interlude, we never kept anything from each other, David.'

'I prefer Jason these days.'

'Yes, I know,' interrupted Conklin. 'I hate it but I understand.'

'*Do* you?'

'Yes,' said Alex softly, nodding as he closed his eyes. 'I'd do anything to change it but I can't.'

'Then *listen* to me. In that serpentine mind of yours – Cactus's description, incidentally – conjure up the worst scenario you can think of and shove those bastards against another wall, one they can't get away from unscathed unless they follow your instructions down to the letter. Those orders will be to stay quiet and wait for you to call and tell them who to reach and what to say.'

Conklin looked over at his damaged friend with guilt and concern. 'There may be a scenario in place that I can't match,' said Alex quietly. 'I won't make another mistake, not in that area. I need more than what I've got.'

Bourne clasped his hands, flesh angrily grinding flesh in frustration. He stared at the scattered printouts in front of him, frowning, wincing, his jaw pulsating. In seconds a sudden passivity came over him; he sat back on the couch and spoke as quietly as Conklin. 'All right, you'll get it. Quickly.'

'How?'

'Me. I'll get it for you. I'll need names, residences, schedules and methods of security, favourite restaurants and bad habits, if any are known. Tell your boys to go to work. Tonight. All night, if necessary.'

'What the hell do you think you're going to *do*?' shouted Conklin, his frail body lurching forward in the armchair. 'Storm their houses? Stick needles in their asses between an appetizer and the entrée?'

'I hadn't thought of the last option,' replied Jason, smiling grimly. 'You've really got a terrific imagination.'

'And you're a *madman*! . . . I'm sorry, I didn't mean that—'

'Why not?' broke in Bourne gently. 'I'm not lecturing on the rise of the Manchu and the Ching dynasty. Considering the accepted state of my mind and memory, the allusion to mental health isn't inappropriate.' Jason paused, then spoke as he leaned slowly forward. 'But let me tell you something, Alex. The memories may not all be there, but the part of my mind that you and Treadstone formed is *all* be there. I proved it in Hong Kong, in Beijing and Macao, and I'll prove it again. I *have* to. There's nothing left for me if I don't . . . Now, get me the information. You mentioned several people who have to be here in Washington. Pentagon supplies or provisions—'

'Procurements,' corrected Conklin. 'It's a lot more expansive and expensive; he's a general named Swayne. Then there's Armbruster, he's head of the Federal Trade Commission, and Burton over at—'

'Chairman of the Joint Chiefs,' completed Bourne. 'Admiral "Joltin" Jack Burton, commander of the Sixth Fleet.'

'One and the same. Formerly the scourge of the South China Sea, now the largest of the large brass.'

'I repeat,' said Jason. 'Tell your boys to go to work. Peter Holland will get you all the help you need. Find me everything there is on each of them.'

'I can't.'

'*What?*'

'I can get us the books on our three Philadelphians because they're part of the immediate Mayflower project – that's the Jackal. I can't touch our five – so far, five – inheritors of Medusa.'

'For Christ's sake, why *not*? You *have* to. We can't waste time!'

'Time wouldn't mean much if both of us were dead. It wouldn't help Marie or the children either.'

'What the hell are you talking about?'

'Why I'm late. Why I didn't want to call you from Virginia. Why I reached Charlie Casset to pick me up at that real estate proprietary in Vienna, and why, until he got there, I wasn't sure I'd ever get here alive.'

'Spell it out, field man.'

'All right, I will . . . I've said nothing to anyone about going after former Medusa personnel – that was between you and me, nobody else.'

'I wondered. When I spoke to you this afternoon you were playing it close. Too close, I thought, considering where you were and the equipment you were using.'

'The rooms and the equipment proved secure. Casset told me later that the Agency doesn't want any traceable records of anything that takes place over there, and that's the best guarantee you can ask for. No bugs, no phone intercepts, nothing. Believe me, I breathed a lot easier when I heard that.'

'Then what's the problem? Why are you *stopping*?'

'Because I have to figure out another admiral before I move any further into Medusa territory . . . Atkinson, our impeccable WASP ambassador to the Court of St James's in London, was very clear. In his panic, he pulled the masks off Burton and Teagarten in Brussels.'

'So?'

'He said Teagarten could handle the Agency if anything about the old Saigon surfaced – because he was very tight with the top max at Langley.'

'*And?*'

'"Top max" is the Washington euphemism for maximum-classified security, and where Langley is concerned that's the director of Central Intelligence . . . That's also Peter Holland.'

'You told me this morning he'd have no problem wasting any *member* of Medusa.'

'Anyone can say anything. But would he?'

Across the Atlantic, in the old Paris suburb of Neuilly-sur-Seine, an old man in a dark threadbare suit trudged up the concrete path towards the entrance of the sixteenth-century cathedral known as the Church of the Blessed Sacrament. The bells in the tower above tolled the first Angelus and the man stopped in the morning sunlight, blessing himself and whispering to the sky.

'*Angelus domini nuntiavit Mariae.*' With his right hand he blew a kiss to the bas-relief crucifix atop the stone archway and proceeded up the steps and through the huge doors of the cathedral, aware that two robed priests eyed him with distaste. *I apologise for defiling your rich parish, you tight-assed snobs,* he thought as he lit a candle and placed it in the prayer rack, *but Christ made it clear that he preferred me to you. 'The meek shall inherit the earth' – what you haven't stolen of it.*

The old man moved cautiously down the centre aisle, his right hand gripping the backs of successive pews for balance, his left fingering the rim of his outsized collar and slipping down to his tie so as to make sure the knot had not somehow come apart. His woman was so weak now that she could barely fold the damn thing together, but, as in the old days, she insisted on putting the finishing touches on his appearance before he went to work. She was still a good woman; they had both laughed, remembering the time she swore at his cuff links over forty years ago because she had put too much starch in his shirt. That night, so long ago, she had wanted him to look the proper bureaucrat when he went to the whore-mongering Oberführer's headquarters on the rue St Lazare carrying a briefcase – a briefcase that, left behind, had blown up half the block. And twenty years later, one winter afternoon she'd had trouble making his expensive stolen overcoat hang properly on his shoulders before he set off to rob the Grande Banque Louis IX on the Madeleine, run by an educated but unappreciative former member of the Résistance who refused him a loan. Those were the good times, followed by bad times and bad health, which led to worse times – in truth, destitute times. Until a man came along, a strange man with an odd calling and an even odder unwritten contract. After that, respect returned in the form of sufficient money for decent food and acceptable wine, for clothes that fit, making his woman look pretty again, and most important, for the doctors who made his woman feel better. The suit and shirt he wore today had been dug out of a closet. In many ways he and his woman were like the actors in a provincial touring company. They had costumes for their various roles. It was their business . . . Today was business. This morning, with the bells of the Angelus, was business.

The old man awkwardly, only partially, genuflected in front of the holy cross and knelt down in the first seat of the sixth row from the altar, his eyes on his watch. Two and a half minutes later he raised his head and, as unobtrusively as possible, glanced around. His weakened sight had adjusted to the dim light of the cathedral; he could see, not well but clearly enough. There were no more than twenty worshippers scattered about, most in prayer, the others staring in meditation at the enormous gold crucifix on the altar. Yet these were not what he was looking for; and then he saw what he was looking for and knew that everything was on schedule. A priest in a priestly black suit walked down the far left aisle and disappeared beyond the dark red drapes of the apse.

The old man again looked at his watch, for everything now was timing; that was the way of the monseigneur. That was the way of the Jackal. Again two minutes passed and the aged courier got unsteadily up from his pew, sidestepped into the aisle, genuflected as best his body would permit, and made his way, step by imperfect step, to the second confessional booth on the left. He pulled back the curtain and went inside.

'Angelus Domini,' he whispered, kneeling and repeating the words he had spoken several hundred times over the past fifteen years.

'Angelus Domini, child of God,' replied the unseen figure behind the black latticework. The blessing was accompanied by a low rattling cough. 'Are your days comfortable?'

'Made more so by an unknown friend . . . my friend.'

'What does the doctor say about your woman?'

'He says to me what he does not say to her, thanks be for the mercy of Christ. It appears that against the odds I will outlive her. The wasting sickness is spreading.'

'My sympathies. How long does she have?'

'A month, no more than two. Soon she will be confined to her bed . . . Soon the contract between us will be void.'

'Why is that?'

'You will have no further obligations to me, and I accept that. You've been good to us and I've saved a little and my wants are few. Frankly, knowing what's facing me, I'm feeling terribly tired—'

'You insufferable *ingrate*!' whispered the voice behind the confessional screen. 'After all I've done, all I've promised you!'

'I beg your pardon?'

'Would you *die* for me?'

'Of course, that's our contract.'

'Then, conversely, you will *live* for me!'

'If that's what you want, naturally I will. I simply wanted you to know that soon I would no longer be a burden to you. I am easily replaced.'

'Do not presume, *never* with me!' The anger erupted in a hollow cough, a cough that seemed to confirm the rumour that had spread through the dark streets of Paris. The Jackal himself was ill, perhaps deathly ill.

'You are our life, our respect. Why should I do that?'

'You just did . . . Nevertheless, I have an assignment for you that will ease your woman's departure for both of you. You will have a holiday in a lovely part of the world, the two of you together. You will pick up the papers and the money at the usual place.'

'Where are we going, if I may ask?'

'To the Caribbean island of Montserrat. Your instructions will be delivered to you there at the Blackburne Airport. Follow them precisely.'

'Of course . . . Again, if I may ask, what is my objective?'

'To find and befriend a mother and two children.'

'Then what?'

'Kill them.'

Brendan Prefontaine, former federal judge of the first circuit court of Massachusetts, walked out of the Boston Five Bank on School Street with fifteen thousand dollars in his pocket. It was a heady experience for a man who had lived an impecunious existence for the past thirty years. Since his release from prison he rarely had more than fifty dollars on his person. This was a very special day.

Yet it was more than very special. It was also very disturbing because he never thought for an instant that Randolph Gates would pay him anywhere near the amount he had demanded. Gates had made an enormous error in doing so; with the money the celebrated attorney had altered the gravity of his endeavours. He had crossed over from ruthless, albeit nonfatal, greed into something potentially quite lethal. Prefontaine had no idea who the woman and the children were or what their relationship was to Lord Randolph of Gates, but whoever they were and whatever it was, Dandy Randy meant them no good.

An irreproachable Zeus-like figure in the legal world did not pay a disbarred, discredited, deniable alcoholic 'scum' like one Brendan Patrick Pierre Prefontaine an outrageous sum of money because his soul was with the archangels of heaven. Rather, that soul was with the disciples of Lucifer. And since this was obviously the case, it might be profitable for the scum to pursue a little knowledge, for as the bromide declared, a little knowledge is a dangerous thing – frequently more so in the eyes of the beholder than in the one possessing scant titbits of information, so slanted as to appear many times more. Fifteen thousand today might well become fifty thousand tomorrow if – if a scum flew to the island of Montserrat and began asking questions.

Besides, thought the judge, the Irish in him chuckling, the French sector in minor rebellion, he had not had a vacation in years. Good *Christ*, it was enough keeping body and soul together; who thought of an unenforced suspension of the hustle?

So Brendan Patrick Pierre Prefontaine hailed a taxi, which he had not done sober for at least ten years, and directed the sceptical driver to take him to Louis's men's store at Faneuil Hall.

'You got the scratch, old man?'

'More than enough to get you a haircut and cure the acne on your pubescent face, young fellow. Drive on, Ben Hur. I'm in a hurry.'

The clothes were off the racks, but they were expensive racks, and after he had shown a roll of hundred-dollar bills, the purple-lipped clerk was extremely cooperative. A midsized suitcase of burnished leather soon held casual apparel, and Prefontaine discarded his worn-out suit, shirt and shoes for a new outfit. Within the hour he looked not unlike a man he had known years ago: the Honourable Brendan P. Prefontaine. (He had always dropped the second *P* for obvious reasons.)

Another taxi took him to his rooming house in Jamaica Plains, where he picked up a few essentials, including his passport, which he always kept active for rapid exits – preferable to prison walls – and then delivered him to Logan Airport, this driver having no concerns regarding his ability to pay the fare. Clothes, of course, never made the man, thought Brendan, but they certainly helped to convience dubious underlings. At Logan's information desk he was told that three airlines out of Boston serviced the island of Montserrat. He asked which counter was the nearest and then bought a ticket for the next available flight. Brendan Patrick Pierre Prefontaine naturally flew first class.

The Air France steward rolled the wheelchair slowly, gently through the ramp and onto the 747 jet in Paris's Orly Airport. The frail woman in the chair was elderly and overly made-up with an imbalance of rouge; she wore an outsized feather hat made of Australian cockatoo. She might have been a caricature except for the large eyes beneath the bangs of grey hair imperfectly dyed red – eyes alive and knowing and filled with humour. It was as if she were saying to all who observed her, Forget it, *mes amis*, he likes me this way and that's all I care about. I don't give a pile of *merde* about you or your opinions.

The *him* in this assumed monologue refered to the old man walking cautiously beside her, every now and then touching her shoulder, lovingly as well as perhaps for balance, but in the touch a volume of poetry that was theirs alone. Closer inspection revealed a sporadic welling of tears in his eyes that he promptly wiped away so she could not see them.

'*Il est ici, mon capitaine*,' announced the steward to the senior pilot, who greeted his two preboarding passengers at the aircraft's entrance. The captain reached for the woman's left hand and touched his lips to her flesh, then stood erect and solemnly saluted the balding grey-haired old man with the small *Légion d'honneur* in his lapel.

'It is an honour, monsieur,' said the captain. 'This aircraft is my command, but you are my commander.' They shook hands and the pilot continued. 'If there's anything the crew and I can do to make the flight most comfortable for you, don't hesitate to ask, monsieur.'

'You're very kind.'

'We are all beholden – all of us, all of France.'

'It was nothing, really—'

'To be singled out by Le Grand Charles himself as a true hero of the Résistance is hardly nothing. Age cannot dull such glory.' The captain snapped his fingers, addressing three stewardesses in the still-empty first-class cabin. 'Quickly, mesdemoiselles! Make everything perfect for a brave warrior of France and his lady.'

So the killer with many aliases was escorted to the wide bulkhead on the left, where his woman was gently transferred from the wheelchair to the seat on the aisle; his was next to the window. Their trays were set up and a chilled bottle of Cristal was brought in their honour and for their enjoyment. The captain raised the first glass and toasted the couple; he returned to the flight deck as the old woman winked at her man, the wink wicked and filled with laughter. In moments, the passengers began boarding the plane, a number of them glancing appreciatively at the elderly 'man and wife' in the front row. For the rumours had spread in the Air France lounge. *A great hero . . . Le Grand Charles himself . . . In the Alps he held off six hundred Boche – or was it a thousand?*

As the enormous jet raced down the runway and with a thump lumbered off the ground into the air, the old 'hero of France' – whose only heroics he could recall from the Résistance were based on theft, survival, insults to his woman, and staying out of whatever army or labour force that might draft him – reached into his pocket for his papers. The passport had his picture duly inserted, but that was the only item he recognized. The rest – name, date and place of birth, occupation – all were unfamiliar, and the attached list of honours, well, they were *formidable.* Totally out of character, but in case anyone should ever refer to them, he had better restudy the 'facts' so he could at least nod in self-effacing modesty. He had been assured that the individual originally possessing the name and the achievements had no living relatives, few friends, and had disappeared from his apartment in Marseilles supposedly on a world trip from which he presumably would not return.

The Jackal's courier looked at the name – he *must* remember it and respond whenever it was spoken. It should not be difficult, for it was such a common name. And so he repeated it silently to himself over and over again.

Jean Pierre Fontaine, Jean Pierre Fontaine, Jean Pierre . . .

A sound! Sharp, abrasive. It was wrong, not *normal*, not part of a hotel's routine noise of hollow drumming at night. Bourne grabbed the weapon by his pillow and rolled out of the bed in his shorts, steadying himself by the wall. It came again! A single, loud knock on the bedroom door of the suite. He shook his head trying to remember . . . Alex? *I'll knock once.* Jason lurched half in sleep to the door, his ear against the wood.

'*Yes?*'

'Open this damn thing before somebody sees me!' came Conklin's muffled voice from the corridor. Bourne did so and the retired field officer limped quickly into the room, treating his cane as if he loathed it. 'Boy, are *you* out of training!' he exclaimed as he sat on the foot of the bed. 'I've been standing there tapping for at least a couple of minutes.'

'I didn't hear you.'

'Delta would have; Jason Bourne would have. David Webb didn't.'

'Give me another day and you won't find David Webb.'

'*Talk.* I want you better than talk!'

'Then stop talking and tell me why you're here – at whatever time it is.'

'When last I looked I met Casset on the road at three-twenty. I had to gimp through a bunch of woods and climb over a goddamned fence—'

'*What?*'

'You heard me. A fence. Try it with your foot in cement . . . You know, I once won the fifty-yard dash when I was in high school.'

'Cut the digression. What happened?'

'Oh, I hear Webb again.'

'What *happened*? And while you're at it, who the hell is this Casset you keep talking about?'

'The only man I trust in Virginia. He and Valentino.'

'*Who*?'

'They're analysts, but they're straight.'

'*What?*'

'Never mind. *Jesus*, there are times when I wish I could get pissed—'

'*Alex*, why are you *here*?'

Conklin looked up from the bed as he angrily gripped his cane. 'I've got the books on our Philadelphians.'

'*That's* why? Who are they?'

'No, that's not why. I mean it's interesting but it's not why I'm here.'

'Then why?' asked Jason, crossing to a chair next to a window and sitting down, frowning, perplexed. 'My erudite friend from Cambodia and beyond doesn't climb over fences with his foot in cement at three o'clock in the morning unless he thinks he has to.'

'I had to.'

'Which tells me nothing. Please tell.'

'It's DeSole.'

'What's the soul?'

'Not "the", *De*Sole.'

'You've lost me.'

'He's the keeper of the keys at Langley. Nothing happens that he doesn't know about and nothing gets done in the area of research that he doesn't pass on.'

'I'm still lost.'

'We're in deep shit.'

'That doesn't help me at all.'

'Webb again.'

'Would you rather I took a nerve out of your neck?'

'All right, all right. Let me get my breath.' Conklin dropped his cane on the rug. 'I didn't even trust the freight elevator. I stopped two floors below and walked up.'

'Because we're in deep shit?'

'Yes.'

'Why? Because of this *De*Sole?'

'Correct, Mr Bourne. Steven DeSole. The man who has his finger on every computer at Langley. The one person who can spin the disks and put your old virginal Aunt Grace in jail as a hooker if he wants her there.'

'What's your point?'

'He's the connection to Brussels, to Teagarten at NATO. Casset learned down in the cellars that he's the *only* connection – they even have an access code bypassing everyone else.'

'What does it mean?'

'Casset doesn't know, but he's goddamned angry.'

'How much did you tell him?'

'The minimum. That I was working on some possibles and Teagarten's name came up in an odd way – most likely a diversion or used by someone trying to impress someone else – but I wanted to know who he talked to at the Agency, frankly figuring it was Peter Holland. I asked Charlie to play it out in the dark.'

'Which I assume means confidentially.'

'Ten times that. Casset is the sharpest knife in Langley. I didn't have to say any more than I did; he got the message. Now he's also got a problem he didn't have yesterday.'

'What's he going to do?'

'I asked him not to do anything for a couple of days and that's what he gave me. Forty-eight hours, to be precise, and then he's going to confront DeSole.'

'He can't do that,' said Bourne firmly. 'Whatever these people are hiding we can use it to pull out the Jackal. Use *them* to pull him out as others like them used me thirteen years ago.'

Conklin stared first down at the floor, then up at Jason Bourne. 'It comes down to the almighty ego, doesn't it?' he said. 'The bigger the ego the bigger the fear—'

'The bigger the bait the bigger the fish,' completed Jason, interrupting. 'A long time back you told me that Carlos's "spine" was as big as his head, which had to be swollen all out of proportion for him to be in the business he's in. That was true then and it's true now. If we can get any one of these high government profiles to send a message to him – namely, to come after me, kill *me* – he'll jump at it. Do you know why?'

'I just told you. Ego.'

'Sure, that's part of it, but there's something else. It's the respect that's eluded Carlos for more than twenty years, starting with Moscow cutting him loose and telling him to get lost. He's made millions, but his clients have mainly been the crud of the earth. For all the fear he's engendered he still remains a punk psychopath. No legends have been built around him, only contempt, and at this stage it's got to be driving him close to the edge. The fact that he's coming after me to settle a thirteen-year-old score supports what I'm saying . . . I'm vital to him – his killing me is vital – because I was the product of our covert operations. That's who he wants to show up, show that he's better than all of us put together.'

'It could also be because he still thinks you can identify him.'

'I thought that at first, too, but after thirteen years and nothing from me – well, I had to think again.'

'So you moved into Mo Panov's territory and came up with a psychiatric profile.'

'It's a free country.'

'Compared with most, yes, but where's all this leading us?'

'Because I know I'm right.'

'That's hardly an answer.'

'*Nothing* can be false or faked,' insisted Bourne, leaning forward in the armchair, his elbows on his bare knees, his hands clasped. 'Carlos would find the contrivance; it's the first thing he'll look for. Our Medusans have to be genuine and genuinely panicked.'

'They're both, I told you that.'

'To the point where they'd actually *consider* making contact with someone like the Jackal.'

'That I don't know—'

'That we'll never know,' broke in Jason, 'until we learn what they're hiding.'

'But if we start the disks spinning at Langley, DeSole will find out. *And*, if he's part of whatever the hell it is, he'll alert the others.'

'Then there'll be no research at Langley. I've got enough to go on anyway, just get me addresses and private telephone numbers. You can do that, can't you?'

'Certainly, that's low-level. What are you going to do?'

Bourne smiled and spoke quietly, even gently. 'How about storming their houses or sticking needles in their asses between the appetizers and the entrées?'

'Now I hear Jason Bourne.'

'So be it.'

7

Marie St Jacques Webb greeted the Caribbean morning by stretching in bed and looking over at the crib several feet away. Alison was deep in sleep, which she had not been four or five hours ago. The little *dear* had been a basket case then, so much so that Marie's brother Johnny had knocked on the door, walked cowardly inside, and asked if he could do anything, which he profoundly trusted he could not.

'How are you at changing a nasty diaper?'

'I don't even want to think about it,' said St Jacques, fleeing.

Now, however, she heard his voice through the shutters outside. She also knew that she was meant to hear it; he was enticing her son, Jamie, into a race in the pool and speaking so loudly he could be heard on the big island of Montserrat. Marie literally crawled out of bed, headed for the bathroom, and four minutes later, ablutions completed, her auburn hair brushed and, wearing a bathrobe, walked out through the shuttered door to the patio overlooking the pool.

'Well, hi there, Mare!' shouted her tanned, dark-haired, handsome younger brother beside her son in the water. 'I hope we didn't wake you up. We just wanted to take a swim.'

'So you decided to let the British coastal patrols in Plymouth know about it.'

'Hey, come on, it's almost nine o'clock. That's late in the islands.'

'Hello, Mommy. Uncle John's been showing me how to scare off sharks with a stick!'

'Your uncle is filled with terribly important information which I hope to God you'll never use.'

'There's a pot of coffee on the table, Mare. And Mrs Cooper will make you whatever you like for breakfast.'

'Coffee's fine, Johnny. The telephone rang last night – was it David?'

'Himself,' replied the brother. 'And you and I are going to talk . . . Come on, Jamie, up we go. Grip the ladder.'

'What about the sharks?'

'You got 'em all, buddy. Go get yourself a drink.'

'*Johnny!*'

'Orange juice, there's a pitcher in the kitchen.' John St Jacques walked around the rim of the pool and up the steps to the bedroom patio as his newphew raced into the house.

Marie watched her brother approach, noting the similarities between him and her husband. Both were tall and muscular; both had in their strides an absence of compromise, but where David usually won, Johnny more often than not lost, and she did not know why. Or why David had such trust in his younger brother-in-law when the two older St Jacques sons would appear to be more responsible. David – or was it Jason Bourne? – never discussed the question in depth; he simply laughed it off and said Johnny had a streak in him that appealed to David – or was it Bourne?

'Let's level,' said the youngest St Jacques sitting down, the water dripping off his body onto the patio. 'What kind of trouble is David in? He couldn't talk on the phone and you were in no shape last night for an extended chat. What's happened?'

'The Jackal . . . The Jackal's what's happened.'

'*Christ!*' exploded the brother. 'After all these *years*?'

'After all these years,' repeated Marie, her voice drifting off.

'How far has that bastard gotten?'

'David's in Washington trying to find out. All we know for certain is that he dug up Alex Conklin and Mo Panov from the horrors of Hong Kong and Kowloon.' She told him about the false telegrams and the trap at the amusement park in Baltimore.

'I presume Alex has them all under protection or whatever they call it.'

'Around the clock, I'm sure. Outside of ourselves and McAllister, Alex and Mo are the only two people still alive who know that David was – oh, *Jesus*, I can't even say the *name*!' Marie slammed the coffee mug down on the patio table.

'Easy, Sis.' St Jacques reached for her hand, placing his on top of hers. 'Conklin knows what he's doing. David told me that Alex was the best – "field man", he called him – that ever worked for the Americans.'

'You don't *understand*, Johnny!' cried Marie, trying to control her voice and emotions, her wide eyes denying the attempt. 'David never said that, David Webb never *knew* that! Jason Bourne said it, and he's back! . . . That ice-cold calculating monster they created is back in David's head. You don't know what it's like. With a look in those unfocused eyes that see things I can't see – or with a tone of voice, a quiet freezing voice I don't *know* – and I'm suddenly with a stranger.'

St Jacques held up his free hand telling her to stop. 'Come on,' he said softly.

'The children? Jamie . . . ?' She looked frantically around.

'No, you. What do you expect David to do? Crawl inside a Wing or Ming dynasty vase and pretend his wife and children aren't in danger – if only because he is? Whether you ladies like it or not, we boys still think it's up to us to keep the big cats from the cave. We honestly believe we're more equipped. We revert to those strengths, the ugliest of them, of course, because we have to. That's what David's doing.'

'When did little brother get so philosophical?' asked Marie, studying John St Jacques's face.

'That ain't philosophy, girl, I just know it. Most men do – apologies to the feminist crowd.'

'Don't apologize; most of us wouldn't have it any other way. Would you believe that your big scholarly sister who called a lot of economic shots in Ottawa still yells like hell when she sees a mouse in our country kitchen, and goes into panic if it's a rat?'

'Certain bright women are more honest than others.'

'I'll accept what you say, Johnny, but you're missing my point. David's been doing so well these last five years, every month just a little bit better than the last. He'll never be totally cured, we all know that – he was damaged too severely – but the furies, his own personal furies, have almost disappeared. The solitary walks in the woods when he'd come back with hands bruised from when he'd attack *tree* trunks; the quiet, stifled tears in his study late at night when he couldn't remember what he was or what he'd done, thinking the worst of himself – they were *gone*, Johnny! There was real sunlight, do you know what I mean?'

'Yes, I do,' said the brother solemnly.

'What's happening now could bring them all back, that's what's frightening me so!'

'Then let's hope it's over quickly.'

Marie stopped, once again studying her brother. 'Hold it, little bro', I know you too well. You're pulling back.'

'Not a bit.'

'Yes, you are . . . You and David – I never understood. Our two older brothers, so solid, so on top of everything, perhaps not intellectually but certainly pragmatically. Yet he turned to you. Why, Johnny?'

'Let's not go into it,' said St Jacques curtly, removing his hand from his sister's.

'But I *have* to. This is my life, *he's* my life! There can't be any more secrets where he's concerned – I can't *stand* any more! . . . Why *you*?'

St Jacques leaned back in the patio chair, his stretched fingers now covering his forehead. He raised his eyes, an unspoken plea in them. 'All right, I know where you're coming from. Do you remember six or seven years ago I left our ranch saying I wanted to try things on my own?'

'Certainly. I think you broke both Mom's and Dad's hearts. Let's face it, you were always kind of the favourite—'

'I was always the *kid*!' interrupted the youngest St Jacques. 'Playing out some moronic *Bonanza* where my thirty-year-old brothers were blindly taking orders from a pontificating, bigoted French Canadian father whose only smarts came with his money and his land.'

'There was more to him than that, but I won't argue – from a "kid's" viewpoint.'

'You couldn't, Marie. You did the same thing, and sometimes you didn't come home for over a year.'

'I was busy.'

'So was I.'

'What did you do?'

'I killed two men. Two animals who'd killed a friend of mine – raped her and killed her.'

'*What?*'

'Keep your voice down—'

'My God, what *happened*?'

'I didn't want to call home, so I reached your husband . . . my friend, David, who didn't treat me like a brain-damaged kid. At the time it seemed like a logical thing to do and it was the best decision I could have made. He was owed favours by his government, and a quiet team of bright people from Washington and Ottawa flew up to James Bay and I was acquitted. Self-defence, and it *was* just that.'

'He never said a *word* to me—'

'I begged him not to.'

'So that's why . . . But I still don't understand!'

'It's not difficult, Mare. A part of him knows I can kill, *will* kill, if I think it's necessary.'

A telephone rang inside the house as Marie stared at her younger brother. Before she could get her voice back, an elderly black woman emerged from the door to the kitchen. 'It's for you, Mr John. It's that pilot over on the big island. He says it's real important, *mon*.'

'Thanks, Mrs Cooper,' said St Jacques, getting out of the chair and walking rapidly down to an extension phone by the pool. He spoke for several moments, looked up at Marie, slammed down the telephone, and rushed back up to his sister. 'Pack up. You're getting out of here!'

'*Why*? Was that the man who flew us—'

'He's back from Martinique and just learned that someone was asking questions at the airport last night. About a woman and two small children. None of the crews said anything, but that may not last. Quickly.'

'My God, where will we go?'

'Over to the inn until we think of something else. There's only one road and my own Tonton Macoute patrols it. No one gets in or out. Mrs Cooper will help you with Alison. *Hurry!*'

The telephone started ringing again as Marie dashed through the bedroom door. St Jacques raced down the steps to the pool extension, reaching it as Mrs Cooper once more stepped out of the kitchen. 'It's Government House over in 'Serrat, Mr John.'

'What the hell do *they* want . . . ?'

'Shall I ask them?'

'Never mind, I'll get it. Help my sister with the kids and pack everything they brought with them into the Rover. They're leaving right away!'

'Oh, a bad time pity, *mon*. I was just getting to know the little babies.'

'"Bad time pity" is right,' mumbled St Jacques, picking up the telephone. 'Yes?'

'Hello, John?' said the chief aide to the Crown governor, a man who had befriended the Canadian developer and helped him through the maze of the colony's Territorial Regulations.

'Can I call you back, Henry? I'm kind of harried at the moment.'

'I'm afraid there's no time, chap. This is straight from the Foreign Office. They want our immediate cooperation, and it won't do you any harm, either.'

'Oh?'

'It seems there's an old fellow and his wife arriving on Air France's connecting flight from Antigua at ten-thirty and Whitehall wants the red-carpet treatment. Apparently the old boy had a splendid war, with a slew of decorations and worked with a lot of our chaps across the Channel.'

'Henry, I'm really in a hurry. What's any of this got to do with *me*?'

'Well, I rather assumed you might have more of an idea about that than we do. Probably one of your rich Canadian guests, perhaps a Frenchie from Montreal who came out of the Résistance and who thought of you—'

'Insults will only get you a bottle of superior French Canadian wine. What do you *want*?'

'Put up our hero and his lady in the finest accommodation you've got, with a room for the French-speaking nurse we've assigned to them.'

'On an hour's *notice*?'

'Well, chap, our buns could be in a collective sling, if you know what I mean – and your so vital but erratic telephone service does depend on a degree of Crown intervention, if you also know what I mean.'

'Henry, you're a terrific negotiator. You so politely kick a person so accurately where it hurts. What's our hero's name? *Quickly*, please!'

'Our names are Jean Pierre and Regine Fontaine, Monsieur le Directeur, and here are our passports,' said the soft-spoken old man inside the immigration officer's glass-enclosed office, the chief aide of the Crown governor at his side. 'My wife can be seen over there,' he added, pointing through the window. 'She is talking with the mademoiselle in the white uniform.'

'Please, Monsieur Fontaine,' protested the stocky black immigration official in a pronounced British accent. 'This is merely an informal formality, a stamping procedure, if you like. Also to remove you from the inconvenience of so many admirers. Rumours have gone throughout the airport that a great man has arrived.'

'Really?' Fontaine smiled; it was a pleasant smile.

'Oh, but not to be concerned, sir. The press has been barred. We know you want complete privacy, and you shall have it.'

'Really?' The old man's smile faded. 'I was to meet someone here, an associate, you might say, I must consult with confidentially. I hope your most considerate arrangements do not prevent him from reaching me.'

'A small, select group with proper standing and credentials will greet you in Blackburne's honoured guest corridor, Monsieur Fontaine,' said the Crown governor's chief aide. 'May we proceed? The reception line will be swift, I assure you.'

'Really? That swift?'

It was, less than five minutes actually, but five seconds would have been enough. The first person the Jackal's courier-killer met was the beribboned Crown governor himself. As the Queen's royal representative embraced the hero in Gallic style, he whispered into Jean Pierre Fontaine's ear.

'We've learned where the woman and her children were taken. We are sending you there. The nurse has your instructions.'

The rest was somewhat anticlimactic for the old man, especially the absence of the press. He had never had his picture in the newspapers except as a felon.

Morris Panov, MD, was a very angry man and he always tried to control his very angry moments because they never helped him or his patients. At the moment, however, sitting at his office desk, he was having difficulty curtailing his emotions. He had not heard from David Webb. He *had* to hear from him, he had to *talk* to him. What was happening could negate thirteen years of therapy, couldn't they *understand* that? . . . No, of course they couldn't; it was not what interested them; they had other priorities and did not care to be burdened by problems beyond their purview. But *he* had to care. The damaged mind was so fragile, so given to setbacks, the horrors of the past were so capable of taking over the present. It could not happen with David! He was so close to being as normal as he would ever be (and who the hell was 'normal' in this fucked-up world). He could function wonderfully as a teacher; he had near total recall where his scholarly expertise was called upon, and he was remembering more and more as each year progressed. But it could all blow apart with a single act of violence, for violence was the way of life for Jason Bourne. *Damn!*

It was crippling enough that they even permitted David to stay around; he had tried to explain the potential damage to Alex but Conklin had an irrefutable reply: *We can't stop him. At least this way we can watch him, protect him.* Perhaps so. 'They' did not stint where protection was involved – the guards down the hall from his office and on the roof of the building, to say nothing of a temporary receptionist bearing arms as well as a strange computer, attested to their concern. Still it would be so much better for David if he was simply sedated and flown down to his island retreat, leaving the hunt for the Jackal to the professionals . . . Panov suddenly caught himself as the realization swept over him: there was no one more professional than Jason Bourne.

The doctor's thoughts were interrupted by the telephone, the telephone he could not pick up until all the security procedures were activated. A trace was placed on the incoming call; a scanner determined whether there were intercepts on the line, and finally the identity of the caller was approved by Panov himself. His intercom buzzed; he flipped the switch on his console. 'Yes?'

'All systems are cleared, sir,' announced the temporary receptionist, who was the only one in the office who would know. 'The man on the line said his name was Treadstone, Mr D. Treadstone.'

'I'll take it,' said Mo Panov firmly. 'And you can remove whatever other "systems" you've got on that machine out there. This is doctor-patient confidentiality.'

'Yes, sir. Monitor is terminated.'

'It's what? . . . Never mind.' The psychiatrist picked up the phone barely able to keep from shouting. 'Why didn't you call me *before* this, you son of a bitch!'

'I didn't want to give you cardiac arrest, is that sufficient?'

'Where are you and what are you doing?'

'At the moment?'

'That'll suffice.'

'Let's see, I rented a car and right now I'm a half a block from a town house in Georgetown owned by the chairman of the Federal Trade Commission, talking to you on a pay phone.'

'For Christ's sake, *why*?'

'Alex will fill you in, but what I want you to do is call Marie on the island. I've tried a couple of times since leaving the hotel but I can't get through. Tell her I'm fine, that I'm perfectly *fine*, and not to worry. Have you got that?'

'I've got it, but I don't buy it. You don't even sound like yourself.'

'You can't tell her that, Doctor. If you're my friend, you can't tell her anything like that.'

'*Stop* it, David. This Jekyll-and-Hyde crap doesn't *wash* any more.'

'Don't tell her that, not if you're my friend.'

'You're *spiralling*, David. Don't let it happen. Come to me, *talk* to me.'

'No time, Mo. The fat cat's limousine is parking in front of his house. I've got to go to work.'

'*Jason!*'

The line went dead.

Brendan Patrick Pierre Prefontaine walked down the jet's metal steps into the hot Caribbean sun of Monstserrat's Blackburne Airport. It was shortly past three o'clock in the afternoon, and were it not for the many thousands of dollars on his person he might have felt lost. It was remarkable how a supply of hundred-dollar bills in various pockets made one feel so secure. In truth, he had to keep reminding himself that his loose change – fifties, twenties and tens – were in his right front trousers pocket so as not to make a mistake and either appear ostentatious or be a mark for some unprincipled hustler. Above all, it was vital for him to keep a low profile to the point of insignificance. He had to insignificantly ask significant questions around the airport regarding a woman and two small children who had arrived on a private aircraft the previous afternoon.

Which was why to his astonishment and alarm he heard the absolutely adorable black female immigration clerk say to him after hanging up a telephone, 'Would you be so kind, sir, as to come with me, please?'

Her lovely face, lilting voice and perfect smile did nothing to allay the former judge's fears. Far too many extremely guilty criminals had such assets. 'Is there something wrong with my passport, young lady?'

'Not that I can see, sir.'

'Then why the delay? Why not simply stamp it and allow me to proceed?'

'Oh, it is stamped and entry is permitted, sir. There is no problem.'

'Then *why* . . . ?'

'Please come with me, sir.'

They approached a large glass-enclosed cubicle with a sign on the left window, the gold letters announcing the occupant: DEPUTY DIRECTOR OF IMMIGRATION SERVICES. The attractive clerk opened the door and, again smiling, gestured for the elderly visitor to go inside. Prefontaine did so, suddenly terrified that he would be searched, the money found, and all manner of charges levelled against him. He did not know which islands were involved in narcotics, but if this was one of them the thousands of dollars in his pockets would be instantly suspect. Explanations raced through his mind as the clerk crossed to the desk handing his passport to the short, heavyset deputy of immigration. The woman gave Brendan a last bright smile and went out the door, closing it behind her.

'Mr Brendan Patrick Pierre Prefontaine,' intoned the immigration official reading the passport.

'Not that it matters,' said Brendan kindly but with summoned authority. 'However, the "Mister" is usually replaced with "Judge" – as I say, I don't believe it's relevant under the circumstances, or perhaps it is, I really don't know. Did one of my law clerks make an error? If so, I'll fly the whole group down to apologize.'

'Oh, not at all, sir – *Judge*,' replied the uniformed, wide-girthed black man with a distinct British accent as he rose from the chair and extended his hand over the desk. 'Actually, it is I who may have made the error.'

'Come now, Colonel, we all do occasionally.' Brendan gripped the official's hand. 'Then perhaps I may be on my way? There's someone here I must meet.'

'That's what *he* said!'

Brendan released the hand. 'I beg your pardon?'

'I may have to beg yours . . . The confidentiality, of course.'

'The what? Could we get to the point, please?'

'I realize that privacy,' continued the official, pronouncing the word as *privvissy*, 'is of utmost importance – that's been explained to us – but whenever we can be of assistance, we try to oblige the Crown.'

'Extremely commendable, Brigadier, but I'm afraid I don't understand.'

The official needlessly lowered his voice. 'A great man arrived here this morning, are you aware of that?'

'I'm sure many men of stature come to your beautiful island. It was highly recommended to me, in fact.'

'Ah, yes, the privacy!'

'Yes, of course, the "privvissy",' agreed the ex-convict judge, wondering if the official had both his oars in the water. 'Could you be clearer?'

'Well, *he* said he was to meet someone, an associate he had to consult with, but after the very private reception line – no press, of course – he was taken directly to the charter that flew him to the out island, and obviously never met the person he was to confidentially meet. *Now*, am I clearer?'

'Like Boston harbour in a squall, General.'

'Very good. I understand. *Privvissy* . . . So all our personnel are alerted to the fact that the great man's friend might be seeking him here at the airport – confidentially, of course.'

'Of course.' *Not even a paddle*, thought Brendan.

'Then I considered another possibility,' said the official in minor triumph. 'Suppose the great man's friend was also flying to our island for a *rendezvous* with the great man?'

'Brilliant.'

'Not without logic. *Then* it struck me to obtain the passenger manifests of all the incoming flights, concentrating, of course, on those in first class, which would be proper for the great man's associate.'

'Clairvoyance,' mumbled the once and former judge. 'And you selected me?'

'The *name*, my good man! Pierre Prefontaine!'

'My pious, departed mother would no doubt take offence at your omitting the "Brendan Patrick". Like the French, the Irish are quite sensitive in such matters.'

'But it was the *family*. I understood that immediately!'

'You did?'

'Pierre *Prefontaine*! . . . Jean *Pierre Fontaine*. I am an expert on immigration procedures, having studied the methods in many countries. Your own name is a fascinating example, most honoured Judge. Wave after wave of immigrants flocked to the United States, the melting pot of nations, races and languages. In the process names were altered, combined or simply misunderstood by armies of confused, overworked clerks. But roots frequently survived and thus it was for you. The family Fontaine became *Prefontaine* in America and the great man's associate was in reality an esteemed member of the American branch!'

'Positively awesome,' muttered Brendan, eyeing the official as if he expected several male nurses to barge into the room with restraining equipment. 'But isn't it possible that this is merely coincidence? Fontaine is a common name throughout France but, as I understand it, the Prefontaines were distinctly centred around Alsace-Lorraine.'

'Yes, of course,' said the deputy, again lowering his voice rather than conceivably winking. 'Yet without any prior word whatsoever, the Quai d'Orsay in Paris calls, then the UK's Foreign Office follows with instructions – a great man is soon to drop out of the sky. Acknowledge him, honour him, spirit him off to a remote resort known for its confidentiality – for that, too, is paramount. The great one is to have total *privvissy* . . . Yet that same great warrior is anxious; he is to confidentially meet with an associate he does not find. Perhaps the great man has secrets – all great men *do*, you know.'

Suddenly, the thousands of dollars in Prefontaine's pockets felt very heavy. Washington's Four Zero clearance in Boston, the Quai d'Orsay in Paris, the Foreign Office in London – Randolph Gates needlessly parting with an extraordinary amount of money out of sheer panic. There was a pattern of strange convergence, the strangest being the inclusion of a frightened, unscrupulous attorney named Gates. Was he an inclusion or an aberration? What did it all mean? 'You are an extraordinary man,' said Brendan quickly, covering his thoughts with rapid words. 'Your perceptions are nothing short of brilliant, but you do understand that confidentiality *is* paramount.'

'I will hear no more, honoured Judge!' exclaimed the deputy. 'Except to add that your appraisal of my abilities might not be lost on my superiors.'

'They will be made clear, I assure you . . . Precisely where did my not too distant and distinguished cousin go?'

'A small out island where the seaplanes must land on the water. Its name is Tranquillity Isle and the resort is called Tranquillity Inn.'

'You will be personally thanked by those above you, be assured of that.'

'And I shall personally clear you through customs.'

Brendan Patrick Pierre Prefontaine, carrying his suitcase of burnished leather, walked out into the terminal of Blackburne Airport a bewildered man. Bewildered, *hell*, he was stunned! He could not decide whether to take the next flight back to Boston or to . . . his feet were apparently deciding for him. He found himself walking towards a counter beneath a large sea-blue sign with white lettering: INTER ISLAND AIRWAYS. It couldn't do any harm to inquire, he mused, *then* he would buy a ticket on the next plane to Boston.

On the wall beyond the counter a list of nearby 'Out Isles' was next to a larger column of the well-known Leeward and Windward Islands from St Kitts and Nevis south to the Grenadines. Tranquillity was sandwiched between Canada Cay and Turtle Rock. Two clerks, both young, one black and one white, the former a young woman, the latter a blond-haired man in his early twenties, were talking quietly. The girl approached. 'May I help you, sir?'

'I'm not really sure,' replied Brendan hesitantly. 'My schedule's so unsettled, but it seems I have a friend on Tranquillity Isle.'

'At the inn, sir?'

'Yes, apparently so. Does it take long to fly over there?'

'If the weather's clear, no more than fifteen minutes, but that would be an amphibious charter. I'm not sure one's available until tomorrow morning.'

'Sure there is, babe,' interrupted the young man with small gold wings pinned crookedly on his white shirt. 'I'm running over some supplies to Johnny St Jay pretty soon,' he added, stepping forward.

'*He's* not scheduled for today.'

'As of an hour ago he is. Pronto.'

At that instant and with those words, Prefontaine's eyes fell in astonishment on two stacks of cartons moving slowly down Inter Island's luggage carousel towards the exterior loading area. Even if he had the time to debate with himself, he knew his decision was made.

'I'd like to purchase a ticket on that flight, if I may,' he said, watching the boxes of Gerber's Assorted Baby Foods and Pampers Medium Diapers disappear into the hold.

He had found the unknown woman with the small male child and the infant.

8

Routine secondhand inquiries at the Federal Trade Commission confirmed the fact that its chairman, Albert Armbruster, did, indeed, have ulcers as well as high blood pressure and under doctor's orders left the office and returned home whenever discomfort struck him. Which was why Alex Conklin telephoned him after a generally overindulgent lunch – also established – with an 'update' of the Snake Lady crisis. As with Alex's initial call, catching Armbruster in the shower, he anonymously told the shaken chairman that someone would be in touch with him later in the day – either at the office or at home. The contact would identify himself simply as Cobra. ('Use all the banal trigger words you can come up with' was the gospel according to St Conklin.) In the meantime, Armbruster was instructed to talk to no one. '*Those are orders from the Sixth Fleet.*'

'*Oh, Christ!*'

Thus Albert Armbruster called for his chariot and was driven home in discomfort. Further nausea was in store for the chairman, however, as Jason Bourne was waiting for him.

'Good afternoon, Mr Armbruster,' said the stranger pleasantly as the chairman struggled out of the limousine, the door held open by the chauffeur.

'Yes, *what*?' Armbruster's response was immediate, unsure.

'I merely said "Good afternoon". My name's Simon. We met at the White House reception for the Joint Chiefs several years ago—'

'I wasn't *there*,' broke in the chairman emphatically.

'Oh?' The stranger arched his brows, his voice still pleasant but obviously questioning.

'Mr Armbruster?' The chauffeur had closed the door and now turned courteously to the chairman. 'Will you be needing—'

'No, *no*,' said Armbruster, again interrupting. 'You're relieved – I won't need you any more today . . . tonight.'

'Same time tomorrow morning, sir?'

'Yes, tomorrow – unless you're told otherwise. I'm not a well man; check with the office.'

'Yes, sir.' The chauffeur tipped his visored cap and climbed back into the front seat.

'I'm sorry to hear that,' said the stranger, holding his place as the limousine's engine was started and the automobile rolled away.

'*What?* . . . Oh, you. I was never at the White House for that damned reception!'

'Perhaps I was mistaken—'

'Yes, well, nice to see you again,' said Armbruster anxiously, impatiently, hurrying to the steps that led up to his Georgetown house.

'Then again I'm quite sure Admiral Burton introduced us—'

'*What?*' The chairman spun around. 'What did you just say?'

'This is a waste of time,' continued Jason Bourne, the pleasantness gone from his voice and his face. 'I'm Cobra.'

'Oh, *Jesus*! . . . I'm not a well man.' Armbruster repeated the statement in a hoarse whisper, snapping his head up to look at the front of his house, to the windows and the door.

'You'll be far worse unless we talk,' added Jason, following the chairman's eyes. 'Shall it be up there? In your house?'

'*No!*' cried Armbruster. 'She yaps all the time and wants to know everything about everybody, then blabs all over town exaggerating everything.'

'I assume you're talking about your wife.'

'All of 'em! They don't know when to keep their traps shut.'

'It sounds like they're starved for conversation.'

'What . . . ?'

'Never mind. I've got a car down the block. Are you up to a drive?'

'I damn well better be. We'll stop at the drugstore down the street. They've got my prescription on file . . . Who the *hell* are you?'

'I told you,' answered Bourne. 'Cobra. It's a snake.'

'Oh, *Jesus*!' whispered Albert Armbruster.

The pharmacist complied rapidly, and Jason quickly drove to a neighbourhood bar he had chosen an hour before should one be necessary. It was dark and full of shadows, the booths deep, the banquettes high, isolating those meeting one another from curious glances. The ambience was important, for it was vital that he stare into the eyes of the chairman when he asked questions, his own eyes ice-cold, demanding . . . threatening. Delta was back, Cain had returned; Jason Bourne was in full command, David Webb forgotten.

'We have to cover ourselves,' said the Cobra quietly after their drinks arrived. 'In terms of damage control that means we have to know how much harm each of us could do under the Amytals.'

'What the hell does *that* mean?' asked Armbruster, swallowing most of his gin and tonic while wincing and holding his stomach.

'Drugs, chemicals, truth serums.'

'*What?*'

'This isn't your normal ball game,' said Bourne, remembering Conklin's words. 'We've got to cover all of the bases because there aren't any constitutional rights in this series.'

'So who are *you*?' The chairman of the Federal Trade Commission belched and brought his glass briefly to his lips, his hand trembling. 'Some kind of one-man *hit* team? John Doe knows something, so he's shot in an alley?'

'Don't be ridiculous. Anything like that would be totally counter-productive. It would only fuel those trying to find us, leave a trail—'

'Then what are you *talking* about?'

'Saving our lives, which includes our reputations and our life-styles.'

'You're one cold prick. How do we do that?'

'Let's take your case, shall we? . . . You're not a well man by your own admission. You could resign under doctor's orders and we take care of you – *Medusa* takes care of you.' Jason's imagination floated, quick sharp forays into reality and fantasy, swiftly searching for the words that might be found in the gospel according to St Alex. 'You're known to be a wealthy man, so a villa might be purchased in your name, or perhaps a Caribbean island, where you'd be completely secure. No one can reach you; no one can talk to you unless you agree, which would mean predetermined interviews, harmless and even favourable results guaranteed. Such things are not impossible.'

'Pretty sterile existence in my opinion,' said Armbruster. 'Me and the yapper all by ourselves? I'd kill her.'

'Not at all,' went on the Cobra. 'There'd be constant distractions. Guests of your choosing could be flown to wherever you are. Other women also – either of your choice or selected by those who respect your tastes. Life goes on much as before, some inconveniences, some pleasant surprises. The point is that you'd be protected, inaccessible and therefore *we're* also protected, the rest of us . . . But, as I say, that option is merely hypothetical at this juncture. In my case, frankly, it's a necessity because there's little I don't know. I leave in a matter of days. Until then I'm determining who goes and who stays . . . How much *do* you know, Mr Armbruster?'

'I'm not involved with the day-to-day operations, naturally. I deal with the big picture. Like the others, I get a monthly coded telex from the banks in Zurich listing the deposits and the companies we're gaining control of – that's about it.'

'So far you don't get a villa.'

'I'll be damned if I want one, and if I do I'll buy it myself. I've got close to a hundred million, American, in Zurich.'

Bourne controlled his astonishment and simply stared at the chairman. 'I wouldn't repeat that,' he said.

'Who am I going to tell? The yapper?'

'How many of the others do you know personally?' asked the Cobra.

'Practically none of the staff, but then they don't know me, either. Hell, they don't know anybody . . . And while we're on the subject, take you, for instance. I've never heard of you. I figure you work for the board and I was told to expect you, but I don't *know* you.'

'I was hired on a very special basis. My background's deep-cover security.'

'Like I said, I figured—'

'What about the Sixth Fleet?' interrupted Bourne, moving away from the subject of himself.

'I see him now and then but I don't think we've exchanged a dozen words. He's military; I'm civilian – very civilian.'

'You weren't once. Where it all began.'

'The hell I wasn't. No uniform ever made a soldier and it sure didn't with me.'

'What about a couple of generals, one in Brussels, the other at the Pentagon?'

'They were career men; they stayed in. I wasn't and I didn't.'

'We have to expect leaks, rumours,' said Bourne almost aimlessly, his eyes now wandering. 'But we can't permit the slightest hint of military orientation.'

'You mean like in junta style?'

'*Never*,' replied Bourne, once more staring at Armbruster. 'That kind of thing creates whirlwinds—'

'*Forget* it!' whispered the chairman of the Federal Trade Commission, angrily interrupting. 'The Sixth Fleet, as you call him, calls the shots only *here* and only because it's convenient. He's a blood-and-guts admiral with a whiz-bang record and a lot of clout where we want it, but that's in *Washington*, not anywhere else!'

'I know that and you know it,' said Jason emphatically, the emphasis covering his bewilderment, 'but someone who's been in a protection programme for over fifteen years is putting together his own scenario and *that* comes out of Saigon – *Command* Saigon.'

'It may have come out of Saigon but it sure as hell didn't stay there. The soldier boys couldn't run with it, we *all* know that . . . But I see what you mean. You tie in Pentagon brass with anything like us, the freaks are in the streets and the bleeding-heart fairies in Congress have a field day. Suddenly a dozen subcommittees are in session.'

'Which we can't tolerate,' added Bourne.

'Agreed,' said Armbruster. 'Are we any closer to learning the name of the bastard who's putting this scenario together?'

'Closer, not close. He's been in contact with Langley but on what level we don't know.'

'*Langley?* For Christ's sake we've *got* someone over there. He can squelch it and find out who the son of a bitch is!'

'DeSole?' offered the Cobra simply.

'That's right.' Armbruster leaned forward. 'There *is* very little you don't know. That connection's very quiet. What does DeSole say?'

'Nothing, we can't touch him,' replied Jason, suddenly, frantically reaching for a credible answer. He had been David Webb too long! Conklin was right; he wasn't thinking fast enough. Then the words came . . . part of the truth, a dangerous part, but credible, and he could *not* lose credibility. 'He thinks he's being watched and we're to stay away from him, no contact whatsoever until he says otherwise.'

'What *happened*?' The chairman gripped his glass, his eyes rigid, bulging.

'Someone in the cellars learned that Teagarten in Brussels has an access fax code directly to DeSole bypassing routine confidential traffic.'

'Stupid goddamned *soldier boys*!' spat out Armbruster. 'Give 'em gold braid and they prance around like debutantes and want every new toy in town! . . . *Faxes, access* codes! Jesus, he probably punched the wrong numbers and got the NAACP.'

'DeSole says he's building a cover and can handle it, but it's no time for him to go around asking questions, especially in this area. He'll check quietly on everything he can, and if he learns something he'll reach us, but we're not to reach him.'

'Wouldn't you *know* it'd be a lousy soldier boy who puts us out on a limb? If it wasn't for that jackass with his *access* code, we wouldn't have a problem. Everything would be taken care of.'

'But he does exist and the problem – the crisis – won't go away,' said Bourne flatly. 'I repeat, we have to cover ourselves. Some of us will have to leave – disappear at least for a while. For the good of all of us.'

The chairman of the Federal Trade Commission leaned back in the booth, his expression pensively disagreeable. 'Yeah, well let me tell you something, Simon, or whatever your name is. You're checking out the wrong people. We're businessmen, some of us rich enough or egotistical enough or for other reasons willing to work for government pay, but first we're *businessmen* with investments all over the place. We're also appointed, not elected, and that means nobody expects full financial disclosures. Do you see what I'm driving at?'

'I'm not sure,' said Jason, instantly concerned that he was losing control, losing the thread. *I've been away too long* . . . and Albert Armbruster was not a fool. He was given to first-level panic but the second level was colder, far more analytical. 'What are you driving at?'

'Get rid of our soldier boys. Buy *them* villas or a couple of Caribbean islands and put *them* out of reach. Give 'em their own little courts and let 'em play kings; that's what they're all about anyway.'

'Operate without them?' asked Bourne, trying to conceal his astonishment.

'You said it and I agree. Any hint of big brass and we're in big trouble. It goes under the heading of "military industrial complex", which freely translated means "military-industrial collusion." Again Armbruster leaned forward over the table. 'We don't need them any more! Get rid of them.'

'There could be very loud objections—'

'No *way*. We've got 'em by their brass balls!'

'I'll have to think about it.'

'There's nothing to think about. In six months we'll have the controls we need in Europe.'

Jason Bourne stared at the chairman of the Federal Trade Commission. *What controls?* he thought to himself. *For what reason? Why?*

'I'll drive you home,' he said.

'I talked to Marie,' said Conklin from the Agency garden apartment in Virginia. 'She's at the inn, not at your house.'

'How *come*?' asked Jason at a gas-station pay phone on the outskirts of Manassas.

'She wasn't too clear . . . I think it was lunchtime or nap time – one of those times when mothers are never clear. I could hear your kids in the background. They were loud, pal.'

'What did she *say*, Alex?'

'It seems your brother-in-law wanted it that way. She didn't elaborate, and other than sounding like one harried mommy, she was the perfectly normal Marie I know and love – which means she only wanted to hear about you.'

'Which means you told her I was perfectly fine, didn't you?'

'Hell, yes. I said you were holed up under guard going over a lot of computer printouts, sort of a variation on the truth.'

'Johnny must have had his talk with her. She told him what's happened, so he moved them all to his exclusive bunker.'

'His what?'

'You never saw Tranquillity Inn, or did you? Frankly, I can't remember whether you did or not.'

'Panov and I saw only the plans and the site; that was four years ago. We haven't been back since, at least I haven't. Nobody's asked me.'

'I'll let that pass because you've had a standing invitation since we got the place . . . Anyway, you know it's on the beach and the only way to get there except by water is up a dirt road so filled with rocks no normal car could make it twice. Everything is flown in by plane or brought over by boat. Almost nothing from the town.'

'And the beach is patrolled,' interrupted Conklin. 'Johnny isn't taking any chances.'

'It's why I sent them down there. I'll call her later.'

'What about now?' said Alex. 'What about Armbruster?'

'Let's put it this way,' replied Bourne, his eyes drifting up at the white plastic shell of the pay phone. 'What does it mean when a man who has a hundred million dollars in Zurich tells me that Medusa – point of origin Command Saigon, emphasis on "command", which is hardly civilian – should get rid of the military because Snake Lady doesn't need them any longer?'

'I don't *believe* it,' said the retired intelligence officer in a quiet, doubting voice. 'He *didn't*.'

'Oh, yes, he did. He even called them soldier boys, and he wasn't memorializing them in song. He verbally dismissed the admirals and the generals as gold-braided debutantes who wanted every new toy in town.'

'Certain senators on the Armed Services Committee would agree with that assessment,' concurred Alex.

'There's more. When I reminded him that Snake Lady came out of Saigon – *Command* Saigon – he was very clear. He said it may have, but it sure as hell didn't stay there because – and this is a direct quote – "The soldier boys couldn't run with it".'

'That's a provocative statement. Did he tell you why they couldn't run with it?'

'No, and I didn't ask. I was supposed to know the answer.'

'I wish you did. I like less and less the sound of what I'm hearing; it's big and it's ugly . . . How did the hundred million come up?'

'I told him Medusa might get him a villa someplace out of the country where he couldn't be reached if we thought it was necessary. He wasn't too interested and said if he wanted one, he'd buy it himself. He had a hundred million, American, in Zurich – a fact I think I was also expected to know.'

'That was all? Just a simple little one hundred million?'

'Not entirely. He told me that like everybody else he gets a monthly telex – in code – from the banks in Zurich listing his deposits. Obviously, they've been growing.'

'Big, ugly and growing,' added Conklin. 'Anything else? Not that I particularly want to hear it, I'm frightened enough.'

'Two more items and you'd better have some fear in reserve . . . Armbruster said that along with the deposit telexes he gets a listing of the companies they're gaining control of.'

'*What* companies? What was he *talking* about? . . . Good *God*.'

'If I had asked, my wife and children might have to attend a private memorial service, no casket in evidence because I wouldn't be there.'

'You've got more to tell me. Tell me.'

'Our illustrious chairman of the Federal Trade Commission said that the ubiquitous "we" could get rid of the military because in six months "we" would have all the controls we needed in Europe . . . Alex, what controls? What are we *dealing* with?'

There was silence on the unbroken line and Jason Bourne did not interrupt. David Webb wanted to shout in defiance and confusion, but there was no point; he was a nonperson. Finally, Conklin spoke.

'I think we're dealing with something we can't handle,' he said softly, his words barely audible over the phone. 'This has to go upstairs, David. We can't keep it to ourselves.'

'*Goddamn* you, you're not talking to David!' Bourne did not raise his voice in anger; he did not have to, its tone was enough. 'This isn't going anywhere unless or until I say it does and I may not ever say it. Understand me, field man, I don't owe anyone anything, especially not the movers and the shakers in this city. They moved and shook my wife and me too much for any concessions where our lives or the lives of our children are concerned! I intend to use everything I can learn for one purpose and one purpose *only*. That's to draw out the Jackal and kill him so we can climb out of our personal hell and go on living . . . I know now that this *is* the way to do it. Armbruster talked tough and he probably is tough, but underneath he's frightened. They're all frightened – panicked, as you put it – and you were right. Present them with the jackal and he's a *solution* they can't refuse. Present Carlos with a client as rich and as powerful as our current Medusa and it's *irresistible* to him – he's got the respect of the international big boys, not just the crud of the world, the fanatics of the left and right . . . Don't stand in my way, *don't*, for God's sake!'

'That's a threat, isn't it?'

'*Stop* it, Alex. I don't want to talk like that.'

'But you just did. It's the reverse of Paris thirteen years ago, isn't it? Only now you'll kill *me* because I'm the one who hasn't a memory, the memory of what we did to you and Marie.'

'That's my *family* out there!' cried David Webb, his voice tight, sweat forming on his hairline as his eyes filled with tears. 'They're a thousand miles away from me and in *hiding*. It can't be any other way because I won't risk letting them be harmed! . . . *Killed*, Alex, because that's what the Jackal will do if he finds them. It's an island this week; where is it *next*? How many thousands of miles more? And after that, where will they go – where will we go? Knowing what we know now, we can't stop – he's after me; that goddamned filthy psychopath is *after* me and everything we've learned about him tells us he wants a maximum kill. His ego demands it, and that kill includes my family! . . . No, field man, don't burden me with things I don't care about – not where they interfere with Marie and the kids – I'm owed that much.'

'I hear you,' said Conklin. 'I don't know whether I'm hearing David or Jason Bourne but I hear you. All right, no reverse Paris, but we have to move fast and I'm talking to Bourne now. What's next? Where are you?'

'I judge about six or seven miles from General Swayne's house,' replied Jason, breathing deeply, the momentary anguish suppressed, the coldness returning. 'Did you make the call?'

'Two hours ago.'

'Am I still "Cobra"?'

'Why not? It's a snake.'

'That's what I told Armbruster. He wasn't happy.'

'Swayne will be less so, but I sense something and I can't really explain it.'

'What do you mean?'

'I'm not sure, but I have an idea that he's answerable to someone.'

'In the Pentagon? Burton?'

'I suppose so, I just don't know. In his partial paralysis he reacted almost as if he was an onlooker, someone involved but not in the middle of the game. He slipped a couple of times and said things like "We'll have to think about this," and "We'll have to confer." Confer with *whom*? It was a one-on-one conversation with my usual warning that he wasn't to talk to *anyone*. His response was a lame editorial "we", meaning that the illustrious general was conferring with himself. I don't buy it.'

'Neither do I,' agreed Jason. 'I'm going to change clothes. They're in the car.'

'What?'

Bourne turned partially in the plastic shell of the pay phone and glanced around the gas station. He saw what he hoped for, a men's room in the side of the building. 'You said that Swayne lives on a large farm west of Manassas—'

'Correction,' interrupted Alex. '*He* calls it a farm, his neighbours and the tax rolls call it a twenty-eight-acre estate. Not bad for a career soldier from a lower-middle-class family in Nebraska who married a hairdresser in Hawaii thirty years ago and supposedly bought his manse ten years ago on the strength of a very sizeable inheritance from an untraceable benefactor, an obscure wealthy uncle I couldn't find. That's what made me curious. Swayne headed up the Quartermaster Corps in Saigon and supplied Medusa . . . What's his place got to do with your changing clothes?'

'I want to look around. I'll get there while it's light to see what it's like from the road, then when it's dark I'll pay him a surprise visit.'

'That'll be effective, but why the looking around?'

'I like farms. They're so spread out and extended and I can't imagine why a professional soldier who knows that he can be transferred anywhere in the world at a moment's notice would saddle himself with such a large investment.'

'The same as my reasoning except I was concerned about the how, not the why. Your approach may be more interesting.'

'We'll see.'

'Be careful. He may have alarms and dogs, things like that.'

'I'm prepared,' said Jason Bourne. 'I did some shopping after I left Georgetown.'

The summer sun was low in the western sky as he slowed down the rental car and lowered the visor to keep from being blinded by the yellow globe of fire. Soon it would drop behind the Shenandoah mountains, twilight descending, prelude to darkness. And it was the darkness that Jason Bourne craved; it was his friend and ally, the blackness in which he moved swiftly, with sure feet and alert hands and arms that served as sensors against all the impediments of nature. The jungles had welcomed him in the past, knowing that although he was an intruder he respected them and used them as a part of him. He did not fear the jungles, he embraced them, for they protected him and allowed him passage to accomplish whatever his objective was; he was at one with the jungles – as he would have to be with the dense woods that flanked the estate of General Norman Swayne.

The main house was set back no less than the distance of two football fields from the country road. A stockade fence separated the entrance on the right from the exit on the left, both with iron gates, fronting a deep drive that was basically an elongated U-turn. Immediately bordering each opening was a profusion of tall trees and shrubbery that was in itself a natural extension of the stockade fence both left and right. All that was missing were guardhouses at each point of entry and exit.

His mind floated back to China, to Beijing and the wild bird sanctuary where he had trapped a killer posing as 'Jason Bourne'. There had been a guardhouse then and a series of armed patrols in the dense forest . . . and a madman, a butcher who controlled an army of killers, foremost among them the false 'Jason Bourne.' He had penetrated that deadly sanctuary, crippled a small fleet of trucks and automobiles by plunging the blade of his knife into every tyre, then proceeded to take out each patrol in the Jing Shan forest until he found the torchlit clearing that held a swaggering maniac and his brigade of fanatics. Could he do it all today? wondered Bourne as he drove slowly past Swayne's property for the third time, his eyes absorbing everything he could see. Five years later, thirteen years after Paris? He tried to evaluate the reality. He was not the younger man that he had been in Paris, nor the more mature man in Hong Kong, Macao and Beijing; he was now fifty and he felt it, every year of it. He would not dwell on it. There was too much else to think about, and the twenty-eight acres of General Norman Swayne's property were not the forest primeval of the Jing Shan sanctuary.

However, as he had done on the primitive outskirts of Beijing, he drove the car off the country road deep into a mass of tall grass and foliage. He climbed out and proceeded to cover the vehicle with bent and broken branches. The rapidly descending darkness would complete the camouflage and with the darkness he would go to work. He had changed his clothes in the men's room at the gas station: black trousers below a black long-sleeved, skintight pullover; and black thick-soled sneakers with heavy tread. These were his working apparel. The items he spread on the ground were his equipment, the shopping he had done after leaving Georgetown. They included a long-bladed hunting knife whose scabbard he threaded into his belt; a dual-chambered CO_2 pistol, encased in a nylon shoulder holster, that silently shot immobilizing darts into attacking animals, such as pit bulls; two flares designed to assist stranded drivers in broken-down cars to attract or deter other motorists; a pair of small Zeiss-Ikon 8 × 10 binoculars attached to his trousers by a Velcro strip; a penlight; raw-hide laces; and finally, pocket-sized wire cutters in case there was a metal fence. Along with the automatic supplied by the Central Intelligence Agency, the gear was either lashed to his belt or concealed in his clothing. The darkness came and Jason Bourne walked into the woods.

The white sheet of ocean spray burst up from the coral reef and appeared suspended, the dark blue waters of the Caribbean serving as a backdrop. It was that hour of early evening, a long sundown imminent, when Tranquillity Isle was bathed in alternating hot tropical colours, pockets of shadows constantly changing with each imperceptible descent of the orange sun. The resort complex of Tranquillity Inn had seemingly been cut out of three adjacent rock-strewn hills above an elongated beach sandwiched between huge natural jetties of coral. Two rows of balconied pink villas with bright red roofs of terracotta extended from each side of the resort's central hub, a large circular building of heavy stone and thick glass, all the structures overlooking the water, the villas connected by a white concrete path bordered by low-cut shrubbery and lined with ground lamps. Waiters in yellow guayabera jackets wheeled room-service tables along the path, delivering bottles and ice and canapes to Tranquillity's guests, the majority of whom sat on their individual balconies savouring the end of the Caribbean day. And as the shadows became more prominent, other people unobtrusively appeared along the beach and on the long dock that extended out over the water. These were neither guests nor service employees; they were armed guards, each dressed in a dark brown tropic uniform and – again unobtrusively – with a MAC-10 machine pistol strapped to his belted waist. On the opposite side of each jacket and hooked to the cloth was a pair of Zeiss-Ikon 8 × 10 binoculars continuously used to scan the darkness. The owner of Tranquillity Inn was determined that it live up to its name.

On the large circular balcony of the villa nearest the main building and the attached glass-enclosed dining room, an elderly infirm woman sat in a wheelchair sipping a glass of Château Carbonnieux '78 while drinking in the splendours of sundown. She absently touched the bangs of her imperfectly dyed red hair as she listened. She heard the voice of her man talking with the nurse inside, then the sound of his less-than-emphatic footsteps as he walked out to join her.

'My God,' she said in French. 'I'm going to get pissed!'

'Why not?' asked the Jackal's courier. 'This is the place for it. I see everything through a haze of disbelief myself.'

'You still will not tell me why the monseigneur sent you here – us here?'

'I told you, I'm merely a messenger.'

'And I don't believe you.'

'Believe. It's important for him but of no consequence for us. Enjoy, my lovely.'

'You always call me that when you won't explain.'

'Then you should learn from experience not to inquire, is it not so?'

'It is *not* so, my dear. I'm dying—'

'We'll hear no more of that!'

'It's true nevertheless; you cannot keep it from me. I don't worry for myself, the pain will end, you see, but I worry about you. *you*, forever better than your circumstances, Michel – No, *no*, you are *Jean Pierre*, I must not forget that . . . Still, I must concern myself. This place, these extraordinary lodgings, this *attention*. I think you will pay a terrible price, my dear.'

'Why do you say that?'

'It's all so grand. Too grand. Something's wrong.'

'You concern yourself too deeply.'

'No, you deceive yourself too easily. My brother, Claude, has always said you take too much from the monseigneur. One day the bill will be presented to you.'

'Your brother, Claude, is a sweet old man with feathers in his head. It's why the monseigneur gives him only the most insignificant assignments. You send him out for a paper in the Montparnasse he ends up in Marseilles not knowing how he got there.' The telephone inside the villa rang, interrupting the Jackal's man. He turned. 'Our new friend will get it,' he said.

'She's a strange one,' added the old woman. 'I don't trust her.'

'She works for the monseigneur.'

'Really?'

'I haven't had time to tell you. She will relay his instructions.'

The uniformed nurse, her light brown hair pulled severely back into a bun, appeared in the doorway. 'Monsieur, it is Paris,' she said, her wide grey eyes conveying an urgency missing in her low, understated voice.

'Thank you.' The Jackal's courier walked inside, following the nurse to the telephone. She picked it up and handed it to him. 'This is Jean Pierre Fontaine.'

'Blessings upon you, child of God,' said the voice several thousand miles away. 'Is everything suitable?'

'Beyond description,' answered the old man. 'It is . . . so grand, so much more than we deserve.'

'You will earn it.'

'However I may serve you.'

'You'll serve me by following the orders given to you by the woman. Follow them precisely with no deviation whatsoever, is that understood?'

'Certainly.'

'Blessings upon you.' There was a click and the voice was no more.

Fontaine turned to address the nurse, but she was not at his side. Instead, she was across the room unlocking the drawer of a table. He walked over to her, his eyes drawn to the contents of the drawer. Side by side were a pair of surgical gloves, a pistol with a cylindrical silencer attached to the barrel, and a straight razor, the blade recessed.

'These are your tools,' said the woman, handing him the key, her flat, expressionless grey eyes boring in on him, 'and the targets are in the last villa on this row. You are to familiarize yourself with the area by taking extended walks on the path, as old men do for circulatory purposes, and you are to kill them. You are to do this wearing the gloves and firing the gun into each skull. It *must* be the head. Then each throat must be slit—'

'Mother of *God*, the *children's*?'

'Those are the orders.'

'They're barbaric!'

'Do you wish me to convey that judgement?'

Fontaine looked over at the balcony door, at his woman in the wheelchair. 'No, no, of course not.'

'I thought not . . . There is a final instruction. With whosever blood is most convenient, you are to write on the wall the following: "Jason Bourne, brother of the Jackal." '

'Oh, my God . . . I'll be caught, of course.'

'That's up to you. Coordinate the executions with me and I'll swear a great warrior of France was in this villa at the time.'

'Time? . . . What is the time? When is this to be done?'

'Within the next thirty-six hours.'

'*Then* what?'

'You may stay here until your woman dies.'

9

Brendan Patrick Pierre Prefontaine was again astonished. Though he had no reservation, the front desk of Tranquillity Inn treated him like a visiting celebrity, then only moments after he had secured a villa told him that he already *had* a villa and asked how was the flight from Paris? Confusion descended for several minutes as the owner of Tranquillity Inn could not be reached for consultation; he was not at his residence and if he was on the premises he could not be found. Ultimately hands were thrown up in equal parts frustration and supplication and the former judge from Boston was taken to his lodgings, a lovely miniature house overlooking the Caribbean. Through accident, hardly design, he had reached into the wrong pocket and given the manager behind the desk a fifty-dollar American bill for his courtesy. Prefontaine was instantly a man to be reckoned with; fingers snapped and bells were palmed downward rapidly. Nothing was too splendid for the bewildering stranger who had suddenly flown in on the seaplane from Montserrat . . . It was the *name* that had thrown everyone behind Tranquillity's front desk into confusion. Could such a coincidence be possible? . . . Still the Crown governor – err on the safe side. Get the man a villa.

Once settled, his casual clothes distributed in the closet and the bureau, the craziness continued. A chilled bottle of Château Carbonnieux 78 accompanied fresh-cut flowers, and a box of Belgian chocolates arrived only to have a confused room-service waiter return to remove the chocolates, apologizing for the fact that they were for another villa down the line – or up the line – he thought, *mon.*

The judge changed into Bermuda shorts, wincing at the sight of his spindly legs, and put on a subdued paisley sport shirt. White loafers and a white cloth cap completed his tropical outfit; it would be dark soon and he wanted a stroll. For several reasons.

'I know who Jean Pierre Fontaine is,' said John St Jacques, reading the register behind the front desk, 'he's the one the CG's office called me about, but who the hell is B. P. *Pre*fontaine?'

'An illustrious judge from the United States,' declared the tall black assistant manager in a distinct British accent. 'My uncle, the deputy director of immigration, phoned me from the airport roughly two hours ago. Unfortunately, I was upstairs when the confusion arose, but our people did the right thing.'

'A judge?' asked the owner of Tranquillity Inn as the assistant manager touched St Jacques's elbow, gesturing for him to move away from the desk and the clerks. Both men did so. 'What did your uncle say?'

'There must be total privvissy where our two distinguished guests are concerned.'

'Why wouldn't there be? What does that mean?'

'My uncle was very discreet but he did allow that he watched the honoured judge go to the Inter Island counter and purchase a ticket. He further permitted himself to say that he knew he had been right. The judge and the French war hero are related and wish to meet confidentially on matters of great import.'

'If that was the case, why didn't the honoured judge have a reservation?'

'There appear to be two possible explanations, sir. According to my uncle, they were originally to meet at the airport but the Crown governor's reception line precluded it.'

'What's the second possibility?'

'An error may have been made in the judge's own offices in Boston, Massachusetts. According to my uncle, there was a brief discussion regarding the judge's law clerks, how they are prone to errors and if one had been made with his passport, he'd fly them all down to apologize.'

'Then judges are paid a lot more in the States than they are in Canada. He's damned lucky we had space.'

'It's the summer season, sir. We usually have available space during these months.'

'Don't remind me . . . All right, so we've got two illustrious relatives who want to meet privately but go about it in a very complicated way. Maybe you should call the judge and tell him what villa Fontaine is in. Or Prefontaine – whichever the hell it is.'

'I suggested that courtesy to my uncle, sir, and he was most adamant. He said we should do and say absolutely nothing. According to my uncle, all great men have secrets and he would not care to have his own brilliant deduction revealed except by the parties themselves.'

'Beg your pardon?'

'If such a call were made to the judge, he would know the information. could only come from my uncle, the deputy director of Montserrat's immigration.'

'Christ, do whatever you want, I've got other things on my mind . . . Incidentally. I've doubled the patrols on the road and the beach.'

'We'll be stretched thin, sir.'

'I've shifted a number off the paths. I know who's *here*, but I don't know who may want to get *in* here.'

'Do we expect trouble, sir?'

John St Jacques looked at the assistant manager. 'Not now,' he said. 'I've been out checking every inch of the grounds and the beach. By the way, I'll be staying with my sister and her children in Villa Twenty.'

The hero of World War II's French Résistance known as Jean Pierre Fontaine walked slowly up the concrete path towards the last villa overlooking the sea. It was similar to the others, with walls of pink stucco and a red tiled roof, but the surrounding lawn was larger, the bordering shrubbery taller and denser. It was a place for prime ministers and presidents, foreign secretaries and secretaries of state, men and women of international stature seeking the peace of pampered isolation.

Fontaine reached the end of the path where there was a four-foot-high white stuccoed wall and beyond it the impenetrable overgrown slope of the hill leading down to the shoreline. The wall itself extended in both directions, curving around the hill below the villas' balconies, at once demarcation and protection. The entrance to Villa Twenty was a pink wrought-iron gate bolted into the wall. Beyond the gate the old man could see a small child running about the lawn in a bathing suit. In moments a woman appeared in the frame of the open front door.

'Come on, Jamie!' she called out. 'Time for dinner.'

'Has Alison eaten, Mommy?'

'Fed and asleep, darling. She won't yell at her brother.'

'I like our house better. Why can't we go back to our house, Mommy?'

'Because Uncle John wants us to stay here . . . The boats are here, Jamie. He can take you fishing and sailing just like he did last April during the spring vacation.'

'We stayed at our house then.'

'Yes, well, Daddy was with us—'

'And we had lots of fun driving over in the truck!'

'*Dinner*, Jamie. Come along now.'

Mother and child went into the house and Fontaine winced thinking about his orders from the Jackal, the bloody executions he was sworn to carry out. And then the child's words came back to him. *Why can't we go back to our house, Mommy? . . . We stayed at our house then.* And the mother's answers: *Because Uncle John wants us to stay here . . . Yes, well, Daddy was with us then.*

There might be any number of explanations for the brief exchange he had overheard, but Fontaine could sense a warning quicker than most men, for his life had been filled with them. He sensed one now, and for that reason an old man would take a number of walks late at night for 'circulatory purposes.'

He turned from the wall and started down the concrete path so absorbed in thought that he nearly collided with a guest at least his own age wearing a foolish-looking little white cap and white shoes.

'Excuse me,' said the stranger, sidestepping out of Fontaine's way.

'Pardon, monsieur!' exclaimed the embarrassed hero of France, unconsciously slipping into his native tongue. '*Je regrette* – that is to say, it is I who must be excused.'

'Oh?' At his words the stranger's eyes briefly widened, almost as if there were recognition in them quickly hidden. 'Not at all.'

'*Pardon*, we have met, monsieur?'

'I don't believe so,' replied the old man in the silly white cap. 'But we've all heard the rumours. A great French hero is among the guests.'

'Foolishness. The accidents of war when we were all much younger. My name is Fontaine. Jean Pierre Fontaine.'

'Mine's . . . Patrick. Brendan Patrick—'

'A pleasure to make your acquaintance, monsieur.' Both men shook hands. 'This is a lovely place, is it not?'

'Simply beautiful.' Again the stranger seemed to be studying him, thought Fontaine, yet oddly enough avoiding any prolonged eye contact. 'Well, I must be on my way,' added the elderly guest in the brand-new white shoes. 'Doctor's orders.'

'*Moi aussi*,' said Jean Pierre, purposely speaking French, which evidently had an effect on the stranger. '*Toujours le médecin à cet âge, n'est-ce pas?*'

'All too true,' replied the old man with the bony legs, nodding and affecting the gesture of a wave as he turned and walked rapidly up the path.

Fontaine stood motionless watching the receding figure, waiting, knowing it would happen. And then it did. The old man stopped and slowly turned around. From a distance their eyes locked; it was enough. Jean Pierre smiled, then proceeded down the concrete path towards his villa.

It was another warning, he mused, and a far more deadly one. For three things were apparent: first, the elderly guest in the foolish white cap spoke French; second, he knew that 'Jean Pierre Fontaine' was in reality someone else – sent to Montserrat by someone else; third . . . he had the mark of the Jackal in his eyes. *Mon Dieu*, how like the monseigneur! Engineer the kill, make sure it is done, then remove all physical traces that could lead back to his methods of operation, in particular his private army of old men. No wonder the nurse had said that after his orders were carried out they could remain here in this paradise until his woman died, a date that was imprecise at best. The Jackal's generosity was not so grand as it appeared; his woman's death, as well as his own, had been scheduled.

John St Jacques picked up the phone in his office. 'Yes?'

'They have *met*, sir!' said the excited assistant manager at the front desk.

'Who's met?'

'The great man and his illustrious relative from Boston, Massachusetts. I would have called you at once but there was a mix-up concerning a box of Belgian chocolates—'

'What *are* you talking about?'

'Several minutes ago, sir, I saw them through the windows. They were conferring on the path. My esteemed uncle, the deputy director, was right in all things!'

'That's nice.'

'The Crown governor's office will be most pleased, and I'm certain we shall be commended, as will, of course, my brilliant uncle.'

'Good for all of us,' said St Jacques wearily. 'Now we don't have to concern ourselves about them any longer, do we?'

'Offhand I would say not, sir . . . Except that as we speak the honoured judge is walking down the path in haste. I believe he's coming inside.'

'I don't think he'll bite you; he probably wants to thank you. Do whatever he says. There's a storm coming up from Basse-Terre and we'll need the CG's input if the phones go out.'

'I shall perform whatever service he requires myself, sir!'

'Well, there are limits. Don't brush his teeth.'

Brendan Prefontaine hurried through the door of the circular glass-walled lobby. He had waited until the old Frenchman had turned into the first villa before reversing direction and heading straight for the main complex. As he had done so many times over the past thirty years, he was forced to think quickly on his feet – usually running feet – building plausible explanations that would support a number of obvious possibilities as well as others not so obvious. He had just committed an unavoidable yet stupid error, unavoidable because he was not prepared to give Tranquillity Inn's desk a false name in case identification was required, and stupid because he *had* given a false name to the hero of France . . . Well, not stupid; the similarity of their surnames might have led to unwanted complications where the purpose of his trip to Montserrat was concerned, which was quite simply extortion – to learn what so frightened Randolph Gates that he would part with fifteen thousand dollars, and having learned it perhaps collect a great deal more. No, the stupidity was in not taking the precautionary step he was about to take. He approached the front desk and the tall, slender clerk behind it.

'Good evening, *sir*,' fairly yelled the inn's employee, causing the judge to look around, grateful that there were very few guests in the lobby. 'However I may assist you, be assured of my perfection!'

'I'd rather be assured of your keeping your voice down, young man.'

'I shall *whisper*,' said the clerk inaudibly.

'What did you say?'

'How may I help you?' intoned the man, now sotto voce.

'Let's just talk quietly, all right?'

'Certainly. I am so very privileged.'

'You are?'

'Of course.'

'Very well,' said Prefontaine. 'I have a favour to ask of you—'

'Anything!'

'*Shhh!*'

'Naturally.'

'Like many men of advanced age I frequently forget things, you can understand that, can't you?'

'A man of your wisdom I doubt forgets anything.'

'What? . . . Never mind. I'm travelling incognito, you *do* know what I mean.'

'Most assuredly, sir.'

'I registered under my name, Prefontaine—'

'You certainly did,' interrupted the clerk. 'I *know*.'

'It was a mistake. My office and those I've told to reach me expect to ask for a "Mr Patrick," my middle name. It's harmless subterfuge to allow me some much needed rest.'

'I *understand*,' said the clerk confidentially, leaning over the counter.

'You do?'

'Of course. If such an eminent person as yourself were known to be a guest here, you might find little rest. As *another*, you must have complete "privvissy"! Be assured, I understand.'

' "Privvissy"? Oh, good Lord . . . '

'I shall myself alter the directory, Judge.'

'Judge . . . ? I said nothing about being a judge.'

An unrevealed blush was apparent on the man's embarrassed face. 'A slip born of wishing to serve you, sir.'

'And of something else – some*one* else.'

'On my word, no one here other than the owner of Tranquillity Inn is aware of the confidential nature of your visit, sir,' whispered the clerk, again leaning over the counter. 'All is total "privvissy"!'

'Holy Mary, that asshole at the airport—'

'My astute uncle,' continued the clerk, overriding and not hearing Prefontaine's soft monotone, 'made it completely clear that we were privileged to be dealing with illustrious men who required total confidentiality. You see, he called me in that spirit—'

'All right, all right, young man, I understand now and appreciate everything you're doing. Just make sure that the name is changed to Patrick, and should anyone here inquire about me, he or she is to be given that name. Do we understand each other?'

'With clairvoyance, honoured Judge!'

'I hope not.'

Four minutes later the harried assistant manager picked up the ringing telephone. 'Front desk,' he intoned, as if giving a benediction.

'This is Monsieur Fontaine in Villa Number Eleven.'

'Yes, sir. The honour is mine . . . ours . . . everyone's!'

'*Merci.* I wondered if you might help me. I met a charming American on the path perhaps a quarter of an hour ago, a man about my own age wearing a white walking cap. I thought I might ask him for an apéritif one day but I'm not sure I heard his name correctly.'

He was being tested, thought the assistant manager. *Great men not only had secrets but concerned themselves with those guarding them.* 'I would have to say from your description, sir, that you met the very charming Mr Patrick.'

'Ah, yes, I believe that was the name. An Irish name, indeed, but he's American, is he not?'

'A very *learned* American, sir, from Boston, Massachusetts. He's in Villa Fourteen, the third west of yours. Simply dial seven-one-four.'

'Yes, well, thank you so much. If you see Monsieur Patrick, I'd prefer you say nothing. As you know, my wife is not well and I must extend the invitation when it is comfortable for her.'

'I would never say *anything*, great sir, unless told to do so. Where you and the learned Mr Patrick are concerned, we follow the Crown governor's confidential instructions to the letter.'

'You do? That's most commendable . . . Adieu.'

He had done it! thought the assistant manager, hanging up the phone. Great men understood subtleties, and he had been subtle in ways his brilliant uncle would appreciate. Not only with the instant offering of the Patrick name, but, more important, by using the word 'learned' which conveyed that of a scholar – or a *judge.* And, finally, by stating that he would not say anything without the Crown governor's instructions. By the use of subtlety he had insinuated himself into the confidentiality of great men. It was a breathtaking experience, and he must call his uncle and share their combined triumph.

Fontaine sat on the edge of the bed, the telephone in its cradle yet still in his hand, staring at his woman out on the balcony. She sat in her wheelchair, her profile to him, the glass of wine on the small table beside the chair, her head bent down in pain . . . *Pain!* The whole terrible world was filled with pain! And he had done his share of inflicting it, he understood that and expected no quarter, but not for his woman. That was never part of the contract. *His* life, yes, of course, but not hers, not while she had breath in her frail body. *Non, monseigneur. Je refus! Ce n'est pas le contrat!*

So the Jackal's army of very old men now extended to America – it was to be expected. And an old Irish American in a foolish white cap, a *learned* man who for one reason or another had embraced the cult of the terrorist, was to be their executioner. A man who had studied him and pretended to speak no French, who had the sign of the Jackal in his eyes. *Where you and the learned Mr Patrick are concerned, we follow the instructions of the Crown governor.* The Crown governor who took his instructions from a master of death in Paris.

A decade ago, after five productive years with the monseigneur, he had been given a telephone number in Argenteuil, six miles north of Paris, that he was never to use except in the most extreme emergency. He had used it only once before, but he would use it now. He studied the international codes, picked up the phone and dialled. After the better part of two minutes, a voice answered.

'Le Coeur de Soldat,' said a flat male voice, martial music in the background.

'I must reach a blackbird,' said Fontaine in French. 'My identity is Paris Five.'

'If such a request is possible, where can such a bird reach you?'

'In the Caribbean.' Fontaine gave the area code, the telephone number and the extension to Villa Eleven. He hung up the phone and sat despondent on the edge of the bed. In his soul he knew that this might be his and his woman's last few hours on earth. If so, he and his woman could face their God and speak the truth. He had killed, no question about that, but he had never harmed or taken the life of a person who had not committed greater crimes against others – with a few minor exceptions that might be called innocent bystanders caught in the heat of fire or in an explosion. All life was pain, did not the Scriptures tell us that? . . . On the other hand, what kind of God allowed such brutalities? *Merde!* Do not think about such things! They are beyond your understanding.

The telephone rang and Fontaine grabbed it, pulling it to his ear. 'This is Paris Five,' he said.

'Child of God, what can be so extreme that you would use a number you have called only once before in our relationship?'

'Your generosity has been absolute, monseigneur, but I feel we must redefine our contract.'

'In what way?'

'My life is yours to do with as you will, as mercifully as you will, but it does not include my woman.'

'*What?*'

'A man is here, a learned man from the city of Boston who studies me with curious eyes, eyes that tell me he has other purposes in mind.'

'That arrogant fool flew down to Montserrat *himself*? He knows *nothing*!'

'Obviously he does, and I beg you, I shall do as you order me to do, but let us go back to Paris . . . I *beg* of you. Let her die in peace. I will ask no more of you.'

'You ask of *me*? I've given you my *word*!'

'Then why is this learned man from America here following me with a blank face and inquisitive eyes, monseigneur?'

The deep, hollow roll of a throated cough filled the silence, and then the Jackal spoke. 'The great professor of law has transgressed, inserted himself where he should not be. He's a dead man.'

Edith Gates, wife of the celebrated attorney and professor of law, silently opened the door of the private study in their elegant town house in Louisburg Square. Her husband sat motionless in his heavy leather armchair staring at the crackling fire, a fire he insisted upon despite the warm Boston night outside and the central air conditioning inside.

As she watched him, Mrs Gates was once again struck by the painful realization that there were . . . *things* . . . about her husband she would never understand. Gaps in his life she could never fill, leaps in his thinking she could not comprehend. She only knew that there were times when he felt a terrible pain and would not share it, and by sharing it lessen the burden on himself. Thirty-three years ago a passably attractive daughter of average wealth had married an extremely tall, gangling, brilliant but impoverished law school graduate whose anxiety and eagerness to please had turned off the major firms in those days of the cool, restrained late fifties. The veneer of sophistication and the pursuit of security were valued over a smouldering, wandering first-rate mind of unsure direction, especially a mind inside a head of unkempt hair and a body dressed in clothes that were cheap imitations of J. Press and Brooks Brothers, made to appear even worse because his bank account precluded any additional expenses for alterations and few discount stores carried his size.

The new Mrs Gates, however, had several ideas that would improve the prospects of their life together. Among them was to lay aside an immediate law career – better none than with an inferior firm, or, God forbid, a private practice with the sort of clients he was bound to attract, namely, those who could not afford established attorneys. Better to use his natural endowments, which were his impressive height and a quick, spongelike intelligence that, combined with his drive, disposed of heavy academic workloads with ease. Using her modest trust fund, Edith shaped the externals of her man, buying the correct clothes and hiring a theatrical vocal coach who instructed his student in the ways of dramatic delivery and effective stage presence. The gangling graduate soon took on a Lincolnesque quality with subtle flashes of John Brown. Too, he was on his way to becoming a legal *expert*, remaining in the milieu of the university, piling one degree upon another while teaching at the graduate level until the sheer depth of his expertise in specific areas was incontestable. And he found himself sought after by the prominent firms that had rejected him earlier.

The strategy took nearly ten years before concrete results appeared, and while the early returns were not earthshaking, still they represented progress. Law reviews, first minor and then major, began publishing his semi-controversial articles as much for their style as for their content, for the young associate professor had a seductive way with the written word, at once riveting and arcane, by turns flowery and incisive. But it was his opinions, latently emerging, that made segments of the financial community take notice. The mood of the nation was changing, the crust of the benevolent Great Society beginning to crack, the lesions initiated with code words coined by the Nixon boys, such as the Silent Majority and Bums-on-Welfare and the pejorative *them*. A meanness was rising out of the ground and spreading, and it was more than the perceptive, decent Ford could stop, weakened as he was by the wounds of Watergate; and too much as well for the brilliant Carter, too consumed by minutiae to exercise compassionate leadership. The phrase '. . . what you can do for your country' was out of fashion, replaced by 'what I can do for *me*.'

Dr Randolph Gates found a relentless wave on which to ride, a mellifluous voice with which to speak, and a growing acerbic vocabulary to match the dawning new era. In his now refined scholarly opinion – legally, economically and socially – *bigger* was better, and *more* far preferable to less. The laws that supported competition in the marketplace he attacked as stifling to the larger agenda of industrial growth from which would flow all manner of benefits for everyone – well, practically everyone. It was, after all, a Darwinian world and, like it or not, the fittest would always survive. The drums went bang and the cymbals clanged and the financial manipulators found a champion, a legal *scholar* who lent respectability to their righteous dreams of merger and consolidation; but out, take over, and sell off, all for the good of the many, of course.

Randolph Gates was summoned, and he ran into their arms with alacrity, stunning one courtroom after another with his elocutionary gymnastics. He had made it, but Edith Gates was not sure what it all meant. She had envisioned a comfortable living, naturally, but not millions, not the private jets flying all over the world, from Palm Springs to the South of France. Nor was she comfortable when her husband's articles and lectures were used to support causes that struck her as unrelated or patently unfair; he waved her arguments aside, stating that the cases in point were legitimate intellectual parallels. Above everything, she had not shared a bed or a bedroom with her husband in over six years.

She walked into the study, abruptly stopping as he gasped, swerving his head around, his eyes glazed and filled with alarm.

'I'm sorry, I didn't mean to startle you.'

'You always knock. Why didn't you knock? You know how it is when I'm concentrating.'

'I said I'm sorry. Something's on my mind and I wasn't thinking.'

'That's a contradiction.'

'Thinking about knocking, I mean.'

'What's on your *mind*,' asked the celebrated attorney as if he doubted his wife had one.

'Please don't be clever with me.'

'What *is* it, Edith?'

'Where were you last night?'

Gates arched his brows in mock surprise. 'My God, are you suspicious? I told you where I was. At the Ritz. In conference with someone I knew years ago, someone I did not care to have at my house. If, at your age, you want confirmation, call the Ritz.'

Edith Gates was silent for a moment; she simply looked at her husband. 'My dear,' she said. 'I don't give a damn if you had an assignation with the most voluptuous whore in the Combat Zone. Somebody would probably have to give her a few drinks to restore her confidence.'

'Not bad, bitch.'

'In that department you're not exactly a stud, bastard.'

'Is there a point to this colloquy?'

'I think so. About an hour ago, just before you came home from your office, a man was at the door. Denise was doing the silver, so I answered it. I must say he looked impressive; his clothes were terribly expensive and his car was a black Porsche—'

'*And?*' broke in Gates, lurching forward in the chair, his eyes suddenly wide, rigid.

'He said to tell you that *le grand professeur* owed him twenty thousand dollars and "he" wasn't where he was supposed to be last night, which I assumed was the Ritz.'

'It wasn't. Something came up . . . Oh, Christ, he doesn't *understand.* What did you say?'

'I didn't like his language or his attitude. I told him I hadn't the vaguest idea where you were. He knew I was lying, but there wasn't anything he could do.'

'Good. Lying's something he knows about.'

'I can't imagine that twenty thousand is such a problem for you—'

'It's not the money, it's the method of payment.'

'For what?'

'*Nothing.*'

'I believe that's what you call a contradiction, Randy.'

'Shut up!' The telephone rang. Gates lunged up from the chair and stared at it. He made no move to go to the desk; instead, he spoke in a guttural voice to his wife. 'Whoever it is, you tell him I'm not here . . . I'm away, out of town – you don't know when I'll be back.'

Edith walked over to the phone. 'It's your very private line,' she said as she picked it up on the third ring. 'The Gates residence,' began Edith, a ploy she had used for years; her friends knew who it was, others did not matter to her any longer. 'Yes . . . Yes? I'm sorry, he's away and we don't know when he'll return.' Gates's wife looked briefly at the phone, then hung up. She turned to her husband. 'That was the operator in Paris . . . It's strange. Someone was calling you, but when I said you weren't here, she didn't even ask where you could be reached. She simply got off the line – very abruptly.'

'Oh, my *God*!' cried Gates, visibly shaken. 'Something happened. . . . something's gone wrong, someone *lied*!' With those enigmatic words the attorney whipped around and raced across the room, fumbling in his trousers pocket. He reached a section of the floor-to-celling book-shelves where the centre of the chest-high shelf had been converted into a safe-like cupboard, a carved wooden door superimposed on the brown steel. In panic, as an afterthought stunned him further, he spun around and screamed at his wife. 'Get *out* of here! Get out, get out, get *out*!'

Edith Gates walked slowly to the study door, where she turned to her husband and spoke quietly. 'It all goes back to Paris, doesn't it, Randy? Seven years ago in Paris. *That's* where something happened, isn't it? You came back a frightened man, a man with a pain you won't share.'

'Get *out of here*!' shrieked the vaunted professor of law, his eyes wild.

Edith went out the door, closing it behind her but not releasing the knob, her hand twisted so the latch would not close. Moments later she opened it barely a few inches and watched her husband.

The shock was beyond anything she could imagine. The man she had lived with for thirty-three years, the legal giant who neither smoked nor drank a drop of alcohol, was plunging a hypodermic needle into his forearm.

10

Darkness had descended on Manassas, the countryside alive with nocturnal undercurrents, as Bourne crept through the woods bordering the 'farm' of General Norman Swayne. Startled birds fluttered out of their black recesses; crows awoke in the trees and cawed their alarms, then, as if calmed by a foraging co-conspirator, kept silent.

He reached it, wondering if indeed *it* would be there. A fence – high, with thick crisscrossing links embedded in green plastic, a coiled-barbed-wire addition above slanting outward. Entry prohibited. *Beijing. The Jing Shan Sanctuary.* There had been things to conceal within that Oriental wildlife preserve, so it was protected by an all but impassable government barrier. But why would a desk-bound general on military pay erect such a barricade around a 'farm' in Manassas, Virginia, an obstruction costing thousands of dollars? It was not designed to fence in livestock; it was, instead, built to keep out human life.

As with the sanctuary in China, there would be no electric alarms threaded through the links, for the animals and the birds of the forest would set them off repeatedly. Nor would there be the unseen beams of trip lights for the same reason; instead, they would be on the flat ground nearer the house, and waist-high, if they existed. Bourne pulled the small wire cutters out of his rear pocket and started with the links at earth level.

With each scissoring cut, he again understood the obvious, the inevitable, confirmed by his heavy breathing and the sweat that had formed on his hairline. No matter how hard he tried – not fanatically but at least assiduously – to keep himself in reasonably good shape, he was now fifty and his body knew it. Again, it was something to think about, not dwell upon, and with every inch of progress not think about at all. There were Marie and the children, his *family*; there was nothing he could not do as long as he willed it. David Webb was gone from his psyche, only the predator Jason Bourne remained.

He was through! The parallel vertical links were cut, the ground wires as well. He gripped the fence and pulled the opening towards him, making each half foot of space an ordeal. He crawled inside this strangely fortified acreage and stood up, listening, his eyes darting in every direction, scanning the darkness – which was not complete darkness. He saw – filtered through the thick branches of the tall overlapping pines bordering the tamed grounds – flickerings of light coming from the large house. Slowly, he made his way towards what he knew was the circular drive. He reached the outer border of the asphalt and lay prone beneath a spreading pine, gathering his thoughts and his breath as he studied the scene in front of him. Suddenly there was a flash of light on his far right, deep inside the grounds at the end of a straight gravelled road that branched off from the circular drive.

A door had been opened; it belonged to what appeared to be a small house or a large cabin and it remained open. Two men and a woman came out and were talking . . . no, they were not just talking, they were arguing – heatedly. Bourne ripped the short powerful binoculars out of their Velcro recess and up to his eyes. Quickly, he focused on the trio, whose voices grew in volume, the words indistinguishable but the anger apparent. As the blurred image sharpened, he studied the three people, knowing instantly that the medium-sized, medium-built, ramrod-straight protesting man on the left was the Pentagon's General Swayne, and the large-breasted woman with streaked dark hair his wife, but what struck him – and fascinated him – was the hulking overweight figure nearest the open door. He *knew* him! Jason could not remember from where or when, which was certainly not unusual, but his visceral reaction to the sight of the man was *not* usual. It was one of instant loathing and he did not know why, since no connection with anything in the past came to him. Only feelings of disgust and revulsion. Where were the images, the brief flashes of time or circumstance that so often illuminated his inner screen? They did not come; he only knew that the man he focused on in the binoculars was his enemy.

Then that huge man did an extraordinary thing. He reached for Swayne's wife, throwing his large left arm protectively around her shoulders, his right hand accusingly jabbing the space between him and the general. Whatever he said – or yelled – caused Swayne to react with what seemed to be stoic resolve mixed with feigned indifference. He turned around, and in military fashion strode back across the lawn towards a rear entrance to the house. Bourne lost him in the darkness and swung back to the couple in the light of the door. The large obese man released the general's wife and spoke to her. She nodded, brushed her lips against his, and ran after her husband. The obvious consort walked back into the small house and slammed the door shut, removing the light.

Jason reattached the binoculars to his trouseres and tried to understand what he had observed. It had been like watching a silent movie minus the subtitles, the gestures far more real and without exaggerated theatricality. That there was in the confines of this fenced acreage a *ménage à trois* was obvious, but this could hardly explain the fence. There was another reason, a reason he had to learn.

Further, instinct told him that whatever it was linked to the huge overweight man who had walked angrily back into the small house. He had to reach that house; he had to reach that man who had been a part of his forgotten past. He slowly got to his feet, and ducking from one pine to the next, he made his way to the end of the circular drive and then continued down the tree-lined border of the narrow gravelled road.

He stopped, lurching to the ground at a sudden intrusion of sound that was no part of the murmuring woods. Somewhere wheels were spinning, crushing stone and displacing it; he rolled over and over into the dark recesses of the low-handing, wide-spreading branches of a pine tree, swinging his body around to locate the disturbance.

Within seconds he saw it racing out of the shadows of the circular drive, rushing over the gravel of the extended road. It was a small odd-shaped vehicle, half three-wheeled motorbike, half miniature golf cart, the tyres large and deeply treaded, capable of both high speed and balance. It was also, in its way, ominous, for in addition to a high flexible antenna, thick curved Plexiglas shields shot up from all sides, bulletproof windows that protected the driver from gunfire while alerting by radio anyone inside the residences of an assault. General Norman Swayne's 'farm' took on an even stranger ambience . . . Then, abruptly, it was macabre.

A second three-wheeled cart swung out from the shadows behind the cabin – and it *was* a cabin with split logs on the exterior – and came to a stop only feet from the first vehicle on the gravelled road. Both drivers' heads swung militarily towards the small house as if they were robots in a public gallery, and then the words shot out from an unseen speaker.

'Secure the gates,' said the amplified voice, a voice in command. 'Release the dogs and resume your rounds.'

As if choreographed, the vehicles swung in unison, each in the opposite direction, the drivers gunning their engines as one, the strange-looking carts racing forward into the shadows. At the mention of dogs Bourne had automatically reached into his back pocket and removed the CO_2 gun; he then crawled laterally, rapidly, through the underbrush to within feet of the extended fence. If the dogs were in a pack, he would have no choice but to scramble up the links and spring over the coiled barbed wire to the other side. His dual-chambered dart pistol could eliminate two animals, not more; there would be no time to reload. He crouched, waiting, ready to leap up on the fence, the sightlines beneath the lower branches relatively clear.

Suddenly a black Doberman raced by on the gravelled road, no hesitation in his pace, no scent picked up, the animal's only objective apparently to reach a given place. Then another dog appeared, this a long-haired shepherd. It slowed down, awkwardly yet instinctively, as if programmed to halt at a specific area; it stopped, an obscure moving silhouette up the road. Standing motionless, Bourne understood. These were trained male attack dogs, each with its own territory, which was constantly urinated upon, forever its possessive turf. It was a behavioural discipline favoured by Oriental peasants and small landowners who knew too well the price of feeding the animals who guarded their minuscule fiefdoms of survival. Train a few, as few as possible, to protect their separated areas from thieves, and if alarms were raised the others would converge. Oriental. Vietnam . . . Medusa. It was coming back to him! Vague, obscure outlines – *images.* A young, powerful man in uniform, driving a Jeep, stepping out, and – through the mists of Jason's inner screen – yelling at what was left of an assault team that had returned from interdicting an ordnance route paralleling the Ho Chi Minh Trail. That *same man*, older, larger, had been in his binoculars only moments ago! And years ago that same man had promised *supplies.* Ammunition, mortars, grenades, *radios.* He had brought *nothing*! Only complaints from Command Saigon that 'you fucking illegals fed us crap.' But they hadn't. Saigon had acted too late, *reacted* too late, and twenty-six men had been killed or captured for nothing.

As if it were an hour ago, a minute ago, Bourne remembered. He had yanked his .45 out of his holster and, without warning, had jabbed the barrel into the approaching noncom's forehead.

'One more word and you're dead, Sergeant.' The man had *been* a sergeant! 'You bring us our requisitions by O-five-hundred tomorrow morning or I'll get to Saigon and personally blow you into the wall of whatever whorehouse you're frequenting. Do I make myself clear or do you care to save me a trip to publicity city? Frankly, in light of our losses, I'd rather waste you now.'

'You'll get what you need.'

'*Très bien!*' had yelled the oldest French member of Medusa, who years later would save his life in a wildlife sanctuary in Beijing. '*Tu es formidable, mon fils!*' How right he was. And how dead he was. D'Anjou, a man legends were written about.

Jason's thoughts were abruptly shattered. The long-haired attack dog was suddenly circling in the road, its snarls growing louder, his nostrils picking up the human scent. Within seconds, as the animal found its directional bearings, a frenzy developed. The dog lunged through the foliage, its teeth bared, the snarls now the throated growls of a kill. Bourne sprang back into the fence, pulling the CO_2 pistol out of its nylon shoulder holster with his right hand; his left arm crooked, extended, prepared for a vital counter-assault that if not executed properly would cost him the night. The crazed animal leaped, a hurling mass of rage. Jason fired, first one cartridge and then the second, and as the darts were embedded, he whipped his left arm around the attack dog's head, yanking the skull counterclockwise, slamming his right knee up into the animal's body to ward off the lashing sharp-nailed paws. It was over in moments – moments of raging, panicked, finally disintegrating fury – but without the howling sounds that might have carried across the lawn of the general's estate. The long-haired dog, its narcotized eyes wide, fell limp in Bourne's arms. He lowered it to the ground and once again waited, afraid to move until he knew that no converging inhuman alarms had been sent to the other animals.

There were none; there was only the constant murmuring of the forest beyond the prohibiting fence. Jason replaced the CO_2 pistol in the holster and crept forward, back to the gravelled road, beads of sweat rolling down his face and into his eyes. He *had* been away too long. Years ago such a feat as silencing an attack dog would have rolled off him – *un exercice ordinaire*, as the legend d'Anjou would have said – but it was no longer ordinary. What permeated his being was fear. Pure, unadulterated *fear.* Where was the man that was? Still, Marie and the children were out there; that man had to be summoned. *Summon* him!

Bourne stripped out the binoculars and raised them to his eyes again. The moonlight was sporadic, low-flying clouds intercepting the rays, but the yellow wash was sufficient. He focused on the shrubbery that fronted the stockade fence that bordered the road outside. Pacing back and forth on a bisecting dirt path like an angry, impatient panther was the black Doberman, stopping now and then to urinate and poke its long snout into the bushes. As he had been programmed to do, the animal roamed between the opposing closed iron gates of the enormous circular drive. At each halting checkpoint it snarled, spinning around several times as if both expecting and loathing the sharp electrical shock it would receive through its collar if it transgressed without cause. Again, the method of training went back to Vietnam; soldiers disciplined the attack dogs around ammunition and matériel depots with such remote-signalling devices. Jason focused the binoculars on the far side of the expansive front lawn. He zeroed in on a third animal, this a huge Weimaraner, gentle in appearance but lethal in attack. The hyperactive dog raced back and forth, aroused perhaps by squirrels or rabbits in the brush, but not by human scent; it did not raise a throated growl, the signal of assault.

Jason tried to analyse what he observed, for that analysis would determine his moves. He had to assume that there was a fourth or a fifth, or even a sixth animal patrolling the perimeters of Swayne's grounds. But why this way? Why not a pack roaming at will and in unison, a far more frightening and inhibiting sight? The expense that concerned the Oriental farmer was no object . . . Then the explanation struck him; it was so basic it was obvious. He shifted the binoculars back and forth between the Weimaraner and the Doberman, the picture of the long-haired German shepherd still all too clear in his mind. Beyond the fact that these were trained attack dogs, they were also something else. They were the top of their breeds, groomed to a fare-thee-well – vicious animals posing as champion show dogs by day, violent predators at night. Of *course.* General Norman Swayne's 'farm' was not unrecorded property, not concealed real estate, but very much out in the open and undoubtedly, jealously perhaps, visited by friends, neighbours and colleagues. During the daylight hours, guests could admire these docile champions in their well-appointed kennels while in the presence of a handler without realizing what they were beneath their glistening coats. Norman Swayne, Pentagon Procurements and alumnus of Medusa, was merely a dog aficionado, attested to by the quality of his animals' bloodlines. He might very well charge stud fees, but there was nothing in the canon of military ethics that precluded the practice.

A sham. If one such aspect of the general's 'farm' was a sham, it had to follow that the estate itself was a sham, as false as the 'inheritance' that made its purchase possible. Medusa.

One of the two strange three-wheeled carts appeared far across the lawn, out of the shadows of the house and down the exit road of the circular drive. Bourne focused on it, not surprised to see the Weimaraner romp over and playfully race beside the vehicle, yapping and seeking approval from the driver. The *driver.* The drivers were the handlers! The familiar scent of their bodies was calming to the dogs, reassuring them. The observation formed the analysis and the analysis determined his next tactic. He had to move, at least more freely than he was moving now, about the general's grounds. To do so he had to be in the company of a handler. He had to take one of the roving patrols; he raced back in the cover of the pine trees to his point of penetration.

The mechanized, bullet-proof vehicle stopped on the narrow path at midpoint between the two front gates nearly obscured by the shrubbery; Jason adjusted his binoculars. The black Doberman was apparently a favoured dog; the driver opened the right panel as the animal sprang up, placing his huge paws on the seat. The man chucked biscuits or pieces of meat into the wide, anticipating jaws, then reached over and massaged the dog's throat.

Bourne knew instantly that he had only moments to put his uncertain strategy together. He had to stop the cart and force the driver outside but without alarming the man, without giving him any reason whatsoever to use his radio and call for help. The *dog*? Lying in the road? No, the driver might assume it had been shot from the other side of the fence and alert the house. What could he *do*? He looked around in the near-total darkness feeling the panic of indecision, his anxiety growing as his eyes swept the area. Then, again, the obvious struck him. The large expanse of close-cropped manicured lawn, the precisely cut shrubbery, the swept circular drive – neatness was the order of the general's turf. Jason could almost hear Swayne commanding his groundskeepers to 'police the area!'

Bourne glanced over at the cart by the Doberman; the driver was playfully pushing the dog away, about to close the shielded panel. Only seconds now! What? *How?*

He saw the outlines of a limb on the ground; a rotted branch had fallen from the pine above him. He crossed quickly to it and crouched, yanking it out of the dirt and debris and dragged it towards the paved asphalt. To lay it across the drive might appear too obvious a trap, but *partially* on the road – an intrusion on the pervasive neatness – would be offensive to the eye, the task of removing it better done now than later in the event the general drove out and saw it upon his return. The men in Swayne's compound were either soldiers or ex-soldiers still under military authority; they would avoid reprimands, especially over the inconsequential. The odds were on Jason's side. He gripped the base of the limb, swung it around, and pushed it roughly five feet into the drive. He heard the panel of the cart slam shut; the vehicle rolled forward, gathering speed as Bourne raced back into the darkness of the pine tree.

The driver steered the vehicle around the dirt curve into the drive. As rapidly as he accelerated, he slowed down, his single headlight beam picking up the new obstruction protruding on the road. He approached it cautiously, at minimum speed, as if he were unsure of what it was; then he was sure and rushed forward. Without hesitation, he opened his side door, the tall Plexiglas shield swinging forward as he stepped out on the drive and walked around the front of the cart.

'Big Rex, you're one bad dog, buddy,' said the driver in a half-loud, very Southern voice. 'What'd you drag out of there, you dumb bastard? The brass-plated asshole would shave your coat for messing up his *ee*state! . . . Rex? *Rex*, you come here, you fuckin' hound!' The man grabbed the limb and pulled it off the road under the pine tree into the shadows. '*Rex*, you hear me! You humpin' knotholes, you horny stud?'

'Stay completely still and put your arms out in front of you,' said Jason Bourne, walking into view.

'Holy shit! Who are *you*?'

'Someone who doesn't give a damn whether you live or die,' replied the intruder calmly.

'You got a gun! I can see it!'

'So do you. Yours is in your holster. Mine's in my hand and it's pointed at your head.'

'The dog! Where the hell's the *dawg*?'

'Indisposed.'

'*What?*'

'He looks like a good dog. He could be anything a trainer wanted him to be. You don't blame the animal, you blame the human who taught it.'

'What are you talkin' about?'

'I guess the bottom line is that I'd rather kill the man than the animal, do I make myself clear?'

'Nothin's clear! I jest know *this* man don't want to get killed.'

'Then let's talk, shall we?'

'I got words, but only one life, mister.'

'Lower your right arm and take out your gun – by the fingers, *mister*.' The guard did so, holding the weapon by his thumb and forefinger. 'Lob it towards me, please.' The man obeyed. Bourne picked it up.

'What the hell's this all *about*?' cried the guard, pleading.

'I want information. I was sent here to get it.'

'I'll give you what I got if you let me get out of here. I don't want nothin' more to do with this place! I figured it was comin' someday, I told Barbie Jo, you ask her! I told her someday people'd be comin' around asking questions. But not this way, not *your* way! Not with guns aimed at our heads.'

'I assume Barbie Jo is your wife.'

'Sort of.'

'Then let's start with why "people" would come out here asking questions. My superiors want to know. Don't worry, you won't be involved, nobody's interested in you. You're just a security guard.'

'That's all I *am*, mister!' interrupted the frightened man.

'Then why did you tell Barbie Jo what you did? That people would someday come out here asking questions.'

'Hell, I'm not sure . . . Jest so many crazy things, y'know?'

'No, I don't know. Like what?'

'Well, like the brass-plated screamer, the general. He's a big wheel, right? He's got Pentagon cars and drivers and even helicopters whenever he wants 'em, right? He owns this place, right?'

'So?'

'So that big mick of a sergeant – a lousy master *sergeant* – orders him around like he wasn't toilet-trained, y'know what I mean? And that big-titty wife of his – she's got a thing goin' with the hulk and she don't give a damn who knows it. It's all crazy, y'see what I mean?'

'I see a domestic mess, but I'm not sure it's anybody's business. Why would people come out here and ask questions?'

'Why are *you* out here, man? You figured there was a meeting tonight, didn't you?'

'A meeting?'

'Them fancy limousines with the chauffeurs and the big shots, right? Well, you picked the wrong night. The dogs are out and they're never let out when there's a meetin.'

Bourne paused, then spoke as he approached the guard. 'We'll continue this in the cart,' he said with authority. 'I'll crouch down and you'll do exactly what I tell you to do.'

'You promised me I could get out of here!'

'You can, you will. Both you and the other fellow making the rounds. The gates over there, are they on an alarm?'

'Not when the dogs are loose. If those hounds see something out on the road and get excited, they'd jump up and set it off.'

'Where's the alarm panel?'

'There are two of 'em. One's in the sergeant's place, the other's in the front hall of the house. As long as the gates are closed, you can turn it on.'

'Come on, let's go.'

'Where are we goin'?'

'I want to see every dog on the premises.'

Twenty-one minutes later, the remaining five attack dogs drugged and carried to their kennels, Bourne unlatched the entrance gate and let the two guards outside. He had given each three hundred dollars. 'This will make up for any pay you lose,' he said.

'Hey, what about my car?' asked the second guard. 'It ain't much but it gets me around. Me and Willie come out here in it.'

'Do you have the keys?'

'Yeah, in my pocket. It's parked in the back by the kennels.'

'Get it tomorrow.'

'Why don't I get it now?'

'You'd make too much noise driving out, and my superiors will be arriving any moment. It's best that they don't see you. Take my word for it.'

'Holy shit! What'd I tell you, Jim-Bob? Jest like I tole Barbie Jo. This place is weird, man!'

'There hundred bucks ain't weird, Willie. C'mon, we'll hitch. T'aint late and some of the boys'll be on the road . . . Hey, mister, who's gonna take care of the hounds when they wake up? They got to be walked and fed before the morning shift, and they'll tear apart any stranger who gets near 'em.'

'What about Swayne's master sergeant? He can handle them, can't he?'

'They don't like him much,' offered the guard named Willie, 'but they obey him. They're better with the general's wife, the horny bastards.'

'What about the general?' asked Bourne.

'He pisses bright yeller at the sight of 'em,' replied Jim-Bob.

'Thanks for the information. Go on now, get down the road a piece before you start hitchhiking. My superiors are coming from the other direction.'

'You know,' said the second guard, squinting in the moonlight at Jason, 'this is the craziest fuckin' night I ever expect to see. You get in here dressed like some gawddamn terrorist, but you talk and act like a shit-kickin' army officer. You keep mentioning these "soopeeriors" of yours; you drug the pups and pay us three hundred bucks to get out. I don't understand nothin'!'

'You're not supposed to. On the other hand, if I was really a terrorist, you'd probably be dead, wouldn't you?'

'He's right, Jim-Bob. Let's get *outta* here!'

'What the hell are we supposed to say?'

'Tell anyone who asks you the truth. Describe what happened tonight. Also, you can add that the code name is Cobra.'

'My *Gawd*!' yelled Willie as both men fled into the road.

Bourne secured the gate and walked back to the patrol cart certain in the knowledge that whatever happened during the next hours, an appendage of Medusa had been thrown into a state of further anxiety. Questions would be asked feverishly – questions for which there were no answers. Nothing. Enigma.

He climbed into the cart, shifted gears and started for the cabin at the end of the gravelled road that branched off from the immaculate circular drive.

He stood by the window peering inside, his face at the edge of the glass. The huge, overweight master sergeant was sitting in a large leather armchair, his feet on an ottoman, watching television. From the sounds penetrating the window, specifically the rapid, high-pitched speech of an announcer, the general's aide was engrossed in a baseball game. Jason scanned the room as best he could; it was typically rustic, a profusion of browns and reds, from dark furniture to checked curtains, comfortable and masculine, a man's cabin in the country. However, there were no weapons in sight, not even the accepted antique rifle over the fireplace, and no general issue .45 automatic either on the sergeant's person or atop the table beside the chair. The aide had no concerns for his immediate safety and why should he? The estate of General Norman Swayne was totally secure – fence, gates, patrols and disciplined roving attack dogs at all points of entry. Bourne stared through the glass at the jowled, strong face of the master sergeant. What secrets did that large head hold? He would find out. Medusa's Delta One would find out if he had to carve that skull apart. Jason pushed himself away from the window and walked around the cabin to the front door. He knocked twice with the knuckles of his left hand; in his right was the untraceable automatic supplied by Alexander Conklin, the crown prince of dark operations.

'It's *open*, Rachel!' yelled the rasping voice from within.

Bourne twisted the knob and shoved the door back; it swung slowly on its hinges and made contact with the wall. He walked inside.

'Jesus *Christ*!' roared the master sergeant, his heavy legs plunging off the ottoman as he wriggled his massive body out of the chair. '*You*! . . . You're a goddamned *ghost*! You're *dead*!'

'Try again,' said Delta of Medusa. 'The name's Flannagan, isn't it? That's what comes to mind.'

'You're *dead*!' repeated the general's aide, screaming, his eyes bulging in panic. 'You bought it in Hong Kong! You were killed in Hong Kong . . . four, five *years* ago!'

'You kept tabs—'

'We know . . . *I* know!'

'You've got connections in the right places, then.'

'You're Bourne!'

'Obviously born again, you might say.'

'I don't *believe* this!'

'Believe, Flannagan. It's the "we" we're going to talk about. Snake Lady, to be precise.'

'*You're* the one – the one Swayne called "Cobra"!'

'It's a snake.'

'I don't *get* it—'

'It's confusing.'

'You're *one* of us!'

'I was. I was also cut out. I snaked back in, as it were.'

The sergeant frantically looked at the door, then the windows. 'How'd you get in here? Where are the guards, the *dogs*? *Jesus!* Where *are* they?'

'The dogs are asleep in the kennels, so I gave the guards the night off.'

'You gave . . . The dogs are on the grounds!'

'Not any longer. They were persuaded to rest.'

'The guards – the goddamned *guards*!'

'They were persuaded to leave. What they think is happening here tonight is even more confusing.'

'What've you done – what are you *doing*?'

'I thought I just mentioned it. We're goint to talk, Sergeant Flannagan. I want to get caught up with some old comrades.'

The frightened man backed awkwardly away from the chair. 'You're the maniac they called Delta before you turned and went in business for yourself!' he cried in a guttural whisper. 'There was a picture, a photograph – you were laid out on a slab, bloodstains all over the sheet from the bullet wounds; your face was uncovered, your eyes wide open, holes still bleeding on your forehead and your throat . . . They asked me who you were and I said, "He's Delta. Delta One from the illegals," and they said, "No, he's not, he's Jason Bourne, the killer, the assassin," so I said, "Then they're one and the same because that man is *Delta* – I *knew* him." They thanked me and told me to go back and join the others.'

'Who were "they"?'

'Some people over at Langley. The one who did all the talking had a limp; he carried a cane.'

'And "the others" – they told you to go back and join?'

'About twenty-five or thirty of the old Saigon crowd.'

'Command Saigon?'

'Yeah.'

'Men who worked with *our* crowd, the "illegals"?'

'Mostly, yeah.'

'When was this?'

'For Christ's sake, I *told* you!' roared the panicked aide. 'Four or five *years* ago! I saw the photograph – you were *dead*!'

'Only a single photograph,' interrupted Bourne quietly, staring at the master sergeant. 'You have a very good memory.'

'You held a gun to my head. Thirty-three years, two wars and twelve combat tours, nobody ever did that to me – nobody but you . . . Yeah. I gotta good memory.'

'I think I understand.'

'I *don't*! I don't understand a goddamned thing! You were dead!'

'You've said that. But I'm not, am I? Or may be I am. Maybe this is the nightmare that's been visited upon you after twenty years of deceit.'

'What kind of crap is that? What the *hell*—'

'Don't move!'

'I'm *not*!'

Suddenly, in the distance, there was a loud report. A *gunshot*! Jason spun around . . . then instinct commanded him to keep turning! *All* around! The massive general's aide was lunging at him, his huge hands like battering rams grazing off Bourne's shoulders as Delta One viciously lashed up his right foot, catching the sergeant's kidney, embedding his shoe deep into the flesh while crashing the barrel of his automatic into the base of the man's neck. Flannagan lurched downwards, splayed on the floor; Jason hammered his left foot into the sergeant's head, stunning him into silence.

A silence that was broken by the continuous hysterical screams of a woman racing outside towards the open door of the cabin. Within seconds, General Norman Swayne's wife burst into the room, recoiling at the sight in front of her, gripping the back of the nearest chair, unable to contain her panic.

'He's *dead*!' she shrieked, collapsing, swerving the chair to her side as she fell to the floor reaching for her lover. 'He *shot* himself, Eddie! Oh, my *God*, he *killed* himself!'

Jason Bourne rose from his crouched position and walked to the door of the strange cabin that held so many secrets. Calmly, watching his two prisoners, he closed it. The woman wept, gasping, trembling, but they were not tears of sorrow, only fear. The sergeant blinked his eyes and shook his huge head, raising it. If any emotion could be defined in his expression, it was an admixture of fury and bewilderment.

11

'Don't *touch* anything,' ordered Bourne as Flannagan and Rachel Swayne haltingly preceded him into the general's photograph-lined study. At the sight of the old soldier's corpse arched back in the chair behind the desk, the ugly gun still in his outstretched hand, and the horror beyond left by the back of his skull that had been blown away, the wife convulsed, falling to her knees as if she might vomit. The master sergeant grabbed her arm, holding her off the floor, his eyes dazed, fixed on the mutilated remains of General Norman Swayne.

'Crazy son of a bitch,' whispered Flannagan, his voice strained and barely audible. Then standing motionless, the muscles of his jaw pulsating, he roared. 'You insane fuckin' son of a *bitch*! What did you do it for – *why*? What do we do *now*?'

'You call the police, sergeant,' answered Jason.

'What?' yelled the aide, spinning around.

'*No!*' screamed Mrs Swayne, lurching to her feet. 'We can't do that!'

'I don't think you've got a choice. You didn't kill him. You may have driven him to kill himself but you didn't kill him.'

'What the hell are you talking about?' asked Flannagan gruffly.

'Better a simple if messy domestic tragedy than a far wider investigation, wouldn't you say? I gather it's no secret that you two have an arrangement that's – well, no secret.'

'He didn't give a shit about our "arrangement", and that was no secret, either.'

'He encouraged us at every opportunity,' added Rachel Swayne, hesitantly smoothing her skirt, oddly, swiftly regaining her composure. She spoke to Bourne but her eyes strayed to her lover. 'He consistently threw us together, often for days at a time . . . Do we *have* to stay in here? My *God*, I was married to that man for twenty-six years! I'm sure you can understand . . . this is *horrible* for me!'

'We have things to discuss,' said Bourne.

'Not in *here*, if you please. The living room; it's across the hall. We'll talk there.' Mrs Swayne, suddenly under control, walked out of the study; the general's aide glanced over at the blood-drenched corpse, grimaced, and followed her. Jason watched them and called out.

'Stay in the hallway where I can see you and don't move!' he shouted, crossing to the desk, his eyes darting from one object to another, taking in the last items Norman Swayne saw before placing the automatic in his mouth. Something was wrong. On the right side of the wide green blotter was a Pentagon memorandum pad, Swayne's rank and name printed below the insignia of the United States Army. Next to the pad, to the left of the blotter's leather border, was a gold ballpoint pen, its sharp silver point protruding, as if recently used, the writer forgetting to twist it back into its recess. Bourne leaned over the desk within inches of the dead body, the acrid smell of the exploded shell and burnt flesh still pungent, and studied the memo pad. It was blank, but Jason carefully tore off the top pages, folded them, and put them into his trousers pocket. He stepped back still bothered . . . what was it? He looked around the room, and as his eyes roamed over the furniture, Master Sergeant Flannagan appeared in the doorway.

'What are you doing?' Flannagan asked suspiciously. 'We're waiting for you.'

'Your friend may find it too difficult to stay in here, but I don't. I can't afford to, there's too much to learn.'

'I thought you said we shouldn't touch anything.'

'Looking isn't touching, Sergeant. Unless you remove something, then no one knows it's been touched because it isn't here.' Bourne suddenly walked over to an ornate brass-topped coffee table, the sort so common to the bazaars in India and the Middle East. It was between two armchairs in front of the study's small fireplace; off centre was a fluted glass ashtray partially filled with the remains of half-smoked cigarettes. Jason reached down and picked it up; he held it in his hand and turned to Flannagan. 'For instance, Sergeant, this ashtray. I've touched it, my fingerprints are on it, but no one will know that because I'm taking it away.'

'What for?'

'Because I smelled something – I mean I really smelled it, with my nose, nothing to do with instincts.'

'What the hell are you talking about?'

'Cigarette smoke, that's what I'm talking about. It hangs around a lot longer than you might think. Ask someone who's given them up more times than he can remember.'

'So what?'

'So let's have a talk with the general's wife. Let's all have a talk. Come on, Flannagan, we'll play show and tell.'

'That weapon in your pocket makes you pretty fuckin' brave, doesn't it?'

'*Move*, Sergeant!'

Rachel Swayne swung her head to her left, throwing back her long, dark streaked hair over her shoulder as she stiffened her posture in the chair. 'That's offensive in the extreme,' she pronounced with wide accusatory eyes, staring at Bourne.

'It certainly is,' agreed Jason, nodding. 'It also happens to be true. There are five cigarette butts in this ashtray and each has lipstick on it.' Bourne sat down across from her, putting the ashtray on the small table next to the chair. 'You were there when he did it, when he put his gun into his mouth and pulled the trigger. Perhaps you didn't think he'd go through with it; maybe you thought it was just another one of his hysterical threats – whatever, you didn't raise a word to stop him. Why should you have? For you and *Eddie* it was a logical and reasonable solution.'

'*Preposterous!*'

'You know, Mrs Swayne, to put it bluntly, that's not a word you should use. You can't carry it off, any more than you're convincing when you say something's "offensive in the extreme." . . . Neither expression is you, Rachel. You're imitating other people – probably rich, vacuous customers a young hairdresser heard repeating such phrases years ago in Honolulu.'

'How *dare* you . . . ?'

'Oh, come on, that's ridiculous, Rachel. Don't even try the "How dare you" bit, it doesn't work at all. Are you, in your nasal twang, going to have my head chopped off by royal decree?'

'Lay *off* her!' shouted Flannagan, standing beside Mrs Swayne. 'You got the iron but you don't have to do this! . . . She's a good woman, a *damn* good woman, and she was shit on by all the crap artists in this town.'

'How could she be? She was the *general's* wife, the mistress of the manor, wasn't she? *Isn't* she?'

'She was *used*—'

'I was laughed at, always laughed at, Mr Delta!' cried Rachel Swayne, gripping the arms of her chair. 'When they weren't leering or drooling. How'd *you* like to be the special piece of meat passed out like a special desert to *very* special people when the dinner and the drinks are over?'

'I don't think I'd like it at all. I might even refuse.'

'I *couldn't*! He made me *do* it!'

'Nobody can make anybody do anything like that.'

'Sure, they can, Mr Delta,' said the general's wife, leaning forward, her large breasts pressing the sheer fabric of her blouse, her long hair partially obscuring her ageing but still soft-featured, sensual face. 'Try an uneducated grammar school dropout from the coal basins in West Virginia when the companies shut down the mines and nobody had no food – excuse me, *any* food. You take what you got and you run with it and that's what I did. I got laid from Aliquippa to Hawaii, but I got there and I learned a trade. That's where I met the Big Boy and I married him, but I didn't have no illusions from day *one*. 'Specially when he got back from 'Nam, y'know what I mean?'

'I'm not sure I do, Rachel.'

'You don't have to explain *nothin'* kiddo!' roared Flannagan.

'No, I wanna, Eddie! I'm sick of the whole shit, *okay*?'

'You watch your tongue!'

'The point is, I don't *know* nothin', Mr Delta. But I can figure things, y'know what I mean?'

'*Stop* it, Rachel!' cried the dead general's aide.

'Fuck off, Eddie! You're not too bright either. This Mr Delta could be our way out. . . . Back to the islands, *right*?'

'Absolutely right, Mrs Swayne.'

'You know what this place is . . . ?'

'Shut *up*!' yelled Flannagan, awkwardly plodding forward, stopped by the sudden ear-shattering explosion of Bourne's gun, the bullet searing into the floor between the sergeant's legs.

The woman screamed. When she stopped, Jason continued: 'What is this place, Mrs Swayne?'

'*Hold* it,' the master sergeant again interrupted, but his objection was not shouted now; instead, it was a plea, a strong man's plea. He looked at the general's wife and then back at Jason. 'Listen, Bourne or Delta or whoever you are, Rachel's right. You could be our way out – there's nothing left for us over here – so what have you got to offer?'

'For what?'

'Say we tell you what we know about this place . . . and *I* tell you where you can start looking for a lot more. How can you help us? How can we get out of here and back to the Pac Islands without being hassled, our names and faces all over the papers?'

'That's a tall order, Sergeant.'

'Goddamn it, she didn't *kill* him – *we* didn't kill him, you said so yourself!'

'Agreed, and I couldn't care less whether you did or not, whether you were responsible or not. I've got other priorities.'

'Like getting "caught up with some old comrades" or whatever the hell it was?'

'That's right, I'm owed.'

'I still can't figure you—'

'You don't have to.'

'You were dead!' broke in the perplexed Flannagan, the words rushing out. 'Delta One from the illegals was *Bourne*, and Bourne was *dead* and Langley proved it to us! But you're *not* dead—'

'I was *taken*, sergeant! That's all you have to know – that and the fact that I'm working alone. I've got a few debts I can call in, but I'm strictly solo. I need information and I need it quickly!'

Flannagan shook his head in bewilderment. 'Well . . . maybe I can help you there,' he said quietly, tentatively, 'better than anyone else would. I was given a special assignment, so I had to learn things, things someone like me wouldn't normally be told.'

'That sounds like the opening notes of a con song, Sergeant. What was your special assignment?'

'Nursemaid. Two years ago Norman began to fall apart. I controlled him, and if I couldn't I was given a number to call in New York.'

'Said number being part of the help you can give me.'

'That and a few licence plate IDs I wrote down just in case—'

'In case,' completed Bourne, 'someone decided your nursemaid's services were no longer required.'

'Something like that. Those pricks never liked us – Norman didn't see it but I did.'

'Us? You and Rachel and Swayne?'

'The *uniform*. They look down their rich civilian noses at us like we're necessary garbage, and they're right about the necessary. They needed Norman. With their eyes they spat on him but they needed him.'

The soldier boys couldn't run with it. Albert Armbruster, chairman of the Federal Trade Commission. Medusa – the civilian inheritors.

'When you say you wrote down the licence plate numbers, I assume that means you weren't part of the meetings that took place – *take* place – here on a fairly regular basis. That is, you didn't mingle with the guests; you weren't one of them.'

'Are you *crazy*?' screeched Rachel Swayne, in her own succinct way answering Jason's question. 'Whenever there was a real meeting and not a lousy drunken dinner party, Norm told me to stay upstairs, or if I wanted to, go over to Eddie's and watch television. Eddie couldn't leave the cabin. We weren't *good* enough for his big fancy asshole friends! It's been that way for years . . . Like I said, he threw us together.'

'I'm beginning to understand, at least I think I am. But you got the licence numbers, Sergeant. How did you do that? I gather you were confined to quarters.'

'I didn't get 'em, my guards did. I called it a confidential security procedure. No one argued.'

'I see. You said Swayne began to fall apart a couple of years ago. How? In what way?'

'Like tonight. Whenever something out of the ordinary happened, he'd freeze; he didn't want to make decisions. If it even smacked of Snake Lady, he wanted to bury his head in the sand until it went away.'

'What *about* tonight? I saw you two arguing . . . it seemed to me the sergeant was giving the general his marching orders.'

'You're damn right I was. Norman was in a panic – over you, over the man they called Cobra who was bringing out this heavy business about Saigon twenty years ago. He wanted me to be with him when you got here and I told him no way. I said I wasn't nuts and I'd have to be nuts to do that.'

'Why? Why would it be nuts for an aide to be with his superior officer?'

'For the same reason noncoms aren't called into situation rooms where the stars and the stripers are figuring out strategy. We're on different levels; it isn't done.'

'Which is another way of saying there are limits to what you should know.'

'You got it.'

'But, you were part of that Saigon twenty years ago, part of Snake Lady – hell, Sergeant, you were *Medusa*, you *are* Medusa.'

'Nickels and dimes' worth, Delta. I sweep up and they take care of me, but I'm only a sweeper in a uniform. When my time comes to turn in that uniform, I go quietly into a nice distant retirement with my mouth shut, or I go out in a body bag. It's all very clear. I'm expendable.'

Bourne watched the master sergeant closely as he spoke, noting Flannagan's brief glances at the general's wife, as if he expected to be applauded or, conversely, to be told with a look to shut up. Either the huge military aide was telling the truth or he was a very convincing actor. 'Then it strikes me,' said Jason finally, 'that this is a logical time to move up your retirement. I can do that, Sergeant. You can fade quietly with your mouth shut and with whatever rewards you're given for sweeping up. A devoted general's aide with over thirty years' service opts for retirement when his friend and superior tragically takes his own life. No one will question you. . . . That's my offer.'

Flannagan again looked at Rachel Swayne; she nodded sharply once, then stared at Bourne. 'What's the guarantee that we can pack up our stuff and get out?' asked the woman.

'Isn't there a little matter of Sergeant Flannagan's discharge and his army pension?'

'I made Norman sign those papers eighteen months ago,' broke in the aide. 'I was posted permanently to his office at the Pentagon and billeted to his residence. I just have to fill in the date, sign my own name, and list a general delivery address which Rachel and I already figured out.'

'That's all?'

'What's left is maybe three or four phone calls. Norman's lawyer, who'll wrap up everything here; the kennels for the dogs; the Pentagon assigned-vehicle dispatcher – and a last call to New York. Then it's Dulles Airport.'

'You must have thought about this for a long time, for years—'

'Nothing but, Mr Delta,' confirmed the general's wife, interrupting. 'Like they say, we paid our dues.'

'But before I can sign those papers or make those calls,' added Flannagan, 'I have to know we can break clean – now.'

'Meaning no police, no newspaper, no involvement with tonight – you simply weren't here.'

'You said it's a tall order. How tall are the debts you can call in?'

'You simply weren't here,' repeated Bourne softly, slowly, looking at the fluted glass ashtray with the lipstick-stained cigarette butts on the table beside him. He pulled his eyes back to the general's aide. 'You didn't touch anything in there; there's nothing to physically tie you in with this suicide . . . Are you really prepared to leave, say, in a couple of hours?'

'Try thirty minutes, Mr Delta,' replied Rachel.

'My God, you had a *life* here, both of you—'

'We don't want anything from this life outside of what we've got.' said Flannagan firmly.

'The estate here is yours, Mrs Swayne—'

'Like hell it is. It's being turned over to some foundation, ask the lawyer. Whatever I get, *if* I get, he'll send on to me. I just want out – we want out.'

Jason looked back and forth at the strange and strangely drawn-together couple. 'Then there's nothing to stop you.'

'How do we *know* that?' pressed Flannagan, stepping forward.

'It'll take a measure of trust on your part, but, believe me, I can do it. On the other hand, look at the alternative. Say you stay here. No matter what you do with *him*, he won't show up in Arlington tomorrow or the next day or the day after that. Sooner or later someone's going to come looking for him. There'll be questions, searches, an investigation, and as sure as God made little Bobby Woodwards, the media will descend with its bellyfull of speculations. In short order your "arrangement" will be picked up – hell, even the guards talked about it – and the newspapers, the magazines and television will have a collective field day . . . Do you want that? Or would it all lead to that body bag you mentioned?'

The master sergeant and his lady stared at each other. 'He's right, Eddie,' said the latter. 'With him we got a chance, the other way we don't.'

'It sounds too easy,' said Flannagan, his breath coming shorter as he glanced towards the door. 'How are you going to handle everything?'

'That's my business,' answered Bourne. 'Give me the telephone numbers, all of them, and then the only call you'll have to make is the one to New York, and if I were you, I'd make it from whatever Pac island you're on.'

'You're *nuts*! The minute the news breaks. I'm on Medusa's rug – so's Rachel! They're going to want to know what happened.'

'Tell them the truth, at least a variation of it, and I think you may even get a bonus.'

'You're a goddamned flake!'

'I wasn't a flake in 'Nam, Sergeant. Nor was I in Hong Kong, and I'm certainly not now . . . You and Rachel came home, saw what had happened, packed up and left – because you didn't want any questions and the dead can't talk and trap themselves. Predate your papers by a day, mail them, and leave the rest to me.'

'I dunno—'

'You don't have a *choice*, Sergeant!' shot back Jason, rising from the chair. 'And I don't care to waste any more time! You want me to go, I'll go – figure it all out for yourselves.' Bourne angrily started for the door.

'No, Eddie, *stop* him! We gotta do it his way, we gotta take the chance! The other way we're dead and you know it.'

'All *right*, all right! . . . Cool it, Delta. We'll do what you say.'

Jason stopped and turned. '*Everything* I say, Sergeant, down to the letter.'

'You got it.'

'First, you and I will go over to your place while Rachel goes upstairs and packs. You'll give me everything you've got – telephone and licence numbers, every name you can remember, anything you can give me that I ask for. Agreed?'

'Yeah.'

'Let's go. And Mrs Swayne, I know that there are probably a lot of little things you'd like to take along, but—'

'*Forget* it, Mr Delta. Mementos I don't have. Whatever I really wanted was long since shipped out of this hell hole. It's all in storage ten thousand miles away.'

'My, you really were prepared, weren't you?'

'Tell me something I don't know. You see, the time had to come, one way or the other, y'know what I mean?' Rachel walked rapidly past the two men and into the hall; she stopped and came back to Master Sergeant Flannagan, a smile on her lips, a glow in her eyes, as she placed her hand on his face. 'Hey, Eddie,' she said quietly. 'It's really gonna happen. We're gonna *live*, Eddie. Y'know what I mean?'

'Yeah, babe. I know.'

As they walked out into the darkness towards the cabin, Bourne spoke. 'I meant what I said about not wasting time, Sergeant. Start talking. What were you going to tell me about Swayne's place here?'

'Are you ready?'

'What does that mean? Of course I'm ready.' But he wasn't. He stopped suddenly on the grass at Flannagan's words.

'For openers, it's a cemetery.'

Alex Conklin sat back in the desk chair, the phone in his hand, stunned, frowning, unable to summon a rational response to Jason's astonishing information. All he could say was, 'I don't *believe* it!'

'Which part?'

'I don't know. Everything, I guess . . . the cemetery on down. But I have to believe it, don't I?'

'You didn't want to believe London or Brussels, either, or a commander of the Sixth Fleet or the keeper of the covert keys in Langley. I'm just adding to the list . . . The point is, once you find out who they all are, we can *move*.'

'You'll have to start from the beginning again; my head's shredded. The telephone number in New York, the licence plates—'

'The *body*, Alex! Flannagan and the general's *wife*! They're on their way; that was the deal and you've got to cover it.'

'Just like that? Swayne kills himself and the two people on the premises who can answer questions, we say *Ciao* to them and let them out of the country? That's only slightly more lunatic than what you've told me!'

'We don't have time for negotiating games – and besides, he can't answer any more questions. They were on different levels.'

'Oh, boy, that's really clear.'

'Do it. Let them go. We may need them both later.'

Conklin sighed, his indecision apparent. 'Are you sure? It's very complicated.'

'*Do* it! For Christ's sake, Alex, I don't give a goddamn about complications or violations or all the manipulations you can dream up! I want *Carlos*! We're building net and we can pull him *in* – *I* can pull him in!'

'All right, all right. There's a doctor in Falls Church that we've used before in special operations. I'll get hold of him, he'll know what to do.'

'Good,' said Bourne, his mind racing. 'Now put me on tape. I'll give you everything Flannagan gave me. Hurry up, I've got a lot to do.'

'You're on tape, Delta One.'

Reading from the list he had written down in Flannagan's cabin, Jason spoke rapidly, enunciating clearly so that there would be no confusion on the tape. There were the names of seven frequent and acknowledged guests at the general's dinner parties, none guaranteed as to accuracy or spelling but with quick-brush descriptions; then came the licence plates, all from the far more serious twice-monthly meetings. Next to last were the telephone numbers of Swayne's lawyer, all of the estate's guards, the dog kennels and the Pentagon extension for assigned vehicles; finally there was the unlisted telephone in New

York, no name here, only a machine that took messages. 'That's got to be a priority one, Alex.'

'We'll break it,' said Conklin, inserting himself on the tape. 'I'll call the kennels and talk Pentagonese – the general's being flown to a hush-factor post and we pay double for getting the animals out first thing in the morning. Open the gates, incidentally . . . The licences are no problem and I'll have Casset run the names through the computers behind DeSole's back.'

'What about Swayne? We've got to keep the suicide quiet for a while.'

'How long?'

'How the hell do I know?' replied Jason, exasperated. 'Until we find out who they all are and I can reach them – or you can reach them – and together we can start the wave of panic rolling. That's when we plant the Carlos solution.'

'Words,' said Conklin, his tone not flattering. 'You could be talking about days, maybe a week or even longer.'

'Then that's what I'm *talking* about.'

'Then we'd better damn well bring in Peter Holland—'

'No, not yet. We don't know what he'd do and I'm not giving him the chance to get in my way.'

'You've got to trust someone besides me, Jason. I can fool the doctor perhaps for twenty-four or forty-eight hours – *perhaps* – but I doubt much longer than that. He'll want higher authorization. And don't forget, I've got Casset breathing down my neck over DeSole—'

'Give me two days, *get* me two days!'

'While tracking down all this information and stalling Charlie, and lying through my teeth to Peter, telling them that we're making progress running down the Jackal's possible couriers at the Mayflower hotel – we *think* . . . Of course, we're doing nothing of the sort because we're up to our credentials in some off-the-wall, twenty-year-old Saigon conspiracy involving who knows *what*, damned if we know, except that the *who* is terribly impressive. Without going into statuses – or is it *statae* – we're now told they have their own private cemetery on the grounds of the general officer in charge of Pentagon procurements who just happened to blow his head off, a minor incident we're sitting on . . . *Jesus*, Delta, back up! The missiles are colliding!'

Though he was standing in front of Swayne's desk, the general's corpse in the chair beside him, Bourne managed a tentative, slow smile. 'That's what we're counting on, isn't it? It's a scenario that could have been written by our beloved Saint Alex himself.'

'I'm only along for the ride, I'm not steering—'

'What about the doctor?' interrupted Jason. 'You've been out of operation for almost five years. How do you know he's still in business?'

'I run into him now and then; we're both museum mavens. A couple of months ago at the Corcoran Gallery he complained that he wasn't given much to do these days.'

'Change that tonight.'

'I'll try. What are you going to do?'

'Delicately pull apart everything in this room.'

'Gloves?'

'Surgical, of course.'

'Don't touch the body.'

'Only the pockets – very delicately . . . Swayne's wife is coming down the stairs. I'll call you back when they're gone. Get hold of that *doctor*!'

Ivan Jax, MD by way of Yale Medical School, surgical training and residency at Massachusetts General, College of Surgeons by appointment, Jamaican by birth, and erstwhile 'consultant' to the Central Intelligence Agency courtesy of a fellow black man with the improbable name of Cactus, drove through the gates of General Swayne's estate in Manassas, Virginia. There were times, thought Ivan, when he wished he had never met old Cactus and this was one of them, but tonight notwithstanding, he never regretted that Cactus had come into his life. Thanks to the old man's 'magic papers', Jax had gotten his brother and sister out of Jamaica during the repressive Manley years when established professionals were all but prohibited from emigrating and certainly not with personal funds.

Cactus, however, using complex mock-ups of government permits, had sprung both young adults out of the country along with bank transfers honoured in Lisbon. All the aged forger requested were stolen blank copies of various official documents, including import/export bills of lading, the two people's passports, separate photographs and copies of several signatures belonging to certain men in positions of authority – easily obtainable through the hundreds of bureaucratic edicts published in the government-controlled press. Ivan's brother was currently a wealthy barrister in London and his sister a research fellow at Cambridge.

Yes, he owed Cactus, thought Dr Jax as he swung his station wagon around the curve to the front of the house, and when the old man had asked him to 'consult' with a few 'friends over in Langley' seven years ago, he had obliged. Some consultation! Still, there were further perks forthcoming in Ivan's silent association with the intelligence agency. When his island home threw out Manley, and Seaga came to power, among the first of the 'appropriated' properties to be returned to their rightful owners were the Jax family's holdings in Montego Bay and Port Antonio. That had been Alex Conklin's doing. but without Cactus there would have been no Conklin, not in Ivan's circle of friends . . . But why did Alex have to call *tonight*? Tonight was his twelfth wedding anniversary and he had sent the kids on an overnight with the neighbours' children so that he and his wife could be alone, alone with grilled Jamaic' ribs on the patio – prepared by the only one who knew how, namely Chef Ivan – a lot of good dark Overton rum, and some highly erotic skinny-dipping in the pool. *Damn* Alex! Double damn the son-of-a-bitch bachelor who could only respond to the event of a wedding anniversary by saying 'What the hell? You made the year, so what's a day count? Get your jollies tomorrow, I need you tonight.'

So he had lied to his wife, the former head nurse at Mass. General. He told her that a patient's life was in the balance – it was, but it had already tipped the wrong way. She had replied that perhaps her next husband would be more considerate of *her* life, but her sad smile and her understanding eyes denied her words. She knew death. *Hurry, my darling!*

Jax turned off the engine, grabbed his medical bag and got out of the car. He walked around the bonnet as the front door opened and a tall man in what appeared to be dark skin-tight clothing stood silhouetted in the frame. 'I'm your doctor,' said Ivan, walking up the steps. 'Our mutual friend didn't give me your name, but I guess I'm not supposed to have it.'

'I guess not,' agreed Bourne, extending a hand in a surgical glove as Jax approached.

'And I guess we're both right,' said Jax, shaking hands with the stranger. 'The mitt you're wearing is pretty familiar to me.'

'Our mutual friend didn't tell me you were black.'

'Is that a problem for you?'

'Good Christ, no. I like our friend even more. It probably never occurred to him to say anything.'

'I think we'll get along. Let's go, no-name.'

Bourne stood ten feet to the right of the desk as Jax swiftly, expertly tended to the corpse, mercifully wrapping the head in gauze. Without explaining, he had cut away sections of the general's clothing, examining those parts of the body beneath the fabric. Finally, he carefully rolled the hooded body off the chair and onto the floor. 'Are you finished in here?' he asked, looking over at Jason.

'I've swept it clean, Doctor, if that's what you mean.'

'It usually is . . . I want this room sealed. No one's to enter it after we leave until our mutual friend gives the word.'

'I certainly can't guarantee that,' said Bourne.

'Then he'll have to.'

'Why?'

'Your general didn't commit suicide, no-name. He was murdered.'

12

'The woman,' said Alex Conklin over the line. 'From everything you told me it had to be Swayne's wife. *Jesus!*'

'It doesn't change anything, but it looks that way,' agreed Bourne half-heartedly. 'She had reason enough to do it, God knows – still, if she did, she didn't tell Flannagan, and *that* doesn't make sense.'

'No, it doesn't . . . ' Conklin paused, then spoke quickly. 'Let me talk to Ivan.'

'Ivan? Your doctor? His name is Ivan?'

'So?'

'Nothing. He's outside . . . "packing the merchandise," was the way he put it.'

'In his wagon?'

'That's right. We carried the body—'

'What makes him so sure it *wasn't* suicide?' broke in Alex.

'Swayne was drugged. He said he'd call you later and explain. He wants to get out of here and no one's to come into this room after we leave – after I leave – until you give the word for the police. He'll tell you that, too.'

'Christ, it must be a mess in there.'

'It's not pretty. What do you want me to do?'

'Pull the curtains, if there are any; check the windows and, if possible, lock the door. If there's no way to lock it, look around for—'

'I found a set of keys in Swayne's pocket,' interrupted Jason. 'I checked; one of them fits.'

'Good. When you leave, wipe the door down clean. Find some furniture polish or a dusting spray.'

'That's not going to keep out anyone who wants to get in.'

'No, but if someone does, we might pick up a print.'

'You're reaching—'

'I certainly am,' concurred the former intelligence officer. 'I've also got to figure out a way to seal up the whole place without using anybody from Langley, *and*, not incidentally, keep the Pentagon at bay just in case someone among those twenty-odd thousand people wants to reach Swayne, and that includes his office and probably a couple of hundred buyers and sellers *a day* in procurements . . . Christ, it's *impossible*!'

'It's perfect,' contradicted Bourne as Dr Ivan Jax suddenly appeared in the doorway. 'Our little game of destabilization will start right here on the "farm". Do you have Cactus's number?'

'Not with me. I think it's probably in a shoebox at home.'

'Call Mo Panov, he's got it. Then reach Cactus and tell him to get to a pay phone and call me here.'

'What the hell have you got in mind? I hear that old man's name, I get nervous.'

'You told me I had to find someone else to trust besides you. I just did. Reach him, Alex.' Jason hung up the telephone. 'I'm sorry, Doctor . . . or maybe under the circumstances I can use your name. Hello, Ivan.'

'Hello, *no*-name, which is the way I'd like to keep it on my end. Especially when I just heard you say another name.'

'Alex? . . . No, of course it wasn't Alex, not our mutual friend.' Bourne laughed quietly, knowingly, as he walked away from the desk. 'It was Cactus, wasn't it?'

'I just came in to ask you if you wanted me to close the gates,' said Jax, bypassing the question.

'Would you be offended if I told you that I didn't think of him until I saw you just now?'

'Certain associations are fairly obvious. The gates, please?'

'Do you owe Cactus as much as I do, Doctor?' Jason held his place, looking at the Jamaican.

'I owe him so much that I could never think of compromising him in a situation like tonight. For God's sake, he's an old man and no matter what deviant conclusions Langley wants to come up with, tonight was *murder*, a particularly brutal killing. No, I wouldn't involve him.'

'You're not me. You see, I have to. He'd never forgive me if I didn't.'

'You don't think much of yourself, do you?'

'Please close the gates, Doctor. There's an alarm panel in the hallway I can activate when they're shut.'

Jax hesitated, as if unsure of what he wanted to say. 'Listen,' he began haltingly, 'most sane people have reasons for saying things – doing things. My guess is you're sane. Call Alex if you need me – if old Cactus needs me.' The doctor left, rushing out of the door.

Bourne turned and glanced around the room. Since Flannagan and Rachel Swayne had left nearly three hours ago, he had searched every foot of the general's study, as well as the dead soldier's separate bedroom on the second floor. He had placed the items he intended to take on the brass coffee table; he studied them now. There were three brown leather-bound covers, each equal in size, each holding inserted spiral pages; they were a desk set. The first was an appointments calendar; the second, a personal telephone book in which the names and numbers were entered in ink; the last was an expense diary, barely touched. Along with these were eleven office messages of the telephone notepad variety, which Jason found in Swayne's pockets, a golf club scorecard, and several memoranda written at the Pentagon. Finally, there was the general's wallet containing a profusion of impressive credentials and very little money. Bourne would turn everything over to Alex and hope further leads would be found, but as far as he could determine, he had turned up nothing startling, nothing dramatically relevant to the modern Medusa. And that bothered him; there had to be *something.* This was the old soldier's home, his sanctum sanctorum inside that home – something! He knew it, he felt it, but he could not find it. So he started again, not foot by foot now; instead, inch by inch.

Fourteen minutes later, as he was removing and turning over the photographs on the wall behind the desk, the wall to the right of the cushioned bay window that overlooked the lawn outside, he recalled Conklin's words about checking the windows and the curtains so that no one could enter or observe the scene inside.

Christ, it must be a mess in there.

It's not very pleasant.

It wasn't. The panes of the central bay window frame were splattered with blood and membrane. And the . . . the small brass *latch*? Not only was it free from its catch, the window itself was open – barely open, but nevertheless it *was open.* Bourne kneeled on the cushioned seat and looked closely at the shiny brass fixture and the surrounding panes of glass. There were smudges among the rivulets of dried blood and tissue, coarse pressings on the stains that appeared to widen and thin them out into irregular shapes. Then below the sill he saw what kept the window from closing. The end of the left drape had been drawn out, a small piece of its tasselled fabric wedged beneath the lower window frame. Jason stepped back bewildered but not really surprised. This was what he had been looking for, the missing piece in the complex puzzle that was the death of Norman Swayne.

Someone had climbed out that window *after* the shot that blew the general's skull apart. Someone who could not risk being seen going through the front hall or out the front door. Someone who knew the house and the grounds . . . and the dogs. A brutal killer from Medusa. *Goddamn* it!

Who? Who had *been* here? Flannagan . . . Swayne's wife! They would know, they *had* to know! Bourne lurched for the telephone on the desk; it began ringing before his hand touched it.

'*Alex?*'

'No, Brer Rabbit, it's just an old friend, and I didn't realize we were so free with names.'

'We're not, we shouldn't be,' said Jason rapidly, imposing a control on himself he could barely exercise. 'Something happened a moment ago – I found something.'

'Calm down, boy. What can I do for you?'

'I need you . . . out here where I am. Are you free?'

'Well, let's see.' Cactus chuckled as he spoke. 'There are several board meetings I should rightfully attend, and the White House wants me for a power breakfast . . . When and where, Brer Rabbit?'

'Not alone, old friend. I want three or four others with you. Is that possible?'

'I don't know. What did you have in mind?'

'That fellow who drove me into town after I saw you. Are there any other like-minded citizens in the neighbourhood?'

'Most are doin' time, frankly, but I suppose I could dig around the refuse and pull up a few. What for?'

'Guard duty. It's pretty simple really. You'll be on the phone and they'll be behind locked gates telling people that it's private property, that visitors aren't welcome. Especially a few honkies probably in limousines.'

'Now that might appeal to the brothers.'

'Call me back and I'll give you directions.' Bourne disconnected the line and immediately released the bar for a dial tone. He touched the numbers for Conklin's phone in Vienna.

'Yes?' answered Alex.

'The doctor was right and I let our Snake Lady executioner get away!'

'Swayne's wife, you mean?'

'No, but she and her fast-talking sergeant know who it was – they had to know who was *here*! Pick them up and hold them. They lied to me, so the deal's off. Whoever staged this gruesome "suicide" had orders from high up in Medusa. I want him. He's our shortcut.'

'He's also beyond our reach.'

'What the hell are you talking about?'

'Because the sergeant and his paramour are beyond our reach. They've disappeared.'

'That's crazy? If I know Saint Alex, and I *do*, you've had them covered since they left here.'

'Electronically, not physically. Remember, you insisted we keep Langley and Peter Holland away from Medusa.'

'What did you do?'

'I sent out a full-toned alert to the central reservations computers of all international airline carriers. As of eight-twenty this evening our subjects had seats on Pan Am's ten o'clock flight to London—'

'*London?*' broke in Jason. 'They were heading the other way, to the Pacific. To Hawaii!'

'That's probably where they're going because they never showed up at Pan Am. Who knows?'

'Damn it, *you* should!'

'How? Two United States citizens flying to Hawaii don't have to present passports to enter our fiftieth state. A driver's licence or a voter's registration card will do. You told me that they've been considering this move for quite a while. How difficult would it be for a master sergeant with over thirty years' service to get a couple of driver's licences using different names?'

'But *why*?'

'To throw off people looking for them – like us, or maybe a few Medusans, very high up.'

'*Shit!*'

'Would you care to talk less in the vulgate, Professor? It was the "vulgate", wasn't it?'

'Shut up, I've got to think.'

'Then think about the fact that we're up to our asses in the Arctic without a heater. It's time for Peter Holland. We need him. We need Langley.'

'No, not *yet*! You're forgetting something. Holland took an oath and everything we know about him says he took it seriously. He may bend a rule now and then, but if he's faced with a Medusa, with hundreds of millions out of Geneva buying up whatever they're buying up in Europe, he may say, "Halt, that's enough!" '

'That's a risk we have to take. We *need* him, David.'

'*Not* David, *goddamn* you! I'm Bourne, Jason Bourne, *your* creation, and I'm owed! My family is owed! I won't have it any other way!'

'And you'll kill me if I go against you.'

Silence. Neither spoke until Delta One of Saigon's Medusa broke the pause. 'Yes, Alex, I'll kill you. Not because you tried to kill me in Paris, but for the same blind assumptions you made back then that led to your decision to come after me. Can you understand that?'

'Yes,' replied Conklin, his voice so low it was barely audible. 'The arrogance of ignorance, it's your favourite Washington theme; you always make it sound so Oriental. But somewhere along the line you're going to have to be a little less arrogant yourself. There's only so much we can do alone.'

'On the other hand, there's so much that can be loused up if we're *not* alone. Look at the progress we've made. From zero to double digits in how long – forty-eight, seventy-two hours? Give me the two days, Alex, *please.* We're closing in on what this whole thing's about, what *Medusa's* all about. One breakthrough, and we present them with the perfect solution to get rid of me. The Jackal.'

'I'll do the best I can. Did Cactus reach you?'

'Yes. He'll call me back and then come out here. I'll explain later.'

'I should tell you. He and our doctor are friends.'

'I know. Ivan told me . . . Alex, I want to get some things over to you – Swayne's telephone book, his wallet, appointments schedule, stuff like that. I'll wrap it all up and have one of Cactus's boys deliver the package to your place, to the security gate. Put everything into your high tech and see what you can find.'

'Cactus's boys? What are you doing?'

'Taking an item off your agenda. I'm sealing this place up. Nobody'll be able to get in but we'll see who tries.'

'That could be interesting. The kennel people are coming for the dogs around seven in the morning, incidentally, so don't make the seals too tight.'

'Which reminds me,' interrupted Jason. 'Be official again and call the guards on the other shifts. Their services are no longer required but each will receive a month's pay by mail in lieu of notice.'

'Who the hell's going to pay it? There's not Langley, remember? No Peter Holland and I'm not independently wealthy.'

'I am. I'll phone my bank in Maine and have them Fed Ex you a cashier's cheque. Ask your friend Casset to pick it up at your apartment in the morning.'

'It's funny, isn't it?' said Conklin slowly, pensively. 'I forgot about your money. I never think about it, actually. I guess I've blocked it out of my mind.'

'That's possible,' added Bourne, a trace of lightness in his voice. 'The official part of you may have visions of some bureaucrat coming up to Marie and saying, "By the way, Mrs Webb or Bourne or whoever you are, while you were in the employ of the Canadian government you made off with over five million dollars belonging to mine." '

'She was only brilliant, David – Jason. You were owed every dollar.'

'Don't press the point, Alex. *She* claimed at least twice the amount.'

'She was right. It's why everyone shut up . . . What are you going to do now?'

'Wait for Cactus's call, then make one of my own.'

'*Oh?*'

'To my wife.'

Marie sat on the balcony of her villa at Tranquillity Inn staring out at the moonlit Caribbean, trying with every controlling instinct in her not to go mad with fear. Strangely, perhaps stupidly or even dangerously, it was not the fear of physical harm that consumed her. She had lived both in Europe and the Far East with the killing machine that was Jason Bourne; she knew what that stranger was capable of and it was brutally efficient. No, it wasn't Bourne, it was David – what Jason Bourne was doing to David Webb. She had to *stop* it! . . . They could go away, far away, to some remote safe haven and start a new life with new names, create a world for themselves that Carlos could never penetrate. They had all the money they would ever need, they could *do* it! It was done all the time – hundreds, thousands of men and women and children whose lives were threatened were shielded by their governments; and if ever a government anywhere had reason to protect a man, that man was David Webb! . . . Thoughts conceived in frenzy, reflected Marie, getting up from her chair and walking to the balcony's railing. It would never happen because David could never accept the solution. Where the Jackal was concerned, David Webb was ruled by Jason Bourne and Bourne was capable of destroying his host body. Oh, *God,* what's *happening* to us?

The telephone rang. Marie stiffened, then rushed into the bedroom and picked it up. 'Yes?'

'Hello, Sis, it's Johnny.'

'*Oh* . . . '

'Which means you haven't heard from David.'

'No, and I'm going a little crazy, Bro.'

'He'll call when he can, you know that.'

'But you're not calling to tell me that.'

'No, I'm just checking in. I'm stuck over here on the big island and it looks like I'll be here for a while. I'm at Government House with Henry, waiting for the CG to personally thank me for accommodating the Foreign Office.'

'I don't understand a word you're saying—'

'Oh, sorry. Henry Sykes is the Crown governor's aide who asked me to take care of that old French war hero down the path from you. When the CG wants to thank you, you wait until you're thanked – when the phones go out, cowboys like me need Government House.'

'You've totally lost me, Johnny.'

'A storm out of Basse-Terre will hit in a few hours.'

'Out of *whom*?'

'It's a what, but I should be back before then. Have the maid make up the couch for me.'

'John, it's not necessary for you to stay here. Good heavens, there are men with guns outside the hedge and down on the beach and God knows where else.'

'That's where they're going to stay. See you later, and hug the kids for me.'

'They're asleep,' said Marie as her younger brother hung up. She looked at the phone as she replaced it, unconsciously saying out loud. 'How little I know about you, little Bro . . . our favourite, incorrigible bro. And how much more does my husband know. Damn the *both* of you!'

The telephone instantly rang again, stunning her. She grabbed it. 'Hello?'

'It's me.'

'Thank *God*!'

'*He's* out of town, but everything's fine. I'm fine, and we're making headway.'

'You don't have to *do* this! *We* don't have to!'

'Yes, we do,' said Jason Bourne, no evidence of David Webb. 'Just know I love you, *he* loves you—'

'*Stop* it! It's *happening*—'

'I'm sorry, I apologize – *forgive* me.'

'You're *David*!'

'Of course I'm David. I was just joking—'

'No, you *weren't*!'

'I was talking to Alex, that's all. We argued, that's *all*!'

'No, it *isn't*! I want you back, I want you *here*!'

'Then I can't talk any longer. I love you.' The line went dead and Marie St Jacques Webb fell on the bed, her cries of futility muffled by the blankets.

Alexander Conklin, his eyes red with strain, kept touching the letters and the numbers of his computer, his head turned to the open pages of the ledgers sent over by Bourne from General Norman Swayne's estate. Two shrill beeps suddenly intruded on the silence of the room. It was the inanimate machine's robotic signal that another dual reference had been calculated. He checked the entry. *R.G.* What did it mean? He back-taped and found nothing. He pressed forward, typing like a mindless automaton. *Three beeps.* He kept punching the irritatingly beige buttons, faster and faster. *Four beeps . . . five . . . six.* Back space – stop – forward. *R.G R.G R.G R.G.* What the hell was *R.G*?

He cross-checked the data with the entries from the three different leather-bound notebooks. A common numeral sprang out in green letters on the screen. *617–202–0011.* A telephone number. Conklin picked up the Langley phone, dialled the night watch, and told the CIA operator to trace it.

'It's unlisted, sir. It's one of three numbers for the same residence in Boston, Massachusetts.'

'The name, please.'

'Gates, Randolph. The residence is—'

'Never mind, Operator,' interrupted Alex, knowing that he had been given the essential information. Randolph Gates, scholar, attorney for the privileged, advocate of the bigger the better, the biggest the best. How right that Gates should be involved with amassing hundreds of millions in Europe controlled by American interests . . . No, wait a moment. It wasn't right at all, it was *wrong*! It was completely illogical for the scholarly attorney to have any connection whatsoever to a highly questionable, indeed illegal, operation like Medusa. It did not make sense! One did not have to admire the celebrated legal giant to grant him just about the cleanest record for propriety in the Bar Association. He was a notorious stickler for the most minute points of law, often using those minutiae of his craft to obtain favourable decisions, but no one ever dared question his integrity. So unpopular were his legal and philosophical opinions to the brightest lawyers in the liberal establishment that he would have been gleefully discredited years ago at the slightest hint of impropriety.

Yet here was his name appearing six times in the appointments calendar of a Medusan responsible for untold millions in the nation's defence expenditures. An unstable Medusan whose apparent suicide was, in fact, murder.

Conklin looked at the screen, at the date of Swayne's last entry referring to R.G. It was on August second, barely a week ago. He picked up the leather-bound diary and turned to the day. He had been concentrating on names not comments, unless the information struck him as relevant – to what he was not sure, but he was trusting to instinct. If he had known up front who R.G was, the abbreviated handwritten notation beside the last entry would have caught his eye.

RG will nt cnsider app't fr Maj. Crft. Need Crft on hs stff. Unlock. Paris – 7 yrs ago. Two file out and bur'd.

The *Paris* should have alerted him, thought Alex, but Swayne's notes throughout were filled with foreign or exotic names and places as if the general were trying to impress whoever might read his personal observations. Also, Conklin regretfully considered, he was terribly tired; were it not for his computer he probably would not have centred in on Dr Randolph Gates, legal Olympian.

Paris – 7 yrs ago. Two file out and bur'd.

The first part was obvious, the second obscure but hardly concealed. The 'Two' referred to the Army's intelligence arm, G-2, and the 'file' was just that, an event or a revelation uncovered by intelligence personnel in *Paris – 7 yrs ago* and removed from the data banks. It was an amateur's attempt to use intelligence gibberish by misusing it. 'Unlock' meant 'key' – *Jesus*, Swayne was an idiot! Using his notepad, Alex wrote out the notation as he knew it to be:

'Randolph Gates will not consider the appointment for a Major Craft or Croft or even Christopher, for the *f* could be an *s*. (But) we need Crft on his staff. The key is to use the information in our G-2 file about Gates in Paris seven years ago, said file removed and in our possession.'

If that was not the exact translation of Swayne's insertion, it was certainly close enough in substance to act upon, mused Conklin, turning his wrist and glancing at his watch. It was twenty past three in the morning, a time when even the most disciplined person would be shaken by the shrill bell of a telephone. Why not? David – *Jason* – was right. Every hour counted now. Alex picked up the phone and touched the numbers for Boston, Massachusetts.

The telephone kept ringing and the *bitch* would not pick it up in her room! Then Gates looked at the lighted square and the blood drained from his head. It was his unlisted number, a number that was restricted to a very few. He thrashed wildly in the bed, his eyes wide; the strange call from Paris unnerved him the more he thought about it. It concerned Montserrat, he *knew* it! The information he had relayed was *wrong* . . . Prefontaine had *lied* to him and now Paris wanted an accounting! My *God*, they'd come after him, *expose* him! . . . No, there was a way, a perfectly acceptable explanation, the *truth.* He would deliver the liars to Paris, to Paris's man here in Boston. He would trap the drunken Prefontaine and the sleazeball detective and force them to tell their lies to the one person who could absolve him . . . The phone! He had to answer it. He could not appear as if he had anything to hide! He reached out and grabbed the incessantly ringing instrument, pulling it to his ear. 'Yes?'

'Seven years ago, Counsellor,' began the quiet voice on the line. 'Do I have to remind you that we've got the entire file. The Deuxième Bureau was extremely cooperative, far more than you have been.'

'For God's sake, I was *lied* to!' cried Gates, swinging his legs onto the floor in panic, his voice hoarse. 'You can't *believe* I'd forward erroneous information. I'd have to be insane!'

'We know you can be obstinate. We made a simple request—'

'I *complied*, I swear I did! Good Christ, I paid fifteen thousand dollars to make certain everything was silent, absolutely untraceable – not that the money matters, of course—'

'You *paid* . . . ?' interrupted the quiet voice.

'I can show you the bank withdrawals.'

'For what?'

'The information, naturally. I hired a former judge who has contacts—'

'For information about Craft?'

'What?'

'Croft . . . Christopher.'

'*Who?*'

'Our major, Counsellor. *The* major.'

'If that's her code name, then yes, yes I did!'

'A code name?'

'The woman. The two children. They flew to the island of Montserrat. I swear that's what I was *told*!'

There was a sudden click and the line went dead.

13

His hand still on the telephone, Conklin broke out in a sweat. He released the phone and got up from his chair, limping away from the computer, looking back at it, down at it, as if it were some monstrous thing that had taken him into a forbidden land where nothing was as it appeared to be or *should* be. What had *happened*? How did Randolph Gates know anything about Montserrat, about Marie and the children? *Why?*

Alex lowered himself into the armchair, his pulse racing, his thoughts clashing, no judgements emerging, only chaos. He gripped his right wrist with his left hand, his nails digging into his flesh. He had to get hold of himself, he had to *think* – he had to act! For David's wife and children.

Associations. What were the conceivable *associations*? It was difficult enough to consider Gates even unwittingly a part of Medusa, but impossible to think he was also connected to Carlos the Jackal. *Impossible!* . . . Yet both appeared to *be*; the connections existed. Was Carlos himself part of Swayne's Medusa? Everything they knew about the Jackal would deny it emphatically. The assassin's strength was in his total *disassociation* with any structured entity, Jason Bourne had proved that thirteen years ago in Paris. No group of people could ever reach *him*; they could only send out a message and he would reach *them.* The single organization the international killer for hire permitted was his army of old men, from the Mediterranean to the Baltic, lost misfits, criminals whose impoverished last days were made better by the assassin's largesse, fealty unto death demanded and received. Where did – *could* – a man like Randolph Gates fit in?

He didn't, concluded Alex as the outer limits of his imagination explored an old territory – be sceptical of the apparent. The celebrated attorney was no more part of Carlos than he was of Medusa. He was the aberration, the flaw in the lens, an otherwise honourable man with a single weakness that had been uncovered by two disparate parties both with extraordinary resources. It was common knowledge that the Jackal could reach into the Sûreté and Interpol, and it took no clairvoyance to assume that Medusa could penetrate the army's G-2. It was the only *possible* explanation, for Gates had been too controversial, too powerful for too long to function as spectacularly as he did in the courts if his vulnerability was easily uncovered. No, it would take predators like the Jackal and the men of Medusa to bore deep enough to dredge up a secret so devastating as to turn Randolph Gates into a valuable pawn. Clearly, Carlos had gotten to him first.

Conklin reflected on a truth that was forever reconfirmed: The world of global corrupters was in reality a small, multi-layered neighbourhood, geometric in design, the irregular avenues of corruption leading into one another. How could it be otherwise? The residents of those lethal streets had services to offer, their clients were a specific breed – the desperate dregs of humanity. Extort, compromise, kill. The Jackal and the men of Medusa belonged to the same fraternal order. The Brotherhood of I-Must-Have-Mine.

Breakthrough. But it was a breakthrough Jason Bourne could handle – not David Webb, and Webb was still too much a part of Bourne. Especially since both parts of the same man were over a thousand miles away from Montserrat, the coordinates of death determined by Carlos. *Montserrat?* . . . Johnny St Jacques! The 'little brother' who had proved himself in a backwater town in the northern regions of Canada, proved himself beyond the knowledge and the understanding of his family, especially his beloved sister. A man who could kill in anger – who had killed in fury – and who would kill again if the sister he adored and her children were under the Jackal's gun. David believed in him – Jason Bourne believed in him, which was far more to the point.

Alex looked over at the telephone console, then quickly got out of the chair. He rushed to the desk, sat down, and touched the buttons that rewound the current tape, adjusting it to the spot where he wanted to pick it up. He went forward and back until he heard Gates's panicked voice.

'. . . *Good Christ, I paid fifteen thousand—*'

No, not there, thought Conklin. Later.

'. . . *I can show you the bank withdrawals—*'

Later!

'. . . *I hired a former judge who has contacts—*'

That's it. A judge.

'. . . *They flew to the island of Montserrat—*'

Alex opened the drawer where he kept a sheet of paper with each number he had called during the past two days on the assumption that he might need specific ones quickly. He saw the number in the Caribbean for Tranquillity Inn, picked up the phone, and dialled. After more rings than seemed necessary, a voice thick with sleep answered.

'Tranquillity—'

'This is an emergency,' broke in Conklin. 'It's urgent that I speak with John St Jacques. Quickly, please.'

'I'm sorry, sir, Mr St Jacques isn't here.'

'I've got to find him. I repeat, it's urgent. Where is he?'

'On the big island—'

'Montserrat?'

'Yes—'

'*Where?* . . . My name's Conklin. He wants to talk to me – he *has* to talk to me. *Please!*'

'A big wind came up from Basse-Terre and all flights are cancelled until morning.'

'A what?'

'A tropical depression—'

'Oh, a storm.'

'We prefer a TD, sir. Mr St Jacques left a telephone number in Plymouth.'

'What's your name?' interrupted Alex suddenly. The clerk replied Pritchard or Pritchen and Conklin continued: 'I'm going to ask you a very delicate question, Mr Pritchard. It's important that you have the right answer, but if it's the wrong one you must do as I tell you. Mr St Jacques will confirm everything I say when I reach him; however, I can't waste time now. Do you understand me?'

'What is your question?' asked the clerk with dignity. 'I'm not a child, *mon.*'

'I'm sorry, I didn't mean to—'

'The question, Mr Conklin. You're in a hurry.'

'Yes, of course . . . Mr St Jacques's sister and her children, are they in a safe place? Did Mr St Jacques take certain precautions?'

'Such as armed guards about the villa and our usual men down on the beach?' said the clerk. 'The answer is yes.'

'It's the right answer.' Alex took a deep breath, his breathing still erratic. 'Now, what's the number where I can reach Mr St Jacques?'

The clerk gave it to Conklin, then added, 'Many phones are out, sir. It might be well if you left a number here. The wind is still strong, but Mr Saint Jay will no doubt come over with the first light if he can.'

'Certainly.' Alex rattled off the number of the sterile telephone in the Vienna apartment and had the man in Montserrat repeat it. 'That's it,' said Conklin. 'I'll try Plymouth now.'

'The spelling of your name, please. It is C-o-n-c-h—'

'C-o-n-*k*,' broke in Alex, snapping off the line and instantly dialling the number in the town of Plymouth, the capital of Montserrat. Once again a startled, drowsy voice answered; it was a barely coherent greeting. 'Who's this?' asked Conklin impatiently.

'Who the hell is *this* – are *you*?' replied an angry Englishman.

'I'm trying to reach John St Jacques. It's an emergency and I was given this number by the desk at Tranquillity Inn.'

'Good Lord, their phones are intact . . . ?'

'Obviously. *Please*, is John there?'

'Yes, yes, of course. He's across the hall, I'll fetch him. Who shall I say—'

'Alex is good enough.'

'Just "Alex"?'

'Hurry, please!' Twenty seconds later the voice of John St Jacques filled the line.

'*Conklin*? Is that *you*?'

'Listen to me. They know Marie and the children flew into Montserrat.'

'We heard that someone was asking questions over at the airport about a woman and two kids—'

'Then that's why you moved them from the house to the inn.'

'That's right.'

'Who was asking questions?'

'We don't know. It was done by telephone . . . I didn't want to leave them, even for a few hours, but I had a command appearance at Government House and by the time that son-of-a-bitch Crown governor showed up, the storm hit.'

'I know. I talked to the desk and got this number.'

'That's one consolation; the phones are still working. In weather like this they usually don't, which is why we suck up to the Crown.'

'I understand you've got guards—'

'You're goddamned right!' cried St Jacques. 'The trouble is I don't know what to look for except strangers in boats or on the beach, and if they don't stop and identify themselves satisfactorily, my orders are to shoot!'

'I may be able to help—'

'Go ahead!'

'We got a break – don't ask how; it's from outer space but that doesn't matter – it's real. The man who traced Marie to Montserrat used a judge who had contacts, presumably in the islands.'

'A *judge*?' exploded the owner of Tranquillity Inn. 'My God, he's there! Christ, he's *there*! I'll kill that *scum* bastard—'

'*Stop* it, Johnny! Get hold of yourself – *who's* there?'

'A judge, and he insisted on using a different *name*! I didn't think anything about it – a couple of whack-a-doo old men with similar names—'

'*Old men?* . . . Slow down, Johnny, this is important. What two old men?'

'The one you're talking about is from Boston—'

'*Yes!*' confirmed Alex emphatically.

'The other flew in from Paris—'

'*Paris?* Jesus *Christ*! The old men of Paris!'

'What . . . ?'

'The Jackal! Carlos has his *old men* in place!'

'Now, *you* slow down, Alex,' said St Jacques, his breathing audible. 'Now *you* be clearer.'

'There's no time, Johnny. Carlos has an army – *his* army – of old men who'll die for him, *kill* for him. There won't be any strangers on the beach, they're already *there*! Can you get back to the island?'

'Somehow, yes! I'll call my people over there. Both those pieces of garbage will be thrown into the cisterns!'

'*Hurry*, John!'

St Jacques pressed down the small bar of the old telephone, released it, and heard the forever-pulsating dial tone. He spun the numbers for the inn on Tranquillity Isle.

'*We are sorry*,' said the recorded voice. '*Due to weather conditions the lines are down to the area you are calling. Government is working very hard to restore communications. Please try your call later. Have a good day*.'

John St Jacques slammed the phone down with such force that he broke it in two. 'A *boat*!' he screamed. 'Get me a *drug* boat!'

'You're crazy,' objected the aide to the Crown governor across the room. 'In these swells?'

'A sea streak, Henry!' said the devoted brother, reaching into his belt and slowly pulling out an automatic. 'Or I'll be forced to do something I don't even want to think about, but I'll get a boat.'

'I simply can't believe this, chap.'

'Neither can I, Henry . . . I mean it, though.'

Jean Pierre Fontaine's nurse sat at her dressing table in front of the mirror and adjusted her tightly knotted blonde hair under the black rain hat. She looked at her watch, recalling every word of the most unusual telephone call she had received several hours ago from Argenteuil in France, from the great man who made all things possible.

'There is an American attorney who calls himself a judge staying near you.'

'I know of no such person, monseigneur.'

'He is there, nevertheless. Our hero rightfully complains of his presence, and a call to his home in the city of Boston confirms that it is he.'

'His presence here is not desirable, then?'

'His presence there is abominable to me. He pretends to be in my debt – an enormous debt, an event that could destroy him – yet his actions tell me that he's ungrateful, that he intends to cancel his debt by betraying me, and by betraying me he betrays you.'

'He's dead.'

'Exactly. In the past he's been valuable to me, but the past is over. Find him, kill him. Make his death appear to be a tragic accident . . . Finally, since we will not speak until you are back on Martinique, are preparations complete for your last act on my behalf?'

'They are, monseigneur. The two syringes were prepared by the surgeon at the hospital in Fort de France. He sends you his devotion.'

'He should. He's alive, as opposed to several dozen of his patients.'

'They know nothing of his other life in Martinique.'

'I'm aware of that . . . Administer the doses in forty-eight hours, when the chaos has begun to subside. Knowing that the hero was my invention – which I'll make sure they know – will put a chameleon to shame.'

'All will be done. You'll be here soon?'

'In time for the shock waves. I'm leaving within the hour and will reach Antigua before it's noon in Montserrat tomorrow. All things being on schedule, I'll arrive in time to observe the exquisite anguish of Jason Bourne before I leave my signature, a bullet in his throat. The Americans will then know who has won. Adieu.'

The nurse, like an ecstatic suppliant, arched her neck in front of the mirror remembering the mystical words of her omniscient lord. It was nearly time, she thought, opening the dresser drawer and picking out a diamond-clustered wire garrote from among her necklaces, a gift from her mentor. It would be so simple. She had easily learned who the judge was and where he was staying – the old, painfully thin man three villas away. Everything now was precision, the 'tragic accident' merely a prelude to the horror that would take place at Villa Twenty in less than an hour. For all of Tranquillity's villas had kerosene lamps in the event of electricity loss and generator malfunction. A panicked old man with loose bowels, or in plain fear, living through such a storm as they were experiencing, might well attempt to light a lamp for additional comfort. How tragic that his upper body would fall into the spilled, flowing kerosene, his neck scorched into black tissue, the neck that had been garroted. *Do it*, insisted the echoing voices of her imagination. *You must obey. Without Carlos you would have been a headless corpse in Algeria.*

She would do it – she would do it now.

The harsh downpour of the rain on the roof and the windows, and the whistling, roaring wind outside were interrupted by a blinding streak of lightning followed by a deafening crack of thunder.

'Jean Pierre Fontaine' wept silently as he knelt beside the bed, his face inches from his woman's, his tears falling on the cold flesh of her arm. She was dead, and the note by her white rigid hand said it all: *Maintenant nous deux sont libres, mon amour.*

They were both free. She from the terrible pain, he from the price demanded by the monseigneur, a price he had not described to her, but one she knew was too horrible to pay. He had known for months that his woman had ready access to pills that would end her life quickly if her living became unendurable; he had frequently, at times frantically, searched for them but he had never found them. Now he knew why as he stared at the small tin of her favourite pastilles, the harmless droplets of liquorice she had popped laughingly into her mouth for years.

'Be thankful, *mon cher*, they might be caviar or those expensive drugs the rich indulge in!' They were not caviar but they were drugs, lethal drugs.

Footsteps. The nurse! She had come out of her room, but she could not see his woman! Fontaine pushed himself up from the bed, wiped his eyes as best he could, and hurried to the door. He opened it, stunned by the sight of the woman; she stood directly in front of him, her arm raised, the knuckles of her hand arcing forward to knock.

'*Monsieur!* . . . You startled me.'

'I believe we startled each other.' Jean Pierre slipped out, rapidly closing the door behind him. 'Regine is finally asleep,' he whispered, bringing his forefinger to his lips. 'This terrible storm has kept her up most of the night.'

'But it is sent from heaven for us – for you – isn't it? There are times when I think the monseigneur can order such things.'

'Then I doubt they come from heaven. It's not the source of his influence.'

'To business,' interrupted the nurse, not amused and walking away from the door. 'Are you prepared?'

'I will be in a matter of minutes,' replied Fontaine, heading for the table where his killing equipment lay in the locked drawer. He reached into his pocket and took out the key. 'Do you want to go over the procedure?' he asked, turning. 'For my benefit, of course. At this age, details are often blurred.'

'Yes, I do, because there is a slight change.'

'*Oh?*' The old Frenchman arched his brows. 'Also at my age sudden changes are not welcome.'

'It's only a question of timing, no more than a quarter of an hour, perhaps much less.'

'An eternity in this business,' said Fontaine as yet another streak of lightning, separated only by milliseconds from its crash of thunder, interrupted the pounding rain on the windows and the roof. 'It's dangerous enough to be outside; that bolt was too near for safety.'

'If you believe that, think how the guards feel.'

'The "slight change," please? Also an explanation.'

'I'll give you no explanation except to say that it is an order from Argenteuil and you were responsible.'

'The *judge*?'

'Draw your own conclusions.'

'Then he was *not* sent to—'

'I'll say no more. The change is as follows. Rather than running up the path from here to the guards at Villa Twenty and demanding emergency assistance for your ill wife, I will say I was returning from the front desk where I was complaining about the telephone and saw a fire in Villa Fourteen, three away from ours. There'll no doubt be a great deal of confusion, what with the storm and everyone yelling and calling for help. That will be your signal. Use the confusion; get through and take out whoever remains at the woman's villa – make sure your silencer is secure. Then go inside and do the work you have sworn to do.'

'So I wait for the fire, for the guards and for you to return to Number Eleven.'

'Exactly. Stay on the porch with the door closed, of course.'

'Of course.'

'It may take me five minutes or perhaps even twenty, but *stay* there.'

'Naturally . . . May I ask, madame – or perhaps mademoiselle, although I see no evidence–'

'What *is* it?'

'It will "take" you five or twenty minutes to do what?'

'You're a fool, old man. What must be done.'

'Of course.'

The nurse pulled her raincoat around her, looped the belt, and walked to the front door of the villa. 'Get your equipment together and be out here in three minutes,' she commanded.

'Of course.' The door swung back with the wind as the woman opened it; she went outside into the torrential rain, pulling it shut behind her. Astonished and confused, the old Frenchman stood motionless, trying to make sense out of the inexplicable. Things were happening too fast for him, blurred in the agony of his woman's death. There was no time to mourn, no time to feel . . . Only think and think quickly. Revelation came hard upon revelation, leaving unanswered questions that *had* to be answered so the whole could be understood – so that Montserrat itself made sense!

The nurse was more than a conduit for instructions from Argenteuil; the angel of mercy was herself an angel of death, a killer in her own right. So why was *he* sent thousands of miles to do the work another could do just as well and without the elaborate charade of his auspicious arrival? An old hero of France, indeed . . . it was all so unnecessary. And speaking of age, there was another – another old man who was no killer at all. Perhaps, thought the false Jean Pierre Fontaine, he had made a terrible mistake. Perhaps, instead of coming to kill him, the other 'old man' had come to *warn* him!

'*Mon Dieu*,' whispered the Frenchman. 'The old men of Paris, the Jackal's army! Too many questions!' Fontaine walked rapidly to the nurse's bedroom door and opened it. With the swiftness developed over a lifetime of practice, impaired only slightly by his years, he began methodically to tear apart the woman's room – suitcase, closet, clothes, pillows, mattress, bureau, dressing table, writing desk . . . the desk. A locked drawer in the desk – a locked drawer in the outer room. The 'equipment'. Nothing mattered now! His woman was gone and there were too many questions!

A heavy lamp on the desk, a thick brass base; he picked it up, pulling out the cord, and smashed it into the drawer. Again and again and again until the wood splintered, shattering the recess that held the tiny vertical latch. He yanked the drawer open and stared in equal parts of horror and comprehension at what he saw.

Next to each other in a cushioned plastic case were two hypodermic needles, their vials filled with an identical yellowish serum. He did not have to know the chemical compounds; there were too many beyond his knowledge that would be effective. Liquid death in the veins.

Nor did he have to be told for whom they were intended. *Côte à côte dans le lit.* Two bodies beside each other in bed. He and his woman in a pact of final deliverance. How thoroughly had the monseigneur thought everything out! Himself dead! One dead old man from the Jackal's army of old men had outwitted all the security procedures, killing and mutilating those dearest to Carlos's ultimate enemy, Jason Bourne. And, naturally, behind that brilliant manipulation was the Jackal himself!

Ce n'est pas le contrat! Myself, *yes*, but not my woman! You promised me!

The *nurse*. The angel not of mercy but of death! The man known on Tranquillity Isle as Jean Pierre Fontaine walked as fast as he could into the other room. To his equipment.

The huge silver racing craft with its two enormous engines crashed through the swells as often above the waves as in them. On the short low bridge, John St Jacques manoeuvred the drug boat through the dangerous reefs he knew by summoned memory, aided by the powerful searchlight that lit up the turbulent waters, now twenty, now two hundred feet in front of the bow. He kept screaming into his radio, the microphone weaving in front of his drenched face, hoping against all logic to raise someone on Tranquillity.

He was within three miles of the island, a shrubbed volcanic intrusion on the water his landmark. Tranquillity Isle was in kilometres much nearer Plymouth than to Blackburne Airport, and if one knew the shoals, not much longer to reach in a drug boat than in a seaplane, which had to bank east out of Blackburne to catch the prevailing west winds in order to land on the sea.

Johnny was not sure why these calculations kept interfering with his concentration except that somehow they made him feel better, that he was doing the best he could – *Damn it!* Why was it always the best he *could* rather than simply the *best*? He couldn't louse up any more, not now, not *tonight*! Christ, he owed everything to Mare and David! Maybe even more to the crazy bastard who was his brother-in-law than to his own sister. David, wild-nuts *David*, a man he sometimes wondered if Marie ever knew existed!

'You back off, little Bro', I'll take care of this.'

'You can't, David, I did it. I killed them!'

'I said back off.'

'I asked for your help, not for you to be me!'

'But you see I am you. I would have done the same thing and that makes me you in my eyes.'

'That's crazy!'

'It's part of it. Someday I may teach you how to kill cleanly, in the dark. In the meantime, listen to the lawyers.'

'Suppose they lose?'

'I'll get you out. I'll get you away.'

'How?'

'I'll kill again.'

'I can't believe you! A teacher, a scholar – I don't believe you, I don't want to believe you – you're my sister's husband.'

'Then don't believe me, Johnny. And forget everything I've said, and never tell your sister I said it.'

'It's that other person inside of you, isn't it?'

'You're very dear to Marie.'

'That's no answer! Here, now, you're Bourne, aren't you? Jason Bourne!'

'We'll never, ever, discuss this conversation, Johnny. Do you understand me?'

No, he had never understood, thought St Jacques, as the swirling winds and the cracks of lighting seemed to envelop the boat. Even when Marie and David appealed to his rapidly disintegrating ego by suggesting he could build a new life for himself in the islands. Seed money, they had said; build us a house and then see where you want to go from there. Within limits, we'll back you. Why would they do that? Why did they?

It was not 'they,' it was he. Jason Bourne.

Johnny St Jacques understood the other morning when he picked up the phone by the pool and was told by an island pilot that someone had been asking questions at the airport about a woman and two children.

Someday I may teach you how to kill cleanly, in the dark. Jason Bourne.

Lights! He saw the beach lights of Tranquillity. He was less than a mile from the shore!

The rain pounded down against the old Frenchman, the blasts of wind throwing him off balance as he made his way up the path towards Villa Fourteen. He angled his head against the elements, squinting, wiping his face with his left hand, his right gripping the weapon, a gun lengthened by the extension of the pocked cylinder that was its silencer. He held the pistol behind him as he had done years ago racing along railroad tracks, sticks of dynamite in one hand, a German Luger in the other, prepared to drop both at the appearance of Nazi patrols.

Whoever they were on the path above, they were no less than the Boche in his mind. All were Boche! He had been subservient to others long enough! His woman was gone; he would be his own man now, for there was nothing left but his own decisions, his own *feelings*, his own very private sense of what was right and what was wrong . . . And the Jackal was wrong! The apostle of Carlos could accept the killing of the woman; it was a debt he could rationalize, but not the children, and certainly not the mutilations. Those acts were against God, and he and his woman were about to face Him; there had to be certain ameliorating circumstances.

Stop the angel of death! What could she be *doing*? What did the fire she talked about *mean*? . . . Then he saw it – a huge burst of flame through the hedges of Villa Fourteen. In a window! The same window that had to be the bedroom of the luxurious pink cottage.

Fontaine reached the flagstone walk that led to the front door as a bolt of lightning shook the ground under him. He fell to the earth, then struggled to his knees, crawling to the pink porch, its fluttering overhead light outlining the door. No amount of twisting or pulling or shoving could release the latch, so he angled his pistol up, squeezed the trigger twice and blew the lock apart. He pushed himself to his feet and went inside.

Inside. The screams came from beyond the door of the master bedroom. The old Frenchman lurched towards it, his legs unsteady, his weapon wavering in his right hand. With what strength he had left, he kicked the door open and observed a scene that he knew had to come from hell.

The nurse, with the old man's head in a metal leash, was forcing her victim down into a raging kerosene fire on the floor.

'*Arrêtez!*' screamed the man called Jean Pierre Fontaine. '*Assez! Maintenant! Vous êtes mort!*'

Through the rising, spreading flames, shots rang out and bodies fell.

The lights of Tranquillity's beach drew nearer as John St Jacques kept yelling into the microphone: 'It's *me*! It's Saint Jay coming in! Don't *shoot*!'

But the sleek silver drug boat was greeted by the staccato gunfire of automatic weapons. St Jacques dived to the deck and kept shouting.

'I'm coming in – I'm *beaching*! Hold your goddamn fire!'

'Is that *you, mon*?' came a panicked voice over the radio.

'You want to get *paid* next week?'

'Oh, yes, Mr Saint Jay!' The loudspeakers on the beach erratically interrupted the winds and the thunder out of Basse-Terre. 'Everyone down on the beach, stop shooting your guns! The *bo-att* is okay, *mon*! It is our *boss mon*, Mr Saint Jay!'

The drug boat shot out of the water and onto the dark sand, its engines screaming, the blades instantly embedded, the pointed hull cracking under the impact. St Jacques leaped up from his crash-protecting foetal position and vaulted over the gunwale. 'Villa *Twenty*!' he roared, racing through the downpour across the beach to the stone steps that ascended to the path. 'All you men get *there*!'

As he ran up the hard, rain-splattered staircase he suddenly gasped, his personal galaxy exploding into a thousand blinding stars of fire. *Gunshots!* One after another. On the east wing of the path! His legs cycled faster and faster, leaping over two and three steps at a time; he reached the path and like a man possessed raced up the path towards Villa Twenty, snapping his head to the right in furious confusion that only added to his panic. *People* – men and women from his *staff* – were clustered around the doorway of Villa Fourteen! . . . Who was there? . . . My *God*, the *judge!*

His lungs bursting, every muscle and tendon in his legs stretched to the breaking point, St Jacques reached his sister's house. He crashed through the gate, and ran to the door, hurling his body against it and bursting through to the room inside. Eyes bulging first in horror, then in unmeasurable pain, he fell to his knees, screaming. On the white wall with terrible clarity were the words scrawled in dark red:

Jason Bourne, brother of the Jackal.

14

'*Johnny!* Johnny, *stop* it!' His sister's voice crashed into his ear as she cradled his head in one arm, the other extended above him, her free hand gripping his hair, nearly pulling it out of his skull. 'Can you *hear me*? We're *all right*, Bro! The children are in another villa – we're *fine*!'

The faces above him and around him came slowly into focus. Among them were the two old men, one from Boston, the other from Paris. 'There they *are*!' screamed St Jacques, lurching up but stopped by Marie who fell across him. 'I'll kill the bastards!'

'*No!*' roared his sister, holding him, helped by a guard whose strong black hands gripped her brother's shoulders. 'At this moment they're two of the best friends we have.'

'You don't know who they *are*!' cried St Jacques, trying to free himself.

'Yes we do,' broke in Marie, lowering her voice, her lips next to his ear. 'Enough to know they can lead us to the Jackal—'

'They *work* for the Jackal!'

'One did,' said the sister. 'The other never heard of Carlos.'

'You don't understand!' whispered St Jacques. 'They're old men – "the old men of Paris", the Jackal's *army*! Conklin reached me in Plymouth and explained . . . they're killers!'

'Again, one was but he's not any more; he has nothing to kill for now. The other . . . well, the other's a mistake, a stupid, outrageous mistake but that's all he is, and thank God for it – for him.'

'It's all crazy . . . !'

'It's crazy,' agreed Marie, releasing his hair and lessening her grip on his neck; she nodded to the guard to help her brother up. 'Come on, Johnny, we have things to talk about.'

The storm had blown away like a violent, unwanted intruder racing off into the night leaving behind the carnage of its rage. The early morning light broke over the eastern horizon, slowly revealing through the mists the blue-green out islands of Montserrat. The first boats cautiously, dolefully lumbered out to the favoured fishing grounds, for the catch of the day meant one more day's survival. Marie, her brother and the two old men were around a table on the balcony of an unoccupied villa. Over coffee, they had been talking for the better part of an hour, treating each point of horror coldly, dissecting facts without feeling. The aged, false hero of France had been assured that all proper arrangements would be made for his woman once phone service had been restored to the big island. If it was possible, he wanted her to be buried in the islands; she would understand. There was nothing left for her in France but the ignominy of a tawdry grave. If it were possible –

'It's possible,' said St Jacques. 'Because of you my sister's alive.'

'Because of me, young man, she might have died.'

'Would you have killed me?' asked Marie, studying the old French-man.

'Certainly not after I saw what Carlos had planned for me and my woman. *He* had broken the contract, not I.'

'Before then.'

'As if I had not seen the needles, understood what was all too obvious?'

'Yes?'

'That's difficult to answer; a contract's a contract. Still, my woman was dead, and a part of her dying was because she sensed that a terrible thing had been demanded of me. To go through with that demand would deny that aspect of her death, don't you see? Yet again, even in her death, the monseigneur could not be totally denied – he had made possible years of relative happiness that would have been impossible without him . . . I simply don't know. I might have reasoned that I owed him your life – your death – but certainly not the children's . . . and most certainly not the rest of it.'

'Rest of what?' asked St Jacques.

'It's best not to inquire.'

'I think you would have killed me,' said Marie.

'I tell you, I simply don't know. There was nothing personal. You were not a person to me, simply an event that was part of a business arrangement . . . Still, as I say, my woman was gone, and I'm an old man with limited time before me. Perhaps a look in your eyes or a plea for your children – who knows, I might have turned the pistol on myself. Then again, I might not have.'

'Jesus, you are a killer,' said the brother quietly.

'I am many things, monsieur. I don't ask forgiveness in this world; the other's another question. There were always circumstances—'

'Gallic logic,' remarked Brendan Patrick Pierre Prefontaine, former judge of the first circuit court in Boston, as he absently touched the raw tender skin of his neck below his singed white hair. 'Thank heavens I never had to argue before *les tribunals*; neither side is ever actually wrong.' The disbarred attorney chuckled. 'You see before you a felon, justly tried and justly convicted. The only exculpatory aspect of my crimes is that I was caught and so many others were not and are not.'

'Perhaps we are related, after all, *Monsieur le Juge.*'

'By comparison, sir, my life is far closer to that of St Thomas Aquinas —'

'Blackmail,' interrupted Marie.

'No, actually the charge was malfeasance. Accepting remunerations for favourable decisions, that sort of thing . . . My God, we're hound's tooth Boston! In New York City it's standard procedure: Leave your money with the bailiff, enough for everyone.'

'I'm not referring to Boston, I'm talking about why you're here. It's blackmail.'

'That's an oversimplification but essentially correct. As I told you, the man who paid me to find out where you'd gone also paid me an additional large sum of money to keep the information to myself. Under the circumstances, and because I have no pressing schedule of appointments, I thought it logical to pursue the inquiry. After all, if the little I knew brought so much, how much more might come to me if I learned a little more?'

'You talk of Gallic logic, monsieur?' inserted the Frenchman.

'It's simple interrogatory progression,' replied the former judge, briefly glancing at Jean Pierre before turning back to Marie. 'However, my dear, I may have glossed over an item that was extremely helpful in negotiations with my client. To put it plainly, your identity was being withheld and protected by the government. It was a strong point that frightened a very strong and influential man.'

'I want his name,' said Marie.

'Then I must have protection, too,' rejoined Prefontaine.

'You'll have it—'

'And perhaps something more,' continued the old disbarred attorney. 'My client has no idea I came here, no knowledge of what's happened, all of which might fuel the fires of his largesse if I described what I've experienced and observed. He'd be frightened out of his mind even to be associated with such events. Also, considering the fact that I was nearly killed by that Teutonic Amazon, I really deserve more.'

'Am I then to be rewarded for saving your life, monsieur?'

'If I had anything of value – other than my legal expertise, which is yours – I'd happily share it. If I'm given anything, that still holds, cousin.'

'*Merci bien, cousin.*'

'*D'accord, mon ami*, but never let the Irish nuns hear us.'

'You don't look like a poor man, Judge,' said John St Jacques.

'Then appearances are as deceiving as a long-forgotten title you so generously use . . . I should add that my wants are not extravagant, for there's no one but myself, and my creature comforts do not require luxury.'

'You've lost your woman, too, then?'

'Not that it's any of your damn business, but my wife left me twenty-nine years ago and my thirty-eight-year-old son, now a successful attorney on Wall Street, uses her name and when questioned by curious people tells them he never knew me. I haven't seen him since he was ten; it was not in his interest, you understand.'

'*Quelle tristesse.*'

'*Quel* bullshit, cousin. That boy got his brains from me, not from the airhead who bore him . . . However, we stray. My French pureblood here has his own reasons – obviously based on betrayal – for cooperating with you. I have equally strong reasons for wanting to help you, too, but I must also consider myself. My aged new friend can go back and live what's left of his life in Paris whereas I have no place to go but Boston and the few opportunities I've developed over the years to eke out a living. Therefore my deep-seated motives for wanting to help must themselves take a backseat. With what I know now I wouldn't last five minutes in the streets of Boston.'

'Breakthrough,' said John St Jacques, staring at Prefontaine. 'I'm sorry, Judge, we don't need you.'

'*What?*' Marie sat forward in her chair. 'Please, Bro, we need all the help we can get!'

'Not in this case. We know who hired him.'

'We *do*?'

'Conklin knows; he called it a "breakthrough". He told me that the man who traced you and the children here used a judge to find you.' The brother nodded across the table at the Bostonian. 'Him. It's why I smashed up a hundred-thousand-dollar boat to get back over here. Conklin knows who his client is.'

Prefontaine again glanced at the old Frenchman. 'Now is the time for "*Quelle tristesse*," Sir Hero. I'm left with nothing. My persistence brought me only a sore throat and a burned scalp.'

'Not necessarily,' interrupted Marie. 'You're the attorney so I shouldn't have to tell you. Corroboration is cooperation. We may want you to tell everything you know to certain people in Washington.'

'Corroboration can be obtained with a subpoena, my dear. Under oath in a courtroom, take my personal as well as my professional word for it.'

'We won't be going to court. Ever.'

'Oh? . . . I see.'

'You couldn't possibly, Judge, not at this juncture. However, if you agree to help us you'll be well paid . . . A moment ago you said that you had strong reasons for wanting to help, reasons that had to be secondary to your own well-being—'

'Are you by any chance a lawyer, my dear?'

'No, an economist.'

'Holy Mary, that's worse . . . About my reasons?'

'Do they concern your client, the man who hired you to trace us?'

'They do. His august persona – as in Caesar Augustus – should be trashed. Slippery intellectuality aside, he's a whore. He had promise once, more than I let him know, but he let it all go by the boards in a flamboyant quest for his own personal grail.'

'What the hell's he talking about, Mare?'

'A man with a great deal of influence or power, neither of which he should have, I think. Our convicted felon here has come to grips with personal morality.'

'Is that an economist speaking?' asked Prefontaine, once more absently touching the blistered flesh of his neck. 'An economist reflecting on her last inaccurate projection that caused inappropriate buying or selling on the stock exchanges, resulting in losses many could afford and many more could not?'

'My voice was never that important, but I'll grant you it's the reflection of a great many others whose projections were, because they never risked, they only theorized. It's a safe position . . . Yours isn't, Judge. You may need the protection we can provide. What's your answer?'

'Jesus, Mary and Joseph, you're a cold one—'

'I have to be,' said Marie, her eyes levelled on the man from Boston. 'I want you with us, but I won't beg, I'll simply leave you with nothing and you can go back to the streets in Boston.'

'Are you *sure* you're not a lawyer – or perhaps a lord high executioner?'

'Take your choice. Just give me your answer.'

'Will somebody tell me what the hell is going on here!' yelled John St Jacques.

'Your sister,' answered Prefontaine, his gentle gaze on Marie, 'has enlisted a recruit. She's made the options clear, which every attorney understands, and the inevitability of her logic, in addition to her lovely face, crowned by that dark red hair, makes my decision also inevitable.'

'What . . . ?'

'He's opted for our side, Johnny. Forget it.'

'What do we need him for?'

'Without a courtroom a dozen different reasons, young man,' answered the judge. 'In certain situations, volunteerism is not the best road to take unless one is thoroughly protected beyond the courts.'

'Is that right, Sis?'

'It's not wrong, Bro, but it's up to Jason – *damn it* – David!'

'No, Mare,' said John St Jacques, his eyes boring into his sister's. 'It's up to Jason.'

'Are these names I should be aware of?' asked Prefontaine. 'The name "Jason Bourne" was sprayed on the wall of your villa.'

'My instructions, cousin,' said the false yet not so false hero of France. 'It was necessary.'

'I don't understand . . . any more than I understand the other name, the "Jackal," or "Carlos," which you both rather brutally questioned me about when I wasn't sure whether I was dead or alive. I thought the "Jackal" was fiction.'

The old man called Jean Pierre Fontaine looked at Marie; she nodded. 'Carlos the Jackal is a legend but he is not fiction. He's a professional killer now in his sixties, rumoured to be ill, but still possessed with a terrible hatred. He's a man of many faces, many sides, some loved by those who have reasons to love him, others detested by those who consider him the essence of evil – and depending on the view, all have their reasons for being correct. I am an example of one who has experienced both viewpoints, but then my world is hardly yours, as you rightfully suggested, St Thomas of Aquinas.'

'*Merci bien.*'

'*D'accord.* But the hatred that obsesses Carlos grows like a cancer in his ageing brain. One man drew him out; one man tricked him, usurped his kills, taking credit for the Jackal's work, kill after kill, driving Carlos mad when he was trying to correct the record, trying to maintain his supremacy as the ultimate assassin. That same man was responsible for the death of his lover – but one far more than a lover, the woman who was his keel, his beloved since childhood in Venezuela, his colleague in all things. That single man, one of hundreds, perhaps thousands sent out by governments everywhere, was the only one who ever saw his face – *as* the Jackal. The man who did all this was a product of American intelligence, a strange man who lived a deadly lie every day of his life for three years. And Carlos will not rest until that man is punished . . . and killed. The man is Jason Bourne.'

Squinting, stunned by the Frenchman's story, Prefontaine leaned forward over the table. 'Who *is* Jason Bourne?' he asked.

'My husband, David Webb,' replied Marie.

'Oh, my *God*,' whispered the judge. 'May I have a drink, please?'

John St Jacques called out. 'Ronald!'

'Yes, boss-*mon*!' cried from within the guard whose strong hands had held his employer's shoulders an hour ago in Villa Twenty.

'Bring us some whisky and brandy, please. The bar should be stocked.'

'Comin', sir.'

The orange sun in the east suddenly took fire, its rays penetrating what was left of the sea mists of dawn. The silence around the table was broken by the soft, heavily accented words of the old Frenchman. 'I am not used to such service,' he said, looking aimlessly beyond the railing of the balcony at the progressively bright waters of the Caribbean. 'When something is asked for, I always think the task should be mine.'

'Not any more,' said Marie quietly, then after a beat, adding, '. . . Jean Pierre.'

'I suppose one could live with that name . . . '

'Why not here?'

'*Qu'est-ce que vous dites, madame?*'

'Think about it. Paris might not be any less dangerous for you than the streets of Boston for our judge.'

The judge in question was lost in his own aimless reverie as several bottles, glasses and a bucket of ice were brought to the table. With no hesitation, Prefontaine reached out and poured himself an extravagant drink from the bottle nearest him. 'I *must* ask a question or two,' he said emphatically. 'Is that proper?'

'Go ahead,' replied Marie. 'I'm not sure I can or will answer you, but try me.'

'The gunshots, the spray paint on the wall – my "cousin" here says the red paint and the words were by his instructions—'

'They were, *mon ami*. The loud firing of the guns as well.'

'Why?'

'Everything must be as it is expected to be. The gunshots were an additional element to draw attention to the event that was to take place.'

'Why?'

'A lesson we learned in the Résistance – not that I was ever a "Jean Pierre Fontaine," but I did my small part. It was called an *accentuation*, a positive statement making clear that the underground was responsible for the action. Everyone in the vicinity knew it.'

'Why *here*?'

'The Jackal's nurse is dead. There is no one to tell him that his instructions have been carried out.'

'Gallic logic. Incomprehensible.'

'French common sense. Incontestable.'

'*Why?*'

'Carlos will be here by noon tomorrow.'

'Oh, dear *God*!'

The telephone rang inside the villa. John St Jacques lurched out of his chair only to be blocked by his sister, who threw her arm in front of his face as she rose and raced through the doors into the living room. She picked up the phone.

'*David?*'

'It's Alex,' said the breathless voice on the line. 'Christ, I've had this goddamned thing on redial for three hours! Are you all right?'

'We're alive but we weren't supposed to be.'

'The old men! The old men of Paris! Did Johnny—'

'Johnny *did*, but they're on our side!'

'Who?'

'The old men—'

'You're not making one damn bit of sense!'

'Yes, I am! We're in control here. What about *David*?'

'I don't know! The telephone lines were cut. Everything's a mess! I've got the police heading out there—'

'*Screw* the police, Alex!' screamed Marie. 'Get the Army, the Marines, the lousy CIA! We're *owed*!'

'Jason won't allow that. I can't turn on him now.'

'Well, try this for size. The Jackal will be here *tomorrow*!'

'Oh, Jesus! I have to get him a jet somewhere.'

'You have to do *something*!'

'You don't understand, Marie. The old Medusa surfaced—'

'You tell that husband of mine that Medusa's *history*! The Jackal *isn't*, and he's flying in here tomorrow!'

'David'll be there, you know that.'

'Yes, I do . . . because he's Jason Bourne now.'

'Brer Rabbit, this ain't thirteen years ago, and you just happen to be thirteen years older. You're not only gonna be useless, you're gonna be a positive liability unless you get some rest, preferably sleep. Turn off the lights and grab some sack time in that big fancy couch in the living room. I'll man the phones, which ain't gonna ring 'cause nobody's callin' at four o'clock in the morning.'

Cactus's voice had faded as Jason wandered into the dark living room, his legs heavy, his lids falling over his eyes like lead weights. He dropped to the couch, swinging his legs slowly, with effort, one at a time, up on the cushions; he stared at the ceiling. *Rest is a weapon, battles won and lost* . . . Philippe d'Anjou. Medusa. His inner screen went blank and sleep came.

A screaming, pulsating siren erupted, deafening, incessant, echoing throughout the cavernous house like a sonic tornado. Bourne spastically whipped his body around and sprang off the couch, at first disoriented, unsure of where he was and for a terrible moment . . . of who he was.

'*Cactus!*' he roared, racing out of the ornate living room into the hallway. '*Cactus!*' he shouted again, hearing his voice lost in the rapid, rhythmic crescendos of the siren-alarm. 'Where *are* you?'

Nothing. He ran to the door of the study, gripping the knob. It was locked! He stepped back and crashed his shoulder against it, once, twice, a third time with all the speed and strength he could summon. The door splintered, then gave way and Jason hammered his foot against the central panel until it collapsed; he went inside and what he found caused the killing machine that was the product of Medusa and beyond to stare in ice-cold fury. Cactus was sprawled over the desk, under the light of the single lamp, in the same chair that had held the murdered general, his blood forming a pool of red on the blotter – a corpse . . . No, *not* a corpse! The right hand moved, Cactus was alive!

Bourne ran to the desk and gently raised the old man's head, the shrill, deafening, all-encompassing alarm making communication – if communication were possible – impossible. Cactus opened his dark eyes, his trembling right hand moving down the blotter, his forefinger curved and tapping the top of the desk.

'What *is* it?' yelled Jason. The hand kept moving back towards the edge of the blotter, the tapping more rapid. 'Below? Underneath?' With minuscule, nearly imperceptible motions of his head, Cactus nodded in the affirmative. '*Under* the desk!' shouted Bourne, beginning to understand. He knelt down to the right of Cactus and felt under the thin top drawer, then to the side – He found it! A button. Again gently, he moved the heavy rolling chair inches to the left and centred his eyes on the button. Beneath it, in tiny white letters on a black plastic strip, was the answer.

Aux. Alarm.

Jason pressed the button; instantly the shrieking pandemonium was cut off. The ensuing silence was nearly as deafening, the adjustment to it nearly as terrifying.

'How were you hit?' asked Bourne. 'How long ago? . . . If you can talk, just whisper, no energy at all, do you understand?'

'Oh, Brer, you're too much,' whispered Cactus, in pain. 'I was a black cabdriver in Washington, man. I've been here before. It ain't fatal, boy, I gotta slug in the upper chest.'

'I'll get a doctor right away – our friend Ivan, incidentally – but if you can tell me what happened while I move you to the floor and look at the damage.' Jason slowly, carefully lowered the old man off the chair and onto the throw rug beneath the bay window. He tore off Cactus's shirt; the bullet had gone through the flesh of the left shoulder. With short, swift movements Bourne ripped the shirt into strips and tightly wrapped a primitive bandage around his friend's chest and between the underarm and the shoulder. 'It's not much,' said Jason, 'but it'll hold you for a while. Go on.'

'He's *out* there, Brer!' coughed Cactus weakly, lying back on the floor. 'He's got a big mother 'fifty-seven magnum with a silencer; he pinned me through the window, then smashed it and climbed inside . . . He – he . . . '

'Easy! Don't talk, never mind—'

'I gotta. The brothers out there, they ain't got no hardware. He'll pick 'em off! . . . I played deep dead and he was in a hurry – oh, was *he* in a hurry! Look over there, will ya?' Jason swung his head in the direction of Cactus's gesture. A dozen or so books had been yanked out of a shelf on the side wall and strewn on the floor. The old man continued, his voice growing weaker. 'He went over to the bookcase like in a panic, until he found what he wanted . . . then to the door, that 'fifty-seven ready for bear, if you follow me . . . I figured it was you he was after, that he'd seen you through the window go out to the other room, and I tell ya, I was workin' my right knee like a runnin' muskrat 'cause I found that alarm button an hour ago and knew I had to stop him—'

'Easy!'

'I gotta tell you . . . I couldn't move my hands 'cause he'd see me, but my knee hit that sucker and the siren damn near blew me out of the chair . . . The honky bastard fell apart. He slammed the door, locked it, and beat his way out of here back through the window.' Cactus's neck arched back, the pain and the exhaustion overtaking him. 'He's out there, Brer Rabbit—'

'That's enough!' ordered Bourne as he cautiously reached up, snapping off the desk lamp, leaving the dim light from the hallway through the shattered door as the only illumination. 'I'm calling Alex; he can send the doctor—'

Suddenly, from somewhere outside, there was a high-pitched scream, a roar of shock and anguish Jason knew only too well. So did Cactus, who whispered, his eyes shut tight: 'He got one. That fucker got one of the brothers!'

'I'm reaching Conklin,' said Jason, pulling the phone off of the desk. 'Then I'll go out and get *him* . . . Oh, Christ! The line's out – it's been *cut*!'

'That honky knows his way around here.'

'So do I, Cactus. Stay as quiet as you can. I'll be back for you—'

There was another scream, this lower, more abrupt, an expulsion of breath more than a roar.

'May sweet Jesus forgive me,' muttered the old black man painfully, meaning the words. 'There's only one brother left—'

'If anyone should ask forgiveness, it's *me*,' cried Bourne, his voice guttural, half choking. '*Goddamn* it! I swear to you, Cactus, I never thought, never even considered, that anything like this would happen.'

'Course you didn't. I know you from back to the old days, Brer, and I never heard of you asking anyone to risk anything for you . . . It's always been the other way around.'

'I'm going to pull you over,' interrupted Jason, tugging on the rug, manoeuvring Cactus to the right side of the desk, the old man's left hand close enough to reach the auxiliary alarm. 'If you hear anything or see anything or *feel* anything, turn on the siren.'

'Where are you going? I mean how?'

'Another room. Another window.'

Bourne crept across the floor to the mutilated door, lurched through it, got to his feet, and ran into the living room. At the far end was a pair of French doors that led to an outside patio; he recalled seeing white wrought-iron lawn furniture on the south end of the house when he was with the guards. He twisted the knob and slipped outside, pulling the automatic from his belt, shutting the right door, and crouching, making his way to the shrubbery at the edge of the grass. He had to move *quickly*. Not only was there a third life in the balance, a third unrelated, unwarranted death, but a killer who could be his shortcut to the crimes of the new Medusa, and those crimes were his bait for the Jackal! A diversion, a magnet, a trap . . . the *flares* – part of the equipment he had brought with him to Manassas. The two emergency 'candles' were in his left rear pocket, each six inches long and bright enough to be seen for miles; ignited together yet spaced apart they would light up Swayne's property like two searchlights. One in the south drive, the other by the kennels, possibly waking the drugged dogs, bewildering them, infuriating them – Do it! *Hurry*.

Jason scrambled across the lawn, his eyes darting everywhere, wondering where the stalking killer was and how the innocent quarry that Cactus had enlisted was evading him. One was experienced, the other not, and Bourne could not permit the latter's life to be wasted.

It *happened*! He had been spotted! Two cracks on either side of him, bullets from a silenced pistol slicing the air. He reached the south leg of the paved drive and, racing across it, dived into the foliage. Ripping a flare from his pocket, he put down the weapon, snapped up the flame of his lighter, ignited the fuse and threw the sizzling candle to his right. It landed on the road; in seconds it would spew out the blinding fire. He ran to his left beneath the pine trees towards the rear of the estate, his lighter and the second flare in one hand, the automatic in the other. He was parallel to the kennels; the flare in the road exploded into bluish-white flames. He ignited the second and threw it end over end, arcing it forty yards away to the front of the kennels. He waited.

The second flare burst into sputtering fire, two balls of blinding white light eerily illuminating the house and grounds of the estate's south side. Three of the dogs began to wail, then made feeble attempts to howl; soon their confused anger would be heard. A *shadow*. Against the west wall of the white house – it *moved*, caught in the light between the flare by the kennels and the house. The figure darted for the protection of the shrubbery; it crouched, an immobile but intrusive part of the silhouetted foliage. Was it the killer or the killer's target, the last 'brother' recruited by Cactus? . . . There was one way to find out, and if it was the former and he was a decent marksman, it was not the best tactic, but still it was the quickest.

Bourne leaped up from the underbrush, yelling in full view as he lunged to his right, at the last half second plunging his foot into the soft dirt and pivoting, lowering his body and diving to his left. 'Head for the *cabin*!' he roared. And he got his answer. Two more spits, two more cracks in the air, the bullets digging up the earth to his right. The killer was good; perhaps not an expert but good enough. A. 357 held six shells; five had been fired but there had been sufficient time to reload the emptied cylinder. Another strategy – *quickly*!

Suddenly another figure appeared, a man running up the road towards the rear of Flannagan's cabin. He was in the open – he could be killed!

'Over here, you *bastard*!' screamed Jason, jumping up and firing his automatic blindly into the shrubbery by the house. And then he got another answer, a welcome one. There was a single spit, a single crack in the air and then no more. The killer had *not* reloaded! Perhaps he had no more shells – *whatever*, the primary target was now on the high ground. Bourne raced out of the bushes and across the lawn through the opposing light of the flares; the dogs began to come to life, the yelps and throated growls of attack becoming louder. The killer ran out of the shrubbery and into the road, racing through shadows towards the front gates. Jason had the bastard, he *knew* it. The gates were closed, the Medusan was cornered. Bourne roared: 'There's no way out, Snake Lady! Make it easy on yourself—'

A spit, a *crack*. The man had reloaded while running! Jason fired; the man fell in the road. And as he did so, the intermittent silence of the night was ripped open by the sound of a powerful, racing engine, the vehicle in question speeding up the outside road, its flashing red and blue lights signifying the police. The police! The alarm must have been wired into the Manassas headquarters, a fact that had never occurred to Bourne; he had assumed that such a measure was impossible where Medusa was concerned. It wasn't logical; the security was *internal*; no external force could be permitted for Snake Lady. There was too much to learn, too much that had to be kept secret – a *cemetery*!

The killer writhed in the road, rolling over and over towards the bordering pine trees. There was something clutched in his hand. Jason approached him as two police officers got out of the patrol car beyond the gate. He lashed his foot out, kicking the man's body, releasing whatever it was in his grip and reaching down to pick it up. It was a leather-bound book, one of a set, like a volume of Dickens or Thackeray, the embossed letters in gold, more for exposure than for reading. It was *crazy*! Then he flipped open a page and understood it was not crazy at all. There was no print inside, only the scrawl of handwritten notes on blank pages. It was a diary, a ledger!

There could be no police! Especially not now. He could not allow them to penetrate his and Conklin's penetration into Medusa any more than Medusa could. The leather-bound book in his hand could not see the official light of day! The Jackal was *everything*. He had to get *rid* of them!

'We got a call, mister,' intoned a laconic, middle-aged patrolman walking towards the grilled gate, a younger associate joining him. 'HQ said he was uptight as hell. We're responding, but like I told dispatch, there've been some pretty wild parties out here, no criticism intended, sir. We all like a good time now and then, right?'

'Absolutely right, Officer,' replied Jason, trying his utmost to control the painful heaving in his chest, his eyes straying to the wounded killer – he had *disappeared*! 'There was a momentary shortage in electricity that somehow interfered with the telephone lines.'

'Happens a lot,' confirmed the younger patrolman. 'Sudden showers and summer heat lightnin'. Someday they'll put all them cables underground. My folks got a place—'

'The point *is*,' interrupted Bourne, 'everything's getting back to normal. As you can see, some of the lights in the house are back on.'

'I can't see nothin' through them flares,' said the young police officer.

'The general always takes the ultimate precautions,' explained Jason. 'I guess he feels he has to,' he added, somewhat lamely. 'Regardless, everything's – as I said – getting back to normal. Okay?'

'Okay by me,' answered the older patrolman, 'but I got a message for someone named Webb. He in there?'

'I'm Webb,' said Jason Bourne, alarmed.

'That makes things easier. You're supposed to call a "Mister Conk" right away. It's urgent.'

'Urgent?'

'An emergency, we were told. It was just radioed to us.'

Jason could hear the rattling of the fence on the perimeter of Swayne's property. The killer was getting away! 'Well, officer, the phones are still out here . . . Do you have one in your car?'

'Not for personal use, sir. Sorry.'

'But you just said it was an emergency.'

'Well, I suppose since you're a guest of the general's I could permit it. If it's long distance though, you'd better have a credit card number.'

'Oh, my *God*.' Bourne unlocked the gate and rushed to the patrol car as the siren-alarm was activated back at the house – activated and then instantly shut off. The remaining brother had apparently found Cactus.

'What the hell was *that*?' yelled the young policeman.

'*Forget* it!' screamed Jason, jumping into the car and yanking an all too familiar patrol phone out of its cradle. He gave Alex's number in Virginia to the police switchboard and kept repeating the phrase: '*It's an emergency, it's an emergency!*'

'Yes?' answered Conklin, acknowledging the police operator.

'It's me!'

'What *happened*?'

'Too involved to go into. What's the emergency?'

'I've got you a private jet out of the Reston airport.'

'Reston? That's north of here—'

'The field in Manassas doesn't have the equipment. I'm sending a car for you.'

'*Why*?'

'Tranquillity. Marie and the kids are okay; they're *okay*! She's in charge.'

'What the hell does *that* mean?'

'Get to Reston and I'll tell you.'

'I want *more*!'

'The Jackal's flying in today.'

'Jesus *Christ*!'

'Wrap things up there and wait for the car.'

'I'll take this one!'

'*No!* Not unless you want to blow everything. We've got time. Wrap it up out there.'

'Cactus . . . he's hurt – shot.'

'I'll call Ivan. He'll get back in a hurry.'

'There's one brother left – only *one*, Alex. I killed the other two – I was responsible.'

'Cut that out. *Stop* it. Do what you have to do.'

'Goddamn you, I *can't*. Someone's got to be here and I *won't* be!'

'You're right. There's too much to keep under wraps out there and you've got to be in Montserrat. I'll drive out with the car and take your place.'

'Alex, tell me what happened on *Tranquillity*!'

'The old men . . . your "old men of Paris", that's what happened.'

'They're dead,' said Jason Bourne quietly, simply.

'Don't be hasty. They've turned – at least I gather the real one turned and the other's a God-given mistake. They're on our side now.'

'They're never on anyone's side but the Jackal's, you don't know them.'

'Neither do you. Listen to your wife. But now you go back to the house and write out everything I should know . . . And Jason, I must tell you something. I hope to Christ you can find your solution – *our* solution – on Tranquillity. Because all things considered, including my life, I can't keep this Medusa on our level much longer. I think you know that.'

'You *promised*!'

'Thirty-six hours. Delta.'

In the woods beyond the fence a wounded man crouched, his frightened face against the green links. In the bright wash of the headlights, he observed the tall man who had gone into the patrol car and now came out, awkwardly, nervously thanking the policemen. He did not, however, permit them inside.

Webb. The killer had heard the name 'Webb'.

It was all they had to know. All Snake Lady had to know.

15

'God, I love you!' said David Webb, leaning into the pay phone in the preboarding room at the private airfield in Reston, Virginia. 'The waiting was the worst part, waiting to talk to you, to hear from *you* that you were all right.'

'How do you think I felt, darling? Alex said the telephone lines had been cut and he was sending the police when I wanted him to send the whole damned army.'

'We can't even allow the police, nothing official anywhere at the moment. Conklin's promised me at least another thirty-six hours . . . We may not need that now. Not with the Jackal in Montserrat.'

'David, what happened? Alex mentioned Medusa—'

'It's a mess and he's right, he has to go higher up with it. *Him*, not us. We stay out. Far away out.'

'What *happened*?' repeated Marie. 'What's the old Medusa got to do with anything?'

'There's a new Medusa – an extension of the old one, actually – and it's big and ugly and it kills – they kill. I saw that tonight; one of their guns tried to kill me after thinking he'd killed Cactus and murdering two innocent men.'

'Good *God*! Alex told me about Cactus when he called me back, but nothing else. How is your Uncle Remus?'

'He'll make it. The Agency doctor came out and took him and the last brother away.'

' "Brother"?'

'I'll tell you when I see you . . . Conklin's out there now. He'll take care of everything and have the telephone fixed. I'll call him from Tranquillity.'

'You're exhausted—'

'I'm tired, but I'm not sure why. Cactus insisted I get some sleep and I must have had all of twelve minutes.'

'My poor darling.'

'I like the tone of your voice,' said David. 'The words even better, except I'm not poor. You took care of that in Paris thirteen years ago.' Suddenly his wife was silent and Webb was alarmed. 'What is it? Are you all right?'

'I'm not sure,' answered Marie softly, but with a strength that was the result of thought, not feeling. 'You say this new Medusa is big and ugly and it tried to kill you – they tried to kill you.'

'They didn't.'

'Yet they, or it, wanted you dead. Why?'

'Because I was there.'

'You don't kill a man because he was at someone's *house*—'

'A lot happened at that house tonight. Alex and I penetrated its circle of secrets and I was seen. The idea was to bait the Jackal with a few rich and all too famous bandits from the old Saigon who would hire him to come after me. It was a hell of a strategy but it spiralled out of control.'

'My God, David, don't you understand? You're marked! They'll come after you *themselves*!'

'How can they? The hit man from Medusa who was there never saw my face except while I was running in shadows, and *they* have no idea who I am. I'm a nonperson who'll simply disappear . . . No, Marie, if Carlos shows up and if I can do what I *know* I can do in Montserrat, we'll be free. To borrow a phrase, "free at last." '

'Your voice changes, doesn't it?'

'My what does which?'

'It really does. I can tell.'

'I don't know what you're talking about,' said Jason Bourne. 'I'm being signalled. The plane's here. Tell Johnny to keep those two old men under guard!'

The whispers spread through Montserrat like rolling pockets of mist. Something terrible had happened on the out island of Tranquillity . . . 'Bad times, *mon*' . . . 'The evil *obeah* come across the Antilles from Jamaic' and there was death and madness' . . . 'And blood on the walls of death, *mon*, a curse put on the family of an animal' . . . '*Sshh!* There was a cat mother and two cat children . . . !'

And there were other voices . . . 'Dear God, keep it *quiet*! It could ruin what tourism we've built!' . . . 'Never anything like this before – an isolated incident, obviously drug-related, brought over from another island!' . . . 'All too true, *mon*! I hear it was a madman. his body filled with dope' . . . 'I'm told a fast boat running like the wind of a hurricane took him out to sea. He's gone!' . . . 'Keep it quiet, I say! Remember the Virgins? The Fountainhead massacre? It took them years to recover. *Quiet*!'

And a single voice. 'It's a trap, sir, and if successful, as we believe it will be, we'll be the talk of the West Indies, the heroes of the Caribbean. It'll be positively *mahvellous* for our image. Law and order and all that.'

'Thank heavens! Was anyone actually killed?'

'One person and she was in the act of taking another's life.'

'*She?* Good God, I don't want to hear another word until it's all over.'

'It's better that you not be available for comment.'

'Damned good idea. I'll go out on the boat; the fish are running well after the storm.'

'Excellent, sir. And I'll stay in radio contact with developments.'

'Perhaps you shouldn't. Anything can be picked up out there.'

'I only meant so as to advise you when to return – at the appropriate moment to make a most advantageous appearance. I'll fill you in, of course.'

'Yes, of course. You're a good man, Henry.'

'Thank you, Crown governor.'

It was ten o'clock in the morning and they held each other fiercely but there was no time for talk, only the brief comfort of being together, safe together, secure in the knowledge that they knew things the Jackal did not know and that knowledge gave them an enormous advantage. Still, it was only an advantage, not a guarantee, not where Carlos was concerned. And both Jason and John St Jacques were adamant: Marie and the children were being flown south to Guadeloupe's Basse-Terre island. They would stay there with the Webbs' regal maid, Mrs Cooper, all under guard until they were called back to Montserrat. Marie objected, but her objections were met with silence; her husband's orders were delivered abruptly, icily.

'You're leaving because I have work to do. We won't discuss it any further.'

'It's Switzerland again . . . Zurich again, isn't it, *Jason*?'

'It's whatever you like,' replied Bourne, now preoccupied as the three of them stood at the base of the dock, two seaplanes bobbing in the water only yards apart at the far end. One had brought Jason directly to Tranquillity from Antigua; the other was fuelled for the flight to Guadeloupe with Mrs Cooper and the children already inside. 'Hurry up, Marie,' added Bourne. 'I want to go over things with Johnny and then grill those two old scumballs.'

'They're not scumballs, David. Because of them we're alive.'

'Why? Because they blew it and had to turn to save their asses?'

'That's not fair.'

'It's fair until I say otherwise, and they're scum until they convince me they're not. You don't know the Jackal's old men. I do. They'll say anything, do anything, lie and snivel to hell and back, and if you turn the other way, they'll shove a knife in your spine. He *owns* them – body, mind and what's left of their souls . . . Now get to the plane, it's waiting.'

'Don't you want to see the children, tell Jamie that—'

'*No*, there isn't time! Take her out there, Johnny. I want to check the beach.'

'There's nothing I haven't checked, David,' said St Jacques, his voice on the edge of defiance.

'*I'll* tell you whether you have or not,' shot back Bourne, his eyes angry as he started across the sand, adding in a loud voice without looking around, 'I'm going to have a dozen questions for you, and I hope to Christ you can answer them!'

St Jacques tensed, taking a step forward but stopped by his sister. 'Leave it alone, Bro,' said Marie, her hand on his arm. 'He's frightened.'

'He's *what*? He's one nasty son of a bitch is what he is!'

'Yes, I know.'

The brother looked at his sister. 'That stranger you were talking about yesterday at the house?'

'Yes, only now it's worse. That's why he's frightened.'

'I don't understand.'

'He's older, Johnny. He's fifty now and he wonders if he can still do the things he did before, years ago – in the war, in Paris, in Hong Kong. It's all gnawing at him, eating into him, because he knows he's got to be better than he ever was.'

'I think he can be.'

'I know he will be, for he has an extraordinary reason going for him. A wife and two children were taken from him once before. He barely remembers them, but they're at the core of his torment; Mo Panov believes that and I do, too . . . Now, years later, another wife and two children are threatened. Every nerve in him has to be on fire.'

Suddenly, from three hundred feet away on the beach, Bourne's voice erupted, splitting through the breezes from the sea. 'Goddamn it, I told you to *hurry*! . . . And you, Mr *Expert*, there's a reef out here with the colour of a sandbar beyond it! Have you *considered* that?'

'Don't answer, Johnny. We'll go out to the plane.'

'A sandbar? What the hell's he talking about? . . . Oh, my God, I *do* see!'

'I don't,' said Marie as they walked rapidly up the pier.

'There are reefs around eighty percent of the island, ninety-five percent where this beach is concerned. They brake the waves, it's why it's called Tranquillity; there's no surf at all.'

'So what?'

'So someone using a tank under water wouldn't risk crashing into a reef, but he would into a sandbar in *front* of a reef. He could watch the beach and the guards and crawl up when his landing was clear, lying in the water only feet from shore until he could take the guard. I never *thought* about that.'

'He did, Bro.'

Bourne sat on the corner of the desk, the two old men on a couch in front of him, his brother-in-law standing by a window fronting the beach in the unoccupied villa.

'Why would I – why would *we* – lie to you, monsieur?' asked the hero of France.

'Because it all sounds like a classic French farce. Similar but different names; one door opening as another closes, look-alikes disappearing and entering on cue. It smells, gentlemen.'

'Perhaps you are a student of Molière or Racine . . . ?'

'I'm a *student* of uncanny coincidence, especially where the Jackal is concerned.'

'I don't think there's the slightest similarity in our appearances,' offered the judge from Boston. 'Except, perhaps, our ages.'

The telephone rang. Jason quickly reached down and picked it up. 'Yes?'

'Everything checks out in Boston,' said Conklin. 'His name's Prefontaine, Brendan Prefontaine. He was a federal judge of the first circuit caught in a government scam and convicted of felonious misconduct on the bench – read that as being very large in the bribery business. He was sentenced to twenty-one years and did ten, which was enough to blow him away in every department. He's what they call a functioning alcoholic, something of a character in Bean Town's shadier districts, but harmless – actually kind of liked in a warped sort of way. He's also considered very bright when he's clearheaded, and I'm told a lot of crumbs wouldn't have gone court-free and others would be doing longer jail terms if he hadn't given shrewd advice to their attorneys of record. You might say he's a behind-the-scenes storefront lawyer, the "stores" in his case being saloons, pool halls and probably warehouses . . . Since I've been where he's at in the booze terrain, he sounds straight arrow to me. He's handling it better than I ever did.'

'You quit.'

'If I could have managed better in that twilight zone, I might not have. There's something to be said for the grape on many occasions.'

'What about his client?'

'Awesome, and our once and former judge was an adjunct professor at Harvard Law, where Gates was a student in two of his classes. No question about it, Prefontaine knows the man . . . Trust him, Jason. There's no reason for him to lie. He was simply after a score.'

'You're following up on the client?'

'With all the quiet ammunition I can pull out of my personal woodwork. He's our link to Carlos . . . The Medusa connection was a false lead, a stupid attempt by a stupid general in the Pentagon to put someone inside Gates's inner legal circle.'

'You're sure of that?'

'I am now. Gates is a highly paid consultant to a law firm representing a megadefence contractor under antitrust scrutiny. He wouldn't even return Swayne's calls, which, if he did, would make him more stupid than Swayne, which he isn't.'

'That's your problem, friend, not mine. If everything goes the way I intend it to go here, I don't even want to hear about Snake Lady. In fact, I can't remember *ever* having heard of it.'

'Thanks for dumping it on my lap – and in a way I guess I mean that. Incidentally, the grammar school notebook you grabbed from the gunslinger in Manassas has some interesting things in it.'

'Oh?'

'Do you remember those three frequent flyers from the Mayflower's registry who flew into Philadelphia eight months ago and just happened to be at the hotel at the same time eight months later?'

'Certainly.'

'Their names are in Swayne's Mickey Mouse loose-leaf. They had nothing to do with Carlos; they're part of Medusa. It's a mother lode of disconnected information.'

'I'm not interested. Use it in good health.'

'We will, and very quietly. That notebook'll be on the most wanted list in a matter of days.'

'I'm happy for you, but I've got work to do.'

'And you refuse any help?'

'Absolutely. This is what I've been waiting thirteen years for. It's what I said at the beginning, it's one on one.'

'*High Noon*, you goddamn fool?'

'No, the logical extension of a very intellectual chess game, the player with the better trap wins, and I've got that trap because I'm using *his*. He'd smell out any deviation.'

'We trained you too well, scholar.'

'Thank you for that.'

'Good hunting, Delta.'

'Goodbye.' Bourne hung up the phone and looked over at the two pathetically curious old men on the couch. 'You passed a sleaze-factored muster, Judge,' he said to Prefontaine. 'And you, "Jean Pierre," what can I say? My own wife, who admits to me that you might very well have killed her without the slightest compunction, tells me that I have to trust you. Nothing makes a hell of a lot of sense, does it?'

'I am what I am, and I did what I did,' said the disgraced attorney with dignity. 'But my client has gone too far. His magisterial persona must come to an end in ashes.'

'My words are not so well phrased as those of my learned, newfound relative,' added the aged hero of France. 'But I know the killing must stop; it's what my woman tried to tell me. I am a hypocrite, of course, for I am no stranger to killing, so I shall only say that *this* kind of killing must stop. There is no business arrangement here, no profit in the kill, only a sick madman's vengeance that demands the unnecessary death of a mother and her children. Where is the profit there? . . . No, the Jackal has gone too far. He, too, must now be stopped.'

'That's the most cold-blooded fucking reasoning I've ever *heard*!' cried John St Jacques by the window.

'I thought your words were very well chosen,' said the former judge to the felon from Paris. '*Très bien*.'

'*D'accord*.'

'And I think I'm out of my mind to have anything to do with either of you,' broke in Jason Bourne. 'But right now I don't have a choice . . . It's eleven-thirty-five, gentlemen. The clock is running.'

'The what?' asked Prefontaine.

'Whatever's going to happen will happen during the next two, five, ten or twenty-four hours. I'm flying back to Blackburne Airport where I'll create a scene, the bereaved husband and father who's gone crazy over the killing of his wife and children. It won't be difficult for me, I assure you; I'll make a hell of a ruckus . . . I'll demand an immediate flight to Tranquillity, and when I get here there'll be three pine coffins on the pier, supposedly containing my wife and children.'

'Everything as it should be,' interrupted the Frenchman. '*Bien*.'

'Very *bien*,' agreed Bourne. 'I'll insist that one be opened, and then I'll scream or collapse or both, whatever comes to mind, so that whoever's watching won't forget what they've seen. St Jacques here will have to control me – be rough, Johnny, be convincing – and finally I'll be taken up to another villa, the one nearest the steps to the beach on the east path . . . Then the waiting begins.'

'For this Jackal?' asked the Bostonian. 'He'll know where you are?'

'Of course he will. A lot of people, including the staff, will have seen where I was taken. He'll find out, that's child's play for him.'

'So you wait for him, monsieur? You think the monseigneur will walk into such a trap? *Ridicule!*'

'Not at all, monsieur,' replied Jason calmly. 'To begin with, I won't be there, and by the time he finds that out, I'll have found him.'

'For Christ's sake, *how*?' half shouted St Jacques.

'Because I'm better than he is,' answered Jason Bourne. 'I always was.'

The scenario went as planned, the personnel at Montserrat's Blackburne Airport still smouldering from the abuse hurled at them by the tall hysterical American who accused them all of murder, of allowing his wife and children to be killed by terrorists – of being willing *nigger* accomplices of filthy killers! Not only were the people of the island quietly furious, but they were also hurt. Quiet because they understood his anguish, hurt because they could not understand how he could blame *them* and use such vicious words, words he had never used before. Was this good *mon*, this wealthy brother of the gregarious Johnny Saint Jay, this rich-rich friend who had put so much money into Tranquillity Isle not a friend at all but, instead, white garbage who blamed them for terrible things they had nothing to do with because their skins were dark? It was an evil puzzle, *mon*. It was part of the madness, the *obeah* that had crossed the waters from the mountains of Jamaic' and put a curse on their islands. *Watch him*, brothers. *Watch his every move.* Perhaps he is another sort of storm, one not born in the south or the east, but whose winds are more destructive. *Watch him, mon.* His anger is dangerous.

So he was watched. By many – the uninformed, civilians and authorities alike – as a nervous Henry Sykes at Government House kept his word. The official investigation was solely under his command. It was quiet, thorough – and nonexistent.

Bourne was far worse on the pier of Tranquillity Inn, striking his own brother, the amiable Saint Jay, until the younger man subdued him and had him carried up the steps to the nearest villa. Servants came and went bringing trays of food and drink to the porch. Selected visitors were permitted to pay their condolences, including the chief aide to the Crown governor who wore his full military regalia, a symbol of the Crown's concern. And an old man who knew death from the brutalities of war and who insisted on seeing the bereaved husband and father; he was accompanied by a woman in a nurse's uniform, properly topped by a hat and a dark mourning veil. And two Canadian guests of the hotel, close friends of the owner, both of whom had met the disconsolate man when Tranquillity Inn opened with great fireworks several years ago; they asked to pay their respects and offer whatever support or comfort they could. John St Jacques agreed, suggesting that their visit be brief and to understand that his brother-in-law remained in a corner of the darkened living room, the drapes having been drawn.

'It's all so horrible, so meaningless!' said the visitor from Toronto softly to the shadowed figure in a chair across the room. 'I hope you're a religious man,

David. I am. Faith helps in such times as these. Your loved ones are in the arms of Christ now.'

'Thank you.' A momentary breeze off the water rustled the drapes, permitting a narrow shaft of sunlight to flash across the room. It was enough.

'Wait a minute,' said the second Canadian. 'You're not – good Lord, *you're* not David Webb. Dave has—'

'Be quiet,' ordered St Jacques, standing at the door behind the two visitors.

'Johnny, I spent seven hours in a fishing boat with Dave and I damn well know him when I see him!'

'Shut up,' said the owner of Tranquillity Inn.

'Oh, dear *God*!' cried the aide to the Crown governor of Montserrat in a clipped British accent.

'Listen to me, both of you,' said St Jacques, rushing forward between the two Canadians and turning to stand in front of the armchair. 'I wish I'd never let you in here but there's nothing we can do about that now . . . I thought you'd add weight, two more observers, if anyone asked you questions, which they will, then that's *exactly* what you're going to do. You've been talking to David Webb, consoling *David Webb*. Do you understand that?'

'I don't understand a damn thing,' objected the bewildered visitor who had spoken of the comfort of faith. 'Who the hell is he?'

'He's the senior aide to the Crown governor,' answered St Jacques. 'I'm telling you this so you *will* understand—'

'You mean the army brass who showed up in full uniform with a squad of black soldiers?' asked the guest who had fished with David Webb.

'Among his duties as chief military aide-de-camp. He's a brigadier—'

'We saw the bastard leave,' protested the fisherman. 'From the dining room, we all saw him *leave*! He was with the old Frenchman and the nurse—'

'You saw someone else leave. Wearing sunglasses.'

'Webb . . . ?'

'*Gentlemen!*' The governor's aide rose from the chair, wearing the ill-fitting jacket worn by Jason Bourne when he had flown back to Tranquillity from Blackburne Airport. 'You are welcome guests on our island but, as guests, you will abide by the Crown's decisions in emergencies. You will either abide by them, or, as we would do in extreme weather, we will be forced to place you in custody.'

'Hey, come on, Henry. They're friends . . .'

'Friends do not call brigadiers "bastards"—'

'You might if you were once a busted corporal, General,' inserted the man of faith. 'My companion here didn't mean anything. Long before the whole damned Canadian army needed his company's engineers, he was a screwed-up infantry grunt. *His* company, incidentally. He wasn't too bright in Korea.'

'Let's cut the crap,' said Webb's fishing companion. 'So we've been in here talking to Dave, right?'

'Right. And that's all I can tell you.'

'It's enough, Johnny. Dave's in trouble, so what can we do?'

'Nothing – absolutely nothing but what's on the inn's agenda. You all got copy delivered to your villas an hour ago.'

'You'd better explain,' said the religious Canadian. 'I never read those goddamn happy-hour schedules.'

'The inn's having a special buffet, everything on the house, and a meteorologist from the Leeward Islands Weather Control will speak for a few minutes on what happened last night.'

'The storm?' asked the fisherman, the former busted corporal and current owner of Canada's largest industrial engineering company. 'A storm's a storm in these islands. What's to explain?'

'Oh, things like why they happen and why they're over so quickly; how to behave – the elimination of fear, basically.'

'You want us all up there, is that what you mean?'

'Yes, I do.'

'That'll help Dave?'

'Yes, it will.'

'Then the whole place'll be up there. I guarantee it.'

'I appreciate that, but how can you?'

'I'll circulate another happy hour notice that Angus MacPherson McLeod, chairman of All Canada Engineering, will award ten thousand dollars to whoever asks the most intelligent question. How about that, Johnny? The rich always want more for nothing, that's our profound weakness.'

'I'll take your word for it,' mumbled St Jacques.

'C'mon,' said McLeod to his religious friend from Toronto. 'We'll circulate with tears in our eyes and spread the word. Then, you idiot colonel – that's what you were, y' bastard – in an hour or so we'll shift gears and only talk of ten thousand dollars and a free-for-all dinner. With the beach and the sun, people's attention spans are roughly two and a half minutes; in cold weather, no more than four. Believe me, I've had it calculated by computer research . . . You'll have a full party tonight, Johnny.' McLeod turned and walked towards the door.

'*Scotty*,' cried the man of faith following the fisherman. 'You're going off half-cocked again! Attention spans, two minutes, four minutes, computer research – I don't believe a *word* of it!'

'Really?' said Angus, his hand on the knob. 'You believe in ten thousand dollars, don't you?'

'I certainly do.'

'You watch, that's my market research . . . That's also why I own the company. And now I intend to summon those tears to my eyes; it's another reason I own the company.'

In a dark storage room on the third floor of Tranquillity Inn's main complex, Bourne, who had shed the military tunic, and the old Frenchman sat on two stools in front of a window overlooking the east and west paths of the shoreline resort. The villas below extended out on both sides of the stone steps leading down to the beach and the dock. Each man held a pair of powerful binoculars to his eyes, scanning the people walking back and forth on the paths and up and down the rock staircase. A hand-held radio with the hotel's private frequency was on the sill in front of Jason.

'He's near us,' said Fontaine softly.

'*What?*' shot out Bourne, yanking the glasses from his face and turning to the old man. 'Where? Tell me *where*!'

'He's not in our vision, monsieur, but he is near us.'

'What do you mean?'

'I can feel it. Like an animal that senses the approach of distant thunder. It's inside of you; it's the fear.'

'That's not very clear.'

'It is to me. Perhaps you wouldn't understand. The Jackal's challenger, the man of many appearances, the Chameleon – the killer known as Jason Bourne – was not given to fear, we are told, only a great bravado that came from his strength.'

Jason smiled grimly, in contradiction. 'Then you were told a lie,' he said softly. 'A part of that man lives with a kind of raw fear few people have ever experienced.'

'I find that hard to believe, monsieur—'

'Believe. I'm he.'

'Are you, Mr Webb? It's not difficult to piece things together. Do you force yourself to assume your other self because of this fear?'

David Webb stared at the old man. 'For God's sake, what choice do I have?'

'You could disappear for a time, you and your family. You could live peacefully, in complete security, your government would see to it.'

'He'd come after me – after us – wherever we were.'

'For how long? A year? Eighteen months? Certainly less than two years. He's a sick man; all Paris – my Paris – knows it. Considering the enormous expense and complexity of the current situation – these events designed to trap you – I would suggest that it's Carlos's last attempt. Leave, monsieur. Join your wife in Basse-Terre and then fly thousands of miles away while you can. Let him go back to Paris and die in frustration. Is it not enough?'

'*No.* He'd come after me, after us! It's got to be settled here, *now*.'

'I will soon join my woman, if such is to be, so I can disagree with certain people, men like you, for instance, *Monsieur Le Caméléon*, whom I would have automatically agreed with before. I do so now, I think you *can* go far away. I think you know that you *can* put the Jackal in a side pocket and get on with your life, altered only slightly for a while, but you won't do it. Something inside stops you; you cannot permit yourself a strategic retreat, no less honourable for its avoidance of violence. Your family is safe but others may die, but even that doesn't stop you. You have to *win*—'

'I think that's enough psychobabble,' interrupted Bourne, bringing the binoculars again to his eyes, concentrating on the scene below beyond the windows.

'That's it, isn't it?' said the Frenchman, studying Le Caméléon, his binoculars still at his side. 'They trained you too well, instilled in you too completely the person you had to become. Jason Bourne against Carlos the Jackal and Bourne must win, it's imperative that he *win* . . . Two ageing lions, each pitted against the other years ago, both with a burning hatred created by far-off strategists who had no idea what the consequences would be. How many have lost their lives because they crossed your converging paths? How many unknowing men and women have been killed—'

'Shut *up*!' cried Jason as flashing images of Paris, even peripherally of Hong Kong, Macao and Beijing – and most recently last night in Manassas, Virginia – assaulted his fragmented inner screen. So much death!

Suddenly, abruptly, the door of the dark storage room opened and Judge Brendan Prefontaine walked rapidly, breathlessly inside. 'He's here,' said the Bostonian. 'One of St Jacques's patrols, a three-man unit a mile down the east shoreline, couldn't be reached by radio. St Jacques sent a guard to find them and he just returned – then ran away himself. All three were killed, each man with a bullet in his throat.'

'The Jackal!' exclaimed the Frenchman. 'It is his *carte de visite* – his calling card. He announces his arrival.'

16

The mid-afternoon sun was suspended, immobile, burning the sky and the land, a ringed globe of fire intent only on scorching everything beneath it. And the alleged 'computerized research' offered by the Canadian industrialist, Angus McLeod, appeared to be confirmed. Although a number of seaplanes flew in to take frightened couples away, the collective attention span of average people after a disturbing event, if certainly longer than two and a half to four minutes, was certainly not more than a few hours. A horrible thing had happened during the predawn storm, an act of terrible vengeance, as they understood it. It involved a single man with a vendetta against old enemies, a killer who had long since fled from the island. With the removal of the ugly coffins as well as the beached, damaged speedboat and the soothing words over the government radio along with the intermittent, unobtrusive appearances of the armed guards, a sense of normality returned – not total, of course, for there was a mourning figure among them, but he was out of sight and would soon leave, they were told, and despite the depth of the horrors, as the rumours had them – naturally exaggerated out of all proportion by the hypersuperstitious island natives – the horrors were not *theirs*. It was an act of violence completely unrelated to them, and after all, life had to go on. Seven couples remained at the inn.

'Christ, we're paying six hundred dollars a day—'

'No one's after *us*—'

'Shit, man, next week it's back to the commodities grind, so we're going to enjoy—'

'No sweat, Shirley, they're not giving out names, they *promised* me—'

With the burning, immobile afternoon sun, a small soiled plot of the vast Caribbean playground came back to its own particular ambience, death receding with the next application of *Bain de Soleil* and another rum punch. Nothing was quite as it had been, but the blue-green waters lapped on the beach, enticing the few bathers to walk into them, immersing their bodies in the cool liquid rhythm of wet constancy. A progressively less tentative peace returned to Tranquillity Isle.

'There!' cried the hero of France.

'*Where?*' shouted Bourne.

'The four priests. Walking down the path in a line.'

'They're black.'

'Colour means nothing.'

'He was a priest when I saw him in Paris, at Neuilly-sur-Seine.'

Fontaine lowered the binoculars and looked at Jason. 'The Church of the Blessed Sacrament?' he asked quietly.

'I can't remember . . . Which one *is* he?'

'You saw him in his priest's habit?'

'And that son of a bitch saw *me*. He knew I *knew* it was him! Which *one*?'

'He's not there, monsieur,' said Jean Pierre, slowly bringing the binoculars back to his eyes. 'It is another *carte de visite*. Carlos anticipates; he is a master of geometry. There is no straight line for him, only many sides, many levels.'

'That sounds damned Oriental.'

'Then you understand. It has crossed his mind that you may not be in that villa, and if you are not, he wants you to know that he knows it.'

'Neuilly-sur-Seine—'

'No, not actually. He can't be sure at the moment. He *was* sure at the Church of the Blessed Sacrament.'

'How should I play it?'

'How does the Chameleon think he should play it?'

'The obvious would be to do nothing,' answered Bourne, his eyes on the scene below. 'And he wouldn't accept that because his uncertainty is too strong. He'd say to himself "he's better than that. I could blow him away with a rocket, so he's somewhere else".'

'I think you're correct.'

Jason reached down and picked up the hand-held radio from the sill. He pressed the button and spoke. 'Johnny?'

'Yes?'

'Those four black priests on the path, do you see them?'

'Yes.'

'Have a guard stop them and bring them into the lobby. Tell him to say the owner wants to see them.'

'Hey, they're not going into the villa, they're just passing by offering prayers to the bereaved inside. The vicar from town called and I gave him permission. They're okay, David.'

'The hell they are,' said Jason Bourne. 'Do as I say.' The Chameleon spun around on the stool, looking at the objects in the storage room. He slid off his perch and walked to an upright bureau with a mirror attached to its top. He yanked the automatic from his belt, smashed the glass, picked up a fragment and brought it to Fontaine. 'Five minutes after I leave, flash this every now and then in the window.'

'I shall do so from the *side* of the window, monsieur.'

'Good thinking.' Jason relented to the point of a brief slight smile. 'It struck me that I didn't really have to suggest that.'

'And what will you do?'

'What he's doing now. Become a tourist in Montserrat, a roving "guest" at Tranquillity Inn.' Bourne again reached down for the radio; he picked it up, pressed the button and gave his orders. 'Go to the men's shop in the lobby and get me three different guayabera jackets, a pair of sandals, two or three wide-brimmed straw hats and grey or tan walking shorts. Then send someone to the tackle shop and bring me a reel of line, hundred pound test, a scaling knife – and two distress flares. I'll meet you on the steps up here. *Hurry*.'

'You will not heed my words, then,' said Fontaine, lowering the binoculars and looking at Jason. '*Monsieur le Caméléon* goes to work.'

'He goes to work,' replied Bourne, replacing the radio on the still.

'If you or the Jackal or both of you are killed, other may die, innocent people slaughtered—'

'Not because of me.'

'Does it matter? Does it matter to the victims or their families who is responsible?'

'I didn't choose the circumstances, old man, they were chosen for me.'

'You can change them, alter them.'

'So can he.'

'He has no conscience—'

'You're one hell of an authority on *that* score.'

'I accept the rebuke, but I have lost something of great value to me. Perhaps it's why I discern a conscience in you – a part of you.'

'Beware the sanctimonious reformer.' Jason started for the door and the beribboned military tunic that hung on an old coatrack alongside the visored officer's hat. 'Among other things he's a bore.'

'Shouldn't you be watching the path below while the priests are detained? It will take some time for St Jacques to get the items you asked for.'

Bourne stopped and turned, his eyes cold on the verbose old Frenchman. He wanted to *leave*, to get away from this old, *old* man who talked too much – said too much! But Fontaine was right. It would be stupid not to watch what happened below. An awkward, unusual reaction on the part of someone, an abrupt, startled glance by someone in an unexpected direction – it was the little things, the sudden involuntary, precisely imprecise small motions that so often pointed to the concealed string that was the fuse leading to the explosive trap. In silence, Jason walked back to the window, picked up the binoculars and put them to his face.

A police officer in the tan and scarlet uniform of Montserrat approached the procession of four priests on the path; he was obviously as bewildered as he was deferential, nodding courteously as the four gathered together to listen, gesturing politely towards the glass doors of the lobby. Bourne's eyes shifted within the frame of vision, studying the black features of each cleric, one after the other in rapid succession. He spoke quietly to the Frenchman. 'Do you see what I see?'

'The fourth one, the priest who was last,' replied Fontaine. 'He's alarmed but the others are not. He's afraid.'

'He was bought.'

'Thirty pieces of silver,' agreed the Frenchman. 'You'll go down and take him, of course.'

'Of course not,' corrected Jason. 'He's right where I want him to be.' Bourne grabbed the radio off the sill. 'Johnny?'

'Yes . . . I'm in the shop. I'll be up in a few minutes—'

'Those priests, do you know them?'

'Only the one who calls himself the "vicar"; he comes around for contributions. And they're not really priests, David, they're more like "ministers" in a religious order. Very religious and very local.'

'Is the vicar there?'

'Yes. He's always first in line.'

'Good . . . Slight change of plans. Bring the clothes to your office, then go and see the priests. Tell them an official of the government wants to meet them and make a contribution in return for their prayers.'

'*What?*'

'I'll explain later. Now hurry up. I'll see you in the lobby.'

'You mean my office, don't you? I've got the clothes, remember?'

'They'll come later – roughly a minute later, after I get out of this uniform. Do you have a camera in your office?'

'Three or four of them. Guests are always leaving them behind—'

'Put all of them with the clothes,' interrupted Jason. 'Get going!' Bourne shoved the radio into his belt, then changed his mind. He pulled it out and handed it to Fontaine. 'Here, you take this. I'll get another and stay in contact . . . What's happening down there?'

'Our alarmed priest looks around as they go to the lobby doors. He's truly frightened now.'

'Where's he looking?' asked Bourne, grabbing the binoculars.

'That's of no help. In every direction.'

'*Damn!*'

'They're at the doors now.'

'I'll get ready—'

'I'll help you.' The old Frenchman got off the stool and went to the coatrack. He removed the tunic and the hat. 'If you are about to do what I think you intend doing, try to stay by a wall and don't turn around. The governor's aide is somewhat stouter than you and we must bunch the jacket in the back.'

'You're pretty good at this, aren't you?' said Jason, holding out his arms so to be helped into the tunic.

'The German soldiers were always much fatter than we were, especially the corporals and the sergeants – all that sausage, you know. We had our tricks.' . . . Suddenly, as if he had been shot or seized by a convulsion, Fontaine gasped, then lurched in front of Bourne. '*Mon Dieu! . . . C'est terrible!* The governor—'

'What?'

'The *Crown governor*!'

'What about him?'

'At the airport, it was so quick, so rapid!' cried the old Frenchman. 'And everything that has happened, my woman, the killing . . . Still, it is *unforgivable* of me!'

'What are you talking about?'

'That man in the villa, the military officer whose uniform you wear. He's his *aide*!'

'We know that.'

'What you do not know, monsieur, is that my very first instructions came from the Crown governor.'

'Instructions?'

'From the Jackal! He is the contact.'

'Oh, my *God*,' whispered Bourne, rushing to the stool where Fontaine had put the radio. He took a deep breath as he picked it up, his thoughts racing, control imperative. 'Johnny?'

'For Christ's sake, my arms are full and I'm on my way to the office and those goddamned monks are in the lobby waiting for me! What the hell do you want *now*?'

'Take it easy and listen very carefully. How well do you know Henry?'

'Sykes? The CG's man?'

'Yes. I've met him a few times but I don't know him, Johnny.'

'I know him very well. You wouldn't have a house and I wouldn't have Tranquillity Inn if it wasn't for him.'

'Is he in touch with the governor? I mean right *now*, is he keeping the CG posted about what's going on here? *Think*, Johnny. It's important. There's a phone in that villa; he could be in contact with Government House. *Is* he?'

'You mean with the CG himself?'

'With *anyone* over there.'

'Believe me, he's not. Everything's so quiet not even the police know what's going on. And as far as the CG is concerned, he's only been given the vaguest scenario, no names, nothing, only a trap. He's also out on his boat and doesn't want to know a damn thing until it's all over . . . Those were his orders.'

'I'll bet they were.'

'Why do you ask?'

'I'll explain later. Hurry *up*!'

'Will you stop *saying* that?'

Jason put down the radio and turned to Fontaine. 'We're clear. The governor isn't one of the Jackal's army of old men. He's a different kind of recruit, probably like that lawyer Gates in Boston – just bought or frightened, no soul involved.'

'You're certain? Your brother-in-law is certain?'

'The man's out on his boat. He was given a bare-bones outline but that's all, and his orders were that he's not to be told anything else until it's all over.'

The Frenchman sighed. 'It's a pity my mind is so old and so filled with salt. If I had remembered, we could have used him. Come, the jacket.'

'How could we have used him?' asked Bourne, again holding out his arms.

'He removed himself to the *gradins* – how is it said?'

'The bleachers. He's out of the game, only an observer.'

'I've known many like him. They want Carlos to lose; *he* wants Carlos to lose. It's his only way out, but he's too terrified to raise a hand against the Jackal.'

'Then how could we turn him?' Jason buttoned the tunic as Fontaine manipulated the belt and the cloth behind him.

'*Le Caméléon* asks such a question?'

'I've been out of practice.'

'Ah, yes,' said the Frenchman, yanking the belt firmly. 'That man I've appealed to.'

'Just shut up . . . How?'

'*Très simple, monsieur.* We tell him the Jackal already knows he's turned – *I* tell him. Who better than the monseigneur's emissary?'

'You *are* good.' Bourne held in his stomach as Fontaine turned him around, pressing the lapels and the ribbons of the jacket.

'I'm a survivor, neither better nor worse than others – except with my woman. Then I was better than most.'

'You loved her very much, didn't you?'

'Love? Oh, I imagine that's taken for granted although rarely expressed. Perhaps it's the comfort of being familiar, although, again, hardly with grand passion. One does not have to finish a sentence to be understood, and a look in the eyes will bring on laughter without a word being said. It comes with the years, I suppose.'

Jason stood motionless for a moment, staring strangely at the Frenchman. 'I want the years you had, old man, I want them very, very much. The years I've had with my . . . woman . . . are filled with scars that won't heal, can't heal, until something inside is changed or cleansed or goes away. That's the way it is.'

'Then you are too strong, or too stubborn or too *stupid*! . . . Don't look at me that way. I told you, I'm not afraid of you, I'm not afraid of anyone any longer. But if what you say is true, that this is the way things really are with you, then I suggest you leave aside all thoughts of love and concentrate on hatred. Since I cannot reason with David Webb, I must prod Jason Bourne. A Jackal filled with hate must die, and only Bourne can kill him . . . Here are your hat and sunglasses. Stay against a wall or you'll look like a military peacock, your khaki tail raised for the purpose of passing *merde*.'

Without speaking, Bourne adjusted the visored hat and sunglasses, walked to the door and let himself out. He crossed to the solid wood staircase and started rapidly down, nearly colliding with a white-jacketed black steward carrying a tray out of the second floor exit. He nodded to the young man, who backed away, allowing him to proceed, when a quiet, ziplike noise along with a sudden movement caught in the corner of his eyes caused him to turn. The waiter was pulling an electronic beeper out of his pocket! Jason spun around, lurching up the steps, his hands lunging into the youngster's body, ripping the device out of his grip as the tray crashed to the floor of the landing. Straddling the youth, with one hand on the beeper and the other grasping the steward's throat, he spoke breathlessly, quietly. 'Who had you do this? *Tell* me!'

'Hey, *mon*, I *fight* you!' cried the youngster, writhing, freeing his right hand and, forming a fist, smashing it up into Bourne's left cheek. 'We don't want no bad *mon* here! Our boss-*mon* the best! You don't scare *me*!' The steward crashed his knee into Jason's groin.

'You young son of a *bitch*!' cried *Le Caméléon*, slapping the youngster's face back and forth while grabbing his aching testicles with his left hand. 'I'm his friend, his *brother*! Will you cut it *out*? . . . Johnny Saint Jay's my brother! In-law, if it makes any goddamned difference!'

'*Oh?* said the large, youthful, obviously athletic steward, a touch of resentment in his wide, embarrassed brown eyes. 'You are the *mon* with Boss Saint Jay's sister?'

'I'm her husband. Who the fuck are you?'

'I am first head steward of the second floor, *sir*! Soon I will be on the first floor because I am very good. I am also a very fine fighter – my father taught me, although he is old now, like you. Do you wish to fight more? I think I can beat you! You have grey in your hair—'

'*Shut* up! . . . What's the beeper all about?' asked Jason, holding up the small brown plastic instrument as he crawled off the young waiter.

'I don't know, *mon* – sir! Bad things have happened. We are told that if we see men running on the staircases we should press the buttons.'

'Why?'

'The lifts, sir. Our very fast elevators. Why would guests use the stairs?'

'What's your name?' asked Bourne, replacing his hat and sunglasses.

'Ishmael, sir.'

'Like in *Moby Dick*?'

'I do not know such a person, sir.'

'Maybe you will.'

'Why?'

'I'm not sure. You're a very good fighter.'

'I see no connection, *mon* – sir.'

'Neither do I.' Jason got to his feet. 'I want you to help me, Ishmael. Will you?'

'Only if your brother permits it.'

'He will. He *is* my brother.'

'I must hear it from him, sir.'

'Very good. You doubt me.'

'Yes, I do, sir,' said Ishmael, getting to his knees and reassembling the tray, separating the broken dishes from the whole ones. 'Would you take the word of a strong man with grey in his hair who runs down the stairs and attacks you and says things anyone could say? . . . If you wish to fight, the loser must speak the truth. Do you wish to fight?'

'No, I do not wish to fight and don't you press it. I'm not that old and you're not that good, young man. Leave the tray and come with me. I'll explain to Mr St Jacques, who, I remind you, is my brother – my wife's brother. To hell with it, come *on*!'

'What do you want me to do, sir?' asked the steward, getting to his feet and following Jason.

'Listen to me,' said Bourne, stopping and turning on the steps above the first-floor landing. 'Go ahead of me into the lobby and walk to the front door. Empty ashtrays or something and look busy but keep glancing around. I'll come out in a few moments and you'll see me go over and talk to Saint Jay and four priests, who'll be with him—'

'Priests?' interrupted the astonished Ishmael. 'Men of the cloth, sir? *Four* of them? What are they doing here, *mon*? More bad things happen. The *obeah*?'

'They came here to pray so the bad things will stop – no more *obeah*. But what's important to me is that I must speak to one of them alone. When they leave the lobby, this priest I have to see may break away from the others to be by himself . . . or possibly to meet someone else. Do you think you could follow him without his seeing you?'

'Would Mr Saint Jay tell me to do that?'

'Suppose I have him look over at you and nod his head.'

'Then I can do it. I am faster than the mongoose and, like the mongoose, I know every foot trail on Tranquillity. He goes one way, I know where he's going and will be there first . . . But how will I know which priest? More than one may go off by himself.'

'I'll talk to all four separately. He'll be the last one.'

'Then I will know.'

'That's pretty fast thinking,' said Bourne. 'You're right; they could separate.'

'I think good, *mon.* I am fifth in my class at 'Serrat's Technical Academy. The four ahead of me are all girls, so they don't have to work.'

'That's an interesting observation—'

'In five or six years I'll have the money to attend the university in Barbados!'

'Maybe sooner. Go on now. Walk into the lobby and head for the door. Later, after the priests leave, I'll come out looking for you, but I won't be in this uniform, from any distance you won't know me. If I don't find you, meet me in an hour – Where? Where's a quiet place?'

'Tranquillity Chapel, sir. The path in the woods above the east beach. No one ever goes there, even on the Sabbath.'

'I remember it. Good idea.'

'There is a remaining subject, sir—'

'Fifty dollars, American.'

'*Thank* you, sir!'

Jason waited by the door for ninety seconds, then opened it barely an inch. Ishmael was in place by the entrance and he could see John St Jacques talking with the four priests several feet to the right of the front desk. Bourne tugged at his jacket, squared his shoulders in military fashion, and walked out into the lobby towards the priests and the owner of Tranquillity Inn.

'It's an honour and a privilege, Fathers,' he said to the four black clerics as a surprised and curious St Jacques watched him. 'I'm new here in the islands and I must say I'm very impressed. The government is particularly pleased that you saw fit to help calm our troubled waters,' continued Jason, his hands clasped firmly behind his back. 'For your efforts, the Crown governor has authorized Mr St Jacques here to issue you a cheque in the amount of one hundred pounds for your church – to be reimbursed by the treasury, of course.'

'It is such a magnificent gesture, I hardly know what to say,' intoned the vicar, his high lilting voice sincere.

'You could tell me whose idea it was,' said the Chameleon. 'Most touching, most touching, indeed.'

'Oh, I cannot take the credit, sir,' replied the vicar, looking, as the two others did, at the fourth man. 'It was Samuel's. Such a good and decent leader of our flock.'

'Good show, Samuel.' Bourne stared briefly, his eyes penetrating, at the fourth man. 'But I should like to thank each of you personally. And know your names.' Jason went down the line shaking the three hands and quietly exchanging pleasantries. He came to the last priest, whose eyes kept straying away from his. 'Of course, I know your name, Samuel,' he said, his voice even lower, barely audible. 'And I should like to know whose idea it was before you took the credit.'

'I don't understand you,' whispered Samuel.

'Certainly you do – such a good and decent man – you must have received another very generous contribution.'

'You mistake me for someone else, sir,' mumbled the fourth priest, his dark eyes for an instant betraying deep fear.

'I don't make mistakes, your friend knows that. I'll find you, Samuel. Maybe not today, but surely tomorrow or the day after that.' Bourne raised his voice as he released the cleric's hand. 'Again, the government's profound thanks, Fathers. The Crown is most grateful. And now I must be on my way; a dozen telephone calls should be answered . . . Your office, St Jacques?'

'Yes, of course, *General*.'

Inside the office, Jason took out his automatic and tore off the uniform as he separated the pile of clothing Marie's brother had brought for him. He slipped on a pair of knee-length grey Bermuda walking shorts, chose a red-and-white-striped guayabera jacket, and the widest-brimmed straw hat. He removed his socks and shoes, put on the sandals, stood up, and swore. '*Goddamn* it!' He kicked off the sandals and shoved his bare feet back into his heavy rubber-soled shoes. He studied the various cameras and their accessories, choosing the lightest but most complicated, and crossed the straps over his chest. John St Jacques walked into the room carrying a small hand-held radio.

'Where the hell did you come from? Miama Beach?'

'Actually, a little north – say, Pompano. I'm not that gaudy. I won't stand out.'

'Actually, you're right. I've got people out there who'd swear you were old-time Key West conservative. Here's the radio.'

'Thanks.' Jason put the compact instrument into his breast pocket.

'Where to now?'

'After Ishmael, the kid I had you nod at.'

'*Ishmael?* I didn't nod at Ishmael, you simply said I should nod my head at the entrance.'

'Same thing.' Bourne squeezed the automatic under his belt beneath the guayabera and looked at the equipment brought from the tackle shop. He picked up the reel of one hundred-test line and the scaling knife, placing both in his pockets, then opened an empty camera case and put the two distress flares inside. It was not everything he wanted but it was enough. He was not who he was thirteen years ago and he was not so young even then. His mind had to work better and faster than his body, a fact he reluctantly accepted. *Damn!*

'That Ishmael's a good boy,' said Marie's brother somewhat pointlessly.

'He's pretty smart and strong as a prize Saskatchewan steer. I'm thinking of making him a guard in a year or so. The pay's better.'

'Try Harvard or Princeton if he does his job this afternoon.'

'Wow, *that's* a wrinkle. Did you know his father was the champion wrestler of the islands? Of course, he's sort of getting on now—'

'Get the hell out of my way,' ordered Jason, heading for the door. 'You're not exactly *eighteen*, either!' he added, turning briefly before he let himself out.

'Never said I was. What's your problem?'

'Maybe it's the sandbar you never saw, Mr *Security*.' Bourne slammed the door as he ran out into the hallway.

'Touchy, touchy.' St Jacques slowly shook his head as he unclenched his thirty-four-year-old fist.

Nearly two hours had passed and Ishmael was nowhere to be found! His leg locked in place as if crippled, Jason limped convincingly from one end of Tranquillity Inn's property to the other, his eye focused through the mirrored lens of the camera, seeing everything, but no sign of young Ishmael. Twice he had gone up the path into the woods to the isolated square structure of logs, thatched roof and stained glass that was the multi-denominational chapel of the resort, a sanctuary for meditation built more for its quaint appearance than for utility. As the young black steward had observed, it was rarely visited but had its place in vacation brochures.

The Caribbean sun was growing more orange, inching its way down towards the water's horizon. Soon the shadows of sundown would crawl across Montserrat and the out islands. Soon thereafter darkness would come, and the Jackal approved of darkness. But then, so did a chameleon.

'Storage room, anything?' said Bourne into his radio.

'*Rien, monsieur.*'

'Johnny?'

'I'm up on the roof with six scouts at all points. Nothing.'

'What about the dinner, the party tonight?'

'Our meteorologist arrived ten minutes ago by boat from Plymouth. He's afraid to fly . . . And Angus tacked a cheque for ten thousand on the bulletin board, signature and payee to be entered. Scotty was right, all seven couples will be there. We're a society of who-gives-a-shit after an appropriate few minutes of silence.'

'Tell me something I don't know, Bro . . . Out. I'm heading back to the chapel.'

'Glad to hear somebody goes there. A travel bastard in New York said it'd be a nice touch, but I haven't heard from him since. Stay in touch, David.'

'I will, Johnny,' replied Jason Bourne.

The path to the chapel was growing dark, the tall palms and dense foliage above the beach hastening nature's process by blocking the rays of the setting sun. Jason was about to turn around and head for the tackle shop and a flashlight when suddenly, as if on photoelectric cue, blue and red floods came alive, shooting their wide circles of light up from the ground into the palms above. For a moment Bourne felt that he had abruptly, too abruptly, entered a lush Technicolor tunnel cut out of tropical forest. It was disorienting, then disturbing. He was a moving, illuminated target in a garishly coloured gallery.

He quickly walked into the underbrush beyond the border of floodlights, the nettles of the wild shrubbery stinging his bare legs. He went deeper into the enveloping foliage and continued in the now semidarkness towards the chapel, his pace slow, difficult, the moist branches and vines tangling about his hands and feet. Instinct. Stay out of the light, the gaudy bombastic lights that belonged more properly to an island *carnivale.*

A blunt sound! A thud that was no part of the shoreline woods. Then the start of a moan growing into a convulsion – stopped, thwarted . . . suppressed? Jason crouched and foot by foot broke through the inhibiting, succeeding walls of bush until he could see the thick cathedral door of the chapel. It was partially open, the soft, pulsating glow of the electric candles penetrating the wash of the red and blue floods on the outside path.

Think. Memory. *Remember!* He had been to the chapel only once before, humourously berating his brother-in-law for spending good money on a useless addition to Tranquillity Inn.

At least it's quaint, had said St Jacques.

It ain't, Bro, Marie had replied. *It doesn't belong. This isn't a retreat.*

Suppose someone gets bad news. You know, really bad –

Get him a drink, David Webb had said.

Come on inside, I've got symbols of five different religions in stained glass, including Shinto.

Don't show your sister the bills on this one, Webb had whispered.

Inside. Was there a door inside? Another exit? . . . No, there was not. Only five or six rows of pews, then a railing of some sort in front of a raised lectern, beneath primitive stained-glass windows done by native artisans.

Inside. Someone was inside. Ishmael? A distraught guest of Tranquillity? A honeymooner who had sudden, deep reservations embarrassingly too late? He again reached into his breast pocket for the miniaturized radio. He brought it to his lips and spoke softly.

'Johnny?'

'Right here on the roof.'

'I'm at the chapel. I'm going inside.'

'Is Ishmael there?'

'I don't know. Someone is.'

'What's wrong, Dave? You sound—'

'Nothing's wrong,' interrupted Bourne. 'I'm just checking in . . . What's behind the building? East of it.'

'More woods.'

'Any paths?'

'There was one several years ago; it's overgrown by now. The construction crews used it to go down to the water . . . I'm sending over a couple of guards—'

'*No!* If I need you, I'll call. Out.' Jason replaced the radio and, still crouching, stared at the chapel door.

Silence now. No sound at all from inside, no human movement, nothing but the flickering 'candlelight'. Bourne crept to the border of the path, removed the camera equipment and the straw hat and opened the case holding the flares. He removed one, inserted it under his belt, and took out the automatic beside it. He reached into the left pocket of his guayabera jacket for his lighter, gripping it in his hand as he got to his feet and walked quietly, rapidly, to the corner of the small building – this unlikely sanctuary in the tropic woods above a tropic beach. Flares and the means to light them went back long before Manassas, Virginia, he considered, as he inched his way around the corner towards the chapel's entrance. They went back to Paris – thirteen years ago to Paris, and a cemetery in Rambouillet. And Carlos . . . He reached the frame of the partially opened door and slowly, cautiously moved his face to the edge and looked inside.

He gasped, his breath suspended, the horror filling him as disbelief and fury spread within him. On the raised platform in front of the rows of glistening wood was the young Ishmael, his body bent forward over the lectern, his arms hanging down, his dark face bruised and lacerated, blood trickling out of his mouth onto the floor. The guilt overwhelmed Jason; it was sudden and complete and devastating, the words of the old Frenchman screaming in his ears. *Others may die, innocent people slaughtered.*

Slaughtered! A child was *slaughtered*! Promises were implied, but death had been delivered. Oh, *Christ*, what have I *done*? . . . What can I *do*?

Sweat pouring down his face, his eyes barely focusing, Bourne ripped the distress flare out of his pocket, snapped the lighter and, trembling, held it to the red tip. Ignition was instant; the white fire spewed out in white heat, hissing like a hundred angry snakes. Jason threw it into the chapel towards the far end, leaped through the frame, pivoted, and slammed the heavy door shut behind him. He lunged to the floor below the last row, pulled the radio from his pocket and pushed the *Send* button.

'Johnny, the chapel. *Surround* it!' He did not wait for St Jacques's reply; that there was a voice was enough. The automatic in his hand, the hissing flare continuously erupting as shafts of colour shot down from the stained-glass windows, Bourne crept to the far aisle, his eyes moving constantly, seeking out everything he no longer remembered about Tranquillity Inn's chapel. The one place where he could not look again was the lectern that held the body of the child he had killed . . . On both sides of the raised platform were narrow draped archways, like scenic doors on a stage leading to minimum wing space, entrances both left and right. Despite the anguish he felt, there welled up in Jason Bourne a deep sense of satisfaction, even of morbid elation. The lethal game was his for the winning. Carlos had mounted an elaborate trap and the Chameleon had reversed it, Medusa's Delta had turned it around! Behind one of those two draped archways was the assassin from Paris.

Bourne got to his feet, his back pressed against the right wall, and raised his gun. He fired twice into the left archway, the drapes fluttering with each shot, as he sprang behind the last row, scrambling to the far side, getting to his knees and firing twice more into the archway on the right.

A figure lunged in panic through the drapes, clutching the cloth as it fell forward, the dark red fabric ripped from the hooks, bunched around the target's shoulders as he fell to the floor. Bourne rushed forward, screaming Carlos's name, firing again and again until the automatic's magazine was empty. Suddenly from above there was an explosion, blowing out a whole section of stained glass high on the left wall. As the coloured fragments shot through the air and down onto the floor, a man on a ledge outside moved into the centre of the open space above the hissing, blinding flare.

'You're out of bullets,' said Carlos to the stunned Jason Bourne below. 'Thirteen years, Delta, thirteen loathsome years. But now they'll know who won.'

The Jackal raised his gun and fired.

17

The searing ice-cold heat ripped through his neck as Bourne lunged over the pews, crashing down between the second and third rows, smashing his head and his hips on the glistening brown wood as he clawed at the floor. His vision spun out of control as a cloud of darkness enveloped him. In the distance, far, far away, he heard the sound of voices shouting hysterically. Then the darkness was complete.

'*David.*' There was no shouting now; the single voice was low and urgent and used a name he did not care to acknowledge. 'David, can you hear me?'

Bourne opened his eyes, instantly aware of two facts. There was a wide bandage around his throat and he was lying fully clothed on a bed. To his right, the anxious face of John St Jacques came into focus; on his left was a man he did not know, a middle-aged man with a level, steady gaze. '*Carlos*,' managed Jason, finding his voice. 'It was the *Jackal*!'

'Then he's still on the island – this island.' St Jacques was emphatic. 'It's been barely an hour and Henry's got Tranquillity ringed. Patrols are hovering offshore, roving back and forth, all in visual and radio contact. He's calling it a "drug exercise", very quiet and very official. A few boats come in but none go out and none will go out.'

'Who's *he*?' asked Bourne, looking at the man on his left.

'A doctor,' answered Marie's brother. 'He's staying at the inn and he's a friend of mine. I was a patient of his in—'

'I think we should be circumspect here,' interrupted the Canadian doctor firmly. 'You asked for my help and my confidence, John, and I give both gladly, but considering the nature of the events and the fact that your brother-in-law won't be under my professional care, let's dispense with my name.'

'I couldn't agree with you more, Doctor,' added Jason wincing, then suddenly snapping his head up, his eyes wide in an admixture of pleading and panic. '*Ishmael!* He's dead – I *killed* him!'

'He isn't and you didn't,' said St Jacques calmly. 'He's a goddamned mess but he's not dead. He's one tough kid, like his father, and he'll make it. We're flying him to the hospital in Martinique.'

'*Christ*, he was a corpse!'

'He was savagely beaten,' explained the doctor. 'Both arms were broken, along with multiple lacerations, contusions, I suspect internal injuries and a severe concussion. However, as John accurately described the young man, he's one tough kid.'

'I want the best for him.'

'Those were my orders.'

'Good.' Bourne moved his eyes to the doctor. 'How damaged am I?'

'Without X-rays or seeing how you move – symptomatically, as it were – I can only give you a cursory judgement.'

'Do that.'

'Outside of the wound, I'd say primarily traumatic shock.'

'Forget it. That's not allowed.'

'Who says?' said the doctor, smiling kindly.

'I do and I'm not trying to be funny. The body, not the head. I'll be the judge of the head.'

'Is he a native?' asked the doctor, looking at the owner of Tranquillity Inn. 'A white but older Ishmael? I'll tell you he's not a physician.'

'Answer him, please.'

'All right. The bullet passed through the left side of your neck, missing by millimetres several vital spots that would certainly have rendered you voiceless and probably dead. I've bathed the wound and sutured it. You'll have difficulty moving your head for a while, but that's only a superficial opinion of the damage.'

'In short words, I've got a very stiff neck, but if I can walk . . . well, I can walk.'

'In shorter words, that's about it.'

'It was the flare that did it after all,' said Jason softly, carefully moving his neck back over the pillow. 'It blinded him just enough.'

'What?' St Jacques leaned over the bed.

'Never mind . . . Let's see how well I walk – symptomatically, that is.' Bourne slid off the bed, swinging his legs cautiously to the floor, shaking his head at his brother-in-law who started to help him. 'No thanks, Bro. This has got to be me-on-me.' He stood up, the inhibiting bandage around his throat progressively becoming more uncomfortable. He stepped forward, pained by the bruises on his thighs, but they *were* bruises; they were minor. A hot bath would reduce the pain, and medication, extra-strength aspirin and liniment, would permit more normal mobility. It was the goddamned dressing around his neck; it not only choked him but forced him to move his shoulders in order to look in any direction . . . Still, he considered, he was far less incapacitated than he might have been – for a man of his age. *Damn.* 'Can we loosen this necklace, Doctor? It's strangling me.'

'A bit, not much. You don't want to risk rupturing those sutures.'

'What about an Ace bandage? It gives.'

'Too much for a neck wound. You'd forget about it.'

'I promise not to.'

'You're very amusing.'

'I don't feel remotely amusing.'

'It's your neck.'

'It certainly is. Can you get one, Johnny?'

'Doctor?' St Jacques looked at the physician.

'I don't think we can stop him.'

'I'll send someone to the pro shop.'

'Excuse me, Doctor,' said Bourne as Marie's brother went to the telephone. 'I want to ask Johnny a few questions and I'm not sure you want to hear them.'

'I've heard more than I care to already. I'll wait in the other room.' The doctor crossed to the door and let himself out.

While St Jacques talked on the phone, Jason moved about the room raising and lowering his arms and shaking his hands to check the functioning of his motor controls. He crouched, then rose to his feet four times in succession, each movement faster than the previous one. He had to be ready – he *had* to be!

'It'll only be a few minutes,' said the brother-in-law, hanging up the phone. 'Pritchard will have to go down and open the shop. He'll bring different sizes of tape.'

'Thanks.' Bourne stopped moving and stood in place. 'Who was the man I shot. Johnny? He fell through the curtains in that archway but I couldn't see his face.'

'No one I know, and I thought I knew every white man in these islands who could afford an expensive suit. He must have been a tourist – a tourist on assignment . . . for the Jackal. Naturally, there wasn't any identification. Henry's shipped him off to 'Serrat.'

'How many here know what's going on?'

'Outside of the staff, there are only fourteen guests and no one's got a clue. I've sealed off the chapel – the word is storm damage. And even those who have to know something – like the doctor and the two guys from Toronto – they don't know the whole story, just pieces, and they're friends. I trust them. The others are heavy into island rum.'

'What about the gunshots at the chapel?'

'What about the loudest and lousiest steel band in the islands? Also, you were a thousand feet away in the woods . . . Look, David, most everyone's left but some diehards who wouldn't stay here if they weren't old Canadian buddies showing me loyalty, and a few casuals who'd probably take a vacation in Teheran. What can I tell you except that the bar is doing a hell of a business.'

'It's like a mystifying charade,' murmured Bourne, again carefully arching his neck and staring at the ceiling. 'Figures in silhouette playing out disconnected, violent events behind white screens, nothing really making sense, everything's whatever you want it to be.'

'That's a little much for me, Professor. What's your point?'

'Terrorists aren't born, Johnny, they're made, schooled in a curriculum you won't find in any academic catalogue. Leaving aside the reasons why they are what they are – which can range from a justifiable cause to the psychopathic megalomania of a Jackal – you keep the charades going because *they're* playing out their own.'

'So?' St Jacques frowned in bewilderment.

'So you control your players, telling them what to act out but not why.'

'That's what we're doing here and that's what Henry's doing out on the water all around Tranquillity.'

'Is he? Are we?'

'Hell, yes.'

'I thought I was too, but I was wrong. I overestimated a big clever kid doing a simple, harmless job and underestimated a humble, frightened priest who took thirty pieces of silver.'

'What *are* you talking about?'

'Ishmael and Brother Samuel. Samuel must have witnessed the torture of a child through the eyes of Torquemada.'

'Turkey who?'

'The point is we don't really know the players. The guards, for instance, the ones you brought to the chapel—'

'I'm not a fool, David,' protested St Jacques, interrupting. 'When you called for us to surround the place, I took a small liberty and chose two men, the only two I would choose, figuring a pair of Uzis made up for the absence of one man and the four points of the compass. They're my head boys and former Royal Commandos; they're in charge of all the security here and, like Henry, I trust them.'

'Henry? He's a good man, isn't he?'

'He's a pain in the ass sometimes, but he's the best in the islands.'

'And the Crown governor?'

'He's just an ass.'

'Does Henry know that?'

'Sure, he does. He didn't get to be a brigadier on his looks, potbelly and all. He's not only a good soldier, he's a good administrator. He covers for a lot around here.'

'And you're certain he hasn't been in touch with the CG?'

'He told me he'd let me know before he reached the pompous idiot and I believe him.'

'I sincerely hope you're right – because that pompous idiot is the Jackal's contact in Montserrat.'

'*What?* I don't *believe* it!'

'Believe. It's confirmed.'

'It's incredible!'

'No, it's not. It's the way of the Jackal. He finds vulnerability and he recruits it, buys it. There are very few in the grey areas beyond his ability to purchase them.'

Stunned, St Jacques wandered aimlessly to the balcony doors coming to terms with the unbelievable. 'I suppose it answers a question a lot of us have asked ourselves. The governor's old-line landed gentry with a brother high up in the Foreign Office who's close to the prime minister. Why at his age was he sent out here, or, maybe more to the point, why did he accept it? You'd think he'd settle for nothing less than Bermuda or the British Virgins. Plymouth can be a stepping-stone, not a final post.'

'He was banished, Johnny. Carlos probably found out why a long time ago and has him on a list. He's been doing it for years. Most people read newspapers and books and magazines for diversion; the Jackal pores over volumes of in-depth intelligence reports from every conceivable source he can unearth, and he's unearthed more than the CIA, the KGB, MI5 and 6, Interpol and a dozen other services even want to think about . . . Those seaplanes flew in four or five times after I got back here from Blackburne. Who was on them?'

'Pilots,' answered St Jacques, turning around. 'They were taking people out, not bringing anyone in, I told you that.'

'Yes, you told me. Were you watching?'

'Watching who?'

'Each plane when it came in.'

'Hey, come on! You had me doing a dozen different things.'

'What about the two black commandos. The ones you trust so much.'

'They were checking and positioning the other guards, for Christ's sake.'

'Then we don't really know who may have come in on those planes, do we? Maybe slipping into the water over the pontoons as they taxied through the reefs – perhaps before the sandbar.'

'For God's sake, David, I've known those charter jocks for years. They wouldn't let anything like that happen. No way!'

'You mean it's kind of unbelievable.'

'You bet your ass.'

'Like the Jackal's contact in Monstserrat. The Crown governor.'

The owner of Tranquillity Inn stared at his brother-in-law. 'What kind of world do you live in?'

'One I'm sorry you ever became a part of. But you are now and you'll play by its rules, my rules.' A fleck, a *flash*, an infinitesimal streak of deep red light from the darkness outside! *Infrared!* Arms extended, Bourne lunged at St Jacques, propelling him off his feet, away from the balcony doors. 'Get *out* of there!' Jason roared in midair as both crashed to the floor, three successive snaps crackling the space above them as bullets thumped with finality into the walls of the villa.

'What the *hell*—'

'He's out there and he wants me to *know* it!' said Bourne, shoving his brother-in-law into the lower moulding, crawling beside him, and reaching into the pocket of his guayabera. 'He knows who you are, so you're the first corpse, the one he realizes will drive me to the edge because you're Marie's brother – you're *family* and that's what he's holding over my head. My *family*!'

'Jesus *Christ*! What do we *do*?'

'*I* do!' replied Jason, pulling the second flare out of his pocket. 'I send him a message. The message that tells him why I'm alive and why I *will* be when he's dead. *Stay* where you are!' Bourne pulled his lighter out of his right pocket, snapped up the flame, and ignited the flare. Scrambling, he raced across the balcony doors hurling the hissing, blinding missile out into the darkness. Two snaps followed, the bullets ricocheting off the tiled ceiling and shattering the mirror of a dressing table. 'He's got a MAC-10 with a silencer,' said Medusa's Delta, rolling into the wall, grabbing his inflamed neck as he did so. 'I have to get *out* of here!'

'David, you're *hurt*!'

'That's nice.' Jason Bourne got to his feet and raced to the door, slamming it back and rushing into the villa's living room, only to face a frowning Canadian physician.

'I heard some noise in there,' said the doctor. 'Is everything all right?'

'I have to leave. Get to the *floor*.'

'Now, see here! There's blood on your bandage, the sutures—'

'Get your ass on the *floor*!'

'You're not twenty-one, Mr Webb—'

'Get out of my *life*!' shouted Bourne, running to the entrance, letting himself outside, and rushing up the lighted path towards the main complex, suddenly aware of the deafening steel band, its sound amplified throughout the grounds by a score of speakers nailed to the trees.

The undulating cacophony was overwhelming and that was not to this disadvantage, thought Jason. Angus McLeod had been true to his word. The huge glass-enclosed circular dining room held the few remaining guests and the fewer staff, and that meant the Chameleon had to change colours. He knew the mind of the Jackal as well as he knew his own, and that meant that the assassin would do exactly what he himself would do under the circumstances. The hungry, salivating wolf went into the cave of its confused, energized quarry and pulled out the prized piece of meat. So would he, shedding the skin of the mythical chameleon, revealing a much larger beast of prey – say a Bengal tiger – which could rip a jackal apart in his jaws . . . Why were the images important? *Why?* He knew why, and it filled him with a feeling of emptiness, a longing for something that had passed – he was no longer Delta, the feared guerrilla of Medusa; nor was he the Jason Bourne of Paris and the Far East. The older, much older, David Webb kept intruding, invading, trying to find reason within insanity and violence.

No! Get *away* from me! You are nothing and I am everything! . . . Go away, David, for Christ's sake, go *away*.

Bourne spun off the path and ran across the harsh, sharp tropical grass towards the side entrance of the inn. Instantly, breathlessly, he cut his pace to a walk at the sight of a figure coming through the door; then upon recognizing the man, he resumed running. It was one of the few members of Tranquillity's staff he remembered and one of the few he wished he could forget. The insufferable snob of an assistant manager named Pritchard, a loquacious bore, albeit hardworking, who never let anyone forget his family's importance in Montserrat – especially an uncle who was Deputy Director of immigration, a not so incidental plus for Tranquillity Inn, David Webb suspected.

'Pritchard!' shouted Bourne, approaching the man. 'Have you got the bandages?'

'Why, *sir*!' cried the assistant manager, genuinely flustered. 'You're *here*. We were told you left this afternoon—'

'Oh, shit!'

'Sir? . . . Such condolences of sorrow so pain my lips—'

'Just keep them shut, Pritchard. Do you understand me?'

'Of course, I was not here this morning to greet you or this afternoon to bid you farewell and express my deepest feelings, for Mr Saint Jay asked me to work this evening, through the night, actually—'

'Pritchard, I'm in a hurry. Give me the bandages and don't tell anyone – *anyone* – that you saw me. I want that very clear.'

'Oh, it is clear, sir,' said Pritchard, handing over the three different rolls of elasticized tape. 'Such privileged information is safe with me, as safe as the knowledge that your wife and children were staying here – oh, God *forgive* me! *Forgive* me, sir!'

'I will and He will if you keep your mouth shut.'

'Sealed. It is sealed. I am so privileged!'

'You'll be shot if you abuse the privilege. Is *that* clear?'

'*Sir*?'

'Don't faint, Pritchard. Go down to the villa and tell Mr Saint Jay that I'll be in touch with him and he's to stay there. Have you got that? He's to *stay* there . . . You, too, for that matter.'

'Perhaps I could —'

'Forget it. Get *out* of here!' The talkative assistant manager ran across the lawn towards the path to the east villas as Bourne raced to the door and went inside. He climbed the steps two at a time – only years before, it would have been three at a time – and again, out of breath, reached St Jacques's office. He entered, closed the door, and quickly went to the closet where he knew his brother-in-law kept several changes of clothing. Both men were approximately the same size – outsized, as Marie claimed – and Johnny had frequently borrowed jackets and shirts from David Webb when visiting. Jason selected the most subdued combination in the closet. Lightweight grey slacks and an all-cotton, dark blue blazer; the only shirt in evidence, again tropic cotton, was thankfully short-sleeved and brown. Nothing would pick up or reflect light.

He started to undress when he felt a sharp, hot jolt on the left side of his neck. He looked in the closet mirror, alarmed, then furious at what he saw. The constricting bandage around his throat was deep red with spreading blood. He tore open the box of the widest tape; it was too late to change the dressing, he could only reinforce it and hope to stem the bleeding. He unravelled the elasticized tape around his neck, tearing it after several revolutions, and applied the tiny clamps to hold it in place. It was more inhibiting than ever; it was also an impediment he would put out of his mind.

He changed clothes, pulling the collar of the brown shirt high over his throat, the automatic in his belt, the reel of fishing line in the blazer's pocket . . . *Footsteps!* The door opened as he pressed his back against the wall, his hand on the weapon. Old Fontaine walked in; he stood for a moment, looking at Bourne, then closed the door.

'I've been trying to find you, frankly not knowing if you were still alive,' said the Frenchman.

'We're not using the radios unless we have to.' Jason walked away from the wall. 'I thought you got the message.'

'I did and it was right. Carlos may have his own radio by now. He's not alone, you know. It's why I've been wandering around looking for you. Then it occurred to me that you and your brother-in-law might be up here in his office, a headquarters, as it were.'

'It's not very smart for you to be walking around out in the open.'

'I'm not an idiot, monsieur. I would have perished long before now if I were. Wherever I walked I did so with great caution . . . in truth, it's why I made up my mind to find you, assuming you were not dead.'

'I'm not and you found me. What is it? You and the judge are supposed to be in an empty villa somewhere, not wandering around.'

'We are; we were. You see, I have a plan, a *stratagème*, I believe would interest you. I discussed it with Brendan—'

'Brendan?'

'His name, monsieur. He thinks my plan has merit and he's a brilliant man, very *sagace*—'

'Shrewd? Yes, I'm sure he is, but he's not in our business.'

'He's a survivor. In that sense we are all in the same business. He thinks there is a degree of risk, but what plan under these circumstances is without risk?'

'What's your plan?'

'It is a means to trap the Jackal with minimum danger to the other people here.'

'That really worries you, doesn't it?'

'I told you why, so there's no reason to repeat it. There are men and women together out there—'

'Go on,' broke in Bourne, irritated. 'What's this strategy of yours, and you'd better understand that I intend to take out the Jackal if I have to hold this whole goddamned island hostage. I'm not in a giving mood. I've given too much.'

'So you and Carlos stalk each other in the night? Two crazed middle-aged hunters obsessed with killing each other, not caring who else is killed or wounded or maimed for life in the bargain?'

'You want compassion, go to a church and appeal to that God of yours who pisses on this planet! He's either got one hell of a warped sense of humour or he's a sadist. Now either talk sense or I'm getting out of here.'

'I've thought this out—'

'*Talk!*'

'I know the monseigneur, know the way he thinks. He planned the death of my woman and me but not to coincide with yours, not in a way that would detract from the high drama of his immediate victory over you. It would come later. The revelation that I, the so-called hero of France, was in reality the Jackal's instrument, his creation, would be the final proof of his triumph. Don't you see?'

Briefly silent, Jason studied the old man. 'Yes, I do,' he replied quietly. 'Not that I ever figured on someone like you, but that approach is the basis of everything I believe. He's a megalomaniac. In his head he's the king of hell and wants the world to recognize him and his throne. By his lights, his genius has been overlooked, relegated to the level of punk killers and Mafia hit men. He wants trumpets and drums when all he hears are tired sirens and weary questions in police lineups.'

'*C'est vrai.* He once complained to me that almost no one in America knew who he was.'

'They don't. They think he's a character out of novels or films, if they think about him at all. He tried to make up for that thirteen years ago, when he flew over from Paris to New York to kill me.'

'Correction, monsieur. You forced him to go after you.'

'It's history. What's all this got to do with now, tonight . . . your plan?'

'It provides us with a way to force the Jackal to come out after *me*, to meet with *me*. Now. Tonight.'

'How?'

'By my wandering around the grounds very much in the open where he or one of his scouts will see me and hear me.'

'Why would that force him to come out after you?'

'Because I will not be with the nurse he had assigned to me. I will be with someone else, unknown to him, someone who would have no reason at all to kill me.'

Again Bourne looked at the old Frenchman in silence. 'Bait,' he said finally.

'A lure so provocative it will drive him into a frenzy until he has it in his possession – has me in his grip so he can question me . . . You see, I'm vital to him – more specifically, my death is vital – and everything is timing to him. Precision is his . . . his *dicton*, how is it said?'

'His byword, his method of operation, I suppose.'

'It is how he has survived, how he has made the most of each kill, each over the years adding to his reputation as the *assassin suprême*. Until a man named Jason Bourne came out of the Far East . . . he has never been the same since. But you know all that—'

'I don't care about all that,' interrupted Jason. 'The "timing". Go on.'

'After I'm gone he can reveal who Jean Pierre Fontaine, the hero of France, really was. An impostor, *his* impostor, *his* creation, the instrument of death who was the snare for Jason Bourne. What a triumph for him! . . . But he cannot do that until I'm dead. Quite simply, it would be too inconvenient. I know too much, too many of my colleagues in the gutters of Paris. No, I must be dead before he has his triumph.'

'Then he'll kill you when he sees you.'

'Not until he has his answers, monsieur. Where is his killer nurse? What has happened to her? Did *Le Caméléon* find her, turn her, do away with her? Have the British authorities got her? Is she on her way to London and MI6 with all their chemicals, to be turned over at last to Interpol? So many questions . . . No, he will not kill me until he learns what he must learn. It may take only minutes to satisfy him, but long before then I trust that you will be at my side insuring my survival, if not his.'

'The nurse? Whoever it is, she'll be shot.'

'No, not at all. I'll order her away in anger, out of my sight at the first sign of contact. As I walk with her I shall lament the absence of my new dear friend, the angel of mercy who takes such good care of my wife, wondering out loud,

What has happened to her? Where has she gone? Why haven't I seen her all *day*? Naturally, I will conceal on my person the radio, activated, of course. Wherever I am taken – for surely one of Carlos's men will make contact first – I will ask an enfeebled old man's questions. Why am I going here? Why are we there? . . . You will follow – in full force, I sincerely hope. If you do so, you'll have the Jackal.'

Holding his head straight, his neck rigid, Bourne walked to St Jacques's desk and sat on the edge. 'Your friend, Judge Brendan what's-his-name, is right—'

'*Pre*fontaine. Although Fontaine is not my true name, we've decided it's all the same family. When the earliest members left Alsace-Lorraine for America in the eighteenth century with Lafayette, they added the *Pre* to distinguish them from the Fontaines who spread out all over France.'

'He told you that?'

'He's a brilliant man, once an honoured judge.'

'Lafayette came from Alsace-Lorraine?'

'I don't know, monsieur. I've never been there.'

'He's a brilliant man . . . More to the point, he's right. Your plan has a lot of merit, but there's also considerable risk. And I'll be honest with you, Fontaine, I don't give a damn about the risk you're taking or about the nurse, whoever it is. I want the Jackal, and if it costs your life or the life of a woman I don't know, it doesn't matter to me. I want you to understand that.'

The old Frenchman stared at Jason with amused rheumy eyes and laughed softly. 'You are such a transparent contradiction. Jason Bourne would never have said what you just did. He would have remained silent, accepting my proposition without comment but knowing the advantage. Mrs Webb's husband, however, must have a voice. *He* objects and must be heard.' Fontaine suddenly spoke sharply. 'Get *rid* of him, Monsieur Bourne. *He* is not my protection, not the death of the Jackal. Send him away.'

'He's gone. I promise you, he's *gone*.' The Chameleon sprang up from the desk, his neck frozen in pain. 'Let's get started.'

The steel band continued its deafening assault, but now restricted to the confines of the glass-enclosed lobby and adjacent dining room. The speakers on the grounds were switched off on St Jacques's orders, the owner of Tranquillity Inn having been escorted up from the unoccupied villa by the two Uzi-bearing former commandos along with the Canadian doctor and the incessantly chattering Mr Pritchard. The assistant manager was instructed to return to the front desk and say nothing to anyone about the things he had witnessed during the past hour.

'Absolutely nothing, sir. If I am asked, I was on the telephone with the authorities over in 'Serrat.'

'About *what*?' objected St Jacques.

'Well, I thought—'

'Don't think. You were checking the maid service on the west path, that's all.'

'Yes, sir.' The deflated Pritchard headed for the office door, which had been opened moments before by the nameless Canadian doctor.

'I doubt it would make much difference what he said,' offered the physician as the assistant manager left. 'That's a small zoo down there. The combination of last night's events, too much sun today and excessive amounts of alcohol this evening, will augur a great deal of guilt in the morning. My wife doesn't think your meteorologist will have much to say, John.'

'Oh?'

'He's having a few himself, and even if he's halfway lucid, there aren't five sober enough to listen to him.'

'I'd better get down there. We may as well turn it into a minor *carnivale.* It'll save Scotty ten thousand dollars, and the more distraction we have, the better. I'll speak to the band and the bar and be right back.'

'We may not be here,' said Bourne as his brother-in-law left and a strapping young black woman in a complete nurse's uniform walked out of St Jacques's private bathroom into the office. At the sight of her, old Fontaine approached.

'Very good, my child, you look splendid,' said the Frenchman. 'Remember now, I'll be holding your arm as we walk and talk, but when I squeeze you and raise my voice, telling you to leave me alone, you'll do as I say, correct?'

'Yes, sir. I am to hurry away quite angry with you for being so unnice.'

'That's it. There's nothing to be afraid of, it's just a game. We want to talk with someone who's very shy.'

'How's the neck?' asked the doctor, looking at Jason, unable to see the bandage beneath the brown shirt.

'It's all right,' answered Bourne.

'Let's take a look at it,' said the Canadian stepping forward.

'Thanks but not now, Doctor. I suggest you go downstairs and rejoin your wife.'

'Yes. I thought you'd say that, but may I say something very quickly?'

'*Very* quickly.'

'I'm a doctor and I've had to do a great many things I didn't like doing and I'm sure this is in that category. But when I think of that young man and what was done to him—'

'*Please*,' broke in Jason.

'Yes, yes, I understand. Nevertheless, I'm here if you need me, I just wanted you to know that . . . I'm not terribly proud of my previous statements. I saw what I saw and I do have a name and I'm perfectly willing to testify in a court of law. In other words, I withdraw my reluctance.'

'There'll be no courts, Doctor, no testimony.'

'Really? But these are serious *crimes*!'

'We *know* what they are,' interrupted Bourne. 'Your help is greatly appreciated, but nothing else concerns you.'

'I see,' said the doctor, staring curiously at Jason. 'I'll go then.' The Canadian went to the door and turned. 'You'd better let me check that neck later. If you've got a neck.' The doctor left and Bourne turned to Fontaine.

'Are we ready?'

'We're ready,' replied the Frenchman, smiling pleasantly at the large, imposing, thoroughly mystified young black woman. 'What are you going to do with all the money you're earning tonight, my dear?'

The girl giggled shyly, her broad smile alive with bright white teeth. 'I have a good boyfriend. I'm going to buy him a fine present.'

'That's lovely. What's your boyfriend's name?'

'Ishmael, sir.'

'Let's go,' said Jason firmly.

The plan was simple to mount and, like most good strategies, however complex, simple to execute. Old Fontaine's walk through the grounds of Tranquillity Inn had been precisely mapped out. The trek began with Fontaine and the young woman returning to his villa presumably to look in on his ill wife before his established, medically required evening stroll. They stayed on the lighted main path, straying now and then across the floodlit lawns always visible, a crotchety old man supposedly walking wherever his whims led him to the annoyance of his companion. It was a familiar sight the world over, an enfeebled, irascible septuagenarian taunting his keeper.

The two former Royal Commandos, one rather short, the other fairly tall, had selected their successive stations between the points where the Frenchman and his 'nurse' would turn and head in different directions. As the old man and the girl proceeded into the next planned leg, the second commando bypassed his colleague in darkness to the next location, using unseen routes only they knew or could negotiate, such as that beyond the coastline wall above the tangled tropical brush that led to the beach below the villas. The black guards climbed like two enormous spiders in a jungle, crawling swiftly, effortlessly from branch and rock to limb and vine, keeping pace with their two charges. Bourne followed the second man, his radio on Receive, the angry words of Fontaine pulsating through the static.

Where is that other nurse? That lovely girl who takes care of my woman? Where is she? I haven't seen her all day! The emphatic phrases were repeated over and over again with growing hostility.

Jason slipped. He was caught! He was behind the coastal wall, his left foot entangled in thick vines. He could not pull his leg loose – the strength was not there! He moved his head – his shoulders – and the hot flashes of pain broke out on his neck. It is *nothing*. Pull, yank, *rip*! . . . His lungs bursting, the blood now drenching his shirt, he worked his way free and crawled on.

Suddenly there were lights, *coloured* lights spilling over the wall. They had reached the path to the chapel, the red and blue floodlights that lit up the entrance to Tranquillity Inn's sealed-off sanctuary. It was the last destination before the return route back to Fontaine's villa, and one they all agreed was designed more to permit the old Frenchman time to catch his breath than for any other purpose. St Jacques had stationed a guard there to prevent entrance into the demolished chapel. There would be no contact here. Then Bourne heard the words over the radio – *the* words that would send the false nurse racing away from her false charge.

'Get *away* from me!' yelled Fontaine. 'I don't like you. Where is our regular nurse? What have you *done* with her?'

Up ahead, the two commandos were side by side, crouching below the wall. They turned and looked at Jason, their expressions in the eerie wash of coloured lights telling him what he knew only too well. From that moment on, all decisions were his; they had led him, escorted him, to his enemy. The rest was up to him.

The unexpected rarely disturbed Bourne; it did now. Had Fontaine made a mistake? Had the old man forgotten about the inn's guard and erroneously presumed he was the Jackal's contact? In his aged eyes had an understandably surprised reaction on the guard's part been misinterpreted as an approach? Anything was possible, but considering the Frenchman's background – the life of a survivor – and the state of his alert mind, such a mistake was not realistic.

Then the possibility of another reality came into focus and it was sickening. Had the guard been killed or bribed, replaced by another? Carlos was a master of the turn-around. It was said he had fulfilled a contract on the assassination of Anwar Sadat without firing a weapon, by merely replacing the Egyptian president's security detail with inexperienced recruits – money dispersed in Cairo returned a hundredfold by the anti-Israel brotherhoods in the Middle East. If it were true, the exercise on Tranquillity Isle was child's play.

Jason rose to his feet, gripped the top of the coastal wall, and slowly, painfully, his neck in agony, pulled himself up over the ledge, again slowly, inch by inch, sending one arm after the other across the surface to grab the opposing edge for support. What he saw stunned him!

Fontaine was immobile, his mouth gaped in shock, his wide eyes disbelieving, as another old man in a tan gabardine suit approached him and threw his arms around the aged hero of France. Fontaine pushed the man away in panic and bewilderment. The words erupted out of the radio in Bourne's pocket. '*Claude! Quelle secousse! Vous êtes ici!*'

The ancient friend replied in a tremulous voice, speaking French. 'It is a privilege our monseigneur permitted me. To see for a final time my sister, and to give comfort to my friend, her husband. I am here and I am with you!'

'With *me*? He brought you *here*? But, of course, he did!'

'I am to take you to him. The great man wishes to speak with you.'

'Do you know what you're doing – what you've *done*?'

'I am with you, with her. What else matters?'

'She's *dead*! She took her own life last night. *He* intended to kill us both.'

Shut off your radio! screamed Bourne in the silence of his thoughts. *Kill the radio!* It was too late. The left door of the chapel opened and the silhouetted figure of a man walked out into the floodlit corridor of coloured lights. He was young, muscular and blond, with blunt features and rigid posture. Was the Jackal training someone else to take his place?

'Come with me, please,' said the blond man, his French gentle but icily commanding. 'You,' he added, addressing the old man in the tan gabardine suit. 'Stay where you are. At the slightest sound, fire your gun . . . Take it out. Hold it in your hand.'

'*Oui, monsieur.*'

Jason watched helplessly as Fontaine was escorted through the door of the chapel. From the pocket of his jacket there was an eruption of static followed by a snap; the Frenchman's radio had been found and destroyed. Yet something was wrong, off-centre, out of balance – or perhaps too symmetrical. It made no sense for Carlos to use the location of a failed trap a second time, no sense at all! The appearance of the brother of Fontaine's wife was an exceptional move, worthy of the Jackal, a truly unexpected move within the swirling winds of confusion, but not this, not again Tranquillity Inn's superfluous chapel. It was too orderly, too repetitive, too obvious. *Wrong.*

And therefore right? considered Bourne. Was it the illogical logic of the assassin who had eluded a hundred special branches of the international intelligence community for nearly thirty years? 'He wouldn't do *that* – it's crazy!' '. . . Oh, yes, he might because he knows we think it's crazy.' Was the Jackal in the chapel or wasn't he? If not, where *was* he? Where had he set his trap?

The lethal chess game was not only supremely intricate, it was sublimely intimate. Others might die, but only one of *them* would live. It was the only way it could end. Death to the seller of death or death to the challenger, one seeking the preservation of a legend, the other seeking the preservation of his family and himself. Carlos had the advantage; ultimately he would risk everything, for, as Fontaine revealed, he was a dying man and he did not care. Bourne had everything to live for, a middle-aged hunter whose life was indelibly marked, split in two by the death of a vaguely remembered wife and children long ago in far-off Cambodia. It could not, *would* not, happen again!

Jason slid down off the coastal wall to the slanting precipice at its base. He crawled forward to the two former commandos and whispered, 'They've taken Fontaine inside.'

'Where is the *guard*?' asked the man nearest Bourne, confusion and anger in his whisper. 'I myself placed him here with specific instructions. *No* one was permitted inside. He was to be on the radio the instant he saw *anyone*!'

'Then I'm afraid he didn't see him.'

'Who?'

'A blond man who speaks French.'

Both commandos whipped their heads towards each other, exchanging glances as the second guard instantly looked at Jason and spoke quietly. 'Describe him, please,' he said.

'Medium height, large chest and shoulders—'

'Enough,' interrupted the first guard. 'Our man saw him, sir. He is third provost of the government police, an officer who speaks several languages and is chief of drug investigations.'

'But why is he here, *mon*?' asked the second commando of his colleague. 'Mr Saint Jay said the Crown police are not told everything, they are not part of us.'

'Sir Henry, *mon*. He has Crown boats, six or seven, running back and forth with orders to stop anyone leaving Tranquillity. They are drug boats, *mon*. Sir Henry calls it a patrol exercise, so naturally the chief of investigations must be—' The lilting whisper of the West Indian trailed off in midsentence as he looked at his companion. '. . . Then why isn't he out on the water, *mon*? On the lead boat, *mon*?'

'Do you like him?' asked Bourne instinctively, surprising himself by his own question. 'I mean, do you respect him? I could be wrong but I seem to sense something—'

'You are not wrong, sir,' answered the first guard, interrupting. 'The provost is a cruel man and he doesn't like the "Punjabis", as he calls us. He's very quick to accuse us and many have lost work because of his rash accusations.'

'Why don't you complain, get rid of him? The British will listen to you.'

'The Crown governor will not, sir,' explained the second guard. 'He's very partial to his strict chief of narcotics. They are good friends and often go out after the big fish together.'

'I see.' Jason did see and was suddenly alarmed, *very* alarmed. 'Saint Jay told me there used to be a path behind the chapel. He said it might be overgrown but he thought it was still there.'

'It is,' confirmed the first commando. 'The help still use it to go down to the water on their off times.'

'How long is it?'

'Thirty-five, forty metres. It leads to an incline where steps have been cut out of the rocks that take one down to the beach.'

'Which of you is faster?' asked Bourne, reaching into his pocket and taking out the reel of fishing line.

'I am.'

'*I* am!'

'I choose you,' said Jason, nodding his head at the shorter first guard, handing him the reel. 'Go down on the border of that path and wherever you can, string this line across it, tying it to limbs or trunks or the strongest branches you can find. You mustn't be seen, so be alert, see in the dark.'

'Is no pro*blem, mon*!'

'Have you got a knife?'

'Do I have eyes?'

'Good. Give me your Uzi. *Hurry!*'

The guard scrambled away along the vine-tangled precipice and disappeared into the dense foliage beyond. The second Royal Commando spoke. 'In truth, sir, I am much faster, for my legs are much longer.'

'Which is why I chose him and I suspect you know it. Long legs are no advantage here, only an impediment, which *I* happen to know. Also, he's much shorter and less likely to be spotted.'

'The smaller ones always get the better assignments. They parade *us* up front and put *us* in boxing rings with rules we don't understand, but the small soldiers get the plumbies.'

' "Plumbies"? The better jobs?'

'Yes, sir.'

'The most dangerous jobs?'

'Yes, *mon*!'

'Live with it, big fella.'

'What do we do now, sir?'

Bourne looked above at the wall and the soft wash of coloured lights. 'It's called the waiting game – no love songs implied, only the hatred that comes from wanting to live when others want to kill you. There's nothing quite like it because you can't *do* anything. All you can do is think about what the enemy may or may not be doing, and whether he's thought of something you haven't considered. As somebody once said, I'd rather be in Philadelphia.'

'Where, *mon*?'

'Nothing. It isn't true.'

Suddenly, filling the air above in chilling horror, came a prolonged excruciating scream, followed by words shrieked in pain. '*Non, non! Vous êtes monstrueux! . . . Arrêtez, arrêtez*!'

'*Now!*' cried Jason, slinging the strap of his Uzi over his shoulder as he leaped onto the wall, gripping the edge, pulling himself up as the blood poured out of his neck. He could not *get* up! He could not get *over*! Then strong hands pulled him and he fell over the top of the wall. 'The *lights*!' he shouted. 'Shoot them out!'

The tall commando's Uzi blazing, the lines of floodlights exploded in the ground on both sides of the chapel's path. Again, strong black hands pulled him to his feet in the new darkness. And then a single shaft of yellow appeared, roving swiftly in all directions; it was a powerful halogen flashlight in the commando's left hand. The figure of a blood-drenched old man in a tan gabardine suit lay curled up in the path, his throat slit.

'*Stop!* In the name of almighty *God*, stop where you *are*!' came Fontaine's voice from inside the chapel, the open half door revealing the flickering light of the electric candles. They approached the entrance, automatic weapons levelled, prepared for continuous fire . . . But not prepared for what they saw. Bourne closed his eyes, the sight was too painful. Old Fontaine, like young Ishmael, was sprawled over the lectern on the raised platform beneath the blown-out, stained-glass windows of the left wall, his face running with blood where he had been slashed, and attached to his body were thin cables that led to various black boxes on both sides of the chapel.

'Go *back*!' screamed Fontaine. '*Run*, you fools! I'm wired—'

'Oh, *Christ*!'

'Mourn not for me, Monsieur le Caméléon. I gladly join my woman! This world is too ugly even for me. It is no longer amusing. *Run*! The charge will go off – they are watching!'

'You, *mon*! *Now!*' roared the second commando, grabbing Jason's jacket and racing him to the wall, holding Bourne in his arms as they plummeted over the stone surface into the thick foliage.

The explosion was massive, blinding and deafening. It was as if this small corner of the small island had been taken out by a heat-seeking nuclear missile. Flames erupted into the night sky, but the burning mass was quickly diffused in the still wind to fiery rubble.

'The *path*!' shouted Jason, in a hoarse whisper, as he crawled to his feet in the sloping brush. 'Get to the path!'

'You're in bad condition, *mon*—'

'I'll take care of *me*, you take care of *you*!'

'I believe I've taken care of both of us.'

'So you've got a fucking medal and I'll add a lot of money to it. Now, get us up to the *path*!'

Pulling, pushing, and finally with Bourne's feet grinding like a machine out of control, the two men reached the border of the path thirty feet behind the smouldering ruins of the chapel. They crept into the weeds and within seconds the first commando found them. 'They're in the south palms,' he said breathlessly. 'They wait until the smoke has cleared to see if anyone is alive, but they cannot stay long.'

'You were *there*?' asked Jason. '*With* them?'

'No problem, *mon*, I told you, sir.'

'What's happening? How many are there?'

'There were four, sir. I killed the man whose place I assumed. He was black, so it made no matter in appearance with the darkness. It was quick and silent. The throat.'

'Who's left?'

''Serrat's chief of narcotics, of course, and two others—'

'*Describe* them!'

'I could not see clearly, but one I think was another black man, tall and without much hair. The third I could not see at all, for he – or she – was wearing strange clothes, with cloth over the head like a woman's sun hat or insect veil.'

'A *woman*?'

'It is possible, sir.'

'A woman . . . ? They've got to get *out* of there – *he's* got to get out of there!'

'Very soon they will run to this path and race down to the beach, where they will hide in the woods of the cove until a boat comes for them. They have no choice. They cannot go back to the inn, for strangers are seen instantly, and even though we are far away and the steel band is loud, the explosion was certainly heard by the guards posted outside. They will report it.'

'Listen to me,' said Bourne, his voice hoarse, tense. 'One of those three people is the man I want and I want him for *myself*! So hold your fire because I'll know him when I see him. I don't give a *damn* about the others; they can be flushed out of that cove later.'

There was a sudden burst of gunfire from the tropical forest accompanied by screams from the once floodlit corridor beyond the ruins of the chapel. Then one after another the figures raced out of the tangled brush into the path. The first to be caught was the blond-haired police officer from Montserrat, the waist-high invisible fishing line tripping him as he fell into the dirt, breaking the thin, taut string. The second man, slender, tall, dark-featured, with only a fringe of hair below his bald head, was hard upon the first, pulling him to his feet, sight or instinct making the second killer wield his automatic weapon in slashing arcs, cutting the impeding lines across the path to the ledge that led down to the beach. The third figure appeared. It was *not* a woman. Instead it was a man, in the robes of a monk. A priest. It was *he*. The *Jackal*!

Bourne rose to his feet and stumbled out of the brush into the path, the Uzi in his hands; the victory was his, his *freedom* his, his *family* his! As the robed figure reached the top of the primitive rock-hewn staircase, Jason pressed his trigger finger, holding it in place, the fusillade of bullets exploding out of the automatic weapon.

The monk arched in silhouette, then fell, his body tumbling, rolling, sprawling down the steps carved out of volcanic rock, finally lurching over the edge and plummeting to the sand below. Bourne raced down the awkward, irregular stone staircase, the two commandos behind him. He reached the beach, raced over to the corpse, and pulled the drenched hood away from the face. In horror, he looked at the black features of Samuel, the brother priest of Tranquillity Isle, the Judas who had sold his soul to the Jackal for thirty pieces of silver.

Suddenly, in the distance, there was the roar of powerful dual engines as a huge speedboat lurched out of a shadowed section of the cove and sped for a break in the reefs. The beam of a searchlight shot out, firing the barriers of rock protruding above the choppy black water, its wash illuminating the fluttering ensign of the government's drug fleet. *Carlos!* . . . The Jackal was no chameleon, but he had changed! He had *aged*, grown thinner and bald – he was not the sharp, broad, full-headed muscular image of Jason's memory. Only the indistinct dark Latin features remained, the face and the unfamiliar expanse of bare skin above burned by the sun. He was *gone*!

The boat's motors screamed in unison as the craft breached a precarious opening in the reef and burst out into open water. Then the words in heavily accented English, metallically spewing from the distant loudspeaker, echoed within the tropical cove.

'*Paris*, Jason Bourne! Paris, if you *dare*! Or shall it be a certain minor university in Maine, *Dr Webb*?'

Bourne, his neck wound ripped open, collapsed in the lapping waves, his blood trickling into the sea.

18

Steven DeSole, keeper of the deepest secrets for the Central Intelligence Agency, forced his overweight frame out of the driver's seat. He stood in the deserted parking lot of the small shopping centre in Annapolis, Maryland, where the only source of light was the storefront neon of a closed gas station, with a large German shepherd sleeping in the window. DeSole adjusted his steel-rimmed glasses and squinted at his watch, barely able to see the radium hands. As near as he could determine, it was between three-fifteen and three-twenty in the morning, which meant he was early and that was good. He had to adjust his thoughts; he was unable to do so while driving, as his severe night blindness necessitated complete concentration on the road, and hiring a taxi or a driver was out of the question.

The information was at first . . . well, merely a name . . . a rather common name. *His name is Webb*, the caller had said. *Thank you*, he had replied. A sketchy description was given, one fitting several million men, so he had thanked the informer again and hung up the phone. But then, in the recesses of his analyst's mind, by profession and training a warehouse for both essential and incidental data, an alarm went off. Webb, Webb . . . *amnesia*? A clinic in Virginia years ago. A man more dead than alive had been flown down from a hospital in New York, the medical file so maximum classified it could not even be shown to the Oval Office. Yet interrogation specialists talk in dark corners, as often to relieve frustration as to impress a listener, and he had heard about a recalcitrant, unmanageable patient, an amnesiac they called 'Davey' and sometimes just a short, sharp, hostile 'Webb', formerly a member of Saigon's infamous Medusa, and a man they suspected of feigning his loss of memory . . . Loss of memory? Alex Conklin had told them that the Medusan they had trained to go out in deep cover for Carlos the Jackal, an *agent provocateur* they called Jason Bourne, had lost his *memory*. Lost his memory and nearly lost his life because his controls disbelieved the story of *amnesia*! That was the man they called 'Davey' . . . David. David Webb was Conklin's Jason Bourne! How could it be otherwise?

David Webb! And he had been at Norman Swayne's house the night the Agency was told that poor cuckolded Swayne had taken his own life, a suicide that had not been reported in the papers for reasons DeSole could not possibly understand! David Webb. The old Medusa. Jason Bourne. Conklin. *Why*?

The headlights of an approaching limousine shot through the darkness at the far end of the parking lot, swerving in a semicircle towards the CIA analyst, causing him to shut his eyes, the refracted light through his thick lenses painful. He had to make the sequence of his revelations clear to these men. They were his means to a life he and his wife had dreamed of – *money*. Not bureaucratic less-than-money, but *real* money. Education at the best universities for their grandchildren, not the state colleges and the begged-for scholarships that came with the government salary of a bureaucrat – a bureaucrat so much better than those around him it was pitiful. *DeSole the Mute Mole*, they called him, but would not pay him for his expertise, the very expertise that prohibited him from going into the private sector, surrounding him with so many legal restrictions that it was pointless to apply. Someday Washington would learn; that day would not come in his lifetime, so six grandchildren had made the decision for him. The empathetic new Medusa had beckoned with generosity, and in his bitterness he had come running.

He rationalized that it was no more an unethical decision on his part than those made every year by scores of Pentagon personnel who walked out of Arlington and into the corporate arms of their old friends the defence contractors. As an army colonel once said to him, 'It's work now and get paid later,' and God knew that one Steven DeSole worked like hell for his country, but his country hardly reciprocated in kind. He hated the name Medusa, though, and rarely if ever used it because it was a symbol from another time, ominous and misleading. The great oil companies and railroads sprang from the chicanery and the venality of the robber barons, but they were not now what they were then. Medusa may have been born in the corruption of a war-ravaged Saigon, its early funding may have been a result of it, but that Medusa no longer existed; it had been replaced by a dozen different names and companies.

'We're not pure, Mr DeSole, no American-controlled international conglomerate is,' said his recruiter, 'and it's true that we seek what some might call unfair economic advantage based on privileged information. Secrets, if you like. You see, we have to because our competitors throughout Europe and the Far East consistently have it. The difference between them and us is that *their* governments support their efforts – ours doesn't . . . Trade, Mr DeSole, trade and profits. They're the healthiest pursuits on earth. Chrysler may not like Toyota, but the astute Mr Iacocca does not call for an air strike against Tokyo. At least not yet. He finds ways to join forces with the Japanese.'

Yes, mused DeSole as the limousine came to a stop ten feet from him. What he did for the 'corporation', which he preferred to call it, as opposed to what he did for the Company, might even be considered benevolent. Profits, after all, were more desirable than bombs . . . and his grandchildren would go to the finest schools and universities in the country. Two men got out of the limousine and approached him.

'What's this Webb look like?' asked Albert Armbruster, chairman of the Federal Trade Commission, as they walked along the edge of the parking lot.

'I only have a description from the gardener who was hiding behind a fence thirty feet away.'

'What did he tell you?' The unidentified associate of the chairman, a short stocky man with dark eyebrows beneath dark hair and with penetrating dark eyes, looked at DeSole. 'Be precise,' he added.

'Now, just a minute,' protested the analyst defensively but firmly. 'I'm precise in everything I say and, frankly, whoever you are, I don't like the tone of your voice one bit.'

'He's upset,' said Armbruster, as if his associate was dismissible. 'He's a spaghetti head from New York and doesn't trust anybody.'

'Who's to trust in New *Yawk*?' asked the short, dark man, laughing and poking his elbow into the wide girth of Albert Armbruster. 'You WASPs are the worst, you got the banks, *amico*!'

'Let's keep it that way and out of the courts . . . The description, please?' The chairman looked at DeSole.

'It's incomplete, but there *is* a long-ago tie-in with Medusa that I'll describe – *precisely*.'

'Go ahead, pal,' said the man from New York.

'He's rather large, tall, that is, and in his late forties or early fifties and—'

'Has he got some grey around his temples?' asked Armbruster, interrupting.

'Well, yes, I think the gardener said something to that effect – greying, or grey in his hair, or something like that. It's obviously why he judged him to be in his forties or fifties.'

'It's Simon,' said Armbruster, looking at the New Yorker.

'*Who*?' DeSole stopped, as the other two stopped and looked at him.

'He called himself Simon, and he knew all about you, Mr CIA,' said the chairman. 'About you and Brussels and our whole thing.'

'What are you *talking* about?'

'For starters, your goddamn fax machine exclusively between you and that fruitcake in Brussels.'

'It's a buried, dedicated line! It's locked up!'

'Someone found the key, Mr Precision,' said the New Yorker, not smiling.

'Oh, my God, that's *terrible*! What should I *do*?'

'Make up a story between you and Teagarten, but do it from public phones,' continued the mafioso. 'One of you will come up with something.'

'*You* know about . . . Brussels?'

'There's very little I don't know.'

'That son of a bitch conned me into thinking he was one of us and he had me by the balls!' said Armbruster angrily, continuing to walk along the edge of the parking lot, the other two joining him, DeSole hesitantly, apprehensively. 'He seemed to know everything, but when I think back, he only brought up bits and pieces – damned *big* bits and pieces like Burton and you and Brussels – and I, like a fucking idiot, filled in a hell of a lot more. *Shit!*'

'Now, just *wait* a minute!' cried the CIA analyst, once again forcing the others to stop. 'I don't understand – I'm a strategist, and I don't *understand*. What was David Webb – Jason Bourne, if he *is* Jason Bourne – doing at Swayne's place the other night?'

'Who the hell is *Jason Bourne*?' roared the chairman of the Federal Trade Commission.

'He's the tie-in with Saigon's Medusa that I just mentioned. Thirteen years ago the Agency gave him the name Jason Bourne, the original Bourne a dead man by then, and sent him out in deep cover on a Four Zero assignment – a termination with extreme prejudice, if you like—'

'A hit, if you want to speak English, *paisan*.'

'Yes, yes, that's what it was . . . But things went wrong; he had a loss of memory and the operation collapsed. It collapsed, but he survived.'

'Holy Christ, what a bunch of *zucchinis*!'

'What can you tell us about this Webb . . . or Bourne – this Simon or the "Cobra"? Jesus, he's a walking vaudeville act!'

'Apparently that's what he did before. He assumed different names, different appearances, different personalities. He was trained to do that when he was sent out to challenge the assassin called the Jackal – to draw him out and kill him.'

'The *Jackal*?' asked the astonished capo supremo of the Cosa Nostra. 'Like in the movie?'

'No, not the movie *or* the book, you idiot—'

'Hey, easy, *amico*.'

'Oh, shut up . . . Ilich Ramirez Sanchez, otherwise known as Carlos the Jackal, is a living person, a professional killer the international authorities have been hunting for over a quarter of a century. Outside of scores of confirmed hits, many think he was the puff of smoke on the grassy knoll in Dallas, the true killer of John Kennedy.'

'You're shittin' me.'

'I can assure you, I am not shitting you. The word we got at the Agency at the highest secure levels was that after all these years Carlos had tracked down the only man alive who could identify him, Jason Bourne – or, as I'm firmly convinced, David Webb.'

'That *word* had to come from somebody!' exploded Albert Armbruster. 'Who *was* it?'

'Oh, yes. Everything's so sudden, so bewildering . . . He's a retired field agent with a crippled leg, a man named Conklin, Alexander Conklin. He and a psychiatrist – Panov, Morris Panov – are close friends of Webb . . . or Jason Bourne.'

'Where are they?' asked the capo supremo grimly.

'Oh, you couldn't reach either one, talk to either of them. They're both under maximum security.'

'I didn't ask for the rules of engagement, *paisan*, I asked where they were.'

'Well, Conklin's at a condominium in Vienna, a proprietary of ours no one could penetrate, and Panov's apartment and office are both under round-the-clock surveillance.'

'You'll give me the addresses, won't you?'

'Certainly, but I guarantee they won't talk to you.'

'Oh, that would be a pity. We're just looking for a guy with a dozen names, asking questions, offering assistance.'

'They won't buy it.'

'Maybe I can sell it.'

'Goddamn it, *why*?' spouted Armbruster, then immediately lowered his voice. 'Why was this Webb or Bourne or whoever the hell he is at *Swayne's*?'

'It's a gap I can't fill,' said DeSole.

'A *what*?'

'That's an Agency term for no answer.'

'No wonder the country's up shit's creek.'

'That's not true—'

'Now *you* shut up!' ordered the man from New York, reaching into his pocket and pulling out a small notepad and a ballpoint pen. 'Write out the addresses of this retired spook and the yid shrink. *Now!*'

'It's difficult to see,' said DeSole, writing, angling the small pad of paper towards the neon lights of the closed gas station. 'There. The apartment number may be wrong but it's close, and Panov's name will be on the mailbox. But I tell you again, he won't talk to you.'

'Then we'll just have to apologize for interrupting him.'

'Yes, you probably will. I gather he's very dedicated where his patients are concerned.'

'Oh? Like that telephone line into your fax machine.'

'No, no, that's a technical term. Number Three wire, to be precise.'

'And you're always precise, aren't you, *paisan*?'

'And you're very irritating—'

'We've got to go,' broke in Armbruster, watching the New Yorker take back the pad and the ballpoint pen. 'Stay calm, Steven,' he added, obviously suppressing his anger and heading back to the limousine. 'Remember, there's nothing we can't handle. When you talk to Jimmy T in Brussels, see if you two can come up with a reasonable explanation, okay? If not, don't worry, we'll figure it out upstairs.'

'Of course, Mr Armbruster. But if I may ask? Is my account in Bern ready for immediate release – in case . . . well, you understand . . . in case —'

'Of course it is, Steven. All you have to do is fly over and write out the numbers of your account in your own handwriting. That's your signature, the one on file, remember?'

'Yes, yes, I do.'

'It must be over two million by now.'

'Thank you. *Thank* you . . . sir.'

'You've earned it, Steven. Good night.'

The two men settled back in the rear seat of the limousine, but there was no lack of tension. Armbruster glanced at the mafioso as the chauffeur, beyond the glass partition, turned on the ignition. 'Where's the other car?'

The Italian switched on the reading light and looked at his watch. 'By now he's parked less than a mile down the road from the gas station. He'll pick up DeSole on his way back and stay with him until the circumstances are right.'

'Your man knows exactly what to do?'

'Come on, a virgin he's not. He's got a searchlight mounted on that car so powerful it can be seen in Miami. He comes alongside, switches it on high, and wiggles the handle. Your two-million-dollar flunky is blinded and out of business, and we're only charging a quarter of that amount for the job. It's your day, Alby.'

The chairman of the Federal Trade Commission sat back in the shadows of the left rear seat, and stared out the window at the dark, rushing images beyond the smoked glass. 'You know,' he said quietly, 'if anyone ever told me twenty years ago that I'd be sitting in this car with someone like you, saying what I'm saying, I would've told him it was impossible.'

'Oh, that's what we like about you class-act characters. You look down your noses and drip your snot on us until you need us. Then all of a sudden we're "associates". Live and be well, Alby, we're eliminating another problem for you. Go back to your big federal commission and decide which companies are clean and which aren't – decisions not necessarily based on soap, right?'

'Shut up!' roared Armbruster, pounding his hand on the armrest. 'This Simon – this *Webb*! Where's he coming from? What's he on our case for? What's he *want*?'

'Something to do with that Jackal character maybe.'

'That doesn't make sense. We don't have anything to do with the Jackal.'

'Why should you?' asked the mafioso, grinning. 'You got us, right?'

'It's a very loose association and don't you forget it . . . Webb – *Simon*, god*damn* it, whoever he is, we've got to find him! With what he already knew, plus what I told him, he's a fucking *menace*!'

'He's a real major item, isn't he?'

'A major item,' agreed the chairman, again staring out the window, his right fist clenched, the fingers of his left hand drumming furiously on the armrest.

'You want to negotiate?'

'*What*?' snapped Armbruster, turning and looking at the calm Sicilian face of his companion.

'You heard me, only I used the wrong word and I apologize for that. I'll give you a *non*negotiable figure and you can either accept it or reject it.'

'A . . . contract? On Simon – *Webb*?'

'No,' replied the mafioso, slowly shaking his head. 'On a character named Jason Bourne. It's cleaner to kill someone who's already dead, isn't it? . . . Since we just saved you one and a half mill, the price of the contract is five.'

'Five *million*?'

'The cost of eliminating problems in the category of major items is high. Menaces are even higher. Five million, Alby, half on acceptance within the usual twenty-four hours.'

'That's outrageous!'

'Then turn me down. You come back, it's seven fifty; and if you come back again, it's double that. Fifteen million.'

'What guarantee do we have that you can even *find* him? You heard DeSole. He's Four Zero, which means he's out of reach, buried.'

'Oh, we'll dig him up just so we can replant him.'

'How? Two and a half million is a lot to pay on your word. *How*?'

Again smiling, the Mafia supremo reached into his pocket and pulled out the small notebook Steven DeSole had returned to him. 'Close friends are the best sources, Alby. Ask the sleazes who write all those gossip books. I got two addresses.'

'You won't get near them.'

'Hey, come on. You think you're dealing with old Chicago and the animals? With Mad Dog Capone and Nitti, the nervous finger? We got sophisticated people on the payroll these days. *Geniuses.* Scientists, electronics whiz kids – doctors. By the time we get finished with the spook and the yid, they won't know what happened. But we'll have Jason Bourne, the character who doesn't exist because he's already dead.'

Albert Armbruster nodded once and returned to the window in silence.

'I'll close up for six months, change the name, then start a promotional campaign in the magazines before reopening,' said John St Jacques, standing by the window as the doctor worked on his brother-in-law.

'There's no one left?' asked Bourne, wincing as he sat in a chair dressed in a bathrobe, the last suture on his neck being pincered.

'Sure there is. Seven crazy Canadian couples, including my old buddy, who's needlepointing your throat at the moment. Would you believe they wanted to start up a brigade, Renfrews of the Mounties, after the evil people.'

'That was Scotty's idea,' interrupted the doctor softly, concentrating on the wound. 'Count me out. I'm too old.'

'So's he but he doesn't know it. Then he wanted to advertise a reward to the tune of a hundred thousand for information leading to the *et cetera*! I finally convinced him that the less said the better.'

'Nothing said is the best,' added Jason. 'That's the way it's got to be.'

'That's a little tough, David,' said St Jacques, misunderstanding the sharp glance *Bourne* levelled at him. 'I'm sorry, but it is. We're deflecting most of the local inquiries with an ersatz story about a massive propane-gas leak, but not too many people are buying it. Of course, to the world outside, an earthquake down here wouldn't rate six lines buried in the last pages of the want ads, but rumours are flying around the Leewards.'

'You said local inquiries . . . what about that world outside? Has there been anything from it?'

'There will be but not about here, not about Tranquillity. Montserrat, yes, and the news will get a column in the London *Times* and maybe an inch in the New York and Washington papers, but I don't think it'll touch us.'

'Stop being so cryptic.'

'We'll talk later.'

'Say whatever you like, John,' broke in the doctor. 'I'm just about finished, so I'm not paying much attention, and even if I heard you, I'm entitled to.'

'I'll make it brief,' said St Jacques, walking to the right of the chair. 'The Crown governor,' he continued. 'You were right, at least I have to assume you were right.'

'Why?'

'The news came in while you were getting cleaned up. The CG's boat was found smashed on one of the nastier reefs off Antigua, halfway to Barbuda. There was no sign of survivors. Plymouth assumes it was one of those whipsaw squalls that can come out of south Nevis, but it's hard to swallow. Not a squall necessarily, but the circumstances.'

'Which were?'

'His usual two crewmen weren't with him. He dismissed them at the yacht club, saying he wanted to take the boat out by himself, yet he told Henry he was going out for the running big fish—'

'Which means he would've had to have a crew,' interrupted the Canadian physician. 'Oh, sorry.'

'Yes, he would've,' agreed the owner of Tranquillity Inn. 'You can't fish the big fellas and skipper a boat at the same time – at least the CG couldn't. He was afraid to take his eyes off the charts.'

'But he could read them, couldn't he?' asked Jason. 'The charts?'

'As a navigator, he was no Captain Bligh sailing by the Pacific stars, but he was good enough to stay out of trouble.'

'He was told to go out alone,' said Bourne. 'Ordered to rendezvous with a boat in waters that called for him to *really* keep his eyes on the charts.' Jason suddenly realized that the doctor's nimble fingers were no longer touching his neck; instead, there was the constricting bandage and the physician was standing beside him looking down. 'How are we doing?' asked Bourne, looking up, an appreciative smile creasing his lips.

'We're done,' said the Canadian.

'Well . . . then I think we'd better meet later, for a drink, all right?'

'Good heavens, you're just getting to the good part.'

'It's not good, Doctor, it's not good at all, and I'd be a very ungrateful patient – which I'm not – if I even unwittingly let you hear things I don't think you should hear.'

The elderly Canadian locked his eyes with Jason's. 'You mean that, don't you? In spite of everything that's happened, you really don't want to involve me any further. And you're not playing melodramatic games, secrecy for secrecy's sake – an old dodge for inferior doctors, incidentally – but you're really concerned, aren't you?'

'I guess I am.'

'Considering what's happened to you, and I don't just mean these past few hours, which I've been a part of, but what the scars on your body tell me you've been through before, it's rather remarkable that you can be concerned for anyone but yourself. You're a strange man, Mr Webb. At times you even sound like two different people.'

'I'm not strange, Doctor,' said Jason Bourne, momentarily closing his eyes, his lids briefly tight. 'I don't want to be strange or different or anything exotic at all. I want to be as normal and ordinary as the next fellow, no *games* at all. I'm just a teacher, and that's all I want to be. But in the present circumstances, I have to do things my way.'

'Which means I leave for my own benefit?'

'Yes, it does.'

'And if I ever learn all the facts, I'll realize that your instructions were very educational.'

'I hope so.'

'I'll bet you're one hell of a teacher, Mr Webb.'

'*Doctor* Webb,' interjected John St Jacques spontaneously, as if the clarification were mandatory. 'My brother-in-law's a doctor, too. Like my sister, he's got a PhD; he speaks a couple of Oriental languages and is a full professor. Places like Harvard, McGill and Yale have been after him for years, but he won't budge—'

'Will you please be *quiet*,' said Bourne, close to laughing, albeit kindly at his wife's brother. 'My entrepreneurial young friend is impressed with any alphabet after a name despite the fact that left to my own resources I couldn't afford one of these villas for more than a couple of days.'

'That's a crock.'

'I said my *own* resources.'

'You've got a point.'

'I've got a rich wife . . . Forgive us, Doctor, it's an old family argument.'

'Not only a good teacher,' the physician repeated, 'but under the grim exterior I suspect a very engaging one.' The Canadian walked to the door; he turned and added, 'I'll take you up on that drink later, I'd really like that.'

'Thanks,' said Jason. 'Thanks for everything.' The doctor nodded and left, closing the door firmly behind him. Bourne turned to his brother-in-law. 'He's a good friend, Johnny.'

'Actually, he's a cold fish but a hell of a doctor. That's the most human I've ever seen him . . . So you figure the Jackal had the Crown governor meet him somewhere off the Antigua coast, got the CG's information, killed him, and fed him to the sharks.'

'Conveniently foundering the boat in reef waters,' completed Jason. 'Perhaps opening the throttle and setting a short high-speed course into the shoals. A tragedy at sea and a link to Carlos vanishes – that's vital to him.'

'That's also something I have trouble with,' said St Jacques. 'I didn't go into it, but the section of reef north of Falmouth where he bought it is called Devil's Mouth, and it's not the kind of place that's advertised. Charters just stay away from it and no one boasts about the number of lives and boats it's claimed.'

'So?'

'So assuming the Jackal told the CG where to rendezvous, some place obviously close to Devil's Mouth, how the hell did the Jackal know about it?'

'Your two commandos didn't tell you?'

'Tell me what? I sent them right over to Henry to give *him* a full report while we took care of you. There wasn't time to sit down and talk and I figured every moment counted.'

'Then Henry knows by now; he's probably in shock. He's lost two drug boats in two days, and only one is likely to be paid for, and he still doesn't know about his boss, the so honourable Crown governor, lackey of the Jackal who made fools of the Foreign Office by passing off a small-time Paris hit man as a venerable hero of France. The wires will be burning all night between Government House and Whitehall.'

'Another *drug* boat? What are you trying to tell me? What does Henry know *now* – what could my guards tell him?'

'Your question a minute ago was how did the Jackal know about the reef off the coast of Antigua called Devil's Mouth.'

'Take my word for it, *Doctor* Webb, I remember the question. How could he?'

'Because he had a third man here, that's what your Royal Commandos have told Henry by now. A blond-haired son of a bitch who heads up Montserrat's drug patrols.'

'*Him*? Rickman? The one-man British Ku Klux Klan? By-the-Rules-Rickman, scourge of anybody who's afraid to yell back at him? Holy *Christ*, Henry won't *believe* it!'

'Why not? You just described a likely disciple of Carlos.'

'I suppose I did but it seems so *un*likely. He's the original sanctimonious deacon. Prayer meetings before work in the morning, calling on God to aid him in his battle against Satan, no alcohol, no women—'

'Savonarola?'

'I'd say that fits – from what I remember reading in history courses.'

'Then I'd say he's prime meat for the Jackal. And Henry *will* believe it when his lead boat doesn't come back to Plymouth and the bodies of the crew float up on shore or simply don't show up for the prayer meetings.'

'That's how Carlos got away?'

'Yes.' Bourne nodded and gestured at the couch several feet in front of him, the space between taken up by a glass-topped coffee table. 'Sit down, Johnny. We have to talk.'

'What have we been doing?'

'Not about what *has* happened, Bro, but about what's going to happen.'

'What's going to happen?' asked St Jacques, lowering himself on the couch.

'I'm leaving.'

'*No!*' cried the younger man, shooting to his feet as if propelled by a bolt of electricity. 'You *can't*!'

'I have to. He knows our names, where we live. Everything.'

'Where are you *going*?'

'Paris.'

'Goddamn it, *no*! You can't *do* that to Marie! Or to the kids, for Christ's sake. I won't *let* you!'

'You can't stop me.'

'For God's sake, David, listen to me! If Washington's too cheap or doesn't give a shit, believe me, Ottawa's cut from better stock. My sister *worked* for the government and *our* government doesn't kiss people off because it's inconvenient or too expensive. I know people – like Scotty, the Doc and others. A few words from them and you'll be put in a fortress in Calgary. No one could touch you!'

'You think my government wouldn't do the same? Let me tell you something, Bro, there are people in Washington who've put their lives on the line to keep Marie and the children and me alive. Selflessly, without any reward for themselves *or* the government. If I wanted a safe house where no one could touch us, I'd probably get an estate in Virginia, with horses and servants and a full platoon of armed soldiers protecting us around the clock.'

'Then that's the answer. *Take* it!'

'To what end, Johnny? To live in our own personal prison? The kids not allowed to go over to friends' houses, guards with them *if* they go to school and not tutored by themselves, no overnights, no pillow fights – no neighbours? Marie and I staring at each other, glancing over at the searchlights outside the windows, hearing the footsteps of the guards, the occasional cough or sneeze, or, heaven forbid, the crack of a rifle bolt because a rabbit disturbed a garden? That's not living, that's imprisonment. Your sister and I couldn't handle it.'

'Neither could I, not the way you describe it. But what can Paris solve?'

'I can find him. I can take him.'

'He's got the manpower over there.'

'I've got Jason Bourne,' said David Webb.

'I don't buy that crap!'

'Neither do I, but it seems to work . . . I'm calling in your debt to me, Johnny. Cover for me. Tell Marie I'm fine, not hurt at all, and that I've got a lead on the Jackal that only old Fontaine could have provided – which is the truth, actually. A café in Argenteuil called Le Coeur du Soldat. Tell her I'm bringing in Alex Conklin and all the help Washington can provide.'

'But you're not, are you?'

'No. The Jackal would hear about it; he's got ears up and down the Quai d'Orsay. Solo's the only way.'

'Don't you think she'll know that?'

'She'll suspect it, but she can't be certain. I'll have Alex call her, confirming that he's in touch with all the heavy covert firepower in Paris. But first it comes from you.'

'Why the lie?'

'You shouldn't have to ask that, Bro. I've put her through enough.'

'All right, I'll tell her, but she won't believe me. She'll see right through me, she always has. Since I was a kid, those big brown eyes would look into mine, most of the time pissed off, but not like our brothers', not – oh, I don't know – not with that disgust in their faces because the "kid" was a screwup. Can you understand that?'

'It's called caring. She's always cared for you – even when you were a screwup.'

'Yeah, Marie's okay.'

'Somewhat more than that, I think. Call her in a couple of hours and bring them back here. It's the safest place they can be.'

'What about you? How are you going to get to Paris? The connections out of Antigua and Martinique are lousy, sometimes booked days in advance.'

'I can't use those airlines anyway. I've got to get in secretly under a shroud. Somehow, a man in Washington will have to figure it out. Somehow. He's *got* to.'

Alexander Conklin limped out of the small kitchen in the CIA's Vienna apartment, his face and hair soaking wet. In the old days, before the old days fell into a distillery vat, he would calmly leave the office – wherever it was –

when things got too heavy too fast and indulge himself in an unwavering ritual. He would seek out the best steak house – again, wherever he was – have two dry martinis and a thick rare slab of meat with the greasiest potatoes on the menu. The combination of the solitude, the limited intake of alcohol, the blood-rare hunk of beef and, in particular, the grease-laden potatoes, had such a calming effect on him that all the rushing, conflicting complexities of the hectic day sorted themselves out and reason prevailed. He would return to his office – whether a smart flat in London's Belgrave Square or the back rooms of a whore house in Katmandu – with multiple solutions. It was how he got the sobriquet of Saint Alex of Conklin. He had once mentioned this gastronomical phenomenon to Mo Panov, who had a succinct reply: 'If your crazy head doesn't kill you, your stomach will.'

These days, however, with postalcoholic vacuum and various other impediments, such as high cholesterol and dumb little triglycerides, whatever the hell *they* were, he had to come up with a different solution. It came about by accident. One morning during the Iran-Contra hearings, which he found to be the finest hours of comedy on television, his set blew out. He was furious, so he turned on his portable radio, an instrument he had not used in months or perhaps years, as the television set had a built-in radio component – also inoperable at the time – but the portable radio's batteries had long since melted into white slime. His artificial foot in pain, he walked to his kitchen telephone – where his defunct portable radio resided – knowing that a call to his television repairman, for whom he had done several favours, would bring the man running to his emergency. Unfortunately, the call only brought forth a hostile diatribe from the repairman's wife, who screamed that her husband, the 'customer-fucker', had run off with a 'horny rich black bitch from Embassy Row!' (Zaire, as it later turned out in the Puerta Vallarta papers.) Conklin, in progressive apoplexy, had rushed to the kitchen sink, where his stress and blood pressure pills stood on the windowsill above the sink, and turned on the cold water. The tap exploded, surging out of its recess into the ceiling as a powerful gush of water inundated his entire head. *Caramba!* The shock calmed him down and he remembered that the Cable Network was scheduled to rebroadcast the hearings in full that evening. A happy man, he called the plumber and went out and bought a new television set.

So, since that morning, whenever his own furies or the state of the world disturbed him – the world he knew – he lowered his head in a kitchen sink and let the cold water pour over his head. He had done so this morning. This *goddamned, fucked-up morning!*

DeSole! *Killed* in an accident on a deserted country road in Maryland at four-thirty that morning. What the hell was Steven DeSole, a man whose driver's licence clearly stated that he was afflicted with night blindness, doing on a backcountry road outside Annapolis at four-thirty in the morning? And then Charlie Casset, a very angry Casset, calling him at six o'clock, yelling his usually cool head off, telling Alex he was going to put the commander of NATO on the goddamned spit and demand an explanation for the buried fax connection between the general and the dead chief of clandestine reports, who was not a victim of an accident, but of murder! Furthermore, one retired field officer named Conklin had better damned well come clean with everything he knew about DeSole and Brussels and related matters, or all bets were off where said retired field agent and his elusive friend Jason Bourne were concerned. Noon at the latest! And *then*, Ivan Jax! The brilliant black doctor from Jamaica phoned, telling him he wanted to put Norman Swayne's body back where he had found it because he did not want to be loused up by another Agency fiasco. But it was *not* Agency, cried Conklin to himself, unable to explain to Ivan Jax the real reason he had asked for his help. *Medusa.* And Jax could *not* simply drive the corpse back to Manassas because the police, on federal orders – the orders of one retired field agent using appropriated codes he was not entitled to use – had sealed off General Norman Swayne's estate without explanation.

'What do I do with the *body*?' Jax had yelled.

'Keep it cold for a while; Cactus would want it that way.'

'*Cactus?* I've been with him at the hospital all night. He's going to be okay, but he doesn't know what the hell is going on any more than *I* do!'

'We in the clandestine services can't always explain things,' Alex said, wincing as he spoke the ridiculous words. 'I'll call you back.'

So he had gone into the kitchen and put his head under a spray of cold water. What else could go wrong? And naturally the telephone rang.

'Dunkin' Doughnuts,' said Conklin, the phone to his ear.

'Get me *out* of here,' said Jason Bourne, not a trace of David Webb in his voice. 'To *Paris*!'

'What happened?'

'He got away, that's what happened, and I have to get to Paris under a cover, no immigration, no customs. He's got them all wired and I can't give him the chance to track me . . . Alex, are you *listening* to me?'

'DeSole was killed last night, killed in an accident that was no accident at four o'clock in the morning. Medusa's closing in.'

'I don't give a *damn* about Medusa! For me it's history; we made a wrong turn. I want the Jackal and I've got a place to start. I can find him, *take* him!'

'Leaving me with Medusa . . .'

'You said you wanted to go higher – you said you'd only give me forty-eight hours until you did. Shove the clock ahead. The forty-eight hours are over, so *go* higher, just get me out of here and over to Paris.'

'They'll want to talk to you.'

'Who?'

'Peter Holland, Casset, whoever else they bring in . . . the attorney general, Christ, the President himself.'

'About *what*?'

'You spoke at length with Armbruster, with Swayne's wife and that sergeant, Flannagan. I didn't. I just used a few code words that triggered responses from Armbruster and Ambassador Atkinson in London, nothing substantive. You've got the fuller picture first hand. I'm too deniable. They'll have to talk to you.'

'And put the Jackal on a back *burner*?'

'Just for a day, two at the most.'

'Goddamn it, *no*. Because it doesn't work that way and you know it! Once I'm back there I'm their only material witness, shunted from one closed interrogation to another; and if I refuse to cooperate, I'm in custody. No *way*, Alex. I've got only one priority and he's in Paris!'

'Listen to me,' said Conklin. 'There are some things I can control, others I can't. We needed Charlie Casset and he helped us, but he's not someone you can con, nor would I want to. He knows DeSole's death was no accident – a man with night blindness doesn't take a five-hour drive at four o'clock in the morning – and he also knows that *we* know a lot more about DeSole and Brussels than we're telling him. If we want the Agency's help, and we need it for things like getting you on a military or a diplomatic flight into France, and God knows what else when you're there, I can't ignore Casset. He'll step on us and by his lights, he should.'

Bourne was silent; only his breathing was heard. 'All right,' he said. 'I see where we're at. You tell Casset that if he gives us whatever we ask for now, we'll give him – no, *I'll* give him; keep yourself cleaner than me – enough information for the Department of Justice to go after some of the biggest fish in the government, assuming Justice isn't part of Snake Lady . . . You might add that'll include the location of a cemetery that might prove enlightening.'

It was Conklin's turn to be silent for a moment. 'He may want more than that, considering your current pursuits.'

'Oh . . . ? Oh, I see. In case I lose. Okay, add that when I get to Paris, I'll hire a stenographer and dictate everything I know, everything I've learned, and send it to *you*. I'll trust Saint Alex to carry it from there. Maybe a page or two at a time to keep them cooperative.'

'I'll handle that part . . . Now Paris, or close by. From what I recall, Montserrat's near Dominica and Martinique, isn't it?'

'Less than an hour to each, and Johnny knows every pilot on the big island.'

'Martinique's French, we'll go with that. I know people in the Deuxième Bureau. Get down there and call me from the airport terminal. I'll have made the arrangements by then.'

'Will do . . . There's a last item, Alex. Marie. She and the children will be back here this afternoon. Call her and tell her I'm covered with all the firepower in Paris.'

'You lying son of a bitch—'

'*Do* it!'

'Of course I will. On that score and not lying, if I live through the day, I'm having dinner with Mo Panov at his place tonight. He's a terrible cook, but he thinks he's the Jewish Julia Child. I'd like to bring him up to date; he'll go crazy if I don't.'

'Sure. Without him we'd both be in padded cells chewing rawhide.'

'Talk to you later. Good luck.'

The next day at 10:25 in the morning, Washington time, Dr Morris Panov, accompanied by his guard, walked out of Walter Reed Hospital after a psychiatric session with a retired army lieutenant suffering from the after effects of a training exercise in Georgia that took the lives of twenty-odd recruits under his command eight weeks ago. There was not much Mo could do; the man was guilty of competitive overachievement, military style, and had to live with his guilt. The fact that he was a financially privileged black and a graduate of West Point did not help. Most of the twenty dead recruits were also black and they had been underprivileged.

Panov, muddling over the available options with his patient, looked at his guard, suddenly startled. 'You're a new man, aren't you? I mean I thought I knew all of you.'

'Yes, sir. We're often reassigned on short notice, keeps all of us on our toes.'

'Habit-oriented anticipation – it can lull anybody.' The psychiatrist continued across the pavement to where his armour-plated car was usually waiting for him. It was a different vehicle. 'This isn't my car,' he said, bewildered.

'Get in!' ordered his guard, politely opening the door.

'What?' A pair of hands from inside the car grabbed him and a uniformed man pulled him into the backseat as the guard followed, sandwiching Panov between them. The two men held the psychiatrist as the one who had been inside yanked Mo's seersucker jacket off his shoulder and shoved up the short sleeve of his summer shirt. He plunged a hypodermic needle into Panov's arm.

'Good night, Doctor,' said the soldier with the insignia of the Medical Corps on the lapels of his uniform. 'Call New York,' he added.

19

The Air France 747 from Martinique circled Orly Airport in the early evening haze over Paris; it was five hours and twenty-two minutes behind schedule because of the severe weather patterns in the Caribbean. As the pilot entered his final approach the flight officer acknowledged their clearance to the tower, then switched to his prescribed sterile frequency and sent a last message in French to an off-limits communications room.

'Deuxième, special cargo. Please instruct your interested party to go to his designated holding area. Thank you. Out.'

'Instructions received and relayed,' was the terse reply.'Out.'

The special cargo in question sat in the left rear bulkhead seat in the first-class section of the aircraft; the seat beside him was unoccupied on orders of the Deuxième Bureau in cooperation with Washington. Impatient, annoyed, and because of the constricting bandage around his neck making sleep impossible, close to exhaustion, Bourne reflected on the events of the past nineteen hours. To put it mildly, they had not gone as smoothly as Conklin anticipated. The Deuxième had balked for over six hours as phone calls went back and forth feverishly between Washington, Paris and, finally, Vienna, Virginia. The stumbling block, and it was more of a hard rock, was the CIA's inability to spell out the covert operation in terms of one Jason Bourne, for only Alexander Conklin could release the name and he refused to do so, knowing the Jackal's penetrations in Paris extended to just about everywhere but the kitchens of the Tour d'Argent. Finally, in desperation and realizing it was lunchtime in Paris, Alex placed ordinary, unsafe overseas telephone calls to several cafés on the Rive Gauche, finding an old Deuxième acquaintance at one on the rue de Vaugirard.

'Do you remember the tinamou and an American somewhat younger than he is now who made things a little simpler for you?'

'Ah, the tinamou, the bird with hidden wings and ferocious legs! They were such better days, younger days. And if the somewhat older American was at the time given the status of a saint, I shall never forget him.'

'Don't now, I need you.'

'It *is* you, Alexander?'

'It is and I've got a problem with D. Bureau.'

'It is solved.'

And it was, but the weather was insoluble. The storm that had battered the central Leeward Islands two nights before was only a prelude to the torrential rain and winds that swept up from the Grenadines, with another storm behind it. The islands were entering the hurricane season, so the weather was not astonishing, merely a delaying factor. Finally, when clearance for takeoff was around the chronological corner, it was discovered that there was a malfunction in the far starboard engine; no one argued while the problem was traced, found and repaired. The elapsed time, however, was an additional three hours.

Except for the churning of his mind, the flight itself was uneventful for Jason; only his guilt interfered with his thoughts of what was before him – Paris, Argenteuil, a café with the provocative name of Le Coeur du Soldat, The Soldier's Heart. The guilt was most painful on the short flight from Montserrat to Martinique when they passed over Guadeloupe and the island of Basse-Terre. He knew that only a few thousand feet below were Marie and his children, unknowing, preparing to fly back to Tranquillity Isle, to the husband and father who would not be there. His infant daughter, Alison, would, of course, know nothing, but Jamie would; his wide eyes would grow larger and cloud over as words tumbled out about fishing and swimming . . . and Marie – *Christ,* I can't think about her! It hurts too much!

She'd think he had betrayed her, run away to seek a violent confrontation with an enemy from long ago in another far-off life that was no longer *their* life. She would think like old Fontaine, who had tried to persuade him to take his family thousands of miles away from where the Jackal prowled, but neither of them understood. The ageing Carlos might die, but on his deathbed he would leave a legacy, a bequest that would hinge on the mandatory death of Jason Bourne – David Webb and his family. *I'm right, Marie! Try to understand me. I have to find him, I have to kill him! We can't live in our personal prison for the rest of our lives!*

'Monsieur Simon?' said the stoutish well-tailored Frenchman, an older man with a close-cropped white chin beard, pronouncing the name *Seemohn.*

'That's right,' replied Bourne, shaking the hand extended to him in a narrow deserted hallway somewhere in Orly Airport.

'I am Bernardine, François Bernardine, an old colleague of our mutual friend, Alexander the Saint.'

'Alex mentioned you,' said Jason, smiling tentatively. 'Not by name, of course, but he told me you might bring up his sainthood. It was how I'd know you were – his colleague.'

'How is he? We hear stories, of course.' Bernardine shrugged. 'Banal gossip, by and large. Wounded in the futile Vietnam, alcohol, dismissed, disgraced, brought back a hero of the Agency, so many contradictory things.'

'Most of them true; he's not afraid to admit that. He's a cripple now, and he doesn't drink, and he *was* a hero. I know.'

'I see. Again stories, rumours, who can believe what? Flights of fancy out of Beijing, Hong Kong – some concerning a man named Jason Bourne.'

'I've heard them.'

'Yes, of course . . . But now Paris. Our saint said you would need lodgings, clothes purchased *en scène,* as it were, French to the core.'

'A small but varied closet,' agreed Jason. 'I know where to go, what to buy, and I have sufficient money.'

'Then we are concerned with lodgings. A hotel of your choice? La Tremoille? George Cinq? Plaza-Athénée?'

'Smaller, much smaller and far less expensive.'

'Money *is* a problem, then?'

'Not at all. Only appearances. I'll tell you what, I know Montmartre. I'll find a place myself. What I will need is a car – registered under another name, preferably a name that's a dead end.'

'Which means a dead man. It's been arranged; it is in the underground garage on the Capucines, near the Place Vendôme.' Bernardine reached into his pocket, pulled out a set of keys, and handed them to Jason. 'An older Peugeot in Section E. There are thousands like them in Paris and the licence number is on the tab.'

'Alex told you I'm travelling deep?'

'He didn't really have to. I believe our saint scoured the cemeteries for useful names when he worked here.'

'I probably learned it from him.'

'We all learned things from that extraordinary mind, the finest in our profession, yet so self-effacing, so . . . *je ne sais quoi* . . . so "why not try it", yes?'

'Yes, why not try it.'

'I must tell you, though,' said Bernardine, laughing. 'He once chose a name, admittedly from a tombstone, that drove the Sûreté *fou* – crazy! It was the alias of an axe murderer the authorities had been hunting for months!'

'That *is* funny,' agreed Bourne, chuckling.

'Yes, very. He told me later that he found it in Rambouillet – in a cemetery on the outskirts of Rambouillet.'

Rambouillet! The cemetery where Alex had tried to kill him thirteen years ago. All traces of a smile left Jason's lips as he stared at Alex's friend from the Deuxième Bureau. 'You know who I am, don't you?' he asked softly.

'Yes,' answered Bernardine. 'It was not so difficult to piece together, not with the rumours and the gossip out of the Far East. After all, it was here in Paris where you made your mark on Europe, Mr Bourne.'

'Does anyone else know?'

'*Mon Dieu, non!* Nor will they. I must explain, I owe my life to Alexander Conklin, our modest saint of *les opérations noires* – the black assignments in your language.'

'That's not necessary, I speak French fluently . . . or didn't Alex tell you that?'

'Oh, my God, you doubt me,' said the Deuxième man, his grey eyebrows arched. 'Take into account, young man – younger man – that I am in my seventieth year, and if I have lapses of language and try to correct them, it is because I mean to be kind, not *subreptice*.'

'*D'accord. Je regrette.* I mean that.'

'*Bien.* Alex is several years younger than I am, but I wonder how he's handling it. The age, that is.'

'Same as you. Badly.'

'There was an English poet – a Welsh poet, to be exact – who wrote, "Do not go gently into that good night". Do you remember it?'

'Yes. His name was Dylan Thomas and he died in his mid-thirties. He was saying fight like a son of a bitch. Don't give in.'

'I mean to do that.' Bernardine again reached into a pocket and pulled out a card. 'Here is my office – merely consultant status, you understand – and on the back I've written down my home phone; it is a special telephone, actually unique. Call me; whatever you need will be provided. Remember, I am the only friend you have in Paris. No one else knows you are here.'

'May I ask you a question?'

'*Mais certainement.*'

'How can you do the things you're doing for me when for all intents and purpose you've been put out to pasture?'

'*Ah,*' exclaimed the consultant to the Deuxième Bureau. 'The younger man grows older! Like Alex, I carry my credentials in my head. I know the *secrets.* How it is otherwise?'

'You could be taken out, neutralized – have an accident.'

'*Stupide*, young man! What is in both our heads we say is written down, locked away, to be revealed should such unnatural acts occur . . . Of course, it's all nonsense, for what do we really know that could not be denied, labelled as the ramblings of old men, but *they* do not know that. *Fear*, monsieur. It is the most potent weapon in our profession. Second, of course, is embarrassment, but that is usually reserved for the Soviet KGB and your Federal Bureau of Investigation, both of which fear embarrassment more than their nations' enemies.'

'You and Conklin come from the same street, don't you?'

'But, of course. To the best of my knowledge, neither of us has a wife or a family, only sporadic lovers to fill our beds, and loud, annoying nephews and nieces to fill our flats on certain holidays; no really close friends except now and then an enemy we respect who, for all we know and in spite of our truce, might shoot us or poison us with a drink. We *must* live alone, you see, for we are the professionals – we have nothing to do with the normal world; we merely use it as a *couverture* – as we slink around in dark alleys, paying or compromising people for secrets that mean nothing where summit conferences are concerned.'

'Then why do you do it? Why not walk away if it's so useless?'

'It's in the blood rushing through our veins. We've been trained. Beat the enemy in the deadly game – he takes you or you take him, and it is better that you take him.'

'That's dumb.'

'But of course. It's all dumb. So why does Jason Bourne go after the Jackal here in Paris? Why doesn't he walk away and say *enough.* Complete protection is yours for the asking.'

'So's prison. Can you get me out of here and into the city? I'll find a hotel and be in touch with you.'

'Before you are in touch with me, reach Alex.'

'What?'

'Alex wants you to call him. Something happened.'

'Where's a *phone*?'

'Not now. Two o'clock, Washington time; you have well over an hour. He won't be back before then.'

'Did he say what it was?'

'I think he's trying to find out. He was very upset.'

The room at the Pont-Royal on the rue Montalembert was small and in a secluded corner of the hotel, reached by taking the slow, noisy brass elevator to the top floor and walking down two narrow intersecting hallways, all of which was satisfactory to Bourne. It reminded him of a mountain cave, remote and secure.

To chew up the minutes before calling Alex, he walked along the nearby Boulevard Saint-Germain, making necessary purchases. Various toiletries joined several articles of clothing; casual denims called for summer shirts and a lightweight safari jacket; dark socks required tennis shoes, to be scuffed and soiled. Whatever he could supply himself now would save time later. Fortunately, there was no need to press old Bernardine for a weapon. During the drive into Paris from Orly, the Frenchman had opened the glove compartment of his car in silence, withdrawn a taped brown box and handed it to Jason. Inside was an automatic with two boxes of shells. Underneath, neatly layered, were thirty thousand francs, in varying denominations, roughly five thousand dollars, American.

'Tomorrow I will arrange a method for you to obtain funds whenever necessary. Within limits, of course.'

'No limits,' Bourne had contradicted. 'I'll have Conklin wire you a hundred thousand, and then another hundred after that, if it's necessary. You just tell him where.'

'Of *contingency* funds?'

'No. Mine. Thanks for the gun.'

With both his hands holding the looped strings of shopping bags, he headed back to the Montalembert and the hotel. In a few minutes it would be two in the afternoon in Washington, eight at night in Paris. As he walked rapidly down the street he tried not to think about Alex's news – an impossible demand on himself. If anything had happened to Marie and the children, he'd go out of his mind! Yet what could have happened? They were back on Tranquillity by now, and there was no safer place for them. There was *not*! He was sure of that. As he entered the old elevator and lowered the bags in his right hands so as to push the number of his floor and remove the hotel key from his pocket, there was a stinging sensation in his neck; he gasped – he had moved too fast, stretched the gut of a suture perhaps. He felt no warm trickle of blood; it was merely a warning this time. He rushed down the two narrow corridors to his room, unlocked the door, threw the shopping bags on the bed, and rapidly took the three necessary steps to the desk and the telephone. Conklin was true to his word; the phone in Vienna, Virginia, was picked up on the first ring.

'Alex, it's me. What happened? *Marie* . . . ?'

'No,' interrupted Conklin curtly. 'I spoke to her around noon. She and the kids are back at the inn and she's ready to kill me. She doesn't believe a word I told her and I'm going to erase the tape. I haven't heard that kind of language since the Mekong Delta.'

'She's upset—'

'So am I,' broke in Alex, making no attempt to make light of Bourne's understatement. 'Mo's disappeared.'

'What?'

'You heard me. Panov's gone, vanished.'

'My God, *how*? He's guarded every minute!'

'We're trying to piece it together; that's where I was, over at the hospital.'

'Hospital?'

'Walter Reed. He was in a psych session with a military this morning, and when it was over he never came out to his detail. They waited twenty minutes or so, then went in to find him and his escort because he was on a tight schedule. They were told he left.'

'That's crazy!'

'It gets crazier and scarier. The head floor nurse said an army doctor, a surgeon, came to the desk, showed his ID, and instructed her to tell Dr Panov that there was a change of routing for him, that he was to use the east-wing exit because of an expected protest march at the main entrance. The east wing has a different hallway to the psych area than the one to the main lobby, yet the army surgeon used the main doors.'

'Come again?'

'He walked right past our escort in the hallway.'

'And obviously out the same way and around to the east wing hall. Nothing on-scene unusual. A doctor with clearance in a restricted area, in and out, and while he's in, he delivers false instructions . . . But Christ, Alex, *who*? Carlos was on his way back here, to Paris! Whatever he wanted in Washington he got. He found me, he found *us*. He didn't *need* any more!'

'DeSole,' said Conklin quietly. 'DeSole knew about me and Mo Panov. I threatened the Agency with both of us, and DeSole was there in the conference room.'

'I'm not with you. What are you telling me?'

'DeSole, Brussels . . . Medusa.'

'All right, I'm slow.'

'It's not *he*, David, it's *they*. DeSole was taken out, our connection removed. It's Medusa.'

'To *hell* with them! They're on *my* back burner!'

'You're not on theirs. You cracked their shell. They want you.'

'I couldn't care *less*. I told you yesterday, I've only got one priority and he's in Paris, *square* one in Argenteuil.'

'Then I haven't been clear,' said Alex, his voice faint, the tone defeated. 'Last night I had dinner with Mo. I told him everything. Tranquillity, your flying to Paris, Bernardine . . . *everything*!'

*

A former judge of the first circuit court, residing in Boston, Massachusetts, United States of America, stood among the small gathering of mourners on the flat surface of the highest hill on Tranquillity Isle. The cemetery was the final resting place – *in voce verbatim via amicus curiae*, as he legally explained to the authorities on Montserrat. Brendan Patrick Pierre Prefontaine watched as the two splendid coffins provided by the generous owner of Tranquillity Inn were lowered into the ground along with the absolutely incomprehensible blessings of the native priest, who no doubt usually clasped the neck of a dead chicken in his mouth while intoning his benediction in voodoo. 'Jean Pierre Fontaine' and his wife were at peace.

Nevertheless, barbarism not withstanding, Brendan, the quasi-alcoholic street lawyer of Harvard Square, had found a cause. A cause beyond his own survival, and that in itself was remarkable. Randolph Gates, Lord Randolph of Gates, Dandy Randy of the Courts of the Elite, was in reality a scumball, a conduit of death in the Caribbean. And the outlines of a scheme were forming in Prefontaine's progressively clearer mind, clearer because among other inhumane deprivations, he had suddenly decided to do without his four shots of vodka upon waking up in the morning. Gates had provided the essential information that led the would-be killers of the Webb family to Tranquillity Isle. *Why?* . . . That was basically, even legally, irrelevant; the fact that he had supplied their whereabouts to known killers, with prior knowledge that they *were* killers, was not. That was accomplice to murder, *multiple* murder. Dandy Randy's testicles were in a vice, and as the plates closed, he would – he *had* to – reveal information that would assist the Webbs, especially the glorious auburn-headed woman he wished to almighty God he had met fifty years ago.

Prefontaine was flying back to Boston in the morning, but he had asked John St Jacques if he might return one day. Perhaps not with a prepaid reservation.

'Judge, my house is your house,' was the reply.

'I might even earn that courtesy.'

Albert Armbruster, chairman of the Federal Trade Commission, got out of his limousine and stood on the pavement before the steep steps of his town house in Georgetown. 'Check with the office in the morning,' he said to the chauffeur, holding the rear door. 'As you know, I'm not a well man.'

'Yes, sir.' The driver closed the door. 'Would you like assistance, sir?'

'*Hell*, no. Get out of here.'

'Yes, sir.' The government chauffeur climbed into the front seat; the sudden roar of his engine was not meant as a courteous exit as he sped down the street.

Armbruster climbed the stone staircase, his stomach and chest heaving with each step, cursing under his breath at the sight of his wife's silhouette beyond the glasss door of their Victorian entrance. 'Shit-kicking *yapper*,' he said to himself as he neared the top, gripping the railing before facing his adversary of thirty years.

A spit exploded out of the darkness from somewhere within the grounds of the property next door. Armbruster's arms flew up, his wrists bent as if trying to locate the bodily chaos; it was too late. The chairman of the Federal Trade Commission tumbled back down the stone staircase, his thumping dead weight landing grotesquely on the pavement below.

Bourne changed into the French denim trousers, slipped on a dark short-sleeved shirt and the cotton safari jacket, put his money, his weapon, and all his identifications – authentic and false – into his pockets and left the Pont-Royal. Before doing so, however, he stuffed the bed with pillows, and hung his travelling clothes in clear view over the chair. He walked casually past the ornate front desk, and once outside on the Montalembert ran to the nearest telephone kiosk. He inserted a coin and dialled Bernardine's home.

'It's Simon,' he said.

'I thought so,' replied the Frenchman. 'I was hoping so. I've just heard from Alex and told him *not* to tell me where you were; one cannot reveal what one does not know. Still, if I were you, I'd go to another place, at least for the night. You may have been spotted at the airport.'

'What about you?'

'I intend to be a *canard*.'

'A duck?'

'The sitting variety. The Deuxième has my flat under watch. Perhaps I'll have a visitor; it would be convenient, *n'est-ce pas*?'

'You didn't tell your office about—'

'About *you*?' interrupted Bernardine. 'How could I, monsieur, I don't *know* you? My protective Bureau believes I had a threatening call from an old adversary known to be a psychopath. Actually I removed him in the Maritimes years ago but I never closed the file—'

'Should you be telling me this on your telephone?'

'I thought I mentioned that it was a unique instrument.'

'You did.'

'Suffice it to say it cannot be tapped and still function . . . You need rest, monsieur. You are no good to anyone, least of all yourself, without it. Find a bed, I cannot help you there.'

'"Rest is a weapon",' said Jason, repeating a phrase he had come to believe was a vital truth, vital for survival in a world he loathed.

'I beg your pardon?'

'Nothing. I'll find a bed and call you in the morning.'

'Tomorrow then. *Bonne chance, mon ami.* For both of us.'

He found a room at the Avenir, an inexpensive hotel on the rue Gay-Lussac. Registering under a false name, promptly forgotten, he climbed the stairs to his room, removed his clothes, and fell into the bed. 'Rest is a weapon,' he said to himself, staring at the ceiling, at the flickering lights of the Paris streets as they travelled across the plaster. Whether rest came in a mountain cave or a rice paddy in the Mekong Delta, it did not matter; it was a weapon frequently more powerful than firepower. That was the lesson drummed into his head by d'Anjou, the man who had given his life in a Beijing forest so that Jason

Bourne might live. Rest *is* a weapon, he considered, touching the bandage around his neck yet not really feeling it, its constricting presence fading as sleep came.

He woke up slowly, cautiously, the noise of the traffic in the streets below pounding up to his window, the metallic horns like the erratic cawing of angry crows amid the irregular bursts of angry engines, full bore one moment, abrupt quiet the next. It was a normal morning in the narrow streets of Paris. Holding his neck rigid, Jason swung his legs to the floor from the inadequate bed and looked at his watch, startled at what he saw, wondering for an instant whether he had adjusted the watch for Paris time. Of course he had. It was ten-seven in the morning– Paris time. He had slept nearly eleven hours, a fact confirmed by the rumbling in his stomach. Exhaustion was now replaced by acute hunger.

Food, however, would have to wait; there were things to take care of, and first on the list was to reach Bernardine, and then to learn the security status of the Pont-Royal hotel. He got to his feet, stiffly, unsteadily, numbness momentarily invading his legs and arms. He needed a hot shower, which was not to be had at the Avenir, then mild exercise to limber up his body, therapies unnecessary only a few years ago. He removed his wallet from his trousers, pulled out Bernardine's card and returned to the bed to use the telephone beside it; he dialled.

'*Le canard* had no visitors, I'm afraid,' said the Deuxième veteran. 'Not even the hint of a hunter, which I presume is favourable news.'

'It's not until we find Panov– *if* we find him. The *bastards*!'

'Yes, that must be faced. It's the ugliest part of our work.'

'Goddamn it, I can't dismiss a man like Mo with "That must be *faced*"!'

'I'm not asking you to. I'm only remarking upon the reality. Your feelings are meaningful to you, but they don't change reality. I did not mean to offend you.'

'And I didn't mean to mouth off. Sorry. It's just that he's a very special person.'

'I understand . . . What are your plans? What do you need?'

'I don't know yet,' answered Bourne. 'I'll pick up the car in the Capucines and an hour or so later I'll know more. Will you be home or at the Deuxième Bureau?'

'Until I hear from you I will stay in my flat and near my very unique telephone. Under the circumstances I prefer that you do not call me at the office.'

'That's an astonishing statement.'

'I don't know everyone these days at the Deuxième, and at my age, caution is not merely the better part of valour, it's frequently a substitute. Besides, to call off my protection so swiftly might generate rumours of senility . . . Speak to you later, *mon ami*.'

Jason replaced the phone, tempted to pick it up again and reach the Pont-Royal but this was Paris, the city of discretion, where hotel clerks were loath to give information over the telephone, and would refuse to do so with guests they did not know. He dressed quickly, went down to pay his bill, and walked out onto the rue Gay-Lussac. There was a taxi stand at the corner; eight minutes later he walked into the lobby of the Pont-Royal and up to the concierge. '*Je m'appelle Monsieur Simon*,' he said to the man, giving his room number. 'I ran into a friend last night,' he continued in flawless French, 'and I stayed at her place. Would you know if anyone came around looking for me, perhaps asking for me.' Bourne removed several large franc notes, his eyes telling the man he would pay generously for confidentiality. 'Or even describing someone like me,' he added softly.

'*Merci bien, monsieur* . . . I understand. I will check further with the night concierge, but I'm sure he would have left a note for my personal attention if someone had come here seeking you.'

'Why are you so sure?'

'Because he *did* leave such a note for me to speak with you. I've been calling your room since seven o'clock this morning when I came on duty.'

'What did the note say?' asked Jason, his breathing on hold.

'It's what I'm to say to you. "Reach his friend across the Atlantic. The man has been phoning all night." I can attest to the accuracy of that, monsieur. The switchboard tells me that last call was less than thirty minutes ago.'

'Thirty minutes ago?' said Jason, looking hard at the concierge and then at his watch. 'It's five a.m. over there . . . all *night*?'

The hotel man nodded as Bourne started for the elevator.

'Alex, for Christ's sake, what *is* it? They told me you've been calling all—'

'Are you at the hotel?' interrupted Conklin quickly.

'Yes, I am.'

'Get to a public phone in the street and call me back. Hurry.'

Again the slow, cumbersome elevator; the faded ornate lobby now half filled with Parisiennes talking manically, many heading for the bar and their prenoon apéritifs; and again the hot bright summer street outside and the maddening congested traffic. Where was a telephone? He walked rapidly down the pavement towards the Seine – where was a *phone*? There! Across the converging rue du Bac, a red-domed booth with posters covering the sides.

Dodging the onslaught of automobiles and small trucks, all with furious drivers, he raced to the other side of the street and down to the booth. He sped inside, deposited a coin, and after an agonizing few moments explaining that he was *not* calling Austria, the international operator accepted his AT&T credit number and put the call through to Vienna, Virginia.

'Why the hell couldn't I talk from the hotel?' asked Bourne angrily. 'I called you last night from there!'

'That was last night, not today.'

'Any news about Mo?'

'Nothing yet, but they may have made a mistake. We may have a line on the army doctor.'

'Break him!'

'With pleasure. I'll take off my foot and smash his face with it until he begs to cooperate – if the line on him is rumb.'

'That's not why you've been calling me all night, though, is it?'

'No. I was with Peter Holland for five hours yesterday. I went over to see him after we talked, and his reaction was exactly what I thought it would be, with a few generous broadsides in the bargain.'

'Medusa?'

'Yes. He insists you fly back immediately; you're the only one with direct knowledge. It's an order.'

'Bullshit! He can't insist I do anything, much less give me an order!'

'He can cut you off and I can't do anything about it. If you need something in a hurry, he won't deliver.'

'Bernardine's offered to help. "Whatever you need," those were his words.'

'Bernardine's limited. Like me, he can call in debts, but without access to the machine he's too restricted.'

'Did you tell Holland I'm writing down everything I know, every statement that was made to me, every answer to every question I asked?'

'Are you?'

'I will.'

'He doesn't buy it. He wants to question you; he says he can't question pages of paper.'

'I'm too close to the Jackal! I won't *do* it. He's an unreasonable son of a bitch!'

'I think he wanted to be reasonable,' said Conklin. 'He knows what you're going through, what you've been through, but after seven o'clock last night he closed the doors.'

'Why?'

'Armbruster was shot to death outside his house. They're calling it a Georgetown robbery, which, of course, it isn't and wasn't.'

'Oh, *Jesus*!'

'There are a couple of other things you ought to know. To begin with, we're releasing Swayne's "suicide".'

'For God's sake, why?'

'To let whoever killed him think he's off the hook, and more important, to see who shows up during the next week or so.'

'At the funeral?'

'No, that's a "closed family affair", no guests, no formal ceremony.'

'Then who's going to show up where?'

'At the estate, in one from or another. We checked with Swayne's attorney, very officially, of course, and he confirmed what Swayne's wife told you about his leaving the whole place to a foundation.'

'Which one?' asked Bourne.

'One you've never heard of, funded privately a few years ago by wealthy close friends of the august "wealthy" general. It's as touching as can be. It goes under the title of the Soldiers, Sailors and Marines Retreat; the board of directors is already in place.'

'Medusans.'

'Or their surrogates. We'll see.'

'Alex, what about the names I gave you, the six or seven names Flannagan gave *me*? And that slew of licence plate numbers from their meetings?'

'Cute, real cute,' said Conklin enigmatically.

'What's cute?'

'Take the names – they're the dregs of the wing-ding social set, no relation to the Georgetown upper crust. They're out of the *National Enquirer*, not the *Washington Post*.'

'But the *licences*, the meetings! That's got to be the ball of wax.'

'Even cuter,' observed Alex. 'A ball of sheep dip . . . Every one of those licences is registered to a limousine company, read that companies. I don't have to tell you how authentic the names would be even if we had the dates to trace them.'

'There's a cemetery out there!'

'Where is it? How big, how small? There are twenty-eight acres—'

'Start looking!'

'And advertise what we know?'

'You're right; you're playing it right . . . Alex, tell Holland you couldn't reach me.'

'You're joking.'

'No, I mean it. I've got the concierge, I can cover. Give Holland the hotel and the name and tell him to call himself, or send over whoever he likes from the embassy to verify. The concierge will swear I checked in yesterday and he hasn't seen me since. Even the switchboard will confirm it. Buy me a few days, *please*.'

'Holland could still pull all the plugs and probably will.'

'He won't if he thinks I'll come back when you find me. I just want him to keep looking for Mo and keep my name out of Paris. Good *or* bad, no Webb, no Simon, no Bourne!'

'I'll try.'

'Was there anything else? I've got a lot to do.'

'Yes. Casset is flying over to Brussels in the morning. He's going to nail Teagarten – *him* we can't allow and it won't touch you.'

'Agreed.'

On a side street in Anderlecht, three miles south of Brussels, a military sedan bearing the flags of a four-star general officer pulled up to the kerb in front of a sidewalk café. General James Teagarten, commander of NATO, his tunic emblazoned with five rows of ribbons, stepped gingerly out of the car into the bright early afternoon sunlight. He turned and offered his hand to a stunning WAC major, who smiled her thanks as she climbed out after him. Gallantly, with military authority, Teagarten released the woman's hand and took her elbow; he escorted her across the wide pavement towards a cluster of umbrella-topped tables behind a row of flowering planter boxes that was the alfresco section of the café. They reached the entrance, a latticework archway profusely covered with baby roses, and walked inside. All the tables were occupied save one at the far end of the enclosed pavement; the hum of luncheon conversation was punctuated by the tinkling of wine bottles gently touching wine glasses and the delicate clatter of utensils lowered on china plates. The decibel level of the conversation was suddenly reduced, and the general, aware that his presence inevitably brought stares, amiable waves and not infrequently mild applause, smiled benignly at no one in particular and yet everyone as he guided his lady to the deserted table where a small folded card read *Réservé.*

The owner, with two waiters trailing behind him like anxious egrets, practically flew between the tables to greet his distinguished guest. When the commander was seated, a chilled bottle of Corton Charlemagne was presented and the menu discussed. A young Belgian child, a boy of five or six, walked shyly up to the table and brought his hand to his forehead; he smiled and saluted the general. Teagarten rose to his feet, standing erect, and saluted the child back.

'*Vous êtes un soldat distingué, mon camarade,*' said the general, his commanding voice ringing through the sidewalk café, his bright smile winning the crowd, who responded with appreciative applause. The child retreated and the meal continued.

A leisurely hour later, Teagarten and his lady were interrupted by the general's chauffeur, a middle-aged army sergeant whose expression conveyed his anxiety. The commander of NATO had received an urgent message over his vehicle's secure phone, and the chauffeur had the presence of mind to write it down and repeat it for accuracy. He handed Teagarten the note.

The general stood up, his tanned face turning pale as he glanced around the now half-empty sidewalk café, his eyes narrowed, angry, afraid. He reached into his pocket and pulled out a folded wad of Belgian franc notes, peeling off several large ones and dropping them on the table. 'Come on,' he said to the woman major. 'Let's go . . . You' – he turned to his driver – 'get the car started!'

'What is it?' asked his luncheon companion.

'London. Over the wire. Armbruster and DeSole are dead.'

'Oh, my God! *How?*'

'It doesn't matter. Whatever they say is a lie.'

'What's happening?'

'I don't know. I just know we're getting out of here. Come *on*!'

The general and his lady rushed through the latticework archway, across the wide pavement, and into the military vehicle. On either side of the bonnet, something was missing. The middle-aged sergeant had removed the two red-and-gold flags denoting the impressive rank of his superior, the commander of NATO. The car shot forward, travelling less than fifty yards when it happened.

A massive explosion blew the military vehicle into the sky, shards of glass and metal, pieces of flesh and streaks of blood filling the narrow street in Anderlecht.

'*Monsieur!*' cried the petrified waiter as crews of police, firemen and sanitation workers went about their grisly business in the road.

'What is it?' replied the distraught owner of the sidewalk café, still shaking from the harsh interrogation he had gone through from the police and the descending hordes of journalists. 'I am ruined. We will be known as the Café de la Mort, the restaurant of death.'

'Monsieur, *look*!' The waiter pointed at the table where the general and his lady had sat.

'The police have gone over it,' said the disconsolate owner.

'No, monsieur. *Now!*'

Across the glass top of the table, the capital letters scrawled in glistening red lipstick, was a name.

JASON BOURNE

20

Stunned, Marie stared at the television set, at the satellite news programme beamed from Miami. Then she screamed as a camera moved in on a glass table in a town called Anderlecht in Belgium and the name printed in red across the top. '*Johnny!*'

St Jacques burst through the bedroom door of the suite he had built for himself on the second floor of Tranquillity Inn. '*Christ*, what *is* it?'

Tears streaming down her face, Marie pointed in silence and in horror at the set. The announcer on the overseas 'feed' was speaking in the monotonic drone peculiar to such satellite transmissions.

'*. . . as if a bloodstained savage from the past had returned to terrorize civilized society. The infamous killer, Jason Bourne, second only to Carlos the Jackal in the assassin-for-hire market, has claimed responsibility for the explosion that took the lives of General James Teagarten and his companions. Conflicting reports have come from Washington and London intelligence circles and police authorities. Sources in Washington claim that the assassin known as Jason Bourne was hunted down and killed in Hong Kong five years ago in a joint British-American operation. However, spokesmen for both the Foreign Office and British intelligence deny any knowledge of such an operation and say that a joint effort as was described is highly unlikely. Still other sources, these from Interpol's headquarters in Paris, have stated that their branch in Hong Kong knew of the supposed death of Jason Bourne, but as the widely circulated reports and photographs were so sketchy and unidentifiable, they did not give much credence to the story. They assumed, as was also reported, that Bourne disappeared into the People's Republic of China for a last contract fatal to himself. All that's clear today is that in the quaint city of Anderlecht in Belgium, General James Teagarten, commander of NATO, was assassinated and someone calling himself Jason Bourne has taken credit for killing this great and popular soldier . . . We now show you an old composite photograph from Interpol's files produced by a consensus of those who purportedly had seen Bourne at close range. Remember, this is a composite, the features put together separately from scores of other photographs and, considering the killer's reputation for changing his appearance, probably not of great value.*'

The screen was suddenly filled with the face of a man, somewhat irregular and lacking definition.

'It's not David!' said John St Jacques.

'It could be, Bro,' said his sister.

'*And now to other news. The drought that has plagued large areas of Ethiopia—*'

'Turn that goddamned thing off!' shouted Marie, lurching out of the chair and heading for the telephone as her brother switched off the set. 'Where's Conklin's number? I wrote it down here on your desk somewhere . . . Here it is, on the blotter. *Saint Alex* has a hell of a lot to explain, that son of a *bitch*!' She dialled angrily but accurately, sitting in St Jacques's chair, tapping her clenched fist as the tears continued to roll down her cheeks. Tears of sorrow and fury. 'It's me, you *bastard*! . . . You've killed him! You let him go – *helped* him to go – and you've *killed* him!'

'I can't talk to you now, Marie,' said a cold, controlled Alexander Conklin. 'I've got Paris on the other line.'

'*Screw* Paris! Where is he? Get him *out*!'

'Believe me, we're trying to find him. All fucking hell has broken out here. The British want Peter Holland's ass for even hinting at a Far East connection, and the French are in an uproar over something they can't figure out but suspect, like special Deuxième cargo on a plane from Martinique, which was originally rejected. I'll call you back, I *swear* it!'

The line was disconnected and Marie slammed down the phone. 'I'm flying to Paris, Johnny,' she said, breathing deeply and wiping the tears from her face.

'You're *what*?'

'You heard me. Bring Mrs Cooper over here. Jamie loves her and she's better with Alison than I could ever be – and why not? She's had seven children, all grown up, who still come back to her every Sunday.'

'You're *crazy*! I won't let you!'

'Somehow,' said Marie, withering her brother with a look, 'I have an idea you probably said something like that to David when he told you *he* was going to Paris.'

'Yes, I did!'

'And you couldn't stop him any more than you can stop me.'

'But *why*?'

'Because I know every place he knows in Paris, every street, every café, every alley, from Sacre-Coeur to Montmartre. He has to *use* them, and I'll find him long before the Deuxième or the Sûreté.' The telephone rang; Marie picked it up.

'I told you I'd call you right back,' said the voice of Alex Conklin. 'Bernardine has an idea that might work.'

'Who's Bernardine?'

'An old Deuxième colleague and a good friend who's helping David.'

'What's his idea?'

'He got Jason – *David* – a rental car. He knows the licence plate number and is having it radioed to all the Paris police patrols to report it if seen, but not to stop the car or harass the driver. Simply keep it in sight and report directly to him.'

'And you think David – *Jason* – won't spot something like that? You've got a terrible memory, worse than my husband's.'

'It's only one possibility, there are others.'

'Such as?'

'Well . . . well, he's bound to call *me.* When he hears the news about Teagarten, he's *got* to call me.'

'Why?'

'Like you say, to get him out!'

'With Carlos in the offing? Fat chance, fathead. I've got a better idea. I'm flying to Paris.'

'You *can't*!'

'I don't want to hear that any more, I *won't* hear that any more. Are you going to help me or do I do it by myself?'

'I couldn't get a postage stamp from a dispensing machine in France, and Holland couldn't get the address of the Eiffel Tower.'

'Then I'm on my own, which, frankly, under the circumstances, makes me feel a lot safer.'

'What can you *do*, Marie?'

'I won't give you a litany, but I can go to all those places he and I went to, *used* when we were running. He'll use them again, somehow, someway. He has to because in your crazy jargon they were "secure", and in his crazy frame of mind he'll return to them because he knows they're secure.'

'God bless, favourite lady.'

'*He* abandoned us, Alex. God doesn't exist.'

Prefontaine walked through the terminal at Boston's Logan Airport and hailed a cab on the crowded platform. Actually looking around, he lowered his hand and stood in line; things had changed in thirty years. Everything, including airports, had become cafeterias; one stood in line for a plate of third-rate mulligan stew, as well as a taxi.

'The Ritz-Carlton,' said the judge to the driver.

'You h'ain'd got no luggage?' asked the man. 'Nudding but d'liddle bag?'

'No, I do not,' replied Prefontaine, and, unable to resist a follow-up, added. 'I keep wardrobes wherever I go.'

'Tutti-fruitee,' said the driver, removing an outsized, wide-toothed comb from his hair as he swung out into the traffic.

'You have a reservation, sir?' asked the tuxedoed clerk behind the counter at the Ritz.

'I trust one of my law clerks made it for me. The name's Scofield, Justice William Scofield of the Supreme Court. I'd hate to think that the Ritz had lost a reservation, especially these days when everyone's screaming for consumer protection.'

'Justice *Scofield* . . . ? I'm sure it's here somewhere, sir.'

'I specifically requested Suite Three-C, I'm sure it's in your computer.'

'Three-C . . . it's booked—'

'*What?*'

'No, no, I'm wrong, Mr Justice. They haven't arrived . . . I mean it's an error . . . they're in another suite.' The clerk pounded his bell with ferocity. 'Bellboy, *bellboy*!'

'No need for that, young fella, I travel light. Just give me the key and point me in the right direction.'

'Yes, *sir*!'

'I trust you've got a few bottles of decent whisky up there, as usual?'

'If they're not, they will be, Mr Justice. Any particular brands?'

'Good rye, good bourbon and good brandy. The white stuff is for sissies, right?'

'*Right*, sir. Right away, sir!'

Twenty minutes later, his face washed and a drink in his hand, Prefontaine picked up the phone and dialled Dr Randolph Gates.

'The Gates residence,' said the woman on the line.

'Oh, come on, Edie, I'd know your voice under water and it's been almost thirty years.'

'I know yours, too, but I simply can't place it.'

'Try a rough adjunct professor at the law school who kept beating the hell out of your husband, which made no impression upon him and he was probably right because I ended up in jail. The first of the local judges to be put away, and rightfully so.'

'*Brendan?* Dear God, it's you! I never believed all those things they said about you.'

'Believe, my sweet, they were true. But right now I have to speak to the lord of the Gates. Is he there?'

'I suppose he is, I don't really know. He doesn't speak to me very much any more.'

'Things are not well, my dear?'

'I'd love to talk to you, Brendan. He's got a problem, a problem I never knew about.'

'I suspect he has, Edie, and of course we'll talk. But at the moment I have to speak with *him*. Right now.'

'I'll call him on the intercom.'

'Don't tell him it's me, Edith. Tell him it's a man named Blackburne, from the island of Montserrat in the Caribbean.'

'What?'

'Do as I say, dear Edie. It's for his sake as well as yours – perhaps more for you, if truth were told.'

'He's *sick*, Brendan.'

'Yes, he is. Let's try to make him well. Get him on the line for me.'

'I'll put you on hold.'

The silence was interminable, the two minutes more like two hours until the gravelled voice of Randolph Gates exploded on the line.'Who *are* you?' whispered the celebrated attorney.

'Relax, Randy, it's Brendan. Edith didn't recognize my voice but I sure remembered hers. You're one lucky fellow.'

'What do you *want*? What's this about Montserrat?'

'Well, I just came back from there—'

'You *what*?'

'I decided I needed a vacation.'

'You *didn't* . . . !' Gates's whisper was now essentially a cry of panic.

'Oh, but I did, and because I did your whole life is going to change. You see, I ran into the woman and her two children that you were so interested in, remember them? It's quite a story and I want to tell it to you in all its fascinating detail . . . You set them up to be killed, Dandy Randy, and that's a no-no. A dreadful no-no.'

'I don't know what you're *talking* about! I've never heard of Montserrat or any woman with two children. You're a desperate snivelling drunk and I'll deny your insane allegations as the alcoholic fantasies of a convicted felon!'

'Well done, Counsellor. But denying any allegations made by me isn't the core of your dilemma. No, that's in Paris.'

'*Paris . . . ?*'

'A certain man in Paris, someone I didn't realize was a living person, but I learned otherwise. It's somewhat murky how it came about, but a strange thing happened in Montserrat. I was mistaken for *you.*'

'You were . . . what?' Gates was barely audible, his thin voice tremulous.

'Yes. Odd, isn't it? I imagine that when this man in Paris tried to reach you here in Boston, someone told him your imperial presence was out or away and that's how the mix-up began. Two brilliant legal minds, both with an elusive connection to a woman and her two children, and Paris thought I was you.'

'What *happened*?'

'Calm down, Randy. At the moment he probably thinks you're dead.'

'*What?*'

'He tried to have me killed – you killed. For transgression.'

'Oh, my God!'

'And when he finds out you're very much alive and eating well in Boston, he won't permit a second attempt to fail.'

'Jesus *Christ* . . . !'

'There may be a way out, Dandy Boy, which is why you must come and see me. Incidentally, I'm in the same suite at the Ritz that you were when I came to see *you.* Three-C; just take the elevator. Be here in thirty minutes, and remember, I have little patience with clients who abuse schedules, for I'm a very busy man. By the way, my fee is twenty thousand dollars an hour or any part thereof, so bring money, Randy. Lots of it. In cash.'

He was ready, thought Bourne, studying himself in the mirror, satisfied with what he saw. He had spent the last three hours getting ready for his drive to Argenteuil, to a restaurant named Le Coeur du Soldat, the message centre for a 'blackbird', for Carlos the Jackal. The Chameleon had dressed for the environment he was about to enter; the clothes were simple, the body and the face less so. The first required a trip to the secondhand stores and pawn shops in Montmartre, where he found faded trousers and a surplus French army shirt, and an equally faded small combat ribbon that denoted a wounded veteran. The second, somewhat more complex, demanded hair colouring, a day's growth of beard, and another constricting bandage, this bound around his right knee so tight he could not forget the limp he had quickly perfected. His hair and eyebrows were now a dull red – dirty, unkempt red, which fit his new surroundings, a cheap hotel in Montparnasse whose front desk wanted as little contact as possible with its clientele.

His neck was more an irritant now than an impediment; either he was adjusting to the stiff, restricted movement or the healing process was doing its mysterious work. And that restricted movement was not a liability where his current appearance was concerned; in truth, it was an asset. An embittered, wounded veteran, a discarded son of France, would be hard pressed to forget his dual immobility. Jason shoved Bernardine's automatic into his trousers pocket, checked his money, his car keys, and his scabbarded hunting knife, the latter purchased at a sporting goods store and strapped inside his shirt, and limped to the door of the small, filthy, depressing room. Next stop, the Capucines and a nondescript Peugeot in an underground garage. He *was* ready.

Out on the street, he knew he had to walk a number of blocks before he found a taxi station; cabs were not the fashion in this section of Montparnasse . . . Neither was the commotion around a newspaper kiosk at the second corner. People were shouting, many waving their arms, clutching papers in their fists, anger and consternation in their voices. Instinctively, he quickened his pace, reached the stand, threw down his coins and grabbed a newspaper.

The breath went out of him as he tried to suppress the shock waves that swept through him. *Teagarten killed!* The assassin, Jason Bourne! *Jason Bourne!* Madness, *insanity*! What had *happened*? Was it a resurrection of *Hong Kong* and *Macao*? Was he losing what was left of his *mind*? Was he in some nightmare so real he had entered its dimensions, the horror of demented sleep, the fantasy of conjured, improvised terror turned into *reality*? He broke away from the crowd, reeled across the pavement, and leaned against the stone wall of a building, gasping for air, his neck now in pain, trying desperately to find a reasonable train of thought. Alex! *A telephone!*

'What *happened*?' he screamed into the mouthpiece to Vienna, Virginia.

'Come down and stay cold,' said Conklin in a low monotone. 'Listen to me. I want to know *exactly* where you are. Bernardine will pick you up and get you out. He'll make the arrangements and put you on the Concorde to New York.'

'Wait a minute – *wait* a minute! . . . The Jackal did this, didn't he?'

'From what we're told, it was a contract from a crazy jihad faction out of Beirut. They're claiming it was their kill. The actual executioner is unimportant. That may be true and it may not. At first I didn't buy it, not after DeSole and Armbruster, but the numbers add up. Teagarten was forever sounding off about sending NATO forces into Lebanon and levelling every suspected Palestinian enclave. He's been threatened before; it's just that the Medusa connection is too *damned* coincidental for me. But to answer your question, of course it was the Jackal.'

'So he laid it on me, *Carlos* laid it on *me*!'

'He's an ingenious fucker, I'll say that for him. You come after him and he uses a contract that freezes you in Paris.'

'Then we turn it *around*!'

'What the hell are you talking about? You get out!'

'No way. While he thinks I'm running, hiding, evading – I'm walking right into his nest.'

'You're nuts! You get out while we can still *get* you out!'

'No, I stay in. Number one, he figures I have to in order to reach him, but, as you say, he's locked me in ice. He thinks that after all these years I'll panic in my fashion and make stupid moves – God knows I made enough on Tranquillity – but so stupid here that his army of old men will find me by looking in the right places and knowing what to look for. *Christ*, he's good! Shake the bastard up so he'll make a mistake. I *know* him, Alex. I know the way he thinks and I'll out-think *him*. I'll stay on course, no prolonged safe cave for me.'

'Cave? *What* cave?'

'A figure of speech, forget it. I was in place *before* the news of Teagarten. I'm okay.'

'You're not okay, you're a fruitcake! Get *out*!'

'Sorry, Saint Alex, this is exactly where I want to be. I'm going after the Jackal.'

'Well, maybe I can move you off that place you're clinging to. I spoke to Marie a couple of hours ago. Guess what, you ageing Neanderthal? She's flying to Paris. To find you.'

'She *can't*!'

'That's what *I* said, but she wasn't in a listening mode. She said she knew all the places you and she used when you were running from us thirteen years ago. That you'd use them again.'

'I have. Several. But she *mustn't*!'

'Tell *her*, not me.'

'What's the Tranquillity number? I've been afraid to call her – to be honest, I've tried like *hell* to put her and the kids out of my mind.'

'That's the most reasonable statement you've made. Here it is.' Conklin recited the 809 area code number and the instant he had done so, Bourne slammed down the phone.

Frantically, Jason went through the agonizing process of relaying destination and credit card numbers, accompanied by the beeps and stutters of an overseas call to the Caribbean, and, finally, after subduing some idiot at the front desk of Tranquillity Inn, got through to his brother-in-law.

'Get Marie for me!' he ordered.

'*David?*'

'Yes . . . David. Get Marie.'

'I can't. She's gone. She left an hour ago.'

'*Where to?*'

'She wouldn't tell me. She chartered a plane out of Blackburne but she wouldn't tell me what international island she was going to. There's only Antigua or Martinique around here, but she could have flown to St Maartens or Puerto Rico. She's on her way to Paris.'

'Couldn't you have *stopped* her?'

'Christ, I tried, David. Goddamn it, I *tried*!'

'Did you ever think about locking her up?'

'*Marie?*'

'I see what you mean . . . She can't get here until tomorrow morning at the earliest.'

'Have you heard the news?' cried St Jacques. 'General *Teagarten* was killed and they say it was Jason—'

'Oh, shut up,'said Bourne, replacing the phone and leaving the booth, walking down the street to collect what thoughts he could generate.

Peter Holland, director of the Central Intelligence Agency, rose to his feet behind his desk and roared at the crippled man seated in front of him. 'Do *nothing*? Have you lost your fucking *senses*?'

'Did you lose yours when you issued that statement about a joint British-American operation in Hong Kong?'

'It was the goddamned truth!'

'There are truths and then again there are other truths, such as denying the truth when it doesn't serve the service.'

'*Shit!* Fairy politicians!'

'I'd hardly say that, Genghis Khan. I've heard of such men going to the wall, accepting execution rather than betraying the current truth they had to live by . . . You're off base, Peter.'

Exasperated, Holland sank back into his chair. 'Maybe I really don't belong here.'

'Maybe you don't, but give yourself a little more time. Maybe you'll become as dirty as the rest of us; it could happen, you know.'

The director leaned back, arching his head over the chair; he spoke in a broken cadence. 'I was dirtier than any of you in the field, Alex. I still wake up at night seeing the faces of young men staring at me as I ripped a knife up their chests, taking their lives away, somehow knowing that they had no idea why they were there.'

'It was either you or them. They would have put a bullet in your head if they could have.'

'Yes, I suppose so.' The DCI shot forward, his eyes locked with Conklin's. 'But that's not what we're talking about, is it?'

'You might say it's a variation on the theme.'

'Cut the horseshit.'

'It's a musician's term. I like music.'

'Then get to the main symphonic line, Alex. I like music, too.'

'All right. Bourne's disappeared. He told me that he thinks he's found a cave – his word, not mine – where he's convinced he can track the Jackal. He didn't say where it is, and God knows when he'll call me again.'

'I sent our man at the embassy over to the Pont-Royal, asking for Simon. What they told you is true. Simon checked in, went out, and never came back. Where *is* he?'

'Staying out of sight. Bernardine had an idea, but it blew up in his face. He thought he could quietly close in on Bourne by circulating the licence number of the rental car, but it wasn't picked up at the garage and we both agree it won't be. He doesn't trust anybody now, not even me, and considering his history, he has every right not to.'

Holland's eyes were cold and angry. 'You're not lying to me, are you, Conklin?'

'Why would I lie at a time like this, about a friend like this?'

'That's not an answer, it's a question.'

'Then no, I'm not lying. I don't know where he is.' And, in truth, Alex did not.

'So your idea is to do nothing.'

'There's nothing we can do. Sooner or later he'll call me.'

'Have you any idea what a Senate investigating committee will say a couple of weeks or months down the road when all this explodes, and it *will* explode? We covertly send a man known to be "Jason Bourne" over to Paris, which is as close to Brussels as New York is to Chicago—'

'Closer, I think.'

'Thanks, I need that . . . The illustrious commander of NATO is assassinated with said "Jason Bourne" taking credit for the kill, and we don't say a goddamned thing to anybody! *Jesus*, I'll be cleaning latrines on a tugboat!'

'But he didn't kill him.'

'You know that and *I* know that, but speaking of his history, there's a little matter of mental illness that'll come out the minute our clinical records are subpoenaed.'

'It's called amnesia; it has nothing to do with violence.'

'Hell, no, it's worse. He can't remember what he did.'

Conklin gripped his cane, his wandering eyes intense. 'I don't give a goddamn what everything appears to be, there's a gap. Every instinct I have tells me Teagarten's assassination is tied to *Medusa.* Somehow, somewhere, the wires crossed; a message was intercepted and a hell of a diversion was put in a game plan.'

'I believe I speak and understand English as well as you do,' said Holland, 'but right now I can't follow you.'

'There's nothing to follow, no arithmetic, no line of progression. I simply don't know . . . But Medusa's there.'

'With your testimony, I can pull in Burton on the Joint Chiefs, and certainly Atkinson in London.'

'No, leave them alone. Watch them but don't sink their dinghies, Admiral. Like Swayne's "retreat"', the bees will flock to the honey sooner or later.'

'Then what are you suggesting?'

'What I said when I came in here. Do nothing; it's the waiting game.' Alex suddenly slammed his cane against the table. 'Son of a bitch, it's *Medusa.* It *has* to be!'

The hairless old man with a wrinkled face struggled to his feet in a pew of the Church of the Blessed Sacrament in Neuilly-sur-Seine on the outskirts of Paris. Step by difficult step he made his painful way to the second confessional booth on the left. He pulled back the black curtain and knelt in front of the black latticework covered with black cloth, his legs in agony.

'*Angelus domini*, child of God,' said the voice from behind the screen. 'Are you well?'

'Far better for your generosity, monseigneur.'

'That pleases me, but I must be pleased more than that, as you know . . . What *happened* in Anderlecht? What does my beloved and well-endowed army *tell* me? Who has *presumed*?'

'We have dispersed and worked for the past eight hours, monseigneur. As near as we can determine, two men flew over from the United States – it is assumed so, for they spoke only American English – and took a room in a *pension de famille* across the street from the restaurant. They left the premises within minutes after the assault.'

'A frequency-detonated explosive!'

'Apparently, monseigneur. We have learned nothing else.'

'But why? *Why*?'

'We cannot see into men's minds, monseigneur.'

Across the Atlantic Ocean, in an opulent apartment in Brooklyn Heights with the lights of the East River and the Brooklyn Bridge seductively pulsating beyond the windows, a capo supremo lounged in an overstuffed couch, a glass of Perrier in his hand. He spoke to his friend sitting across from him in an armchair, drinking a gin and tonic. The young man was slender, dark-haired and striking.

'You know, Frankie, I'm not just bright, I'm brilliant, you know what I mean? I pick up on nuances – that's hints of what could be important and what couldn't – and I got a hell of a sense. I hear a spook *paisan* talk about things and I put four and four together and instead of eight, I get twelve. *Bingo!* It's the answer. There's this cat who calls himself "Bourne" a creep who makes like he's a major hit man but who isn't – he's a lousy *esca*, bait to pull in someone else, but *he's* the hot cannoli *we* want, see? Then the Jew shrink, being very under the weather, spits out everything I need. This cannoli's got only half a head, a *testa balzana;* a lot of the time he don't know who he is, or maybe what he does, right?'

'That's right, Lou.'

'And there this Bourne is in Paris, France, a couple of blocks away from a real big impediment, a fancy general the quiet boys across the river want taken out, like the two fatsoes already planted. *Capisce*?'

'I *capisco*, Lou,' said the clean-cut young man from the chair. 'You're real intelligent.'

'You don't know what the fuck I'm talking about, you *zabaglione.* I could be talking to myself, so why not? . . . So I get my twelve and I figure let's slam the loaded dice right into the felt, *see*?'

'I see, Lou.'

'We got to eliminate this asshole general because he's the impediment to the fancy crowd who needs us, right?'

'Right on, Lou. An imped – an im*ped*—'

'Don't bother, *zabaglione.* So I say to myself, let's blow him away and say the hot cannoli did it, *got* it?'

'Oh, yeah, Lou. You're *real* intelligent.'

'So we get rid of the impediment and put the cannoli, this Jason Bourne, who's not all there, in everybody's gun sights, right? If we don't get him, and this Jackal don't get him, the federals will, *right*?'

'Hey, that's terrific, Lou. I gotta say it, I really respect you.'

'Forget respect, *bello ragazzo*. The rules are different in this house. Come on over and make good love to me.'

The young man got up from the chair and walked over to the couch.

Marie sat in the back of the plane drinking coffee from a plastic cup, trying desperately to recall every place – every hiding and resting place – she and David had used thirteen years ago. There were the rock-bottom cafés in Montparnasse, the cheap hotels as well; and a motel – where was it? – ten miles outside of Paris, and an inn with a balcony in Argenteuil where David – *Jason* – first told her he loved her but could not stay with her *because* he loved her – the goddamned ass! And there was the Sacre-Coeur, far up on the steps where Jason – *David* – met the man in a dark alley who gave them the information they needed – what *was* it, who *was* he?

'*Mesdames et monsieurs*,' came the voice over the flight deck's loudspeaker. '*Je suis votre capitaine. Bienvenu.*' The pilot continued first in French, then he and his crew repeated the information in English, German, Italian and, finally with a female interpreter, in Japanese. 'We anticipate a very smooth flight to Marseilles. Our estimated flight time is seven hours and fourteen minutes, landing on or before schedule at six o'clock in the morning, Paris time. Enjoy.'

The moonlight outside bathed the ocean below as Marie St Jacques Webb looked out the window. She had flown to San Juan, Puerto Rico, and taken the night flight to Marseilles, where French immigration was at best a mass of confusion and, at worst, intentionally lax. At least that was the way it was thirteen years ago, a time she was re-entering. She would then take a domestic flight to Paris and she would find him. As she had done thirteen years ago, she *would find* him. She had to! As it had been thirteen years ago, if she did not, the man she loved was a dead man.

21

Morris Panov sat listlessly in a chair by a window looking out over the pasture of a farm somewhere, he assumed, in Maryland. He was in a small second-floor bedroom dressed in a hospital nightshirt, his bare right arm confirming the story he knew only too well. He had been drugged repeatedly, taken up to the moon, in the parlance of those who usually administered such narcotics. He had been mentally raped, his mind penetrated, violated, his innermost thoughts and secrets brought chemically to the surface and exposed.

The damage he had done was incalculable, he understood that; what he did not understand was why he was still alive. Even more perplexing was why he was being treated so deferentially. Why was his guard with the foolish black mask so courteous, the food plentiful and decent? It was as if the present imperative of his captivity was to restore his strength – profoundly sapped by the drugs – and make him as comfortable as possible under the extraordinarily difficult circumstances. *Why?*

The door opened and his masked guard walked in, a short heavyset man with a rasping voice Panov placed somewhere in the northeastern United States or possibly Chicago. In another situation he might have appeared comic, his large head too massive for the asinine Lone Ranger eye-covering, which would certainly not impede instant identification. However, in the current state of affairs, he was not comic at all; his obsequiousness was in itself menacing. Over his left arm were the psychiatrist's clothes.

'Okay, Doc, you gotta get dressed. I made sure everything was cleaned and pressed, even the undershorts. How about that?'

'You mean you have your own laundry and dry cleaners out here?'

'Fuck no, we take 'em over to – *oh*, no, you don't get me *that* way, Doc.' The guard grinned with slightly yellowed teeth beneath the black mask. 'Pretty smart, huh? You figure I'll tell you where we are, huh?'

'I was simply curious.'

'Yeah, sure. Like I got a nephew, my sister's kid, who's always "simply curious", askin' me questions I don't wanna answer. Like, "Hey, Unc, how'd you put me through medical school, huh." *Yeah!* He's a *doctor*, like *you*, what do you think of *that*?'

'I'd say his mother's brother is a very generous person.'

'Yeah, well, wadda you gonna do, huh? . . . Come on, put on the threads, Doc, we're going on a little trip.' The guard handed Mo his clothes.

'I suppose it would be foolish to ask where,' said Panov, getting out of the chair, removing his hospital nightshirt and putting on his shorts.

'Very foolish.'

'I hope not as foolish as your nephew not telling you about a symptom you have that I'd find somewhat alarming if I were you.' Mo casually pulled up his trousers.

'Wadda you talkin'?'

'Perhaps nothing,' replied Panov, putting on his shirt and sitting down to pull up his socks. 'When did you last see your nephew?'

'A couple of weeks ago. I put in some bread to cover his insurance. Shit, those mothers are *bleeders*! . . . Wadda you mean when did I last see the prick?'

'I just wondered if he said anything to you.'

'About *what*?'

'About your mouth.' Mo laced his shoes and gestured with his head. 'There's a mirror over the bureau, go take a look.'

'At what?' The capo subordinato walked quickly to the mirror.

'Smile.'

'At *what*?'

'Yourself . . . See the yellow on your teeth, the fading red of your gums and how the gums recede the higher they go?'

'So? They always been like that —'

'It might be nothing, but he should have spotted it.'

'Spotted *what*, for Christ's sake?'

'Oral ameloblastoma. Possibly.'

'What the hell is *that*? I don't brush too good and I don't like dentists. They're butchers!'

'You mean you haven't seen a dentist or an oral surgeon in quite a while?'

'So?' The capo bared his teeth again in front of the mirror.

'That could explain why your nephew didn't say anything.'

'Why?'

'He probably figures you have regular dental checkups, so let those people explain it to you.' Shoes tied, Panov stood up.

'I don't getcha.'

'Well, he's grateful for everything you've done for him, appreciative of your generosity. I can understand why he'd hesitate telling you.'

'Telling me *what*?' The guard spun away from the mirror.

'I could be wrong but you really ought to see a periodontist.' Mo put on his jacket. 'I'm ready,' he said. 'What do we do now?'

The capo subordinato, his eyes squinting, his forehead creased in ignorance and suspicion, reached into his pocket and pulled out a large black kerchief. 'Sorry, Doc, but I gotta blindfold you.'

'Is that so you can put a bullet in my head when, mercifully, I don't know it's going to happen?'

'No, doctor. No bam-bam for you. You're too valuable.'

'*Valuable?*' asked the capo supremo rhetorically in his opulent living room in

Brooklyn Heights. 'Like a gold mine just popped out of the ground and landed in your minestrone. This Jew has worked on the heads of some of the biggest lasagnas in Washington. His files have got to be worth the price of Detroit.'

'You'll never get them, Louis,' said the attractive middle-aged man dressed in an expensive tropical worsted suit sitting across from his host. 'They'll be sealed and carted off out of your reach.'

'Well, we're working on that, Mr Park Avenue, Manhattan. Say – just for laughs – say we got 'em. What are they worth to you?'

The guest permitted himself a thin aristocratic smile. 'Detroit?' he replied.

'*Va bene!* I like you, you got a sense of humour.' As abruptly as he had grinned, the mafioso became serious, even ugly. 'The five mill still holds for this Bourne-Webb character, right?'

'With a proviso.'

'I don't like provisos, Mr Lawyer. I don't like them at *all.*'

'We can go elsewhere. You're not the only game in town.'

'Let me explain something to you, Signor Avvocato. In a lot of ways, we – all of *we* – *are* the only game in town. We don't mess with other families' hits, you know what I mean? Our councils have decided hits are too personal; it makes for bad blood.'

'Will you listen to the proviso? I don't think you'll be offended.'

'Shoot.'

'I wish you'd use another word—'

'Go ahead.'

'There'll be a two-million-dollar bonus because we insist you include Webb's wife and his government friend Conklin.'

'Done, Mr Park Avenue, Manhattan.'

'Good. Now to the rest of our business.'

'I want to talk about the Jew.'

'We'll get to him—'

'*Now.*'

'Please don't give orders to me,' said the attorney from one of Wall Street's most prestigious firms. 'You're really not in a position to do that, *wop.*'

'Hey, *farrabutto*! You don't talk to me like that!'

'I'll talk to you any way I like . . . On the outside, and to your credit in negotiations, you're a very masculine, very macho fellow.' The lawyer calmly uncrossed and crossed his legs. 'But the inside's quite different, isn't it? You've got a soft heart, or should I say hard loins, for pretty young men.'

'*Silenzio!*' The Italian shot forward on the couch.

'I have no wish to exploit the information. On the other hand, I don't believe Gay Rights are very high on the Cosa Nostra's agenda, do you?'

'You son of a *bitch*!'

'You know, when I was a young army lawyer in Saigon, I defended a career lieutenant who was caught *in flagrante delicto* with a Vietnamese boy, a male prostitute obviously. Through legal manoeuvres, using ambiguous phrases in the military code regarding civilians, I saved him from a dishonourable discharge, but it was obvious that he had to resign from the service. Unfortunately, he never went on to a productive life; he shot himself two hours after the verdict. You see, he'd become a pariah, a disgrace before his peers and he couldn't handle the burden.'

'Get on with your business,' said the capo supremo named Louis, his voice low and flat and filled with hatred.

'Thank you . . . First, I left an envelope on your foyer table. It contains payment for Armbruster's tragic confrontation in Georgetown and Teagarten's equally tragic assassination in Brussels.'

'According to the yid head doctor,' interrupted the mafioso, 'you got two more they know about. An ambassador in London and that admiral on the Joint Chiefs. You wanna add another bonus?'

'Possibly later, not now. They both know very little and nothing about the financial operations. Burton thinks that we're essentially an ultraconservative veterans' lobbying effort that grew out of the Vietnam disgrace – legally borderline for him, but then he has strong patriotic feelings. Atkinson's a rich dilettante; he does what he's told, but he doesn't know why or by whom. He'd do anything to hold on to the Court of Saint James's and has; his only connection was with Teagarten . . . Conklin hit pay dirt with Swayne and Armbruster, Teagarten and, of course, DeSole, but the other two are window dressing, quite respectable window dressing. I wonder how it happened.'

'When I find out, and I *will* find out, I'll let you know, gratis.'

'Oh?' The attorney raised his eyebrows. 'How?'

'We'll get to it. What's your other business?'

'Two items, both vital, and the first I'll give *you* – gratis. Get rid of your current boyfriend. He goes to places he shouldn't and throws money around like a cheap hoodlum. We're told he boasts about his connection in high places. We don't know what else he talks about or what he knows or what he's pieced together, but he concerns us. I'd think he'd concern you, too.'

'*Il prostituto!*' roared Louis, slamming his clenched fist down on the arm of the couch. '*Il pinguino!* He's dead.'

'I accept your thanks. The other item is far more important, certainly to us. Swayne's house in Manassas. A book was removed, an office diary, which Swayne's lawyer in Manassas – our lawyer in Manassas – could not find. It was on a bookshelf, its binding identical to all the other books in that row, the entire row on the shelf. A person would have to know *exactly* which one to take.'

'So what do you want from me?'

'The gardener was your man. He was put in place to do his job, and he was given the only number we knew was totally secure, namely, DeSole's.'

'*So?*'

'To do his job, to mount the suicide authentically, he had to study Swayne's every move. You yourself explained that to me ad nauseam when you demanded your outrageous fee. It's not hard to picture your man peering through the window at Swayne in his study, the place where Swayne supposedly would take his life. Gradually your man realizes that the general keeps taking a specific book from off his shelf, writes in it, and returns it to the same spot. That has to intrigue him; that particular book has to be valuable. Why wouldn't he take it? I would, *you* would. So where is it?'

The mafioso got slowly, menacingly to his feet. 'Listen to me, Avvocato, you gotta lot of fancy words that make for conclusions, but we ain't got no book like that and I'll tell you how I can *prove it*! If there was anything anywhere written down that could burn your ass, I'd be shoving it in your face right now, *capisce*?'

'That's not illogical,' said the well-dressed attorney, once again uncrossing and crossing his legs as the resentful capo sullenly returned to the couch. 'Flannagan,' added the Wall Street lawyer. 'Naturally . . . of course, *Flannagan.* He and his hairdresser bitch had to have their insurance policy, no doubt with minor extortion in the bargain. Actually, I'm relieved. They could never use it without exposing themselves. Accept my apologies, Louis?'

'Your business finished?'

'I believe so.'

'Now, the Jew shrink.'

'What about him?'

'Like I said, he's a gold mine.'

'Without his patients' files, less than twenty-four carat, I think.'

'Then you think wrong,' countered Louis. 'Like I told Armbruster before he became another big impediment for you, we got doctors, too. Specialists in all kinds of medical things, including what they call motor responses and, get this, "triggered mental recall under states of external control" – I remembered that one especially. It's a whole different kind of gun at your head, only no blood.'

'I assume there's a point to this.'

'You can bet your country club on it. We're moving the Jew to a place in Pennsylvania, a kind of nursing home where only the richest people go to get dried out or straightened out, if ya know what I mean.'

'I believe I do. Advanced medical equipment, superior staff – well-patrolled grounds.'

'Yeah, sure you do. A lot of your crowd passes through—'

'Go on,' interrupted the attorney, looking at his gold Rolex watch. 'I haven't much time.'

'Make time for this. According to my specialists – and I purposely used the word "my", if you follow me – on a prearranged schedule, say every fourth or fifth day, the new patient is "shot up to the moon" – that's the phrase they use, it's not mine, Christ knows. Between times he's been treated real good. He's been fed the right neutermints or whatever they are, given the proper exercise, a lot of sleep and all the rest of that shit . . . We should all be so careful of our bodies, right, Avvocato?'

'Some of us play squash every other day.'

'Well, you'll forgive me, Mr Park Avenue, Manhattan, but squash to me is zucchini and I eat it.'

'Linguistic and cultural differences do crop up, don't they?'

'Yeah, I can't fault you there, Consigliere.'

'Hardly. And my title is attorney.'

'Give me time. It could be Consigliere.'

'There's not enough years in our lifetimes, Louis. Do you go on or do I leave?'

'I go on, Mr Attorney . . . So each time the Jew shrink is shot up to that moon my specialist talks about, he's in pretty good shape, right?'

'I see the periodic remissions to normalcy, but then I'm not a doctor.'

'I don't know what the fuck you're talking about, but then I'm not a doctor, either, so I'll take my specialist's word for it. You see, every time he's shot up, his mind is pretty clear inside, and then he's fed name after name after name. A lot, maybe most, won't mean a thing, but every now and then one will, and then another, and another. With each, they start what they call a probe, finding out bits and pieces of information, just enough to get a sketch of the patient he's talking about – just enough to scare the shit out of that lasagna when he's reached. Remember, these are stressful times and this Hebe doctor treats some of the fattest cats in Washington, in and outside the government. How does that grab you, Mr Attorney?'

'It's certainly unique,' replied the guest slowly, studying the capo supremo. 'His files, of course, would be infinitely preferable.'

'Yeah, well, like I say, we're working on that, but it'll take time. This is now, *immediato*. He'll be in Pennsylvania in a couple of hours. You want to deal? You and me?'

'Over what? Something you don't have and may never get?'

'Hey, come on, what do you think I am?'

'I'm sure you don't want to hear that—'

'Cut the crap. Say in a day or so, maybe a week, we meet and I give you a list of names I think you might be interested in, all of which we got information on – let's say information not readily available. You pick one or two or maybe none, what can you lose? We're talkin' spitballs anyway, 'cause the deal's between you and me only. No one else is involved except my specialist and his assistant who don't know you and you don't know them.'

'A side arrangement, as it were?'

'Not as it were, like it is. Depending on the information. I'll figure out the charge. It may only be a thou or two, or it may go to twenty, or it may be gratis, who knows? I'd be fair because I want your business, *capisce?*'

'It's very interesting.'

'You know what my specialist says? He says we could start our own cottage industry, he called it. Snatch a dozen shrinks, all with heavy government connections, like in the Senate or even the White House—'

'I understand fully,' interrupted the attorney, getting to his feet, 'but my time's up . . . Bring me a list, Louis.' The guest walked towards the short marble foyer.

'No fancy attaché case, Signor Avvocato?' said the capo, rising from the couch.

'And upset the not so delicate mechanisms in your doorway?'

'Hey, it's a violent world out there.'

'I wouldn't know about that.'

The Wall Street attorney left, and at the sound of the closing door, Louis rushed across the room to the inlaid Queen Anne desk and virtually pounced on the ivory French telephone – as usual, tipping over the tall thin instrument twice before securing the stem with one hand while dialling with the other. 'Fucking swish horn!' he mumbled. 'Goddamned fairy decorator! . . . *Mario?*'

'Hello, Lou,' said the pleasant voice in New Rochelle. 'I'll bet you called to wish Anthony a happy birthday, huh?'

'Who?'

'My kid, Anthony. He's fifteen today, did you forget? The whole family's out in the garden and we miss you, Cousin. And hey, Lou, what a garden this year. I'm a real artist.'

'You also may be something else.'

'What?'

'Buy Anthony a present and send me the bill. At fifteen, maybe a broad. He's ready for manhood.'

'Lou, you're too much. There are other things—'

'There's only *one* thing now, Mario, and I want the truth from your lips or I'll carve them out of your face!'

There was a brief pause from New Rochelle before the pleasant-sounding executioner spoke. 'I don't deserve to be talked to that way, *cugino.*'

'Maybe, maybe not. There was a book taken from that general's place in Manassas, a very valuable book.'

'They found out it was missing, huh?'

'Holy *shit*! You got it?'

'I *had* it, Lou. It was going to be a present to you, but I lost it.'

'You *lost* it? What the fuck did you do, leave it in a *taxi*?'

'No, I was running for my life, that maniac with the flares, what's his name, Webb, unloading at me in the driveway. He grazed me and I fell and the lousy book flew out of my hand – just as the police car arrived. He picked it up and I ran like hell for the fence.'

'*Webb's* got it?'

'I guess so.'

'Christ on a trampoline . . . !'

'Anything else, Lou? We're about to light the candles on the cake.'

'Yeah, Mario, I may need you in Washington – a big cannoli without a foot but with a book.'

'Hey, wait a minute, *cugino*, you know my rules. Always a month between business trips. What did Manassas take? Six weeks? And last May in Key West, three, almost four weeks? I can't call, I can't write a postcard – no, Lou, always a month. I got responsibilities to Angie and the children. I'm not going to be an absentee parent; they've got to have a role model, you know what I mean?'

'I got Ozzie Nelson for a fuckin' cousin!' Louis slammed down the phone, and instantly grabbed it as it crashed over on the desk. its delicate ivory stem displaying a crack. 'The best hit man in the business and he's a freak,' mumbled the capo supremo as he dialled frantically. When the line was picked up, the anxiety and the anger disappeared from his voice; it was not apparent but it had not gone away. 'Hello, Frankie baby, how's my closest friend?'

'Oh, hi, Lou,' came the floating, but hesitant, languorous tones from an expensive apartment in Greenwich Village. 'Can I call you back in two minutes? I'm just putting my mother into a cab to take her back to Jersey. Okay?'

'Sure, kid. Two minutes.' *Mother?* The whore! *Il pinguino!* Louis walked to his mirrored marbled bar with the pink angles flying over the Lalique inset above the whisky bottles. He poured himself a drink and took several calming swallows. The bar phone rang. 'Yeah?' he said, carefully picking up the fragile crystal instrument.

'It's me, Lou. Frankie. I said goodbye to Mama.'

'That's a good boy, Frankie. Never forget your mama.'

'Oh, I never do, Lou. You taught me that. You told me you gave your mama the biggest funeral they ever saw in East Hartford.'

'Yeah, I bought the fuckin' church, man.'

'Real nice, real nice.'

'Now let's get to something else real nice, okay? It's been one of those days, Frankie, lots of turmoil, you know what I mean?'

'Sure, Lou.'

'So I got an itch. I gotta get some relief. Come on over here, Frankie.'

'As fast as a cab can take me, Lou.'

Prostituto! It would be Frankie the Big Mouth's last service for him.

Out on the street, the well-dressed attorney walked two blocks south and a block east to his waiting limousine parked beneath the canopy of another impressive residence in Brooklyn Heights. His stocky chauffeur of middle years was talking pleasantly with the uniformed doorman, whom he had generously tipped by now. Spotting his employer, the driver walked rapidly to the limousine's rear door and opened it. Several minutes later they were in traffic heading for the bridge.

In the quiet of the backseat, the lawyer undid his alligator belt, pressed the upper and lower rims of the buckle, and a small cartridge fell out between his legs. He picked it up and refastened the belt.

Holding the cartridge up to the filtered light from the window, he studied the miniaturized voice-activated recording device. It was an extraordinary machine, tiny enough and with an acrylic mechanism that permitted it to fly through the most sophisticated detectors. The attorney leaned forward in his seat and spoke to the driver. '*William*?'

'Yes, sir.' The chauffeur glanced up at his rearview mirror and saw his employer's outstretched hand; he reached back.

'Take this over to the house and put it on a cassette, will you, please?'

'Right, Major.'

The Manhattan lawyer reclined in the seat, smiling to himself. Louis would give him anything he wanted from now on. A capo did not make side arrangements where the family was concerned, say nothing of acknowledging certain sexual preferences.

Morris Panov sat blindfolded in the front seat of the sedan with his guard, his hands loosely, almost courteously bound, as if the capo subordinato felt he was following unnecessary orders. They had been driving for about thirty minutes in silence when the guard spoke.

'What's a perry-oh-dentist?' he asked.

'An oral surgeon, a doctor trained to operate inside patients' mouths on problems relating to teeth and gum tissue.'

Silence. Then seven minutes later: 'What kind of problems?'

'Any number of them, from infections to scraping the roots to more complicated surgery usually in tandem with an oncologist.'

Silence. Four minutes later: 'What was that last – the tandy-uncle stuff?'

'Oral cancer. If it's caught in time, it can be arrested with minor bone removal . . . If not, the entire jaw might have to go.' Panov could feel the car briefly swerve as the driver momentarily lost control.

Silence. A minute and a half later: 'The whole fuckin' jaw? Half the face?'

'It's either that or the whole of the patient's life.'

Thirty seconds later: 'You think I could *have* something like that?'

'I'm a doctor, not an alarmist. I merely noted a symptom, I did not make a diagnosis.'

'So *bullshit*! So make a dagassnossis!'

'I'm not qualified!'

'Bullshit! You're a doctor, ain't you? I mean a real doctor, not a *fasullo* who says he is but ain't got no shingle that's legit.'

'If you mean medical school, yes, I'm that kind of doctor.'

'So look at me!'

'I can't. I'm blindfolded.' Panov suddenly felt the guard's thick strong hand clawing at his head, yanking the kerchief off him. The dark interior of the automobile answered a question for Mo: How could anyone travel in a car with a blindfolded passenger? In that car it was no problem; except for the windshield, the windows were not merely tinted, they were damn near opaque, which meant from the outside they *were* opaque. No one could see inside.

'Go on, *look*!'

'What?' The capo subordinato, his eyes on the road, his large head tilted grotesquely towards Panov; his thick lips parted and his teeth bared like those of a child playing monster in the mirror, he shouted again. 'So tell me what you see!'

'It's too dark in here,' replied Mo, seeing essentially what he wanted to see in the front window; they were on a country road, so narrow and so country the next step lower was dirt. Wherever he was being taken, he was being driven there by an extremely circuitous route.

'Open the fuckin' *window*!' yelled the guard, his head still twisted, his eyes still on the road, his gaping mouth approaching a caricature of Orca, the about-to-vomit whale. 'Don't hold nothin' back. I'll break every goddamn finger in that prick's hands! He can do his fuckin' surgery with his elbows! . . . I told that stupid sister of mine he was no fuckin' good, that fairy. Always readin' books, no action on the street, y'know what I mean?'

'If you'll stop shouting for a few seconds, I can get a closer look,' said Panov, having lowered the window at his side, seeing nothing but trees and the coarse underbrush of a *distinctly* backcountry road, one he doubted was on too many maps. 'There we are,' continued Mo, raising his loosely bound hands to the capo's mouth, his eyes, however, not on that mouth but on the road ahead.

'Oh, my God!' cried Panov.

'*What?*' screamed the guard.

'Pus. Pockets of pus everywhere. In the upper and lower mandibles. The worst sign.'

'Oh, *Christ*!' The car swerved with the shock of revelation – but it did not swerve enough.

A huge *tree*. Up ahead. On the left-hand side of the deserted road! Morris Panov surged his bound hands over to the wheel, lifting his body off the seat as he propelled the steering wheel to the left. Then at the last second before the car hit the tree, he hurled himself to the right, curling into a foetal position for protection.

The crash was enormous. Shattered glass and crushed metal accompanied the rising mists of steam from burst cylinders, and the growing fires of viscous fluids underneath that soon would reach a gas tank. The guard was moaning, not dead, his face bleeding; Panov pulled him out of the wreck and into the grass as far as he could until exhaustion overtook him, just before the car exploded.

In the moist overgrowth, his breath somewhat restored but his fear still at the forefront, Mo released his loosely bound hands and picked the fragments of glass out of his guard's face. He then checked for broken bones – the right arm and the left leg were candidates – and with stolen stationery from a hotel he had never heard of from the capo's pocket, he used the guard's pen to write out his diagnosis. Among the items he removed was a gun – what kind, he had no idea – but it was heavy and too large for his pocket and sagged in his belt.

Enough. Hippocrates had his limits.

Panov searched the guard's clothing, astonished at the money that was there – some six thousand dollars – and the various driver's licences – five different identities from five different states. He took the money and the licences to turn them over to Alex Conklin, but he left the capo's wallet otherwise intact. There were photographs of his family, his children, grandchildren and assorted relatives – and somewhere among them a young surgeon he had put through medical school. Ciao, *amico*, thought Mo as he crawled over to the road, stood up and smoothed his clothes, trying to look as respectable as possible.

Standing on the hard coarse surface, common sense dictated that he continue north, in the direction the car was heading; to return south was not only pointless, it was conceivably dangerous. Suddenly, it struck him.

Good God! Did I just do what I just did?

He began to tremble, the trained psychiatrically oriented part of him telling him it was postpartum trauma.

Bullshit, you asshole. It wasn't you!

He started walking, and then kept walking and walking and walking. He was not on a backcountry road, he was on *Tobacco* Road. There were no signs of civilization, not a car in either direction, not a house – not even the ruins of an old farmhouse – or a primitive stone wall that would at least have proved that humans had visited the environs. Mile after mile passed and Mo fought off the effects of the drug-induced exhaustion. How long had it been? They had taken his watch, his watch with the day and date in impossible small print, so he had no idea of either the present time or the time that had elapsed since he had been taken from the Walter Reed Hospital. He had to find a telephone. He had to reach Alex Conklin! Something had to happen soon!

It did.

He heard the growing roar of an engine and spun around. A red car was speeding up the road from the south – no, not speeding, but racing, with its accelerator flat to the floor. He waved his arms wildly, gestures of helplessness and appeal. To no avail; the vehicle rushed past him in a blur . . . then to his delighted surprise the air was filled with dust and screeching brakes. The car *stopped*! He ran ahead as the automobile actually backed up, the tyres still screaming. He remembered the words his mother incessantly repeated when he was a youngster in the Bronx: *Always tell the truth, Morris. It's the shield God gave us to keep us righteous.*

Panov did not precisely subscribe to the admonition, but there were times when he felt it had socially interactive validity. This might be one of them. So, somewhat out of breath he approached the opened passenger window of the red automobile. He looked inside at the woman driver, a platinum blonde in her mid-thirties with an overly made-up face and large breasts encased in decolletage more fitting to an X-rated film than a backcountry road in Maryland. Nevertheless, his mother's words echoed in his ears, so he spoke the truth.

'I realize that I look rather shabby, madam, but I assure you it's purely an exterior impression. I'm a doctor and I've been in an accident—'

'Get in, for Christ's sake!'

'Thank you so very much.' No sooner had Mo closed the door than the woman slammed the car into gear, gunned the engine to its maximum, and seemingly launched off the rough pavement and down the road. 'You're obviously in a hurry,' offered Panov.

'So would you be, pal, if you were me. I gotta husband back there who's puttin' his truck together to come after my ass!'

'Oh, really?'

'Stupid fuckin' jerk! He rolls across the country three weeks outta the month layin' every broad on the highways, then blows his keister when he finds out I had a little fun of my own.'

'Oh, I'm terribly sorry.'

'You'll be a hell of a lot sorrier if he catches up with us.'

'I beg your pardon?'

'You really a doctor?'

'Yes, I am.'

'Maybe we can do business.'

'I *beg* your pardon?'

'Can you handle an abortion?'

Morris Panov closed his eyes.

22

Bourne walked for nearly an hour through the streets of Paris trying to clear his head, ending up at the Seine, on the Pont de Solferino, the bridge that led to the Quai des Tuileries and the gardens. As he leaned against the railing absently watching the boats lazily ploughing the waters below, the question kept assaulting him. Why, why, *why*? What did Marie think she was *doing*? Flying over to Paris! It wasn't just foolish, it was stupid – yet his wife was neither a fool nor an idiot. She was a very bright lady with reserves of control and a quick, analytical mind. That's what made her decision so untenable; what could she possibly hope to accomplish? She had to know he was far safer working alone rather than worrying about her while tracking the Jackal. Even if she found him, the risk was doubled for both of them, and *that* she had to completely understand. Figures and projections were her profession. So *why*?

There was only one conceivable answer, and it infuriated him. She thought he might slip back over the edge as he had done in Hong Kong, where she alone had brought him to his senses, to the reality that was uniquely his own, a reality of frightening half truths and only partial remembrances, episodic moments she lived with every day of their lives together. *God*, how he adored her; he loved her so! And the fact that she had made this foolish, stupid, *untenable* decision only fuelled that love because it was so – so giving, so outrageously unselfish. There were moments in the Far East when he had craved his own death, if only to expunge the guilt he felt at putting her in such dangerous – untenable? – positions. The guilt was still there, *always* there, but the ageing man in him recognized another reality. Their children. The cancer of the Jackal had to be ripped out of *all* their lives. Couldn't she realize that and leave him *alone*?

No. For she was not flying to Paris to save his life – she had too much confidence in Jason Bourne for that. She was coming to Paris to save his mind. *I'll handle it, Marie. I can and will handle it!*

Bernardine. He could do it. The Deuxième could find her at Orly or De Gaulle. Find her and take her, put her under guard at a hotel and claim no one knew where he was. Jason ran from the Pont de Solferino to the Quai des Tuileries and to the first telephone he could find.

'Can you *do* it?' asked Bourne. 'She's only got one updated passport and it's American, not Canadian.'

'I can try on my own,' answered Bernardine, 'but not with any help from the

Deuxième. I don't know how much Saint Alex told you, but at the moment my consultant status has been cancelled and I think my desk has been thrown out the window.'

'*Shit!*'

'*Merde* to the triple, *mon ami.* The Quai d'Orsay wants my underwear burned with me in it, and were it not for certain information I possess regarding several members of the Assembly, they would no doubt revive the guillotine.'

'Can you pass around some money at immigration?'

'It would be better if I acted in my former official capacity on the assumption that the Deuxième does not so swiftly advertise its embarrassments. Her full name, please.'

'Marie Elise St Jacques Webb—'

'Ah, yes, I recall now, at least the St Jacques,' broke in Bernardine. 'The celebrated Canadian economist. The newspapers were filled with her photograph. *La belle mademoiselle.*'

'It was exposure she could have done without.'

'I'm certain it was.'

'Did Alex say anything about Mo Panov?'

'Your doctor friend?'

'Yes.'

'I'm afraid not.'

'*Goddamn* it!'

'If I may, you must think of yourself now.'

'I understand.'

'Will you pick up the car?'

'Should I?'

'Frankly, I wouldn't, if I were you. It's unlikely, but the invoice might be traced back to me. There's risk, however minor.'

'That's what I thought. I bought a *métro* map. I'll use the trains . . . When can I call you?'

'Give me four, perhaps five hours to get back here from the airports. As our saint explained, your wife could be leaving from several different points of embarkation. To get all those passenger manifests will take time.'

'Concentrate on the flights arriving early tomorrow morning. She can't fake a passport, she wouldn't know how to do it.'

'According to Alex, one does not underestimate Marie Elise St Jacques. He even spoke French. He said she was *formidable.*'

'She can come at you from the outer limits, I'll tell you that.'

'*Qu'est-ce que c'est?*'

'She's an original, let's leave it there.'

'And you?'

'I'm taking the subway. It's getting dark. I'll call you after midnight.'

'*Bonne chance.*'

'*Merci.*'

Bourne left the booth knowing his next move as he limped down the Quai, the bandage around his knee forcing him to assume a damaged leg. There was a *métro* station by the Tuileries where he would catch a train to Havre-Caumartin and switch to the Regional Express north line past St Denis Basilique to Argenteuil. Argenteuil, a town of the Dark Ages founded by Charlemagne in honour of a nunnery fourteen centuries ago, now a city that housed the message centre of a killer as brutal as any man who roamed the bloody fields with a broadsword in Charlemagne's barbaric days, then as now celebrating and sanctifying brutality in the shadows of religiosity.

Le Coeur du Soldat was not on a street or a boulevard or an avenue. Instead, it was in a dead-end alleyway around the corner and across from a long-since closed factory whose faded signs indicated a once flourishing metallurgical refining plant in what had to be the ugliest part of the city. Nor was the Soldat listed in the telephone directory; it was found by innocently asking strangers where it was, as the inquirer was to meet *une grosse secousse* at this undiscoverable *pissoir.* The more dilapidated the buildings and the filthier the streets, the more cogent were the directions.

Bourne stood in the dark narrow alley leaning against the aged rough brick of the opposing structure across from the bistro's entrance. Above the thick massive door in square block letters, several missing, was a dull red sign: L C eur d Soldat. As the door was sporadically opened for entering or departing clientele, metallic martial music blared forth into the alley; and the clientele were not candidates for an haute couture cotillion. His appearance was in keeping, thought Jason, as he struck a wooden match against the brick, lighting a thin black cigar as he limped towards the door.

Except for the language and the deafening music, it might have been a waterfront bar in Sicily's Palermo, reflected Bourne as he made his way to the crowded bar, his squinting eyes roaming, absorbing everything he could observe – briefly confused, wondering when he had been in Palermo, Sicily. A heavyset man in a tank shirt got off a stool; Jason slid on top of it.

The clawlike hand gripped his shoulder; Bourne slapped his right hand up, grabbing the wrist and twisting it clockwise, pushing the barstool away and rising to his full height. 'What's your problem?' he asked calmly in French but loud enough to be heard.

'That's my seat, *pig*! I'm just taking a piss!'

'So maybe when you're finished, I'll take one,' said Jason, his gaze boring into the man's eyes, the strength of his grip unmistakable – emphasized by pressing his adversary's nerve with his thumb which had nothing to do with strength.

'*Ah*, you're a fucking *cripple* . . . !' cried the man, trying not to wince. 'I don't pick on invalids.'

'I'll tell you what,' said Bourne, releasing his thumb. 'You come back, we'll take turns, and I'll buy you a drink each time you let me get off this bum leg of mine, okay?'

Looking up at Jason, the heavyset man slowly grinned. 'Hey, you're all right.'

'I'm not all right, but I'm certainly not looking for a fight, either. Shit, you'd hammer me to the floor.' Bourne released the muscular Tank Shirt's arm.

'I'm not so sure of *that*,' said the man, now laughing and holding his wrist. 'Sit, *sit*! I'll take a piss and come back and buy *you* a drink. You don't look like you're loaded with francs.'

'Well, like they say, appearances are deceiving,' replied Jason, sitting down. 'I've got different, better clothes and an old friend told me to meet him here but not to wear them . . . I just got back from good money in Africa. You know, training the savages—'

Cymbals crashed in the metallic, deafening martial music as Tank Shirt's eyes widened. '*Africa?*' interrupted the stranger. 'I knew it! That grip – *LPN*.'

What remained of the Chameleon's memory data banks expanded into the code. LPN – *Légion Patria Nostra*. France's Foreign Légion, the mercenaries of the world. It was not what he had in mind, but it would certainly do. 'Christ, you too?' he asked, again coarsely but innocently.

'La Légion étrangère! "The Légion is our Fatherland"!'

'This is crazy!'

'We don't announce ourselves, of course. There's great jealousy, naturally, because we were the best and we were paid for it, but still these are our people. *Soldiers!*'

'When did you leave the Légion?' asked Bourne, sensing a cloud that could be troublesome.

'*Ah*, nine years ago! They threw me out before my second conscription for overweight. They were right and they probably saved my life. I'm from Belgique, a corporal!'

'I was discharged a month ago, before my first term was over. Wounds during our incursion into Angola and the fact that they figured I was older than my papers said. They don't pay for extended recoveries.' How easily the words came.

'Angola? We did *that*? What was the d'Orsay *thinking* about.'

'I don't know. I'm a soldier, I follow orders and don't question those I can't understand.'

'*Sit!* My kidneys are bursting. I'll be right back. Maybe we know friends . . . I never heard of any Angola operation.'

Jason leaned forward over the bulging bar and ordered *une bière*, grateful that the bartender was too busy and the music too loud for the man to have overheard the conversation. However, he was infinitely more grateful to Saint Alex of Conklin, whose primary advice to a field agent was to 'get in bad with a mark first before you get in good,' the theory being that the reversal from hostility to amiability was far stronger for the change. Bourne swallowed the beer in relief. He had made a friend at Le Coeur du Soldat. It was an inroad, minor but vital, and perhaps not so minor.

Tank Shirt returned, his thick arm around the shoulders of a younger man in his early twenties, of medium height and with the physique of a large safe; he was wearing an American field jacket. Jason started to get off the barstool. 'Sit, *sit*!' cried his new friend, leaning forward to be heard through the crowds and the music. 'I brought us a virgin.'

'*What?*'

'You forgot so quickly? He's on his way to becoming a Légion recruit.'

'Oh, that,' laughed Bourne, covering his gaffe. 'I wondered in a place like this—'

'In a place like this,' broke in Tank Shirt, 'half will take it or give it either way as long as it's rough. But that's neither here nor there, I thought he should talk to you. He's American and his French is *grotesque*, but if you speak slow, he'll catch on.'

'No need to,' said Jason in faintly accented English. 'I grew up in Neufchâtel but I spent several years in the States.'

'That's nice to heah.' The American's speech was distinctly Deep South, his smile genuine, his eyes wary but unafraid.

'Then let us start again,' said the Belgian in heavily accented English. 'My name is . . . Maurice, it's as good a name as any. My young friend here is Ralph, at least he says it is. What's yours, my wounded hero?'

'François,' replied Jason, thinking of Bernardine and wondering briefly how he was doing at the airports. 'And I'm no hero; they die too quickly . . . Order your drinks, I'm paying.' They did and Bourne did, his mind racing, trying to recall the little he knew about the French Foreign Legion. 'A lot has changed in nine years, Maurice.' *How very easily the words came,* thought the Chameleon. 'Why are you enlisting, Ralph?'

'Ah figure it's the wisest thing I can do – kinda disappear for a few years, and I understand five is the minimum.'

'If you last the first, *mon ami*,' interjected the Belgian.

'Maurice is right. Listen to him. The officers are tough and difficult—'

'All *French*!' added the Belgian. 'Ninety percent, at least. Only one in perhaps three hundred *étrangers* reach the officer corps. Have no illusions.'

'But Ah'm a college man. An engineer.'

'So you'll build fine latrines for the camps and design perfect shit holes in the field,' laughed Maurice. 'Tell him, François. Explain how the *savants* are treated.'

'The educated ones must first know how to fight,' said Jason, hoping he was right.

'*Always* first!' exclaimed the Belgian. 'For their schooling is suspicious. Will they doubt? Will they think when they are paid only to follow orders? . . . Oh, no, *mon ami*, I would not emphasize your *érudition*.'

'Let it come out gradually,' added Bourne. 'When they need it, not when you want to offer it.'

'*Bien!*' cried Maurice. 'He knows what he's talking about. A true *légionnaire*!'

'Can you fight?' asked Jason. 'Could you go after someone to kill him?'

'Ah killed mah *feeancee* and her two brothers and a cousin, all with a knife and my bare hands. She was fuckin' a big banker in Nashville and they were coverin' for her because he was payin all of 'em a lot of money . . . Yeah, I can kill, Mr François.'

Manhunt for Crazed Killer in Nashville

Young Engineer with Promising Future Escapes Dragnet . . .

Bourne remembered the newspaper headlines of only weeks ago, as he stared at the face of the young American. 'Go for the Légion,' he said.

'If push comes to shove, Mr François, could I use you as a reference?'

'It wouldn't help you, young man, it might only hurt. If you're pressed, just tell the truth. It's your credentials.'

'*Aussi bien!* He knows the Legion. They will not take maniacs if they can help it, but they – how do you say it, François?'

'Look the other way, I think.'

'*Oui.* They look the other way when there are – *encore*, François?'

'When there are extenuating circumstances.'

'*See?* My friend François also has brains. I wonder how he survived.'

'By not showing them, Maurice.'

A waiter wearing about the filthiest apron Jason had ever seen clapped the Belgian on the neck. '*Votre table, René.*'

'So?' shrugged Tank Shirt. 'Just another name. *Quelle difference?* We eat and with good fortune we will not be poisoned.'

Two hours later, with four bottles of rough *vin ordinaire* consumed by Maurice and Ralph, along with suspicious fish, Le Coeur du Soldat settled in for its nightly endurance ritual. Fights episodically broke out, broken up by muscular waiters. The blaring music marshalled memories of battles won and lost, engendering arguments between old soldiers who had basically been the assault troops, cannon fodder, at once resentful and filled with the pride of survival because they *had* survived the blood and horror their gold-braided superiors knew nothing about. It was the collective roar of the underprivileged foot soldiers heard from the time of the Pharaoh's legions to the grunts of Korea and Vietnam. The properly uniformed officers decreed from far behind the lines, and the foot soldiers died to preserve their superiors' wisdom. Bourne remembered Saigon and could not fault the existence of Le Coeur du Soldat.

The head bartender, a massive bald man with steel-rimmed glasses, picked up a telephone concealed below the far end of the bar and brought it to his ear. Jason watched him between the roving figures. The man's eyes spun around the crowded room – what he heard appeared to be important; what he saw, dismissible. He spoke briefly, plunged his hand below the bar and kept it there for several moments; he had dialled. Again, he spoke quickly, then calmly replaced the phone out of sight. It was the kind of sequence described by old Fontaine on Tranquillity Isle. Message received, message relayed. And at the end of that receiving line was the Jackal.

It was all he wanted to see that evening; there were things to consider, perhaps men to hire, as he had hired men in the past. Expendable men who meant nothing to him, people who could be paid or bribed, blackmailed or threatened into doing what he wanted them to do without explanation.

'I just spotted the man I was to meet here,' he said to the barely conscious Maurice and Ralph. 'He wants me to go outside.'

'You're *leaving* us?' whined the Belgian.

'Hey, man, you shouldn't do *thay-at*,' added the young American from the south.

'Only for tonight.' Bourne leaned over the table. 'I'm working with another legionnaire, someone who's on to something that involves a lot of money. I don't know you, but you seem like decent men.' Bourne pulled out his roll of bills and peeled off a thousand francs, five hundred for each of his companions. 'Take this, both of you – shove it in your pockets, *quickly*!'

'Holy *shee-itt*!'

'*Merde!*'

'It's no guarantee, but maybe we can use you. Keep your mouths shut and get out of here ten or fifteen minutes after I leave. Also, no more wine. I want you sober tomorrow . . . When does this place open, Maurice?'

'I'm not sure it closes. I myself have been here at eight o'clock in the morning. Naturally, it is not so crowded—'

'Be here around noon. But with clear heads, all right?'

'I shall be *le caporal extraordinaire* of the Légion. The man that I once was! Should I wear my uniform?' Maurice belched.

'Hell, no.'

'Ah'll wear a suit and a tie. I got a suit and a tie, honest!' The American hiccupped.

'*No.* Both of you be like you are now, but with your heads straight. Do you understand me?'

'You sound *très américain, mon ami.*'

'He sure do.'

'I'm not, but then the truth's not a commodity here, is it?'

'*Où est-ce que—*'

'Ah know what he means. I learned it real well. You kinda fib with a tie on.'

'No tie, Ralph. See you tomorrow.' Bourne slid out of the booth, and suddenly a thought struck him. Instead of heading for the door, he cautiously made his way to the far end of the bar and the huge bald bartender. No seats were available, so he, again cautiously, politely, squeezed sideways between two customers, ordered a Pernod, and asked for a napkin on which to write a message, ostensibly personal, to no one who might concern the establishment. On the back of the napkin's crude coat of arms, he wrote the following with his ballpoint pen in French.

The nest of a blackbird is worth a million francs. Object: confidential business advice. If interested, be at the old factory around the corner in thirty minutes. Where is the harm? An additional 5000 F for being there alone.

Bourne palmed the napkin along with a hundred-franc note and signalled the bartender, who adjusted his steel-rimmed glasses as if the unknown patron's gesture was an impertinence. Slowly he moved his large body forward, and leaned his thick tattooed arms on the bar.

'What is it?' he asked gruffly.

'I have written out a message for you,' replied the Chameleon, his eyes steady, focused on the bartender's glasses. 'I am by myself and hope you will consider the request. I am a man who carries wounds but I am not a poor man.' Bourne quickly but gently – very gently – reached for the bartender's hand, passing the napkin and the franc note. With a final imploring look at the astonished man, Jason turned and headed for the door, his limp pronounced.

Outside, Bourne hurried up the distressed pavement towards the alley's entrance. He judged that his interlude at the bar had taken between eight and twelve minutes. Knowing the bartender was watching him, he had purposely not tried to see if his two companions were still at the table, but he assumed they were. Tank Shirt and Field Jacket were not at their sharpest, and in their condition minutes did not count; he could only hope five hundred francs apiece might bring about a degree of responsibility and that they would leave soon as instructed. Oddly enough, he had more faith in Maurice-René than in the young American who called himself Ralph. A former corporal in the Foreign Legion was imbued with an automatic reflex where orders where concerned; he followed them blind drunk or blind sober. Jason hoped so; it was not mandatory, but he could use their assistance – if, *if* the bartender at Le Coeur du Soldat had been sufficiently intrigued by the excessive sums of money, as well as by a solitary conversation with a cripple he could obviously kill with one tattooed arm.

Bourne waited in the street, the wash of the streetlights diminishing in the alley, fewer and fewer people going in or coming out, those arriving in better shape than those departing, all passing Jason without a glance at the derelict weaving against the brick.

Instinct prevailed. Tank Shirt pulled the much younger Field Jacket through the heavy door, and at one point after the door had swung shut, slapped the American across the face, telling him in unclear words to follow orders, for they were rich and could become much richer.

'It is better than being shot in Angola!' cried the former *légionnaire,* loud enough for Bourne to hear. 'Why did they do that?'

Jason stopped them at the entrance to the alley, pulling both men around the edge of the brick building. 'It's *me,*' he said, his voice commanding.

'*Sacrebleu . . . !*'

'*What the Gawdamn hell . . . !*'

'Be *quiet*! You can make another five hundred francs tonight, if you want to. If not, there are twenty other men who will.'

'We are comrades!' protested Maurice-René.

'And Ah could bust your ass for scarin' us like *thay*-at . . . But mah buddy's right, we're comrades – that ain't Commie stuff, is it, Maurice?'

'*Taisez-vous!*'

'That means shut up,' explained Bourne.

'Ah know *thay*-at. I hear it a lot—'

'Listen to me. Within the next few minutes the bartender in there may come out looking for me. He *may*; he also may not, I simply don't know. He's the large bald man wearing glasses. Do either of you know him?'

The American shrugged, but the Belgian nodded his floating head, his lips flat until he spoke. 'His name is Santos and he is *espagnol.*'

'Spanish?'

'Or *latino-américain.* No one knows.'

Ilich Ramirez Sanchez, thought Jason. *Carlos the Jackal*, Venezuelan by birth, rejected terrorist, whom even the Soviets could not handle. Of course he would return to his own. 'How well do you know him?'

It was the Belgian's turn to shrug. 'He is the complete authority where Le Coeur du Soldat is concerned. He has been known to crush men's heads if they behave too badly. He always takes off his glasses first, and that is the first sign that something will happen that even proven soldiers do not care to witness . . . If he is coming out here to see you, I would advise you to leave.'

'He may come because he *wants* to see me, not because he wants to harm me.'

'That is not Santos—'

'You don't have to know the particulars, they don't concern you. But if he does come out that door, I want you to engage him in conversation, can you do that?'

'*Mais, certainement.* On several occasions I have slept on his couch upstairs, personally carried there by Santos himself when the cleaning women came in.'

'Upstairs?'

'He lives above the café on the second floor. It is said that he never leaves, never goes into the streets, even to the markets. Other people purchase all the supplies, or they are simply delivered.'

'I see.' Jason pulled out his money and distributed another five hundred francs to each weaving man. 'Go back into the alley, and if Santos comes out, stop him and behave like you've had too much to drink. Ask him for money, a bottle, whatever.'

Like children, Maurice-René and Ralph clutched the franc notes, glancing at each other both as conspirators and as victors. François, the crazy *légionnaire*, was passing out money as if he printed it himself! Their collective enthusiasm grew.

'How long do you want us to hassle this turkey?' asked the American from the Deep South.

'I will talk the ears off his bald head!' added the Belgian.

'No, just long enough for me to see that he's alone,' said Bourne, 'that no one else is with him or comes out after him.'

'Piece a' cake, man.'

'We shall earn not only your francs but your respect. You have the word of a Légion corporal!'

'I'm touched. Now, get back in there.' The two inebriated men lurched down the alley, Field Jacket slapping Tank Shirt triumphantly across the shoulders. Jason pressed his back against the street-side brick inches from the edge of the building and waited. Six minutes passed, and then he heard the words he so desperately wanted to hear.

'*Santos!* My great and good friend Santos!'

'What are you doing here, René?'

'My young American friend was sick to his stomach but it has gone – he vomited.'

'American . . . ?'

'Let me introduce you, Santos. He's about to become a great soldier.'

'There is a Children's Crusade somewhere?' Bourne peered around the corner as the bald bartender looked at Ralph. 'Good luck, baby face. Go find your war in a playground.'

'You talk French awful fast, mistuh, but I caught some of that. You're a big mother, but *I* can be a mean son of a bitch!'

The bartender laughed and switched effortlessly to English. 'Then you'd better be mean someplace else, baby face. We only permit peaceable gentlemen in Le Coeur du Soldat . . . Now I must go.'

'*Santos!*' cried Maurice-René. 'Lend me ten francs. I left my billfold back at my flat.'

'If you ever had a billfold, you left it back in North Africa. You know my policy. Not a sou for any of you.'

'What money I had went for your lousy fish! It made my friend vomit!'

'For your next meal, go down to Paris and dine at the Ritz . . . Ah, *yes*! You did have a meal – but you did not pay for it.' Jason pulled quickly back as the bartender snapped his head around and looked up the alley. 'Good night, René. You too, baby warrior. I have business.'

Bourne ran down the pavement towards the gates of the old factory. Santos was coming to meet him. *Alone.* Crossing the street into the shadows of the shut-down refinery, he stood still, moving only his hand so as to feel the hard steel and the security of his automatic. With every step Santos took the Jackal was closer! Moments later, the immense figure emerged from the alley, crossed the dimly lit street and approached the rusted gates.

'I am here, monsieur,' said Santos.

'And I am grateful.'

'I'd rather you'd keep your word first. I believe you mentioned five thousand francs in your note.'

'It's here.' Jason reached into his pocket, removed the money, and held it out for the manager of Le Coeur du Soldat.

'Thank you,' said Santos, walking forward and accepting the bills. '*Take* him!' he added.

Suddenly, from behind Bourne, the old gates of the factory burst open. Two men rushed out, and before Jason could reach his weapon, a heavy blunt instrument crashed down on his skull.

23

'We're alone,' said the voice across the dark room as Bourne opened his eyes. Santos's huge frame minimized the size of his large armchair, and the low wattage of the single floor lamp heightened the white scalp of his immense bald head. Jason arched his neck and felt the angry swelling on top of his skull; he was angled into the corner of a sofa. 'There's no break, no blood, only what I imagine is a very painful lump,' commented the Jackal's man.

'Your diagnosis is accurate, especially the last part.'

'The instrument was hard rubber and cushioned. The results are predictable except where concussions are concerned. At your side, on a tray, is an ice bag. It might be well to use it.'

Bourne reached down in the dim light, grabbed the bulky cold bag and brought it to his head. 'You're very considerate,' he said flatly.

'Why not? We have several things to discuss . . . perhaps a million, if broken down into francs.'

'It's yours under the conditions stated.'

'Who *are* you?' asked Santos sharply.

'That's not one of the conditions.'

'You're not a young man.'

'Not that it matters, but neither are you.'

'You carried a gun and a knife. The latter is for younger men.'

'Who said so?'

'Our reflexes . . . What do you know about a blackbird?'

'You might as well ask me how I knew about Le Coeur du Soldat.'

'How did you?'

'Someone told me.'

'*Who?*'

'Sorry, not one of the conditions. I'm a broker and that's the way I work. My clients expect it.'

'Do they also expect you to bind your knee so as to feign an injury? As your eyes opened. I pressed the area; there was no sign of pain, no sprain, no break. Also, you carry no identification but considerable amounts of money?'

'I don't explain my methods, I only clarify my restrictions as I understand them to be. I got my message through to you, didn't I? Since I had no telephone number, I doubt I could have done so very successfully had I arrived at your establishment in a business suit carrying an attaché case.'

Santos laughed. 'You never would have gotten inside. You would have been rudely stopped in the alley and stripped.'

'The thought occurred to me . . . Do we do business, say a million francs' worth?'

The Jackal's man shrugged. 'It would seem to me that if a buyer mentions such an amount in his first offer, he will go higher. Say a million and a half. Perhaps even two.'

'But I'm not the buyer, I'm the broker. I was authorized to pay one million, which is far too much in my opinion, but time is of the essence. Take it or leave it, I have other options.'

'Do you really?'

'Certainly.'

'Not if you're a corpse found floating in the Seine without any identification.'

'I see.' Jason looked around the darkened flat; it bore little relationship to the shabby café below. The furniture was large, as required by the owner, but tastefully selected, not elegant but certainly not cheap. What was mildly astonishing were the bookshelves covering the wall between the two front windows. The academic in Bourne wished he could read the titles; they might give him a clearer picture of this strange, huge man whose speech might have been formed at the Sorbonne – a committed brute on the outside, perhaps someone else inside. His eyes returned to Santos. 'Then my leaving here freely under my own power is not a given, is it?'

'No,' answered the Jackal's conduit. 'It might have been had you answered my simple questions, but you tell me that your conditions, or should I say your restrictions, forbid you to do so . . . Well, I, too, have conditions and you will live or die by them.'

'That's succinct.'

'There's no reason not to be.'

'Of course, you're forfeiting any chance of collecting a million francs – or, as you suggested, perhaps a great deal more.'

'Then may I also suggest,' said Santos, crossing his thick arms in front of him as if he were a cleric, absently glancing at the large tattoos on his skin, vaguely wondering how they got there, 'that a man with such funds available will not only part with them in exchange for his life, but will happily deliver the information requested so as to avoid unnecessary and excruciating pain.' The Jackal's man suddenly slammed his clenched right first down on the armrest and shouted, 'What do you know about a *blackbird*? Who told you about Le Coeur du Soldat? Where do you come from and who *are* you and who is your *client*?'

Bourne froze, his body rigid but his mind spinning, whirling, racing. He had to get *out*! He had to reach Bernardine – how many hours was his call overdue? Where was *Marie*? Yet what he wanted to do, *had* to do, could not be done by opposing the giant across the room. Santos was neither a liar nor a fool. He would and could kill his prisoner handily and without hesitation . . . and he would not be duped by outright false or convoluted information. The Jackal's man was protecting two turfs – his own and his mentor's. The

Chameleon had only one option open: to expose a part of the truth so dangerous as to be credible, the ring of authenticity so plausible that the risk of rejecting it was unacceptable. Jason put the ice bag on the tray and spoke slowly from the shadows of the large couch.

'Obviously I don't care to die for a client or be tortured to protect his information, so I'll tell you what I know, which isn't as much as I'd like under the present circumstances. I'll take your points in order if I'm not too damned frightened to forget the sequence. To begin with, the funds are not available to me personally. I meet with a man in London to whom I deliever the information and he releases an account in Bern, Switzerland, to a name and a number – any name, any number – that I give him . . . We'll skip over my life and the "excruciating pain" – I've answered both. Let's see, what do I know about a blackbird? The Coeur du Soldat is part of that question, incidentally . . . I was told that an old man – name and nationality unknown, at least to me, but I suspect French – approached a well-known public figure and told him he was the target of an assassination. Who believes a drunken old man, especially one with a long police record looking for a reward? Unfortunately the assassination took place, but fortunately an aide to the deceased was by his side when the old man warned him. Even more fortunate, the aide was and is extremely close to my client and the assassination was a welcome event to both. The aide secretly passed on the old man's information. A blackbird is sent a message through a café known as Le Coeur du Soldat in Argenteuil. This blackbird must be an extraordinary man and now my client wants to reach him . . . As for myself, my offices are hotel rooms in various cities. I'm currently registered under the name of Simon at the Pont-Royal, where I keep my passport and other papers.' Bourne paused, his palms outstretched. 'I've just told you the entire truth as I know it.'

'*Not* the entire truth,' corrected Santos, his voice low and guttural. 'Who is your client?'

'I'll be killed if I tell you.'

'I'll kill you right now if you don't,' said the Jackal's conduit, removing Jason's hunting knife from his wide leather belt, the blade glistening in the light of the floor lamp.

'Why not give me the information my client wants along with a name and a number – any name, any number – and I'll guarantee you two million francs. All my client asks is for me to be the *only* intermediary. Where's the harm? The blackbird can turn me down and tell me to go to hell . . . *Three* million!'

Santos's eyes wavered as if the temptation were almost too much for his imagination. 'Perhaps we'll do business later—'

'Now.'

'*No!*' Carlos's man pushed his immense body out of the chair and walked towards the couch, the knife held threateningly in front of him. 'Your client.'

'Plural,' replied Bourne. 'A group of powerful men in the United States.'

'Who?'

'They guard their names like nuclear secrets, but I know of one and he should be enough for you.'

'*Who?*'

'Find out for yourself – at least learn the enormity of what I'm trying to tell you. *Protect* your blackbird by all means! Ascertain that I'm telling you the truth and in the process make yourself so rich you can do anything you want to do for the rest of your life. You could travel, disappear, perhaps have time for those books of yours rather than being concerned with all that garbage downstairs. As you pointed out, neither of us is young. I make a generous brokering fee and you're a wealthy man, free of care, of unpleasant drudgery . . . Again, where's the harm? I can be turned down, my clients turned down. There's no trap. My clients don't ever want to see him. They want to *hire* him.'

'How could this be done? How could I be satisfied?'

'Invent some high position for yourself and reach the American ambassador in London – the name is Atkinson. Tell him you've received confidential instructions from Snake Lady. Ask him if you should carry them out.'

'Snake Lady? What's that?'

'Medusa. They call themselves Medusa.'

Mo Panov excused himself and slid out of the booth. He made his way through the crowded highway diner towards the men's room, frantically scanning the wall at the far end for a pay phone. There was none! The only goddamned phone was ten feet from the booth and in clear sight of the wild-eyed platinum blonde whose paranoia was as deeply embedded as the dark roots of her hair. He had casually mentioned that he thought he should call his office and tell his staff about the accident and where he was, and was instantly met with invective.

'And have a swarm of cops coming out to pick you *up*! Not on your fuckin' life, Medicine Man. Your office calls the fuzz, they call my devoted Chief Fork-in-Mouth, and my ass is bouncing into every barbed-wire fence in the country. He's in with every cop on the roads. I think he tells 'em where to get laid.'

'There'd be no reason for me to mention you and I certainly wouldn't. If you recall, you said he might resent me.'

'Resent don't count. He'd just cut your cute little nose off. I'm not takin' any chances – you don't look like you're too with-it. You'd blurt out about your accident – next thing the cops.'

'You know, you're not really making sense.'

'All right, I'll make sense. I'll yell "Rape!" and tell these not-so-pansy truckers I picked you up on the road two days ago and I've been a sex slave ever since. How does that grab you?'

'Very firmly. May I at least go to the men's room? It's urgent that I do.'

'Be my guest. They don't put phones in the cans in these places.'

'Really? . . . No, honestly, I'm not chagrined – not disappointed – just curious. Why don't they? Truckers make good money; they're not interested in stealing dimes or quarters.'

'Boy, you're from La La Land, Doc. Things happen on the highways, things get switched or snitched, you dig? If people make phone calls, other people want to know who makes them.'

'Really . . . ?'

'Oh, *Jesus.* Hurry up. We only got time for a couple of greasies, so I'll order. He'll head up Seventy, not Ninety-seven. He wouldn't figure.'

'Figure what? What are Seventy and Ninety-seven?'

'Routes, for Christ's sake! There are routes and there are *routes.* You are one dumb medicine man. Hit the head then maybe later we'll stop at a motel where we can continue our business discussion while you get an advance bonus.'

'I beg your pardon?'

'I'm pro-choice. Is that against your religion?'

'Good Lord, no. I'm a firm advocate.'

'Good. Hurry *up*!'

So Panov headed for the men's room and indeed the woman was right. There was no phone and the window to the outside was too small for anyone but a small cat or a large rat to crawl through . . . But he had money, a great deal of money, along with five driver's licences from five different states. In Jason Bourne's lexicon these were weapons, especially the money. Mo went to the urinal – long overdue – and then to the door; he pulled it back several inches to observe the blonde. Suddenly, the door swung violently back several feet and Panov crashed into the wall.

'Hey, *sorry*, pal!' cried a short heavyset man who grabbed the psychiatrist by the shoulders as Mo grabbed his face. 'You okay, buddy?'

'Oh, certainly. Yes, of course.'

'The hell you are, you got a nosebleed! C'mon over here by the towels,' ordered the T-shirted trucker, his left half-sleeve rolled up to hold a pack of cigarettes. 'C'mon, put your head back while I get some cold water on your schnoz . . . Loosen up and lean against the wall. There, that's better; we'll stop this sucker in a moment or two.' The short man reached up and gently pressed the wet paper towels across Panov's face while holding the back of his neck, and every few seconds checking the flow of blood from Mo's nostrils. 'There y'are, buddy, it's damned near stopped. Just breathe through your mouth, deep breaths, you got me? Head tilted, okay?'

'Thank you,' said Panov, holding the towels and amazed that a nosebleed could be stopped so quickly. 'Thank you very much.'

'Don't thank me, I bashed you one by mistake,' answered the trucker, relieving himself. 'Feel better now?' he asked, zipping up his trousers.

'Yes, I do.' And against the advice of his dear deceased mother, Mo decided to take advantage of the moment and forgo righteousness. 'But I should explain that it was my mistake, not yours.'

'Wadda ya mean?' asked the short heavyest trucker, washing his hands.

'Frankly, I was hiding behind the door looking at a woman I'm trying to get away from – if that makes sense to you.'

Panov's personal medic laughed as he dried his hands. 'Whose sense wouldn't it make? It's the story of mankind, pal! They getcha in their clutches and *whammo*, they whine and you don't know what to do, they scream and you're at their feet. Now me, I got it different. I married a real Eur'pean, you know? She don't speak so good English but she's grateful . . . Great with the kids, great with me, and I still get excited when I see her. Not like these fuckin' princesses over here.'

'That's an extremely interesting, even visceral, statement,' said the psychiatrist.

'It's who?'

'Nothing. I still want to get out of here without her seeing me leave. I have some money—'

'Hold the money, who is she?'

Both men went to the door and Panov pulled it back a few inches. 'She's the one over there, the blonde who keeps looking in this direction and at the front door. She's getting very agitated—'

'Holy shit,' interrupted the short trucker. 'That's the Bronk's wife! She's way off course.'

'Off course? The *Bronk*?'

'He trucks the eastern routes, not these. What the *hell* is she doing here?'

'I think she's trying to avoid him.'

'Yeah,' agreed Mo's companion. 'I heard she's been messing around and don't charge no money.'

'Do you know her?'

'Hell, yeah. I been to a couple of their barbecues. He makes a hell of a sauce.'

'I have to get *out* of here. As I told you, I have some money—'

'So you told me and we'll discuss it later.'

'Where?'

'In my truck. It's a red semi with white stripes, like the flag. It's parked out front, on the right. Get around the cab and stay out of sight.'

'She'll see me leave.'

'No she won't. I'm goin' over and give her a big surprise. I'll tell her all the CBs are hummin' and the Bronk is headin' south to the Carolinas – at least that's what I heard.'

'How can I ever repay you?'

'Probably with some of that money you keep talkin' about. Not too much, though. The Bronk's an animal and I'm a born-again Christian.' The short trucker swung back the door, nearly shoving Panov back into the wall again. Mo watched as his conspiratorial colleague approached the booth, his conspiratorial arms extended as the trucker embraced an old friend and started talking rapidly; the woman's eyes were attentive – she was mesmerized. Panov rushed out of the men's room, through the diner's entrance, and towards the huge red-and-white-striped truck. He crouched breathlessly behind the cab, his chest pounding, and waited.

Suddenly, the Bronk's wife came racing out of the diner, her platinum hair rising grotesquely in the air behind her as she ran to her bright red automobile. She climbed inside and in seconds the engine roared; she continued north as Mo watched, astonished.

'How are y' doing, buddy – wherever the hell you are?' shouted the short man with no name who had not only amazingly stopped a nosebleed but had rescued him from a manic wife whose paranoid mood swings were rooted in equal parts of vengeance and guilt.

Stop it, asshole, cried Panov to himself as he raised his voice. 'Over here . . . buddy!'

Thirty-five minutes later, they reached the outskirts of an unidentified town and the trucker stopped in front of a cluster of stores that bordered the highway. 'You'll find a phone there, buddy. Good luck.'

'Are you sure?' asked Mo. 'About the money, I mean.'

'Sure I'm sure,' replied the short man behind the wheel. 'Two hundred dollars is fine – maybe even what I earned – but more than that corrupts, don't it? I been offered fifty times that to haul stuff I won't haul, and you know what I tell 'em?'

'What do you tell them?'

'I tell 'em to go piss into the wind with their poison. It's gonna flash back and blind 'em.'

'You're a good person,' said Panov, climbing out onto the pavement.

'I got a few things to make up for.' The door of the cab slammed shut and the huge truck shot forward as Mo turned, looking for a telephone.

'Where the hell *are* you?' shouted Alexander Conklin in Virginia.

'I don't *know*!' answered Panov. 'If I were a patient, I'd ponderously explain that it was an extension of some Freudian dream sequence because it never *happens*, but it happened to *me*. They shot me up, Alex!'

'Stay cold. We assumed that. We have to know where you are. Let's face it, others are looking for you, too.'

'All right, all right . . . Wait a minute! There's a drugstore across the street. The sign says "Battle Ford's Best," will that help?'

The sigh on the line from Virginia was the reply. 'Yes, it does. If you were a socially productive Civil War buff rather than an insignificant shrink, you'd know it, too.'

'What the hell does that mean?'

'Head for the old battleground at Ford's Bluff. It's a national landmark; there are signs everywhere. A helicopter will be there in thirty minutes, and don't say a goddamned thing to *anybody*!'

'Do you know how extreme you sound? Yet *I* was the object of hostility—'

'*Out*, coach!'

Bourne walked into the Pont-Royal and immediately approached the night concierge, peeling off a five-hundred-franc note and placing it quietly in the man's hand. 'The name is Simon,' he said, smiling. 'I've been away. Any messages?'

'No messages, Monsieur Simon,' was the quiet reply, 'but two men are outside, one on the Montalembert, the other across on the rue du Bac.'

Jason removed a thousand-franc note and palmed it to the man. 'I pay for such eyes and I pay well. Keep it up.'

'Of course, monsieur.'

Bourne crossed to the brass elevator. Reaching his floor, he walked rapidly down the intersecting corridors to his room. Nothing was disturbed; everything was as he had left it, except the bed had been made up. The bed. Oh, God, he needed to rest, to sleep. He couldn't *do* it any longer. Something was happening inside him – less energy, less breath. Yet he had to have both, now more than ever. Oh, Christ, he wanted to lie down . . . *No.* There was Marie. There was Bernardine. He went to the telephone and dialled the number he had committed to memory.

'I'm sorry I'm late,' he said.

'Four hours late, *mon ami.* What happened?'

'No time. What about Marie?'

'There is nothing. Absolutely nothing. She is not on any international flight currently in the air or scheduled for departure. I even checked the transfers from London, Lisbon, Stockholm and Amsterdam – nothing. There is no Marie Elise St Jacques Webb en route to Paris.'

'There *has* to be. She wouldn't change her mind, it's not like her. And she wouldn't know how to bypass immigration.'

'I repeat. She's not listed on any flight from any country coming into Paris.'

'*Damn!*'

'I will keep trying, my friend. The words of Saint Alex keep ringing in my ears. Do not underestimate *la belle mademoiselle.*'

'She's not a goddamned mademoiselle, she's my wife . . . She's not one of us, Bernardine; she's not an agent in the field who can cross and double-cross and triple-cross. That's not *her.* But she's on her way to Paris. I know it!'

'The airlines do not, what more can I say?'

'Just what you said,' said Jason, his lungs seemingly incapable of absorbing the air he needed, his eyelids heavy. 'Keep trying.'

'What happened tonight? *Tell* me.'

'Tomorrow,' replied David Webb, barely audible. 'Tomorrow . . . I'm so tired and I have to be somebody else.'

'What are you talking about? You don't even sound like yourself.'

'Nothing. Tomorrow. I have to think . . . Or maybe I shouldn't think.'

Marie stood in Marseilles's immigration line, mercifully short because of the early hour, and assumed an air of boredom, the last thing she felt. It was her turn to go to the passport counter.

'*Américaine,*' said the half-awake official. 'Are you heer on bizziness or playseeoor, madame?'

'*Je parle français, monsieur. Je suis canadienne d'origine – Quebec. Séparatiste.*'

'*Ah, bien!*' The sleepy clerk's eyes opened somewhat wider as he proceeded in French. 'You are in business?'

'No, I'm not. This is a journey of memories. My parents came from Marseilles and both died recently. I want to see where they came from, where they lived – perhaps what I missed.'

'How extraordinarily touching, lovely lady,' said the immigration official, appraising the most appealing traveller. 'Perhaps also you might need a guide? There is no part of this city that is not indelibly printed on my mind.'

'You're most kind. I'll be at the Sofitel Vieux Port. What's your name? You have mine.'

'Lafontaine, madame. At your service!'

'*Lafontaine?* You don't say?'

'I do indeed!'

'How interesting.'

'I am *very* interesting,' said the official, his eyelids half closed but not with sleepiness, as his rubber stamps flew recklessly down through the air processing the tourist. 'I am at your every service, madame!'

It must run in that very peculiar clan, though Marie as she headed for the luggage area. From there she would board a domestic flight to Paris under any name she chose.

François Bernardine awoke with a start, shooting up on his elbows, frowning, disturbed. *She's on her way to Paris, I know it!* The words of the husband who knew her best. *She's not listed on any flight from any other country coming into Paris.* His own words. Paris. The operative word was *Paris!*

But suppose it was *not* Paris?

The Deuxième veteran crawled rapidly out of bed in the early morning light shining through the tall narrow windows of his flat. In fewer minutes than his face appreciated, he shaved, then completed his ablutions, dressed, and walked down into the street to his Peugeot, where there was the inevitable ticket on the windshield; alas, it was no longer officially dismissible with a quiet phone call. He sighed, picked it off the glass, and climbed in behind the wheel.

Fifty-eight minutes later he swung the car into the parking lot of a small nondescript brick building in the huge cargo complex of Orly Airport. The building was nondescript; the work inside was not. It was a branch of the Department of Immigration, an all-important arm known simply as the Bureau of Air Entries, where sophisticated computers kept up-to-the-minute records of every traveller flying into France at all the international airports. It was vital to immigration but not often consulted by the Deuxième, for there were far too many other points of entry used by the people in which the Deuxième was interested. Nevertheless, over the years, Bernardine, operating on the theory of the obvious being unnoticed, had sought information from the Bureau of Air Entries. Every now and then he had been rewarded. He wondered if that would be the case this morning.

Nineteen minutes later he had his answer. It was the case, but the reward was considerably diminished in value for the information came too late. There was a pay phone in the bureau's lobby; Bernardine inserted a coin and dialled the Pont-Royal.

'Yes?' coughed the voice of Jason Bourne.

'I apologize for waking you.'

'François?'

'Yes.'

'I was just getting up. There are two men down in the street far more tired than I am, unless they're replacements.'

'Relative to last night? All night?'

'Yes. I'll tell you about it when I see you. Is that why you called?'

'No. I'm out at Orly and I'm afraid I have bad news, information that proves me an *idiot.* I should have considered it . . . Your wife flew into Marseilles slightly over two hours ago. Not Paris. Marseilles.'

'Why is that *bad* news?' cried Jason. 'We know where she *is*! We can – Oh, Christ, I see what you mean.' Subdued, Bourne's words trailed off. 'She can take a train, hire a car . . .'

'She can even fly up to Paris under any name she cares to,' added Bernardine. 'Still I have an idea. It's probably as worthless as my brain but I suggest it anyway . . . Do you and she have special – how do you say it? – nicknames for each other? *Sobriquets* of endearment perhaps?'

'We're not much for the cute stuff, frankly . . . Wait a minute. A couple of years ago, Jamie, that's our son, had trouble with "mommy". He turned it around and called her "Meemom". We kidded about it and I called her that for a few months off and on until he got it right.'

'I know she speaks French fluently. Does she read the papers?'

'Religiously, at least the financial pages. I'm not sure she goes seriously much beyond them; it's her morning ritual.'

'Even in a crisis?'

'Especially in a crisis. She claims it calms her.'

'Let's send her a message – on the financial pages.'

Ambassador Phillip Atkinson settled in for a morning of dreary paperwork at the American embassy in London. The dreariness was compounded by a dull throbbing at his temples and a sickening taste in his mouth. It was hardly a typical hangover because he rarely drank whisky and for over twenty-five years had never been drunk. He had learned a long time ago, roughly thirty months after Saigon fell, the limits of his talents, his opportunities and, above all, his resources. When he returned from the war with reasonable, if not exceptional, commendations at twenty-nine, his family had purchased him an available seat on the New York Stock Exchange, where in thirty additional months he had lost something over three million dollars.

'Didn't you ever learn a goddamned *thing* at Andover and Yale?' his father had roared. 'At least make a few connections on the *Street*?'

'Dad, they were all jealous of me, you know that. My looks, the girls – I look like you, Dad – they all conspired against me. Sometimes I think they were really getting at you through *me*! You know how they talk. Senior and Junior, dashing socialites and all that crap . . . Remember the column in the *Daily News* when they compared us to the Fairbanks?'

'I've known Doug for forty years!' yelled the father. 'He's got it upstairs, one of the best.'

'He didn't go to Andover and Yale, Dad.'

'He didn't *have* to, for Christ's sake! . . . Hold it. Foreign Service . . . ? What the hell was that degree you got at Yale?'

'Bachelor of Arts.'

'Screw that! There was something else. The courses or something.'

'I majored in English literature and minored in political science.'

'*That's* it! Shove the fairy stuff on the back burner. You were outstanding in the other one – the political science bullshit.'

'Dad, it wasn't my strongest course.'

'You passed?'

'Yes . . . Barely.'

'*Not* barely, with *honours*! That's *it*!'

And so Phillip Atkinson III began his career in the Foreign Service by way of a valuable political contributor who was his father, and never looked back. And although that illustrious man had died eight years ago, he never forgot the old war horse's last admonition: 'Don't fuck this up, son. You want to drink or you want to whore around, you do it inside your own house or in a goddamned desert somewhere, understand? And you treat that wife of yours, whatever the hell her name is, with real affection wherever anybody can see you, *got* it?'

'Yes, Dad.'

Which was why Phillip Atkinson felt so *blah* on this particular morning. He had spent the previous evening at a dinner party with unimportant royals who drank until the drink flowed out of their nostrils, and with his wife who excused their behaviour because they *were* royals, all of which he could tolerate only with seven glasses of Chablis. There were times when he longed for the freewheeling, free-drinking days of the old Saigon.

The telephone rang, causing Atkinson to slur his signature on a document that made no sense to him. 'Yes?'

'The high commissioner from the Hungarian Central Committee is on the line, sir.'

'*Oh?* Who's that – who *are* they? Do we recognize them – it – *him*?'

'I don't know, Mr Ambassador. I really can't pronounce his name.'

'Very well, put him through.'

'Mr Ambassador?' said the deep accented voice on the phone. 'Mr Atkinson?'

'Yes, this is Atkinson. Forgive me, but I don't recollect either your name or the Hungarian affiliation you speak for.'

'It does not matter. I speak on behalf of Snake Lady—'

'*Stop!* cried the ambassador to the Court of St James's. 'Stay on the line and we'll resume talking in twenty seconds.' Atkinson reached down, snapped on his scrambler, and waited until the spiralling sounds of the pre-intercepter subsided. 'All right, continue.'

'I have received instructions from Snake Lady and was told to confirm the origin from you.'

'Confirmed!'

'And therefore I am to carry out these instructions?'

'Good Lord, *yes*! Whatever they say. My God, look what happened to Teagarten in Brussels, Armbruster in Washington! Protect me! Do whatever they *say*!'

'Thank you, Mr Ambassador.'

Bourne first sat in the hottest tub he could endure, then took the coldest shower he could tolerate. He then changed the dressing around his neck, walked back into the small hotel room and fell on the bed . . . So Marie had found a simple, ingenious way to reach Paris. Goddamn it! How could he find her, *protect* her? Had she any idea what she was *doing*? David would go out of his mind. He'd panic and make a thousand mistakes . . . Oh, my God, I *am* David!

Stop it. Control. Pull back.

The telephone rang; he grabbed it off the bedside table. 'Yes?'

'Santos wants to see you. With peace in his heart.'

24

The Emergency Medical Service helicopter was lowered into its threshhold; the rotors were cut and the blades thumped to a stop. Following EMS procedure when disembarking ambulatory patients, only then did the exit door open and the metal steps slap down to the ground. A uniformed paramedic preceded Panov, turning and assisting the doctor to the tarmac, where a second man in civilian clothes escorted him to a waiting limousine. Inside were Peter Holland, director of the CIA, and Alex Conklin, the latter in the right jump seat, obviously for conversational purposes. The psychiatrist climbed in beside Holland; he took several deep breaths, sighed audibly and fell back into the seat.

'I am a maniac,' he stated, emphasizing each word. 'Certifiably insane and I'll sign the papers of commitment myself.'

'You're safe, that's all that matters, Doctor,' said Holland.

'Good to see you, Crazy Mo,' added Conklin.

'Have you any idea what I *did*? . . . I purposely crashed a car into a tree with me *in* it! Then after walking at least half the distance to the Bronx, I was picked up by the only person I know who may have more loose bananas in her head than *I* do. Her libido is unhinged and she's running away from her trucker husband – hot on her French heels – who I subsequently learned has the cuddly name of the Bronk. My hooker chauffeur proceeds to hold me hostage with such wiles as threatening to yell "Rape!" in a diner filled with a collection of the NFL's most carnivorous linebackers . . . except for one who got me out.' Panov abruptly stopped and reached into his pocket. 'Here,' he continued, thrusting the five driver's licences and the roughly six thousand dollars into Conklin's hands.

'What's this?' asked the bewildered Alex.

'I robbed a bank and decided to become a professional driver! . . . What do you think it is? I took it from the man who was guarding me. I described as best I could to the chopper's crew where the crash took place. They're flying back to find him. They will; he's not walking anywhere.'

Peter Holland reached for the limousine's telephone, pushing three buttons. In less than two seconds, he spoke. 'Get word to EMS-Arlington, Equipment Fifty-seven. The man they're picking up is to be brought directly to Langley. To the infirmary. And keep me informed as to their progress . . . Sorry, Doctor. Go on.'

'Go on? What's to go on to? I was kidnapped and held in some farmhouse and injected with enough sodium pentothal, if I'm not mistaken, to make me a resident of – of La La Land, which I was recently accused of being by Madame Scylla Charybdis.'

'What the hell are you talking about?' said Holland flatly.

'Nothing, Admiral, or Mr Director or—'

'Peter's fine, Mo,' completed Holland. 'I simply didn't understand you.'

'There's nothing to understand but the facts. My allusions are compulsive attempts at false erudition. It's called postpartum anxiety.'

'Of course, now you're perfectly clear.'

Panov turned to the DCI with a nervous smile. 'It's my turn to be sorry, Peter. I'm still wound up. This last day or so hasn't exactly been representative of my normal life-style.'

'I don't think it's anybody's,' concurred Holland. 'I've seen my share of rotten stuff, but nothing like this, nothing that tampers with the mind. I missed all that.'

'There's no hurry, Mo,' added Conklin. 'Don't press yourself; you've taken a lot of punishment. If you like, we can postpone the briefing for a few hours so you can rest, calm down.'

'Don't be a damn fool, Alex!' protested the psychiatrist sharply. 'For the *second* time I've put David's life in jeopardy. The knowledge of *that* is far worse punishment. There's not a minute to lose . . . Forget Langley, Peter. Take me to one of your clinics. Free-floating, I want to get out everything I can recall, consciously or unconsciously. *Hurry*. I'll tell the doctors what to do.'

'You've got to be joking,' said Holland, staring at Panov.

'I'm not joking for an instant. You both have to know what I know – whether I realize I know it or not. Can't you *understand* that?'

The director again reached for the telephone and pressed a single button. In the front seat, beyond the glass partition, the driver picked up the phone recessed in the seat beside him. 'There's been a change of plans,' said Holland. 'Head for Sterile Five.'

The limousine slowed down, and at the next intersection turned right towards the rolling hills and verdant fields of the Virginia hunt country. Morris Panov closed his eyes, as if in a trance or as a man might do facing some appalling ordeal – his own execution perhaps. Alex looked at Peter Holland; they both glanced at Mo, then back at each other. Whatever Panov was doing, there was a reason for it. Until they reached the gates of the estate that was Sterile House Five thirty minutes later, no one spoke.

'DCI and company,' announced the driver to the guard wearing the uniform of a private security firm, in reality a CIA proprietary. The limousine proceeded down the long tree-lined entrance.

'Thanks,' said Mo, opening his eyes and blinking. 'As I'm sure you gathered, I'm trying to clear my head and with any luck bring down my blood pressure.'

'You don't have to do this,' insisted Holland.

'Yes, I do,' said Panov. 'Maybe with time I could piece things together with a degree of clarity, but I can't now and we don't *have* the time.' Mo turned to Conklin. 'How much can you tell me?'

'Peter knows everything. For the sake of that blood pressure of yours, I won't fill you in on all the details, but the bottom line is that David's all right. At least we haven't heard otherwise.'

'Marie? The children?'

'On the island,' replied Alex, avoiding Holland's eyes.

'What about this Sterile Five?' asked Panov, now looking at Holland. 'I assume there's a specialist, or specialists, the kind I need.'

'In relays and around the clock. You probably know a few of them.'

'I'd rather not.' The long dark vehicle swung around the circular drive and stopped in front of the stone steps of the pillared Georgian mansion that was the focal point of the estate. 'Let's go,' said Mo quietly, stepping outside.

The sculptured white doors, the rose-coloured marble floors and the elegant winding staircase in the great hall all combined to furnish a superb cover for the work done at Sterile Five. Defectors, double and triple agents, and field officers returned from complex assignments for rest and debriefing were continuously processed through its various agendas. The staff, each with a Four Zero clearance, consisted of two doctors and three nurses in relay units, cooks and domestic attendants recruited from the foreign service – in the main overseas embassies – and guards, all with Ranger training or its equivalent. They moved about the house and grounds unobtrusively, eyes constantly alert, each with either a concealed or an unconcealed weapon, except for the medical personnel. Visitors without exception were given small lapel pins by the well-spoken, dark-suited house steward, who admitted them and directed them to the locations of their scheduled appointments. The man was a retired grey-haired interpreter for the Central Intelligence Agency, but he suited his position so well in appearance he might have come from Central Casting.

Naturally, at the sight of Peter Holland, the steward was astonished. He prided himself on committing to memory every schedule at Sterile Five. 'A surprise visit, sir?'

'Good to see you, Frank.' The DCI shook hands with the former interpreter. 'You may remember Alex Conklin—'

'Good Lord, is that you, Alex? It's been years!' Again hands were shaken. 'When was the last time? . . . That crazy woman from Warsaw, wasn't it?'

'The KGB's been chuckling ever since,' laughed Conklin. 'The only secret she had was the recipe for the worst *golumpki* I've ever tasted . . . Still keeping your hand in, Frank?'

'Every now and then,' replied the steward, grimacing in mock disapproval. 'These young translators don't know a quiche from a *kluski*.'

'Since I don't either,' said Holland, 'may I have a word with you, Frank?' The two older men walked off to the side speaking quietly as Alex and Mo Panov held their places, the latter frowning and sporadically breathing deeply. The director returned, handing lapel pins to his colleagues. 'I know where to go now,' he said. 'Frank will call ahead.'

The three of them walked up the curving ornate staircase, Conklin limping, and down a lushly carpeted hallway on the left to the rear of the enormous house. On the right wall was a door unlike any of the doors they had passed; it was made of thick varnished oak with four small windows in the upper recessed panels and two black buttons set in an outlet casing beside the knob.

Holland inserted a key, twisted it and pressed the lower button; instantly a red light appeared in the small stationary camera mounted on the ceiling. Twenty seconds later there was the familiar muffled metallic clanking of an elevator coming to a stop. 'Inside, gentlemen,' ordered the DCI. The door closed and the elevator began its descent.

'We walked up to go *down*?' asked Conklin.

'Security,' answered the director. 'It's the only way to get where we're going. There's no elevator on the first floor.'

'Why not, may the man with one foot missing ask?' said Alex.

'I'd think you'd be able to answer that better than me,' retorted the DCI. 'Apparently all accesses to the cellars are sealed off except for two elevators that bypass the first floor and for which you need a key. This one and another on the other side; this takes us to where we want to go, the other leads to the furnaces, air-conditioning units and all the rest of the normal basement equipment. Frank gave me the key, incidentally. If it doesn't return to its slot within a given period of time, another alarm goes off.'

'It all strikes me as unnecessarily complicated,' said Panov curtly, nervously. 'Expensive games.'

'Not necessarily, Mo,' interrupted Conklin gently. 'Explosives can be concealed pretty easily in heating pipes and ducts. And did you know that during the last days of Hitler's bunker a few of his saner aides tried to insert poison gas into the air-filtering machinery? These are just precautions.'

The elevator stopped and the door opened. 'To your left, Doctor,' Holland said. The hallway was a glistening pristine white, antiseptic in its way, which was altogether proper, as this underground complex was a highly sophisticated medical centre. It was devoted not only to the healing of men and women, but also to the process of breaking them down, crippling their resistance so that information might be revealed, truths learned that could prevent the penetration of high-risk operations, frequently saving lives as a result.

They entered a room that was in stark contrast to the fluorescent antiseptic quality of the bright hallway. There were heavy armchairs and soft indirect lighting, a coffee urn on a table with cups and saucers; newspapers and magazines were folded neatly on other tables, all the comforts of a lounge designed for those waiting for someone or something. From an inner door, a man in a white medical jacket appeared; he was frowning, uncertain.

'Director Holland?' he said, approaching Peter, extending his hand. 'I'm Dr Walsh, second shift. Needless to say, we didn't expect you.'

'I'm afraid it's an emergency and hardly one of my choosing. May I introduce you to Dr Morris Panov – unless you know him?'

'*Of* him, of course.' Walsh again extended his hand. 'A pleasure, Doctor, also a privilege.'

'You may take both back before we're finished, Doctor. May we talk privately?'

'Certainly. My office is inside.' The two men disappeared through the inner door.

'Shouldn't you go with them?' asked Conklin, looking at Peter.

'Why not you?'

'Goddamn it, you're the *director*. You should insist!'

'You're his closest friend. So should you.'

'I don't have any clout here.'

'Mine disappeared when Mo dismissed us. Come on, let's have some coffee. This place gives me the proverbial creeps.' Holland went to the table with the coffee urn and poured two cups. 'How do you like it?'

'With more milk and sugar than I'm supposed to have. I'll do it.'

'I still take it black,' said the director, moving away from the table and removing a pack of cigarettes from his shirt pocket. 'My wife says the acid will kill me one day.'

'Other people say tobacco will.'

'What?'

'Look.' Alex pointed at the sign on the opposite wall. It read THANK YOU FOR NOT SMOKING.

'That I've got enough clout for,' announced Holland quietly as he snapped his lighter and lit a cigarette.

Nearly twenty minutes passed. Every now and then one or the other of them picked up a magazine or a newspaper only to put it down moments later and look up at the inner door. Finally, twenty-eight minutes after he had disappeared with Panov, the doctor named Walsh reappeared.

'He tells me you know what he's requesting and that you have no objections, Director Holland.'

'I've got plenty of objections, but it seems he's overruled them . . . Oh, excuse me, Doctor, this is Alex Conklin. He's one of us and a close friend of Panov.'

'How do *you* feel, Mr Conklin?' asked Walsh, nodding at Alex as he returned the greeting.

'I hate what he's doing – what he wants to do – but he says it makes sense. If it does, it's right for him and I understand why he insists on doing it. If it doesn't make sense, I'll pull him out of there myself, one foot and all. *Does* it make sense, Doctor? And what's the risk of damage?'

'There's always a risk where drugs are concerned, especially in terms of chemical balance, and he knows that. It's why he's designed an intravenous flow that prolongs his own psychological pain but somewhat reduces the potential damage.'

'*Somewhat?*' cried Alex.

'I'm being honest. So is he.'

'Bottom line, Doctor,' said Holland.

'If things go wrong, two or three months of therapy, not permanent.'

'And the sense?' insisted Conklin. 'Does it make *sense*?'

'Yes,' replied Walsh. 'What happened to him is not only recent, it's consumed him. It's obsessed his conscious, which can only mean that it's inflamed his subconscious. He's right. His unreachable recall is on the cutting edge . . . I came in here as a courtesy. He's insisted we proceed, and from what he's told me, I'd do the same thing. Each of us would.'

'What's the security?' asked Alex.

'The nurse will be dismissed and stay outside the door. There'll be only a single battery-operated tape recorder and me . . . and one or both of you.' The doctor turned to the door, then glanced back. 'I'll send for you at the proper time,' he added, again disappearing inside.

Conklin and Peter Holland looked at each other. The second period of waiting began.

To their astonishment, it ended barely ten minutes later. A nurse came out into the lounge and asked them to follow her. They walked through what appeared to be a maze of antiseptic white walls broken up only by recessed white panels with glass knobs that denoted doors. Only once on their brief journey did they see another human being; it was a man in a white smock, wearing a white surgical mask who walked out of yet another white door, his sharp, intense eyes above the white cloth somehow accusing, determining them to be aliens from some different world that had not been cleared for Sterile House Five.

The nurse opened a door; there was a blinking red light above its top frame. She put her index finger to her lips, indicating silence. Holland and Conklin walked quietly inside a dark room and confronted a drawn white curtain concealing a bed or an examining table beyond, a small circle of intense light shining through the cloth. They heard the softly spoken words of Dr Walsh.

'You are going back, Doctor, not far back, just a day or so, just when you began to feel the dull, constant pain in your arm . . . your *arm*, Doctor. Why are they inflicting pain on your *arm*? You were in a farmhouse, a small farmhouse with fields outside your window and then they put a blindfold on you and began hurting your arm. Your *arm*, Doctor.'

Suddenly, there was a muted flashing of green light reflected on the ceiling. The curtain parted electronically several feet, revealing the bed, the patient and the doctor. Walsh took his finger off a bedside button and looked at them, gesturing slowly with his hands as if to say: 'There's no one else here. Confirmed?'

Both witnesses nodded, at first mesmerized, then repelled at the sight of Panov's grimacing pale face and the tears that began to flow from his wide-open eyes. Then, as one, they saw the white straps that emerged from under the white sheet, holding Mo in place; the order had to be his.

'The *arm*, Doctor. We have to begin with the *physically* invasive procedure, don't we? Because you know what it does, Doctor, don't you? It leads to another invasive procedure that you cannot permit. You must stop its progression.'

The ear-shattering scream was a prolonged shriek of defiance and horror. 'No, *no! I won't tell you*! I *killed* him once, I won't kill him *again*! Get away from *meeeee* . . . !'

Alex slumped, falling to the floor. Peter Holland grabbed him and gently the strong, broad-shouldered admiral, a veteran of the darkest operations in the Far East, led Conklin silently through the door to the nurse. 'Get him away from here, please.'

'Yes, sir.'

'*Peter*,' coughed Alex, trying to stand, collapsing on his false foot. 'I'm sorry, Christ, I'm *sorry*!'

'What for?' whispered Holland.

'I should watch but I *can't* watch!'

'I understand. It's all too close. If I were you, I probably couldn't either.'

'No, you *don't* understand! Mo said he killed David, but of course he didn't. But *I* meant to, I really *wanted* to kill him! I was wrong, but I tried with all the expertise in my bones to *kill* him! And now I've done it again. I sent him to Paris . . . It's not Mo, it's *me*!'

'Put him against the wall, miss. Let him sink to the floor and leave us alone.'

'Yes, *sir*!' The nurse did as she was ordered and fled, leaving Holland and Alex alone in the antiseptic maze.

'Now, you listen to me, Field Man,' whispered the grey-haired director of the Central Intelligence Agency, kneeling in front of Conklin. 'This fucking merry-go-round of guilt had better stop – has *got* to stop – or nobody's going to be any good to *anybody*. I don't give a good goddamn what you or Panov did thirteen years ago, or five years ago, or *now*! We're all reasonably bright people, and we did what each of us did because we thought they were the right moves at the time . . . Guess what, *Saint* Alex? Yes, I've heard the term. We make *mistakes*. Fucking inconvenient, isn't it? Maybe we're not so *brilliant* after all. Maybe Panov isn't the greatest behavioural whatever-the-hell-it-is; maybe you're not the shrewdest son of a bitch in the field, the one who got canonized, and maybe *I'm* not the superjock behind-the-lines strategist they've made me out to be. So *what*? We take our baggage and go where we have to go.'

'Oh, for *Christ's* sake, *shut* up!' yelled Conklin, struggling against the wall.

'*Shhh!*'

'Oh, shit! The last thing I need is a sermon from you! If I had a foot, I'd take you.'

'Now we're physical?'

'I was Black Belt. First class, Admiral.'

'Golly, gee. I don't even know how to wrestle.'

Their eyes met and Alex was the first to laugh quietly. 'You're too much, Peter. I got your message. Help me up, will you? I'll go back to the lounge and wait for you. Come on, give me a hand.'

'The hell I will,' said Holland, getting to his feet and standing over Conklin. 'Help yourself. Someone told me that the Saint made it back through a hundred and forty miles in enemy territory, through rivers and streams and jungle, and arrived at the Foxtrot base camp asking if anybody had a bottle of bourbon.'

'Yeah, well, that was different. I was a hell of a lot younger and I had another foot.'

'Pretend you got one now, Saint Alex.' Holland winked. 'I'm going back inside. One of us has to be there.'

'*Bastard!*'

For an hour and forty-seven minutes, Conklin sat in the lounge. His attachable footless foot never throbbed, but it was throbbing now. He did not know what the impossible feeling meant, but he could not dismiss the beat that surged through his leg. If nothing else, it was something to think about, and he thought wistfully of the younger days, when he had both feet, and before. Oh, how he had wanted to change the world! And how he had felt so *right* in a destiny that forced him to become the youngest valedictorian in his high school's history, the youngest freshman ever accepted at Georgetown, a bright, *bright* light that shimmered at the end of the tunnels of academe. His decline started when someone, somewhere, found out that his name at birth was not Alexander Conklin but Aleksei Nikolae Konsolikov. That now faceless man had casually asked him a question, the answer to which changed Conklin's life.

'Do you by any chance speak Russian?'

'Of course,' he had replied, amused that his visitor would think otherwise. 'As you obviously know, my parents were immigrants. I grew up not only in a Russian home but in a Russian neighbourhood – at least in the early years. You couldn't buy a loaf of bread at the *ovoshchnoi otdel* if you didn't. And at church school the older priests and nuns, like the Poles, held ferociously on to the language . . . I'm sure it contributed to my leaving the faith.'

'Those were the early years, however, as I believe you mentioned.'

'Yes.'

'What changed?'

'I'm sure it's in your government report somewhere and will hardly satisfy your iniquitous Senator McCarthy.'

The face came back to Alex with the memory of those words. It was a middle-aged face and it had suddenly become expressionless, the eyes clouded but with suppressed anger in them. 'I assure you, Mr Conklin, I am in no way associated with the senator. You call him iniquitous, I have other terms, but they're not pertinent here . . . What changed?'

'Quite late in his life my father became what he had been in Russia, a highly successful merchant, a capitalist. At last count he owned seven supermarkets in upscale malls. They're called Conklin's Corners. He's over eighty now, and although I love him dearly, I regret to say he's an ardent supporter of the senator. I simply consider his years, his struggles, his hatred of the Soviets, and avoid the subject.'

'You're very bright and very diplomatic.'

'Bright and diplomatic,' Alex had agreed.

'I've shopped at a couple of Conklin's Corners. Kind of expensive.'

'Oh, yes.'

'Where did the "Conklin" come from?'

'My father. My mother says he saw it on a billboard advertising motor oil, she thinks, about four or five years after they got here. And, of course, the Konsolikov had to go. As my considerably bigoted father once said, "Only the Jews with Russian names can make money over here." Again, I avoid the subject.'

'*Very* diplomatic.'

'It's not difficult. He has his share of good points as well.'

'Even if he didn't, I'm sure you could be convincing in your diplomacy, in the concealment of your feelings.'

'Why do I think that's a leading statement?'

'Because it is, Mr Conklin. I represent a government agency that's extremely interested in you, and one in which your future would be as unlimited as that of any potential recruit I've spoken to in a decade . . .'

That conversation had taken place nearly thirty years ago, mused Alex, his eyes drifting up once again to the inner door of Sterile Five's waiting lounge in its own private medical centre. And how crazy the intervening years had been. In a stress-defying bid for unrealistic expansion, his father had overextended himself, committing enormous sums of money that existed only in his imagination and in the minds of avaricious bankers. He lost six of his seven supermarkets, the smallest and last supporting a life-style that he found unacceptable, so he conveniently had a massive stroke and died as Alex's own adult life was about to begin.

Berlin – East and West. Moscow, Leningrad, Tashkent and Kamchatka. Vienna, Paris, Lisbon and Istanbul. Then back across the world to stations in Tokyo, Hong Kong, Seoul, Cambodia, Laos, and finally Saigon and the tragedy that was Vietnam. Over the years, with his facile mastery of languages and the expertise that came with survival, he had become the Agency's point man in clandestine operations, its primary scout and often the on-scene strategist for covert activities. Then one morning with the mists hanging over the Mekong Delta, a land mine shattered his life as well as his foot. There was little left for a field man who depended on mobility in his chosen work; the rest was down hill and out of the field. His excessive drinking he accepted, and excused as genetic. The Russian's winter of depression carried over into spring, summer and autumn. The skeletal, trembling wreck of a man who was about to go under was given a reprieve. David Webb – Jason Bourne – came back into his life.

The door opened, mercifully cutting short his reverie, and Peter Holland walked slowly into the lounge. His face was pale and drawn, his eyes glazed, and in his left hand were two small plastic containers, each presumably holding a cassette tape.

'As long as I live,' said Peter, his voice low and hollow, barely above a whisper, 'I hope to Christ I never go through anything like this again, never witness anything like this again.'

'How's Mo?'

'I didn't think he'd live . . . I thought he'd kill himself. Every now and then Walsh would stop. Let me tell you, he was one frightened doctor.'

'Why didn't he call it *off*, for God's sake?'

'I asked him that. He said Panov's instructions were not only explicit but that he'd written them out and signed them and expected them to be followed to the letter. Maybe there's some kind of unwritten code of ethics between doctors, I don't know, but I do know Walsh hooked him up to an EKG that he rarely took his eyes off. Neither did I; it was easier than looking at Mo. Jesus, let's get *out* of here!'

'Wait a minute. What about Panov?'

'He's not ready for a welcome-home party. He'll stay here for a couple of days under observation. Walsh will call me in the morning.'

'I'd like to see him. I want to see him.'

'There's nothing to see but a human dishrag. Believe me, you don't and he wouldn't want you to. Let's go.'

'Where?'

'Your place in Vienna – our place in Vienna. I assume you've got a cassette machine.'

'I've got everything but a moon rocket, most of which I can't operate.'

'I want to stop and get a bottle of whisky.'

'There's whatever you want at the apartment.'

'It doesn't bother you?' asked Holland, studying Alex.

'Would it matter if it did?'

'Not a bit . . . If I remember, there's an extra bedroom, isn't there?'

'Yes.'

'Good. We may be up most of the night listening to these.' The director held up the cassettes. 'The first couple of times won't mean anything. All we'll hear is the pain, not the information.'

It was shortly past five o'clock in the afternoon when they left the estate known within the Agency as Sterile House Five. The days were growing shorter, September on the cusp, the descending sun announcing the forthcoming change with an intensity of colour that was the death of one season and the birth of another.

'The light's always brightest before we die,' said Conklin, leaning back in the seat beside Holland in the limousine, staring out of the window.

'I find that not only inappropriate but quite possibly sophomoric,' declared Peter wearily. 'I won't commit to the latter until I know who said it. Who was it?'

'Jesus, I think.'

'The scriptures were never edited. Too many campfires, no on-scene confirmation.'

Alex laughed softly, reflectively. 'Did you ever actually read them? The Scriptures, I mean.'

'Most of it – most of them.'

'Because you had to?'

'Hell, no. My father and mother were as agnostic as any two people could be without being branded godless pariahs. They shut up about it and sent me and my two sisters to a Protestant service one week, a Catholic mass on another, and a synagogue after that. Never with any regularity, but I guess they figured we should catch the whole scene. *That's* what makes kids want to read. Natural curiosity wrapped in mysticism.'

'Irresistible,' agreed Conklin. 'I lost my faith, and now after years of proclaiming my spiritual independence, I wonder if I'm missing something.'

'Like what?'

'Comfort, Peter. I have no comfort.'

'For what?'

'I don't know. Things I can't control, maybe.'

'You mean you don't have the comfort of an excuse, a metaphysical excuse. Sorry, Alex, we part company. We're accountable for what we do, and no confessional absolution can change that.'

Conklin turned his head, his eyes wide open, and looked at Holland. 'Thank you,' he said.

'For what?'

'For sounding like me, even using a variation of the words I've used . . . I came back from Hong Kong five years ago with the banner of Accountability on my lance.'

'You've lost me.'

'Forget it. I'm back on track . . . "Beware the pitfalls of ecclesiastical presumption and self-absorbed thought." '

'Who the hell said that?'

'Either Savonarola or Salvador Dali, I can't remember who.'

'Oh, for Christ's sake, cut the crap!' laughed Holland.

'Why should I? It's the first chuckle we've had. And what about your two sisters? What happened to them?'

'It's a better joke,' replied Peter, his head angled down into his chin, a mischievous smile on his lips. 'One's a nun in New Delhi, and the other's president of her own public relations firm in New York and uses better Yiddish than most of her colleagues in the profession. A couple of years ago she told me they stopped calling her *shiksa*. She loves her life; so does my other sister in India.'

'Yet you chose the military.'

'Not *yet*, Alex . . . *And* I chose it. I was an angry young man who really believed this country was being dumped on. I came from a privileged family – money, influence, an expensive prep school – that guaranteed me – *me*, not the black kid on the streets of Philadelphia or Harlem – automatic admittance to Annapolis. I simply figured I had to somehow earn that privilege. I had to show that people like me didn't just use our advantages to avoid, but instead to extend, our responsibilities.'

'Aristocracy reborn,' said Conklin. 'Noblesse oblige – nobility imposes obligations.'

'That's not fair,' protested Holland.

'Yes, it is, in a very real sense. In Greek, *aristo* means the "best", and *kratia* is the word for "rule." In ancient Athens such young men led armies, their swords up front, not behind, if only to prove to the troops that they would sacrifice with the lowliest of them, for the lowliest were under their commands, the commands of the finest.'

Peter Holland's head arched back into the top of the velvet seat, his eyes half closed. 'Maybe that was part of it, I'm not sure – I'm not sure at all. We were asking so much . . . for what? Pork Chop Hill? Unidentifiable, useless terrain in the Mekong? Why? For Christ's sake, *why*? Men shot, their stomachs and chests blown away by an enemy two feet in front of them, by a 'Cong who knew jungles they didn't know? What kind of war was that? . . . If guys like me didn't go up with the kids and say, "Look, here I am, I'm with you," how the hell do you think we could have lasted as long as we did? There might have been mass revolts and maybe there should have been. Those kids were what some people call niggers, and spics and the foul-ups who couldn't read or write beyond a third-grade level. The privileged had deferments – deferments from getting soiled – or service that damn near guaranteed no combat. The others didn't. And if my being with them – this privileged son of a bitch – meant anything, it was the best gig I ever did in my life.' Holland suddenly stopped talking and shut his eyes.

'I'm sorry, Peter. I didn't mean to rough up past roads, I really didn't. Actually, I started with my guilt, not yours . . . It's crazy how it all dovetails and feeds upon itself, isn't it? What did you call it? The merry-go-round of guilt. Where does it stop?'

'*Now*,' said Holland, sitting up in the seat, straightening his back and shoulders. He picked up the limousine telephone, punched two numbers and spoke. 'Drop us off in Vienna, please. And when you've done that, go find a Chinese restaurant and bring us back the best they've got . . . Frankly, I'm partial to spare ribs and lemon chicken.'

Holland proved to be half right. The first hearing of Panov's session under the serum was agonizing to listen to, the voice devastating, the emotional content blurring the information, especially for anyone who knew the psychiatrist. The second hearing, however, produced instantaneous concentration, engendered without question by the very pain they heard. There was no time to indulge in personal feelings; the information was suddenly everything. Both men began taking copious notes on legal pads, frequently stopping and replaying numerous sections for clarity and understanding. The third hearing refined the salient points further; by the end of the fourth, both Alex and Peter Holland had thirty to forty pages of notes apiece. They spent an additional hour in silence, each going over his own analysis.

'Are you ready?' asked the CIA's director from the couch, a pencil in his hand.

'Sure,' said Conklin, seated at the desk with his various electronic equipment, the tape machine at his elbow.

'Any opening remarks?'

'Yes,' replied Alex. 'Ninety-nine point forty-four per cent of what we listened to gives us nothing, except to tell us what a terrific prober this Walsh is. He hopscotched around picking up cues faster than I could find them, and I wasn't exactly an amateur when it came to interrogations.'

'Agreed,' said Holland. 'I wasn't so bad either, especially with a blunt instrument. Walsh is good.'

'Better than that, but that doesn't concern us. What he pulled out of Mo does – again with a "but". It's not in Panov's recapturing what he revealed because we have to assume he revealed almost everything I told him. Instead, it's in what he repeated having *heard*.' Conklin separated several pages. 'Here's an example. "The family will be pleased . . . our supreme will give us his blessing." He's repeating someone else's words, not his own. Now, Mo isn't familiar with criminal jargon, certainly not to the point where he would automatically make a connection, but the connection's there. Take the word "supreme" and change it by removing one vowel and inserting another. "Supremo" – capo supremo, hardly a heavenly supreme being. Suddenly "the family" is light years away from Norman Rockwell, and "blessing" is interchangeable with a reward or a bonus.'

'Mafia,' said Peter, his eyes steady and clear despite a number of drinks that had obviously been burned out of his system. 'I hadn't thought that one through, but I marked it instinctively . . . Okay, here's something else along the same lines, the same lines because I also picked up on the unlike-Panov phrases.' Holland flipped through his legal pad and stopped at a specific page. 'Here. "New York wants it all." Peter continued slapping over the pages. 'Again here. "That Wall Street is something." ' Once more the DCI progressed through his legal pad. 'And this one. "Blondie fruits" – the rest is garbled.'

'I missed that. I heard it, but it didn't make any sense to me.'

'Why should it, Mr Aleksei Konsolikov?' Holland smiled. 'Underneath that Anglo-Saxon exterior, education and all, beats the heart of a Russian. You're not sensitive to what some of us have to endure.'

'Huh?'

'I'm a WASP and "blondie fruits" is but one more pejorative description given us by, I must admit, other trampled-upon minorities. Think about it. Armbruster, Swayne, Atkinson, Burton, Teagarten – "blondies" all. And Wall Street, certain firms in that orginally WASP financial bastion, at any rate.'

'Medusa,' said Alex, nodding. 'Medusa and the Mafia . . . Holy Christ.'

'We've got a *telephone* number!' Peter leaned forward on the couch. 'It was in the ledger Bourne brought out of Swayne's house.'

'I've tried it, remember? It's an answering machine, that's all it is.'

'And that's enough. We can get a location.'

'To what end? Whoever picks up the messages does it by remote, and if he or she has half a brain, it's done from a public phone. The relay is not only untraceable but capable of erasing all other messages, so we can't tap in.'

'You're not very into high tech, are you, Field Man?'

'Let's put it this way,' replied Conklin. 'I bought a VCR so I could watch old movies, and I can't figure out how to turn off the goddamn blinking clock. I called the dealer and he said, "Read the instructions on the interior panel." I can't find the interior panel.'

'Then let me explain what we can do to an answering machine . . . We can jam it externally.'

'Gee willikers, Sandy, what's next for Orphan Annie? What the hell is that going to do? Other than kill the source.'

'You're forgetting. We have the location from the numbers.'

'Oh?'

'Someone has to come and repair the machine.'

'*Oh.*'

'We take him and find out who sent him there.'

'You know, Peter, you've got possibilities. For a neophyte, you understand, your current outrageously undeserved position notwithstanding.'

'Sorry I can't offer you a drink.'

Bryce Ogilvie, of the law firm Ogilvie, Spofford, Crawford and Cohen, was dictating a highly complex reply to the Justice Department's antitrust division when his very private telephone line rang; it rang only at his desk. He picked up the phone, pressed the green button and spoke rapidly. 'Hold on,' he ordered, looking up at his secretary. 'Would you excuse me, please?'

'Certainly, sir.' The secretary got out of her chair, walked across the large impressive office, and disappeared beyond the door.

'Yes, what is it?' asked Ogilvie, returning to the phone.

'The machine isn't working,' said the voice on the sacrosanct line.

'What happened?'

'I don't know. All I get is a busy signal.'

'That's the best equipment available. Perhaps someone was calling in when *you* called.'

'I've been trying for the past two hours. There's a glitch. Even the best machines break down.'

'All right, send someone up to check it out. Use one of the niggers.'

'Naturally. No white man would go up there.'

25

It was shortly past midnight when Bourne got off the *métro* in Argenteuil. He had divided the day into segments, splitting the hours between the arrangements he had to make and looking for Marie, going from one arrondissement to another, scouting every café, every shop, every large and small hotel he could recall having been a part of their fugitive nightmare thirteen years ago. More than once he had gasped, seeing a woman in the distance or across a café; the back of a head, a quick profile, and twice a crown of dark red hair, any of which from a distance or in a café's dim light might have been his wife. None were, but he began to understand his own anxiety and, by understanding it, was better able to control it. These were the most impossible parts of the day; the rest was merely filled with difficulty and frustration.

Alex! Where the hell was *Conklin*? He could not reach him in Virginia! Because of the time difference, he had counted on Alex to take care of the details, swiftly expediting the transfer of funds, primarily. The business day on the eastern seaboard of the United States began at four o'clock, Paris time, and the business day in Paris stopped at five o'clock or before, Paris time. That left barely an hour to release and transfer over a million American dollars to one Mr Simon at his chosen bank in Paris, and *that* meant said Mr Simon had to make himself known to the aforementioned, as yet unchosen, Paris bank. Bernardine had been helpful. Helpful, *hell*! He had made it possible.

'There's a bank on the rue de Grenelle that the Deuxième frequently uses. They can be accommodating in terms of hours and the absence of an authentic signature or two, but they give nothing for nothing, and they trust no one. Especially anyone associated with our benevolent socialist government.'

'You mean regardless of the teletypes, if the money's not there you don't get it.'

'Not a sou. The President, himself, could call and he would be told to pick it up in Moscow, where they firmly believe he belongs.'

'Since I can't reach Alex, I've bypassed the bank in Boston and called our man in the Cayman Islands, where Marie put the bulk of the money. He's Canadian and so's the bank. He's waiting for instructions.'

'I'll make a phone call. Are you at the Pont-Royal?'

'No. I'll call you back.'

'Where are you?'

'I suppose you could say I'm an anxious and confused butterfly going from one vaguely remembered place to another.'

'You are looking for her.'

'Yes. But then that wasn't a question, was it?'

'Forgive me, but in some ways I hope you do not find her.'

'Thanks. I'll call you back in twenty minutes.'

He had gone to yet another point of recall, the Trocadéro, and the Palais de Chaillot. He had been shot at in the past on one of the terraces; there had been gunfire and men running down the endless stone steps, intermittently obscured by the huge gilded statues and the great sprays of the fountains, disappearing into the formal gardens, finally out of sight, out of range. What had happened? Why did he remember the Trocadéro? . . . But Marie had been there – *somewhere.* Where had she been in that enormous complex? Where? . . . A terrace! She had been on a *terrace.* Near a statue – *what* statue? . . . Descartes? Racine? Talleyrand? The statue of Descartes came to his mind first. He would find it.

He had found it and there was no Marie. He had looked at his watch; it had been nearly forty-five minutes since he had talked to Bernardine. Like the men in his inner screen, he had raced down the steps. To a telephone.

'Go to the Banque Normandie and ask for Monsieur Tabouri. He understands that a Monsieur Simon intends to transfer over seven million francs from the Caymans by way of voice authorization through his private banker in the islands. He is most happy to let you use his phone, but believe me, he'll charge you for the call.'

'Thanks, François.'

'Where are you now?'

'The Trocadéro. It's crazy. I have the damnedest feelings, like vibrations, but she's not there. It's probably the things I can't remember. Hell, I may have taken a bullet here, I simply don't know.'

'Go to the bank.'

He had done so, and within thirty-five minutes after his call to the Caymans, the olive-skinned, perpetually smiling Monsieur Tabouri confirmed that his funds were in place. He requested 750,000 francs in the largest notes possible. They were delivered to him, and the grinning obsequious banker took him confidentially aside, away from the desk – which was rather foolish, as there was no one else in the office – and spoke quietly by a window.

'There are some marvellous real estate opportunities in Beirut, believe me, I *know.* I am the expert on the Middle East and these stupid conflagrations cannot last much longer. *Mon Dieu,* no one will be left alive! It will once again rise as the Paris of the Mediterranean. Estates for a fraction of their value, hotels for *le ridicule*!'

'It sounds interesting. I'll be in touch.'

He had fled the Banque Normandie as if its confines held the germs of a lethal disease. He had returned to the Pont-Royal, and again tried to reach Alex Conklin in the United States. It was then close to one o'clock in the afternoon in Vienna, Virginia, and still all he had heard was an answering machine with Alex's disembodied voice instructing the caller to leave a message. For any number of reasons, Jason had chosen not to do so.

And now he was in Argenteuil, walking up the steps of the *métro* to the pavement, where he would slowly, cautiously make his way into the uglier streets and the vicinity of Le Coeur du Soldat. His instructions were clear. He was not to be the man he was last night, no limp, no ragged cast-off army clothing, no image that anyone might recognize. He was to be a simple labourer and reach the gates of the old closed-down refinery and smoke cigarettes while leaning against the wall. This was to take place between twelve-thirty and one o'clock in the morning. No sooner and no later.

When he had asked Santos's messengers – after giving them several hundred francs for their inconvenience – why these late-night precautions, the less inhibited man had replied, 'Santos never leaves Le Coeur du Soldat.'

'He left last evening.'

'For minutes only,' rejoined the more voluble messenger.

'I understand.' Bourne nodded, but he had not understood, he could only speculate. Was Santos in some way the Jackal's prisoner, confined to the sleazy café night and day? It was a fascinating query in light of the manager's size and sheer raw power, both combined with a far-above-average intellect.

It was 12:37 when Jason, in blue jeans, cap and a dark, tattered V-necked sweater, reached the gates of the old factory. He took out a pack of Gauloise cigarettes and leaned against the wall, lighting one with a match, holding the flame longer than necessary before he blew it out. His thoughts returned to the enigmatic Santos, the premier conduit in Carlos's army, the most trusted satellite in the Jackal's orbit, a man whose French might have been formed at the Sorbonne, yet Santos was a Latin American. A Venezuelan, if Bourne's instincts had merit. *Fascinating.* And Santos wanted to see him 'with peace in his heart.' Bravo, *amigo*, thought Jason. Santos had reached a terrified ambassador in London with a question so loaded it made a political party's private poll look like the essence of nonpartisan neutrality. Atkinson had no choice but to state emphatically, if not in panic, that whatever instructions Snake Lady issued were to be carried out. The power of Snake Lady was the ambassador's only protection, his ultimate refuge.

So Santos could bend; that decision was rooted in intellect, not loyalty, not obligation. The conduit wanted to crawl out of his sewer, and with three million francs in the offing, combined with a multitude of faraway places across the globe to choose from, the conduit's mind told him to listen, to consider. There were alternatives in life if opportunities were presented. One had been presented to Santos, vassal to Carlos, whose fealty to his lord had perhaps run its suffocating course. It was this instinctive projection that made Bourne include in his plea – calmly but firmly, the emphasis in understatement – such phrases as: *You could travel, disappear . . . a wealthy man, free of care and unpleasant drudgery.* The key words were 'free' and 'disappear' and Santos's eyes had responded. He was ready to take the three-million-franc bait, and Bourne was perfectly happy to let him break the line and swim with it.

Jason looked at his watch; fifteen minutes had passed. No doubt Santos's minions were checking the streets, a final inspection before the high priest of conduits appeared. Bourne thought briefly of Marie, of the sensations he felt at the Trocadero, remembering old Fontaine's words when the two of them watched the paths of Tranquillity Inn from the high storage room, waiting for

Carlos. *He's near; I feel it. Like the approach of distant thunder.* In a different – far different – way, Jason had like feelings at the Trocadéro. *Enough!* Santos! The Jackal!

His watch read one o'clock, and the two messengers from the Pont-Royal walked out of the alley and across the street to the gates of the old refinery.

'Santos will see you now,' said the voluble one.

'I don't see him.'

'You are to come with us. He does not leave Le Coeur du Soldat.'

'Why do I find that not to my liking?'

'There's no reason for such feelings. He has peace in his heart.'

'What about his knife?'

'He has no knife, no weapon. He never carries either.'

'That's nice to hear. Let's go.'

'He has no need for such weapons,' added the messenger, disquietingly.

He was escorted down the alley, past the neon-lit entrance, to a barely negotiable break in the buildings. One by one, Jason between the two men, they made their way to the rear of the café, where there was just about the last thing Bourne expected to see in this run-down section of the city. It was . . . well, an English garden. A plot of ground perhaps thirty feet in length, twenty in depth, and trellises supporting a variety of flowering vines, a barrage of colour in the French moonlight.

'That's quite a sight,' commented Jason. 'It didn't come about through neglect.'

'Ah, it is a passion with Santos! No one understands it, but no one touches a single flower, either.'

Fascinating.

Bourne was led to a small outside elevator whose steel frame was attached to the stone wall of the building. There was no other access in sight. The conveyance barely held the three of them, and once the iron gate was closed, the silent messenger pressed a button in the darkness and spoke. 'We are here, Santos. *Camellia.* Bring us up.'

'Camellia?' asked Jason.

'He knows everything is all right. If not, my friend might have said "lily" or "rose".'

'What would happen then?'

'You don't want to think about it. *I* don't care to think about it.'

'Naturally. Of course.'

The outside elevator stopped with a disturbing double jerk, and the quiet messenger opened a thick, steel door that required his full weight to open. Bourne was led into the familiar room with the tasteful, expensive furniture, the bookcases, and the single floor lamp that illuminated Santos in his outsized armchair.

'You may leave, my friends,' said the large man, addressing the messengers. 'Pick up your money from the faggot, and for God's sake, tell him to give René and the American who calls himself Ralph fifty francs apiece and get them out of here. They're pissing in the corners . . . Say the money's from their friend from last night who forgot about them.'

'Oh, *shit*!' exploded Jason.

'You did forget, didn't you?' Santos grinned.

'I've had other things on my mind.'

'Yes, sir! Yes, Santos!' The two messengers, instead of heading for the back of the room and the elevator, opened a door in the left wall and disappeared. Bourne looked after them, bewildered.

'There is a staircase leading to our kitchen, such as it is,' said Santos, answering Jason's unspoken question. 'The door can be opened from this side, not from the steps below except by me . . . Sit down, Monsieur Simon. You are my guest. How is your head?'

'The swelling's gone down, thank you.' Bourne sat on the large couch, sinking into the pillows; it was not an authoritative position, nor was it meant to be. 'I understand you have peace in your heart.'

'And a desire for three million francs in the avaricious section of that heart.'

'Then you were satisfied with your call to London?'

'No one could have programmed that man into reacting the way he did. There *is* a Snake Lady and she instils extraordinary devotion and fear in high places – which means that female serpent is not without power.'

'That's what I tried to tell you.'

'Your word is accepted. Now, let me recapitulate your request, your demand, as it were—'

'My restrictions,' interrupted Jason.

'Very well, your restrictions,' agreed Santos. 'You and you *alone* must reach the blackbird, correct?'

'It's an absolute.'

'Again, I must ask why?'

'Speaking frankly, you already know too much, more than my clients realize, but then none of them was about to lose his own life on the second floor of a café in Argenteuil. They want nothing to do with you, they want no traces, and in that area you're vulnerable.'

'*How?*' Santos crashed his fist against the arm of the chair.

'An old man in Paris with a police record who tried to warn a member of the Assembly that he was to be assassinated. He was the one who mentioned the blackbird; he was the one who spoke of Le Coeur du Soldat. Fortunately, our man heard him and silently passed the word to my clients, but that's not good enough. How many other old men in Paris in their senile delusions may mention Le Coeur du Soldat – and *you*? . . . No, you can have nothing to do with my clients.'

'Even through *you*?'

'I disappear, you don't. Although, in all honesty, I believe you should think about doing so . . . Here, I brought you something.' Bourne sat forward on the couch and reached into his back pocket. He pulled out a roll of tightly wound franc notes held together by a thick elastic band. He threw it over to Santos, who caught it effortlessly in midair. 'Two hundred thousand francs on account – I was authorized to give this to you. On a best-efforts basis. You give me the information I need, I deliver it to London, and whether or not the blackbird accepts my clients' offer, you still receive the balance of the three million.'

'But you could disappear before then, couldn't you?'

'Have me watched as you've been doing, have me followed to London and back. I'll even call you with the names of the airlines and the flight numbers. What could be fairer?'

'One thing more could be fairer, Monsieur Simon,' replied Santos, pushing his immense frame out of the chair and baronially striding to a card table against the lacquered brick wall of his flat. 'If you will, please come over here.'

Jason rose from the couch and walked over to the card table, instantly astonished. 'You're thorough, aren't you?'

'I try to be . . . Oh, don't blame the concierges, they belong to you. I'm much further below scale. Chambermaids and stewards are more to my liking. They're not so spoiled and nobody really misses them if they don't show up one day.'

Spread across the table were Bourne's three passports, courtesy of Cactus in Washington, as well as the gun and the knife taken from him last night. 'You're very convincing, but it doesn't solve anything, does it?'

'We'll see,' answered Santos. 'I'll accept your money now – for my best efforts – but instead of your flying to London, have London fly to Paris. Tomorrow morning. When he arrives at the Pont-Royal, you'll call me – I'll give you my private number, of course – and we'll play the Soviets' game. Exchange for exchange, like walking across a bridge with our respective prisoners in tow. The money for the information.'

'You're crazy, Santos. My clients don't expose themselves that way. You just lost the rest of the three million.'

'Why not try them? They could always hire a blind, couldn't they? An innocent tourist with a false bottom in his or her Louis Vuitton carry-on? No alarms are set off with paper. *Try* it! It is the only way you'll get what you want, monsieur.'

'I'll do what I can,' said Bourne.

'Here is my telephone.' Santos picked up a prearranged card from the table with numbers scrawled across it. 'Call me when London arrives. In the meantime, I assure you, you *will* be watched.'

'You're a real swell guy.'

'I'll escort you to the elevator.'

Marie sat up in bed, sipping hot tea in the dark room, listening to the sounds of Paris outside the windows. Sleep was not only impossible, it was intolerable, a waste of time when every hour counted. She had taken the earliest flight from Marseilles to Paris and had gone directly to the Meurice on the rue de Rivoli, the same hotel where she had waited thirteen years ago, waited for a man to listen to reason or lose his life, and in doing so, losing a large part of hers. She had ordered a pot of tea then, and he had come back to her; she ordered tea now from the night floor steward, absently perhaps, as if the repeated ritual might bring about a repetition of his appearance so long ago.

Oh, God, she had *seen* him! It was no illusion, no mistake, it was *David*! She had left the hotel at midmorning and began wandering, going down the list she had made on the plane, heading from one location to another without any logical sequence in mind, simply following the succession of places as they had come to her – that was her sequence. It was a lesson she had learned from Jason Bourne thirteen years ago: *When running or hunting, analyse your options but remember your first. It's usually the cleanest and the best. Most of the time you'll take it.*

So she had followed the list, from the pier of the Bateau Mouche at the base of the avenue George V to the bank on the Madeleine . . . to the Trocadéro. She had wandered aimlessly along the terraces of the last, as if in a trance, looking for a statue she could not remember, jostled by the intermittent groups of tourists led by loud, officious guides. The huge statues all began to look alike; she had felt light-headed. The late August sun was blinding. She was about to sit down on a marble bench, remembering yet another dictate from Jason Bourne: *Rest is a weapon.* Suddenly, up ahead, she saw a man wearing a cap and a dark V-necked sweater; he had turned and raced towards the palatial stone steps that led to the avenue Gustave V. She knew that run, that stride; she knew it better than *anyone*! How often had she watched him – frequently from behind bleachers, unseen – as he had pounded around the university track, ridding himself of the furies that had gripped him. It was *David*! She had leaped up from the bench and raced after him.

'*David!* David, it's me . . . *Jason!*'

She had collided with a tour guide leading a group of Japanese. The man was incensed; she was furious, so she furiously pummelled her way through the astonished Orientals, the majority shorter than she was, but her superior sightlines were no help. Her husband had disappeared. Where had he *gone*? Into the gardens? Into the street with the crowds and the traffic from the Pont d'Iéna? For Christ's sake, *where*?

'*Jason!*' she had screamed at the top of her voice. 'Jason, come *back*!'

People had looked at her, some with the empathetic glances of lovers burned, most simply disapproving. She had run down the never-ending steps to the street, spending – how long a time she could not recall – searching for him. Finally, in exhaustion, she had taken a taxi back to the Meurice. In a daze, she reached her room and fell on the bed, refusing to let the tears come. It was no time for tears. It was a time for a brief rest and food; energy to be restored, the lessons of Jason Bourne. Then back into the streets, the hunt to continue. And as she lay there, staring at the wall, she felt a swelling in her chest, in her lungs perhaps, and it was accompanied by a sense of passive elation. As she was looking for David, *he* was looking for *her*. Her husband had not run away, even Jason Bourne had not run away. Neither part of the same man could have seen her. There had been another unknown reason for the sudden, hurried exit from the Trocadéro, but there was only one reason for his being *at* the Trocadéro. He, too, was searching what memories he had of Paris thirteen years ago. He, too, understood that somewhere, someplace in those memories he would *find* her.

She had rested, ordered room service and two hours later gone out again into the streets.

Now, at the moment, as she drank her tea, she could not wait for the light to come. The day ahead was meant for searching.

'Bernardine!'

'*Mon Dieu*, it is four o'clock in the morning so I can assume you have something vital to tell this seventy-year-old man.'

'I've got a problem.'

'I think you have many problems, but I suppose it's a minor distinction. What is it?'

'I'm as close as I can be but I need an end man.'

'Please speak clearer English, or if you will, far clearer French. It must be an American term, this "end man". But then you have so many esoteric phrases. I'm sure someone sits in Langley and thinks them up.'

'Come on, I haven't time for your *bon mots*.'

'You come on, my friend. I'm not trying to be clever, I'm trying to wake up . . . *There*, my feet are on the floor and a cigarette's in my mouth. *Now* what is it?'

'My access to the Jackal expects an Englishman to fly over from London this morning with two million eight hundred thousand francs—'

'Far less than you have at your disposal, I assume,' interrupted Bernardine. 'The Banque Normandie was accommodating, was it not?'

'Very. The money's there, and that Tabouri of yours is a beaut. He tried to sell me real estate in Beirut.'

'That Tabouri is a thief – but Beirut is interesting.'

'*Please.*'

'Sorry, Go ahead.'

'I'm being watched, so I can't go to the bank, and I don't have any Englishman to bring what I can't get to the Pont-Royal.'

'*That's* your problem?'

'Yes.'

'Are you willing to part with, say, fifty thousand francs?'

'What for?'

'Tabouri.'

'I suppose so.'

'You signed papers, of course.'

'Of course.'

'Sign another paper, handwritten by you and also signed, releasing the money to – Wait a moment, I must go to my desk.' There was silence on the line as Bernardine obviously went to another room in his flat; his voice returned. '*Allo?*'

'I'm here.'

'Oh, this is lovely,' intoned the former Deuxième specialist. 'I sunk him in his sailboat off the shoals of the Costa Brava. The sharks had a feeding frenzy; he was so fat and delectable. The name is Antonio Scarzi, a Sardinian who traded drugs for information, but you know nothing about that, of course.'

'Of course.' Bourne repeated the last name, spelling it out.

'Correct. Seal the envelope, rub a pencil or a pen over your thumb and press your prints along the seal. Then give it to the concierge for Mr Scarzi.'

'Understood. What about the Englishman? This morning? It's only a few hours away.'

'The Englishman is not a problem. The morning is – the few hours are. It's a simple matter to transfer funds from one bank to another – buttons are pressed, computers instantly cross-check the data, and, poof, figures are entered on paper. It's quite another thing to collect nearly three million francs in cash, and your access certainly won't accept pounds or dollars for fear of being caught exchanging them or depositing them. Add to this the problem of collecting notes large enough to be part of a bundle small enough to be concealed from customs inspectors . . . Your access, *mon ami*, has to be aware of these difficulties.'

Jason looked aimlessly at the wall, his thoughts on Bernardine's words. 'You think he's testing me?'

'He has to.'

'The money could be gotten together from the foreign departments of different banks. A small private plane could hop across the Channel and land in a pasture where a car's waiting to bring the man to Paris.'

'*Bien.* Of course. However, these logistics take time even for the most influential people. Don't make it all appear too simple, that would be suspect. Keep your access informed as to the progress being made, emphasizing the secrecy, how there can be no risk of exposure, explain the delays. If there were none, he might think it's a trap.'

'I see what you mean. It comes down to what you just said – don't make it seem so easy because that's not credible.'

'There's something else, *mon ami.* A chameleon may be many things in daylight; still, he is safer in darkness.'

'You forgot something,' said Bourne. 'What about the Englishman?'

'Tallyho, old *chap*,' said Bernardine.

The operation went as smoothly as any Jason had ever engineered or been witness to, perhaps thanks to the flair of a resentful, talented man who had been sent to the pastures too soon. While throughout the day Bourne made progress calls to Santos, Bernardine had someone other than himself pick up the sealed instructions from the concierge and bring them to him, at which point he made his appointment with Monsieur Tabouri. Shortly after four-thirty in the afternoon, the Deuxième veteran walked into the Pont-Royal dressed in a dark pin-striped suit so obviously British that it screamed Savile Row. He went to the elevator and eventually, after two wrong turns, reached Bourne's room.

'Here's the money,' he said, dropping the attaché case on the floor and going straight to Jason's hotel wet bar; he removed two miniature bottles of Tanqueray gin, snapped them open and poured the liquor into a questionably clean glass. '*A votre santé*,' he added, swallowing half his drink before breathing heavily through his mouth and then rapidly swallowing the rest. 'I haven't done anything like that in years.'

'You haven't?'

'Frankly, no. I had others do such things. It's far too dangerous . . . Nevertheless, Tabouri is forever in your debt, and, frankly, he's convinced me I should look into Beirut.'

'What?'

'Of course, I haven't your resources, but a percentage of forty years of *les fonds de contingence* have found their way to Geneva on my behalf. I'm not a poor man.'

'You may be a dead man if they pick you up leaving here.'

'Oh, but I shan't go,' said Bernardine, once again searching the small refrigerator. 'I shall stay in this room until you have concluded your business.' François ripped open two additional bottles and, holding them in the fingers of one hand, poured them into his glass. 'Now, perhaps, my old heart will beat slower,' he added as he walked to the inadequate desk, placed his drink on the blotter, and proceeded to take out two automatics and three grenades from his pockets, placing them all in a row in front of his glass. 'Yes, I will relax now.'

'What the hell is *that* – are *they*?' cried Jason.

'I think you Americans call it deterrence,' replied Bernardine. 'Although I frankly believe both you and the Soviets are playing with yourselves as you both put so much money into weaponry that doesn't work. Now, I come from a different era. When you go out to do your business, you will leave the door open. If someone comes down that narrow corridor, he will see a grenade in my hand. That is not nuclear abstraction, *that* is deterrence.'

'I'll buy it,' said Bourne, going to the door. 'I want to get this over with.'

Out on the Montalembert, Jason walked to the corner, and as he had done at the old factory in Argenteuil, leaned against the wall and lit a cigarette. He waited, his posture casual, his mind in high gear.

A man walked across from the bisecting rue du Bac towards him. It was the talkative messenger from last night; he approached, his hand in his jacket pocket.

'Where's the money?' said the man in French.

'Where's the information?' answered Bourne.

'The money first.'

'That's not the arrangement.' Without warning, Jason grabbed the minion from Argenteuil by his lapel, yanking him forward off his feet. Bourne whipped up his free hand and gripped the messenger's throat, his fingers digging into the man's flesh. 'You go back and tell Santos he's got a one-way ticket to hell. I don't *deal* this way.'

'*Enough!*' said the low voice, its owner rounding the corner on Jason's right. The huge figure of Santos approached. 'Let him go, Simon. He is nothing. It is now only you and me.'

'I thought you never left Le Coeur du Soldat?'

'You've changed that, haven't you?'

'Apparently.' Bourne released the messenger, who looked at Santos. With a gesture of his large head, the man raced away.

'Your Englishman arrived,' said Santos when they were alone. 'He carried a valise, I saw for myself.'

'He arrived carrying a valise,' agreed Jason.

'So London capitulates, no? London is very anxious.'

'The stakes are very high and that's all I'll say about it. The information, please.'

'Let us first again define the procedure, shall we?'

'We've defined it several times . . . You give me the information, my client tells me to act upon it; and if satisfactory contact is made, I bring you the remainder of the three million francs.'

'You say "satisfactory contact". What will satisfy you? How will you know the contact is firm? How do *I* know that you will not claim it is unsatisfactory and steal my money when, indeed, you have made the connection your clients have paid for?'

'You're a suspicious fellow, aren't you?'

'Oh, *very* suspicious. Our world, Mr Simon, is not peopled with saints, is it?'

'Perhaps more than you realize.'

'That would astonish me. Please answer my questions.'

'All right, I'll try . . . How will I know the contact's firm? That's easy. I'll simply *know* because it's my business to know. It's what I'm paid for, and a man in my position does not make mistakes at this level and live to apologize. I've refined the process, done my research, and I'll ask two or three questions myself. Then I'll know – one way or another.'

'That's an elusive reply.'

'In our world, Mr Santos, being elusive is hardly a negative, is it? . . . As to your concern that I would lie to you and take your money, let me assure you I don't cultivate enemies like you and the network your blackbird obviously controls any more than I would make enemies of my clients. That way is madness and a much shorter life.'

'I admire your perspicacity as well as your caution,' said the Jackal's intermediary.

'The bookcases didn't lie. You're a learned man.'

'That's neither here nor there, but I have certain credentials. Appearances can be a liability as well as an asset . . . What I am about to tell you, Mr Simon, is known by only four men on the face of the earth, all of whom speak French fluently. How you wish to use that information is up to you. However, if you even hint at Argenteuil, I'll know it instantly and you will never leave the Pont-Royal alive.'

'The contact can be made so quickly?'

'With a telephone number. But you will not place the call for at least an hour from the moment we part. If you do, again I will know it, and again I tell you you're a dead man.'

'An hour. Agreed . . . Only three other people have this number? Why not pick one you're not particularly fond of so I might peripherally allude to him – if it's necessary.'

Santos permitted himself a small, flat smile. 'Moscow,' he said softly. 'High up in Dzerzhinsky Square.'

'The *KGB*?'

'The blackbird is building a cadre in Moscow, always Moscow, it's an obsession with him.'

Ilich Ramirez Sanchez, thought Bourne. *Trained at Novgorod. Dismissed by the Komitet as a maniac. The Jackal!*

'I'll bear it in mind – if it's called for. The number, please?'

Santos recited it twice along with the words Bourne was to say. He spoke slowly, obviously impressed that Bourne wrote nothing down. 'Is it all clear?'

'Indelibly, no pencil or paper required . . . If everything goes as I trust it will, how do you want me to get you the money?'

'Phone me; you've got my number. I will leave Argenteuil and come to you. And never return to Argenteuil.'

'Good luck, Santos. Something tells me you deserve it.'

'No one more so. I have drunk the hemlock far too many times.'

'Socrates,' said Jason.

'Not directly. Plato's dialogues, to be precise. *Au revoir*.'

Santos walked away and Bourne, his chest pounding, headed back to the Pont-Royal, desperately suppressing his desire to run. *A running man is an object of curiosity, a target.* A lesson from the cantos of Jason Bourne.

'*Bernardine!*' he yelled, racing down the narrow, deserted hallway to his room, all too aware of the open door and the old man seated at the desk, a grenade in one hand, a gun in the other. 'Put the hardware away, we've hit pay dirt!'

'Who's paying?' asked the Deuxième veteran as Jason closed the door.

'I am,' answered Bourne. 'If this works out the way I think it will, you can add to your account in Geneva.'

'I do not do what I'm doing for that, my friend. It has never been a consideration.'

'I know, but as long as we're passing out francs like we're printing them in the garage, why shouldn't you get a fair share?'

'I can't argue with that, either.'

'An *hour*,' announced Jason. 'Forty-three minutes now, to be exact.'

'For what?'

'To find out if it's real, actually *real*.' Bourne fell on the bed, his arms behind his head on the pillow, his eyes alive. 'Write this down, François.' Jason recited the telephone number given him by Santos. 'Buy, bribe, or threaten every high-level contact you've ever had in the Paris telephone service, but get me the location of that number.'

'It's not such an expensive request—'

'Yes, it *is*,' countered Bourne. 'He's got it guarded, inviolate; he wouldn't do it any other way. Only four people in his entire network have it.'

'Then, perhaps, we do not go high-level, but, instead, far lower to the ground, underground actually. Into the tunnels of the telephone service beneath the streets.'

Jason snapped his head over at Bernardine. 'I hadn't thought of that.'

'Why should you? You are not Deuxième. The technicians are the source, not the bureaucrats behind the desks . . . I know several. I will find one and give him a quiet call at home later tonight—'

'Tonight?' broke in Bourne, raising himself off the bed.

'It will cost a thousand francs or so, but you'll get the location of the telephone.'

'I can't wait until later tonight.'

'Then you add a risk by trying to reach such a man at work. These men are monitored; no one trusts anyone in the telephone service. It's the Socialists' paradox: Give its labouring forces responsibility but no individual authority.'

'*Hold* it!' said Jason from the bed. 'You have the home phone numbers, right?'

'They're in the book, yes. These people don't keep private listings.'

'Have someone's wife call. An emergency. Someone's got to get home.'

Bernardine nodded his head. 'Not bad, my friend. Not bad at all.'

The minutes turned into quarter hours as the retired Deuxième officer went to work, unctuously, with promises of reward for the wives of telephone technicians, if they would do what he asked them to do. Two hung up on him, three turned him down with epithets born of the suspicious Paris kerbsides; but the sixth, amid obscenities, declared, 'Why not?' As long as the rodent she had married understood that the money was hers.

The hour was over, and Jason left the hotel, walking slowly, deliberately, down the pavement, crossing four streets until he saw a public phone on the Quai Voltaire by the Seine. A blanket of darkness was slowly floating down over Paris, the boats on the river and the bridges over it dotted with lights. As he approached the red kiosk, he breathed steadily, inhaling deeply, exercising a control over himself that he never thought possible. He was about to place the most important phone call of his life, but he could not let the Jackal know that, if, indeed, it was the Jackal. He went inside, inserted the coin, and dialled.

'Yes?' It was a woman's voice, the French *oui* sharp and harsh. A Parisienne.

'Blackbirds circle in the sky,' said Bourne, repeating Santos's words in French. 'They make a great deal of noise, all but one. He is silent.'

'Where do you call from?'

'Here in Paris, but I am not from Paris.'

'From where, then?'

'Where the winters are far colder,' answered Jason, feeling the moisture on his hairline. Control. *Control!* 'It is urgent that I reach a blackbird.'

The line was suddenly filled with silence, a sonic void, and Bourne stopped breathing. Then came the voice, low, steady, and as hollow as the previous silence. 'We speak to a Muscovite?'

The *Jackal!* It *was* the Jackal! The smooth, swift French could not hide the Latino trace. 'I did not say that,' answered Bourne; his own French dialect was one he employed frequently, with the guttural tinge of Gascony. 'I merely said the winters were colder than Paris.'

'Who is this?'

'Someone who is considered by someone who knows you sufficiently impressive to be given this number along with the proper words to go with it. I can offer you the contract of your career, of your *life*. The fee is immaterial – name your own – but those who pay are among the most powerful men in the United States. They control much of American industry, as well as that country's financial institutions, and have direct access to the nerve centres of the government.'

'This is also a very strange call. Very unorthodox.'

'If you're not interested, I'll forget this number and go elsewhere. I'm merely the broker. A simple yes or no will suffice.'

'I do not commit to things I know nothing about, to people I never heard of.'

'You'd recognize their positions, if I were at liberty to reveal them, believe that. However, I'm not seeking a commitment, only your interest at this point. If the answer is yes, I can reveal more. If it's no, well, I tried, but am forced to go elsewhere. The newspapers say he was in Brussels only yesterday. I'll find him.' There was a short, sharp intake of breath at the mention of Brussels and the unspoken Jason Bourne. 'Yes or no, blackbird?'

Silence. Finally the Jackal spoke. 'Call me back in two hours,' he ordered, hanging up the phone.

It was *done*! Jason leaned against the pay phone, the sweat pouring down his face and breaking out on his neck. The Pont-Royal. He had to get back to Bernardine!

'It was Carlos!' he announced, closing the door and crossing directly to the bedside phone while taking Santos's card out of his pocket. He dialled; in seconds, he spoke. 'The bird's confirmed,' he said. 'Give me a name, any name.' The pause was brief. 'I've got it. The merchandise will be left with the concierge. It'll be locked and taped; count it and send my passports back to me. Have your best boy pick everything up and call off the dogs. They could lead a blackbird to you.' Jason hung up and turned to Bernardine.

'The telephone number is in the fifteenth arrondissement,' said the Deuxième veteran. 'Our man knew that, or at least assumed it when I gave it to him.'

'What's he going to do?'

'Go back into the tunnels and refine things further.'

'Will he call us here?'

'Fortunately, he drives a motorbike. He said he would be back at work in ten minutes or so and reach us by this room number within the hour.'

'Perfect!'

'Not entirely. He wants five thousand francs.'

'He could have asked ten times that . . . What's "within the hour"? How long before he calls?'

'You were gone perhaps thirty, thirty-five minutes, and he reached me shortly after you left. I'd say within the next half hour.'

The telephone rang. Twenty seconds later they had an address on the Boulevard Lefebvre.

'I'm leaving,' said Jason Bourne, taking Bernardine's automatic off the desk and putting two grenades in his pocket. 'Do you mind?'

'Be my guest,' replied the Deuxième, reaching under his jacket and removing a second weapon from his belt. 'Pickpockets so abound in Paris one should always carry a backup . . . But what for?'

'I've got at least a couple of hours and I want to look around.'

'*Alone?*'

'How else? If we call for support, I risk being gunned down or spending the rest of my life in jail for an assassination I had nothing to do with in Belgium.'

Former judge of the first circuit court in Boston, the once Honourable Brendan Patrick Prefontaine, watched the weeping, disconsolate Randolph Gates as he sat forward on the couch at the Ritz-Carlton hotel, his face in his widespread hands.

'Oh, good Christ, how the mighty fall with such a thud of finality,' observed Brendan, pouring himself a short bourbon on the rocks. 'So you got snookered, Randy. French style. Your facile brain and your imperial presence didn't help you very much when you saw *Paree*, huh? You should have stayed "down on the farm", soldier boy.'

'My *God*, Prefontaine, you don't know what it was *like*! I was setting up a cartel – Paris, Bonn, London and New York with the Far East labour markets – an enterprise worth billions when I was taken from the Plaza-Athénée and put in a car and *blindfolded*. Then I was thrown into a plane and flown to Marseilles, where the most horrible things *happened* to me. I was kept in a room, and every few hours I was injected – for over six weeks! Women were brought in, films taken – I wasn't *myself*!'

'Maybe you were the self you never recognized, Dandy Boy. The same self that learned to anticipate instant gratification, if I use the phrase correctly. Make your clients extraordinary profits on paper, which they trade on the exchanges while thousands of jobs are lost in buy-outs. Oh, yes, my dear royalist, that's instant gratification.'

'You're *wrong*, Judge—'

'So lovely to hear that term again. Thank you, Randy.'

'The unions became too strong. Industry was being crippled. Many companies had to go overseas to survive!'

'And not talk? Oddly enough, you may have a point, but you never considered an alternative . . . Regardless, we stray. You emerged from your confinement in Marseilles an addict – and, of course, there were the films of the eminent attorney in compromising situations.'

'What could I *do*?' screamed Gates. 'I was ruined!'

'We know what you did. You became this Jackal's confidence man in the world of high finance, a world where competition is undesirable baggage better lost along the way.'

'It's how he found me to begin with. The cartel we were forming was opposed by Japanese and Taiwanese interests. They hired him . . . Oh, my God, he'll *kill* me!'

'Again?' asked the judge.

'What?'

'You forget. He thinks you're already dead – thanks to me.'

'I have cases coming up, a congressional hearing next week. He'll know I'm alive!'

'Not if you don't show up.'

'I *have* to! My clients expect—'

'Then I agree,' interrupted Prefontaine. 'He'll kill you. Sorry about that, Randy.'

'What am I going to *do*?'

'There's a way, Dandy Boy, not only out of your current dilemma but for years to come. Of course it will require some sacrifice on your part. For starters, a long convalescence at a private rehabilitation centre, but even before that, your complete cooperation right now. The first ensures your imminent disappearance, the second – the capture and elimination of Carlos the Jackal. You'll be free, Randy.'

'*Anything!*'

'How do you reach him?'

'I have a telephone number!' Gates fumbled for his wallet, yanking it out of his pocket and with trembling fingers digging into a recess. 'Only four people alive have it!'

Prefontaine accepted his first $20,000-an-hour fee, instructed Randy to go home, beg Edith's forgiveness, and be prepared to leave Boston tomorrow. Brendan had heard of a private treatment centre in Minneapolis, he thought, where the rich sought help incognito; he would refine the details in the morning and call him, naturally expecting a second payment for his services. The instant a shaken Gates left the room, Prefontaine went to the phone and called John St Jacques at Tranquillity Inn.

'John, it's the judge. Don't ask me questions, but I have urgent information that could be invaluable to your sister's husband. I realize I can't reach him, but I know he's dealing with someone in Washington—'

'His name is Alex Conklin,' interrupted St Jacques. 'Wait a minute, Judge, Marie wrote the number down on the desk blotter. Let me get over there.' The sound of one phone being placed on a hard surface preceded the clicks of another being picked up. 'Here it is,' Marie's brother recited the number.

'I'll explain everything later. Thank you, John.'

'An awful lot of people keep telling me that, goddamn it!' said St Jacques.

Prefontaine dialled the number with a Virginia area code. It was answered with a short, brusque 'Yes?'

'Mr Conklin, my name is Prefontaine and I was given this number by John St Jacques. What I have to tell you is in the nature of an emergency.'

'You're the judge,' broke in Alex.

'Past tense, I'm afraid. Very past.'

'What is it?'

'I know how to reach the man you call the Jackal.'

'*What?*'

'Listen to me.'

Bernardine stared at the ringing telephone, briefly debating with himself whether or not to pick it up. There was no question; he had to. 'Yes?'

'Jason? It's you, isn't it? . . . Perhaps I have the wrong room.'

'*Alex?* This is you?'

'François? What are *you* doing there? Where's Jason?'

'Things have happened so fast. I know he's been trying to reach you.'

'It's been a rough day. We've got Panov back.'

'That's good news.'

'I've got other news. A telephone number where the Jackal can be reached.'

'We've *got* it! And a location. Our man left an hour ago.'

'For Christ's sake, how did you *get* it?'

'A convoluted process I sincerely believe only your man could have negotiated. He's brilliantly imaginative, a true *caméléon*.'

'Let's compare,' said Conklin. 'What's yours?'

Bernardine complied, reciting the number he had written down on Bourne's instructions.

The silence on the phone was a silent scream. 'They're different,' said Alex finally, his voice choked. 'They're *different*!'

'A trap,' said the Deuxième veteran. 'God in heaven, it's a *trap*!'

26

Twice Bourne had passed the dark, quiet row of old stone houses on the Boulevard Lefebvre in the concrete backwater of the fifteenth arrondissement. He then doubled back to the rue d'Alesia and found a sidewalk café. The outdoor tables, their candles flickering under glass, were peopled mostly by gesturing argumentative students from the nearby Sorbonne and Montparnasse. It was nearly ten o'clock and the aproned waiters were growing irritable; the majority of customers were not full of largesse, either in their hearts or in their pockets. Jason wanted only a strong espresso, but the perpetual scowl on the face of the approaching *garçon* convinced him he would get mud if he ordered only the coffee, so he added the most expensive brandy he could recall by name.

As the waiter returned to the service bar, Jason pulled out his small notebook and ballpoint pen, shutting his eyes for a moment, then opening them and sketching out everything he could envision from the row of houses on his inner screen. There were three structures of two attached houses each, separated by two narrow alleyways. Each double complex was three storeys high, each front entrance reached by climbing a steep flight of brick steps, and at either end of the row were vacant lots covered with rubble, the remains of demolished adjacent buildings. The address of the Jackal's buried telephone number – the address was available in the underground tunnels solely for repair purposes – was the final structure on the right, and it took no imagination to know he occupied the entire building, if not the entire row.

Carlos was the consummate self-protector, so one had to assume that his Paris command post would be a fortress, employing every human and electronic security device that loyalty and high technology could provide. And the seemingly isolated, all but deserted, section of the outlying fifteenth arrondissement served his purposes far better than any crowded section of the city. For that reason, Bourne had first paid a drunken tramp to walk with him during his initial foray past the houses, he himself limping unsteadily in the shadows beside his companion; and for his second appraisal, he had hired a middle-aged whore as his cover, with no limp or stagger in his gait, only the shadows remaining. He knew the terrain now, for all the good it did him, but it was the beginning of the end. He *swore* himself to that!

The waiter arrived with his espresso and the cognac, and only when Jason placed a hundred-frane note on the table, accompanied by a wave of his hand, did the man's hostile countenance move to neutral ground. '*Merci*,' he mumbled.

'Is there a pay phone nearby?' asked Bourne, removing an additional ten-franc note.

'Down the street, fifty, sixty metres,' replied the waiter, his eyes on the new money.

'Nothing closer?' Jason peeled off another note, twenty francs. 'I'm calling right here within a few blocks.'

'Come with me,' said the aproned *garçon*, gingerly picking up the franc notes and leading Bourne through the open doors of the café to a cashier seated on high at the far end of the restaurant. The gaunt, sallow-faced woman looked annoyed; obviously she assumed that Bourne was a discontented customer.

'Let him use your telephone,' said the waiter.

'Why?' spat out the harridan. 'So he can call *China*?'

'He calls up the street. He will pay.'

Jason proffered a ten-franc note, his innocent eyes looking blankly into a highly suspicious pair. '*Augh*, take it,' said the woman, removing a phone from under her cash-register stand and grasping the money. 'It has an extension so you can move to the wall, as they all do. *Men!* Business and the bed, it's all you think about!'

He dialled the Pont-Royal and asked for his room, expecting Bernardine to pick up on the first or second ring. By the fourth, he was concerned; by the eighth, he was profoundly disturbed. Bernardine was not there! Had *Santos* . . . ? No, the Deuxième veteran was armed and knew how to use his 'deterrence' – there would have been at the least loud gunfire, at the last a room blown apart by a grenade. Bernardine had left under his own control. *Why?*

There could be any one of several reasons, thought Bourne, handing back the telephone and returning to his table outside. The first and most wished for was news of Marie; the old intelligence officer would not raise false hopes by detailing the nets he had spread throughout the city, but they were there, Jason was sure of it . . . Bourne could not think of another reason, so it was best not to think about Bernardine. He had other pressing considerations, the most intensely pressing of his life. He returned to the strong coffee and his notebook; every detail had to be exact.

An hour later he finished his espresso, taking a sip of the cognac and spilling the rest on the pavement under the usual soiled red tablecloth. He left the café and the rue d'Alesia, turning right and walking slowly, as a far older man might walk, towards the Boulevard Lefebvre. The closer he came to the last corner, the more he became aware of the undulating, erratic sounds from apparently different directions. *Sirens!* The two-note sirens of the Paris police! What had happened? What was *happening*? Jason abandoned his elderly gait and ran to the edge of the building fronting the Lefebvre and the row of old stone houses. Instantly, he was in shock, fury and astonishment joining together in panic. What were they *doing*?

Five patrol cars converged on the row of stone houses, each successively screeching to a halt in front of the structure on the right. Then a large black police van appeared, swinging directly around to face the two entrances of the building, its searchlight shooting out as a squad of black-uniformed men with automatic weapons leaped into the street and took up crouching attack positions only partially concealed by the patrol cars – an assault was in the making!'

Fools. Goddamned *fools*! To give Carlos a warning was to lose the Jackal! Killing was his profession; escape, his *obsession*. Thirteen years ago Bourne had been told that Carlos's huge retreat in the village hills of Vitry-sur-Seine outside Paris had more false walls and concealed staircases than a nobleman's Loire château in the time of Louis XIV. The fact that no one had ever determined which estate it was, or whom it was assigned to, did not vitiate the all too acceptable rumours. And with three supposedly separated structures on the Boulevard Lefebvre, it was also all too acceptable to presuppose hidden underground tunnels linking each to the others.

For Christ's sake, who had *done* this? Had a terrible error been made? Had he and Bernardine been so obtuse as to think the Deuxième *or* Peter Holland's Paris station of the CIA had overlooked tapping into his Pont-Royal telephone or bribed or enlisted the various relays of operators on the hotel's switchboard? If so, that obtuseness was rooted in an absolute: It was next to impossible to tap a phone on short notice in a relatively small hotel without being detected. Technology required a stranger on the premises, and bribe money spread around was countered with larger bribes by the subject under surveillance. *Santos?* Bugs placed in the room by a chambermaid or a bellman? Not likely. The huge conduit to the Jackal, especially if he had reneged on their contract, would not *expose* the Jackal. *Who? How?* The questions burned into Jason's imagination as he watched in horror and dismay the scene taking place on the Boulevard Lefebvre.

'*On police authority, all residents will evacuate the building.*' The orders over the loudspeaker metallically echoed throughout the street. '*You have one minute before we take aggressive procedures.*'

What aggressive *procedures*? screamed Bourne into the silent void of his mind. You've lost him. *I've* lost him. Insanity! *Who? Why?*

The door at the top of the brick steps on the left side of the building opened first. A petrified man, short, obese, in an undershirt, his trousers held up by suspenders, cautiously walked out into the flood of the searchlight, spreading his hands in front of his face and turning his head away from the blinding beam. 'What is it, messieurs?' he cried, his voice tremulous. 'I am merely a baker – a *good* baker – but I know nothing about this street except that the rent is cheap! Is that a crime for the *police*?'

'Our concerns are not with you, monsieur,' continued the amplified voice.

'Not with *me*, you say? You arrive here like an army, frightening my wife and children into thinking it is their last minutes on earth, and yet you say we don't *concern* you? What kind of reasoning is that? We live among *fascists*?'

Hurry up! thought Jason. *For God's sake, hurry! Every second is a minute in escape time, an hour for the Jackal!*

The door above the flight of brick steps on the right now opened, and a nun in the full flowing black robe of a religious habit appeared. She stood defiantly in the frame, no fear whatsoever in her almost operatic voice. 'How *dare* you?' she roared. 'These are the hours of vespers and you intrude. Better you should be asking forgiveness for your sins than interrupting those who plead with *God* for theirs!'

'Nicely said, Sister,' intoned the unimpressed police officer over the loudspeaker. 'But we have other information and we respectfully insist on searching your house. If you refuse, we shall disrespectfully carry out our orders.'

'We are the Magdalen Sisters of Charity!' exclaimed the nun. 'These are the sacrosanct quarters of women devoted to Christ!'

'We respect your position, Sister, but we are still coming inside. If what you say is so, I'm sure the authorities will make a generous contribution to your cause.'

You're wasting time! screamed Bourne to himself. *He's getting away!*

'Then may your souls be damned for transgression, but come ahead and invade this holy ground!'

'*Really*, Sister?' asked another official over the loudspeaker. 'I don't believe there's anything in the canons that gives you the right to condemn souls to hell on such a flimsy excuse . . . Go ahead, Monsieur Inspector. Under the habit, you may find lingerie more suited to the Faubourg.'

He knew that voice! It was Bernardine! What had happened? Was Bernardine no friend after all? Was it all an act, the smooth talk of a traitor? If so, there would be another death that night!

The black-uniformed squad of anti-terrorists, their automatic weapons bolted into firing modes, raced to the base of the brick steps as the *gendarmes* blocked off the Boulevard Lefebvre, north and south, while the red and blue lights of the patrol cars incessantly blinked their bright warnings to all beyond the area: *Stay away.*

'May I go *inside*?' screamed the baker. No one replied, so the obese man ran through his door clutching his trousers.

An official in civilian clothes, the obvious leader of the assault, joined his invading unit on the pavement below the steps. With a nod of his head, he and his men raced up the brick staircase through the door held open by the defiant nun.

Jason held his place at the edge of the building, his body pressed against the stone, the sweat pouring from his hairline and his neck, his eyes on the incomprehensible scene being played out on the Lefebvre. He knew the *who* now, but *why*? Was it true? Was the man most trusted by Alex Conklin and himself in reality another pair of eyes and ears for the Jackal? *Christ*, he did not want to *believe* it!

Twelve minutes passed, and with the re-emergence of Paris's version of a SWAT team and its leader, several members bowing and kissing the hand of the real or would-be abbess, Bourne understood that his and Conklin's instincts had been on true course.

'*Bernardine!*' screamed the official approaching the first patrol car. 'You are finished! *Out!* Never are you to talk to the lowest recruit in the Deuxième, even the man who cleans the *toilets*! You are *ostracized*! . . . If I had my way, you'd be *shot*! . . . International murder in the Boulevard Lefebvre! A friend of the *Bureau*! An agent we must *protect*! . . . A fucking *nunnery*, you miserable son of a bitch! *Shit*! A *nunnery* . . . Get out of my car, you smelly pig. Get *out* before a weapon goes off by mistake and your stomach's on the street, where it belongs!'

Bernardine lurched out of the patrol car, his old unsteady legs barely able to maintain balance, twice falling into the street. Jason waited, wanting to rush to his friend, but knowing he had to wait. The patrol cars and the van raced away; *still* Bourne had to wait, his eyes alternately watching Bernardine and the front entrance of the Jackal's house. And it *was* the Jackal's house, the nun proved it. Carlos could never let go of his lost faith; he consistently used it as a viable cover, but it was much more than that. Much more.

Bernardine staggered into the shadows of a long-abandoned storefront across from the house on the Boulevard Lefebvre. Jason breached the corner and ran down the pavement, racing into the recess and grabbing the Deuxième veteran as he leaned against a long glass window, breathing heavily.

'For God's sake, what *happened*?' cried Bourne, supporting Bernardine by both shoulders.

'Easy, *mon ami*,' choked Bernardine. 'The pig I sat next to – a politician, no doubt, looking for an issue – punched me in the chest before he threw me out of the car . . . I told you, I don't know all the new people who attach themselves to the Bureau these days. You have the same problems in America, so, please, do not give me a lecture.'

'It's the last thing I'm about to do . . . This is the *house*, Bernardine. Right *here*, right in front of us!'

'This is also a trap.'

'*What?*'

'Alex and I confirmed it. The telephone numbers were different. I gather you did not make your call to Carlos, as he instructed you to.'

'No. I had the address and I wanted him stretched. What's the difference? This is the *house*!'

'Oh, this is where your Mr *Simon* was to go, and if he was truly *Mr Simon*, he would be taken to another rendezvous. But if he was *not* Monsieur Simon but someone else, then he would be shot – poof – another corpse in search of the Jackal.'

'You're *wrong*!' insisted Jason, shaking his head and speaking quietly, rapidly. 'This may be a detour, but Carlos is still on the switch. He's not going to allow anyone to waste me but himself. That's his commandment.'

'As yours is regarding him?'

'Yes. I have a family; he has a borderline legend. Mine is complete for me, but his is a vacuum – without any real meaning for him any longer. He's gone as far as he can go. The only way he can go further is to move into my territory – David Webb's territory – and eliminate Jason Bourne.'

'*Webb?* David *Webb*? Who in the name of almighty God is *that*?'

'Me,' replied Bourne, smiling forlornly and leaning beside Bernardine against the window. 'It's nuts, isn't it?'

'*Nuts?*' cried the former Deuxième. 'It is *fou! Insane*, not to be *believed*!'

'Believe it.'

'You are a family man with children and you *do* this work?'

'Alex never told you?'

'If he did so, I passed it off as a cover – one goes along with anything.' Shaking his head, the older man looked up at his taller companion. 'You *really* have a family whom you do not wish to escape from?'

'On the contrary, I want to get back to them as soon as I can. They're the only people on earth I really care about.'

'But you are *Jason Bourne*, the killer Chameleon. The deepest recesses of the criminal world tremble at your name!'

'Oh, come on, that's a bit much, even from you.'

'Not for an instant! You are *Bourne*, second only to the Jackal—'

'*No!*' shouted the suddenly forgotten David Webb. 'He's no *match* for me! I'll *take* him! I'll *kill* him!'

'Very well, very well, *mon ami*,' said Bernardine calmly, reassuringly, staring at the man he could not understand. 'What do you want me to do?'

Jason Bourne turned and breathed heavily against the glass window for several moments – and then through the mists of indecision the Chameleon's strategy became clear. He swung around and looked across the dark street at the stone building on the right. 'The police are gone,' he said quietly.

'Of course, I realize that.'

'Did you also realize that no one from the other two buildings came outside? Yet there are lights on in a number of the windows.'

'I was preoccupied, what can I say? I did not notice.' Bernardine raised his eyebrows in sudden recollection. 'But there were faces at the windows, several faces, I saw them.'

'Yet no one came outside.'

'Very understandable. The police . . . men with weapons racing around. Best to barricade oneself, no?'

'Even after the police and the weapons and the patrol cars have left? They all just go back to their television sets as if nothing had happened? No one comes out to check with the neighbours? That's not natural, François; it's not even unnaturally natural. It's been orchestrated.'

'What do you mean? How?'

'One man walks out on the porch and shouts into a searchlight. Attention is drawn to him and precious seconds of a minute's warning evaporate. Then a nun emerges on the other side draping herself in holy indignation – more seconds lost, more hours for Carlos. The assault's mounted and the Deuxième comes up with zero . . . And when it's all over, everything's back to normal – an abnormal normalcy. A job was done according to a predesigned plan, so there's no call for really normal curiosity – no gathering in the street, no excitement, not even a collective postcrisis indignation. Simply people inside undoubtedly checking with one another. Doesn't it all tell you something?'

Bernardine nodded. 'A prearranged strategy carried out by professionals,' said the veteran field officer.

'That's what I think, too.'

'It's what you saw and I did not,' countered Bernardine. 'Stop being kind,

Jason. I've been too long away from the cold. Too soft, too old, too unimaginative.'

'So have I,' said Bourne. 'It's just that the stakes are so high for me that I have to force myself into thinking like a man I wanted to forget.'

'This is Monsieur Webb speaking?'

'I guess it is.'

'So where does that leave us?'

'With an irate baker and an angry nun, and if they prove to be ciphers, several faces in various windows. At this juncture the pickings are ours but that won't last long, I doubt through the morning.'

'I beg your pardon?'

'Carlos will close up shop here and he'll do it quickly. He hasn't got a choice now. Someone in his Praetorian guard gave someone else the location of his Paris headquarters, and you can bet your pension – if you've still got one – that he's climbing the walls trying to figure out who betrayed him—'

'Get *back*!' cried Bernardine, interrupting and grabbing Jason by the cloth of his black jacket, yanking him into the farthest recess of the dark storefront. 'Get out of sight! Flat on the pavement.'

Both men threw themselves down, lying prone on the broken concrete, Bourne's face against the short wall below the glass, his head angled to see the street. A second dark van appeared from the right, but it was not police equipment. Instead, it was shinier and smaller, somehow thicker, lower to the ground and more powerful. The one glaring, blinding similarity it had to the police van was the searchlight . . . No, not one, but *two* searchlights, one on either side of the windshield, both beams swinging back and forth scanning the vehicle's flanks. Jason reached for the weapon in his belt – the gun he had borrowed from Bernardine – knowing that his companion already had his backup automatic out of his pocket. The beam of the left searchlight shot over their bodies as Bourne whispered.

'Good work, but how did you spot it?' he asked.

'The moving reflections of the lamps on the side windows,' replied old François. 'I thought for a moment it was my former colleague returning to finish the job he had contemplated. Namely, my stomach in the street . . . My God, *look*!'

The van swept past the first two buildings, then suddenly swerved into the kerb and stopped in front of the last structure, nearly two hundred feet from the storefront, the building farthest from the Jackal's telephone. The instant the vehicle came to a halt the rear door opened and four men jumped out, automatic weapons in their hands, two running to the street side, one racing down the pavement to the front, the last guard standing menacingly by the open doors, his MAC-10 ready to fire. A dull wash of yellow light appeared at the top of the brick steps; the door had been opened and a man in a black raincoat came outside. He stood for a moment looking up and down the Boulevard Lefebvre.

'Is that *him*?' whispered François.

'No, not unless he's wearing high heels and a wig,' answered Jason, reaching into his jacket pocket. 'I'll know him when I see him – because I *see* him every day of my life!' Bourne took out one of the grenades he had also borrowed from Bernardine. He checked the release, laying down his gun and gripping the pockmarked steel oval, tugging at the pin to make certain it was free of corrosion.

'What the hell do you think you're *doing*?' asked the old Deuxième veteran.

'That man up there is a decoy,' replied Jason, his soft voice suspended in a cold monotone. 'In moments another will take his place, run down the steps and get into the van, either in the front seat or through the rear doors – I hope the latter, but it won't make much difference.'

'You're *mad*! You'll be killed! What good is a corpse to that family of yours?'

'You're not thinking, François. The guards will run back and climb up through the rear doors because there's no room in front. There's a lot of difference between climbing into a truck and jumping out of it. For starters, it's a slower sequence . . . By the time the last man gets in and reaches out to close those wide doors, I'll have a primed grenade inside that van . . . And I have no intention of becoming a corpse. Stay *here*!'

Before Bernardine could object further, Medusa's Delta crawled out into the dark boulevard, dark but for the harsh stationary beams of the searchlights, which were now angled on the flanks, thus actually enhancing Bourne's concealment. The hot white light around the vehicle obscured the darkness beyond; his only extreme risk was the guard posted by the open doors. Hugging the shadows of the successive storefronts as though he were threading his way through the high grass of the Mekong Delta towards a floodlit prisoner compound, Jason crept slowly forward with each wayward glance of the rear guard, his eyes darting continuously up to the man by the door above the brick steps.

Suddenly another figure emerged; it was a woman carrying a small suitcase in one hand, a large purse in the other. She spoke to the man in the black raincoat as the guard's attention was drawn to both of them. Bourne scrambled, his elbows and knees silently pounding the hard pavement, until he reached that point nearest the van where he could observe the scene on the staircase with minimum risk of being spotted. He was relieved to see that the two guards in the street continuously winced and blinked under the beam of the searchlight. His status was as clean as it could be under the tenuous circumstances. Everything now was timing, precision, and all the expertise he could summon from times too often unremembered or too vague too long ago. He had to remember now; instinct had to propel him through his personal mists. *Now.* The end of the nightmare was at hand.

It was happening! There was suddenly furious activity at the door as a third figure came rushing out, joining the other two. The man was shorter than his male colleague, wearing a beret and carrying a briefcase. He obviously issued orders that included the rear guard, who ran up to the pavement as the new arrival hurled his briefcase down over the brick steps. The guard instantly clutched his weapon under his left arm and effortlessly caught the leather missile in midair.

'*Allez. Nous partons! Vite!*' shouted the second man, gesturing for the other two on the brick steps to precede him down to the van. They did so, the man in the raincoat joining the guard at the rear doors, the woman accompanying the one who gave the orders. The . . . The *Jackal*? Was it *Carlos*? *Was* it?

Bourne desperately wanted to believe that it was – therefore, it *was*! The sound of the vehicle's kerbside door slamming shut was followed rapidly by the gunning of the vehicle's powerful engine; both were a signal. The three other guards raced from their posts to the rear doors of the van. One by one they climbed up inside after the man in the black raincoat, their legs stretched, arms bracing shoulders, curved hands gripping the two metal frames that with instant muscular strain propelled them inside as their weapons were thrown in front of them. Then a pair of hands reached out for the interior door handles –

Now! Bourne pulled the pin of the grenade and lurched to his feet, running as he had never run in his life towards the swinging rear doors of the van. He dived, twisting his body in flight, landing on his back as he gripped the left panel and threw the grenade inside, the bomb's release in his hand. *Six seconds* and it would detonate. Jason got to his knees, arms extended, and crashed the doors shut. A fusillade of gunfire erupted; it was an unintended *miracle*. As the Jackal's van was bulletproof, it was also impervious to bullets shot from within! There were no penetrations of the steel, only thuds and the screaming whistles of ricochets . . . and the screams of the wounded inside.

The glistening vehicle shot forward on the Boulevard Lefebvre as Bourne sprang to a crouch and raced towards the deserted storefronts on the east side of the street. He was nearly across the wide avenue when the impossible happened. The *impossible*!

The Jackal's van blew up, the explosion firing the dark Paris sky, and the moment it happened a brown limousine screeched around the nearest corner, the windows open, men in the black spaces, weapons in their grips, spraying the entire area with thunderous, indiscriminate fire. Jason lunged into the nearest recess, curling up into a foetal position in the shadows, accepting the fact – not in fear but in fury – that it might well be his last moment of life. He had failed. Failed Marie and his children! . . . But not *this* way. He spun off the concrete, the weapon in his hand. He would kill, *kill*! That was the way of Jason Bourne.

Then the incredible happened. The *incredible*. A siren? The *police*? The brown limousine shot forward, skirting the flaming wreck of the Jackal's van and disappeared into the dark streets as a patrol car raced out of the opposing darkness, its siren screaming, the tyres screeching as it skidded to a stop only yards from the flames of the demolished vehicle. Nothing made sense! thought Jason. Where before there had been five patrol cars, only one had returned. *Why?* And even that question was superfluous. Carlos had mounted a strategy employing not one but seven, conceivably eight, decoys, all *expendable*, all led to their terrible death by the consummate self-protector. The Jackal had sprung himself from the trap that had been reversed by his hated quarry – Delta, the product of the Medusa, a creation of American intelligence. Once again, the assassin had out-thought him, but he had not killed him. There would be another day, another night.

*

'*Bernardine!*' screamed the Deuxième official who less than thirty minutes ago had officially disowned his colleague. Leaping out of the patrol car, the man shouted again. 'Bernardine! Where are you? . . . My God, where *are* you? I came back, old friend, for I could not *leave* you! My God, you were *right*, I see that now for myself! Oh *Christ*, tell me you're alive! *Answer* me!'

'Another is dead,' came the reply from Bernardine as his gaunt figure walked slowly, with difficulty, out of the storefront two hundred feet north of Bourne. 'I tried to tell you but you would not listen—'

'I was perhaps too *hasty*!' roared the official, running to the old man and embracing him as the others in the patrol car, their arms crossed in front of their faces, surrounded the burning van but at a considerable distance. 'I've radioed for our people to return!' added the official. 'You must believe me, old friend, I came back because I couldn't leave you in anger, not my old comrade . . . I had no idea that pig from the newspaper actually assaulted you, *struck* you. He told me and I threw him out! . . . I came back for you, you see that, don't you? But, my *God*, I never expected anything like this!'

'It's horrible,' said the Deuxième veteran, while cautiously, his eyes straying rapidly up and down the boulevard, he surveyed the area. He specifically noted the many frightened, intense faces in the windows of the three stone buildings. The scenario had blown apart with the van's explosion and the disappearance of the brown limousine. The minions were without their leader and filled with anxiety. 'It's not entirely your error alone – my old comrade,' he continued, a note of apology in his voice. 'I had the wrong building.'

'Ah *ha*,' cried the Deuxième associate, relishing a minor triumph, self-vindication. 'The wrong building? That is indeed a mistake of consequence, *eh*, François?'

'The consequences might have been far less tragic had you not abandoned me so hastily, as you so aptly phrased it. Instead of listening to a man with my vast experience, you ordered me out of your car only to have me witness the horror moments after you fled.'

'We followed your orders! We searched the building – the *wrong* building!'

'Had you remained, if only for a brief conference, this might have been avoided and a friend might be alive. I shall have to include that judgement in my report—'

'*Please*, old friend,' broke in the associate. 'Let us reason together for the good of the Bureau—' The interruption now came with the shrill appearance of a fire truck. Bernardine held up his hand and led his protesting former comrade across the boulevard, ostensibly to get out of the way of the firemen, more purposefully to be within earshot of Jason Bourne. 'When our people arrive,' went on the associate of the Deuxième, his voice rising with authority, 'we shall empty the buildings and detain every resident for thorough interrogation!'

'My *God*,' exclaimed Bernardine, 'don't add asininity to incompetence!'

'What?'

'The limousine, the brown limousine – surely you saw it.'

'Yes, of course. The driver said it raced away.'

'That's all he told you?'

'Well, the truck was in flames and there was so much confusion radioing for personnel—'

'Look at the shattered glass!' commanded François, pointing at the storefronts away from the recess where Bourne was hiding. 'Look at the pits on the pavement and in the street. Gunfire, my old comrade. Those involved escaped believing they had killed me! . . . Say *nothing, do* nothing. Leave these people alone.'

'You are incomprehensible—'

'And you are a fool. If for any reason whatsoever there is the slightest possibility that even one of those killers is ordered to return here, there can be no impediments.'

'Now you are inscrutable.'

'Not at all,' protested Bernardine as the firemen hosed down the flames of the van, their efforts augmented by giant extinguishers. 'Send your people into each building, inquiring if everything is all right, explaining that the authorities have determined the terrible events on the boulevard were criminally oriented. The crisis has passed; there is no further alarm.'

'But is that true?'

'It's what we want them to believe.' An ambulance stormed into the street followed by two additional patrol cars, all the sirens at maximum volume. From the rue d'Alésia, apartment dwellers had gathered at both corners, many in hastily pulled-on street attire – trousers and undershirts – while others were in night clothes – frayed bathrobes and worn slippers. Noting that the Jackal's van was now a smouldering mass of twisted steel and shattered glass, Bernardine continued: 'Give the crowds time to satisfy their morbid viewing, then send men to disperse them. In an hour or so, when the rubble is under control and the bodies carted away, proclaim loudly to your police detachment that the emergency is over, ordering all but one man back to the precinct. That man is to remain here on duty until the debris is cleared from the boulevard. He is also to be instructed not to interfere with anyone leaving the buildings, is that clear?'

'Not for a moment. You said that someone might be hiding—'

'I know what I said,' pressed the former Deuxième consultant. 'It changes nothing.'

'You will stay here, then?'

'Yes. I will move slowly, inconspicuously, around the area.'

'I see . . . What about the police report? And my report?'

'Use some of the truth, not all of it, of course. Word was passed to you – informer's name withheld – that an act of violence related to the Bureau's narcotics division was to take place on the Boulevard Lefebvre at precisely this hour. You commandeered a police contingent and found nothing, but shortly thereafter your highly professional instincts sent you back beyond the time span, unfortunately too late to stop the carnage.'

'I might even be commended,' said the associate, suddenly frowning, wary. 'And *your* report?' he asked quietly.

'We'll see if one is necessary, won't we?' replied the newly reinstated Deuxième consultant.

*

The medical team wrapped the bodies of the victims, placing them in the ambulance as a wrecker hoisted what was left of the destroyed vehicle into the huge attached dumpster. The crew swept the street, several remarking that they should not sweep too thoroughly or no one would recognize the Lefebvre. A quarter of an hour later the job was finished; the wrecker departed, the lone patrolman joining the crew to be dropped off at the nearest police phone several blocks away. It was well past four o'clock in the morning and soon the dawn would light up the sky over Paris, preceding the boisterous human carnival below. Now, however, the only signs of life on the Boulevard Lefebvre were five lighted windows in the row of stone buildings controlled by Carlos the Jackal. Inside those rooms were men and women for whom sleep was not permitted. They had work to do for their monseigneur.

Bourne sat on the pavement, his legs outstretched, his back against the inside wall of a storefront across from the building where the frightened yet argumentative baker and the indignant nun had confronted the police. Bernardine was in a similar recess several hundred feet away, opposite the first building where the Jackal's van had stopped for its condemned cargo. Their agreement was firm: Jason would follow and take by force whoever left first from any building; the old Deuxième veteran would follow whoever left second, ascertain his or her destination, but make no contact. Bourne's judgement was that either the baker or the nun would be the assassin's messenger, so he had selected the north end of the row of stone houses.

He was partially right, but he had not anticipated an embarrassment of personnel and conveyances. At five-seventeen, two bicycles ridden by nuns in full habits and white hats wheeled up from the south side of the boulevard, ringing the muted bells on their handlebars as they stopped in front of the house that was supposedly the quarters of the Magdalen Sisters of Charity. The door opened and three additional nuns, each carrying a bicycle, walked out and down the brick steps to join their charitable sisters. They discreetly mounted their saddles and the procession started up the street; the one consoling fact for Jason was that Carlos's indignant nun took up the single rear position. Not knowing how it would happen, knowing only that it *would* happen, Bourne lurched out of the storefront and ran across the dark boulevard. As he reached the shadows of the deserted lot adjacent to the Jackal's house, another door opened. He crouched, watching the overweight irate baker waddle rapidly down his brick steps and head south. Bernardine had his work cut out for him, too, thought Jason as he got to his feet and ran after his procession of cycling nuns.

Paris traffic is an endless enigma regardless of the hour of day or night. It also provides palpable excuses for anyone wishing to be early or late, or having arrived at the right destination or the wrong one. In a phrase, Parisians behind a steering wheel embody the last civilized vestiges of lethal abandon – possibly outdone by their counterparts in Rome or Athens. And so it was for the Magdalen Sisters of Charity, especially for the officious superior hen on the single rear point. At an intersection of the rue Lecourbe in Montparnasse, a congestion of produce trucks prevented her from keeping up with her religious colleagues. Benignly, she waved them on and abruptly turned into a narrow side street, suddenly pedalling faster than before. Bourne, his wound from Tranquillity Isle now pulsating throughout his neck, did not increase his pace; he did not have to. The white-lettered blue sign on the building fronting the street read IMPASSE, a dead end; there was no other way out.

He found the bicycle chained to an extinguished street lamp and waited in the darkness of a doorway no more than fifteen feet away. He raised his hand and touched the warm moistness of the bandage around his neck; the bleeding was slight. With luck, no more than one suture had burst . . . Oh, *Christ*, his legs were tired – no, 'tired' was inadequate. They ached with the pain that came with unused and abused muscles; the rhythmic strides of jogging, even running, were no preparation for lurching or weaving, or for violently sudden stops and starts. He leaned against the stone, breathing heavily, his eyes on the bicycle, trying to suppress a thought that kept recurring with infuriating regularity: Only a few short years ago, he would never have noticed the discomfort in his legs. There would have been none.

The sound of an unlatched bolt broke the stillness of the predawn narrow street, followed rapidly by the grating noise of a heavy door being opened. It was the entrance to the flat in front of the chained bicycle. His back against the wall, Jason removed the gun from his belt and watched the woman in the nun's habit rush to the lamppost. She fumbled with a key in the dim light, awkwardly trying to insert it into the base of the lock. Bourne stepped out on the pavement and walked swiftly, silently forward.

'You'll be late for early Mass,' he said.

The woman spun around, the key flying into the street, her black cloth snapping in the turn as she plunged her right hand between the folds of her habit. Jason lurched, gripping her arm with his left hand and tearing off the large white hat with his right. At the sight of the exposed face in front of him, he gasped.

'My *God*,' he whispered. 'It's *you*!'

27

'I *know* you!' cried Bourne. 'Paris . . . years ago . . . your name is Lavier . . . Jacqueline *Lavier.* You had one of those dress shops . . . Les Classiques – St Honoré – Carlos's drop in the Faubourg! I found you in a confessional booth in Neuilly-sur-Seine. I thought you were *dead.*' The woman's sharp, creased, middle-aged face was contorted in frenzy. She tried to twist out of his grip but Jason stepped sideways as she pivoted, yanking her away in a sweeping circular motion, crashing her against the wall, pinning her, his left forearm across her throat. 'But you *weren't* dead. You were part of the trap that ended at the Louvre, blew apart at the Louvre! . . . By Christ, you're coming with me. Men died in that trap – *Frenchmen* died – and I couldn't stay around and tell them how it happened or who was responsible . . . In my country, you kill a cop, it doesn't go off the books. It's no different over here; and when it's *cops,* they don't stop looking. Oh, they'll remember the Louvre, they'll remember their men!'

'You're wrong!' choked the woman, her wide green eyes bulging above the black habit. 'I'm not who you think I am—'

'You're Lavier! Queen of the Faubourg, sole contact to the Jackal's woman, the general's wife. Don't tell me I'm wrong . . . I followed the two of you out to Neuilly – to that church with the bells ringing and priests everywhere – one of them *Carlos*! Moments later his whore came back out, but you didn't. She left in a hurry, so I ran inside and described you to an old priest – if he was a priest – and he told me you were in the second confessional from the left. I walked over and pulled the curtain and there you were. *Dead.* I thought you'd just been *killed* and everything was happening so fast. Carlos had to *be* there! He was within my reach, my gun – or maybe I was within his. I raced around like a maniac and finally I saw him! Out in the street in his priestly black clothes – I *saw* him, I *knew* it was him because he saw me and started to run through the traffic. And then I lost him, I *lost* him! . . . But I had a card to play. *You.* I passed the word – Lavier's dead . . . It was just what I was supposed to do, wasn't it? *Wasn't* it?'

'I tell you again, you are *wrong*!' The woman no longer struggled; it was pointless. Instead, she remained rigid against the wall, no part of her body moving, as if by doing so she might be permitted to speak. 'Will you listen to me?' she asked with difficulty, Jason's forearm still pressed against her throat.

'Forget it, lady,' answered Bourne. 'You're going out of here limp – a Sister of Charity being helped, not assaulted, by a stranger. You're about to have a fainting spell. At your age it's a fairly common occurrence, isn't it?'

'*Wait.*'

'Too late.'

'We must talk!'

'We will.' Releasing his arm, Jason instantly crashed both his hands simultaneously into the woman's shoulder blades where the tendons weave into the neck muscles. She collapsed and he caught her in the fall, picking her up in his arms, and carrying her out of the narrow street as an adoring supplicant might a religious social worker. The dawn light was beginning to fill the sky and several early risers, one a young jogger in shorts, converged on the man carrying the nun. 'She's been with my wife and sick children for nearly two days without sleep!' pleaded the Chameleon in street French. 'Will someone please find me a taxi so I can take her back to her convent in the ninth arrondissement?'

'*I* shall!' roared the young runner. 'There's an all-night stand on the rue de Sèvres, and I'm very fast!'

'You are a gift, monsieur,' said Jason, appreciating but instantly disliking the all too confident, all too young jogger.

Six minutes later the taxi arrived, the youth inside. 'I told the driver you have money,' he said, climbing out. 'I trust it's so.'

'Of course. And thanks.'

'Tell the sister what I did,' added the young man in running shorts, helping Bourne gently insert the unconscious woman into the back of the taxi. 'I'll need all the help I can get when my time comes.'

'I trust that's not imminent,' said Jason, trying to return the youth's grin.

'Not likely! I represent my firm in the marathon.' The overgrown child began running in place.

'Thanks again. I hope you win the next one.'

'Tell the sister to pray for me!' cried the infantile athlete, racing away.

'The Bois de Boulogne,' said Bourne, closing the door and addressing the driver.

'The Bois? That ventilating nut told me it was an emergency! You had to get the nun to a hospital.'

'She drank too much wine, what can I tell you?'

'The Bois de Boulogne,' said the driver, nodding his head. 'Let her walk it off. I have a second cousin in the Lyons convent. She gets out for a week she's soused to the temples. Who can blame her?'

The bench on the gravelled path of the Bois progressively received the warm rays of the early sun as the middle-aged woman in the religious habit began shaking her head. 'How are you doing, *Sister*?' asked Jason, sitting beside his prisoner.

'I believe I was struck by an army tank,' replied the woman, blinking and opening her mouth to swallow air. 'At least a tank.'

'Which I suspect you know more about than a welfare wagon from the Magdalen Sisters of Charity.'

'Quite so,' agreed the woman.

'Don't bother to look for your gun,' said Bourne. 'I removed it from the very expensive belt under your habit.'

'I'm glad you recognized the value. It's part of what we must talk about . . . Since I am not in a police station, I assume you've granted me my request to talk.'

'Only if what you say suits my purpose, I assume you understand that.'

'But it must, you see. Suit your purpose, as you say. I've failed. I've been taken. I'm not where I should be, and whatever the time is, the light tells me I'm too late for excuses. Also, my bicycle has either disappeared or is still chained to the lamppost.'

'I didn't take it.'

'Then I'm a dead woman. And if it's gone I'm just as dead, don't you see?'

'Because you've disappeared? Not where you're supposed to be?'

'Of course.'

'You're *Lavier*!'

'That's true. I'm Lavier. But I'm not the woman you knew. You knew my sister Jacqueline – I am Dominique Lavier. We were close in age and since we were children strongly resembled each other. But you are not wrong about Neuilly-sur-Seine or what you saw there. My sister was killed because she broke a cardinal rule, committed a mortal sin, if you like. She panicked and led *you* to Carlos's woman, his most cherished and useful secret.'

'Me? . . . You know who I am?'

'All Paris – the Jackal's Paris – knows who you are, Monsieur Bourne. Not by sight, I grant you, but they know you are here and they know you're tracking Carlos.'

'And you're part of that Paris?'

'I am.'

'Good Christ, lady, he killed your *sister*!'

'I'm aware of that.'

'Still you work for him?'

'There are times when a person's choices are considerably reduced. Say, to live or die. Until six years ago when Les Classiques changed ownership, it was vital to the monseigneur. I took Jacqui's place—'

'Just like that?'

'It wasn't difficult. I was younger, and more to the point I looked younger.' The lines in the middle-aged Lavier's face cracked with a brief pensive smile. 'My sister always said it came with living on the Mediterranean . . . At any rate, cosmetic surgery is commonplace in the world of haute couture. Jacqui supposedly went to Switzerland for a facial . . . and I returned to Paris after eight weeks of preparation.'

'How could you? Knowing what you knew, how the hell *could* you?'

'I did not know earlier what I learned later, by which time it was irrelevant. By then I had the choice I just mentioned. To live or to die.'

'It never occurred to you to go to the police or the Sûreté?'

'Regarding Carlos?' The woman looked at Bourne as if rebuking a foolish child. 'As the British say in Cap Ferrat, Surely you jest.'

'So you blithely went into the killing game.'

'Not consciously. I was gradually led into it, my education slow, piecemeal . . . In the beginning I was told Jacqueline had died in a boating accident with her lover of the month and that I would be enormously well paid to carry on in her place. Les Classiques was far more than a grand salon—'

'*Far* more,' agreed Jason, interrupting. 'It was the drop for France's most highly classified military and intelligence secrets funnelled to the Jackal by his woman, a celebrated general's wife.'

'I was not aware of that until long after the general killed her. Villiers was his name, I believe.'

'It was.' Jason looked across the path at the still dark waters of a pond, white lilies floating in clusters. Images came back to him. 'I'm the one who found him, found them. Villiers was in a high-backed brocaded chair, a gun in his hand, his wife lying on the bed, naked, bleeding, dead. He was going to kill himself. It was a proper execution for a traitor, he said, for his devotion to his wife had blinded his judgement and in that blindness he had betrayed his beloved France . . . I convinced him there was another way; it almost worked – thirteen years ago. In a strange house on Seventy-first Street in New York.'

'I don't know what happened in New York, but General Villiers left instructions that after his death what happened in *Paris* was to be made part of the public record. When he died and the truth was known, it was said that Carlos went mad with fury, killing several high-ranking military commanders simply because they were generals.'

'It's all an old story,' interrupted Bourne sharply, no passive tone of remembrance in his voice. 'This is now, thirteen years later. What happens *now*?'

'I don't know, monsieur. My choices are zero, aren't they? One or the other of you will kill me, I suppose.'

'Maybe not. Help me take him and you're free of both of us. You can go back to the Mediterranean and live in peace. You won't even have to disappear – you merely return to wherever it is after a number of profitable years in Paris.'

'Disappear?' asked Lavier, studying the haggard face of her captor. 'As in the word "vanish"?'

'No need for that. Carlos can't reach you because he'll be dead.'

'Yes, I understand that part. It's the disappearance that interests me along with the "profitable" years. Does this profit come from you?'

'Yes.'

'I see . . . Is that what you offered Santos? A profitable disappearance?'

It was as if the words were hard flesh and had slapped him across the face. Jason looked at his prisoner. 'So it was Santos after all,' he said softly. 'The Lefebvre *was* a trap. Christ, he's good.'

'He's dead, Le Coeur du Soldat cleaned out and closed down.'

'What?' Stunned, Bourne again stared at the Lavier woman. 'That was his reward for cornering me?'

'No, for betraying Carlos.'

'I don't understand.'

'The monseigneur has eyes everywhere, I'm sure that's no surprise to you.

Santos, the total recluse, was observed sending several heavy boxes out with his main food supplier, and yesterday morning he did not clip and water his precious garden, a summer ritual as predictable as the sun. A man was sent to the supplier's warehouse and opened the boxes.'

'Books,' broke in Jason quietly.

'Placed in storage until further instructions,' completed Dominique Lavier. 'Santos's departure was to be swift and secret.'

'And Carlos knew there was no one in Moscow giving out a telephone number.'

'I beg your pardon?'

'Nothing . . . What kind of man was Santos?'

'I never knew him, never even saw him. I've only heard the downstairs rumours, which weren't many.'

'I haven't time for many. What were they?'

'Apparently he was a very large man—'

'I know that,' interrupted Jason impatiently. 'And from the books we both know that he was well read, probably well educated, if his speech was indicative. Where did he come from and why did he work for the Jackal?'

'They say he was Cuban and fought in Fidel's revolution, that he was a deep thinker, as well as a law student with Castro, and once a great athlete. Then, of course, as in all revolutions, the internal strife sours the victories – at least that's what my old friends from the May Day barricades tell me.'

'Translation, please?'

'Fidel was jealous of the leaders of certain cadres, especially Che Guevara and the man you knew as Santos. Where Castro was larger than life, those two were larger than he was, and Fidel could not tolerate the competition. Che was sent on a mission that ended his life, and trumped up counter-revolutionary charges were brought against Santos. He was within an hour of being executed when Carlos and his men broke into the prison and spirited him away.'

'Spirited? Dressed as priests, no doubt.'

'I have no doubts. The Church with all its medieval lunacies once held sway over Cuba.'

'You sound bitter.'

'I'm a woman, the Pontiff is not; he's merely medieval.'

'Judgement decreed . . . So Santos joined forces with Carlos, two disillusioned Marxists in search of their personal cause – or maybe their own personal Hollywood.'

'That's beyond me, monsieur, but if I vaguely understand you, the fantasy belongs to the brilliant Carlos; the bitter disillusion was Santos's fate. He owed his life to the Jackal, so why not give it? What was left for him? . . . Until you came along.'

'That's all I need. Thanks. I just wanted a few gaps filled in.'

'Gaps?'

'Things I didn't know.'

'What do we do now, Monsieur Bourne? Wasn't that your original question?'

'What do you *want* to do, Madame Lavier?'

'I know I don't want to die. And I am not Madame Lavier in the marital sense. The restrictions never appealed to me and the benefits seemed unnecessary. For years I was a high-priced call girl in Monte Carlo, Nice and Cap Ferrat until my looks and my body deserted me. Still, I once had friends from the old days, intermittent lovers who took care of me for old time's sake. Most are dead now, a pity, really.'

'I thought you said you were enormously well paid for assuming your sister's identity.'

'Oh, I was and to a degree I still am, for I'm still valuable. I move among the elite of Paris, where gossip abounds, and that's often helpful. I have a beautiful flat on the Montaigne. Antiques, fine paintings, servants, charge accounts – everything a woman once in high fashion should be expected to have for the circles she still travels in. And money. Every month my bank receives eighty thousand francs from Geneva – somewhat more than enough for me to pay the bills. For, you see, *I* have to pay them, no one else can do so.'

'So then you've got money.'

'No, monsieur. I have a *life*-style, not money. That's the way of the Jackal. Except for the old men, he pays only for what he gets in terms of immediate service. If the money from Geneva did not arrive at my bank on the tenth of every month, I'd be thrown out in thirty days. But then if Carlos decided to get rid of me, there would be no need for Geneva. I'd be finished – as I am no doubt finished now. If I returned to my flat in the Montaigne this morning, I'd never come out . . . as my sister never came out of that church in Neuilly-sur-Seine. At least not alive.'

'You're convinced of that?'

'Of course. The stop where I chained the bicycle was made to receive instructions from one of the old men. The orders were precise and to be precisely followed. A woman I know would meet me in twenty minutes at a bakery in the St Germain where we were to exchange clothes. She was to proceed to the Magdalen mission and I was to meet a courier from Athens in a room at the Hotel Tremoille.'

'The Magdalen mission . . . ? You mean those women on the bicycles were actually nuns?'

'Complete with vows of chastity and poverty, monsieur. I am a frequent visiting superior from the convent at St Malo.'

'And the woman at the bakery. Is she—'

'She falls from grace now and then, but she's a perfectly splendid administrator.'

'Jesus,' mumbled Bourne.

'He's frequently on their lips . . . Do you see now the hopelessness of my position?'

'I'm not sure I do.'

'Then I am forced to wonder if you really are the Chameleon. I was *not* at the bakery. The meeting with the Greek courier never took place. Where was I?'

'You were delayed. The bicycle chain broke; you got grazed by one of those trucks on the rue Lecourbe. Hell, you got mugged. What's the difference? You were delayed.'

'How long has it been since you rendered me unconscious?'

Jason looked at his watch, now easily seen in the bright morning sunlight. 'Something over an hour-plus, I think; perhaps an hour and a half. Considering how you were dressed, the taxi driver cruised around trying to find a place to park where we could help you to a bench on the path with as little scrutiny as possible. He was well paid for his assistance.'

'An hour and a half?' asked Lavier pointedly.

'So?'

'So why didn't I call the bakery or the Hotel Tremoille?'

'Complications? . . . No, too easily verified,' added Bourne, shaking his head.

'Or?' Lavier locked her creased, large green eyes with his. '*Or*, monsieur?'

'The Boulevard Lefebvre,' replied Jason slowly, softly. 'The trap. As I reversed his on me, he reversed mine for him three hours later. Then I broke the strategy and took *you*.'

'Exactly.' The once and former whore of Monte Carlo nodded. 'And he cannot know what transpired between us . . . therefore, I'm marked for execution. A pawn is removed, for she is merely a pawn. She can tell the authorities nothing of substance; she's never seen the Jackal; she can only repeat the gossip of lowly subordinates.'

'You've never *seen* him?'

'I may have, but not to my knowledge. Again, the rumours fly around Paris. This one with swarthy Latin skin, or that one with black eyes and a dark moustache – "He is really Carlos, you know" – how often have I heard the phrases! But no, no man has ever come up to me and said, "I am he and I make your life pleasant, you ageing elegant prostitute." I simply report to old men who every now and then convey information that I must have – such as this evening on the Boulevard Lefebvre.'

'I see.' Bourne got to his feet, stretching his body above the bench, looking down at his prisoner. 'I can get you out,' he said quietly. 'Out of Paris, out of Europe. Beyond Carlos's reach. Do you want that?'

'As eagerly as Santos did,' answered Lavier, her eyes imploring. 'I willingly trade my allegiance from him to you.'

'Why?'

'Because he is old and grey-faced and is no match for you. You offer me life; he offers death.'

'That's a reasonable decision, then,' said Jason, a tentative but warm smile on his lips. 'Do you have any money? With you, I mean?'

'Nuns are sworn to poverty, monsieur,' replied Dominique Lavier, returning his smile. 'Actually, I have several hundred francs. Why?'

'It's not enough,' continued Bourne, reaching into his pocket and taking out his impressive roll of franc notes. 'Here's three thousand,' he said, handing her the money. 'Buy some clothes somewhere – I'm sure you know how – and take a room at the . . . the Meurice on the rue de Rivoli.'

'What name should I use?'

'What suits you?'

'How about Brielle? A lovely seaside town.'

'Why not? . . . Give me ten minutes to get out of here and then leave. I'll see you at the Meurice at noon.'

'With all my *heart*, Jason Bourne!'

'Let's forget that name.'

The Chameleon walked out of the Bois de Boulogne to the nearest taxi station. Within minutes an ecstatic cabdriver accepted a hundred francs to remain in place at the end of the three-vehicle line, his passenger slumped in the rear seat waiting to hear the words.

'The nun comes out, monsieur!' cried the driver. 'She enters the first taxi!'

'Follow it,' said Jason, sitting up.

On the avenue Victor Hugo, Lavier's taxi slowed down and pulled up in front of one of Paris's few exceptions to tradition – an open plastic-domed public telephone. 'Stop *here*,' ordered Bourne, who climbed out the instant the driver swung into the kerb. Limping, the Chameleon walked swiftly, silently, to the telephone directly behind and unseen by the frantic nun under the plastic booth. He was not seen, but he could hear clearly as he stood several feet behind her.

'The *Meurice*!' she shouted into the phone. 'The name is *Brielle.* He'll be there at noon . . . Yes, yes, I'll stop at my flat, change clothes, and be there in an hour.' Lavier hung up and turned, gasping at the sight of Jason. '*No!*' she screamed.

'Yes, I'm afraid,' said Bourne. 'Shall we take my taxi or yours? . . . "He's old and grey-faced" – those were your words, Dominique. Pretty goddamned descriptive for someone who never met Carlos.'

A furious Bernardine walked out of the Pont-Royal with the doorman, who had summoned him. 'This is *preposterous*! he shouted as he approached the taxi. 'No, it's not,' he amended, looking inside. 'It's merely insane.'

'Get in,' said Jason on the far side of the woman dressed in the habit of a nun. François did so, staring at the black clothes, the white pointed hat and the pale face of the reluctant religious female between them. 'Meet one of the Jackal's more talented performers,' added Bourne. 'She could make a fortune in your *cinéma-vérité*, take my word for it.'

'I'm not a particularly religious man, but I trust you have not made a mistake . . . I did – or should I say we did – with that pig of a baker.'

'Why?'

'He's a *baker*, that's all he is! I damn near put a grenade in his ovens but no one but a French *baker* could plead the way *he* did!'

'It fits,' said Jason. 'The illogical logic of Carlos – I can't remember who said that, probably me.' The taxi made a U-turn and entered the rue du Bac. 'We're going to the Meurice,' added Bourne.

'I'm sure there's a reason,' stated Bernardine, still looking at the enigmatically passive face of Dominique Lavier. 'I mean, this sweet old lady says nothing.'

'I'm not *old*!' cried the woman vehemently beneath her pointed white hat.

'Of course not, my dear,' agreed the Deuxième veteran. 'Only more desirable in your mature years.'

'Boy, did *you* hit it!'

'Why the Meurice?' asked Bernardine.

'It's the Jackal's final trap for me,' answered Bourne. 'Courtesy of our persuasive Magdalen Sister of Charity here. He expects me to be there and I'll be there.'

'I'll call in the Deuxième. Thanks to a frightened bureaucrat, they'll do anything I ask. Don't endanger yourself, my friend.'

'I don't mean to insult you, François, but you yourself told me you didn't know all of the people in the Bureau these days. I can't take the chance of a leak. One man could send out an alarm.'

'Let me help.' The low soft-spoken voice of Dominique Lavier broke the hum of the outside traffic like the initial burr of a chain saw. 'I *can* help.'

'I listened to your help before, lady, and it was leading me to my own execution. No thanks.'

'That was before, not now. As must be obvious to you, my position now is truly hopeless.'

'Didn't I hear those words recently?'

'No, you did not. I just added the word "now" . . . For God's sake, put yourself in my place. I can't pretend to understand, but this ancient boulevardier beside me casually mentions that he'll call in the Deuxième – the *Deuxième*, Monsieur Bourne! For some that is no less than France's Gestapo! Even if I survived I'm marked by that infamous branch of the government. I'd no doubt be sent to some horrible penal colony halfway across the world – oh, I've heard the stories of the Deuxième!'

'Really?' said Bernardine. 'I haven't. Sounds positively marvellous. How *wonderful*.'

'Besides,' continued Lavier, looking hard at Jason as she yanked the starched pointed white hat off her head, a gesture that caused the driver to raise his eyebrows in the rearview mirror. '*Without* me, without my presence in decidedly different clothing at the Meurice, Carlos won't come near the rue de Rivoli.' Bernardine tapped the woman's shoulder, bringing his index finger to his lips and nodding towards the front seat. Dominique quickly added, 'The man you wish to *confer* with will not be there.'

'She's got a point,' said Bourne, leaning forward and looking past Lavier at the Deuxième veteran. 'She's also got an apartment on the Montaigne, where she's supposed to change clothes and neither of us can go in with her.'

'That poses a dilemma, doesn't it?' responded Bernardine. 'There's no way we can monitor the telephones from outside in the street, is there?'

'You *fools*! . . . I have no *choice* but to cooperate with you, and if you can't see that you should be led around by trained dogs! This old, *old* man here will have my name in the Deuxième files the first chance he gets, and as the notorious Jason Bourne has even a nodding acquaintance with the Deuxième, several profound questions are raised – once raised by my sister, Jacqueline, incidentally. Who is this Bourne? Is he real or unreal? Is he the assassin of Asia or is he a fraud, a *plant*? She phoned me herself one night in Nice after too many brandies – a night perhaps you recall, Monsieur Le Caméléon – a terribly expensive restaurant outside Paris. You threatened her . . . in the name of powerful, *unnamed* people you *threatened* her! You demanded that she reveal what she knew about a certain acquaintance of hers – who it was at the time I had no idea – but you frightened her. She said you appeared deranged, that your eyes became glazed and you uttered words in a language she could not understand.'

'I remember,' interrupted Bourne icily. 'We had dinner and I threatened her and she was frightened. She went to the ladies' room, paid someone to make a phone call, and I had to get out of there.'

'And now the Deuxième is allied with those powerful unnamed people?' Dominique Lavier shook her head repeatedly and lowered her voice. 'No, messieurs, I am a survivor and I do not fight against such odds. One knows when to pass the shoe in baccarat.'

After a short period of silence, Bernardine spoke. 'What's your address on the avenue Montaigne? I'll give it to the driver, but before I do, understand me, madame. If your words prove false, all the true horrors of the Deuxième will be visited upon you.'

Marie sat at the room-service table in her small suite at the Meurice reading the newspapers. Her attention constantly strayed; concentration was out of the question. Her anxiety had kept her awake after she returned to the hotel shortly past midnight, having made the rounds of five cafés she and David had frequented so many years ago in Paris. Finally by four-something in the morning, exhaustion had short-circuited her tossing and turning; she fell asleep with the bedside lamp switched on and was awakened by the same light nearly six hours later. It was the longest she had slept since that first night on Tranquillity Isle, itself a distant memory now except for the very real pain of not seeing or hearing the children. *Don't think about them, it hurts too much. Think about David . . . No, think about Jason Bourne! Where? Concentrate!*

She put down the *Paris Tribune* and poured herself a third cup of black coffee, glancing over at the French doors that led to a small balcony overlooking the rue de Rivoli. It disturbed her that the once bright morning had turned into a dismal grey day. Soon the rain would come, making her search in the streets even more difficult. Resigned, she sipped her coffee and replaced the elegant cup in the elegant saucer, annoyed that it was not one of the simple pottery mugs favoured by David and her in their rustic country kitchen in Maine. Oh, God, would they ever be back there again? *Don't think about such things! Concentrate!* Out of the question.

She picked up the *Tribune*, aimlessly scanning the pages, seeing only isolated words, no sentences or paragraphs, no continuity of thought or meaning, merely words. Then one stood out on the bottom of a meaningless column, a single meaningless line bracketed at the bottom of a meaningless page.

The word was *Memom*, followed by a telephone number; and despite the fact that the *Tribune* was printed in English, the French in her switchable French-thinking brain absently translated the word as *Maymohm*. She was about to turn the page when a signal from another part of her brain screamed *Stop*!

Memom . . . *mommy* – turned around by a child struggling with his earliest attempts at language. *Meemom!* Jamie – their *Jamie*! The funny inverted name he had called her for several weeks! David had joked about it while she, frightened, had wondered if their son had dyslexia.

'He could also just be confused, *memom*,' David had laughed.

David! She snapped up the page; it was the financial section of the paper, the section she instinctively gravitated to every morning over coffee. David was sending her a message! She pushed back her chair, crashing it to the floor as she grabbed the paper and rushed to the telephone on the desk. Her hands trembling, she dialled the number. There was no answer, and thinking that in her panic she had made an error or had not used the local Paris digit, she dialled again, now slowly, precisely.

No answer. But it *was* David, she felt it, she *knew* it! He had been looking for her at the Trocadero and now he was using a briefly employed nickname only the two of them would know! My love, my *love*, I've found you! . . . She also knew she could not stay in the confining quarters of the small hotel suite, pacing up and down and dialling every other minute, driving herself crazy with every unanswered ring. *When you're stressed out and spinning until you think you'll blow apart, find someplace where you can keep moving without being noticed. Keep moving! That's vital. You can't let your head explode.* One of the lessons from Jason Bourne. Her head spinning, Marie dressed more rapidly than she had ever done in her life. She tore out the message from the *Tribune* and left the oppressive suite, trying not to run to the bank of elevators but needing the crowds of the Paris streets where she could keep moving without being noticed. From one telephone kiosk to another.

The ride down to the lobby was both interminable and insufferable, the latter because of an American couple – he laden with camera equipment, she with purple eyelids and a peroxide bouffant apparently set in concrete – who kept complaining that not enough people in Paris, France, spoke English. The elevator doors thankfully opened and Marie walked rapidly out into the crowded Meurice lobby.

As she crossed the marble floor towards the large glass doors of the ornate, filigreed entrance, she suddenly, involuntarily stopped as an elderly man in a dark pin-striped suit gasped, his slender body lurching forward in a heavy leather chair below on her right. The old man stared at her, his thin lips parted in astonishment, his eyes in shock.

'Marie St Jacques!' he whispered. 'My *God*, get *out* of here!'

'I beg your . . . *What?*'

The aged Frenchman quickly, with difficulty, rose to his feet, his head subtly, swiftly, jerking in short movements as he scanned the lobby. 'You cannot be seen here, Mrs Webb,' he said, his voice still a whisper but no less harsh and commanding. 'Don't look at me! Look at your watch. Keep your head down.' The Deuxième veteran glanced away, nodding aimlessly at several people in nearby chairs as he continued, his lips barely moving. 'Go out the door on the far left, the one used for luggage. *Hurry!*'

'*No!*' replied Marie, her head down, her eyes on her watch. 'You know me but I don't know you! Who *are* you?'

'A friend of your husband.'

'My God, is he *here*?'

'The question is why are *you* here?'

'I stayed at this hotel once before. I thought he might remember it.'

'He did but in the wrong context, I'm afraid. *Mon Dieu*, he never would have chosen it otherwise. Now, *leave*.'

'I won't! I have to find him. Where *is* he?'

'You *will* leave or you may find only his corpse. There's a message for you in the Paris *Tribune*—'

'It's in my purse. The financial page. "*Memom*—" '

'Call in several hours.'

'You can't *do* this to me.'

'You cannot do this to *him*. You'll kill him! Get out of here. *Now!*'

Her eyes half blinded with fury and fear and tears, Marie started towards the left side of the lobby, desperately wanting to look back, but just as desperately knowing she could not do so. She reached the narrow set of glass double doors, colliding with a uniformed bellhop carrying suitcases inside.

'*Pardon, madame!*'

'*Moi aussi*,' she stammered, manoeuvring again blindly around the luggage and out to the pavement. What could she do – what *should* she do? David was somewhere in the hotel – *in* the hotel! And a strange man recognized her and warned her and told her to get out – *get away*! What was happening? . . . My God, someone's trying to kill David! The old Frenchman had said as much – who *was* it . . . who were *they*? *Where* were they?

Help me! For God's sake, Jason, tell me what to do. *Jason?* . . . Yes, Jason . . . *help* me! She stood, frozen, as taxis and limousines broke off from the noonday traffic and pulled up to the Meurice's kerb, where a gold-braided doorman under the huge canopy greeted newcomers and old faces and sent bellboys scurrying in all directions. A large black limousine with a small discreet religious insignia on its passenger door, the cruciform standard of some high office of the Church, inched its way to the canopied area. Marie stared at the small emblem; it was circular and no more than six inches in diameter, a globe of royal purple surrounding an elongated crucifix of gold. She winced and held her breath; her panic now had a disturbing new dimension. She had seen that insignia before, and all she remembered was that it had filled her with horror.

The limousine stopped; both kerbside doors were opened by the smiling, bowing doorman as five priests emerged, one from the front seat, four from the spacious rear section. The latter four prelates immediately, oddly, threaded their way into the noonday crowds of strollers on the pavement, two forward in front of the vehicle, two behind it, one of the priests whipping past Marie, his black coat making contact with her, his face so close she could see the blazing unpriestly eyes of a man who was no part of a religious order . . . Then the association with the emblem, the religious insignia, came back to her!

Years ago, when David – when *Jason* – was in maximum therapy with Panov, Mo had him sketch, draw, doodle whatever images came to him. Time and again that terrible circle with the thin crucifix appeared . . . invariably torn apart or stabbed repeatedly with the pencil point. *The Jackal!*

Suddenly, Marie's eyes were drawn to a figure crossing the rue de Rivoli. It was a tall man in dark clothes – a dark sweater and trousers – and he was limping, dodging the traffic, his face covered by a hand shielding his face from the drizzle that soon would turn into rain. The limp was *false*! The leg straightened if only for an instant and the swing of the shoulder that compensated was a defiant gesture she knew only too well. It was David!

Another, no more than eight feet from her, also saw what she saw. A miniature radio was instantly brought to the man's lips. Marie rushed forward, her extended hands the claws of a tigress as she lunged at the killer in priest's clothing.

'*David!*' she screamed, drawing blood from the face of the Jackal's man.

Gunshots filled the rue de Rivoli. The crowds panicked, many running into the hotel, many more racing away from the canopied entrance, all shrieking, yelling, seeking safety from the murderous insanity that had suddenly exploded in the civilized street. In the violent struggle with the man-priest who would kill her husband, the strong Canadian ranch girl ripped the automatic out of his belt and fired it into his head; blood and membrances were blown into the air.

'*Jason!*' she screamed again as the killer fell, instantly realizing that she stood alone with only the corpse beneath her; she was a *target*! Then from death she knew she had been granted life. The old aristocratic Frenchman who had recognized her in the lobby came crashing out of the front entrance, his automatic weapon on repeat fire as he sprayed the black limousine, stopping for an instant to switch his aim and shattering the legs of a 'priest' whose weapon was levelled at him.

'*Mon ami!*' roared Bernardine.

'*Here!*' shouted Bourne. 'Where *is* she?'

'*A votre droite! Auprès de—*' A single gunshot exploded from the glass double doors of the Meurice. As he fell, the Deuxième veteran cried out, '*Les Capucines, mon ami. Les Capucines!*' Bernardine slumped to the pavement; a second gunshot ended his life.

Marie was paralysed, she could not *move*! Everything was a blizzard, a hurricane of iced particles crashing with such force against her face she could neither think nor find meaning. Weeping out of control, she fell to her knees, then collapsed in the street, her screams of despair clear to the man who suddenly was above her. 'My children . . . oh *God*, my *children*!'

'*Our* children,' said Jason Bourne, his voice not the voice of David Webb. 'We're getting out of here, can you understand that?'

'Yes . . . *yes*!' Marie awkwardly, painfully, swung her legs behind her and lurched to her feet, held by the husband she either knew or did not know. '*David*?'

'Of course I'm David. Come on!'

'You frighten me—'

'I frighten myself. Let's *go*! Bernardine gave us our exit. Run with me; hold my hand!'

They raced down the rue de Rivoli, swinging east into the Boulevard St Michel until the Parisian strollers in their *nonchalance de jour* made it clear that the fugitives were safe from the horrors of the Meurice. They stopped in an alleyway and held each other.

'Why did you *do* it?' asked Marie, cupping his face. 'Why did you run away from us?'

'Because I'm better without you, you know that.'

'You weren't before, David – or should I say Jason?'

'Names don't matter, we have to move!'

'Where to?'

'I'm not sure. But we *can* move, that's the important thing. There's a way out. Bernardine gave it to us.'

'He was the old Frenchman?'

'Let's not talk about him, okay? At least not for a while. I'm shredded enough.'

'All right, we won't talk about him. Still, he mentioned Les Capucines – what did he mean?'

'It's our way out. There's a car waiting for me in the Boulevard des Capucines. That's what he was telling me. Let's *go*!'

They raced south out of Paris in the nondescript Peugeot taking the Barbizon highway to Villeneuve-St Georges. Marie sat close to her husband, their bodies touching, her hand clutching his arm. She was, however, sickeningly aware that the warmth she intended was not returned in equal measure. Only a part of the intense man behind the wheel was her David; the rest of him was Jason Bourne and he was now in command.

'For God's sake, talk to me!' she cried.

'I'm thinking . . . Why did you come to Paris?'

'Good *Christ*!' exploded Marie. 'To find you, to *help* you!'

'I'm sure you thought it was right . . . It wasn't, you know.'

'That voice again,' protested Marie. 'That goddamned disembodied tone of voice! Who the hell do you think you are to make that judgement? *God*? To put it bluntly – no, not bluntly, but brutally – there are things you have trouble remembering, my darling.'

'Not about Paris,' objected Jason. 'I remember everything about Paris. Everything.'

'Your friend Bernardine didn't think so! He told me you never would have chosen the Meurice if you did.'

'What?' Bourne briefly, harshly glanced at his wife.

'Think. Why did you choose – and you *did* choose – the Meurice?'

'I don't know . . . I'm not sure. It's a hotel; the name just came to me.'

'*Think.* What happened years ago at the Meurice – right outside the Meurice?'

'I – I know something happened . . . *You*?'

'Yes, my love, *me.* I stayed there under a false name and you came to meet me, and we walked to the newsstand on the corner where in one horrible moment we both knew my life could never be the same again – with you or without you.'

'Oh, Jesus, I forgot! The newspapers – your photograph on all the front pages. You were the Canadian government official—'

'The *escaped* Canadian economist,' broke in Marie, 'hunted by the authorities all over Europe for multiple killings in Zurich in tandem with the theft of millions from Swiss banks! Those kinds of headlines never leave a person, do they? They can be refuted, proved to be totally false, yet still there is that lingering doubt. "Where there's smoke there must be fire," I believe is the bromide. My own colleagues in Ottawa . . . dear, dear friends I'd worked with for years . . . were afraid to *talk* to me!'

'*Wait* a minute!' shouted Bourne, his eyes again flashing at David's wife. 'They *were* false – it was a Treadstone ploy to pull me in – you were the one who understood it, *I* didn't!'

'Of course I did, because you were so stretched you couldn't see it. It didn't matter to me then because I'd made up my mind, my very precise analytical mind, a mind I'd match against yours any day of the week, my sweet scholar.'

'*What?*'

'Watch the *road*! You missed the turn, just the way you missed the one to our cabin only days ago – or was it years ago?'

'What the hell are you talking about?'

'That small inn we stayed at outside the Barbizon. You politely asked them to please light the fire in the dining room – we were the only people there. It was the third time I saw through the mask of Jason Bourne to someone else, someone I was falling deeply in love with.'

'Don't do this to me.'

'I have to, David. If only for myself now. I have to know you're there.'

Silence. A U-turn on the *grand-route* and the driver pressed the accelerator to the floor. 'I'm here,' whispered the husband, lifting his right arm and pulling his wife to him. 'I don't know for how long, but I'm here.'

'Hurry, my darling.'

'I will. I just want to hold you in my arms.'

'And I want to call the children.'

'Now I know I'm here.'

28

'You'll tell us everything we want to know voluntarily or we'll send you up into a chemical orbit your hacks never dreamed of with Dr Panov,' said Peter Holland, director of the Central Intelligence Agency, his quiet monotone as hard and as smooth as polished granite. 'Furthermore, I should elaborate on the extremes to which I'm perfectly willing to go because I'm from the old school, *paisan.* I don't give a shit for rules that favour garbage. You play cipher with me, I'll deep-six you still breathing a hundred miles off Hatteras in a torpedo casing. Am I clear?'

The capo subordinato, thick plaster casts around his left arm and right leg, lay on the bed in Langley's deserted infirmary room, deserted since the DCI had ordered the medical staff to get out of hearing range for their own good. The mafioso's naturally puffed face was additionally enlarged by swellings around both eyes, as well as his generous lips, the result of his head having smashed into the dashboard when Mo Panov sent the car into a Maryland oak. He looked up at Holland, his heavy-lidded gaze travelling over to Alexander Conklin seated in a chair, the ever-present cane gripped in anxious hands.

'You got no right, Mr Big Shot,' said the capo gruffly. ''Cause *I* got rights, you know what I mean?'

'So did the doctor, and you violated them – *Jesus,* did you violate them!'

'I don't gotta talk without my lawyer.'

'Where the hell was *Panov's* lawyer?' shouted Alex, thumping his cane on the floor.

'That's not the way the system works,' protested the patient, attempting to raise his eyebrows in indignation. 'Besides, I was good to the doc. He took advantage of my goodness, s'help me God!'

'You're a cartoon,' said Holland. 'You're a hot sketch but you're not remotely amusing. There are no lawyers here, linguine, just the three of us, and a torpedo casing is very much in your future.'

'What d'ya *want* from me?' cried the mafioso. 'What do *I* know? I just do what I'm told, like my older brother did – my he rest in peace – and my father – may he also rest in peace – and probably *his* father, which I don't know nothin' about.'

'It's like succeeding generations on welfare, isn't it?' observed Conklin. 'The parasites never get off the dole.'

'Hey, that's my family you're talkin' about – whatever the fuck you're talkin' about.'

'My apologies to your heraldry,' added Alex.

'And it's that family of yours we're interested in, Augie,' broke in the DCI. 'It *is* Augie, isn't it? That was the name on one of the five driver's licences and we thought it seemed most authentic.'

'Well, you're not so authentically bright, Mr Big Shot!' spat out the immobilized patient through his painfully swollen lips. 'I got none of them names.'

'We have to call you something,' said Holland. 'If only to burn it into the casing down at Hatteras so that some scale-headed archaeologist several thousand years from now can give an identity to the teeth he's measuring.'

'How about Chauncy?' asked Conklin.

'Too ethnic,' replied Peter. 'I like "Asshole" because that's what he is. He's going to be strapped into a tube and dropped over the continental shelf into six miles of seawater for crimes other people committed. I mean, that's being an asshole.'

'Cut it out!' roared the asshole. 'Awright, my name's Nicolo . . . Nicholas Dellacroce, and for even giving you that you gotta get me protection! Like with Vallachi, that's part of the deal.'

'It is?' Holland frowned. 'I don't remember mentioning it.'

'Then you don't get *nuthin'*!'

'You're wrong, Nicky,' broke in Alex from across the small room. 'We're going to get everything we want, the only drawback being that it's a one-time shot. We won't be able to cross-examine you, or bring you into a federal court, or even have you sign a deposition.'

'Huh?'

'You'll come out a vegetable with a refried brain. Of course, I suppose it's a blessing in a way. You'll hardly know it when you're packed into that shell casing in Hatteras.'

'Hey, wadda ya *talkin'*?'

'Simple logic,' answered the former naval commando and present head of the Central Intelligence Agency. 'After our medical team gets finished with you, you can't expect us to keep you around, can you? An autopsy would railroad us to a rock pile for thirty years and, frankly, I haven't got that kind of time . . . What'll it be, Nicky? You want to talk to us or do you want a priest?'

'I gotta think—'

'Let's go, Alex,' said Holland curtly, walking away from the bed towards the door. 'I'll send for a priest. This poor son of a bitch is going to need all the comfort he can get.'

'It's times like this,' added Conklin, planting his cane on the floor and rising, 'when I seriously ponder man's inhumanity to man. Then I rationalize. It's not brutality, for that's only a descriptive abstraction; it's merely the custom of the trade we're all in. Still, there's the individual – his mind and his flesh and his all too sensitive nerve endings. It's the excruciating pain. Thank heavens I've always been in the background, out of reach – like Nicky's associates. They dine in elegant restaurants and he goes over in a tube beyond the continental shelf, six miles down in the sea, his body imploding into itself.'

'Awright, *awright*!' screamed Nicolo Dellacroce, twisting on the bed, his obese frame tangling the sheets. 'Ask your fuckin' questions, but you give me protection, *capisce*?'

'That depends on the truthfulness of your answers,' said Holland, returning to the bed.

'I'd be very truthful, Nicky,' observed Alex, limping back to the chair. 'One misstatement and you sleep with the fishes – I believe that's the customary phrase.'

'I don't need no coaching, I know where it's at.'

'Let's begin, Mr Dellacroce,' said the CIA chief, taking a small tape recorder out of his pocket, checking the charge and placing it on the high white table by the patient's bed. He drew up a chair and continued speaking, addressing his opening remarks to the thin silver recorder. 'My name is Admiral Peter Holland, currently director of the Central Intelligence Agency, voice confirmation to be verified if necessary. This is an interview with an informer we'll call John Smith, voice distortion to follow on interagency master tape, identification in the DCI's classified files . . . All right, Mr Smith, we're going to cut through the bullshit to the essential questions. I'll generalize them as much as possible for your protection, but you'll know exactly what I'm referring to and I expect specific answers . . . Whom do you work for, Mr Smith?'

'Atlas Coin Vending Machines, Long Island City,' replied Dellacroce, his words slurred and spoken gruffly.

'Who owns it?'

'I dunno who owns it. Most of us work from home – some fifteen, maybe twenty guys, you know what I mean? We service the machines and send in our reports.'

Holland glanced over at Conklin; both men smiled. With one answer the mafioso had placed himself within a large circle of potential informers. Nicolo was not new to the game. 'Who signs your pay cheques, Mr Smith?'

'A Mr Louis DeFazio, a very legitimate businessman, to d'best of my knowledge. He gives us our assignments.'

'Do you know where he lives?'

'Brooklyn Heights. On the river, I think someone told me.'

'What was your destination when our personnel intercepted you?'

Dellacroce winced, briefly closing his swollen eyes before answering. 'One of those drunk-and-dope tanks somewhere south of Philly – which you already know, Mr Big Shot, 'cause you found the map in the car.'

Holland angrily reached for the recorder, snapping it off. 'You're on your way to Hatteras, you son of a bitch!'

'*Hey*, you get your info your way, I give it mine, okay? There *was* a map – there's *always* a map – and each of us has to take those cockamamy back roads to the joint like we were driving the President or even a don superiore to an Appalachian meet . . . You gimme that message pad and the pencil, I'll give you the location right down to the brass plate on the stone gate.' The mafioso raised his uncased right arm and jabbed his index finger at the DCI. 'It'll be accurate, Mr Big Shot, because I don't wanna sleep with no fishes, *capisce*?'

'But you won't put it on tape,' said Holland, a disturbed inflection in his voice. 'Why not?'

'Tape, shit! What did you call it? An interagency *master* bullshit? What do you think . . . our people can't tap into this place? Hoo-*hah*! That fuckin' doctor of yours could be one of us!'

'He's not, but we're going to get to an army doctor who is.' Peter Holland picked up the message pad and pencil from the bedside table, handing both to Dellacroce. He did not bother to switch on the tape recorder. They were beyond props and into hardball.

In New York City, on 138th Street between Broadway and Amsterdam Avenue, the hard core of Harlem, a large dishevelled black man in his mid-thirties staggered up the sidewalk. He bounced off the chipped brick wall of a run-down apartment building and slumped down on the pavement, his legs extended, his unshaven face angled into the right collar of his torn army surplus shirt.

'With the looks I'm getting,' he said quietly into the miniaturized micro-phone under the cloth, 'you'd think I'd invaded the high colonic white shopping district of Palm Springs.'

'You're doing beautifully,' came the metallic voice over the tiny speaker sewn into the back of the agent's collar. 'We've got the place covered; we'll give you plenty of notice. That answering machine's so jammed it's sending out whistling smoke.'

'How did you two lily boys get into that trap over there?'

'Very early this morning, so early no one noticed what we looked like.'

'I can't wait to watch you get out; it's a needle condo if I ever saw one. Speaking of which, which we are in a way, are the cops on this beat alerted? I'd hate like hell to get hauled in after growing this bristle on my face. It itches like crazy and my new wife of three weeks doesn't dig it.'

'You should have stayed with the first one, buddy.'

'Funny little white boy. She didn't like the hours or the geography. Like in being away for weeks at a time playing games in Zimbabwe. Answer me, please?'

'The blue coats have your description and the scenario. You're part of a federal bust, so they'll leave you alone . . . *Hold* it! Conversation's over. This has to be our man; he's got a telephone satchel strapped to his belt . . . It *is*. He's heading for the doorway. It's all yours, Emperor Jones.'

'Funny little white boy . . . I've got him and I can tell you now he's a soft chocolate mousse. He's scared shitless to go into this place.'

'Which means he's legitimate,' said the metallic voice in the collar. 'That's good.'

'That's bad, junior,' countered the black agent instantly. 'If you're right, he doesn't know anything, and the layers between him and the source will be as thick as southern molasses.'

'Oh? Then how do you read it?'

'On-scene tech. I have to see the numbers when he programmes them into his troubleshooter.'

'What the hell does that mean?'

'He may be legit, but he's also been frightened and not by the premises.'

'What does *that* mean?'

'It's all over his face, man. He could enter in false numbers if he thinks he's being followed or watched.'

'You've lost me, buddy.'

'He has to duplicate the digits that correspond to the remote so the beeps can be relayed—'

'Forget it,' said the voice from the back of the collar. 'That high tech I'm not. Besides, we got a man down at that company, Reco-something-or-other, now. He's waiting for you.'

'Then I've got work to do. Out, but keep me monitored.' The agent rose from the pavement and unsteadily made his way into the dilapidated building. The telephone repairman had reached the second floor, where he turned right in the narrow, filthy corridor; he had obviously been there before, as there was no hesitation, no checking the barely legible numbers on the doors. Things were going to be a little easier, considered the CIA man, grateful because his assignment was beyond the purview of the Agency. Purview, shit, it was illegal.

He took the steps three at a time, his soft double-soled rubber shoes reducing the noise to the inevitable creaks of an old staircase. His back against the wall, he peered around the corner of the trash-filled hall-way and watched the repairman insert three separate keys into three vertical locks, turning each in succession and entering the last door on the left. *Things*, reconsidered the agent, might not be so easy after all. The instant the man closed the door, he ran silently down the corridor and stood motionless, listening. Not wonderful, but not the worst, he thought as he heard the sound of only one lock being latched; the repairman was in a hurry. He placed his ear against the peeling paint of the door and held his breath, no echo from his lungs disturbing his hearing. Thirty seconds later he turned his head, exhaled, then took a deep breath and went back to the door. Although muffled, he heard the words clearly enough to piece together the meaning.

'Central, this is Mike up on a Hundred Thirty-eighth Street, section twelve, machine sixteen. Is there another unit in this building, which I wouldn't believe if you said there was.' The following silence lasted perhaps twenty additional seconds. '. . . We don't, huh? Well, we got a frequency interference and it don't make no sense to me . . . The what? Cable TV? Ain't no one in this neighbourhood got the bread for that . . . Oh, I gotcha, brother. *Area* cable. The drug boys live high, don't they? Their addresses may be shit, but inside them homes they got theyselves a pile of fancy crap . . . So clear the line and reroute it. I'll stay here until I get a clean signal, okay, brother?'

The agent again turned away from the door and again breathed, now in relief. He could leave without a confrontation; he had all he needed. One Hundred Thirty-eighth Street, section *twelve*, machine *sixteen*, and they knew the firm that installed the equipment. The Reco-Metropolitan Company, Sheridan Square, New York. The lily-whites could handle it from there. He walked back to the questionable staircase and lifted the collar of his army-surplus shirt. 'In case I get run over by a truck, here's the input. Are you reading me?'

'Loud and clear, Emperor Jones.'

'It's machine sixteen in what they call section twelve.'

'Got it! You've earned your pay cheque.'

'You might at least say "Outstanding, old chap."'

'Hey, you're the guy who went to college over there, not me.'

'Some of us are overachievers . . . *Hold* it! I've got *company*!'

Below on the bottom of the staircase a small compact black man appeared, his dark eyes bulging, staring up at the agent, a gun in his hand. The CIA man spun behind the edge of the wall as four successive gunshots shattered the corridor. Lunging across the open space, his revolver ripped from its holster, the agent fired twice, but once was enough. His assailant fell to the floor of the soiled lobby.

'I caught a ricochet in my leg!' cried the agent, 'but he's down – deep dead or not I can't tell. Sweep up the vehicle and get us both out. *Pronto*.'

'On its way. Stay put!'

It was shortly past eight o'clock the next morning when Alex Conklin limped into Peter Holland's office, the guards at the CIA gates impressed with his immediate access to the director.

'Anything?' asked the DCI, looking up from the papers on his desk.

'Nothing,' answered the retired field officer angrily, heading for the couch against the wall rather than a chair. 'Not a goddamned thing. Jesus, what a fucked-up day and it hasn't even begun! Casset and Valentino are down in the cellars sending out queries all over the Paris sewers but so far *nothing* . . . Christ, look at the scenario and find me a thread! Swayne, Armbruster, DeSole – our mute son of a bitch, the *mole*. Then for God's sake, *Teagarten* with Bourne's calling card when we know damned well it's a trap for Jason set by the Jackal. But there's no logic anywhere that ties Carlos to Teagarten and by extension to *Medusa*. Nothing makes sense, Peter. We've lost the spine – everything's gone off the wire!'

'Calm down,' said Holland gently.

'How the hell *can* I? Bourne's disappeared – I mean really disappeared, if he isn't dead. And there's no trace of Marie, no word from her, and then we learn that Bernardine was killed in a shoot-out only hours ago on the Rivoli – *Christ*, shot in broad daylight! And that means Jason was there – he had to be *there*!'

'But since none of the dead or wounded fits his description, we can assume he got away, can't we?'

'We can hope, yes.'

'You asked for a thread,' mused the DCI. 'I'm not sure I can actually provide one but I can give you something like it.'

'*New York*?' Conklin sat forward on the couch. 'The answering machine? That DeFazio hood in Brooklyn Heights?'

'We'll get to New York, to all of that – them. Right now let's concentrate on that thread of yours, that spine you mentioned.'

'I'm not the slowest kid on the block, but where is it?'

Holland leaned back in his chair, gazing first at the papers on his desk then up at Alex. 'Seventy-two hours ago, when you decided to come clean with me about everything, you said that the idea behind Bourne's strategy was to convince the Jackal and this latter-day Medusa to join forces, with Bourne as the common target, one feeding the other. Wasn't that basically the premise? Both sides wanted him killed. Carlos had two reasons – revenge and the fact that he believes Bourne could identify him; the Medusans because Bourne had pieced together so much about them?'

'That was the premise, yes,' agreed Conklin, nodding. 'It's why I dug around and made those phone calls, never expecting to find what I did. *Jesus*, a global cartel born twenty years ago in Saigon, peopled by some of the biggest fish in and out of the government and the military. It was the kind of pay dirt I didn't want and wasn't looking for. I thought I might dig up maybe ten or twelve hotshot millionaires with post-Saigon bank accounts that couldn't bear scrutiny, but not this, not *this* Medusa.'

'To put it as simply as possible,' continued Holland, frowning, his eyes again straying down to the papers in front of him, then up at Alex. 'Once the connection was made between Medusa and Carlos, word would be passed to the Jackal that there was a man Medusa wanted eliminated, and cost was no object. So far, yes?'

'The key here was the calibre and the status of those reaching Carlos,' explained Conklin. 'They had to be as close to bona fide Olympians as we could find, the kind of clients the Jackal doesn't get and never got.'

'Then the name of the target is revealed – say, in a way such as "John Smith, once known years ago as Jason Bourne" – and the Jackal is hooked. Bourne, the one man he wants dead above all others.'

'Yes. That's why the Medusans reaching Carlos had to be so solid, so above questioning that Carlos accepts them and dismisses any sort of a trap.'

'Because,' added the CIA's director, 'Jason Bourne came out of Saigon's Medusa – a fact known to Carlos – but he never shared in the riches of the later, postwar Medusa. That's the background scenario, isn't it?'

'The logic's as clean as it can be. For three years he was used and damn near killed in a black operation, and along the way he supposedly discovered that more than a few undistinguished Saigon pricks were driving Jaguars and were sailing yachts and pulling down six-figure retainers while he went on a government pension. That could try the patience of John the Baptist, to say nothing of Barabbas.'

'It's a terrific libretto,' allowed Holland, a slow smile breaking across his face. 'I can hear the tenors soaring in triumph and the bassos slinking off stage in Machiavellian defeat . . . Don't *scowl* at me, Alex, I mean it! It's really ingenious. It's so inevitable it became a self-fulfilling prophecy.'

'What the hell are you talking about?'

'Your Bourne was right from the beginning. It all took place the way he saw it, but not in *any* way he could have imagined. Because it was inevitable; somewhere there had to be a cross-pollinator.'

'Please come down from Mars and explain to an earthling, Peter.'

'Medusa's *using* the Jackal! *Now.* Teagarten's assassination proves it unless you want to concede that Bourne actually blew up that car outside of Brussels.'

'Of course not.'

'Then Carlos's name had to surface for someone in Medusa who already knew about Jason Bourne. It couldn't be otherwise. You didn't mention either one to Armbruster, or Swayne, or Atkinson in London, did you?'

'Again, of course not. The time wasn't right; we weren't ready to pull those triggers.'

'Who's left?' asked Holland.

Alex stared at the DCI. 'Good Lord,' he said softly. 'DeSole?'

'Yes, DeSole, the grossly underpaid specialist who complained amusingly but incessantly that there was no way a man could properly educate his children and grandchildren on government pay. He was brought in on everything we discussed, starting with your assault on us in the conference room.'

'He certainly was, but that was limited to Bourne and the Jackal. There was no mention of Armbruster or Swayne, no Teagarten or Atkinson – the new Medusa wasn't even in the picture. Hell, Peter, *you* didn't know about it until seventy-two hours ago.'

'Yes, but DeSole did because he'd sold out; he was part of it. He had to have been alerted. ". . . *Watch* it. We've been penetrated. Some maniac says he's going to expose us, blow us apart." . . . You told me yourself that panic buttons were punched from the Trade Commission to Pentagon Procurements to the embassy in London.'

'They were punched,' agreed Conklin. 'So hard that two of them had to be taken out along with Teagarten and our disgruntled Mole. Snake Lady's elders quickly decided who their vulnerable people were. But where does Carlos or Bourne fit in? There's no attribution.'

'I thought we agreed that there was.'

'DeSole?' Conklin shook his head. 'It's a provocative thought, but it doesn't wash. He couldn't have presumed that I knew about Medusa's penetration because we hadn't even started it.'

'But when you did, the sequence had to bother him if only in the sense that although they were poles apart, one crisis followed too quickly upon another. What was it? A matter of hours?'

'Less than twenty-four . . . Still they *were* poles apart.'

'Not for an analyst's analyst,' countered Holland. 'If it walks like an odd duck and sounds like an odd duck, look for an odd duck. I submit that somewhere along the line DeSole made the connection between Jason Bourne and the madman who had infiltrated Medusa – the new Medusa.'

'For Christ's sake, *how*?'

'I don't know. Maybe because you told us Bourne came out of the old *Saigon* Medusa – that's one hell of a connection to begin with.'

'My God, you may be right,' said Alex, falling back on the couch. 'The driving force we gave our unnamed madman was that he'd been cut *off* from the new Medusa. I used the words myself with every phone call. "He's spent years putting it together . . ." "He's got names and ranks and banks in

Zurich . . ." Jesus, I'm *blind*! I said those things to total strangers on a telephone fishing expedition and never even thought about having mentioned Bourne's origins in Medusa at that meeting when DeSole was *here*.'

'Why should you have thought about it? You and your man decided to play a separate game all by yourselves.'

'The reasons were goddamned valid,' broke in Conklin. 'For all I knew, *you* were a Medusan.'

'Thanks a bunch.'

'Come on, don't give me that shit. "We've got a top max out at Langley" . . . those were the words I heard from London. What would you have thought, what would you have done?'

'Exactly what you did,' answered Holland, a tight grin on his lips. 'But you're supposed to be so bright, so much smarter than I'm supposed to be.'

'Thanks a bunch.'

'Don't be hard on yourself; you did what any of us would have done in your place.'

'For that I do thank you. And you're right, of course. It had to be DeSole; how he did it, I don't know, but it had to be him. It probably went back years inside his head – he never really forgot anything, you know. His mind was a sponge that absorbed everything and never let a recollection drip away. He could remember words and phrases, even spontaneous grunts of approval or disapproval the rest of us forgot . . . And I gave him the whole Bourne-Jackal history – and then someone from Medusa used it in Brussels.'

'They did more than that, Alex,' said Holland, leaning forward in his chair and picking up several papers from his desk. 'They stole your scenario, usurped your strategy. They've pitted Jason Bourne against Carlos the Jackal, but instead of the controls being in your hands, Medusa has them. Bourne's back where he was in Europe thirteen years ago, maybe with his wife, maybe not, the only difference being that in addition to Carlos and Interpol and every other police authority on the Continent ready to waste him on sight, he's got another lethal monkey on his back.'

'That's what's in those pages you're holding, isn't it? The information from New York?'

'I can't guarantee it, but I think so. It's the cross-pollinator I spoke about before, the bee that went from one rotten flower to another carrying poison.'

'Deliver, please.'

'Nicolo Dellacroce and the higher-ups above him.'

'Mafia?'

'It's consistent, if not socially acceptable. Medusa grew out of Saigon's officer corps and it still relegates its dirty work to the hungry grunts and corrupt NCOs. Check out Nicky D. and men like Sergeant Flannagan. When it comes to killing or kidnapping or using drugs on prisoners, the starched-shirt boys stay far in the background; they're nowhere to be found.'

'But I gather you found them,' said the impatient Conklin.

'Again, we think so – we being our people in quiet consultation with New York's anti-crime division, especially a unit called the US platoon.'

'Never heard of it.'

'They're mostly Italian Americans; they gave themselves the name Untouchable Sicilians. Thus the US initials with a dual connotation.'

'Nice touch.'

'Unnice work . . . According to the Reco-Metropolitan's billing files—'

'The *who*?'

'The company that installed the answering machine on One Hundred Thirty-eighth Street in Manhattan.'

'Sorry. Go on.'

'According to the files, the machine was leased to a small importing firm on Eleventh Avenue several blocks from the piers. An hour ago we got the telephone records for the past two months for the company, and guess what we found?'

'I'd rather not wait,' said Alex emphatically.

'Nine calls to a reasonably acceptable number in Brooklyn Heights, and three in the space of an hour to an extremely unlikely telephone on Wall Street.'

'Someone was excited—'

'That's what we thought – we in this case being our own unit. We asked the Sicilians to give us what they had on Brooklyn Heights.'

'DeFazio?'

'Let's put it this way. He lives there, but the phone is registered to the Atlas Coin Vending Machine Company in Long Island City.'

'It fits. Dumb, but it fits. What about DeFazio?'

'He's a middle-level but ambitious capo in the Giancavallo family. He's very close, very underground, very vicious . . . and very gay.'

'*Holy Christ . . . !*'

'The Untouchables swore us to secrecy. They intend to spring it themselves.'

'Bullshit,' said Conklin softly. 'One of the first things we learn in this business is to lie to anyone and everyone, especially anyone who's foolish enough to trust us. We'll use it any time it gets us a square forward . . . What's the other telephone number, the unlikely one?'

'Just about the most powerful law firm on Wall Street.'

'Medusa,' concluded Alex firmly.

'That's the way I read it. They've got seventy-six lawyers on two floors of the building. Which one is it – or who among them are they?'

'I don't *give* a goddamn! We go after DeFazio and whatever controls he's sending over to Paris. To Europe to feed the Jackal. They're the guns after Jason and that's all I care about. Go to work on *DeFazio*. He's the one under contract!'

Peter Holland leaned back in his chair, rigid, intense. 'It had to come to this, didn't it, Alex?' he asked quietly. 'We both have our priorities . . . I'd do anything within my sworn capacity to save the lives of Jason Bourne and his wife, but I will not violate my oath to defend this country first. I can't do it and I suspect you know that. My priority is Medusa, in your words a global cartel that intends to become a government within our government over here. That's whom I have to go after. First and immediately and without regard to casualties. To put it plainly, my friend – and I hope you're my friend – the Bournes, or whoever they are, are expendable. I'm sorry, Alex.'

'That's really why you asked me to come over here this morning, isn't it?' said Conklin, planting his cane on the floor and awkwardly getting to his feet.

'Yes, it is.'

'You've got your own game plan against Medusa – and we can't be a part of it.'

'No, you can't. It's a fundamental conflict of interest.'

'I'll grant you that. We'd louse you up in a minute if it'd help Jason and Marie. Naturally, my personal and professional opinion is that if the whole fucking United States government can't rip out a Medusa without sacrificing a man and a woman who've given so much, I'm not sure it's *worth* a damn!'

'Neither am I,' said Holland, standing up behind the desk. 'But I swore an oath to try – in order of my sworn priorities.'

'Have I got any perks left?'

'Anything I can get you that doesn't compromise our going after Medusa.'

'How about two seats on a military aircraft, Agency-cleared, to Paris.'

'*Two* seats?'

'Panov and me. We went to Hong Kong together, why not Paris?'

'*Alex*, you're out of your goddamned *mind*!'

'I don't think you understand, Peter. Mo's wife died ten years after they were married, and I never had courage to give it a try. So you see, "Jason Bourne" and Marie are the only family we have. She makes a hell of a meat loaf, let me tell you.'

'Two tickets to Paris,' said Holland, his face ashen.

29

Marie watched her husband as he walked back and forth, the pacing deliberate, energized. He tramped angrily between the writing table and the sunlit curtains of the two windows overlooking the front lawn of the Auberge des Artistes in Barbizon. The country inn was the one Marie remembered, but it was not part of David Webb's memory; and when he said as much, his wife briefly closed her eyes, hearing another voice from years ago.

'Above everything, he's got to avoid extreme stress, the kind of tension that goes with survival under life-threatening circumstances. If you see him regressing into that state of mind – and you'll know it when you see it – stop him. Seduce him, slap him, cry, get angry . . . anything, just stop him.' *Morris Panov, dear friend, doctor and the guiding force behind her husband's therapy.*

She had tried seduction within minutes after they were alone together. It was a mistake, even a touch farcical, awkward for both of them. Neither was remotely aroused. Yet there was no embarrassment; they held each other on the bed, both understanding.

'We're a couple of real sexpots, aren't we?' said Marie.

'We've been there before,' replied David Webb gently, 'and I've no doubt we'll be there again.' Then Jason Bourne rolled away and stood up. 'I have to make a list,' he said urgently, heading for the quaint country table against the wall that served as a desk and a depository for the telephone. 'We have to know where we are and where we're going.'

'And I have to call Johnny on the island,' added Marie, rising to her feet and smoothing her skirt. 'After I talk to him I'll speak to Jamie. I'll reassure him and tell him we'll be back soon.' The wife crossed to the table; she stopped, blocked by her husband – her husband yet not her husband.

'No,' said Bourne quietly, shaking his head.

'Don't *say* that to me,' protested the mother, anger flashing in her eyes.

'Three hours ago in the Rivoli changed everything. Nothing's the same now. Don't you understand that?'

'I understand that my children are several thousand miles away from me and I intend to reach them. Don't you understand *that*?'

'Of course I do, I just can't allow it,' answered Jason.

'*Goddamn* you, Mr Bourne!'

'Will you listen to me? . . . You'll talk to Johnny and to Jamie – we'll both talk to them – but not from here and not while they're on the island.'

'What . . . ?'

'I'm calling Alex in a few minutes and telling him to get all of them out of there, including Mrs Cooper, of course.'

Marie had stared at her husband, suddenly understanding. 'Oh, my God, *Carlos*!'

'Yes. As of this noon he's got only one place to zero in on – Tranquillity. If he doesn't know now, he'll learn soon enough that Jamie and Alison are with Johnny. I trust your brother and his personal Tonton Macoute, but I still want them away from there before it's night in the islands. I also don't know if Carlos has sources in the island's trunk lines that could trace a call between there and here, but I do know that Alex's phone is sterile. That's why you can't call now. From here to there.'

'Then, for God's sake, call Alex! What the hell are you *waiting* for?'

'I'm not sure.' For a moment there was a blank, panicked look in her husband's eyes – they were the eyes of David Webb, not Jason Bourne. 'I have to decide – where do I send the kids?'

'Alex will know, *Jason*,' said Marie, her own eyes levelled steadily on his. 'Now.'

'Yes . . . yes, of course. Now.' The veiled, vacuous look passed and Bourne reached for the phone.

Alexander Conklin was not in Vienna, Virginia, USA. Instead, there was the monotonic voice of a recorded operator that had the effect of crashing thunder. 'The telephone number you have called is no longer in service.'

He had placed the call twice again, believing in desperate hope that an error had been made by the French telephone service. Then bolts of lightning followed: 'The telephone number you have called is no longer in service.' For a third time.

The pacing had begun; from the table to the windows and back again. Over and over, the curtains were pulled aside, anxious eyes nervously peering out, then seconds later poring over a growing list of names and places. Marie suggested lunch; he did not hear her, so she watched him in silence from across the room.

The quick, abrupt movements of her husband were like those of a large disquieted cat, smooth, fluid, alert for the unexpected. They were the movements of Jason Bourne and, before him, Medusa's Delta, not David Webb. She remembered the medical records compiled by Mo Panov in the early days of David's therapy. Many were filled with wildly divergent descriptions from people who claimed to have seen the man known as the Chameleon, but among the most reliable was a common reference to the catlike mobility of the 'assassin'. Panov had been looking for clues to Jason Bourne's identity then, for all they had at the time were a first name and fragmented images of painful death in Cambodia. Mo often wondered aloud if there was more to his patient's physical dexterity than mere athleticism; oddly enough, there was not.

As Marie looked back, the subtle physical differences between the two men who were her husband both fascinated and repelled her. Each was muscular and graceful, each capable of performing difficult tasks requiring physical coordination; but where David's strength and mobility came from an easy sense of accomplishment, Jason's was filled with an inner malice, no pleasure in the accomplishment, only a hostile purpose. When she had mentioned this to Panov, his reply was succinct: 'David couldn't kill. Bourne can; he was trained to.'

Still, Mo was pleased that she had spotted the different 'physical manifestations', as he called her observation. 'It's another signpost for you. When you see Bourne, bring David back as fast as you can. If you can't, call me.'

She could not bring David back now, she thought. For the sake of the children and herself *and* David, she dared not try.

'I'm going out for a while,' announced Jason by the window.

'You can't!' cried Marie. 'For God's sake, don't leave me alone.'

Bourne frowned, lowering his voice, somewhere an undefined conflict within him. 'I'm just driving out on the highway to find a phone, that's all.'

'Take me with you. *Please.* I can't stay by myself any longer.'

'All right . . . As a matter of fact, we'll need a few things. We'll find one of those malls and buy some clothes – toothbrushes, a razor . . . whatever else we can think of.'

'You mean we can't go back to Paris.'

'We can and probably will go back to Paris, but not to our hotels. Do you have your passport?'

'Passport, money, credit cards, everything. They were all in my purse which I *didn't* know I had until you gave it to me in the car.'

'I didn't think it was such a good idea to leave it at the Meurice. Come on. A phone first.'

'Who are you calling?'

'Alex.'

'You just tried him.'

'At his apartment; he was thrown out of his security tent in Virginia. Then I'll reach Mo Panov. Let's go.'

They drove south again to the small city of Corbeil-Essonnes, where there was a relatively new shopping centre several miles west of the highway. The crowded merchandising complex was a blight on the French countryside but a welcome sight for the fugitives. Jason parked the car, and like any husband and wife out for late-afternoon shopping, they strolled down the central mall while frantically looking for a public telephone.

'Not a goddamned one on the highway!' said Bourne through clenched teeth. 'What do they think people are supposed to do if they have an accident or a flat tyre?'

'Wait for the police,' answered Marie, 'and there *was* a phone only it was broken into. Maybe that's why there aren't more – *There's* one.'

Once again Jason went through the irritating process of placing an overseas call with local operators who found it irritating to ring through to the international branch of the system. And then the thunder returned, distant but implacable.

'This is Alex,' said the recorded voice over the line. 'I'll be away for a while, visiting a place where a grave error was made. Call me in five or six hours. It's now nine-thirty in the morning, Eastern Standard time. Out, Juneau.'

Stunned, his mind spinning, Bourne hung up the phone and stared at Marie. 'Something's happened and I have to make sense out of it. His last words were – "Out, Juneau." '

'*Juneau?*' Marie squinted, her eyes blocking out the light, then she opened them and looked at her husband. 'Alpha, Bravo, Charlie,' she began softly, adding, 'Alternating military alphabets?' Then she spoke rapidly. 'Foxtrot, Gold . . . India, *Juneau*! Juneau's for J and J is for *Jason*! . . . What was the rest?'

'He's visiting someplace—'

'Come on, let's walk,' she broke in, noticing the curious faces of two men waiting to use the phone; she grabbed his arm and pulled him away from the booth. 'He couldn't be clearer?' she asked as they entered the flow of the crowds.

'It was a recording. " . . . where a grave error was made." '

'The *what*?'

'He said to call him in five or six hours – he was visiting a place where a grave error – grave? – my God, it's *Rambouillet*!'

'The cemetery . . . ?'

'Where he tried to kill me thirteen years ago. That's *it*! Rambouillet!'

'Not in five or six hours,' objected Marie. 'No matter when he left the message he couldn't fly to Paris and then drive to Rambouillet in five hours. He was in Washington.'

'Of course he could; we've both done it before. An army jet out of Andrews Air Force Base under diplomatic cover to Paris. Peter Holland threw him out but he gave him a going-away present. Immediate separation, but a bonus for bringing him Medusa.' Bourne suddenly whipped his wrist up and looked at his watch. 'It's still only around noon in the islands. Let's find another phone.'

'Johnny? Tranquillity? You really think—'

'I can't *stop* thinking!' interrupted Jason, rushing ahead, holding Marie's hand as she trippingly kept up with him. '*Glace*,' he said, looking up to his right.

'Ice cream?'

'There's a phone inside, over there,' he answered, slowing them both down and approaching the huge windows of a *pâtisserie* that had a red banner over its door announcing an ice cream counter with several dozen flavours. 'Get me a vanilla,' he said, ushering them both into the crowded store.

'Vanilla what?'

'Whatever.'

'You won't be able to hear—'

'He'll hear *me*, that's all that matters. Take your time, give *me* time.' Bourne crossed to the phone, instantly understanding why it was not used; the noise of the store was nearly unbearable. '*Mademoiselle, s'il vous plaît, c'est urgent!*' Three minutes later, holding his palm against his left ear, Jason had the unexpected comfort of hearing Tranquillity Inn's most irritating employee over the phone.

'This is Mr Pritchard, Tranquillity Inn's associate manager. My switchboard informs me that you have an emergency, sir. May I inquire as to the nature of your—'

'You can shut *up*!' shouted Jason from the cacophonous ice cream parlour in Corbeil-Essonnes in France. 'Get Jay St Jay on the phone, *now*. This is his brother-in-law.'

'Oh, it is such a pleasure to hear from you, sir! Much has happened since you left. Your lovely children are with us and the handsome young boy plays on the beach – with *me*, sir – and all is—'

'Mr St Jacques, please. *Now!*'

'Of course, sir. He is upstairs . . .'

'*Johnny?*'

'David, where *are* you?'

'That doesn't matter. Get out of there. Take the kids and Mrs Cooper and get *out*!'

'We know all about it, Dave—'

'Who?'

'I said, Dave. *You*.'

'Yes . . . yes, of course . . . What do you know?'

'Alex Conklin called several hours ago and said somebody named Holland would reach us . . . I gather he's the chief honcho of your intelligence service.'

'He is. Did he?'

'Yeah, about twenty minutes after I talked to Alex. He told us we were being choppered out around two o'clock this afternoon. He needed the time to clear a military aircraft in here. Mrs Cooper was my idea; your backward son says he doesn't know how to change diapers sport . . . David, what the hell is going on? Where's *Marie*?'

'She's all right – I'll explain everything later. Just do as Holland says. Did he say where you were being taken?'

'He didn't want to, I'll tell you that. But no fucking American's going to order me and your kids around – my *Canadian* sister's kids – and I told him that in a seven spade flush.'

'That's nice, Johnny. Make friends with the director of the CIA.'

'I don't give a shit on that score. In my country we figure those initials mean Caught In the Act, and I told him so!'

'That's even nicer . . . What did he say?'

'He said we were going to a safe house in Virginia, and I said mine's pretty goddamned safe right here and we had a restaurant and room service and a beach and ten guards who could shoot his balls off at two hundred yards.'

'You're filled with tact. And what did he say to that?'

'Actually, he laughed. Then he explained that his place had twenty guards who could take out one of my balls at four hundred yards, along with a kitchen and room service and television for the kids that I couldn't match.'

'That's pretty persuasive.'

'Well, he said something else that was even more persuasive that I *really* couldn't match. He told me there was no public access to the place, that it was an old estate in Fairfax turned over to the government by a rich ambassador who had more money than Ottawa, with its own airfield and an entrance road four miles from the highway.'

'I know the place,' said Bourne, wincing at the noise of the *pâtisserie.* 'It's the Tannenbaum estate. He's right; it's the best of the sterile houses. He likes us.'

'I asked you before – where's *Marie*?'

'She's with me.'

'She *found* you!'

'Later, Johnny. I'll reach you in Fairfax.' Jason hung up the phone as his wife awkwardly made her way through the crowd and handed him a pink plastic cup with a blue plastic spoon plunged into a mound of dark brown.

'The *children*?' she asked, raising her voice to be heard, her eyes on fire.

'Everything's fine, better than we might have expected. Alex reached the same conclusion about the Jackal as I did. Peter Holland's flying them all up to a safe house in Virginia, Mrs Cooper included.'

'Thank God!'

'Thank Alex.' Bourne looked at the pink plastic cup with the thin blue spoon. 'What the hell is this? They didn't have vanilla?'

'It's a hot fudge sundae. It was meant for the man beside me but he was yelling at his wife, so I took it.'

'I don't *like* hot fudge.'

'So yell at your wife. Come on, we've got to buy clothes.'

The early afternoon Caribbean sun burned down on Tranquillity Inn as John St Jacques descended the staircase into the lobby carrying a LeSport duffle bag in his right hand. He nodded to Mr Pritchard, whom he had spoken to over the phone only moments ago, explaining that he was leaving for several days and would be in touch within hours after he reached Toronto. What remained of the staff had been apprised of his sudden, quite necessary departure, and he had full confidence in the executive manager and his valuable assistant, Mr Pritchard. He assumed that no problems would arise beyond their combined expertise. Tranquillity Inn, for all intents and purposes, was virtually shut down. However, Sir Henry Sykes at Government House on the big island should be contacted in the event of difficulties.

'There shall be none beyond *my* expertise!' Pritchard had replied. 'The repair and maintenance crews will work every bit as hard in your absence.'

St Jacques walked out the glass doors of the circular building towards the first villa on the right, the one nearest the stone steps to the pier and the two beaches. Mrs Cooper and the two children waited inside for the arrival of the United States Navy long-range seagoing helicopter that would take them to Puerto Rico, where they would board a military jet to Andrews Air Force Base outside Washington.

Through the huge glass windows, Mr Pritchard watched his employer disappear through the doors of Villa One. At that same moment he heard the growing sounds of a large helicopter's rotors thumping in the air above the inn. In minutes it would circle the water beyond the pier and descend, awaiting its passengers. Apparently, those passengers heard what he had heard, thought Mr Pritchard as he saw St Jacques, gripping his young nephew's hand, and the insufferably arrogant Mrs Cooper, who was holding a blanketed infant in her arms, come out of the villa, followed by the two favourite guards carrying their luggage. Pritchard reached below the counter for the telephone that bypassed the switchboard. He dialled.

'This is the office of the deputy director of immigration, himself speaking.'

'Esteemed uncle—'

'It is you?' broke in the official from Blackburne Airport, abruptly lowering his voice. 'What have you learned?'

'Everything is of immense value, I assure you. I heard it all on the telephone!'

'We shall both be greatly rewarded, I have that on the highest authority. They may all be undercover terrorists, you know, St Jacques himself the leader. It is said they may even fool Washington. What can I pass on, brilliant nephew?'

'They are being taken to what is called a "safe" house in Virginia. It is known as the Tannenbaum estate and has its own airport, can you *believe* such a thing?'

'I can believe anything where these animals are concerned.'

'Be sure to include my name and position, esteemed uncle.'

'Would I do otherwise, *could* I do otherwise? We shall be the heroes of Montserrat! . . . But remember, my intelligent nephew, everything must be kept in utmost secrecy. We are both sworn to silence, never forget that. Just think! We've been selected to render service to a great international organization. Leaders the world over will know of our contributions.'

'My heart bursts with pride . . . May I know what this august organization is called?'

'*Shhh!* It has no name; that is part of the secrecy. The money was wired through a bank computer transfer directly from Switzerland; that is the proof.'

'A sacred trust,' added Mr Pritchard.

'Also well paid, trusted Nephew, and it is only the beginning. I myself am monitoring all aircraft arriving here and sending the manifests on to Martinique, to a famous surgeon, no less! Of course, at the moment all flights are on hold, orders from Government House.'

'The American military helicopter?' asked the awed Pritchard.

'*Shhh!* It, too, is a secret, *everything* is secret.'

'Then it is a very loud and apparent secret, my esteemed uncle. People are on the beach watching it now.'

'*What?*'

'It's here. Mr Saint Jay and the children are boarding as we speak. Also that dreadful Mrs Cooper—'

'I must call Paris at once,' interrupted the immigration officer, disconnecting the line.

'*Paris?*' repeated Mr Pritchard. 'How inspiring. How privileged we are!'

'I didn't tell him everything,' said Peter Holland quietly, shaking his head as he spoke. 'I wanted to – I intended to – but it was in his eyes, in his own words actually. He said that he'd louse us up in a minute if it would help Bourne and his wife.'

'He would, too.' Charles Casset nodded; he sat in the chair in front of the director's desk, a computer printout of a long-buried classified file in his hand. 'When you read this you'll understand. Alex really did try to kill Bourne in Paris years ago – his closest friend and he tried to put a bullet in his head for all the wrong reasons.'

'Conklin's on his way to Paris now. He and Morris Panov.'

'That's on *your* head, Peter. I wouldn't have done it, not without strings.'

'I couldn't refuse him.'

'Of course you could. You didn't want to.'

'We owed him. He brought us Medusa – and from here on, Charlie, that's *all* that concerns us.'

'I understand, Director Holland,' said Casset coldly. 'And I assume that due to foreign entanglements you're working backwards into a domestic conspiracy that should be incontestably established before you alert the guardians of domestic accord, namely, the Federal Bureau.'

'Are you threatening me, you lowlife?'

'I certainly am, Peter,' Casset dropped the ice from his expression, replacing it with a calm, thin smile. 'You're breaking the law, Mr Director . . . That's regrettable, old boy, as my predecessors might have said.'

'What the hell do you *want* from me?' cried Holland.

'Cover one of our own, one of the best we ever had. I not only want it, I insist upon it.'

'If you think I'm going to give him everything, including the name of Medusa's law firm on Wall Street, you're out of your fucking mind. It's our *keystone*!'

'For God's sake, go back into the navy, Admiral,' said the deputy director, his voice level, again cold, without emphasis. 'If you think that's what I'm suggesting, you haven't learned very much in that chair.'

'Hey, come on, smart ass, that's pretty close to insubordination.'

'Of course it is, because I'm insubordinate – but this isn't the navy. You can't keelhaul me, or hang me from the yardarm, or withhold my ration of rum. All you can do is fire me, and if you do, a lot of people will wonder why, which wouldn't do the Agency any good. But that's not necessary.'

'What the *hell* are you talking about, Charlie?'

'Well, to begin with, I'm *not* talking about that law firm in New York because you're right, it is our keystone, and Alex with his infinite imagination would probe and threaten to the point where the shredding begins and our paper trail here and abroad ends.'

'I had something like that in mind—'

'Then again you were right,' interrupted Casset, nodding. 'So we keep Alex away from our keystone, as far away from *us* as possible, but we give him our marker. Something tangible he can plug into, knowing its value.'

Silence. Then Holland spoke. 'I don't understand a word you're saying.'

'You would if you knew Conklin better. He knows now that there's a connection between Medusa and the Jackal. What did you call it? A self-fulfilling prophecy?'

'I said the strategy was so perfect it was inevitable and therefore self-fulfilling. DeSole was the unexpected catalyst who moved everything ahead of schedule – him and whatever the hell happened down in Montserrat . . . What's this marker of yours, this tangible item of value?'

'The string, Peter. Knowing what he knows, you can't let Alex bounce around Europe like a loose cannon any more than you could give him the name of that law firm in New York. We need a pipeline to him so we have some idea what he's up to – more than an idea, if we can manage it. Someone like his friend Bernardine, only someone who can also be our friend.'

'Where do we find such a person?'

'I have a candidate – and I hope we're not being taped.'

'Count on it,' said Holland with a trace of anger. 'I don't believe in that crap and this office is swept every morning. Who's the candidate?'

'A man at the Soviet embassy in Paris,' replied Casset calmly. 'I think we can deal.'

'A mole?'

'Not for a minute. A KGB officer whose first priority never changes. Find Carlos. Kill Carlos. Protect Novgorod.'

'Novgorod . . . ? The Americanized village or town where the Jackal was initially trained in Russia?'

'Half trained and escaped from before he could be shot as a maniac. Only it's not just an American compound – that's a mistake we make so often. There are British and French compounds, too, also Israeli, Dutch, Spanish, West German and God knows how many others. Dozens of square miles cut out of the forests along the Volkhov River, dotted with settlements so that you'd swear you were in a different country with each one you entered – if you could get inside, which you couldn't. Like the Aryan breeding farms, the *Lebensborn* of Nazi Germany, Novgorod is one of Moscow's most closely guarded secrets. They want the Jackal as badly as Jason Bourne does.'

'And you think this KGB fellow will cooperate, keep us informed about Conklin if they make contact?'

'I can try. After all, we have a common objective, and I know Alex would accept him because he knows how much the Soviets want Carlos on the dead list.'

Holland leaned forward in his chair. 'I told Conklin I'd help him any way I could as long as it didn't compromise our going after Medusa . . . He'll be landing in Paris within the hour. Shall I leave instructions at the diplomatic counter for him to reach you?'

'Tell him to call Charlie Bravo Plus One,' said Casset, getting up and dropping the computer printout on the desk. 'I don't know how much I can give him in an hour but I'll go to work. I've got a secure channel to our Russian, thanks to an outstanding "consultant" of ours in Paris.'

'Give him a bonus.'

'She's already asked for one – harassed me is more appropriate. She runs the cleanest escort service in the city; the girls are checked weekly.'

'Why not hire them all?' asked the director, smiling.

'I believe seven are already on the payroll, sir,' answered the deputy director, his demeanour serious, in contrast to his arched eyebrows.

Dr Morris Panov, his legs unsteady, was helped down the metal steps of the diplomatically cleared jet by a strapping marine corporal in starched summer khakis carrying his suitcase. 'How do you people manage to look so presentable after such a perfectly horrendous trip?' asked the psychiatrist.

'None of us will look this presentable after a couple of hours of liberty in Paris, sir.'

'Some things never change, Corporal. Thank God . . . Where's that crippled delinquent who was with me?'

'He was vehicled off for a diplograph, sir.'

'Come again? A noun's a verb leading to the incomprehensible?'

'It's not so hard, Doctor,' laughed the marine, leading Panov to a motorized cart complete with a uniformed driver and a stencilled American flag on the side. 'During our descent, the tower radioed the pilot that there was an urgent message for him.'

'I thought he went to the bathroom.'

'That, too, I believe, sir.' The corporal put the suitcase on a rear rack and helped Mo into the cart. 'Easy now, Doctor, lift your leg up a little higher.'

'That's the other one, not me,' protested the psychiatrist. 'He's the one without a foot.'

'We were told you'd been ill, sir.'

'Not in my goddamned legs . . . Sorry, young man, no offence. I just don't like flying in small tubes a hundred and ten miles up in the sky. Not too many astronauts come from Tremont Avenue in the Bronx.'

'Hey, you're kidding, Doc!'

'What?'

'I'm from *Garden* Street, you know, across from the *zoo*! The name's Fleishman, Morris Fleishman. Nice to meet a fellow Bronxite.'

'Morris?' said Panov, shaking hands. 'Morris the Marine? I should have had a talk with your parents . . . Stay well, Mo. And thank you for your concern.'

'You get better, Doc, and when you see Tremont Avenue again, give it my best, okay?'

'I will, indeed, Morris,' replied Morris, raising his hand as the diplomatic cart shot forward.

Four minutes later, escorted by the driver, Panov entered the long grey corridor that was the immigration-free access to France for government functionaries of nations accredited by the Quai d'Orsay. They walked in to the large holding lounge where men and women were gathered in small groups, conversing quietly, the sounds of different languages filling the room. Alarmed, Mo saw that Conklin was nowhere in sight; he turned to the driver-escort as a young woman dressed in the neutral uniform of a hostess approached.

'*Docteur?*' she asked, addressing Panov.

'Yes,' replied Mo, surprised. 'But I'm afraid my French is pretty rusty if not nonexistent.'

'It's of no matter, sir. Your companion requested that you remain here until he returns. It will be no more than a few minutes, he was quite sure . . . Please, sit down. May I bring you a drink?'

'Bourbon with ice, if you'd be so kind,' answered Panov, lowering himself into the armchair.

'Certainly, sir.' The hostess retreated as the driver placed Mo's suitcase beside him.

'I have to get back to my vehicle,' said the diplomatic escort. 'You'll be fine here.'

'I wonder where he went,' mused Panov, glancing at his watch.

'Probably to an outside phone, Doctor. They come in here, get messages at the counters, then go like hell into the terminal to find public pay phones; they don't like the ones in here. The Russkies always walk the fastest; the Arabs, the slowest.'

'Must be their respective climates,' offered the psychiatrist, smiling.

'Don't bet your stethoscope on it.' The driver laughed and brought his hand up for an informal salute. 'Take care, sir, and get some rest. You look tired.'

'Thank you, young man. Goodbye.' *I am tired,* thought Panov as the escort disappeared into the grey corridor. *So tired, but Alex was right. If he'd flown here alone, I would never have forgiven him . . . David! We've got to find him! The damage to him could be incalculable – none of them understands. With a single act his fragile, damaged mind could regress years – thirteen years – to where he was a functioning killer, and for him nothing else!* . . . A voice. The figure above was talking to him. 'I'm sorry, forgive me.'

'Your drink, Doctor,' said the hostess pleasantly. 'I debated whether to wake you, but then you moved and sounded as though you were in pain—'

'No, not at all, my dear. Just tired.'

'I understand, sir. Sudden flights can be so exhausting, and if they are long and uncomfortable, even worse.'

'You touched on all three points, miss,' agreed Panov, taking his drink. 'Thank you.'

'You are American, of course.'

'How could you tell? I'm not wearing cowboy boots or a Hawaiian shirt.'

The woman laughed charmingly. 'I know the driver who brought you in here. He's American security, and quite nice, *very* attractive.'

'Security? You mean like in "police"?'

'Oh, very much so, but we never use the word . . . Oh, here's your companion coming back inside.' The hostess lowered her voice. 'May I ask quickly, Doctor? Does he require a wheelchair?'

'Good heavens, no. He's walked like that for years.'

'Very well. Enjoy your stay in Paris, sir.' The woman left as Alex, limping, weaved around several groups of chattering Europeans to the chair next to Panov. He sat down and leaned awkwardly forward in the soft leather. He was obviously disturbed.

'What's the matter?' asked Mo.

'I just talked to Charlie Casset in Washington.'

'He's the one you like, the one you trust, isn't he?'

'He's the best there is when he has personal access, or at least human intelligence. When he can see and hear and look for himself, and not simply read words on paper or a computer screen without asking questions.'

'Are you, perchance, moving into my territory again, *Doctor* Conklin?'

'I accused David of that last week and I'll tell you what he told me. It's a free country, and your training notwithstanding, you don't have a franchise on common sense.'

'*Mea culpa*,' agreed Panov, nodding. 'I gather your friend did something you don't approve of.'

'He did something *he* wouldn't approve of if he had more information on whom he did it with.'

'That sounds positively Freudian, even medically imprudent.'

'Both are part of it, I guess. He made an outside unsanctioned deal with a man named Dimitri Krupkin at the Russian embassy here in Paris. We'll be working with the local KGB – you, me, Bourne and Marie – if and when we find them. Hopefully, in Rambouillet in an hour or so.'

'What are you *saying*?' asked Mo, astonished and barely audible.

'Long story, short time. Moscow wants the Jackal's head, the rest of him separated from it. Washington can't feed us or protect us, so the Soviets will act as our temporary paterfamilias if we find ourselves in a bind.'

Panov frowned, then shook his head as though absorbing very strange information, then spoke. 'I suppose it's not your run-of-the-mill development, but there's a certain logic, even comfort, to it.'

'On paper, Mo,' said Conklin. 'Not with Dimitri Krupkin. I know him. Charlie doesn't.'

'Oh? He's one of the evil people?'

'Kruppie evil? No, not really—'

'*Kruppie*?'

'We go way back as young hustlers to Istanbul in the late sixties and Athens after that, then Amsterdam later . . . Krupkin's not malevolent, and he works like a son of a bitch for Moscow with a damn good second-rate mind, better than eighty per cent of the clowns in our business, but he's got a problem. He's fundamentally on the wrong side, in the wrong society. His parents should have come over with mine when the Bolsheviks took the throne.'

'I forget. Your family was Russian.'

'Speaking the language helps with Kruppie. I can nail his nuances. He's the quintessential capitalist. Like the economic ministers in Beijing, he doesn't just like money, he's obsessed with it – and everything that *goes* with it. Out of sight and out of sanction, he could be bought.'

'You mean by the Jackal?'

'I saw him bought in Athens by Greek developers selling additional airstrips to Washington when they knew the Communists were going to throw us out. They paid him to shut up. Then I watched him broker diamonds in Amsterdam between the merchants on the Nieuwmarkt and the dacha-elite in Moscow. We had drinks one night in the Kattengat and I asked him,

"Kruppie, what the fuck are you *doing*?" You know what he said? He said in clothes I couldn't afford, "Aleksei, I'll do everything I can to outsmart you, to help the supreme Soviet to gain world dominance, but in the meantime, if you'd like a holiday, I have a lovely house on the lake in Geneva." That's what he *said*, Mo.'

'He's remarkable. Of course, you told your friend Casset all this—'

'Of course I didn't,' broke in Conklin.

'Good God, why *not*?'

'Because Krupkin obviously never told Charlie that he knew *me*. Casset may have the deal, but I'm dealing.'

'With what? How?'

'David – Jason – has over five million in the Caymans. With only a spit of that amount I'll turn Kruppie so he'll be working *only* for us, if we need him or want him to.'

'Which means you don't trust Casset.'

'Not so,' said Alex. 'I trust Charlie with my life. It's just that I'm not sure I want it in his hands. He and Peter Holland have their priorities and we have ours. Theirs is Medusa; ours are David and Marie.'

'*Messieurs?*' The hostess returned and addressed Conklin. 'Your car has arrived, sir. It is on the south platform.'

'You're sure it's for me?' asked Alex.

'Forgive me, monsieur, but the attendant said a Mr Smith had a difficult leg.'

'He's certainly right about that.'

'I've called a porter to carry your luggage, messieurs. It's a rather long walk. He'll meet you on the platform.'

'Thanks very much.' Conklin got to his feet and reached into his pocket, pulling out money.

'*Pardon, monsieur*,' interrupted the hostess. 'We are not permitted to accept gratuities.'

'That's right. I forgot . . . My suitcase is behind your counter, isn't it?'

'Where your escort left it, sir. Along with the doctor's, it will be at the platform within minutes.'

'Thanks again,' said Alex. 'Sorry about the tip.'

'We are well paid, sir, but thank you for the thought.'

As they walked to the door that led into the main terminal of Orly Airport, Conklin turned to Panov. 'How did she know you were a doctor?' he asked. 'You soliciting couch business?'

'Hardly. The commuting would be a bit strenuous.'

'Then how? I never said anything about your being a doctor.'

'She knows the security escort who brought me into the lounge. In fact, I think she knows him quite well. She said in that delectable French accent of hers that he was "verry attractiefe".'

'Oh,' said Alex as they looked up at the signs in the crowded terminal and started towards the south platform.

What neither of them saw was a distinguished-looking, olive-skinned man with wavy black hair and large dark eyes walk quickly out of the diplomatic lounge, his steady gaze directed at the two Americans. He crossed to the wall, rushing past the crowds until he was diagonally in front of Conklin and Panov near the taxi platform. Then, squinting, as if unsure, he removed a small photograph from his pocket and kept glancing at it as he raised his eyes and looked up at the departing passengers from the United States. The photograph was of Dr Morris Panov, dressed in a white hospital gown, a glazed, unearthly expression on his face.

The Americans went out on the platform; the dark-haired man did the same. The Americans looked around for an unfamiliar taxi; the dark-haired man signalled a familiar private car. A driver got out of a cab; he approached Conklin and Panov, speaking quietly, as a porter arrived with their luggage; the two Americans climbed into the taxi. The stranger who followed them slipped into the private car two vehicles behind the cab.

'*Pazzo!* said the dark-haired man in Italian to the fashionably dressed middle-aged woman behind the wheel. 'I tell you it's crazy! For three days we wait, all incoming American planes watched, and we are about to give up when that fool in New York turns out to be right. It's *them*! . . . Here, I'll drive. You get out and reach our people over there. Tell them to call DeFazio; instruct him to go to his other favourite restaurant and await my call to him. He is not to leave until we speak.'

'Is this you, old man?' asked the hostess in the diplomatic lounge, speaking softly into the telephone at her counter.

'It is I,' replied the quivering voice at the other end of the line. 'And the Angelus rings for eternity in my ears.'

'It is you, then.'

'I told you that, so get on with it.'

'The list we were given last week included a slender, middle-aged American with a limp, possibly accompanied by a doctor. Is this correct?'

'Correct! *And?*'

'They have passed through. I used the title "doctor" with the cripple's companion and he responded to it.'

'Where have they gone? It's vital that I *know*!'

'It was not disclosed, but I will soon learn enough for you to find out, old man. The porter who took their luggage to the south platform will get the description and the licence of the car that meets them.'

'In the name of *God*, call me back with the information!'

Three thousand miles from Paris, Louis DeFazio sat alone at a rear table in Trafficante's Clam House on Prospect Avenue in Brooklyn, New York. He finished his late afternoon lunch of *vitello tonnato* and dabbed his lips with the bright red napkin, trying to look his usual jovial, if patronizing, self. However, if the truth were known, it was all he could do to stop from gnawing on the napkin rather than caressing his mouth with it. *Maledetto!* He had been at Trafficante's for nearly two hours – *two hours*! And it had taken him forty-five minutes to get there after the call from Garafola's Pasta Palace in Manhattan, so that meant it was actually *over* two hours, almost *three*, since the gumball in

Paris, France, spotted two of the targets. How long could it take for two *bersaglios* to get to a hotel in the city from the airport? Like three *hours*? Not unless the Palermo gumball drove to London, England, which was not out of the question, not if one knew Palermo.

Still, DeFazio knew he had been right! The way the Jew shrink talked under the needle there was no other route he and the ex-spook could take *but* to Paris and their good buddy, the fake hit man . . . So Nicolo and the shrink disappeared, went *poof-zam*, so what the fuck? The Jew got away and Nicky would do time. But Nicolo wouldn't talk; he understood that bad trouble, like a knife in the kidney, was waiting for him wherever he went if he did. Besides, Nicky didn't know anything so specific the lawyers couldn't wipe away as secondhand horseshit from a fifth-rate horse's ass. And the shrink only knew he was in a room in some farmhouse, if he could even remember that. He never saw anybody but Nicolo when he was 'compass mantis', as they say.

But Louis DeFazio knew he was *right*. And because he was right, there were more than seven million big ones waiting for him in Paris. *Seven million! Holy Christ!* He could give the Palermo gumballs in Paris more than they ever expected and still walk away with a bundle.

An old waiter from the old country, an uncle of Trafficante, approached the table and Louis held his breath. 'There's a telephone call for you, Signor DeFazio.'

As was usual, the capo supremo went to a pay phone at the end of a narrow dark corridor outside the men's room. 'This is New York,' said DeFazio.

'This is Paris, Signor New York. This is also *pazzo*!'

'Where've you been? You *pazzo* enough to drive to London, England? I've been waitin' three hours!'

'Where I've *been* is on a number of unlit country roads, which is important only to my nerves. Where I am now is crazy!'

'So where?'

'I'm using a gatekeeper's telephone for which I'm paying roughly a hundred American dollars and the French *buffone* keeps looking through the window to see that I don't steal anything – perhaps his lunch pail, who knows?'

'You don't sound too stupid for a gumball. So what gatekeeper's that? What are you talking about?'

'I'm at a cemetery about twenty-five miles from Paris. I tell you—'

'A *cimitero*?' interrupted Louis. 'What the hell *for*?'

'Because your two acquaintances drove here from the airport, you *ignorante*! At the moment there is a burial in progress – a night burial with a candlelight procession which will soon be drowned out by rain – and if your two acquaintances flew over here to attend this barbaric ceremony, then the air in America is filled with brain-damaging pollutants! We did not bargain for this *sciocchezze*, New York. We have our own work to do.'

'They went there to meet the big cannoli,' said DeFazio quietly, as if to himself. 'As to work, gumball, if you ever want to work with us, or Philadelphia, or Chicago, or Los Angeles again, you'll do what I tell you. You'll also be terrifically paid for it, *capisce*?'

'That makes more sense, I admit.'

'Stay out of sight but stay with them. Find out where they go and who they see. I'll get over there as soon as I can, but I gotta go by way of Canada or Mexico, just to make sure no one's watching. I'll be there late tomorrow or early the next day.'

'*Ciao*,' said Paris.

'*Omerta*,' said Louis DeFazio.

30

The hand-held candles flickered in the night drizzle as the two parallel lines of mourners walked solemnly behind the white casket borne on the shoulders of six men; several began to slip on the increasingly wet gravel of the cemetery's path. Flanking the procession were four drummers, two on each side, their snare drums snapping out the slow cadence of the death march, erratically out of sequence because of the unexpected rocks and the unseen flat grave markers in the darkness of the bordering grass. Shaking his head slowly in bewilderment, Morris Panov watched the strange nocturnal burial rite, relieved to see Alex Conklin limping, threading his way between the tombstones towards their meeting ground.

'Any sign of them?' asked Alex.

'None,' replied Panov. 'I gather you didn't do any better.'

'Worse. I got stuck with a lunatic.'

'How?'

'A light was on in the gatehouse, so I went over thinking David or Marie might have left us a message. There was a clown outside who kept looking into a window and said he was the watchman and did I want to rent his telephone.'

'His telephone?'

'He said there were special rates for the night, as the nearest pay phone was ten kilometres down the road.'

'A lunatic,' agreed Panov.

'I explained that I was looking for a man and a woman I was to meet here and wondered if they'd left a message. There was no message but there *was* the telephone. Two hundred francs – crazy.'

'I might do a flourishing business in Paris,' said Mo, smiling. 'Did he by any chance see a couple wandering around?'

'I asked him that and he nodded affirmative, saying there were dozens. Then he pointed to that candlelight parade over there before going back to his goddamn window.'

'What *is* that parade, incidentally?'

'I asked him that, too. It's a religious cult; they only bury their dead at night. He thinks they may be gypsies. He said *that* while blessing himself.'

'They're going to be wet gypsies,' observed Panov, pulling up his collar as the drizzle turned into rain.

'Christ, why didn't I *think* of it?' exclaimed Conklin, looking over his shoulder.

'The rain?' asked the bewildered psychiatrist.

'No, the large tomb halfway up the hill beyond the gatehouse. It's where it happened!'

'Where you tried to—' Mo did not finish the question; he did not have to.

'Where he could have killed me but didn't,' completed Alex. 'Come on!'

The two Americans retreated down the gravel path past the gatehouse and into the darkness of the rising hill of grass punctuated by white gravestones now glistening in the rain. '*Easy*,' cried Panov, out of breath. 'You're used to that non-existent foot of yours, but I haven't quite adjusted to my pristine body having been raped by chemicals.'

'Sorry.'

'*Mo!*' shouted a woman's voice from under a marble portico above. The figure waved her arms beneath the pillared, overhanging roof of a grave so large it looked like a minor mausoleum.

'*Marie?*' yelled Panov, rushing ahead of Conklin.

'That's nice!' roared Alex, limping with difficulty up the wet slippery grass. 'You hear the sound of a female and suddenly you're *unraped*. You need a shrink, you phony!'

The embraces were meant; a family was together. While Panov and Marie spoke quietly, Jason Bourne took Conklin aside to the edge of the short marble roof, the rain now harsh. The former candlelight procession below, the flickering flames now gone, was half scattered, half holding its position by a gravesite. 'I didn't mean to choose this place, Alex,' said Jason. 'But with that crowd down there I couldn't think of another.'

'Remember the gatehouse and that wide path to the parking lot? . . . You'd won. I was out of ammunition and you could have blown my head apart.'

'You're wrong, how many times have I told you? I *couldn't* have killed you. It was in your eyes; even though I wan't able to see them clearly I knew what was there. Anger and confusion, but, above all, confusion.'

'That's never been a reason not to kill a man who tries to kill you.'

'It is if you can't remember. The memory may be gone but not the fragments, not the – well, for me they were . . . pulsating images. In and out, in and out, but there.'

Conklin looked up at Bourne, a sad grin on his face. 'The pulsating bit,' he said. 'That was Mo's term. You stole it.'

'Probably,' said Jason as both men in unison looked back at Marie and Panov. 'She's talking about me, you know that, don't you?'

'Why not? She's concerned and he's concerned.'

'I hate to think how many more concerns I'll give them both. You, too, I imagine.'

'What are you trying to tell me, David?'

'Just that. *Forget* David. David Webb doesn't exist, not here, not now. He's an act I put on for his wife, and I do it badly. I want her to go back to the States, to her children.'

'*Her* children? She won't do it. She came over to find you and she found you. She remembers Paris thirteen years ago and she won't leave you. Without her then you wouldn't be alive today.'

'She's an impediment. She has to go. I'll find a way.'

Alex looked up at the cold eyes of the creation once known as the Chameleon and spoke quietly. 'You're a fifty-year-old man, *Jason*. This isn't Paris thirteen years ago or Saigon years before that. It's *now*, and you need all the help you can get. If she thinks she can provide a measure of it, I for one believe her.'

Bourne snapped his head down at Conklin. 'I'll be the judge of who believes what.'

'That's a touch extreme, pal.'

'You know what I mean,' said Jason, softening his tone. 'I don't want to have happen here what happened in Hong Kong. That can't be a problem for you.'

'Maybe not . . . Look, let's get out of here. Our driver knows a little country restaurant in Epernon, about six miles from here, where we can talk. We've got several things to go over.'

'Tell me,' said Bourne, holding his place. 'Why Panov? Why did you bring Mo with you?'

'Because if I hadn't he would have put strychnine in my flu shot.'

'What the hell does that mean?'

'Exactly what it says. He's a part of us, and you know it better than Marie or myself.'

'Something happened to him, didn't it? Something happened to him because of me.'

'It's over with and he's back, that's all you have to know now.'

'It was Medusa, wasn't it?'

'Yes, but I repeat, he's back, and outside of being a little tired, he's okay.'

'Little . . . ? A little country restaurant six miles from here, isn't that what your driver said?'

'Yes, he knows Paris and everything around it thoroughly.'

'Who is he?'

'A French Algerian who's worked for the Agency for years. Charlie Casset recruited him for us. He's tough, knowledgeable and very well paid for both. Above all, he can be trusted.'

'I suppose that's good enough.'

'Don't suppose, accept it.'

They sat in a booth at the rear of the small country inn, complete with a worn canopy, hard pine banquettes and perfectly acceptable wine. The owner, an expansive, florid fat man, proclaimed the cuisine to be extraordinary, but since no one could summon hunger, Bourne paid for four entrées to keep the proprietor happy. It did. The owner sent over two large carafes of good *vin ordinaire* along with a bottle of mineral water, and stayed away from the table.

'All right, Mo,' said Jason, 'you won't tell me what happened, or who did it, but you're still the same functioning, overbearing, verbose medicine man with a chicken in his mouth we've known for thirteen years, am I correct?'

'Correct, you schizophrenic escapee from Bellevue. And in case you think I'm being heroic, let me make it absolutely clear that I'm here only to protect my nonmedical civil rights. My paramount interest is with my adorable Marie, who I trust you'll notice is sitting beside me, not you. I positively salivate thinking about her meat loaf.'

'Oh, how I do love you, Mo,' said David Webb's wife, squeezing Panov's arm.

'Let me count the ways,' responded the doctor, kissing her cheek.

'I'm here,' said Conklin. 'My name is Alex and I have a couple of things to talk about and they don't include meat loaf . . . Although I should tell you, Marie, I told Peter Holland yesterday that it was terrific.'

'What's with my damned meat loaf?'

'It's the red sauce,' interjected Panov.

'May we get to what we're here for,' said Jason Bourne, his voice a monotone.

'Sorry, darling.'

'We'll be working with the Soviets.' Conklin spoke quickly, his rush of words countering the immediate reaction from Bourne and Marie. 'It's all right, I know the contact, I've known him for years, but Washington doesn't know I know him. His name is Krupkin, Dimitri Krupkin, and as I told Mo, he can be bought for five pieces of silver.'

'Give him thirty-one,' interrupted Bourne, 'to make sure he's on our side.'

'I figured you'd say that. Do you have a ceiling?'

'None.'

'Not so fast,' said Marie. 'What's a negotiable starting point?'

'Our economist speaks,' proclaimed Panov, drinking his wine.

'Considering his position in the Paris KGB, I'd say around fifty thousand, American.'

'Offer him thirty-five and escalate to seventy-five under pressure. Up to a hundred, if necessary, of course.'

'For Christ's *sake*,' cried Jason, controlling his voice. 'We're talking about *us*, about the *Jackal*. Give him anything he wants!'

'Too easily bought, too easily turned to another source. To a counter-offer.'

'Is she right?' asked Bourne, staring at Conklin.

'Normally, of course, but in this case it would have to be the equivalent of a workable diamond mine. No one wants Carlos in the dead file more than the Soviets, and the man who brings in his corpse will be the hero of the Kremlin. Remember, he was trained at Novgorod. Moscow never forgets that.'

'Then do as she says, only *buy* him,' said Jason.

'I understand,' Conklin leaned forward, turning his glass of water. 'I'll call him tonight, pay phone to pay phone, and get it settled. Then I'll arrange a meeting tomorrow, maybe lunch somewhere outside of Paris. Very early, before the regulars come in.'

'Why not here?' asked Bourne. 'You can't get much more remote and I'll know the way.'

'Why not?' agreed Alex. 'I'll talk to the owner. But not the four of us, just – Jason and me.'

'I assumed that,' said Bourne coldly. 'Marie's not to be involved. She's not to be seen or heard, is that clear?'

'David, really—'

'Yes, *really*.'

'I'll go over and stay with her,' interrupted Panov quickly. 'Meat loaf?' he added, obviously to lesson the tension.

'I don't have a kitchen, but there's a lovely restaurant that serves fresh trout.'

'One sacrifices,' sighed the psychiatrist.

'I think you should eat in the room.' Bourne's voice was now adamant.

'I will *not* be a prisoner,' said Marie quietly, her gaze fixed on her husband. 'Nobody knows who we are or where we are, and I submit that someone who locks herself in her room and is never seen draws far more attention than a perfectly normal Frenchwoman who goes about her normal business of living.'

'She's got a point,' observed Alex. 'If Carlos has his network calling around, someone behaving abnormally could be picked up. Besides, Panov's from left field – pretend you're a doctor or something, Mo. Nobody'll believe it, but it'll add a touch of class. For reasons that escape me, doctors are usually above suspicion.'

'Psychopathic ingrate,' mumbled Panov.

'May we get back to business,' said Bourne curtly.

'You're very rude, David.'

'I'm very impatient, do you mind?'

'Okay, cool it,' said Conklin. 'We're all uptight, but things have got to be clear. Once Krupkin's on board, his first job will be to trace the number Gates gave Prefontaine in Boston.'

'Who gave what *where*?' asked the bewildered psychiatrist.

'You were out of it, Mo. Prefontaine's an impeached judge who fell into a Jackal contact. To cut it short, the contact gave our judge a number here in Paris to reach the Jackal, but it didn't coincide with the one Jason already had. But there's no question that the contact, a lawyer named Gates, reached Carlos.'

'*Randolph* Gates? Boston's gift to the boardrooms of Genghis Khan?'

'That's the one.'

'Holy *Christ* – I'm sorry, I shouldn't say that. I'm not a gentile. What the hell, I'm nothing, but you'll admit it's a shock.'

'A large one, and we have to know who owns that number here in Paris. Krupkin can find out for us. It's corkscrew, I grant you, but there it is.'

'*Corkscrew*?' asked Panov. 'Are you now going to produce a Rubik's cube in Arabic? Or, perhaps, a Double-Crostic from the London *Times*? What in heaven's name is a Prefontaine, judge, jury or otherwise? It sounds like a bad early wine.'

'It's a late, very good vintage,' broke in Marie. 'You'd like him, Doctor. You could spend months studying him because he's got more brights than most of us, and that grand intellect of his is still intact despite such inconveniences as alcohol, corruption, loss of family and prison. He's an original, Mo, and where the majority of felons in his league blame everyone but themselves, he doesn't. He retains a gloriously ironic sense of humour. If the American judiciary had any brains – which on the surface the Justice Department would seem to refute

– they'd put him back on the bench . . . He went after the Jackal's people on principle first, because they wanted to kill me and my children. If, on the second round, he makes a dollar, he deserves every penny and I'll see that he gets it.'

'You're succinct. You like him.'

'I *adore* him, as I adore you and Alex. You've all taken such risks for us—'

'*May* we get back to what we're here for?' said the Chameleon angrily. 'The past doesn't interest me, tomorrow does.'

'You're not only rude, my dear, you're terribly ungrateful.'

'So be it. Where were we?'

'At the moment with Prefontaine,' replied Alex sharply, looking at Bourne. 'But he may not matter because he probably won't survive Boston . . . I'll call you at the inn at Barbizon tomorrow and set up a time for lunch. Out here. Clock yourself on the drive back so we're not hanging around like mateless snow geese. Also, if that fat guy's right about his "cuisine", Kruppie will love it and tell everybody he discovered it.'

'*Kruppie?*'

'Relax. I told you, we go back a long time.'

'And don't go into it,' added Panov. 'You really don't want to hear about Istanbul and Amsterdam. They're both a couple of thieves.'

'We pass,' said Marie. 'Go on, Alex, what about tomorrow?'

'Mo and I will take a taxi out to your place, and your husband and I will drive back here. We'll call you after lunch.'

'What about that driver of yours, the one Casset got you?' asked the Chameleon, his eyes cold, inquiring.

'What about him? He'll be paid double what he can make in a month with his taxi for tonight, and after he drops us off at a hotel, he'll disappear. We won't see him again.'

'Will he see anyone else?'

'Not if he wants to live and send money to his relatives in Algeria. I told you, Casset cleared him. He's granite.'

'Tomorrow, then,' said Bourne grimly, looking across the table at Marie and Morris Panov. 'After we leave for Paris you're to stay out at Barbizon, and you're not to leave the inn. Do you both understand that?'

'You know, David,' answered Marie, bristling and rigid on the pine banquette. 'I'm going to tell you something. Mo and Alex are as much a part of our family as the children, so I'll say it in front of them. We all, *all* of us, humour you and in some ways pamper you because of the horrible things you went through. But you cannot and you will not order us around as if we were inferior beings in your august presence. Do *you* understand *that*?'

'Loud and clear, lady. Then maybe you should go back to the States so you won't have to put up with my *august* presence.' Jason Bourne rose from the table, pushing the chair behind him. 'Tomorrow's going to be a busy day, so I have to get some sleep – I haven't had much lately – and a better man than any of us here once told me that rest was a weapon. I believe that . . . I'll be in the car for two minutes. Take your choice. I'm sure Alex can get you out of France.'

'You *bastard*,' whispered Marie.

'So be it,' said the Chameleon, walking away.

'Go to him,' interjected Panov quickly. 'You know what's happening.'

'I can't *handle* it, Mo!'

'*Don't* handle it, just be with him. You're the only rope he's got. You don't even have to talk, just be there. With him.'

'He's become the killer again.'

'He'd never harm you—'

'Of course not, I know that.'

'Then provide him with that link to David Webb. It *has* to be there, Marie.'

'Oh, *God*, I love him so!' cried the wife, rushing to her feet and racing after her husband – yet not her husband.

'Was that the right advice, Mo?' asked Conklin.

'I don't know, Alex. I just don't think he should be alone with his nightmares, none of us should. That's not psychiatry, it's just common sense.'

'Sometimes you sound like a real doctor, you know that?'

The Algerian section of Paris lies between the tenth and eleventh arrondissements, barely three blocks, where the low buildings are Parisian but the sounds and the smells are Arabic. A long black limousine entered this ethnic enclave, the insignia of the high church small but emblazoned in gold on the doors. It stopped in front of a wood-framed, three-storeyed house, where an old priest got out and walked to the door. He selected a name on the mail plate and pressed the button that rang a bell on the second floor.

'*Oui?*' said the metallic voice on the primitive intercom.

'I am a messenger from the American embassy,' answered the visitor in religious garb, his French partially ungrammatical as was all too frequent with Americans. 'I can't leave my vehicle, but we have an urgent message for you.'

'I'll be right down,' said the French-Algerian driver recruited by Charles Casset in Washington. Three minutes later the man emerged from the building and walked out on the short narrow pavement. 'What are you dressed like that for?' he asked the messenger who stood by the large automobile, covering the insignia on the rear door.

'I'm the Catholic chaplain, my son. Our military chargé d'affaires would like a word with you.' He opened the door.

'I'll do many things for you people,' laughed the driver as he bent down to look inside the limousine, 'but being drafted into your army isn't one of them . . . Yes, sir, what can I do for you?'

'Where did you take our people?' asked the shadowed figure in the backseat, his features in darkness.

'What people?' said the Algerian, sudden concern in his voice.

'The two you picked up at the airport several hours ago. The cripple and his friend.'

'If you're from the embassy and they want you to know, they'll call and tell you, won't they?'

'*You'll* tell me!' A third, powerfully built man in a chauffeur's uniform appeared from behind the boot of the car. He walked rapidly forward, raising his arm and crashing a thick ugly blackjack down on the Algerian's skull. He shoved his victim inside; the old man in the guise of a chaplain climbed in behind him, pulling the door shut as the chauffeur ran around the bonnet to the front seat. The limousine raced away down the street.

An hour later on the deserted rue Houdon, a block from Place Pigalle, the Algerian's bruised and bleeding corpse was disgorged from the large automobile. Inside, the figure in shadows addressed his aged, personally ordained priest.

'Get your car and remain outside the cripple's hotel. Stay awake, for you'll be relieved in the morning and can rest all day. Report any movements and go where he goes. Don't fail me.'

'Never, monseigneur.'

Dimitri Krupkin was not a tall man but he appeared taller than he was, nor was he particularly heavy yet he seemed to possess a much fuller figure than he carried. He had a pleasant if somewhat fleshy face and a generous head held erect; his full eyebrows and well-groomed pepper-and-salt hair and chin beard combined attractively with alert blue eyes and a seemingly perpetual smile, defining a man who enjoyed his life and his work, an intellect behind both. At the moment he was seated in a booth, facing the rear wall, in the all but empty country restaurant in Epernon staring across the table at Alex Conklin, who sat beside the unidentified Bourne and had just explained that he no longer drank alcohol.

'The world is coming to an end!' exclaimed the Russian in heavily accented English. 'You see what happens to a good man in the self-indulgent West? Shame on your parents. They should have stayed with us.'

'I don't think you want to compare the rates of alcoholism in our two countries.'

'Not for a wager of money,' said Krupkin, grinning. 'Speaking of money, my dear old enemy, how and where am I to be paid according to our agreement last night on the telephone?'

'How and where do you want to be paid?' asked Jason.

'Ah ha, you are my benefactor, sir?'

'I'll be paying you, yes.'

'*Hold* it!' whispered Conklin, his attention drawn to the restaurant's entrance. He leaned towards the open side of the booth, his hand on his forehead, then quickly moved back as a couple were shown to a table in the corner to the left of the door.

'What is it?' asked Bourne.

'I don't know . . . I'm not sure.'

'Who came in, Aleksei?'

'That's just it, I think I should know him but I don't.'

'Where is he seated? In a booth?'

'No, a table. In the corner beyond the bar. He's with a woman.'

Krupkin moved to the edge of his seat, took out his billfold and removed a small mirror the size and thickness of a credit card from its recess. Cupping it in both hands, he cautiously angled the glass in front of him. 'You must be addicted to the society pages of the Paris tabloids,' said the Russian, chuckling as he replaced the mirror and returned the billfold to his jacket pocket. 'He's with the Italian embassy; that's his wife. Paolo and Davinia something-or-other, with pretensions to nobility, I believe. Strictly *corpo diplomatico* on the protocol level. They dress up a party quite nicely and they're obviously stinking rich.'

'I don't travel in those circles but I've seen him somewhere before.'

'Of course you have. He looks like every middle-aged Italian screen star or any one of those vineyard owners who extol the virtues of the Chianti Classico on television commercials.'

'Maybe you're right.'

'I am.' Krupkin turned to Bourne. 'I shall write out the name of a bank and the number of an account in Geneva.' The Soviet reached into his pocket for a pen as he pulled a paper napkin in front of him. He was not able to use either for a man in his early thirties, dressed in a tight-fitting suit, walked rapidly up to the table.

'What is it, Sergei?' asked Krupkin.

'Not you, sir,' replied the Soviet aide. '*Him*,' he added, nodding at Bourne.

'What is it?' repeated Jason.

'You have been followed. At first we were not sure, for it is an old man with a urinary problem. He rapidly left the car twice to relieve himself, but once settled he used the car telephone and squinted through the windscreen to read the name of the restaurant. That was barely minutes ago.'

'How do you know he was following me?'

'Because he arrived shortly after you did, and we were here a half hour before that securing the area.'

'Securing the area!' erupted Conklin, looking at Krupkin. 'I thought this conference was strictly between us.'

'Dear Aleksei, benevolent Aleksei, who would save me from myself. Can you really believe I'd meet with you without considering my own protection. Not you personally, old friend, but your aggressors in Washington. Can you imagine? A deputy director of the CIA negotiates with me over a man he pretends to think I do not *know*. A rank amateur ploy.'

'Goddamn you, I never *told* him!'

'Oh, dear me, then the error's mine. I apologize, Aleksei.'

'Don't,' interrupted Jason firmly. 'That old man's from the Jackal—'

'*Carlos!*' cried Krupkin, his face flushed, his alert blue eyes now intense, angry. 'The Jackal's after *you*, Aleksei?'

'No, him,' answered Conklin. 'Your benefactor.'

'Good God! With what we've picked up, it's all falling into place. So I have the distinct honour to meet the infamous Jason Bourne. A great *pleasure*, sir! We have the same objective where Carlos is concerned, do we not?'

'If your men are any good, we may reach that objective before the next hour's up. Come *on*! Let's get out of here and use the back way, the kitchen, a window, whatever. He's found me and you can bet your ass he's coming out here for me. Only he doesn't know we know that. Let's *go*!'

As the three men rose from the table Krupkin gave instructions to his aide.

'Have the car brought around to the rear, the service entrance, if there is one, but do it *casually*, Sergei. No sense of urgency, you understand me?'

'We can drive half a mile down the road and turn into a pasture that will lead to the rear of the building. We will not be seen by the old man in his car.'

'*Very* good, Sergei. And have our backup remain in place but be prepared.'

'Of course, comrade.' The aide hurried back to the front entrance.

'A backup?' exploded Alex. 'You had a *backup*?'

'Please, Aleksei, why quibble? It's your own fault, after all. Even last night on the phone you did not tell me about your conspiracy against your own deputy director.'

'It wasn't a conspiracy, for Christ's sake!'

'It wasn't exactly a pure rapport between the home office and the field, was it? No, Aleksei Nikolae Kousolikov, you knew you could – shall we say – use me and you did. Never forget, my fine old adversary, you *are* Russian.'

'Will you two shut up and get *out* of here?'

They waited in Krupkin's armour-plated Citroën on the edge of an overgrown field a hundred feet behind the old man's car, the front of the restaurant in clear sight. To Bourne's annoyance, Conklin and the KGB officer reminisced like two ageing professionals dissecting each other's strategies in past intelligence operations, pointing out the deficiencies each held to be with the other's. The Soviet backup was a nondescript sedan on the far shoulder of the road diagonally across from the restaurant. Two armed men were ready to leap out, their automatic weapons prepared to fire.

Suddenly, a Renault station wagon pulled up to the kerb in front of the inn. Three couples were inside; all but the driver got out, all laughing, playfully entwining their arms. They walked with abandon towards the entrance as their companion drove the car into the small side parking lot.

'*Stop* them,' said Jason. 'They could be killed.'

'Yes, they could be, Mr Bourne, but if we stop them we will lose the Jackal.'

Jason stared at the Russian, unable to speak, the harsh winds of anger and confusion clouding his thoughts. He started to utter a protest but could not do so; the words would not come. Then it was too late for words. A dark brown limousine shot up the road from the highway to Paris and Bourne found his voice.

'It's the one from the Boulevard Lefebvre, the one that got away!'

'The one from *where*?' asked Conklin.

'There was trouble on Lefebvre several days ago,' said Krupkin. 'An automobile or a truck was blown up. Do you refer to that?'

'It was a trap. For me . . . A van, then a limo and a double for Carlos – a trap. That's the second one; it raced out of a dark side street, I think, and tried to cut us down with firepower.'

'Us?' Alex watched Jason; he saw the undisguised fury in the Chameleon's eyes, the tight, rigid set of his mouth, the slow spreading and contraction of his strong fingers.

'Bernardine and me,' whispered Bourne in reply, suddenly raising his voice. 'I want a *weapon*,' he cried. 'The gun in my pocket isn't a goddamned weapon!'

The driver was Krupkin's powerfully built Soviet aide Sergei; he reached across his seat and pulled up a Russian AK-47. He held it over his shoulder as Jason grabbed it.

The limousine, its tyres skidding on the backcountry road, screamed to a stop in front of the faded, worn canopy; and like trained commandos, two men leaped out of the side door, their faces encased in stocking masks, their hands holding automatic weapons. They raced to the entrance, each spinning his body to either side of the double doors. A third man emerged from the vehicle, a balding man in a priest's black clothing. With a gesture of his weapon, the two assault troops spun back towards the doors, their hands on the thick brass knobs. The driver of the limousine gunned his engine in place.

'*Go!*' yelled Bourne. 'It's him! It's *Carlos*!'

'*No!*' roared Krupkin. 'Wait. It's our trap now, and he must be trapped – *inside.*'

'For Christ's sake, there are people in there!' countered Jason.

'All wars have casualties, Mr Bourne, and in case you don't realize it, this is war. Yours and mine. Yours is far more personal than mine, incidentally.'

Suddenly, there was an ear-splitting scream of vengeance from the Jackal as the double doors were crashed back and the terrorists rushed inside, their weapons on automatic fire.

'*Now!*' cried Sergei, the ignition started, the accelerator on the floor. The Citroën swung out on the road, rushing towards the limousine, but in a split half second its progress was derailed. A massive explosion took place on the right. The old man and the nondescript grey car in which he sat was blown apart, sending the Citroën swerving to the left into the ancient post-and-rail fence that bordered the sunken parking lot on the side of the inn. The instant it happened the Jackal's dark brown limousine, instead of racing forward, lurched backward, jerking to a halt as the driver jumped out of the cab, concealing himself behind it; he had spotted the Soviet backup. As the two Russians ran towards the restaurant, the Jackal's driver killed one with a burst from his weapon. The other threw himself into the bordering, sloping grass, watching helplessly as Carlos's driver shot out the tyres and the windows of the Soviet vehicle.

'Get *out*!' yelled Sergei, pulling Bourne from the seat onto the dirt by the fence, as his stunned superior and Alex Conklin crawled out behind him.

'Let's *go*!' cried Jason, gripping the AK-47 and getting to his feet. 'That son of a bitch blew up the car by remote.'

'I'll go first!' said the Soviet.

'Why?'

'Frankly, I'm younger and stronger—'

'Shut up!' Bourne raced ahead, zigzagging to draw fire, then plummeting to the ground when it came from the driver of Carlos's limousine. He raised his weapon in the grass, knowing that the Jackal's man believed his fusillade had been accurate; the head appeared and then was no more as Jason squeezed the trigger.

The second Russian backup, hearing the death cry from behind the limousine, rose from the sloping grass and continued towards the restaurant's entrance. From inside came the sound of erratic gunfire, sudden bursts accompanied by screams of panic, followed by additional bursts. A living nightmare of terror and blood was taking place within the confines of a once bucolic country inn. Bourne got to his feet, Sergei at his side; running, they joined the other surviving Soviet aide. At Jason's nod, the Russians pulled back the doors and as one they burst inside.

The next sixty seconds presented a scene like the shrieking hell imagined by Käthe Kollwitz. A waiter and two of the men who were among the three couples were dead, the waiter and one man sprawled on the floor, their skulls shattered, what was left of their faces lying in blood; the third man was splayed back in the banquette, his eyes wide and glass-dead, his clothes riddled with bullets, rivulets of blood rolling down the fabric. The women were in total shock, alternately moaning and screaming as they kept trying to crawl over the pine walls of the booth. The well-dressed man and wife from the Italian Embassy were nowhere in sight.

Sergei suddenly rushed forward, his weapon on auto fire; in a rear corner of the room he had spotted a figure whom Bourne had not seen. The stocking-faced killer sprang out of the shadows, his machine rifle swinging into position, but before he could exercise his advantage, the Soviet cut him down . . . *Another!* A body lurching behind the short counter that served as a bar. Was it the *Jackal*? Jason pivoted into the diagonal wall, crouching, his eyes darting into every recess in the vicinity of the wine racks. He lunged to the base of the bar as the second Russian backup, assessing the situation, ran to the hysterical women, spinning around, his gun swinging back and forth protecting them. The stocking-faced head shot up from behind the counter, his weapon surging out over the wood. Bourne sprang to his feet, gripping the hot barrel with his left hand, his right commanding the AK-47; he fired point blank into the terrorist's contorted face beyond the silk. It was *not* Carlos. Where was the *Jackal*?

'In *there*!' shouted Sergei as if he had heard Jason's furious question.

'*Where?*'

'Those doors!'

It was the country restaurant's kitchen. Both men converged on the swinging doors. Again Bourne nodded, the signal for them to crash inside, but before they could move, both were partially blown back by an explosion from within; a grenade had been set off, with fragments of metal and glass embedded in the doors. The smoke billowed, wafting out into the dining room; the smell was acrid, sickening.

Silence.

Jason and Sergei once more approached the kitchen's entrance, and once again they were stopped by a second sudden explosion followed by staccato gunfire, the bullets piercing the thin, louvred panels of the swinging doors.

Silence.

Stand off.

Silence.

It was too much for the furious, impassioned Chameleon. He cracked the bolt of his AK-47, pulled the selective lever and then the trigger for auto fire, and crashed the doors open, lunging for the floor.

Silence.

Another scene from another hell. A section of the outside wall had been blown away, the obese owner and his hatted chef were dead, corpses pinned against the lower shelves of the kitchen, blood streaming across and down the wood.

Bourne slowly rose to his feet, his legs in agony, every nerve in his body frayed, the edge of hysteria not far away. As if in a trance, he looked around through the smoke and the debris, his eyes finally settling on a large, ominous fragment of brown butcher's paper nailed to the wall by a heavy cleaver. He approached it, yanking out the cleaver and reading the words printed in a black butcher's pencil.

The trees of Tannenbaum will burn and children will be the kindling. Sleep well, Jason Bourne.

The mirrors of his life were shattered into a thousand pieces of glass. There was nothing else to do but scream.

31

'*Stop it*, David!'

'My God, he's insane, Aleksei, Sergei, grab him, hold him . . . *You*, help Sergei! Put him on the ground so I can talk to him. We must leave here quickly!'

It was all the two Russian aides could do to wrestle the screaming Bourne to the grass. He had raced out through the exploded hole in the wall, running into the high grass in a futile attempt to find the Jackal, firing his AK-47 into the field beyond until his magazine was empty. Sergei and the surviving backup had rushed after him, the former ripping the weapon out of Jason's hands, together leading the hysterical man back to the rear of the mutilated country inn, where Alex and Krupkin were waiting for them. Forcibly, their charge in a sweating, erratically breathing trance, the five men walked rapidly to the front of the restaurant; there the uncontrollable hysteria again seized the Chameleon.

The Jackal's limousine was gone. Carlos had reversed his line of flight and escaped and Jason Bourne had gone mad.

'*Hold* him!' roared Krupkin, kneeling beside Jason as the two aides pinned Bourne to the ground. The KGB officer reached down and spread his hand across the American's face, gouging his cheeks with thumb and forefinger, forcing Treadstone Seventy-one to look at him. 'I'll say this *once*, Mr Bourne, and if it doesn't sink in, you may stay here by yourself and take the consequences! But we must leave. If you get hold of yourself, we'll be in touch with the proper officials of your government within the hour from Paris. I've read the warning to you and I can assure you your own people are capable of protecting your family – as your family was explained to me by Aleksei. But you, *yourself*, must be part of that communication. You can become rational, Mr Bourne, or you can go to hell. Which will it be?'

The Chameleon, straining against the knees pinning him to the ground, exhaled as if it were his final breath. His eyes came into focus and he replied. 'Get these bastards off me,' he said.

'One of those bastards saved your life,' said Conklin.

'And I saved one of theirs. So be it.'

The armour-plated Citroën sped down the country road towards the Paris highway. On the scrambled cellular telephone, Krupkin ordered a team to Epernon for the immediate removal of what was left of the Russian backup vehicle. The body of the slain man had been placed carefully in the Citroën's boot, and the official Soviet comment, if asked for, was one of non-involvement: Two lower-level diplomatic staff had gone out for a country lunch when the massacre occurred. Several killers were in stocking masks, the others barely seen as the staff members escaped through a back door, running for their lives. When it was over they returned to the restaurant, covering the victims, trying to calm the hysterical women and the lone surviving man. They had called their superiors to report the hideous incident and were instructed to inform the local police and return at once to the embassy. Soviet interests could not be jeopardized by the accidental presence at the scene of an act of French criminality.

'It sounds so *Russian*,' Krupkin said.

'Will anyone believe it?' Alex wondered.

'It doesn't matter,' answered the Soviet. 'Epernon reeks of a Jackal reprisal. The blown-apart old man, two subordinate terrorists in stocking masks – the Sûreté knows the signs. If we were involved, we were on the correct side so they won't pursue our presence.'

Bourne sat silently by the window. Krupkin was beside him with Conklin in the jump seat in front of the Russian. Jason broke his angry silence, taking his eyes off the rushing scenery and slamming his fist on the armrest. 'Oh, Christ, the *kids*!' he shouted. 'How could that *bastard* have *learned* about the Tannenbaum house?'

'Forgive me, Mr Bourne,' broke in Krupkin gently. 'I realize it's far easier for me to say than for you to accept, but very soon now you'll be in touch with Washington. I know something about the Agency's ability to protect its own and I guarantee you it's maddeningly effective.'

'It can't be so goddamned great if Carlos can penetrate this far!'

'Perhaps he didn't,' said the Soviet. 'Perhaps he had another source.'

'There weren't any.'

'One never knows, sir.'

They sped through the streets of Paris in the blinding afternoon sun as the pedestrians sweltered in the summer heat. Finally, they reached the Soviet embassy on the Boulevard Lannes and raced through the gates, the guards waving them on, instantly recognizing Krupkin's grey Citroën. They swung around the cobblestone courtyard, stopping in front of the imposing marble steps and the sculptured arch that formed the entrance.

'Stay available, Sergei,' ordered the KGB officer. 'If there's to be any contact with the Sûreté, you're selected.' Then, as if it were an afterthought, Krupkin addressed the aide sitting next to Sergei in the front seat. 'No offence, young man,' he added, 'but over the years my old friend and driver has become highly resourceful in these situations. However, you also have work to do. Process the body of our loyal deceased comrade for cremation. Internal Operations will explain the paperwork.' With a nod of his head, Dimitri Krupkin instructed Bourne and Alex Conklin to get out of the car.

Once inside, Dimitri explained to the army guard that he did not care for his guests to be subjected to the metal detecting trellises through which all visitors to the Soviet Embassy were expected to pass. As an aside, he whispered in English to his guests. 'Can you imagine the alarms that would go off? Two armed Americans from the savage CIA roaming the halls of this bastion of the proletariat? Good heavens, I can feel the cold of Siberia in my testicles.'

They walked through the ornate, richly decorated nineteenth-century lobby to a typical brass-grilled French elevator; they entered and proceeded to the third floor. The grille opened and Krupkin continued as he led the way down a wide corridor. 'We'll use an in-house conference room,' he said. 'You'll be the only Americans who have ever seen it or will ever see it, as it's one of the few offices without listening devices.'

'You wouldn't want to submit that statement to a polygraph, would you?' asked Conklin, chuckling.

'Like you, Aleksei, I learned long ago how to fool those idiot machines; but even if that were not so, in this case I would willingly submit it, for it's true. In all honesty, it's to protect ourselves from ourselves. Come along now.'

The conference room was the size of an average suburban dining room but with a long heavy table and dark masculine furniture, the chairs thick, unwieldy and quite comfortable. The walls were covered with deep brown panelling, the inevitable portrait of Lenin centred ostentatiously behind the head chair, beside which was a low table designed for the telephone console within easy reach. 'I know you're anxious,' said Krupkin, going to the console, 'so I'll authorize an international line for you.' Lifting the phone, touching a button, and speaking rapidly in Russian, Dimitri did so, then hung up and turned to the Americans. 'You're assigned number twenty-six; it's the last button on the right, second row.'

'Thanks.' Conklin nodded and reached into his pocket, pulling out a scrap of paper and handing it to the KGB officer. 'I need another favour, Kruppie. That's a telephone number here in Paris. It's supposed to be a direct line to the Jackal, but it didn't match the one Bourne was given that *did* reach him. We don't know where it fits in, but wherever it is, it's tied to Carlos.'

'And you don't want to call it for fear of exposing your possession of the number – initial codes, that sort of thing. I understand, of course. Why send out an alert when it's unnecessary? I'll take care of it.' Krupkin looked at Jason, his expression that of an older, understanding colleague. 'Be of good and firm heart, Mr Bourne, as the Czarists would say facing no discernible harm whatsoever. Despite your apprehensions, I have enormous faith in Langley's abilities. They've harmed my not insignificant operations more than I care to dwell upon.'

'I'm sure you've done your share of damage to them,' said Jason impatiently, glancing at the telephone console.

'That knowledge keeps me going.'

'Thanks, Kruppie,' said Alex. 'In your words, you're a fine old enemy.'

'Again, shame on your parents! If they had stayed in Mother Russia, just think. By now you and I would be running the Komitet.'

'And have two lakefront houses?'

'Are you crazy, Aleksei? We would own the entire Lake Geneva!' Krupkin turned and walked to the door, letting himself out with quiet laughter.

'It's all a damned game with you people, isn't it?' said Bourne.

'Up to a point,' agreed Alex, 'but not when stolen information can lead to the loss of life – on both sides, incidentally. That's when the weapons come out and the games are over.'

'Reach Langley,' said Jason abruptly, nodding at the console. 'Holland's got some explaining to do.'

'Reaching Langley wouldn't help—'

'*What?*'

'It's too early; it's barely seven o'clock in the States, but not to worry, I can bypass.' Conklin again reached into a pocket and withdrew a small notebook.

'*Bypass?*' cried Bourne. 'What kind of double talk is *that*? I'm close to the edge, Alex, those are my *children* over there!'

'Relax, all it means is that I've got his unlisted home number.' Conklin sat down and picked up the phone; he dialled.

'"Bypass," for Christ's sake. You relics of outmoded ciphers can't use the English language. *Bypass!*'

'Sorry, Professor, it's habit . . . *Peter?* It's Alex. Open your eyes and wake up, sailor. We've got complications.'

'I don't have to wake up,' said the voice from Fairfax, Virginia. 'I just got back from a five-mile jog.'

'Oh, you people with feet think you're so smart.'

'Jesus, I'm sorry, Alex . . . I didn't mean—'

'Of course you didn't, Ensign Holland, but we've got a problem.'

'Which means at least you've made contact. You reached Bourne.'

'He's standing over my shoulder and we're calling from the Soviet embassy in Paris.'

'*What?* Holy *shit*!'

'Not holy, just Casset, remember?'

'Oh, yes, I forgot . . . What about his wife?'

'Mo Panov's with her. The good doctor's covering the medical bases, for which I'm grateful.'

'So am I. Any other progress?'

'Nothing you want to hear, but you're going to hear it loud and clear.'

'What are you talking about?'

'The Jackal knows about the Tannenbaum estate.'

'You're *nuts*!' shouted the director of the Central Intelligence Agency so loud that there was a metallic ring on the transoceanic line. '*Nobody* knows! Only Charlie Casset and myself. We built up a chrono with false names and Central American bios so far removed from Paris that *no* one could make a connection. Also, there was no *mention* of the Tannenbaum place in the orders! S'help me, Alex, it was airtight because we wouldn't let anyone else *handle* it!'

'Facts are facts, Peter. My friend got a note saying the trees of Tannenbaum would burn, the children with them.'

'Son of a *bitch*!' yelled Holland. 'Stay on the line,' he ordered. 'I'll call St Jacques over there, then max-security and have them moved this morning. Stay on the line!' Conklin looked up at Bourne, the telephone between them, the words heard by both men.

'If there's a leak, and there *is* a leak, it can't come from Langley,' said Alex.

'It *has* to! He hasn't looked deep enough.'

'Where does he look?'

'Christ, *you're* the experts. The helicopter that flew them out: the crew, the people who cleared an American aircraft flying into UK territory. My *God*! Carlos bought the lousy Crown governor of Montserrat and his head drug chief. What's to prevent him from owning the communications between our military and Plymouth?'

'But you *heard* him,' insisted Conklin. 'The names were fake, the chronologies oriented to Central America, and above all, no one on the relay flights knew about the Tannenbaum estate. *No* one . . . We've got a gap.'

'Please spare me that crypto-jargon.'

'It's not cryptic at all. A gap's a space that hasn't been filled—'

'*Alex?*' The angry voice of Peter Holland was back on the line.

'Yes, Peter?'

'We're moving them out and I won't even tell *you* where they're going. St Jacques is pissed off because Mrs Cooper and the kids are settled but I told him he's got an hour.'

'I want to talk to Johnny,' said Bourne, bending over and speaking loud enough to be heard.

'Nice to meet you, if only on the phone,' broke in Holland.

'Thanks for all you're doing for us,' managed Jason quietly, sincerely. 'I mean that.'

'Quid pro quo, Bourne. In your hunt for the Jackal you pulled a big ugly rabbit out of a filthy hat nobody knew was there.'

'What?'

'Medusa, the new one.'

'How's it going?' interrupted Conklin.

'We're doing our own cross-pollinating between the Sicilians and a number of European banks. It's dirtying up everything it touches, but we've now got more wires into that high-powered law firm in New York than in a NASA lift-off. We're closing in.'

'Good hunting,' said Jason. 'May I have the number at Tannenbaum's so I can reach John St Jacques?'

Holland gave it to him; Alex wrote it down and hung up. 'The horn's all yours,' said Conklin, awkwardly getting out of the chair by the console and moving to the one at the right corner of the table.

Bourne sat down and concentrated on the myriad buttons below him. He picked up the telephone and, reading the numbers Alex had recorded in his notebook, touched the appropriate digits on the console.

The greetings were abrupt, Jason's questions harsh, his voice demanding. 'Who did you talk to about the Tannenbaum house?'

'Back up, David,' said St Jacques instinctively defensive. 'What do you mean who did I talk to?'

'Just that. From Tranquillity to Washington, who did you speak to about Tannenbaum's?'

'You mean after Holland told me about it?'

'For Christ's sake, Johnny, it couldn't be before, could it?'

'No, it couldn't, Sherlock Holmes.'

'Then *who*?'

'You. Only you, esteemed brother-in-law.'

'What?'

'You heard me. Everything was happening so fast I probably forgot Tannenbaum's name anyway, and if I remembered it, I certainly wasn't going to advertise it.'

'You *must* have. There was a leak and it didn't come from Langley.'

'It didn't come from me, either. Look, Dr Academic, I may not have an alphabet after my name, but I'm not exactly an idiot. That's my niece and nephew in the other room and I fully expect to watch them grow up . . . The leak's why we're being moved, isn't it?'

'Yes.'

'How severe?'

'Maximum. The Jackal.'

'*Jesus!*' exploded St Jacques. 'That bastard shows up in the neighbourhood, he's *mine*!'

'Easy, Canada,' said Jason, his voice now softer, conveying thought, not anger. 'You say, and I believe you, that you described the Tannenbaum place only to me and, if I recall, *I* was the one who identified it.'

'That's right. I remember because when Pritchard told me you were on the phone, I was on the other line with Henry Sykes in 'Serrat. Remember Henry, the CG's aide?'

'Of course.'

'I was asking him to keep half an eye on Tranquillity because I had to leave for a few days. Naturally, he knew that because he had to clear the US aircraft in here, and I distinctly recall his asking me where I was going and all I said was Washington. It never even occurred to me to say anything about Tannenbaum's place, and Sykes didn't press me because he obviously figured it had something to do with the horrible things that had happened. I suppose you could say he's a professional in these matters.' St Jacques paused, but before Bourne could speak he uttered hoarsely, 'Oh, my *God*!'

'Pritchard,' supplied Jason. 'He stayed on the line.'

'*Why*? Why would he *do* it?'

'You forget,' explained Bourne. 'Carlos bought your Crown governor and his Savonarola drug chief. They had to cost heavy money; he could have bought Pritchard for a lot less.'

'No, you're wrong, David. Pritchard may be a deluded, self-inflated jackass but he wouldn't turn on me for money. It's not that important in the islands – prestige is. And except when he drives me up the wall, I feed it to him; actually he does a pretty damn good job.'

'There's no one else, Bro.'

'There's also one way to find out. I'm here, not there, and I'm not about to leave here.'

'What's your point?'

'I want to bring in Henry Sykes. Is that all right with you?'

'Do it.'

'How's Marie?'

'As well as can be expected under the circumstances . . . And, Johnny, I don't want her to know a thing about any of this, do you understand me? When she reaches you, and she will, just tell her you're settled in and everything's okay, nothing about the move or Carlos.'

'I understand.'

'Everything *is* all right, isn't it? How are the kids – how's Jamie taking everything?'

'You may resent this but he's having a grand time, and Mrs Cooper won't even let me touch Alison.'

'I don't resent either piece of information.'

'Thanks. What about you? Any progress?'

'I'll be in touch,' said Bourne, hanging up and turning to Alex. 'It doesn't make sense, and Carlos always makes sense if you look hard enough. He leaves me a warning that drives me crazy with fear, but he has no means of carrying out his threat. What do you make of it?'

'The sense is in driving you crazy,' replied Conklin. 'The Jackal's not going to take on an installation like Tannenbaum's sterile house long distance. That message was meant to panic you and it did. He wants to throw you off so you'll make mistakes. He wants the controls in his hands.'

'It's another reason for Marie to fly back to the States as soon as possible. She's *got* to. I want her inside a fortress, not having lunch out in the open in Barbizon.'

'I'm more sympathetic to that view than I was last night.' Alex was interrupted by the sound of the door opening. Krupkin walked into the room carrying several computer printouts.

'The number you gave me is disconnected,' he said, a slight hesitancy in his voice.

'Who *was* it connected to?' asked Jason.

'You will not like this any more than I do, and I'd lie to you if I could invent a plausible alternative, but I cannot and I undoubtedly should not . . . As of five days ago it was transferred from an obviously false organization to the name of Webb. David Webb.'

Conklin and Bourne stared in silence at the Soviet intelligence officer, but in that silence were the unheard static cracks of high voltage electricity. 'Why are you so certain we won't like the information?' asked Alex quietly.

'My fine old enemy,' began Krupkin, his gentle voice no louder than Conklin's. 'When Mr Bourne came out of that café of horror with the brown paper clasped in his hand, he was hysterical. In trying to calm him, to bring him under control, you called him David . . . I now have a name I sincerely wish I did not possess.'

'*Forget* it,' said Bourne.

'I shall do my best to, but there are ways—'

'That's not what I mean,' broke in Jason. 'I have to live with the fact that you know it and I'll manage. Where was that phone installed, the *address*?'

'According to the billing computers, it's a mission home run by an organization called the Magdalen Sisters of Charity. Again obviously false.'

'Obviously not,' corrected Bourne. 'It exists. They exist. It's legitimate down to their religious helmets, and it's also a usable drop. Or was.'

'Fascinating,' mused Krupkin. 'So many of the Jackal's various façades are tied to the Church. A brilliant if overdone modus operandi. It's said that he once studied for the priesthood.'

'Then the Church is one up on you,' said Alex, angling his head in a humourously mocking rebuke. 'They thew him out before you did.'

'I never underestimate the Vatican,' laughed Dimitri. 'It ultimately proved that our mad Joseph Stalin misunderstood priorities when he asked how many battalions the Pope had. His Holiness doesn't need them; he achieves more than Stalin ever did with all his purges. Power goes to the one who instils the greatest fear, not so, Aleksei? All the princes of this earth use it with brutal effectiveness. And it all revolves around death – the fear of it, before and after. When will we grow up and tell them all to go to the devil?'

'*Death*,' whispered Jason, frowning. 'Death in the Rivoli, at the Meurice, the Magdalen Sisters . . . my *God*, I completely forgot! Dominique Lavier! She was at the Meurice – she may still be *there*. She said she'd work with me!'

'Why would she?' asked Krupkin sharply.

'Because Carlos killed her sister and she had no choice but to join him or be killed herself.' Bourne turned to the console. 'I need the telephone number of the Meurice—'

'Four two six zero three eight six zero,' offered Krupkin as Jason grabbed a pencil and wrote down the numbers on Alex's notepad. 'A lovely place, once known as the hotel of kings. I especially like the grill.'

Bourne touched the buttons, holding up his hand for quiet. Remembering, he asked for Madame Brielle's room, the name they had agreed upon, and when the hotel operator said '*Mais, oui*,' he nodded rapidly in relief to Alex and Dimitri Krupkin. Lavier answered.

'Yes?'

'It is *I*, madame,' said Jason, his French just slightly coarse, ever so minimally Anglicized; the Chameleon was in charge. 'Your housekeeper suggested we might reach you here. Madame's dress is ready. We apologize for the delay.'

'It was to have been brought to me yesterday – by *noon* – you ass! I intended to wear it last evening at Le Grand Véfour. I was mortified!'

'A thousand apologies. We can deliver it to the hotel immediately.'

'You are again an ass! I'm sure my maid also told you I was here for only two days. Take it to my flat in the Montaigne and it had better be there by four o'clock or your bill will not be paid for six months!' The conversation was believably terminated by a loud crack at the other end of the line.

Bourne replaced the phone; perspiration had formed at his slightly greying hairline. 'I've been out of this too long,' he said, breathing deeply. 'She has a flat on the Montaigne and she'll be there after four o'clock.'

'Who the *hell* is Dominique whatever-her-name-is?' fairly yelled the frustrated Conklin.

'Lavier,' answered Krupkin, 'only she uses her dead sister's name, Jacqueline. She's been posing as her sister for years.'

'You *know* about that?' asked Jason, impressed.

'Yes, but it never did us much good. It was an understandable ruse – look-alikes, several months' absence, minor surgery and programming – all quite normal in the abnormal world of haute couture. Who looks or listens to anyone in that superficial orbit? We watch her, but she's never led us to the Jackal, she wouldn't know how. She has no direct access; everything she reports to Carlos is filtered, stone walls at every relay. That's the way of the Jackal.'

'It's not always the way,' said Bourne. 'There was a man named Santos who managed a run-down café in Argenteuil called Le Coeur du Soldat. He had access. He gave it to me and it was very special.'

'*Was?*' Krupkin raised his eyebrows. '*Had?* You employ the past tense?'

'He's dead.'

'And that run-down café in Argenteuil, is it still flourishing?'

'It's cleaned out and closed down,' admitted Jason, no defeat in his admission.

'So the access is terminated, no?'

'Sure, but I believe what he told me because he was killed for telling it to me. You see, he was getting out, just as this Lavier woman wants to get out – only, *his* association went back to the beginning. To Cuba, where Carlos saved a misfit like himself from execution. He knew he could use that man, that huge imposing giant who could operate inside the dregs of humanity and be his primary relay. Santos *had* direct access. He proved it because he gave me an alternate number that did reach the Jackal. Only a very few men could do that.'

'Fascinating,' said Krupkin, his eyes firmly focused on Bourne. 'But as my fine old enemy, Aleksei, who is now looking at you as I look at you, might inquire, what are you leading up to, Mr Bourne? Your words are ambiguous but your implied accusations appear dangerous.'

'To you. Not to us.'

'I beg your pardon?'

'Santos told me that only four men in the world have direct access to the Jackal. One of them is in Dzerzhinsky Square. "Very high in the Komitet" were Santos's words, and believe me, he didn't think much of your superior.'

It was as if Dimitri Krupkin had been struck in the face by a director of the Politburo in the middle of Red Square during a May Day parade. The blood drained from his head, his skin taking on the pallor of ash, his eyes steady, unblinking. 'What else did this Santos tell you? I have to *know*!'

'Only that Carlos had a thing about Moscow, that he was making contact with people in high places. It was an obsession with him . . . If you can find that contact in the Dzerzhinsky, it would be a big leap forward. In the meantime, all we've got is Dominique Lavier—'

'Damn, *damn*!' roared Krupkin, cutting off Jason. 'How *insane*, yet how perfectly logical! You've answered several questions, Mr Bourne, and how they've burned into my mind. So many times I've come so close – so many, so close – and always *nothing.* Well, let me tell you, gentlemen, the games of the devil are not restricted to those confined to hell. Others can play them. My *God,* I've been a pearl to be flushed from one oyster to another, always the bigger fool! . . . Make no more calls from that telephone!'

It was three-thirty in the afternoon, Moscow time, and the elderly man in the uniform of a Soviet army officer walked as rapidly as his age permitted down the hallway on the fifth floor of KGB headquarters in Dzerzhinsky Square. It was a hot day, and as usual the air conditioning was only barely and erratically adequate so General Grigorie Rodchenko permitted himself a privilege of rank: his collar was open. It did not stop the occasional rivulet of sweat from sliding in and out of the crevices of his deeply lined face on its way down to his neck, but the absence of the tight, red-bordered band of cloth around his throat was a minor relief.

He reached the bank of elevators, pressed the button and waited, gripping a key in his hand. The doors to his right opened and he was pleased to see that there was no one inside. It was easier than having to order everyone out – at least, far less awkward. He entered, inserted the key in the uppermost lock-release above the panel, and again waited while the mechanism performed its function. It did so quickly, and the elevator shot directly down to the lowest underground levels of the building.

The doors opened and the general walked out, instantly aware of the pervasive silence that filled the corridors both left and right. In moments, that would change, he thought. He proceeded down the left hallway to a large steel door with a metal sign riveted in the centre.

ENTRANCE FORBIDDEN

AUTHORIZED PERSONNEL ONLY

It was a foolish admonition, he considered, as he took out a thin plastic card from his pocket and shoved it slowly, carefully, into a slot on the right. Without the pass card – and sometimes even with it if inserted too quickly – the door would not open. There were two clicks and Rodchenko removed his card as the heavy, knobless door swung back, a television monitor recording his entry.

The hum of activity was pronounced from dozens of lighted cubicles within the huge, dark low-ceilinged complex the size of a czar's grand ballroom, but without the slightest attempt at decor. A thousand pieces of equipment in black and grey, several hundred personnel in pristine white coveralls within white-walled cubicles. And, thankfully, the air was cool, almost cold in fact. The machinery demanded it, for this was the KGB's communications centre. Information poured in twenty-four hours a day from all over the world.

The old soldier trudged up the familiar path to the farthest aisle on the right, then left to the last cubicle at the far end of the enormous room. It was a long walk, and the general's breath was short, his legs were tired. He entered the small enclosure, nodding at the middle-aged operator who looked up at his visitor and removed the cushioned headset from his ears. On the white counter in front of him was a large electronic console with myriad switches, dials and a keyboard. Rodchenko sat down in a steel chair next to the man; catching his breath, he spoke.

'You have word from Colonel Krupkin in Paris?'

'I have words *concerning* Colonel Krupkin, General. In line with your instructions to monitor the colonel's telephone conversations, including those international lines authorized by him, I received a tape from Paris several minutes ago that I thought you should listen to.'

'As usual, you are most efficient and I am most grateful; and as always, I'm sure Colonel Krupkin will inform us of events, but as you know, he's so terribly busy.'

'No explanations are necessary, sir. The conversations you are about to hear were recorded within the past half hour. The earphones, please?'

Rodchenko slipped on the headset and nodded. The operator placed a pad and a container of sharpened pencils in front of the general; he touched a number on the keyboard and sat back as the powerful third *direktor* of the Komitet leaned forward listening. In moments the general began taking notes; minutes later he was writing furiously. The tape came to an end and Rodchenko removed the headset. He looked sternly at the operator, his narrow Slavic eyes rigid between the folds of lined flesh, the crevices in his face seemingly more pronounced than before.

'Erase the tape, then destroy the reel,' he ordered, getting out of the chair. 'As usual, you have heard nothing.'

'As usual, General.'

'And, as usual, you will be rewarded.'

It was four-seventeen when Rodchenko returned to his office and sat down at his desk, studying his notes. It was *incredible*! It was beyond *belief*, yet there it was – he had heard for himself the words and the voices saying those words! . . . Not those concerning the monseigneur in Paris; he was secondary now and could be reached in minutes, if it was necessary. That could wait, but the other could not wait, not an instant longer! The general picked up his phone and rang his secretary.

'I want an immediate satellite transmission to our consulate in New York. All maximum scramblers in place and operational.'

How could it happen?

Medusa!

32

Frowning, Marie listened to her husband's voice over the telephone, nodding at Mo Panov across the hotel room. 'Where are you now?' she asked.

'At a pay phone in the Plaza-Athénée,' answered Bourne. 'I'll be back in a couple of hours.'

'What's happening?'

'Complications, but also some progress.'

'That doesn't tell me anything.'

'There's not that much to tell.'

'What's this Krupkin like?'

'He's an original. He brought us to the Soviet Embassy and I talked to your brother on one of their lines.'

'*What?* . . . How are the *children*?'

'Fine. Everything's fine. Jamie's thoroughly enjoying himself and Mrs Cooper won't let Johnny touch Alison.'

'Which means Bro doesn't want to touch Alison.'

'So be it.'

'What's the number? I want to call.'

'Holland's setting up a secure line. We'll know in an hour or so.'

'Which means you're lying.'

'So be it. You should be with them. If I'm delayed, I'll call you.'

'Wait a minute. Mo wants to talk to you—'

The line went dead. Across the room, Panov slowly shook his head as he watched Marie's reaction to the suddenly terminated conversation. 'Forget it,' he said. 'I'm the last person he wants to talk to.'

'He's back there, Mo. He's not David any longer.'

'He has a different calling now,' added Panov softly. 'David can't handle it.'

'I think that's the most frightening thing I've ever heard you say.'

The psychiatrist nodded. 'It may well be.'

The grey Citroën was parked several hundred feet diagonally across from the canopied entrance of Dominique Lavier's apartment building on the fashionable Avenue Montaigne. Krupkin, Alex and Bourne sat in the back, Conklin again in the jump seat, his size and disabled leg making the position more feasible. Conversation was at a minimum as the three men anxiously kept glancing over at the glass doors of the apartment.

'Are you sure this is going to work?' asked Jason.

'I am only sure that Sergei is an immensely talented professional,' replied Krupkin. 'He was trained in Novgorod, you know, and his French is impeccable. He also carries on him a variety of identifications that would fool the Division of Documents at the Deuxième Bureau.'

'What about the other two?' pressed Bourne.

'Silent subordinates, controlled by and subservient to their superior. They're also experts at their craft . . . Here he comes!'

Sergei could be seen walking out of the glass doors; he turned left, and within moments crossed the wide boulevard towards the Citroën. He reached the car, went around the bonnet and climbed in behind the wheel. 'Everything is in order,' he said, angling his head over the front seat. 'Madame has not returned and the flat is number twenty-one, second floor, right front side. It has been swept thoroughly; there are no intercepts.'

'Are you *certain*?' asked Conklin. 'There's no room for error here, Sergei.'

'Our instruments are the best, sir,' answered the KGB aide, smiling. 'It pains me to say it, but they were developed by the General Electronics Corporation under contract to Langley.'

'Two points for our side,' said Alex.

'Minus twelve for permitting the technology to be stolen,' concluded Krupkin. 'Besides, I'm sure a number of years ago our Madame Lavier might have had bugs sewn into her mattress—'

'Checked,' broke in Sergei.

'Thank you, but my point is that the Jackal could hardly have monitoring personnel all over Paris. It all gets so complicated.'

'Where are your other two men?' asked Bourne.

'In the lobby corridors, sir. I'll join them shortly and we have a support vehicle down the street, all in radio contact, of course . . . I'll drive you over now.'

'Wait a minute,' interrupted Conklin. 'How do we get in? What do we say?'

'It's been said, sir, you need say nothing. You are authorized covert personnel from the French SEDCE—'

'The what?' broke in Jason.

'The Service of External Documentation and Counterespionage,' answered Alex. 'It's the nearest thing here to Langley.'

'What about the Deuxième?'

'Special Branch,' said Conklin offhandedly, his mind elsewhere. 'Some say it's an elite corps, others say otherwise . . . Sergei, won't they check?'

'They already have, sir. After showing the concierge and his assistant my identification, I gave them an unlisted telephone number that confirmed the Service and my status. I subsequently described the three of you and requested no conversation, merely access to Madame Lavier's flat . . . I'll drive over now. It will make a better impression on the doorman.'

'Sometimes simplicity backed by authority is best in deception,' observed Krupkin as the Citroën was manoeuvred between the sparse, erratic traffic across the wide avenue to the entrance of the white stone apartment complex. 'Take the car around the corner out of sight, Sergei,' ordered the KGB officer, reaching for the door handle. 'And my radio, if you please?'

'Yes, sir,' replied the aide, handing Krupkin a miniaturized electronic intercom over the seat. 'I'll signal you when I'm in position.'

'I can reach all of you with this?'

'Yes, comrade. Beyond a hundred and fifty metres the frequency is undetectable.'

'Come along, gentlemen.'

Inside the marble lobby, Krupkin nodded at the formally dressed concierge behind the counter, Jason and Alex on the Soviet's right. '*La porte est ouverte*,' said the concierge, his gaze downward, avoiding direct eye contact. 'I shall not be in evidence when madame arrives,' he continued in French. 'How you got in is unknown to me; however, there is a service entrance at the rear of the building.'

'But for official courtesy it is the one we would have used,' said Krupkin, looking straight ahead as the threesome walked to the elevator.

Lavier's flat was a testament to the world of haute couture chic. The walls were dotted with photographs of notables of fashion attending important showings and events, as well as framed original sketches by celebrated designers. Like a Mondrian, the furniture was stark in its simplicity, the colours bold and predominantly red, black and deep green; the chairs, sofas and tables only vaguely resembled chairs, sofas and tables – they seemed more suitable for use in spacecraft.

As if by rote, both Conklin and the Russian immediately began examining the tables, ferreting out handwritten notes, a number of which were beside a mother-of-pearl telephone on top of a curved, thick dark green table of sorts.

'If this is a desk,' said Alex, 'where the hell are the drawers or the handles?'

'It's the newest thing from Leconte,' replied Krupkin.

'The tennis player?' interrupted Conklin.

'No, Aleksei, the furniture designer. You press in and they shoot out.'

'You're kidding.'

'Try it.'

Conklin did so and a barely discernible drawer sprang loose from an all but invisible crack. 'I'll be damned—'

Krupkin's miniaturized radio suddenly erupted with two sharp beeps from inside his breast pocket. 'It must be Sergei checking in,' said Dimitri, removing the instrument. 'You're in place, comrade?' he continued, speaking into the base of the radio.

'More than that,' came the aide's quiet voice accompanied by minor static. 'The Lavier woman has just entered the building.'

'The concierge?'

'Nowhere in sight.'

'Good. Out . . . Aleksei, get away from there. Lavier is on her way up.'

'You want to hide?' asked Conklin facetiously, turning the pages of a telephone notebook.

'I'd rather not start off with instant hostility, which will be the case if she sees you rifling through her personal effects.'

'All right, all right.' Alex returned the notebook to the drawer and closed it. 'But if she isn't going to cooperate. I'm taking that little black book.'

'She'll cooperate,' said Bourne. 'I told you, she wants out and the only way out for her is with a dead Jackal. The money's secondary – not inconsequential, but getting out comes first.'

'Money?' asked Krupkin. 'What money?'

'I offered to pay her and I will.'

'And I can assure you, money is not secondary to Madame Lavier,' added the Russian.

The sound of a key being inserted into a latch echoed throughout the living room. The three men turned to the door as a startled Dominique Lavier walked inside. Her astonishment, however, was so brief as to be fleeting; there were no cracks whatsoever in her composure. Brows arched in the manner of a regal mannequin, she calmly replaced the key in her beaded purse, looked over at the intruders and spoke in English.

'Well, Kruppie, I might have known you were somewhere in this bouillabaisse.'

'Ah, the charming Jacqueline, or may we drop the pretence, Domie?'

'*Kruppie?*' cried Alex. 'Domie? . . . Is this old home week?'

'Comrade Krupkin is one of the more advertised KGB officers in Paris,' said Lavier, walking to the long, cubed red table behind the white silk sofa and putting down her purse. 'Knowing him is derigueur in certain circles.'

'It has its advantages, dear Domie. You can't imagine the disinformation I'm fed in those circles by the Quai d'Orsay, and once having tasted it, knowing it's false. By the way, I understand you've met our tall American friend and even had certain negotiations with him, so I think it's only proper I introduce you to his colleague . . . Madame, Monsieur Aleksei Konsolikov.'

'I don't believe you. He's no Soviet. One's nostrils become attuned to the approach of the unwashed bear.'

'Ah, you *destroy* me, Domie! But you're right, it was a parental error of judgement. He may therefore introduce himself, if he cares to.'

'The name's Conklin, Alex Conklin, Miss Lavier, and I'm American. However, our mutual acquaintance "Kruppie" is right in one sense. My parents were Russian and I speak it fluently, so he's at a loss to mislead me when we're in Soviet company.'

'I think that's delicious.'

'Well, it's at least appetizing, if you know Kruppie.'

'I'm wounded, fatally wounded!' exclaimed Krupkin. 'But my injuries are not essential to this meeting. You will work with us, Domie?'

'I'll work with you, Kruppie. My *God*, will I work with you! I ask only that Jason Bourne clarifies his offer to me. With Carlos I'm a caged animal, but without him I'm a near destitute ageing courtesan. I want him to pay for my sister's death and for everything he's done to me, but I don't care to sleep in the gutter.'

'Name your price,' said Jason.

'*Write* it down,' clarified Conklin, glancing at Krupkin.

'Let me see,' said Lavier, walking around the sofa and crossing to the Leconte desk. 'I'm within a few years of sixty – from one direction or another, it's immaterial – and without the Jackal, and the absence of some other fatal disease, I will have perhaps fifteen to twenty years.' She bent down over the desk and wrote a figure on a notepad, tore it off, then stood up and looked at the tall American. 'For you, Mr Bourne, and I'd rather not argue. I believe it's fair.'

Jason took the paper and read the amount: *$1,000,000.00, American.* 'It's fair,' said Bourne, handing the note back to Lavier. 'Add how and where you want it paid and I'll make the arrangements when we leave here. The money will be there in the morning.'

The ageing courtesan looked into Bourne's eyes. 'I believe you,' she said, again bending over the desk and writing out her instructions. She rose and gave the paper back to Jason. 'The deal is made, monsieur, and may God grant us the kill. If He does not, we are dead.'

'You're speaking as a Magdalen sister?'

'I'm speaking as a sister who's terrified, no more and certainly no less.'

Bourne nodded. 'I've several questions,' he said. 'Do you want to sit down?'

'*Oui.* With a cigarette.' Lavier crossed to the sofa, and sinking into the cushions, reached for her purse on the red table. She took out a pack of cigarettes, extracted one, and picked up a gold lighter from the coffee table. 'Such a filthy habit but at times so damned necessary,' she said, snapping the flame and inhaling deeply. 'Your questions, monsieur?'

'What happened at the Meurice? *How* did it happen?'

'The woman happened – I assume it was *your* woman – that was my understanding. As we agreed, you and your friend from Deuxième were positioned so that when Carlos arrived to trap you, you would kill him. For reasons no one can fathom, your woman screamed as you crossed the Rivoli – the rest you saw for yourself . . . How *could* you have told me to take a room at the Meurice knowing she was there?'

'That's easy to answer. I didn't know she was there. Where do we stand now?'

'Carlos still trusts me. He blames everything on the woman, your wife, I'm told, and has no reason to hold me responsible. After all, you were there, which proves my allegiance. Were it not for the Deuxième officer, you'd be dead.'

Again Bourne nodded. 'How can you reach him?'

'I cannot myself. I never have, nor have I cared to. He prefers it that way, and, as I told you, the cheques arrive on time so I have no reason to.'

'But you send him messages,' pressed Jason. 'I heard you.'

'Yes, I do, but never directly. I call several old men at cheap cafés – the names and numbers vary weekly and quite a few have no idea what I'm talking about, but for those that do, they call others immediately, and *they* call others beyond themselves. Somehow the messages get through. Very quickly, I might add.'

'What did I tell you?' said Krupkin emphatically. 'All the relays end with false names and filthy cafés. Stone walls!'

'Still the messages get through,' said Alex Conklin, repeating Lavier's words.

'Yet Kruppie's correct.' The ageing but still striking woman dragged heavily, nervously on her cigarette. 'The routings are convoluted to the point of being untraceable.'

'I don't care about that,' said Alex, squinting at nothing the others could see. 'They also reach Carlos quickly, you made that clear.'

'It's true.'

Conklin widened his eyes and fixed them on Lavier. 'I want you to send the most urgent message you've ever relayed to the Jackal. You *must* talk to him directly. It's an emergency that you can entrust to no one but Carlos himself.'

'About *what*?' erupted Krupkin. 'What could be so urgent that the Jackal will comply? Like our Mr Bourne, he is obsessed with traps, and under the circumstances, any direct communication smells of one!'

Alex shook his head and limped to a side window, squinting again, deep in thought, his intense eyes reflecting his concentration. Then gradually, slowly, once more his eyes opened. He gazed at the street below. 'My God, it could *work*,' he whispered to himself.

'What could work?' asked Bourne.

'Dimitri, hurry! Call the embassy and have them send over the biggest, fanciest diplomatic limousine you proletarians own.'

'*What?*'

'Just do as I say! Quickly!'

'Aleksei . . . ?'

'*Now!*'

The force and urgency of Conklin's command had its effect. The Russian walked rapidly to the mother-of-pearl telephone and dialled, his questioning eyes on Alex, who kept staring down at the street. Lavier looked at Jason; he shook his head in bewilderment as Krupkin spoke into the phone, his Russian a short series of clipped phrases.

'It's done,' said the KGB officer, hanging up. 'And now I think you should give me an extremely convincing reason for doing it.'

'*Moscow*,' replied Conklin, still looking out the window.

'Alex, for Christ's sake—'

'What are you *saying*?' roared Krupkin.

'We've got to get Carlos out of Paris,' said Conklin, turning. 'Where better than Moscow?' Before the astonished men could respond, Alex looked at Lavier. 'You say he still trusts you?'

'He has no reason not to.'

'Then two words should do it. "Moscow, emergency," that's the basic message you're sending him. Put it any way you like, but add that the crisis is of such a nature that you must speak only with him.'

'But I never *have*. I know men who have spoken to him – some claim personally – who in drunken moments try to describe him, but to me he's a complete stranger.'

'All the stronger for it,' broke in Conklin, turning to Bourne and Krupkin. 'In this city he's got all the cards, *all* of them. He's got firepower, an untraceable network of gunslingers and couriers, and for every crevice he can crawl into and burst out from, there are dozens more available to him. Paris is his territory, his protection – we could run blindly all over the city for days, weeks, even months, getting nowhere until the moment comes when he's got you and Marie in his gun sights . . . you can also add Mo and me to that scenario, London, Amsterdam, Brussels, Rome – they'd all be better for us than Paris, but the best is Moscow. Oddly enough, it's the one place in the world that has a hypnotic hold on him – and also the one that's the least hospitable.'

'Aleksei, *Aleksei*,' cried Dimitri Krupkin. 'I really think you should reconsider alcohol, for it's obvious you've lost your senses! Say Domie actually reaches Carlos and tells him what you say. Do you really believe that on the basis of an "emergency" in Moscow he'll up and take the next plane there? Insanity!'

'You can bet your last black market ruble, I do,' replied Conklin. 'That message is only to convince him to get in touch with her. Once he does, she explodes the bomb . . . She's just heard an extraordinary piece of information that she knew should only be conveyed to him, not sent through the message tunnels.'

'And what in God's name might *that* be?' asked Lavier, extracting another cigarette and instantly lighting it.

'The KGB in Moscow is closing in on the Jackal's man in Dzerzhinsky Square. They've narrowed it down to, say, ten or fifteen officers in the highest ranks. Once they find him, Carlos is neutralized in the Komitet – worse, he's about to lose an informer who knows far too much about him to the Lubyanka interrogators.'

'But how would *she* know that?' said Jason.

'Who would *tell* her?' added Krupkin.

'It's the truth, isn't it?'

'So are your very secret substations in Beijing, Kabul and – forgive my impertinence – Canada's Prince Edward Island, but you don't advertise them,' said Krupkin.

'I didn't know about Prince Edward,' admitted Alex. 'Regardless, there are times when advertisements aren't necessary, only the means to convey the information credibly. A few minutes ago I didn't have any means, only authenticity, but that gap has just been filled . . . Come over here, Kruppie – just you for the moment, and stay away from the window. Look between the corner of the drapes.' The Soviet did as he was told, going to Conklin's side and parting the fold of lace fabric from the wall. 'What do you see?' asked Alex, gesturing at a shabby, nondescript brown car below on the Avenue Montaigne. 'Doesn't do much for the neighbourhood, does it?'

Krupkin did not bother to reply. Instead, he whipped the miniaturized radio from his pocket and pressed the transmitter button. 'Sergei, there's a brown automobile roughly eighty metres down the street from the building's entrance—'

'We know, sir,' interrupted the aide. 'We've got it covered and if you'll notice, our backup is parked across the way. It's an old man who barely moves except to look out the window.'

'Does he have a car telephone?'

'No, comrade, and should he leave the automobile he'll be followed, so there can be no outside calls unless you direct otherwise.'

'I shall not direct otherwise. Thank you, Sergei. Out.' The Russian looked at Conklin. 'The old man,' he said. 'You saw him.'

'Bald head and all,' affirmed Alex. 'He's not a fool; he's done this before and knows he's being watched. He can't leave for fear of missing something, and if he had a phone there'd be others down in the Montaigne.'

'The Jackal,' said Bourne, stepping forward, then stopping, remembering Conklin's order to stay away from the window.

'Now, do you understand?' asked Alex, addressing the question to Krupkin.

'Of course,' conceded the KGB official, smiling. 'It's why you wanted an ostentatious limousine from our embassy. After we leave, Carlos is told that a Soviet diplomatic vehicle was sent to pick us up, and for what other reason would we be here but to interrogate Madame Lavier? Naturally, in my well-advertised presence was a tall man who might or might not be Jason Bourne, and another shorter individual with a disabled leg – thus confirming that it *was* Jason Bourne . . . Our unholy alliance is therefore established and observed, and again, naturally, during our harsh questioning of Madame Lavier, tempers flared and references were made to the Jackal's informer in Dzerzhinsky Square.'

'Which only I'd known about through my dealing with Santos at Le Coeur du Soldat,' said Jason quietly. 'So Dominique has a credible observer – an old man from Carlos's army of old men – to back up the information she delivers . . . I've got to say it, St Alex, that serpentine brain of yours hasn't lost its cunning.'

'I hear a professor I once knew . . . I thought he'd left us.'

'He has.'

'Only for a while, I hope.'

'Well done, Aleksei. You still have the touch; you may remain abstemious, if you must, much as it pains me . . . It's always the nuances, isn't it?'

'Not always by any means,' disagreed Conklin simply, shaking his head. 'Most of the time it's foolish mistakes. For instance, our new colleague here, "Domie", as you affectionately call her, was told she was still trusted, but she wasn't, not completely. So an old man was dispatched to watch her apartment – no big deal, just a little insurance in a car that doesn't belong in a street with Jaguars and Rolls-Royces. So we pay off on the small policy, and with luck cash in on the big one. Moscow.'

'Let me intellectualize,' said Krupkin. 'Although you were always far better in that department than I, Aleksei. I prefer the best wine to the most penetrating thoughts, although the latter – in both our countries – invariably leads to the former.'

'*Merde!*' yelled Dominique Lavier, crushing out her cigarette. 'What are you two idiots talking about?'

'They'll tell us, believe me,' answered Bourne.

'As has been reported and repeated in secure circles too often for comfort,' continued the Soviet, 'years ago we trained a madman in Novgorod, and years ago we would have put a bullet in his head had he not escaped. His methods, if sanctioned by any legitimate government, especially the two superpowers, would lead to confrontations neither of us can ever permit. Yet, withal, in the beginning he was a true revolutionary with a capital *R*, and we, the world's *truest* revolutionaries, disinherited him . . . By his lights, it was a great injustice and he never forgets it. He will always yearn to come back to the mother's breast for that's where he was born . . . Good *God*, the people he's killed in the name of "aggressors" while he made fortunes is positively *revolting*!'

'But you denied him,' said Jason flatly, 'and he wants that denial reversed. He has to be acknowledged as the master killer you trained. That psychopathic ego of his is the basis for everything Alex and I mounted . . . Santos said he continuously bragged about the cadre he was building in Moscow – "always Moscow, it's an obsession with him" – those were Santos's words. The only specific person he knew about, and not by name, was Carlos's mole high up in the KGB, but he said Carlos claimed to have others in key positions at various powerful departments, that as the monseigneur he'd been sending them money for years.'

'So the Jackal thinks he forms a core of supporters within our government,' observed Krupkin. 'Despite everything he still believes he can come back. He is, indeed, an egomaniac but he's never understood the Russian mind. He may temporarily corrupt a few cynical opportunists but these will cover themselves and turn on him. No one looks forward to a stay at the Lubyanka or a Siberian gulag. The Jackal's Potemkin village will burn to the ground.'

'All the more reason for him to race to Moscow and put out the brushfires,' said Alex.

'What do you mean?' asked Bourne.

'The burning will start with the exposure of Carlos's man in Dzerzhinsky Square; he'll know that. The only way to prevent it is for him to reach Moscow and make a determination. Either his informer will elude internal security or the Jackal will have to kill him.'

'I forgot,' interrupted Bourne. 'Something else Santos said . . . most of the Russians on Carlos's payroll spoke French. Look for a man high up in the Komitet who speaks French.'

Krupkin's radio again intruded, the two piercing beeps barely muffled by his jacket. He pulled it out and spoke. 'Yes?'

'I don't know how or why, comrade,' said the tense voice of Sergei, 'but the ambassador's limousine has just arrived at the building. I *swear* to you I have no idea what happened!'

'I do. I called for it.'

'But the embassy flags will be seen by everyone!'

'Including, I trust, an alert old man in a brown automobile. We'll be down shortly. Out,' Krupkin turned to the others. 'The car's here, gentlemen. Where shall we meet, Domie? And when?'

'Tonight,' replied Lavier. 'There's a showing at La Galerie d'Or in the rue de Paradis. The artist's a young upstart who wants to be a rock star or something, but he's the rage and everyone will be there.'

'Tonight then . . . Come, gentlemen. Against our instincts, we must be very observable outside on the pavement.'

*

The crowds moved in and out of the shafts of light while the music was provided by an ear-shattering rock band mercifully placed in a side room away from the main viewing area. Were it not for the paintings on the walls and the beams of the small spotlights illuminating them, a person might think he was in a discotheque rather than in one of Paris's elegant art galleries.

Through a series of nods, Dominique Lavier manoeuvred Krupkin to a corner of the large room. Their graceful smiles, arched brows and intermittently mimed laughter covered their quiet conversation.

'The word passed among the old men is that the monseigneur will be away for a few days. However, they are all to continue searching for the tall American and his crippled friend and list wherever they are seen.'

'You must have done your job well.'

'As I relayed the information, he was utterly silent. In his breathing, however, there was utter loathing. I felt my bones grow cold.'

'He's on his way to Moscow,' said the Russian. 'No doubt through Prague.'

'What will you do now?'

Krupkin arched his neck and raised his eyes to the ceiling in false, silent laughter. Levelling his gaze on her, he answered, smiling. 'Moscow,' he said.

33

Bryce Ogilvie, managing partner of Ogilvie, Spofford, Crawford and Cohen, prided himself on his self-discipline. That was to say, not merely the outward appearance of composure, but the cold calm he forced upon his deepest fears in times of crisis. However, when he arrived at his office barely fifty minutes ago and found his concealed private telephone ringing, he experienced a twinge of apprehension at such an early morning call over that particular line. Then when he heard the heavily accented voice of the Soviet consul general of New York demanding an immediate conference, he had to acknowledge a sudden void in his chest . . . and when the Russian instructed him – *ordered* him – to be at the Carlyle Hotel, Suite 4-C, in one hour, rather than their usual meeting place at the apartment on Thirty-second and Madison, Bryce felt a searing-hot pain filling that void in his chest. *And* when he had mildly objected to the suddenness of the proposed, unscheduled conference, the pain in his chest had burst into fire, the flames travelling up to his throat at the Soviet's reply.

'What I have to show you will make you devoutly wish we never knew each other, much less had any occasion to meet this morning. *Be* there!'

Ogilvie sat back in his limousine, as far back as the upholstery could be pressed, his legs stretched, rigid on the carpeted floor. Abstract, swirling thoughts of personal wealth, power and influence kept circling in his mind; he had to get hold of himself! After all, he was Bryce Ogilvie, *the* Bryce Ogilvie, perhaps the most successful corporate attorney in New York, and arguably second only to Boston's Randolph Gates in the fast track of corporate and antitrust law.

Gates! The mere thought of that son of a bitch was a welcome diversion. Medusa had asked a minor favour of the celebrated Gates, an inconsequential, perfectly acceptable staff appointment on an ad hoc government-oriented commission, and he had not even answered their phone calls! Calls put through by another perfectly acceptable source, the supposedly irreproachable, impartial head of Pentagon procurements, an asshole named General Norman Swayne, who only wanted the best information. Well, perhaps more than information, but Gates could not have known about that . . . Gates? There was something in the *Times* the other morning about his bowing out of a hostile takeover proceeding. What was it?

The limousine pulled up to the kerb in front of the Carlyle Hotel, once the Kennedy family's favoured New York City address, now the temporary clandestine favourite of the Soviets. Ogilvie waited until the uniformed doorman opened the left rear door of the car before he stepped out onto the pavement. He normally would not have done so, believing the delay was an unnecessary affectation, but this morning he did; he *had* to get hold of himself. He had to be the Ice-Cold Ogilvie his legal adversaries feared.

The elevator's ascent to the fourth floor was swift, the walk over the blue-carpeted hallway to Suite 4-C far slower, the distance much closer. *The* Bryce Ogilvie breathed deeply, calmly, and stood erect as he pressed the bell. Twenty-eight seconds later, irritatingly clocked by the attorney as he silently counted 'one one-thousand, two one-thousand,' ad nauseam, the door was opened by the Soviet consul general, a slender man of medium height whose aquiline face had taut white skin and large brown eyes.

Vladimir Sulikov was a wiry seventy-three-year-old full of nervous energy, a scholar and former professor of history at Moscow University, a committed Marxist, yet oddly enough, considering his position, not a member of the Communist Party. In truth, he was not a member of any political orthodoxy, preferring the passive role of the unorthodox individual within a collectivist society. That, and his singularly acute intellect, had served him well; he was sent to posts where more conformist men would not have been half so effective. The combination of these attributes, along with a dedication to physical exercise, made Sulikov appear ten to fifteen years younger than his age. His was an unsettling presence for those negotiating with him for somehow he radiated the wisdom acquired over the years and the vitality of youth to implement it.

The greetings were abrupt. He offered nothing but a stiff, cold handshake and a stiffly upholstered armchair. Sulikov stood in front of the suite's narrow mantel of white marble as though it were a classroom blackboard, his hands clasped behind him, an agitated professor about to question and lecture simultaneously an annoying, disputatious graduate student.

'To our business,' said the Russian curtly. 'You are aware of Admiral Peter Holland?'

'Yes, of course. He's the director of the Central Intelligence Agency. Why do you ask?'

'Is he one of you?'

'No.'

'Are you quite sure?'

'Of course I am.'

'Is it possible he became one of you without your knowledge?'

'Certainly not, I don't even know the man. And if this is some kind of amateurish interrogatory, Soviet style, practise on someone else.'

'Ohh, the fine expensive American attorney objects to being asked simple questions?'

'I object to being insulted. You made an astonishing statement over the phone. I'd like it explained, so please get to it.'

'I'll get to it, Counsellor, believe me, I'll get to it, but in my own fashion. We Russians protect our flanks; it's a lesson we learned from the tragedy and the triumph of Stalingrad – an experience you Americans never had to endure.'

'I came from another war, as you well know,' said Ogilvie coolly, 'but if the history books are accurate, you had some help from your Russian winter.'

'That's difficult to explain to thousands upon thousands of frozen Russian corpses.'

'Granted, and you have both my condolences and my congratulations, but it's not the explanation – or even the lack of one – that I requested.'

'I'm only trying to explain a truism, young man. As has been said, it's the painful lessons of history we don't know about that we are bound to repeat . . . You see, we *do* protect our flanks, and if some of us in the diplomatic arena suspect that we have been duped into international embarrassment, we reinforce those flanks. It's a simple lesson for one so erudite as yourself, Counsellor.'

'And so obvious, it's trivial. What about Admiral Holland?'

'In a moment . . . First, let me ask you about a man named Alexander Conklin?'

Bryce Ogilvie bolted forward in the chair, stunned. 'Where did you *get* that name?' he asked, barely audible.

'There's more . . . Someone called Panov, Mortimer or Moishe Panov, a Jewish physician, we believe. And finally, Counsellor, a man and a woman we assume are the assassin Jason Bourne and his wife.'

'My *God*!' exclaimed Ogilvie, his body angled and tense, his eyes wide. 'What have these people got to do with *us*?'

'That's what we have to know,' answered Sulikov, staring at the Wall Street lawyer. 'You're obviously aware of each one, aren't you?'

'Well, yes – *no*!' protested Ogilvie, his face flushed, his words spilling over one another. 'It's an entirely different situation. It has nothing to do with *our* business – a business we've poured millions into, developed for twenty years!'

'And made millions in return, Counsellor, may I be permitted to remind you of that?'

'Venture capital in the international markets!' cried the attorney. 'That's no crime in this country. Money flows across the oceans with the touch of a computer button. *No* crime!'

'Really?' The Soviet consul general arched his brows. 'I thought you were a better attorney than that statement suggests. You've been buying up companies all over Europe through mergers and acquisitions using surrogate and misleading corporate entities. The firms you acquire represent sources of supply, often in the same markets, and you subsequently determine prices between former competitors. I believe that's called collusion and restraint of trade, legal terms that we in the Soviet Union have no problems with, as the state sets prices.'

'There's no evidence *whatsoever* to support such charges!' declared Ogilvie.

'Of course not, as long as there are liars and unscrupulous lawyers to bribe and advise the liars. It's a labyrinthian enterprise, brilliantly executed, and we've both profited from it. You've sold us anything we've wanted or needed for years, including every major item on your government's restricted lists under so many names our computers broke down trying to keep track of them.'

'No *proof*!' insisted the Wall Street attorney emphatically.

'I'm not interested in such proof, Counsellor. I'm only interested in the names I mentioned to you. In order, they are Admiral Holland, Alexander Conklin, Dr Panov, and lastly Jason Bourne and his wife. Please tell me about them.'

'*Why?*' pleaded Ogilvie. 'I've just explained they have nothing to *do* with you and me, nothing to do with our arrangements!'

'We think they might have, so why not start with Admiral Holland?'

'Oh, for God's sake . . . !' The agitated lawyer shook his head back and forth, stammered several times and let the words rush out. 'Holland – all right, you'll see . . . We recruited a man at the CIA, an analyst named DeSole who panicked and wanted to sever his relations with us. Naturally, we couldn't permit that, so we had him eliminated – *professionally* eliminated – as we were forced to do with several others who we believed were dangerously unstable. Holland may have had his suspicions and probably speculated on foul play, but he couldn't do any more than speculate – the professionals we employed left no traces; they never do.'

'Very well,' said Sulikov, holding his place by the mantel and gazing down at the nervous Ogilvie. 'Next, Alexander Conklin.'

'He's a former CIA station chief and tied in with Panov, a psychiatrist – they're both connected to the man they call Jason Bourne and his wife. They go back years, to Saigon, in fact. You see, we had been penetrated, several of our people were reached and threatened, and DeSole came to the conclusion that this Bourne, with Conklin's help, was the one responsible for the penetration.'

'How could he do that?'

'I don't know. I only know that he has to be eliminated and our professionals have accepted the contract – contracts. They all have to go.'

'You mentioned Saigon.'

'Bourne was part of the old Medusa,' admitted Ogilvie quietly. 'And like most of that crowd in the field a thieving misfit . . . It could be something as simple as his having recognized someone from twenty years ago. The story DeSole heard was that this trash Bourne – that's not his real name, incidentally – was actually trained by the Agency to pose as an international assassin for the purpose of drawing out a killer they call the Jackal. Ultimately, the strategy failed and Bourne was pensioned off – gold watch time: "Thanks for trying, old sport, but it's over now." Obviously, he wanted a great deal more than that so he came after us . . . You can see now, can't you? The two issues are completely separate; there's no linkage. One has nothing to do with the other.'

The Russian unclasped his hands and took a step forward away from the mantel. His expression was more one of concern than of alarm. 'Can you really be so blind, or is your vision so tunnelled that you see nothing but your enterprise?'

'I reject your insult out of hand. What the hell are you talking about?'

'The connection is there because it was engineered, created for one purpose only. You were merely a by-product, a side issue that suddenly became immensely important to the authorities.'

'I don't . . . understand,' whispered Ogilvie, his face growing pale.

'You just said "*a* killer they call the Jackal", and before that you alluded to Bourne as a relatively insignificant rogue agent trained to pose as an assassin, a strategy that failed, so he was pensioned off – "gold watch time", I believe you said.'

'It's what I was told—'

'And what else were you told about Carlos the Jackal? About the man who uses the name Jason Bourne? What do you *know* about them?'

'Very little, frankly. Two ageing killers, scum who've been stalking each other for years. Again, frankly, who gives a damn? My only concern is the complete confidentiality of our organization – which you've seen fit to question.'

'You still don't see, do you?'

'See *what*, for God's sake?'

'Bourne may not be the lowly scum you think he is, not when you consider his associates.'

'Please be clearer,' said Ogilvie in a flat monotone.

'He's using Medusa to hunt the Jackal.'

'Impossible! *That* Medusa was destroyed years ago in Saigon!'

'Obviously he thought otherwise. Would you care to remove your well-tailored jacket, roll up your sleeve, and display the small tattoo on your inner forearm?'

'No relevance! A mark of honour in a war no one supported but *we* had to fight!'

'Oh, come, Counsellor. From the piers and the supply depots in Saigon? Stealing your forces blind and routing couriers to the banks in Switzerland. Medals aren't issued for those heroics.'

'Pure speculation without foundation!' exclaimed Ogilvie.

'Tell that to Jason Bourne, a graduate of the original Snake Lady . . . Oh, yes, Counsellor, he looked for you and he found you and he's using you to go after the Jackal.'

'For Christ's sake, *how*?'

'I honestly don't know, but you'd better read these.' The consul general crossed rapidly to the hotel desk, picked up a sheaf of stapled, typewritten pages, and brought them over to Bryce Ogilvie. 'These are decoded telephone conversations that took place four hours ago at our embassy in Paris. The identities are established, the destinations as well. Read them carefully, Counsellor, then render me your legal opinion.'

The celebrated attorney, *the* Ice-Cold Ogilvie, grabbed the papers and with swift, practised eyes began reading. As he flipped from one page to another, the blood drained from his face to the pallor of death. 'My *God*, they know it all. My offices are *wired*! How? *Why?* It's insane! We're *impenetrable*!'

'Again, I suggest you tell that to Jason Bourne and his old friend and station chief from Saigon, Alexander Conklin. They found you.'

'They couldn't have!' roared Ogilvie. 'We paid off or eliminated everyone in Snake Lady who even suspected the extent of our activities. *Jesus*, there weren't that many and goddamned few in the field! I told you, they were scum and we knew better – they were the thieves of the world and wanted for crimes all over Australia and the Far East. The ones in combat we knew and we *reached*!'

'You missed a couple, I believe,' observed Sulikov.

The lawyer returned to the typed pages, beads of sweat breaking out at his hairline and rolling down his temples. 'God in heaven, I'm *ruined*,' he whispered, choking.

'The thought occurred to me,' said the Soviet consul general of New York, 'but then, there are always options, aren't there? . . . Naturally, there's only one course of action for us. Like much of the continent, we were taken in by ruthless, capitalist privateers. Lambs led to the slaughter on the altars of greed as this American cartel of financial plunderers cornered markets, selling inferior goods and services at inflated prices, claiming by way of false documents to have Washington's approval to deliver thousands of restricted items to us and our satellites.'

'You son of a *bitch*!' exploded Ogilvie. 'You – *all* of you – cooperated every step of the way. You brokered millions for us out of the bloc countries, rerouted, renamed – Christ, *repainted* – ships throughout the Mediterranean, the Aegean, up the Bosporus and into Marmara, to say nothing about ports in the Baltic!'

'Prove it, Counsellor,' said Sulikov, laughing quietly. 'If you wish, I could make a laudable case for your defection. Moscow would welcome your expertise.'

'*What?*' cried the attorney as panic spread across his face.

'Well, you certainly can't stay here an hour longer than absolutely necessary. Read those words, Mr Ogilvie. You're in the last stages of electronic surveillance before being picked up by the authorities.'

'Oh, my *God*—'

'You might try to operate from Hong Kong or Macao – they'd welcome your money, but with the problems they currently have with the Mainland's markets and the Sino-British Treaty of '97, they'd probably frown on your indictments. I'd say Switzerland's out; the reciprocal laws are so narrow these days, as Vesco found out. Ahh, Vesco. You could join him in Cuba.'

'*Stop it!*' yelled Ogilvie.

'Then again you could turn state's evidence; there's so much to unravel. They might even take, say, ten years off your thirty-year sentence.'

'Goddamn it, I'll *kill* you!'

The bedroom door suddenly opened as a consulate guard appeared, his hand menacingly under his jacket. The attorney had lurched to his feet; trembling helplessly, he returned to the chair and leaned forward, his head in his hands.

'Such behaviour would not be looked upon favourably,' said Sulikov. 'Come, Counsellor, it's a time for cool heads, not emotional outbursts.'

'How the hell can you say that?' asked Ogilvie, a catch in his voice, a prelude to tears. 'I'm *finished*.'

'That's a harsh judgement from such a resourceful man as you. I mean it. It's true you can't remain here but still your resources *are* immense. Act from that position of strength. Force concessions; it's the art of survival. Eventually the authorities will see the value of your contributions as they did with Boesky, Levine, and several dozen others who endure their minimal sentences playing tennis and backgammon while still possessing fortunes. Try it.'

'How?' said the lawyer, looking up at the Russian, his eyes red, pleading.

'The where comes first,' explained Sulikov. 'Find a neutral country that has no extradition treaty with Washington, one where there are officials who can be persuaded to grant you temporary residence so you can carry on your business activities – the term "temporary" is extremely elastic, of course. Bahrain, the Emirates, Morocco, Turkey, Greece – there's no lack of attractive possibilities. All with rich English-speaking settlements . . . We might even be able to help you, very quietly.'

'Why would you?'

'Your blindness returns, Mr Ogilvie. For a price, naturally . . . You have an extraordinary operation in Europe. It's in place and functioning, and under our control we could derive considerable benefits from it.'

'Oh . . . my . . . *God*,' said the leader of Medusa, his voice trailing off as he stared at the consul general.

'Do you really have a choice, Counsellor? . . . Come now, we must hurry. Arrangements have to be made. Fortunately, it's still early in the day.'

It was three twenty-five in the afternoon when Charles Casset walked into Peter Holland's office at the Central Intelligence Agency. 'Breakthrough,' said the deputy director, then added less enthusiastically, 'of sorts.'

'The Ogilvie firm?' asked the DCI.

'From left field,' replied Casset, nodding and placing several stock photographs on Holland's desk. 'These were faxed down from Kennedy Airport an hour ago. Believe me, it's been a heavy sixty minutes since then.'

'From Kennedy?' Frowning, Peter studied the facsimiled duplicates. They comprised a sequence of photographs showing a crowd of people passing through metal detectors in one of the airport's international terminals. The head of a single man was circled in red in each photo. 'What is it? Who is it?'

'They're passengers heading for the Aeroflot lounge, Moscow bound, Soviet carrier, of course. Security routinely photographs US nationals taking those flights.'

'So? Who is he?'

'Ogilvie himself.'

'*What?*'

'He's on the two o'clock nonstop to Moscow . . . Only he's not supposed to be.'

'Come again?'

'Three separate calls to his office came up with the same information. He was out of the country, in London, at the Dorchester, which we know he isn't. However, the Dorchester desk confirmed that he was booked but hadn't arrived, so they were taking messages.'

'I don't understand, Charlie.'

'It's a smoke screen and pretty hastily contrived. In the first place, why would someone as rich as Ogilvie settle for Aeroflot when he could be on the

Concorde to Paris and Air France to Moscow? Also, why would his office volunteer that he was either in or on his way to London when he was *heading* for Moscow?'

'The Aeroflot flight's obvious,' said Holland. 'It's the state airline and he's under Soviet protection. The London-Dorchester bit isn't too hard, either. It's to throw people off – my God, to throw *us* off!'

'Right on, master. So Valentino did some checking with all that fancy equipment in the cellars and guess what? . . . Mrs Ogilvie and their two teenage children are on a Royal Air Maroc flight to Casablanca with connections to Marrakesh.'

'Marrakesh? . . . Air Maroc – Morocco, *Marrakesh.* Wait a minute. In those computer sheets Conklin had us work up on the Mayflower hotel's registers, there was a woman – one of three people he tied to Medusa – who had been in Marrakesh.'

'I commend your memory, Peter. That woman and Ogilvie's wife were roommates at Bennington in the early seventies. Fine old families; their pedigrees ensure a large degree of sticking together and giving advice to one another.'

'Charlie, what the *hell* is going on?'

'The Ogilvies were tipped off and have gotten out. Also, if I'm not mistaken and if we could sort out several hundred accounts, we'd learn that millions have been transferred from New York to God knows where beyond these shores.'

'*And?*'

'Medusa's now in Moscow, Mr Director.'

34

Louis DeFazio wearily dragged his small frame out of the taxi in the Boulevard Masséna followed by his larger, heavier, far more muscular cousin Mario from Larchmont, New York. They stood on the pavement in front of a restaurant, its name in red-tubed script across a green tinted window: *Tetrazzini's.*

'This is the place,' said Louis. 'They'll be in a private room in the back.'

'It's pretty late.' Mario looked at his watch under the wash of a street lamp. 'I set the time for Paris; it's almost midnight here.'

'They'll wait.'

'You still haven't told me their names, Lou. What do we call them?'

'You don't,' answered DeFazio, starting for the entrance. 'No names – they wouldn't mean anything anyway. All you gotta do is be respectful, you know what I mean?'

'I don't have to be told that, Lou, I really don't,' reprimanded Mario in his soft-spoken voice. 'But for my own information, why do you even bring it up?'

'He's a high-class *diplomatico,*' explained the capo supremo, stopping briefly on the pavement and looking up at the man who had nearly killed Jason Bourne in Manassas, Virginia. 'He operates out of Rome from fancy government circles, but he's the direct contact with the dons in Sicily. He and his wife are very, *very* highly regarded, you understand what I'm saying?'

'I do and I don't,' admitted the cousin. 'If he's so grand, why would he accept such a menial assignment as following our targets?'

'Because he *can.* He can go places some of our *pagliacci* can't get near, you know what I mean? Also, I happen to let our people in New York know who our clients were, especially one, *capisce*? The dons all the way from Manhattan to the estates south of Palermo have a language they use exclusively between themselves, did you know that, *cugino*? . . . It comes down to a couple of orders: "Do it" and "Don't do it".'

'I think I understand, Lou. We render respect.'

'Respect, *yes,* my fancy rendering cousin, but not no weakness, *capisce*? No weakness! The word's got to go up and down the line that this is an operation Lou DeFazio took control of and ran from beginning to end. You *got* that?'

'If that's the case, maybe I can go home to Angie and the kids,' said Mario, grinning.

'What? . . . You shut up, *cugino*! With this one job you got annuities for your whole passel of *bambini.*'

'Not a passel, Lou, just five.'

'Let's go. Remember, respect, but we don't take no shit.'

The small private dining room was a miniature version of Tetrazzini's decor. The ambience was Italian in all things. The walls were papered with dated, now-faded murals of Venice, Rome and Florence; the softly piped-in music was predominantly operatic arias and tarantellas, and the lighting indirect with pockets of shadows. If a patron did not know he was in Paris, he might think he was dining on Rome's Via Frascati, at one of the many commercialized family *ristoranti* lining that ancient street.

There was a large round table in the centre covered by a deep red tablecloth, with a generous overhang, and four chairs equidistant from one another. Additional chairs were against the walls, allowing for an expanded conference of principals or for the proper location of secondary subalterns, usually armed. Seated at the far end of the table was a distinguished-looking olive-skinned man with wavy dark hair; on his left was a fashionably dressed, well-coiffed middle-aged woman. A bottle of Chianti Classico was between them, the crude thick-stemmed wineglasses in front of them not the sort one would associate with such aristocratic diners. On a chair behind the *diplomatico* was a black leather suitcase.

'I'm DeFazio,' said the capo supremo from New York, closing the door. 'This is my cousin Mario, who you may have heard of – a very talented man who takes precious time away from his family to be with us.'

'Yes, of course,' said the aristocratic mafioso. 'Mario, *il boia, esecuzione garantito* – deadly with any weapon. Sit down, gentlemen.'

'I find such descriptions meaningless,' responded Mario, approaching a chair. 'I'm skilled in my craft, that's all.'

'Spoken like a professional, signore,' added the woman as DeFazio and his cousin sat down. 'May I order you wine, drinks?' she continued.

'Not yet,' replied Louis. 'Maybe later – maybe . . . My talented relative on my mother's side, may she rest in the arms of Christ, asked a good question outside. What do we call you, Mr and Mrs Paris, France? Which is by way of saying I don't need no real names.'

'*Conte* and *Contessa* is what we're known by,' answered the husband smiling, the tight smile more appropriate to a mask than a human face.

'See what I mean, *cugino*? These are people of high regard . . . So, Mr Count, bring us up to date, how about it?'

'There's no question about it, Signor DeFazio,' replied the Roman, his voice as tight as his previous smile, which had completely disappeared. 'I will bring you up to date, and were it in my powers I would leave you in the far distant past.'

'Hey, what kind of fuckin' talk is that?'

'Lou, *please*!' intruded Mario, quietly but firmly. 'Watch your language.'

'What about *his* language? What kind of language is that? He wants to leave me in some kind of *dirt*?'

'You asked me what has happened, Signor DeFazio, and I'm telling you,' said the count, his voice as strained as before. 'Yesterday at noon my wife and I were nearly killed – *killed*, Signor DeFazio. It's not the sort of experience we're used to or can tolerate. Have you any idea what you've gotten yourself *into*?'

'You . . . ? They *marked* you?'

'If you mean by that, did they know who we were, happily they did not. Had they known, it's doubtful we'd be sitting at this table!'

'Signor DeFazio,' interrupted the contessa, glancing at her husband, her look telling him to calm down. 'The word we received over here is that you have a contract on this cripple and his friend, the doctor. Is that true?'

'Yeah,' confirmed the capo supremo cautiously. 'As far as that goes but it goes further, you know what I mean?'

'I haven't the vaguest idea,' replied the count icily.

'I tell you this because it's possible I could use your help, for which, like I told you, you'll be paid good, real good.'

'How does the contract go "further"?' asked the wife, again interrupting.

'There's someone else we have to hit. A third party these two came over here to meet.'

The count and his countess instantly looked at each other. 'A "third party",' repeated the man from Rome, raising the wine glass to his lips. 'I see . . . A three target contract is generally quite profitable. *How* profitable, Signor DeFazio?'

'Hey, come on, do I ask you what you make a week in Paris, France? Let's just say it's a lot and you two personally can count on six figures, if everything goes according to the book.'

'Six figures encompass a wide spectrum,' observed the countess. 'It also indicates that the contract is worth over seven figures.'

'*Seven* . . . ?' DeFazio looked at the woman, his breathing on hold.

'Over a million dollars,' concluded the countess.

'Yeah, well, you see, it's important to our clients that these people leave this world,' said Louis, breathing again as seven figures had not been equated with seven million. 'We don't ask why, we just do the job. In situations like this, our dons are generous; we keep most of the money and "our thing" keeps its reputation for efficiency. Isn't that right, Mario?'

'I'm sure it is, Lou, but I don't involve myself in those matters.'

'You get paid, don't you, *cugino*?'

'I wouldn't be here if I didn't, Lou.'

'See what I mean?' said DeFazio, looking at the aristocrats of the European Mafia, who showed no reaction at all except to stare at the capo supremo, 'Hey, what's the matter? . . . Oh, this bad thing that happened yesterday, huh? What was it – they saw you, *right*? They spotted you and some gorilla got off a couple of shots to scare you away, that's it, isn't it? I mean what else could it be, right? They didn't know who you were but you were there – a couple of times too often, maybe – so a little muscle was used, okay? It's an old scam: Scare the shit out of strangers you see more than once.'

'Lou, I asked you to temper your language.'

'Temper? I'm *losing* my temper. I want to deal!'

'In plain words,' said the count, disregarding DeFazio's words with a soft voice and arched brows, 'you say you must kill this cripple and his friend the doctor, as well as a third party, is that correct?'

'In plain words, you got it right.'

'Do you know who this third party is – outside of a photograph or a detailed description?'

'Sure, he's a government slime who was sent out years ago to make like he was a Mario here, an *esecuzione*, can you believe it? But these three individuals have injured our clients, I mean really *hurt* them. That's why the contract, what else can I tell you?'

'We're not sure,' said the countess, gracefully sipping her wine. 'Perhaps you don't really know.'

'Know what?'

'Know that there is someone else who wants this third party dead far more than you do,' explained the count. 'Yesterday noon he assaulted a small café in the countryside with murderous gunfire, killing a number of people, because your third party was inside. So were we . . . We saw them – *him* – warned by a guard and race outside. Certain emergencies are communicated. We left immediately, only minutes before the massacre.'

'*Condannare!*' choked DeFazio. 'Who is this bastard who wants the kill? *Tell* me!'

'We've spent yesterday afternoon and all day today trying to find out,' began the woman, leaning forward, delicately fingering the indelicate glass as though it were an affront to her sensibilities. 'Your targets are never alone. There are always men around them, armed guards, and at first we didn't know where they came for them, and the Avenue Montaigne we saw a Soviet limousine come for them, and your third man in the company of a well-known KGB officer, and now we think we *do* know.'

'Only you, however,' broke in the count, 'can confirm it for us. What is the name of this third man on your contract? Surely we have a right to know.'

'Why not? He's a loser named Bourne, Jason Bourne, who's blackmailing our clients.'

'*Ecco*,' said the husband quietly.

'*Ultimo*,' added the wife. 'What do you know of this Bourne?' she asked.

'What I told you. He went out under cover for the government and got shafted by the big boys in Washington. He gets pissed off, so he ends up shafting our clients. A real slime.'

'You've never heard of Carlos the Jackal?' said the count, leaning back in the chair, studying the capo supremo.

'Oh, yeah, sure, I heard of him, and I see what you mean. They say this Jackal character has a big thing against this Bourne and vice versa, but it don't cut no ice with me. You know, I thought that fox-cat was just in books, in the movies, you know what I mean? Then they tell me he's a real hit man, wadda y' know?'

'Very real,' agreed the countess.

'But like I said, him I couldn't care less about. I want the Jew shrink, the cripple, and this rot-gut Bourne, that's all. And I *really* want them.'

The diplomat and his wife looked at each other; they shrugged in mild astonishment, then the *contessa* nodded, deferring to her husband. 'Your sense of fiction has been shattered by reality,' said the count.

'Come again?'

'There *was* a Robin Hood, you know, but he wasn't a noble of Locksley. He was a barbaric Saxon chief who opposed the Normans, a murdering, butchering thief, extolled only in legends. And there *was* an Innocent the Third, a pope who was hardly innocent and who followed the savage policies of a predecessor, Saint Gregory the Seventh, who was hardly a saint. Between them they split Europe asunder, into rivers of blood for political power and to enrich the coffers of the "Holy Empire". Centuries before there *was* the gentle Quintus Cassius Longinus of Rome, beloved protector of the Further Spain, yet he tortured and mutilated a hundred thousand Spaniards.'

'What the *hell* are you talkin' about?'

'These men were fictionalized, Signor DeFazio, into many different shadings of what they may actually have been, but regardless of the distortions, they were real. Just as the Jackal is real, and is a deadly problem for you. As, unfortunately, he is a problem for us, for he's a complication we cannot accept.'

'*Huh?*' The capo supremo, mouth gaping, stared at the Italian aristocrat.

'The presence of the Soviets was both alarming and enigmatic,' continued the count. 'Then finally we perceived a possible connection which you just confirmed . . . Moscow has been hunting Carlos for years, solely for the purpose of executing him, and all they've gotten for their efforts is one dead hunter after another. Somehow – God *knows* how – Jason Bourne negotiated with the Russians to pursue their common objective.'

'For Christ's sake, speak English *or* Italian, but with words that make sense! I didn't exactly go to Harvard City College, gumball. I didn't have to, *capisce*?'

'The Jackal stormed that country inn yesterday. He's the one hunting down Jason Bourne, who was foolish enough to come back to Paris and persuade the Soviets to work with him. Both were stupid, for this *is* Paris and Carlos will win. He'll kill Bourne and your other targets and laugh at the Russians. Then he'll proclaim to the clandestine departments of all governments that he *has* won, that he's the *padrone*, the *maestro*. You in America have never been exposed to the whole story, only bits and pieces, for your interest in Europe stops at the money line. But we have lived through it, watching in fascination, and now we are mesmerized. Two ageing master assassins obsessed with hatred, each wanting only to cut the other's throat.'

'Hey, back up, gumball!' shouted DeFazio. 'This slime Bourne's a fake, a *contraffazione*. He never *was* an executioner!'

'You're quite wrong, signore,' said the countess. 'He may not have entered the arena with a gun, but it became his favourite instrument. Ask the Jackal.'

'*Fuck* the Jackal!' cried DeFazio, getting up from the chair.

'*Lou!*'

'Shut *up*, Mario! This Bourne is *mine*, ours! *We* deliver the corpse, *we* take the pictures with me – *us* – standing over all three with a dozen ice picks in their bodies, their heads pulled up by the hair, so nobody can say it ain't our kills!'

'Now you're the one who's *pazzo*,' said the Mafia count quietly, in counterpoint to the capo supremo's raucous yelling. 'And please keep your voice down.'

'Then don't get me excited—'

'He's trying to explain things, Lou,' said DeFazio's relative, the killer. 'I want to hear what the gentleman has to say because it could be vital to my approach. Sit *down*, cousin.' Louis sat down. 'Please continue, Count.'

'Thank you, Mario. You don't object to my calling you Mario.'

'Not at all, sir.'

'Perhaps you should visit Rome—'

'Perhaps we should get back to *Paris*,' again choked the capo supremo.

'Very well,' agreed the Roman, now dividing his attention between DeFazio and his cousin, but favouring the latter. 'You might take out all three targets with a long-range rifle but you won't get near the bodies. The Soviet guards will be indistinguishable from any other people in the area, and if they see the two of you coming in to the killing ground, they'll open fire, assuming you're from the Jackal.'

'Then we must create a diversion where we can isolate the targets,' said Mario, his elbows on the table, his intelligent eyes on the count. 'Perhaps an emergency in the early hours of the morning. A fire in their lodgings, perhaps, that necessitates their coming outside. I've done it before; in the confusion of fire trucks and police sirens and the general panic, one can pull targets away and complete the assignments.'

'It's a fine strategy, Mario, but there are still the Soviet guards.'

'We take them out!' cried DeFazio.

'You are only two men,' said the diplomat, 'and there are at least three in Barbizon, to say nothing of the hotel in Paris where the cripple and the doctor are staying.'

'So we outmatch the numbers.' The capo supremo pulled the back of his hand over the sweat that had gathered on his forehead. 'We hit this Barbizon first, *right*?'

'With only two men?' asked the countess, her cosmeticized eyes wide in surprise.

'*You* got men!' exclaimed DeFazio. 'We'll use a few . . . I'll pay additional.'

The count shook his head slowly and spoke softly. 'We will not go to war with the Jackal,' he said. 'Those are my instructions.'

'Fairy *bastards*!'

'An interesting comment coming from you,' observed the countess, a thin insulting smile on her lips.

'Perhaps our dons are not as generous as yours,' continued the diplomat. 'We are willing to cooperate up to a point but no further.'

'You'll never make another shipment to New York, *or* Philly, *or* Chicago!'

'We'll let our superiors debate those issues, won't we?' There was a sudden knocking at the door, four raps in a row, harsh and intrusive. '*Avanti*,' called out the count, instantly reaching under his jacket and ripping an automatic out of his belt; he lowered it beneath the overhang of the red tablecloth and smiled as the manager of Tetrazzini's entered.

'*Emergenza*,' said the grossly overweight man, walking rapidly to the well-tailored mafioso and handing him a note.

'*Grazie*.'

'*Prego*,' replied the manager, crossing back to the door and exiting as quickly as he had arrived.

'The anxious gods of Sicily may be smiling down on you after all,' said the count, reading. 'This communication is from the man following your targets. They are outside Paris and they are alone, and for reasons I cannot possibly explain, there are no guards. They have no protection.'

'*Where?*' cried DeFazio, leaping to his feet.

Without answering, the diplomat calmly reached for his gold lighter, ignited it, and fired the small piece of paper, lowering it into an ashtray. Mario sprang up from his chair; the man from Rome dropped the lighter on the table and swiftly retrieved the gun from his lap. 'First, let us discuss the fee,' he said as the note coiled into flaming black ash. 'Our dons in Palermo are definitely not as generous as yours. Please talk quickly, as every minute counts.'

'You motherfucking *bastard*!'

'My Oedipal problems are not your concern. How much, Signor DeFazio?'

'I'll go the limit,' replied the capo supremo, lowering himself into the chair, staring at the charred remnants of the information. 'Three hundred thousand, American. That's it.'

'That's *excremento*,' said the countess. 'Try again. Seconds become minutes and you cannot afford them.'

'All right, all *right*! Double it!'

'Plus expenses,' added the woman.

'What the fuck can *they* be?'

'Your cousin Mario is right,' said the diplomat. 'Please watch your language in front of my wife.'

'Holy *shit*—'

'I warned you, signore. The expenses are an additional quarter of a million, American.'

'What are you, *nuts*?'

'No, you're vulgar. The total is one million one hundred fifty thousand dollars, to be paid as our couriers in New York so instruct you . . . If not, you will be missed in – what is it? – Brooklyn Heights, Signor DeFazio?'

'Where are the targets?' said the beaten capo supremo, his defeat painful to him.

'At a small private airfield in Pontcarré, about forty-five minutes from Paris. They're waiting for a plane that was grounded in Poitiers due to bad weather. It can't possibly arrive for at least an hour and a quarter.'

'Did you bring the equipment we requested?' asked Mario rapidly.

'It's all there,' answered the countess, gesturing at the large black suitcase on a chair against the wall.

'A car, a *fast* car!' cried DeFazio as his executioner retrieved the suitcase.

'Outside,' replied the count. 'The driver will know where to take you. He's been to that field.'

'Come on, *cugino*. Tonight we collect and you can settle a score!'

Except for a single clerk behind the counter in the small one-room terminal and an air controller hired to stay the extra hours in the radio tower, the private airport in Pontcarré was deserted. Alex Conklin and Mo Panov stayed discreetly behind as Bourne led Marie outside to the gate area fronting the field beyond a waist-high metal fence. Two strips of receding amber ground lights defined the long runway for the plane from Poitiers; they had been turned on only a short time ago.

'It won't be long now,' said Jason.

'This whole damn thing's stupid,' retorted Webb's wife. '*Everything.*'

'There's no reason for you to stay and every reason for you to leave. For you to be alone here in Paris would be stupid. Alex is right. If Carlos's people found you, you'd be taken hostage, so why risk it?'

'Because I'm capable of staying out of sight and I don't want to be ten thousand miles away from you. You'll forgive me if I worry about you, Mr *Bourne.* And care for you.'

Jason looked at her in the shadows, grateful for the darkness; she could not clearly see his eyes. 'Then be reasonable and use your head,' he said coldly, suddenly feeling so old, too old for such a transparently false lack of feeling. 'We know Carlos is in Moscow and Krupkin isn't far behind him. Dimitri's flying us there in the morning, and we'll be under the protection of the KGB in the tightest city in the world. What more could we want?'

'You were under the protection of the United States government on a short East Side block in New York thirteen years ago and it didn't do you much good.'

'There's a great deal of difference. Back then the Jackal knew exactly where I was going and when I'd be there. Right now he has no idea we even know he's in Moscow. He's got other problems, big ones for him, and he thinks we're here in Paris – he's ordered his people to keep searching for us.'

'What will you do in Moscow?'

'We won't know until we get there, but whatever it is, it's better than here in Paris. Krupkin's been busy. Every ranking officer in Dzerzhinsky Square who speaks French is being watched and is under surveillance. He said the French narrowed down the possibilities and that something should break . . . Something *will* break; the odds are on our side. And when it does, I can't be worried about you back here.'

'That's the nicest thing you've said in the past thirty-six hours.'

'So be it. You should be with the children and you know that. You'll be out of reach and safe . . . and the kids need you. Mrs Cooper's a terrific lady but she's not their mother. Besides, your brother probably has Jamie smoking his Cuban cigars and playing Monopoly with real money by now.'

Marie looked up at her husband, a gentle smile apparent in the darkness as well as in her voice. 'Thanks for the laugh. I need it.'

'It's probably the truth – your brother, I mean. If there are good-looking women on the staff, it's quite possible our son's lost his virginity.'

'*David!*' Bourne was silent. Marie chuckled briefly, then went on. 'I suppose I really can't argue with you.'

'And you would if my argument was flawed, Dr St Jacques. That's something I've learned over the past thirteen years.'

'I still object to this *crazy* trip back to Washington! From here to Marseilles, then to London, *then* on a flight to Dulles. It'd be so much simpler just to get on a plane from Orly to the States.'

'It's Peter Holland's idea. He'll meet you himself so ask him; he doesn't say an awful lot on the phone. I suspect he doesn't want to deal with the French authorities for fear of a leak to Carlos's people. A single woman with a common name on crowded flights is probably best.'

'I'll spend more time sitting in airports than in the air.'

'Probably, so cover those great legs of yours and carry a Bible.'

'That's sweet,' said Marie, touching his face. 'I suddenly hear you, David.'

'What?' Again Bourne did not respond to the warmth.

'Nothing . . . Do me a favour, will you?'

'What is it?' asked Jason, in a distant monotone.

'Bring that David back to me.'

'Let's get an update on the plane,' said Bourne, his voice flat and abrupt as he touched her elbow and led her back inside. *I'm getting older – old – and I cannot be what I am not much longer. The Chameleon is slipping away; the imagination isn't there the way it used to be. But I cannot stop! Not now! Get away from me, David Webb!*

No sooner had they re-entered the small terminal than the telephone on the counter rang. The lone clerk picked it up. '*Oui?*' He listened for no more than five seconds. '*Merci*,' he said, hanging up and addressing the four interested parties in French. 'That was the tower. The plane from Poitiers will be on the ground in approximately four minutes. The pilot requests that you be ready, madame, as he would like to fly ahead of the weather front moving east.'

'So would I,' agreed Marie, rushing to Alex Conklin and Mo Panov. The farewells were brief, the embraces strong, the words heartfelt. Bourne led his wife back outside. 'I just remembered – where are Krupkin's guards?' she asked as Jason unlatched the gate and they walked towards the lighted runway.

'We don't need them or want them,' he answered. 'The Soviet connection was made in the Montaigne, so we have to assume the embassy's being watched. No guards rushing out into cars, therefore no movement on our part for Carlos's people to report.'

'I see.' The sound of a small decelerating jet could be heard as the plane circled the airfield once and made its descent onto the four-thousand-foot runway. 'I love you so much, David,' said Marie, raising her voice to be heard over the roar of the aircraft, rolling towards them.

'He loves you so much,' said Bourne, images colliding in his mind. '*I* love you so much.'

The jet loomed clearly into view between the rows of amber lights, a white bulletlike machine with short delta wings sweeping back from the fuselage, giving it the appearance of an angry flying insect. The pilot swung the plane around in a circle, coming to a jarring stop as the automatic passenger door sprang out and up while metal steps slapped down to the ground. Jason and Marie ran towards the jet's entrance.

It happened with the sudden impact of a murderous wind shear, at once unstoppable, enveloping, the swirling winds of death! *Gunfire.* Automatic weapons – two of them; one nearby, one farther away – shattering windows, ripping into wood, a piercing screech of pain erupting from the terminal, announcing a mortal hit.

With both hands Bourne gripped Marie by the waist, heaving her up and propelling her into the plane as he shouted to the pilot. 'Shut the door and get *out* of here!'

'*Mon Dieu!*' cried the man from the open flight deck. '*Allez-vous-en!* (Escape! Get away!)' he roared, ordering Jason away from the spring-hinged door and the metal steps, gunning the jet's engine as the plane lurched forward. Jason plunged to the ground and raised his eyes. Marie's face was pressed against the window; she was screaming hysterically. The plane thundered down the runway; it was free.

Bourne was not. He was caught in the wash of the amber lights, the glowing rows a cyclorama of yellowish orange. No matter where he stood or knelt or crouched he was in silhouette. So he pulled out the automatic from his belt, the weapon, he reflected, given to him by Bernardine, and began slithering, snaking his way across the asphalt towards the bordering grass outside the fenced-gate area.

The gunfire erupted again, but now they were three scattered single shots from within the terminal, where the lights had been extinguished. They had to have come from Conklin's gun, or possibly the clerk's if he had a weapon; Panov did not. Then who had been hit? . . . No *time*! A shattering fusillade burst out of the nearer automatic rifle; it was steady, prolonged and deadly, spraying the side of the small building and the gate area.

Then the second automatic weapon commenced firing; from the sound it was on the opposite side of the terminal's waiting room. Moments later there were two single shots, the last one accompanied by a scream . . . again on the other side of the building.

'I've been hit!' The voice was the cry of a man in pain . . . on the *other side* of the *building*. The automatic rifle! Jason slowly rose to a low crouch in the grass and peered into the darkness. A fragment of blacker darkness moved. He raised his automatic and fired into the moving mass, getting to his feet and racing across the gate area, turning and squeezing the trigger until he was both out of bullets and out of sight on the east side of the building, where the runway ended and the amber lights stopped. He crawled cautiously to the section of the waist-high fence that paralleled the corner of the small terminal. The greyish-white gravel of the parking area was a gratifying sight; he was able to make out the figure of a man writhing on the stones. The figure gripped a weapon in his hands, then pushing it into the gravel, raised himself to a half-sitting position.

'*Cugino!*' he screamed. 'Help me!' His answer was another burst of gunfire from the west side of the building, diagonally to the right of the wounded man. 'Holy Christ!' he shrieked. 'I'm hit *bad*!' Again the reply was yet another fusillade from the automatic rifle, these rounds simultaneous with crashing glass. The killer on the west side of the building had smashed the windows and was blowing apart everything inside.

Bourne dropped the useless automatic and grabbed the top of the fence, vaulting over it, his left leg landing in agony on the ground. *What's happened to me? Why do I hurt? Goddamn it!* He limped to the wood-framed corner of the building and edged his face to the open space beyond. The figure on the gravel fell back, unable to support himself on the automatic rifle. Jason felt the ground, found a large rock, and threw it with all his strength beyond the wounded man. It crashed, bouncing into the gravel, for an instant like the sound of approaching footsteps. The killer spastically rose and spun his body to the rear, gripping his weapon, which twice fell out of his grasp.

Now! Bourne raced across the stones of the parking lot and lunged off his feet down into the man with the gun. He tore the weapon from the killer's grip and crashed the metal stock into his skull. The short, slender man went limp. And, again, suddenly, there was another crescendo of gunfire from the west exterior of the terminal building, again accompanied by the shattering of glass. The first and nearer killer was narrowing down his targets. *He had to be stopped!* thought Jason, his breath gone, every muscle in his body in pain. *Where was the man from yesterday? Where was Delta from Medusa? The Chameleon from Treadstone Seventy-one?* Where *was* that man?

Bourne grabbed the MAC-10 submachine gun from the unconscious figure on the gravel and raced towards the side door of the terminal.

'*Alex!*' he roared. 'Let me *in*! I've got the weapon!'

The door crashed open. 'My God, you're alive!' shouted Conklin in the darkness of the shadows as Jason ran inside. 'Mo's in bad shape – he was shot in the chest. The clerk's dead and we can't raise the tower out on the field. They must have reached it first.' Alex slammed the door shut. 'Get down on the floor!' A fusillade raked the walls. Bourne got to his knees and fired back, then threw himself down beside Conklin.

'What *happened*?' cried Jason, breathless, his voice strained, the sweat dripping down his face and stinging his eyes.

'The Jackal happened.'

'How did he *do* it?'

'He fooled us all. You, me, Krupkin, and Lavier – worst of all *me*. He sent the word out that he'd be away, no explanation even with you here in Paris, just that he'd be gone for a while. We thought the trap had worked; everything pointed to Moscow . . . He sucked us into his own trap. Oh, Christ, did he suck us in! I should have known better, I should have seen through it! It was too clean . . . I'm sorry, David. Oh, God, I'm sorry!'

'That's *him* out there, isn't it? He wants the kill all to himself – nothing else matters to him.'

Suddenly a flashlight, its powerful beam blinding, was thrown through a shattered window. Instantly, Bourne raised the MAC-10 and blew the shiny metal tube away, extinguishing the light. The damage, however, had been done; their bodies had been seen.

'Over *here*!' screamed Alex, grabbing Jason and diving behind the counter as a murderous barrage came from the blurred silhouette in the window. It stopped; there was the crack of a bolt.

'He has to *reload*!' whispered Bourne, with the break in the fire. '*Stay* here!' Jason stood up and raced to the gate doors, crashing through them, his weapon gripped in his right hand, his body prone, tense, prepared to kill – if the years would permit it. They *had* to permit it!

He crawled through the gate he had opened for Marie and spun on the ground to his right, scrambling along the fence. He *was* Delta – of Saigon's *Medusa* . . . he could *do* it! There was no friendly jungle now, but there was everything he could use – *Delta* could use – the darkness, the intermittent blocks of shadows from the myriad clouds intercepting the moonlight. Use *everything*! It was what you were trained to use . . . so many years ago – so many. Forget it, forget time! *Do* it! The animal only yards away wants you dead – your wife dead, your children dead. *Dead!*

It was the quickness born of pure fury that propelled him, obsessed him, and he knew that to win he had to win quickly, with all the speed that was in him. He crept swiftly along the fence that enclosed the airfield, and past the corner of the terminal, prepared for the instant of exposure. The lethal submachine gun was still gripped in his hand, his index finger now on the trigger. There was a cluster of wild shrubbery preceding two thick trees no more than thirty feet away; if he could reach them, the advantage was his. He would have the 'high ground', the Jackal in the valley of death, if only because he was behind the assassin and unseen.

He reached the shrubbery. And at that moment he heard a massive smashing of glass followed by yet another fusillade – this time so prolonged that the entire magazine had to be emptied. He had *not* been seen; the figure by the window had backed away to reload, his concentration on that task, not on the possibility of an escape. Carlos, too, was growing old and losing his finesse, thought Jason Bourne. Where were the flares intrinsic to such an operation? Where were the alert, roving eyes that loaded weapons in total darkness?

Darkness. A cloud cover blocked the yellow rays of the moon; there *was* darkness. He vaulted over the fence, concealing himself behind the shrubbery, then raced to the first of the two trees where he could stand upright, view the scene, and consider his options.

Something was wrong. There was a primitiveness he could not associate with the Jackal. The assassin had isolated the terminal, *ad valorem*, and the price was high, but there was an absence of the finer points of the deadly equation. The subtlety was not there; instead, there was a brute force, hardly to be denied, but not when employed against the man they called Jason Bourne who had escaped from the trap.

The figure by the shattered window had spent his ammunition; he reeled back against the building, pulling another magazine out of his pocket. Jason raced out of the cover of the trees, his MAC-10 on automatic fire, exploding the dirt in front of the killer, then circling the bullets around his frame.

'That's *it*!' he shouted, closing in on the assassin. 'You're dead, *Carlos*, with one pull of my finger – if you *are* the Jackal!'

The man by the shattered window threw down his weapon. 'I am not he, Mr Bourne,' said the executioner from Larchmont, New York. 'We've met before but I am not the person you think I am.'

'Hit the ground, you son of a bitch!' The killer did so as Jason approached. 'Spread your legs and your arms!' The command was obeyed. 'Raise your *head*!'

The man did so and Bourne stared at the face, vaguely illuminated by the distant glow of the amber lights on the airfield's runway. 'You see now?' said Mario. 'I'm not who you think I am.'

'My *God*,' whispered Jason, his incredulity all too apparent. 'You were in the driveway in Manassas, Virginia. You tried to kill Cactus, then *me*!'

'Contracts, Mr Bourne, nothing more.'

'What about the tower? The air controller here in the *tower*!'

'I do not kill indiscriminately. Once the plane from Poitiers was given clearance to land, I told him to leave . . . Forgive me, but your wife was also on the list. Fortunately, as she is a mother, it was beyond my abilities.'

'Who the hell *are* you?'

'I just told you. A contract employee.'

'I've seen better.'

'I'm not, perhaps, in your league, but I serve my organization well.'

'Jesus, you're *Medusa*!'

'I've heard the name but that's all I can tell you . . . Let me make one thing clear, Mr Bourne. I will not leave my wife a widow, or my children orphans for the sake of a contract. That position simply isn't viable. They mean too much to me.'

'You'll spend a hundred and fifty years in prison, and that's only if you're prosecuted in a state that doesn't have the death penalty.'

'Not with what I know, Mr Bourne. My family and I will be well taken care of – a new name, perhaps a nice farm in the Dakotas or Wyoming. You see, I knew this moment had to come.'

'What's come now, you *bastard*, is that a friend of mine inside there is shot up! You *did* it!'

'A truce, then?' said Mario.

'What the hell do you mean by that?'

'I have a very fast car a half mile away.' The killer from Larchmont, New York, pulled a square instrument from his belt. 'It can be here in less than a minute. I'm sure the driver knows the nearest hospital.'

'*Do* it!'

'It's done, Jason Bourne,' said Mario, pressing a button.

Morris Panov had been rolled into the operating room; Louis DeFazio was still on a gurney, as it was determined that his wound was superficial. And through back-channel negotiations between Washington and Quai d'Orsay, the criminal known only as Mario was securely in the custody of the American embassy in Paris.

A white-frocked doctor came out into the hospital's waiting room; both Conklin and Bourne got to their feet, frightened. 'I will not pretend to be a bearer of glad tidings,' said the physician in French, 'for it would be quite wrong. Both lungs of your friend were punctured, as well as the wall of his heart. He has at best a forty-sixty chance of survival – against him, I'm afraid.

Still, he is a strong-willed man who wants to live. At times that means more than all the medical negatives. What else can I tell you?'

'Thank you, Doctor.' Jason turned away.

'I have to use a telephone,' said Alex to the surgeon. 'I should go to our embassy but I haven't the time. Do I have any guarantee that I won't be tapped, overheard?'

'I imagine you have every guarantee,' replied the physician. 'We wouldn't know how to do it. Use my office, please.'

'Peter?'

'*Alex!*' cried Holland from Langley, Virginia. 'Everything go all right? Did Marie get off?'

'To answer your first question, no, everything did not go all right; and as far as Marie goes, you can expect a panicked phone call from her the minute she reaches Marseilles. That pilot won't touch his radio.'

'What?'

'Tell her we're okay, that David's not hurt—'

'What are you *talking* about?' broke in the director of Central Intelligence.

'We were ambushed while waiting for the plane from Poitiers. I'm afraid Mo Panov's in bad shape, so bad I don't want to think about it right now. We're in a hospital and the doctor's not encouraging.'

'Oh, God, Alex, I'm *sorry*.'

'In his way, Mo's a fighter. I'll still bet on him. Incidentally, don't tell Marie. She thinks too much.'

'Of course not. Is there anything I can do?'

'Yes, there is, Peter. You can tell me why Medusa's here in Paris.'

'In *Paris*? It's not according to everything I know and I know a hell of a lot.'

'Our identification's positive. The two guns that hit us an hour ago were sent over by Medusa. We've even got a confession of sorts.'

'I don't *understand*!' protested Holland. 'Paris never entered into our thinking. There's no linkage in the scenario.'

'Sure there is,' contradicted the former station chief. 'You said it yourself. You called it a self-fulfilling prophecy, remember? The ultimate logic that Bourne conceived as a theory. Medusa joining up with the Jackal, the target Jason Bourne.'

'That's the point, Alex. It *was* only a theory, hypothetically convincing, but still just a theory, the basis for a sound strategy. But it never happened.'

'It obviously did.'

'Not from this end. As far as we're concerned, Medusa's now in Moscow.'

'*Moscow?*' Conklin nearly dropped the phone on the doctor's desk.

'That's right. We've concentrated on Ogilvie's law firm in New York, tapping everything that could be tapped. Somehow – and we don't know how – Ogilvie was tipped off and got out of the country. He took an Aeroflot to Moscow, and the rest of his family headed to Marrakesh.'

'Ogilvie . . . ?' Alex could barely be heard; frowning, his memory peeled away the years. 'From Saigon? A legal officer from *Saigon*?'

'That's right. We're convinced he runs Medusa.'

'And you withheld that information from me?'

'Only the name of the firm. I told you we had our priorities and you had yours. For us, Medusa came first.'

'You simple swab-jockey!' exploded Conklin. 'I *know* Ogilvie – more precisely, I *knew* him. Let me tell you what they called him in Saigon: Ice-Cold Ogilvie, the smoothest-talking legal scumball in Vietnam. With a few subpoenas and some research, I could have told you where a few of his courtroom skeletons were buried – you blew it! You could have pulled him in for fixing the army courts in a couple of killings – there are no statutes, civilian or military, on those crimes. Jesus, why didn't you *tell* me?'

'In all honesty, Alex, you never asked. You simply assumed – rightly so – that I wouldn't tell you.'

'All right, all right, it's done; to hell with it. By tomorrow or the next day you'll have our two Medusans, so go to work on them. They both want to save their asses – the capo's a slime, but his sharpshooter keeps praying for his family and it's not organizational.'

'What are you going to do?' pressed Holland.

'We're on our way to Moscow.'

'After *Ogilvie*?'

'No, the Jackal. But if I see Bryce, I'll give him your regards.'

35

Buckingham Pritchard sat next to his uniformed uncle, Cyril Sylvester Pritchard, deputy director of immigration, in the office of Sir Henry Sykes at Government House in Montserrat. Beside them, on the deputy's right, was their attorney, the finest native solicitor Sykes could persuade to advise the Pritchards in the event that the Crown brought a case against them as accessories to terrorism. Sir Henry sat behind the desk and glanced in partial shock at the lawyer, one Jonathan Lemuel, who raised his head and eyes to the ceiling, not to have the benefit of the tropic fan that stirred the humid air, but to show disbelief. Lemuel was a Cambridge-educated attorney, once a 'scholarship boy' from the colonies, who years ago had made his money in London and returned in the autumn of his life to his native 'Serrat to enjoy the fruits of his labours. Actually, Sir Henry had persuaded his retired black friend to give assistance to a couple of idiots who might have involved themselves in a serious international matter.

The cause of Sir Henry's shock and Jonathan Lemuel's disbelief cum exasperation came about through the following exchange between Sykes and the deputy director of immigration.

'Mr Pritchard, we've established that your nephew overheard a telephone conversation between John St Jacques and his brother-in-law, the American, Mr David Webb. Further, your nephew Buckingham Pritchard here, freely, even enthusiastically, admits calling you with certain information contained in that conversation and that you in turn emphatically stated that you had to reach Paris immediately. Is this true?'

'It is all *completely* true, Sir Henry.'

'Whom did you reach in Paris? What's the telephone number?'

'With respect, sir, I am sworn to secrecy.'

At that succinct and totally unexpected reply, Jonathan Lemuel had lifted his astonished eyes to the ceiling.

Sykes, regaining his composure, put an end to the brief pause of amazement. '*What* was that, Mr Pritchard?'

'My nephew and I are part of an international organization involving the great leaders of the world, and we have been sworn to secrecy.'

'Good God, he believes it,' muttered Sir Henry.

'Oh, for heaven's sake,' said Lemuel, lowering his head. 'Our telephone service here is not the most sophisticated, especially where pay phones are concerned, which I presume you were instructed to use, but within a day or so that number can be traced. Why not simply give it to Sir Henry now. He obviously needs to know quickly, so where is the harm?'

'The harm, sir, is to our superiors in the organization, that was made explicitly clear to me personally.'

'What's the name of this international organization?'

'I don't know, Sir Henry. That is part of the confiden*sheeal*ity, do you not see?'

'I'm afraid *you're* the one who doesn't see, Mr Pritchard,' said Sykes, his voice clipped, his anger surfacing.

'Oh, but I *do*, Sir Henry, and I shall prove it to you!' interrupted the deputy, looking at each man as if to draw the sceptical Sykes and the astonished attorney, as well as his adoring nephew, into his confidence. 'A large sum of money was wired from a private banking institution in Switzerland directly to my own account here in Montserrat. The instructions were clear, if flexible. The funds were to be used liberally in pursuit of the assignments delegated to me . . . Transportation, entertainment, lodgings – I was told I had complete discretion but, of course, I keep a record of all expenditures, as I do as the second highest officer of immigration . . . Who but vastly superior people would put such trust in a man they knew only by an enviable reputation and position?'

Henry Sykes and Jonathan Lemuel again looked at each other, astonishment and disbelief now joined by total fascination. Sir Henry leaned forward over the desk. 'Beyond this – shall we say – in-depth observation of John St Jacques requiring the obvious services of your nephew, have you been given other assignments?'

'Actually not, sir, but I'm sure that as soon as the leaders see how expeditiously I have performed, others will follow.'

Lemuel raised his hand calmly a few inches off the arm of his chair to inhibit a red-faced Sykes. 'Tell me,' he said quickly, gently. 'This large sum of money sent from Switzerland, just how large was it? The amount doesn't matter legally and Sir Henry can always call your bank under the laws of the Crown, so please tell us.'

'Three hundred pounds!' replied the elder Pritchard, the pride of his value in his voice.

'Three *hundred* . . . ?' The solicitor's words trailed off.

'Not exactly staggering, eh?' mumbled Sir Henry, leaning back, speechless.

'Roughly,' continued Lemuel, 'what's been your expenses?'

'Not roughly, but precisely,' affirmed the deputy Director of immigration, removing a small notebook from the breast pocket of his uniform.

'My brilliant uncle is always precise,' offered Buckingham Pritchard.

'Thank you, Nephew.'

'How much?' insisted the attorney.

'Precisely twenty-six pounds, twenty-five pence, English, or the equivalent of one hundred thirty-two East Caribbean dollars, the EC's rounded off to the nearest double zero at the latest rate of exchange – in this case I absorbed forty-seven cents, so entered.'

'Amazing,' intoned Sykes, numbed.

'I've scrupulously kept every receipt,' went on the deputy, gathering steam as he continued reading. 'They're locked in a strongbox at my flat on Old Road Bay, and include the following: A total of seven dollars and eighteen cents for local calls to Tranquillity – I would not use my official phone; twenty-three dollars and sixty-five cents for the long-distance call to Paris; sixty-eight dollars and eighty cents . . . dinner for myself and my nephew at Vue Point, a business conference, naturally—'

'That will do,' interrupted Jonathan Lemuel, wiping his perspiring black brow with a handkerchief, although the tropic fan was perfectly adequate for the room.

'I am prepared to submit everything at the proper time—'

'I said that will do, Cyril.'

'You should know that I refused a taxi driver when he offered to inflate the price of a receipt and soundly criticized him in my official position.'

'*Enough!*' thundered Sykes, the veins in his neck pronounced. 'You both have been damn fools of the first magnitude! To have even considered John St Jacques a criminal of any sort is preposterous!'

'Sir Henry,' broke in the younger Pritchard. 'I myself *saw* what happened at Tranqillity Inn! It was so *horrible.* Coffins on the dock, the chapel blown up, government boats around our peaceful isle – *gun*shots, sir! It will be months before we're back in full operation.'

'Exactly!' roared Sykes. 'And do you believe Johnny St Jay would willingly destroy his own property, his own business?'

'Stranger things have happened in the outside criminal world, Sir Henry,' said Cyril Sylvester Pritchard knowingly. 'In my official capacity I've heard many, many stories. The incidents my nephew described are called diversionary tactics employed to create the illusion that the scoundrels are victims. It was all thoroughly explained to me.'

'Oh, it *was,* was it?' cried the former brigadier of the British Army. 'Well, let me explain something else, shall I? You've been duped by an international terrorist wanted the world over! Do you know the universal penalty for aiding and abetting such a killer? I'll make it plain, in case it's escaped your attention – in your official capacity, of course . . . It is death by firing squad or, less charitably, a public hanging! Now, what's that goddamned number in Paris?'

'Under the circumstances,' said the deputy, summoning what dignity he could despite the fact that his trembling nephew clutched his left arm and his hand shook as he reached for his notebook. 'I'll write it out for you . . . One asks for a blackbird. In French, Sir Henry. I speak a few words, Sir Henry. In French – Sir Henry.'

Summoned by an armed guard dressed casually as a weekend guest in white slacks and a loose, bulky white linen jacket, John St Jacques walked into the library of their new safe house, an estate on Chesapeake Bay. The guard, a muscular, medium-sized man with clean-cut Hispanic features, stood inside the doorway; he pointed to the telephone on the large cherry-wood desk. 'It's for you, Mr Jones. It's the director.'

'Thanks, Hector,' said Johnny, pausing briefly. 'Is that Mr Jones stuff really necessary?'

'As necessary as "Hector". My real name's Roger . . . or Daniel. Whatever.'

'Gotcha.' St Jacques crossed to the desk and picked up the phone. 'Holland?'

'That number your friend Sykes got is a blind, but useful.'

'As my brother-in-law would say, please speak English.'

'It's the number of a café in the Marais waterfront on the Seine. The routine is to ask for a blackbird – *un oiseau noir* – and somebody shouts out. If the blackbird's there, contact is made. If he isn't, you try again.'

'Why is it useful?'

'We'll try again – and again and again – with a man inside.'

'What's happening otherwise?'

'I can only give you a limited answer.'

'Goddamn you!'

'Marie can fill you in—'

'*Marie?*'

'She's on her way home. She's mad as hell but she's also one relieved wife and mother.'

'Why is she mad?'

'I've booked her low-key on several long flights back—'

'For Christ's sake, *why*?' broke in the brother angrily. 'You send a god-damned *plane* for her! She's been more valuable to you than anyone in your dumb Congress or your corkscrew administration, and you send planes for *them* all over the place. I'm not joking, Holland!'

'*I* don't send those planes,' replied the director firmly. 'Others do. The ones I send involve too many questions and too much curiosity on foreign soil and that's all I'll say about it. Her safety is more important than her comfort.'

'We agree on that, honcho.'

The director paused, his irritation apparent. 'You know something? You're not really a very pleasant fellow, are you?'

'My sister puts up with me, which more than offsets your opinion. Why is she relieved – as a wife and mother, I think you said?'

Again Holland paused, not in irritation now, but searching for the words. 'A disagreeable incident took place, one none of us could predict or even contemplate.'

'Oh, I hear those famous fucking words from the American establishment!' roared St Jacques. 'What did you miss *this* time? A truckload of US missiles to the Ayatollah's agents in Paris? What *happened*?'

For a third time, Peter Holland employed a moment of silence, although his heavy breathing was audible. 'You know, young man, I could easily hang up the phone and dismiss your existence, which would be quite beneficial for my blood pressure.'

'Look, honcho, that's my sister out there, and a guy she's married to who I think is pretty terrific. Five years ago, you bastards – I repeat, you *bastards* – damn near killed them both over in Hong Kong and points east. I don't know all the facts because they're too decent or too dumb to talk about them, but I know enough to know I wouldn't trust you with a waiter's payroll in the islands!'

'Fair enough,' said Holland, subdued. 'Not that it matters, but I wasn't here then.'

'It *doesn't* matter. It's your subterranean system. You would have done the same thing.'

'Knowing the circumstances, I might have. So might you, if you knew them. But that doesn't matter, either. It's history.'

'And now is now,' broke in St Jacques. 'What happened in Paris, this "disagreeable incident"?'

'According to Conklin, there was an ambush at a private airfield in Pontcarré. It was aborted. Your brother-in-law wasn't hurt and neither was Alex. That's all I can tell you.'

'It's all I want to hear.'

'I spoke to Marie a little while ago. She's in Marseilles and will be here late tomorrow morning. I'll meet her myself and we'll be driven out to Chesapeake.'

'What about David?'

'Who?'

'My brother-in-law!'

'Oh . . . yes, of course. He's on his way to Moscow.'

'*What?*'

The Aeroflot jetliner reversed engines and swung off the runway at Moscow's Sheremetyevo Airport. The pilot taxied down the adjacent exit lane, then stopped a quarter of a mile from the terminal as an announcement was made in both Russian and French.

'There will be a five- to seven-minute delay before disembarkation. Please remain seated.'

No explanation accompanied the information, and those passengers on the flight from Paris who were not Soviet citizens returned to their reading material, assuming the delay was caused by a backup of departing aircraft. However, those who *were* citizens, as well as a few others familiar with Soviet arrival procedures, knew better. The curtained-off front section of the huge Ilyushin jet, a small seating area that was reserved for special unseen passengers, was in the process of being evacuated, if not totally, at least in part. The custom was for an elevated platform with a shielded metal staircase to be rolled up to the front exit door. Several hundred feet away there was always a government limousine, and while the backs of those disembarked special passengers were briefly in view on their way to the vehicles, flight attendants roamed through the aircraft making sure no cameras were in evidence. There never were. These travellers were the property of the KGB, and for reasons known only to the Komitet, they were not to be observed in Sheremetyevo's international terminal. It was the case this late afternoon on the outskirts of Moscow.

Alex Conklin limped out of the shielded staircase followed by Bourne, who carried the two outsized flight bags that served as their minimum luggage.

Dimitri Krupkin emerged from the limousine and hurried towards them as the steps were rolled away from the aircraft and the huge jet engines began growing in volume.

'How is your friend the *doctor*?' asked the Soviet intelligence officer, shouting to be heard over the roar.

'Holding his own!' yelled Alex. 'He may not make it but he's fighting like hell!'

'It's your own fault, Aleksei!' The jet rolled away and Krupkin lowered his voice accordingly, still loud but not shouting. 'You should have called Sergei at the embassy. His unit was prepared to escort you wherever you wished to go.'

'Actually, we thought that if we did, we'd be sending out an alert.'

'Better a prohibiting alert than inviting an assault!' countered the Russian. 'Carlos's men would never have dared to attack you under our protection.'

'It wasn't the *Jackal* – the Jackal,' said Conklin, abruptly resuming a conversational tone as the roar of the aircraft became a hum in the distance.

'Of course it wasn't him – he's here. It was his goons following orders.'

'Not his goons, not his orders.'

'What are you talking about?'

'We'll go into it later. Let's get out of here.'

'Wait.' Krupkin arched his brows. 'We'll talk first – and first, welcome to Mother Russia. Second, it would be most appreciated if you would refrain from discussing certain aspects of my life-style while in the service of my government in the hostile, war-mongering West with anyone you might meet.'

'You know, Kruppie, one of these days they'll catch up with you.'

'Never. They adore me for I feed the Komitet more useful gossip about the upper ranks of the debauched, so-called free world than any other officer in a foreign post. I also entertain my superiors in that same debauched world far better than any other office *anywhere.* Now, if we corner the Jackal here in Moscow, I'll no doubt be made a member of the Politburo, hero status.'

'Then you can really steal.'

'Why not? They all do.'

'If you don't mind,' interrupted Bourne curtly, lowering the two flight bags to the ground. 'What's happened? Have you made any progress in Dzerzhinsky Square?'

'It's not inconsiderable for less than thirty hours. We've narrowed down Carlos's mole to thirteen possibles, all of whom speak French fluently. They're under total surveillance, human and electronic; we know exactly where they are every minute, also who they meet and who they talk to over the telephone . . . I'm working with two ranking commissars, neither of whom can remotely speak French – they can't even speak a literate Russian, but that's the way it is sometimes. The point is they're both fail-safe and dedicated; they'd rather be instrumental in capturing the Jackal than re-fight the Nazi. They've been very cooperative in mounting surveillance.'

'Your surveillance is rotten and you know it,' said Alex. 'They fall over toilet seats in the women's room when they're chasing a guy.'

'Not this time, for I chose them myself,' insisted Krupkin. 'Outside of four of our own people, each trained in Novgorod, they're defectors from the UK,

America, France, and South Africa – all with intelligence backgrounds – who could lose their dachas if they screw up, as you Westerners say. I really would like to be appointed to the Presidium, perhaps even the Central Committee. I might be posted to Washington or New York.'

'Where you could really steal,' said Conklin.

'You're wicked, Aleksei, very, very wicked. Still, after a vodka or six, remind me to tell you about some real estate our chargé d'affaires picked up in Virginia two years ago. For a *song*, and financed by his lover's bank in Richmond. Now a developer wants the property at ten times the price! . . . Come, the car.'

'I don't *believe* this conversation,' said Bourne, picking up the flight bags.

'Welcome to the real world of high-tech intelligence,' explained Conklin, laughing quietly. 'At least from one point of view.'

'From *all* points of view, however,' continued Krupkin as they started towards the limousine, 'we will dispense with this conversation while riding in an official vehicle, won't we, gentlemen? Incidentally, you have a two-bedroom suite at the Metropole on the Marx Prospekt. It's convenient and I've personally shut down all listening devices.'

'I can understand why but how did you manage it?'

'Embarrassment, as you well know, is the Komitet's greatest enemy. I explained to internal security that what might be recorded could prove most embarrassing to the wrong people who would undoubtedly transfer any who overheard the tapes to Kamchatka.' They reached the car, the left rear door opened by a driver in a dark brown business suit identical to the one worn by Sergei in Paris. 'The fabric's the same,' said Krupkin in French, noting his companions' reaction to the similar apparel. 'Unfortunately the tailoring is not. I insisted Sergei have his refitted in the Faubourg.'

The Hotel Metropole is a renovated, pre-revolutionary structure built in the ornate style of architecture favoured by the czar who had visited fin-de-siècle Vienna and Paris. The ceilings are high, the marble profuse, and the occasional tapestries priceless. Intrinsic to the elaborate lobby is a defiance aimed at a government that would permit so many shabby citizens to invade the premises. The majestic walls and the glittering, filigreed chandeliers seem to stare at the unworthy trespassers with disdain. These impressions, however, did not apply to Dimitri Krupkin, whose baronial figure was very much at ease and at home in the surroundings.

'Comrade!' cried the manager sotto voce as the KGB officer accompanied his guests to the elevators. 'There is an urgent message for you,' he continued, walking rapidly up to Dimitri and thrusting a folded note into Krupkin's hand. 'I was told to deliver it to you personally.'

'You have done so and I thank you.' Dimitri watched the man walk away, then opened the paper as Bourne and Conklin stood behind him. 'I must reach Dzerzhinsky immediately,' he said, turning. 'It's the extension of my second commissar. Come, let us hurry.'

The suite, like the lobby, belonged to another time, another era, indeed, another country, marred only by the faded fabrics and the less-than-perfect restoration of the original mouldings. These imperfections served to accentuate the distance between the past and the present. The doors of the two bedrooms were opposite each other, the space between a large sitting room complete with a copper dry bar and several bottles of spirits rarely seen on Moscow shelves.

'Help yourselves,' said Krupkin, heading for a telephone on an ersatz antique desk that appeared to be a cross between Queen Anne and a later Louis. 'Oh, I forgot, Aleksei, I'll order some tea or spring water—'

'Forget it,' said Conklin, taking his flight bag from Jason and heading into the left bedroom. 'I'm going to wash up; that plane was filthy.'

'I trust you found the fare agreeable,' responded Krupkin, raising his voice and dialling. 'Incidentally, you ingrate, you'll find your weapons in your bedside table drawers. Each is a .38 calibre Graz Burya automatic . . . Come, Mr Bourne,' he added. 'You're not abstemious and it was a long trip – this may be a long conversation. My commissar number two is a windy fellow.'

'I think I will,' said Jason, dropping his bag by the door to the other bedroom. He crossed to the bar and chose a familiar bottle, pouring himself a drink as Krupkin began talking in Russian. It was not a language he understood so Bourne walked to a pair of tall cathedral windows overlooking the wide avenue known as the Marx Prospekt.

'*Dobryi den . . . Da, da – pochemu? . . . Sadovaya togda. Dvadsat minut.*' Krupkin shook his head in weary irritation as he hung up the telephone. The movement caused Jason to turn towards the Soviet. 'My second commissar was not talkative on this occasion, Mr Bourne. Haste and orders took precedent.'

'What do you mean?'

'We must leave immediately.' Krupkin glanced at the bedroom to the left and raised his voice. '*Aleksei*, come out here! Quickly! . . . I tried to tell him that you'd just this second arrived,' continued the KGB man, turning back to Jason, 'but he was having none of it. I even went so far as to say that one of you was already taking a shower, and his only comment was "Tell him to get out and get dressed."' Conklin limped through the bedroom door, his shirt unbuttoned and blotting his wet face with a towel. 'Sorry, Aleksei, we must go.'

'Go where? We just got here.'

'We've appropriated a flat on the Sadovaya – that's Moscow's "Grand Boulevard", Mr Bourne. It's not the Champs-Elysées, but neither is it inconsequential. The czars knew how to build.'

'What's over there?' pressed Conklin.

'Commissar number one,' replied Krupkin. 'We'll be using it as our, shall we say, our headquarters. A smaller and rather delightful annexe of Dzerzhinsky Square, only nobody knows about it but the five of us. Something's come up and we're to go there immediately.'

'That's good enough for me,' said Jason, putting his drink down on the copper dry bar.

'Finish it,' said Alex, rushing awkwardly back into the bedroom. 'I've got to get the soap out of my ears and restrap my lousy boot.'

Bourne picked up the glass, his eyes straying to the Soviet field officer who looked after Conklin, his brow lined, his expression curiously sad. 'You knew him before he lost his foot, didn't you?' asked Jason quietly.

'Oh, yes, Mr Bourne. We go back twenty-five, twenty-six years. Istanbul, Athens, Rome . . . Amsterdam. He was a remarkable adversary. Of course, we were young then, both slender and quick and so taken with ourselves, wanting so desperately to live up to the images we envisioned for ourselves. It was all so long ago. We were both terribly good, you know. He was actually better than me, but don't you ever tell him I said so. He always saw the broader picture, the longer road than I saw. It was the Russian in him, of course.'

'Why do you use the word "adversary"?' asked Jason. 'It's so athletic, as if you'd been playing a game. Wasn't he your enemy?'

Krupkin's large head snapped towards Bourne, his eyes glass, not warm at all. 'Of course he was my enemy, Mr Bourne, and to clarify the picture for you, he still *is* my enemy. Don't, I beg you, mistake my indulgences for what they are not. A man's weaknesses may intrude on his faith but they do not diminish it. I may not have the convenience of the Roman confession to expiate my sins so as to go forth and sin again despite my belief, but I *do* believe . . . My grandfathers *and* grandmothers were hanged – *hanged*, sir, for stealing chickens from a Romanov prince's estate. Few, if any, of my ancestors were ever given the privilege of the most rudimentary schooling, forget *education*. The Supreme Soviet revolution of Karl Marx and Vladimir Lenin made possible the *beginning* of all things. Thousands upon thousands of mistakes have been made – many inexcusable, many more brutal – but a beginning *was* made. I, myself, am both the proof and the error of it.'

'I'm not sure I understand that.'

'Because you and your feeble intellectuals have never understood what we have understood from the start. *Das Kapital*, Mr Bourne, envisages *stages* towards a just society, economic and political, but it does not and never *did* state what specific form the nuts-and-bolts government will ultimately be. Only that it could not be as it was.'

'I'm not a scholar in that department.'

'One does not have to be. In a hundred years you may be the socialists, and with luck, we'll be the capitalists, *da*?'

'Tell me something,' said Jason, hearing, as they both heard, the water faucets in Conklin's room turned off. 'Could you kill Alex – Aleksei?'

'As surely as he could kill me – with deep regrets – if the value of the information called for it. We are professionals. We understand that, often reluctantly.'

'I can't understand either one of you.'

'Don't even try, Mr Bourne, you're not there yet – you're getting closer, but you're not there.'

'Would you explain that, please?'

'You're at the cusp, Jason – may I call you Jason?'

'Please do.'

'You're fifty years of age or thereabouts, give or take a year or two, correct?'

'Correct. I'll be fifty-one in a few months. So what?'

'Aleksei and I are in our sixties – have you any idea what a leap that is?'

'How could I?'

'Let me tell you. You still visualize yourself as the younger man, the post-adolescent man who sees himself doing the things you did only moments ago in your mind, and in many ways you are right. The motor controls are there, the will is there; you are still the master of your body. Then suddenly, as strong as the will is and as strong as the body remains, the mind slowly, insidiously begins to reject the necessity to make an immediate decision – both intellectually and physically. Simply put, we care less. Are we to be condemned or congratulated on having survived?'

'I think you just said you couldn't kill Alex.'

'Don't count on it, Jason Bourne – or David whoever-you-are.'

Conklin came through the door, his limp pronounced, wincing in pain. 'Let's go,' he said.

'Did you strap it wrong again?' asked Jason. 'Do you want me to—'

'Forget it,' broke in Alex irritably. 'You have to be a contortionist to get the goddamned thing right all the time.'

Bourne understood; he forgot about any attempt on his part to adjust the prosthesis. Krupkin again looked at Alex with that strange admixture of sadness and curiosity, then spoke rapidly. 'The car is parked up the street in the Sverdlov. It's less obvious over there, I'll have a lobby steward fetch it.'

'Thanks,' said Conklin, gratitude in his glance.

The opulent apartment on the busy Sadovaya was one among many in an aged stone building that, like the Metropole, reflected the grand architectural excesses of the old Russian Empire. The flats were primarily used – and bugged – for visiting dignitaries, and the chambermaids, doormen and concierges were all frequently questioned by the KGB when not directly employed by the Komitet. The walls were covered with red velour; the sturdy furniture was reminiscent of the ancien régime. However, to the right of the gargantuan ornate living-room fireplace was an item that stood out like a decorator's nightmare: a large jet-black television console complete with an assortment of tape decks compatible with the various sizes of video cassettes.

The second contradiction to the decor, and undoubtedly an affront to the memory of the elegant Romanovs, was a heavyset man in a rumpled uniform, open at the neck and stained with vestiges of recent meals. His blunt face was full, his greyish hair cut close to his skull, and a missing tooth surrounded by discoloured companions bespoke an aversion to dentistry. It was the face of a peasant, the narrow, perpetually squinting eyes conveying a peasant's shrewd intelligence. He was Krupkin's Commissar Number One.

'My English not good,' announced the uniformed man, nodding at his visitors, 'but is understanding. Also, for you I have no name, no official position. Call me colonel, yes? It is below my rank, but all Americans think all Soviets in Komitet are "colonel", *da*? Okay?'

'I speak Russian,' replied Alex. 'If it's easier for you, use it, and I'll translate for my colleague.'

'*Hah!*' roared the colonel, laughing. 'So Krupkin cannot fool you, yes?'

'Yes, he can't fool me, no.'

'Is good. He talks too fast, *da*? Even in Russian his words come like stray bullets.'

'In French, also, Colonel.'

'Speaking of which,' intruded Dimitri, 'may we get to the issue at hand, comrade? Our associate in the Dzerzhinsky said we were to come over immediately.'

'*Da!* Immediate.' The KGB officer walked to the huge ebony console, picked up a remote control, and turned to the others. 'I will speak English – is good practice . . . Come. Watch. Everything is on one cartridge. All material taken by men and women Krupkin select to follow our people who speak the French.'

'People who could not be compromised by the Jackal,' clarified Krupkin.

'*Watch!*' insisted the peasant-colonel, pressing a button on the remote control.

The screen came alive on the console, the opening shots crude and choppy. Most had been taken with hand-held video cameras from car windows. One scene after another showed specific men walking in the Moscow streets or getting into official vehicles, driving or being driven throughout the city and, in several cases, outside the city over country roads. In every case the subjects under surveillance met with other men and women, whereupon the zoom lenses enlarged the faces. A number of shots took place inside buildings, the scenes murky and dark, the result of insufficient light and awkwardly-held concealed cameras.

'That one is expensive *whore*!' laughed the colonel as a man in his late sixties escorted a much younger woman into an elevator. 'It is the Solnechy Hotel on the Varshavkoye. I will personally check the general's vouchers and find a loyal ally, *da*?'

The choppy, cross-cutting tape continued as Krupkin and the two Americans grew weary of the seemingly endless and pointless visual record. Then, suddenly, there was an exterior shot of a huge cathedral, crowds on the pavement, the light indicating early evening.

'St Basil's Cathedral in Red Square,' said Krupkin. 'It's a museum now and a very fine one, but every now and then a zealot – usually foreign – holds a small service. No one interferes, which, of course, the zealots want us to do.'

The screen became murky again, the vibrating focus briefly and wildly swaying; the camcorder had moved inside the cathedral as the agent operating it was jostled by the crowds. Then it became steady, held perhaps against a pillar. The focus now was on an elderly man, his hair white in contrast to the lightweight black raincoat he was wearing. He was walking down a side aisle pensively glancing at the succession of icons and the higher majestic stained-glass windows.

'Rodchenko,' said the peasant-colonel, his voice guttural. 'The *great* Rodchenko.'

The man on the screen proceeded into what appeared to be a large stone corner of the cathedral where two thick pedestalled candles threw moving shadows against the walls. The video camera jerkily moved upward, the agent, again perhaps, standing on a portable stool or a hastily obtained box. The picture grew suddenly more detailed, the figures larger as the zoom lens was activated, thrusting through the crowds of tourists. The white-haired subject approached another man, a priest in priestly garb – balding, thin, his complexion dark.

'It's him!' cried Bourne. 'It's *Carlos*!'

Then a third man appeared on the screen, joining the other two, and Conklin shouted.

'*Jesus!*' he roared as all eyes were riveted on the television set. 'Hold it there!' The KGB commissar instantly complied with his remote; the picture remained stationary, shaky but constant. 'The *other* one! Do you recognize him, David?'

'I know him but I don't know him,' replied Bourne, barely audible, as images going back years began filling his inner screen. There were explosions, white blinding lights with blurred figures running in a jungle . . . and then a man, an Oriental, being shot repeatedly, screaming as he was hammered into the trunk of a thick tree by an automatic weapon. The mists of confusion swelled, dissolving into a barracks-like room with soldiers sitting behind a long table, a wooden chair on the right, a man sitting there, fidgeting, nervous. And without warning, Jason suddenly knew that man – it was himself! A younger, much younger self, and there was another figure, in uniform, pacing like a caged ferret back and forth in front of the chair, savagely berating the man then known as Delta One . . . Bourne gasped, his eyes frozen on the television screen as he realized he was staring at an older version of that angry, pacing figure in his mind's eyes. 'A courtroom in a base camp north of Saigon,' he whispered.

'It's *Ogilvie*,' said Conklin, his voice distant, hollow. 'Bryce Ogilvie . . . My God, they *did* link up. Medusa found the Jackal!'

36

'It was a trial, wasn't it, Alex?' said Bourne, bewildered, the words floating, hesitant. 'A *military* trial.'

'Yes, it was,' agreed Conklin. 'But it wasn't *your* trial, you weren't the accused.'

'I wasn't?'

'No. You were the one who brought charges, a rare thing for any of your group to do then, in or out of the field. A number of the army people tried to stop you but they couldn't . . . We'll go into it later, discuss it later.'

'I want to discuss it now,' said Jason firmly. 'That man is with the Jackal, right there in front of our eyes. I want to know who he is and what he is and why he's here in Moscow – *with* the Jackal.'

'Later—'

'*Now*. Your friend Krupkin is helping us, which means he's helping Marie and me and I'm grateful for his help. The colonel here is also on our side or we wouldn't be seeing what's on that screen at this moment. I want to know what happened between that man and me and all of Langley's security measures can go to hell. The more I know about him – now – the better I know what to ask for, what to expect.' Bourne suddenly turned to the Soviets. 'For your information, there's a period in my life I can't completely remember, and that's all you have to know. Go on, Alex.'

'I have trouble remembering last night,' said the colonel.

'Tell him what he wants to know, Aleksei. It can have no bearing on our interests. The Saigon chapter is closed, as is Kabul.'

'All right.' Conklin lowered himself into a chair and massaged his right calf; he tried to speak casually but the attempt was not wholly successful. 'In December of 1970 one of your men was killed during a search-and-destroy patrol. It was called an accident of "friendly fire", but you knew better. You knew he was marked by some horseshit artists down south at headquarters; they had it in for him. He was a Cambodian and no saint by any means, but he knew all the contraband trails so he was your point.'

'Just images,' interrupted Bourne. 'All I get are fragments. I see but I can't remember.'

'The facts aren't important any more; they're buried along with several thousand other questionable events. Apparently a large narcotics deal went sour in the Triangle and your scout was held responsible, so a few hotshots in Saigon thought a lesson should be taught their gook runners. They flew up to your territory, went into the grass, and took him out like they were a VC advance unit. But you saw them from a piece of high ground and blew all your gaskets. You tracked them back to the helicopter pad and gave them a choice: Get in and you'd storm the chopper leaving no survivors, or they could come back with you to the base camp. They came back under your men's guns and you forced Field Command to accept your multiple charges of murder. That's when Ice-Cold Ogilvie showed up looking after his Saigon boys.'

'Then something happened, didn't it? Something crazy – everything got confused, twisted.'

'It certainly did. Bryce got you on the stand and made you look like a maniac, a sullen pathological liar and a killer who, except for the war and your expertise, would be in a maximum security prison. He called you everything in the rotten black book and demanded that you reveal your real name – which you wouldn't do, *couldn't* do, because your first wife's Cambodian family would have been slaughtered. He tried to tie you in verbal knots, and, failing that, threatened the military court with exposing the whole bastard battalion, which it also couldn't allow . . . Ogilvie's thugs got off for lack of credible testimony, and after the trial you had to be physically restrained in the barracks until Ogilvie was airborne back to Saigon.'

'His name was Kwan Soo,' said Bourne dreamily, his head moving back and forth as if rejecting a nightmare. 'He was a kid, maybe sixteen or seventeen, sending the drug money back to three villages so they could eat. There wasn't any other way . . . oh, *shit*! What would *any* of us have done if our families were *starving*?'

'That wasn't anything you could say at the trial and you knew it. You had to hold your tongue and take Ogilvie's vicious crap. I came up and watched you and I never saw a man exercise such control over his hatred.'

'That isn't the way I seem to recall it – what I can recall. Some of it's coming back, not much, but some.'

'During that trial you adapted to the necessities of your immediate surroundings – you might say like a chameleon.' Their eyes locked, and Jason turned back to the television screen.

'And there he is with Carlos. It's a small rotten world, isn't it? Does he know I'm Jason Bourne?'

'How could he?' asked Conklin, getting out of the chair. 'There was no Jason Bourne then. There wasn't even a David, only a guerrilla they called Delta One. No names were used, remember?'

'I keep forgetting; what else is new?' Jason pointed at the screen. 'Why is he in Moscow? Why did you say Medusa found the Jackal? *Why?*'

'Because he's the law firm in New York.'

'*What?*' Bourne whipped his head towards Conklin. '*He's* the—'

'The chairman of the board,' completed Alex, interrupting. 'The Agency closed in and he got out. Two days ago.'

'Why the hell didn't you *tell* me?' cried Jason angrily.

'Because I never thought for a moment we'd be standing here looking at that picture on the screen. I still can't understand it, but I can't deny it, either. Also, I saw no reason to bring up a name you might or might not remember, a personally very disturbing occurrence you might or might not remember. Why add an unnecessary complication? There's enough stress.'

'All right, Aleksei!' said an agitated Krupkin, stepping forward. 'I've heard words and names that evoke certain unpleasant memories for *me*, at any rate, and I think it behoves me to ask a question or two – specifically one. Just who is this Ogilvie that concerns you so? You've told us who he was in Saigon, but who is he now?'

'Why not?' Conklin asked himself quietly. 'He's a New York attorney who heads up an organization that's spread throughout Europe and the Mediterranean. Initially, by pushing the right buttons in Washington, they bought up companies through extortion and leveraged buy-outs; they've cornered markets and set prices, and in the bargain they've moved into the killing game, employing some of the best professionals in the business. There's hard evidence that they've contracted for the murder of various officials in the government and the military, the most recent example – with which you're no doubt familiar – is General Teagarten, supreme commander of NATO.'

'*Unbelievable!*' whispered Krupkin.

'*Jeez-Chrize!*' intoned the peasant-colonel, his eyes bulging.

'Oh, they're very creative, and Ogilvie's the most inventive of all. He's Superspider and he's spun a hell of a web from Washington through every capital in Europe. Unfortunately for him, and thanks to my associate here, he was caught like a fly in his own spinning. He was about to be pounced on by people in Washington he couldn't possibly corrupt, but he was tipped off and got out the day before yesterday . . . Why he came to Moscow, I haven't the vaguest idea.'

'I may be able to answer that for you,' said Krupkin, glancing at the KGB colonel and nodding, as if to say *it's all right*. 'I know nothing – absolutely *nothing* – about any such killing as you speak of, indeed of any killing whatsoever. However, you could be describing an American enterprise in Europe that's been servicing our interests for years.'

'In what way?' asked Alex.

'With all manner of restricted American technology, as well as armaments, matériel, spare parts for aircraft and weapons systems – even the aircraft and the weapons systems themselves on various occasions through the bloc countries. I tell you this knowing that *you* know I'd vehemently deny ever having said it.'

'Understood,' nodded Conklin. 'What's the name of this enterprise?'

'There's no single name. Instead, there are fifty or sixty companies apparently under one umbrella but with so many different titles and origins it's impossible to determine the specific relationships.'

'There's a name and Ogilvie runs it,' said Alex.

'That crossed my mind,' said Krupkin, his eyes suddenly glass-cold, his expression that of an unrelenting zealot. 'However, what appears to disturb you so about your American attorney, I can assure you is far, *far* outweighed by our own concerns.' Dimitri turned to the television set and the shakily stationary picture, his eyes now filled with anger. 'The Soviet intelligence officer on that screen is General Rodchenko, second in command of the KGB and close adviser to the premier of the Soviet Union. Many things may be done in the name of Russian interests and without the premier's knowledge, but in this day and age *not* in the areas you describe. My *God*, the Supreme Commander of *NATO*! And never – *never* – using the services of Carlos the Jackal! These embarrassments are no less than dangerous and frightening catastrophes.'

'Have you got any suggestions?' asked Conklin.

'A foolish question,' answered the colonel gruffly. 'Arrest, then the Lubyanka . . . then silence.'

'There's a problem with that solution,' said Alex. 'The Central Intelligence Agency knows Ogilvie's in Moscow.'

'So where is the problem? We rid us both of an unhealthy person and his crimes and go about our business.'

'It may seem strange to you, but the problem isn't only with the unhealthy person and his crimes, even where the Soviet Union is concerned. It's with the cover-up – where Washington's concerned.'

The Komitet officer looked at Krupkin and spoke in Russian. 'What is this one talking about?'

'It's difficult for us to understand,' answered Dimitri in his native language, 'still, for them it *is* a problem. Let me try to explain.'

'What's he saying?' asked Bourne, annoyed.

'I think he's about to give a civics lesson, US style.'

'Such lessons more often than not fall on deaf ears in Washington,' interrupted Krupkin in English, then immediately resuming Russian, he addressed his KGB superior. 'You see, comrade, no one in America would blame us for taking advantage of this Ogilvie's criminal activities. They have a proverb they repeat so frequently that it covers oceans of guilt: "One does not look a gift horse in the mouth." '

'What has a horse's mouth got to do with gifts? From its tail comes manure for the farms; from its mouth, only spittle.'

'It loses something in the translation . . . Nevertheless, this attorney, Ogilvie, obviously had a great many government connections, officials who overlooked his questionable practices for large sums of money, practices that entailed millions upon millions of dollars. Laws were circumvented, men killed, lies accepted as the truth; in essence, there was considerable corruption and, as we know, the Americans are obsessed with corruption. They even label every progressive accommodation as potentially "corrupt", and there's nothing older, more knowledgeable peoples can do about it. They hang out their soiled linen for all the world to see like a badge of honour.'

'Because it is,' broke in Alex, speaking English. 'That's something a lot of people here wouldn't understand because you cover every accommodation you make, every crime you commit, every mouth you shut with a basket of roses . . . However, considering pots and kettles and odious comparisons, I'll dispense with a lecture. I'm just telling you that Ogilvie has to be sent back and all the accounts settled; that's the "progressive accommodation" you have to make.'

'I'm sure we'll take it under advisement.'

'Not good enough,' said Conklin. 'Let's put it this way. Beyond accountability, there's simply too much known – or will be in a matter of days – about his enterprise, including the connection to Teagarten's death, for you to keep him here. Not only Washington, but the entire European community would dump on you. Talk of embarrassments, this is a beaut, to say nothing about the effects on trade, or your imports and exports—'

'You've made your point, Aleksei,' interrupted Krupkin. 'Assuming this accommodation can be made, will it be clear that Moscow cooperated fully in bringing this American criminal back to American justice?'

'We obviously couldn't do it without you. As the temporary field officer of record, I'll swear to it before both intelligence committees of Congress, if need be.'

'And that we had nothing – absolutely *nothing* – to do with the killings you mentioned, specifically the assassination of the supreme commander of NATO.'

'Absolutely clear. It was one of the major reasons for your cooperation. Your government was horrified by the assassination.'

Krupkin looked hard at Alex, his voice lower but stronger for it. He turned slowly, his eyes briefly on the television screen, then back to Conklin. 'General Rodchenko?' he said. 'What shall we do with General Rodchenko?'

'What you do with General Rodchenko is your business,' replied Alex quietly. 'Neither Bourne nor I ever heard the name.'

'*Da*,' said Krupkin, nodding, again slowly. 'And what you do with the Jackal in Soviet territory is your business, Aleksei. However, be assured we shall cooperate to the fullest degree.'

'How do we begin?' asked Jason impatiently.

'First things first.' Dimitri looked over at the KGB commissar. 'Comrade, have you understood what we've said?'

'Enough so, Krupkin,' replied the heavyset peasant-colonel, walking to a telephone on an inlaid marble table against the wall. He picked up the phone and dialled; his call was answered immediately. 'It is I,' said the commissar in Russian. 'The third man in tape seven with Rodchenko and the priest, the one New York identified as the American named Ogilvie. As of now he is to be placed under our surveillance and he is not to leave Moscow.' The colonel suddenly arched his thick brows, his face growing red. '*That* order is countermanded! He is no longer the responsibility of Diplomatic Relations, he is now the sole property of the KGB . . . A *reason*? Use your skull, potato head! Tell them we are convinced he is an American double agent who those fools did not uncover. Then the usual garbage; harbouring enemies of the state due to laxness, their exalted positions once again protected by the Komitet – that sort of thing. Also, you might mention that they should not look a gift horse in the mouth . . . I don't understand any more than you do, comrade, but those butterflies over there in their tight-fitting suits probably will. Alert the airports.' The commissar hung up.

'He did it,' said Conklin, turning to Bourne. 'Ogilvie stays in Moscow.'

'I don't give a *goddamn* about Ogilvie!' exploded Jason, his voice intense, his jaw pulsating. 'I'm here for Carlos!'

'The priest?' asked the colonel, walking away from the table.

'That's exactly who I mean.'

'Is simple. We put General Rodchenko on a very long rope that he cannot see or feel. You will be at the other end. He will meet his Jackal priest again.'

'That's all I ask,' said Jason Bourne.

General Grigorie Rodchenko sat at a window table in the Lastochka restaurant by the Krymsky Bridge on the Moskva River. It was his favourite place for a midnight dinner; the lights on the bridge and on the slow-moving boats in the water were relaxing to the eye and therefore to the metabolism. He needed the calming atmosphere, for during the past two days *things* had been so unsettling. Had he been right or had he been wrong? Had his instincts been correct or far off the mark? He could not know at the moment, but those same instincts had enabled him to survive the mad Stalin as a youth, the blustering Khrushchev in middle age, and the inept Brezhnev a few years later. Now there was yet a new Russia under Gorbachev, a new Soviet, in fact, and his old age welcomed it. Perhaps *things* would relax a bit and long-standing enmities fade into a once hostile horizon. Still, horizons did not really change; they were always horizons, distant, flat, fired with colour or darkness, but still distant, flat and unreachable.

He was a survivor, Rodchenko understood that, and a survivor protected himself on as many points of the compass as he could read. He also insinuated himself into as many degrees of that compass as possible. Therefore, he had laboured diligently to become a trusted mouth to the chairman; he was an expert at gathering information for the Komitet; he was the initial conduit to the American enterprise known to him alone in Moscow as Medusa, through which extraordinary shipments had been made throughout Russia and the bloc nations. On the other hand, he was also a liaison to the monseigneur in Paris, Carlos the Jackal, whom he had either persuaded or bought off from contracts that might point to the Soviet Union. He had been the ultimate bureaucrat, working behind the scenes on the international stage, seeking neither applause nor celebrity, merely survival. Then why had he done what he did? Was it mere impetuousness born of weariness and fear and a plague-on-both-your-houses? No, it was a logical extension of events, consistent with the needs of his country and, above all, the absolute necessity that Moscow disassociate itself from both Medusa and the Jackal.

According to the consul general in New York, Bryce Ogilvie was finished in America. The consul's suggestion was to find him asylum somewhere and, in exchange, gradually absorb his myriad assets in Europe. What worried the consul general in New York was not Ogilvie's financial manipulations that broke more laws than there were courts to prosecute, but rather the killings, which as far as the consul could determine were widespread and entailed the murder of high US government officials, and, unless he was grossly mistaken, the assassination of the Supreme Commander of NATO. Compounding this chain of horrors was New York's opinion that in order to save a number of his companies from confiscation, Ogilvie might have ordered additional killings in Europe, primarily of those few powerful executives in various firms who understood the complex international linkages that led back to a great law firm and the unspoken code name Medusa. Should those contracted murders take place while Ogilvie was in Moscow, questions might arise that Moscow could not tolerate. Therefore, get him in and out of the Soviet Union as fast as possible, a recommendation more easily made than accomplished.

Suddenly, Rodchenko reflected, into this *danse macabre* had come the paranoid monseigneur from Paris. *It was imperative they meet immediately!* Carlos had fairly screamed his demand over the arranged public telephone communication they employed, but every precaution had to be taken. The Jackal, as always, demanded a public place, with crowds, and numerous available exits, where he could circle like a hawk, never showing himself until his professional eyes were satisfied. Two calls later, from two different locations, the rendezvous was set. St Basil's Cathedral in Red Square during the height of the early evening's summer tourist onslaught. In a darkened corner to the right of the altar where there were outside exits through the curtained walkways to the sacristy. *Done!*

Then, during that third telephone call, like a crack of thunder over the Black Sea, Grigorie Rodchenko was struck by an idea so dramatically bold, yet so patently obvious and simple, that he had momentarily lost his breath. It was the solution that would totally distance the Soviet government from any involvement or complicity with either the Jackal or Medusa's Ogilvie should such distance be necessary in the eyes of the civilized world.

Quite simply, unknown to each other, bring the Jackal and Ogilvie together, if only for an instant, just long enough to get photographic evidence of their being seen within the same frame. It was all that was needed.

He had gone to Diplomatic Relations yesterday afternoon, having requested a short routine meeting with Ogilvie. During the extremely innocuous and very friendly conference, Rodchenko had waited for his opening – an opening he had engineered with precision, having done his research.

'You spend summers on Cape Cod, *da*?' the general had said.

'For me, it's weekends mainly. My wife and the children are there for the season.'

'When I was posted in Washington, I had two great American friends on Cape Cod. I spent several lovely, as you say, weekends with them. Perhaps you know my friends, the Frosts – Hardleigh and Carol Frost?'

'Of course I do. Like myself, he's an attorney, specializes in maritime law. They live down the shore road in Dennis.'

'A very attractive lady, the Frost woman.'

'Very.'

'*Da.* Did you ever attempt to recruit her husband for your firm?'

'No. He has his own. Frost, Goldfarb and O'Shaunessy; they cover the waterfront, as it were, in Massachusetts.'

'I feel I almost know you, Mr Ogilvie, if only through mutual friends.'

'I'm sorry we never met at the Cape.'

'Well, perhaps, I can take advantage of our near meeting – through mutual friends – and ask of you a favour, far less than the convenience I understand my government willingly affords you.'

'I've been given to understand the convenience is mutual,' said Ogilvie.

'*Ahh*, I know nothing of such diplomatic matters, but it is conceivable that I could intervene on your behalf if you would cooperate with us – with my small, although not insignificant, department.'

'What is it?'

'There is a priest, a socially oriented militant priest, who claims to be a Marxist agitator well known to the courts of New York City. He arrived only hours ago and demands a clandestine meeting only hours from now. There is simply no time to verify his claims, but as he insists he has a history of legal "persecutions" in the courts of New York, as well as many photographs in the newspapers, you might recognize him.'

'I probably could, if he is who he says he is.'

'*Da!* And one way or another, we will certainly let it be known how you cooperated with us.'

It had been arranged. Ogilvie would be in the crowds at St Basil's Cathedral close to the meeting ground. When he saw Rodchenko approach a priest in the far corner to the right of the altar, he was to 'come across' the KGB general casually, as if surprised. Their greeting would be brief to the point of discourtesy, so rapid and blurred as to be meaningless, the sort of encounter civilized but hostile acquaintances cannot avoid when they run into one another in a public place. Close proximity was also required, as the light was so dim and so cluttered with shadows that the attorney might not get a good look at the priest.

Ogilvie had performed with the expertise of an accomplished trial lawyer verbally trapping a prosecution's witness with an objectionable inquiry, then shouting 'I withdraw the question,' leaving the prosecutor speechless.

The Jackal had instantly turned furiously away but not before an obese elderly female, a miniature camera in the handle of her purse, had snapped a series of automatically advanced photographs with ultra high-speed film. That evidence was now in a vault in Rodchenko's office. The file was titled *Surveillance of the American Male B. Ogilvie.*

On the page below the photograph showing the assassin and the American attorney together was the following: *Subject with as yet unidentified contact during covert meeting at St Basil's Cathedral. Meeting covered eleven minutes and thirty-two seconds. Photographs sent to Paris for any possible verification. It is believed that the unidentified contact may be Carlos the Jackal.*

Needless to say, Paris was working up a reply that included several photographic composites from the Deuxième Bureau and the Sûreté. The answer: *Confirmed. Definitely the Jackal.*

How shocking! And on Soviet soil.

The assassin, on the other hand, had proved to be less accommodating. After the brief, awkward confrontation with the American, Carlos had resumed his ice-cold inquisition, his burning savage self just below the frozen surface.

'They're closing in on you!'

'Who is?'

'The Komitet.'

'I *am* the Komitet!'

'Perhaps you're mistaken.'

'Nothing goes on in the KGB without my knowledge. Where did you get this information?'

'Paris. Krupkin's the source.'

'Krupkin will do anything to further himself, including the spreading of false information, even where I am concerned. He's an enigma – one moment an efficient multilingual intelligence officer, the next a gossiping clown in French feathers, still again a pimp for travelling ministers. He can't be taken seriously, not where serious matters are concerned.'

'I hope you're right. I'll reach you tomorrow, late in the evening. Will you be at home?'

'Not for a phone call from you. I'll dine alone at the Lastochka, a late supper. What will you be doing tomorrow?'

'Making certain you *are* right.' The Jackal had disappeared into the crowds of the cathedral.

That was over twenty-four hours ago and Rodchenko had heard nothing to upset the schedule. Perhaps the psychopath had returned to Paris, somehow convinced that his paranoid suspicions were groundless, his need to keep moving, racing, flying all over Europe superseding his momentary panic. Who knew? Carlos, too, was an enigma. Part of him was a retarded sadist, a savant perhaps in the darkest methods of cruelty and killing, yet another part revealed a sick, twisted romantic, a brain-damaged adolescent reaching for a vision that wanted nothing to do with him. Who knew? The time was approaching when a bullet in his head was the answer.

Rodchenko raised his hand for the waiter; he would order coffee and brandy – the decent French brandy reserved for the true heroes of the Revolution, especially the survivors. Instead, the manager of Lastochka came rushing to the table, carrying a telephone.

'There is an urgent call for you, General,' said the man in the loose-fitting black suit, placing the phone on the table and holding out the plastic knob of the extension cord that was to be placed into the walled receptacle.

'Thank you.' The manager left and Rodchenko inserted the device. 'Yes?'

'You're being watched wherever you go,' said the voice of the Jackal.

'By whom?'

'Your own people.'

'I don't believe you.'

'I've been watching all day. Would you like me to describe the places you've been for the past thirty hours? Starting with drinks at a café on the Kalinin, a kiosk in the Arbat, the Slavyanky for lunch, an afternoon walk along the Luznekaya?'

'Stop it! Where are you?'

'Come outside the Lastochka. Slowly, casually. I'll prove it to you.' The line went dead.

Rodchenko hung up and signalled the waiter for his bill. The aproned man's instant reaction was due less to the general's status than to the fact that he was the last diner in the restaurant. Leaving his money on top of the bill, the old soldier said good night, walked through the dimly lit foyer to the entrance and let himself out. It was nearly one-thirty in the morning, and except for a few stragglers with too much vodka in them, the street was deserted. In moments an upright figure, silhouetted in the wash of a street lamp, emerged from a storefront, perhaps thirty metres away on the right. It was the Jackal, still in the black cloth and the white collar of a priest. He beckoned the general to join him as he walked slowly to a dark brown car parked directly across the street. Rodchenko caught up with the assassin, now standing on the kerb side of the vehicle, which faced the direction of the Lastochka restaurant.

Suddenly, the Jackal snapped on a flashlight, its powerful beam shooting through the open window of the car. The old soldier momentarily stopped breathing, his heavy-lidded eyes scanning the horrible scene in front of him. Across the seat, the KGB agent behind the wheel was arched back, his throat cut, a river of blood drenching his clothes. Immediately beyond the window was the second surveillant, his wrists and feet bound by wire, a thick rope strapped around his face, yanked taut against his gaping mouth, gagging him, permitting only a rattling, gasping cough. He was alive, his eyes wide in terror.

'The driver was trained at Novgorod,' said the general, no comment in his voice.

'I know,' replied Carlos. 'I have his papers. That training's not what it was, comrade.'

'This other one is Krupkin's liaison here in Moscow. The son of a good friend, I'm told.'

'He's mine now.'

'What are you going to do?' asked Rodchenko, staring at the Jackal.

'Correct a mistake,' answered Carlos as he raised his gun, the silencer in place, and fired three bullets into the general's throat.

37

The night sky was angry, the storm clouds over Moscow swirling, colliding, promising rain and thunder and lightning. The brown sedan sped down the country road, racing past overgrown fields, the driver maniacally gripping the wheel and sporadically glancing at his bound prisoner, a young man who kept straining at his wire-bound hands and feet, his rope-strapped face causing him enormous pain, attested to by his constant grimace and his bulging, frightened eyes.

In the rear seat, the upholstery covered with blood, were the corpses of General Grigorie Rodchenko and the KGB Novgorod graduate who headed the old soldier's surveillance team. Suddenly, without slowing down the car or giving any indication of his action, the Jackal saw what he was looking for and swerved off the road. Tyres shrieking in the sidewinding turn, the sedan plunged into a field of tall grass and in seconds came to a shatteringly abrupt stop, the bodies in the rear crashing into the back of the front seat. Carlos opened his door and lurched outside; he proceeded to yank the blood-drenched corpses from their upholstered crypts and dragged them into the high grass, leaving the general partially on top of the Komitet officer, their life fluids now mingling as they soiled the ground.

He returned to the car and brutally pulled the young KGB agent out of the front seat with one hand, the glistening blade of a hunting knife in the other.

'We have a lot to talk about, you and I,' said the Jackal in Russian. 'And you would be foolish to withhold anything . . . You won't, you're too soft, too young.' Carlos whipped the man to the ground, the tall grass bending under the fall. He withdrew his flashlight and knelt beside his captive, the knife going towards the agent's eyes.

The bloodied, lifeless figure below had spoken his last words, and they were words that reverberated like kettledrums in the ears of Ilich Ramirez Sanchez. Jason Bourne was in *Moscow*! It had to be Bourne, for the terrified, youthful KGB surveillant had blurted out the information in a gushing, panicked stream of phrases and half phrases, saying anything and everything that might possibly save his life. *Comrade Krupkin – two Americans, one tall, the other with a limp! We took them to the hotel, then to the Sadovaya for a conference.*

Krupkin and the hated Bourne had turned his people in Paris – in *Paris*, his impenetrable armed camp! – and had traced him to Moscow. How? *Who?* . . .

It did not matter now. All that mattered was that the Chameleon himself was at the Metropole; the traitors in Paris could wait. At the *Metropole*! His enemy of enemies was barely an hour away back in Moscow, no doubt sleeping the night away, without any idea that Carlos the Jackal knew he was there. The assassin felt the exhilaration of triumph – over life *and* death. The doctors said he was dying, but doctors were as often wrong as they were right, and at this moment they were wrong! The death of Jason Bourne would *renew* his life.

However, the hour was not right. Three o'clock in the morning was not the time to be seen prowling the streets or the hotels in search of a kill in Moscow, a city in the grip of permanent suspicion, darkness itself contributing to its wariness. It was common knowledge that the night-floor stewards in the major hotels were armed, selected as much for their marksmanship as for their aptitude for service. Daylight brought a relaxation of the night's concerns; the bustling activity of the early morning was the time to strike – and strike he would.

But the hour *was* right for another kind of strike, at least the prelude to it. The time had come to call together his disciples in the Soviet government and let them know the monseigneur had arrived, that their personal messiah was here to set them free. Before leaving Paris he had collected the dossiers, and the dossiers behind those dossiers, all seemingly innocuous pages of blank paper in file folders until they were exposed to infrared light, the heat waves bringing up the typewritten script. He had selected a small deserted store in the Vavilova for his meeting ground. He would reach each of his people by public telephone and instruct them to be there by five-thirty, all taking back streets and alleyways to the rendezvous. By six-thirty his task would be finished, each disciple armed with the information that would elevate him – and her – to the highest ranks of Moscow's elite. It was one more invisible army, far smaller than Paris, but equally effective and as dedicated to Carlos, the unseen monseigneur who made life infinitely more comfortable for his converts. And by seven-thirty, the mighty Jackal would be in place at the Metropole, ready for the early movements of awakening guests, the time for the rushing trays and tables of room-service waiters and the hectic confusion of a lobby alive with chatter, anxiety and bureaucracy. It was at the Metropole where he would be ready for Jason Bourne.

One by one, like wary stragglers in the early light, the five men and three women arrived at the run-down entrance of the abandoned store in the back street known only as the Vavilova. Their caution was understandable; it was a district to be avoided, although not necessarily because of unsavoury inhabitants, for the Moscow police were ruthlessly thorough in such areas, but because of the stretch of decrepit buildings. The area was in the process of renovation; however, like similar projects in urban blights the world over, the progress had two speeds: slow and stop. The only constant, which was at best a dangerous convenience, was the existence of electricity, and Carlos used it to his advantage.

He stood at the far end of the bare concrete room, a lamp on the floor behind him, silhouetting him, leaving his features undefined and further obscured by the upturned collar of his black suit. To his right was a wreck of a low wooden table with file folders spread across the top, and to his left, under a pile of newspapers, unseen by his 'disciples,' was a cut-down Type 56, AK-47 assault weapon. A forty-round magazine was inserted, a second magazine in the Jackal's belt. The only reason for the weapon was the normal custom of his trade; he expected no difficulty whatsoever. Only adoration.

He surveyed his audience, noting that all eight kept glancing furtively at one another. No one talked; the dank air in the eerily lit abandoned store was tense with apprehension. Carlos understood that he had to dispel that fear, that furtiveness, as rapidly as possible, which was why he had gathered eight distressed chairs from the various deserted office rooms in the rear of the store. Seated, people were less tense; it was a truism. However, none of the chairs was being used.

'Thank you for coming here this morning,' said the Jackal in Russian, raising his voice. 'Please, each of you take a chair and sit down. Our discussion will not be long, but will require the utmost concentration . . . Would the comrade nearest the door close it, please. Everyone is here.'

The old, heavy door was creaked shut by a stiffly walking bureaucrat as the rest reached for chairs, each distancing his and hers from others that were nearby. Carlos waited until the scraping sounds of wood against cement subsided and all were seated. Then, like a practised orator-actor, the Jackal paused before formally addressing his captive audience. He looked briefly at each person with his penetrating dark eyes as if conveying to each that he or she was special to him. There were short, successive hand movements, mostly female, as those he gazed at in turn smoothed their respective garments. The clothes they wore were characteristic of the ranks of upper-level government officials – in the main drab and conservative, but well pressed and spotless.

'I am the monseigneur from Paris,' began the assassin in priestly garb. 'I am he who has spent several years seeking each of you out – with the assistance of comrades here in Moscow and beyond – and sent you large sums of money, asking only that you silently await my arrival and render me the loyalty I have shown to you . . . By your faces, I can anticipate your questions, so let me amplify. Years ago I was among the elite few selected to be trained at Novgorod.' There was a quiet yet audible reaction from the chosen eight. The myth of Novgorod matched its reality; it was, indeed, an advanced indoctrination centre for the most gifted of comrades – as they were given to understand, yet none really understood, for Novgorod was rarely spoken about except in whispers. With several silent nods, Carlos acknowledged the impact of his revelation and continued.

'The years since have been spent in many foreign countries promulgating the interests of the great Soviet revolution, an undercover commissar with a flexible portfolio that called for many trips back here to Moscow and extensive research into the specific departments in which each of you holds a responsible position.' Again the Jackal paused, then spoke suddenly, sharply. 'Positions of responsibility but without the authority that should be *yours*. Your abilities are undervalued and under-rewarded, for there is *deadwood* above you.'

The small crowd's reaction was now somewhat more audible, definitely less constrained. 'Compared to similar departments in the governments of our adversaries,' went on Carlos, 'we here in Moscow have lagged far behind when we should be ahead, and we are behind because *your* talents have been suppressed by entrenched office-holders who care more for their office privileges than they do for the functions of their departments!'

The response was immediate, even electric, with the three women openly if softly applauding. 'It is for that reason, *these* reasons, that I and my associate comrades here in Moscow have sought you out. Further, it is why I have sent you funds – to be used totally at your discretion – for the money you've received is the approximate value of the privileges your superiors enjoy. Why should you not receive them and enjoy them as *they* do?'

The rumble of *why not's*? and *he's right* rippled through the audience, now actually looking at one another, eyes locked, and heads nodding firmly. The Jackal then began to reel off the eight major departments in question, and as each was named successively, there was an enthusiastic nodding of heads. 'The ministries of Transport, Information, Finance, Import/Export, Legal Procedures, Military Supply, Scientific Research . . . and hardly the least, Presidium Appointments . . . These are your domains but you have been *cut out* from all final decisions. That is no longer acceptable – changes must be made!'

The assembled listeners rose almost as one, no longer strangers but, instead, people united in a cause. Then *one*, the obviously cautious bureaucrat who had closed the door, spoke. 'You appear to know our situations well, sir, but what can change them?'

'*These*,' announced Carlos, gesturing dramatically at the file folders spread out across the low table. Slowly the small crowd sat down, singly and in couples, looking at one another when not staring at the folders. 'On this table are secretly gathered confidential dossiers of your superiors in each of the departments represented here. They contain such injurious information that when presented by you individually will guarantee your immediate promotions, and in several cases your succession to those high offices. Your superiors will have no choice, for these files are daggers aimed at their throats – exposure would result in disgrace and execution.'

'Sir?' A middle-aged woman in a neat but nondescript plain blue dress cautiously stood up. Her blonde-grey hair was swept back into a stern bun; she touched it briefly, self-consciously, as she spoke. 'I evaluate personnel files on a daily basis . . . and frequently discover errors . . . how can you be certain these dossiers are accurate? For if they are not accurate we could be placed in extremely dangerous situations, is that not so?'

'That you should even question their accuracy is an affront, madame,' relied the Jackal coldly. 'I am the monseigneur from Paris. I have accurately described your individual situations and *accurately* depicted the inferiority of your superiors. Further, and at great expense and risk to myself and my associates here in Moscow, I have covertly funnelled monies to you so as to make your lives more comfortable.'

'Speaking for myself,' interrupted a gaunt man wearing glasses and a brown business suit, 'I appreciate the money – I assigned mine to our collective fund and expect a moderate return – but does one have anything to do with the *other*? I am with the Ministry of Finance, of course, and having admitted that, I absolve myself of complicity for being clear about my status.'

'Whatever that means, accountant, you're about as clear as your paralysed ministry,' interrupted an obese man in a black suit too small for his girth. 'You also cast doubt on your ability to recognize a decent return! Naturally, I'm with Military Supply, and you consistently shortchange *us*.'

'As you do *constantly* with Scientific Research!' exclaimed a short, tweedy professorial member of the audience, the irregularity of his clipped beard due, no doubt, to poor vision, despite the thick spectacles bridging his nose. '*Returns*, indeed! What about *allocations*?'

'More than sufficient for your grade-school scientists! The money is better spent stealing from the West!'

'*Stop* it!' cried the priest-assassin, raising his arms like a messiah. 'We are not here to discuss interdepartmental conflicts, for they will all be resolved with the emergence of our new elite. Remember! I am the monseigneur from Paris, and together we will bring about a new, cleansed order for our great revolution! Complacency is *over*.'

'It is a thrilling concept, sir,' said a second woman, a female in her early thirties, her skirt expensively pleated, her compact features obviously recognized by the others as a popular newscaster on television. 'However, may we return to the issue of accuracy?'

'It is *settled*,' said the dark-eyed Carlos, staring in turn at each person. 'How else would I know all about you?'

'I do not doubt you, sir,' continued the newscaster. 'But as a journalist I must always seek a second source of verification unless the ministry determines otherwise. Since you are not with the Ministry of Information, sir, and knowing that whatever you say will remain confidential, can you give us a secondary source?'

'Am I to be hounded by manipulated journalists when I speak the *truth*?' The assassin caught his breath in anger. 'Everything I've told you *is* the truth and you know it.'

'So were the crimes of Stalin, sir, and they were buried along with twenty million corpses for thirty years.'

'You want proof, *journalist*? I'll give you *proof*. I have the eyes and the ears of the leaders of the KGB – namely, the great General Grigorie Rodchenko himself. *He is my eyes* and *my* ears, and if you care to know a harsher truth, he is beholden to me! For I am his monseigneur from Paris as well.'

There was a rustling among the captive audience, a collective hesitancy, a wave of quiet throat-clearing. The television newscaster spoke again, now softly, her wide brown eyes riveted on the man in priest's clothes.

'You may be whatever you say you are, sir,' she began, 'but you do not listen to Radio Moscow's all-night station. It was reported over an hour ago that General Rodchenko was shot to death this morning by foreign criminals . . . It was also reported that all high officers of the Komitet have been called into an emergency session to evaluate the circumstances of the general's murder. The speculation is that there had to be extraordinary reasons for a man of General Rodchenko's experience to be lured into a trap by these foreign criminals.'

'They will tear apart his files,' added the cautious bureaucrat, stiffly getting to his feet. 'They will put everything under a KGB microscope, searching for those "extraordinary reasons".' The circumspect public official looked at the killer in priest's clothes. 'Perhaps they will find you, sir. And your dossiers.'

'No,' said the Jackal, perspiration breaking out on his high forehead. '*No!* That is *impossible.* I have the only copies of these dossiers – there are no others!'

'If you believe that, priest,' said the obese man from the Ministry of Military Supply, 'you do not know the Komitet.'

'*Know* it?' cried Carlos, a tremor developing in his left hand. 'I have its *soul*! No secrets are kept from me, for I am the repository of *all* secrets! I have volumes on governments everywhere, on their leaders, their generals, their highest officials – I have sources all over the *world*!'

'You don't have Rodchenko any more,' continued the black-suited man from Military Supply, he, too, getting out of his chair. 'And come to think of it, you weren't even surprised.'

'*What?*'

'For most of us, perhaps all of us, the first thing we do upon rising in the morning is to turn on our radios. It's always the same foolishness and I suppose there's comfort in that, but I'd guess most of us knew about Rodchenko's death . . . But you didn't, priest, and when our television lady told you, you weren't astonished, you weren't shocked – as I say, you weren't even surprised.'

'*Certainly* I was!' shouted the Jackal. 'What you don't understand is that I have extraordinary *control.* It's why I'm trusted, *needed* by the leaders of world Marxism!'

'That's not even fashionable,' mumbled the middle-aged, greyish-blonde woman whose expertise was in personnel files; she also stood up.

'What are you *saying*?' Carlos's voice was now a harsh, condemning whisper, rising rapidly in intensity and volume. 'I am the monseigneur from Paris. I have made your lives comfortable far beyond your miserable expectations and now you *question* me? How would I know the things I know – how could I have poured my concentration and my resources into you here in this room if I were not among the most privileged in *Moscow*? Remember who I *am*!'

'But we don't know who you are,' said another man, rising. Like the other males, his clothes were neat, sombre and well pressed, but there was a difference in that they were better tailored, as though he took considerable pains with his appearance. His face, too, was different; it was paler than the others and his eyes were more intense, more focused somehow, giving the impression that when he spoke he weighed his words with great care. 'Beyond the clerical title you've appropriated, we have no knowledge as to your identity and you obviously do not care to reveal it. As to what you know, you've recounted blatant weaknesses and subsequent injustices in our departmental systems, but they are rampant throughout the ministries. You might as well have picked a dozen others like us from a dozen other divisions, and I dare say the complaints would have been the same. Nothing new there—'

'How *dare* you?' screamed Carlos the Jackal, the veins in his neck pronounced. 'Who are you to say such things to *me*? I am the monseigneur from Paris, a true son of the Revolution!'

'And I am a judge advocate in the Ministry of Legal Procedures, Comrade Monseigneur, and a much younger product of that revolution. I may not know the heads of the KGB, who you claim are your minions, but I know the penalties for taking the legal processes in our own hands and personally – secretly – confronting our superiors rather than reporting directly to the Bureau of Irregularities. They are penalties I'd rather not face without far more thorough evidentiary materials than unsolicited dossiers from unknown sources, conceivably invented by discontented officials below even our levels . . . Frankly, I don't care to see them for I will not be compromised by gratuitous pre-trial testimony that could be injurious to my position.'

'You are an insignificant *lawyer*!' roared the assassin in priest's clothing, now repeatedly clenching his hands into fists, his eyes becoming bloodshot. 'You are all twisters of the truth! You are sworn companions of the prevailing winds of *convenience*!'

'Nicely said,' said the attorney from Legal Procedures, smiling. 'Except, comrade, you stole the phrase from the English Blackstone.'

'I will not *tolerate* your insufferable insolence!'

'You don't have to, Comrade *Priest*, for I intend to leave, and my legal advice to all here in this room is to do the same.'

'You *dare*?'

'I certainly do,' replied the Soviet attorney, granting himself a moment of humour as he looked around the gathering and grinned. 'I might have to prosecute myself, and I'm far too good at my job.'

'The *money*!' shrieked the Jackal. 'I've sent you all *thousands*!'

'Where is it recorded?' asked the lawyer with an air of innocence. 'You, yourself, made sure it was untraceable. Paper bags in our mail slots, or in our office drawers – notes attached instructing us to burn them. Who among our citizens would admit to having placed them there? That way lies the Lubyanka . . . Goodbye, Comrade Monseigneur,' said the attorney for the Ministry of Legal Procedures, scraping his chair in place and starting for the door.

One by one, as they had arrived, the assembled group followed the lawyer, each looking back at the strange man who had so exotically, so briefly, interrupted their tedious lives, all knowing instinctively that in his path was disgrace and execution. Death.

Yet none was prepared for what followed. The killer in priest's clothing suddenly snapped; visceral bolts of lightning electrified his madness. His dark eyes burned with a raging fire that could be extinguished only by soul-satisfying violence – relentless, brutal, savage vengeance for all the wrongs done to his pure purpose to kill the unbelievers! The Jackal swept away the dossiers from the table and lurched down to the pile of newspapers; he grabbed the deadly automatic weapon from beneath the scattered pages and roared.

'*Stop! All* of you!'

None did, and the outer regions of psychopathic energy became the order of the moment. The killer squeezed the trigger and men and women died. Amid screams from the shattered bodies nearest the door, the assassin raced outside, leaping over the corpses, his assault rifle on automatic fire, cutting down the figures in the street, screaming curses, condemning the unbelievers to a hell only he could imagine.

'Traitors! Filth! *Garbage!*' screamed the crazed Jackal as he leaped over the dead bodies, racing to the car he had commandeered from the Komitet and its inadequate surveillance unit. The night had ended; the morning had begun.

The Metropole's telephone did not ring, it erupted. Startled, Alex Conklin snapped open his eyes, instantly shaking the sleep from his head as he clawed for the strident instrument on the bedside table. 'Yes?' he announced, wondering briefly if he was speaking into the conically shaped mouthpiece or into the receiver.

'Aleksei, stay put! Admit no one to your rooms and have your weapons ready!'

'Krupkin? . . . What the hell are you talking about.'

'A crazed dog is loose in Moscow.'

'*Carlos?*'

'He's gone completely mad. He killed Rodchenko and butchered the two agents who were following him. A farmer found their bodies around four o'clock this morning – it seems the dogs woke him up with their barking, downwind of the blood scents, I imagine.'

'Christ, he's gone over the edge . . . But why do you think—'

'One of our agents was tortured before being killed,' broke in the KGB officer, fully anticipating Alex's question. 'He was our driver from the airport, a protégé of mine and the son of a classmate I roomed with at the university. A fine young man from a rational family but not trained for what he was put through.'

'You're saying you think he may have told Carlos about us, aren't you?'

'Yes . . . There's more, however. Approximately an hour ago in the Vavilova, eight people were cut down by automatic fire. They were slaughtered; it was a massacre. One of the dying, a woman with the Ministry of Information, a *direktor*, second class, and a television journalist, said the killer was a priest from Paris who called himself the "monseigneur".'

'*Jesus!*' exploded Conklin, whipping his legs over the edge of the bed, absently staring at the stump of flesh where once there had been a foot. 'It was his cadre.'

'So called and past tense,' said Krupkin. 'If you remember, I told you such recruits would abandon him at the first sign of peril.'

'I'll get Jason—'

'*Aleksei*, listen to me!'

'What?' Conklin cupped the telephone under his chin as he reached down for the hollowed-out prosthetic boot.

'We've formed a tactical assault squad, men and women in civilian clothes – they're being given instructions now and will be there shortly.'

'Good move.'

'But we have purposely *not* alerted the hotel staff or the police.'

'You'd be idiots if you did,' broke in Alex. 'We'll settle for taking the son of a bitch here! We'd never do it with uniforms prowling around or clerks in hysterics. The Jackal has eyes in his kneecaps.'

'Do as I say,' ordered the Soviet. 'Admit no one, stay away from the windows, and take all precautions.'

'Naturally . . . What do you mean, the windows? He'll need time to find out where we are . . . question the maids, the stewards.'

'Forgive me, old friend,' interrupted Krupkin, 'but an angelic priest inquiring at the desk about two Americans, one with a pronounced limp, during the early morning rush in the lobby?'

'Good point, even if you're paranoid.'

'You're on a high floor, and directly across the Marx Prospekt is the roof of an office building.'

'You also think pretty fast.'

'Certainly faster than that fool in the Dzerzhinsky. I would have reached you long before now but my commissar *Kartoshki* over there didn't call *me* until two minutes ago.'

'I'll wake up Bourne.'

'Be *careful.*'

Conklin did not hear the Soviet's final admonition. Instead, he swiftly replaced the telephone and pulled on his boot, carelessly lashing the Velcro straps around his calf. He then opened the bedside table drawer and took out the Graz Burya automatic, a specially designed KGB weapon with three clips of ammunition. The Graz, as it was commonly known, was unique insofar as it was the only automatic known that would accept a silencer. The cylindrical instrument had rolled to the front of the drawer; he removed it and spun it into the short barrel. Unsteadily, he got into his trousers, shoved the weapon into his belt and crossed to the door. He opened it and limped out only to find Jason, fully dressed, standing in front of a window in the ornate Victorian sitting room.

'That had to be Krupkin,' said Bourne.

'It was. Get away from the window.'

'*Carlos?*' Bourne instantly stepped back and turned to Alex. 'He knows we're in Moscow?' he asked. Then added, 'He knows where we *are*?'

'The odds are yes to both questions.' In short concise statements, Conklin related Krupkin's information. 'Does all this tell you something?' asked Alex when he had finished.

'He's blown apart,' answered Jason quietly. 'It had to happen. The time bomb in his head finally went off.'

'That's what I think. His Moscow cadre turned out to be a myth. They probably told him to pound sand and he exploded.'

'I regret the loss of life and I mean that,' said Bourne. 'I wish it could have happened another way, but I can't regret his state of mind. What's happened to him is what he wanted for me – to crack wide open.'

'Kruppie said it,' added Conklin. 'He's got a psychopathic death wish to return to the people who first found out he was a maniac. Now if he knows you're here, and we have to assume that he does, the obsession's compounded, your death replacing his – giving him some kind of symbolic triumph maybe.'

'You've been talking to Panov too much . . . I wonder how Mo is.'

'Don't. I called the hospital at three o'clock this morning – five o'clock, Paris time. He may lose the use of his left arm and suffer partial paralysis of his right leg, but they think he'll make it now.'

'I don't give a goddamn about his arms or his legs. What about his *head*?'

'Apparently it's intact. The chief nurse on the floor said that for a doctor he's a terrible patient.'

'Thank *Christ*!'

'I thought you were an agnostic.'

'It's a symbolic phrase, check with Mo.' Bourne noticed the gun in Alex's belt; he gestured at the weapon. 'That's a little obvious, isn't it?'

'For whom?'

'Room service,' replied Jason. 'I phoned for whatever gruel they've got and a large pot of coffee.'

'No way. Krupkin said we don't let anyone in here and I gave him my word.'

'That's a crock of paranoia—'

'Almost my words, but this is his turf, not ours. Just like the windows.'

'*Wait* a minute!' exclaimed Bourne. 'Suppose he *is* right?'

'Unlikely, but possible, except that—' Conklin could not finish his statement. Jason reached under the right rear flap of his jacket, yanked out his own Graz Burya, and started for the hallway door of the suite. 'What are you *doing*?' cried Alex.

'Probably giving your friend "Kruppie" more credit than he deserves, but it's worth a try . . . Get over there,' ordered Bourne, pointing to the far left corner of the room. 'I'll leave the door unlocked, and when the steward gets here, tell him to come in – in Russian.'

'What about you?'

'There's an ice machine down the hall; it doesn't work, but it's in a cubicle along with a Pepsi machine. That doesn't work either, but I'll slip inside.'

'Thank God for capitalists, no matter how misguided. Go *on*!'

The Medusan once known as Delta unlatched the door, opened it, glanced up and down the Metropole's corridor and rushed outside. He raced down the hallway to the cut-out alcove that housed the two convenience machines and crouched by the right interior wall. He waited, his knees and legs aching – pains he never *felt* only years ago – and then he heard the sounds of rolling wheels. They grew louder and louder as the cart draped with a tablecloth passed and proceeded to the door of the suite. He studied the floor steward; he was a young man in his twenties, blonde, short of stature, and with the posture of an obsequious servant; cautiously, he knocked on the door. No Carlos he, thought Bourne, getting painfully to his feet. He could hear Conklin's muffled voice telling the steward to enter; and as the young man opened the door, shoving the table inside, Jason calmly inserted his weapon into its concealed place. He bent over and massaged his right calf; he could feel the swelling cluster of a muscle cramp.

It happened with the impact of a single furious wave against a shoal of rock. A figure in black lurched out of an unseen recess in the corridor, racing past the machines. Bourne spun back into the wall. It was the *Jackal*!

38

Madness! At full force Carlos slammed his right shoulder into the blond-haired waiter, propelling the young man across the hallway and crashing the room-service table over on its side; dishes and food splattered the walls and the carpeted floor. Suddenly the waiter lunged to his left, spinning in midair as, astonishingly, he yanked a weapon from his belt. The Jackal either sensed or caught the movement in the corner of his eye. He whipped around, his automatic weapon on rapid fire, savagely pinning the blond Russian into the wall, bullets puncturing the waiter's head and torso. At that prolonged, horrible moment, the enlarged sightline on the barrel of Bourne's Graz Burya caught in the waistline of his trousers. He tore the fabric as the eyes of Carlos swept up centring on his own, fury and triumph in the assassin's stare.

Jason ripped the gun loose, spinning, crouching back into the wall of the small alcove as the Jackal's fusillade blew apart the gaudy panelling of the soft-drink machine and tore into the sheets of heavy plastic that fronted the broken-down icemaker. On his stomach, Bourne surged across the opening, the Graz Burya raised and firing as fast as he could squeeze the trigger. Simultaneously, there were other gunshots, *not* those of a machine pistol. Alex was firing from inside the suite! They had Carlos in their cross fire! It was possible – it could all end in a hotel corridor in Moscow! Let it happen, let *it happen*!

The Jackal roared; it was a defiant shriek at having been hit. Bourne lunged back across the opening, pivoting once again into the wall, momentarily distracted by the sounds of a now-functioning ice machine. Again he crouched, inching his face towards the corner of the archway when the murderous insanity in the hallway erupted into the fever pitch of close combat. Like an enraged caged animal, the wounded Carlos kept spinning around in place, continuous bursts from his weapon exploding as if he were firing through unseen walls that were closing in on him. Two piercing, hysterical screams came from the far end of the hallway, one male, one female; a couple had been wounded or killed in the panicked fusillade of stray bullets.

'Get *down*!' Conklin's scream from across the corridor was an instant command for what Jason could not know. 'Take *cover*! Grab the fucking walls!' Bourne did as he was told, understanding only that the order meant he was to shove himself into as small a place as possible, protecting his head as much as possible. The *corner*. He lunged as the first explosion rocked the walls

– somewhere – and then a second, this much nearer, far more thunderous, in the hallway itself. *Grenades!*

Smoke mingled with falling plaster and shattered glass. *Gunshots.* Nine, one after another – a Graz Burya automatic . . . *Alex!* Jason spun up and away from the corner of the recess and lurched for the opening. Conklin stood outside the door of their suite in front of the upturned room-service table; he snapped out his empty clip and furiously searched his trousers pockets. 'I haven't got one!' he shouted angrily, referring to the extra clips of ammunition supplied by Krupkin. 'He ran around the corner into the other corridor, and I don't have any goddamned *shells*!'

'I do and I'm a lot faster than you,' said Jason, removing his spent magazine and inserting a fresh clip from his pocket. 'Get back in there and call the lobby. Tell them to clear it.'

'Krupkin said—'

'I don't *give* a damn what he said! Tell them to shut down the elevators, barricade all staircase exits, and stay the hell away from this floor!'

'I see what you mean—'

'*Do* it!' Bourne raced down the hallway, wincing as he approached the couple who lay on the carpet; each moved, groaning. Their clothes were spotted with blood, but they *moved*! He turned and yelled to Alex, who was limping around the room-service table. 'Get help up here!' he ordered, pointing at an exit door directly down the corridor. 'They're alive! Use that exit and *only* that one!'

The hunt began, compounded and impeded by the fact that the word had been spread throughout these adjacent wings of the Metropole's tenth floor. It took no imagination to realize that behind the closed doors, along both sides of the hallways, panicked calls were being made to the front desk as the sound of nearby gunfire echoed throughout the corridors. Krupkin's strategy for a KGB assault team in civilian clothes had been nullified with the first burst from the Jackal's weapon.

Where *was* he? There was another exit door at the far end of the long hallway Jason had entered, but there were perhaps fifteen to eighteen guest-room doors lining that hallway. Carlos was no fool, and a wounded Carlos would call upon every tactic he could summon from a long life of violence and survival to survive, if only long enough to achieve the kill he wanted more than life itself . . . Bourne suddenly realized how accurate his analysis was, for he was describing himself. What had old Fontaine said on Tranquillity Isle, in that faraway storeroom from which they had stared down at the procession of priests knowing that one had been bought by the Jackal? '. . . Two ageing lions stalking each other, not caring who's killed in the cross fire' – those had been Fontaine's words, a man who had sacrificed his life for another he barely knew because his own life was over, for the woman he loved was gone. As Jason started cautiously, silently down the hall towards the first door on the left, he wondered if he could do the same. He wanted desperately to live – with Marie and their children – but if she was gone . . . if they were gone . . . would life really matter? Could he throw it away if he recognized something in another man that reflected something in himself?

No *time.* Meditate on your *own* time, David Webb! I have no use for you, you weak, soft son of a *bitch.* Get *away* from me! I have to flush out a bird of prey I've wanted for thirteen years. His claws are razor-sharp and he's killed too often, too many, and now he wants to kill my own – *your* own. Get away from me!

Bloodstains. On the dull, dark brown carpet, wet driblets glistening in the dim overhead light. Bourne crouched and felt them; they *were* wet; they were red – blood red. Unbroken, they passed the first door, then the second, remaining on the left – then they crossed the hall, the pattern now altered, no longer steady, instead zigzagging, as if the wound had been located, the bleeding partially stemmed. The trail passed the sixth door on the right, and the seventh . . . then abruptly the shining red drops stopped – *no,* not entirely. There was a trickle heading left, barely visible, and again, across the hallway – there it *was*! A faint smudge of red just above the knob on the eighth door on the left, no more than twenty feet from the corridor's exit staircase. Carlos was behind that door holding hostage whoever was inside.

Precision was everything now, every movement, every sound concentrated on the capture or the kill. Breathing steadily while imposing a suspension of the muscular spasms he felt everywhere throughout his body, Bourne once more walked silently, now retracing his steps up the hallway. He reached a point roughly thirty paces away from the eighth door on the left and turned around, suddenly aware of a muted chorus of sporadic sobs and cries that came from closed doorways along the hotel corridor. Orders had been given couched in languages far removed from Krupkin's instructions: *Stay inside your rooms, please. Admit no one. Our people are investigating.* It was always 'our people', never 'the police', never 'the authorities'; with those names came panic. And panic was precisely what Medusa's Delta One had in mind. Panic and diversion, eternal components for the human snare, lifelong allies in the springing trap.

He raised the Graz Burya automatic, aiming at one of the ornate hallway chandeliers, and fired twice, simultaneously shouting furiously as the earsplitting explosions accompanied the shattered glass that plummeted from the ceiling.

'There he *goes*! A black suit!' His feet pounding, Bourne ran with loud emphatic strides down the corridor to the eighth door on the left, then *past* the door, shouting once again. 'The exit . . . the *exit*! He abruptly stopped, firing a third shot into another chandelier, the jarring cacophony covering the absence of his pounding feet as he spun around, throwing his back against the opposing wall of the eighth door, then pushing himself away, hurling his body at the door and crashing into it, smashing it off its hinges as he lurched inside, plunging to the floor, his weapons raised, prepared for rapid fire.

He was *wrong*! He knew it instantly – a final reverse trap was in the making! He heard another door opening somewhere outside – he either heard it or he instinctively *knew* it! He rolled furiously to his right, over and over again, his legs crashing into a floor lamp, sending it towards the door, his panicked darting eyes catching a glimpse of an elderly couple clutching each other, crouching in a far corner.

The white-gowned figure burst into the room, his automatic pistol spitting indiscriminately, the staccato reports deafening. Bourne fired repeatedly into the mass of white as he sprang into the left wall, knowing that if for only a split second he was positioned on the killer's blind right flank. It was *enough*!

The Jackal was caught in his shoulder – his *right* shoulder! The weapon literally snapped out of his grip as he jerked up his forearm, his fingers spastically uncurled under the impact of the Graz Burya's penetration. With no cessation of movement, the Jackal swung around, the bloody long white robe separating, billowing like a sail as he grabbed the massive flesh wound with his left hand and violently kicked the floor lamp into Jason's face.

Bourne fired again, half blinded by the flying, approaching shade of the heavy lamp, his weapon deflected by its thick stem. The shot went wild; steadying his hand, he squeezed the trigger again, only to hear the sickening finality of a sharp metallic click – the gun's magazine was empty! Struggling to a crouch, he lunged for the blunt, ugly automatic weapon as the white-robed Carlos raced through the shattered doorway into the corridor. Jason got to his feet; his knee collapsed! It had buckled under his own weight. Oh, *Christ*! He crawled to the edge of the bed and dived over the pulled-down sheets towards the bedside telephone – it had been demolished, the Jackal had shot it apart! Carlos's demented mind *was* summoning up every tactic, every counteraction he had ever used.

Another sound! This loud and abrupt. The crash bar on the hallway's stairway exit had been slammed into the opening position, the heavy metal door smashed back into the concrete wall of the landing. The Jackal was heading down the flight of steps to the lobby. If the front desk had listened to Conklin, he was *trapped*!

Bourne looked at the elderly couple in the corner, affected by the fact that the old man was covering the woman with his own body. 'It's all right,' he said, trying to calm them by lowering his voice. 'I know you probably don't understand me – I don't speak Russian – but you're safe now.'

'We don't speak Russian either,' admitted the man, obviously an Englishman, in clipped, guarded tones, straining his neck as he looked at Jason while trying to rise. 'Thirty years ago I would have been standing at that door! Eighth Army with Monty, y'know. Rather grand at El Alamein – all of us, of course. To paraphrase, age doth wither, as they say.'

'I'd rather not hear it, General—'

'No, no, merely a brigadier—'

'Fine!' Bourne crept over the bed, testing his knee; whatever it was had snapped back. 'I have to get to a phone!'

'Actually, what outraged me was the goddamned robe!' went on the veteran of El Alamein. 'Fucking *disgraceful*, I say – forgive me, darling.'

'What are you talking about?'

'The white *robe*, lad! It had to be Binky's – the couple across the hall we're travelling with – he must have copped it from that lovely Beau-Rivage in Lausanne. The rotten theft is bad enough, but to have given it to that *swine* is unforgivable!'

In seconds, Jason had grabbed the Jackal's weapon and crashed his way into the room across the hall, immediately knowing that 'Binky' deserved more admiration than the brigadier afforded him. He lay on the floor bleeding from silent knife wounds across his stomach and his throat.

'*I can't reach* anyone!' screamed the woman with thinning grey hair; she was on her knees above the victim, weeping hysterically. 'He fought like a madman – somehow he knew that priest wouldn't fire his gun!'

'Hold the skin together wherever you *can*,' yelled Bourne, looking over at the telephone. It was untouched! He ran to it, and instead of calling the front desk or the operator, he dialled the numbers for the suite.

'*Krupkin?*' cried Alex.

'No, me! *First.* Carlos is on the staircase – the hallway I went into! *Second.* A man's cut up, same hallway, seventh door on the right! *Hurry.*'

'As fast as I can. I've got a clear line to the office.'

'Where the hell is the KGB team?'

'They just got here. Krupkin called only seconds ago from the lobby – it's why I thought you were—'

'I'm going to the staircase!'

'For God's sake, *why*?'

'Because he's *mine*!'

Jason raced to the door, offering no words of comfort for the hysterical wife; he could not summon them. He crashed his way through the exit door, the Jackal's weapon in his hand. He started down the staircase, suddenly hearing the sound of his own shoes; he stopped on the seventh step and removed both, and then his ankle-length socks. The cool surface of the stone on his feet somehow reminded him of the jungles, flesh against the cold morning underbrush; for some abstract, foolish memory he felt more in command of his fears – the jungles were always the friend of Delta One.

Floor by floor he descended, following the inevitable rivulets of blood, larger now, no longer to be stemmed, for the last wound was too severe to stop by exerting pressure. Twice the Jackal had applied such pressure, once at the fifth and again at the third-floor hallway doors, only to be followed by streaks of dark red, as he could not manipulate the exterior locks without the security keys.

The second floor, then the first, there *were no more*! Carlos *was* trapped! Somewhere in the shadows below was the death of the killer who would set him *free*! Silently, Bourne removed a book of Metropole matches from his pocket; he huddled against the concrete wall, tore out a single match and, cupping his hands, fired the packet. He threw it over the railing, the weapon in his hand ready to explode with continuous rounds of bullets at anything that moved below!

There was nothing – *nothing*! The cement floor was empty – there was no one there! Impossible! Jason raced down the last flight of steps and pounded on the door to the lobby.

'*Shto?*' yelled a Russian inside. '*Kto tam?*'

'I'm an *American*! I'm working with the KGB! Let me *in*!'

'*Shto . . . ?*'

'I understand,' shouted another voice. 'And, please, you understand that many guns are directed at you when I open the door. It is understand?'

'Understand!' shouted Bourne, at the last second remembering to drop Carlos's weapon on the concrete floor. The door opened.

'*Da!*' said the Soviet police officer, instantly correcting himself as he spotted the machine pistol at Jason's feet. '*Nyet!*' he yelled.

'*Ne za shto,*' said the breathless Krupkin, urging his heavyset body forward.

'*Pochemu?*'

'*Komitet!*'

'*Prekrasno.*' The policeman nodded obsequiously, but stayed in place.

'What are you *doing*?' demanded Krupkin. 'The lobby is cleared and our assault squad is in place!'

'He was *here*!' whispered Bourne, as if his intense quiet voice further obscured his incomprehensible words.

'The *Jackal*?' asked Krupkin, astonished.

'He came down this *staircase*! He couldn't have gone out on any other floor. Every fire door is dead-bolted from the inside – only the crash bars release them.'

'*Skazhi,*' said the KGB official to the hotel guard. 'Has anyone come through this door within the past ten minutes since the orders were given to seal them off?'

'No, sir!' replied the *mititsiya.* 'Only an hysterical woman in a soiled bathrobe. In her panic, she fell in the bathroom and cut herself. We thought she might have a heart attack, she was screaming so. We escorted her immediately to the nurse's office.'

Krupkin turned to Jason, switching back to English, 'Only a woman came through, a woman in panic who had injured herself.'

'A *woman*? Is he certain? . . . What colour was her hair?'

Dimitri asked the guard; with the man's reply he again looked at Bourne. 'He says it was reddish and quite curly.'

'*Reddish?*' An image came to Jason, a very unpleasant one. 'A house phone – no, the front desk! Come *on*, I may need your help.' With Krupkin following, the barefoot Bourne ran across the lobby to a clerk at the reception counter. 'Can you speak English?'

'Certainly most good, even many veniculars, mister sir.'

'A room plan for the tenth floor. *Quickly.*'

'Mister sir?'

Krupkin translated; a large loose-leaf notebook was placed on the counter, the plastic-enclosed page turned to – '*This* room!' said Jason, pointing at a square and doing his best not to alarm the frightened clerk. 'Get it on the telephone! If the line's busy, knock off anybody on it.'

Again Krupkin translated as a phone was placed in front of Bourne. He picked it up and spoke. 'This is the man who came into your room a few minutes ago—'

'Oh, yes, of course, dear fellow. *Thank* you *so* much! The doctor's here and Binky's—'

'I have to know something, and I have to know it right now . . . Do you carry hairpieces, or wigs, with you when you travel?'

'I'd say that's *rather* impertinent—'

'Lady, I don't have *time* for amenities, I have to *know*! *Do* you?'

'Well, yes I do. It's no secret, actually, all my friends know it and they forgive the artifice. You see, dear boy, I have diabetes . . . my grey hair is painfully thin.'

'Is one of those wigs *red*?'

'As a matter of fact, yes, I rather fancy changing—'

Bourne slammed down the phone and looked over at Krupkin. 'The son of a bitch lucked out. It was *Carlos*!'

'Come with me!' said Krupkin as they both raced across the empty lobby to the complex of back-room offices of the Metropole. They reached the nurse's infirmary door and went inside. They both stopped; both gasped and then winced at what they saw.

There were rolls of torn, unwound gauze and reels of tape in various widths, and broken syringes and tubes of antibiotics scattered about the examining table and the floor, as if all were somehow administered in panic. These, however, the two men barely noticed, for their eyes were riveted on the woman who had tended to her crazed patient. The Metropole's nurse was arched back in her chair, her throat surgically punctured, and over her immaculate white uniform ran a thin stream of blood. *Madness!*

Standing beside the living room table, Dimitri Krupkin spoke on the phone as Alex Conklin sat on the brocaded couch massaging his bootless leg and Bourne stood by the window staring out on the Marx Prospekt. Alex looked over at the KGB officer, a thin smile on his gaunt face as Krupkin nodded, his eyes on Conklin. An acknowledgement was being transmitted between the two of them. They were worthy adversaries in a never-ending, essentially futile war in which only battles were won, the philosophical conflicts never resolved.

'I have your assurance then, comrade,' said Krupkin in Russian, 'and, frankly, I will hold you to it . . . Of course I'm taping this conversation! Would you do otherwise? . . . Good! We understand each other as well as our respective responsibilities, so let me recapitulate. The man is seriously wounded, therefore the city taxi service as well as all doctors and all hospitals in the Moscow area have been alerted. The description of the stolen automobile has been circulated and any sightings of man or vehicle are to be reported only to you. The penalty for disregarding these instructions is the Lubyanka, that must be clear . . . Good! We have a mutual understanding and I expect to hear from you the minute you have any information, yes? . . . Don't have a cardiac arrest, comrade. I am well aware that you are my superior, but then this *is* a proletarian society, yes? Simply follow the advice of an extremely experienced subordinate. Have a pleasant day . . . No, that is not a threat, it is merely a phrase I picked up in Paris – American origin, I believe.' Krupkin hung up the phone and sighed. 'There's something to be said for our vanished, educated aristocracy, I'm afraid.'

'Don't say it out loud,' observed Conklin, nodding at the telephone. 'I gather nothing's coming down.'

'Nothing to act upon immediately but something rather interesting, even fascinating in a macabre sort of way.'

'By which you mean it concerns Carlos, I assume.'

'No one else.' Krupkin shook his head as Jason looked over at him from the window. 'I stopped at my office to join the assault squad and on my desk were eight large manila envelopes, only one of which had been opened. The police found them in the Vavilova and, true to form, having read the contents of only one, wanted nothing to do with them.'

'What were they?' asked Alex, chuckling. 'State secrets describing the entire Politburo as gay?'

'You're probably not far off the mark,' interrupted Bourne. 'That was the Jackal's Moscow cadre in the Vavilova. He was either showing them the dirt he had on them, or giving them the dirt on others.'

'The latter in this case,' said Krupkin. 'A collection of the most preposterous allegations directed at the ranking heads of our major ministries.'

'He's got vaults of that garbage. It's standard operating procedure for Carlos; it's how he buys his way into circles he shouldn't be able to penetrate.'

'Then I'm not being clear, Jason,' continued the KGB officer. 'When I say preposterous, I mean exactly that – beyond belief. Lunacy.'

'He's almost always on target. Don't take that judgement to the bank.'

'If there were such a bank I certainly would, and I'd negotiate a sizeable loan on its efficacy as collateral. Most of the information is the stuff of the lowest grade tabloids – nothing unusual there, of course – but along with such nonsense are outright distortions of times, places, functions and even identities. For example, the Ministry of Transport is not where a particular file says, but a block away, and a certain comrade *direktor* is not married to the lady named but to someone else – the woman mentioned is their daughter and is not in Moscow but rather in Cuba, where she's been for six years. Also, the man listed as head of Radio Moscow and accused of just about everything short of having intercourse with dogs, died eleven months ago and was a known closet orthodox Catholic, who would have been far happier as a truly devout priest . . . These blatant falsehoods I picked up in a matter of minutes, time being at a premium, but I'm sure there are dozens more.'

'You're saying that a scam was pulled on Carlos?' said Conklin.

'One so garish – albeit compiled with extreme conviction – it would be laughed out of our most rigidly doctrinaire courts. Whoever fed him these melodramatic "exposés" wanted built-in deniabilities.'

'Rodchenko?' asked Bourne.

'I can't think of anyone else. Grigorie – I say "Grigorie" but I never called him that to his face; it was always "'General" – was a consummate strategist, the ultimate survivor, as well as a deeply committed Marxist. Control was his byword, his addiction, really, and if he could control the infamous Jackal for the Motherland's interests, what a profound exhilaration for the old man. Yet the Jackal killed him with those symbolic bullets in his throat. Was it betrayal, or was it carelessness on Rodchenko's part at having been discovered? Which?

We'll never know.' The telephone rang and Krupkin's hand shot down, picking it up. '*Da?*' Shifting to Russian, Dimitri gestured for Conklin to restrap the prosthetic boot as he spoke. 'Now listen to me very carefully, comrade. The police are to make no moves – above all, they are to remain out of sight. Call in one of our unmarked vehicles to replace the patrol car, am I clear? . . . Good. We'll use the Moray frequency.'

'Breakthrough?' asked Bourne, stepping away from the window as Dimitri slammed down the phone.

'Maximum!' replied Krupkin. 'The car was spotted on the Nemchinovka road heading towards Odintsovo.'

'That doesn't mean anything to me. What's in Odintsovol, or whatever it's called?'

'I don't know specifically but I must assume he does. Remember, he knows Moscow and its environs. Odintsovo is what you might call an industrial suburb about thirty-five minutes from the city—'

'*Goddamn* it!' yelled Alex, struggling with the Velcro straps of his boot.

'Let me do that,' said Jason, his tone of voice brooking no objection as he knelt down and swiftly manipulated the thick strips of coarse cloth. 'Why is Carlos still using the Dzerzhinsky car?' continued Bourne, addressing Krupkin. 'It's not like him to take that kind of risk.'

'It is if he has no choice. He has to know that all Moscow taxis are a silent arm of the state, and he is, after all, severely wounded and undoubtedly now without a gun or he would have used it on you. He's in no condition to threaten a driver or steal an automobile . . . Besides, he reached the Nemchinovka road quickly; that the car was even seen is pure chance. The road is not well travelled, which I assume he also knows.'

'Let's get *out* of here!' cried Conklin, annoyed both by Jason's attention and his own infirmity. He stood up, wavered, angrily rejected Krupkin's hand, and started for the door. 'We can talk in the car. We're wasting time.'

'Moray, come in, please,' said Krupkin in Russian, sitting beside the assault squad driver in the front seat, the microphone at his lips, his hand on the frequency dial of the vehicle's radio. 'Moray, respond, if I'm reaching you.'

'What the hell's he talking about?' asked Bourne, in the back seat with Alex.

'He's trying to make contact with the unmarked KGB patrol following Carlos. He keeps switching from one ultrahigh frequency to another. It's the Moray code.'

'The what?'

'It's an eel, Jason,' replied Krupkin, glancing over the seat. 'Of the Muraenidae family with porelike gills and capable of descending to great depths. Certain species can be quite deadly.'

'Thank you, Peter Lorre,' said Bourne.

'Very good,' laughed the KGB man. 'But you'll admit it's aptly descriptive. Very few radios can either send it or receive it.'

'When did you steal it from us?'

'Oh, not you, not you at all. From the British, truthfully. As usual, London is very quiet about these things, but they're far ahead of you and the Japanese in certain areas. It's that damned MI6. They dine in their clubs in Knightsbridge, smoke their odious pipes, play the innocents, and send us defectors trained at the Old Vic.'

'They've had their gaps,' said Conklin defensively.

'More so in their high-dudgeon revelations than in reality, Aleksei. You've been away too long. We've both lost more than they have in that department, but they can cope with public embarrassment – we haven't learned that time-honoured trait. We bury our "gaps", as you put it; we try too hard for that respectability which too often eludes us. Then, I suppose, we're historically young by comparison.' Krupkin again switched back into Russian. '*Moray*, come in, please! I'm reaching the end of the spectrum. Where are you, Moray?'

'Stop *there*, comrade!' came the metallic voice over the loudspeaker. 'We're in contact. Can you hear me?'

'You sound like a castrato but I can hear you.'

'This must be Comrade Krupkin—'

'Were you expecting the Pope? Who's this?'

'Orlov.'

'Good! You know what you're doing.'

'I hope you do, Dimitri.'

'Why do you say that?'

'Your insufferable orders to do nothing, *that's* why. We're two kilometres away from the building – I drove up through the grass on a small hill – and we have the vehicle in sight. It's parked in the lot and the suspect's inside.'

'What building? What hill? You tell me nothing.'

'The Kubinka Armoury.'

At the sound of the Russian words, Conklin bolted forward in the seat. 'Oh, my God!' he cried.

'What is it?' asked Bourne.

'He reached an armoury.' Alex saw the frown of confusion on Jason's face. 'Over here armouries are a hell of a lot more than enclosed parade grounds for legionnaires and reservists. They're serious training quarters and warehouses for weapons.'

'He wasn't heading for Odintsovo,' broke in Krupkin. 'The armoury's farther south, on the outskirts of the town, another four or five kilometres. He's been there before.'

'Those places must have tight security,' said Bourne. 'He can't just walk inside.'

'He already has,' corrected the KGB officer from Paris.

'I mean into restricted areas – like storerooms filled with weapons.'

'That's what concerns me,' went on Krupkin, fingering the microphone in his hand. 'Since he's been there before – and he obviously has – what does he know about the installation . . . *who* does he know?'

'Get on a radio patch, call the place, and have him stopped, held!' insisted Jason.

'Suppose I reach the wrong person, or suppose he already has weapons and we set him off? With one phone call, one hostile confrontation or even the appearance of a strange automobile, there would be wholesale slaughter of several dozen men and women. We saw what he did at the Metropole, in the Vavilova. He's lost all control, he's utterly mad.'

'*Dimitri*,' came the metallic Soviet voice over the radio speaking Russian. 'Something's happening. The man just came out of a side door with a burlap sack and is heading for the car . . . Comrade, I'm not sure it's the *same* man. It probably is, but there's something different about him.'

'What do you mean? The clothes?'

'No, he's wearing a dark suit and his right arm is in a black sling as before . . . yet he's moving more rapidly, his pace firmer, his posture erect.'

'You're saying he does not appear to be wounded, yes?'

'I guess that's what I'm saying, yes.'

'He could be faking it,' said Conklin. 'That son of a bitch could be taking his last breath and convince you he's ready for a marathon.'

'For what purpose, Aleksei? Why any pretence at all?'

'I don't know, but if your man in that car can see him, he can see the car. Maybe he's just in a hell of a hurry.'

'What's going on?' asked Bourne angrily.

'Someone's come outside with a bagful of goodies and going to the car,' said Conklin in English.

'For Christ's sake, *stop* him!'

'We're not sure it's the Jackal,' interrupted Krupkin. 'The clothes are the same, even to the arm sling, but there are physical differences—'

'Then he wants you to think it *isn't* him!' said Jason emphatically.

'*Shto?* . . . What?'

'He's putting himself in your place, thinking like you're thinking now and by doing that *out-thinking* you. He may or may not know that he's been spotted, the car picked up, but he has to assume the worst and act accordingly. How long before we get there?'

'The way my outrageously reckless young comrade is driving, I'd say three or four minutes.'

'*Krupkin!*' The voice burst from the radio speaker. 'Four other people have come outside – three men and a woman. They're running to the car!'

'What did he say?' asked Bourne. Alex translated and Jason frowned. 'Hostages?' he said quietly, as if to himself. 'He just *blew* it!' Medusa's Delta leaned forward and touched Krupkin's shoulder. 'Tell your man to get out of there the moment that car takes off and he knows where it's heading. Tell him to be obvious, to blow the hell out of his horn while he passes the armoury, which he *must* pass from one way or the other.'

'My *dear* fellow!' exploded the Soviet intelligence officer. 'Would you mind telling *me* why I should issue such an order?'

'Because your colleague was right and I was wrong. The man in the sling isn't Carlos. The Jackal's inside, waiting for the cavalry to pass the fort so he can get away in another car – if there is a cavalry.'

'In the name of our revered Karl Marx, *do* explain how you reached this contradictory conclusion!'

'Simple. He made a mistake . . . Even if you could, you wouldn't shoot up that car on the road, would you?'

'Agreed. There are four other people inside, all no doubt innocent Soviet citizens forced to appear otherwise.'

'Hostages?'

'Yes, of course.'

'When was the last time you heard of people running like hell into a situation where they could *become* hostages? Even if they were under a gun from a doorway, one or two, if not all of them, would try to race behind other cars for protection.'

'My *word—*'

'But you were right about one thing. Carlos has a contact inside that armoury – the man in the sling. He may only be an innocent Russian with a brother or a sister living in Paris, but the Jackal owns him.'

'*Dimitri!*' shouted the metallic voice in Russian. 'The car is speeding out of the parking lot!'

Krupkin pressed the button on his microphone and gave his instructions. Essentially, they were to follow that automobile to the borders of Finland, if necessary, but to take it without violence, calling in the police, if they had to. The last order was to pass the armoury, blowing his horn repeatedly. In the Russian vernacular, the agent named Orlov asked, 'What the fuck for?'

'Because I've had a vision from St Nickolai the Good! Also, I'm your charitable superior. *Do* it!'

'You're not well, Dimitri.'

'Do you wish a superb service report or one that will send you to Tashkent?'

'I'm on my way, comrade.'

Krupkin replaced the microphone in the dashboard receptacle. 'Everything proceeds,' he said haltingly, partially over his shoulder. 'If I'm to go down with either a crazed assassin or a convoluted lunatic who displays certain decencies, I imagine it's best to choose the latter. Contrary to the most enlightened sceptics, there might be a God, after all . . . Would you care to buy a house on the lake in Geneva, Aleksei?'

'*I* might,' answered Bourne. 'If I live through the day and do what I have to do, give me a price. I won't quibble.'

'Hey, David,' interjected Conklin. 'Marie made that money, *you* didn't.'

'She'll listen to me. To him.'

'What now, whoever you are?' asked Krupkin.

'Give me all the firepower I need from this trunk of yours and let me off in the grass just before the armoury. Give me a couple of minutes to get in place, then pull into the parking lot and obviously – very obviously – see that the car is missing and get out of there fast, gunning your engine.'

'And leave you *alone*?' cried Alex.

'It's the only way I can take him. The only way he can be taken.'

'*Lunacy!*' spat out Krupkin, his jowls vibrating.

'No, Kruppie, reality,' said Jason Bourne simply. 'It's the same as it was in the beginning. One on one, it's the only way.'

'*That* is sophomoric heroics!' roared the Russian, slamming his hand down on the back of the seat. 'Worse, it's ridiculous strategy. If you're right, I can surround the armoury with a thousand troops!'

'Which is exactly what he'd want – what *I'd* want, if I were Carlos. Don't you see? He could get away in the confusion, in the sheer numbers – that's not a problem for either of us, we've both done it too many times before. Crowds and anxiety are our protection – they're child's play. A knife in a uniform, the uniform ours; toss a grenade into the troops, and after the explosion we're one of the staggering victims – that's amateur night for paid killers. Believe me, I know – I became one in spite of myself.'

'So what do you think you can do by yourself, *Batman*?' asked Conklin, furiously massaging his useless leg.

'Stalk the killer who wants to kill me – and I'll take him.'

'You're a fucking megalomaniac!'

'You're absolutely right. It's the only way to be in the killing game. It's the only edge you've got.'

'*Insanity!*' yelled Krupkin.

'So allow me; I'm entitled to a little craziness. If I thought the entire Russian army would ensure my survival, I'd scream for it. But it wouldn't – it couldn't. There's only this way . . . Stop the car and let me choose the weapons.'

39

The dark green KGB sedan rounded the final curve in the sloping road cut out of the countryside. The descent had been gradual. The ground below was flat and summer-green with fields of wild grass bordering the approach to the massive brown building that was the Kubinka Armoury. It seemed to rise out of the earth, a huge boxlike intrusion on the pastoral scene, an ugly man-made interruption of heavy brown wood and miserly windows reaching three storeys high and covering two acres of land. Like the structure itself, the front entrance was large, square and unadorned except for the dull bas-relief profiles above the door of three Soviet soldiers rushing into the deadly winds of battle, their rifles at port arms, about to blow one another's heads off.

Armed with an authentic Russian AK-47 and five standard thirty-round magazine clips, Bourne jumped out the far side of the silent, coasting government car, using the bulk of the rolling vehicle to conceal himself in the grass directly across the road from the entrance. The armoury's huge dirt parking area was to the right of the long building; a single row of unkempt shrubbery fronted the entrance lawn, in the centre of which stood a tall white pole, the Soviet flag hanging limp in the breezeless morning air. Jason ran across the road, his body low, and crouched by the hedgerow; he had only moments to peer through the bushes and ascertain the existence or nonexistence of the armoury's security procedures. At best, they appeared lax to the point of being informal, if not irrelevant. There was a glass window in the right wall of the entrance similar to that of a theatre's box office; behind it sat a uniformed guard reading a magazine, and alongside him, less visible but seen clearly enough, was another, his head on the counter, asleep. Two other soldiers emerged from the immense armoury door – double doors – both casual, unconcerned, as one glanced at his watch and the other lighted a cigarette.

So much for Kubinka's security; no sudden assault was anticipated nor had one taken place, at least none that had set off alarms reaching the front patrols, usually the first to be alerted. It was eerie, unnatural, beyond the unexpected. The Jackal was inside this military installation, yet there was no sign that he had penetrated it, no indication that somewhere within the complex he was controlling a minimum of five personnel – a man impersonating him, three other men, and a woman.

The parking area itself? He had not understood the exchanges between Alex, Krupkin and the voice over the radio, but now it was clear to him that when they had collectively spoken in Russian and English of people coming outside and running to the stolen car, they were *not* referring to the front entrance! There had to be an exit on the parking area! *Christ*, he had only seconds before the driver of the Komitet car started up the engine and roared into the huge dirt lot, circling it, and racing out, both actions announcing the government vehicle's arrival and swift, calamitous departure. If Carlos was going to make his break, it would be then! After waiting for the standard radio backup, every moment of distance he put between himself and the armoury would make it more difficult to pick up his trail. And *he*, the efficient killing machine from Medusa, was in the wrong *place*! Further, the sight of a civilian running across a lawn or down a road carrying an automatic weapon within a military compound was to invite disaster. It was a small, stupid omission! Three or four additional words translated *and* a less arrogant, more probing listener would have avoided the error. It was always the little things, the seemingly insignificant that crippled grey to black operations. *Goddamn it!*

Five hundred feet away the KGB sedan suddenly thundered as it swerved into the dirt parking area raising clouds of dry dust while crushing and spitting out pieces of rock from its spinning tyres. There was no time to think, time only to act. Bourne held the AK-47 against his right leg, concealing it as much as possible as he rose to his feet, his left hand skimming the top of the low hedgerow – a gardener, perhaps, surveying an anticipated assignment, or an indolent stroller aimlessly touching the roadside shrubbery, nothing remotely threatening, just a gesture, a sign of the commonplace; to the casual observer, he might have been walking down that road for several minutes without being noticed.

He glanced over at the armoury's entrance. The two soldiers were laughing quietly, the one without a cigarette again looking at his watch. Then the object of their minor conspiracy came out of the left front door, an attractive dark-haired girl, barely in her twenties. She humourously, meaninglessly, clapped both her hands over her ears, made a grotesque face and walked rapidly to the time-conscious man in uniform, kissing him on the lips. The threesome linked arms, the woman in the centre, and started to their right, away from the entrance.

A *crash*! Metal colliding with metal, glass shattering glass, the loud harsh sound coming from the distant parking area. Something had happened to the Komitet car with Alex and Krupkin; the young driver from the assault squad had either smashed or skidded into another vehicle in the dry dirt of the lot. Using the sound as an excuse, Jason started down the road, the image of Conklin coming instantly to his mind, producing a limp in his own rapid strides the better to keep his weapon in minimum view. He turned his head, expecting to see the two soldiers and the woman running down the armoury path towards the accident, only to realize that the three of them were running the *other* way, removing themselves from any involvement. Obviously, precious breaks in a military schedule were jealously protected.

Bourne discarded the limp, crashed through the hedgerow, and raced to the concrete path that stretched to the corner of the huge building. Gathering speed and breathing heavily with increasing frequency, Jason's weapon was now in plain sight, slashing the air as he gripped it in the hand of his swinging right arm. He reached the end of the path, his chest heaving, the veins in his neck seemingly prepared to burst as the sweat ran down his skin, drenching his face, his collar and his shirt. Gasping, he steadied the AK-47, his back pressed against the wall of the building, then spun around the corner into the parking area, stunned by what he saw. His pounding feet, coupled with the anxiety that caused his hair-soaked temples to throb, had blocked out all sound up ahead. What he observed now, what sickened him now, he knew had to be the result of multiple gunshots muted by a weapon equipped with a silencer. Dispassionately, Medusa's Delta understood; he had been there many times many years before. There were circumstances under which kills had to be made quietly – utter silence was the unreachable goal, but at least minimal noise was crucial.

The young KGB driver from the assault squad was sprawled on the ground by the boot of the dark green sedan, the wounds in his head certifying death. The car had swerved into the side of a government bus, the sort used to haul workers to and from their places of employment. How or why the accident had happened, Bourne could not know. Neither could he know whether Alex or Krupkin had survived; the car's windows had been pierced repeatedly and there was no sign of movement inside, both facts suggesting the worst but nothing conclusive. Above all, at this moment, the Chameleon also understood that he could not be affected by what he saw – emotions were *out*! If the worst had happened, mourning the dead would come later, vengeance and taking the killer came now.

Think! How? *Quickly!*

Krupkin had said there were 'several dozen men and women' working at the armoury. If so, where the hell *were* they? The Jackal was not acting in a vacuum; it was impossible! Yet a collision had occurred, its violent crash heard over a hundred yards away – well over the distance of a football field – and a man had been shot dead at the site of that crash, his lifeless body bleeding in the dirt, yet no one – *no one* – had appeared, either accidentally or intentionally. With the exception of Carlos and five unknown people, was the entire armoury operating in a vacuum? Nothing made sense!

And then he heard the muffled but emphatic strains of music from deep inside the building. Martial music, drums and trumpets predominating, swelling to crescendos that Bourne could only imagine were deafening within the echoing confines of the huge structure. The image of the young woman emerging from the front entrance returned; she had playfully clapped her hands over her ears and grimaced, and Jason had not understood. He did now. She had come from the armoury's inner staging area, where the decibel level of the music was overpowering. An event was taking place at the Kubinka, a decently attended affair, which accounted for the profusion of automobiles, small vans and buses in the vast parking area – profusion at any rate in the Soviet Union where such vehicles were not in oversupply. Altogether there were perhaps twenty conveyances in the dirt lot, parked in a semicircle. The activity inside was both the Jackal's diversion and his protection; he knew how to orchestrate both to his advantage. So did his enemy. Checkmate.

Why didn't Carlos come out? Why *hadn't* he come out? What was he waiting for? The circumstances were optimal; they couldn't be better. Had his wounds slowed him to the point that he had lost the advantages he had created? It was possible, not likely. The assassin had gotten this far, and if escape was in the offing, it was in him to go further, much further. Then *why*? Irreversible logic, a killer's *survival* logic demanded that after taking out the backup the Jackal had to race away as fast as humanly possible. It was his only chance! Then why was he still *inside*? Why hadn't his escape car fled from the area speeding him to freedom?

His back once again pressed against the wall, Jason sidestepped to his left, closely observing everything he could see. Like most armouries the world over, Kubinka had no windows on the first floor, at least not for the first fifteen feet from the ground; he presumed it was because the occasional wildly galloping horses and glass did not go together. He could see a window frame on what appeared to be the second floor but close enough to the slain driver to afford maximum accuracy for a silenced high-powered weapon. Another frame on ground level had a knob protruding; it was the rear exit no one had bothered to mention. *The little things, the insignificant things! Goddamn!*

The muted music inside swelled again, but now the swelling was different, the drums louder, the trumpets more sustained, more piercing. It was the unmistakable ending of a symphonic march, martial music at its most intense . . . That was *it*! The end of the event inside was at hand and the Jackal would use the emerging crowds to cover his escape. He would mingle, and when panic spread through the parking area with the sight of the dead man and the shot-up sedan, he would disappear – with whom and with what vehicle would take hours to determine.

Bourne had to get inside; he had to stop him, *take* him! Krupkin had worried about the lives of 'several dozen men and women' – he had no idea that in reality there were several hundred! Carlos would use whatever fire-power he had stolen, including grenades, to create mass hysteria so that he could escape. Lives meant nothing, if further killing was required to save his own, *nothing*. Abandoning caution, Delta raced to the door, gripping his AK-47 laterally in his arm, the safety unlatched, his index finger on the trigger. He grabbed the knob and twisted it – it would not *turn*. He fired his weapon into the plated metal around the lock, then a second fusillade into the opposing frame, and as he reached for the smoking knob, his personal world went mad!

Out of the line of vehicles a heavy truck suddenly shot forward, coming straight towards him, wildly accelerating as it approached. Simultaneously, successive bursts of automatic gunfire erupted, the bullets thumping into the wood to his right. He lunged to his left, rolling on the ground, the dust and dirt filling his eyes as he kept rolling, his body a tube spinning away, *away* from the terrifying thing that was happening.

And then it happened! The massive explosion tore apart the door, blowing away a large section of the wall above, and through the black smoke and settling debris he could see a figure lurching awkwardly towards the semi-circle of vehicles. His killer was getting away after all. But *he* was alive! And the reason for it was obvious – the Jackal had made a mistake. Not in the trap, that was extraordinary; Carlos *knew* his enemy was with Krupkin and the KGB and so he *had* gone outside and waited for him. Instead, his error was in the placement of the explosives. He had wired the bomb or bombs to the top of the truck's engine, not *underneath*. Explosive compounds seek release through the least resistant barriers; the relatively thin bonnet of a vehicle is far less solid than the iron beneath it. The bomb actually blew up; it did not blow out on ground level, sending death-inducing metal fragments along the surface.

No *time*! Bourne struggled to his feet and staggered to the Komitet sedan, a horrible fear coming into focus. He looked through the shattered windows, his eyes suddenly drawn to the front seat as a heavily fleshed hand was raised. He yanked the door open and saw Krupkin, his large body squeezed below the seat under the dashboard, his right shoulder half torn away, bleeding flesh apparent through the fabric of his jacket.

'We are hurt,' said the KGB officer weakly, but calmly. 'Aleksei somewhat more seriously than I am, so attend to him first, if you please.'

'The crowd's coming out of the armoury—'

'*Here!*' interrupted Krupkin, painfully reaching into his pocket and pulling out his plastic identification case. 'Get to the idiot in charge and bring him to me. We must get a doctor. For *Aleksei*, you damn fool. *Hurry!*'

The two wounded men lay alongside each other on examining tables in the armoury's infirmary as Bourne stood across the room, leaning against the wall, watching but not understanding what was being said. Three doctors had been dispatched by helicopter from the roof of the People's Hospital on the Serova Prospekt – two surgeons and an anaesthetist, the last, however, proving unnecessary. Severe invasive procedures were not called for; local anaesthetics were sufficient for the cleansing and suturing, followed by generous injections of antibiotics. The foreign objects had passed through their bodies, explained the chief doctor.

'I presume you mean bullets when you speak so reverently of "foreign objects",' said Krupkin in high dudgeon.

'He means bullets,' confirmed Alex hoarsely in Russian. The retired CIA station chief was unable to move his head because of his bandaged throat. Wide adhesive straps extended down across his collarbone and upper right shoulder.

'Thank you,' said the surgeon. 'You were both fortunate, especially you, our American patient for whom we must compile confidential medical records. Incidentally, give our people the name and address of your physician in the United States. You'll need attention for some weeks ahead.'

'Right now he's in a hospital in Paris.'

'I beg your pardon?'

'Well, whenever something's wrong with me, I tell him and he sends me to the doctor he thinks I should see.'

'That's not exactly socialized medicine.'

'For me it is. I'll give his name and address to a nurse. With luck he'll be back soon.'

'I repeat, you were very fortunate.'

'I was very fast, Doctor, and so was your comrade. We saw that son of a bitch running out towards us, so we locked the doors and kept moving in the seats and firing at him as he tried to get close enough to put us away, which he damned near did . . . I'm sorry about the driver; he was a brave young man.'

'He was an angry young man as well, Aleksei,' broke in Krupkin from the other table. 'Those first shots from the doorway sent him into that bus.'

The door of the infirmary burst open, which was to say it was not *opened* so much as it was invaded, submitting to the august presence of the KGB commissar from the flat in Slavyansky. The blunt-featured, blunt-spoken Komitet officer in the dishevelled uniform lived up to his appearance. 'You,' he said to the doctor, 'I've spoken to your associates outside. You are finished here, they say.'

'Not entirely, comrade. There are minor items to attend to such as therapeutical—'

'Later,' interrupted the commissar. 'We talk privately. Alone.'

'The Komitet speaks?' asked the surgeon, his contempt minor but evident.

'It speaks.'

'Sometimes too often.'

'*What?*'

'You heard me,' replied the doctor, heading for the door.

The KGB man shrugged and waited for the infirmary door to close. He then walked to the foot of both examining tables, his squinting flesh-encased eyes darting between the two wounded men, and spat out one word. '*Novgorod!*' he said.

'What?'

'*What* . . . ?'

The responses were simultaneous; even Bourne snapped himself away from the wall.

'You, *asmyehrekee*,' he added, switching to his limited English. 'Understand I say?'

'If you said what I think you said, I think I do, but only the name.'

'I explain good enough. We question the nine men-women he locked in weapons storage. He kill two guards who do not stop him, okay? He take automobile keys from four men but uses no automobiles, okay?'

'I saw him head for the cars!'

'Which? Three other people at Kubinka shot dead, automobile papers taken. Which?'

'For Christ's sake, check with your vehicle bureau, or whatever you call it!'

'Take time. Also in Moskva, automobiles under different names, different tag plates – Leningrad, Smolensk, who knows – all to not look for automobile laws broken.'

'What the hell is he *talking* about?' shouted Jason.

'Automobile ownership is regulated by the state,' explained Krupkin weakly from the table. 'Each major centre has its own registration and is frequently reluctant to cooperate with another centre.'

'*Why?*'

'Individual ownership under different family names – even non-family names. It's forbidden. There are only so many vehicles available for purchase.'

'So?'

'Local bribery is a fact of life. No one in Leningrad wants a finger pointed at him from a bureaucrat in Moscow. He's telling you that it could take several days to learn what automobile the Jackal's driving.'

'That's *crazy*!'

'You said it, Mr Bourne, I didn't. I'm an upstanding citizen of the Soviet Union, please remember that.'

'But what's it all got to do with Novgorod – that *is* what he said, isn't it?'

'*Novgorod. Shto eto znachit?*' said Krupkin to the KGB official. In rapid, clipped Russian, the peasant commissar gave the pertinent details to his colleague from Paris. Krupkin turned his head on the table and translated in English. 'Try to follow this, Jason,' he said, his voice intermittently fading, his breathing becoming increasingly more difficult. 'Apparently there is a walk-around gallery above the armoury's arena. He used it and saw you through a window on the road by the hedges and came back to the weapons room screaming like the maniac he is. He shouted to his bound hostages that you were *his* and you were dead . . . And there was only one last thing he had to accomplish.'

'*Novgorod*,' interrupted Conklin, whispering, his head rigid, staring at the ceiling.

'Precisely,' said Krupkin, his eyes focused on Alex's profile beside him. 'He's going back to the place of his birth . . . where Ilich Ramirez Sanchez became Carlos the Jackal because he was disinherited, marked for execution as a madman. He held his gun against everyone's throat, quietly demanding to know the best roads to Novgorod, threatening to kill whoever gave him the wrong answer. None did, of course, and all who knew told him it was five to six hundred kilometres away, a full day's drive.'

'Drive?' interjected Bourne.

'He knows he cannot use any other means of transportation. The railroads, the airports – even the small airfields – all will be watched, he understands that.'

'What will he do in Novgorod?' asked Jason quickly.

'Dear God in heaven, which, of course, there is neither, who *knows*? He intends to leave his mark, a highly destructive memorial to himself, no doubt, in answer to those he believes betrayed him thirty-odd years ago, as well as the poor souls who fell under his gun this morning in the Vavilova . . . He took the papers from our agent trained at Novgorod; he thinks they'll get him inside. They won't – we'll stop him.'

'Don't even try,' said Bourne. 'He may or may not use them, depending upon what he sees, what he senses. He doesn't need papers to get in there any more than I do, but if he senses something wrong, and he will, he'll kill a number of good men and still get inside.'

'What are you driving at?' asked Krupkin warily, eyeing Bourne, the American with alternate identities and apparently conflicting life-styles.

'Get me inside ahead of him with a detailed map of the whole complex and some kind of document that gives me free access to go wherever I want to go.'

'You've lost your *senses*!' cried Dimitri. 'A nondefecting American, an assassin hunted by every NATO country in Europe, inside *Novgorod*?'

'*Nyet, nyet, nyet!*' roared the Komitet commissar. 'I understand good, *okay*? You are lunatic, *okay*?'

'Do you want the Jackal?'

'Naturally, but there are limits to the cost.'

'I haven't the slightest interest in Novgorod or in any of the compounds – you should know that by now. Your little infiltrating operations and *our* little infiltrating operations can go on and on and it doesn't matter because none of it means a goddamned thing in the long run. It's all adolescent game playing. We either live together on this planet or there is no planet . . . My only concern is Carlos. I want him dead so *I* can go on living.'

'Of course, I personally agree with much of what you say, although the adolescent games do keep some of us rather gracefully employed. However, there's no way I could convince my more rigid superiors, starting with the one standing above me.'

'All right,' said Conklin from his table, his eyes still on the ceilling. 'Down and dirty – we deal. You get him into Novgorod and you keep Ogilvie.'

'We've already got him, Aleksei.'

'Not clean, you haven't. Washington knows he's here.'

'So?'

'So *I* can say you lost him and they'll believe me. They'll take my word for it that he flew out of your nest and you're mad as hell, but you can't get him back. He's operating from points unknown or unreachable, but obviously under the sovereign protection of a United Nations country. As a matter of conjecture, I suspect that's how you got him over here in the first place.'

'You're cryptic, my fine old enemy. To what purpose should I entertain your suggestion?'

'No World Court embarrassments, no charges of harbouring an American accused of international crimes . . . You win the stakes in Europe. You take over the Medusa operation with no complications – in the person of one Dimitri Krupkin, a proven sophisticate from the cosmopolitan world of Paris. Who better to guide the enterprise? . . . The newest hero of the Soviet, a member of the inner economic council of the Presidium. Forget the lousy house in Geneva, Kruppie, how about a mansion on the Black Sea?'

'It is a most intelligent and attractive offer, I grant you,' said Krupkin. 'I know two or three men on the Central Committree whom I can reach in a matter of minutes – everything confidential, of course.'

'*Nyet, nyet!*' shouted the KGB commissar, slamming his fist down on Dimitri's table. 'I understand some – you talk too fast – but all is lunatic!'

'Oh, for God's sake, *shut up*!' roared Krupkin. 'We're discussing things far beyond your grasp.'

'*Shto?*' Like a young child reprimanded by an adult, the Komitet officer, his puffed eyes widened, was both astonished and frightened by his subordinate's incomprehensible rebuke.

'Give my friend his chance, Kruppie,' said Alex. 'He's the best there is and he may bring you the Jackal.'

'He may also bring about his own death, Aleksei.'

'He's been there before. I believe in him.'

'Belief,' whispered Krupkin, his own eyes now on the ceiling. 'Such a luxury it is . . . Very well, the order will be issued secretly, its origins untraceable, of course. You'll enter your own American compound. It's the one least understood.'

'How fast can I get there?' asked Bourne. 'There's a lot I have to put together.'

'We have an airport in Vnokova under our control, no more than an hour away. First, I must make arrangements. Hand me a telephone . . . *You* my imbecilic *commissar*! I will hear no more from you! A *telefone*!' The once all-powerful, now subdued superior who had really only understood such words as *Presidium* and *Central Committee*, moved with alacrity, bringing an extension phone to Krupkin's table.

'One more thing,' said Bourne. 'Have Tass put out an immediate bulletin with heavy coverage in the newspapers, radio, and television that the assassin known as Jason Bourne died of wounds here in Moscow. Make the details sketchy but have them parallel what happened here this morning.'

'That's not difficult. Tass is an obedient instrument of the state.'

'I haven't finished,' continued Jason. 'I want you to include in those sketch details that among the personal effects found on Bourne's body was a road map of Brussels and its environs. The town of Anderlecht was circled in red – that has to appear.'

'The assassination of the supreme commander of NATO – very good, very convincing. However, Mr Bourne or Webb or whatever your name may be, you should know that this story will splash across the world like a giant tidal wave.'

'I understand that.'

'Are you prepared for it?'

'Yes, I am.'

'What about your wife? Don't you think you should reach her first, before the civilized world learns that Jason Bourne is dead?'

'No. I don't even want the slightest risk of a leak.'

'*Jesus!*' exploded Alex, coughing. 'That's *Marie* you're talking about. She'll fall apart!'

'It's a risk I'll accept,' said Delta coldly.

'You son of a *bitch*!'

'So be it,' agreed the Chameleon.

John St Jacques, tears welling in his eyes, walked into the bright, sunlit room at the sterile house in the Maryland countryside; in his hand was a page of computer printout. His sister was on the floor in front of the couch playing with an exuberant Jamie, she having put the infant Alison back into the crib upstairs. She looked worn and haggard, her face pale with dark circles under her eyes; she was exhausted from the tension and the jet lag of the long, idiotically routed flights from Paris to Washington. In spite of arriving late last night, she had gotten up early to be with the children and no amount of friendly persuasion on the part of the motherly Mrs Cooper could dissuade her. The brother would have given years of his life not to do what had to be done during the next few minutes, but he could not risk the alternatives. He had to be with her when she found out.

'Jamie,' said St Jacques gently. 'Go find Mrs Cooper, will you please? I think she's in the kitchen.'

'Why, Uncle John?'

'I want to talk to your mother for a few minutes.'

'Johnny, *please*,' objected Marie.

'I have to, Sis.'

'What . . . ?' The child left, and as children will often do, he obviously sensed something beyond his understanding; he stared at his uncle before heading to the door. Marie got to her feet and looked hard at her brother, at the tears that began to roll down his cheeks. The terrible message was conveyed. 'No . . . !' she whispered, her pallid face growing paler. 'Dear God, *no*,' she cried, her hands and then her shoulders starting to tremble. 'No . . . *no*!' she roared.

'He's gone, Sis. I wanted you to hear it from me, not over a radio or a TV set. I want to be with you.'

'You're wrong, *wrong*!' screamed Marie, rushing towards him. grabbing his shirt and clenching the fabric in her fists. 'He's protected! . . . He promised me he was *protected*!'

'This just came from Langley,' said the younger brother, holding up the page of computer printout. 'Holland called me a few minutes ago and said it was on its way over. He knew you had to see it. It was picked up from Radio Moscow during the night and will be on all the broadcasts and in the morning papers.'

'*Give* it to me!' she shouted defiantly. He did so and gently held her shoulders, prepared to take her in his arms and give what comfort he could. She read the copy rapidly, then shook off his hands, frowning, and walked back to the couch and sat down. Her concentration was absolute; she placed the paper on the coffee table and studied it as though it were an archaeological find, a scroll perhaps.

'He's gone, Marie. I don't know what to say – you know how I felt about him.'

'Yes, I know, Johnny,' Then to St Jacques's astonishment, his sister looked up at him, a thin, wan smile appearing on her lips. 'But it's a little early for our tears, Bro. He's alive. Jason Bourne's alive and up to his tricks and that means David's alive too.'

My God, she can't accept it, thought the brother, walking to the couch and kneeling beside the coffee table in front of Marie, taking her hands in his. 'Sis, honey, I don't think you understand. I'll do everything possible to help you, but you've got to understand.'

'Bro, you're very sweet but you haven't read this closely – really closely. The impact of the message detracts from the subtext. In economics we call it obfuscation with a cloud of smoke and a couple of mirrors.'

'*Huh?*' St Jacques released her hands and stood up. 'What are you talking about?'

Marie picked up the Langley communiqué and scanned it. 'After several confused, even contradictory, accounts of what happened,' she said, 'described by people on the scene at this armoury, or whatever it is, the following is buried in the last paragraph. "Among the personal effects found on the slain assassin's body was a map of Brussels and the surrounding area with the town of Anderlecht circled in red." Then it goes on to make the obvious connection with Teagarten's assassination. It's a wash, Johnny, from two points of view . . . First, David would never carry such a map. Second, and far more telling, the fact that the Soviet media would give such prominence to the story is unbelievable enough, but to include the assassination of General Teagarten is simply too much.'

'What do you mean? Why?'

'Because the presumed assassin was *in* Russia, and Moscow wants no conceivable linkage to the killing of a NATO commander . . . No, Bro, someone bent the rules and persuaded Tass to put out the story, and I suspect heads will roll. I don't know where Jason Bourne is, but I know he's not dead. David made sure I'd know that.'

Peter Holland picked up the phone and touched the buttons on his console for Charles Casset's private line.

'Yes?'

'Charlie, it's Peter.'

'I'm relieved to hear that.'

'Why?'

'Because all I'm getting on this phone is trouble and confusion. I just got off with our source in Dzerzhinsky Square and he told me the KGB's after blood.'

'The Tass release on Bourne?'

'Right. Tass and Radio Moscow assumed the story was officially sanctioned because it was faxed by the Ministry of Information using the proper immediate-release codes. When the shit hit the fan, no one owned up, and whoever programmed the codes can't be traced.'

'What do you make of it?'

'I'm not sure, but from what I've learned about Dimitri Krupkin, it could be his style. He's now working with Alex and if this isn't something out of the Conklin textbook, I don't know Saint Alex. And I do.'

'That dovetails with what Marie thinks.'

'Marie?'

'Bourne's wife. I just spoke to her and her argument's pretty strong. She says Moscow's report is a wash for all the right reasons. Her husband's alive.'

'I agree. Is that what you called to tell me?'

'No,' answered the director, taking a deep breath. 'I'm adding to your trouble and confusion.'

'I'm not relieved to hear that. What is it?'

'The Paris telephone number, the link to the Jackal we got from Henry Sykes in Montserrat that reached a café on the Marais waterfront in Paris.'

'Where someone would answer a call for a blackbird. I remember.'

'Someone did and we followed him. You're not going to like this.'

'Alex Conklin is about to earn the prick-of-the-year award. He put us on to Sykes, didn't he?'

'Yes.'

'Do tell.'

'The message was delivered to the home of the director of the Deuxième Bureau.'

'My God! We'd better turn that over to the SED branch of French intelligence with a restricted chronology.'

'I'm not turning anything over to anybody until we hear from Conklin. We owe him that much – I think.'

'What the hell are they *doing*?' shouted a frustrated Casset over the phone. 'Putting out false death notices – from *Moscow*, no less! What *for*?'

'Jason Bourne's gone hunting,' said Peter Holland. 'And when the hunt is over – if it's over and *if* the kill is made – he's going to have to get out of the woods before anyone turns on him . . . . I want every station and listening post on the borders of the Soviet Union on full alert. Code name: Assassin. Get him back.'

40

Novgorod. To say it was incredible was to obliquely recognize the existence of credibility and that was nearly impossible. It was the ultimate fantasy, its optical illusions seemingly more real than reality, the phantasmagoria there to be touched, felt, used, entered into and departed from; it was a collective masterpiece of invention cut out of the immense forests along the Volkhov River. From the moment Bourne emerged from the deep underground tunnel below the water with its guards, gates and myriad cameras, he was close to being in a state of shock while still being able to keep walking, observing, absorbing – thinking.

The American compound, presumably like those of the different countries, was broken up into sections, built on areas anywhere from two to five acres, each distinctly separate from the others. One area, erected on the banks of the river, might be the heart of a Maine waterfront village; another, farther inland, a small Southern town; yet another, a busy metropolitan city street. Each was completely 'authentic' with the appropriate vehicular traffic, police, dress codes, shops, grocery and drugstores, gas stations and mock structures of buildings – many of which rose two storeys high and were so real they had American hardware on the doors and windows. Obviously, as vital as the physical appearances was language – not merely the fluent use of English but the mastery of linguistic idiosyncrasies, the dialects that were characteristic of specific locations. As Jason wandered from one section to another he heard all around him the distinctive sounds. From New England Down East with its 'eeahh' to Texas's drawl and its familiar 'you-alls'; from the gentle nasality of the Midwest to the loud abrasiveness of the large Eastern cities with the inevitable 'know what I mean?' tacked on to conversational sentences, whether questions or statements. It *was* all incredible. It was not simply beyond belief, it made the true suspension of disbelief frighteningly viable.

He had been briefed on the flight from Vnokova by a late-middle-aged Novgorod graduate who had been urgently summoned from his Moscow apartment by Krupkin. The small, bald man was not only garrulously instructive, but in his own way mesmerizing. If anyone had ever told Jason Bourne that he was going to be briefed in depth by a Soviet espionage agent whose English was so laced with the Deep South that it sonorously floated out of his mouth with the essence of magnolias, he would have deemed the information preposterous.

'*Good Lawd*, Ah do miss those barbecues, especially the ribs. You know who grilled 'em best? That black fellow who I believed was such a good friend until he exposed me. Can you *imagine*? I thought he was one of those radicals. He turned out to be a boy from Dartmouth workin' for the FBI. A *lawyer*, no less . . . Hell, the exchange was made at Aeroflot in New York and we still write each other.'

'Adolescent games,' had mumbled Bourne.

'Games? . . . Oh yes, he was a mighty fine coach.'

'Coach?'

'Sure n'uff. A few of us started a Little League in East Point. That's right outside Atlanta.'

Incredible.

'May we concentrate on Novgorod, please?'

'Suttn'ly. Dimitri may have told you, I'm semi-retired, but my pension requires that I spend five days a month there as a *tak govorya* – a "trainer", as you would say.'

'I didn't understand what he meant.'

'Ah'll explain.' The strange man whose voice belonged to the old Confederacy had been thorough.

Each compound at Novgorod was divided into three classes of personnel. The trainers, the candidates, and operations. The last category included the KGB staff, guards, and maintenance. The practical implementation of the Novgorod process was simple in structure. A compound's staff created the daily training schedules for each individual section, and the trainers, both permanent and part-time retirees, commandeered all individual and group activities while the candidates carried them out, using only the language of the compound and the dialects of the specific areas in which they were located. No Russian was permitted, the rule tested frequently by the trainers who would suddenly bark orders or insults in the native language; there could be no acknowledgement of understanding on the candidates' part.

'When you say assignments,' Bourne had asked, 'what do you mean?'

'Situations, mah friend. Jest about anything you might think of. Like ordering lunch or dinner, or buying clothes, or fillin' the tank of your car, requesting a specific gasoline . . . leaded or unleaded and the degrees of octane – all of which we don't know a thing about here. Then, of course, there are the more dramatic events often *un*scheduled so as to test the candidates' reactions. Say, an automobile accident necessitating conversations with "American" police and the resulting insurance forms that must be filled out – you can give yourself away if you appear too ignorant.'

The little things, the insignificant things – they were vital. A back door at the Kubinka Armoury. 'What else?'

'So many inconsequential things that a person might not consider significant, but they can be. Say, being mugged in a city street at night – what should you do, what shouldn't you do? Remember, many of our candidates, and all of the younger ones, are trained in self-defence, but depending upon the circumstances, it may not be advisable to use those skills. Questions of background could be raised. Discretion, always discretion . . . For me, as an experienced part-time *tak govorya*, of course, I've always preferred the more imaginative situations which we are permitted to implement whenever we care to as long as they fall within the guidelines of environmental penetration.'

'What does that mean?'

'Learn always, but never appear to be learning. For example, a favourite of mine is to approach several candidates, say, at a bar in some "location" near a military testing ground. I pretend to be a disgruntled government worker or perhaps an inebriated defence contractor – obviously someone with access to information – and start ladlin' out classified material of recognized value.'

'Just for curiosity,' Bourne had interrupted, 'under those circumstances how should candidates react?'

'Listen carefully and be prepared to write down every salient fact, all the while feigning total disinterest and offering such remarks as . . . ' Here the Novgorod graduate's Southern dialect became so rough-mountain South that the magnolias were replaced by sour mash. '. . . "Who gives a barrel a' hogshit 'bout that stuff?" and "They got any of them whoors over there lak people say they got?" or "Don't understand a fuckin' word you're talkin' about, asshole – all Ah knows is that you're borin' the holy be-Jesus outta me!" . . . that sort of thing.'

'Then what?'

'Later, each man is called in and told to list everything he learned – fact by salient fact.'

'What about passing along the information? Are there training procedures for that?'

Jason's Soviet instructor had stared at him in silence for several moments from the adjacent seat in the small plane. 'I'm sorry you had to ask the question,' he said slowly. 'I'll have to report it.'

'I didn't *have* to ask it, I was simply curious. Forget I asked it.'

'I can't do that. I won't do that.'

'Do you trust Krupkin?'

'Of course I do. He's brilliant, a multilingual phenomenon. A true hero of the Komitet.'

You don't know the half of it, thought Bourne, but he said, with even a trace of reverence, 'Then report it only to him. He'll tell you it *was* just curiosity. I owe absolutely nothing to my government; instead, it owes me.'

'Very well . . . Speakin' of yourself, let's get to you. With Dimitri's authority I've made arrangements for your visit to Novgorod – please don't tell me your objective; it's not in my purview any more than the question you asked is in yours.'

'Understood. The arrangements?'

'You will make contact with a young trainer named Benjamin in the manner I will describe in a few moments. I'll tell you this much about Benjamin so you'll perhaps understand his attitude. His parents were Komitet officers assigned to the consulate in Los Angeles for nearly twenty years. He's basically American-educated, his freshman and sophomore years at UCLA; in fact, until he and his father were hurriedly recalled to Moscow four years ago—'

'He and his *father*?'

'Yes. His mother was caught in an FBI sting operation at the naval base in

San Diego. She has three more years to serve in prison. There is no clemency and no exchanges for a Russian "momma".'

'Hey, *wait* a minute. Then it can't be all *our* fault.'

'I didn't say it was, Ah'm just relayin' the facts.'

'Understood. I make contact with Benjamin.'

'He's the only one who knows who you are – not by name, of course, you'll use the name "Archie" – and he'll furnish you with the necessary clearance to go from one compound to the other.'

'Papers?'

'He'll explain. He'll also watch you, be with you at all times, and, frankly, he's been in touch with Comrade Krupkin and knows far more than I do – which is precisely the way this retired Georgia cracker likes it . . . Good huntin', polecat, if it's huntin' you're after. Don't rape no wooden Indians.'

Bourne followed the signs – everything was in English – to the city of *Rockledge, Florida*, fifteen miles southwest of NASA's Cape Canaveral. He was to meet Benjamin at a luncheon counter in the local Woolworth store, looking for a man in his mid-twenties wearing a red-checkered shirt, with a Budweiser baseball cap on the stool beside him, saving it. It was the hour, within the time span of minutes: three thirty-five in the afternoon.

He saw him. The sandy-haired, California-educated Russian was seated at the far right end of the counter, the baseball cap on the stool to his left. There were half a dozen men and women along the row talking to one another and consuming soft drinks and snacks. Jason approached the empty seat, glanced down at the cap and spoke politely. 'Is this taken?' he asked.

'I'm waiting for someone.' replied the young KGB trainer, his voice neutral, his grey eyes straying up to Bourne's face.

'I'll find another place.'

'She may not get here for another five minutes.'

'Hell, I'm just having a quick vanilla Coke. I'll be out of here by then—'

'Sit down,' said Benjamin, removing the hat and casually putting it on his head. A gum-chewing counterman came by and Jason ordered; his drink arrived, and the Komitet trainer continued quietly, his eyes now on the foam of his milk shake, which he sipped through a straw. 'So you're Archie, like in the comics.'

'And you're Benjamin. Nice to know you.'

'We'll both find out if that's a fact, won't we?'

'Do we have a problem?'

'I want the ground rules clear so there won't be one,' said the West Coast-bred Soviet. 'I don't approve of your being permitted in here. Regardless of my former address and the way I may sound, I haven't much use for Americans.'

'Listen to me, Ben,' interrupted Bourne, his eyes forcing the trainer to look at him. 'All things considered, I don't approve of your mother still being in prison, either, but I didn't put her there.'

'We free the dissidents and the Jews, but you insist on keeping a fifty-eight-year-old woman who was at best a simple courier!' whispered the Russian, spitting out the words.

'I don't know the facts and I wouldn't be too quick to call Moscow the mercy capital of the world, but if you can help me – *really* help me – maybe I can help your mother.'

'Goddamned bullshit promises. What the hell can *you* do?'

'To repeat what I said an hour ago to a bald-headed friend of yours in the plane, I don't owe my government a thing, but it sure as hell owes me. Help me, Benjamin.'

'I will because I've been ordered to, not because of your con. But if you try to learn things that have nothing to do with your purpose here – you won't get out. *Clear?*'

'It's not only clear, it's irrelevant and unnecessary. Beyond normal astonishment and curiosity, both of which I will suppress to the best of my ability, I haven't the slightest interest in the objectives of Novgorod. Ultimately, in my opinion, they lead nowhere . . . Although, I grant you, the whole complex beats the hell out of Disneyland.'

Benjamin's involuntary laugh through the straw caused the foam on his milk shake to swell and burst. 'Have you been to Anaheim?' he asked mischievously.

'I could never afford it.'

'We had diplomatic passes.'

'Christ, you're human, after all. Come on, let's take a walk and talk some turkey.'

They crossed over a miniature bridge into *New London, Connecticut*, home of America's submarine construction, and strolled down to the Volkhov River, which in this area had been turned into a maximum security naval base – again, all in realistic miniature. High fences and armed 'US Marine' guards were stationed at the gates and patrolled the grounds fronting the concrete slips that held enormous mock-ups of the stallions of America's nuclear undersea fleet.

'We have all the stations, all the schedules, every device and every reduced inch of the piers,' said Benjamin. 'And we've yet to break the security procedures. Isn't that crazy?'

'Not for a minute. We're pretty good.'

'Yes, but we're better. Except for minor pockets of discontent, we believe. You merely accept.'

'What?'

'Your crap notwithstanding, white America was never in slavery. We were.'

'That's not only long-past history, young man, but rather selective history, isn't it?'

'You sound like a professor.'

'Suppose I were?'

'I'd argue with you.'

'Only if you were in a sufficiently broad-minded environment that allowed you to argue with authority.'

'Oh, come on, cut the bullshit, man! The academic-freedom bromide *is* history. Check out our campuses. We've got rock and blue jeans and more grass than you can find the right paper to roll it in.'

'That's progress?'

'Would you believe it's a start?'

'I'll have to think about it.'

'Can you really help my mother?'

'Can you really help me?'

'Let's try . . . Okay, this Carlos the Jackal. I've heard of him but he's not large in my vocabulary. *Direktor* Krupkin says he's one very bad dude.'

'I hear California checking in.'

'It comes back. Forget it. I'm where I want to be and don't for a moment think otherwise.'

'I wouldn't dare.'

'What?'

'You keep protesting—'

'Shakespeare said it better. My minor at UCLA was English lit.'

'What was your major?'

'American history. What else, grandpa?'

'Thanks, kid.'

'This Jackal,' said Benjamin, leaning against the New London fence as several guards began to run towards him. '*Prahsteetye!*' he yelled. 'No, *no*! I mean, excuse me. *Tak govorya!* I'm a trainer! . . . Oh, *shit*!'

'Will you be reported?' asked Jason as they quickly walked away.

'No, they're too damned dumb. They're maintenance personnel in uniforms; they walk their posts but they don't really know what's going on. Only who and what to stop.'

'Pavlov's dogs?'

'Who better? Animals don't rationalize; they go for the throats and plug up the holes.'

'Which brings us back to the Jackal,' said Bourne.

'I don't understand.'

'You don't have to, it's symbolic. How could he get in here?'

'He couldn't. Every guard in every tunnel up the line has the name and serial numbers of the Novgorod papers he took from the agent he killed in Moscow. If he shows up, they'll stop him and shoot him on sight.'

'I told Krupkin not to do that.'

'For Christ's sake, why?'

'Because it won't *be* him and lives could be lost. He'll send in others, maybe two or three or four into different compounds, always testing, confusing, until he finds a way to get through.'

'You're nuts. What happens to the men he sends in?'

'It wouldn't matter. If they're shot, he watches and learns something.'

'You're really crazy. Where would he find people like that?'

'Any place where there are people who think they're making a month's salary for a few minutes' work. He could call each one a routine security check – remember, he's got the papers to prove he's official. Combined with money, people are impressed with such documents and aren't too sceptical.'

'And at the first gate he loses those papers,' insisted the trainer.

'Not at all. He's driving over five hundred miles through a dozen towns and cities. He could easily have copies made in any number of places. Your business centres have Xerox machines; they're all over the place, and touching up those papers to look like the real items is no sweat.' Bourne stopped and looked at the Americanized Soviet. 'You're talking details, Ben, and take my word for it, they don't count. Carlos is coming here to leave his mark, and we have one advantage that blows away all his expertise. If Krupkin was able to get the news out properly, the Jackal thinks I'm dead.'

'The whole *world* thinks you're dead . . . Yes, Krupkin told me; it would've been dumb not to. In here, you're a recruit named "Archie", but I know who you are, Bourne. Even if I'd never heard of you before, I sure as hell have now. You're all Radio Moscow's been talking about for hours.'

'Then we can assume Carlos has heard the news, too.'

'No question. Every vehicle in Russia is equipped with a radio; it's standard. In case of an American attack, incidentally.'

'That's good marketing.'

'Did you really assassinate Teagarten in Brussels?'

'Get off my case—'

'Off-limits, okay. What's your point?'

'Krupkin should have left it to me.'

'Left what?'

'The Jackal's penetration.'

'What the hell are you talking about?'

'Use Krupkin, if necessary, but send the word up to every tunnel, every entrance to Novgorod, to let in anyone using those papers. My guess is three or four, maybe five. They're to watch them, but they're to let everyone come inside.'

'You just got awarded a room made of thick sponge rubber. You're certifiable, Archie.'

'No, I'm not. I said that everyone should be watched, followed, that the guards maintain constant contact with us here in this compound.'

'So?'

'One of those men will disappear in a matter of minutes. No one will know where he is or where he went. That man will be Carlos.'

'*And?*'

'He'll convince himself he's invulnerable, free to do whatever he wants to do, because he thinks I'm dead. That sets him free.'

'Why?'

'Because he knows and I know that we're the only ones who can track each other, whether it's in the jungles or the cities or a combination of both. Hatred does that, Benjamin. Or desperation.'

'That's pretty emotional, isn't it? Also abstract.'

'No way,' answered Jason. 'I have to think like he thinks – I was trained to do that years ago . . . Let's examine the alternatives. How far up the Volkhov does Novgorod extend? Thirty, forty kilometres?'

'Forty-seven, to be exact, and every metre is impenetrable. There are magnesium pipes crisscrossing the water, spaced above and below the surface to permit the free flow of underwater life but capable of setting off alarms. On the east bank are interlocking ground grids, all weight-sensing. Anything over ninety pounds instantly sets off sirens, and television monitors and spotlights zero in on any intruder over that weight. And even if an eighty-nine-pound wonder reached the fence, he'd be electrically rendered unconscious on the first touch; that also goes for the magnesium pipes in the river. Of course, falling trees or floating logs and the heavier animals keep our security forces on the run. It's good discipline, I suppose.'

'Then there are only the tunnels,' said Bourne, 'is that right?'

'You came through one, what can I tell you that you didn't see? Except that iron gates literally crash down at the slightest irregularity, and in emergencies all the tunnels can be flooded.'

'All of which Carlos knows. He was trained here.'

'Many years ago, Krupkin told me.'

'Many years,' agreed Jason. 'I wonder how much things have changed.'

'Technologically you could probably fill a few volumes, especially in communications and security, but not the basics. Not the tunnels or the miles of grids in and out of the water; they're built for a couple of centuries. As far as the compounds go, there're always some minor adjustments, but I don't think they'd tear up the streets or the buildings. It'd be easier to move a dozen cities.'

'So whatever the changes, they're essentially internal.'

They reached a miniature intersection where an argumentative driver of an early seventies Chevrolet was being given a ticket for a traffic violation by an equally disagreeable policeman. 'What's that all about?' asked Bourne.

'The purpose of the assignment is to instil a degree of contentiousness on the part of the one driving the car. In America a person will frequently, often loudly, argue with a police officer. It's not the case here.'

'Like in questioning authority, such as a student contradicting his professor? I don't imagine that's too popular, either.'

'That's also entirely different.'

'I'm glad you think so.' Jason heard a distant hum and looked up at the sky. A light, single-engine seaplane was flying south following the Volkhov River. 'My God, airborne,' he said, as if to himself.

'Forget it,' countered Benjamin. 'It's ours . . . Technology again. One, there's no place to land except patrolled helicopter pads; and two, we're shielded by radar. An unidentified plane coming within thirty miles of here, the air base at Belopol is alerted and it's shot down.' Across the street a small crowd had gathered, watching the disagreeable policeman and the argumentative driver, who had slammed his hand down on the roof of the Chevrolet as the crowd vocally encouraged him. 'Americans can be very foolish,' mumbled the young trainer, his embarrassment showing.

'At least someone's idea of Americans can be,' said Bourne, smiling.

'Let's go,' said Benjamin, starting to walk away. 'I personally pointed out that the assignment wasn't very realistic, but it was explained to me that instilling the attitude was important.'

'Like telling a student that he can actually argue with a professor, or a citizen that he can publicly criticize a member of the Politburo? They *are* strange attitudes, aren't they?'

'Pound sand, Archie.'

'Relax, young Lenin,' said Jason, coming alongside the trainer. 'Where's your LA cool?'

'I left it in the Labrea Tar Pits.'

'I want to study the maps. All of them.'

'It's been arranged. Also the other ground rules.'

They sat in a conference room at staff headquarters, the large rectangular table covered with maps of the entire Novgorod complex. Bourne could not help himself; even after nearly four hours of concentration, he frequently shook his head in sheer astonishment. The series of deep-cover training grounds along the Volkhov were more expansive and more intricate than he had thought possible. Benjamin's remark that it would 'be easier to move a dozen cities' rather than drastically alter Novgorod was a simple statement of fact, not an exaggeration. Scaled-down replicas of towns and cities, water-fronts and airports, military and scientific installations from the Mediterranean to the Atlantic, north to the Baltic and up the Gulf of Bothnia, were represented within its parameters, all in addition to the American acreage. Yet for all the massive detail, suggestion and miniaturization made it possible to place everything within barely thirty miles of riverfront wilderness, at a depth ranging from three to five miles.

'Egypt, Israel, Italy,' began Jason, circling the table, staring down at the maps. 'Greece, Portugal, Spain, France, the UK—' He rounded the corner as Benjamin interrupted, leaning wearily back in a chair.

'Germany, the Netherlands, and the Scandinavian countries,' he completed. 'As I explained, most of the compounds included two separate and distinct countries, usually where there are common boundaries, cultural similarities, or just to conserve space. There are basically nine major compounds, representing all the major nations – major to our interests – and therefore nine tunnels, approximately seven kilometres apart starting with the one here and heading north along the river.'

'Then the first tunnel next to ours is the UK, right?'

'Yes, followed by France, then Spain – which includes Portugal – then across the Mediterranean beginning with Egypt along with Israel—'

'It's clear,' broke in Jason, sitting down at the end of the table, bringing his clasped hands together in thought. 'Did you get word up the line that they're to admit anyone with those papers Carlos has, no matter what he looks like?'

'No.'

'*What?*' Bourne snapped his head towards the young trainer.

'I had Comrade Krupkin do that. He's in a Moscow hospital, so they can't lock him up here for training fatigue.'

'How can I cross over into another compound? Quickly if necessary.'

'Then you're ready for the rest of the ground rules?'

'I'm ready. There's only so much these maps can tell me.'

'Okay.' Benjamin reached into his pocket and withdrew a small black object the size of a credit card but somewhat thicker. He tossed it to Jason, who caught it in midair and studied it. 'That's your passport,' continued the Soviet. 'Only the senior staff have them and if one's lost or misplaced for even a few minutes, it's reported immediately.'

'There's no ID, no writing or marking at all.'

'It's all inside, computerized and coded. Each compound checkpoint has a clearing lock. You insert it and the barriers are raised, admitting you and telling the guards that you're cleared from headquarters – and noted.'

'Damned clever, these backward Marxists.'

'They had the same little dears for just about every hotel room in Los Angeles, and that was four years ago . . . Now for the rest.'

'The ground rules?'

'Krupkin calls them protective measures – for us as well as you. Frankly, he doesn't think you'll get out of here alive; and if you don't, you're to be deep-fried and lost.'

'How nicely realistic.'

'He likes you, Bourne . . . Archie.'

'Go on.'

'As far as the senior staff is concerned, you're undercover personnel from the inspector general's office in Moscow, an American specialist sent in to check on Novgorod leaks to the West. You're to be given whatever you need, including weapons, but no one is to talk to you unless you talk to him first. Considering my own background, I'm your liaison; anything you want you relay through me.'

'I'm grateful.'

'Maybe not entirely,' said Benjamin. 'You don't go anywhere without me.'

'That's unacceptable.'

'That's the way it is.'

'No, it's not.'

'Why not?'

'Because I won't be impeded . . . and if I do get out of here, I'd like a certain Benjamin's mother to find him alive and well and commuting to Moscow.'

The young Russian stared at Bourne, strength mingled with no little pain in his eyes. 'You really think you can help my father and me?'

'*I know* I can . . . so help *me*. Play by my rules, Benjamin.'

'You're a strange man.'

'I'm a hungry man. Can we get some food around here? And maybe a little bandage? I got hit a while back, and after today my neck and shoulders are letting me know it.' Jason removed his jacket; his shirt was drenched in blood.

'Jesus *Christ*! I'll call a doctor—'

'No, you won't. Just a medic, that's all . . . My rules, Ben.'

'Okay – Archie. We're staying at the Visiting Commissars Suite; it's on the top floor. We've got room service and I'll ring the infirmary for a nurse.'

'I said I'm hungry and uncomfortable, but they're not my major concerns.'

'Not to worry,' said the Soviet Californian. 'The instant anything unusual happens anywhere, we'll be reached. I'll roll up the maps.'

*

It happened at precisely 12:02 a.m. directly after the universal changing of the guard, during the darkest darkness of the night. The telephone in the Commissars Suite screamed, propelling Benjamin off the couch. He raced across the room to the jangling, insistent instrument and yanked it off its cradle. 'Yes? . . . *Gde? Kodga? Shto eto znachit? . . . Da!*' He slammed the phone down and turned to Bourne at the dinner table, the maps of Novgorod having replaced the room-service dishes. 'It's *unbelievable.* At the Spanish tunnel – across the river two guards are dead, and on this side the officer of the watch was found fifty yards away from his post, a bullet in his throat. They ran the video tapes and all they saw was an unidentified man walking through carrying a *duffel* bag! In a guard's *uniform*!'

'There was something else, wasn't there?' asked Delta coldly.

'Yes, and you may be right. On the other side was a dead farmhand clutching torn papers in his hand. He was lying between the two murdered guards, one of them stripped to his shorts and shoes . . . How did he *do* it?'

'He was the good guy, I can't think of anything else,' mused Bourne, rising quickly, and reaching, pouncing on the map of the Spanish compound. 'He must have sent in his paid impostor with the rotten mocked-up papers, then ran in himself, the wounded Komitet officer at the last moment exposing the fraud and speaking the foreign language which his impostor couldn't do and couldn't understand . . . I told you, Ben. Probe, test, agitate, confuse and find a way in. Stealing a uniform is standard, and in the confusion it got him through the tunnel.'

'But anyone using those papers was to be watched, followed. They were your instructions and Krupkin sent the word up the line!'

'The Kubinka,' said Jason, now pensive as he studied the map.

'The armoury? The one mentioned in the news bulletins from Moscow?'

'Exactly. Just as he had done at the Kubinka, Carlos has someone inside here. Someone with enough authority to order an expendable officer of the guard to bring anyone penetrating the tunnel to him before sending out alarms and raising headquarters.'

'That's possible,' agreed the young trainer rapidly, firmly. 'Involving headquarters with false alarms can be embarrassing, and as you say, there must have been a lot of confusion.'

'In Paris,' said Bourne, glancing up from the compound map. 'I was told that embarrassment was the KGB's worst enemy. True?'

'On a scale of one to ten, at least eight,' replied Benjamin. 'But who would he have in here, who *could* he have? He hasn't been here in over thirty years!'

'If we had a couple of hours and a few computers programmed with the records of everyone in Novgorod, we might be able to feed in several hundred names and come up with possibilities, but we don't have hours. We don't even have minutes! Also, if I know the Jackal, it won't matter.'

'I think it matters one whole hell of a lot!' cried the Americanized Soviet. 'There's a traitor here and we should know who it is.'

'My guess is that you'll find out soon enough . . . *Details*, Ben. The point is, he's *here*! Let's go, and when we get outside we stop somewhere and you get me what I need.'

'Okay.'

'Everything I need.'

'I'm cleared for that.'

'And then you disappear. I know what I'm talking about.'

'No way, José!'

'California checking in again?'

'You heard me.'

'Then young Benjamin's mother may find a corpse for a son when she gets back to Moscow.'

'So be it!'

'So *be* . . . ? Why did you have to say that?'

'I don't know. It just seemed right.'

'Shut up! Let's get out of here.'

41

Ilich Ramirez Sanchez snapped his fingers twice in the shadows as he climbed the short steps of the miniaturized entrance to a small church in 'Madrid's' Paseo del Prado, the duffel bag in his left hand. From behind a fluted mock pillar a figure emerged, a heavyset man in his early sixties who walked partially into the dim light of a distant street lamp. He was dressed in the uniform of a Spanish army officer, a lieutenant general with three rows of ribbons affixed to his tunic. He was carrying a leather suitcase; he raised it slightly and spoke in the compound's language.

'Come inside, to the vestry. You can change there. That ill-fitting guard's jacket is an invitation for sharpshooters.'

'It's good to speak our language again,' said Carlos, following the man inside the tiny church and turning stiffly to close the heavy door. 'I'm in your debt, Enrique,' he added, glancing around at the empty rows of pews and the soft lights playing upon the altar, the gold crucifix gleaming.

'You've been in my debt for over thirty years, Ramirez, and a lot of good it does me,' laughed the soldier quietly as they proceeded across to the right aisle and down towards the sacristy.

'Then perhaps you're out of touch with what remains of your family in Baracoa. Fidel's own brothers and sisters don't live half so well.'

'Neither does crazy Fidel, but he doesn't care. They say he bathes more frequently now and I suppose that's progress. However, you're talking about my family in Baracoa; what about *me*, my fine international assassin? No yachts, no racing colours, shame on you! Were it not for my warning you, you would have been executed in this very compound thirty-three years ago. Come to think of it, it was right outside this idiotic dollhouse church on the Prado that you made your escape – dressed as a priest, a figure that perpetually bewilders the Russians, like most everyone else.'

'Once I was established, did you ever lack for anything?' They entered a small panelled room where supposed prelates prepared the sacraments. 'Did I ever refuse you?' Carlos added, placing the heavy duffel bag on the floor.

'I'm joking with you, of course,' objected Enrique, smiling good-naturedly and looking at the Jackal. 'Where is that lusty humour of yours, my infamous old friend?'

'I have other things on my mind.'

'I'm sure you do, and, in truth, you were never less than generous where my family in Cuba was concerned, and I thank you. My father and mother lived out their lives in peace and comfort, bewildered naturally, but so much better off than anyone they knew . . . It was all so insane. Revolutionaries thrown out by their own revolution's leaders.'

'You were threats to Castro, as was Che. It's past.'

'A great deal has passed,' agreed Enrique, studying Carlos. 'You've aged poorly, Ramirez. Where's that once full head of dark hair and the handsome strong face with the clear eyes?'

'We won't talk about it.'

'Very well. I grow fat, you grow thin; that tells me something. How badly are you wounded?'

'I can function well enough for what I intend to do – what I must do.'

'Ramirez, what else *is* there?' asked the costumed soldier suddenly. 'He's *dead*! Moscow takes credit over the radio for his death, but when you reached me I knew the credit was yours, the kill yours. Jason Bourne is dead! Your enemy is gone from this world. You're not well; go back to Paris and heal yourself. I'll get you out the same way I got you in. We'll head into "France" and I'll clear the way. You will be a courier from the commandant of "Spain" and "Portgual" who's sending a confidential message to Dzerzhinsky Square. It's done all the time; no one trusts anyone here, especially his own gates. You won't even have to take the risk of killing a single guard.'

'No! A lesson must be *taught*.'

'Then let me phrase it another way. When you called with your emergency codes, I did what you demanded, for by and large you have fulfilled your obligations to me, obligations that go back thirty-three years. But now there is another risk involved – *risks*, to be precise – and I'm not sure I care to take them.'

'You speak this way to *me*?' cried the Jackal, removing the dead guard's jacket, his clean white bandages taut, holding his right shoulder firm with no evidence of blood.

'Stop your theatrics,' said Enrique softly. 'We go back long before that. I'm speaking to a young revolutionary I followed out of Cuba with a great athlete named Santos . . . How is he, by the way? He was the real threat to Fidel.'

'He's well,' answered Carlos, his voice flat. 'We're moving Le Coeur du Soldat.'

'Does he still tend to his gardens – his English gardens?'

'Yes, he does.'

'He should have been a landscaper, or a florist, I think. And I should have been a fine agricultural engineer, an agronomist, as they say – that's how Santos and I met, you know . . . Melodramatic politics changed our lives, didn't they?'

'Political *commitments* changed them. Everywhere the fascists changed them.'

'And now we want to be like the fascists, and they want to take what's not so terrible about us Communists and spread a little money around – which doesn't really work, but it's a nice thought.'

'What has this to do with me – your monseigneur?'

'Horse droppings, Ramirez. As you may or may not know, my Russian wife died a number of years ago and I have three children in the Moscow University. Without my position they would not be there and I want them there. They will be scientists, doctors . . . You see, those are the risks you ask of me. I've covered myself up until this moment – and you deserve this moment – but perhaps no more. In a few months I will retire, and in recognition of my years of service in southern Europe and the Mediterranean, I will share a fine dacha on the Black Sea where my children will come and visit me. I will not unduly risk what life I have before me. So be specific, Ramirez, and I'll tell you whether you're on your own or not . . . I repeat, your getting in here cannot be traced to me, and, as I say, you deserved that much, but this is where I may be forced to stop.'

'I see,' said Carlos, approaching the suitcase Enrique had placed on the sacristy table.

'I hope you do and, further, I hope you understand. Over the years you've been good to my family in ways that I could never be, but then I've served you well in ways that I could. I led you to Rodchenko, fed you names in ministries where rumours abounded, rumours Rodchenko himself investigated for you. So, my old revolutionary comrade, I've not been idle on your behalf either. However, things are different now; we're not young firebrands in search of a cause any longer, for we've lost our appetites for causes – you long before me, of course.'

'My cause remains constant,' interrupted the Jackal sharply. 'It is myself and all those who serve me.'

'*I've* served you—'

'You've made that clear, as well as my generosity to you and yours. And now that I'm here you wonder if I deserve further assistance, that's it, isn't it?'

'I must protect myself. Why *are* you here?'

'I told you. To teach a lesson, to leave a message.'

'They are one and the same?'

'Yes.' Carlos opened the suitcase; it held a coarse shirt, a Portuguese fisherman's cap with the appropriate rope-belted trousers, and a seaman's shoulder-strapped canvas satchel. 'Why these?' asked the Jackal.

'They're loose-fitting and I haven't seen you in years – not since Málaga in the early seventies, I think. I couldn't very well have clothes tailored for you, and I'm glad I didn't try – you are not as I remembered you, Ramirez.'

'You're not much larger than I remember you,' countered the assassin. 'A little thicker around the stomach, perhaps, but we're still the same height, the same basic frame.'

'So? What does that mean?'

'In a moment . . . Have things changed a great deal since we were together here?'

'Constantly. Photographs arrive and construction crews follow a day later. The Prado here in "Madrid" has new shops, new signs, even a few new sewers as they are changed in that city. Also "Lisbon" and the piers along the "Bay" and "Tagus River" have been altered to conform to the changes that have taken place. We are nothing if not authentic. The candidates who complete the training are literally at home wherever they're initially sent. Sometimes I really believe it's all excessive, then I recall my first assignment at the naval base in Barcelona and realize how comfortable I was. I went right to work because the psychological orientation had already taken place; there were no major surprises.'

'You're describing appearance,' broke in Carlos.

'Of course, what else is there?'

'More permanent structures that are not so apparent, not so much in evidence.'

'Such as?'

'Warehouses, fuel depots, fire stations, that are not part of the duplicated scenery. Are they still where they were?'

'By and large, yes. Certainly the major warehouses and the fuel depots with their underground tanks. Most are still west of the "San Roque" district, the "Gibraltar" access.'

'What about going from one compound to another?'

'Now that *has* changed.' Enrique withdrew a small flat object from the pocket of his tunic. 'Each border crossing has a computerized registration release that permits entry when this is inserted.'

'No questions are asked?'

'Only at Novgorod's Capital Headquarters, if there are any questions.'

'I don't understand.'

'If one of these is lost or stolen, it's reported instantly and the internal codes are nullified.'

'I see.'

'*I* don't! Why these questions? Again, why are you *here*? What is this lesson, this message?'

'The "San Roque" district . . . ?' said Carlos, as if remembering. 'That's about three or four kilometres south of the tunnel, isn't it? A small waterfront village, no?'

'The "Gibraltar" access, yes.'

'And the next compound is "France," of course, and then "England" and finally the largest, the "United States". Yes, it's all clear to me, everything's come back.' The Jackal turned away, his right hand awkwardly disappearing beneath his trousers.

'Yet nothing is clear to *me*,' said Enrique, his low voice threatening. 'And it must be. Answer me, Ramirez. Why are you here?'

'How dare you question me like this?' continued Carlos, his back to his old associate. 'How dare *any* of you question the monseigneur from Paris.'

'You listen to me, Priest Piss Ant. You answer me or I walk out of here and you're a dead monseigneur in a matter of minutes!'

'Very well, Enrique,' answered Ilich Ramirez Sanchez, addressing the panelled wall of the sacristy. 'My message will be triumphantly clear and will shake the very foundations of the Kremlin. Not only did Carlos the Jackal kill the weak pretender Jason Bourne on Soviet soil, he left a reminder to all Russia that the Komitet made a colossal error in not utilizing my extraordinary talents.'

'Really now,' said Enrique, laughing softly, as if humouring a far less than extraordinary man. 'More melodramatics, Ramirez? And how will you convey this reminder, this *message*, this supreme statement of yours?'

'Quite simply,' replied the Jackal, turning, a gun in his hand, the silencer intact. 'We have to change places.'

'*What?*'

'I'm going to burn Novgorod.' Carlos fired a single shot into the upper throat of Enrique. He wanted as little blood as possible on the tunic.

Dressed in combat fatigues with the insignias of an army major on the shoulders of his field jacket, Bourne blended in with the sporadic appearances of military personnel as they crisscrossed the American compound from one sector to another on their night patrols. There were not many, perhaps thirty men, covering the entire acreage of the eight square miles, according to Benjamin. In the 'metropolitan' areas they were generally on foot, in twosomes; in the 'rural' districts they drove military vehicles. The young trainer had requisitioned a jeep.

From the Commissars Suite at US headquarters, they had been taken to a military warehouse west of the river where Benjamin's papers gained them entrance and the jeep. Inside, the astonished interior guards watched as the silent Bourne was outfitted with a field uniform complete with a carbine bayonet, a standard .45 automatic and five clips of live ammunition, this last obtained only after an authorization call was placed to Krupkin's unknowing subordinates at Capital HQ. Once again outside, Jason complained: 'What about the flares I wanted and at least three or four grenades? You agreed to get me everything I needed, not half of it!'

'They're coming,' answered Benjamin, speeding out of the warehouse parking lot. 'The flares are over at motor vehicles and grenades aren't part of normal ordnance. They're in steel vaults down at the tunnel – all the tunnels – under Emergency Weapons.' The young trainer glanced at Bourne, a glimmering of humour seen on his face in the glow of the headlights washing over the roofless jeep. 'In anticipation of a NATO assault, most likely.'

'That's stupid. We'd come in from the sky.'

'Not with the air base ninety seconds' flying time away.'

'Hurry up, I want those grenades. Will we have any trouble getting them?'

'Not if Krupkin keeps up the good work.' Krupkin had; with the flares in hand, the tunnel was their last supply stop. Four Russian army grenades were counted out and countersigned by Benjamin. 'Where to?' he asked as the soldier in an American uniform returned to the concrete guardhouse.

'These aren't exactly US general issue,' said Jason, putting the grenades carefully, one by one, into the pockets of his field jacket.

'They're not for training, either. The compounds aren't military-oriented but basically civilian. If those are ever used, it's not for indoctrination purposes . . . Where do we go now?'

'Check with headquarters first. See if anything's happened at any of the border checkpoints.'

'My beeper would have gone off—'

'I don't trust beepers, I like words,' interrupted Jason. 'Get on the radio.'

Benjamin did so, switching to the Russian language and using the codes that only senior staff were assigned. The terse Soviet reply came over the speaker; the young trainer replaced the microphone and turned to Bourne. 'No activity at all,' he said. 'Just some inter-compound fuel deliveries.'

'What are they?'

'Petrol distribution mainly. Some compounds have larger tanks than others, so logistics call for routine apportionments until the main supplies are shipped downriver.'

'They distribute at night?'

'It's far better than those trucks clogging up the streets during the day. Remember, everything's scaled down here. Also, we've been driving through the back roads but there's a maintenance army in the central locations cleaning up stores and offices and restaurants, getting ready for tomorrow's assignments. Large trucks wouldn't help.'

'Christ, it *is* Disneyland . . . All right, head for the Spanish border, Pedro.'

'To get there we have to pass through England and France. I don't suppose it matters much, but I don't speak French. Or Spanish. Do you?'

'French fluently, Spanish acceptably. Anything else?'

'Maybe you'd better drive.'

The Jackal braked the huge fuel truck at the 'West German' border; it was as far as he intended to go. The remaining northernmost areas of Scandinavia and the Netherlands were the lesser satellites; the impact of their destruction was not comparable to that of the lower compounds and the time element spared them. Everything was timing now, and 'West Germany' would initiate the wholesale conflagrations. He adjusted the coarse Portuguese shirt that covered a Spanish general's tunic beneath, and as the guard came out of the gatehouse Carlos spoke in Russian, using the same words he had used at every other crossing.

'Don't ask me to speak the stupid language you talk here. I deliver petrol, I don't spend time in classrooms! Here's my key.'

'I barely speak it myself, comrade,' said the guard, laughing as he accepted the small, flat, cardlike object and inserted it into the computerized machine. The heavy iron barrier arced up into the vertical position; the guard returned the key and the Jackal sped through into a miniaturized 'West Berlin.'

He raced through the narrow replica of the Kurfürstendamm to the Budapesterstrasse, where he slowed down and pulled out the petcock release. The fuel flowed into the street. He then reached into the open duffel bag on the seat beside him, ripped out the small pretimed plastique explosives, and as he had done throughout the southern compounds to the border of 'France', hurled them through the lowered windows on both sides of the truck into the foundations of the wooden buildings he thought most flammable. He sped into the 'Munich' sector, then to the port of 'Bremerhaven' on the river, and finally into 'Bonn' and the scaled-down versions of the embassies in 'Bad Godesberg,' flooding the streets, distributing the explosives. He looked at his watch; it was time to head back. He had barely fifteen minutes before the first detonations took place in all of 'West Germany,' followed by the explosions in the combined compounds of 'Italy-Greece', 'Israel-Egypt' and 'Spain-Portugal,' each spaced eight minutes apart, timed to create maximum chaos.

There was no way the individual fire brigades could contain the flaming streets and buildings in the disparate sectors of their compounds north of 'France'. Others would be ordered in from adjacent compounds only to be recalled when the fires erupted on their own grounds. It was a simple formula for cosmic confusion, the cosmos being the false universe of Novgorod. The border gates would be flagged open, frantic traffic unimpeded, and to complete the devastation, the genius that was llich Ramirez Sanchez – brought into the world of terror as Carlos the Jackal by the errors of that same Novgorod – had to be in 'Paris.' Not *his* Paris, but the hated Novgorod's 'Paris,' and he would burn it to the ground in ways the maniacs of the Third Reich never dreamed of. Then would come 'England,' and finally, ultimately, the largest compound in the despised, isolated, illusionist Novgorod, where he would leave his triumphant message – the 'United States of America,' breeder of the apostate assassin Jason Bourne. The statement would be as pure and as clear as Alpine water washing over the blood of a destroyed false universe.

I alone have done this. My enemies are dead and I live.

Carlos checked his duffel bag; what remained were the most lethal instrument of death found in the arsenal of Kubinka. Four layered rows of short-packaged, heat-seeking missiles, twenty in all, each capable of blowing up the entire base of the Washington monument; and once fused and unshielded, each would seek the sources of fire and do its work. Satisfied, the Jackal shut off the fuel release, turned around and sped back to the border gate.

The sleepy technician at Capital Headquarters blinked his eyes and stared at the green letters on the screen in front of him. What he read did not really make sense, but the clearances went unchallenged. For the fifth time the 'commandant' of the 'Spanish' compound had crossed and recrossed the north borders up into 'Germany' and was now heading back into 'France'. Twice before, when the codes were transmitted and in accord with the maximim alert that was in force, the technician had phoned the gates of 'Israel' and 'Italy' and was told that only a fuel truck had passed through. That was the information he had given to a code-cleared trainer named Benjamin, but now he wondered. Why would such a high-ranking offical be driving a fuel truck? . . . On the other hand, why not? Novgorod was rife with corruption, everyone suspected that, so perhaps the 'commandant' was either seeking out the corrupters or collecting his fees at night. Regardless, since there was no report of a lost or stolen card, and the computers raised no objections, it was better to leave the odd occurrence well enough alone. One never knew who his next superior might be.

'*Voici ma carte*,' said Bourne to the guard at the border crossing as he handed the man his computerized card. '*Vite, s'il vous plaît!*'

'*Da . . . oui*,' replied the guard, walking rapidly to the clearance machine as an enormous fuel truck, heading the other way, passed through into 'England.'

'Don't press the French too much,' said Benjamin, in the front seat beside Jason. 'These cats do their best, but they're not linguists.'

'*Cal-if-fornia* . . . here I come,' sang Bourne softy. 'You sure you and your father don't want to join your mother in LA?'

'*Shut* up!'

The guard returned, saluted, and the iron barrier was raised. Jason accelerated, and saw in a matter of moments, bathed in floodlights, a three-storey replica of the Eiffel Tower. In the distance, to the right, was a miniature Champs-Elysees with a wooden reproduction of the Arc de Triomphe, high enough to be unmistakable. Absently, Bourne's mind wandered back to those fitful, terrible hours when he and Marie had raced all over Paris trying desperately to find each other . . . Marie, oh God, *Marie! I want to come back. I want to be David again. He and I – we're so much older now. He doesn't frighten me any longer and I don't anger him . . . Who? Which of us? Oh, Christ!*

'Hold it,' said Benjamin, touching Jason's arm. 'Slow down.'

'What is it?'

'*Stop*,' cried the young trainer. 'Pull over and shut off the engine.'

'What's the matter with you?'

'I'm not sure.' Benjamin's neck was arched back, his eyes on the clear night sky and the shimmering lights of the stars. 'No clouds,' he said cryptically. 'No storms.'

'It's not raining, either. So what? I want to get up to the Spanish compound!'

'There it goes again—'

'What the *hell* are you talking about?' And then Bourne heard it . . . far away, the sound of distant thunder, yet the night *was* clear. It happened again – and again and again, one deep rumble after another.

'*There!*' shouted the young Soviet from Los Angeles, standing up in the jeep and pointing to the north. 'What *is* it?'

'That's fire, young man,' answered Jason softly, hesitantly, as he also stood up and stared at the pulsating yellow glow that lit up the distant sky. 'And my guess is that it's the Spanish compound. He was initially trained there and that's what he came back to do – to blow the place *up*! It's his revenge! . . . *Get* down, we've got to get up there!'

'No, you're wrong,' broke in Benjamin, quickly lowering himself into the seat as Bourne started the engine and yanked the jeep into gear. '"Spain's" no more that five or six miles from here. Those fires are a lot farther away.'

'Just show me the fastest route,' said Jason, pressing the accelerator to the floor.

Under the trainer's swiftly roving eyes accompanied by sudden shouts of 'Turn here!' and 'Go right!' and 'Straight down this road!' they raced through 'Paris,' and north into successive sectors labelled 'Marseilles,' 'Montbéliard', 'Le Havre', 'Strasbourg,' and so many others, circling town squares and passing quaint streets and miniaturized city blocks, until finally they were in sight of the 'Spanish' border. The closer they came, the louder were the booms in the distance, the brighter the yellow night sky. The guards at the gate were furiously manning their telephones and hand-held radios; the two-note blasts of sirens joined the shouting and the screaming as police cars and fire engines appeared seemingly out of nowhere, racing into the streets of 'Madrid' on their way to the next northern border crossing.

'What's *happening?*' yelled Benjamin, leaping from the jeep and dropping all pretence of Novgorod training by speaking Russian. 'I'm senior staff!' he added, slipping the card into the release equipment, snapping the barrier up. '*Tell* me!'

'*Insanity*, comrade!' shouted an officer from the gatehouse window. 'Unbelievable! . . . It's as if the earth went crazy! First "Germany," all over there are explosions and fires in the streets and buildings going up in flames. The ground trembles and we are told it's some kind of massive earthquake. Then it happens in "Italy" – "Rome" is torched, and in the "Greek" sector "Athens" and the port of "Piraeus" are filled with fires everywhere and still the explosions continue, the streets in flames!'

'What does Capital Headquarters say?'

'They don't know *what* to say! The earthquake nonsense was just that – *nonsense.* Everyone's in panic, issuing orders, then countermanding them.' Another wall phone rang inside the gatehouse; the officer of the guard picked it up and listened, then instantly screamed at the top of his lungs. 'Madness, it's complete *madness*! Are you certain?'

'What is it?' roared Benjamin, rushing to the window.

'"Egypt"!' he screamed, his ear pressed to the telephone. '"*Israel*"! . . . "Cairo" and "Tel Aviv" – fires *everywhere*, bombs everywhere! No one can keep up with the devastation; the trucks crash into one another in the narrow streets. The hydrants are blown up; water flows in the gutters but the streets are still in flames . . . And some idiot just got on the line and asked if the No Smoking signs were properly placed as the wooden buildings are on their way to becoming rubble! Idiots. They are all *idiots*!'

'Get back here!' yelled Bourne, having made the jeep lurch through the gate. 'He's *in* here somewhere! You drive and I'll—' Jason's words were cut off by a deafening explosion up ahead in the centre of 'Madrid's' Paseo del Prado. It was an enormous detonation, lumber and stone arcing up into the flaming sky. Then, as if the Paseo del Prado itself were a living, throbbing immense wall of fire, the flames rolled forwards, swinging to the left out of the 'city' into the road that was the approach to the border gate. '*Look!*' shouted Bourne, reaching down out of the jeep, his hand scraping the gravelled surface beneath; he brought his fingers to his face, his nostrils. '*Christ*,' he roared. 'The whole goddamned road's soaked with *gasoline*!' A burst of fire imploded thirty yards in front of the jeep, sending stones and dirt smashing into the metal grille, and propelling the flames forward with increasing speed. '*Plastics!*' said Jason to himself, then yelled at Benjamin, who was running to the jeep, 'Go back there! Get everyone out of here! The son of a bitch has the place ringed with plastics! Head for the river.'

'I'm going with *you*!' shouted the young Soviet, grabbing the edge of the door.

'Sorry, Junior,' cried Bourne, gunning the engine and swerving the army vehicle back into the open gate, sending Benjamin sprawling onto the gravel. 'This is for grown-ups.'

'What are you *doing*?' screamed Benjamin, his voice fading as the jeep sped across the border.

'The fuel truck, that lousy *fuel* truck!' whispered Jason as he raced into 'Strasbourg, France.'

It happened in 'Paris' – where else but *Paris*! The huge duplicate of the Eiffel Tower blew up with such force that the earth shook. Rockets? Missiles? The Jackal had stolen *missiles* from the Kubinka Armoury! Seconds later, starting far behind him, the explosions began as the streets burst into flames. *Everywhere.* All 'France' was being destroyed – as the madman Adolf Hitler could only have envisaged in his most twisted dreams. Panicked men and women ran through the alleyways and the streets, screaming, falling, praying to gods their leaders had forsworn.

'*England!*' He had to get into 'England' and then ultimately into 'America', where all his instincts told him the end would come – one way or another. He had to find the truck that was being driven by the Jackal and destroy both. He could do it – he *could do* it! Carlos thought he was dead and that was the key, for the Jackal would do what he had to do, what *he*, Jason Bourne, would do if he were Carlos. When the holocaust he had set in motion was at its zenith, the Jackal would abandon the truck and put into play his means of escape – his escape to Paris, the *real* Paris, where his army of old men would spread the word of their monseigneur's triumph over the ubiquitous, disbelieving Soviets. It would be somewhere near the tunnel; that was a given.

The race through 'London', 'Coventry' and 'Portsmouth' could only be likened to the newsreel footage from World War II depicting the carnage hurled down on Great Britain by the Luftwaffe, compounded by the screaming then silent terror of the V-1 and V-2 rockets. But the residents of Novgorod were not British – forbearance gave way to mass hysteria, concern for all became survival for self alone. As the impressive reproductions of Big Ben and the Houses of Parliament crashed down in flames and the aircraft factories of 'Coventry' were reduced to raging fires, the streets swelled with screaming, horrified crowds racing through the roads that led to the Volkhov River and the shipyards of 'Portsmouth'. There, from the scaled-down piers and slips, scores threw themselves into rushing waters only to be caught in the magnesium grids where sharp, jagged bolts of electricity blazingly zigzagged through the air, leaving limp bodies floating towards the next metal traps above and below the angry surface. In paralysed fragments, the crowds watched and turned in panic, fighting their way back into the miniaturized city of 'Portsea'; the guards had abandoned their posts and chaos ruled the night.

Snapping on the jeep's searchlight, Bourne drove in sudden spurts down alleyways and the less-crowded narrow streets – south, always south. He grabbed a flare from the army vehicle's floor, pulled the release string, and proceeded to thrust the spitting, hissing, blinding burst of fire into the hands and faces of the hysterical racing stragglers who tried to climb on board. The sight of the constantly pulsating flame so close to their eyes was enough; each screamed and recoiled in terror, no doubt thinking yet another explosive had detonated in his or her immediate vicinity.

A gravelled road! The gates to the American compound were less than a hundred yards away . . . The *gravelled road*? Soaked with fuel! The plastic charges had not gone off – but they would in a matter of moments, creating a wall of fire, enveloping the jeep and its driver! With the accelerator pressed to the floor, Jason raced to the gate. It was deserted – and the iron barrier was *down*! He slammed on the brakes, skidding to a stop, hoping beyond reasonable hope that no sparks would fly out and ignite the gravel. Placing the spewing flare on the metal floor, he swiftly removed two grenades from his pockets – grenades he was loath to part with – pulled the pins, and hurled both towards the gate. The massive explosions blew the barricade away and instantly set the gravelled road on fire, the leaping flames immediate – enveloping him! He had no choice: he threw the hot flare away and sped through the tunnel of fire into Novgorod's final largest compound. As he did so the concrete guardhouse of the 'English' border exploded; glass, stone and shards of metal shot out and up everywhere.

He had been so filled with anxiety on their way to the crossing into 'Spain' that he barely recalled the diminutive replicas of the 'American' cities and towns, much less the fastest routes that led to the tunnel. He had merely followed young Benjamin's harsh, shouted commands, but he did remember that the California-bred trainer kept referring to the 'coast road – like Route One, man, up to Carmel!' It was, of course, those streets closest to the Volkhov, which in turn became, in no order of geographical sequence, a shoreline in 'Maine', the Potomac River of 'Washington', and the northern waters of Long Island Sound that housed the naval base at 'New London'.

The madness had reached 'America'. Police cars, their sirens wailing, sped through the streets, men shouting into radios as people in various stages of dress and undress ran out of buildings and stores, screaming about the terrible earthquake that had hit this leg of the Volkhov, one even more severe than the castastrophe in Armenia. Even with the surest knowledge of devastating infiltration, the leaders of Novgorod could not reveal the truth. It was as if the seismic geologists of the world were forgotten, their discoveries unfounded. The giant forces beneath the earth did not collide and erupt in terrible swift immediacy; instead, they worked in relays, sending a series of crippling body blows from north to south. Who questions authority in the panic of survival? Everyone in 'America' was being prepared, primed for what they knew not.

They found out roughly ten minutes after the destruction of a large part of the diminutive 'Great Britain'. Bourne reached the compressed miniaturized outlines of 'Washington, DC' when the conflagration began. The first to plunge into flames, the sound of its detonation delayed only by milliseconds, was the wooden duplicate of the Capitol dome; it blew into the yellowed sky like the thin, hollow replica it was. Moments later – only *moments* – the Washington Monument, centred in its patch of grassy park, crumpled with a distant boom as if its false base had been shovelled away by a thunderous ground-moving machine. In seconds, the artificial set piece that was the White House collapsed in flames, the explosions dulled both audibly and visibly, for 'Pennsylvania Avenue' was awash in fire.

Bourne *knew* where he was now. The tunnel was between 'Washington' and

'New London, Connecticut'! It was no more than five minutes away! He drove the jeep down to the street paralleling the river, and again there were frightened, hysterical crowds. The police were shouting through loudspeakers, first in English and then in Russian, explaining the terrible consequences if anyone tried to swim across the water, the searchlights swinging back and forth, picking up the floating bodies of those who had tried in the northern compounds.

'The tunnel, the *tunnel! Open the tunnel*!'

The screams from the excited crowds became a chant that could not physically be denied; the underground pipeline was about to be assaulted. Jason leaped out of the surrounded jeep, pocketing the remaining three flares, and propelled his way, arms and shoulders working furiously, often fruitlessly, through the crushing, crashing bodies. There was nothing else for it; he pulled out a flare and ripped the release from its recess. The spewing flame had its effect; heat and fire were catalysts. He ran through the crowd, pummelling everyone in front of him, shoving the blinding, spitting flare into terrified faces, until he reached the front and faced a cordon of guards in the uniforms of the United States Army. It was crazy, *insane*! The world had gone *nuts*!

No! *There!* In the fenced-off parking lot was the fuel truck! He broke through the cordon of guards, holding up his computerized release card, and ran up to the soldier with the highest-ranking insignia on his uniform, a colonel with an AK-47 strapped to his waist who was as panicked as any officer of high rank he had ever seen since Saigon.

'My identification is with the name "Archie" and you can clear it immediately. Even now I refuse to speak our language, only *English*! Is that understood? Discipline is *discipline*!'

'*Togda?*' yelled the officer, questioning the moment, then instantly returning to English in a maddeningly Boston accent. 'Of course, we know of you,' he cried, 'but what can I *do*? This is an uncontrollable riot!'

'Has anyone passed through the tunnel in the last, say, half hour?'

'No one, absolutely, *no* one! Our orders are to keep the tunnel closed at all costs!'

'Good . . . Get on the loudspeakers and disperse the crowds. Tell them the crisis has passed and the danger with it.'

'How *can* I? The fires are everywhere, the explosions *everywhere*!'

'They'll stop soon.'

'How do you know that?'

'I *know*! Do as I say!'

'Do as he *says*!' roared a voice behind Bourne; it was Benjamin, his face and shirt drenched with sweat. 'And I hope to hell you know what you're *talking* about!'

'Where did *you* come from?'

'Where, you know; how is another question. Try scaring the shit out of Capital HQ for a chopper ordered by an apoplectic Krupkin from a hospital bed in Moscow.'

' "Apoplectic" – not bad for a Russian—'

'Who *gives* me such orders?' yelled the officer of the guard. 'You are only a young man!'

'Check me out, buddy, but do it quick,' answered Benjamin, holding out his card. 'Otherwise I think I'll have you transferred to Tashkent. Nice scenery, but no private toilets . . . *Move*, you asshole!'

'Cal-if-fornia, here I—'

'Shut *up*!'

'He's *here*! There's the fuel truck. Over there.' Jason pointed to the huge vehicle that dwarfed the scattered cars and vans in the fenced parking area.

'A fuel truck? How did you figure it out?' asked the astonished Benjamin.

'That tank's got to hold close to a hundred thousand pounds. Combined with the plastics, strategically placed, it's enough for the streets and those fake structures of old, dried wood.'

'*Mozhnon*,' blared the myriad loudspeakers around the tunnel, demanding attention, as indeed the explosions began to diminish. The colonel climbed on top of the low, concrete gatehouse, a microphone in his hand, his figure outlined in the harsh beams of powerful searchlights. 'The earthquake has passed,' he cried in Russian, 'and although the damage is extensive and the fires will continue throughout the night, the crisis has *passed*! . . . Stay by the banks of the river and our comrades in the maintenance crews will do their best to provide for your needs . . . These are orders from our superiors, comrades. Do not give us reason to use force, I *plead* with you!'

'*What* earthquake?' shouted a man in the front ranks of the panicked multitude. '*You* say it's an earthquake and we are all *told* it is an earthquake but your brains are in your bowels! I've lived through an earthquake and this is *no* earthquake. It is an armed attack!'

'Yes, yes! An attack!'

'We are being *attacked*!'

'Invaded! It's an *invasion*!'

'Open the tunnel and let us out or you'll have to shoot us down! Open the *tunnel*!'

The protesting chorus grew from all sections of the desperate crowd as the soldiers held firm, their bayonets unsheathed and affixed to their rifles. The colonel continued, his features contorted, his voice nearly matching the hysteria of his frenzied audience.

'*Listen* to me and ask yourselves a question!' he screamed. 'I'm telling you, as I have been told, that this is an earthquake and I know it's true. Further, I will tell you *how* I know it's true! . . . Have you heard a single gunshot? Yes, that is the *question*! A single *gunshot*! No, you have not! . . . Here, as in all the compounds and in every sector of those compounds, there are police and soldiers and trainers who carry weapons. Their orders are to repel by force any unwarranted displays of violence, to say *nothing* of armed invaders! Yet nowhere has there been any gunfire—'

'What's he shouting about?' asked Jason, turning to Benjamin.

'He's trying to convince them it is – or *was* – an earthquake. They don't believe him; they think it's an invasion. He's telling them it couldn't be because there's been no gunfire.'

'Gunfire?'

'That's his proof. Nobody's shooting at anybody and they sure as hell would be if there was an armed attack. No gunshots, no attack.'

'*Gunshots* . . . ?' Bourne suddenly grabbed the young Soviet and spun him around. 'Tell him to stop! For God's sake, *stop* him!'

'What?'

'He's giving the Jackal the opening he wants – he needs!'

'Now what are *you* talking about?'

'Gunfire . . . gunshots, confusion!'

'*Nyet!*' screamed a woman, breaking through the crowd and shouting at the officer in the centre of the searchlight beams. 'The explosions are bombs! They come from bombers above!'

'You are foolish,' cried the colonel, replying in Russian. 'If it was an air raid, our fighter planes from Belopol would fill the sky! . . . The explosions come out of the earth, the fires out of the earth, from the gases *below*—' These false words were the last words the Soviet officer would ever speak.

A staccato volley of automatic gunfire burst from the shadows of the tunnel's parking area cutting the Russian down, his instantly limp, punctured body collapsing and falling off the roof of the gatehouse, plummeting to the ground out of sight at the rear. The already frantic crowd went rabid; the ranks of uniformed 'American' soldiers broke, and if chaos had ruled previously nihilistic mobocracy now reigned supreme. The narrow, fenced entrance to the tunnel was virtually stormed, racing figures colliding, pummelling, climbing over one another, rushing en masse towards the mouth of the underwater access. Jason pulled his young trainer to the side of the stampeding hordes, never for an instant taking his eyes off the darkened parking area.

'Can you operate the tunnel's machinery?' he shouted.

'Yes! Everyone on the senior staff can, it's part of the job!'

'The iron gates you told me about?'

'Of course.'

'Where are the mechanisms?'

'The guardhouse.'

'Get in there!' yelled Bourne, taking one of the three remaining flares out of his field-jacket pocket and handing it to Benjamin. 'I've got two more of these and two other grenades . . . . When you see one of my flares go over the crowd, lower those gates on *this side* – *only* this side, understood?'

'What for?'

'*My rules*, Ben! *Do* it! Then ignite this flare and throw it out the window so I'll know it's done.'

'Then what?'

'Something you may not want to do, but you have to . . . Take the "forty-seven" from the colonel's body and force the crowd, *shoot* it back into the street. Rapid fire into the ground in front of them – or above them – do whatever you have to do, even if it means wounding a few. Whatever the cost, it must be *done.* I have to find him, isolate him, above all, cut him off from everyone else trying to get out.'

'You're a goddamned *maniac*,' broke in Benjamin, the veins pronounced in his forehead. 'I could kill "*a few*" – *more* than a few! You're crazy!'

'At this moment I'm the most rational man you've ever met,' interrupted Jason harshly, rapidly, as the panicked residents of Novgorod kept rushing by. 'There's not a sane general in the Soviet army – the *same* army that retook Stalingrad – who wouldn't agree with me . . . It's called the "calculated estimate of losses", and there's a very good reason for that lousy verbiage. It simply means you're paying a lot less for what you're getting now than you'd pay later.'

'You're asking too *much*! These people are my comrades, my friends; they're Russians. Would you fire into a crowd of Americans? One recoil of my hands – an inch, two inches with a "forty-seven" – and I could maim or kill a half a dozen people! The risk's too great!'

'You don't have a choice. If the Jackal gets by me – and I'll *know* it if he does – I'll throw in a grenade and kill twenty.'

'You son of a bitch!'

'Believe it, Ben. Where Carlos is concerned I'm a son of a bitch. I can't afford him any longer, the world can't afford him. *Move!*'

The trainer named Benjamin spat in Bourne's face, then turned and began fighting his way to the guardhouse and the unseen corpse of the colonel beyond. Almost unconsciously Jason wiped his face with the back of his hand, his concentration solely on the fenced parking area, his eyes darting from one pocket of shadows to another, trying to centre in on the origins of the automatic gunfire, yet knowing it was pointless; the Jackal had changed positions by then. He counted the other vehicles in addition to the fuel truck; there were nine parked by the fence – two station wagons, four sedans, and three suburban vans, all American made or simulated as such. Carlos was concealed beyond one of them or possibly the fuel truck, the last unlikely as it was the farthest away from the open gate in the fence that permitted access to the guardhouse and thus to the tunnel.

Jason crouched and crawled forward; he reached the waist-high fence, the pandemonium behind him continuous, deafening. Every muscle and joint in his legs and arms pounded with pain; *cramps* were developing everywhere, everywhere! *Don't think about them, don't acknowledge them. You're too close, David! Keep going. Jason Bourne knows what to do. Trust him!*

Aaughh! He spun his body over the fence; the handle of his sheathed bayonet embedded itself in his kidney. *There is no pain! You're too close, David – Jason. Listen to Jason!*

The searchlights – someone had pressed something and they went crazy, spinning around in circles, abrupt, blinding, out of control! Where would Carlos go? Where could he *hide*? The beams were erratically piercing everywhere! Then, from an opening that he could not see from across the fenced-in area, two police cars raced inside, their sirens blaring. Uniformed men leaped out from every door, and contrary to anything he expected to see, each scrambled to the borders of the fence, behind the cars and the vans, one after another dashing from one vehicle to another to the open gate that led to the guardhouse and the tunnel.

There was a break in space, in *time*. In *men*! The last four escapes from the second car were suddenly three – and only moments later did the fourth appear – but he was not the same – the uniform was not the *same*! There were specks of orange and red, and the visored officer's cap was laced with gold ribbing, the visor itself too prominent for the American army, the crown of the cap too pointed. What *was* it? . . . And, suddenly, Bourne understood. Fragments of his memories spiralled back years to Madrid or Casavieja, when he was tracing the Jackal's contracts with the Falangists. It was a *Spanish* uniform! That was it! Carlos had infiltrated through the Spanish compound, and as his Russian was fluent, he was using the high-ranking uniform to make his escape from Novgorod.

Jason lurched to his feet, his automatic drawn, and ran across the gravelled lot, his left hand reaching into his field jacket pocket for his second-to-last flare. He pulled the release, and hurled the fired stalk above the cars, beyond the fence. Benjamin would not see it from the guardhouse and mistake it for the signal to close the gates of the tunnel; that signal would come shortly – in seconds, perhaps – but at the moment it was premature.

'*Eto srochno!*' roared one of the escaping men, spinning around and panicked at the sight of the hissing, blinding flare.

'*Skoryeye!*' shouted another, passing three companions and racing towards the open section of the fence. As the whirling searchlights continued their maniacal spinning, Bourne counted the seven figures as one by one they dashed away from the last car and passed through the opening, joining the excited crowds at the mouth of the tunnel. The eighth man did not appear; the high-ranking Spanish uniform was nowhere in sight. The Jackal was trapped!

Now! Jason whipped out his last flare, yanked the release, and threw it with all his strength over the stream of rushing men and women at the guardhouse. *Do it, Ben!* he screamed in silence as he removed the next-to-last grenade from the pocket of his field jacket. *Do it now!*

As if the answer to his fevered plea was immediate, a thunderous roar came from the tunnel, round after round of hysterical protestations punctuated by screams and shrieks and wailing chaos. Two rapid, deafening bursts of automatic gunfire preceded unintelligible commands over the speakers, shouted in Russian . . . Another burst and the same voice continued, louder, even more authoritative, as the crowd momentarily but perceptibly quieted down, only to suddenly resume screaming at full volume. Bourne glanced over, astonished to see through the beams of the spinning searchlights the figure of Benjamin now standing on the roof of the concrete guardhouse. The young trainer was shouting into the microphone, exhorting the crowd to follow his instructions, whatever they were . . . And whatever they were, they were being obeyed! The multitude gradually, then gathering momentum, began reversing direction – then, as a single unit, started racing back into the street! Benjamin ignited his flare and waved it, pointing to the north. He was sending Jason his own signal. Not only was the tunnel shut down but the crowds were being dispersed without anyone being shot with the AK-47. There had been a better way.

Bourne dropped to the ground, his eyes scanning the undersides of the stationary vehicles, the spewing flame beyond lighting up the open spaces . . . A pair of legs – in *boots*! Behind the third automobile on the left, no more than twenty yards from the break in the fence that led to the tunnel. Carlos was *his*! The end *was* at last in sight! No *time*! *Do what you have to do and do it quickly!* He dropped his weapon on the gravel, gripped the grenade in his right hand, pulled the pin, grabbed the .45 with his left hand, and lurched off the ground, racing forward. Roughly thirty feet from the car he dived back down into the gravel, turned sideways and heaved the grenade under the automobile – only at the last instant, the small bomb having left his hand, realizing that he had made a terrible *error*! The legs behind the car did not move – the boots remained in place, for they were just that, *boots*! He lunged to his right, rolling furiously over the sharp stones, shielding his face, curling his body into the smallest mass he could manage.

The explosion was deafening, the lethal debris joining the whirling beams of the searchlights in the night sky, fragments of metal and glass stinging Jason's back and legs. Move, *move*! screamed the voice in his mind's ears as he lurched to his knees, then to his feet in the smoke and fire of the burning automobile. As he did so, the gravel erupted all around him; he zigzagged wildly towards the protection of the nearest vehicle, a square-shaped van. He was hit twice, in his shoulder and thigh! He spun around the wall of the van at the precise moment when the large windshield was blown away.

'You're no *match* for me, Jason Bourne!' screamed Carlos the Jackal, his automatic weapon on rapid fire. 'You never *were*! You are a pretender, a *fraud*!'

'So be it,' roared Bourne. 'Then come and get me!' Jason raced to the driver's door, yanked it open, then ran to the back of the vehicle where he crouched, his face to the edge, his Colt .45 angled straight up next to his cheek. With a final hissing expulsion, the flare beyond the fence burned itself out as the Jackal stopped his continuous fire. Bourne understood. Carlos faced the open door, unsure, indecisive . . . only seconds to go. Metal against metal; a gun barrel was rammed against the door, slamming it shut. *Now!*

Jason spun around the edge of the van, his weapon exploding, firing into the Spanish uniform, blowing the gun out of the Jackal's hands. *One, two, three*; the shells flew in the air – and then they stopped! They *stopped*, the explosions replaced by a sickening, jamming click as the round in the chamber failed to eject. Carlos lurched to the ground for his weapon, his left arm limp and bleeding but his right hand still strong, clutching the gun like the claw of a crazed animal.

Bourne whipped his bayonet out of its scabbard and sprang forward, slicing the blade down towards the Jackal's forearm. He was too *late*! Carlos held the weapon! Jason lunged up, his left hand clasping the hot barrel – hold on, hold *on*! *You can't let it go! Twist it! Clockwise! Use the bayonet – no don't! Drop it! Use both hands!* The conflicting commands clashed in his head, *madness*. He had no breath, no strength; his eyes could not focus – the *shoulder*. Like Bourne himself, the Jackal was wounded in his right shoulder!

Hold on! Reach the shoulder but *hold on*! With a last, gasping final surge, Bourne shot up and crashed Carlos back into the side of the van, pummelling the wounded area. The Jackal screamed, dropping the weapon, then kicked it under the vehicle.

Where the blow came from, Jason at first did not know; he only knew that the left side of his skull seemed suddenly split in two. Then he realized that he had done it to himself! He had slipped on the blood-covered gravel, and had crashed into the metal grille of the van. It did not matter – *nothing* mattered!

Carlos the Jackal was racing away! With the rampant confusion everywhere, there were a hundred ways he could get out of Novgorod. It had all been for *nothing*!

Still, there was his last grenade. Why not? Bourne removed it, pulled the pin, and threw it over the van into the centre of the parking area. The explosion followed and Jason got to his feet; perhaps the grenade would tell Benjamin something, warn him to keep his eyes on the area.

Staggering and barely able to walk, Jason started for the break in the fence that led to the guardhouse and the tunnel. *Oh, God, Marie, I failed! I'm so sorry. Nothing! It was for nothing!* And then, as if all Novgorod were having a final laugh at his expense, he saw that someone had opened the iron gates to the tunnel, giving the Jackal his invitation to freedom.

'*Archie . . .?*' Benjamin's astonished voice floated over the sounds of the river, followed by the sight of the young Soviet running out of the guardhouse towards Bourne. 'Christ almighty, I thought you were *dead*!'

'So you opened the gates and let my executioner walk away,' yelled Jason weakly. 'Why didn't you send a limousine for him?'

'I suggest you look again, Professor,' replied a breathless Benjamin as he stopped in front of Bourne, studying Jason's battered face and bloodstained clothing. 'Old age has withered your eyesight.'

'What?'

'You want gates, you'll have gates.' The trainer shouted an order towards the guardhouse in Russian. Seconds later the huge iron gates descended, covering the mouth of the tunnel. But something was strange. Bourne had not actually seen the lowered gates before, yet these were not like anything he might have imagined. They appeared to be . . . swollen somehow, distorted perhaps. 'Glass,' said Benjamin.

'Glass?' asked a bewildered Jason.

'At each end of the tunnel, five-inch-thick walls of glass, locked and sealed.'

'What are you talking about?' It was not necessary for the young Russian to explain. Suddenly, like a series of gigantic waves crashing against the walls of a huge aquarium, the tunnel was being filled with the waters of the Volkhov River. Then within the violence of the growing, swirling liquid mass, there was an object . . . a thing, a form, a *body*! Bourne stared in shock, his eyes bulging, his mouth gaped, frozen in place, unable to disgorge the cry that was in him. He summoned what strength he had left, running unsteadily, twice falling to his knees, but gathering speed with each stride, and raced to the massive wall of glass that sealed the entrance beyond it. Breathlessly, his chest heaving, he placed his hands against the glass wall and leaned into it, bearing witness to the macabre scene barely inches in front of him. The grotesquely uniformed corpse of Carlos the Jackal kept crashing back and forth into the steel bars of the gate, his dark features twisted in hate, his eyes two glass orbs reviling death as it overtook him.

The cold eyes of Jason Bourne watched in satisfaction, his mouth taut, rigid, the face of a killer, a killer among killers, who had won. Briefly, however, the softer eyes of David Webb intruded, his lips parted, forming the face of a man for whom the weight of a world he loathed had been removed.

'He's gone, Archie,' observed Benjamin at Jason's side. 'That bastard can't come back.'

'You flooded the tunnel,' said Bourne simply. 'How did you know it was him?'

'You didn't have an automatic weapon, but he did. Frankly, I thought Krupkin's prophecy was – shall we say – borne out? You were dead, and the man who killed you would take the quickest way out. This was it and the uniform confirmed it. Everything suddenly made sense from the Spanish compound down.'

'How did you get that crowd away?'

'I told them barges were being sent to take them across the river – about two miles north . . . Speaking of Krupkin, I've got to get you out of here. *Now.* Come on, the helicopter pad's about a half a mile away. We'll use the jeep. Hurry up, for God's sake!'

'Krupkin's instructions?'

'Choked from his hospital bed, in as much anger as in shock.'

'What do you mean?'

'You might as well know. Someone up in the rarefied circle – Krupkin doesn't know who – issued the order that you weren't to leave here under any conditions. Put plainly, it was unthinkable, but then no one ever thought that the whole goddamned Novgorod would go up in flames, either, and that's our cover.'

'*Ours?*'

'I'm not your executioner, somebody else is. The word never reached me and in this mess, it won't now.'

'*Wait* a minute! Where's the chopper taking me?'

'Cross your fingers, Professor, and hope Krupkin and your American friend know what they're doing. The helicopter takes you to Yelsk, and from there a plane to Zomosc across the Polish border, where an ungrateful satellite has apparently permitted a CIA listening post.'

'Christ, I'll still be in Soviet bloc territory!'

'The implication was that your people are ready for you. Good luck.'

'Ben,' said Jason, studying the young man. 'Why are you doing this? You're disobeying a direct order—'

'I *received* no order!' broke in the Russian. 'And even if I had, I'm no unthinking robot. You had an arrangement and you fulfilled your end . . . Also, if there's a chance for my mother—'

'There's more than a chance,' interrupted Bourne.

'Come on, let's go! We're wasting time. Yelsk and Zomosc are only the beginning for you. You face a long and dangerous journey, Archie.'

42

Sundown, and the out islands of Montserrat were growing darker, becoming patches of deep green surrounded by a shimmering blue sea and never-ending sprays of white foam erupting from coral reefs off the shorelines; all were bathed in the diaphanous orange of the Caribbean horizon. On Tranquillity Isle, lamps were gradually turned on inside the last four villas in the row above the beach at Tranquillity Inn, and figures could be seen, by and large walking slowly between the rooms and out on the balconies where the rays from the setting sun washed over the terraces. The soft breezes carried the scents of hibiscus and poinciana across the tropical foliage as a lone fishing boat weaved its way through the reefs with its late afternoon catch for the inn's kitchen.

Brendan Patrick Pierre Prefontaine carried his Perrier out to the balcony of Villa Seventeen, where Johnny St Jacques stood by the railing sipping a rum and tonic. 'How long do you think it will take before you reopen?' asked the former judge of the Boston court, sitting down at the white wrought-iron table.

'The structural damage can be repaired in a matter of weeks,' replied the owner of Tranquillity Inn, 'but the aftertaste of what happened here will take longer, a lot longer.'

'Again, how long?'

'I'll give it four or five months before I send out the initial brochures – it'll be late for the season's bookings, but Marie agrees. To do anything earlier would not only be tasteless, but the urgency would fuel all the gossip again . . . Terrorists, drug runners, corrupt island government – we don't need that and we don't deserve it.'

'Well, as I mentioned, I can pay my freight,' said the once-honourable justice of the federal district court in Massachusetts. 'Perhaps not to the extent of your highest seasonal prices, dear man, but certainly sufficient to cover the costs of a villa, plus a little for the inn's kitty.'

'I told you, forget it. I owe you more than I can ever repay. Tranquillity's yours as long as you want to stay.' St Jacques turned from the railing, his eyes lingering on the fishing boat below, and sat down opposite Prefontaine. 'I worry about the people down there, in the boats and on the beach. I used to have three or four boats bringing in the freshest fish with crews to match. Now, I've only got one coming in for us and what's left of the staff – all of which are on half salary.'

'Then you need my money.'

'Come on, Judge, *what* money? I don't want to appear intrusive, but Washington gave me a pretty complete rundown on you. You've been living off the streets for years.'

'Ah, yes, Washington,' pronounced Prefontaine, raising his glass to the orange and azure sky. 'As usual, it is twelve steps behind the crime – twenty steps where its *own* criminality is concerned.'

'What are you talking about?'

'Randolph Gates, that's what I'm talking about – *who* I'm talking about.'

'That bastard from *Boston*? The one who put the Jackal on David's trail?'

'The touchingly reformed Randolph Gates, Johnny. Reformed in all ways but monetary restitution, I might add . . . Still, nevertheless, with the mind and the conscience that I knew at Harvard years ago. Not the brightest, not the best, but with the literary and oratorical skills that camouflaged a brilliance that was never really there.'

'Now what the *hell* are you talking about?'

'I visited him the other day at his rehabilitation centre in Minnesota, or Michigan, I can't actually remember which, for I flew first class and the drinks were delivered on request. Regardless, we met and our arrangement was concluded. He's changing *sides*, Johnny. He's now going to fight – legally – for the people, *not* for the conglomerates who buy and sell on *paper*. He told me he's going after the raiders and the merger brokers who make billions in the markets and cost thousands upon thousands in jobs.'

'How can he do that?'

'Because he was there. He did it all; he knows all the tricks and is willing to commit his considerable talents to the cause.'

'Why would he do it?'

'Because he's got Edith back.'

'Who in God's name is *Edith*?'

'His wife . . . Actually, I'm still in love with her. I was from the time we first met, but in those days a distinguished judge with a wife and a child, regardless of how repulsive both might be, did not pursue such longings. Randy the Grand never deserved her; perhaps now he'll make up for all the lost years.'

That's very interesting, but what's it got to do with your arrangement?'

'Did I mention that Lord Randolph of Gates made great sums of money during those lost but productive years?'

'Several times. So?'

'Well, in recognition of the services I rendered that undoubtedly contributed to the removal of a life-threatening situation in which he found himself, said threat emanating from Paris, he saw clearly the validity of compensating me. Especially in light of the knowledge I possess . . . You know, after a number of bloodletting courtroom battles, I think he's going after a judgeship. Far higher than mine, I think.'

'*So?*'

'So, if I keep my own counsel, get out of Boston, and for the sake of a loose tongue stay off the sauce, his bank will forward me fifty thousand dollars a year for the rest of my life.'

'Jesus *Christ*!'

'That's what I said to myself when he agreed. I even went to Mass for the first time in thirty-odd years.'

'Still, you won't be able to go home again.'

'Home?' Prefontaine laughed softly. 'Was it really? No matter, I may have found another. Through a gentleman named Peter Holland at the Central Intelligence Agency, I was given an introduction to your friend, Sir Henry Sykes over in Montserrat, who in turn introduced me to a retired London barrister named Jonathan Lemuel, originally a native islander. We're both getting on but neither of us is ready for a different sort of "home". We may open a consulting firm, specialists in American and UK laws where export and import licensing is concerned. Of course, we'll have to do some boning up but we'll manage. I expect I'll be here for years.'

St Jacques rose quickly from the table to replenish his drink, his eyes warily on the former, disbarred judge.

Morris Panov walked slowly, cautiously out of his bedroom and into the sitting room of Villa Eighteen where Alex Conklin sat in a wheelchair. The bandages across the psychiatrist's chest were visible under the light fabric of his white guayabera; they extended down his exposed left arm below the elbow. 'It took me damn near twenty minutes to lift this useless appendage through the sleeve!' he complained angrily but without self-pity.

'You should have called me,' said Alex, spinning himself around in the chair, away from the telephone. 'I can still roll this thing pretty damned fast. Of course, I had a couple of years' experience prior to my Quasimodo's boot.'

'Thank you, but I prefer to dress myself – as I believe you preferred to walk by yourself once the prosthesis was fitted.'

'That's the first lesson, Doctor. I expect there's something about it in your head books.'

'There is. It's called dumb, or, if you like, obstinate stupidity.'

'No, it's not,' countered the retired intelligence officer, his eyes levelled with Panov's as the psychiatrist lowered himself slowly into a chair.

'No . . . it's not,' agreed Mo, returning Conklin's look. 'The first lesson is independence. Take as much as you can handle and keep grabbing for more.'

'There's a good side, too,' said Alex, smiling, and adjusting the bandage around his throat. 'It gets easier, not harder. You learn new tricks every day; it's surprising what our little grey cells come up with.'

'Do tell? I must explore that field one day . . . I heard you on the phone, who was it?'

'Holland. The wires have been burning on all the back channels between Moscow and Washington, every covert phone on both sides damn near paralysed thinking there could be a leak and theirs would be held responsible.'

'Medusa?'

'You never heard that name, *I* never heard that name, and nobody we *know* has ever heard it. There's been enough bloodletting in the international marketplace – to say nothing of a few buckets of real blood spilled – to call into question the sanity of both governments' controlling institutions, which were obviously blind or just plain stupid.'

'How about just plain guilty?' asked Panov.

'Too few at the top to warrant the destruction of the whole – that's the verdict of Langley and Dzerzhinsky Square. The chief pin-stripers at the State Department in the Kremlin's Council of Ministers agree. Nothing can be served by pursuing or exposing the extent of the malfeasance – how do you like that, *malfeasance*? Murder, assassination, kidnapping, extortion and large-scale corruption using organized crime on both sides of the Atlantic are now conveniently slotted as "malfeasance"! They say it's better to salvage what we can as quietly and as expeditiously as possible.'

'That's obscene.'

'That's reality, Doctor. You're about to witness one of the biggest cover-ups in modern history, certainly among powerful sovereign nations . . . And the real obscenity is that they're probably right. If Medusa were exposed to the fullest – and it would be fully exposed if it was exposed at all – the people in their righteous indignation would throw the bastards out – many of them the wrong bastards, tainted only by association. That sort of thing produces vacuums in high places, and these are not the times for vacuums of any kind. Better the Satans you know than the ones you don't who come later.'

'So what's going to happen?'

'Trade off,' said Conklin pensively. 'The scope of Medusa's operations is so far-ranging geographically and structurally that it's almost impossible to unravel. Moscow's sending Ogilvie back with a team of financial analysts, and with our own people they'll start the process of dismantling. Eventually Holland foresees a quiet, unannounced economic mini-summit, calling together various financial ministers of the NATO and Eastern bloc countries. Wherever Medusa's assets can be self-sustaining or absorbed by their individual economies, that'll be the case with restrictive covenants on all parties. The main point is to prevent financial panics through mass factory closings and wholesale company collapses.'

'Thus burying Medusa,' offered Panov. 'It's again history, unwritten and unacknowledged, the way it was from the beginning.'

'Above all, that,' conceded Alex. 'By omission and commission there's enough sleaze to go around for everybody.'

'What about men like Burton on the Joint Chiefs, and Atkinson in London?'

'No more than messengers and fronts; they're out for reasons of health, and believe me, they understand.'

Panov winced as he adjusted his wounded, uncomfortable body in the chair. 'It hardly compensates for his crimes, but the Jackal served a purpose of sorts, didn't he? If you hadn't been hunting him, you wouldn't have found Medusa.'

'The coincidence of evil, Mo,' said Conklin. 'I'm not about to recommend a posthumous medal.'

'I'd say it's more than coincidence,' interrupted Panov, shaking his head. 'In the final analysis, David was right. Whether forced or leaped upon, a connection was there after all. Someone in Medusa had a killer or killers using the name of "Jason Bourne" assassinate a high-visibility target in the Jackal's own backyard; that someone knew what he was doing.'

'You mean Teagarten, of course.'

'Yes. Since Bourne was on Medusa's death list, our pathetic turncoat, DeSole, had to tell them about the Treadstone operation, perhaps not by name but its essentials. When they learned that Jason – David – was in Paris, they used the original scenario; Bourne against the Jackal. By killing Teagarten the way they did, they accurately assumed they were enlisting the most deadly partner they could find to hunt down and kill David.'

'We know that. So?'

'Don't you see, Alex? When you think about it, Brussels was the beginning of the end, and at the end, David used that false accusation to tell Marie he was still alive, to tell Peter Holland that he was still alive. The map circling Anderlecht in red.'

'He gave hope, that's all. Hope isn't something I put much trust in, Mo,'

'He did more than give hope. That message made Holland prepare every station in Europe to expect Jason Bourne, assassin, and to use every extreme to get him back here.'

'It worked. Sometimes that kind of thing doesn't.'

'It worked because weeks ago a man called Jason Bourne knew that to catch Carlos there had to be a link between himself and the Jackal, a long-forgotten connection that had to be brought to the surface. He *did* it, you did it!'

'In a hell of a roundabout way,' admitted Conklin. 'We were reaching, that's all. Possibilities, probabilities, abstractions – it's all we had to work with,'

'Abstractions?' asked Panov, gently. 'That's such an erroneously passive term. Have you any idea what thunder in the mind abstractions provoke?'

'I don't even know what you're talking about.'

'Those grey cells, Alex. They go crazy, spinning around like infinitesimal Ping-Pong balls trying to find tiny tunnels to explode through, drawn by their own inherent compulsions.'

'You've lost me.'

'You said it yourself, the coincidence of evil. But I'd suggest another conductor – the *magnet* of evil. That's what you and David created, and within that magnetic field was Medusa.'

Conklin spun around in the chair and wheeled himself towards the balcony and the descending orange glow on the horizon beyond the deep green out islands of Montserrat. 'I wish everything was as simple as you put it, Mo,' he said rapidly. 'I'm afraid it's not.'

'You'll have to be clearer.'

'Krupkin's a dead man.'

'*What?*'

'I mourn him as a friend and one hell of an enemy. He made everything possible for us and when it was all over, he did what was right, not what was ordered. He let David live and now he's paying for it.'

'What happened to him?'

'According to Holland, he disappeared from the hospital in Moscow five days ago – he simply took his clothes and walked out. No one knows how he did it or where he went, but an hour after he left, the KGB came to arrest him and move him to the Lubyanka.'

'Then they haven't caught him—'

'They will. When the Kremlin issues a Black Alert, every road, train station, airport and border crossing is put under a microscope. The incentives are irresistible: whoever lets him out will spend ten years in a gulag. It's just a question of time. *Goddamn it.*'

There was a knock on the front door and Panov called out. 'It's open because it's easier! Come in.'

The be-blazered, immaculately dressed assistant manager, Mr Pritchard, entered, preceded by a room-service table that he was capable of pushing while standing completely erect. He smiled broadly and announced his presence as well as his mission. 'Buckingham Pritchard at your service, gentlemen. I've brought a few delicacies from the sea for your collegial gathering before the evening meal which I have personally attended to at the side of the chef who has been known to be prone to errors without expert guidance which I was all too happy to provide.'

'Collegial?' said Alex. 'I got out of college damn near thirty-five years ago.'

'It obviously didn't take where the nuances of English are concerned,' mumbled Morris Panov. '*Tell* me, Mr Pritchard, aren't you terribly hot in those clothes? I'd be sweating like a pig.'

'No nuances there, only an unproven cliché,' muttered Conklin.

'I do not perspire, sir,' replied the assistant manager.

'I'll bet my pension you "perspired" when Mr St Jacques came back from Washington,' offered Alex. 'Christ almighty, Johnny a "terrorist"!'

'The incident has been forgotten, sir,' said Pritchard stoically. 'Mr Saint Jay and Sir Henry understand that my brilliant uncle and I had only the children's interests at heart.'

'Savvy, very savvy,' observed Conklin.

'I'll set up the canapés, gentlemen, and check the ice. The others should be here in a matter of minutes.'

'That's very kind of you,' said Panov.

David Webb leaned against the balcony archway watching his wife as she read the last pages of a children's story to their son. The outstanding Mrs Cooper was dozing in a chair, her magnificent black head, crowned by a fleece of silver and grey, kept nodding above her full chest as if she expected at any moment to hear sounds from the infant Alison beyond the half-closed door that was only feet from where she was sitting. The inflections of Marie's quiet voice matched the words of the story, confirmed by Jamie's wide eyes and parted lips. But for an analytical mind that found music in figures, his wife might have been an actress, mused David. She had the surface attributes of that precarious profession – striking features, a commanding presence, the sine qua non that forced both men and women to fall silent and pensively appraise her when she walked down a street or entered a room.

'You can read to me tomorrow, Daddy!'

The story was over, attested to by his son jumping off the couch and Mrs

Cooper flashing her eyes open. 'I wanted to read that one tonight,' said Webb defensively, moving away from the arch.

'Well, you still kind of smell,' said the boy, frowning.

'Your father doesn't smell, Jamie,' explained Marie, smiling. 'I told you, it's the medicine the doctor said he had to use on his injuries from the accident.'

'He still smells.'

'You can't argue with an analytical mind when it's right, can you?' asked David.

'It's too early to go to bed, Mommy! I might wake up Alison and she'll start crying again.'

'I know, dear, but Daddy and I have to go over and see all your uncles—'

'And my new grandfather!' cried the child exuberantly. 'Grandpa Brendan said he was going to teach me how to be a judge some day.'

'God help the boy,' interjected Mrs Cooper. 'That man dresses like a peacock flowering to mate.'

'You may go into our room and watch television,' overrode Marie quickly. 'But only for a half hour—'

'*Aww!*'

'All right, perhaps an hour, but Mrs Cooper will select the channels.'

'Thanks, Mommy!' cried the child, racing into his parents' bedroom as Mrs Cooper got out of the chair and followed him.

'Oh, I can start him off,' said Marie, getting up from the couch.

'No, Miss Marie,' protested Mrs Cooper. 'You stay with your husband. That man hurts but he won't say anything.' She disappeared into the bedroom.

'Is that true, my darling?' asked Marie, walking to David. 'Do you hurt?'

'I hate to dispel the myth of a great lady's incontestable perceptions, but she's wrong.'

'Why do you have to use a dozen words when one will suffice?'

'Because I'm supposed to be a scholar. We academicians never take a direct route because it doesn't leave us any offshoots to claim if we're wrong. What are you, anti-intellectual?'

'No,' answered Marie. 'You see, that's a simple, one word declarative.'

'What's a declarative?' asked Webb, talking his wife in his arms and kissing her, their lips enveloping, so meaningful to each, arousing to each.

'It's a shortcut to the truth,' said Marie, arching her head back and looking at him. 'No offshoots, no circumlocutions, just fact. As in five and five equals ten, not nine or eleven, but ten.'

'You're a ten.'

'That's banal, but I'll take it . . . You *are* more relaxed, I can feel you again. Jason Bourne's leaving you, isn't he?'

'Just about. While you were with Alison, Ed McAllister called me from the National Security Agency. Benjamin's mother is on her way back to Moscow.'

'Hey, that's *wonderful*, David!'

'Both Mac and I laughed, and as we laughed I thought to myself I'd never heard McAllister laugh before. It was nice.'

'He wore his guilt on his sleeve – no, all over him. He sent us both to Hong Kong and he never forgave himself. Now you're back and alive and free. I'm not sure *I'll* ever forgive him, but at least I won't hang up on him when he calls.'

'He'd like that. As a matter of fact I told him to call. I said you might even ask him to dinner some day.'

'I didn't go that far.'

'Benjamin's mother? That kid saved my life.'

'Maybe a quick brunch.'

'Take your hands off me, woman. In another fifteen seconds I'm going to throw Jamie and Mrs Cooper out of our bedroom and demand my connubials.'

'I'm tempted, Attila, but I think Bro's counting on us. Two feisty invalids and an overimaginative disbarred judge are more than an Ontario ranch boy can handle.'

'I love them all.'

'So do I. Let's go.'

The Caribbean sun had disappeared; only faint sprays of orange barely illuminated the western horizon. The flames of the glass-encased candles were steady, pointed, sending streams of grey smoke through their funnels, their glows producing warm light and comfortable shadows around the terraced balcony of Villa Eighteen. The conversation, too, had been warm and comfortable – survivors relishing their deliverance from a nightmare.

'I emphatically explained to Handy Randy that the doctrine of *stare decisis* has to be challenged if the times have altered the perceptions that existed when the original decisions were rendered,' expounded Prefontaine. 'Change, *change* – the inevitable result of the calendar.'

'That's so obvious, I can't imagine anyone debating it,' said Alex.

'Oh, Flood-the-Gates used it incessantly, confusing juries with his erudition and confounding his peers with multiple *decises*.'

'Mirrors and smoke,' added Marie, laughing. 'We do the same in economics. Remember, Bro, I told you that?'

'I didn't understand a word. Still don't.'

'No mirrors and no smoke where medicine's involved,' said Panov. 'At least not where the labs are monitored and the pharmaceutical money boys are prohibited. Legitimate advances are validated every day.'

'In many ways it's the purposely undefined core of our Constitution,' continued the former judge. 'It's as though the Founders had read Nostradamus but didn't care to admit their frivolity, or perhaps studied the drawings of Da Vinci, who foresaw aircraft. They understood that they could not legislate the future, for they had no idea what it would hold, or what society would demand for its future liberties. They created brilliant omissions.'

'Unaccepted as such by the brilliant Randolph Gates, if memory serves,' said Conklin.

'Oh, he'll change quickly now,' interrupted Prefontaine, chuckling. 'He was always a sworn companion of the wind and he's smart enough to adjust his sails when he has to buck it.'

'I keep wondering whatever happened to the truck driver's wife, the one in the diner who was married to the man they called "Bronk",' said the psychiatrist.

'Try to imagine a small house and a white picket fence, et cetera,' offered Alex. 'It's easier that way.'

'What truck driver's wife?' asked St Jacques.

'Leave it alone, Bro, I'd rather not find out.'

'Or that son-of-a-bitch army doctor who pumped me full of Amytal!' pressed Panov.

'He's running a clinic in Leavenworth,' replied Conklin. 'I forgot to tell you . . . So many, so crazy. And Krupkin. Crazy old Kruppie, elegance and all. We owe him, but we can't help him.'

There was a moment of silence as each in his or her own way thought of a man who had selflessly opposed a monolithic system that demanded the death of David Webb, who stood by the railing staring out at the darkened sea, somehow separated in mind and body from the others. It would take time, he understood that. Jason Bourne had to vanish; he had to *leave* him. *When?*

Not now! Out of the early night, the madness began again! From the sky the roar of multiple engines broke the silence like approaching sharp cracks of lightning. Three military helicopters swooped down towards the Tranquillity dock, fusillades of gunfire chewing up the shoreline as a powerful bullet speedboat swung through the reefs towards the beach. St Jacques was on his intercom. '*Shore alarm!*' he screamed. 'Grab your weapons!'

'Christ, the Jackal's *dead*!' yelled Conklin.

'His goddamned *disciples* aren't!' shouted Jason Bourne – no trace of David Webb – as he shoved Marie to the floor and took a gun out of his belt, a weapon his wife knew nothing about. 'They were told he was here!'

'It's insane!'

'That's *Carlos*,' replied Jason, racing to the balcony railing. 'He *owns* them! They're his for life!'

'*Shit!*' roared Alex as he wheeled his chair furiously and pushed Panov away from the table and the lighted candles.

Suddenly a deafening loudspeaker from the lead helicopter crackled with static, followed by the words of the pilot. 'You saw what we did to the beach, *mon*! We'll cut you in two if you don't stop your engine! . . . That's better, *mon.* Drift into shore – *drift*, no motor at all and both of you come on deck, your hands on the gunwale, leaning forward! Do it *now*!'

The searchlight beams of the two circling helicopters centred on the boat as the lead aircraft dropped to the beach, the rotors swirling up the sand, producing an outline of a threshold for its landing. Four men leaped out, their weapons trained on the drifting speedboat as the inhabitants of Villa Eighteen stood by the railing, staring down in astonishment at the unbelievable scene below.

'*Pritchard!*' yelled St Jacques. 'Bring me the binoculars!'

'They're in my hands. Mr Saint Jay – oh, there they are.' The assistant manager rushed out with the powerful magnifiers and handed them to his employer. 'I managed to clean the lenses, sir!'

'What do you *see*?' asked Bourne sharply.

'I don't know. Two men.'

'Some *army*!' said Conklin.

'Give them to me,' ordered Jason, grabbing the binoculars from his brother-in-law.

'What *is* it, David?' shouted Marie, seeing the shock on her husband's face.

'It's Krupkin,' he said.

Dimitri Krupkin sat at the white wrought-iron table, his face pale – and it was his full face, as his chin beard had been removed – and refused to speak to anyone until he had finished his third brandy. Like Panov, Conklin and David Webb, he was clearly a hurt man, a wounded man, a man in considerable physical pain, which, like the others, he did not care to dwell upon, as what lay ahead was infinitely better than what he had left behind. His decidedly inferior clothes seemed to annoy him whenever he glanced down at them, but he shrugged continually in silence, the shrugs conveying the fact that soon he would be back in sartorial splendour. His first words were to the elderly Brendan Prefontaine as he appraised the former judge's intricately laced peach guayabera above the royal-blue trousers. 'I like that outfit,' he said admiringly. 'Very tropical and in good taste for the climate.'

'Thank you.'

Introductions were made, and the instant they were over, a barrage of questions was hurled at the Soviet. He held up both hands, as a pope might from his balcony in St Peter's Square, and spoke.

'I will not bore you or disturb you with the trivial details of my flight from Mother Russia, other than to say I'm aghast at the high price of corruption and will neither forget nor forgive the filthy accommodations I was forced to endure for the exorbitant sums of money I spent . . . That said, thank God for Crédit Suisse and those lovely green coupons they issue.'

'Just tell us what happened,' said Marie.

'*You*, dear lady, are even lovelier than I had imagined. Had we met in Paris I would have whisked you away from this Dickensian ragamuffin you call a husband. *My*, look at your hair – glorious!'

'He probably couldn't tell you what colour it is,' said Marie, smiling. 'You'll be the threat I hold over his peasant head.'

'Still, for his age he's remarkably competent.'

'That's because I feed him a lot of pills, all kinds of pills, Dimitri. Now tell us, what happened?'

'What *happened*? They found me out, that's what happened! They confiscated my lovely house in Geneva! It's now an adjunct to the Soviet embassy. The loss is heartbreaking!'

'I think my wife's talking about the peasant *me*,' said Webb. 'You were in the hospital in Moscow and you found out what someone intended for me – namely my execution. Then you told Benjamin to get me out of Novgorod.'

'I have sources, Jason, and errors are made in high places and I'll incriminate no one by using names. It was simply wrong. If Nuremberg taught us all nothing else, it was that obscene commands should not be obeyed. That lesson crosses borders and penetrates minds. We in Russia suffered far, far more than anyone in America during the last war. Some of us remember that and we will not emulate that enemy.'

'Well spoken,' said Prefontaine, raising his glass of Perrier to the Soviet. 'When everything's said and done, we're all part of the same thinking, feeling human race, aren't we?'

'Well,' choked Krupkin, swallowing his fourth brandy, 'beyond that very attractive if overused observation, there are divisions of commitment, Judge. Not serious, of course, but nevertheless varied. For instance, although my house on the lake in Geneva is no longer mine, my accounts in the Cayman Islands remain intensely personal. Incidentally, how far are those islands from here?'

'Roughly twelve hundred miles due west,' replied St Jacques. 'A jet out of Antigua will get you there in three hours plus.'

'That's what I thought,' said Krupkin. 'When we were in the hospital in Moscow, Alex frequently spoke of Tranquillity Isle and Montserrat, so I checked the map in the hospital library. Everything seems to be on course . . . Incidentally, the man with the boat, he won't be dealt with too harshly, will he? My outrageously expensive ersatz papers are very much in order.'

'His crime was in his appearance, not in bringing you over here,' answered St Jacques.

'I was in a hurry, it goes with running for your life.'

'I've already explained to Government House that you're an old friend of my brother-in-law.'

'Good. Very good.'

'What will you do now, Dimitri?' asked Marie.

'My options are limited, I'm afraid. Our Russian bear not only has more claws than a centipede has legs, she's also computerized with a global network. I shall have to remain buried for quite some time while I construct another existence. From birth, of course.' Krupkin turned to the owner of Tranquillity Inn. 'Would it be possible to lease one of these lovely cottages, Mr St Jacques?'

'After what you did for David and my sister, don't give it a second thought. This house is your house, Mr Krupkin, all of it.'

'How very kind. First, naturally, there'll be the trip to the Caymans, where, I'm told, there are excellent tailors; then perhaps a clever little yacht and a small charter business that can be substantiated as having been moved from Tierra del Fuego or the Malvinas, some godforsaken place where a little money can produce an identity and a highly credible if obscure past. After these are set in motion, there's a doctor in Buenos Aires who does wonders with fingerprints – quite painlessly, I'm told – and then minor cosmetic surgery – Rio has the best, you know, far better than New York – just enough to alter the profile and perhaps remove a few years . . . For the past five days and nights, I've had nothing to do but think and plan, enduring situations of passage I would not describe in front of the lovely Mrs Webb.'

'You certainly have been thinking,' agreed David's wife, impressed. 'And please call me Marie. How can I hold you over the peasant's head if I'm Mrs Webb?'

'Ah, the adorable Marie.'

'What about these adorable plans of yours?' asked Conklin pointedly. 'How long will they take to implement?'

'You of all people should ask that question?' Krupkin's eyes were wide in disbelief.

'I think I'd better,' broke in Alex.

'*You*, who were instrumental in building the dossier of the greatest impersonator the international world of terrorism has ever *known*? The incomparable Jason Bourne?'

'If that includes me,' said Webb, 'I'm out. I'm heavy into interior decorating.'

'How long, Kruppie?'

'For heaven's sake, man, you were training a recruit for an assignment, a single mission, *I'm* altering a life!'

'How *long*?'

'You tell me, Alex. It's my life we're talking about now – as worthless as that life may be in the geopolitical scheme of things – it's still my life.'

'Whatever he needs,' interrupted David Webb, the unseen image of Jason Bourne looking over his wounded shoulder.

'Two years to do it well, three years to do it better,' said Dimitri Krupkin.

'They're yours,' said Marie.

'*Pritchard*,' said St Jacques, angling his head. 'Fix my drink, if you please.'

Epilogue

They walked along the moonlit beach, alternately touching and not touching, the embarrassment of intimacy intermittently intruding as if a world that had separated them had not let them escape its terrible orbit, constantly pulling them into its fiery nucleus.

'You carried a gun,' said Marie softly. 'I had no idea you had one. I hate guns.'

'So do I. I'm not sure I knew I had one, either. It was just there.'

'Reflex? Compulsion?'

'Both, I guess. It didn't matter, I didn't use it.'

'But you wanted to, didn't you?'

'Again, I'm not sure. If you and the children were threatened, of course I would, but I don't think I'd fire indiscriminately.'

'Are you sure, David? Would the appearance of danger to us make you pick up a gun and shoot at shadows?'

'No, I don't shoot at shadows.'

Footsteps. In the sand! Waves lapping over the unmistakable intrusion of a human being, breaks in the flow of the natural rhythm – sounds Jason Bourne knew from a hundred beaches! He spun around, violently propelling Marie off her feet, sending her out of the line of fire as he crouched, his weapon in his hand.

'Please don't kill me, David,' said Morris Panov, the beam of his flashlight illuminating the area. 'It simply wouldn't make sense.'

'*Jesus*, Mo!' cried Webb. 'What were you *doing*?'

'Trying to find you, that's all . . . Would you please help Marie?'

Webb did so, pulling his wife to her feet, both half blinded by the flashlight. 'My *God*, you're the *mole*!' cried Jason Bourne, raising his weapon. 'You knew every move I was making!'

'I'm *what*?' roared the psychiatrist, throwing down his flashlight. 'If you believe that, gun me down, you *son of a bitch*!'

'I don't know, Mo. I don't know anything any more . . . !' David's head arched back in pain.

'Then cry your heart out, you *bastard*! Cry like you've never cried *before*! Jason Bourne is dead, cremated in Moscow, and that's the way it is! You either accept that or I don't want a goddamned thing to do with you any more! Have you got that, you arrogant, brilliant *creation*! You *did* it, and it's *over*!'

Webb fell to his knees, the tears welling in his eyes, trembling and trying not to make a sound.

'We're going to be okay, Mo,' said Marie, kneeling beside her husband, holding him.

'I know that,' acknowledged Panov, nodding in the glow of the grounded flashlight. 'Two lives in one mind, none of us can know what it's like. But it's over now. It's really over.'